THE STORY AND ITS WRITER

An Introduction to Short Fiction

THE STORY AND ITS WRITER

An Introduction to Short Fiction

Edited by

Ann Charters

University of Connecticut

A Bedford Book

ST. MARTIN'S PRESS ❧ NEW YORK

Acknowledgments

Sherwood Anderson. "Hands" from *Winesburg, Ohio*, by Sherwood Anderson. Copyright 1919 by
    B. W. Huebsch. Copyright 1947 by Eleanor Copenhaver Anderson. Reprinted by permission of
    Viking Penguin Inc. "Death in the Woods" copyright © 1926 by the American Mercury, Inc.
    Renewed 1953 by Eleanor Copenhaver Anderson. "On Form, Not Plot, in the Short Story" copy-
    right © 1924 by B. W. Huebsch, Inc. Renewed 1952 by Eleanor Copenhaver Anderson. Both re-
    printed by permission of Harold Ober Associates Incorporated.
Isaac Babel. "My First Goose," trans. Walter Morison, and "Guy de Maupassant," trans. Raymond Ro-
    senthal and Waclaw Selski, from *Collected Stories*, copyright 1961. Reprinted by permission of
    S. G. Phillips, Inc.
Imamu Amiri Baraka. "Uncle Tom's Cabin: Alternate Ending" copyright © 1967 by Leroi Jones. Re-
    printed by permission of The Sterling Lord Agency, Inc.
John Barth. "Lost in the Funhouse" from *Lost in the Funhouse* by John Barth. Copyright © 1967 by
    The Atlantic Monthly Company. Reprinted by permission of Doubleday & Company, Inc.
Ann Beattie. "Waiting," copyright © 1979 by Ann Beattie. Reprinted from *The Burning House: Short
    Stories*, by Ann Beattie, by permission of Random House, Inc.
Jorge Luis Borges. "The End of the Duel" and "Borges and I" copyright © 1967 by Grove Press, Inc.
    Translated from the Spanish by Anthony Kerrigan. Reprinted by permission of Grove Press, Inc.
    "On the Meaning and Form of 'The End of the Duel' " from *Borges on Writing*, by Jorge Luis
    Borges. Copyright © 1972, 1973 by Jorge Luis Borges, Norman Thomas di Giovanni, Daniel
    Halpern, and Frank MacShane. Reprinted by permission of the publisher, E. P. Dutton, Inc.
Willa Cather. "Paul's Case" reprinted from *Youth and the Bright Medusa*, by Willa Cather, courtesy of
    Alfred A. Knopf, Inc. "On Katherine Mansfield" copyright 1936 by Willa Cather. Reprinted
    from *Willa Cather on Writing: Critical Studies on Writing as an Art*, by Willa Cather, by per-
    mission of Alfred A. Knopf, Inc.
John Cheever. "The Enormous Radio" and "The Swimmer" copyright 1947, © 1964 by John Cheever.
    Reprinted from *The Stories of John Cheever*, by John Cheever, by permission of Alfred A. Knopf,
    Inc.

Acknowledgments and copyrights continue at the back of the book on pages 1237–1239,
which constitute an extension of the copyright page.

Preface

The Story and Its Writer came into existence because I wanted my students to learn about the literary genre of the short story as much as possible from the writers themselves. In my years of teaching classes in the short story, most of the anthologies I used were either textbooks with a limited number of stories and a great deal of editorial discussion — categorizing the stories by plot, character, theme, and the like, and often restricting the students' interpretation and my classroom presentation — or anthologies collecting a hundred or so stories with almost no editorial apparatus except brief biographies of the writers that did not suggest their significance as *story* writers.

I have assembled a book that includes a wide selection of short story masterpieces, arranged so they help students understand the historical development of this literary form and the lively interaction between short story writers themselves over its 150-year history. In the first part of *The Story and Its Writer*, sixty writers and their works receive primary attention. The eighty-one stories include dual selections from the work of several major writers of short fiction. Here the book's chronological organization (by author's date of birth) reflects important stages in the evolution of the genre. In the second part, almost half of the writers included in the anthology — and one or two other literary figures — comment on the form of the short story and on specific stories included in the first part.

Because in my classroom experience I have found that students often need guidance in learning how to read stories intelligently and how to write about them coherently, this book opens with a general introduction discussing the elements of short fiction. I have concentrated on one story, Hawthorne's "Young Goodman Brown," the first story in the volume: students understandably grow restive if literary analysis refers to a flock of stories they have not read yet. In this introductory chapter I present much of the terminology used later in the headnotes, which provide biographical information and discuss each author's significance as a story writer, suggesting his or her place in the development of the form. An appendix on writing about short fiction (which also draws primarily on "Young Goodman Brown") and a glossary of literary terms conclude the book.

I wish to acknowledge the help of several people in the preparation of this book. The staff of the reference section of the University of Connecticut library, especially Leeanne Pander, Pamela Skinner, and David McChesney, gave unflagging assistance. My colleagues in the English department—Lee Jacobus, Barbara Rosen, William Sheidley (who cowrote the instructors' manual), William Curtin, Milton Stern, Jack Davis, Jack Manning, and Feenie Ziner — generously contributed suggestions and advice at every stage of this volume's preparation. Students in my short story classes diligently produced sample essays illustrating the various ways to write about stories. I thank them all for their help and encouragement, which made my work on *The Story and Its Writer* much easier.

Contents

Edith Wharton

Rudyard Kipling

Stephen Crane

Willa Cather

Gertrude Stein

Jack London

Sherwood Anderson

A. E. Coppard

James Joyce

Virginia Woolf

Franz Kafka

Part Two

The Commentaries

Flannery O'Connor

John Updike

WRITING ABOUT SHORT STORIES
1203

GLOSSARY OF LITERARY TERMS
1227

Alphabetical Listing
of Writers and Their Stories

THE STORY AND ITS WRITER

An Introduction to Short Fiction

INTRODUCTION

THE FORM OF THE SHORT STORY

Read literature for the pleasure of reading it, Ernest Hemingway once told an interviewer, adding "Whatever else you find will be the measure of what you brought to the reading." The stories in this anthology have been chosen because — if you bring an alert intelligence and a lively imagination to the reading — they are a pleasure to read. We all have different personalities, and we all read for different reasons, depending on our moods and circumstances, but we always look forward to being entertained by what we read. In an exciting story, we are offered the pleasant exercise of letting our imagination enter into a fictional situation, or of identifying with a character in a story because that character experiences or understands something very much like what has actually happened to us or what we fantasize might happen to us. Being acquisitive as well as inquisitive creatures, we can emerge from our encounter with literature with more than just entertainment. We gather information that helps us understand ourselves and others better.

Beyond these important reasons for reading literature, however, reading short fiction attentively and imaginatively promises further pleasure — the pleasure of enjoying the way the storyteller uses language to create a work of art. It is this way of reading that brings us closest to understanding the full achievement of the story and its writer. Literature is invention, and the storyteller is an inventor, whether he or she appears in the guise of entertainer, teacher, or enchanter. The sixty authors of the short stories in this anthology are experts in the art of invention, and you will be most enchanted by their art if you try to come closer to the individual magic of their genius by looking attentively at the ways in which they have shaped and selected the patterns and the details of their fiction.

What Is a Short Story?

The literary form *short story* is usually defined as a short fictional prose narrative, often involving one connected episode. Early in the nineteenth century the American writer Edgar Allan Poe was one of the first to attempt an analysis of its aesthetic properties. He stressed the element of *unity* of a single effect as its most characteristic feature. If all narration is a reconstruction of experience, imaginative or real, then a short story is condensation of experience to the highest degree. Real life is rarely that unified, so in a sense all fiction is "lies" — whether short stories, long stories, or novels. Paradoxically, however, the measure of success for all fiction is how *true* it is to our emotions, how accurately it shows the life that is lived by all of us.

One criticism of the short story as a form has been that, unlike the novel, it is too short for readers to get involved in, but this shorter length is actually one of the strengths of the form when the reader is responsive to the way the author uses language to create a work of art. Every detail adds to the unity of the final impression, so no aspect of the story can be extraneous or can detract from the single, vivid impression of the whole. Language is often used on the page of a story with the force and strength of poetry. Writers of short stories may forego the comprehensiveness of the novel but, like poets, they can impress upon the reader the unity of their vision of life by focusing on a single effect.

The novel and the short story are considered related forms because each is a prose narrative, but they are not close relations, as Edith Wharton, A. E. Coppard, and Nadine Gordimer have explained (to mention only a few writers included in this anthology who have discussed the difference between the two forms). Sometimes a writer like D. H. Lawrence employs both forms equally well; in other instances, a writer like Nathaniel Hawthorne needs the longer form to express his genius most fully. Once William Faulkner, probably half-joking, told an interviewer from the *Paris Review*, "Maybe every novelist wants to write poetry first, finds he can't, and then tries the short story, which is the most demanding form after poetry. And, failing at that, only then does he take up novel writing."

Stories and tales have existed since human beings felt the inborn and universal need to turn actual or imagined events into words and tell those words to themselves and others, but they have developed through many different stages in their long history. Telling stories is an ancient art, originating, as A. E. Coppard has said, "in the folk tale, which was a thing of joy even before writing, not to mention printing, was invented." The earliest folk tales were the myths and legends of the oral tradition, like the creation myths of primitive peoples, explaining how things got started. The next important stage was the great beast fables, stories in which animals are shown acting like humans in order to teach a moral lesson. The fables of the Greek slave Aesop (620?–560? B.C.) are still well known today. Another very early form of the short story is the religious parable and allegory, short and pithy stories with a moral twist, such as the parable of the wise and foolish virgins in the New Testament. Around the fourteenth century, a great variety of secular tales in prose and verse became popular, most notably the short prose tales of Giovanni Boccaccio (1313–1375), whose best-known book, *The Decameron*, is a series of 100 tales told by seven ladies and three men who have fled the plague that devastated Florence in 1348. In the same century, Geoffrey Chaucer (d. 1400) wrote *The Canterbury Tales*, a collection of religious and secular tales, most in verse and often bawdy and irreverent. Coming closer to modern times, the short story reached a further stage of development in the seventeenth and eighteenth centuries, with several new prose forms appearing in the periodicals that became popular with the emerging middle class — character sketches, satires, gothic tales, rogue stories, simple adventure stories, and vapid, sentimental sketches with predictable moral outcomes where the hero or heroine is rewarded, and the villain is punished. What is known as the modern short story did not appear until the early years of the nineteenth century. Its vitality was shaped by the spirit of the age, the Romantic movement in literature, which valued imagination and originality above all other qualities in writing.

This anthology begins with stories from the early nineteenth century, when printed short fictional narrative first emerged as a separate and recognizable literary form: carefully constructed prose works in which every word chosen in the structure of the plot, and every detail of description and characterization, contributes to a vivid and unified impression. The attempt of professional writers to create such an impression through short narrative developed nearly simultaneously in Europe and in America, with Nathaniel Hawthorne and Edgar Allan Poe two of our earliest authors to achieve success in the form. As the introductions to the various writers included in this anthology explain, the short story was explored by most of the great prose writers of the nineteenth century and the twentieth century. The form was developed into maturity in the work of Guy de Maupassant and Anton Chekhov in the last years of the nineteenth century. It flowered into its most intense expression in the stories of the great Modernist writers of the early twentieth century — James Joyce, D. H. Lawrence, Katherine Mansfield, Franz Kafka, and Isaac Babel, to name only a few of the great innovators who experimented with the structure and texture of literature and challenged its conventions. In our own time, the short story continues to flourish throughout the world in the work of many contemporary writers, even as fewer magazines print short fiction and the market for it diminishes.

All stories are created out of an author's personal act of vision, and the elements of fiction — plot, characters, setting, point of view, style, and theme — are set in motion by the impulse of the writer to use language to express the mystery and magic of real life. Without the act of human understanding, experience is "the worst kind of emptiness," wrote the short story writer Eudora Welty in her essay "Words into Fiction." The shape taken by the work of fiction as it is being written is only limited by the range and quality of the writer's mind; but when the story is completed, this shape must make its own impression on readers so that they feel some design in life, that is, some meaning communicated through the pattern of the story. Fiction created by the imagination of the writer for the imagination of the reader is an illusion come full circle, an illusion made by art to show an important human truth. If the story is well told, your imagination will be involved. If the story is a success, your imagination will be ignited.

To understand the effect of a story, you must understand the way the writer achieved it. Showing what life is like by finding words for human experience and organizing these words into a narrative pattern — transferring real or imagined events into fiction — gives the storyteller the advantage of revealing connections and coherence in experiences. This is the basic appeal of all storytelling. When writers go beyond this basic function and invent stories that ignite our imagination, they do so by touching us emotionally through language, by creating a pattern that enchants us, by evoking our feelings about the mysterious nature of experience. It is this enchantment, created by the writer's inspired use of the elements of short fiction to involve our emotions, that makes the miracle happen. It moves us to catch a glimpse of what life is *like* from its reflection in the story.

The Elements of Fiction

PLOT

The short story can be defined as a prose narrative usually involving one connected episode or a sequence of related events, so the element of plot may be seen as basic to this literary form. *Plot* is the action of the story. This means not only an action whose end a reader must not foresee if the story is to hold interest, but also an action whose end must appear inevitable (or be foreshadowed) from the start, if the story is to appear well crafted. The plot of a story usually involves a conflict or struggle between opposing forces, and the discerning reader can see it proceed in a pattern during the course of the narration. A plot always includes the basic pattern of a beginning, a middle, and an end: setting up the problem or conflict, introducing various complications that prolong suspense and make the struggle more meaningful, and finally resolving the conflict to a greater or lesser degree. But these stages may also be shaped by the writer into a complex structure that impresses the reader with its qualities of balance and proportion.

The first part of the plot, called the *exposition*, introduces characters, scene, time, and situation. The particular pattern of short fiction varies from story to story, of course, and from author to author. Hawthorne begins "Young Goodman Brown," for example, with only a few short paragraphs of exposition, the leave-taking between Goodman Brown and his wife Faith. Herman Melville devotes pages to exposition in his much longer story, "Bartleby the Scrivener," describing the lawyer, his two eccentric copyists, and his office boy before introducing the title character. The second part of the plot is called the *rising action*, the dramatization of events that complicate the situation and gradually intensify the conflict. In "Young Goodman Brown," Goodman Brown's walk through the forest with the devil, in which he meets Goody Cloyse and then hides to spy on the minister and the deacon, is the rising action of the story, culminating in the scene when Goodman Brown looks to heaven, hears a young woman's lamentations, and sees a pink ribbon flutter through the air and catch on the branch of a tree. After this, he shouts "My Faith is gone," and Hawthorne tells the reader that he has become "the chief horror of the scene."

From this point in the story, the narration proceeds to the third stage, the *climax* of the plot or *turning point* of the story, its emotional high point. Goodman Brown speeds through the forest and joins the devil's congregation inside the ring of fire formed by the four blazing pines. He stands be-side his wife and prepares to participate in an unholy communion, the scene illuminated by Hawthorne's descriptive powers. There Goodman Brown summons the courage to beseech his wife to "resist the Wicked One," the climax of the plot. The pace of the narration breaks off dramati-cally at this point, and in one sentence Hawthorne changes the scenery to show us Goodman Brown alone "amid calm night and solitude." Now begins the fourth stage of the narration, called the *falling action* of the plot, where the problem or conflict that was presented in the earlier sections pro-ceeds toward resolution. This last section of the plot, and the *conclusion* in the final paragraph, are comparatively brief in this story, balancing the short exposition at the beginning of the tale. Nevertheless, in these last parts of the story, Hawthorne is careful to settle all the unstable elements of the sit-uation and bring the sequence of related events to an end.

A story's ending often contains an element of surprise, just as the other four stages of narration engage the reader's curiosity and prolong his expec-tation of a satisfying conclusion. There is little surprise in finding Goodman Brown a "distrustful, if not a desperate man" after his fearful night in the forest, but Hawthorne gives the story a final, unexpected twist in the last sentence describing the funeral, when he writes that Goodman Brown's survivors "carved no hopeful verse upon his tombstone, for his dying hour was gloom." Brown's vision was *not* the final word, as the author suddenly makes clear. Hawthorne's continuation of the narrative to a point in time beyond his main character's death places the conflict that was dramatized in the story into a larger human context and reveals to the reader a deeper perception of what life is like.

Plot can work in any of several ways. It can be propelled by apparent accident of fate, as when the two mustachioed thieves appear out of no-where on a winter night in Nikolai Gogol's "The Overcoat" and steal Akakii Akakiievich's new overcoat off his back. It can be an outgrowth of a character's personality or drives, as in Montresor's insane scheme of revenge against Fortunato in Poe's "The Cask of Amontillado." Or it can be con-trolled by the setting, as in Stephen Crane's tale of a shipwrecked crew in "The Open Boat." Plot does not emerge only through the description of events in the story. It can also be carried forward in dialogue, as when Hawthorne introduces the characters, the time, and the situation through the conversation between Goodman Brown and his wife in the beginning of the story.

Regardless of the method, the goal is always the same: The writer of short stories must *show* the reader what is important through the dramatic action of the plot and the other elements of the story, and not just explicitly *tell* the reader what to think. Invention, not preaching, enchants the modern reader and sustains the illusion of reality in short fiction. Haw-thorne dramatizes his own final judgment of Goodman Brown by inventing the detail of his tombstone, not by concluding with an explicit, solemn announcement about the necessity of keeping faith in human nature alive. Of course Hawthorne is also telling us something by showing us the villagers' attitude toward Goodman Brown as revealed on the tombstone, but he maintains the important illusion that the story is continuing meanwhile. The plot must not cease to move forward, and it must always be interesting. The events of the story must unfold with the easy forward movement of an apparently endless silk handkerchief drawn from a skillful magician's innocent coat sleeve.

CHARACTER

The action of the plot is performed by the *characters* in the story, the persons who make something happen or produce an effect. (And not always just persons. Various authors have experimented with other animals, such as cows, cats, and bugs, and even with trees, chairs, and shoes, as characters — even as narrators — with varying degrees of success. But when we say *character*, we usually mean a person.) With a plot we do not ask only, What next? We also ask, Why? This is usually answered by the characters in the story, who are only plausible if they have reasons for doing what they do. The reader instinctively wants to connect the events of a story by more than their simple chronological sequence. A relationship between the events and the characters makes the story seem coherent.

How are the characters in a short story to be understood? Any discussion of characters tends to drift sooner or later into a value judgment, since our principles of definition and evaluation for fictional characters are based on the ones we use for real people, a topic of considerable controversy and confusion for most of us. The important distinction to remember is that we are reading about *fictional* characters in a short story, not real ones. We are on firmer ground in literary discussions when we analyze the writer's methods of characterization as well as the character's personality. We know that Montresor is a homicidal maniac in Poe's "The Cask of Amontillado," but merely pigeonholing his character in a neat category does not bring us very close to the miracle of horror that Poe accomplishes in the story. We can get this closeness more readily by relishing the language Poe uses in dialogue and description to show us the specific mental processes of his main character, which involves us emotionally in Montresor's plot for revenge.

In all successful fiction, characters come alive as individuals. They must materialize on the page, through the accumulation of details about their appearance, actions, and responses, as seen, heard, and felt physical realities. Hawthorne tells us little about the physical appearance of Goodman Brown except that he is young and newly married. We do not even know his first name — "Goodman" was used as a title of respect by the Puritans for those below the rank of gentleman. We know more about his wife — her name is Faith, she is pretty, and she wears pink ribbons on her cap. The lack of physical details about the main character in Hawthorne's story makes Goodman Brown less than flesh and blood to most readers. He remains an abstraction, the figure of a man on trial for his belief in good and evil. This is what Hawthorne intended. He was not trying to write a realistic narrative. Yet as we read the story we suspend our disbelief in the physical existence of the abstract character named Goodman Brown because his actions as a fictional "person" provoke our curiosity and his responses arouse our alarm. If he continues to interest us after we finish reading the story, it is because we are fascinated, like Hawthorne, with the moral dilemma that the narrative dramatizes.

Characters in fiction are sometimes called *round* or *flat* in literary discussions. For characters in a story to emerge as round, the reader must feel the play and pull of their alternative actions and responses to situations. If the reader sees the characters as capable of alternatives, then the characters become more real. As an abstraction, Goodman Brown never truly becomes a round character, but because he is on the brink of a significant change when the story begins, we think of him as more rounded than Faith. By comparison she is a flat character, a minor person on the periphery of the action of the story, without much dimension beyond her name and her pink ribbons. A truly round character is one whose essential nature changes and develops in the course of the story, like Ivan Ilych in Leo Tolstoy's "The Death of Ivan Ilych," who acts at the end of the story in a way that was not predictable from what we learned earlier about his personality and his past actions, yet is consistent with them.

Flat characters, though less psychologically complex than round characters, are not always inferior artistically. Nor is a character who changes during the course of the narration necessarily convincing as a round or psychologically developed character. Each writer of short fiction puts his or her own emphasis on character. Encountering stories in this anthology by writers of different historical periods, from different countries, or with different philosophical beliefs, an attentive reader can perceive that Anton Chekhov and Jorge Luis Borges, for example, are not developing characters in the same way in their stories. Chekhov, a great nineteenth-century realist, places the highest emphasis in his stories on character, believing that it determines our fate. Borges, a contemporary teller of philosophical tales, believes that our subjective nature as human beings makes it impossible for us to understand the essential riddle of human action, so he makes plot more important than character when he writes a story. Different fictional worlds make different demands on the reader, who realizes that the importance given to characterization by the different storytellers is an indication of their vision of life. Regardless of the emphasis on character, what is most important is the truth of the fictional character, flat or round. Avoiding *sentimentality* (emotional overindulgence) or *stereotyping* (generalized, oversimplified judgment) in the creation of the characters, the writer must be able to suggest enough complexity in the human situation to engage the emotions of the reader, or the story will not be a success.

SETTING

Setting is the place and time of the story. To set the scene in a story, the writer attempts to create in the reader's visual imagination the illusion of a solid world in which the story takes place. With a few deft strokes in the opening paragraph of "Young Goodman Brown," Hawthorne sketches a street of Salem village during Puritan times, but the mass of details about the physical landscape are not given to us until Goodman Brown enters the forest. Then Hawthorne paints a gloomy growth of "innumerable trunks and . . . thick boughs overhead" that serves as the main scene for his character's troubled journey. Sometimes the setting is merely the backdrop for the action, as it is while Goodman Brown talks with Faith in the first scene; at other times it is central to the action, as it becomes when Goodman Brown enters the forest.

When the writer locates the narrative in a physical setting, the reader is moved along step by step toward the acceptance of the fiction. The *external* reality of the setting is always an appearance, an illusion, a mirage of language as insubstantial as a shimmering oasis in a desert or a Puritan wilderness evoked in 1837 on the page of a young author's manuscript; yet this invented setting is essential if the reader is to be given the opportunity to glimpse a vision of truth about *internal* life from the characters and the plot. When Goodman Brown enters the dark, tangled world of the seventeenth-century forest surrounding Salem village, the attentive reader perceives that he really enters the dreary, evil world of his own mind, which has brought him to exchange the companionship of his young wife for the dubious attractions of his older, less trustworthy companion, the devil.

The setting of a story furnishes the location for the story's world of feeling, whether it is the different emotional associations awakened in the reader's mind by a Puritan forest in a Hawthorne story or by the stifling despotism of the Russian council office suggested in Gogol's "The Overcoat." A sense of place is essential if readers are to begin to engage themselves in the fictional characters' situations. Place helps make the characters seem real, but to be most effective, the setting must also have a dramatic use. It must be shown, or at least felt, to affect character or plot. The gloom of the Puritan forest increases the doubt and uncertainty in Goodman Brown's mind that he has taken the right path on his journey. The miserly wages paid to clerks in the council office make it a struggle and a sacrifice for Akakii Akakiievich to afford a decent, warm overcoat.

In the most basic sense, place is where writers have their roots. It provides the experience of life out of which they write. Hawthorne was rooted in the Puritan setting of many of his stories through his ancestral connections in Salem. Gogol knew at first hand about the arrogance of bureaucratic officials and the corruption of legal process in Russia. Selecting, choosing, combining, superimposing, and altering the details of the outside world in the creation of a story, the writer must exert his talent to make the reader see only the fictional world that emerges on the printed page, under the illusion that while the story unfolds, it is the real world itself.

POINT OF VIEW

The point of view of the narration always shapes our response to the characters and events presented in a story. From whose authority, whose point of view, is the story told? In one sense the answer is simple: the author's, of course. Even when a story is not autobiographical, or when it appears to be narrated objectively, the writer's point of view is always present in his use of language. Hawthorne's point of view toward his main character in "Young Goodman Brown," for instance, is not immediately apparent, but the careful reader will find it indicated close to the beginning of the tale. At first the exposition of the story is carefully manipulated so that we only know Hawthorne's attitude toward the young wife — we are told she has a "pretty head," and we are shown that she is attached to her husband, giving him a parting kiss and "peeping after him with a melancholy air" as he leaves the village. The words Hawthorne uses to tell us about Goodman Brown, on the other hand, are neutral for the most part. We know that he is fond of his wife, "for his heart smote him" as he left sight of her, but we are not told what Hawthorne thinks of him or his errand in the forest until we sense a subtle irony in the description of Goodman Brown's thoughts while turning the corner by the meeting-house.

Then Hawthorne tells us that Goodman Brown promises himself that after one night away from Faith he will cling to her skirts and follow her to heaven. Hawthorne adds drily, "With this excellent resolve for the future, Goodman Brown felt himself justified in making more haste on his present evil purpose." Here Hawthorne's point of view is evident for the first time in giving the sentence a double meaning. Goodman Brown thinks he has justified his errand to himself with his "excellent resolve," but Hawthorne sees his character's resolution as a form of rationalization, a sign of his moral weakness. Hawthorne lets us know his point of view through the irony implied in writing "this *excellent* resolve," the opposite of what he actually means, knowing it to be only a feeble rationalization. He makes this clearer at the end of the sentence by referring explicitly to his "evil purpose."

A reader who is attentive to the details and nuances of language in a short story, as in this ironic sentence from "Young Goodman Brown," can probably sense the author's point of view, especially if, like Hawthorne, the author is making a moral judgment, which modern writers often do not do. In the contemporary author Milan Kundera's "The Hitchhiking Game," a story about two lovers driving along a road on their way to their summer vacation, the reader must search the text as closely as a radar scan to understand Kundera's attitude toward his subject, since it is not immediately clear from either the dialogue or his description of the incidents.

As a specific literary term, the words *point of view* have another meaning, referring to the way the story is told. In giving an account of the events in a story, the author must decide whether to employ a first-person narrator, using the pronoun "I," or a third-person narrator, using the pronouns "he," "she," and "they." (The second-person narrator, "you," is rarely used, since a forced identification of the reader with the fictional world is usually difficult to maintain successfully.) If the chosen point of view is not the right one for the complete dramatic ordering of the subject, the narrative will not reveal all its possibilities to the writer, and the pattern of the story will be incomplete. If Hawthorne had chosen to tell his story from the point of view of Goodman Brown, for example, using the first-person narrator to describe how an evening in the forest with the devil ruined his life forever, it is likely that the resulting story would have struck the reader as the gloomy ruminations of a religious fanatic. It would also necessarily have ended with Goodman Brown's death, and its larger meaning would not have emerged so explicitly.

A useful scheme that classifies the most frequently used ways of telling stories is to group them into two major categories:

First-person narrator (narrator a participant in the story)
    a. A major character
    b. A minor character
Third-person narrator (narrator a nonparticipant in the story)
    a. Omniscient — seeing into all characters
    b. Limited Omniscient — seeing into one or two characters

First-Person Narrator

When the narrator is one of the characters in the story, he or she can be either a minor or a major character in the action. Poe's "The Cask of Amontillado" and Turgenev's "Byezhin Prairie," for example, are both first-person narratives; but in Poe's tale the narrator is the central character, and in Turgenev's the narrator is placed on the outskirts of the story, which only begins to emerge as he listens to the conversation of the boys he meets on the prairie during the night. A first-person narrator can move freely within the fictional world created by the writer, and he can approach other fictional characters as closely as one human being can approach another, but he has no way of arriving at an understanding of these characters except by his observation of what they say and do. By making his narrator a major character in the action, Poe intensifies Montresor's insane behavior, showing us his continued imperviousness to the horror of what he is doing.

Turgenev's narrator, on the other hand, is less completely realized as a personality. His shadowy character fits his role as an observer in the story.

The authority of a first-person narrator is limited, though it is immediate and compelling as far as it goes. He is an eyewitness. He can also summarize less important events or back off from the immediate scene and meditate on its significance, since he is usually telling a story that happened in the past, but his meditations, like Montresor's, are not always trustworthy. The biased report of the first-person narrator must have a dramatic significance in the story, since there is often a discrepancy between the way he sees characters and events, and the reader's sense of what really happened. At the end of "The Cask of Amontillado," Montresor says that his heart "grew sick — on account of the dampness of the catacombs." The reader may perceive the truth differently, and feel that Montresor has at least subconsciously realized the horror of what he has just done to Fortunato.

Third-Person Narrator

The third-person narrator is not a participant in the story. There are two general kinds of third-person narration. The *omniscient* point of view is most clearly apparent in fairy tales beginning "Once upon a time," when the teller knows everything there is to know about all of the characters, both inside and out — what they think and feel as well as what they do. The great virtue of this third-person narration is the sense it gives the reader of the broad scope of human life. This is achieved by a continual shifting of focus from the close view to a larger perspective. In the hands of a master like Hawthorne, a feeling for the complexity of human life emerges through the controlling authority of the omniscient narrator. When this type of narration is used by a writer who is also a genius at the realistic rendering of experience, like Tolstoy in "The Death of Ivan Ilych," the powerful combination of the author's great imaginative ability and his moral genius invests the various characters and scenes with such reality that we accept them unquestionably.

Limited omniscient narration usually confines itself to revealing the thoughts of one or two characters. This method was first developed in fiction by Gustave Flaubert, who exchanged the distancing of "once upon a time" (with its implied moral view) for an interior, more subjective view of characters and events. Flaubert's story "A Simple Heart" is an example of limited omniscient narration, concentrating on one character. Flaubert's omniscient narrator also sticks to *impartial* (not judgmental) *omniscience;* he tells the story without really evaluating or commenting on the actions, which speak for themselves. Henry James formulated another theory about limited omniscient narration. He referred to certain characters in his stories as the "central intelligence," a term that sounds today as if it would fit best in a James Bond thriller. Stories told by this method of narration are not always about a single central character. They do, however, involve a character, placed at the center of the story's action, through whose "intelligence" the author evaluates everything that happens in the story, including what happens to and within that character. In this kind of story, like James Joyce's "The Dead," this character's psyche is the stage for the drama. Having established this single evaluating intelligence, the writer may range over the whole cast of characters and dramatize their views of the action. They will, however, always be perceived through or measured against the thoughts and feelings of the central intelligence, who may not understand what is going on at the time, but will finally perceive the truth. In Joyce's "The Dead," the central character Gabriel Conroy sees himself as a very different man at the end of the story from the fellow he fancied himself at the beginning. The actual drama of the story is not the series of events described, but rather his growth in moral awareness.

The stories of Stephen Crane are another variant of the limited omniscient point of view. The narration may at any given moment in a Crane story reveal a different character's perceptions and feelings. In "The Open Boat," Crane renders the sensations of the various participants in the shipwreck, constantly changing his point of view to borrow the eyes, ears, tactile senses of all four men in the boat. If the war correspondent has the last word in the story, it is because the author finds him the best person to say what the pattern of the story requires at this point.

Various types of narration can be classified into tidy groups, but the different ways of telling stories available to writers are always more flexible than the categories imply. Different points of view are not always mutually exclusive within a story, either. Guy de Maupassant shifts point of view in the opening pages of "Miss Harriet," and Franz Kafka, who uses Gregor Samsa as his "central intelligence" through most of "The Metamorphosis," continues the story well beyond Gregor's death. What is important is not the theory of how short stories are constructed, but the story itself. Awareness of an abstract pattern of narration, whether first-person or third-person, helps the reader become sensitive to the pattern of language that is the story, because the way the story is written is an essential part of what it is saying.

STYLE

Style is the language the author uses in his narration. It is made up of various topics, including the writer's *tone*, or the way he uses words to convey unstated attitudes. The tone of dry restraint in Hawthorne's comment about Goodman Brown's "excellent resolve" is an example of the way tone contributes to his dignified, lofty prose style. An understated *irony*, drawing attention to the differences between what is said and what really happens, helps him keep an emotional distance from his characters suitable to the level of abstraction he has created in the narrative. This tone is completely unlike the less formal tone of a writer like Sherwood Anderson, who uses the language of everyday speech to set up a feeling of intimacy with the reader. This suggests a sympathy for the fictional characters in his realistic stories about frustrated, small-town lives, like "Hands" and "Death in the Woods." (Be careful in judging the tone of stories that have been translated into English from foreign languages. It is nearly impossible for a translation to capture the exact tone of the original language, even if it renders most other details of the story accurately.)

Another aspect of a writer's literary style is the use of *symbols*, a type of figurative, not literal language. A symbol is usually defined as something that stands for something else. In the final memory of a story, after closing the book and thinking about it, the reader will often recall the author's use of symbols most vividly — the way language can suggest deeper meaning by bringing together different images to elicit emotional responses. Sometimes the entire story will seem to exist in the reader's imagination more on an abstract, symbolic level than on a realistic level. "Young Goodman Brown" is such a story. Hawthorne employs such an extended use of symbols throughout the story that the narrative becomes an *allegory*, with a whole system of correspondences of characters and events to mythical religious experience. Shirley Jackson's "The Lottery" is another such completely symbolic story, although its point is less explicit than Hawthorne's. Most readers take Kafka's "The Metamorphosis" both literally and symbolically, not precisely sure what the monstrous insect symbolizes.

Symbols are not always understood the same way by different readers. Faith's pink ribbons in "Young Goodman Brown," an apparently realistic detail in an otherwise clearly allegorical story (the devil has a walking stick that turns into a snake before Goodman Brown's eyes), may symbolize her youth and innocence to one reader, and her femininity and coquettishness to another. She is such an abstract character that either interpretation is possible; we can never know for sure whether she actually was present at the witches' coven in the forest, or whether her presence there was part of her husband's hallucination while she spent the night quietly at home in her own bed. Regardless of how the symbol of the ribbons is interpreted, both readers experience them as a dominant image in the dark, dreary landscape of Hawthorne's fiction. Symbols are more eloquent as a specific image — a visual idea — than any paraphrase into language; this is the source of their appeal to storytellers.

THEME

Theme is a generalization about the meaning of a story. While the plot of a story can be summarized by saying what happened in the action (a young Puritan husband loses his faith in God and mankind after attending a witches' coven), the theme is an even more general statement of the meaning of the story (losing faith destroys a person's life). It is often difficult for readers to find words to describe what a story means. Sometimes out of frustration, after many futile minutes of trying to "boil down" a story to a one-sentence essence, the words that come irresistibly to mind are the ones written in another context by the American poet Archibald MacLeish: "A poem should not mean/But be."

What makes the statement of a theme so difficult is that the theme must be true to any and all of the specific details in the narrative. This is the test to apply to a theme, once it has been stated. Reading a summary of the plot or a statement of the theme does not mean that you understand a story and so can skip reading it, however. The theme or meaning of any good story is inseparable from the language of the complete story. In fact, the way the writer fleshes out a dramatic structure to embody the theme is, in the final sense, the most important achievement of the story, infinitely more important than the bare theme standing and shivering alone in its unconvincing nakedness on a sheet of notebook paper. A reader who does not know this should try to recreate a story from memory after writing a one-sentence summary of its theme.

Most writers do not like to tell what their stories are "about." Even when they do, as Flannery O'Connor did in her intelligent explanation of the theme of her story "A Good Man Is Hard to Find," some readers agree intellectually but not emotionally with the writer's interpretation of the work. O'Connor said that she understood the story might be read in different ways by different people, but as for her, she could only have written it with the one meaning she had in mind. Theme comes last in a discussion of the elements of fiction because all the other elements must be accounted for in determining it. The structure and theme of a story are fused like the body and soul of a reader; their interaction creates a living pattern. While the various actions of the plot must strike the reader as realistic and inevitable, the complete truth that it reveals is in essence indefinable and untranslatable outside the story. Trying to arrive at the theme of a story teaches us that no statement of it can be final, except the story itself. As Leo Tolstoy once told a friend:

> The most important thing in a work of art is that it should have a kind of focus, i.e., there should be some place where all the rays meet or from which they issue. *And this focus must not be able to be completely explained in words.* This indeed is one of the significant facts about a true work of art — that its content in its entirety can be expressed only by itself.

Many readers tend to look for moral judgments about life when they think about the meaning of a story, but literature does not demand that they do. It is possible that an interesting, well-constructed story will also contain a meaning with moral implications, as Hawthorne's "Young Goodman Brown" does. It is equally possible that an interesting, well-constructed story will be without a moral, existing as a complete and satisfactory aesthetic pattern in itself. Ultimately, all great literature makes a statement beyond morality. The innate impulse to create a story does not originate in an awareness of a moral sense or a conscience. It arises from the mysterious and inexplicable urge to *create*.

Reading Short Stories

Vladimir Nabokov once described the best temperament for a reader to develop as being "a combination of the artistic and the scientific one. The enthusiastic artist alone is apt to be too subjective in his attitude toward a book, and so a scientific coolness of judgment will temper the intuitive heat." Read a story first for the pleasure of reading it; bring out your "scientific coolness" when you study it a second time. Then you can use Nabokov's formula to test the *quality* of a literary text, whether it merges "the precision of poetry with the intuition of science." The ideal reader should keep a little aloof, a little detached when reading the story a second time. Cherish the details that create the pattern within the story, and wait (if you are fortunate) for the sensual and intellectual pleasure that results when you begin to understand its individual magic. Once upon a time another wise man said that the great majority of people need more often to be reminded than instructed. It may be necessary, as the last word, to remind you to read each story in its entirety. The best way to read short stories so that they have a chance to enchant you is to give them your full attention and read carefully, without skipping, straight through to the end.

PART ONE

THE STORIES

NATHANIEL HAWTHORNE (1804–1864), *the novelist and short story writer, was born into a distinguished family in Salem, Massachusetts. His Puritan great-grandfather had been a judge who persecuted the Quakers; his grandfather had been one of the judges who presided over the infamous Salem witch trials; and his father was a sea captain who died in the East Indies when Nathaniel was four years old. After the death of the father, the family led a secluded, pious life. After his graduation from Bowdoin College in Brunswick, Maine, in 1825, Hawthorne, who had already decided to become a writer, returned to Salem. He lived frugally at home, undergoing a self-imposed literary apprenticeship, studying literature and the legends and history of his native New England. He also wrote short stories, which he tried to sell to American magazines. Magazines of the time were mostly interested in publishing ghost stories, Indian legends, and "village tales" based on historical anecdotes; Hawthorne (like Edgar Allan Poe at the same time) brought his powers of genius to the young literary form of the popular magazine story and raised it above the conventional level that most readers had come to expect.*

Hawthorne's first collection of stories, Twice-Told Tales, was published in 1837, and he published another collection, Mosses from an Old Manse, in 1846. That year he stopped writing and took more lucrative employment as surveyor of customs for the port of Salem. This was a political appointment, and after the Whigs won the presidency in 1848, Hawthorne — a Democrat — found himself out of a job in 1849. He returned to writing fiction, and sketched his "official life" at the Custom House in introducing his novel The Scarlet Letter in 1850. He also wrote three other novels — The House of the Seven Gables (1851), The Blithedale Romance (1852), and The Marble Faun (1860) — several books for children, and another collection of tales.

In "The Custom House," Hawthorne suggested that his chosen life as a writer would not have impressed his Puritan ancestors:

> *"What is he?" murmurs one grey shadow of my forefathers to the other. "A writer of story-books! What kind of business in life, what manner of glorifying God, or being serviceable to mankind in his day and generation, may that be? Why, the degenerate fellow might as well have been a fiddler!" Such are the compliments bandied between my great-grandsires and myself across the gulf of time! And yet, let them scorn me as they will, strong traits of their nature have intertwined themselves with mine.*

Despite Hawthorne's portrait of himself as an object of misunderstanding and his earlier sketches about the futility of writing (which include "The Devil in Manuscript"), he was recognized by contemporaries like

Edgar Allan Poe as a "genius of a very lofty order." Hawthorne wrote about 120 short tales and sketches in addition to his novels. His notebooks are filled with ideas for stories. They show that his imagination was fired more by a curious passage in his reading or by an abstract idea from one of his speculative reveries than by an anecdote he had been told or by detailed observation of a "real" individual. In his writing Hawthorne demonstrated what he himself called "an inveterate love of allegory," as in the story "Young Goodman Brown." If he inherited the old Puritan custom of using explicit moral imagery to reveal human guilt and human evil, he also dramatized his own sense of humanity in his fiction, often finding a transcendent meaning in physical objects, using symbols to express what would otherwise be inexpressible.

Nathaniel Hawthorne

ಐಐ

Young Goodman Brown

Young Goodman Brown came forth at sunset into the street at Salem village; but put his head back, after crossing the threshold, to exchange a parting kiss with his young wife. And Faith, as the wife was aptly named, thrust her own pretty head into the street, letting the wind play with the pink ribbons of her cap while she called to Goodman Brown.

"Dearest heart," whispered she, softly and rather sadly, when her lips were close to his ear, "prithee put off your journey until sunrise and sleep in your own bed to-night. A lone woman is troubled with such dreams and such thoughts that she's afeared of herself sometimes. Pray tarry with me this night, dear husband, of all nights in the year."

"My love and my Faith," replied young Goodman Brown, "of all nights in the year, this one night must I tarry away from thee. My journey, as thou callest it, forth and back again, must needs be done 'twixt now and sunrise. What, my sweet, pretty wife, dost thou doubt me already, and we but three months married?"

"Then God bless you!" said Faith, with the pink ribbons; "and may you find all well when you come back."

"Amen!" cried Goodman Brown. "Say thy prayers, dear Faith, and go to bed at dusk, and no harm will come to thee."

So they parted; and the young man pursued his way until, being about to turn the corner by the meeting-house, he looked back and saw the head of Faith still peeping after him with a melancholy air, in spite of her pink ribbons.

"Poor little Faith!" thought he, for his heart smote him. "What a wretch am I to leave her on such an errand! She talks of dreams, too. Methought as she spoke there was trouble in her face, as if a dream had warned her what work is to be done to-night. But no, no; 't would kill her to think it. Well, she's a blessed angel on earth; and after this one night I'll cling to her skirts and follow her to heaven."

With this excellent resolve for the future, Goodman Brown felt himself justified in making more haste on his present evil purpose. He had taken a dreary road, darkened by all the gloomiest trees of the forest, which barely stood aside to let the narrow path creep through, and closed immediately behind. It was all as lonely as could be; and there is this peculiarity in such a solitude, that the traveller knows not who may be concealed by the innumerable trunks and the thick boughs overhead; so that with lonely footsteps he may yet be passing through an unseen multitude.

"There may be a devilish Indian behind every tree," said Goodman Brown to himself; and he glanced fearfully behind him as he added, "What if the devil himself should be at my very elbow!"

His head being turned back, he passed a crook of the road, and, looking forward again, beheld the figure of a man, in grave and decent attire, seated at the foot of an old tree. He arose at Goodman Brown's approach and walked onward side by side with him.

"You are late, Goodman Brown," said he. "The clock of the Old South was striking as I came through Boston, and that is full fifteen minutes agone."

"Faith kept me back a while," replied the young man, with a tremor in his voice, caused by the sudden appearance of his companion, though not wholly unexpected.

It was now deep dusk in the forest, and deepest in that part of it where these two were journeying. As nearly as could be discerned, the second traveller was about fifty years old, apparently in the same rank of life as Goodman Brown, and bearing a considerable resemblance to him, though perhaps more in expression than features. Still they might have been taken for father and son. And yet, though the elder person was as simply clad as the younger, and as simple in manner too, he had an indescribable air of one who knew the world, and who would not have felt abashed at the governor's dinner table or in King William's court, were it possible that his affairs should call him thither. But the only thing about him that could be fixed upon as remarkable was his staff, which bore the likeness of a great black snake, so curiously wrought that it might almost be seen to twist and wriggle itself like a living serpent. This, of course, must have been an ocular deception, assisted by the uncertain light.

"Come, Goodman Brown," cried his fellow-traveller, "this is a dull pace for the beginning of a journey. Take my staff, if you are so soon weary."

"Friend," said the other, exchanging his slow pace for a full stop, "having kept covenant by meeting thee here, it is my purpose now to return whence I came. I have scruples touching the matter thou wot'st of."

"Sayest thou so?" replied he of the serpent, smiling apart. "Let us walk on, nevertheless, reasoning as we go; and if I convince thee not thou shalt turn back. We are but a little way in the forest yet."

"Too far! too far!" exclaimed the goodman, unconsciously resuming his walk. "My father never went into the woods on such an errand, nor his father before him. We have been a race of honest men and good Christians since the days of the martyrs; and shall I be the first of the name of Brown that ever took this path and kept" —

"Such company, thou wouldst say," observed the elder person, interpreting his pause. "Well said, Goodman Brown! I have been as well acquainted with your family as with ever a one among the Puritans; and that's no trifle to say. I helped your grandfather, the constable, when he lashed the Quaker woman so smartly through the streets of Salem; and it was I that brought your father a pitch-pine knot, kindled at my own hearth, to set fire to an Indian village, in King Philip's war. They were my good friends, both; and many a pleasant walk have we had along this path, and returned merrily after midnight. I would fain be friends with you for their sake."

"If it be as thou sayest," replied Goodman Brown, "I marvel they never spoke of these matters; or, verily, I marvel not, seeing that the least rumor of the sort would have driven them from New England. We are a people of prayer, and good works to boot, and abide no such wickedness."

"Wickedness or not," said the traveller with the twisted staff, "I have a very general acquaintance here in New England. The deacons of many a church have drunk the communion wine with me; the selectmen of divers towns make me their chairman; and a majority of the Great and General Court are firm supporters of my interest. The governor and I, too — But these are state secrets."

"Can this be so?" cried Goodman Brown, with a stare of amazement at his undisturbed companion. "Howbeit, I have nothing to do with the governor and council; they have their own ways, and are no rule for a simple husbandman like me. But, were I to go on with thee, how should I meet the eye of that good old man, our minister, at Salem village? Oh, his voice would make me tremble both Sabbath day and lecture day."

Thus far the elder traveller had listened with due gravity; but now burst into a fit of irrepressible mirth, shaking himself so violently that his snake-like staff actually seemed to wriggle in sympathy.

"Ha! ha! ha!" shouted he again and again; then composing himself, "Well, go on, Goodman Brown, go on; but, prithee, don't kill me with laughing."

"Well, then, to end the matter at once," said Goodman Brown, considerably nettled, "there is my wife, Faith. It would break her dear little heart; and I'd rather break my own."

"Nay, if that be the case," answered the other, "e'en go thy ways, Goodman Brown. I would not for twenty old women like the one hobbling before us that Faith should come to any harm."

As he spoke he pointed his staff at a female figure on the path, in whom Goodman Brown recognized a very pious and exemplary dame, who had taught him his catechism in youth, and was still his moral and spiritual adviser, jointly with the minister and Deacon Gookin.

"A marvel, truly that Goody Cloyse should be so far in the wilderness at nightfall," said he. "But with your leave, friend, I shall take a cut through the woods until we have left this Christian woman behind. Being a stranger to you, she might ask whom I was consorting with and whither I was going."

"Be it so," said his fellow-traveller. "Betake you to the woods, and let me keep the path."

Accordingly the young man turned aside, but took care to watch his companion, who advanced softly along the road until he had come within a staff's length of the old dame. She, meanwhile, was making the best of her way, with singular speed for so aged a woman, and mumbling some indistinct words — a prayer, doubtless — as she went. The traveller put forth his staff and touched her withered neck with what seemed the serpent's tail.

"The devil!" screamed the pious old lady.

"Then Goody Cloyse knows her old friend?" observed the traveller, confronting her and leaning on his writhing stick.

"Ah, forsooth, and is it your worship indeed?" cried the good dame. "Yea, truly is it, and in the very image of my old gossip, Goodman Brown, the grandfather of the silly fellow that now is. But — would your worship believe it? — my broomstick hath strangely disappeared, stolen, as I suspect, by that unhanged witch, Goody Cory, and that, too, when I was all anointed with the juice of smallage, and cinquefoil, and wolf's bane" —

"Mingled with fine wheat and the fat of a new-born babe," said the shape of old Goodman Brown.

"Ah, your worship knows the recipe," cried the old lady, cackling aloud. "So, as I was saying, being all ready for the meeting, and no horse to ride on, I made up my mind to foot it; for they tell me there is a nice young man to be taken into communion to-night. But now your good worship will lend me your arm, and we shall be there in a twinkling."

"That can hardly be," answered her friend. "I may not spare you my arm, Goody Cloyse; but here is my staff, if you will."

So saying, he threw it down at her feet, where, perhaps, it assumed life, being one of the rods which its owner had formerly lent to the Egyptian magi. Of this fact, however, Goodman Brown could not take cognizance.

He had cast up his eyes in astonishment, and, looking down again, beheld neither Goody Cloyse nor the serpentine staff, but his fellow-traveller alone, who waited for him as calmly as if nothing had happened.

"That old woman taught me my catechism," said the young man; and there was a world of meaning in this simple comment.

They continued to walk onward, while the elder traveller exhorted his companion to make good speed and persevere in the path, discoursing so aptly that his arguments seemed rather to spring up in the bosom of his auditor than to be suggested by himself. As they went, he plucked a branch of maple to serve for a walking stick, and began to strip it of the twigs and little boughs, which were wet with evening dew. The moment his fingers touched them they became strangely withered and dried up as with a week's sunshine. Thus the pair proceeded, at a good free pace, until suddenly, in a gloomy hollow of the road, Goodman Brown sat himself down on the stump of a tree and refused to go any farther.

"Friend," he said, stubbornly, "my mind is made up. Not another step will I budge on this errand. What if a wretched old woman do choose to go to the devil when I thought she was going to heaven: is that any reason why I should quit my dear Faith and go after her?"

"You will think better of this by and by," said his acquaintance, composedly. "Sit here and rest yourself a while; and when you feel like moving again, there is my staff to help you along."

Without more words, he threw his companion the maple stick, and was as speedily out of sight as if he had vanished into the deepening gloom. The young man sat a few moments by the roadside, applauding himself greatly, and thinking with how clear a conscience he should meet the minister in his morning walk, nor shrink from the eye of good old Deacon Gookin. And what calm sleep would be his that very night, which was to have been spent so wickedly, but so purely and sweetly now, in the arms of Faith! Amidst these pleasant and praiseworthy meditations, Goodman Brown heard the tramp of horses along the road, and deemed it advisable to conceal himself within the verge of the forest, conscious of the guilty purpose that had brought him thither, though now so happily turned from it.

On came the hoof tramps and the voices of the riders, two grave old voices, conversing soberly as they drew near. These mingled sounds appeared to pass along the road, within a few yards of the young man's hiding-place; but, owing doubtless to the depth of the gloom at that particular spot, neither the travellers nor their steeds were visible. Though their figures brushed the small boughs by the wayside, it could not be seen that they intercepted, even for a moment, the faint gleam from the strip of bright sky athwart which they must have passed. Goodman Brown alternately crouched and stood on tiptoe, pulling aside the branches and thrusting forth his head as far as he durst without discerning so much as a shadow. It vexed him the more, because he could have sworn, were such a thing possible, that he recognized the voices of the minister and Deacon Gookin, jogging along quietly, as they were wont to do, when bound to some ordination or ecclesiastical council. While yet within hearing, one of the riders stopped to pluck a switch.

"Of the two, reverend sir," said the voice like the deacon's, "I had rather miss an ordination dinner than to-night's meeting. They tell me that some of our community are to be here from Falmouth and beyond, and others from Connecticut and Rhode Island, besides several of the Indian powwows, who, after their fashion, know almost as much deviltry as the best of us. Moreover, there is a goodly young woman to be taken into communion."

"Mighty well, Deacon Gookin!" replied the solemn old tones of the minister. "Spur up, or we shall be late. Nothing can be done, you know, until I get on the ground."

The hoofs clattered again; and the voices, talking so strangely in the empty air, passed on through the forest, where no church had ever been gathered or solitary Christian prayed. Whither, then, could these holy men be journeying so deep into the heathen wilderness? Young Goodman Brown caught hold of a tree for support, being ready to sink down on the ground, faint and overburdened with the heavy sickness of his heart. He looked up to the sky, doubting whether there really was a heaven above him. Yet there was the blue arch, and the stars brightening in it.

"With heaven above and Faith below, I will yet stand firm against the devil!" cried Goodman Brown.

While he still gazed upward into the deep arch of the firmament and had lifted his hands to pray, a cloud, though no wind was stirring, hurried across the zenith and hid the brightening stars. The blue sky was still visible, except directly overhead, where this black mass of cloud was sweeping swiftly northward. Aloft in the air, as if from the depths of the cloud, came a confused and doubtful sound of voices. Once the listener fancied that he could distinguish the accents of towns-people of his own, men and women, both pious and ungodly, many of whom he had met at the communion table, and had seen others rioting at the tavern. The next moment, so indistinct were the sounds, he doubted whether he had heard aught but the murmur of the old forest, whispering without a wind. Then came a stronger swell of those familiar tones, heard daily in the sunshine at Salem village, but never until now from a cloud of night. There was one voice, of a young woman, uttering lamentations, yet with an uncertain sorrow, and entreating for some favor, which, perhaps, it would grieve her to obtain; and all the unseen multitude, both saints and sinners, seemed to encourage her onward.

"Faith!" shouted Goodman Brown, in a voice of agony and desperation; and the echoes of the forest mocked him, crying, "Faith! Faith!" as if bewildered wretches were seeking her all through the wilderness.

The cry of grief, rage, and terror was yet piercing the night, when the unhappy husband held his breath for a response. There was a scream, drowned immediately in a louder murmur of voices, fading into far-off laughter, as the dark cloud swept away, leaving the clear and silent sky above Goodman Brown. But something fluttered lightly down through the air and caught on the branch of a tree. The young man seized it, and beheld a pink ribbon.

"My Faith is gone!" cried he after one stupefied moment. "There is no good on earth; and sin is but a name. Come, devil; for to thee is this world given."

And, maddened with despair, so that he laughed loud and long, did Goodman Brown grasp his staff and set forth again, at such a rate that he seemed to fly along the forest path rather than to walk or run. The road grew wilder and drearier and more faintly traced, and vanished at length, leaving him in the heart of the dark wilderness, still rushing onward with the instinct that guides mortal man to evil. The whole forest was peopled with frightful sounds — the creaking of the trees, the howling of wild beasts, and the yell of Indians; while sometimes the wind tolled like a distant church bell, and sometimes gave a broad roar around the traveller, as if all Nature were laughing him to scorn. But he was himself the chief horror of the scene, and shrank not from its other horrors.

"Ha! ha! ha!" roared Goodman Brown when the wind laughed at him. "Let us hear which will laugh loudest. Think not to frighten me with your deviltry. Come witch, come wizard, come Indian powwow, come devil himself, and here comes Goodman Brown. You may as well fear him as he fear you."

In truth, all through the haunted forest there could be nothing more frightful than the figure of Goodman Brown. On he flew among the black pines, brandishing his staff with frenzied gestures, now giving vent to an inspiration of horrid blasphemy, and now shouting forth such laughter as set all the echoes of the forest laughing like demons around him. The fiend in his own shape is less hideous than when he rages in the breast of man. Thus sped the demoniac on his course, until, quivering among the trees, he saw a red light before him, as when the felled trunks and branches of a clearing have been set on fire, and throw up their lurid blaze against the sky, at the hour of midnight. He paused, in a lull of the tempest that had driven him onward, and heard the swell of what seemed a hymn, rolling solemnly from a distance with the weight of many voices. He knew the tune; it was a familiar one in the choir of the village meeting-house. The verse died heavily away, and was lengthened by a chorus, not of human voices, but of all the sounds of the benighted wilderness pealing in awful harmony together. Goodman Brown cried out, and his cry was lost to his own ear by its unison with the cry of the desert.

In the interval of silence he stole forward until the light glared full upon his eyes. At one extremity of an open space, hemmed in by the dark wall of the forest, arose a rock, bearing some rude, natural resemblance either to an altar or a pulpit, and surrounded by four blazing pines, their tops aflame, their stems untouched, like candles at an evening meeting. The mass of foliage that had overgrown the summit of the rock was all on fire, blazing high into the night and fitfully illuminating the whole field. Each pendent twig and leafy festoon was in a blaze. As the red light arose and fell, a numerous congregation alternately shone forth, then disappeared in shadow, and again grew, as it were, out of the darkness, peopling the heart of the solitary woods at once.

"A grave and dark-clad company," quoth Goodman Brown.

In truth they were such. Among them, quivering to and fro between gloom and splendor, appeared faces that would be seen next day at the council board of the province, and others which, Sabbath after Sabbath, looked devoutly heavenward, and benignantly over the crowded pews, from the holiest pulpits in the land. Some affirm that the lady of the governor was there. At least there were high dames well known to her, and wives of honored husbands, and widows, a great multitude, and ancient maidens, all of excellent repute, and fair young girls, who trembled lest their mothers should espy them. Either the sudden gleams of light flashing over the obscure field bedazzled Goodman Brown, or he recognized a score of the church members of Salem village famous for their especial sanctity. Good old Deacon Gookin had arrived, and waited at the skirts of that venerable saint, his revered pastor. But, irreverently consorting with these grave, reputable, and pious people, these elders of the church, these chaste dames and dewy virgins, there were men of dissolute lives and women of spotted fame, wretches given over to all mean and filthy vice, and suspected even of horrid crimes. It was strange to see that the good shrank not from the wicked, nor were the sinners abashed by the saints. Scattered also among their pale-faced enemies were the Indian priests, or powwows, who had often scared their native forest with more hideous incantations than any known to English witchcraft.

"But where is Faith?" thought Goodman Brown; and, as hope came into his heart, he trembled.

Another verse of the hymn arose, a slow and mournful strain, such as the pious love, but joined to words which expressed all that our nature can conceive of sin, and darkly hinted at far more. Unfathomable to mere mortals is the lore of fiends. Verse after verse was sung; and still the chorus of the desert swelled between like the deepest tone of a mighty organ; and with the final peal of that dreadful anthem there came a sound, as if the roaring wind, the rushing streams, the howling beasts, and every other voice of the unconcerted wilderness were mingling and according with the voice of guilty man in homage to the prince of all. The four blazing pines threw up a loftier flame, and obscurely discovered shapes and visages of horror on the smoke wreaths above the impious assembly. At the same moment the fire on the rock shot redly forth and formed a glowing arch above its base,

where now appeared a figure. With reverence be it spoken, the figure bore
no slight similitude, both in garb and manner, to some grave divine of the
New England churches.

"Bring forth the converts!" cried a voice that echoed through the field
and rolled into the forest.

At the word, Goodman Brown stepped forth from the shadow of the
trees and approached the congregation, with whom he felt a loathful brotherhood by the sympathy of all that was wicked in his heart. He could have
well-nigh sworn that the shape of his own dead father beckoned him to advance, looking downward from a smoke wreath, while a woman, with dim
features of despair, threw out her hand to warn him back. Was it his
mother? But he had no power to retreat one step, nor to resist, even in
thought, when the minister and good old Deacon Gookin seized his arms
and led him to the blazing rock. Thither came also the slender form of a
veiled female, led between Goody Cloyse, that pious teacher of the catechism, and Martha Carrier, who had received the devil's promise to be
queen of hell. A rampant hag was she. And there stood the proselytes beneath the canopy of fire.

"Welcome, my children," said the dark figure, "to the communion of
your race. Ye have found thus young your nature and your destiny. My
children, look behind you!"

They turned; and flashing forth, as it were, in a sheet of flame, the
fiend worshippers were seen; the smile of welcome gleamed darkly on every
visage.

"There," resumed the sable form, "are all whom ye have reverenced
from youth. Ye deemed them holier than yourselves and shrank from your
own sin, contrasting it with their lives of righteousness and prayerful aspirations heavenward. Yet here are they all in my worshipping assembly. This
night it shall be granted you to know their secret deeds: how hoary-bearded
elders of the church have whispered wanton words to the young maids of
their households; how many a woman, eager for widows' weeds, has given
her husband a drink at bedtime and let him sleep his last sleep in her
bosom; how beardless youths have made haste to inherit their fathers'
wealth; and how fair damsels — blush not, sweet ones — have dug little
graves in the garden, and bidden me, the sole guest, to an infant's funeral.
By the sympathy of your human hearts for sin ye shall scent out all the
places — whether in church, bedchamber, street, field, or forest — where
crime has been committed, and shall exult to behold the whole earth one
stain of guilt, one mighty blood spot. Far more than this. It shall be yours to
penetrate, in every bosom, the deep mystery of sin, the fountain of all
wicked arts, and which inexhaustibly supplies more evil impulses than
human power — than my power at its utmost — can make manifest in
deeds. And now, my children, look upon each other."

They did so; and, by the blaze of the hell-kindled torches, the wretched man beheld his Faith, and the wife her husband, trembling before that unhallowed altar.

"Lo, there ye stand, my children," said the figure, in a deep and solemn tone, almost sad with its despairing awfulness, as if his once angelic nature could yet mourn for our miserable race. "Depending upon one another's hearts, ye had still hoped that virtue were not all a dream. Now are ye undeceived. Evil is the nature of mankind. Evil must be your only happiness. Welcome again, my children, to the communion of your race."

"Welcome," repeated the fiend worshippers, in one cry of despair and triumph.

And there they stood, the only pair, as it seemed, who were yet hesitating on the verge of wickedness in this dark world. A basin was hollowed, naturally, in the rock. Did it contain water, reddened by the lurid light? or was it blood? or, perchance, a liquid flame? Herein did the shape of evil dip his hand and prepare to lay the mark of baptism upon their foreheads, that they might be partakers of the mystery of sin, more conscious of the secret guilt of others, both in deed and thought, than they could now be of their own. The husband cast one look at his pale wife, and Faith at him. What polluted wretches would the next glance show them to each other, shuddering alike at what they disclosed and what they saw!

"Faith! Faith!" cried the husband, "look up to heaven, and resist the wicked one."

Whether Faith obeyed he knew not. Hardly had he spoken when he found himself amid calm night and solitude, listening to a roar of the wind which died heavily away through the forest. He staggered against the rock, and felt it chill and damp; while a hanging twig, that had been all on fire, besprinkled his cheek with the coldest dew.

The next morning young Goodman Brown came slowly into the street of Salem village, staring around him like a bewildered man. The good old minister was taking a walk along the graveyard to get an appetite for breakfast and meditate his sermon, and bestowed a blessing, as he passed, on Goodman Brown. He shrank from the venerable saint as if to avoid an anathema. Old Deacon Gookin was at domestic worship, and the holy words of his prayer were heard through the open window. "What God doth the wizard pray to?" quoth Goodman Brown. Goody Cloyse, that excellent old Christian, stood in the early sunshine at her own lattice, catechizing a little girl who had brought her a pint of morning's milk. Goodman Brown snatched away the child as from the grasp of the fiend himself. Turning the corner by the meeting-house, he spied the head of Faith, with the pink ribbons, gazing anxiously forth, and bursting into such joy at sight of him that she skipped along the street and almost kissed her husband before the whole village. But Goodman Brown looked sternly and sadly into her face, and passed on without a greeting.

Had Goodman Brown fallen asleep in the forest and only dreamed a wild dream of a witch-meeting?

Be it so if you will; but, alas! it was a dream of evil omen for young Goodman Brown. A stern, a sad, a darkly meditative, a distrustful, if not a desperate man did he become from the night of that fearful dream. On the Sabbath day, when the congregation were singing a holy psalm, he could not listen because an anthem of sin rushed loudly upon his ear and drowned all the blessed strain. When the minister spoke from the pulpit with power and fervid eloquence, and, with his hand on the open Bible, of the sacred truths of our religion, and of saint-like lives and triumphant deaths, and of future bliss or misery unutterable, then did Goodman Brown turn pale, dreading lest the roof should thunder down upon the gray blasphemer and his hearers. Often, awaking suddenly at midnight, he shrank from the bosom of Faith; and at morning or eventide, when the family knelt down at prayer, he scowled and muttered to himself, and gazed sternly at his wife, and turned away. And when he had lived long, and was borne to his grave a hoary corpse, followed by Faith, an aged woman, and children and grand-children, a goodly procession, besides neighbors not a few, they carved no hopeful verse upon his tombstone, for his dying hour was gloom.

[1835]

Nathaniel Hawthorne

ༀ

THE DEVIL IN MANUSCRIPT

On a bitter evening of December, I arrived by mail in a large town, which was then the residence of an intimate friend, one of those gifted youths who cultivate poetry and the belles lettres, and call themselves students at law. My first business, after supper, was to visit him at the office of his distinguished instructor. As I have said, it was a bitter night, clear starlight, but cold as Nova Zembla — the shop-windows along the street being frosted, so as almost to hide the lights, while the wheels of coaches thundered equally loud over frozen earth and pavements of stone. There was no snow, either on the ground or the roofs of the houses. The wind blew so violently, that I had but to spread my cloak like a mainsail, and scud along the street at the rate of ten knots, greatly envied by other navigators who were beating slowly up, with the gale right in their teeth. One of these I capsized, but was gone on the wings of the wind before he could even vociferate an oath.

After this picture of an inclement night, behold us seated by a great blazing fire, which looked so comfortable and delicious that I felt inclined to lie down and roll among the hot coals. The usual furniture of a lawyer's office was around us — rows of volumes in sheepskin, and a multitude of writs, summonses, and other legal papers, scattered over the desks and tables. But there were certain objects which seemed to intimate that we had little dread of the intrusion of clients, or of the learned counsellor himself, who, indeed, was attending court in a distant town. A tall, decanter-shaped bottle stood on the table, between two tumblers, and beside a pile of blotted manuscripts, altogether dissimilar to any law documents recognized in our courts. My friend, whom I shall call Oberon — it was a name of fancy and friendship between him and me — my friend Oberon looked at these papers with a peculiar expression of disquietude.

"I do believe," said he, soberly, "or, at least, I would believe, if I chose, that there is a devil in this pile of blotted papers. You have read them, and know what I mean — that conception, in which I endeavored to embody the character of a fiend, as represented in our traditions and the written records of witchcraft. Oh! I have a horror of what was created in my own brain, and shudder at the manuscripts in which I gave that dark idea a sort of material existence. Would they were out of my sight!"

"And of mine too," thought I.

"You remember," continued Oberon, "how the hellish thing used to suck away the happiness of those who, by a simple concession that seemed almost innocent, subjected themselves to his power. Just so my peace is gone, and all by these accursed manuscripts. Have you felt nothing of the same influence?"

"Nothing," replied I, "unless the spell be hid in a desire to turn novelist, after reading your delightful tales."

"Novelist!" exclaimed Oberon, half seriously. "Then, indeed, my devil has his claw on you! You are gone! You cannot even pray for deliverance! But we will be the last and only victims: for this night I mean to burn the manuscripts, and commit the fiend to his retribution in the flames."

"Burn your tales!" repeated I, startled at the desperation of the idea.

"Even so," said the author, despondingly. "You cannot conceive what an effect the composition of these tales has had on me. I have become ambitious of a bubble, and careless of solid reputation. I am surrounding myself with shadows, which bewilder me, by aping the realities of life. They have drawn me aside from the beaten path of the world, and led me into a strange sort of solitude — a solitude in the midst of men — where nobody wishes for what I do, nor thinks nor feels as I do. The tales have done all this. When they are ashes, perhaps I shall be as I was before they had existence. Moreover, the sacrifice is less than you may suppose; since nobody will publish them."

"That does make a difference, indeed," said I.

"They have been offered, by letter," continued Oberon, reddening with vexation, "to some seventeen booksellers. It would make you stare to read their answers; and read them you should, only that I burnt them as fast as they arrived. One man publishes nothing but school-books; another has five novels already under examination —"

"What a voluminous mass the unpublished literature of America must be!" cried I.

"Oh! the Alexandrian manuscripts were nothing to it," said my friend. "Well; another gentleman is just giving up business, on purpose, I verily believe, to escape publishing my book. Several, however, would not absolutely decline the agency, on my advancing half the cost of an edition, and giving bonds for the remainder, besides a high percentage to themselves, whether the book sells or not. Another advises a subscription."

"The villain!" exclaimed I.

"A fact!" said Oberon. "In short, of all the seventeen booksellers, only one has vouchsafed even to read my tales; and he — a literary dabbler himself, I should judge — has the impertinence to criticize them, proposing what he calls vast improvements, and concluding, after a general sentence of condemnation, with the definitive assurance that he will not be concerned on any terms."

"It might not be amiss to pull that fellow's nose," remarked I.

"If the whole 'trade' had one common nose, there would be some satisfaction in pulling it," answered the author. "But, there does seem to be one honest man among these seventeen unrighteous ones, and he tells me fairly, that no American publisher will meddle with an American work, seldom if by a known writer, and never if by a new one, unless at the writer's risk."

"The paltry rogues!" cried I. "Will they live by literature, and yet risk nothing for its sake? But, after all, you might publish on your own account."

"And so I might," replied Oberon. "But the devil of the business is this. These people have put me so out of conceit with the tales, that I loathe the very thought of them, and actually experience a physical sickness of the stomach, whenever I glance at them on the table. I tell you there is a demon in them! I anticipate a wild enjoyment in seeing them in the blaze; such as I should feel in taking vengeance on an enemy or destroying something noxious."

I did not very strenuously oppose this determination, being privately of opinion, in spite of my partiality for the author, that his tales would make a more brilliant appearance in the fire than anywhere else. Before proceeding to execution, we broached the bottle of champagne, which Oberon had provided for keeping up his spirits in this doleful business. We swallowed each a tumblerfull, in sparkling commotion; it went bubbling down our throats, and brightened my eyes at once, but left my friend sad and heavy as before. He drew the tales towards him, with a mixture of natural affection and natural disgust, like a father taking a deformed infant into his arms.

"Pooh! Pish! Pshaw!" exclaimed he, holding them at arm's length. "It was Gray's idea of Heaven, to lounge on a sofa and read new novels. Now, what more appropriate torture would Dante himself have contrived, for the sinner who perpetrates a bad book, than to be continually turning over the manuscript?"

"It would fail of effect," said I, "because a bad author is always his own great admirer."

"I lack that one characteristic of my tribe, the only desirable one," observed Oberon. "But how many recollections throng upon me, as I turn over these leaves! This scene came into my fancy as I walked along a hilly road, on a starlight October evening; in the pure and bracing air, I became all soul, and felt as if I could climb the sky and run a race along the Milky Way. Here is another tale, in which I wrapt myself during a dark and dreary night-ride in the month of March, till the rattling of the wheels and the voices of my companions seemed like faint sounds of a dream, and my visions a bright reality. That scribbled page describes shadows which I summoned to my bedside at midnight; they would not depart when I bade them; the gray dawn came, and found me wide awake and feverish, the victim of my own enchantments!"

"There must have been a sort of happiness in all this," said I, smitten with a strange longing to make proof of it.

"There may be happiness in a fever fit," replied the author. "And then the various moods in which I wrote! Sometimes my ideas were like precious stones under the earth, requiring toil to dig them up, and care to polish and brighten them; but often, a delicious stream of thought would gush out upon the page at once, like water sparkling up suddenly in the desert; and when it had passed, I gnawed my pen hopelessly, or blundered on with cold and miserable toil, as if there were a wall of ice between me and my subject."

"Do you now perceive a corresponding difference," inquired I, "between the passages which you wrote so coldly, and those fervid flashes of the mind?"

"No," said Oberon, tossing the manuscripts on the table. "I find no traces of the golden pen, with which I wrote in characters of fire. My treasure of fairy coin is changed to worthless dross. My picture, painted in what seemed the loveliest hues, presents nothing but a faded and indistinguishable surface. I have been eloquent and poetical and humorous in a dream — and behold! it is all nonsense, now that I am awake."

My friend now threw sticks of wood and dry chips upon the fire, and seeing it blaze like Nebuchadnezzar's furnace, seized the champagne bottle, and drank two or three brimming bumpers, successively. The heady liquor combined with his agitation to throw him into a species of rage. He laid violent hands on the tales. In one instant more, their faults and beauties would alike have vanished in a glowing purgatory. But, all at once, I remembered passages of high imagination, deep pathos, original thoughts, and points of such varied excellence, that the vastness of the sacrifice struck me most forcibly. I caught his arm.

"Surely, you do not mean to burn them!" I exclaimed.

"Let me alone!" cried Oberon, his eyes flashing fire. "I will burn them! Not a scorched syllable shall escape! Would you have me a damned author? — To undergo sneers, taunts, abuse, and cold neglect, and faint praise, bestowed, for pity's sake, against the giver's conscience! A hissing and a laughing stock to my own traitorous thoughts! An outlaw from the protection of the grave — one whose ashes every careless foot might spurn, unhonored in life, and remembered scornfully in death! Am I to bear all this, when yonder fire will ensure me from the whole? No! There go the tales! May my hand wither when it would write another!"

The deed was done. He had thrown the manuscripts into the hottest of the fire, which at first seemed to shrink away, but soon curled around them, and made them a part of its own fervent brightness. Oberon stood gazing at the conflagration, and shortly began to soliloquize, in the wildest strain, as if Fancy resisted and became riotous, at the moment when he would have compelled her to ascend that funeral pile. His words described objects which he appeared to discern in the fire, fed by his own precious thoughts; perhaps the thousand visions, which the writer's magic had incorporated with those pages, became visible to him in the dissolving heat, brightening forth ere they vanished forever; while the smoke, the vivid sheets of flame, the ruddy and whitening coals, caught the aspect of a varied scenery.

"They blaze," said he, "as if I had steeped them in the intensest spirit of genius. There I see my lovers clasped in each other's arms. How pure the flame that bursts from their glowing hearts! And yonder the features of a villain, writhing in the fire that shall torment him to eternity. My holy men, my pious and angelic women, stand like martyrs amid the flames, their mild eyes lifted heavenward. Ring out the bells! A city is on fire. See! — destruction roars through my dark forests, while the lakes boil up in steaming billows, and the mountains are volcanoes, and the sky kindles with a lurid brightness! All elements are but one pervading flame! Ha! The fiend!"

I was somewhat startled by this latter exclamation. The tales were almost consumed, but just then threw forth a broad sheet of fire, which flickered as with laughter, making the whole room dance in its brightness, and then roared portentously up the chimney.

"You saw him? You must have seen him!" cried Oberon. "How he glared at me and laughed, in that last sheet of flame, with just the features that I imagined for him! Well! The tales are gone."

The papers were indeed reduced to a heap of black cinders, with a multitude of sparks hurrying confusedly among them, the traces of the pen being now represented by white lines, and the whole mass fluttering to and fro, in the draughts of air. The destroyer knelt down to look at them.

"What is more potent than fire!" said he, in his gloomiest tone. "Even thought, invisible and incorporeal as it is, cannot escape it. In this little time, it has annihilated the creations of long nights and days, which I could no more reproduce, in their first glow and freshness, than cause ashes and whitened bones to rise up and live. There, too, I sacrificed the unborn children of my mind. All that I had accomplished — all that I planned for future years — has perished by one common ruin, and left only this heap of embers. The deed has been my fate. And what remains? A weary and aimless life — a long repentance of this hour — and at last an obscure grave, where they will bury and forget me."

As the author concluded his dolorous moan, the extinguished embers arose and settled down and arose again, and finally flew up the chimney, like a demon with sable wings. Just as they disappeared, there was a loud and solitary cry in the street below us. "Fire! Fire!" Other voices caught up that terrible word, and it speedily became the shout of a multitude. Oberon started to his feet, in fresh excitement.

"A fire on such a night!" cried he. "The wind blows a gale, and wherever it whirls the flames, the roofs will flash up like gunpowder. Every pump is frozen up, and boiling water would turn to ice the moment it was flung from the engine. In an hour, this wooden town will be one great bonfire! What a glorious scene for my next —— Pshaw!"

The street was now all alive with footsteps, and the air full of voices. We heard one engine thundering round a corner, and another rattling from a distance over the pavements. The bells of three steeples clanged out at once, spreading the alarm to many a neighboring town, and expressing hurry, confusion, and terror, so inimitably that I could almost distinguish in their peal the burthen of the universal cry — "Fire! Fire! Fire!"

"What is so eloquent as their iron tongues!" exclaimed Oberon. "My heart leaps and trembles, but not with fear. And that other sound, too — deep and awful as a mighty organ — the roar and thunder of the multitude on the pavement below! Come! We are losing time. I will cry out in the loudest of the uproar, and mingle my spirit with the wildest of the confusion, and be a bubble on the top of the ferment!"

From the first outcry, my forebodings had warned me of the true object and centre of alarm. There was nothing now but uproar — above, beneath, and around us; footsteps stumbling pell-mell up the public stair-case, eager shouts and heavy thumps at the door, the whiz and dash of water from the engines, and the crash of furniture thrown upon the pavement. At once, the truth flashed upon my friend. His frenzy took the hue of joy, and, with a wild gesture of exultation he leaped almost to the ceiling of the chamber.

"My tales!" cried Oberon. "The chimney! The roof! The Fiend has gone forth by night, and startled thousands in fear and wonder from their beds! Here I stand — a triumphant author! Huzza! Huzza! My brain has set the town on fire! Huzza!"

[1838]

EDGAR ALLAN POE *(1809–1849), the son of poor traveling actors, was adopted after his mother's death by the merchant John Allan of Richmond, Virginia. Poe took his adoptive father's surname for his middle name. He was educated in Virginia and England, served two years in the army as an enlisted man, and then entered the military academy at West Point. He was expelled after a year. When John Allan disowned him because of his dissolute living habits, Poe had to earn his own living. He turned to writing as a profession. In 1833 his story, "Ms. Found in a Bottle," won a fifty-dollar prize for the best story in a popular Baltimore periodical, and he obtained an editorial position on the* Southern Literary Messenger. *He became its editor in 1835. The following year he married his cousin Virginia Clemm, who was thirteen years old; she died of tuberculosis in 1847. Poe's reviews, poems, and stories attracted wide attention, but he was fired from the* Southern Literary Messenger *in 1837 because of his unstable temperament. His remaining years were a struggle with poverty, depression, poor health aggravated by indulgence in drugs and alcohol, and grief over the death of his wife. The writer Jorge Luis Borges has observed that Poe's life "was short and unhappy, if unhappiness can be short."*

Although in his personal life Poe was a man torn by the most contradictory passions, as a writer he professed a belief in reason and championed lucidity. He claimed that rhymed poetry was the highest literary form, but conceded that the prose tale "affords unquestionably the fairest field for the exercise of the loftiest talent which can be afforded by the wide domains of mere prose." Most of his stories can be divided into two categories: tales of terror, like "The Cask of Amontillado," where unity of effect or a single impression is of the greatest importance; and stories of intellect or ratiocination, analytic tales that are precursors of the modern detective story. When Poe was accused of imitating German Romantic writers in his tales of horror, he answered, "Terror is not of Germany, but of the soul."

Poe has been labeled a Romantic writer, and most readers encounter his fiction when they are adolescents, seeking thrills from his macabre horror stories. Yet he also had a philosophic perspective and wrote stories and essays containing serious ideas about life and art. "The Oval Portrait" is a tale illustrating Poe's theory that in order to give life artistic form, the artist must feed on the spirit of life itself. Poe's most extensive comments on the short story form are contained in his reviews of Hawthorne's tales (1842 and 1847), in which he also described his own practices as a short story writer. (See Part II of this anthology, page 1123.)

Edgar Allan Poe

රාරා

THE CASK OF AMONTILLADO

The thousand injuries of Fortunato I had borne as I best could; but when he ventured upon insult, I vowed revenge. You, who so well know the nature of my soul, will not suppose, however, that I gave utterance to a threat. *At length* I would be avenged; this was a point definitely settled — but the very definitiveness with which it was resolved precluded the idea of risk. I must not only punish, but punish with impunity. A wrong is unredressed when retribution overtakes its redresser. It is equally unredressed when the avenger fails to make himself felt as such to him who has done the wrong.

It must be understood, that neither by word nor deed had I given Fortunato cause to doubt my good-will. I continued, as was my wont, to smile in his face, and he did not perceive that my smile *now* was at the thought of his immolation.

He had a weak point — this Fortunato — although in other regards he was a man to be respected and even feared. He prided himself on his connoisseurship in wine. Few Italians have the true virtuoso spirit. For the most part their enthusiasm is adopted to suit the time and opportunity — to practise imposture upon the British and Austrian *millionnaires*. In painting and gemmary Fortunato, like his countrymen, was a quack — but in the matter of old wines he was sincere. In this respect I did not differ from him materially: I was skilful in the Italian vintages myself, and bought largely whenever I could.

It was about dusk, one evening during the supreme madness of the carnival season, that I encountered my friend. He accosted me with excessive warmth, for he had been drinking much. The man wore motley. He had on a tight-fitting parti-striped dress, and his head was surmounted by the conical cap and bells. I was so pleased to see him, that I thought I should never have done wringing his hand.

I said to him: "My dear Fortunato, you are luckily met. How remarkably well you are looking to-day! But I have received a pipe[1] of what passes for Amontillado, and I have my doubts."

[1] a large cask or keg.

"How?" said he. "Amontillado? A pipe? Impossible! And in the middle of the carnival!"

"I have my doubts," I replied; "and I was silly enough to pay the full Amontillado price without consulting you in the matter. You were not to be found, and I was fearful of losing a bargain."

"Amontillado!"

"I have my doubts."

"Amontillado!"

"And I must satisfy them."

"Amontillado!"

"As you are engaged, I am on my way to Luchesi. If any one has a critical turn, it is he. He will tell me —— "

"Luchesi cannot tell Amontillado from Sherry."

"And yet some fools will have it that his taste is a match for your own."

"Come, let us go."

"Whither?"

"To your vaults."

"My friend, no; I will not impose upon your good nature. I perceive you have an engagement. Luchesi —— "

"I have no engagement; — come."

"My friend, no. It is not the engagement, but the severe cold with which I perceive you are afflicted. The vaults are insufferably damp. They are encrusted with nitre."

"Let us go, nevertheless. The cold is merely nothing. Amontillado! You have been imposed upon. And as for Luchesi, he cannot distinguish Sherry from Amontillado."

Thus speaking, Fortunato possessed himself of my arm. Putting on a mask of black silk, and drawing a *roquelaire*[2] closely about my person, I suffered him to hurry me to my palazzo.

There were no attendants at home; they had absconded to make merry in honor of the time. I had told them that I should not return until the morning, and had given them explicit orders not to stir from the house. These orders were sufficient, I well knew, to insure their immediate disappearance, one and all, as soon as my back was turned.

I took from their sconces two flambeaux, and giving one to Fortunato, bowed him through several suites of rooms to the archway that led into the vaults. I passed down a long and winding staircase, requesting him to be cautious as he followed. We came at length to the foot of the descent, and stood together on the damp ground of the catacombs of the Montresors.

The gait of my friend was unsteady, and the bells upon his cap jingled as he strode.

"The pipe?" said he.

[2] a short cloak.

"It is farther on," said I; "but observe the white web-work which gleams from these cavern walls."

He turned toward me, and looked into my eyes with two filmy orbs that distilled the rheum of intoxication.

"Nitre?" he asked, at length.

"Nitre," I replied. "How long have you had that cough?"

"Ugh! ugh! ugh! — ugh! ugh! ugh! — ugh! ugh! ugh! — ugh! ugh! ugh! — ugh! ugh! ugh!"

My poor friend found it impossible to reply for many minutes.

"It is nothing," he said, at last.

"Come," I said, with decision, "we will go back; your health is precious. You are rich, respected, admired, beloved; you are happy, as once I was. You are a man to be missed. For me it is no matter. We will go back; you will be ill, and I cannot be responsible. Besides, there is Luchesi ———— "

"Enough," he said; "the cough is a mere nothing; it will not kill me. I shall not die of a cough."

"True — true," I replied; "and, indeed, I had no intention of alarming you unnecessarily; but you should use all proper caution. A draught of this Medoc will defend us from the damps."

Here I knocked off the neck of a bottle which I drew from a long row of its fellows that lay upon the mould.

"Drink," I said, presenting him the wine.

He raised it to his lips with a leer. He paused and nodded to me familiarly, while his bells jingled.

"I drink," he said, "to the buried that repose around us."

"And I to your long life."

He again took my arm, and we proceeded.

"These vaults," he said, "are extensive."

"The Montresors," I replied. "were a great and numerous family."

"I forget your arms."

"A huge human foot d'or,[3] in a field azure; the foot crushes a serpent rampant whose fangs are imbedded in the heel."

"And the motto?"

"*Nemo me impune lacessit.*"[4]

"Good!" he said.

The wine sparkled in his eyes and the bells jingled. My own fancy grew warm with the Medoc. We had passed through walls of piled bones, with casks and puncheons intermingling, into the inmost recesses of the catacombs. I paused again, and this time I made bold to seize Fortunato by an arm above the elbow.

"The nitre!" I said; "see, it increases. It hangs like moss upon the

---

[3] of gold.
[4] "No one wounds me with impunity"; the motto of the royal arms of Scotland.

vaults. We are below the river's bed. The drops of moisture trickle among the bones. Come, we will go back ere it is too late. Your cough —— "

"It is nothing," he said; "let us go on. But first, another draught of the Medoc."

I broke and reached him a flagon of De Grâve. He emptied it at a breath. His eyes flashed with a fierce light. He laughed and threw the bottle upward with a gesticulation I did not understand.

I looked at him in surprise. He repeated the movement — a grotesque one.

"You do not comprehend?" he said.

"Not I," I replied.

"Then you are not of the brotherhood."

"How?"

"You are not of the masons."

"Yes, yes," I said; "yes, yes."

"You? Impossible! A mason?"

"A mason," I replied.

"A sign," he said.

"It is this," I answered, producing a trowel from beneath the folds of my *roquelaire.*

"You jest," he exclaimed, recoiling a few paces. "But let us proceed to the Amontillado."

"Be it so," I said, replacing the tool beneath the cloak, and again offering him my arm. He leaned upon it heavily. We continued our route in search of the Amontillado. We passed through a range of low arches, descended, passed on, and descending again, arrived at a deep crypt, in which the foulness of the air caused our flambeaux rather to glow than flame.

At the most remote end of the crypt there appeared another less spacious. Its walls had been lined with human remains, piled to the vault overhead, in the fashion of the great catacombs of Paris. Three sides of this interior crypt were still ornamented in this manner. From the fourth the bones had been thrown down, and lay promiscuously upon the earth, forming at one point a mound of some size. Within the wall thus exposed by the displacing of the bones, we perceived a still interior recess, in depth about four feet, in width three, in height six or seven. It seemed to have been constructed for no especial use within itself, but formed merely the interval between two of the colossal supports of the roof of the catacombs, and was backed by one of their circumscribing walls of solid granite.

It was in vain that Fortunato, uplifting his dull torch, endeavored to pry into the depth of the recess. Its termination the feeble light did not enable us to see.

"Proceed," I said; "herein is the Amontillado. As for Luchesi —— "

"He is an ignoramus," interrupted my friend, as he stepped unsteadily forward, while I followed immediately at his heels. In an instant he had reached the extremity of the niche, and finding his progress arrested by the rock, stood stupidly bewildered. A moment more and I had fettered him to the granite. In its surface were two iron staples, distant from each other about two feet, horizontally. From one of these depended a short chain, from the other a padlock. Throwing the links about his waist, it was but the work of a few seconds to secure it. He was too much astounded to resist. Withdrawing the key I stepped back from the recess.

"Pass your hand," I said, "over the wall; you cannot help feeling the nitre. Indeed it is *very* damp. Once more let me *implore* you to return. No? Then I must positively leave you. But I must first render you all the little attentions in my power."

"The Amontillado!" ejaculated my friend, not yet recovered from his astonishment.

"True," I replied; "the Amontillado."

As I said these words I busied myself among the pile of bones of which I have before spoken. Throwing them aside, I soon uncovered a quantity of building stone and mortar. With these materials and with the aid of my trowel, I began vigorously to wall up the entrance of the niche.

I had scarcely laid the first tier of the masonry when I discovered that the intoxication of Fortunato had in a great measure worn off. The earliest indication I had of this was a low moaning cry from the depth of the recess. It was *not* the cry of a drunken man. There was then a long and obstinate silence. I laid the second tier, and the third, and the fourth; and then I heard the furious vibrations of the chain. The noise lasted for several minutes, during which, that I might hearken to it with the more satisfaction, I ceased my labors and sat down upon the bones. When at last the clanking subsided, I resumed the trowel, and finished without interruption the fifth, the sixth, and the seventh tier. The wall was now nearly upon a level with my breast. I again paused, and holding the flambeaux over the masonwork, threw a few feeble rays upon the figure within.

A succession of loud and shrill screams, bursting suddenly from the throat of the chained form, seemed to thrust me violently back. For a brief moment I hesitated — I trembled. Unsheathing my rapier, I began to grope with it about the recess; but the thought of an instant reassured me. I placed my hand upon the solid fabric of the catacombs, and felt satisfied. I reapproached the wall. I replied to the yells of him who clamored. I re-echoed — I aided — I surpassed them in volume and in strength. I did this, and the clamorer grew still.

It was now midnight, and my task was drawing to a close. I had completed the eighth, the ninth, and the tenth tier. I had finished a portion of the last and the eleventh; there remained but a single stone to be fitted and plastered in. I struggled with its weight; I placed it partially in its destined position. But now there came from out the niche a low laugh that erected the hairs upon my head. It was succeeded by a sad voice, which I had difficulty in recognizing as that of the noble Fortunato. The voice said —

"Ha! ha! ha! — he! he! — a very good joke indeed — an excellent jest. We will have many a rich laugh about it at the palazzo — he! he! he! — over our wine — he! he! he!"

"The Amontillado!" I said.

"He! he! he! — he! he! he! — yes, the Amontillado. But is it not getting late? Will not they be awaiting us at the palazzo, the Lady Fortunato and the rest? Let us be gone."

"Yes," I said, "let us be gone."

"For the love of God, Montresor!"

"Yes," I said, "for the love of God!"

But to these words I hearkened in vain for a reply. I grew impatient. I called aloud:

"Fortunato!"

No answer. I called again:

"Fortunato!"

No answer still. I thrust a torch through the remaining aperture and let it fall within. There came forth in return only a jingling of the bells. My heart grew sick — on account of the dampness of the catacombs. I hastened to make an end of my labor. I forced the last stone into its position; I plastered it up. Against the new masonry I re-erected the old rampart of bones. For the half of a century no mortal has disturbed them. *In pace requiescat!*

[1846]

Edgar Allan Poe

ଚୢ

THE OVAL PORTRAIT

The chateau in which my valet had ventured to make forcible entrance, rather than permit me, in my desperately wounded condition, to pass a night in the open air, was one of those piles of commingled gloom and grandeur which have so long frowned among the Apennines, not less in fact than in fancy of Mrs. Radcliffe. To all appearance it had been temporarily and very lately abandoned. We established ourselves in one of the smallest and least sumptuously furnished apartments. It lay in a remote turret of the building. Its decorations were rich, yet tattered and antique. Its walls were hung with tapestry and bedecked with manifold and multiform armorial trophies, together with an unusually great number of very spirited modern paintings in frames of rich golden arabesque. In these paintings, which depended from the walls not only in their main surfaces, but in very many nooks which the bizarre architecture of the chateau rendered necessary — in these paintings my incipient delirium, perhaps, had caused me to take deep interest; so that I bade Pedro to close the heavy shutters of the room — since it was already night — to light the tongues of a tall candelabrum which stood by the head of my bed — and to throw open far and wide the fringed curtains of black velvet which enveloped the bed itself. I wished all this done that I might resign myself, if not to sleep, at least alternately to the contemplation of these pictures, and the perusal of a small volume which had been found upon the pillow, and which purported to criticise and describe them.

Long — long I read — and devoutly, devotedly I gazed. Rapidly and gloriously the hours flew by, and the deep midnight came. The position of the candelabrum displeased me, and outstretching my hand with difficulty, rather than disturb my slumbering valet, I placed it so as to throw its rays more fully upon the book.

But the action produced an effect altogether unanticipated. The rays of the numerous candles (for there were many) now fell within a niche of the room which had hitherto been thrown into deep shade by one of the bed-posts. I thus saw in vivid light a picture all unnoticed before. It was the portrait of a young girl just ripening into womanhood. I glanced at the painting hurriedly, and then closed my eyes. Why I did this was not at first apparent even to my own perception. But while my lids remained thus shut, I ran over in mind my reason for so shutting them. It was an impulsive movement to gain time for thought — to make sure that my vision had not deceived me — to calm and subdue my fancy for a more sober and more certain gaze. In a very few moments I again looked fixedly at the painting.

That I now saw aright I could not and would not doubt; for the first flashing of the candles upon that canvas had seemed to dissipate the dreamy stupor which was stealing over my senses, and to startle me at once into waking life.

The portrait, I have already said, was that of a young girl. It was a mere head and shoulders, done in what is technically termed a *vignette* manner; much in the style of the favorite heads of Sully.[1] The arms, the bosom and even the ends of the radiant hair, melted imperceptibly into the vague yet deep shadow which formed the background of the whole. The frame was oval, richly gilded and filagreed in *Moresque*.[2] As a thing of art nothing could be more admirable than the painting itself. But it could have been neither the execution of the work, nor the immortal beauty of the countenance, which had so suddenly and so vehemently moved me. Least of all,

---

[1] Thomas Sully (1783–1872), one of the best-known American portrait painters of the nineteenth century.

[2] in the Moorish style.

could it have been that my fancy, shaken from its half slumber, had mistaken the head for that of a living person. I saw at once that the peculiarities of the design, of the *vignetting*, and of the frame, must have instantly dispelled such idea — must have prevented even its momentary entertainment. Thinking earnestly upon these points, I remained, for an hour perhaps, half sitting, half reclining, with my vision riveted upon the portrait. At length, satisfied with the true secret of its effect, I fell back within the bed. I had found the spell of the picture in an absolute *life-likeliness* of expression, which at first startling, finally confounded, subdued and appalled me. With deep and reverent awe I replaced the candelabrum in its former position. The cause of my deep agitation being thus shut from view, I sought eagerly the volume which discussed the paintings and their histories. Turning to the number which designated the oval portrait, I there read the vague and quaint words which follow:

"She was a maiden of rarest beauty, and not more lovely than full of glee. And evil was the hour when she saw, and loved, and wedded the painter. He, passionate, studious, austere, and having already a bride in his Art; she a maiden of rarest beauty, and not more lovely than full of glee; all light and smiles, and frolicksome as the young fawn: loving and cherishing all things: hating only the Art which was her rival: dreading only the palette and brushes and other untoward instruments which deprived her of the countenance of her lover. It was thus a terrible thing for this lady to hear the painter speak of his desire to portray even his young bride. But she was humble and obedient, and sat meekly for many weeks in the dark high turret-chamber where the light dripped upon the pale canvas only from overhead. But he, the painter, took glory in his work, which went on from hour to hour and from day to day. And he was a passionate, and wild and moody man, who became lost in reveries; so that he *would* not see that the light which fell so ghastly in that lone turret withered the health and the spirits of his bride, who pined visibly to all but him. Yet she smiled on and still on, uncomplainingly, because she saw that the painter, (who had high renown,) took a fervid and burning pleasure in his task, and wrought day and night to depict her who so loved him, yet who grew daily more dispirited and weak. And in sooth some who beheld the portrait spoke of its resemblance in low words, as of a mighty marvel, and a proof not less of the power of the painter than of his deep love for her whom he depicted so surpassingly well. But at length, as the labor drew nearer to its conclusion, there were admitted none into the turret; for the painter had grown wild with the ardor of his work, and turned his eyes from the canvas rarely, even to regard the countenance of his wife. And he *would* not see that the tints which he spread upon the canvas were drawn from the cheeks of her who sate beside him. And when many weeks had passed, and but little remained to do, save one brush upon the mouth and one tint upon the eye, the spirit of the lady again flickered up as the flame within the socket of the lamp.

And then the brush was given, and then the tint was placed; and, for one moment, the painter stood entranced before the work which he had wrought; but in the next, while he yet gazed, he grew tremulous and very pallid, and aghast, and crying with a loud voice, 'This is indeed *Life* itself!' turned suddenly to regard his beloved: — *She was dead!*"

[1842]

NIKOLAI GOGOL (1809–1852) broke through the eighteenth-century literary conventions that prevailed in his time. He is considered the father of Russian realism — "We all came out from under Gogol's 'Overcoat' " is a remark variously attributed to Ivan Turgenev, Leo Tolstoy, and Fyodor Dostoevsky, and that literary critics feel any of these writers might have said it indicates the story's importance. But Gogol brilliantly used techniques of romanticism and fantasy in his fiction as well.

Born in the town of Sorochintsky in the Russian Ukraine, the son of a deeply religious mother and a father who was a small landowner, Gogol attended a provincial grammar school. At the age of twelve he was sent away to a boarding school, where he was so sickly and unattractive that the other students gave him the name "the mysterious dwarf." In 1828, after he left school, Gogol's health improved. He moved to St. Petersburg (then the capital of Russia), passed the civil service examinations, and held various government jobs, but he also entered the literary life of the city, becoming a friend of Alexander Pushkin, the great Russian poet. In 1831 and 1832 Gogol published a two-volume collection of stories, Evenings on a Farm near Dikanka, and in 1835 a historical novel about the Ukrainian Cossacks, Taras Bulba. In 1836 his play The Inspector General, a satire ridiculing Russian officials, was considered so dangerously critical of the government that Gogol was forced to leave the country for a more or less permanent exile in Rome. There he worked on what he considered his most important book, the novel Dead Souls, which was published in 1842. In his long years abroad Gogol made several hectic visits to Russia, despite his worsening illness. He died, insane, in 1852.

In The Lonely Voice, his study of the short story, Frank O'Connor maintains that the expression "We all came out from under Gogol's 'Overcoat' " has a general validity beyond its relevance for Russian writers. Written in 1840, "The Overcoat" is neither satiric nor heroic, but ultimately transcends both modes. O'Connor identifies it as "the first appearance in fiction of the Little Man." He goes on to define the special impact of the short story as the literary form that offers the reader an intense awareness of human loneliness. To O'Connor, the short story (unlike the novel) never has a true hero. Instead it features "a submerged population group," which changes its character from writer to writer and generation to generation. "It may be Gogol's officials, Turgenev's serfs, Maupassant's prostitutes, Chekhov's doctors and teachers, Sherwood Anderson's provincials, always dreaming of escape." Everything about Akakii Akakiievich in "The Overcoat," from his absurd name to his absurd family to his absurd job, is on the same level of mediocrity, and yet something about the little

*clerk moves us to pity and sympathy. When others torment him, we seem
to hear him say, "Leave me alone! Why do you pick on me? I am your
brother."*

Nikolai Gogol

ʋʊ

THE OVERCOAT

–translated by Bernard G. Guerney

In the Bureau of . . . but it might be better not to mention the Bureau
by its precise name. There is nothing more touchy than all these Bureaus,
Regiments, Chancelleries of every sort, and, in a word, every sort of person
belonging to the administrative classes. Nowadays every civilian, even, considers all of society insulted in his own person. Quite recently, so they say, a
petition came through from a certain Captain of Rural Police in some town
or other (I can't recall its name), in which he explained clearly that the
whole social structure was headed for ruin and that his sacred name was actually being taken entirely in vain, and, in proof, he documented his petition with the enormous tome of some romantic work or other wherein,
every ten pages or so, a Captain of Rural Police appeared — in some passages even in an out-and-out drunken state. And so, to avoid any and all
unpleasantnesses, we'd better call the Bureau in question *a certain Bureau.*
And so, in *a certain Bureau* there served *a certain clerk* — a clerk whom one
could hardly style very remarkable: quite low of stature, somewhat pock-
marked, somewhat rusty-hued of hair, even somewhat purblind, at first
glance; rather bald at the temples, with wrinkles along both cheeks, and his
face of that complexion which is usually called hemorrhoidal. Well, what
would you? It's the Petersburg climate that's to blame. As far as his rank is
concerned (for among us the rank must be made known first of all), why, he
was what they call a Perpetual Titular Councilor a rank which, as everybody knows, various writers who have a praiseworthy wont of throwing their
weight about among those who are in no position to hit back, have twitted
and exercised their keen wits against often and long. This clerk's family
name was Bashmachkin. It's quite evident, by the very name, that it sprang
from *bashmak* or shoe, but at what time, just when and how it sprang from
a shoe — of that nothing is known. For not only this clerk's father but his
grandfather and even his brother-in-law, and absolutely all the Bashmach-
kins, walked about in boots, merely resoling them three times a year.

His name and patronymic were Akakii Akakiievich. It may, perhaps,
strike the reader as somewhat odd and out of the way, but the reader may

rest assured that the author has not gone out of his way at all to find it, but
that certain circumstances had come about of themselves in such fashion
that there was absolutely no way of giving him any other name. And the
precise way this came about was as follows. Akakii Akakiievich was born —
unless my memory plays me false — on the night of the twenty-third of
March. His late mother, a government clerk's wife, and a very good woman,
was all set to christen her child, all fit and proper. She was still lying in bed,
facing the door, while on her right stood the godfather, a most excellent
man by the name of Ivan Ivanovich Eroshkin, who had charge of some Department or other in a certain Administrative Office, and the godmother,
the wife of the precinct police officer, a woman of rare virtues, by the name
of Arina Semenovna Byelobrushkina. The mother was offered the choice of
any one of three names: Mokii, Sossii — or the child could even be given
the name of that great martyr, Hozdavat. "No," the late lamented had reflected, "what sort of names are these?" In order to please her they opened
the calendar at another place — and the result was again three names: Triphilii, Dula, and Varahasii. "What a visitation!" said the elderly woman.
"What names all these be! To tell you the truth, I've never even heard the
likes of them. If it were at least Baradat or Baruch, but why do Triphilii and
Varahasii have to turn up?" They turned over another page — and came
up with Pavsikahii and Vahtissii. "Well, I can see now," said the mother,
"that such is evidently his fate. In that case it would be better if he were
called after his father. His father was an Akakii — let the son be an Akakii
also." And that's how Akakii Akakiievich came to be Akakii Akakiievich.

The child was baptized, during which rite he began to bawl and made
terrible faces as if anticipating that it would be his lot to become a Perpetual Titular Councilor. And so that's the way it had all come about. We
have brought the matter up so that the reader might see for himself that all
this had come about through sheer inevitability and it had been utterly impossible to bestow any other name upon Akakii Akakiievich.

When, at precisely what time, he entered the Bureau, and who gave
him the berth, were things which no one could recall. No matter how many
Directors and his superiors of one sort or another came and went, he was
always to be seen in the one and the same spot, in the same posture, in the
very same post, always the same Clerk of Correspondence, so that subsequently people became convinced that he evidently had come into the
world just the way he was, all done and set, in a uniform frock and bald at
the temples. No respect whatsoever was shown him in the Bureau. The por-
ters not only didn't jump up from their places whenever he happened to
pass by, but didn't even as much as glance at him, as if nothing more than a
common housefly had passed through the reception hall. His superiors
treated him with a certain chill despotism. Some assistant or other of some
Head of a Department would simply shove papers under his nose, without
as much as saying "Transcribe these," or "Here's a rather pretty, interesting
little case," or any of those small pleasantries that are current in well-

conducted administrative institutions. And he would take the work, merely glancing at the paper, without looking up to see who had put it down before him and whether that person had the right to do so; he took it and right then and there went to work on it. The young clerks made fun of him and sharpened their wits at his expense, to whatever extent their quill-driving wittiness sufficed, retailing in his very presence the various stories made up about him; they said of his landlady, a crone of seventy, that she beat him, and asked him when their wedding would take place, they scattered torn paper over his head, maintaining it was snow.

But not a word did Akakii Akakiievich say in answer to all this, as if there were actually nobody before him. It did not even affect his work: in the midst of all these annoyances he did not make a single clerical error. Only when the jest was past all bearing, when they jostled his arm, hindering him from doing his work, would he say: "Leave me alone! Why do you pick on me?" And there was something odd about his words and in the voice with which he uttered them. In that voice could be heard something that moved one to pity — so much so that one young man, a recent entrant, who, following the example of the others, had permitted himself to make fun of Akakii Akakiievich, stopped suddenly, as if pierced to the quick, and from that time on everything seemed to change in his eyes and appeared in a different light. Some sort of preternatural force seemed to repel him from the companions he had made, having taken them for decent, sociable people. And for a long time afterward, in the very midst of his most cheerful moments, the little squat clerk would appear before him, with the small bald patches on each side of his forehead, and he would hear his heart-piercing words "Leave me alone! Why do you pick on me?" And in these heart-piercing words he caught the ringing sound of others: "I am your brother." And the poor young man would cover his eyes with his hand, and many a time in his life thereafter did he shudder, seeing how much inhumanity there is in man, how much hidden ferocious coarseness lurks in refined, cultured worldliness and, O God! even in that very man whom the world holds to be noble and honorable. . . .

It is doubtful if you could find anywhere a man whose life lay so much in his work. It would hardly do to say that he worked with zeal; no, it was a labor of love. Thus, in this transcription of his, he visioned some sort of diversified and pleasant world all its own. His face expressed delight; certain letters were favorites of his and whenever he came across them he would be beside himself with rapture: he'd chuckle, and wink, and help things along by working his lips, so that it seemed as if one could read on his face every letter his quill was outlining. If rewards had been meted out to him commensurately with his zeal, he might have, to his astonishment, actually found himself among the State Councilors; but, as none other than those wits, his own co-workers, expressed it, all he'd worked himself up to was a button in a buttonhole too wide, and piles in his backside.

However, it would not be quite correct to say that absolutely no attention was paid him. One Director, being a kindly man and wishing to reward him for his long service, gave orders that some work of a more important nature than the usual transcription be assigned to him; to be precise, he was told to make a certain referral to another Administrative Department out of a docket already prepared: the matter consisted, all in all, of changing the main title as well as some pronouns here and there from the first person singular to the third person singular. This made so much work for him that he was all of a sweat, kept mopping his forehead, and finally said: "No, better let me transcribe something." Thenceforth they left him to his transcription for all time. Outside of this transcription, it seemed, nothing existed for him.

He gave no thought whatsoever to his dress; the uniform frock coat on him wasn't the prescribed green at all, but rather of some rusty-flour hue. His collar was very tight and very low, so that his neck, even though it wasn't a long one, seemed extraordinarily long emerging therefrom, like those gypsum kittens with nodding heads which certain outlanders balance by the dozen atop their heads and peddle throughout Russia. And, always, something was bound to stick to his coat: a wisp of hay or some bit of thread; in addition to that, he had a peculiar knack whenever he walked through the streets of getting under some window at the precise moment when garbage of every sort was being thrown out of it, and for that reason always bore off on his hat watermelon and cantaloupe rinds and other such trifles. Not once in all his life had he ever turned his attention to the everyday things and doings out in the street — something, as everybody knows, that is always watched with eager interest by Akakii Akakiievich's confrère, the young government clerk, the penetration of whose lively gaze is so extensive that he will even take in somebody on the opposite sidewalk who has ripped loose his trouser strap — a thing that never fails to evoke a sly smile on the young clerk's face. But even if Akakii Akakiievich did look at anything, he saw thereon nothing but his own neatly, evenly penned lines of script, and only when some horse's nose, bobbing up from no one knew where, would be placed on his shoulder and let a whole gust of wind in his face through its nostrils, would he notice that he was not in the middle of a line of script but, rather, in the middle of the roadway.

On coming home he would immediately sit down at the table, gulp down his cabbage soup and bolt a piece of veal with onions, without noticing in the least the taste of either, eating everything together with the flies and whatever else God may have sent at that particular time of the year. On perceiving that his belly was beginning to swell out, he'd get up from the table, take out a small bottle of ink, and transcribe the papers he had brought home. If there were no homework, he would deliberately, for his own edification, make a copy of some paper for himself, especially if the document were remarkable not for its beauty of style but merely addressed to some new or important person.

Even at those hours when the gray sky of Petersburg became entirely extinguished and all the pettifogging tribe has eaten its fill and finished dinner, each as best he could, in accordance with the salary he receives and his own bent, when everybody has already rested up after the scraping of quills in various departments, the running around, the unavoidable cares about their own affairs and the affairs of others, and all that which restless man sets himself as a task voluntarily and to an even greater extent than necessary — at a time when the petty bureaucrats hasten to devote whatever time remained to enjoyment: he who is of the more lively sort hastening to the theater; another for a saunter through the streets, devoting the time to an inspection of certain pretty little hats; still another to some evening party, to spend that time in paying compliments to some comely young lady, the star of a small bureaucratic circle; a fourth (and this happened most frequently of all) would simply go for a call on a confrère in a flat up three or four flights of stairs, consisting of two small rooms with an entry and a kitchen and one or two attempts at the latest improvements — a kerosene lamp instead of candles, or some other elegant little thing that had cost many sacrifices, such as going without dinners or good times — in short, even at the time when all the petty bureaucrats scatter through the small apartments of their friends for a session of dummy whist, sipping tea out of tumblers and nibbling at cheap zwieback, drawing deep at their pipes, the stems thereof as long as walking sticks, retailing, during the shuffling and dealing, some bit of gossip or other from high society that had reached them at long last (something which no Russian, under any circumstances, and of whatever estate he be, can ever deny himself), or even, when there was nothing whatsoever to talk about, retelling the eternal chestnut of the commandant to whom people came to say that the tail of the horse on the Falconetti monument had been docked — in short, even at the time when every soul yearns to be diverted, Akakii Akakiievich did not give himself up to any diversion. No man could claim having ever seen him at any evening gathering. Having had his sweet fill of quill-driving, he would lie down to sleep, smiling at the thought of the next day: just what would God send him on the morrow?

Such was the peaceful course of life of a man who, with a yearly salary of four hundred, knew how to be content with his lot, and that course might even have continued to a ripe old age had it not been for sundry calamities, such as are strewn along the path of life, not only of Titular, but even Privy, Actual, Court, and all other sorts of Councilors, even those who never give any counsel to anybody nor ever accept any counsel from others for themselves.

There is, in Petersburg, a formidable foe of all those whose salary runs to four hundred a year or thereabouts. This foe is none other than our northern frost — even though, by the bye, they do say that it's the most healthful thing for you. At nine in the morning, precisely at that hour when the streets are thronged with those on their way to sundry bureaus, it begins dealing out such powerful and penetrating fillips to all noses, without any discrimination, that the poor bureaucrats absolutely do not know how to hide them. At this time, when even those who fill the higher posts feel their foreheads aching because of the frost and the tears come to their eyes, the poor Titular Councilors are sometimes utterly defenseless. The sole salvation, if one's overcoat is of the thinnest, lies in dashing, as quickly as possible, through five or six blocks and then stamping one's feet plenty in the porter's room, until the faculties and gifts for administrative duties, which have been frozen on the way, are thus thawed out at last.

For some time Akakii Akakiievich had begun to notice that the cold was somehow penetrating his back and shoulders with especial ferocity, despite the fact that he tried to run the required distances as quickly as possible. It occurred to him, at last, that there might be some defects about this overcoat. After looking it over rather thoroughly at home he discovered that in two or three places — in the back and at the shoulders, to be exact — it had become no better than the coarsest of sacking; the cloth was rubbed to such an extent that one could see through it, and the lining had crept apart. The reader must be informed that Akakii Akakiievich's overcoat, too, was a butt for the jokes of the petty bureaucrats; it had been deprived of the honorable name of an overcoat, even, and dubbed a *negligée*. And, really, it was of a rather queer cut; its collar grew smaller with every year, inasmuch as it was utilized to supplement the other parts of the garment. This supplementing was not at all a compliment to the skill of the tailor, and the effect really was baggy and unsightly.

Perceiving what the matter was, Akakii Akakiievich decided that the overcoat would have to go to Petrovich the tailor, who lived somewhere up four flights of backstairs and who, despite a squint-eye and pockmarks all over his face, did quite well at repairing bureaucratic as well as all other trousers and coats — of course, be it understood, when he was in a sober state and not hatching some nonsartorial scheme in his head. One shouldn't, really, mention this tailor at great length, but since there is already a precedent for each character in a tale being clearly defined, there's no help for it, and so let's trot out Petrovich as well. In the beginning he had been called simply Gregory and had been the serf of some squire or other; he had begun calling himself Petrovich only after obtaining his freedom papers and taking to drinking rather hard on any and every holiday — at first on the red-letter ones and then, without any discrimination, on all those designated by the church: wherever there was a little cross marking the day on the calendar. In this respect he was loyal to the customs of our grandsires, and, when bickering with his wife, would call her a worldly woman and a German frau. And, since we've already been inadvertent enough to mention his wife, it will be necessary to say a word or two about her as well; but, regrettably, little was known about her — unless, perhaps, the fact that Petrovich had a wife, or that she even wore a house-cap and not a kerchief: but as for beauty, it appears that she could hardly boast of any; at least the soldiers in the Guards were the only ones with hardihood enough to bend down for a peep under her cap, twitching their mustache as they did so and emitting a certain peculiar sound.

As he clambered up the staircase that led to Petrovich — the staircase, to render it its just due, was dripping all over from water and slops and thoroughly permeated with that alcoholic odor which makes the eyes smart and is, as everybody knows, unfailingly present on all the backstairs of all the houses in Petersburg — as he clambered up this staircase Akakii Akakiievich was already conjecturing how stiff Petrovich's asking-price would be and mentally determined not to give him more than two rubles. The door was open, because the mistress of the place, being busy preparing some fish, had filled the kitchen with so much smoke that one actually couldn't see the very cockroaches for it. Akakii Akakiievich made his way through the kitchen, unperceived even by the mistress herself, and at last entered the room wherein he beheld Petrovich, sitting on a wide table of unpainted deal with his feet tucked in under him like a Turkish Pasha. His feet, as is the wont of tailors seated at their work, were bare, and the first thing that struck one's eyes was the big toe of one, very familiar to Akakii Akakiievich, with some sort of deformed nail, as thick and strong as a turtle's shell. About Petrovich's neck were loops of silk and cotton thread, while some sort of ragged garment was lying on his knees. For the last three minutes he had been trying to put a thread through the eye of a needle, couldn't hit the mark, and because of that was very wroth against the darkness of the room and even the thread itself, grumbling under his breath: "She won't go through, the heathen! You've spoiled my heart's blood, you damned good-for-nothing!"

Akakii Akakiievich felt upset because he had come at just the moment when Petrovich was very angry; he liked to give in his work when the latter was already under the influence or, as his wife put it, "He's already full of rot-gut, the one-eyed devil." In such a state Petrovich usually gave in willingly and agreed to everything; he even bowed and was grateful every time. Afterward, true enough, his wife would come around and complain weepily that, now, her husband had been drunk and for that reason had taken on the work too cheaply; but all you had to do was to tack on another ten kopecks — and the thing was in the bag. But now, it seemed, Petrovich was in a sober state, and for that reason on his high horse, hard to win over, and bent on boosting his prices to the devil knows what heights. Akakii Akakiievich surmised this and, as the saying goes, was all set to make back tracks, but the deal had already been started. Petrovich puckered up his one good eye against him very fixedly and Akakii Akakiievich involuntarily said, "Greetings, Petrovich!" "Greetings to you, Sir," said Petrovich and looked askance at Akakii Akakiievich's hands, wishing to see what sort of booty the other bore.

"Well, now, I've come to see you, now, Petrovich!"

Akakii Akakiievich, the reader must be informed, explained himself for the most part in prepositions, adverbs, and such verbal oddments as have absolutely no significance. But if the matter was exceedingly difficult, he actually had a way of not finishing his phrase at all, so that, quite frequently, beginning his speech with such words as "This, really, is perfectly, you know —" — he would have nothing at all to follow up with, and he himself would be likely to forget the matter, thinking that he had already said everything in full.

"Well, just what is it?" asked Petrovich, and at the same time, with his one good eye, surveyed the entire garment, beginning with the collar and going on to the sleeves, the back, the coat-skirts, and the buttonholes, for it was all very familiar to him, inasmuch as it was all his own handiwork. That's a way all tailors have; it's the first thing a tailor will do on meeting you.

"Why, what I'm after, now, Petrovich . . . the overcoat, now, the cloth . . . there, you see, in all the other places it's strong as can be . . . it's gotten a trifle dusty and only seems to be old, but it's really new, there's only one spot . . . a little sort of . . . in the back . . . and also one shoulder, a trifle rubbed through — and this shoulder, too, a trifle — do you see? Not a lot of work, really —"

Petrovich took up the *negligée,* spread it out over the table as a preliminary, examined it for a long time, shook his head, and then groped with his hand on the window sill for a round snuffbox with the portrait of some general or other on its lid — just which one nobody could tell, inasmuch as the place occupied by the face had been holed through with a finger and then pasted over with a small square of paper. After duly taking tobacco, Petrovich held the *negligée* taut in his hands and scrutinized it against the light, and again shook his head; after this he turned it with the lining up and again shook his head, again took off the lid with the general's face pasted over with paper and, having fully loaded both nostrils with snuff, covered the snuffbox, put it away, and at long last, gave his verdict:

"No, there's no fixin' this thing: your wardrobe's in a bad way!"

Akakii Akakiievich's heart skipped a beat at these words.

"But why not, Petrovich?" he asked, almost in the imploring voice of a child. "All that ails it, now . . . it's rubbed through at the shoulders. Surely you must have some small scraps of cloth or other —"

"Why, yes, one could find the scraps — the scraps will turn up," said Petrovich. "Only there's no sewing them on: the whole thing's all rotten: touch a needle to it — and it just crawls apart on you."

"Well, let it crawl — and you just slap a patch right on to it."

"Yes, but there's nothing to slap them little patches on to; there ain't nothing for the patch to take hold on — there's been far too much wear. It's cloth in name only, but if a gust of wind was to blow on it it would scatter."

"Well, now, you just fix it up. That, really, now . . . how can it be?"

"No," said Petrovich decisively, "there ain't a thing to be done. The whole thing's in a bad way. You'd better, when the cold winter spell comes, make footcloths out of it, because stockings ain't so warm. It's them Germans that invented them stockings, so's to rake in more money for themselves." (Petrovich loved to needle the Germans whenever the chance turned up.) "But as for that there overcoat, it looks like you'll have to make yourself a new one."

At the word *new* a mist swam before Akakii Akakiievich's eyes and everything in the room became a hotchpotch. All he could see clearly was the general on the lid of Petrovich's snuffbox, his face pasted over with a piece of paper.

"A new one? But how?" he asked, still as if he were in a dream. "Why, I have no money for that."

"Yes, a new one," said Petrovich with a heathenish imperturbability.

"Well, if there's no getting out of it, how much, now —"

"You mean, how much it would cost?"

"Yes."

"Why, you'd have to cough up three fifties and a bit over," pronounced Petrovich and significantly pursed up his lips at this. He was very fond of strong effects, was fond of somehow nonplusing somebody, utterly and suddenly, and then eyeing his victim sidelong, to see what sort of wry face the nonplusee would pull after his words.

"A hundred and fifty for an overcoat!" poor Akakii Akakiievich cried out — cried out perhaps for the first time since he was born, for he was always distinguished for his low voice.

"Yes, Sir!" said Petrovich. "And what an overcoat, at that! If you put a marten collar on it and add a silk-lined hood it might stand you even two hundred."

"Petrovich, please!" Akakii Akakiievich was saying in an imploring voice, without grasping and without even trying to grasp the words uttered by Petrovich and all his effects. "Fix it somehow or other, now, so's it may do a little longer, at least —"

"Why, no, that'll be only having the work go to waste and spending your money for nothing," said Petrovich, and after these words Akakii Akakiievich walked out annihilated. But Petrovich, after his departure, remained as he was for a long time, with meaningfully pursed lips and without resuming his work, satisfied with neither having lowered himself nor having betrayed the sartorial art.

Out in the street, Akakii Akakiievich walked along like a somnambulist. "What a business, now, what a business," he kept saying to himself. "Really, I never even thought that it, now . . . would turn out like that. . . ." And then, after a pause, added: "So that's it! That's how it's turned out after all. Really, now, I couldn't even suppose that it . . . like that, now —" This was followed by another long pause, after which he uttered aloud: "So that's how it is! This, really, now, is something that's beyond all, now, expectation . . . well, I never! What a fix, now!"

Having said this, instead of heading for home, he started off in an entirely different direction without himself suspecting it. On the way a chimneysweep caught him square with his whole sooty side and covered his whole shoulder with soot; enough quicklime to cover his whole hat tumbled down on him from the top of a building under construction. He noticed nothing of all this and only later, when he ran up against a policeman near his sentry box (who, having placed his halberd near him, was shaking some tobacco out of a paper cornucopia on to his calloused palm), did Akakii Akakiievich come a little to himself, and that only because the policeman said: "What's the idea of shoving your face right into mine? Ain't the sidewalk big enough for you?" This made him look about him and turn homeward.

Only here did he begin to pull his wits together; he perceived his situation in its clear and real light; he started talking to himself no longer in snatches but reasoningly and frankly, as with a judicious friend with whom one might discuss a matter most heartfelt and intimate. "Well, no," said Akakii Akakiievich, "there's no use reasoning with Petrovich now; he's, now, that way. . . . His wife had a chance to give him a drubbing, it looks like. No, it'll be better if I come to him on a Sunday morning; after Saturday night's good time he'll be squinting his eye and very sleepy, so he'll have to have a hair of the dog that bit him, but his wife won't give him any money, now, and just then I'll up with ten kopecks or so and into his hand with it — so he'll be more reasonable to talk with, like, and the overcoat will then be sort of. . . ."

That was the way Akakii Akakiievich reasoned things out to himself, bolstering up his spirits. And, having bided his time till the next Sunday and spied from afar that Petrovich's wife was going off somewhere out of the house, he went straight up to him. Petrovich, sure enough, was squinting his eye hard after the Saturday night before, kept his head bowed down to the floor, and was no end sleepy; but, found that, as soon as he learned what was up, it was as though the Devil himself nudged him.

"Can't be done," said he. "You'll have to order a new overcoat."

Akakii Akakiievich thrust a ten-kopeck coin on him right then and there.

"I'm grateful to you, Sir; I'll have a little something to get me strength back and will drink to your health," said Petrovich, "but as for your overcoat, please don't fret about it; it's of no earthly use any more. As for a new overcoat, I'll tailor a glorious one for you; I'll see to that."

Just the same, Akakii Akakiievich started babbling again about fixing the old one, but Petrovich simply would not listen to him and said: "Yes, I'll tailor a new one for you without fail; you may rely on that, I'll try my very best. We might even do it the way it's all the fashion now — the collar will button with silver catches under appliqué."

It was then that Akakii Akakiievich perceived that there was no doing without a new overcoat, and his spirits sank utterly. Really, now, with what means, with what money would he make this overcoat? Of course he could rely, in part, on the coming holiday bonus, but this money had been apportioned and budgeted ahead long ago. There was an imperative need of outfitting himself with new trousers, paying the shoemaker an old debt for a new pair of vamps to an old pair of bootlegs, and he had to order from a sempstress three shirts and two pair of those nethergarments which it is impolite to mention in print: in short, all the money was bound to be expended entirely, and even if the Director was so gracious as to decide on giving him five and forty, or even fifty rubles as a bonus, instead of forty, why, even then only the veriest trifle would be left over, which, in the capital sum required for the overcoat, would be as a drop in a bucket. Even though Akakii Akakiievich was, of course, aware of Petrovich's maggot of popping out with the devil knows how inordinate an asking price, so that even his wife herself could not restrain herself on occasion from crying out: "What, are you going out of your mind, fool that you are! There's times when he won't take on work for anything, but the Foul One has egged him on to ask a bigger price than all of him is worth" — even though he knew, of course, that Petrovich would probably undertake the work for eighty rubles, nevertheless and notwithstanding where was he to get those eighty rubles? Half of that sum might, perhaps, be found: half of it could have been found, maybe even a little more — but where was he going to get the other half?

But first the reader must be informed where the first half was to come from. Akakii Akakiievich had a custom of putting away a copper or so from every ruble he expended, into a little box under lock and key, with a small opening cut through the lid for dropping money therein. At the expiration of every half-year he made an accounting of the entire sum accumulated in coppers and changed it into small silver. He had kept this up a long time, and in this manner, during the course of several years, the accumulated sum turned out to be more than forty rubles. And so he had half the sum for the overcoat on hand; but where was he to get the other half? Where was he to get the other forty rubles? Akakii Akakiievich mulled the matter over and over and decided that it would be necessary to curtail his ordinary expenses, for the duration of a year at the very least; banish the indulgence in tea of evenings; also, of evenings, to do without lighting candles, but, if there should be need of doing something, to go to his landlady's room and work by her candle; when walking along the streets he would set his foot as lightly and carefully as possible on the cobbles and flagstones, walking almost on tiptoes, and thus avoid wearing out his soles prematurely; his linen would have to be given as infrequently as possible to the laundress and, in order that it might not become too soiled, every time he came home all of it must be taken off, the wearer having to remain only in his jean bathrobe, a most ancient garment and spared even by time itself.

It was, the truth must be told, most difficult for him in the beginning to get habituated to such limitations, but later it did turn into a matter of habit, somehow, and everything went well; he even became perfectly trained to going hungry of evenings; on the other hand, however, he had spiritual sustenance, always carrying about in his thoughts the eternal idea of the new overcoat. From this time forth it seemed as if his very existence had become somehow fuller, as though he had taken unto himself a wife, as though another person was always present with him, as though he were not alone but as if an amiable feminine helpmate had consented to traverse the path of life side by side with him — and this feminine helpmate was none other than this very same overcoat, with a thick quilting of cotton wool, with a strong lining that would never wear out.

He became more animated, somehow, even firmer of character, like a man who has already defined and set a goal for himself. Doubt, indecision — in a word, all vacillating and indeterminate traits — vanished of themselves from his face and actions. At times a sparkle appeared in his eyes; the boldest and most daring of thoughts actually flashed through his head: Shouldn't he, after all, put marten on the collar? Meditations on this subject almost caused him to make absentminded blunders. And on one occasion, as he was transcribing a paper, he all but made an error, so that he emitted an almost audible "Ugh," and made the sign of the cross.

During the course of each month he would make at least one call on Petrovich, to discuss the overcoat: Where would it be best to buy the cloth, and of what color and at what price — and even though somewhat preoccupied he always came home satisfied, thinking that the time would come, at last, when all the necessary things would be bought and the overcoat made.

The matter went even more quickly than he had expected. Contrary to all his anticipations, the Director designated a bonus not of forty or forty-five rubles for Akakii Akakiievich, but all of sixty. Whether he had a premonition that Akakii Akakiievich needed a new overcoat, or whether this had come about of its own self, the fact nevertheless remained: Akakii Akakiievich thus found himself the possessor of an extra twenty rubles. This circumstance hastened the course of things. Some two or three months more of slight starvation — and lo! Akakii Akakiievich had accumulated around eighty rubles. His heart, in general quite calm, began to palpitate. On the very first day possible he set out with Petrovich to the shops. The cloth they bought was very good, and no great wonder, since they had been thinking over its purchase as much as half a year before and hardly a month had gone by without their making a round of the shops to compare prices; but then, Petrovich himself said that there couldn't be better cloth than that. For lining they chose calico, but of such good quality and so closely woven that, to quote Petrovich's words, it was still better than silk and, to look at, even more showy and glossy. Marten they did not buy, for, to be sure, it was expensive, but instead they picked out the best catskin the shop boasted — catskin that could, at a great enough distance, be taken for marten.

Petrovich spent only a fortnight in fussing about with the making of the overcoat, for there was a great deal of stitching to it, and if it hadn't been for that it would have been ready considerably earlier. For his work

Petrovich took twelve rubles — he couldn't have taken any less; everything was positively sewn with silk thread, with a small double stitch, and after the stitching Petrovich went over every seam with his own teeth, pressing out various figures with them.

It was on . . . it would be hard to say on precisely what day, but it was, most probably, the most triumphant day in Akakii Akakiievich's life when Petrovich, at last, brought the overcoat. He brought it in the morning, just before Akakii Akakiievich had to set out for his Bureau. Never, at any other time, would the overcoat have come in so handy, because rather hard frosts were already setting in and, apparently, were threatening to become still more severe. Petrovich's entrance with the overcoat was one befitting a good tailor. Such a portentous expression appeared on his face as Akakii Akakiievich had never yet beheld. Petrovich felt to the fullest, it seemed, that he had performed no petty labor and that he had suddenly evinced in himself that abyss which lies between those tailors who merely put in linings and alter and fix garments and those who create new ones.

He extracted the overcoat from the bandanna in which he had brought it. (The bandanna was fresh from the laundress; it was only later on that he thrust it in his pocket for practical use.) Having drawn out the overcoat, he looked at it quite proudly and, holding it in both hands, threw it deftly over the shoulders of Akakii Akakiievich, pulled it and smoothed it down the back with his hand, then draped it on Akakii Akakiievich somewhat loosely. Akakiievich, as a man along in his years, wanted to try it on with his arms through the sleeves. Petrovich helped him on with it: it turned out to be fine, even with his arms through the sleeves. In a word, the overcoat proved to be perfect and had come in the very nick of time. Petrovich did not let slip the opportunity of saying that he had done the work so cheaply only because he lived in a place without a sign, on a side street, and, besides, had known Akakii Akakiievich for a long time; *but* on the Nevski Prospect they would have taken seventy-five rubles from him for the labor alone. Akakii Akakiievich did not feel like arguing the matter with Petrovich and, besides, he had a dread of all the fancy sums with which Petrovich liked to throw dust in people's eyes. He paid the tailor off, thanked him, and walked right out in the new overcoat on his way to the Bureau. Petrovich walked out at his heels and, staying behind on the street, for a long while kept looking after the overcoat from afar, and then deliberately went out of his way so that, after cutting across a crooked lane, he might run out again into the street and have another glance at his overcoat from a different angle — that is, full front.

In the meantime Akakii Akakiievich walked along feeling in the most festive of moods. He was conscious every second of every minute that he had a new overcoat on his shoulders, and several times even smiled slightly because of his inward pleasure. In reality he was a gainer on two points: for one, the overcoat was warm, for the other, it was a fine thing. He did not notice the walk at all and suddenly found himself at the Bureau; in the porter's room he took off his overcoat, looked it all over, and entrusted it to the particular care of the doorman. None knows in what manner everybody in the Bureau suddenly learned that Akakii Akakiievich had a new overcoat, and that the *negligée* was no longer in existence. They all immediately ran out into the vestibule to inspect Akakii Akakiievich's new overcoat. They fell to congratulating him, to saying agreeable things to him, so that at first he could merely smile, and in a short time became actually embarrassed. And when all of them, having besieged him, began telling him that the new overcoat ought to be baptized and that he ought, at the least, to get up an evening party for them, Akakii Akakiievich was utterly at a loss, not knowing what to do with himself, what answers to make, nor how to get out of inviting them. It was only a few minutes later that he began assuring them, quite simple-heartedly, that it wasn't a new overcoat at all, that it was just an ordinary overcoat, that in fact it was an old overcoat. Finally one of the bureaucrats — some sort of an Assistant to a Head of a Department actually — probably in order to show that he was not at all a proud stick and willing to mingle even with those beneath him, said: "So be it, then; I'm giving a party this evening and ask all of you to have tea with me; today, appropriately enough, happens to be my birthday."

The clerks, naturally, at once thanked the Assistant to a Head of a Department and accepted the invitation with enthusiasm. Akakii Akakiievich attempted to excuse himself at first, but all began saying that it would show disrespect to decline, that it would be simply a shame and a disgrace, and after that there was absolutely no way for him to back out. However, when it was all over, he felt a pleasant glow as he reminded himself that this would give him a chance to take a walk in his new overcoat even in the evening. The whole day was for Akakii Akakiievich something in the nature of the greatest and most triumphant of holidays.

Akakii Akakiievich returned home in the happiest mood, took off the overcoat, and hung it carefully on the wall, once more getting his fill of admiring the cloth and the lining, and then purposely dragged out, for comparison, his former *negligée*, which by now had practically disintegrated. He glanced at it and he himself had to laugh, so great was the difference! And for a long while thereafter, as he ate dinner, he kept on smiling slightly whenever the present state of the *negligée* came to his mind. He dined gaily, and after dinner did not write a single stroke; there were no papers of any kind, for that matter; he just simply played the sybarite a little, lounging on his bed, until it became dark. Then, without putting matters off any longer, he dressed, threw the overcoat over his shoulders, and walked out into the street.

We are, to our regret, unable to say just where the official who had extended the invitation lived; our memory is beginning to play us false — very much so — and everything in Petersburg, no matter what, including all its streets and houses, has become so muddled in our mind that it's quite hard to get anything out therefrom in any sort of decent shape. But wherever it may have been, at least this much is certain: that official lived in the best part of town; consequently a very long way from Akakii Akakiievich's quarters. First of all Akakii Akakiievich had to traverse certain deserted streets with but scant illumination; however, in keeping with his progress toward the official's domicile, the streets became more animated; the pedestrians flitted by more and more often; he began meeting even ladies, handsomely dressed; the men he came upon had beaver collars on their overcoats; more and more rarely did he encounter jehus[1] with latticed wooden sleighs, studded over with gilt nails — on the contrary, he kept coming across first-class drivers in caps of raspberry-hued velvet, their sleighs lacquered and with bearskin robes, while the carriages had decorated seats for the drivers and raced down the roadway, their wheels screeching over the snow.

Akakii Akakiievich eyed all this as a novelty — it was several years by now since he had set foot out of his house in the evening. He stopped with curiosity before the illuminated window of a shop to look at a picture, depicting some handsome woman or other, who was taking off her shoe, thus revealing her whole leg (very far from ill-formed), while behind her back some gentleman or other, sporting side whiskers and a handsome goatee, was poking his head out of the door of an adjoining room. Akakii Akakiievich shook his head and smiled, after which he went on his way. Why had he smiled? Was it because he had encountered something utterly unfamiliar, yet about which, nevertheless, everyone preserves a certain instinct? Or did he think, like so many other petty clerks, "My, the French they are a funny race! No use talking! If there's anything they get a notion of, then, sure enough, there it is!" And yet, perhaps, he did not think even that; after all, there's no way of insinuating one's self into a man's soul, of finding out all that he might be thinking about.

At last he reached the house in which the Assistant to a Head of a Department lived. The Assistant to a Head of a Department lived on a grand footing; there was a lantern on the staircase: his apartment was only one flight up. On entering the foyer of the apartment Akakii Akakiievich beheld row after row of galoshes. In their midst, in the center of the room, stood a samovar, noisy and emitting clouds of steam. The walls were covered with hanging overcoats and capes, among which were even such as had beaver collars or lapels of velvet. On the other side of the wall he could hear much noise and talk, which suddenly became distinct and resounding when the door opened and a flunky came out with a tray full of empty tumblers, a cream pitcher, and a basket of biscuits. It was evident that the bureaucrats had gathered long since and had already had their first glasses of tea.

Akakii Akakiievich, hanging up his overcoat himself, entered the room and simultaneously all the candles, bureaucrats, tobacco-pipes and card tables flickered before him, and the continuous conversation and the scraping of moving chairs, coming from all sides, struck dully on his ears. He

[1] coach-drivers.

halted quite awkwardly in the center of the room, at a loss and trying to think what he ought to do. But he had already been noticed, was received with much shouting, and everyone immediately went to the foyer and again inspected his overcoat. Akakii Akakiievich, even though he was somewhat embarrassed, still could not but rejoice on seeing them all bestow such praises on his overcoat, since he was a man with an honest heart. Then, of course, they all dropped him and his overcoat and, as is usual, directed their attention to the whist tables.

All this — the din, the talk, and the throng of people — all this was somehow a matter of wonder to Akakii Akakiievich. He simply did not know what to do, how to dispose of his hands, his feet, and his whole body; finally he sat down near the card-players, watched their cards, looked now at the face of this man, now of that, and after some time began to feel bored, to yawn — all the more so since his usual bedtime had long since passed. He wanted to say good-bye to his host but they wouldn't let him, saying that they absolutely must toast his new acquisition in a goblet of champagne. An hour later supper was served, consisting of mixed salad, cold veal, meat pie, patties from a pastry cook's, and champagne. They forced Akakii Akakiievich to empty two goblets, after which he felt that the room had become ever so much more cheerful. However, he absolutely could not forget that it was already twelve o'clock and that it was long since time for him to go home. So that his host might not somehow get the idea of detaining him, he crept out of the room, managed to find his overcoat — which, not without regret, he saw lying on the floor; then, shaking the overcoat and taking every bit of fluff off it, he threw it over his shoulders and made his way down the stairs and out of the house.

It was still dusk out in the street. Here and there small general stores, those round-the-clock clubs for domestics and all other servants, were still open; other shops, which were closed, nevertheless showed, by a long streak of light along the crack either at the outer edge or the bottom, that they were not yet without social life and that, probably, the serving wenches and lads were still winding up their discussions and conversations, thus throwing their masters into utter bewilderment as to their whereabouts. Akakii Akakiievich walked along in gay spirits; he even actually made a sudden dash, for some unknown reason, after some lady or other, who had passed by him like a flash of lightning, and every part of whose body was filled with buoyancy. However, he stopped right then and there and resumed his former exceedingly gentle pace, actually wondering himself at the sprightliness that had come upon him from none knows where.

Soon he again was passing stretch after stretch of those desolate streets which are never too gay even in the daytime, but are even less so in the evening. Now they had become still more deserted and lonely; he came upon glimmering street lamps more and more infrequently — the allotment of oil was now evidently decreasing; there was a succession of wooden houses and fences, with never another soul about; the snow alone glittered on the street, and the squat hovels, with their shutters closed in sleep, showed like depressing dark blotches. He approached a spot where the street was cut in two by an unending square, with the houses on the other side of it barely visible — a square that loomed ahead like an awesome desert.

Far in the distance, God knows where, a little light flickered in a policeman's sentry box that seemed to stand at the end of the world. Akakii Akakiievich's gay mood somehow diminished considerably at this point. He set foot in the square, not without a premonition of something evil. He looked back and on each side of him — it was as though he were in the midst of a sea. "No, it's better even not to look," he reflected and went on with his eyes shut. And when he did open them to see if the end of the square were near, he suddenly saw standing before him, almost at his very nose, two strangers with mustaches — just what sort of men they were was something he couldn't even make out. A mist arose before his eyes and his heart began to pound.

"Why, that there overcoat is mine!" said one of the men in a thunderous voice, grabbing him by the collar. Akakii Akakiievich was just about to yell "Police!" when the other put a fist right up to his mouth, a fist as big as any government clerk's head, adding: "There, you just let one peep out of you!"

All that Akakii Akakiievich felt was that they had taken the overcoat off him, given him a kick in the back with the knee, and that he had fallen flat on his back in the snow, after which he felt nothing more. In a few minutes he came to and got up on his feet, but there was no longer anybody around. He felt that it was cold out in that open space and that he no longer had the overcoat, and began to yell; but his voice, it seemed, had no intention whatsoever of reaching the other end of the square. Desperate, without ceasing to yell, he started off at a run across the square directly toward the sentry box near which the policeman was standing and, leaning on his halberd, was watching the running man, apparently with curiosity, as if he wished to know why the devil anybody should be running toward him from afar and yelling. Akakii Akakiievich, having run up to him, began to shout in a stifling voice that he, the policeman, had been asleep, that he was not watching and couldn't see that a man was being robbed. The policeman answered that he hadn't seen anything, that he had seen two men of some sort stop him in the middle of the square, but he had thought they were friends of Akakii Akakiievich's, and that instead of cursing him out for nothing he'd better go on the morrow to the Inspector, and the Inspector would find out who had taken his overcoat.

Akakii Akakiievich ran home in utter disorder; whatever little hair still lingered on his temples and the nape of his neck was all disheveled; his side and his breast and his trousers were all wet with snow. The old woman, his landlady, hearing the dreadful racket at the door, hurriedly jumped out of bed, and, with a shoe on only one foot, ran down to open the door, modestly holding the shift at her breast with one hand; but, on opening the door and seeing Akakii Akakiievich in such a state, she staggered back. When he had told her what the matter was, however, she wrung her hands and said that he ought to go directly to the Justice of the Peace; the District Officer of Police would take him in, would make promises to him and then lead him about by the nose; yes, it would be best of all to go straight to the Justice. Why, she was even acquainted with him, seeing as how Anna, the Finnish woman who had formerly been her cook, had now gotten a place as a nurse at the Justice's; that she, the landlady herself, sees the Justice often when he drives past her house, and also that he went to church every Sunday, praying, yet at the same time looking so cheerfully at all the folks, and that consequently, as one could see by all the signs, he was a kindhearted man. Having heard this solution of his troubles through to the end, the saddened Akakii Akakiievich shuffled off to his room, and how he passed the night there may be left to the discernment of him who can in any degree imagine the situation of another.

Early in the morning he set out for the Justice's, but was told there that he was sleeping; he came at ten o'clock, and was told again, "He's sleeping." He came at eleven; they told him, "Why, His Honor's not at home." He tried at lunchtime, but the clerks in the reception room would not let him through to the presence under any circumstances and absolutely had to know what business he had come on and what had occurred, so that, at last, Akakii Akakiievich for once in his life wanted to evince firmness of character and said sharply and categorically that he had to see the Justice personally, that they dared not keep him out, that he had come from his own Bureau on a Government matter, and that now, when he'd lodge a complaint against them, why, they would see, then. The clerks dared not say anything in answer to this and one of them went to call out the Justice of the Peace.

The Justice's reaction to Akakii Akakiievich's story of how he had been robbed of his overcoat was somehow exceedingly odd. Instead of turning his attention to the main point of the matter, he began interrogating Akakii Akakiievich: Just why had he been coming home at so late an hour? Had he, perhaps, looked in at, or hadn't he actually visited, some disorderly house? Akakii Akakiievich became utterly confused and walked out of the office without himself knowing whether the investigation about the overcoat would be instituted or not.

This whole day he stayed away from his Bureau (the only time in his life he had done so). On the following day he put in an appearance, all pale and in his old *negligée,* which had become more woebegone than ever. The recital of the robbery of the overcoat, despite the fact that there proved to be certain ones among his co-workers who did not let pass even this opportunity to make fun of Akakii Akakiievich, nevertheless touched many. They decided on the spot to make up a collection for him, but they collected the utmost trifle, inasmuch as the petty officials had spent a lot even without this, having subscribed for a portrait of the Director and for some book or

other, at the invitation of the Chief of the Department, who was a friend of
the writer's; and so the sum proved to be most trifling. One of them, moved
by compassion, decided, at the least, to aid Akakii Akakiievich with good
advice telling him that he oughtn't to go to the precinct officer of the police, because, even though it might come about that the precinct officer,
wishing to merit the approval of his superiors, might locate the overcoat in
some way, the overcoat would in the end remain with the police, if Akakii
Akakiievich could not present legal proofs that it belonged to him; but that
the best thing of all would be to turn to a *certain important person*; that this
important person, after conferring and corresponding with the proper people in the proper quarters, could speed things up.

There was no help for it; Akakii Akakiievich summoned up his courage
to go to the important person. Precisely what the important person's post
was and what the work of that post consisted of, has remained unknown up
to now. It is necessary to know that the certain important person had only
recently become an Important Person, but, up to then, had been an unimportant person. However, his post was not considered an important one
even now in comparison with more important ones. But there will always be
found a circle of people who perceive the importance of that which is unimportant in the eyes of others. However, he tried to augment his importance by many other means, to wit: he inaugurated the custom of having
the subordinate clerks meet him while he was still on the staircase when he
arrived at his office; another, of no one coming directly into his presence,
but having everything follow the most rigorous precedence: a Collegiate
Registrar was to report to the Provincial Secretary, the Provincial Secretary
to a Titular one, or whomever else it was necessary to report to, and only
thus was any matter to come to him. For it is thus in our Holy Russia that
everything is infected with imitativeness; everyone apes his superior and
postures like him. They even say that a certain Titular Councilor, when
they put him at the helm of some small individual chancellery, immediately
had a separate room for himself partitioned off, dubbing it the Reception
Center, and had placed at the door some doormen or other with red collars
and gold braid, who turned the doorknob and opened the door for every visitor, even though there was hardly room in the Reception Center to hold
even an ordinary desk.

The manners and ways of the important person were imposing and
majestic, but not at all complex. The chief basis of his system was strictness.
"Strictness, strictness, and — strictness," he was wont to say, and when uttering the last word he usually looked very significantly into the face of the
person to whom he was speaking, even though, by the way, there was no
reason for all this, inasmuch as the half-score of clerks constituting the
whole administrative mechanism of his chancellery was under the proper
state of fear and trembling even as it was: catching sight of him from afar
the staff would at once drop whatever it was doing and wait, at attention,
until the Chief had passed through the room. His ordinary speech with his

subordinates reeked of strictness and consisted almost entirely of three phrases: "How dare you? Do you know whom you're talking to? Do you realize in whose presence you are?" However, at soul he was a kindly man, treated his friends well, and was obliging; but the rank of General had knocked him completely off his base. Having received a General's rank he had somehow become muddled, had lost his sense of direction, and did not know how to act. If he happened to be with his equals he was still as human as need be, a most decent man, in many respects — even a man not at all foolish; but whenever he happened to be in a group where there were people even one rank below him, why, there was no holding him; he was taciturn, and his situation aroused pity, all the more since he himself felt that he could have passed the time infinitely more pleasantly. In his eyes one could at times see a strong desire to join in some circle and its interesting conversation, but he was stopped by the thought: Wouldn't this be too much unbending on his part, wouldn't it be a familiar action, and wouldn't he lower his importance thereby? And as a consequence of such considerations he remained forever aloof in that invariably taciturn state, only uttering some monosyllabic sounds at rare intervals, and had thus acquired the reputation of a most boring individual.

It was before such an *important person* that our Akakii Akakiievich appeared, and he appeared at a most inauspicious moment, quite inopportune for himself — although, by the bye, most opportune for the important person. The important person was seated in his private office and had gotten into very, very jolly talk with a certain recently arrived old friend and childhood companion whom he had not seen for several years. It was at this point that they announced to the important person that some Bashmachkin or other had come to see him. He asked abruptly, "Who is he?" and was told, "Some petty clerk or other." "Ah. He can wait; this isn't the right time for him to come," said the important man.

At this point it must be said that the important man had fibbed a little; he had the time; he and his old friend had long since talked over everything and had been long eking out their conversation with protracted silences, merely patting each other lightly on the thigh from time to time and adding, "That's how it is, Ivan Abramovich!" and "That's just how it is, Stepan Varlaamovich!" But for all that he gave orders for the petty clerk to wait a while just the same, in order to show his friend, a man who had been long out of the Civil Service and rusticating in his village, how long petty clerks had to cool their heels in his anteroom.

Finally, having had his fill of talk, yet having had a still greater fill of silences, and after each had smoked a cigar to the end in a quite restful armchair with an adjustable back, he at last appeared to recall the matter and said to his secretary, who had halted in the doorway with some papers for a report, "Why, I think there's a clerk waiting out there. Tell him he may come in."

On beholding the meek appearance of Akakii Akakiievich and his rather old, skimpy frock coat, he suddenly turned to him and asked, "What is it you wish?" — in a voice abrupt and firm, which he had purposely rehearsed beforehand in his room at home in solitude and before a mirror, actually a week before he had received his present post and his rank of General.

Akakii Akakiievich already had plenty of time to experience the requisite awe, was somewhat abashed, and, as best he could, insofar as his poor freedom of tongue would allow him, explained, adding even more *nows* than he would have at another time, that his overcoat had been perfectly new, and that, now, he had been robbed of it in a perfectly inhuman fashion, and that he was turning to him, now, so that he might interest himself through his . . . now . . . might correspond with the Head of Police or somebody else, and find his overcoat, now. . . . Such conduct, for some unknown reason, appeared familiar to the General.

"What are you up to, my dear Sir?" he resumed abruptly. "Don't you know the proper procedure? Where have you come to? Don't you know how matters ought to be conducted? As far as this is concerned, you should have first of all submitted a petition to the Chancellery; it would have gone from there to the head of the proper Division, then would have been transferred to the Secretary, and the Secretary would in due time have brought it to my attention —"

"But, Your Excellency," said Akakii Akakiievich, trying to collect whatever little pinch of presence of mind he had, yet feeling at the same time that he was in a dreadful sweat. "I ventured to trouble you, Your Excellency, because secretaries, now . . . aren't any too much to be relied upon —"

"What? What? What?" said the important person. "Where did you get such a tone from? Where did you get such notions? What sort of rebellious feeling has spread among the young people against the administrators and their superiors?" The important person had, it seems, failed to notice that Akakii Akakiievich would never see fifty again, consequently, even if he could have been called a young man it could be applied only relatively, that is, to someone who was already seventy. "Do you know whom you're saying this to? Do you realize in whose presence you are? Do you realize? Do you realize, I'm asking you!" Here he stamped his foot, bringing his voice to such an overwhelming note that even another than an Akakii Akakiievich would have been frightened. Akakii Akakiievich was simply bereft of his senses, swayed, shook all over, and simply could not stand on his feet. If a couple of doormen had not run up right then and there to support him he would have slumped to the floor; they carried him out in a practically cataleptic state. But the important person, satisfied because the effect had surpassed even anything he had expected, and inebriated by the idea that a word from him could actually deprive a man of his senses, looked out of the corner of his eye to learn how his friend was taking this and noticed, not without satisfaction, that his friend was in a most indeterminate state and was even beginning to experience fear on his own account.

How he went down the stairs, how he came out into the street — that was something Akakii Akakiievich was no longer conscious of. He felt neither his hands nor his feet; never in all his life had he been dragged over such hot coals by a General — and a General outside his bureau, at that! With his mouth gaping, stumbling off the sidewalk, he breasted the blizzard that was whistling and howling through the streets; the wind, as is its wont in Petersburg, blew upon him from all the four quarters, from every cross lane. In a second it had blown a quinsy down his throat, and he crawled home without the strength to utter a word; he became all swollen and took to his bed. That's how effective a proper hauling over the coals can be at times!

On the next day he was running a high fever. Thanks to the magnanimous all-round help of the Petersburg climate, the disease progressed more rapidly than could have been expected, and when the doctor appeared he, after having felt the patient's pulse, could not strike on anything to do save prescribing hot compresses, and that solely so that the sick man might not be left without the beneficial help of medicine; but, on the whole, he announced on the spot that in another day and a half it would be curtains for Akakii Akakiievich, after which he turned to the landlady and said, "As for you, Mother, don't you be losing any time for nothing; order a pine coffin for him right now, because a coffin of oak will be beyond his means."

Whether Akakii Akakiievich heard the doctor utter these words, so fateful for him, and, even if he did hear them, whether they had a staggering effect on him, whether he felt regrets over his life of hard sledding — about that nothing is known, inasmuch as he was all the time running a temperature and was in delirium. Visions, each one stranger than the one before, appeared before him ceaselessly: now he saw Petrovich and was ordering him to make an overcoat with some sort of traps to catch thieves, whom he ceaselessly imagined to be under his bed, at every minute calling his landlady to pull out from under his blanket one of them who had actually crawled under there; then he would ask why his old *negligée* was hanging in front of him, for he had a new overcoat; then once more he had a hallucination that he was standing before the General, getting a proper raking over the coals, and saying, "Forgive me, Your Excellency!"; then, finally, he actually took to swearing foully, uttering such dreadful words that his old landlady could do nothing but cross herself, having never in her life heard anything of the sort from him, all the more so since these words followed immediately after "Your Excellency!"

After that he spoke utter nonsense, so that there was no understanding anything; all one could perceive was that his incoherent words and thoughts all revolved about that overcoat and nothing else.

Finally poor Akakii Akakiievich gave up the ghost. Neither his room nor his things were put under seal; in the first place because he had no heirs, and in the second because there was very little left for anybody to inherit, to wit: a bundle of goose quills, a quire of white governmental paper, three pairs of socks, two or three buttons that had come off his trousers, and the *negligée* which the reader is already familiar with. Who fell heir to all this treasure-trove, God knows; I confess that even the narrator of this tale was not much interested in the matter. They bore Akakii Akakiievich off and buried him. And Petersburg was left without Akakii Akakiievich, as if he had never been therein. There vanished and disappeared a being protected by none, endeared to no one, of no interest to anyone, a being that actually had failed to attract to itself the attention of even a naturalist who wouldn't let a chance slip of sticking an ordinary housefly on a pin and of examining it through a microscope; a being that had submissively endured the jests of the whole chancellery and that had gone to its grave without any extraordinary fuss, but before which, nevertheless, even before the very end of its life, there had flitted a radiant guest in the guise of an overcoat, which had animated for an instant a poor life, and upon which being calamity had come crashing down just as unbearably as it comes crashing down upon the heads of the mighty ones of this earth!

A few days after his death a doorman was sent to his house from the Bureau with an injunction for Akakii Akakiievich to appear immediately; the Chief, now, was asking for him; but the doorman had to return empty-handed, reporting back that "he weren't able to come no more," and to the question, "Why not?" expressed himself in the words, "Why, just so; he up and died; they buried him four days back." Thus did they learn at the Bureau about the death of Akakii Akakiievich, and the very next day a new pettifogger, considerably taller than Akakii Akakiievich, was already sitting in his place and putting down the letters no longer in such a straight hand, but considerably more on the slant and downhill.

But whoever could imagine that this wouldn't be all about Akakii Akakiievich, that he was fated to live for several noisy days after his death, as though in reward for a life that had gone by utterly unnoticed? Yet that is how things fell out, and our poor history is taking on a fantastic ending.

Rumors suddenly spread through Petersburg that near the Kalinkin Bridge, and much farther out still, a dead man had started haunting of nights, in the guise of a petty government clerk, seeking for some overcoat or other that had been purloined from him and, because of that stolen overcoat, snatching from all and sundry shoulders, without differentiating among the various ranks and titles, all sorts of overcoats: whether they had collars of catskin or beaver, whether they were quilted with cotton wool, whether they were lined with raccoon, with fox, with bear — in a word, every sort of fur and skin that man has ever thought of for covering his own hide. One of the clerks in the Bureau had seen the dead man with his own eyes and had immediately recognized in him Akakii Akakiievich. This had inspired him with such horror, however, that he started running for all his legs were worth and for that reason could not make him out very well but had merely seen the other shake his finger at him from afar. From all sides came an uninterrupted flow of complaints that backs and shoulders — it wouldn't matter so much if they were merely those of Titular Councilors, but even those of Privy Councilors were affected — were exposed to the danger of catching thorough colds, because of this oft-repeated snatching-off of overcoats.

An order was put through to the police to capture the dead man, at any cost, dead or alive, and to punish him in the severest manner as an example to others — and they all but succeeded in this. To be precise, a policeman at a sentry box on a certain block of the Kirushkin Lane had already gotten a perfect grip on the dead man by his coat collar, at the very scene of his malefaction, while attempting to snatch off the frieze overcoat of some retired musician, who in his time had tootled a flute. Seizing the dead man by the collar, the policeman had summoned two of his colleagues by shouting and had entrusted the ghost to them to hold him, the while he himself took just a moment to reach down in his bootleg for his snuffbox, to relieve temporarily a nose that had been frostbitten six times in his life; but the snuff, probably, was of such a nature as even a dead man could not stand. Hardly had the policeman, after stopping his right nostril with a finger, succeeded in drawing half a handful of rapee up his left, than the dead man sneezed so heartily that he completely bespattered the eyes of all the three myrmidons. While they were bringing their fists up to rub their eyes, the dead man vanished without leaving as much as a trace, so that they actually did not know whether he had really been in their hands or not.

From then on the policemen developed such a phobia of dead men that they were afraid to lay hands even on living ones and merely shouted from a distance, "Hey, there, get going!" and the dead government clerk began to do his haunting even beyond the Kalinkin Bridge, inspiring not a little fear in all timid folk.

However, we have dropped entirely a certain *important person*, who, in reality, had been all but the cause of the fantastic trend taken by what is, by the bye, a perfectly true story. First of all, a sense of justice compels us to say that the *certain important person*, soon after the departure of poor Akakii Akakiievich, done to a turn in the raking over the hot coals, had felt something in the nature of compunction. He was no stranger to compassion; many kind impulses found access to his heart, despite the fact that his rank often stood in the way of their revealing themselves. As soon as the visiting friend had left his private office, he actually fell into a brown study over Akakii Akakiievich. And from that time on, almost every day, there appeared before him the pale Akakii Akakiievich, who had not been able to stand up under an administrative hauling over the coals. The thought concerning him disquieted the certain important person to such a degree that, a week later, he even decided to send a clerk to him to find out what the man had wanted, and how he was, and whether it were really possible to help him in some way. And when he was informed that Akakii Akakiievich had died suddenly in a fever he was left actually stunned, hearkening to the reproaches of conscience, and was out of sorts the whole day.

Wishing to distract himself to some extent and to forget the unpleasant impression this news had made upon him, he set out for an evening party to one of his friends, where he found a suitable social gathering, and, what was best of all, all the men there were of almost the same rank, so that he absolutely could not feel constrained in any way. This had an astonishing effect on the state of his spirits. He relaxed, became amiable and pleasant to converse with — in a word, he passed the time very agreeably. At supper he drank off a goblet or two of champagne — a remedy which, as everybody knows, has not at all an ill effect upon one's gaiety. The champagne predisposed him to certain extracurricular considerations; to be precise, he decided not to go home yet but to drop in on a certain lady of his acquaintance, a Caroline Ivanovna — a lady of German extraction, apparently, toward whom his feelings and relations were friendly. It must be pointed out the important person was no longer a young man, that he was a good spouse, a respected *paterfamilias.* He had two sons, one of whom was already serving in a chancellery, and a pretty daughter of sixteen, with a somewhat humped yet very charming little nose, who came to kiss his hand every day, adding, "*Bonjour,* papa," as she did so. His wife, a woman who still had not lost her freshness and was not even in the least hard to look at, would allow him to kiss her hand first, then, turning her own over, kissed the hand that was holding hers.

Yet *the important person,* who, by the bye, was perfectly contented with domestic tendernesses, found it respectable to have a lady friend in another part of the city. This lady friend was not in the least fresher or younger than his wife, but such are the enigmas that exist in this world, and to sit in judgment upon them is none of our affair. And so the important person came down the steps, climbed into his sleigh, and told his driver, "To Caroline Ivanovna's!" — while he himself, after muffling up rather luxuriously in his warm overcoat, remained in that pleasant state than which no better could even be thought of for a Russian — that is, when one isn't even thinking of his own volition, but the thoughts in the meanwhile troop into one's head by themselves, each more pleasant than the other, without giving one even the trouble of pursuing them and seeking them. Filled with agreeable feelings, he lightly recalled all the gay episodes of the evening he had spent, all his *mots*[2] that had made the select circle go off into peals of laughter; many of them he even repeated in a low voice and found that they were still just as amusing as before, and for that reason it is not to be wondered at that even he chuckled at them heartily.

Occasionally, however, he became annoyed with the gusty wind which, suddenly escaping from God knows where and no one knows for

---

[2] witticisms (French; literally, "words").

what reason, simply cut the face, tossing tatters of snow thereat, making the collar of his overcoat belly out like a sail, or suddenly, with unnatural force, throwing it over his head and in this manner giving him ceaseless trouble in extricating himself from it.

Suddenly the important person felt that someone had seized him rather hard by his collar. Turning around, he noticed a man of no great height, in a old, much worn frock coat, and, not without horror, recognized in him Akakii Akakiievich. The petty clerk's face was wan as snow and looked utterly like the face of a dead man. But the horror of the important person passed all bounds when he saw that the mouth of the man became twisted and, horribly wafting upon him the odor of the grave, uttered the following speech: "Ah, so there you are, now, at last! At last I have collared you, now! Your overcoat is just the one I need! You didn't put yourself out any about mine, and on top of that hauled me over the coals — so now let me have yours!"

The poor important person almost passed away. No matter how firm of character he was in his chancellery and before his inferiors in general, and although after but one look merely at his manly appearance and his figure everyone said, "My, what character he has!" — in this instance, nevertheless, like quite a number of men who have the appearance of doughty knights, he experienced such terror that, not without reason, he even began to fear an attack of some physical disorder. He even hastened to throw his overcoat off his shoulders himself and cried out to the driver in a voice that was not his own. "Go home — fast as you can!"

The driver, on hearing the voice that the important person used only at critical moments and which he often accompanied by something of a far more physical nature, drew his head in between his shoulders just to be on the safe side, swung his whip, and flew off like an arrow. In just a little over six minutes the important person was already at the entrance to his own house. Pale, frightened out of his wits, and minus his overcoat, he had come home instead of to Caroline Ivanovna's, somehow made his way stumblingly to his room, and spent the night in quite considerable distress, so that the next day, during the morning tea, his daughter told him outright, "You're all pale today, papa." But papa kept silent and said not a word to anybody of what had befallen him, and where he had been, and where he had intended to go.

This adventure made a strong impression on him. He even badgered his subordinates at rarer intervals with his, "How dare you? Do you realize in whose presence you are?" — and even if he did utter these phrases he did not do so before he had first heard through to the end just what was what. But still more remarkable is the fact that from that time forth the apparition of the dead clerk ceased its visitations utterly; evidently the General's overcoat fitted him to a t; at least, no cases of overcoats being snatched off anybody were heard of any more, anywhere. However, many energetic and solicitous people simply would not calm down and kept on saying from

time to time that the dead government clerk was still haunting the remoter
parts of the city.

And, sure enough, one policeman at a sentry box in Colomna had with
his own eyes seen the apparition coming out of a house; but, being by nature somewhat puny, so that on one occasion an ordinary well-grown shoat,
darting out of a private yard, had knocked him off his feet, to the profound
amusement of the cab drivers who were standing around, from whom he
had exacted a copper each for humiliating him so greatly, to buy snuff
with — well, being puny, he had not dared to halt him but simply followed
him in the dark until such time as the apparition suddenly looked over its
shoulder, and, halting, asked him, "What are you after?" and shook a fist at
him whose like for size was not to be found among the living. The policeman said, "Nothing," and at once turned back. The apparition, however,
was considerably taller by now and was sporting a pair of enormous mustachios; setting its steps apparently in the direction of the Obuhov Bridge, it
disappeared utterly in the darkness of night.

[1840]

IVAN TURGENEV (1818–1883) was born in the city of Orel, south of Moscow, and spent his early childhood at Spasskoye, the estate of his mother, a wealthy, domineering heiress who was capable of great cruelty to her servants and to her three sons. His father was a handsome, impecunious former cavalry officer who neglected his children, and Turgenev was raised by his mother. At the age of fifteen Turgenev entered the University of Moscow, but the following year he transferred to the University of St. Petersburg. In 1838 he continued his studies at the University of Berlin, where he met other "westernizers," young Russians who were eager for political reforms in their homeland and believed that Russia's progress lay in adopting the best features of European civilization.

Returning to Russia in 1841, Turgenev decided to make literature his career. His first success came in 1847, when the magazine The Contemporary published his short story about two serfs, "Khor and Kalinych." Turgenev continued to write short stories, many of which appeared together in book form in 1852 as A Sportsman's Sketches. These won him acclaim as an artist. They also had considerable effect on public opinion: the stories consistently presented the Russian serf — at that time a peasant owned by his master — as a human being, often superior in humanity to his owner. Some believe that A Sportsman's Sketches was partially responsible for the decision of Czar Alexander II to abolish serfdom a decade later. But oppressive conditions in Russia and problems with official censors caused Turgenev to leave the country in 1855, and he spent most of the rest of his life abroad. All of his six novels — including his most famous, Fathers and Sons (1862) — are concerned with the country's social and political issues, even though they were written in exile.

Turgenev was a tireless craftsman, and he is famous for his descriptions of Russian nature, full of varied, subtle, lyrical detail. Living in Paris, he would often meet other émigré writers in the cafés and talk about Russia. The American writer Henry James, who was sometimes present, has described their conversations. To Turgenev, James wrote, the "germ of a story" was never the plot, but rather the "representation of certain persons. The first form in which a tale appeared to him was as the figure of an individual or a combination of individuals, whom he wished to see in action." Turgenev reported that "Byezhin Prairie" took shape in his mind in the following sequence. First he thought of describing the peasant boys driving the horses; then he wrote the campfire tales; he composed the opening section, where the narrator gets lost, third. Then he published the story in a magazine, but readers complained it lacked a theme or a "general thread," so Turgenev added the conclusion announcing Pavel's death when he included the story in A Sportsman's Sketches the following year.

Ivan Turgenev

ၰၰ

BYEZHIN PRAIRIE

—*translated by Constance Garnett*

It was a glorious July day, one of those days which only come after many days of fine weather. From earliest morning the sky is clear; the sunrise does not glow with fire; it is suffused with a soft roseate flush. The sun, not fiery, not red-hot as in time of stifling drought, not dull purple as before a storm, but with a bright and genial radiance, rises peacefully behind a long and narrow cloud, shines out freshly, and plunges again into its lilac mist. The delicate upper edge of the strip of cloud flashes in little gleaming snakes; their brilliance is like polished silver. But, lo! the dancing rays flash forth again, and in solemn joy, as though flying upward, rises the mighty orb. About midday there is wont to be, high up in the sky, a multitude of rounded clouds, golden-grey, with soft white edges. Like islands scattered over an overflowing river, that bathes them in its unbroken reaches of deep transparent blue, they scarcely stir; farther down the heavens they are in movement, packing closer; now there is no blue to be seen between them, but they are themselves almost as blue as the sky, filled full with light and heat. The color of the horizon, a faint pale lilac, does not change all day, and is the same all round; nowhere is there storm gathering and darkening; only somewhere rays of bluish color stretch down from the sky; it is a sprinkling of scarce-perceptible rain. In the evening these clouds disappear; the last of them, blackish and undefined as smoke, lie streaked with pink, facing the setting sun; in the place where it has gone down, as calmly as it rose, a crimson glow lingers long over the darkening earth, and, softly flashing like a candle carried carelessly, the evening star flickers in the sky. On such days all the colors are softened, bright but not glaring; everything is suffused with a kind of touching tenderness. On such days the heat is sometimes very great; often it is even "steaming" on the slopes of the fields, but a wind dispels this growing sultriness, and whirling eddies of dust — sure sign of settled, fine weather — move along the roads and across the fields in high white columns. In the pure dry air there is a scent of wormwood, rye in blossom, and buckwheat; even an hour before nightfall there is no moisture in the air. It is for such weather that the farmer longs, for harvesting his wheat. . . .

On just such a day I was once out grouse-shooting in the Tchern district of the province of Tula. I started and shot a fair amount of game; my full game-bag cut my shoulder mercilessly, but already the evening glow had faded, and the cool shades of twilight were beginning to grow thicker, and to spread across the sky, which was still bright, though no longer lighted up by the rays of the setting sun, when I at last decided to turn back homewards. With swift steps I passed through the long "square" of underwoods, clambered up a hill, and instead of the familiar plain I expected to see, with the oakwood on the right and the little white church in the distance, I saw before me a scene completely different, and quite new to me. A narrow valley lay at my feet, and directly facing me a dense wood of aspen trees rose up like a thick wall. I stood still in perplexity, looked round me. . . . "Aha!" I thought, "I have somehow come wrong; I kept too much to the right," and surprised at my own mistake, I rapidly descended the hill. I was at once plunged into a disagreeable clinging mist, exactly as though I had gone down into a cellar; the thick high grass at the bottom of the valley, all drenched with dew, was white like a smooth tablecloth; one felt afraid somehow to walk on it. I made haste to get on the other side, and walked along beside the aspenwood, bearing to the left. Bats were already hovering over its slumbering treetops, mysteriously flitting and quivering across the clear obscure of the sky; a young belated hawk flew in swift, straight course upwards, hastening to its nest. "Here, directly I get to this corner," I thought to myself, "I shall find the road at once; but I have come a mile out of my way!"

I did at last reach the end of the wood, but there was no road of any sort there; some kind of low bushes overgrown with long grass extended far and wide before me; behind them in the far, far distance could be discerned a tract of waste land. I stopped again. "Well? Where am I?" I began ransacking my brain to recall how and where I had been walking during the day. . . . "Ah! but these are the bushes at Parahin," I cried at last; "of course! then this must be Sindyev wood. But how did I get here? So far? . . . Strange! Now I must bear to the right again."

I went to the right through the bushes. Meantime the night had crept close and grown up like a storm cloud; it seemed as though, with the mists of evening, darkness was rising up on all sides and flowing down from overhead. I had come upon some sort of little, untrodden, overgrown path; I walked along it, gazing intently before me. Soon all was blackness and silence around — only the quail's cry was heard from time to time. Some small night-bird, flitting noiselessly near the ground on its soft wings, almost flapped against me and scurried away in alarm. I came out on the further side of the bushes, and made my way along a field by the hedge. By now I could hardly make out distant objects; the field showed dimly white around; beyond it rose up a sullen darkness, which seemed moving up closer in huge masses every instant. My steps gave a muffled sound in the air, that grew colder and colder. The pale sky began again to grow blue — but it was the blue of night. The tiny stars glimmered and twinkled in it.

What I had been taking for a wood turned out to be a dark round hillock. "But where am I, then?" I repeated again aloud, standing still for the third time and looking inquiringly at my spot and tan English dog, Dianka by name, certainly the most intelligent of four-footed creatures. But the most intelligent of four-footed creatures only wagged her tail, blinked her weary eyes dejectedly, and gave me no sensible advice. I felt myself disgraced in her eyes and pushed desperately forward, as though I had suddenly guessed which way I ought to go; I scaled the hill, and found myself in a hollow of no great depth, ploughed round.

A strange sensation came over me at once. This hollow had the form of an almost perfect cauldron, with sloping sides; at the bottom of it were some great white stones standing upright — it seemed as though they had crept there for some secret council — and it was so still and dark in it, so dreary and weird seemed the sky, overhanging it, that my heart sank. Some little animal was whining feebly and piteously among the stones. I made haste to get out again on to the hillock. Till then I had not quite given up all hope of finding the way home; but at this point I finally decided that I was utterly lost, and without any further attempt to make out the surrounding objects, which were almost completely plunged in darkness, I walked straight forward, by the aid of the stars, at random. . . . For about half an hour I walked on in this way, though I could hardly move one leg before the other. It seemed as if I had never been in such a deserted country in my life; nowhere was there the glimmer of a fire, nowhere a sound to be heard. One sloping hillside followed another; fields stretched endlessly upon fields; bushes seemed to spring up out of the earth under my very nose. I kept walking and was just making up my mind to lie down somewhere till morning, when suddenly I found myself on the edge of a horrible precipice.

I quickly drew back my lifted foot, and through the almost opaque darkness I saw far below me a vast plain. A long river skirted it in a semicircle, turned away from me; its course was marked by the steely reflection of the water still faintly glimmering here and there. The hill on which I found myself terminated abruptly in an almost overhanging precipice, whose gigantic profile stood out black against the dark blue waste of sky, and directly below me, in the corner formed by this precipice and the plain near the river, which was there a dark, motionless mirror, under the lee of the hill, two fires side by side were smoking and throwing up red flames. People were stirring round them, shadows hovered, and sometimes the front of a little curly head was lighted up by the glow.

I found out at last where I had got to. This plain was well known in our parts under the name of Byezhin Prairie. . . . But there was no possibility of returning home, especially at night; my legs were sinking under me from weariness. I decided to get down to the fires and to wait for the dawn in the company of these men, whom I took for drovers. I got down successfully, but I had hardly let go of the last branch I had grasped, when suddenly two large shaggy white dogs rushed angrily barking upon me. The sound of ringing boyish voices came from round the fires; two or three boys quickly got up from the ground. I called back in response to their shouts of inquiry. They ran up to me, and at once called off the dogs, who were specially struck by the appearance of my Dianka. I came down to them.

I had been mistaken in taking the figures sitting round the fires for drovers. They were simply peasant boys from a neighboring village, who were in charge of a drove of horses. In hot summer weather with us they drive the horses out at night to graze in the open country: the flies and gnats would give them no peace in the daytime; they drive out the drove towards evening, and drive them back in the early morning: it's a great treat for the peasant boys. Bareheaded, in old fur capes, they bestride the most spirited nags, and scurry along with merry cries and hooting and ringing laughter, swinging their arms and legs, and leaping into the air. The fine dust is stirred up in yellow clouds and moves along the road; the tramp of hoofs in unison resounds afar; the horses race along, pricking up their ears; in front of all, with his tail in the air and thistles in his tangled mane, prances some shaggy chestnut, constantly shifting his paces as he goes.

I told the boys I had lost my way, and sat down with them. They asked me where I came from, and then were silent for a little and turned away. Then we talked a little again. I lay down under a bush, whose shoots had been nibbled off, and began to look round. It was a marvelous picture; about the fire a red ring of light quivered and seemed to swoon away in the embrace of a background of darkness; the flame flaring up from time to time cast swift flashes of light beyond the boundary of this circle; a fine tongue of light licked the dry twigs and died away at once; long thin shadows, in their turn breaking in for an instant, danced right up to the very fires; darkness was struggling with light. Sometimes, when the fire burnt low and the circle of light shrank together, suddenly out of the encroaching darkness a horse's head was thrust in, bay, with striped markings or all white, stared with intent blank eyes upon us, nipped hastily the long grass, and drawing back again, vanished instantly. One could only hear it still munching and snorting. From the circle of light it was hard to make out what was going on in the darkness; everything close at hand seemed shut off by an almost black curtain; but farther away hills and forests were dimly visible in long blurs upon the horizon.

The dark unclouded sky stood, inconceivably immense, triumphant, above us in all its mysterious majesty. One felt a sweet oppression at one's heart, breathing in that peculiar, overpowering, yet fresh fragrance — the fragrance of a summer night in Russia. Scarcely a sound was to be heard around. . . . Only at times, in the river near, the sudden splash of a big fish leaping, and the faint rustle of a reed on the bank, swaying lightly as the ripples reached it . . . the fires alone kept up a subdued crackling.

The boys sat round them: there too sat the two dogs, who had been so eager to devour me. They could not for long after reconcile themselves to my presence, and, drowsily blinking and staring into the fire, they growled now and then with an unwonted sense of their own dignity; first they growled, and then whined a little, as though deploring the impossibility of carrying out their desires. There were altogether five boys: Fedya, Pavlusha, Ilyusha, Kostya and Vanya. (From their talk I learnt their names, and I intend now to introduce them to the reader.)

The first and eldest of all, Fedya, one would take to be about fourteen. He was a well-made boy, with good-looking, delicate, rather small features, curly fair hair, bright eyes, and a perpetual half-merry, half-careless smile. He belonged, by all appearances, to a well-to-do family, and had ridden out to the prairie, not through necessity, but for amusement. He wore a gay print shirt, with a yellow border; a short new overcoat slung round his neck was almost slipping off his narrow shoulders; a comb hung from his blue belt. His boots, coming a little way up the leg, were certainly his own — not his father's. The second boy, Pavlusha, had tangled black hair, grey eyes, broad cheekbones, a pale face pitted with smallpox, a large but well-cut mouth; his head altogether was large — "a beer-barrel head," as they say — and his figure was square and clumsy. He was not a good-looking boy — there's no denying it! — and yet I liked him; he looked very sensible and straightforward, and there was a vigorous ring in his voice. He had nothing to boast of in his attire; it consisted simply of a homespun shirt and patched trousers. The face of the third, Ilyusha, was rather uninteresting; it was a long face, with shortsighted eyes and a hook nose; it expressed a kind of dull, fretful uneasiness; his tightly drawn lips seemed rigid; his contracted brow never relaxed; he seemed continually blinking from the firelight. His flaxen — almost white — hair hung out in thin wisps under his low felt hat, which he kept pulling down with both hands over his ears. He had on new bast-shoes and leggings; a thick string, wound three times round his figure, carefully held together his neat black smock. Neither he nor Pavlusha looked more than twelve years old. The fourth, Kostya, a boy of ten, aroused my curiosity by his thoughtful and sorrowful look. His whole face was small, thin, freckled, pointed at the chin like a squirrel's; his lips were barely perceptible; but his great black eyes, that shone with liquid brilliance, produced a strange impression; they seemed trying to express something for which the tongue — his tongue, at least — had no words. He was undersized and weakly, and dressed rather poorly. The remaining boy, Vanya, I had not noticed at first; he was lying on the ground, peacefully curled up under a square rug, and only occasionally thrust his curly brown head out from under it: this boy was seven years old at the most.

So I lay under the bush at one side and looked at the boys. A small pot was hanging over one of the fires; in it potatoes were cooking. Pavlusha was looking after them, and on his knees he was trying them by poking a splinter of wood into the boiling water. Fedya was lying leaning on his elbow, and smoothing out the skirts of his coat. Ilyusha was sitting beside Kostya, and still kept blinking constrainedly. Kostya's head drooped despondently, and he looked away into the distance. Vanya did not stir under his rug. I pretended to be asleep. Little by little, the boys began talking again.

At first they gossiped of one thing and another, the work of tomorrow, the horses; but suddenly Fedya turned to Ilyusha, and, as though taking up again an interrupted conversation, asked him:

"Come then, so you've seen the domovoy?"[1]

"No, I didn't see him, and no one ever can see him," answered Ilyusha, in a weak hoarse voice, the sound of which was wonderfully in keeping with the expression of his face; "I heard him. . . . Yes, and not I alone."

"Where does he live — in your place?" asked Pavlusha.

"In the old paper mill."

"Why, do you go to the factory?"

"Of course we do. My brother Avdushka and I, we are paper-glazers."

"I say — factory hands!"

"Well, how did you hear it, then?" asked Fedya.

"It was like this. It happened that I and my brother Avdushka, with Fyodor of Mihyevska, and Ivashka the squint-eyed, and the other Ivashka who comes from the Red Hills, and Ivashka of Suhorukov too — and there were some other boys there as well — there were ten of us boys there altogether — the whole shift, that is — it happened that we spent the night at the paper mill; that's to say, it didn't happen, but Nazarov, the overseer, kept us. 'Why,' said he, 'should you waste time going home, boys; there's a lot of work tomorrow, so don't go home, boys.' So we stopped, and were all lying down together, and Avdushka had just begun to say, 'I say, boys, suppose the domovoy were to come?' And before he'd finished saying so, some one suddenly began walking over our heads; we were lying down below, and he began walking upstairs overhead, where the wheel is. We listened: he walked; the boards seemed to be bending under him, they creaked so; then he crossed over, above our heads; all of a sudden the water began to drip and drip over the wheel; the wheel rattled and rattled and again began to turn, though the sluices of the conduit above had been let down. We wondered who could have lifted them up so that the water could run; any way, the wheel turned and turned a little, and then stopped. Then he went to the door overhead and began coming downstairs, and came down like this, not hurrying himself; the stairs seemed to groan under him too. . . . Well, he came right down to our door, and waited and waited . . . and all of a sudden the door simply flew open. We were in a fright; we looked — there was nothing. . . . Suddenly what if the net on one of the vats didn't begin moving; it got up, and went rising and ducking and moving in the air as though some one were stirring with it, and then it was in its place again. Then, at another vat, a hook came off its nail, and then was on its nail again; and

---

[1] the demon or spirit who haunts a particular house or building.

then it seemed as if some one came to the door, and suddenly coughed and choked like a sheep, but so loudly! . . . We all fell down in a heap and huddled against one another. . . . Just weren't we in a fright that night!"

"I say!" murmured Pavel, "what did he cough for?"

"I don't know; perhaps it was the damp."

All were silent for a little.

"Well," inquired Fedya, "are the potatoes done?"

Pavlusha tried them.

"No, they are raw. . . . My, what a splash!" he added, turning his face in the direction of the river; "that must be a pike. . . . And there's a star falling."

"I say, I can tell you something, brothers," began Kostya, in a shrill little voice; "listen what my dad told me the other day."

"Well, we are listening," said Fedya with a patronizing air.

"You know Gavrila, I suppose, the carpenter up in the big village?"

"Yes, we know him."

"And do you know why he is so sorrowful always, never speaks? Do you know? I'll tell you why he's so sorrowful; he went one day, daddy said, he went, brothers, into the forest nutting. So he went nutting into the forest and lost his way; he went on — God only can tell where he got to. So he went on and on, brothers — but 'twas no good! — he could not find the way; and so night came on out of doors. So he sat down under a tree. 'I'll wait till morning,' thought he. He sat down and began to drop asleep. So as he was falling asleep, suddenly he heard some one call him. He looked up; there was no one. He fell asleep again; again he was called. He looked and looked again; and in front of him there sat a russalka[2] on a branch, swinging herself and calling him to her, and simply dying with laughing; she laughed so. . . . And the moon was shining bright, so bright, the moon shone so clear — everything could be seen plain, brothers. So she called him, and she herself was as bright and as white sitting on the branch as some dace or a roach, or like some little carp so white and silvery. . . . Gavrila the carpenter almost fainted, brothers, but she laughed without stopping, and kept beckoning him to her like this. Then Gavrila was just getting up; he was just going to yield to the russalka, brothers, but — the Lord put it into his heart, doubtless — he crossed himself like this. . . . And it was so hard for him to make that cross, brothers; he said, 'My hand was simply like a stone; it would not move.' . . . Ugh! the horrid witch. . . . So when he made the cross, brothers, the russalka, she left off laughing, and all at once how she did cry. . . . She cried, brothers, and wiped her eyes with her hair, and her hair was green as any hemp. So Gavrila looked and looked at her, and at last he fell to questioning her. 'Why are you weeping, wild thing of the woods?' And the russalka began to speak to him like this: 'If you had not crossed yourself, man,' she says, 'you should have lived with me in gladness of heart

---

[2] a water-nymph.

to the end of your days; and I weep, I am grieved at heart because you crossed yourself; but I will not grieve alone; you too shall grieve at heart to the end of your days.' Then she vanished, brothers, and at once it was plain to Gavrila how to get out of the forest. . . . Only since then he goes always sorrowful, as you see."

"Ugh!" said Fedya after a brief silence; "but how can such an evil thing of the woods ruin a Christian soul — he did not listen to her?"

"And I say!" said Kostya. "Gavrila said that her voice was as shrill and plaintive as a toad's."

"Did your father tell you that himself?" Fedya went on.

"Yes. I was lying in the loft; I heard it all."

"It's a strange thing. Why should he be sorrowful? . . . But I suppose she liked him, since she called him."

"Ay, she liked him!" put in Ilyusha. "Yes, indeed! she wanted to tickle him to death, that's what she wanted. That's what they do, those russalkas."

"There ought to be russalkas here too, I suppose," observed Fedya.

"No," answered Kostya, "this is a holy open place. There's one thing, though: the river's near."

All were silent. Suddenly from out of the distance came a prolonged, resonant, almost wailing sound, one of those inexplicable sounds of the night, which break upon a profound stillness, rise upon the air, linger, and slowly die away at last. You listen: it is as though there were nothing, yet it echoes still. It is as though some one had uttered a long, long cry upon the very horizon, as though some other had answered him with shrill harsh laughter in the forest, and a faint, hoarse hissing hovers over the river. The boys looked round about shivering. . . .

"Christ's aid be with us!" whispered Ilyusha.

"Ah, you craven crows!" cried Pavel, "what are you frightened of? Look, the potatoes are done." They all came up to the pot and began to eat the smoking potatoes; only Vanya did not stir. "Well, aren't you coming?" said Pavel.

But he did not creep out from under his rug. The pot was soon completely emptied.

"Have you heard, boys," began Ilyusha, "what happened with us at Varnavitsi?"

"Near the dam?" asked Fedya.

"Yes, yes, near the dam, the broken-down dam. That is a haunted place, such a haunted place, and so lonely. All round there are pits and quarries, and there are always snakes in pits."

"Well, what did happen? Tell us."

"Well, this is what happened. You don't know, perhaps, Fedya, but there a drowned man was buried; he was drowned long, long ago, when the water was still deep; only his grave can still be seen, though it can only just be seen . . . like this — a little mound. . . . So one day the bailiff called the huntsman Yermil, and says to him, 'Go to the post, Yermil.' Yermil always goes to the post for us; he has let all his dogs die; they never will live with him, for some reason, and they have never lived with him, though he's a good huntsman, and everyone liked him. So Yermil went to the post, and he stayed a bit in the town, and when he rode back, he was a little tipsy. It was night, a fine night; the moon was shining. . . . So Yermil rode across the dam; his way lay there. So, as he rode along, he saw, on the drowned man's grave, a little lamb, so white and curly and pretty, running about. So Yermil thought, 'I will take him,' and he got down and took him in his arms. But the little lamb didn't take any notice. So Yermil goes back to his horse, and the horse stares at him, and snorts and shakes his head; however, he said 'wo' to him and sat on him with the lamb, and rode on again; he held the lamb in front of him. He looks at him, and the lamb looks him straight in the face, like this. Yermil the huntsman felt upset. 'I don't remember,' he said, 'that lambs ever look at any one like that'; however, he began to stroke it like this on its wool, and to say, 'Chucky! chucky!' And the lamb suddenly showed its teeth and said too, 'Chucky! chucky!' "

The boy who was telling the story had hardly uttered this last word, when suddenly both dogs got up at once, and, barking convulsively, rushed away from the fire and disappeared in the darkness. All the boys were alarmed. Vanya jumped up from under his rug. Pavlusha ran shouting after the dogs. Their barking quickly grew fainter in the distance. . . . There was the noise of the uneasy tramp of the frightened drove of horses. Pavlusha shouted aloud: 'Hey Grey! Beetle!' . . . In a few minutes the barking ceased; Pavel's voice sounded still in the distance. . . . A little time more passed; the boys kept looking about in perplexity, as though expecting something to happen. . . . Suddenly the tramp of a galloping horse was heard; it stopped short at the pile of wood, and, hanging on to the mane, Pavel sprang nimbly off it. Both the dogs also leaped into the circle of light and at once sat down, their red tongues hanging out.

"What was it? What was it?" asked the boys.

"Nothing," answered Pavel, waving his hand to his horse; "I suppose the dogs scented something. I thought it was a wolf," he added, calmly drawing deep breaths into his chest.

I could not help admiring Pavel. He was very fine at that moment. His ugly face, animated by his swift ride, glowed with hardihood and determination. Without even a switch in his hand, he had, without the slightest hesitation, rushed out into the night alone to face a wolf. . . . "What a splendid fellow!" I thought, looking at him.

"Have you seen any wolves, then?" asked the trembling Kostya.

"There are always a good many of them here," answered Pavel; "but they are only troublesome in the winter."

He crouched down again before the fire. As he sat down on the ground, he laid his hand on the shaggy head of one of the dogs. For a long while the flattered brute did not turn his head, gazing sidewise with grateful pride at Pavlusha.

Vanya lay down under his rug again.

"What dreadful things you were telling us, Ilyusha!" began Fedya, whose part it was, as the son of a well-to-do peasant, to lead the conversation. (He spoke little himself, apparently afraid of lowering his dignity.) "And then some evil spirit set the dogs barking. . . . Certainly I have heard that place was haunted."

"Varnavitsi? . . . I should think it was haunted! More than once, they say, they have seen the old master there — the late master. He wears, they say, a long skirted coat, and keeps groaning like this, and looking for something on the ground. Once grandfather Trofimitch met him. 'What,' says he, 'your honor, Ivan Ivanitch, are you pleased to look for on the ground?' "

"He asked him?" put in Fedya in amazement.

"Yes, he asked him."

"Well, I call Trofimitch a brave fellow after that. . . . Well, what did he say?"

" 'I am looking for the herb that cleaves all things,' says he. But he speaks so thickly, so thickly. 'And what, your honor, Ivan Ivanitch, do you want with the herb that cleaves all things?' 'The tomb weighs on me; it weighs on me, Trofimitch: I want to get away — away.' "

"My word!" observed Fedya, "he didn't enjoy his life enough, I suppose."

"What a marvel!" said Kostya. "I thought one could only see the departed on All Hallows' day."

"One can see the departed any time," Ilyusha interposed with conviction. From what I could observe, I judged he knew the village superstitions better than the others. . . . "But on All Hallows' day you can see the living too; those, that is, whose turn it is to die that year. You need only sit in the church porch, and keep looking at the road. They will come by you along the road; those, that is, who will die that year. Last year old Ulyana went to the porch."

"Well, did she see anyone?" asked Kostya inquisitively.

"To be sure she did. At first she sat a long, long while, and saw no one and heard nothing . . . only it seemed as if some dog kept whining and whining like this somewhere. . . . Suddenly she looks up: a boy comes along the road with only a shirt on. She looked at him. It was Ivashka Fedosyev."

"He who died in the spring?" put in Fedya.

"Yes, he. He came along and never lifted up his head. But Ulyana knew him. And then she looks again: a woman came along. She stared and stared at her. . . . Ah, God Almighty! . . . it was herself coming along the road; Ulyana herself."

"Could it be herself?" asked Fedya.

"Yes, by God, herself."

"Well, but she is not dead yet, you know?"

"But the year is not over yet. And only look at her; her life hangs on a thread."

All were still again. Pavel threw a handful of dry twigs on to the fire. They were soon charred by the suddenly leaping flame; they cracked and smoked, and began to contract, curling up their burning ends. Gleams of light in broken flashes glanced in all directions, especially upwards. Suddenly a white dove flew straight into the bright light, fluttered round and round in terror, bathed in the red glow, and disappeared with a whirr of its wings.

"It's lost its home, I suppose," remarked Pavel. "Now it will fly till it gets somewhere, where it can rest till dawn."

"Why, Pavlusha," said Kostya, "might it not be a just soul flying to heaven?"

Pavel threw another handful of twigs on to the fire.

"Perhaps," he said at last.

"But tell us, please, Pavlusha," began Fedya, "what was seen in your parts of Shalamovy at the heavenly portent?"[3]

"When the sun could not be seen? Yes, indeed."

"Were you frightened then?"

"Yes; and we weren't the only ones. Our master, though he talked to us beforehand, and said there would be a heavenly portent, yet when it got dark, they say he himself was frightened out of his wits. And in the house-serfs' cottage the old woman, directly it grew dark, broke all the dishes in the oven with the poker. 'Who will eat now?' she said; 'the last day has come.' So the soup was all running about the place. And in the village there were such tales about among us: that white wolves would run over the earth, and would eat men, that a bird of prey would pounce down on us, and that they would even see Trishka."[4]

"What is Trishka?" asked Kostya.

"Why, don't you know?" interrupted Ilyusha warmly. "Why, brother, where have you been brought up, not to know Trishka? You're a stay-at-home, one-eyed lot in your village, really! Trishka will be a marvelous man, who will come one day, and he will be such a marvelous man that they will never be able to catch him, and never be able to do anything with him; he will be such a marvelous man. The people will try to take him; for example, they will come after him with sticks, they will surround him, but he will blind their eyes so that they fall upon one another. They will put him in prison, for example; he will ask for a little water to drink in a bowl; they will bring him the bowl, and he will plunge into it and vanish from their sight. They will put chains on him, but he will only clap his hands — they will

---

[3] This is what the peasants call an eclipse. [Turgenev's note]

[4] The popular belief in Trishka is probably derived from some tradition of Antichrist. [Turgenev's note]

fall off him. So this Trishka will go through villages and towns; and this Trishka will be a wily man; he will lead astray Christ's people . . . and they will be able to do nothing to him. . . . He will be such a marvelous, wily man."

"Well, then," continued Pavel, in his deliberate voice, "that's what he's like. And so they expected him in our parts. The old men declared that directly the heavenly portent began, Trishka would come. So the heavenly portent began. All the people were scattered over the street, in the fields, waiting to see what would happen. Our place, you know, is open country. They look; and suddenly down the mountainside from the big village comes a man of some sort; such a strange man, with such a wonderful head . . . that all scream: 'Oy, Trishka is coming! Oy, Trishka is coming!' and all run in all directions! Our elder crawled into a ditch; his wife stumbled on the door-board and screamed with all her might; she terrified her yard-dog, so that he broke away from his chain and over the hedge and into the forest; and Kuzka's father, Dorofyitch, ran into the oats, lay down there, and began to cry like a quail. 'Perhaps' says he, 'the Enemy, the Destroyer of Souls, will spare the birds, at least.' So they were all in such a scare! But he that was coming was our cooper Vavila; he had bought himself a new pitcher, and had put the empty pitcher over his head."

All the boys laughed; and again there was a silence for a while, as often happens when people are talking in the open air. I looked out into the solemn, majestic stillness of the night; the dewy freshness of late evening had been succeeded by the dry heat of midnight; the darkness still had long to lie in a soft curtain over the slumbering fields; there was still a long while left before the first whisperings, the first dewdrops of dawn. There was no moon in the heavens; it rose late at that time. Countless golden stars, twinkling in rivalry, seemed all running softly toward the Milky Way, and truly, looking at them, you were almost conscious of the whirling, never-resting motion of the earth. . . . A strange, harsh, painful cry sounded twice together over the river, and a few moments later was repeated farther down. . . .

Kostya shuddered. "What was that?"

"That was a heron's cry," replied Pavel tranquilly.

"A heron," repeated Kostya. . . . "And what was it, Pavlusha, I heard yesterday evening," he added, after a short pause; "you perhaps will know."

"What did you hear?"

"I will tell you what I heard. I was going from Stony Ridge to Shashkino; I went first through our walnut wood, and then passed by a little pool — you know where there's a sharp turn down to the ravine — there is a water-pit there, you know; it is quite overgrown with reeds; so I went near this pit, brothers, and suddenly from this came a sound of someone groaning, and piteously, so piteously; oo-oo, oo-oo! I was in such a fright, my brothers; it was late, and the voice was so miserable. I felt as if I should cry myself. . . . What could that have been, eh?"

"It was in that pit the thieves drowned Akim the forester, last summer," observed Pavel; "so perhaps it was his soul lamenting."

"Oh, dear, really, brothers," replied Kostya, opening wide his eyes, which were round enough before, "I did not know they had drowned Akim in that pit. Shouldn't I have been frightened if I'd known!"

"But they say there are little, tiny frogs," continued Pavel, "who cry piteously like that."

"Frogs? Oh, no, it was not frogs, certainly not. (A heron again uttered a cry above the river.) Ugh, there it is!" Kostya cried involuntarily; "it is just like a wood-spirit shrieking."

"The wood-spirit does not shriek; it is dumb," put in Ilyusha; "it only claps its hands and rattles."

"And have you seen it then, the wood-spirit?" Fedya asked him ironically.

"No, I have not seen it, and God preserve me from seeing it; but others have seen it. Why, one day it misled a peasant in our parts, and led him through the woods and all in a circle in one field. . . . He scarcely got home till daylight."

"Well, and did he see it?"

"Yes. He says it was a big, big creature, dark, wrapped up, just like a tree; you could not make it out well; it seemed to hide away from the moon, and kept staring and staring with its great eyes, and winking and winking with them. . . ."

"Ugh!" exclaimed Fedya with a slight shiver, and a shrug of the shoulders; "pfoo."

"And how does such an unclean brood come to exist in the world?" said Pavel; "it's a wonder."

"Don't speak ill of it; take care, it will hear you," said Ilyusha.

Again there was a silence.

"Look, look, brothers," suddenly came Vanya's childish voice; "look at God's little stars; they are swarming like bees!"

He put his fresh little face out from under his rug, leaned on his little fist, and slowly lifted up his large soft eyes. The eyes of all the boys were raised to the sky, and they were not lowered quickly.

"Well, Vanya," began Fedya caressingly, "is your sister Anyutka well?"

"Yes, she is very well," replied Vanya with a slight lisp.

"You ask her, why doesn't she come to see us?"

"I don't know."

"You tell her to come."

"Very well."

"Tell her I have a present for her."

"And a present for me too?"

"Yes, you too."

Vanya sighed.

"No; I don't want one. Better give it to her; she is so kind to us at home."

And Vanya laid his head down again on the ground. Pavel got up and took the empty pot in his hand.

"Where are you going?" Fedya asked him.

"To the river, to get water; I want some water to drink."

The dogs got up and followed him.

"Take care you don't fall into the river!" Ilyusha cried after him.

"Why should he fall in?" said Fedya. "He will be careful."

"Yes, he will be careful. But all kinds of things happen; he will stoop over, perhaps, to draw the water, and the water-spirit will clutch him by the hand, and drag him to him. Then they will say, 'The boy fell into the water.' . . . Fell in, indeed! . . . There, he has crept in among the reeds," he added, listening.

The reeds certainly "shished," as they call it among us, as they were parted.

"But is it true," asked Kostya, "that crazy Akulina has been mad ever since she fell into the water?"

"Yes, ever since. . . . How dreadful she is now! But they say she was a beauty before then. The water-spirit bewitched her. I suppose he did not expect they would get her out so soon. So down there at the bottom he bewitched her."

(I had met this Akulina more than once. Covered with rags, fearfully thin, with face as black as a coal, blear-eyed and forever grinning, she would stay whole hours in one place in the road, stamping with her feet, pressing her fleshless hands to her breast, and slowly shifting from one leg to the other, like a wild beast in a cage. She understood nothing that was said to her, and only chuckled spasmodically from time to time.)

"But they say," continued Kostya, "that Akulina threw herself into the river because her lover had deceived her."

"Yes, that was it."

"And do you remember Vasya?" added Kostya, mournfully.

"What Vasya?" asked Fedya.

"Why, the one who was drowned," replied Kostya, "in this very river. Ah, what a boy he was! What a boy he was! His mother, Feklista, how she loved him, her Vasya! And she seemed to have a foreboding, Feklista did, that harm would come to him from the water. Sometimes, when Vasya went with us boys in the summer to bathe in the river, she used to be trembling all over. The other women did not mind; they passed by with the pails, and went on, but Feklista put her pail down on the ground, and set to calling him, 'Come back, come back, my little joy; come back, my darling!' And no one knows how he was drowned. He was playing on the bank, and his mother was there haymaking; suddenly she hears, as though some one was blowing bubbles through the water, and behold! there was only Vasya's little cap to be seen swimming on the water. You know since then Feklista has not been right in her mind: she goes and lies down at the place where he was drowned; she lies down, brothers, and sings a song — you remember Vasya was always singing a song like that — so she sings it too, and weeps and weeps, and bitterly rails against God."

"Here is Pavlusha coming," said Fedya.

Pavel came up to the fire with a full pot in his hand.

"Boys," he began, after a short silence, "something bad happened."

"Oh, what?" asked Kostya hurriedly.

"I heard Vasya's voice."

They all seemed to shudder.

"What do you mean? What do you mean?" stammered Kostya.

"I don't know. Only I went to stoop down to the water; suddenly I hear my name called in Vasya's voice, as though it came from below water: 'Pavlusha, Pavlusha, come here.' I came away. But I fetched the water, though."

"Ah, God have mercy upon us!" said the boys, crossing themselves.

"It was the water-spirit calling you, Pavel," said Fedya; "we were just talking of Vasya."

"Ah, it's a bad omen," said Ilyusha, deliberately.

"Well, never mind, don't bother about it," Pavel declared stoutly, and he sat down again; "no one can escape his fate."

The boys were still. It was clear that Pavel's words had produced a strong impression on them. They began to lie down before the fire as though preparing to go to sleep.

"What is that?" asked Kostya, suddenly lifting his head.

Pavel listened.

"It's the curlews flying and whistling."

"Where are they flying to?"

"To a land where, they say, there is no winter."

"But is there such a land?"

"Yes."

"Is it far away?"

"Far, far away, beyond the warm seas."

Kostya sighed and shut his eyes.

More than three hours had passed since I first came across the boys. The moon at last had risen; I did not notice it at first; it was such a tiny crescent. This moonless night was as solemn and hushed as it had been at first. . . . But already many stars, that not long before had been high up in the heavens, were setting over the earth's dark rim; everything around was perfectly still, as it is only still towards morning; all was sleeping the deep unbroken sleep that comes before daybreak. Already the fragrance in the air was fainter; once more a dew seemed falling. . . . How short are nights in summer! . . . The boys' talk died down when the fires did. The dogs even were dozing; the horses, so far as I could make out, in the hardly perceptible, faintly shining light of the stars, were asleep with downcast heads. . . . I fell into a state of weary unconsciousness, which passed into sleep.

A fresh breeze passed over my face. I opened my eyes; the morning was beginning. The dawn had not yet flushed the sky, but already it was growing light in the east. Everything had become visible, though dimly visible, around. The pale grey sky was growing light and cold and bluish; the stars twinkled with a dimmer light, or disappeared; the earth was wet, the leaves covered with dew, and from the distance came sounds of life and voices, and a light morning breeze went fluttering over the earth. My body responded to it with a faint shudder of delight. I got up quickly and went to the boys. They were all sleeping as though they were tired out round the smouldering fire; only Pavel half rose and gazed intently at me.

I nodded to him, and walked homewards beside the misty river. Before I had walked two miles, already all around me, over the wide dew-drenched prairie, and in front from forest to forest, where the hills were growing green again, and behind, over the long dusty road and the sparkling bushes, flushed with the red glow, and the river faintly blue now under the lifting mist, flowed fresh streams of burning light, first pink, then red and golden. . . . All things began to stir, to awaken, to sing, to flutter, to speak. On all sides thick drops of dew sparkled in glittering diamonds; to welcome me, pure and clear as though bathed in the freshness of morning, came the notes of a bell, and suddenly there rushed by me, driven by the boys I had parted from, the drove of horses, refreshed and rested. . . .

Sad to say, I must add that in that year Pavel met his end. He was not drowned; he was killed by a fall from his horse. Pity! he was a splendid fellow!

[1852]

HERMAN MELVILLE (1819–1891) made his first attempt at the short story form in "Bartleby, the Scrivener: A Story of Wall Street." Behind him were seven years of writing novels, which began with a burst of creative energy that produced his early novels of sea adventure: Typee (1846), Omoo (1847), Mardi (1849), Redburn (1849), and White-Jacket (1850). All of these were based on his own experiences on board ship. Melville had been left in poverty at the age of fifteen when his father went bankrupt, and in 1839 he went to sea as a cabin boy. Two years later he sailed on a whaler bound for the Pacific, but he deserted in the Marquesas Islands and lived for a time with cannibals. Having little formal education, Melville later boasted that "a whale ship was my Yale College and my Harvard." His most ambitious book was Moby Dick (1851), a work of romantic and allegorical complexity heavily indebted to the influence of Nathaniel Hawthorne, his neighbor in the Berkshires at the time he wrote it. Moby Dick was not as great a commercial success as Melville's earlier books, however, and the novel that followed it, Pierre (1852), was dismissed as incomprehensible trash by the critics, one of whom protested that Melville was allowing his mind to "run riot amid remote analogies, where the chain of association is invisible to mortal minds."

It was at this point that Melville turned to the short story. Between 1853 and 1856 he published fifteen sketches and stories and a serialized historical novel, promising the popular magazines that his stories would "contain nothing of any sort to shock the fastidious." But when these pieces, and another novel (The Confidence Man, 1857), failed to restore interest in him as a writer, Melville ceased trying to make his living by his pen. He left his farm in the Berkshires, moved with his family to a house in New York City bought for them by his father-in-law, and worked in that city from 1866 to 1888 as an inspector of customs. He published a few books of poems in his later years, and wrote a short novel, Billy Budd, which critics acclaimed as one of his greatest works when it was published — thirty years after his death.

Melville's stories dropped into oblivion after their first publication, but modern critics regard many of them as among his best works of fiction. The meaning of "Bartleby the Scrivener" is much disputed by readers, but it is often regarded as a parable illustrating Melville's own fate as a writer who refused to conform to the demands of the reading public. Melville himself never commented on the tale, or analyzed the fictional form of the short story. In Moby Dick he had explored the mysterious relationship between the individual and God; in "Bartleby the Scrivener" he shifted ground to dramatize the complexities of the bond between the individual and society.

Herman Melville

თივ

BARTLEBY THE SCRIVENER

A Story of Wall Street

I am a rather elderly man. The nature of my avocations, for the last thirty years, has brought me into more than ordinary contact with what would seem an interesting and somewhat singular set of men, of whom, as yet, nothing, that I know of, has ever been written — I mean, the law-copyists, or scriveners. I have known very many of them, professionally and privately, and, if I pleased, could relate divers histories, at which good-natured gentlemen might smile, and sentimental souls might weep. But I waive the biographies of all other scriveners, for a few passages in the life of Bartleby, who was a scrivener, the strangest I ever saw, or heard of. While, of other law-copyists, I might write the complete life, of Bartleby nothing of that sort can be done. I believe that no materials exist, for a full and satisfactory biography of this man. It is an irreparable loss to literature. Bartleby was one of those beings of whom nothing is ascertainable, except from the original sources, and, in his case, those are very small. What my own astonished eyes saw of Bartleby, *that* is all I know of him, except, indeed, one vague report, which will appear in the sequel.

Ere introducing the scrivener, as he first appeared to me, it is fit I make some mention of myself, my *employés*, my business, my chambers, and general surroundings, because some such description is indispensable to an adequate understanding of the chief character about to be presented. Imprimis:[1] I am a man who, from his youth upwards, has been filled with a profound conviction that the easiest way of life is the best. Hence, though I belong to a profession proverbially energetic and nervous, even to turbulence, at times, yet nothing of that sort have I ever suffered to invade my peace. I am one of those unambitious lawyers who never address a jury, or in any way draw down public applause; but, in the cool tranquillity of a snug retreat, do a snug business among rich men's bonds, and mortgages, and title-deeds. All who know me, consider me an eminently *safe* man. The late John Jacob Astor, a personage little given to poetic enthusiasm, had no

[1] in the first place (Latin).

hesitation in pronouncing my first grand point to be prudence; my next, method. I do not speak it in vanity, but simply record the fact, that I was not unemployed in my profession by the late John Jacob Astor; a name which, I admit, I love to repeat; for it hath a rounded and orbicular sound to it, and rings like unto bullion. I will freely add, that I was not insensible to the late John Jacob Astor's good opinion.

Some time prior to the period at which this little history begins, my avocations had been largely increased. The good old office, now extinct in the State of New York, of a Master in Chancery, had been conferred upon me. It was not a very arduous office, but very pleasantly remunerative. I seldom lose my temper; much more seldom indulge in dangerous indignation at wrongs and outrages; but I must be permitted to be rash here and declare, that I consider the sudden and violent abrogation of the office of Master in Chancery, by the new Constitution, as a —— premature act; inasmuch as I had counted upon a life-lease of the profits, whereas I only received those of a few short years. But this is by the way.

My chambers were up stairs, at No. — Wall Street. At one end, they looked upon the white wall of the interior of a spacious skylight shaft, penetrating the building from top to bottom.

This view might have been considered rather tame than otherwise, deficient in what landscape painters call "life." But, if so, the view from the other end of my chambers offered, at least, a contrast, if nothing more. In that direction, my windows commanded an unobstructed view of a lofty brick wall, black by age and everlasting shade; which wall required no spy-glass to bring out its lurking beauties, but, for the benefit of all near-sighted spectators, was pushed up to within ten feet of my window-panes. Owing to the great height of the surrounding buildings, and my chambers being on the second floor, the interval between this wall and mine not a little resembled a huge square cistern.

At the period just preceding the advent of Bartleby, I had two persons as copyists in my employment, and a promising lad as an office-boy. First, Turkey; second, Nippers; third, Ginger Nut. These may seem names, the like of which are not usually found in the Directory. In truth, they were nicknames, mutually conferred upon each other by my three clerks, and were deemed expressive of their respective persons or characters. Turkey was a short, pursy Englishman, of about my own age — that is, somewhere not far from sixty. In the morning, one might say, his face was of a fine florid hue, but after twelve o'clock, meridian — his dinner hour — it blazed like a grate full of Christmas coals; and continued blazing — but, as it were, with a gradual wane — till six o'clock, P.M., or thereabouts; after which, I saw no more of the proprietor of the face, which, gaining its meridian with the sun, seemed to set with it, to rise, culminate, and decline the following day, with the like regularity and undiminished glory. There are many singular coincidences I have known in the course of my life, not the least among which was the fact, that, exactly when Turkey displayed his fullest beams from his red and radiant countenance, just then, too, at that critical moment, began the daily period when I considered his business capacities as seriously disturbed for the remainder of the twenty-four hours. Not that he was absolutely idle, or averse to business then; far from it. The difficulty was, he was apt to be altogether too energetic. There was a strange, inflamed, flurried, flighty recklessness of activity about him. He would be incautious in dipping his pen into his inkstand. All his blots upon my documents were dropped there after twelve o'clock, meridian. Indeed, not only would he be reckless, and sadly given to making blots in the afternoon, but, some days, he went further, and was rather noisy. At such times, too, his face flamed with augmented blazonry, as if cannel coal had been heaped on anthracite. He made an unpleasant racket with his chair; spilled his sand-box; in mending his pens, impatiently split them all to pieces, and threw them on the floor in a sudden passion; stood up, and leaned over his table, boxing his papers about in a most indecorous manner, very sad to behold in an elderly man like him. Nevertheless, as he was in many ways a most valuable person to me, and all the time before twelve o'clock, meridian, was the quickest, steadiest creature, too, accomplishing a great deal of work in a style not easily to be matched — for these reasons, I was willing to overlook his eccentricities, though, indeed, occasionally, I remonstrated with him. I did this very gently, however, because, though the civilest, nay, the blandest and most reverential of men in the morning, yet, in the afternoon, he was disposed, upon provocation, to be slightly rash with his tongue — in fact, insolent. Now, valuing his morning services as I did, and resolved not to lose them — yet, at the same time, made uncomfortable by his inflamed ways after twelve o'clock — and being a man of peace, unwilling by my admonitions to call forth unseemly retorts from him, I took upon me, one Saturday noon (he was always worse on Saturdays) to hint to him, very kindly, that, perhaps, now that he was growing old, it might be well to abridge his labors; in short, he need not come to my chambers after twelve o'clock, but, dinner over, had best go home to his lodgings, and rest himself till tea-time. But no; he insisted upon his afternoon devotions. His countenance became intolerably fervid, as he oratorically assured me — gesticulating with a long ruler at the other end of the room — that if his services in the morning were useful, how indispensable, then, in the afternoon?

"With submission, sir," said Turkey, on this occasion, "I consider myself your right-hand man. In the morning I but marshal and deploy my columns; but in the afternoon I put myself at their head, and gallantly charge the foe, thus" — and he made a violent thrust with the ruler.

"But the blots, Turkey," intimated I.

"True; but, with submission, sir, behold these hairs! I am getting old. Surely, sir, a blot or two of a warm afternoon is not to be severely urged against gray hairs. Old age — even if it blot the page — is honorable. With submission, sir, we *both* are getting old."

This appeal to my fellow-feeling was hardly to be resisted. At all events, I saw that go he would not. So, I made up my mind to let him stay, resolving, nevertheless, to see to it that, during the afternoon, he had to do with my less important papers.

Nippers, the second on my list, was a whiskered, sallow, and, upon the whole, rather piratical-looking young man, of about five-and-twenty. I always deemed him the victim of two evil powers — ambition and indigestion. The ambition was evinced by a certain impatience of the duties of a mere copyist, an unwarrantable usurpation of strictly professional affairs such as the original drawing up of legal documents. The indigestion seemed betokened in an occasional nervous testiness and grinning irritability, causing the teeth to audibly grind together over mistakes committed in copying; unnecessary maledictions, hissed, rather than spoken, in the heat of business; and especially by a continual discontent with the height of the table where he worked. Though of a very ingenious mechanical turn, Nippers could never get this table to suit him. He put chips under it, blocks of various sorts, bits of pasteboard, and at last went so far as to attempt an exquisite adjustment, by final pieces of folded blotting-paper. But no invention would answer. If, for the sake of easing his back, he brought the table-lid at a sharp angle well up towards his chin, and wrote there like a man using the steep roof of a Dutch house for his desk, then he declared that it stopped the circulation in his arms. If now he lowered the table to his waistbands, and stooped over it in writing, then there was a sore aching in his back. In short, the truth of the matter was, Nippers knew not what he wanted. Or, if he wanted anything, it was to be rid of a scrivener's table altogether. Among the manifestations of his diseased ambition was a fondness he had for receiving visits from certain ambiguous-looking fellows in seedy coats, whom he called his clients. Indeed, I was aware that not only was he, at times, considerable of a ward-politician, but he occasionally did a little business at the justices' courts, and was not unknown on the steps of the Tombs.[2] I have good reason to believe, however, that one individual who called upon him at my chambers, and who, with a grand air, he insisted was his client, was no other than a dun, and the alleged title-deed, a bill. But, with all his failings, and the annoyances he caused me, Nippers, like his compatriot Turkey, was a very useful man to me; wrote a neat, swift hand; and, when he chose, was not deficient in a gentlemanly sort of deportment. Added to this, he always dressed in a gentlemanly sort of way; and so, incidentally, reflected credit upon my chambers. Whereas, with respect to Turkey, I had much ado to keep him from being a reproach to me. His clothes were apt to look oily, and smell of eating-houses. He wore his pantaloons very loose and baggy in summer. His coats were execrable, his hat not to be handled. But

---

[2] maximum-security prison in New York City.

while the hat was a thing of indifference to me, inasmuch as his natural civility and deference, as a dependent Englishman, always led him to doff it
the moment he entered the room, yet his coat was another matter. Concerning his coats, I reasoned with him; but with no effect. The truth was, I
suppose, that a man with so small an income could not afford to sport such
a lustrous face and a lustrous coat at one and the same time. As Nippers
once observed, Turkey's money went chiefly for red ink. One winter day, I
presented Turkey with a highly respectable-looking coat of my own — a
padded gray coat, of a most comfortable warmth, and which buttoned
straight up from the knee to the neck. I thought Turkey would appreciate
the favor, and abate his rashness and obstreperousness of afternoons. But
no; I verily believe that buttoning himself up in so downy and blanket-like a
coat had a pernicious effect upon him — upon the same principle that too
much oats are bad for horses. In fact, precisely as a rash, restive horse is said
to feel his oats, so Turkey felt his coat. It made him insolent. He was a man
whom prosperity harmed.

Though, concerning the self-indulgent habits of Turkey, I had my own
private surmises, yet, touching Nippers, I was well persuaded that, whatever
might be his faults in other respects, he was, at least, a temperate young
man. But, indeed, nature herself seemed to have been his vintner, and, at
his birth, charged him so thoroughly with an irritable, brandy-like disposition, that all subsequent potations were needless. When I consider how,
amid the stillness of my chambers, Nippers would sometimes impatiently
rise from his seat, and stooping over his table, spread his arms wide apart,
seize the whole desk, and move it, and jerk it, with a grim, grinding motion
on the floor, as if the table were a perverse voluntary agent, intent on
thwarting and vexing him, I plainly perceive that, for Nippers, brandy-and-
water were altogether superfluous.

It was fortunate for me that, owing to its peculiar cause — indigestion — the irritability and consequent nervousness of Nippers were mainly
observable in the morning, while in the afternoon he was comparatively
mild. So that, Turkey's paroxysms only coming on about twelve o'clock, I
never had to do with their eccentricities at one time. Their fits relieved each
other, like guards. When Nippers' was on, Turkey's was off; and *vice versa.*
This was a good natural arrangement, under the circumstances.

Ginger Nut, the third on my list, was a lad, some twelve years old. His
father was a carman, ambitious of seeing his son on the bench instead of a
cart, before he died. So he sent him to my office, as student at law, errand-
boy, cleaner and sweeper, at the rate of one dollar a week. He had a little
desk to himself, but he did not use it much. Upon inspection, the drawer
exhibited a great array of the shells of various sorts of nuts. Indeed, to this
quick-witted youth, the whole noble science of the law was contained in a
nutshell. Not the least among the employments of Ginger Nut, as well as
one which he discharged with the most alacrity, was his duty as cake and
apple purveyor for Turkey and Nippers. Copying lawpapers being prover-

bially a dry, husky sort of business, my two scriveners were fain to moisten their mouths very often with Spitzenbergs, to be had at the numerous stalls nigh the Custom House and Post Office. Also, they sent Ginger Nut very frequently for that peculiar cake — small, flat, round, and very spicy — after which he had been named by them. Of a cold morning, when business was but dull, Turkey would gobble up scores of these cakes, as if they were mere wafers — indeed, they sell them at the rate of six or eight for a penny — the scrape of his pen blending with the crunching of the crisp particles in his mouth. Of all the fiery afternoon blunders and flurried rash-ness of Turkey, was his once moistening a ginger-cake between his lips, and clapping it on to a mortgage, for a seal. I came within an ace of dismissing him then. But he mollified me by making an oriental bow, and saying —

"With submission, sir, it was generous of me to find you in stationery on my own account."

Now my original business — that of a conveyancer and title hunter, and drawer-up of recondite documents of all sorts — was considerably in-creased by receiving the Master's office. There was now great work for scriv-eners. Not only must I push the clerks already with me, but I must have additional help.

In answer to my advertisement, a motionless young man one morning stood upon my office threshold, the door being open, for it was summer. I can see that figure now — pallidly neat, pitiably respectable, incurably for-lorn! It was Bartleby.

After a few words touching his qualifications, I engaged him, glad to have among my corps of copyists a man of so singularly sedate an aspect, which I thought might operate beneficially upon the flighty temper of Tur-key, and the fiery one of Nippers.

I should have stated before that ground-glass folding-doors divided my premises into two parts, one of which was occupied by my scriveners, the other by myself. According to my humor, I threw open these doors, or closed them. I resolved to assign Bartleby a corner by the folding-doors, but on my side of them, so as to have this quiet man within easy call, in case any trifling thing was to be done. I placed his desk close up to a small side-window in that part of the room, a window which originally had afforded a lateral view of certain grimy brickyards and bricks, but which, owing to subsequent erections, commanded at present no view at all, though it gave some light. Within three feet of the panes was a wall, and the light came down from far above, between two lofty buildings, as from a very small opening in a dome. Still further to a satisfactory arrangement, I procured a high green folding screen, which might entirely isolate Bartleby from my sight, though not remove him from my voice. And thus, in a manner, pri-vacy and society were conjoined.

At first, Bartleby did an extraordinary quantity of writing. As if long famishing for something to copy, he seemed to gorge himself on my docu-ments. There was no pause for digestion. He ran a day and night line, copying by sunlight and by candle-light. I should have been quite delighted with his application, had he been cheerfully industrious. But he wrote on silently, palely, mechanically.

It is, of course, an indispensable part of a scrivener's business to verify the accuracy of his copy, word by word. Where there are two or more scriveners in an office, they assist each other in this examination, one reading from the copy, the other holding the original. It is a very dull, wearisome, and lethargic affair. I can readily imagine that, to some sanguine temperaments, it would be altogether intolerable. For example, I cannot credit that the mettlesome poet, Byron, would have contentedly sat down with Bartleby to examine a law document of, say five hundred pages, closely written in a crimpy hand.

Now and then, in the haste of business, it had been my habit to assist in comparing some brief document myself, calling Turkey or Nippers for this purpose. One object I had, in placing Bartleby so handy to me behind the screen, was, to avail myself of his services on such trivial occasions. It was on the third day, I think, of his being with me, and before any necessity had arisen for having his own writing examined, that, being much hurried to complete a small affair I had in hand, I abruptly called to Bartleby. In my haste and natural expectancy of instant compliance, I sat with my head bent over the original on my desk, and my right hand sideways, and somewhat nervously extended with the copy, so that, immediately upon emerging from his retreat, Bartleby might snatch it and proceed to business without the least delay.

In this very attitude did I sit when I called to him, rapidly stating what it was I wanted him to do — namely, to examine a small paper with me. Imagine my surprise, nay, my consternation, when, without moving from his privacy, Bartleby, in a singularly mild, firm voice, replied, "I would prefer not to."

I sat awhile in perfect silence, rallying my stunned faculties. Immediately it occurred to me that my ears had deceived me, or Bartleby had entirely misunderstood my meaning. I repeated my request in the clearest tone I could assume; but in quite as clear a one came the previous reply, "I would prefer not to."

"Prefer not to," echoed I, rising in high excitement, and crossing the room with a stride. "What do you mean? Are you moonstruck? I want you to help me compare this sheet here — take it," and I thrust it towards him.

"I would prefer not to," said he.

I looked at him steadfastly. His face was leanly composed; his gray eye dimly calm. Not a wrinkle of agitation rippled him. Had there been the least uneasiness, anger, impatience or impertinence in his manner; in other words, had there been anything ordinarily human about him, doubtless I should have violently dismissed him from the premises. But as it was, I should have as soon thought of turning my pale plaster-of-paris bust of Cicero out of doors. I stood gazing at him awhile, as he went on with his own writing, and then reseated myself at my desk. This is very strange, thought I. What had one best do? But my business hurried me. I concluded to forget the matter for the present, reserving it for my future leisure. So, calling Nippers from the other room, the paper was speedily examined.

A few days after this, Bartleby concluded four lengthy documents, being quadruplicates of a week's testimony taken before me in my High Court of Chancery. It became necessary to examine them. It was an important suit, and great accuracy was imperative. Having all things arranged, I called Turkey, Nippers, and Ginger Nut, from the next room, meaning to place the four copies in the hands of my four clerks, while I should read from the original. Accordingly, Turkey, Nippers, and Ginger Nut had taken their seats in a row, each with his document in his hand, when I called to Bartleby to join this interesting group.

"Bartleby! quick, I am waiting."

I heard a slow scrape of his chair legs on the uncarpeted floor, and soon he appeared standing at the entrance of his hermitage.

"What is wanted?" said he, mildly.

"The copies, the copies," said I, hurriedly. "We are going to examine them. There" — and I held towards him the fourth quadruplicate.

"I would prefer not to," he said, and gently disappeared behind the screen.

For a few moments I was turned into a pillar of salt, standing at the head of my seated column of clerks. Recovering myself, I advanced towards the screen, and demanded the reason for such extraordinary conduct.

"*Why* do you refuse?"

"I would prefer not to."

With any other man I should have flown outright into a dreadful passion, scorned all further words, and thrust him ignominiously from my presence. But there was something about Bartleby that not only strangely disarmed me, but, in a wonderful manner, touched and disconcerted me. I began to reason with him.

"These are your own copies we are about to examine. It is labor saving to you, because one examination will answer for your four papers. It is common usage. Every copyist is bound to help examine his copy. Is it not so? Will you not speak? Answer!"

"I prefer not to," he replied in a flute-like tone. It seemed to me that, while I had been addressing him, he carefully revolved every statement that I made; fully comprehended the meaning; could not gainsay the irresistible conclusion; but, at the same time, some paramount consideration prevailed with him to reply as he did.

"You are decided, then, not to comply with my request — a request made according to common usage and common sense?"

He briefly gave me to understand, that on that point my judgment was sound. Yes: his decision was irreversible.

It is not seldom the case that, when a man is browbeaten in some unprecedented and violently unreasonable way, he begins to stagger in his own plainest faith. He begins, as it were, vaguely to surmise that, wonderful as it may be, all the justice and all the reason is on the other side. Accordingly, if any disinterested persons are present, he turns to them for some reinforcement for his own faltering mind.

"Turkey," said I, "what do you think of this? Am I not right?"

"With submission, sir," said Turkey, in his blandest tone, "I think that you are."

"Nippers," said I, "what do *you* think of it?"

"I think I should kick him out of the office."

(The reader of nice perceptions will have perceived that, it being morning, Turkey's answer is couched in polite and tranquil terms, but Nippers replies in ill-tempered ones. Or, to repeat a previous sentence, Nippers' ugly mood was on duty, and Turkey's off.)

"Ginger Nut," said I, willing to enlist the smallest suffrage in my behalf, "what do *you* think of it?"

"I think, sir, he's a little *luny*," replied Ginger Nut, with a grin.

"You hear what they say," said I, turning towards the screen, "come forth and do your duty."

But he vouchsafed no reply. I pondered a moment in sore perplexity. But once more business hurried me. I determined again to postpone the consideration of this dilemma to my future leisure. With a little trouble we made out to examine the papers without Bartleby, though at every page or two Turkey deferentially dropped his opinion, that this proceeding was quite out of the common; while Nippers, twitching in his chair with a dyspeptic nervousness, ground out, between his set teeth, occasional hissing maledictions against the stubborn oaf behind the screen. And for his (Nippers') part, this was the first and the last time he would do another man's business without pay.

Meanwhile Bartleby sat in his hermitage, oblivious to everything but his own peculiar business there.

Some days passed, the scrivener being employed upon another lengthy work. His late remarkable conduct led me to regard his ways narrowly. I observed that he never went to dinner; indeed, that he never went anywhere. As yet I had never, of my personal knowledge, known him to be outside of my office. He was a perpetual sentry in the corner. At about eleven o'clock though, in the morning, I noticed that Ginger Nut would advance toward the opening in Bartleby's screen, as if silently beckoned thither by a gesture invisible to me where I sat. The boy would then leave the office, jingling a few pence, and reappear with a handful of ginger-nuts, which he delivered in the hermitage, receiving two of the cakes for his trouble.

He lives, then, on ginger-nuts, thought I; never eats a dinner, properly speaking; he must be a vegetarian, then, but no; he never eats even vegetables, he eats nothing but ginger-nuts. My mind then ran on in reveries

concerning the probable effects upon the human constitution of living entirely on ginger-nuts. Ginger-nuts are so called, because they contain ginger
as one of their peculiar constituents, and the final flavoring one. Now, what
was ginger? A hot, spicy thing. Was Bartleby hot and spicy? Not at all. Ginger, then, had no effect upon Bartleby. Probably he preferred it should have
none.

Nothing so aggravates an earnest person as a passive resistance. If the
individual so resisted be of a not inhumane temper, and the resisting one
perfectly harmless in his passivity, then, in the better moods of the former,
he will endeavor charitably to construe to his imagination what proves impossible to be solved by his judgment. Even so, for the most part, I regarded
Bartleby and his ways. Poor fellow! thought I, he means no mischief; it is
plain he intends no insolence; his aspect sufficiently evinces that his eccentricities are involuntary. He is useful to me. I can get along with him. If I
turn him away, the chances are he will fall in with some less indulgent employer, and then he will be rudely treated, and perhaps driven forth miserably to starve. Yes. Here I can cheaply purchase a delicious self-approval.
To befriend Bartleby; to humor him in his strange wilfulness, will cost me
little or nothing, while I lay up in my soul what will eventually prove a
sweet morsel for my conscience. But this mood was not invariable with me.
The passiveness of Bartleby sometimes irritated me. I felt strangely goaded
on to encounter him in new opposition — to elicit some angry spark from
him answerable to my own. But, indeed, I might as well have essayed to
strike fire with my knuckles against a bit of Windsor soap. But one afternoon the evil impulse in me mastered me, and the following little scene ensued:

"Bartleby," said I, "when those papers are all copied, I will compare
them with you."

"I would prefer not to."

"How? Surely you do not mean to persist in that mulish vagary?"

No answer.

I threw open the folding-doors nearby, and turning upon Turkey and
Nippers, exclaimed:

"Bartleby a second time says, he won't examine his papers. What do
you think of it, Turkey?"

It was afternoon, be it remembered. Turkey sat glowing like a brass
boiler; his bald head steaming; his hands reeling among his blotted papers.

"Think of it?" roared Turkey. "I think I'll just step behind his screen,
and black his eyes for him!"

So saying, Turkey rose to his feet and threw his arms into a pugilistic
position. He was hurrying away to make good his promise, when I detained
him, alarmed at the effect of incautiously rousing Turkey's combativeness
after dinner.

"Sit down, Turkey," said I, "and hear what Nippers has to say. What do you think of it, Nippers? Would I not be justified in immediately dismissing Bartleby?"

"Excuse me, that is for you to decide, sir. I think his conduct quite unusual, and, indeed, unjust, as regards Turkey and myself. But it may only be a passing whim."

"Ah," exclaimed I, "you have strangely changed your mind, then — you speak very gently of him now."

"All beer," cried Turkey; "gentleness is effects of beer — Nippers and I dined together to-day. You see how gentle *I* am, sir. Shall I go and black his eyes?"

"You refer to Bartleby, I suppose. No, not to-day, Turkey," I replied; "pray, put up your fists."

I closed the doors, and again advanced towards Bartleby. I felt additional incentives tempting me to my fate. I burned to be rebelled against again. I remembered that Bartleby never left the office.

"Bartleby," said I, "Ginger Nut is away; just step around to the Post Office, won't you?" (it was but a three minutes' walk) "and see if there is anything for me."

"I would prefer not to."

"You *will* not?"

"I *prefer* not."

I staggered to my desk, and sat there in a deep study. My blind inveteracy returned. Was there any other thing in which I could procure myself to be ignominiously repulsed by this lean, penniless wight? — my hired clerk? What added thing is there, perfectly reasonable, that he will be sure to refuse to do?

"Bartleby!"

No answer.

"Bartleby," in a louder tone.

No answer.

"Bartleby," I roared.

Like a very ghost, agreeably to the laws of magical invocation, at the third summons, he appeared at the entrance of his hermitage.

"Go to the next room, and tell Nippers to come to me."

"I prefer not to," he respectfully and slowly said, and mildy disappeared.

"Very good, Bartleby," said I, in a quiet sort of serenely-severe self-possessed tone, intimating the unalterable purpose of some terrible retribution very close at hand. At the moment I half intended something of the kind. But upon the whole, as it was drawing towards my dinner-hour, I thought it best to put on my hat and walk home for the day, suffering much from perplexity and distress of mind.

Shall I acknowledge it? The conclusion of this whole business was, that it soon became a fixed fact of my chambers, that a pale young scriv-

ener, by the name of Bartleby, had a desk there; that he copied for me at
the usual rate of four cents a folio (one hundred words); but he was permanently exempt from examining the work done by him, that duty being
transferred to Turkey and Nippers, out of compliment, doubtless, to their
superior acuteness; moreover, said Bartleby was never, on any account, to
be dispatched on the most trivial errand of any sort; and that even if entreated to take upon him such a matter, it was generally understood that he
would "prefer not to" — in other words, that he would refuse point-blank.

As days passed on, I became considerably reconciled to Bartleby. His
steadiness, his freedom from all dissipation, his incessant industry (except
when he chose to throw himself into a standing revery behind his screen),
his great stillness, his unalterableness of demeanor under all circumstances,
made him a valuable acquisition. One prime thing was this — *he was always there* — first in the morning, continually through the day, and the last
at night. I had a singular confidence in his honesty. I felt my most precious
papers perfectly safe in his hands. Sometimes, to be sure, I could not, for
the very soul of me, avoid falling into sudden spasmodic passions with him.
For it was exceeding difficult to bear in mind all the time those strange peculiarities, privileges, and unheard-of exemptions, forming the tacit stipula-
tions on Bartleby's part under which he remained in my office. Now and
then, in the eagerness of dispatching pressing business, I would inadvertently summon Bartleby, in a short, rapid tone, to put his finger, say, on the
incipient tie of a bit of red tape with which I was about compressing some
papers. Of course, from behind the screen the usual answer, "I prefer not
to," was sure to come; and then, how could a human creature, with the
common infirmities of our nature, refrain from bitterly exclaiming upon
such perverseness — such unreasonableness? However, every added repulse
of this sort which I received only tended to lessen the probability of my repeating the inadvertence.

Here it must be said, that, according to the custom of most legal gentlemen occupying chambers in densely populated law buildings, there were
several keys to my door. One was kept by a woman residing in the attic,
which person weekly scrubbed and daily swept and dusted my apartments.
Another was kept by Turkey for convenience sake. The third I sometimes
carried in my own pocket. The fourth I knew not who had.

Now, one Sunday morning I happened to go to Trinity Church, to
hear a celebrated preacher, and finding myself rather early on the ground I
thought I would walk round to my chambers for a while. Luckily I had my
key with me; but upon applying it to the lock, I found it resisted by something inserted from the inside. Quite surprised, I called out; when to my
consternation a key was turned from within; and thrusting his lean visage at
me, and holding the door ajar, the apparition of Bartleby appeared, in his
shirt-sleeves, and otherwise in a strangely tattered *deshabille,* saying quietly
that he was sorry, but he was deeply engaged just then, and — preferred not

admitting me at present. In a brief word or two, he moreover added, that perhaps I had better walk round the block two or three times, and by that time he would probably have concluded his affairs.

Now, the utterly unsurmised appearance of Bartleby, tenanting my law-chambers of a Sunday morning, with his cadaverously gentlemanly *nonchalance*, yet withal firm and self-possessed, had such a strange effect upon me, that incontinently I slunk away from my own door, and did as desired. But not without sundry twinges of impotent rebellion against the mild effrontery of this unaccountable scrivener. Indeed, it was his wonderful mildness chiefly, which not only disarmed me, but unmanned me, as it were. For I consider that one, for the time, is a sort of unmanned when he tranquilly permits his hired clerk to dictate to him, and order him away from his own premises. Furthermore, I was full of uneasiness as to what Bartleby could possibly be doing in my office in his shirt-sleeves, and in an otherwise dismantled condition of a Sunday morning. Was anything amiss going on? Nay, that was out of the question. It was not to be thought of for a moment that Bartleby was an immoral person. But what could he be doing there? — copying? Nay again, whatever might be his eccentricities, Bartleby was an eminently decorous person. He would be the last man to sit down to his desk in any state approaching to nudity. Besides, it was Sunday; and there was something about Bartleby that forbade the supposition that he would by any secular occupation violate the proprieties of the day.

Nevertheless, my mind was not pacified; and full of a restless curiosity, at last I returned to the door. Without hindrance I inserted my key, opened it, and entered. Bartleby was not to be seen. I looked round anxiously, peeped behind his screen; but it was very plain that he was gone. Upon more closely examining the place, I surmised that for an indefinite period Bartleby must have ate, dressed, and slept in my office, and that too without plate, mirror, or bed. The cushioned seat of a rickety old sofa in one corner bore the faint impress of a lean, reclining form. Rolled away under his desk, I found a blanket; under the empty grate, a blacking box and brush; on a chair, a tin basin, with soap and a ragged towel; in a newspaper a few crumbs of ginger-nuts and a morsel of cheese. Yes, thought I, it is evident enough that Bartleby has been making his home here, keeping bachelor's hall all by himself. Immediately then the thought came sweeping across me, what miserable friendlessness and loneliness are here revealed! His poverty is great; but his solitude, how horrible! Think of it. Of a Sunday, Wall Street is deserted as Petra;[3] and every night of every day it is an emptiness. This building, too, which of week-days hums with industry and life, at nightfall echoes with sheer vacancy, and all through Sunday is forlorn. And here Bartleby makes his home; sole spectator of a solitude which he has

---

[3] A city in what is now Jordan, once the center of an Arab kingdom. It was deserted for more than ten centuries, until its rediscovery by explorers in 1812.

seen all populous — a sort of innocent and transformed Marius[4] brooding among the ruins of Carthage!

For the first time in my life a feeling of overpowering stinging melancholy seized me. Before, I had never experienced aught but a not unpleasing sadness. The bond of a common humanity now drew me irresistibly to gloom. A fraternal melancholy! For both I and Bartleby were sons of Adam. I remembered the bright silks and sparkling faces I had seen that day, in gala trim, swan-like sailing down the Mississippi of Broadway; and I contrasted them with the pallid copyist, and thought to myself, Ah, happiness courts the light, so we deem the world is gay; but misery hides aloof, so we deem that misery there is none. These sad fancyings — chimeras, doubtless, of a sick and silly brain — led on to other and more special thoughts, concerning the eccentricities of Bartleby. Presentiments of strange discoveries hovered round me. The scrivener's pale form appeared to me laid out, among uncaring strangers, in its shivering winding-sheet.

Suddenly I was attracted by Bartleby's closed desk, the key in open sight left in the lock.

I mean no mischief, seek the gratification of no heartless curiosity, thought I; besides, the desk is mine, and its contents, too, so I will make bold to look within. Everything was methodically arranged, the papers smoothly placed. The pigeon-holes were deep, and removing the files of documents, I groped into their recesses. Presently I felt something there, and dragged it out. It was an old bandanna handkerchief, heavy and knotted. I opened it, and saw it was a saving's bank.

I now recalled all the quiet mysteries which I had noted in the man. I remembered that he never spoke but to answer; that, though at intervals he had considerable time to himself, yet I had never seen him reading — no, not even a newspaper; that for long periods he would stand looking out, at his pale window behind the screen, upon the dead brick wall; I was quite sure he never visited any refectory or eating-house; while his pale face clearly indicated that he never drank beer like Turkey; or tea and coffee even, like other men; that he never went anywhere in particular that I could learn; never went out for a walk, unless, indeed, that was the case at present; that he had declined telling who he was, or whence he came, or whether he had any relatives in the world; that though so thin and pale, he never complained of ill-health. And more than all, I remembered a certain unconscious air of pallid — how shall I call it? — of pallid haughtiness, say, or rather an austere reserve about him, which has positively awed me into my tame compliance with his eccentricities, when I had feared to ask him to do the slightest incidental thing for me, even though I might know, from his

---

[4] Gaius Marius (157?–86 B.C.), a Roman general, several times elected consul. Marius's greatest military successes came in the Jugurthine War, in Africa. Later, when his opponents gained power and he was banished, he fled to Africa. Carthage was a city in North Africa.

long-continued motionlessness, that behind his screen he must be standing in one of those dead-wall reveries of his.

Revolving all these things, and coupling them with the recently discovered fact, that he made my office his constant abiding place and home, and not forgetful of his morbid moodiness; revolving all these things, a prudential feeling began to steal over me. My first emotions had been those of pure melancholy and sincerest pity; but just in proportion as the forlornness of Bartleby grew and grew to my imagination, did that same melancholy merge into fear, that pity into repulsion. So true it is, and so terrible, too, that up to a certain point the thought or sight of misery enlists our best affections; but, in certain special cases, beyond that point it does not. They err who would assert that invariably this is owing to the inherent selfishness of the human heart. It rather proceeds from a certain hopelessness of remedying excessive and organic ill. To a sensitive being, pity is not seldom pain. And when at last it is perceived that such pity cannot lead to effectual succor, common sense bids the soul be rid of it. What I saw that morning persuaded me that the scrivener was the victim of innate and incurable disorder. I might give alms to his body; but his body did not pain him; it was his soul that suffered, and his soul I could not reach.

I did not accomplish the purpose of going to Trinity Church that morning. Somehow, the things I had seen disqualified me for the time from church-going. I walked homeward, thinking what I would do with Bartleby. Finally, I resolved upon this — I would put certain calm questions to him the next morning, touching his history, etc., and if he declined to answer them openly and unreservedly (and I supposed he would prefer not), then to give him a twenty dollar bill over and above whatever I might owe him, and tell him his services were no longer required; but that if in any other way I could assist him, I would be happy to do so, especially if he desired to return to his native place, wherever that might be, I would willingly help to defray the expenses. Moreover, if, after reaching home, he found himself at any time in want of aid, a letter from him would be sure of a reply.

The next morning came.

"Bartleby," said I, gently calling to him behind his screen.

No reply.

"Bartleby," said I, in a still gentler tone, "come here; I am not going to ask you to do anything you would prefer not to do — I simply wish to speak to you."

Upon this he noiselessly slid into view.

"Will you tell me, Bartleby, where you were born?"

"I would prefer not to."

"Will you tell me *anything* about yourself?"

"I would prefer not to."

"But what reasonable objection can you have to speak to me? I feel friendly towards you."

He did not look at me while I spoke, but kept his glance fixed upon my bust of Cicero, which, as I then sat, was directly behind me, some six inches above my head.

"What is your answer, Bartleby?" said I, after waiting a considerable time for a reply, during which his countenance remained immovable, only there was the faintest conceivable tremor of the white attenuated mouth.

"At present I prefer to give no answer," he said, and retired into his hermitage.

It was rather weak in me I confess, but his manner, on this occasion, nettled me. Not only did there seem to lurk in it a certain calm disdain, but his perverseness seemed ungrateful, considering the undeniable good usage and indulgence he had received from me.

Again I sat ruminating what I should do. Mortified as I was at his behavior, and resolved as I had been to dismiss him when I entered my office, nevertheless I strangely felt something superstitious knocking at my heart, and forbidding me to carry out my purpose, and denouncing me for a villain if I dared to breathe one bitter word against this forlornest of mankind. At last, familiarly drawing my chair behind his screen, I sat down and said: "Bartleby, never mind, then, about revealing your history; but let me entreat you, as a friend, to comply as far as may be with the usages of this office. Say now, you will help to examine papers tomorrow or next day: in short, say now, that in a day or two you will begin to be a little reasonable: — say so, Bartleby."

"At present I would prefer not to be a little reasonable," was his mildly cadaverous reply.

Just then the folding-doors opened, and Nippers approached. He seemed suffering from an unusually bad night's rest, induced by severer indigestion than common. He overheard those final words of Bartleby.

"*Prefer not*, eh?" gritted Nippers — "I'd *prefer* him, if I were you, sir," addressing me — "I'd *prefer* him; I'd give him preferences, the stubborn mule! What is it, sir, pray, that he *prefers* not to do now?"

Bartleby moved not a limb.

"Mr. Nippers," said I, "I'd prefer that you would withdraw for the present."

Somehow, of late, I had got into the way of involuntarily using this word "prefer" upon all sorts of not exactly suitable occasions. And I trembled to think that my contact with the scrivener had already and seriously affected me in a mental way. And what further and deeper aberration might it not yet produce? This apprehension had not been without efficacy in determining me to summary measures.

As Nippers, looking very sour and sulky, was departing, Turkey blandly and deferentially approached.

"With submission, sir," said he, "yesterday I was thinking about Bartleby here, and I think that if he would but prefer to take a quart of good ale every day, it would do much towards mending him, and enabling him to assist in examining his papers."

"So you have got the word, too," said I, slightly excited.

"With submission, what word, sir?" asked Turkey, respectfully crowding himself into the contracted space behind the screen, and by so doing, making me jostle the scrivener. "What word, sir?"

"I would prefer to be left alone here," said Bartleby, as if offended at being mobbed in his privacy.

"*That's* the word, Turkey," said I — "*that's* it."

"Oh, *prefer?* oh yes — queer word. I never use it myself. But, sir, as I was saying, if he would but prefer — "

"Turkey," interrupted I, "you will please withdraw."

"Oh certainly, sir, if you prefer that I should."

As he opened the folding-door to retire, Nippers at his desk caught a glimpse of me, and asked whether I would prefer to have a certain paper copied on blue paper or white. He did not in the least roguishly accent the word "prefer." It was plain that it involuntarily rolled from his tongue. I thought to myself, surely I must get rid of a demented man, who already has in some degree turned the tongues, if not the heads of myself and clerks. But I thought it prudent not to break the dismission at once.

The next day I noticed that Bartleby did nothing but stand at his window in his dead-wall revery. Upon asking him why he did not write, he said that he had decided upon doing no more writing.

"Why, how now? what next?" exclaimed I, "do no more writing?"

"No more."

"And what is the reason?"

"Do you not see the reason for yourself?" he indifferently replied.

I looked steadfastly at him, and perceived that his eyes looked dull and glazed. Instantly it occurred to me, that his unexampled diligence in copying by his dim window for the first few weeks of his stay with me might have temporarily impaired his vision.

I was touched. I said something in condolence with him. I hinted that of course he did wisely in abstaining from writing for a while; and urged him to embrace that opportunity of taking wholesome exercise in the open air. This, however, he did not do. A few days after this, my other clerks being absent, and being in a great hurry to dispatch certain letters by the mail, I thought that, having nothing else earthly to do, Bartleby would surely be less inflexible than usual, and carry these letters to the Post Office. But he blankly declined. So, much to my inconvenience, I went myself.

Still added days went by. Whether Bartleby's eyes improved or not, I could not say. To all appearance, I thought they did. But when I asked him if they did, he vouchsafed no answer. At all events, he would do no copying. At last, in replying to my urgings, he informed me that he had permanently given up copying.

"What!" exclaimed I; "suppose your eyes should get entirely well — better than ever before — would you not copy then?"

"I have given up copying," he answered, and slid aside.

He remained as ever, a fixture in my chamber. Nay — if that were possible — he became still more of a fixture than before. What was to be done? He would do nothing in the office; why should he stay there? In plain fact, he had now become a millstone to me, not only useless as a necklace, but afflictive to bear. Yet I was sorry for him. I speak less than truth when I say that, on his own account, he occasioned me uneasiness. If he would but have named a single relative or friend, I would instantly have written, and urged their taking the poor fellow away to some convenient retreat. But he seemed alone, absolutely alone in the universe. A bit of wreck in the mid-Atlantic. At length, necessities connected with my business tyrannized over all other considerations. Decently as I could, I told Bartleby that in six days' time he must unconditionally leave the office. I warned him to take measures, in the interval, for procuring some other abode. I offered to assist him in this endeavor, if he himself would but take the first step towards a removal. "And when you finally quit me, Bartleby," added I, "I shall see that you go not away entirely unprovided. Six days from this hour, remember."

At the expiration of that period, I peeped behind the screen, and lo! Bartleby was there.

I buttoned up my coat, balanced myself; advanced slowly towards him, touched his shoulder, and said, "The time has come; you must quit this place; I am sorry for you; here is money; but you must go."

"I would prefer not," he replied, with his back still towards me.

"You *must*."

He remained silent.

Now I had an unbounded confidence in this man's common honesty. He had frequently restored to me sixpences and shillings carelessly dropped upon the floor, for I am apt to be very reckless in such shirt-button affairs. The proceeding, then, which followed will not be deemed extraordinary.

"Bartleby," said I, "I owe you twelve dollars on account; here are thirty-two; the odd twenty are yours — Will you take it?" and I handed the bills towards him.

But he made no motion.

"I will leave them here, then," putting them under a weight on the table. Then taking my hat and cane and going to the door, I tranquilly turned and added — "After you have removed your things from these offices, Bartleby, you will of course lock the door — since every one is now gone for the day but you — and if you please, slip your key underneath the mat, so that I may have it in the morning. I shall not see you again; so good-bye to you. If, hereafter, in your new place of abode, I can be of any service to you, do not fail to advise me by letter. Good-bye, Bartleby, and fare you well."

But he answered not a word; like the last column of some ruined temple, he remained standing mute and solitary in the middle of the otherwise deserted room.

As I walked home in a pensive mood, my vanity got the better of my pity. I could not but highly plume myself on my masterly management in getting rid of Bartleby. Masterly I call it, and such it must appear to any dispassionate thinker. The beauty of my procedure seemed to consist in its perfect quietness. There was no vulgar bullying, no bravado of any sort, no choleric hectoring, and striding to and fro across the apartment, jerking out vehement commands for Bartleby to bundle himself off with his beggarly traps. Nothing of the kind. Without loudly bidding Bartleby depart — as an inferior genius might have done — I *assumed* the ground that depart he must; and upon that assumption built all I had to say. The more I thought over my procedure, the more I was charmed with it. Nevertheless, next morning, upon awakening, I had my doubts — I had somehow slept off the fumes of vanity. One of the coolest and wisest hours a man has, is just after he awakes in the morning. My procedure seemed as sagacious as ever — but only in theory. How it would prove in practice — there was the rub. It was truly a beautiful thought to have assumed Bartleby's departure; but, after all, that assumption was simply my own, and none of Bartleby's. The great point was, not whether I had assumed that he would quit me, but whether he would prefer to do so. He was more a man of preferences than assumptions.

After breakfast, I walked down town, arguing the probabilities *pro* and *con.* One moment I thought it would prove a miserable failure, and Bartleby would be found all alive at my office as usual; the next moment it seemed certain that I should find his chair empty. And so I kept veering about. At the corner of Broadway and Canal Street, I saw quite an excited group of people standing in earnest conversation.

"I'll take odds he doesn't," said a voice as I passed.

"Doesn't go? — done!" said I, "put up your money."

I was instinctively putting my hand in my pocket to produce my own, when I remembered that this was an election day. The words I had overheard bore no reference to Bartleby, but to the success or non-success of some candidate for the mayoralty. In my intent frame of mind, I had, as it were, imagined that all Broadway shared in my excitement, and were debating the same question with me. I passed on, very thankful that the uproar of the street screened my momentary absent-mindedness.

As I had intended, I was earlier than usual at my office door. I stood listening for a moment. All was still. He must be gone. I tried the knob. The door was locked. Yes, my procedure had worked to a charm; he indeed must be vanished. Yet a certain melancholy mixed with this: I was almost sorry for my brilliant success. I was fumbling under the door mat for the key, which Bartleby was to have left there for me, when accidentally my knee knocked against a panel, producing a summoning sound, and in response a voice came to me from within — "Not yet; I am occupied."

It was Bartleby.

I was thunderstruck. For an instant I stood like the man who, pipe in mouth, was killed one cloudless afternoon long ago in Virginia, by summer lightning; at his own warm open window he was killed, and remained leaning out there upon the dreamy afternoon, till some one touched him, when he fell.

"Not gone!" I murmured at last. But again obeying that wondrous ascendancy which the inscrutable scrivener had over me, and from which ascendancy, for all my chafing, I could not completely escape, I slowly went down stairs and out into the street, and while walking round the block, considered what I should next do in this unheard-of perplexity. Turn the man out by an actual thrusting I could not; to drive him away by calling him hard names would not do; calling in the police was an unpleasant idea; and yet, permit him to enjoy his cadaverous triumph over me — this, too, I could not think of. What was to be done? or, if nothing could be done, was there anything further that I could *assume* in the matter? Yes, as before I had prospectively assumed that Bartleby would depart, so now I might retrospectively assume that departed he was. In the legitimate carrying out of this assumption, I might enter my office in a great hurry, and pretending not to see Bartleby at all, walk straight against him as if he were air. Such a proceeding would in a singular degree have the appearance of a home-thrust. It was hardly possible that Bartleby could withstand such an application of the doctrine of assumption. But upon second thoughts the success of the plan seemed rather dubious. I resolved to argue the matter over with him again.

"Bartleby," said I, entering the office, with a quietly severe expression, "I am seriously displeased. I am pained, Bartleby. I had thought better of you. I had imagined you of such a gentlemanly organization, that in any delicate dilemma a slight hint would suffice — in short, an assumption. But it appears I am deceived. Why," I added, unaffectedly starting, "you have not even touched that money yet," pointing to it, just where I had left it the evening previous.

He answered nothing.

"Will you, or will you not, quit me?" I now demanded in a sudden passion, advancing close to him.

"I would prefer *not* to quit you," he replied, gently emphasizing the *not.*

"What earthly right have you to stay here? Do you pay any rent? Do you pay my taxes? Or is this property yours?"

He answered nothing.

"Are you ready to go on and write now? Are your eyes recovered? Could you copy a small paper for me this morning? or help examine a few lines? or step round to the Post Office? In a word, will you do anything at all, to give a coloring to your refusal to depart the premises?"

He silently retired into his hermitage.

I was now in such a state of nervous resentment that I thought it but prudent to check myself at present from further demonstrations. Bartleby and I were alone. I remembered the tragedy of the unfortunate Adams and the still more unfortunate Colt in the solitary office of the latter; and how poor Colt, being dreadfully incensed by Adams, and imprudently permitting himself to get wildly excited, was at unawares hurried into his fatal act — an act which certainly no man could possibly deplore more than the actor himself.[5] Often it had occurred to me in my ponderings upon the subject that had that altercation taken place in the public street, or at a private residence, it would not have terminated as it did. It was the circumstance of being alone in a solitary office, up stairs, of a building entirely unhallowed by humanizing domestic associations — an uncarpeted office, doubtless, of a dusty, haggard sort of appearance — this it must have been, which greatly helped to enhance the irritable desperation of the hapless Colt.

But when this old Adam of resentment rose in me and tempted me concerning Bartleby, I grappled him and threw him. How? Why, simply by recalling the divine injunction: "A new commandment give I unto you, that ye love one another." Yes, this it was that saved me. Aside from higher considerations, charity often operates as a vastly wise and prudent principle — a great safeguard to its possessor. Men have committed murder for jealousy's sake, and anger's sake, and hatred's sake, and selfishness' sake, and spiritual pride's sake; but no man, that ever I heard of, ever committed a diabolical murder for sweet charity's sake. Mere self-interest, then, if no better motive can be enlisted, should, especially with high-tempered men, prompt all beings to charity and philanthropy. At any rate, upon the occasion in question, I strove to drown my exasperated feelings towards the scrivener by benevolently construing his conduct. Poor fellow, poor fellow! thought I, he don't mean anything; and besides, he has seen hard times, and ought to be indulged.

I endeavored, also, immediately to occupy myself, and at the same time to comfort my despondency. I tried to fancy, that in the course of the morning, at such time as might prove agreeable to him, Bartleby, of his own free accord, would emerge from his hermitage and take up some decided line of march in the direction of the door. But no. Half-past twelve o'clock came; Turkey began to glow in the face, overturn his inkstand, and become generally obstreperous; Nippers abated down into quietude and courtesy; Ginger Nut munched his noon apple; and Bartleby remained standing at his window in one of his profoundest dead-wall reveries. Will it be credited? Ought I to acknowledge it? That afternoon I left the office without saying one further word to him.

[5] John C. Colt murdered Samuel Adams in January 1842. Later that year, after his conviction, Colt committed suicide a half-hour before he was to be hanged. The case received wide and sensationalistic press coverage at the time.

Some days now passed, during which, at leisure intervals I looked a little into "Edwards[6] on the Will," and "Priestley[7] on Necessity." Under the circumstances, those books induced a salutary feeling. Gradually I slid into the persuasion that these troubles of mine, touching the scrivener, had been all predestined from eternity, and Bartleby was billeted upon me for some mysterious purpose of an all-wise Providence, which it was not for a mere mortal like me to fathom. Yes, Bartleby, stay there behind your screen, thought I; I shall persecute you no more; you are harmless and noiseless as any of these old chairs; in short, I never feel so private as when I know you are here. At last I see it, I feel it; I penetrate to the predestined purpose of my life. I am content. Others may have loftier parts to enact; but my mission in this world, Bartleby, is to furnish you with office-room for such period as you may see fit to remain.

I believe that this wise and blessed frame of mind would have continued with me, had it not been for the unsolicited and uncharitable remarks obtruded upon me by my professional friends who visited the rooms. But thus it often is, that the constant friction of illiberal minds wears out at last the best resolves of the more generous. Though to be sure, when I reflected upon it, it was not strange that people entering my office should be struck by the peculiar aspect of the unaccountable Bartleby, and so be tempted to throw out some sinister observations concerning him. Sometimes an attorney, having business with me, and calling at my office, and finding no one but the scrivener there, would undertake to obtain some sort of precise information from him touching my whereabouts; but without heeding his idle talk, Bartleby would remain standing immovable in the middle of the room. So after contemplating him in that position for a time, the attorney would depart, no wiser than he came.

Also, when a reference was going on, and the room full of lawyers and witnesses, and business driving fast, some deeply-occupied legal gentleman present, seeing Bartleby wholly unemployed, would request him to run round to his (the legal gentleman's) office and fetch some papers for him. Thereupon, Bartleby would tranquilly decline, and yet remain idle as before. Then the lawyer would give a great stare, and turn to me. And what could I say? At last I was made aware that all through the circle of my professional acquaintance, a whisper of wonder was running round, having reference to the strange creature I kept at my office. This worried me very

---

[6] Jonathan Edwards, *Freedom of the Will* (1754). Edwards was an important American theologian, a rigidly orthodox Calvinist who believed in the doctrine of predestination, and a leader of the Great Awakening, the religious revival that swept the North American colonies in the 1740s.

[7] Joseph Priestley, eighteenth-century English scientist and clergyman. Priestley began as a Unitarian, but developed his own radical ideas on "natural determinism." As a scientist, he did early experiments with electricity and was one of the first to discover the existence of oxygen. As a political philosopher, he championed the French Revolution — a cause so unpopular in England that he had to flee that country and spend the last decade of his life in the United States.

much. And as the idea came upon me of his possibly turning out a long-lived man, and keeping occupying my chambers, and denying my authority; and perplexing my visitors; and scandalizing my professional reputation; and casting a general gloom over the premises; keeping soul and body together to the last upon his savings (for doubtless he spent but half a dime a day), and in the end perhaps outlive me, and claim possession of my office by right of his perpetual occupancy: as all these dark anticipations crowded upon me more and more, and my friends continually intruded their relentless remarks upon the apparition in my room; a great change was wrought in me. I resolved to gather all my faculties together, and forever rid me of this intolerable incubus.

Ere revolving any complicated project, however, adapted to this end, I first simply suggested to Bartleby the propriety of his permanent departure. In a calm and serious tone, I commended the idea to his careful and mature consideration. But, having taken three days to meditate upon it, he apprised me, that his original determination remained the same; in short, that he still preferred to abide with me.

What shall I do? I now said to myself, buttoning up my coat to the last button. What shall I do? what ought I to do? what does conscience say I *should* do with this man, or, rather, ghost. Rid myself of him, I must; go, he shall. But how? You will not thrust him, the poor, pale, passive mortal — you will not thrust such a helpless creature out of your door? you will not dishonor yourself by such cruelty? No, I will not, I cannot do that. Rather would I let him live and die here, and then mason up his remains in the wall. What, then, will you do? For all your coaxing, he will not budge. Bribes he leaves under your own paper-weight on your table; in short, it is quite plain that he prefers to cling to you.

Then something severe, something unusual must be done. What! surely you will not have him collared by a constable, and commit his innocent pallor to the common jail? And upon what ground could you procure such a thing to be done? — a vagrant, is he? What! he a vagrant, a wanderer, who refuses to budge? It is because he will *not* be a vagrant, then, that you seek to count him *as* a vagrant. That is too absurd. No visible means of support: there I have him. Wrong again: for indubitably he *does* support himself, and that is the only unanswerable proof that any man can show of his possessing the means so to do. No more, then. Since he will not quit me, I must quit him. I will change my offices; I will move elsewhere, and give him fair notice, that if I find him on my new premises I will then proceed against him as a common trespasser.

Acting accordingly, next day I thus addressed him: "I find these chambers too far from the City Hall; the air is unwholesome. In a word, I propose to remove my offices next week, and shall no longer require your services. I tell you this now, in order that you may seek another place."

He made no reply, and nothing more was said.

On the appointed day I engaged carts and men, proceeded to my chambers, and, having but little furniture, everything was removed in a few hours. Throughout, the scrivener remained standing behind the screen, which I directed to be removed the last thing. It was withdrawn; and, being folded up like a huge folio, left him the motionless occupant of a naked room. I stood in the entry watching him a moment, while something from within me upbraided me.

I re-entered, with my hand in my pocket — and — and my heart in my mouth.

"Good-bye, Bartleby; I am going — good-bye, and God some way bless you; and take that," slipping something in his hand. But it dropped upon the floor, and then — strange to say — I tore myself from him whom I had so longed to be rid of.

Established in my new quarters, for a day or two I kept the door locked, and started at every footfall in the passages. When I returned to my rooms, after any little absence, I would pause at the threshold for an instant, and attentively listen, ere applying my key. But these fears were needless. Bartleby never came nigh me.

I thought all was going well, when a perturbed-looking stranger visited me, inquiring whether I was the person who had recently occupied rooms at No. — Wall Street.

Full of forebodings, I replied that I was.

"Then, sir," said the stranger, who proved a lawyer, "you are responsible for the man you left there. He refuses to do any copying; he refuses to do anything; he says he prefers not to; and he refuses to quit the premises."

"I am very sorry, sir," said I, with assumed tranquillity, but an inward tremor, "but, really, the man you allude to is nothing to me — he is no relation or apprentice of mine, that you should hold me responsible for him."

"In mercy's name, who is he?"

"I certainly cannot inform you. I know nothing about him. Formerly I employed him as a copyist; but he has done nothing for me now for some time past."

"I shall settle him, then — good morning, sir."

Several days passed, and I heard nothing more; and, though I often felt a charitable prompting to call at the place and see poor Bartleby, yet a certain squeamishness, of I know not what, withheld me.

All is over with him, by this time, thought I, at last, when, through another week, no further intelligence reached me. But, coming to my room the day after, I found several persons waiting at my door in a high state of nervous excitement.

"That's the man — here he comes," cried the foremost one, whom I recognized as the lawyer who had previously called upon me alone.

"You must take him away, sir, at once," cried a portly person among them, advancing upon me, and whom I knew to be the landlord of No. — Wall Street. "These gentlemen, my tenants, cannot stand it any longer; Mr. B———," pointing to the lawyer, "has turned him out of his room, and he now persists in haunting the building generally, sitting upon the banisters of the stairs by day, and sleeping in the entry by night. Everybody is concerned; clients are leaving the offices; some fears are entertained of a mob; something you must do, and that without delay."

Aghast at this torrent, I fell back before it, and would fain have locked myself in my new quarters. In vain I persisted that Bartleby was nothing to me — no more than to any one else. In vain — I was the last person known to have anything to do with him, and they held me to the terrible account. Fearful, then, of being exposed in the papers (as one person present obscurely threatened), I considered the matter, and, at length, said, that if the lawyer would give me a confidential interview with the scrivener, in his (the lawyer's) own room, I would, that afternoon, strive my best to rid them of the nuisance they complained of.

Going up stairs to my old haunt, there was Bartleby silently sitting upon the banister at the landing.

"What are you doing here, Bartleby?" said I.

"Sitting upon the banister," he mildly replied.

I motioned him into the lawyer's room, who then left us.

"Bartleby," said I, "are you aware that you are the cause of great tribulation to me, by persisting in occupying the entry after being dismissed from the office?"

No answer.

"Now one of two things must take place. Either you must do something, or something must be done to you. Now what sort of business would you like to engage in? Would you like to re-engage in copying for some one?"

"No; I would prefer not to make any change."

"Would you like a clerkship in a dry-goods store?"

"There is too much confinement about that. No, I would not like a clerkship; but I am not particular."

"Too much confinement," I cried, "why, you keep yourself confined all the time!"

"I would prefer not to take a clerkship," he rejoined, as if to settle that little item at once.

"How would a bar-tender's business suit you? There is no trying of the eye-sight in that."

"I would not like it at all; though, as I said before, I am not particular."

His unwonted wordiness inspirited me. I returned to the charge.

"Well, then, would you like to travel through the country collecting bills for the merchants? That would improve your health."

"No, I would prefer to be doing something else."

"How, then, would going as a companion to Europe, to entertain some young gentleman with your conversation — how would that suit you?"

"Not at all. It does not strike me that there is anything definite about that. I like to be stationary. But I am not particular."

"Stationary you shall be, then," I cried, now losing all patience, and, for the first time in all my exasperating connection with him, fairly flying into a passion. "If you do not go away from these premises before night, I shall feel bound — indeed, I *am* bound — to — to — to quit the premises myself!" I rather absurdly concluded, knowing not with what possible threat to try to frighten his immobility into compliance. Despairing of all further efforts, I was precipitately leaving him, when a final thought occurred to me — one which had not been wholly unindulged before.

"Bartleby," said I, in the kindest tone I could assume under such exciting circumstances, "will you go home with me now — not to my office, but my dwelling — and remain there till we can conclude upon some convenient arrangement for you at our leisure? Come, let us start now, right away."

"No: at present I would prefer not to make any change at all."

I answered nothing; but, effectually dodging every one by the suddenness and rapidity of my flight, rushed from the building, ran up Wall Street towards Broadway, and, jumping into the first omnibus, was soon removed from pursuit. As soon as tranquillity returned, I distinctly perceived that I had now done all that I possibly could, both in respect to the demands of the landlord and his tenants, and with regard to my own desire and sense of duty, to benefit Bartleby, and shield him from rude persecution. I now strove to be entirely care-free and quiescent; and my conscience justified me in the attempt; though, indeed, it was not so successful as I could have wished. So fearful was I of being again hunted out by the incensed landlord and his exasperated tenants, that, surrendering my business to Nippers, for a few days, I drove about the upper part of the town and through the suburbs, in my rockaway; crossed over to Jersey City and Hoboken, and paid fugitive visits to Manhattanville and Astoria. In fact, I almost lived in my rockaway for the time.

When again I entered my office, lo, a note from the landlord lay upon the desk. I opened it with trembling hands. It informed me that the writer had sent to the police, and had Bartleby removed to the Tombs as a vagrant. Moreover, since I knew more about him than any one else, he wished me to appear at that place, and make a suitable statement of the facts. These tidings had a conflicting effect upon me. At first I was indignant; but, at last, almost approved. The landlord's energetic, summary disposition, had led him to adopt a procedure which I do not think I would have decided upon myself; and yet, as a last resort, under such peculiar circumstances, it seemed the only plan.

As I afterwards learned, the poor scrivener, when told that he must be conducted to the Tombs, offered not the slightest obstacle, but, in his pale, unmoving way, silently acquiesced.

Some of the compassionate and curious by-standers joined the party;

and headed by one of the constables arm-in-arm with Bartleby, the silent procession filed its way through all the noise, and heat, and joy of the roaring thoroughfares at noon.

The same day I received the note, I went to the Tombs, or, to speak more properly, the Halls of Justice. Seeking the right officer, I stated the purpose of my call, and was informed that the individual I described was, indeed, within. I then assured the functionary that Bartleby was a perfectly honest man, and greatly to be compassionated, however unaccountably eccentric. I narrated all I knew, and closed by suggesting the idea of letting him remain in as indulgent confinement as possible, till something less harsh might be done — though, indeed, I hardly knew what. At all events, if nothing else could be decided upon, the alms-house must receive him. I then begged to have an interview.

Being under no disgraceful charge, and quite serene and harmless in all his ways, they had permitted him freely to wander about the prison, and, especially, in the inclosed grass-platted yards thereof. And so I found him there, standing all alone in the quietest of the yards, his face towards a high wall, while all around, from the narrow slits of the jail windows, I thought I saw peering out upon him the eyes of murderers and thieves.

"Bartleby!"

"I know you," he said, without looking round — "and I want nothing to say to you."

"It was not I that brought you here, Bartleby," said I, keenly pained at his implied suspicion. "And to you, this should not be so vile a place. Nothing reproachful attaches to you by being here. And see, it is not so sad a place as one might think. Look, there is the sky, and here is the grass."

"I know where I am," he replied, but would say nothing more, and so I left him.

As I entered the corridor again, a broad meat-like man, in an apron, accosted me, and, jerking his thumb over his shoulder, said — "Is that your friend?"

"Yes."

"Does he want to starve? If he does, let him live on the prison fare, that's all."

"Who are you?" asked I, not knowing what to make of such an unofficially speaking person in such a place.

"I am the grub-man. Such gentlemen as have friends here, hire me to provide them with something good to eat."

"Is this so?" said I, turning to the turnkey.

He said it was.

"Well, then," said I, slipping some silver into the grub-man's hands (for so they called him), "I want you to give particular attention to my friend there; let him have the best dinner you can get. And you must be as polite to him as possible."

"Introduce me, will you?" said the grub-man, looking at me with an expression which seemed to say he was all impatience for an opportunity to give a specimen of his breeding.

Thinking it would prove of benefit to the scrivener, I acquiesced; and, asking the grub-man his name, went up with him to Bartleby.

"Bartleby, this is a friend; you will find him very useful to you."

"Your sarvant, sir, your sarvant," said the grub-man, making a low salutation behind his apron. "Hope you find it pleasant here, sir; nice grounds — cool apartments — hope you'll stay with us some time — try to make it agreeable. What will you have for dinner to-day?"

"I prefer not to dine to-day," said Bartleby, turning away. "It would disagree with me; I am unused to dinners." So saying, he slowly moved to the other side of the inclosure, and took up a position fronting the dead-wall.

"How's this?" said the grub-man, addressing me with a stare of astonishment. "He's odd, ain't he?"

"I think he is a little deranged," said I, sadly.

"Deranged? deranged is it? Well, now, upon my word, I thought that friend of yourn was a gentleman forger; they are always pale and genteel-like, them forgers. I can't help pity 'em — can't help it, sir. Did you know Monroe Edwards?" he added, touchingly, and paused. Then, laying his hand piteously on my shoulder, sighed, "he died of consumption at Sing-Sing. So you weren't acquainted with Monroe?"

"No, I was never socially acquainted with any forgers. But I cannot stop longer. Look to my friend yonder. You will not lose by it. I will see you again."

Some few days after this, I again obtained admission to the Tombs, and went through the corridors in quest of Bartleby; but without finding him.

"I saw him coming from his cell not long ago," said a turnkey, "may be he's gone to loiter in the yards."

So I went in that direction.

"Are you looking for the silent man?" said another turnkey, passing me. "Yonder he lies — sleeping in the yard there. 'Tis not twenty minutes since I saw him lie down."

The yard was entirely quiet. It was not accessible to the common prisoners. The surrounding walls, of amazing thickness, kept off all sounds behind them. The Egyptian character of the masonry weighed upon me with its gloom. But a soft imprisoned turf grew under foot. The heart of the eternal pyramids, it seemed, wherein, by some strange magic, through the clefts, grass-seed, dropped by birds, had sprung.

Strangely huddled at the base of the wall, his knees drawn up, and lying on his side, his head touching the cold stones, I saw the wasted Bartleby. But nothing stirred. I paused; then went close up to him; stooped over, and saw that his dim eyes were open; otherwise he seemed profoundly sleeping. Something prompted me to touch him. I felt his hand, when a tingling shiver ran up my arm and down my spine to my feet.

The round face of the grub-man peered upon me now. "His dinner is ready. Won't he dine to-day, either? Or does he live without dining?"

"Lives without dining," said I, and closed the eyes.

"Eh! — He's asleep, ain't he?"

"With kings and counselors,"[8] murmured I.

There would seem little need for proceeding further in this history. Imagination will readily supply the meagre recital of poor Bartleby's interment. But, ere parting with the reader, let me say, that if this little narrative has sufficiently interested him, to awaken curiosity as to who Bartleby was, and what manner of life he led prior to the present narrator's making his acquaintance, I can only reply, that in such curiosity I fully share, but am wholly unable to gratify it. Yet here I hardly know whether I should divulge one little item of rumor, which came to my ear a few months after the scrivener's decease. Upon what basis it rested, I could never ascertain; and hence, how true it is I cannot now tell. But, inasmuch as this vague report has not been without a certain suggestive interest to me, however sad, it may prove the same with some others; and so I will briefly mention it. The report was this: that Bartleby had been a subordinate clerk in the Dead Letter Office at Washington, from which he had been suddenly removed by a change in the administration. When I think over this rumor, hardly can I express the emotions which seize me. Dead letters! does it not sound like dead men? Conceive a man by nature and misfortune prone to a pallid hopelessness, can any business seem more fitted to heighten it than that of continually handling these dead letters, and assorting them for the flames? For by the cart-load they are annually burned. Sometimes from out the folded paper the pale clerk takes a ring — the finger it was meant for, perhaps, moulders in the grave; a bank-note sent in swiftest charity — he whom it would relieve, nor eats nor hungers any more; pardon for those who died despairing; hope for those who died unhoping; good tidings for those who died stifled by unrelieved calamities. On errands of life, these letters speed to death.

Ah, Bartleby! Ah, humanity!

[1853]

---

[8] A reference to Job 3:14. Job, who has lost his family and all his property and been stricken by a terrible disease, wishes he had never been born: "then had I been at rest with kings and counselors of the earth, which built desolate places for themselves."

GUSTAVE FLAUBERT (1821–1880) said that in writing, everything is a matter of style, of the particular turn and aspect one gives to things. Flaubert led a singularly uneventful life, remarkable mostly for the intensity with which he devoted himself to writing fiction. He once told a friend, "I have more imagination than heart." Born into a prosperous bourgeois family in Rouen, Flaubert was the son of a surgeon. His mother encouraged him to read literature and write plays while he was still a child. He attended school in Rouen and began to study law in Paris, but in 1844 his health failed and he suffered the first of many attacks of unconsciousness — possibly epilepsy. Like his contemporary Charles Baudelaire and his relative Guy de Maupassant, he was also afflicted with syphilis; in his Dictionary of Accepted Opinions, Flaubert defined syphilis as being in his time as common as the cold.

Returning to live with his widowed mother in the family home on the Seine, Flaubert began to write his books. His most famous novel is Madame Bovary (1857), which he worked on with complete absorption for more than four years, struggling to rewrite it and polish it constantly. His attention to subtly nuanced verbal images rather than dramatic action set a new standard of perfection in fiction. The poet Baudelaire later imaginatively reconstructed what went on in Flaubert's mind as he wrote the book: "We shall employ a style that is terse, vivid, subtle, and exact on a subject that is banal. We shall imprison the most burning and passionate feelings within the most commonplace intrigue. The most solemn utterances will come from the most imbecile mouths."

Flaubert considered himself "a bourgeois living retired in the country," but he kept himself apart from the provincial society that surrounded him in Normandy. In his story "A Simple Heart" (included in his last book, Three Tales, published in 1877), his narration of the life of a humble maidservant conveys his emotional distance from the central character; his language, in its precisely observed detail, is detached. His aim was to show that "there are no noble subjects or ignoble subjects; from the standpoint of pure Art one might almost establish the axiom that there is no such thing as subject — style in itself being an absolute manner of seeing things." In keeping with his impartial point of view, Flaubert never moralized. He let the tale speak for itself, believing that "the artist ought not to appear in the work any more than God in nature."

Henry James, who was introduced to Flaubert by Turgenev, understood that for Flaubert "beauty comes with expression, that expression is creation, that it makes the reality, and only in the degree in which it is, exquisitely, expression." Flaubert sought perfection, trying to make his prose *"as rhythmical as verse and as precise as the language of science." He died of a sudden cerebral hemorrhage at age fifty-nine, and was buried in the cemetery at Rouen.*

Gustave Flaubert

ཉ

A SIMPLE HEART

—translated by Robert Baldick

I

For half a century the women of Pont-l'Évêque envied Mme Aubain her maidservant Félicité.

In return for a hundred francs a year she did all the cooking and the housework, the sewing, the washing, and the ironing. She could bridle a horse, fatten poultry, and churn butter, and she remained faithful to her mistress, who was by no means an easy person to get on with.

Mme Aubain had married a young fellow who was good-looking but badly-off, and who died at the beginning of 1809, leaving her with two small children and a pile of debts. She then sold all her property except for the farms of Toucques and Geffosses, which together brought in five thousand francs a year at the most, and left her house at Saint-Melaine for one behind the covered market which was cheaper to run and had belonged to her family.

This house had a slate roof and stood between the alley-way and a lane leading down to the river. Inside there were differences in level which were the cause of many a stumble. A narrow entrance-hall separated the kitchen from the parlor, where Mme Aubain sat all day long in a wicker easy-chair by the window. Eight mahogany chairs were lined up against the white-painted wainscoting, and under the barometer stood an old piano loaded with a pyramid of boxes and cartons. On either side of the chimney-piece, which was carved out of yellow marble in the Louis Quinze style, there was a tapestry-covered arm-chair, and in the middle was a clock designed to look like a temple of Vesta.[1] The whole room smelt a little musty, as the floor was on a lower level than the garden.

On the first floor was "Madame's" bedroom — very spacious, with a patterned wallpaper of pale flowers and a portrait of "Monsieur" dressed in

---

[1] Roman goddess of the hearth.

what had once been the height of fashion. It opened into a smaller room in which there were two cots, without mattresses. Then came the drawing-room, which was always shut up and full of furniture covered with dust-sheets. Next there was a passage leading to the study, where books and papers filled the shelves of a book-case in three sections built round a big writing-table of dark wood. The two end panels were hidden under pen-and-ink drawings, landscapes in gouache, and etchings by Audran,[2] souvenirs of better days and bygone luxury. On the second floor a dormer window gave light to Félicité's room, which looked out over the fields.

Every day Félicité got up at dawn, so as not to miss Mass, and worked until evening without stopping. Then, once dinner was over, the plates and dishes put away, and the door bolted, she piled ashes on the log fire and went to sleep in front of the hearth, with her rosary in her hands. Nobody could be more stubborn when it came to haggling over prices, and as for cleanliness, the shine on her saucepans was the despair of all the other servants. Being of a thrifty nature, she ate slowly, picking up from the table the crumbs from her loaf of bread — a twelve pound loaf which was baked specially for her and lasted twenty days.

All the year round she wore a kerchief of printed calico fastened behind with a pin, a bonnet which covered her hair, grey stockings, a red skirt, and over her jacket a bibbed apron such as hospital nurses wear.

Her face was thin and her voice was sharp. At twenty-five she was often taken for forty; once she reached fifty, she stopped looking any age in particular. Always silent and upright and deliberate in her movements, she looked like a wooden doll driven by clock-work.

II

Like everyone else, she had had her love-story.

Her father, a mason, had been killed when he fell off some scaffolding. Then her mother died, and when her sisters went their separate ways, a farmer took her in, sending her, small as she was, to look after the cows out in the fields. She went about in rags, shivering with cold, used to lie flat on the ground to drink water out of the ponds, would be beaten for no reason at all, and was finally turned out of the house for stealing thirty sous, a theft of which she was innocent. She found work at another farm, looking after the poultry, and as she was liked by her employers the other servants were jealous of her.

One August evening — she was eighteen at the time — they took her off to the fête at Colleville. From the start she was dazed and bewildered by the noise of the fiddles, the lamps in the trees, the medley of gaily colored dresses, the gold crosses and lace, and the throng of people jigging up and down. She was standing shyly on one side when a smart young fellow, who

[2] family name of several famous French engravers.

had been leaning on the shaft of a cart, smoking his pipe, came up and asked her to dance. He treated her to cider, coffee, girdle-cake, and a silk neckerchief, and imagining that she knew what he was after, offered to see her home. At the edge of a field of oats, he pushed her roughly to the ground. Thoroughly frightened, she started screaming for help. He took to his heels.

Another night, on the road to Beaumont, she tried to get past a big, slow-moving wagon loaded with hay, and as she was squeezing by she recognized Théodore.

He greeted her quite calmly, saying that she must forgive him for the way he had behaved to her, as "it was the drink that did it."

She did not know what to say in reply and felt like running off.

Straight away he began talking about the crops and the notabilities of the commune, saying that his father had left Colleville for the farm at Les Écots, so that they were now neighbors.

"Ah!" she said.

He added that his family wanted to see him settle but that he was in no hurry and was waiting to find a wife to suit his fancy. She lowered her head. Then he asked her if she was thinking of getting married. She answered with a smile that it was mean of him to make fun of her.

"But I'm not making fun of you!" he said. "I swear I'm not!"

He put his left arm round her waist, and she walked on supported by his embrace. Soon they slowed down. There was a gentle breeze blowing, the stars were shining, the huge load of hay was swaying about in front of them, and the four horses were raising clouds of dust as they shambled along. Then, without being told, they turned off to the right. He kissed her once more and she disappeared into the darkness.

The following week Théodore got her to grant him several rendezvous.

They would meet at the bottom of a farm-yard, behind a wall, under a solitary tree. She was not ignorant of life as young ladies are, for the animals had taught her a great deal; but her reason and an instinctive sense of honor prevented her from giving way. The resistance she put up inflamed Théodore's passion to such an extent that in order to satisfy it (or perhaps out of sheer naïveté) he proposed to her. At first she refused to believe him, but he swore that he was serious.

Soon afterwards he had a disturbing piece of news to tell her: the year before, his parents had paid a man to do his military service for him, but now he might be called up again any day, and the idea of going into the army frightened him. In Félicité's eyes this cowardice of his appeared to be a proof of his affection, and she loved him all the more for it. Every night she would steal out to meet him, and every night Théodore would plague her with his worries and entreaties.

In the end he said that he was going to the Prefecture himself to make inquiries, and that he would come and tell her how matters stood the following Sunday, between eleven and midnight.

At the appointed hour she hurried to meet her sweetheart, but found one of his friends waiting for her instead.

He told her that she would not see Théodore again. To make sure of avoiding conscription, he had married a very rich old woman, Mme Lehoussais of Toucques.

Her reaction was an outburst of frenzied grief. She threw herself on the ground, screaming and calling on God, and lay moaning all alone in the open until sunrise. Then she went back to the farm and announced her intention of leaving. At the end of the month, when she had received her wages, she wrapped her small belongings up in a kerchief and made her way to Pont-l'Évêque.

In front of the inn there, she sought information from a woman in a widow's bonnet, who, as it happened, was looking for a cook. The girl did not know much about cooking, but she seemed so willing and expected so little that finally Mme Aubain ended up by saying: "Very well, I will take you on."

A quarter of an hour later Félicité was installed in her house.

At first she lived there in a kind of fearful awe caused by "the style of the house" and the memory of "Monsieur" brooding over everything. Paul and Virginie, the boy aged seven and the girl barely four, seemed to her to be made of some precious substance. She used to carry them about pick-a-back, and when Mme Aubain told her not to keep on kissing them she was cut to the quick. All the same, she was happy now, for her pleasant surroundings had dispelled her grief.

On Thursdays, a few regular visitors came in to play Boston, and Félicité got the cards and the footwarmers ready beforehand. They always arrived punctually at eight, and left before the clock struck eleven.

Every Monday morning the second-hand dealer who lived down the alley put all his junk out on the pavement. Then the hum of voices began to fill the town, mingled with the neighing of horses, the bleating of lambs, the grunting of pigs, and the rattle of carts in the streets.

About midday, when the market was in full swing, a tall old peasant with a hooked nose and his cap on the back of his head would appear at the door. This was Robelin, the farmer from Geffosses. A little later, and Liébard, the farmer from Toucques, would arrive — a short, fat, red-faced fellow in a grey jacket and leather gaiters fitted with spurs.

Both men had hens or cheeses they wanted to sell to "Madame." But Félicité was up to all their tricks and invariably outwitted them, so that they went away full of respect for her.

From time to time Mme Aubain had a visit from an uncle of hers, the Marquis de Grémanville, who had been ruined by loose living and was now living at Falaise on his last remaining scrap of property. He always turned up at lunch-time, accompanied by a hideous poodle who dirtied all the furniture with its paws. However hard he tried to behave like a gentleman, even going so far as to raise his hat every time he mentioned "my late fa-ther" the force of habit was usually too much for him, for he would start pouring himself one glass after another and telling bawdy stories. Félicité used to push him gently out of the house, saying politely: "You've had quite enough, Monsieur de Grémanville. See you another time!" and shut-ting the door on him.

She used to open it with pleasure to M. Bourais, who was a retired so-licitor. His white tie and his bald head, his frilled shirt-front and his ample brown frock-coat, the way he had of rounding his arm to take a pinch of snuff, and indeed everything about him made an overwhelming impression on her such as we feel when we meet some outstanding personality.

As he looked after "Madame's" property, he used to shut himself up with her for hours in "Monsieur's" study. He lived in dread of compromis-ing his reputation, had a tremendous respect for the Bench, and laid claim to some knowledge of Latin.

To give the children a little painless instruction, he made them a pres-ent of a geography book with illustrations. These represented scenes in dif-ferent parts of the world, such as cannibals wearing feather head-dresses, a monkey carrying off a young lady, Bedouins in the desert, a whale being harpooned, and so on.

Paul explained these pictures to Félicité, and that indeed was all the education she ever had. As for the children, they were taught by Guyot, a poor devil employed at the Town Hall, who was famous for his beautiful handwriting, and who had a habit of sharpening his penknife on his boots.

When the weather was fine the whole household used to set off early for a day on the Geffosses farm.

The farm-yard there was on a slope, with the house in the middle; and the sea, in the distance, looked like a streak of grey. Félicité would take some slices of cold meat out of her basket, and they would have their lunch in a room adjoining the dairy. It was all that remained of a country house which had fallen into ruin, and the wallpaper hung in shreds, fluttering in the draught. Mme Aubain used to sit with bowed head, absorbed in her memories, so that the children were afraid to talk. "Why don't you run along and play?" she would say, and away they went.

Paul climbed up into the barn, caught birds, played ducks and drakes on the pond, or banged with a stick on the great casks, which sounded just like drums.

Virginie fed the rabbits, or scampered off to pick cornflowers, showing her little embroidered knickers as she ran.

One autumn evening they came home through the fields. The moon, which was in its first quarter, lit up part of the sky, and there was some mist floating like a scarf over the winding Toucques. The cattle, lying out in the middle of the pasture, looked peacefully at the four people walking by. In the third field a few got up and made a half circle in front of them.

"Don't be frightened!" said Félicité, and crooning softly, she stroked the back of the nearest animal. It turned about and the others did the same. But while they were crossing the next field they suddenly heard a dreadful bellowing. It came from a bull which had been hidden by the mist, and which now came towards the two women.

Mme Aubain started to run.

"No! No!" said Félicité. "Not so fast!"

All the same they quickened their pace, hearing behind them a sound of heavy breathing which came nearer and nearer. The bull's hooves thudded like hammers on the turf, and they realized that it had broken into a gallop. Turning round, Félicité tore up some clods of earth and flung them at its eyes. It lowered its muzzle and thrust its horns forward, trembling with rage and bellowing horribly.

By now Mme Aubain had got to the end of the field with her two children and was frantically looking for a way over the high bank. Félicité was still backing away from the bull, hurling clods of turf which blinded it, and shouting: "Hurry! Hurry!"

Mme Aubain got down into the ditch, pushed first Virginie and then Paul up the other side, fell once or twice trying to climb the bank, and finally managed it with a valiant effort.

The bull had driven Félicité back against a gate, and its slaver was spurting into her face. In another second it would have gored her, but she just had time to slip between two of the bars, and the great beast halted in amazement.

This adventure was talked about at Pont-l'Évêque for a good many years, but Félicité never prided herself in the least on what she had done, as it never occurred to her that she had done anything heroic.

Virginie claimed all her attention, for the fright had affected the little girl's nerves, and M. Poupart, the doctor, recommended sea-bathing at Trouville.

In those days the resort had few visitors. Mme Aubain made inquiries, consulted Bourais, and got everything ready as though for a long journey.

Her luggage went off in Liébard's cart the day before she left. The next morning he brought along two horses, one of which had a woman's saddle with a velvet back, while the other carried a cloak rolled up to make a kind of seat on its crupper. Mme Aubain sat on this, with Liébard in front. Félicité looked after Virginie on the other horse, and Paul mounted M. Lechaptois's donkey, which he had lent them on condition they took great care of it.

The road was so bad that it took two hours to travel the five miles to Toucques. The horses sank into the mud up to their pasterns and had to jerk their hind-quarters to get out; often they stumbled in the ruts, or else they had to jump. In some places, Liébard's mare came to a sudden stop, and while he waited patiently for her to move off again, he talked about the people whose properties bordered the road, adding moral reflections to each story. For instance, in the middle of Toucques, as they were passing underneath some windows set in a mass of nasturtiums, he shrugged his shoulders and said:

"There's a Madame Lehoussais lives here. Now instead of taking a young man, she. . . ."

Félicité did not hear the rest, for the horses had broken into a trot and the donkey was galloping along. All three turned down a bridle-path, a gate swung open, a couple of boys appeared, and everyone dismounted in front of a manure-heap right outside the farm-house door.

Old Mother Liébard welcomed her mistress with every appearance of pleasure. She served up a sirloin of beef for lunch, with tripe and black pudding, a fricassee of chicken, sparkling cider, a fruit tart and brandy-plums, garnishing the whole meal with compliments to Madame, who seemed to be enjoying better health, to Mademoiselle, who had turned into a "proper little beauty," and to Monsieur Paul, who had "filled out a lot." Nor did she forget their deceased grandparents, whom the Liébards had known personally, having been in the family's service for several generations.

Like its occupants, the farm had an air of antiquity. The ceiling-beams were worm-eaten, the walls black with smoke, and the window-panes grey with dust. There was an oak dresser laden with all sorts of odds and ends — jugs, plates, pewter bowls, wolf-traps, sheep-shears, and an enormous syringe which amused the children. In the three yards outside there was not a single tree without either mushrooms at its base or mistletoe in its branches. Several had been blown down and had taken root again in the middle; all of them were bent under the weight of their apples. The thatched roofs, which looked like brown velvet and varied in thickness, weathered the fiercest winds, but the cart-shed was tumbling down. Mme Aubain said that she would have it seen to, and ordered the animals to be reharnessed.

It took them another half-hour to reach Trouville. The little caravan dismounted to make their way along the Écores, a cliff jutting right out over the boats moored below; and three minutes later they got to the end of the quay and entered the courtyard of the Golden Lamb, the inn kept by Mère David.

After the first few days Virginie felt stronger, as a result of the change of air and the sea-bathing. Not having a costume, she went into the water in her chemise and her maid dressed her afterwards in a customs officer's hut which was used by the bathers.

In the afternoons they took the donkey and went off beyond the Roches-Noires, in the direction of Hennequeville. To begin with, the path went uphill between gentle slopes like the lawns in a park, and then came out on a plateau where pastureland and ploughed fields alternated. On

either side there were holly-bushes standing out from the tangle of bram-
bles, and here and there a big dead tree spread its zigzag branches against
the blue sky.

They almost always rested in the same field, with Deauville on their
left, Le Havre on their right, and the open sea in front. The water glittered
in the sunshine, smooth as a mirror, and so still that the murmur it made
was scarcely audible; unseen sparrows could be heard twittering, and the
sky covered the whole scene with its huge canopy. Mme Aubain sat doing
her needlework, Virginie plaited rushes beside her, Félicité gathered lavender, and Paul, feeling profoundly bored, longed to get up and go.

Sometimes they crossed the Toucques in a boat and hunted for shells.
When the tide went out, sea-urchins, ormers, and jelly-fish were left behind;
and the children scampered around, snatching at the foam-flakes carried on
the wind. The sleepy waves, breaking on the sand, spread themselves out
along the shore. The beach stretched as far as the eye could see, bounded
on the land side by the dunes which separated it from the Marais, a broad
meadow in the shape of an arena. When they came back that way, Trouville, on the distant hillside, grew bigger at every step, and with its medley
of oddly assorted houses seemed to blossom out in gay disorder.

On exceptionally hot days they stayed in their room. The sun shone in
dazzling bars of light between the slats of the blind. There was not a sound
to be heard in the village, and not a soul to be seen down in the street.
Everything seemed more peaceful in the prevailing silence. In the distance
caulkers were hammering away at the boats, and the smell of tar was wafted
along by a sluggish breeze.

The principal amusement consisted in watching the fishingboats come
in. As soon as they had passed the buoys, they started tacking. With their
canvas partly lowered and their foresails blown out like balloons they glided
through the splashing waves as far as the middle of the harbor, where they
suddenly dropped anchor. Then each boat came alongside the quay, and
the crew threw ashore their catch of quivering fish. A line of carts stood
waiting, and women in cotton bonnets rushed forward to take the baskets
and kiss their men.

One day one of these women spoke to Félicité, who came back to the
inn soon after in a state of great excitement. She explained that she had
found one of her sisters — and Nastasie Barette, now Leroux, made her appearance, with a baby at her breast, another child holding her right hand,
and on her left a little sailor-boy, his arms akimbo and his cap over one ear.

Mme Aubain sent her off after a quarter of an hour. From then on
they were forever hanging round the kitchen or loitering about when the
family went for a walk, though the husband kept out of sight.

Félicité became quite attached to them. She bought them a blanket,
several shirts, and a stove; and it was clear that they were bent on getting all
they could out of her.

This weakness of hers annoyed Mme Aubain, who in any event disliked the familiar way in which the nephew spoke to Paul. And so, as Virginie had started coughing and the good weather was over, she decided to go back to Pont-l'Évêque.

M. Bourais advised her on the choice of a school; Caen was considered the best, so it was there that Paul was sent. He said good-bye bravely, feeling really rather pleased to be going to a place where he would have friends of his own.

Mme Aubain resigned herself to the loss of her son, knowing that it was unavoidable. Virginie soon got used to it. Félicité missed the din he used to make, but she was given something new to do which served as a distraction; from Christmas onwards she had to take the little girl to catechism every day.

III

After genuflecting at the door, she walked up the center aisle under the nave, opened the door of Mme Aubain's pew, sat down, and started looking about her.

The choir stalls were all occupied, with the boys on the right and the girls on the left, while the curé stood by the lectern. In one of the stained-glass windows in the apse the Holy Ghost looked down on the Virgin; another window showed her kneeling before the Infant Jesus; and behind the tabernacle there was a wood-carving of St. Michael slaying the dragon.

The priest began with a brief outline of sacred history. Listening to him, Félicité saw in imagination the Garden of Eden, the Flood, the Tower of Babel, cities burning, peoples dying, and idols being overthrown; and his dazzling vision left her with a great respect for the Almighty and profound fear of His wrath.

Then she wept as she listened to the story of the Passion. Why had they crucified Him, when He loved children, fed the multitudes, healed the blind, and had chosen out of humility to be born among the poor, on the litter of a stable? The sowing of the seed, the reaping of the harvest, the pressing of the grapes — all those familiar things of which the Gospels speak had their place in her life. God had sanctified them in passing, so that she loved the lambs more tenderly for love of the Lamb of God, and the doves for the sake of the Holy Ghost.

She found it difficult, however, to imagine what the Holy Ghost looked like, for it was not just a bird but a fire as well, and sometimes a breath. She wondered whether that was its light she had seen flitting about the edge of the marshes at night, whether that was its breath she had felt driving the clouds across the sky, whether that was its voice she had heard in the sweet music of the bells. And she sat in silent adoration, delighting in the coolness of the walls and the quiet of the church.

Of dogma she neither understood nor even tried to understand anything. The curé discoursed, the children repeated their lesson, and she finally dropped off to sleep, waking up suddenly at the sound of their sabots[3] clattering across the flagstones as they left the church.

It was in this manner, simply by hearing it expounded, that she learnt her catechism, for her religious education had been neglected in her youth. From then on she copied all Virginie's observances, fasting when she did and going to confession with her. On the feast of Corpus Christi the two of them made an altar of repose together.

The preparations for Virginie's first communion caused her great anxiety. She worried over her shoes, her rosary, her missal, and her gloves. And how she trembled as she helped Mme Aubain to dress the child!

All through the Mass her heart was in her mouth. One side of the choir was hidden from her by M. Bourais, but directly opposite her she could see the flock of maidens, looking like a field of snow with their white crowns perched on top of their veils; and she recognized her little darling from a distance by her dainty neck and her rapt attitude. The bell tinkled. Every head bowed low, and there was a silence. Then, to the thunderous accompaniment of the organ, choir and congregation joined in singing the *Agnus Dei.* Next the boys' procession began, and after that the girls got up from their seats. Slowly, their hands joined in prayer, they went towards the brightly lit altar, knelt on the first step, received the Host one by one, and went back to their places in the same order. When it was Virginie's turn, Félicité leant forward to see her, and in one of those imaginative flights born of real affection, it seemed to her that she herself was in the child's place. Virginie's face became her own, Virginie's dress clothed her, Virginie's heart was beating in her breast; and as she closed her eyes and opened her mouth, she almost fainted away.

Early next morning she went to the sacristy and asked M. le Curé to give her communion. She received the sacrament with all due reverence, but did not feel the same rapture as she had the day before.

Mme Aubain wanted her daughter to possess every accomplishment, and since Guyot could not teach her English or music, she decided to send her as a boarder to the Ursuline Convent at Honfleur.

Virginie raised no objection, but Félicité went about sighing at Madame's lack of feeling. Then she thought that perhaps her mistress was right: such matters, after all, lay outside her province.

Finally the day arrived when an old wagonette stopped at their door, and a nun got down from it who had come to fetch Mademoiselle. Félicité hoisted the luggage up on top, gave the driver some parting instructions, and put six pots of jam, a dozen pears, and a bunch of violets in the boot.

At the last moment Virginie burst into a fit of sobbing. She threw her arms round her mother, who kissed her on the forehead, saying: "Come now, be brave, be brave." The step was pulled up and the carriage drove away.

---

[3] wooden shoes.

Then Mme Aubain broke down, and that evening all her friends, M. and Mme Lormeau, Mme Lechaptois, the Rochefeuille sisters, M. de Houppeville, and Bourais, came in to console her.

To begin with she missed her daughter badly. But she had a letter from her three times a week, wrote back on the other days, walked round her garden, did a little reading, and thus contrived to fill the empty hours.

As for Félicité, she went into Virginie's room every morning from sheer force of habit and looked round it. It upset her not having to brush the child's hair any more, tie her bootlaces, or tuck her up in bed; and she missed seeing her sweet face all the time and holding her hand when they went out together. For want of something to do, she tried making lace, but her fingers were too clumsy and broke the threads. She could not settle to anything, lost her sleep, and, to use her own words, was "eaten up inside."

To "occupy her mind," she asked if her nephew Victor might come and see her, and permission was granted.

He used to arrive after Mass on Sunday, his cheeks flushed, his chest bare, and smelling of the countryside through which he had come. She laid a place for him straight away, opposite hers, and they had lunch together. Eating as little as possible herself, in order to save the expense, she stuffed him so full of food that he fell asleep after the meal. When the first bell for vespers rang, she woke him up, brushed his trousers, tied his tie, and set off for church, leaning on his arm with all a mother's pride.

His parents always told him to get something out of her — a packet of brown sugar perhaps, some soap, or a little brandy, sometimes even money. He brought her his clothes to be mended, and she did the work gladly, thankful for anything that would force him to come again.

In August his father took him on a coasting trip. The children's holidays were just beginning, and it cheered her up to have them home again. But Paul was turning capricious and Virginie was getting too old to be addressed familiarly — a state of affairs which put a barrier of constraint between them.

Victor went to Morlaix, Dunkirk, and Brighton in turn, and brought her a present after each trip. The first time it was a box covered with shells, the second a coffee cup, the third a big gingerbread man. He was growing quite handsome, with his trim figure, his little moustache, his frank open eyes, and the little leather cap that he wore on the back of his head like a pilot. He kept her amused by telling her stories full of nautical jargon.

One Monday — it was the fourteenth of July 1819, a date she never forgot — Victor told her that he had signed on for an ocean voyage, and that on the Wednesday night he would be taking the Honfleur packet to join his schooner, which was due to sail shortly from Le Havre. He might be away, he said, for two years.

The prospect of such a long absence made Félicité extremely unhappy, and she felt she must bid him godspeed once more. So on the

Wednesday evening, when Madame's dinner was over, she put on her clogs and swiftly covered the ten miles between Pont-l'Évêque and Honfleur.

When she arrived at the Calvary she turned right instead of left, got lost in the shipyards, and had to retrace her steps. Some people she spoke to advised her to hurry. She went right round the harbor, which was full of boats, constantly tripping over moorings. Then the ground fell away, rays of light criss-crossed in front of her, and for a moment, she thought she was going mad, for she could see horses up in the sky.

On the quayside more horses were neighing, frightened by the sea. A derrick was hoisting them into the air and dropping them into one of the boats, which was already crowded with passengers elbowing their way between barrels of cider, baskets of cheese, and sacks of grain. Hens were cackling and the captain swearing, while a cabin-boy stood leaning on the cats-head, completely indifferent to it all. Félicité, who had not recognized him, shouted: "Victor!" and he raised his head. She rushed forward, but at that very moment the gangway was pulled ashore.

The packet moved out of the harbor with women singing as they hauled it along, its ribs creaking and heavy waves lashing its bows. The sail swung round, hiding everyone on board from view, and against the silvery, moonlit sea the boat appeared as a dark shape that grew ever fainter, until at last it vanished in the distance.

As Félicité was passing the Calvary, she felt a longing to commend to God's mercy all that she held most dear; and she stood there praying for a long time, her face bathed in tears, her eyes fixed upon the clouds. The town was asleep, except for the customs officers walking up and down. Water was pouring ceaselessly through the holes in the sluice-gate, making as much noise as a torrent. The clocks struck two.

The convent parlor would not be open before daybreak, and Madame would be annoyed if she were late; so, although she would have liked to give a kiss to the other child, she set off for home. The maids at the inn were just waking up as she got to Pont-l'Évêque.

So the poor lad was going to be tossed by the waves for months on end! His previous voyages had caused her no alarm. People came back from England and Brittany; but America, the Colonies, the Islands, were all so far away, somewhere at the other end of the world.

From then on Félicité thought of nothing but her nephew. On sunny days she hoped he was not too thirsty, and when there was a storm she was afraid he would be struck by lightning. Listening to the wind howling in the chimney or blowing slates off the roof, she saw him being buffeted by the very same storm, perched on the top of a broken mast, with his whole body bent backwards under a sheet of foam; or again — and these were reminiscences of the illustrated geography book — he was being eaten by savages, captured by monkeys in the forest, or dying on a desert shore. But she never spoke of her worries.

Mme Aubain had worries of her own about her daughter. The good nuns said that she was an affectionate child, but very delicate. The slightest emotion upset her, and she had to give up playing the piano.

Her mother insisted on regular letters from the convent. One morning when the postman had not called, she lost patience and walked up and down the room, between her chair and the window. It was really extraordinary! Four days without any news!

Thinking her own example would comfort her, Félicité said:

"I've been six months, Madame, without news."

"News of whom?"

The servant answered gently:

"Why — of my nephew."

"Oh, your nephew!" And Mme Aubain started pacing up and down again, with a shrug of her shoulders that seemed to say: "I wasn't thinking of him — and indeed, why should I? Who cares about a young, good-for-nothing cabin-boy? Whereas my daughter — why, just think!"

Although she had been brought up the hard way, Félicité was indignant with Madame, but she soon forgot. It struck her as perfectly natural to lose one's head where the little girl was concerned. For her, the two children were of equal importance; they were linked together in her heart by a single bond, and their destinies should be the same.

The chemist told her that Victor's ship had arrived at Havana: he had seen this piece of information in a newspaper.

Because of its association with cigars, she imagined Havana as a place where nobody did anything but smoke, and pictured Victor walking about among crowds of Negroes in a cloud of tobacco-smoke. Was it possible, she wondered, "in case of need" to come back by land? And how far was it from Pont-l'Évêque? To find out she asked M. Bourais.

He reached for his atlas, and launched forth into an explanation of latitudes and longitudes, smiling like the pedant he was at Félicité's bewilderment. Finally he pointed with his pencil at a minute black dot inside a ragged oval patch, saying:

"There it is."

She bent over the map, but the network of colored lines meant nothing to her and only tired her eyes. So when Bourais asked her to tell him what was puzzling her, she begged him to show her the house where Victor was living. He threw up his hands, sneezed, and roared with laughter, delighted to come across such simplicity. And Félicité — whose intelligence was so limited that she probably expected to see an actual portrait of her nephew — could not make out why he was laughing.

It was a fortnight later that Liébard came into the kitchen at market-time, as he usually did, and handed her a letter from her brother-in-law. As neither of them could read, she turned to her mistress for help.

Mme Aubain, who was counting the stitches in her knitting, put it down and unsealed the letter. She gave a start, and, looking hard at Félicité, said quietly:

"They have some bad news for you. . . . Your nephew. . . ."

He was dead. That was all the letter had to say.

Félicité dropped on to a chair, leaning her head against the wall and closing her eyelids, which suddenly turned pink. Then, with her head bowed, her hands dangling, and her eyes set, she kept repeating:

"Poor little lad! Poor little lad!"

Liébard looked at her and sighed. Mme Aubain was trembling slightly. She suggested that she should go and see her sister at Trouville, but Félicité shook her head to indicate that there was no need for that.

There was a silence. Old Liébard thought it advisable to go.

Then Félicité said:

"It doesn't matter a bit, not to them it doesn't."

Her head fell forward again, and from time to time she unconsciously picked up the knitting needles lying on the work table.

Some women went past carrying a tray full of dripping linen.

Catching sight of them through the window, she remembered her own washing; she had passed the lye through it the day before and today it needed rinsing. So she left the room.

Her board and tub were on the bank of the Toucques. She threw a pile of chemises down by the water's edge, rolled up her sleeves, and picked up her battledore. The lusty blows she gave with it could be heard in all the neighboring gardens.

The fields were empty, the river rippling in the wind; at the bottom long weeds were waving to and fro, like the hair of corpses floating in the water. She held back her grief, and was very brave until the evening; but in her room she gave way to it completely, lying on her mattress with her face buried in the pillow and her fists pressed against her temples.

Long afterwards she learnt the circumstances of Victor's death from the captain of his ship. He had gone down with yellow fever, and they had bled him too much at the hospital. Four doctors had held him at once. He had died straight away, and the chief doctor had said:

"Good! There goes another!"

His parents had always treated him cruelly. She preferred not to see them again, and they made no advances, either because they had forgotten about her or out of the callousness of the poor.

Meanwhile Virginie was growing weaker. Difficulty in breathing, fits of coughing, protracted bouts of fever, and mottled patches on the cheekbones all indicated some deepseated complaint. M. Poupart had advised a stay in Provence. Mme Aubain decided to follow this suggestion, and, if it had not been for the weather at Pont-l'Évêque, she would have brought her daughter home at once.

She arranged with a jobmaster to drive her out to the convent every Tuesday. There was a terrace in the garden, overlooking the Seine, and there Virginie, leaning on her mother's arm, walked up and down over the fallen vineleaves. Sometimes, while she was looking at the sails in the distance, or at the long stretch of horizon from the Château de Tancarville to the lighthouses of Le Havre, the sun would break through the clouds and make her blink. Afterwards they would rest in the arbor. Her mother had secured a little cask of excellent Malaga, and, laughing at the idea of getting tipsy, Virginie used to drink a thimbleful, but no more.

Her strength revived. Autumn slipped by, and Félicité assured Mme Aubain that there was nothing to fear. But one evening, coming back from some errand in the neighborhood, she found M. Poupart's gig standing at the door. He was in the hall, and Mme Aubain was trying on her bonnet.

"Give me my foot-warmer, purse, gloves. Quickly now!"

Virginie had pneumonia and was perhaps past recovery.

"Not yet!" said the doctor; and the two of them got into the carriage with snowflakes swirling around them. Night was falling and it was very cold.

Félicité rushed into the church to light a candle, and then ran after the gig. She caught up with it an hour later, jumped lightly behind, and hung on to the fringe. But then a thought struck her: the courtyard had not been locked up, the burglars might get in. So she jumped down again.

At dawn the next day she went to the doctor's. He had come home and gone out again on his rounds. Then she waited at the inn, thinking that somebody who was a stranger to the district might call there with a letter. Finally, when it was twilight, she got into the coach for Lisieux.

The convent was at the bottom of a steep lane. When she was halfway down the hill, she heard a strange sound which she recognized as a death-bell tolling.

"It's for somebody else," she thought, as she banged the door-knocker hard.

After a few minutes she heard the sound of shuffling feet, the door opened a little way, and a nun appeared.

The good sister said with an air of compunction that "she had just passed away." At that moment the bell of Saint-Léonard was tolled more vigorously than ever.

Félicité went up to the second floor. From the doorway of the room she could see Virginie lying on her back, her hands clasped together, her mouth open, her head tilted back under a black crucifix that leant over her, her face whiter than the curtains that hung motionless on either side. Mme Aubain was clinging to the foot of the bed and sobbing desperately. The Mother Superior stood on the right. Three candlesticks on the chest of drawers added touches of red to the scene, and fog was whitening the windows. Some nuns led Mme Aubain away.

For two nights Félicité never left the dead girl. She said the same prayers over and over again, sprinkled holy water on the sheets, then sat down again to watch. At the end of her first vigil she noticed that the child's face had gone yellow, the lips were turning blue, the nose looked sharper, and the eyes were sunken. She kissed them several times, and would not have been particularly surprised if Virginie had opened them again: to minds like hers the supernatural is a simple matter. She laid her out, wrapped her in a shroud, put her in her coffin, placed a wreath on her, and spread out her hair. It was fair and amazingly long for her age. Félicité cut off a big lock, half of which she slipped into her bosom, resolving never to part with it.

The body was brought back to Pont-l'Évêque at the request of Mme Aubain, who followed the hearse in a closed carriage.

After the Requiem Mass, it took another three-quarters of an hour to reach the cemetery. Paul walked in front, sobbing. Then came M. Bourais, and after him the principal inhabitants of the town, the women all wearing long black veils, and Félicité. She was thinking about her nephew; and since she had been unable to pay him these last honors, she felt an added grief, just as if they were burying him with Virginie.

Mme Aubain's despair passed all bounds. First of all she rebelled against God, considering it unfair of Him to have taken her daughter from her — for she had never done any harm, and her conscience was quite clear. But was it? She ought to have taken Virginie to the south; other doctors would have saved her life. She blamed herself, wished she could have joined her daughter, and cried out in anguish in her dreams. One dream in particular obsessed her. Her husband, dressed like a sailor, came back from a long voyage, and told her amid tears that he had been ordered to take Virginie away — whereupon they put their heads together to discover somewhere to hide her.

One day she came in from the garden utterly distraught. A few minutes earlier — and she pointed to the spot — father and daughter had appeared to her, doing nothing, but simply looking at her.

For several months she stayed in her room in a kind of stupor. Félicité scolded her gently, telling her that she must take care of herself for her son's sake, and also in remembrance of "her."

"Her?" repeated Mme Aubain, as if she were waking from a sleep. "Oh, yes, of course! You don't forget her, do you!" This was an allusion to the cemetery, where she herself was strictly forbidden to go.

Félicité went there every day. She would set out on the stroke of four, going past the houses, up the hill, and through the gate, until she came to Virginie's grave. There was a little column of pink marble with a tablet at its base, and a tiny garden enclosed by chains. The beds were hidden under a carpet of flowers. She watered their leaves and changed the sand, going down on her knees to fork the ground thoroughly. The result was that when Mme Aubain was able to come here, she experienced a feeling of relief, a kind of consolation.

Then the years slipped by, each one like the last, with nothing to vary the rhythm of the great festivals: Easter, the Assumption, All Saints' Day. Domestic events marked dates that later served as points of reference. Thus in 1825 a couple of glaziers whitewashed the hall; in 1827 a piece of the roof fell into the courtyard and nearly killed a man; and in the summer of 1828 it was Madame's turn to provide the bread for consecration. About this time Bourais went away in a mysterious fashion; and one by one the old acquaintances disappeared: Guyot, Liébard, Mme Lechaptois, Robelin, and Uncle Grémanville, who had been paralyzed for a long time.

One night the driver of the mail-coach brought Pont-l'Évêque news of the July Revolution.[4] A few days later a new subprefect was appointed. This was the Baron de Larsonnière, who had been a consul in America, and who brought with him, besides his wife, his sister-in-law and three young ladies who were almost grown-up. They were to be seen on their lawn, dressed in loose-fitting smocks; and they had a Negro servant and a parrot. They paid a call on Mme Aubain, who made a point of returning it. As soon as Félicité saw them coming, she would run and tell her mistress. But only one thing could really awaken her interest, and that was her son's letters.

He seemed to be incapable of following any career and spent all his time in taverns. She paid his debts, but he contracted new ones, and the sighs Mme Aubain heaved as she knitted by the window reached Félicité at her spinning wheel in the kitchen.

The two women used to walk up and down together beside the espalier,[5] forever talking of Virginie and debating whether such and such a thing would have appealed to her, or what she would have said on such and such an occasion.

All her little belongings were in a cupboard in the children's bedroom. Mme Aubain went through them as seldom as possible. One summer day she resigned herself to doing so, and the moths were sent fluttering out of the cupboard.

Virginie's frocks hung in a row underneath a shelf containing three dolls, a few hoops, a set of toy furniture, and the wash-basin she had used. Besides the frocks, they took out her petticoats, her stockings and her handkerchiefs, and spread them out on the two beds before folding them up again. The sunlight streamed in on these pathetic objects, bringing out the stains and showing up the creases made by the child's movements. The air was warm, the sky was blue, a blackbird was singing, and everything seemed to be utterly at peace.

They found a little chestnut-colored hat, made of plush with a long nap; but the moths had ruined it. Félicité asked if she might have it. The two women looked at each other and their eyes filled with tears. Then the mistress opened her arms, the maid threw herself into them, and they clasped each other in a warm embrace, satisfying their grief in a kiss which made them equal.

---

[4] Popular rebellion of July and August 1830 in response to the attempt of King Charles X to dissolve the elected Chamber of Deputies and repeal certain freedoms granted in the Charter of 1814. It took just over a week for the rebels to force Charles to abdicate and to replace him with Louis-Philippe, the duke of Orleans.

[5] a trellis against which shrubs and fruit trees grow flat.

It was the first time that such a thing had happened, for Mme Aubain was not of a demonstrative nature. Félicité was as grateful as if she had received a great favor, and henceforth loved her mistress with dog-like devotion and religious veneration.

Her heart grew softer as time went by.

When she heard the drums of a regiment coming down the street she stood at the door with a jug of cider and offered the soldiers a drink. She looked after the people who went down with cholera. She watched over the Polish refugees, and one of them actually expressed a desire to marry her. But they fell out, for when she came back from the Angelus one morning, she found that he had got into her kitchen and was calmly eating an oil-and-vinegar salad.

After the Poles it was Père Colmiche, an old man who was said to have committed fearful atrocities in '93.[6] He lived by the river in a ruined pig-sty. The boys of the town used to peer at him through the cracks in the walls, and threw pebbles at him which landed on the litter where he lay, constantly shaken by fits of coughing. His hair was extremely long, his eyelids inflamed, and on one arm there was a swelling bigger than his head. Félicité brought him some linen, tried to clean out his filthy hovel, and even wondered if she could install him in the wash-house without annoying Madame. When the tumor had burst, she changed his dressings every day, brought him some cake now and then, and put him out in the sun on a truss of hay. The poor old fellow would thank her in a faint whisper, slavering and trembling all the while, fearful of losing her and stretching his hands out as soon as he saw her moving away.

He died, and she had a Mass said for the repose of his soul.

That same day a great piece of good fortune came her way. Just as she was serving dinner, Mme de Larsonnière's Negro appeared carrying the parrot in its cage, complete with perch, chain, and padlock. The Baroness had written a note informing Mme Aubain that her husband had been promoted to a Prefecture and they were leaving that evening; she begged her to accept the parrot as a keepsake and a token of her regard.

This bird had engrossed Félicité's thoughts for a long time, for it came from America, and that word reminded her of Victor. So she had asked the Negro all about it, and once she had even gone so far as to say:

"How pleased Madame would be if it were hers!"

The Negro had repeated this remark to his mistress, who, unable to take the parrot with her, was glad to get rid of it in this way.

IV

His name was Loulou. His body was green, the tips of his wings were pink, his poll blue, and his breast golden.

---

[6] in 1793, during the Reign of Terror in the French Revolution.

Unfortunately he had a tiresome mania for biting his perch, and also used to pull his feathers out, scatter his droppings everywhere, and upset his bath water. He annoyed Mme Aubain, and so she gave him to Félicité for good.

Félicité started training him, and soon he could say: "Nice boy! Your servant, sir! Hail, Mary!" He was put near the door, and several people who spoke to him said how strange it was that he did not answer to the name of Jacquot, as all parrots were called Jacquot. They likened him to a turkey or a block of wood, and every sneer cut Félicité to the quick. How odd, she thought, that Loulou should be so stubborn, refusing to talk whenever anyone looked at him!

For all that, he liked having people around him, because on Sundays, while the Rochefeuille sisters, M. Houppeville, and some new friends — the apothecary Onfroy, M. Varin, and Captain Mathieu — were having their game of cards, he would beat on the window-panes with his wings and make such a din that it was impossible to hear oneself speak.

Bourais's face obviously struck him as terribly funny, for as soon as he saw it he was seized with uncontrollable laughter. His shrieks rang round the courtyard, the echo repeated them, and the neighbors came to their windows and started laughing too. To avoid being seen by the bird, M. Bourais used to creep along by the wall, hiding his face behind his hat, until he got to the river, and then come into the house from the garden. The looks he gave the parrot were far from tender.

Loulou had once been cuffed by the butcher's boy for poking his head into his basket; and since then he was always trying to give him a nip through his shirt. Fabu threatened to wring his neck, although he was not a cruel fellow, in spite of his tattooed arms and bushy whiskers. On the contrary, he rather liked the parrot, so much so indeed that in a spirit of jovial camaraderie he tried to teach him a few swear-words. Félicité, alarmed at this development, put the bird in the kitchen. His little chain was removed and he was allowed to wander all over the house.

Coming downstairs, he used to rest the curved part of his beak on each step and then raise first his right foot, then his left; and Félicité was afraid that this sort of gymnastic performance would make him giddy. He fell ill and could neither talk nor eat for there was a swelling under his tongue such as hens sometimes have. She cured him by pulling this pellicule[7] out with her finger-nails. One day M. Paul was silly enough to blow the smoke of his cigar at him; another time Mme Lormeau started teasing him with the end of her parasol, and he caught hold of the ferrule with his beak. Finally he got lost.

Félicité had put him down on the grass in the fresh air, and left him there for a minute. When she came back, the parrot had gone. First of all she looked for him in the bushes, by the river and on the rooftops, paying

[7] a thin skin or piece of skin.

no attention to her mistress's shouts of: "Be careful, now! You must be mad!" Next she went over all the gardens in Pont-l'Évêque, stopping passersby and asking them: "You don't happen to have seen my parrot by any chance?" Those who did not know him already were given a description of the bird. Suddenly she thought she could make out something green flying about behind the mills at the foot of the hill. But up on the hill there was nothing to be seen. A pedlar told her that he had come upon the parrot a short time before in Mère Simon's shop at Saint-Melaine. She ran all the way there, but no one knew what she was talking about. Finally she came back home, worn out, her shoes falling to pieces, and death in her heart. She was sitting beside Madame on the garden-seat and telling her what she had been doing, when she felt something light drop on her shoulder. It was Loulou! What he had been up to, no one could discover: perhaps he had just gone for a little walk round the town.

Félicité was slow to recover from this fright, and indeed never really got over it.

As the result of a chill she had an attack of quinsy, and soon after that her ears were affected. Three years later she was deaf, and she spoke at the top of her voice, even in church. Although her sins could have been proclaimed over the length and breadth of the diocese without dishonor to her or offense to others, M. le Curé thought it advisable to hear her confession in the sacristy.

Imaginary buzzings in the head added to her troubles. Often her mistress would say: "Heavens, how stupid you are!" and she would reply: "Yes, Madame," at the same time looking all around her for something.

The little circle of her ideas grew narrower and narrower, and the pealing of bells and the lowing of cattle went out of her life. Every living thing moved about in a ghostly silence. Only one sound reached her ears now, and that was the voice of the parrot.

As if to amuse her, he would reproduce the click-clack of the turn-spit, the shrill call of a man selling fish, and the noise of the saw at the joiner's across the way; and when the bell rang he would imitate Mme Aubain's "Félicité! The door, the door!"

They held conversations with each other, he repeating *ad nauseam* the three phrases in his repertory, she replying with words which were just as disconnected but which came from the heart. In her isolation, Loulou was almost a son or a lover to her. He used to climb up her fingers, peck at her lips, and hang on to her shawl; and as she bent over him, wagging her head from side to side as nurses do, the great wings of her bonnet and the wings of the bird quivered in unison.

When clouds banked up in the sky and there was a rumbling of thunder, he would utter piercing cries, no doubt remembering the sudden downpours in his native forests. The sound of the rain falling roused him to frenzy. He would flap excitedly around, shoot up to the ceiling, knocking everything over, and fly out of the window to splash about in the garden. But he would soon come back to perch on one of the firedogs, hopping about to dry his feathers and showing tail and beak in turn.

One morning in the terrible winter of 1837, when she had put him in front of the fire because of the cold she found him dead in the middle of his cage, hanging head down with his claws caught in the bars. He had probably died of a stroke, but she thought he had been poisoned with parsley, and despite the absence of any proof, her suspicions fell on Fabu.

She wept so much that her mistress said to her: "Why don't you have him stuffed?"

Félicité asked the chemist's advice, remembering that he had always been kind to the parrot. He wrote to Le Havre, and a man called Fellacher agreed to do the job. As parcels sometimes went astray on the mail-coach, she decided to take the parrot as far as Honfleur herself.

On either side of the road stretched an endless succession of apple trees, all stripped of their leaves, and there was ice in the ditches. Dogs were barking around the farms; and Félicité, with her hands tucked under her mantlet, her little black sabots and her basket, walked briskly along the middle of the road.

She crossed the forest, passed Le Haut-Chêne, and got as far as Saint-Gatien.

Behind her, in a cloud of dust, and gathering speed as the horses galloped downhill, a mail-coach swept along like a whirlwind. When he saw this woman making no attempt to get out of the way, the driver poked his head out above the hood, and he and the postilion shouted at her. His four horses could not be held in and galloped faster, the two leaders touching her as they went by. With a jerk of the reins the driver threw them to one side, and then, in a fury, he raised his long whip and gave her such a lash, from head to waist, that she fell flat on her back.

The first thing she did on regaining consciousness was to open her basket. Fortunately nothing had happened to Loulou. She felt her right cheek burning, and when she touched it her hand turned red; it was bleeding.

She sat down on a heap of stones and dabbed her face with her handkerchief. Then she ate a crust of bread which she had taken the precaution of putting in her basket, and tried to forget her wound by looking at the bird.

As she reached the top of the hill at Ecquemauville, she saw the lights of Honfleur twinkling in the darkness like a host of stars, and the shadowy expanse of the sea beyond. Then a sudden feeling of faintness made her stop; and the misery of her childhood, the disappointment of her first love, the departure of her nephew, and the death of Virginie all came back to her at once like the waves of a rising tide, and, welling up in her throat, choked her.

When she got to the boat she insisted on speaking to the captain, and without telling him what was in her parcel, asked him to take good care of it.

Fellacher kept the parrot a long time. Every week he promised it for the next; after six months he announced that a box had been sent off, and nothing more was heard of it. It looked as though Loulou would never come back, and Félicité told herself: "They've stolen him for sure!"

At last he arrived — looking quite magnificent, perched on a branch screwed into a mahogany base, one foot in the air, his head cocked to one side, and biting a nut which the taxidermist, out of love of the grandiose, had gilded.

Félicité shut him up in her room.

This place, to which few people were ever admitted, contained such a quantity of religious bric-à-brac and miscellaneous oddments that it looked like a cross between a chapel and a bazaar.

A big wardrobe prevented the door from opening properly. Opposite the window that overlooked the garden was a little round one looking on to the courtyard. There was a table beside the bed, with a water-jug, a couple of combs, and a block of blue soap in a chipped plate. On the walls there were rosaries, medals, several pictures of the Virgin, and a holy-water stoup made out of a coconut. On the chest of drawers, which was draped with a cloth just like an altar, was the shell box Victor had given her, and also a watering-can and a ball, some copy-books, the illustrated geography book, and a pair of ankle-boots. And on the nail supporting the looking-glass, fastened by its ribbons, hung the little plush hat.

Félicité carried this form of veneration to such lengths that she even kept one of Monsieur's frock-coats. All the old rubbish Mme Aubain had no more use for, she carried off to her room. That was how there came to be artificial flowers along the edge of the chest of drawers, and a portrait of the Comte d'Artois in the window-recess.

With the aid of a wall-bracket, Loulou was installed on a chimney-breast that jutted out into the room. Every morning when she awoke, she saw him in the light of the dawn, and then she remembered the old days, and the smallest details of insignificant actions, not in sorrow but in absolute tranquillity.

Having no intercourse with anyone, she lived in the torpid state of a sleep-walker. The Corpus Christi processions roused her from this condition, for she would go round the neighbors collecting candlesticks and mats to decorate the altar of repose which they used to set up in the street.

In church she was forever gazing at the Holy Ghost, and one day she noticed that it had something of the parrot about it. This resemblance struck her as even more obvious in a colorprint depicting the baptism of Our Lord. With its red wings and its emerald-green body, it was the very image of Loulou.

She bought the print and hung it in the place of the Comte d'Artois, so that she could include them both in a single glance. They were linked together in her mind, the parrot being sanctified by this connection with the Holy Ghost, which itself acquired new life and meaning in her eyes. God the Father could not have chosen a dove as a means of expressing Himself, since doves cannot talk, but rather one of Loulou's ancestors. And although Félicité used to say her prayers with her eyes on the picture, from time to time she would turn slightly towards the bird.

She wanted to join the Children of Mary, but Mme Aubain dissuaded her from doing so.

An important event now loomed up — Paul's wedding.

After starting as a lawyer's clerk, he had been in business, in the Customs, and in Inland Revenue, and had even begun trying to get into the Department of Woods and Forests, when, at the age of thirty-six, by some heaven-sent inspiration, he suddenly discovered his real vocation — in the Wills and Probate Department. There he proved so capable that one of the auditors had offered him his daughter in marriage and promised to use his influence on his behalf.

Paul, grown serious-minded, brought her to see his mother. She criticized the way things were done at Pont-l'Évêque, put on airs, and hurt Félicité's feelings. Mme Aubain was relieved to see her go.

The following week came news of M. Bourais's death in an inn in Lower Brittany. Rumors that he had committed suicide were confirmed, and doubts arose as to his honesty. Mme Aubain went over her accounts and was soon conversant with the full catalogue of his misdeeds — embezzlement of interest, secret sales of timber, forged receipts, etc. Besides all this, he was the father of an illegitimate child, and had had "relations with a person at Dozule."

These infamies upset Mme Aubain greatly. In March 1853 she was afflicted with a pain in the chest; her tongue seemed to be covered with a film; leeches failed to make her breathing any easier; and on the ninth evening of her illness she died. She had just reached the age of seventy-two.

She was thought to be younger because of her brown hair, worn in bandeaux round her pale, pock-marked face. There were few friends to mourn her, for she had a haughty manner which put people off. Yet Félicité wept for her as servants rarely weep for their masters. That Madame should die before her upset her ideas, seemed to be contrary to the order of things, monstrous and unthinkable.

Ten days later — the time it took to travel hot-foot from Besançon — the heirs arrived. The daughter-in-law ransacked every drawer, picked out some pieces of furniture, and sold the rest; and then back they went to the Wills and Probate Department.

Madame's arm-chair, her pedestal table, her foot-warmer, and the eight chairs had all gone. Yellow squares in the center of the wall-panels showed where the pictures had hung. They had carried off the two cots with their mattresses, and no trace remained in the cupboard of all Virginie's things. Félicité climbed the stairs to her room, numbed with sadness.

The next day there was a notice on the door, and the apothecary shouted in her ear that the house was up for sale.

She swayed on her feet, and was obliged to sit down.

What distressed her most of all was the idea of leaving her room, which was so suitable for poor Loulou. Fixing an anguished look on him as she appealed to the Holy Ghost, she contracted the idolatrous habit of kneeling in front of the parrot to say her prayers. Sometimes the sun, as it came through the little window, caught his glass eye, so that it shot out a great luminous ray which sent her into ecstasies.

She had a pension of three hundred and eighty francs a year which her mistress had left her. The garden kept her in vegetables. As for clothes, she had enough to last her till the end of her days, and she saved on lighting by going to bed as soon as darkness fell.

She went out as little as possible, to avoid the second-hand dealer's shop where some of the old furniture was on display. Ever since her fit of giddiness, she had been dragging one leg; and as her strength was failing, Mère Simon, whose grocery business had come to grief, came in every morning to chop wood and pump water for her.

Her eyes grew weaker. The shutters were not opened any more. Years went by, and nobody rented the house and nobody bought it.

For fear of being evicted, Félicité never asked for any repairs to be done. The laths in the roof rotted, and all through one winter her bolster was wet. After Easter she began spitting blood.

When this happened Mère Simon called in a doctor. Félicité wanted to know what was the matter with her, but she was so deaf that only one word reached her: "Pneumonia." It was a word she knew, and she answered gently: "Ah! like Madame," thinking it natural that she should follow in her mistress's footsteps.

The time to set up the altars of repose was drawing near.

The first altar was always at the foot of the hill, the second in front of the post office, the third about halfway up the street. There was some argument as to the siting of this one, and finally the women of the parish picked on Mme Aubain's courtyard.

The fever and the tightness of the chest grew worse. Félicité fretted over not doing anything for the altar. If only she could have something put on it! Then she thought of the parrot. The neighbors protested that it would not be seemly, but the curé gave his permission, and this made her so happy that she begged him to accept Loulou, the only thing of value she possessed, when she died.

From Tuesday to Saturday, the eve of Corpus Christi, she coughed more and more frequently. In the evening her face looked pinched and drawn, her lips stuck to her gums, and she started vomiting. At dawn the next day, feeling very low, she sent for a priest.

Three good women stood by her while she was given extreme unction. Then she said that she had to speak to Fabu.

He arrived in his Sunday best, very ill at ease in this funereal atmosphere.

"Forgive me," she said, making an effort to stretch out her arm. "I thought it was you who had killed him."

What could she mean by such nonsense? To think that she had suspected a man like him of murder! He got very indignant and was obviously going to make a scene.

"Can't you see," they said, "that she isn't in her right mind any more?"

From time to time Félicité would start talking to shadows. The women went away. Mère Simon had her lunch.

A little later she picked Loulou up and held him out to Félicité, saying:

"Come now, say good-bye to him."

Although the parrot was not a corpse, the worms were eating him up. One of his wings was broken, and the stuffing was coming out of his stomach. But she was blind by now, and she kissed him on the forehead and pressed him against her cheek. Mère Simon took him away from her to put him on the altar.

V

The scents of summer came up from the meadows; there was a buzzing of flies; the sun was glittering in the river and warming the slates of the roof. Mère Simon had come back into the room and was gently nodding off to sleep.

The noise of church bells woke her up; the congregation was coming out from vespers. Félicité's delirium abated. Thinking of the procession, she could see it as clearly as if she had been following it.

All the school-children, the choristers, and the firemen were walking along the pavements, while advancing up the middle of the street came the church officer armed with his halberd, the beadle carrying a great cross, the schoolmaster keeping an eye on the boys, and the nun fussing over her little girls — three of the prettiest, looking like curly-headed angels, were throwing rose-petals into the air. Then came the deacon, with both arms outstretched, conducting the band, and a couple of censer-bearers who turned round at every step to face the Holy Sacrament, which the curé, wearing his splendid chasuble, was carrying under a canopy of poppy-red velvet held aloft by four churchwardens. A crowd of people surged along behind, between the white cloths covering the walls of the houses, and eventually they got to the bottom of the hill.

A cold sweat moistened Félicité's temples. Mère Simon sponged it up with a cloth, telling herself that one day she would have to go the same way.

The hum of the crowd increased in volume, was very loud for a moment, then faded away.

A fusillade shook the window-panes. It was the postilions saluting the monstrance. Félicité rolled her eyes and said as loud as she could: "Is he all right?" — worrying about the parrot.

She entered into her death-agony. Her breath, coming ever faster, with a rattling sound, made her sides heave. Bubbles of froth appeared at the corners of her mouth, and her whole body trembled.

Soon the booming of the ophicleides,[8] the clear voices of the children, and the deep voices of the men could be heard near at hand. Now and then everything was quiet, and the tramping of feet, deadened by a carpet of flowers, sounded like a flock moving across pasture-land.

The clergy appeared in the courtyard. Mère Simon climbed on to a chair to reach the little round window, from which she had a full view of the altar below.

It was hung with green garlands and adorned with a flounce in English needlepoint lace. In the middle was a little frame containing some relics, there were two orange-trees at the corners, and all the way along stood silver candlesticks and china vases holding sunflowers, lilies, peonies, foxgloves, and bunches of hydrangea. This pyramid of bright colors stretched from the first floor right down to the carpet which was spread out over the pavement. Some rare objects caught the eye: a silver-gilt sugar-basin wreathed in violets, some pendants of Alençon gems gleaming on a bed of moss, and two Chinese screens with landscape decorations. Loulou, hidden under roses, showed nothing but his blue poll, which looked like a plaque of lapis lazuli.

The churchwardens, the choristers, and the children lined up along the three sides of the courtyard. The priest went slowly up the steps and placed his great shining gold sun on the lace altar-cloth. Everyone knelt down. There was a deep silence. And the censers, swinging at full tilt, slid up and down their chains.

A blue cloud of incense was wafted up into Félicité's room. She opened her nostrils wide and breathed it in with a mystical, sensuous fervor. Then she closed her eyes. Her lips smiled. Her heart-beats grew slower and slower, each a little fainter and gentler, like a fountain running dry, an echo fading away. And as she breathed her last, she thought she could see, in the opening heavens, a gigantic parrot hovering above her head.

[1877]

---

[8] an early brass wind instrument.

LEO TOLSTOY (1828–1910) is generally considered the greatest Russian writer of prose fiction. His supreme quality as a storyteller is a narrative gift that enables him to describe with minute fidelity and richness exactly what his characters are doing and thinking.

Tolstoy was born on his parents' estate in the province of Tula, Russia. His early years were unpromising. Like most noblemen, he spent his time at the university drinking and gambling; but in his twenties he joined the Russian army, and he began writing sketches of military life during the Crimean War (1853–1856). After he left the army and traveled in Europe, he settled down to writing. He married in 1862, and produced his two great novels, War and Peace in 1869 and Anna Karenina in 1877.

As Tolstoy grew older, he lost the temporary peace of mind he had possessed while absorbed in his writing and his family life, and began to live according to strict principles of his own view of rational Christian morality. He grew dissatisfied with literature and reached the conclusion that art was ungodly because it was founded on imagination. Vladimir Nabokov has described Tolstoy's obsession thus: "Somehow, the process of seeking the Truth seemed more important to him than the easy, vivid, brilliant discovery of the illusion of truth through the medium of his artistic genius." In his eighties, Tolstoy decided that by continuing to live with his wife and family on his country estate he was betraying his idea of simple, saintly existence. Finally he left his home and family and wandered away, his destination a monastery he never reached, dying in the waiting room of a little railway station.

Tolstoy's fiction is so powerfully written that it usually transcends the sermon that motivated it, but he insisted that it is always the writer's obligation to tell the reader how to live. Describing "The Soul of the Artist" in 1896, Tolstoy wrote:

> The cement which binds together every work of art into a whole and thereby produces the effect of lifelike illusion, is not the unity of persons and places, but that of the author's independent moral relation to the subject. In reality, when we read or examine the work of a new author, the fundamental questions which arise in our mind are always of this kind: "Well, what sort of a man are you? What distinguishes you from all the people I know, and what information can you give me, as to how we must look upon our life?" Whatever the artist depicts, whether it be saints or robbers, kings or lackeys, we seek and see only the soul of the artist himself. And if he is an established writer, with whom we are already acquainted, the question is no longer "Who are you?" but "Well, what more can you tell me that is new? From what standpoint will you now illuminate life for me?" Therefore, a writer who has not a clear, definite, and fresh view of the

universe, and especially a writer who does not even consider this neces-
sary, cannot produce a work of art. He may write much and beautifully,
but a work of art will not result.

The chief theme of Tolstoy's writing, as in his great story "The Death
of Ivan Ilych," is that the only certain happiness in life is to live for others.
This helps to explain the tragedy of the life of Ivan Ilych, who just before
his death concludes that he has not lived as he ought to have lived. The
story took Tolstoy two years to finish. In its first version, the narrative was
mostly told in the first person singular by one of Ivan Ilych's colleagues,
who was given the diary Ivan Ilych kept during his fatal illness by his
widow. The narrator begins, "It is impossible, absolutely impossible, to live
as I have lived, and as we all live. I realized that as a result of the death of an
acquaintance of mine, Ivan Ilych, and of the diary he left behind." Then
Tolstoy changed his approach to the story and started it again in the third
person, without using the form of a diary.

Leo Tolstoy

ις

THE DEATH OF IVAN ILYCH

–translated by Louise and
Aylmer Maude

I

During an interval in the Melvinski trial in the large building of the
Law Courts, the members and public prosecutor met in Ivan Egorovich
Shebek's private room, where the conversation turned on the celebrated
Krasovski case. Fëdor Vasilievich warmly maintained that it was not subject
to their jurisdiction, Ivan Egorovich maintained the contrary, while Peter
Ivanovich, not having entered into the discussion at the start, took no part
in it but looked through the *Gazette* which had just been handed in.

"Gentlemen," he said, "Ivan Ilych has died!"

"You don't say so!"

"Here, read it yourself," replied Peter Ivanovich, handing Fëdor Vasilievich the paper still damp from the press. Surrounded by a black border
were the words: "Praskovya Fëdorovna Golovina, with profound sorrow, informs relatives and friends of the demise of her beloved husband
Ivan Ilych Golovin, Member of the Court of Justice, which occurred on

February the 4th of this year 1882. The funeral will take place on Friday at one o'clock in the afternoon."

Ivan Ilych had been a colleague of the gentlemen present and was liked by them all. He had been ill for some weeks with an illness said to be incurable. His post had been kept open for him, but there had been conjectures that in case of his death Alexeev might receive his appointment, and that either Vinnikov or Shtabel would succeed Alexeev. So on receiving the news of Ivan Ilych's death the first thought of each of the gentlemen in that private room was of the changes and promotions it might occasion among themselves or their acquaintances.

"I shall be sure to get Shtabel's place or Vinnikov's," thought Fëdor Vasilievich. "I was promised that long ago, and the promotion means an extra eight hundred rubles a year for me besides the allowance."

"Now I must apply for my brother-in-law's transfer from Kaluga," thought Peter Ivanovich. "My wife will be very glad, and then she won't be able to say that I never do anything for her relations."

"I thought he would never leave his bed again," said Peter Ivanovich aloud. "It's very sad."

"But what really was the matter with him?"

"The doctors couldn't say — at least they could, but each of them said something different. When last I saw him I thought he was getting better."

"And I haven't been to see him since the holidays. I always meant to go."

"Had he any property?"

"I think his wife had a little — but something quite trifling."

"We shall have to go to see her, but they live so terribly far away."

"Far away from you, you mean. Everything's far away from your place."

"You see, he never can forgive my living on the other side of the river," said Peter Ivanovich, smiling at Shebek. Then, still talking of the distances between different parts of the city, they returned to the Court.

Besides considerations as to the possible transfers and promotions likely to result from Ivan Ilych's death, the mere fact of the death of a near acquaintance aroused, as usual, in all who heard of it the complacent feeling that, "it is he who is dead and not I."

Each one thought or felt, "Well, he's dead but I'm alive!" But the more intimate of Ivan Ilych's acquaintances, his so-called friends, could not help thinking also that they would now have to fulfill the very tiresome demands of propriety by attending the funeral service and paying a visit of condolence to the widow.

Fëdor Vasilievich and Peter Ivanovich had been his nearest acquaintances. Peter Ivanovich had studied law with Ivan Ilych and had considered himself to be under obligations to him.

Having told his wife at dinner-time of Ivan Ilych's death and of his conjecture that it might be possible to get her brother transferred to their circuit, Peter Ivanovich sacrificed his usual nap, put on his evening clothes, and drove to Ivan Ilych's house.

At the entrance stood a carriage and two cabs. Leaning against the wall in the hall downstairs near the cloak-stand was a coffin-lid covered with cloth of gold, ornamented with gold cord and tassels, that had been polished up with metal powder. Two ladies in black were taking off their fur cloaks. Peter Ivanovich recognized one of them as Ivan Ilych's sister, but the other was a stranger to him. His colleague Schwartz was just coming downstairs, but on seeing Peter Ivanovich enter he stopped and winked at him, as if to say: "Ivan Ilych has made a mess of things — not like you and me."

Schwartz's face, with his Piccadilly whiskers and his slim figure in evening dress, had as usual an air of elegant solemnity which contrasted with the playfulness of his character and had a special piquancy here, or so it seemed to Peter Ivanovich.

Peter Ivanovich allowed the ladies to precede him and slowly followed them upstairs. Schwartz did not come down but remained where he was, and Peter Ivanovich understood that he wanted to arrange where they should play bridge that evening. The ladies went upstairs to the widow's room, and Schwartz, with seriously compressed lips but a playful look in his eyes, indicated by a twist of his eyebrows the room to the right where the body lay.

Peter Ivanovich, like everyone else on such occasions, entered feeling uncertain what he would have to do. All he knew was that at such times it is always safe to cross oneself. But he was not quite sure whether one should make obeisances while doing so. He therefore adopted a middle course. On entering the room he began crossing himself and made a slight movement resembling a bow. At the same time, as far as the motion of his head and arm allowed, he surveyed the room. Two young men — apparently nephews, one of whom was a high-school pupil — were leaving the room, crossing themselves as they did so. An old woman was standing motionless, and a lady with strangely arched eyebrows was saying something to her in a whisper. A vigorous, resolute Church Reader, in a frock-coat, was reading something in a loud voice with an expression that precluded any contradiction. The butler's assistant, Gerasim, stepping lightly in front of Peter Ivanovich, was strewing something on the floor. Noticing this, Peter Ivanovich was immediately aware of a faint odor of a decomposing body.

The last time he had called on Ivan Ilych, Peter Ivanovich had seen Gerasim in the study. Ivan Ilych had been particularly fond of him and he was performing the duty of a sick nurse.

Peter Ivanovich continued to make the sign of the cross slightly inclining his head in an intermediate direction between the coffin, the Reader, and the icons on the table in a corner of the room. Afterwards, when it seemed to him that this movement of his arm in crossing himself had gone on too long, he stopped and began to look at the corpse.

The dead man lay, as dead men always lie, in a specially heavy way, his rigid limbs sunk in the soft cushions of the coffin, with the head forever bowed on the pillow. His yellow waxen brow with bald patches over his sunken temples was thrust up in the way peculiar to the dead, the protruding nose seeming to press on the upper lip. He was much changed and had grown even thinner since Peter Ivanovich had last seen him, but, as is always the case with the dead, his face was handsomer and above all more dignified than when he was alive. The expression on the face said that what was necessary had been accomplished, and accomplished rightly. Besides this there was in that expression a reproach and a warning to the living. This warning seemed to Peter Ivanovich out of place, or at least not applicable to him. He felt a certain discomfort and so he hurriedly crossed himself once more and turned and went out the door — too hurriedly and too regardless of propriety, as he himself was aware.

Schwartz was waiting for him in the adjoining room with legs spread wide apart and both hands toying with his top-hat behind his back. The mere sight of that playful, well-groomed, and elegant figure refreshed Peter Ivanovich. He felt that Schwartz was above all these happenings and would not surrender to any depressing influences. His very look said that this incident of a church service for Ivan Ilych could not be a sufficient reason for infringing the order of the session — in other words, that it would certainly not prevent his unwrapping a new pack of cards and shuffling them that evening while a footman placed four fresh candles on the table: in fact, that there was no reason for supposing that this incident would hinder their spending the evening agreeably. Indeed he said this in a whisper as Peter Ivanovich passed him, proposing that they should meet for a game at Fëdor Vasilievich's. But apparently Peter Ivanovich was not destined to play bridge that evening. Praskovya Fëdorovna (a short, fat woman who despite all efforts to the contrary had continued to broaden steadily from her shoulders downwards and who had the same extraordinarily arched eyebrows as the lady who had been standing by the coffin), dressed all in black, her head covered with lace, came out of her own room with some other ladies, conducted them to the room where the dead body lay, and said: "The service will begin immediately. Please go in."

Schwartz, making an indefinite bow, stood still, evidently neither accepting nor declining this invitation. Praskovya Fëdorovna, recognizing Peter Ivanovich, sighed, went close up to him, took his hand, and said: "I know you were a true friend to Ivan Ilych . . ." and looked at him awaiting some suitable response. And Peter Ivanovich knew that, just as it had been the right thing to cross himself in that room, so what he had to do here was to press her hand, sigh, and say, "Believe me. . . ." So he did all this and as he did it felt that the desired result had been achieved: that both he and she were touched.

"Come with me. I want to speak to you before it begins," said the widow. "Give me your arm."

Peter Ivanovich gave her his arm and they went to the inner rooms, passing Schwartz, who winked at Peter Ivanovich compassionately.

"That does for our bridge! Don't object if we find another player. Perhaps you can cut in when you do escape," said his playful look.

Peter Ivanovich sighed still more deeply and despondently, and Praskovya Fëdorovna pressed his arm gratefully. When they reached the drawing-room, upholstered in pink cretonne and lighted by a dim lamp, they sat down at the table — she on a sofa and Peter Ivanovich on a low pouffe, the springs of which yielded spasmodically under his weight. Praskovya Fëdorovna had been on the point of warning him to take another seat, but felt that such a warning was out of keeping with her present condition and so changed her mind. As he sat down on the pouffe Peter Ivanovich recalled how Ivan Ilych had arranged this room and had consulted him regarding this pink cretonne with green leaves. The whole room was full of furniture and knick-knacks, and on her way to the sofa the lace of the widow's black shawl caught on the carved edge of the table. Peter Ivanovich rose to detach it, and the springs of the pouffe, relieved of his weight, rose also and gave him a push. The widow began detaching her shawl herself, and Peter Ivanovich again sat down, suppressing the rebellious springs of the pouffe under him. But the widow had not quite freed herself and Peter Ivanovich got up again, and again the pouffe rebelled and even creaked. When this was all over she took out a clean cambric handkerchief and began to weep. The episode with the shawl and the struggle with the pouffe had cooled Peter Ivanovich's emotions and he sat there with a sullen look on his face. This awkward situation was interrupted by Sokolov, Ivan Ilych's butler, who came to report that the plot in the cemetery that Praskovya Fëdorovna had chosen would cost two hundred rubles. She stopped weeping and, looking at Peter Ivanovich with the air of a victim, remarked in French that it was very hard for her. Peter Ivanovich made a silent gesture signifying his full conviction that it must indeed be so.

"Please smoke," she said in a magnanimous yet crushed voice, and turned to discuss with Sokolov the price of the plot for the grave.

Peter Ivanovich while lighting his cigarette heard her inquiring very circumstantially into the price of different plots in the cemetery and finally decided which she would take. When that was done she gave instructions about engaging the choir. Sokolov then left the room.

"I look after everything myself," she told Peter Ivanovich, shifting the albums that lay on the table; and noticing that the table was endangered by his cigarette-ash, she immediately passed him an ashtray, saying as she did so: "I consider it an affectation to say that my grief prevents my attending to practical affairs. On the contrary, if anything can — I won't say console me, but — distract me, it is seeing to everything concerning him." She again took out her handkerchief as if preparing to cry, but suddenly, as if mastering her feeling, she shook herself and began to speak calmly. "But there is something I want to talk to you about."

Peter Ivanovich bowed, keeping control of the springs of the pouffe, which immediately began quivering under him.

"He suffered terribly the last few days."

"Did he?" said Peter Ivanovich.

"Oh, terribly! He screamed unceasingly, not for minutes but for hours. For the last three days he screamed incessantly. It was unendurable. I cannot understand how I bore it; you could hear him three rooms off. Oh, what I have suffered!"

"Is it possible that he was conscious all that time?" asked Peter Ivanovich.

"Yes," she whispered. "To the last moment. He took leave of us a quarter of an hour before he died, and asked us to take Vasya away."

The thought of the sufferings of this man he had known so intimately, first as a merry little boy, then as a school-mate, and later as a grown-up colleague, suddenly struck Peter Ivanovich with horror, despite an unpleasant consciousness of his own and this woman's dissimulation. He again saw that brow, and that nose pressing down on the lip, and felt afraid for himself.

"Three days of frightful suffering and then death! Why, that might suddenly, at any time, happen to me," he thought, and for a moment felt terrified. But — he did not himself know how — the customary reflection at once occurred to him that this had happened to Ivan Ilych and not to him, and that it should not and could not happen to him, and that to think that it could would be yielding to depression which he ought not to do, as Schwartz's expression plainly showed. After which reflection Peter Ivanovich felt reassured, and began to ask with interest about the details of Ivan Ilych's death, as though death was an accident natural to Ivan Ilych but certainly not to himself.

After many details of the really dreadful physical sufferings Ivan Ilych had endured (which details he learnt only from the effect those sufferings had produced on Praskovya Fëdorovna's nerves) the widow apparently found it necessary to get to business.

"Oh, Peter Ivanovich, how hard is it! How terribly, terribly hard!" and she again began to weep.

Peter Ivanovich sighed and waited for her to finish blowing her nose. When she had done so he said, "Believe me . . ." and she again began talking and brought out what was evidently her chief concern with him — namely, to question him as to how she could obtain a grant of money from the government on the occasion of her husband's death. She made it appear that she was asking Peter Ivanovich's advice about her pension, but he soon saw that she already knew about that to the minutest detail, more even than he did himself. She knew how much could be got out of the government in consequence of her husband's death, but wanted to find out whether she could not possibly extract something more. Peter Ivanovich tried to think of some means of doing so, but after reflecting for a while and, out of propriety, condemning the government for its niggardliness, he said he thought that nothing more could be got. Then she sighed and evidently began to devise means of getting rid of her visitor. Noticing this, he put out his cigarette, rose, pressed her hand, and went out into the anteroom.

In the dining-room where the clock stood that Ivan Ilych had liked so much and had bought at an antique shop, Peter Ivanovich met a priest and a few acquaintances who had come to attend the service, and he recognized Ivan Ilych's daughter, a handsome young woman. She was in black and her slim figure appeared slimmer than ever. She had a gloomy, determined, almost angry expression, and bowed to Peter Ivanovich as though he were in some way to blame. Behind her, with the same offended look, stood a wealthy young man, an examining magistrate, whom Peter Ivanovich also knew and who was her fiancé, as he had heard. He bowed mournfully to them and was about to pass into the death-chamber, when from under the stairs appeared the figure of Ivan Ilych's schoolboy son, who was extremely like his father. He seemed a little Ivan Ilych, such as Peter Ivanovich remembered when they studied law together. His tear-stained eyes had in them the look that is seen in the eyes of boys of thirteen or fourteen who are not pure-minded. When he saw Peter Ivanovich he scowled morosely and shamefacedly. Peter Ivanovich nodded to him and entered the death-chamber. The service began: candles, groans, incense, tears, and sobs. Peter Ivanovich stood looking gloomily down at his feet. He did not look once at the dead man, did not yield to any depressing influence, and was one of the first to leave the room. There was no one in the anteroom, but Gerasim darted out of the dead man's room, rummaged with his strong hands among the fur coats to find Peter Ivanovich's and helped him on with it.

"Well, friend Gerasim," said Peter Ivanovich, so as to say something. "It's a sad affair, isn't it?"

"It's God's will. We shall all come to it some day," said Gerasim, displaying his teeth — the even, white teeth of a healthy peasant — and, like a man in the thick of urgent work, he briskly opened the front door, called the coachman, helped Peter Ivanovich into the sledge, and sprang back to the porch as if in readiness for what he had to do next.

Peter Ivanovich found the fresh air particularly pleasant after the smell of incense, the dead body, and carbolic acid.

"Where to, sir?" asked the coachman.

"It's not too late even now. . . . I'll call round on Fëdor Vasilievich."

He accordingly drove there and found them just finishing the first rubber, so that it was quite convenient for him to cut in.

II

Ivan Ilych's life had been most simple and most ordinary and therefore most terrible.

He had been a member of the Court of Justice, and died at the age of forty-five. His father had been an official who after serving in various ministries and departments in Petersburg had made the sort of career which brings men to positions from which by reason of their long service they cannot be dismissed, though they were obviously unfit to hold any responsible position, and for whom therefore posts are specially created, which though fictitious carry salaries of from six to ten thousand rubles that are not fictitious, and in receipt of which they live on to a great age.

Such was the Privy Councillor and superfluous member of various superfluous institutions, Ilya Epimovich Golovin.

He had three sons, of whom Ivan Ilych was the second. The eldest son was following in his father's footsteps only in another department, and was already approaching that stage in the service at which a similar sinecure would be reached. The third son was a failure. He had ruined his prospects in a number of positions and was now serving in the railway department. His father and brothers, and still more their wives, not merely disliked meeting him, but avoided remembering his existence unless compelled to do so. His sister had married Baron Greff, a Petersburg official of her father's type. Ivan Ilych was *le phénix de la famille*[1] as people said. He was neither as cold and formal as his elder brother nor as wild as the younger, but was a happy mean between them — an intelligent, polished, lively and agreeable man. He had studied with his younger brother at the School of Law, but the latter had failed to complete the course and was expelled when he was in the fifth class. Ivan Ilych finished the course well. Even when he was at the School of Law he was just what he remained for the rest of his life: a capable, cheerful, good-natured, and sociable man, though strict in the fulfillment of what he considered to be his duty: and he considered his duty to be what was so considered by those in authority. Neither as a boy nor as a man was he a toady, but from early youth was by nature attracted to people of high station as a fly is drawn to the light, assimilating their ways and views of life and establishing friendly relations with them. All the enthusiasms of childhood and youth passed without leaving much trace on him; he succumbed to sensuality, to vanity, and latterly among the highest classes to liberalism, but always within limits which his instinct unfailingly indicated to him as correct.

At school he had done things which had formerly seemed to him very horrid and made him feel disgusted with himself when he did them; but when later on he saw that such actions were done by people of good position and that they did not regard them as wrong, he was able not exactly to regard them as right, but to forget about them entirely or not be at all troubled at remembering them.

---

[1] the pride of the family. (Unless otherwise indicated, all foreign phrases are in French — often the everyday language of middle-class and upper-class Russians of Tolstoy's time.)

Having graduated from the School of Law and qualified for the tenth rank of the civil service, and having received money from his father for his equipment, Ivan Ilych ordered himself clothes at Scharmer's, the fashionable tailor, hung a medallion inscribed *respice finem*[2] on his watch-chain, took leave of his professor and the prince who was patron of the school, had a farewell dinner with his comrades at Donon's first-class restaurant, and with his new and fashionable portmanteau, linen, clothes, shaving and other toilet appliances, and a traveling rug, all purchased at the best shops, he set off for one of the provinces where, through his father's influence, he had been attached to the Governor as an official for special service.

In the province Ivan Ilych soon arranged as easy and agreeable a position for himself as he had had at the School of Law. He performed his official tasks, made his career, and at the same time amused himself pleasantly and decorously. Occasionally he paid official visits to country districts, where he behaved with dignity both to his superiors and inferiors, and performed the duties entrusted to him, which related chiefly to the sectarians,[3] with an exactness and incorruptible honesty of which he could not but feel proud.

In official matters, despite his youth and taste for frivolous gaiety, he was exceedingly reserved, punctilious, and even severe; but in society he was often amusing and witty, and always good-natured, correct in his manner, and *bon enfant*,[4] as the governor and his wife — with whom he was like one of the family — used to say of him.

In the province he had an affair with a lady who made advances to the elegant young lawyer, and there was also a milliner; and there were carousals with aides-de-camp who visited the district, and after-supper visits to a certain outlying street of doubtful reputation; and there was too some obsequiousness to his chief and even to his chief's wife, but all this was done with such a tone of good breeding that no hard names could be applied to it. It all came under the heading of the French saying: "*Il faut que jeunesse se passe.*"[5] It was all done with clean hands, in clean linen, with French phrases, and above all among people of the best society and consequently with the approval of people of rank.

So Ivan Ilych served for five years and then came a change in his official life. The new and reformed judicial institutions were introduced, and new men were needed. Ivan Ilych became such a new man. He was offered the post of examining magistrate, and he accepted it though the post was in another province and obliged him to give up the connections he had formed and to make new ones. His friends met to give him a send-off; they had a group-photograph taken and presented him with a silver cigarette-case, and he set off to his new post.

---

[2] "Consider your end," that is, your death (Latin).
[3] "Old Believers," dissenters from the Orthodox Church.
[4] one of the boys (literally, "a good child").
[5] "Youth will have its day."

As examining magistrate Ivan Ilych was just as *comme il faut*[6] and decorous a man, inspiring general respect and capable of separating his official duties from his private life, as he had been when acting as an official on special service. His duties now as examining magistrate were far more interesting and attractive than before. In his former position it had been pleasant to wear an undress uniform made by Scharmer, and to pass through the crowd of petitioners and officials who were timorously awaiting an audience with the governor, and who envied him as with free and easy gait he went straight into his chief's private room to have a cup of tea and a cigarette with him. But not many people had then been directly dependent on him — only police officials and the sectarians when he went on special missions — and he liked to treat them politely, almost as comrades, as if he were letting them feel that he who had the power to crush them was treating them in this simple, friendly way. There were then but few such people. But now, as an examining magistrate, Ivan Ilych felt that everyone without exception, even the most important and self-satisfied, was in his power, and that he need only write a few words on a sheet of paper with a certain heading, and this or that important, self-satisfied person would be brought before him in the role of an accused person or a witness, and if he did not choose to allow him to sit down, would have to stand before him and answer his questions. Ivan Ilych never abused his power; he tried on the contrary to soften its expression, but the consciousness of it and of the possibility of softening its effect, supplied the chief interest and attraction of his office. In his work itself, especially in his examinations, he very soon acquired a method of eliminating all considerations irrelevant to the legal aspect of the case, and reducing even the most complicated case to a form in which it would be presented on paper only in its externals, completely excluding his personal opinion of the matter, while above all observing every prescribed formality. The work was new and Ivan Ilych was one of the first men to apply the new Code of 1864.[7]

On taking up the post of examining magistrate in a new town, he made new acquaintances and connections, placed himself on a new footing, and assumed a somewhat different tone. He took up an attitude of rather dignified aloofness towards the provincial authorities, but picked out the best circle of legal gentlemen and wealthy gentry living in the town and assumed a tone of slight dissatisfaction with the government, of moderate liberalism, and of enlightened citizenship. At the same time, without at all altering the elegance of his toilet, he ceased shaving his chin and allowed his beard to grow as it pleased.

Ivan Ilych settled down very pleasantly in this new town. The society there, which inclined towards opposition to the Governor, was friendly, his

---

[6] proper (literally, "as it should be").
[7] The emancipation of the serfs in 1861 was followed by a thorough all-round reform of judicial proceedings. [Translators' note]

salary was larger, and he began to play *vint*,[8] which he found added not a little to the pleasure of life, for he had a capacity for cards, played good-humoredly, and calculated rapidly and astutely, so that he usually won.

After living there for two years he met his future wife, Praskovya Fëdorovna Mikhel, who was the most attractive, clever, and brilliant girl of the set in which he moved, and among other amusements and relaxations from his labors as examining magistrate, Ivan Ilych established light and playful relations with her.

While he had been an official on special service he had been accustomed to dance, but now as an examining magistrate it was exceptional for him to do so. If he danced now, he did it as if to show that though he served under the reformed order of things, and had reached the fifth official rank, yet when it came to dancing he could do it better than most people. So at the end of an evening he sometimes danced with Praskovya Fëdorovna, and it was chiefly during these dances that he captivated her. She fell in love with him. Ivan Ilych had at first no definite intention of marrying, but when the girl fell in love with him he said to himself: "Really, why shouldn't I marry?"

Praskovya Fëdorovna came of a good family, was not bad looking, and had some little property. Ivan Ilych might have aspired to a more brilliant match, but even this was good. He had his salary, and she, he hoped, would have an equal income. She was well connected, and was a sweet, pretty, and thoroughly correct young woman. To say that Ivan Ilych married because he fell in love with Praskovya Fëdorovna and found that she sympathized with his views of life would be as incorrect as to say that he married because his social circle approved of the match. He was swayed by both these considerations: the marriage gave him personal satisfaction, and at the same time it was considered the right thing by the most highly placed of his associates.

So Ivan Ilych got married.

The preparations for marriage and the beginning of married life, with its conjugal caresses, the new furniture, new crockery, and new linen, were very pleasant until his wife became pregnant — so that Ivan Ilych had begun to think that marriage would not impair the easy, agreeable, gay and always decorous character of his life, approved of by society and regarded by himself as natural, but would even improve it. But from the first months of his wife's pregnancy, something new, unpleasant, depressing, and unseemly, and from which there was no way of escape, unexpectedly showed itself.

His wife, without any reason — *de gaieté de coeur*[9] as Ivan Ilych expressed it to himself — began to disturb the pleasure and propriety of their life. She began to be jealous without any cause, expected him to devote his

---

[8] a form of bridge. [Translators' note]
[9] from sheer exuberance (literally, "from happiness of heart").

whole attention to her, found fault with everything, and made coarse and ill-mannered scenes.

At first Ivan Ilych hoped to escape from the unpleasantness of this state of affairs by the same easy and decorous relation to life that had served him heretofore: he tried to ignore his wife's disagreeable moods, continued to live in his usual easy and pleasant way, invited friends to his house for a game of cards, and also tried going out to his club or spending his evenings with friends. But one day his wife began upbraiding him so vigorously, using such coarse words, and continued to abuse him every time he did not fulfil her demands, so resolutely and with such evident determination not to give way till he submitted — that is, till he stayed at home and was bored just as she was — that he became alarmed. He now realized that matrimony — at any rate with Praskovya Fëdorovna — was not always conducive to the pleasures and amenities of life, but on the contrary often infringed both comfort and propriety, and that he must therefore entrench himself against such infringement. And Ivan Ilych began to seek for means of doing so. His official duties were the one thing that imposed upon Praskovya Fëdorovna, and by means of his official work and the duties attached to it he began struggling with his wife to secure his own independence.

With the birth of their child, the attempts to feed it and the various failures in doing so, and with the real and imaginary illnesses of mother and child, in which Ivan Ilych's sympathy was demanded but about which he understood nothing, the need of securing for himself an existence outside his family life became still more imperative.

As his wife grew more irritable and exacting and Ivan Ilych transferred the center of gravity of his life more and more to his official work so did he grow to like his work better and became more ambitious than before.

Very soon, within a year of his wedding, Ivan Ilych had realized that marriage, though it may add some comforts to life, is in fact a very intricate and difficult affair towards which in order to perform one's duty, that is, to lead a decorous life approved of by society, one must adopt a definite attitude just as towards one's official duties.

And Ivan Ilych evolved such an attitude towards married life. He only required of it those conveniences — dinner at home, housewife, and bed — which it could give him, and above all that propriety of external forms required by public opinion. For the rest he looked for light-hearted pleasure and propriety, and was very thankful when he found them, but if he met with antagonism and querulousness he at once retired into his separate fenced-off world of official duties, where he found satisfaction.

Ivan Ilych was esteemed a good official, and after three years was made Assistant Public Prosecutor. His new duties, their importance, the possibility of indicting and imprisoning anyone he chose, the publicity his speeches received, and the success he had in all these things made his work still more attractive.

More children came. His wife became more and more querulous and ill-tempered, but the attitude Ivan Ilych had adopted towards his home life rendered him almost impervious to her grumbling.

After seven years' service in that town he was transferred to another province as Public Prosecutor. They moved, but were short of money and his wife did not like the place they moved to. Though the salary was higher the cost of living was greater, besides which two of their children died and family life became still more unpleasant for him.

Praskovya Fëdorovna blamed her husband for every inconvenience they encountered in their new home. Most of the conversations between husband and wife, especially as to the children's education, led to topics which recalled former disputes, and those disputes were apt to flare up again at any moment. There remained only those rare periods of amorousness which still came to them at times but did not last long. These were islets at which they anchored for a while and then again set out upon that ocean of veiled hostility which showed itself in their aloofness from one another. This aloofness might have grieved Ivan Ilych had he considered that it ought not to exist, but he now regarded the position as normal, and even made it the goal at which he aimed in family life. His aim was to free himself more and more from those unpleasantnesses and to give them a semblance of harmlessness and propriety. He attained this by spending less and less time with his family, and when obliged to be at home he tried to safeguard his position by the presence of outsiders. The chief thing however was that he had his official duties. The whole interest of his life now centered in the official world and that interest absorbed him. The consciousness of his power, being able to ruin anybody he wished to ruin, the importance, even the external dignity of his entry into court, or meetings with his subordinates, his success with superiors and inferiors, and above all his masterly handling of cases, of which he was conscious — all this gave him pleasure and filled his life, together with chats with his colleagues, dinners, and bridge. So that on the whole Ivan Ilych's life continued to flow as he considered it should do — pleasantly and properly.

So things continued for another seven years. His eldest daughter was already sixteen, another child had died, and only one son was left, a schoolboy and a subject of dissension. Ivan Ilych wanted to put him in the School of Law, but to spite him Praskovya Fëdorovna entered him at the High School. The daughter had been educated at home and had turned out well: the boy did not learn badly either.

III

So Ivan Ilych lived for seventeen years after his marriage. He was already a Public Prosecutor of long standing, and had declined several proposed transfers while awaiting a more desirable post, when an unanticipated and unpleasant occurrence quite upset the peaceful course of his life. He was expecting to be offered the post of presiding judge in a University town, but Happe somehow came to the front and obtained the appointment instead. Ivan Ilych became irritable, reproached Happe, and quarreled both with him and with his immediate superiors — who became colder to him and again passed him over when other appointments were made.

This was in 1880, the hardest year of Ivan Ilych's life. It was then that it became evident on the one hand that his salary was insufficient for them to live on, and on the other that he had been forgotten, and not only this, but that what was for him the greatest and most cruel injustice appeared to others a quite ordinary occurrence. Even his father did not consider it his duty to help him. Ivan Ilych felt himself abandoned by everyone, and that they regarded his position with a salary of 3,500 rubles as quite normal and even fortunate. He alone knew that with the consciousness of the injustices done him, with his wife's incessant nagging, and with the debts he had contracted by living beyond his means, his position was far from normal.

In order to save money that summer he obtained leave of absence and went with his wife to live in the country at her brother's place.

In the country, without his work, he experienced *ennui* for the first time in his life, and not only *ennui* but intolerable depression, and he decided that it was impossible to go on living like that, and that it was necessary to take energetic measures.

Having passed a sleepless night pacing up and down the veranda, he decided to go to Petersburg and bestir himself, in order to punish those who had failed to appreciate him and to get transferred to another ministry.

Next day, despite many protests from his wife and her brother, he started for Petersburg with the sole object of obtaining a post with a salary of five thousand rubles a year. He was no longer bent on any particular department, or tendency, or kind of activity. All he now wanted was an appointment to another post with a salary of five thousand rubles, either in the administration, in the banks, with the railways, in one of the Empress Marya's Institutions,[10] or even in the customs — but it had to carry with it a salary of five thousand rubles and be in a ministry other than that in which they had failed to appreciate him.

And this quest of Ivan Ilych's was crowned with remarkable and unexpected success. At Kursk an acquaintance of his, F. I. Ilyin, got into the first-class carriage, sat down beside Ivan Ilych, and told him of a telegram just received by the Governor of Kursk announcing that a change was about to take place in the ministry: Peter Ivanovich was to be superseded by Ivan Semënovich.

The proposed change, apart from its significance for Russia, had a special significance for Ivan Ilych, because by bringing forward a new man, Peter Petrovich, and consequently his friend Zachar Ivanovich, it was highly favorable for Ivan Ilych, since Zachar Ivanovich was a friend and colleague of his.

---

[10] orphanages founded by the wife of Tsar Paul I, who ruled from 1796 to 1801.

In Moscow this news was confirmed, and on reaching Petersburg Ivan Ilych found Zachar Ivanovich and received a definite promise of an appointment in his former department of Justice.

A week later he telegraphed to his wife: "Zachar in Miller's place. I shall receive appointment on presentation of report."

Thanks to this change of personnel, Ivan Ilych had unexpectedly obtained an appointment in his former ministry which placed him two stages above his former colleagues besides giving him five thousand rubles salary and three thousand five hundred rubles for expenses connected with his removal. All his ill humor towards his former enemies and the whole department vanished, and Ivan Ilych was completely happy.

He returned to the country more cheerful and contented than he had been for a long time. Praskovya Fëdorovna also cheered up and a truce was arranged between them. Ivan Ilych told of how he had been fêted by everybody in Petersburg, how all those who had been his enemies were put to shame and now fawned on him, how envious they were of his appointment, and how much everybody in Petersburg had liked him.

Praskovya Fëdorovna listened to all this and appeared to believe it. She did not contradict anything, but only made plans for their life in the town to which they were going. Ivan Ilych saw with delight that these plans were his plans, that he and his wife agreed, and that, after a stumble, his life was regaining its due and natural character of pleasant lightheartedness and decorum.

Ivan Ilych had come back for a short time only, for he had to take up his new duties on the 10th of September. Moreover, he needed time to settle into the new place, to move all his belongings from the province, and to buy and order many additional things: in a word, to make such arrangements as he had resolved on, which were almost exactly what Praskovya Fëdorovna too had decided on.

Now that everything had happened so fortunately, and that he and his wife were at one in their aims and moreover saw so little of one another, they got on together better than they had done since the first years of marriage. Ivan Ilych had thought of taking his family away with him at once, but the insistence of his wife's brother and her sister-in-law, who had suddenly become particularly amiable and friendly to him and his family, induced him to depart alone.

So he departed, and the cheerful state of mind induced by his success and by the harmony between his wife and himself, the one intensifying the other, did not leave him. He found a delightful house, just the thing both he and his wife had dreamt of. Spacious, lofty reception rooms in the old style, a convenient and dignified study, rooms for his wife and daughter, a study for his son — it might have been specially built for them. Ivan Ilych himself superintended the arrangements, chose the wallpapers, supplemented the furniture (preferably with antiques which he considered particularly *comme il faut*), and supervised the upholstering. Everything progressed and progressed and approached the ideal he had set himself: even when things were only half completed they exceeded his expectations. He saw what a refined and elegant character, free from vulgarity, it would all have when it was ready. On falling asleep he pictured to himself how the reception-room would look. Looking at the yet unfinished drawing-room he could see the fireplace, the screen, the what-not, the little chairs dotted here and there, the dishes and plates on the walls, and the bronzes, as they would be when everything was in place. He was pleased by the thought of how his wife and daughter, who shared his taste in this matter, would be impressed by it. They were certainly not expecting as much. He had been particularly successful in finding, and buying cheaply, antiques which gave a particularly aristocratic character to the whole place. But in his letters he intentionally understated everything in order to be able to surprise them. All this so absorbed him that his new duties — though he liked his official work — interested him less than he had expected. Sometimes he even had moments of absent-mindedness during the Court Sessions, and would consider whether he should have straight or curved cornices for his curtains. He was so interested in it all that he often did things himself, rearranging the furniture, or rehanging the curtains. Once when mounting a step-ladder to show the upholsterer, who did not understand, how he wanted the hangings draped, he made a false step and slipped, but being a strong and agile man he clung on and only knocked his side against the knob of the window frame. The bruised place was painful but the pain soon passed, and he felt particularly bright and well just then. He wrote: "I feel fifteen years younger." He thought he would have everything ready by September, but it dragged on till mid-October. But the result was charming not only in his eyes but to everyone who saw it.

In reality it was just what is usually seen in the houses of people of moderate means who want to appear rich, and therefore succeed only in resembling others like themselves: there were damasks, dark wood, plants, rugs, and dull and polished bronzes — all the things people of a certain class have in order to resemble other people of that class. His house was so like the others that it would never have been noticed, but to him it all seemed to be quite exceptional. He was very happy when he met his family at the station and brought them to the newly furnished house all lit up, where a footman in a white tie opened the door into the hall decorated with plants, and when they went on into the drawing-room, and the study uttering exclamations of delight. He conducted them everywhere, drank in their praises eagerly, and beamed with pleasure. At tea that evening, when Praskovya Fëdorovna among other things asked him about his fall, he laughed and showed them how he had gone flying and had frightened the upholsterer.

"It's a good thing I'm a bit of an athlete. Another man might have been killed, but I merely knocked myself, just here; it hurts when it's touched, but it's passing off already — it's only a bruise."

So they began living in their new home — in which, as always happens, when they got thoroughly settled in they found they were just one room short — and with the increased income, which as always was just a little (some five hundred rubles) too little, but it was all very nice.

Things went particularly well at first, before everything was finally arranged and while something had still to be done: this thing bought, that thing ordered, another thing moved, and something else adjusted. Though there were some disputes between husband and wife, they were both so well satisfied and had so much to do that it all passed off without any serious quarrels. When nothing was left to arrange it became rather dull and something seemed to be lacking, but they were then making acquaintances, forming habits, and life was growing fuller.

Ivan Ilych spent his mornings at the law court and came home to dinner, and at first he was generally in a good humor, though he occasionally became irritable just on account of his house. (Every spot on the tablecloth or the upholstery, and every broken windowblind string, irritated him. He had devoted so much trouble to arranging it all that every disturbance of it distressed him.) But on the whole his life ran its course as he believed life should do: easily, pleasantly, and decorously.

He got up at nine, drank his coffee, read the paper, and then put on his undress uniform and went to the law courts. There the harness in which he worked had already been stretched to fit him and he donned it without a hitch: petitioners, inquiries at the chancery, the chancery itself, and the sittings public and administrative. In all this the thing was to exclude everything fresh and vital, which always disturbs the regular course of official business, and to admit only official relations with people, and then only on official grounds. A man would come, for instance, wanting some information. Ivan Ilych, as one in whose sphere the matter did not lie, would have nothing to do with him: but if the man had some business with him in his official capacity, something that could be expressed on officially stamped paper, he would do everything, positively everything he could within the limits of such relations, and in doing so would maintain the semblance of friendly human relations, that is, would observe the courtesies of life. As soon as the official relations ended, so did everything else. Ivan Ilych possessed this capacity to separate his real life from the official side of affairs and not mix the two, in the highest degree, and by long practice and natural aptitude had brought it to such a pitch that sometimes, in the manner of a virtuoso, he would even allow himself to let the human and official relations mingle. He let himself do this just because he felt that he could at any time he chose resume the strictly official attitude again and drop the human relation. And he did it all easily, pleasantly, correctly, and even artistically. In the intervals between the sessions he smoked, drank tea, chatted a little about politics, a little about general topics, a little about cards, but most of all about official appointments. Tired, but with the feelings of a virtuoso — one of the first violins who has played his part in an orchestra with precision — he would return home to find that his wife and daughter had been out paying calls, or had a visitor, and that his son had been to school, had done his homework with his tutor, and was duly learning what is taught at High Schools. Everything was as it should be. After dinner, if they had no visitors, Ivan Ilych sometimes read a book that was being much discussed at the time, and in the evening settled down to work, that is, read official papers, compared the depositions of witnesses, and noted paragraphs of the Code applying to them. This was neither dull nor amusing. It was dull when he might have been playing bridge, but if no bridge was available it was at any rate better than doing nothing or sitting with his wife. Ivan Ilych's chief pleasure was giving little dinners to which he invited men and women of good social position, and just as his drawing-room resembled all other drawing-rooms so did his enjoyable little parties resemble all other such parties.

Once they even gave a dance. Ivan Ilych enjoyed it and everything went off well, except that it led to a violent quarrel with his wife about the cakes and sweets. Praskovya Fëdorovna had made her own plans, but Ivan Ilych insisted on getting everything from an expensive confectioner and ordered too many cakes, and the quarrel occurred because some of those cakes were left over and the confectioner's bill came to forty-five rubles. It was a great and disagreeable quarrel. Praskovya Fëdorovna called him "a fool and an imbecile," and he clutched at his head and made angry allusions to divorce.

But the dance itself had been enjoyable. The best people were there, and Ivan Ilych had danced with Princess Trufonova, a sister of the distinguished founder of the Society "Bear My Burden."

The pleasures connected with his work were pleasures of ambition; his social pleasures were those of vanity; but Ivan Ilych's greatest pleasure was playing bridge. He acknowledged that whatever disagreeable incident happened in his life, the pleasure that beamed like a ray of light above everything else was to sit down to bridge with good players, not noisy partners, and of course to four-handed bridge (with five players it was annoying to have to stand out, though one pretended not to mind), to play a clever and serious game (when the cards allowed it) and then to have supper and drink a glass of wine. After a game of bridge, especially if he had won a little (to win a large sum was unpleasant), Ivan Ilych went to bed in specially good humor.

So they lived. They formed a circle of acquaintances among the best people and were visited by people of importance and by young folk. In their views as to their acquaintances, husband, wife, and daughter were entirely agreed, and tacitly and unanimously kept at arm's length and shook off the various shabby friends and relations who, with much show of affection, gushed into the drawing-room with its Japanese plates on the walls. Soon these shabby friends ceased to obtrude themselves and only the best people remained in the Golovins' set.

Young men made up to Lisa, and Petrishchev, an examining magistrate and Dmitri Ivanovich Petrishchev's son and sole heir, began to be so attentive to her that Ivan Ilych had already spoken to Praskovya Fëdorovna about it, and considered whether they should not arrange a party for them, or get up some private theatricals.

So they lived, and all went well, without change, and life flowed pleasantly.

IV

They were all in good health. It could not be called ill health if Ivan Ilych sometimes said that he had a queer taste in his mouth and felt some discomfort in his left side.

But this discomfort increased and, though not exactly painful, grew into a sense of pressure in his side accompanied by ill humor. And his irritability became worse and worse and began to mar the agreeable, easy, and correct life that had established itself in the Golovin family. Quarrels between husband and wife became more and more frequent, and soon the ease and amenity disappeared and even the decorum was barely maintained. Scenes again became frequent, and very few of those islets remained on which husband and wife could meet without an explosion. Praskovya Fëdorovna now had good reason to say that her husband's temper was trying. With characteristic exaggeration she said he had always had a dreadful temper, and that it had needed all her good nature to put up with it for twenty years. It was true that now the quarrels were started by him. His bursts of temper always came just before dinner, often just as he began to eat his soup. Sometimes he noticed that a plate or dish was chipped, or the food was not right, or his son put his elbow on the table, or his daughter's hair was not done as he liked it, and for all this he blamed Praskovya Fëdorovna. At first she retorted and said disagreeable things to him, but once or twice he fell into such a rage at the beginning of dinner that she realized it was due to some physical derangement brought on by taking food, and so she restrained herself and did not answer, but only hurried to get the dinner over. She regarded this self-restraint as highly praiseworthy. Having come to the conclusion that her husband had a dreadful temper and made her life miserable, she began to feel sorry for herself, and the more she pitied herself the more she hated her husband. She began to wish he would die; yet she did not want him to die because then his salary would cease. And this irritated her against him still more. She considered herself dreadfully unhappy just because not even his death could save her, and though she concealed her exasperation, that hidden exasperation of hers increased his irritation also.

After one scene in which Ivan Ilych had been particularly unfair and after which he had said in explanation that he certainly was irritable but that it was due to his not being well, she said that if he was ill it should be attended to, and insisted on his going to see a celebrated doctor.

He went. Everything took place as he had expected and as it always does. There was the usual waiting and the important air assumed by the doctor, with which he was so familiar (resembling that which he himself assumed in court), and the sounding and listening, and the questions which called for answers that were foregone conclusions and were evidently unnecessary, and the look of importance which implied that "if only you put yourself in our hands we will arrange everything — we know indubitably how it has to be done, always in the same way for everybody alike." It was all just as it was in the law courts. The doctor put on just the same air towards him as he himself put on towards an accused person.

The doctor said that so-and-so indicated that there was so-and-so inside the patient, but if the investigation of so-and-so did not confirm this, then he must assume that and that. If he assumed that and that, then . . . and so on. To Ivan Ilych only one question was important: was his case serious or not? But the doctor ignored that inappropriate question. From his point of view it was not the one under consideration, the real question was to decide between a floating kidney, chronic catarrh, or appendicitis. It was not a question of Ivan Ilych's life or death, but one between a floating kidney and appendicitis. And that question the doctor solved brilliantly, as it seemed to Ivan Ilych, in favor of the appendix, with the reservation that should an examination of the urine give fresh indications the matter would be reconsidered. All this was just what Ivan Ilych had himself brilliantly accomplished a thousand times in dealing with men on trial. The doctor summed up just as brilliantly, looking over his spectacles triumphantly and even gaily at the accused. From the doctor's summing up Ivan Ilych concluded that things were bad, but that for the doctor, and perhaps for everybody else, it was a matter of indifference, though for him it was bad. And this conclusion struck him painfully, arousing in him a great feeling of pity for himself and of bitterness towards the doctor's indifference to a matter of such importance.

He said nothing of this, but rose, placed the doctor's fee on the table, and remarked with a sigh: "We sick people probably often put inappropriate questions. But tell me, in general, is this complaint dangerous, or not? . . ."

The doctor looked at him sternly over his spectacles with one eye, as if to say: "Prisoner, if you will not keep to the questions put to you, I shall be obliged to have you removed from the court."

"I have already told you what I consider necessary and proper. The analysis may show something more." And the doctor bowed.

Ivan Ilych went out slowly, seated himself disconsolately in his sledge, and drove home. All the way home he was going over what the doctor had said, trying to translate those complicated, obscure, scientific phrases into plain language and find in them an answer to the question: "Is my condition bad? Is it very bad? Or is there as yet nothing much wrong?" And it seemed to him that the meaning of what the doctor had said was that it was very bad. Everything in the streets seemed depressing. The cabmen, the houses, the passers-by, and the shops, were dismal. His ache, this dull gnawing ache that never ceased for a moment, seemed to have acquired a new and more serious significance from the doctor's dubious remarks. Ivan Ilych now watched it with a new and oppressive feeling.

He reached home and began to tell his wife about it. She listened, but in the middle of his account his daughter came in with her hat on, ready to go out with her mother. She sat down reluctantly to listen to this tedious story, but could not stand it long, and her mother too did not hear him to the end.

"Well, I am very glad," she said. "Mind now to take your medicine regularly. Give me the prescription and I'll send Gerasim to the chemist's." And she went to get ready to go out.

While she was in the room Ivan Ilych had hardly taken time to breathe, but he sighed deeply when she left it.

"Well," he thought, "perhaps it isn't so bad after all."

He began taking his medicine and following the doctor's directions, which had been altered after the examination of the urine. But then it happened that there was a contradiction between the indications drawn from the examination of the urine and the symptoms that showed themselves. It turned out that what was happening differed from what the doctor had told him, and that he had either forgotten, or blundered, or hidden something from him. He could not, however, be blamed for that, and Ivan Ilych still obeyed his orders implicitly and at first derived some comfort from doing so.

From the time of his visit to the doctor, Ivan Ilych's chief occupation was the exact fulfilment of the doctor's instructions regarding hygiene and the taking of medicine, and the observation of his pain and his excretions. His chief interests came to be people's ailments and people's health. When sickness, deaths, or recoveries were mentioned in his presence, especially when the illness resembled his own, he listened with agitation which he tried to hide, asked questions, and applied what he heard to his own case.

The pain did not grow less, but Ivan Ilych made efforts to force himself to think that he was better. And he could do this so long as nothing agitated him. But as soon as he had any unpleasantness with his wife, any lack of success in his official work, or held bad cards at bridge, he was at once acutely sensible of his disease. He had formerly borne such mischances, hoping soon to adjust what was wrong, to master it and attain success, or make a grand slam. But now every mischance upset him and plunged him into despair. He would say to himself: "There now, just as I was beginning to get better and the medicine had begun to take effect, comes this accursed misfortune, or unpleasantness. . . ." And he was furious with the mishap, or with the people who were causing the unpleasantness and killing him, for he felt that this fury was killing him but could not restrain it. One would have thought that it should have been clear to him that this exasperation with circumstances and people aggravated his illness, and that he ought therefore to ignore unpleasant occurrences. But he drew the very opposite conclusion: he said that he needed peace, and he watched for everything that might disturb it and became irritable at the slightest infringement of it. His condition was rendered worse by the fact that he read medical books and consulted doctors. The progress of his disease was so gradual that he could deceive himself when comparing one day with another — the difference was so slight. But when he consulted the doctors it seemed to him that he was getting worse, and even very rapidly. Yet despite this he was continually consulting them.

That month he went to see another celebrity, who told him almost the same as the first had done but put his questions rather differently, and the interview with this celebrity only increased Ivan Ilych's doubts and fears. A friend of a friend of his, a very good doctor, diagnosed his illness again quite differently from the others, and though he predicted recovery, his questions and suppositions bewildered Ivan Ilych still more and increased his doubts. A homoeopathist diagnosed the disease in yet another way, and prescribed medicine which Ivan Ilych took secretly for a week. But after a week, not feeling any improvement and having lost confidence both in the former doctor's treatment and in this one's, he became still more despondent. One day a lady acquaintance mentioned a cure effected by a wonder-working icon. Ivan Ilych caught himself listening attentively and beginning to believe that it had occurred. This incident alarmed him. "Has my mind really weakened to such an extent?" he asked himself. "Nonsense! It's all rubbish. I mustn't give way to nervous fears but having chosen a doctor must keep strictly to his treatment. That is what I will do. Now it's all settled. I won't think about it, but will follow the treatment seriously till summer, and then we shall see. From now there must be no more of this wavering!" This was easy to say but impossible to carry out. The pain in his side oppressed him and seemed to grow worse and more incessant, while the taste in his mouth grew stranger and stranger. It seemed to him that his breath had a disgusting smell, and he was conscious of a loss of appetite and strength. There was no deceiving himself: something terrible, new, and more important than anything before in his life, was taking place within him of which he alone was aware. Those about him did not understand or would not understand it, but thought everything in the world was going on as usual. That tormented Ivan Ilych more than anything. He saw that his household, especially his wife and daughter who were in a perfect whirl of visiting, did not understand anything of it and were annoyed that he was so depressed and so exacting, as if he were to blame for it. Though they tried to disguise it he saw that he was an obstacle in their path, and that his wife had adopted a definite line in regard to his illness and kept to it regardless of anything he said or did. Her attitude was this: "You know," she would say to her friends, "Ivan Ilych can't do as other people do, and keep to the treatment prescribed for him. One day he'll take his drops and keep strictly to his diet and go to bed in good time, but the next day unless I watch him he'll suddenly forget his medicine, eat sturgeon — which is forbidden — and sit up playing cards till one o'clock in the morning."

"Oh, come, when was that?" Ivan Ilych would ask in vexation. "Only once at Peter Ivanovich's."

"And yesterday with Shebek."

"Well, even if I hadn't stayed up, this pain would have kept me awake."

"Be that as it may you'll never get well like that, but will always make us wretched."

Praskovya Fëdorovna's attitude to Ivan Ilych's illness, as she expressed it both to others and to him, was that it was his own fault and was another of the annoyances he caused her. Ivan Ilych felt that this opinion escaped her involuntarily — but that did not make it easier for him.

At the law courts too, Ivan Ilych noticed, or thought he noticed, a strange attitude towards himself. It sometimes seemed to him that people were watching him inquisitively as a man whose place might soon be vacant. Then again, his friends would suddenly begin to chaff him in a friendly way about his low spirits, as if the awful, horrible, and unheard-of thing that was going on within him, incessantly gnawing at him and irresistibly drawing him away, was a very agreeable subject for jests. Schwartz in particular irritated him by his jocularity, vivacity, and *savior-faire*, which reminded him of what he himself had been ten years ago.

Friends came to make up a set and they sat down to cards. They dealt, bending the new cards to soften them, and he sorted the diamonds in his hand and found he had seven. His partner said "No trumps" and supported him with two diamonds. What more could be wished for? It ought to be jolly and lively. They would make a grand slam. But suddenly Ivan Ilych was conscious of that gnawing pain, that taste in his mouth, and it seemed ridiculous that in such circumstances he should be pleased to make a grand slam.

He looked at his partner Mikhail Mikhaylovich, who rapped the table with his strong hand and instead of snatching up the tricks pushed the cards courteously and indulgently towards Ivan Ilych that he might have the pleasure of gathering them up without the trouble of stretching out his hand for them. "Does he think I am too weak to stretch out my arm?" thought Ivan Ilych, and forgetting what he was doing he over-trumped his partner, missing the grand slam by three tricks. And what was most awful of all was that he saw how upset Mikhail Mikhaylovich was about it but did not himself care. And it was dreadful to realize why he did not care.

They all saw that he was suffering, and said: "We can stop if you are tired. Take a rest." Lie down? No, he was not at all tired, and he finished the rubber. All were gloomy and silent. Ivan Ilych felt that he had diffused this gloom over them and could not dispel it. They had supper and went away, and Ivan Ilych was left alone with the consciousness that his life was poisoned and was poisoning the lives of others, and that this poison did not weaken but penetrated more and more deeply into his whole being.

With this consciousness, and with physical pain besides the terror, he must go to bed, often to lie awake the greater part of the night. Next morning he had to get up again, dress, go to the law courts, speak, and write; or if he did not go out, spend at home those twenty-four hours a day each of which was a torture. And he had to live thus all alone on the brink of an abyss, with no one who understood or pitied him.

V

So one month passed and then another. Just before the New Year his brother-in-law came to town and stayed at their house. Ivan Ilych was at the law courts and Praskovya Fëdorovna had gone shopping. When Ivan Ilych came home and entered his study he found his brother-in-law there — a healthy, florid man — unpacking his portmanteau himself. He raised his head on hearing Ivan Ilych's footsteps and looked up at him for a moment without a word. That stare told Ivan Ilych everything. His brother-in-law opened his mouth to utter an exclamation of surprise but checked himself, and that action confirmed it all.

"I have changed, eh?"

"Yes, there is a change."

And after that, try as he would to get his brother-in-law to return to the subject of his looks, the latter would say nothing about it. Praskovya Fëdorovna came home and her brother went out to her. Ivan Ilych locked the door and began to examine himself in the glass, first full face, then in profile. He took up a portrait of himself taken with his wife, and compared it with what he saw in the glass. The change in him was immense. Then he bared his arms to the elbow, looked at them, drew the sleeves down again, sat down on an ottoman, and grew blacker than night.

"No, no, this won't do!" he said to himself, and jumped up, went to the table, took up some law papers and began to read them, but could not continue. He unlocked the door and went into the reception-room. The door leading to the drawing-room was shut. He approached it on tiptoe and listened.

"No, you are exaggerating!" Praskovya Fëdorovna was saying.

"Exaggerating! Don't you see it? Why, he's a dead man! Look at his eyes—there's no light in them. But what is it that is wrong with him?"

"No one knows. Nikolaevich said something, but I don't know what. And Leshchetitsky[11] said quite the contrary. . . ."

---

[11] two doctors, the latter a celebrated specialist. [Translators' note]

Ivan Ilych walked away, went to his own room, lay down, and began musing: "The kidney, a floating kidney." He recalled all the doctors had told him of how it detached itself and swayed about. And by an effort of imagination he tried to catch that kidney and arrest it and support it. So little was needed for this, it seemed to him. "No, I'll go to see Peter Ivanovich again." He rang, ordered the carriage, and got ready to go.

"Where are you going, Jean?" asked his wife, with a specially sad and exceptionally kind look.

This exceptionally kind look irritated him. He looked morosely at her. "I must go to see Peter Ivanovich."[12]

He went to see Peter Ivanovich, and together they went to see his friend, the doctor. He was in, and Ivan Ilych had a long talk with him.

Reviewing the anatomical and physiological details of what in the doctor's opinion was going on inside him, he understood it all.

There was something, a small thing, in the vermiform appendix. It might all come right. Only stimulate the energy of one organ and check the activity of another, then absorption would take place and everything would come right. He got home rather late for dinner, ate his dinner, and conversed cheerfully, but could not for a long time bring himself to go back to work in his room. At last, however, he went to his study and did what was necessary, but the consciousness that he had put something aside — an important, intimate matter which he would revert to when his work was done — never left him. When he had finished his work he remembered that this intimate matter was the thought of his vermiform appendix. But he did not give himself up to it, and went to the drawing-room for tea. There were callers there, including the examining magistrate who was a desirable match for his daughter, and they were conversing, playing the piano, and singing. Ivan Ilych, as Praskovya Fëdorovna remarked, spent that evening more cheerfully than usual, but he never for a moment forgot that he had postponed the important matter of the appendix. At eleven o'clock he said good-night and went to his bedroom. Since his illness he had slept alone in a small room next to his study. He undressed and took up a novel by Zola,[13] but instead of reading it he fell into thought, and in his imagination that desired improvement in the vermiform appendix occurred. There were the absorption and evacuation and the re-establishment of normal activity. "Yes, that's it!" he said to himself. "One need only assist nature, that's all." He remembered his medicine, rose, took it, and lay down on his back watching for the beneficent action of the medicine and for it to lessen the pain. "I need only take it regularly and avoid all injurious influences. I am already feeling better, much better." He began touching his side: it was not painful to the touch. "There, I really don't feel it. It's much better al-

---

[12] That was the friend whose friend was a doctor. [Translators' note]
[13] Émile Zola (1840–1902), French novelist.

ready." He put out the light and turned on his side. . . . "The appendix is getting better, absorption is occurring." Suddenly he felt the old, familiar, dull, gnawing pain, stubborn and serious. There was the same familiar loathsome taste in his mouth. His heart sank and he felt dazed. "My God! My God!" he muttered. "Again, again! and it will never cease." And suddenly the matter presented itself in a quite different aspect. "Vermiform appendix! Kidney!" he said to himself. "It's not a question of appendix or kidney, but of life and . . . death. Yes, life was there and now it is going, going and I cannot stop it. Yes. Why deceive myself? Isn't it obvious to everyone but me that I'm dying, and that it's only a question of weeks, days . . . it may happen this moment. There was light and now there is darkness. I was here and now I'm going there! Where?" A chill came over him, his breathing ceased, and he felt only the throbbing of his heart.

"When I am not, what will there be? There will be nothing. Then where shall I be when I am no more? Can this be dying? No, I don't want to!" He jumped up and tried to light the candle, felt for it with trembling hands, dropped candle and candlestick on the floor, and fell back on his pillow.

"What's the use? It makes no difference," he said to himself, staring with wide-open eyes into the darkness. "Death. Yes, death. And none of them know or wish to know it, and they have no pity for me. Now they are playing." (He heard through the door the distant sound of a song and its accompaniment.) "It's all the same to them, but they will die too! Fools! I first, and they later, but it will be the same for them. And now they are merry . . . the beasts!"

Anger choked him and he was agonizingly, unbearably miserable. "It is impossible that all men have been doomed to suffer this awful horror!" He raised himself.

"Something must be wrong. I must calm myself — must think it all over from the beginning." And he again began thinking. "Yes, the beginning of my illness: I knocked my side, but I was still quite well that day and the next. It hurt a little, then rather more. I saw the doctors, then followed despondency and anguish, more doctors, and I drew nearer to the abyss. My strength grew less and I kept coming nearer and nearer, and now I have wasted away and there is no light in my eyes. I think of the appendix — but this is death! I think of mending the appendix, and all the while here is death! Can it really be death?" Again terror seized him and he gasped for breath. He leant down and began feeling for the matches, pressing with his elbow on the stand beside the bed. It was in his way and hurt him, he grew furious with it, pressed on it still harder, and upset it. Breathless and in despair he fell on his back, expecting death to come immediately.

Meanwhile the visitors were leaving. Praskovya Fëdorovna was seeing them off. She heard something fall and came in.

"What has happened?"

"Nothing. I knocked it over accidentally."

She went out and returned with a candle. He lay there panting heavily, like a man who has run a thousand yards, and stared upwards at her with a fixed look.

"What is it, Jean?"

"No . . . no . . . thing. I upset it." ("Why speak of it? She won't understand," he thought.)

And in truth she did not understand. She picked up the stand, lit his candle, and hurried away to see another visitor off. When she came back he still lay on his back, looking upwards.

"What is it? Do you feel worse?"

"Yes."

She shook her head and sat down.

"Do you know, Jean, I think we must ask Leshchetitsky to come and see you here."

This meant calling in the famous specialist, regardless of expense. He smiled malignantly and said "No." She remained a little longer and then went up to him and kissed his forehead.

While she was kissing him he hated her from the bottom of his soul and with difficulty refrained from pushing her away.

"Good-night. Please God you'll sleep."

"Yes."

VI

Ivan Ilych saw that he was dying, and he was in continual despair.

In the depth of his heart he knew he was dying, but not only was he not accustomed to the thought, he simply did not and could not grasp it.

The syllogism he had learnt from Kiezewetter's Logic:[14] "Caius is a man, men are mortal, therefore Caius is mortal," had always seemed to him correct as applied to Caius, but certainly not as applied to himself. That Caius — man in the abstract — was mortal, was perfectly correct, but he was not Caius, not an abstract man, but a creature quite, quite separate from all others. He had been little Vanya, with a mama and a papa, with Mitya and Volodya, with the toys, a ˜oachman and a nurse, afterwards with Katenka and with all the joys, griefs, and delights of childhood, boyhood, and youth. What did Caius know of the smell of that striped leather ball Vanya had been so fond of? Had Caius kissed his mother's hand like that, and did the silk of her dress rustle so for Caius? Had he rioted like that at school when the pastry was bad? Had Caius been in love like that? Could Caius preside at a session as he did? "Caius really was mortal, and it was right for him to die; but for me, little Vanya, Ivan Ilych, with all my

---

[14] Klaus Kiezewetter (1766–1819), *The Outline of Logic According to Kantian Principles,* a popular text in Russia, based on the teachings of German philosopher Immanuel Kant (1722–1804).

thoughts and emotions, it's altogether a different matter. It cannot be that I ought to die. That would be too terrible."

Such was his feeling.

"If I had to die like Caius I should have known it was so. An inner voice would have told me so, but there was nothing of the sort in me and I and all my friends felt that our case was quite different from that of Caius. And now here it is!" he said to himself. "It can't be. It's impossible! But here it is. How is this? How is one to understand it?"

He could not understand it, and tried to drive this false, incorrect, morbid thought away and to replace it by other proper and healthy thoughts. But that thought, and not the thought only but the reality itself, seemed to come and confront him.

And to replace that thought he called up a succession of others, hoping to find in them some support. He tried to get back into the former current of thoughts that had once screened the thought of death from him. But strange to say, all that formerly shut off, hidden, and destroyed, his consciousness of death, no longer had that effect. Ivan Ilych now spent most of his time in attempting to re-establish that old current. He would say to himself: "I will take up my duties again — after all I used to live by them." And banishing all doubts he would go to the law courts, enter into conversation with his colleagues, and sit carelessly as was his wont, scanning the crowd with a thoughtful look and leaning both his emaciated arms on the arms of his oak chair; bending over as usual to a colleague and drawing his papers nearer he would interchange whispers with him, and then suddenly raising his eyes and sitting erect would pronounce certain words and open the proceedings. But suddenly in the midst of those proceedings the pain in his side, regardless of the stage the proceedings had reached, would begin its own gnawing work. Ivan Ilych would turn his attention to it and try to drive the thought of it away, but without success. *It* would come and stand before him and look at him, and he would be petrified and the light would die out of his eyes, and he would again begin asking himself whether *It* alone was true. And his colleagues and subordinates would see with surprise and distress that he, the brilliant and subtle judge, was becoming confused and making mistakes. He would shake himself, try to pull himself together, manage somehow to bring the sitting to a close, and return home with the sorrowful consciousness that his judicial labors could not as formerly hide from him what he wanted them to hide, and could not deliver him from *It*. And what was worst of all was that *It* drew his attention to itself not in order to make him take some action but only that he should look at *It*, look it straight in the face: look at it and without doing anything, suffer inexpressibly.

And to save himself from this condition Ivan Ilych looked for consolations — new screens — and new screens were found and for a while seemed to save him, but then they immediately fell to pieces or rather became transparent, as if *It* penetrated them and nothing could veil *It*.

In these latter days he would go into the drawing-room he had arranged — that drawing-room where he had fallen and for the sake of which (how bitterly ridiculous it seemed) he had sacrificed his life — for he knew that his illness originated with that knock. He would enter and see that something had scratched the polished table. He would look for the cause of this and find that it was the bronze ornamentation of an album, that had got bent. He would take up the expensive album which he had lovingly arranged, and feel vexed with his daughter and her friends for their untidiness — for the album was torn here and there and some of the photographs turned upside down. He would put it carefully in order and bend the ornamentation back into position. Then it would occur to him to place all those things in another corner of the room, near the plants. He could call the footman, but his daughter or wife would come to help him. They would not agree, and his wife would contradict him, and he would dispute and grow angry. But that was all right, for then he did not think about *It*. *It* was invisible.

But then, when he was moving something himself, his wife would say: "Let the servants do it. You will hurt yourself again." And suddenly *It* would flash through the screen and he would see it. It was just a flash, and he hoped it would disappear, but he would involuntarily pay attention to his side. "It sits there as before, gnawing just the same!" And he could no longer forget *It*, but could distinctly see it looking at him from behind the flowers. "What is it all for?"

"It really is so! I lost my life over that curtain as I might have done when storming a fort. Is that possible? How terrible and how stupid. It can't be true! It can't, but it is."

He would go to his study, lie down, and again be alone with *It*: face to face with *It*. And nothing could be done with *It* except to look at it and shudder.

VII

How it happened it is impossible to say because it came about step by step, unnoticed, but in the third month of Ivan Ilych's illness, his wife, his daughter, his son, his acquaintances, the doctors, the servants, and above all he himself, were aware that the whole interest he had for other people was whether he would soon vacate his place, and at last release the living from the discomfort caused by his presence and be himself released from his sufferings.

He slept less and less. He was given opium and hypodermic injections of morphine, but this did not relieve him. The dull depression he experienced in a somnolent condition at first gave him a little relief, but only as something new, afterwards it became as distressing as the pain itself or even more so.

Special foods were prepared for him by the doctors' orders, but all those foods became increasingly distasteful and disgusting to him.

For his excretions also special arrangements had to be made, and this was a torment to him every time — a torment from the uncleanliness, the unseemliness, and the smell, and from knowing that another person had to take part in it.

But just through this most unpleasant matter, Ivan Ilych obtained comfort. Gerasim, the butler's young assistant, always came in to carry the things out. Gerasim was a clean, fresh peasant lad, grown stout on town food and always cheerful and bright. At first the sight of him, in his clean Russian peasant costume, engaged on that disgusting task embarrassed Ivan Ilych.

Once when he got up from the commode too weak to draw up his trousers, he dropped into a soft armchair and looked with horror at his bare, enfeebled thighs with the muscles so sharply marked on them.

Gerasim with a firm light tread, his heavy boots emitting a pleasant smell of tar and fresh winter air, came in wearing a clean Hessian apron, the sleeves of his print shirt tucked up over his strong bare young arms; and refraining from looking at his sick master out of consideration for his feelings, and restraining the joy of life that beamed from his face, he went up to the commode.

"Gerasim!" said Ivan Ilych in a weak voice.

Gerasim started, evidently afraid he might have committed some blunder, and with a rapid movement turned his fresh, kind, simple young face which just showed the first downy signs of a beard.

"Yes, sir?"

"That must be very unpleasant for you. You must forgive me. I am helpless."

"Oh, why, sir," and Gerasim's eyes beamed and he showed his glistening white teeth, "what's a little trouble? It's a case of illness with you, sir."

And his deft strong hands did their accustomed task, and he went out of the room stepping lightly. Five minutes later he as lightly returned.

Ivan Ilych was still sitting in the same position in the armchair.

"Gerasim," he said when the latter had replaced the freshly-washed utensil. "Please come here and help me." Gerasim went up to him. "Lift me up. It is hard for me to get up, and I have sent Dmitri away."

Gerasim went up to him, grasped his master with his strong arms deftly but gently, in the same way that he stepped — lifted him, supported him with one hand, and with the other drew up his trousers and would have set him down again, but Ivan Ilych asked to be led to the sofa. Gerasim, without an effort and without apparent pressure, led him, almost lifting him, to the sofa and placed him on it.

"Thank you. How easily and well you do it all!"

Gerasim smiled again and turned to leave the room. But Ivan Ilych felt his presence such a comfort that he did not want to let him go.

"One thing more, please move up that chair. No, the other one — under my feet. It is easier for me when my feet are raised."

Gerasim brought the chair, set it down gently in place, and raised Ivan Ilych's legs on to it. It seemed to Ivan Ilych that he felt better while Gerasim was holding up his legs.

"It's better when my legs are higher," he said. "Place that cushion under them."

Gerasim did so. He again lifted the legs and placed them, and again Ivan Ilych felt better while Gerasim held his legs. When he set them down Ivan Ilych fancied he felt worse.

"Gerasim," he said. "Are you busy now?"

"Not at all, sir," said Gerasim, who had learnt from the townsfolk how to speak to gentlefolk.

"What have you still to do?"

"What have I to do? I've done everything except chopping the logs for tomorrow."

"Then hold my legs up a bit higher, can you?"

"Of course I can. Why not?" And Gerasim raised his master's legs higher and Ivan Ilych thought that in that position he did not feel any pain at all.

"And how about the logs?"

"Don't trouble about that, sir. There's plenty of time."

Ivan Ilych told Gerasim to sit down and hold his legs, and began to talk to him. And strange to say it seemed to him that he felt better while Gerasim held his legs up.

After that Ivan Ilych would sometimes call Gerasim and get him to hold his legs on his shoulders, and he liked talking to him. Gerasim did it all easily, willingly, simply, and with a good nature that touched Ivan Ilych. Health, strength, and vitality in other people were offensive to him, but Gerasim's strength and vitality did not mortify but soothed him.

What tormented Ivan Ilych most was the deception, the lie, which for some reason they all accepted, that he was not dying but was simply ill, and that he only need keep quiet and undergo a treatment and then something very good would result. He however knew that do what they would nothing would come of it, only still more agonizing suffering and death. This deception tortured him — their not wishing to admit what they all knew and what he knew, but wanting to lie to him concerning his terrible condition, and wishing and forcing him to participate in that lie. Those lies — lies enacted over him on the eve of his death and destined to degrade this awful, solemn act to the level of their visitings, their curtains, their sturgeon for dinner — were a terrible agony for Ivan Ilych. And strangely enough, many times when they were going through their antics over him he had been within a hairbreadth of calling out to them: "Stop lying! You know and I know that I am dying. Then at least stop lying about it!" But he had never had the spirit to do it. The awful, terrible act of his dying was, he could see, reduced by those about him to the level of a casual, unpleasant, and almost indecorous incident (as if someone entered a drawing-room diffusing an unpleasant odor) and this was done by that very decorum which he had served all his life long. He saw that no one felt for him, because no one even wished to grasp his position. Only Gerasim recognized it and pitied him. And so Ivan Ilych felt at ease only with him. He felt comforted when Gerasim supported his legs (sometimes all night long) and refused to go to bed, saying: "Don't you worry, Ivan Ilych. I'll get sleep enough later on," or when he suddenly became familiar and exclaimed: "If you weren't sick it would be another matter, but as it is, why should I grudge a little trouble?" Gerasim alone did not lie; everything showed that he alone understood the facts of the case and did not consider it necessary to disguise them, but simply felt sorry for his emaciated and enfeebled master. Once when Ivan Ilych was sending him away he even said straight out: "We shall all of us die, so why should I grudge a little trouble?" — expressing the fact that he did not think his work burdensome, because he was doing it for a dying man and hoped someone would do the same for him when his time came.

Apart from this lying, or because of it, what most tormented Ivan Ilych was that no one pitied him as he wished to be pitied. At certain moments after prolonged suffering he wished most of all (though he would have been ashamed to confess it) for someone to pity him as a sick child is pitied. He longed to be petted and comforted. He knew he was an important functionary, that he had a beard turning grey, and that therefore what he longed for was impossible, but still he longed for it. And in Gerasim's attitude towards him there was something akin to what he wished for, and so that attitude comforted him. Ivan Ilych wanted to weep, wanted to be petted and cried over, and then his colleague Shebek would come, and instead of weeping and being petted, Ivan Ilych would assume a serious, severe, and profound air, and by force of habit would express his opinion on a decision of the Court of Cassation and would stubbornly insist on that view. This falsity around him and within him did more than anything else to poison his last days.

VIII

It was morning. He knew it was morning because Gerasim had gone, and Peter the footman had come and put out the candles, drawn back one of the curtains, and begun quietly to tidy up. Whether it was morning or evening, Friday or Sunday, made no difference, it was all just the same: the gnawing, unmitigated, agonizing pain, never ceasing for an instant, the consciousness of life inexorably waning but not yet extinguished, the approach of that ever dreaded and hateful Death which was the only reality, and always the same falsity. What were days, weeks, hours, in such a case?

"Will you have some tea, sir?"

"He wants things to be regular, and wishes the gentlefolk to drink tea in the morning," thought Ivan Ilych, and only said "No."

"Wouldn't you like to move onto the sofa, sir?"

"He wants to tidy up the room, and I'm in the way. I am uncleanliness and disorder," he thought, and said only:

"No, leave me alone."

The man went on bustling about. Ivan Ilych stretched out his hand. Peter came up, ready to help.

"What is it, sir?"

"My watch."

Peter took the watch which was close at hand and gave it to his master.

"Half-past eight. Are they up?"

"No, sir, except Vasily Ivanich" (the son) "who has gone to school. Praskovya Fëdorovna ordered me to wake her if you asked for her. Shall I do so?"

"No, there's no need to." "Perhaps I'd better have some tea," he thought, and added aloud: "Yes, bring me some tea."

Peter went to the door, but Ivan Ilych dreaded being left alone. "How can I keep him here? Oh yes, my medicine." "Peter, give me my medicine." "Why not? Perhaps it may still do me some good." He took a spoonful and swallowed it. "No, it won't help. It's all tomfoolery, all deception," he decided as soon as he became aware of the familiar, sickly, hopeless taste. "No, I can't believe in it any longer. But the pain, why this pain? If it would only cease just for a moment!" And he moaned. Peter turned towards him. "It's all right. Go and fetch me some tea."

Peter went out. Left alone Ivan Ilych groaned not so much with pain, terrible though that was, as from mental anguish. Always and for ever the same, always these endless days and nights. If only it would come quicker! If only *what* would come quicker? Death, darkness? . . . No, no! Anything rather than death!

When Peter returned with the tea on a tray, Ivan Ilych stared at him for a time in perplexity, not realizing who and what he was. Peter was disconcerted by that look and his embarrassment brought Ivan Ilych to himself.

"Oh, tea! All right, put it down. Only help me to wash and put on a clean shirt."

And Ivan Ilych began to wash. With pauses for rest, he washed his hands and then his face, cleaned his teeth, brushed his hair, and looked in the glass. He was terrified by what he saw, especially by the limp way in which his hair clung to his pallid forehead.

While his shirt was being changed he knew that he would be still more frightened at the sight of his body, so he avoided looking at it. Finally he was ready. He drew on a dressing-gown, wrapped himself in a plaid, and sat down in the armchair to take his tea. For a moment he felt refreshed, but as soon as he began to drink the tea he was again aware of the same taste, and the pain also returned. He finished it with an effort, and then lay down stretching out his legs, and dismissed Peter.

Always the same. Now a spark of hope flashes up, then a sea of despair rages, and always pain; always pain, always despair, and always the same. When alone he had a dreadful and distressing desire to call someone, but he knew beforehand that with others present it would be still worse. "Another dose of morphine — to lose consciousness. I will tell him, the doctor, that he must think of something else. It's impossible, impossible, to go on like this."

An hour and another pass like that. But now there is a ring at the door bell. Perhaps it's the doctor? It is. He comes in fresh, hearty, plump, and cheerful, with that look on his face that seems to say: "There now, you're in a panic about something, but we'll arrange it all for you directly!" The doctor knows this expression is out of place here, but he has put it on once for all and can't take it off — like a man who has put on a frock-coat in the morning to pay a round of calls.

The doctor rubs his hands vigorously and reassuringly.

"Brr! How cold it is! There's such a sharp frost; just let me warm myself!" he says, as if it were only a matter of waiting till he was warm, and then he would put everything right.

"Well now, how are you?"

Ivan Ilych feels that the doctor would like to say: "Well, how are our affairs?" but that even he feels that this would not do, and says instead: "What sort of a night have you had?"

Ivan Ilych looks at him as much as to say: "Are you really never ashamed of lying?" But the doctor does not wish to understand this question, and Ivan Ilych says: "Just as terrible as ever. The pain never leaves me and never subsides. If only something. . . ."

"Yes, you sick people are always like that. . . . There, now I think I am warm enough. Even Praskovya Fëdorovna, who is so particular, could find no fault with my temperature. Well, now I can say good-morning," and the doctor presses his patient's hand.

Then, dropping his former playfulness, he begins with a most serious face to examine the patient, feeling his pulse and taking his temperature, and then begins the sounding and auscultation.

Ivan Ilych knows quite well and definitely that all this is nonsense and pure deception, but when the doctor, getting down on his knee, leans over him, putting his ear first higher then lower, and performs various gymnastic movements over him with a significant expression on his face, Ivan Ilych submits to it all as he used to submit to the speeches of the lawyers, though he knew very well that they were all lying and why they were lying.

The doctor, kneeling on the sofa, is still sounding him when Praskovya Fëdorovna's silk dress rustles at the door and she is heard scolding Peter for not having let her know of the doctor's arrival.

She comes in, kisses her husband, and at once proceeds to prove that she has been up a long time already, and only owing to a misunderstanding failed to be there when the doctor arrived.

Ivan Ilych looks at her, scans her all over, sets against her the whiteness and plumpness and cleanness of her hands and neck, the gloss of her hair, and the sparkle of her vivacious eyes. He hates her with his whole soul. And the thrill of hatred he feels for her makes him suffer from her touch.

Her attitude towards him and his disease is still the same. Just as the doctor had adopted a certain relation to his patient which he could not abandon, so had she formed one towards him — that he was not doing something he ought to do and was himself to blame, and that she reproached him lovingly for this — and she could not now change that attitude.

"You see he doesn't listen to me and doesn't take his medicine at the proper time. And above all he lies in a position that is no doubt bad for him — with his legs up."

She described how he made Gerasim hold his legs up.

The doctor smiled with a contemptuous affability that said: "What's to be done? These sick people do have foolish fancies of that kind, but we must forgive them."

When the examination was over the doctor looked at his watch, and then Praskovya Fëdorovna announced to Ivan Ilych that it was of course as he pleased, but she had sent today for a celebrated specialist who would examine him and have a consultation with Michael Danilovich (their regular doctor).

"Please don't raise any objections. I am doing this for my own sake," she said ironically, letting it be felt that she was doing it all for his sake and only said this to leave him no right to refuse. He remained silent, knitting his brows. He felt that he was so surrounded and involved in a mesh of falsity that it was hard to unravel anything.

Everything she did for him was entirely for her own sake, and she told him she was doing for herself what she actually was doing for herself, as if that was so incredible that he must understand the opposite.

At half-past eleven the celebrated specialist arrived. Again the sounding began and the significant conversations in his presence and in another room, about the kidneys and the appendix, and the questions and answers, with such an air of importance that again, instead of the real question of life and death which now alone confronted him, the question arose of the kidney and appendix which were not behaving as they ought to and would now be attacked by Michael Danilovich and the specialist and forced to amend their ways.

The celebrated specialist took leave of him with a serious though not hopeless look, and in reply to the timid question Ivan Ilych, with eyes glistening with fear and hope, put to him as to whether there was a chance of recovery, said that he could not vouch for it but there was a possibility. The look of hope with which Ivan Ilych watched the doctor out was so pathetic that Praskovya Fëdorovna, seeing it, even wept as she left the room to hand the doctor his fee.

The gleam of hope kindled by the doctor's encouragement did not last long. The same room, the same pictures, curtains, wallpaper, medicine bottles, were all there, and the same aching suffering body, and Ivan Ilych began to moan. They gave him a subcutaneous injection and he sank into oblivion.

It was twilight when he came to. They brought him his dinner and he swallowed some beef tea with difficulty, and then everything was the same again and night was coming on.

After dinner, at seven o'clock, Praskovya Fëdorovna came into the room in evening dress, her full bosom pushed up by her corset, and with traces of powder on her face. She had reminded him in the morning that they were going to the theater. Sarah Bernhardt was visiting the town and they had a box, which he had insisted on their taking. Now he had forgotten about it and her toilet offended him, but he concealed his vexation when he remembered that he had himself insisted on their securing a box and going because it would be an instructive and aesthetic pleasure for the children.

Praskovya Fëdorovna came in, self-satisfied but yet with a rather guilty air. She sat down and asked how he was, but, as he saw, only for the sake of asking and not in order to learn about it, knowing that there was nothing to learn — and then went on to what she really wanted to say: that she would not on any account have gone but that the box had been taken and Helen and their daughter were going, as well as Petrishchev (the examining magistrate, their daughter's fiancé) and that it was out of the question to let them go alone; but that she would have much preferred to sit with him for a while; and he must be sure to follow the doctor's orders while she was away.

"Oh, and Fëdor Petrovich" (the fiancé) "would like to come in. May he? And Lisa?"

"All right."

Their daughter came in in full evening dress, her fresh young flesh exposed (making a show of that very flesh which in his own case caused so much suffering), strong, healthy, evidently in love, and impatient with illness, suffering, and death, because they interfered with her happiness.

Fëdor Petrovich came in too, in evening dress, his hair curled *à la Capoul,*[15] a tight stiff collar round his long sinewy neck, an enormous white shirt-front and narrow black trousers tightly stretched over his strong thighs.

---

[15] An elaborate hair styling for men. Capoul was a famous French singer.

He had one white glove tightly drawn on, and was holding his opera hat in his hand.

Following him the schoolboy crept in unnoticed, in a new uniform, poor little fellow, and wearing gloves. Terribly dark shadows showed under his eyes, the meaning of which Ivan Ilych knew well.

His son had always seemed pathetic to him, and now it was dreadful to see the boy's frightened look of pity. It seemed to Ivan Ilych that Vasya was the only one besides Gerasim who understood and pitied him.

They all sat down and again asked how he was. A silence followed. Lisa asked her mother about the opera-glasses, and there was an altercation between mother and daughter as to who had taken them and where they had been put. This occasioned some unpleasantness.

Fëdor Petrovich inquired of Ivan Ilych whether he had ever seen Sarah Bernhardt. Ivan Ilych did not at first catch the question, but then replied: "No, have you seen her before?"

"Yes, in *Adrienne Lecouvreur*.[16]

Praskovya Fëdorovna mentioned some rôles in which Sarah Bernhardt was particularly good. Her daughter disagreed. Conversation sprang up as to the elegance and realism of her acting — the sort of conversation that is always repeated and is always the same.

In the midst of the conversation Fëdor Petrovich glanced at Ivan Ilych and became silent. The others also looked at him and grew silent. Ivan Ilych was staring with glittering eyes straight before him, evidently indignant with them. This had to be rectified, but it was impossible to do so. The silence had to be broken, but for a time no one dared to break it and they all became afraid that the conventional deception would suddenly become obvious and the truth become plain to all. Lisa was the first to pluck up courage and break that silence, but by trying to hide what everybody was feeling, she betrayed it.

"Well, if we are going it's time to start," she said, looking at her watch, a present from her father, and with a faint and significant smile at Fëdor Petrovich relating to something known only to them. She got up with a rustle of her dress.

They all rose, said good-night, and went away.

When they had gone it seemed to Ivan Ilych that he felt better; the falsity had gone with them. But the pain remained — that same pain and that same fear that made everything monotonously alike, nothing harder and nothing easier. Everything was worse.

Again minute followed minute and hour followed hour. Everything remained the same and there was no cessation. And the inevitable end of it all became more and more terrible.

"Yes, send Gerasim here," he replied to a question Peter asked.

---

[16] comedy by French playwrights Eugène Scribe and Ernest Legouvé.

IX

His wife returned late at night. She came in on tiptoe, but he heard her, opened his eyes, and made haste to close them again. She wished to send Gerasim away and to sit with him herself, but he opened his eyes and said: "No, go away."

"Are you in great pain?"

"Always the same."

"Take some opium."

He agreed and took some. She went away.

Till about three in the morning he was in a state of stupefied misery. It seemed to him that he and his pain were being thrust into a narrow, deep black sack, but though they were pushed further and further in they could not be pushed to the bottom. And this, terrible enough in itself, was accompanied by suffering. He was frightened yet wanted to fall through the sack, he struggled but yet co-operated. And suddenly he broke through, fell, and regained consciousness. Gerasim was sitting at the foot of the bed dozing quietly and patiently, while he himself lay with his emaciated stockinged legs resting on Gerasim's shoulders; the same shaded candle was there and the same unceasing pain.

"Go away, Gerasim," he whispered.

"It's all right, sir. I'll stay a while."

"No. Go away."

He removed his legs from Gerasim's shoulders, turned sideways onto his arm, and felt sorry for himself. He only waited till Gerasim had gone into the next room and then restrained himself no longer but wept like a child. He wept on account of his helplessness, his terrible loneliness, the cruelty of man, the cruelty of God, and the absence of God.

"Why hast Thou done all this? Why hast Thou brought me here? Why, why dost Thou torment me so terribly?"

He did not expect an answer and yet wept because there was no answer and could be none. The pain again grew more acute, but he did not stir and did not call. He said to himself: "Go on! Strike me! But what is it for? What have I done to Thee? What is it for?"

Then he grew quiet and not only ceased weeping but even held his breath and became all attention. It was as though he were listening not to an audible voice but to the voice of his soul, to the current of thoughts arising within him.

"What is it you want?" was the first clear conception capable of expression in words, that he heard.

"What do you want? What do you want?" he repeated to himself.

"What do I want? To live and not to suffer," he answered.

And again he listened with such concentrated attention that even his pain did not distract him.

"To live? How?" asked his inner voice.

"Why, to live as I used to — well and pleasantly."

"As you lived before, well and pleasantly?" the voice repeated.

And in imagination he began to recall the best moments of his pleasant life. But strange to say none of those best moments of his pleasant life now seemed at all what they had then seemed — none of them except the first recollections of childhood. There, in childhood, there had been something really pleasant with which it would be possible to live if it could return. But the child who had experienced that happiness existed no longer, it was like a reminiscence of somebody else.

As soon as the period began which had produced the present Ivan Ilych, all that had then seemed joys now melted before his sight and turned into something trivial and often nasty.

And the further he departed from childhood and the nearer he came to the present the more worthless and doubtful were the joys. This began with the School of Law. A little that was really good was still found there — there was light-heartedness, friendship, and hope. But in the upper classes there had already been fewer of such good moments. Then during the first years of his official career, when he was in the service of the Governor, some pleasant moments again occurred: they were the memories of love for a woman. Then all became confused and there was still less of what was good; later on again there was still less that was good, and the further he went the less there was. His marriage, a mere accident, then the disenchantment that followed it, his wife's bad breath and the sensuality and hypocrisy: then the deadly official life and those preoccupations about money, a year of it, and two, and ten, and twenty, and always the same thing. And the longer it lasted the more deadly it became. "It is as if I had been going downhill while I imagined I was going up. And that is really what it was. I was going up in public opinion, but to the same extent life was ebbing away from me. And now it is all done and there is only death."

"Then what does it mean? Why? It can't be that life is so senseless and horrible. But if it really has been so horrible and senseless, why must I die and die in agony? There is something wrong!"

"Maybe I did not live as I ought to have done," it suddenly occurred to him. "But how could that be, when I did everything properly?" he replied, and immediately dismissed from his mind this, the sole solution of all the riddles of life and death, as something quite impossible.

"Then what do you want now? To live? Live how? Live as you lived in the law courts when the usher proclaimed 'The judge is coming!' The judge is coming, the judge!" he repeated to himself. "Here he is, the judge. But I am not guilty!" he exclaimed angrily. "What is it for?" And he ceased crying, but turning his face to the wall continued to ponder on the same question: Why, and for what purpose, is there all this horror? But however much he pondered he found no answer. And whenever the thought occurred to him, as it often did, that it all resulted from his not having lived as he ought to have done, he at once recalled the correctness of his whole life and dismissed so strange an idea.

X

Another fortnight passed. Ivan Ilych now no longer left his sofa. He would not lie in bed but lay on the sofa, facing the wall nearly all the time. He suffered ever the same unceasing agonies and in his loneliness pondered always on the same insoluble question: "What is this? Can it be that it is Death?" And the inner voice answered: "Yes, it is Death."

"Why these sufferings?" And the voice answered, "For no reason — they just are so." Beyond and besides this there was nothing.

From the very beginning of his illness, ever since he had first been to see the doctor, Ivan Ilych's life had been divided between two contrary and alternating moods: now it was despair and the expectation of this uncomprehended and terrible death, and now hope and an intently interested observation of the functioning of his organs. Now before his eyes there was only a kidney or an intestine that temporarily evaded its duty, and now only that incomprehensible and dreadful death from which it was impossible to escape.

These two states of mind had alternated from the very beginning of his illness, but the further it progressed the more doubtful and fantastic became the conception of the kidney, and the more real the sense of impending death.

He had but to call to mind what he had been three months before and what he was now, to call to mind with what regularity he had been going downhill, for every possibility of hope to be shattered.

Latterly during that loneliness in which he found himself as he lay facing the back of the sofa, a loneliness in the midst of a populous town and surrounded by numerous acquaintances and relations but that yet could not have been more complete anywhere — either at the bottom of the sea or under the earth — during that terrible loneliness Ivan Ilych had lived only in memories of the past. Pictures of his past rose before him one after another. They always began with what was nearest in time and then went back to what was most remote — to his childhood — and rested there. If he thought of the stewed prunes that had been offered him that day, his mind went back to the raw shrivelled French plums of his childhood, their peculiar flavor and the flow of saliva when he sucked their stones, and along with the memory of that taste came a whole series of memories of those days: his nurse, his brother, and their toys. "No, I mustn't think of that. . . . It is too painful," Ivan Ilych said to himself, and brought himself back to the present — to the button on the back of the sofa and the creases in its morocco. "Morocco is expensive, but it does not wear well: there had been a quarrel about it. It was a different kind of quarrel and a different kind of morocco that time when we tore father's portfolio and were punished, and mama brought us some tarts. . . ." And again his thoughts dwelt on his childhood, and again it was painful and he tried to banish them and fix his mind on something else.

Then again together with that chain of memories another series passed through his mind — of how his illness had progressed and grown worse. There also the further back he looked the more life there had been. There had been more of what was good in life and more of life itself. The two merged together. "Just as the pain went on getting worse and worse, so my life grew worse and worse," he thought. "There is one bright spot there at the back, at the beginning of life, and afterwards all becomes blacker and blacker and proceeds more and more rapidly — in inverse ratio to the square of the distance from death," thought Ivan Ilych. And the example of a stone falling downwards with increasing velocity entered his mind. Life, a series of increasing sufferings, flies further and further towards its end — the most terrible suffering. "I am flying. . . ." He shuddered, shifted himself, and tried to resist, but was already aware that resistance was impossible, and again with eyes weary of gazing but unable to cease seeing what was before them, he stared at the back of the sofa and waited — awaiting that dreadful fall and shock and destruction.

"Resistance is impossible!" he said to himself. "If I could only understand what it is all for! But that too is impossible. An explanation would be possible if it could be said that I have not lived as I ought to. But it is impossible to say that," and he remembered all the legality, correctitude, and propriety of his life. "That at any rate can certainly not be admitted," he thought, and his lips smiled ironically as if someone could see that smile and be taken in by it. "There is no explanation! Agony, death. . . . What for?"

XI

Another two weeks went by in this way and during that fortnight an event occurred that Ivan Ilych and his wife had desired. Petrishchev formally proposed. It happened in the evening. The next day Praskovya Fëdorovna came into her husband's room considering how best to inform him of it, but that very night there had been a fresh change for the worse in his condition. She found him still lying on the sofa but in a different position. He lay on his back, groaning and staring fixedly straight in front of him.

She began to remind him of his medicines, but he turned his eyes towards her with such a look that she did not finish what she was saying; so great an animosity, to her in particular, did that look express.

"For Christ's sake let me die in peace!" he said.

She would have gone away, but just then their daughter came in and went up to say good morning. He looked at her as he had done at his wife, and in reply to her inquiry about his health said dryly that he would soon free them all of himself. They were both silent and after sitting with him for a while went away.

"Is it our fault?" Lisa said to her mother. "It's as if we were to blame! I am sorry for papa, but why should we be tortured?"

The doctor came at his usual time. Ivan Ilych answered "Yes" and "No," never taking his angry eyes from him, and at last said: "You know you can do nothing for me, so leave me alone."

"We can ease your sufferings."

"You can't even do that. Let me be."

The doctor went into the drawing-room and told Praskovya Fëdorovna that the case was very serious and that the only resource left was opium to allay her husband's sufferings, which must be terrible.

It was true, as the doctor said, that Ivan Ilych's physical sufferings were terrible, but worse than the physical sufferings were his mental sufferings, which were his chief torture.

His mental sufferings were due to the fact that that night, as he looked at Gerasim's sleepy, good-natured face with its prominent cheek-bones, the question suddenly occurred to him: "What if my whole life has really been wrong?"

It occurred to him that what had appeared perfectly impossible before, namely that he had not spent his life as he should have done, might after all be true. It occurred to him that his scarcely perceptible attempts to struggle against what was considered good by the most highly placed people, those scarcely noticeable impulses which he had immediately suppressed, might have been the real thing, and all the rest false. And his professional duties and the whole arrangement of his life and of his family, and all his social and official interests, might all have been false. He tried to defend all those things to himself and suddenly felt the weakness of what he was defending. There was nothing to defend.

"But if that is so," he said to himself, "and I am leaving this life with the consciousness that I have lost all that was given me and it is impossible to rectify it — what then?"

He lay on his back and began to pass his life in review in quite a new way. In the morning when he saw first his footman, then his wife, then his daughter, and then the doctor, their every word and movement confirmed to him the awful truth that had been revealed to him during the night. In them he saw himself — all that for which he had lived — and saw clearly that it was not real at all, but a terrible and huge deception which had hidden both life and death. This consciousness intensified his physical suffering tenfold. He groaned and tossed about, and pulled at his clothing which choked and stifled him. And he hated them on that account.

He was given a large dose of opium and became unconscious, but at noon his sufferings began again. He drove everybody away and tossed from side to side.

His wife came to him and said:

"Jean, my dear, do this for me. It can't do any harm and often helps. Healthy people often do it."

He opened his eyes wide.

"What? Take communion? Why? It's unnecessary! However. . . ."

She began to cry.

"Yes, do, my dear. I'll send for our priest. He is such a nice man."

"All right. Very well," he muttered.

When the priest came and heard his confession, Ivan Ilych was softened and seemed to feel a relief from his doubts and consequently from his sufferings, and for a moment there came a ray of hope. He again began to think of the vermiform appendix and the possibility of correcting it. He received the sacrament with tears in his eyes.

When they laid him down again afterwards he felt a moment's ease, and the hope that he might live awoke in him again. He began to think of the operation that had been suggested to him. "To live! I want to live!" he said to himself.

His wife came in to congratulate him after his communion, and when uttering the usual conventional words she added:

"You feel better, don't you?"

Without looking at her he said "Yes."

Her dress, her figure, the expression of her face, the tone of her voice, all revealed the same thing. "This is wrong, it is not as it should be. All you have lived for and still live for is falsehood and deception, hiding life and death from you." And as soon as he admitted that thought, his hatred and his agonizing physical suffering again sprang up, and with that suffering a consciousness of the unavoidable, approaching end. And to this was added a new sensation of grinding shooting pain and a feeling of suffocation.

The expression of his face when he uttered that "yes" was dreadful. Having uttered it, he looked her straight in the eyes, turned on his face with a rapidity extraordinary in his weak state and shouted:

"Go away! Go away and leave me alone!"

XII

From that moment the screaming began that continued for three days, and was so terrible that one could not hear it through two closed doors without horror. At the moment he answered his wife he realized that he was lost, that there was no return, that the end had come, the very end, and his doubts were still unsolved and remained doubts.

"Oh! Oh! Oh!" he cried in various intonations. He had begun by screaming "I won't!" and continued screaming on the letter O.

For three whole days, during which time did not exist for him, he struggled in that black sack into which he was being thrust by an invisible, resistless force. He struggled as a man condemned to death struggles in the hands of the executioner, knowing that he cannot save himself. And every moment he felt that despite all his efforts he was drawing nearer and nearer to what terrified him. He felt that his agony was due to his being thrust into that black hole and still more to his not being able to get right into it. He was hindered from getting into it by his conviction that his life had been a good one. That very justification of his life held him fast and prevented his moving forward, and it caused him most torment of all.

Suddenly some force struck him in the chest and side, making it still harder to breathe, and he fell through the hole and there at the bottom was a light. What had happened to him was like the sensation one sometimes experiences in a railway carriage when one thinks one is going backwards while one is really going forwards and suddenly becomes aware of the real direction.

"Yes, it was all not the right thing," he said to himself, "but that's no matter. It can be done. But what *is* the right thing?" he asked himself, and suddenly grew quiet.

This occurred at the end of the third day, two hours before his death. Just then his schoolboy son had crept softly in and gone up to the bedside. The dying man was still screaming desperately and waving his arms. His hand fell on the boy's head, and the boy caught it, pressed it to his lips, and began to cry.

At that very moment Ivan Ilych fell through and caught sight of the light, and it was revealed to him that though his life had not been what it should have been, this could still be rectified. He asked himself, "What *is* the right thing?" and grew still, listening. Then he felt that someone was kissing his hand. He opened his eyes, looked at his son, and felt sorry for him. His wife came up to him and he glanced at her. She was gazing at him open-mouthed, with undried tears on her nose and cheek and a despairing look on her face. He felt sorry for her too.

"Yes, I am making them wretched," he thought. "They are sorry, but it will be better for them when I die." He wished to say this but had not the strength to utter it. "Besides, why speak? I must act," he thought. With a look at his wife he indicated his son and said: "Take him away . . . sorry for him . . . sorry for you too. . . ." He tried to add, "forgive me," but said "forgo" and waved his hand, knowing that He whose understanding mattered would understand.

And suddenly it grew clear to him that what had been oppressing him and would not leave him was all dropping away at once from two sides, from ten sides, and from all sides. He was sorry for them, he must act so as not to hurt them: release them and free himself from these sufferings. "How good and how simple!" he thought. "And the pain?" he asked himself. "What has become of it? Where are you, pain?"

He turned his attention to it.

"Yes, here it is. Well, what of it? Let the pain be."

"And death . . . where is it?"

He sought his former accustomed fear of death and did not find it. "Where is it? What death?" There was no fear because there was no death.

In place of death there was light.

"So that's what it is!" he suddenly exclaimed aloud. "What joy!"

To him all this happened in a single instant, and the meaning of that instant did not change. For those present his agony continued for another two hours. Something rattled in his throat, his emaciated body twitched, then the gasping and rattle became less and less frequent.

"It is finished!" said someone near him.

He heard these words and repeated them in his soul.

"Death is finished," he said to himself. "It is no more!"

He drew in a breath, stopped in the midst of a sigh, stretched out, and died.

[1886]

M̶ARK TWAIN *was the name under which Samuel Langhorne Clemens (1835–1910) published his works. Clemens was born in the village of Florida, Missouri, the son of a lawyer from Virginia. When he was five, the family moved to Hannibal, Missouri, on the west bank of the Mississippi River — "a heavenly place for a boy," he later remembered. His formal schooling ended at age twelve, when his father died and he was apprenticed to his brother Orion, who edited a country newspaper. At this time he saw his first story printed — "The Dandy Frightening the Squatter," a typical piece of frontier humor. For years he worked as a journeyman printer in St. Louis, New York City, Philadelphia, and Cincinnati. Then he became an apprentice steamboat pilot on the Mississippi in 1857, and remained on the river until the Civil War. In his book* Life on the Mississippi *(1883), Twain wrote that on the river he became "acquainted with all the different types of human nature that are to be found in fiction, biography or history." After considering enlisting in the Confederate Army, he joined his brother Orion in the Nevada territory, first prospecting for gold and then working for the Virginia City* Enterprise. *It was in his writing for this newspaper that Samuel Clemens first used the pseudonym Mark Twain, a call of the Mississippi pilots signifying a depth of two fathoms (twelve feet), just barely safe water for riverboats.*

Twain's early work for the newspapers was influenced by the topical humorists of his time. He first achieved recognition as a writer in 1865 with a tall tale, the story "The Celebrated Jumping Frog of Calaveras County." Twain later said he didn't think much of the story, but it was published in book form with other sketches in 1867. Two years later his career was established with the travel book The Innocents Abroad. *He achieved further fame (and fortune) with the popular success of his novels,* The Adventures of Tom Sawyer *(1876),* The Prince and the Pauper *(1882),* A Connecticut Yankee in King Arthur's Court *(1889),* and many other books, including his masterpiece, *The Adventures of Huckleberry Finn *(1884).* Twain's life was a strange compound of public glory and private tragedy, but he was one of the greatest American writers. "I am persuaded," the Irish dramatist Bernard Shaw wrote to him, "that the future historian of America will find your works as indispensable to him as a French historian finds the political tracts of Voltaire."*

The classic humorous situation involving a man (often a harassed traveler) who gets into an unsolvable predicament appears often in Twain's work, from his earliest travel pieces in newspapers to A Tramp Abroad *in 1880 and* Following the Equator *in 1897. "A Story without an End" appeared in the latter of these. In his essay "How to Tell a Story," he distinguished between the humorous story (American), the comic story*

(English), and the witty story (French). According to Twain, only one kind was difficult — the humorous — because it depended for its effect upon the manner of the telling, while the comic story and the witty story depended upon the matter. *Structure was not Twain's strong point, although he turned this weakness to good account in "A Story without an End," where the plot is built on his inability to finish the story. In his plots he seldom looked far ahead, mixing trivial and farcical events and relying on hunches for inspiration, inventing as he wrote. Organizing his stories according to a formal scheme was as appealing to him as wearing a tight collar, although he revised his work carefully: "The difference between the* right *word and the* almost *right word is the difference between lightning and the lightning bug," he once wrote. Twain had a sensitive ear for the varied riches of American regional dialects, and he was our first author to write great books using a genuinely colloquial and native American speech. He published collections of short stories throughout his life, beginning with his first book,* The Celebrated Jumping Frog of Calaveras County and Other Sketches *(1867), and including such titles as* Mark Twain's Sketches *(1875),* Merry Tales *(1892), and* My Debut as a Literary Person, with Other Essays and Stories *(1903). A volume of the* Complete Stories of Mark Twain, *sixty stories in all, was published in 1957.*

Mark Twain

ಌಌ

A STORY WITHOUT AN END

We had one game in the ship which was a good time-passer — at least it was at night in the smoking-room when the men were getting freshened up from the day's monotonies and dullnesses. It was the completing of non-complete stories. That is to say, a man would tell all of a story except the finish, then the others would try to supply the ending out of their own invention. When every one who wanted a chance had had it, the man who had introduced the story would give it its original ending — then you could take your choice. Sometimes the new endings turned out to be better than the old one. But the story which called out the most persistent and determined and ambitious effort was one which *had* no ending, and so there was nothing to compare the new-made endings with. The man who told it said he could furnish the particulars up to a certain point only, because that was as much of the tale as he knew. He had read it in a volume of sketches twenty-five years ago, and was interrupted before the end was reached. He would give any one fifty dollars who would finish the story to the satisfaction of a jury to be appointed by ourselves. We appointed a jury and wrestled with the tale. We invented plenty of endings, but the jury voted them all down. The jury was right. It was a tale which the author of it may possibly have completed satisfactorily, and if he really had that good fortune I would like to know what the ending was. Any ordinary man will find that the story's strength is in its middle, and that there is apparently no way to transfer it to the close, where of course it ought to be. In substance the storiette was as follows:

John Brown, aged thirty-one, good, gentle, bashful, timid, lived in a quiet village in Missouri. He was superintendent of the Presbyterian Sunday-school. It was but a humble distinction; still, it was his only official one, and he was modestly proud of it and was devoted to its work and its interests. The extreme kindliness of his nature was recognized by all; in fact, people said that he was made entirely out of good impulses and bashfulness; that he could always be counted upon for help when it was needed, and for bashfulness both when it was needed, and when it wasn't.

Mary Taylor, twenty-three, modest, sweet, winning, and in character and person beautiful, was all in all to him. And he was very nearly all in all to her. She was wavering, his hopes were high. Her mother had been in opposition from the first. But she was wavering, too; he could see it. She was being touched by his warm interest in her two charity protégés and by his contributions toward their support. These were two forlorn and aged sisters who lived in a log hut in a lonely place up a cross-road four miles from Mrs. Taylor's farm. One of the sisters was crazy, and sometimes a little violent, but not often.

At last the time seemed ripe for a final advance, and Brown gathered his courage together and resolved to make it. He would take along a contribution of double the usual size, and win the mother over; with her opposition annulled, the rest of the conquest would be sure and prompt.

He took to the road in the middle of a placid Sunday afternoon in the soft Missourian summer, and he was equipped properly for his mission. He was clothed all in white linen, with a blue ribbon for a necktie, and he had on dressy tight boots. His horse and buggy were the finest that the livery-stable could furnish. The lap-robe was of white linen, it was new, and it had a hand-worked border that could not be rivaled in that region for beauty and elaboration.

When he was four miles out on the lonely road and was walking his horse over a wooden bridge, his straw hat blew off and fell in the creek, and floated down and lodged against a bar. He did not quite know what to do. He must have the hat, that was manifest; but how was he to get it?

Then he had an idea. The roads were empty, nobody was stirring. Yes, he would risk it. He led the horse to the roadside and set it to cropping the grass; then he undressed and put his clothes in the buggy, petted the horse a moment to secure its compassion and its loyalty, then hurried to the stream.

He swam out and soon had the hat. When he got to the top of the bank the horse was gone!

His legs almost gave way under him. The horse was walking leisurely along the road. Brown trotted after it, saying, "Whoa, whoa, there's a good fellow"; but whenever he got near enough to chance a jump for the buggy, the horse quickened its pace a little and defeated him. And so this went on, the naked man perishing with anxiety, and expecting every moment to see people come in sight. He tagged on and on, imploring the horse, beseeching the horse, till he had left a mile behind him, and was closing up on the Taylor premises; then at last he was successful, and got into the buggy. He flung on his shirt, his necktie, and his coat; then reached for — but he was too late; he sat suddenly down and pulled up the lap-robe, for he saw some one coming out of the gate — a woman, he thought. He wheeled the horse to the left, and struck briskly up the cross-road. It was perfectly straight, and exposed on both sides; but there were woods and a sharp turn three miles ahead, and he was very grateful when he got there. As he passed around the turn he slowed down to a walk, and reached for his tr — too late again.

He had come upon Mrs. Enderby, Mrs. Glossop, Mrs. Taylor, and Mary. They were on foot, and seemed tired and excited. They came at once to the buggy and shook hands, and all spoke at once, and said, eagerly and earnestly, how glad they were that he was come, and how fortunate it was. And Mrs. Enderby said, impressively:

"It *looks* like an accident, his coming at such a time; but let no one profane it with such a name; he was sent — sent from on high."

They were all moved, and Mrs. Glossop said in an awed voice:

"Sarah Enderby, you never said a truer word in your life. This is no accident, it is a special Providence. He *was* sent. He is an angel — an angel as truly as ever angel was — an angel of deliverance. I say *angel*, Sarah Enderby, and will have no other word. Don't let any one ever say to me again, that there's no such thing as special Providences; for if this isn't one, let them account for it that can."

"I *know* it's so," said Mrs. Taylor, fervently. "John Brown, I could worship you; I could go down on my knees to you. Didn't something tell you — didn't you *feel* that you were sent? I could kiss the hem of your lap-robe."

He was not able to speak; he was helpless with shame and fright. Mrs. Taylor went on:

"Why, just look at it all around, Julia Glossop. *Any* person can see the hand of Providence in it. Here at noon what do we see? We see the smoke rising. I speak up and say, 'That's the Old People's cabin afire.' Didn't I, Julia Glossop?"

"The very words you said, Nancy Taylor. I was as close to you as I am now, and I heard them. You may have said hut instead of cabin, but in substance it's the same. And you were looking pale, too."

"Pale? I was that pale that if — why, you just compare it with this lap-robe. Then the next thing I said was, 'Mary Taylor, tell the hired man to rig up the team — we'll go to the rescue.' And she said, 'Mother, don't you know you told him he could drive to see his people, and stay over Sunday?' And it was just so. I declare for it, I had forgotten it. 'Then,' said I, 'we'll go afoot.' And go we did. And found Sarah Enderby on the road."

"And we all went together," said Mrs. Enderby. "And found the cabin set fire and burnt down by the crazy one, and the poor old things so old and feeble that they couldn't go afoot. And we got them to a shady place and made them as comfortable as we could, and began to wonder which way to turn to find some way to get them conveyed to Nancy Taylor's house. And I spoke up and said — now what did I say? Didn't I say, 'Providence will provide'?"

"Why sure as you live, so you did! I had forgotten it."

"So had I," said Mrs. Glossop and Mrs. Taylor; "but you certainly *said* it. Now wasn't that remarkable?"

"Yes, I said it. And then we went to Mr. Moseley's, two miles, and all of them were gone to the camp-meeting over on Stony Fork; and then we came all the way back, two miles, and then here, another mile — and Providence *has* provided. You see it yourselves."

They gazed at each other awe-struck, and lifted their hands and said in unison:

"It's per-fectly wonderful."

"And then," said Mrs. Glossop, "what do you think we had better do — let Mr. Brown drive the Old People to Nancy Taylor's one at a time, or put both of them in the buggy, and him lead the horse?"

Brown gasped.

"Now, then, that's a question," said Mrs. Enderby. "You see, we are all tired out, and any way we fix it it's going to be difficult. For if Mr. Brown takes both of them, at least one of us must go back to help him, for he can't load them into the buggy by himself, and they so helpless."

"That is so," said Mrs. Taylor. "It doesn't look — oh, how would this do! — one of us drive there *with* Mr. Brown, and the rest of you go along to my house and get things ready. I'll go with him. He and I together can lift one of the Old People into the buggy; then drive her to my house and — "

"But who will take care of the other one?" said Mrs. Enderby. "We mustn't leave her there in the woods alone, you know — especially the crazy one. There and back is eight miles, you see."

They had all been sitting on the grass beside the buggy for a while, now, trying to rest their weary bodies. They fell silent a moment or two, and struggled in thought over the baffling situation; then Mrs. Enderby brightened and said:

"I think I've got the idea, now. You see, we can't *walk* any more. Think what we've done; four miles there, two to Moseley's, is six, then back to here — nine miles since noon, and not a bite to eat; I declare I don't see how we've done it; and as for me, I am just famishing. Now, somebody's got to go back, to help Mr. Brown — there's no getting around that; but whoever goes has got to ride, not walk. So my idea is this: one of us to ride back with Mr. Brown, then ride to Nancy Taylor's house with one of the Old People, leaving Mr. Brown to keep the other old one company, you all to go now to Nancy's and rest and wait; then one of you drive back and get the other one and drive *her* to Nancy's, and Mr. Brown walk."

"Splendid!" they all cried. "Oh, that will do — that will answer perfectly." And they all said that Mrs. Enderby had the best head for planning in the company; and they said that they wondered that they hadn't thought of this simple plan themselves. They hadn't meant to take back the compliment, good simple souls, and didn't know they had done it. After a consultation it was decided that Mrs. Enderby should drive back with Brown, she being entitled to the distinction because she had invented the plan. Everything now being satisfactorily arranged and settled, the ladies rose, relieved and happy, and brushed down their gowns, and three of them started homeward; Mrs. Enderby set her foot on the buggy step and was about to climb in, when Brown found a remnant of his voice and gasped out —

"Please, Mrs. Enderby, call them back — I am very weak; I can't walk, I can't indeed."

"Why, dear Mr. Brown! You *do* look pale; I am ashamed of myself that I didn't notice it sooner. Come back — all of you! Mr. Brown is not well. Is there anything I can do for you, Mr. Brown — I'm real sorry. Are you in pain?"

"No, madam, only weak; I am not sick, but only just weak — lately; not long, but just lately."

The others came back, and poured out their sympathies and commiserations, and were full of self-reproaches for not having noticed how pale he was. And they at once struck out a new plan, and soon agreed that it was by far the best of all. They would all go to Nancy Taylor's house and see to Brown's needs first. He could lie on the sofa in the parlor, and while Mrs. Taylor and Mary took care of him the other two ladies would take the buggy and go and get one of the Old People, and leave one of themselves with the other one, and —

By this time, without any solicitation, they were at the horse's head and were beginning to turn him around. The danger was imminent, but Brown found his voice again and saved himself. He said —

"But, ladies, you are overlooking something which makes the plan impracticable. You see, if you bring *one* of them home, and one remains behind with the other, there will be three persons there when one of you comes back for that other, for some one must drive the buggy back, and *three* can't come home in it."

They all exclaimed, "Why, sure-ly, that is so!" and they were all perplexed again.

"Dear, dear, what *can* we do?" said Mrs. Glossop; "it is the most mixed-up thing that ever was. The fox and the goose and the corn and things — oh, dear, they are nothing to it."

They sat wearily down once more, to further torture their tormented heads for a plan that would work. Presently Mary offered a plan; it was her first effort. She said:

"I am young and strong, and am refreshed, now. Take Mr. Brown to our house, and give him help — you see how plainly he needs it. I will go back and take care of the Old People; I can be there in twenty minutes. You can go on and do what you first started to do — wait on the main road at our house until somebody comes along with a wagon; then send and bring away the three of us. You won't have to wait long; the farmers will soon be coming back from town now. I will keep old Polly patient and cheered up — the crazy one doesn't need it."

This plan was discussed and accepted; it seemed the best that could be done, in the circumstances, and the Old People must be getting discouraged by this time.

Brown felt relieved, and was deeply thankful. Let him once get to the main road and he would find a way to escape.

Then Mrs. Taylor said:

"The evening chill will be coming on, pretty soon, and those poor old burnt-out things will need some kind of covering. Take the lap-robe with you, dear."

"Very well, Mother, I will."

She stepped to the buggy and put out her hand to take it —

That was the end of the tale. The passenger who told it said that when he read the story twenty-five years ago in a train he was interrupted at that point — the train jumped off a bridge.

At first we thought we could finish the story quite easily, and we set to work with confidence; but it soon began to appear that it was not a simple thing, but difficult and baffling. This was on account of Brown's character — great generosity and kindliness, but complicated with unusual shyness and diffidence, particularly in the presence of ladies. There was his love for Mary, in a hopeful state but not yet secure — just in a condition, indeed, where its affair must be handled with great tact, and no mistakes made, no offense given. And there was the mother — wavering, half willing — by adroit and flawless diplomacy to be won over, now, or perhaps never at all. Also, there were the helpless Old People yonder in the woods waiting — their fate and Brown's happiness to be determined by what Brown should do within the next two seconds. Mary was reaching for the lap-robe; Brown must decide — there was no time to be lost.

Of course none but a happy ending of the story would be accepted by the jury; the finish must find Brown in high credit with the ladies, his behavior without blemish, his modesty unwounded, his character for self-sacrifice maintained, the Old People rescued through him, their benefactor, all the party proud of him, happy in him, his praises on all their tongues.

We tried to arrange this, but it was beset with persistent and irreconcilable difficulties. We saw that Brown's shyness would not allow him to give up the lap-robe. This would offend Mary and her mother; and it would surprise the other ladies, partly because this stinginess toward the suffering Old People would be out of character with Brown, and partly because he was a special Providence and could not properly act so. If asked to explain his conduct, his shyness would not allow him to tell the truth, and lack of invention and practice would find him incapable of contriving a lie that would wash. We worked at the troublesome problem until three in the morning.

Meantime Mary was still reaching for the lap-robe. We gave it up, and decided to let her continue to reach. It is the reader's privilege to determine for himself how the thing came out.

[1897]

AMBROSE BIERCE (1842–1914?) *was born in a log cabin in Horse Cave Creek, Meiggs County, Ohio, the youngest of nine children. His father was a poverty-stricken farmer, and Bierce had only one year of formal education at the Kentucky Military Institute when he was seventeen. During the Civil War he enlisted with the 9th Indiana Infantry as a drummer boy. He fought bravely all through the war, was wounded at Kenesaw Mountain, Georgia, in 1864, and was discharged with the title of major. Then Bierce lived with a brother in San Francisco, working briefly as a night watchman at the United States Mint there. He also began his career as a newspaper writer at this time, and published his first story, "The Haunted Valley," in the* Overland Magazine *in 1871. When Bierce married the daughter of a wealthy Nevada miner, his father-in-law gave the young couple a wedding gift of $10,000, and they settled in London for five years. There Bierce worked as a journalist, an experience that polished his writing skills and turned him from a rough western humorist to a wit who wrote with great stylistic finish. Homesick for California, he returned there with his wife and wrote columns and short stories for various newspapers, including William Randolph Hearst's San Francisco* Examiner. *In the 1880s he became very influential in his profession, although in literary circles outside California he was not widely known. Then his wife separated from him, his two sons died tragically, and he became embittered. In his seventies, Bierce supervised the publication of the twelve volumes of his* Collected Works, *revisited the Civil War battlefields of his youth, and then disappeared across the Mexican border, leaving the facts of his life after 1914 to trail off into legend.*

Bierce is well known as the author of the philosophical epigrams in The Devil's Dictionary *(1906), but his two volumes of short stories are his finest achievement as a writer. He is considered a notable forerunner of such American realists as Stephen Crane. "An Occurrence at Owl Creek Bridge" was included in Bierce's first story collection,* In the Midst of Life, *published privately in San Francisco under the original title of* Tales of Soldiers and Civilians *(1891). The second collection,* Can Such Things Be?, *was published in New York two years later. Bierce preferred the short story to the novel, defining the novel as a "short story padded" and saying that it lacked the story's totality of effect. He modeled his technique of creating suspense that leads up to a dramatic crisis on Poe's, but Bierce gave a more realistic motivation to his horrors. His obsession with sudden, violent death cuts through the twists of conventional magazine fiction to give a darker reality to his stories. Dreams, flashbacks, and hallucinations, as in "An Occurrence at Owl Creek Bridge," provide irony and vivid imagery, but offer no escape. After four years on the battlefields of the Civil War, Bierce was* fascinated with death, although he came to doubt the justice of the cause for which he had fought. He declined a large sum of back pay from the United States government, saying, "When I hired out as an assassin for my country, that wasn't part of the contract." Bierce seems entirely indifferent to human suffering in his stories, but his unemotional depictions of the horrors of war have a strong effect on most readers.

Ambrose Bierce

ଧ୍ୟ

AN OCCURRENCE AT OWL CREEK BRIDGE

I

A man stood upon a railroad bridge in Northern Alabama, looking down into the swift waters twenty feet below. The man's hands were behind his back, the wrists bound with a cord. A rope loosely encircled his neck. It was attached to a stout cross-timber above his head, and the slack fell to the level of his knees. Some loose boards laid upon the sleepers supporting the metals of the railway supplied a footing for him and his executioners — two private soldiers of the Federal army, directed by a sergeant, who in civil life may have been a deputy sheriff. At a short remove upon the same temporary platform was an officer in the uniform of his rank, armed. He was a captain. A sentinel at each end of the bridge stood with his rifle in the position known as "support," that is to say, vertical in front of the left shoulder, the hammer resting on the forearm thrown straight across the chest — a formal and unnatural position, enforcing an erect carriage of the body. It did not appear to be the duty of these two men to know what was occurring at the centre of the bridge; they merely blockaded the two ends of the foot plank which traversed it.

Beyond one of the sentinels nobody was in sight; the railroad ran straight away into a forest for a hundred yards, then, curving, was lost to view. Doubtless there was an outpost further along. The other bank of the stream was open ground — a gentle acclivity crowned with a stockade of vertical tree trunks, loop-holed for rifles, with a single embrasure through which protruded the muzzle of a brass cannon commanding the bridge. Midway of the slope between bridge and fort were the spectators — a single company of infantry in line, at "parade rest," the butts of the rifles on the ground, the barrels inclining slightly backward against the right shoulder, the hands crossed upon the stock. A lieutenant stood at the right of the line, the point of his sword upon the ground, his left hand resting upon his right. Excepting the group of four at the centre of the bridge not a man moved. The company faced the bridge, staring stonily, motionless. The sentinels, facing the banks of the stream, might have been statues to adorn the bridge. The captain stood with folded arms, silent, observing the work of his subordinates but making no sign. Death is a dignitary who, when he comes announced, is to be received with formal manifestations of respect, even by those most familiar with him. In the code of military etiquette silence and fixity are forms of deference.

The man who was engaged in being hanged was apparently about thirty-five years of age. He was a civilian, if one might judge from his dress, which was that of a planter. His features were good — a straight nose, firm mouth, broad forehead, from which his long, dark hair was combed straight back, falling behind his ears to the collar of his well-fitting frock coat. He wore a moustache and pointed beard, but no whiskers; his eyes were large and dark grey and had a kindly expression which one would hardly have expected in one whose neck was in the hemp. Evidently this was no vulgar assassin. The liberal military code makes provision for hanging many kinds of people, and gentlemen are not excluded.

The preparations being complete, the two private soldiers stepped aside and each drew away the plank upon which he had been standing. The sergeant turned to the captain, saluted and placed himself immediately behind that officer, who in turn moved apart one pace. These movements left the condemned man and the sergeant standing on the two ends of the same plank, which spanned three of the cross-ties of the bridge. The end upon which the civilian stood almost, but not quite, reached a fourth. This plank had been held in place by the weight of the captain; it was now held by that of the sergeant. At a signal from the former, the latter would step aside, the plank would tilt and the condemned man go down between two ties. The arrangement commended itself to his judgment as simple and effective. His face had not been covered nor his eyes bandaged. He looked a moment at his "unsteadfast footing," then let his gaze wander to the swirling water of the stream racing madly beneath his feet. A piece of dancing driftwood caught his attention and his eyes followed it down the current. How slowly it appeared to move! What a sluggish stream!

He closed his eyes in order to fix his last thoughts upon his wife and children. The water, touched to gold by the early sun, the brooding mists under the banks at some distance down the stream, the fort, the soldiers, the piece of drift — all had distracted him. And now he became conscious of a new disturbance. Striking through the thought of his dear ones was a sound which he could neither ignore nor understand, a sharp, distinct, metallic percussion like the stroke of a blacksmith's hammer upon the anvil; it had the same ringing quality. He wondered what it was, and whether immeasurably distant or near by — it seemed both. Its recurrence was regular, but as slow as the tolling of a death knell. He awaited each stroke with impatience and — he knew not why — apprehension. The intervals of silence grew progressively longer; the delays became maddening. With their greater infrequency the sounds increased in strength and sharpness. They hurt his ear like the thrust of a knife; he feared he would shriek. What he heard was the ticking of his watch.

He unclosed his eyes and saw again the water below him. "If I could free my hands," he thought, "I might throw off the noose and spring into the stream. By diving I could evade the bullets, and, swimming vigorously, reach the bank, take to the woods, and get away home. My home, thank God, is as yet outside their lines; my wife and little ones are still beyond the invader's farthest advance."

As these thoughts, which have here to be set down in words, were flashed into the doomed man's brain rather than evolved from it, the captain nodded to the sergeant. The sergeant stepped aside.

II

Peyton Farquhar was a well-to-do planter, of an old and highly-respected Alabama family. Being a slave owner, and, like other slave owners, a politician, he was naturally an original secessionist and ardently devoted to the Southern cause. Circumstances of an imperious nature which it is unnecessary to relate here, had prevented him from taking service with the gallant army which had fought the disastrous campaigns ending with the fall of Corinth, and he chafed under the inglorious restraint, longing for the release of his energies, the larger life of the soldier, the opportunity for distinction. That opportunity, he felt, would come, as it comes to all in war time. Meanwhile he did what he could. No service was too humble for him to perform in aid of the South, no adventure too perilous for him to undertake if consistent with the character of a civilian who was at heart a soldier, and who in good faith and without too much qualification assented to at least a part of the frankly villainous dictum that all is fair in love and war.

One evening while Farquhar and his wife were sitting on a rustic bench near the entrance to his grounds, a grey-clad soldier rode up to the gate and asked for a drink of water. Mrs. Farquhar was only too happy to serve him with her own white hands. While she was gone to fetch the water, her husband approached the dusty horseman and inquired eagerly for news from the front.

"The Yanks are repairing the railroads," said the man, "and are getting ready for another advance. They have reached the Owl Creek bridge, put it in order, and built a stockade on the other bank. The commandant has issued an order, which is posted everywhere, declaring that any civilian caught interfering with the railroad, its bridges, tunnels, or trains, will be summarily hanged. I saw the order."

"How far is it to the Owl Creek bridge?" Farquhar asked.

"About thirty miles."

"Is there no force on this side the creek?"

"Only a picket post half a mile out, on the railroad, and a single sentinel at this end of the bridge."

"Suppose a man — a civilian and student of hanging — should elude the picket post and perhaps get the better of the sentinel," said Farquhar, smiling, "what could he accomplish?"

The soldier reflected. "I was there a month ago," he replied. "I observed that the flood of last winter had lodged a great quantity of driftwood against the wooden pier at this end of the bridge. It is now dry and would burn like tow."

The lady had now brought the water, which the soldier drank. He thanked her ceremoniously, bowed to her husband, and rode away. An hour later, after nightfall, he repassed the plantation, going northward in the direction from which he had come. He was a Federal scout.

III

As Peyton Farquhar fell straight downward through the bridge, he lost consciousness and was as one already dead. From this state he was awakened — ages later, it seemed to him — by the pain of a sharp pressure upon his throat, followed by a sense of suffocation. Keen, poignant agonies seemed to shoot from his neck downward through every fibre of his body and limbs. These pains appeared to flash along well-defined lines of ramification, and to beat with an inconceivably rapid periodicity. They seemed like streams of pulsating fire heating him to an intolerable temperature. As to his head, he was conscious of nothing but a feeling of fullness — of congestion. These sensations were unaccompanied by thought. The intellectual part of his nature was already effaced; he had power only to feel, and feeling was torment. He was conscious of motion. Encompassed in a luminous cloud, of which he was now merely the fiery heart, without material substance, he swung through unthinkable arcs of oscillation, like a vast pendulum. Then all at once, with terrible suddenness, the light about him shot upward with the noise of a loud plash; a frightful roaring was in his ears, and all was cold and dark. The power of thought was restored; he knew that the rope had broken and he had fallen into the stream. There was no additional strangulation; the noose about his neck was already suffocating him, and kept the water from his lungs. To die of hanging at the bottom of a river — the idea seemed to him ludicrous. He opened his eyes in the blackness and saw above him a gleam of light, but how distant, how inaccessible! He was still sinking, for the light became fainter and fainter until it was a mere glimmer. Then it began to grow and brighten, and he knew that he was rising toward the surface — knew it with reluctance, for he was now very comfortable. "To be hanged and drowned," he thought, "that is not so bad; but I do not wish to be shot. No; I will not be shot; that is not fair."

He was not conscious of an effort, but a sharp pain in his wrist apprised him that he was trying to free his hands. He gave the struggle his attention, as an idler might observe the feat of a juggler, without interest in the outcome. What splendid effort! — what magnificent, what superhuman strength! Ah, that was a fine endeavor! Bravo! The cord fell away; his arms parted and floated upward, the hands dimly seen on each side in the growing light. He watched them with a new interest as first one and then the other pounced upon the noose at his neck. They tore it away and thrust it fiercely aside, its undulations resembling those of a water-snake. "Put it back, put it back!" He thought he shouted these words to his hands, for the undoing of the noose had been succeeded by the direst pang which he had yet experienced. His neck arched horribly; his brain was on fire; his heart, which had been fluttering faintly, gave a great leap, trying to force itself out at his mouth. His whole body was racked and wrenched with an insupportable anguish! But his disobedient hands gave no heed to the command. They beat the water vigorously with quick, downward strokes, forcing him to the surface. He felt his head emerge; his eyes were blinded by the sunlight; his chest expanded convulsively, and with a supreme and crowning agony his lungs engulfed a great draught of air, which instantly he expelled in a shriek!

He was now in full possession of his physical senses. They were, indeed, preternaturally keen and alert. Something in the awful disturbance of his organic system had so exalted and refined them that they made record of things never before perceived. He felt the ripples upon his face and heard their separate sounds as they struck. He looked at the forest on the bank of the stream, saw the individual trees, the leaves and the veining of each leaf — saw the very insects upon them, the locusts, the brilliant-bodied flies, the grey spiders stretching their webs from twig to twig. He noted the prismatic colors in all the dewdrops upon a million blades of grass. The humming of the gnats that danced above the eddies of the stream, the beating of the dragon flies' wings, the strokes of the water spiders' legs, like oars which had lifted their boat — all these made audible music. A fish slid along beneath his eyes and he heard the rush of its body parting the water.

He had come to the surface facing down the stream; in a moment the visible world seemed to wheel slowly round, himself the pivotal point, and he saw the bridge, the fort, the soldiers upon the bridge, the captain, the sergeant, the two privates, his executioners. They were in silhouette against the blue sky. They shouted and gesticulated, pointing at him; the captain had drawn his pistol, but did not fire; the others were unarmed. Their movements were grotesque and horrible, their forms gigantic.

Suddenly he heard a sharp report and something struck the water smartly within a few inches of his head, spattering his face with spray. He heard a second report, and saw one of the sentinels with his rifle at his shoulder, a light cloud of blue smoke rising from the muzzle. The man in the water saw the eye of the man on the bridge gazing into his own through the sights of the rifle. He observed that it was a grey eye, and remembered having read that grey eyes were keenest and that all famous marksmen had them. Nevertheless, this one had missed.

A counter swirl had caught Farquhar and turned him half round; he was again looking into the forest on the bank opposite the fort. The sound of a clear, high voice in a monotonous singsong now rang out behind him and came across the water with a distinctness that pierced and subdued all other sounds, even the beating of the ripples in his ears. Although no soldier, he had frequented camps enough to know the dread significance of that deliberate, drawling, aspirated chant; the lieutenant on shore was taking a part in the morning's work. How coldly and pitilessly — with what an even, calm intonation, presaging and enforcing tranquillity in the men — with what accurately-measured intervals fell those cruel words:

"Attention, company.... Shoulder arms.... Ready.... Aim.... Fire."

Farquhar dived — dived as deeply as he could. The water roared in his ears like the voice of Niagara, yet he heard the dulled thunder of the volley, and rising again toward the surface, met shining bits of metal, singularly flattened, oscillating slowly downward. Some of them touched him on the face and hands, then fell away, continuing their descent. One lodged between his collar and neck; it was uncomfortably warm, and he snatched it out.

As he rose to the surface, gasping for breath, he saw that he had been a long time under water; he was perceptibly farther down stream — nearer to safety. The soldiers had almost finished reloading; the metal ramrods flashed all at once in the sunshine as they were drawn from the barrels, turned in the air, and thrust into their sockets. The two sentinels fired again, independently and ineffectually.

The hunted man saw all this over his shoulder; he was now swimming vigorously with the current. His brain was as energetic as his arms and legs; he thought with the rapidity of lightning.

"The officer," he reasoned, "will not make the martinet's error a second time. It is as easy to dodge a volley as a single shot. He has probably already given the command to fire at will. God help me, I cannot dodge them all!"

An appalling plash within two yards of him, followed by a loud rushing sound, *diminuendo*, which seemed to travel back through the air to the fort and died in an explosion which stirred the very river to its deeps! A rising sheet of water, which curved over him, fell down upon him, blinded him, strangled him! The cannon had taken a hand in the game. As he shook his head free from the commotion of the smitten water, he heard the deflected shot humming through the air ahead, and in an instant it was cracking and smashing the branches in the forest beyond.

"They will not do that again," he thought; "the next time they will use a charge of grape. I must keep my eye upon the gun; the smoke will apprise me — the report arrives too late; it lags behind the missile. It is a good gun."

Suddenly he felt himself whirled round and round — spinning like a top. The water, the banks, the forest, the now distant bridge, fort and men — all were commingled and blurred. Objects were represented by their colors only; circular horizontal streaks of color — that was all he saw. He had been caught in a vortex and was being whirled on with a velocity of advance and gyration which made him giddy and sick. In a few moments he was flung upon the gravel at the foot of the left bank of the stream — the southern bank — and behind a projecting point which concealed him from his enemies. The sudden arrest of his motion, the abrasion of one of his hands on the gravel, restored him and he wept with delight. He dug his fingers into the sand, threw it over himself in handfuls and audibly blessed it. It looked like gold, like diamonds, rubies, emeralds; he could think of nothing beautiful which it did not resemble. The trees upon the bank were giant garden plants; he noted a definite order in their arrangement, inhaled the fragrance of their blooms. A strange, roseate light shone through the spaces among their trunks, and the wind made in their branches the music of æolian harps. He had no wish to perfect his escape, was content to remain in that enchanting spot until retaken.

A whizz and rattle of grapeshot among the branches high above his head roused him from his dream. The baffled cannoneer had fired him a random farewell. He sprang to his feet, rushed up the sloping bank, and plunged into the forest.

All that day he travelled, laying his course by the rounding sun. The forest seemed interminable; nowhere did he discover a break in it, not even a woodman's road. He had not known that he lived in so wild a region. There was something uncanny in the revelation.

By nightfall he was fatigued, footsore, famishing. The thought of his wife and children urged him on. At last he found a road which led him in what he knew to be the right direction. It was as wide and straight as a city street, yet it seemed untravelled. No fields bordered it, no dwelling anywhere. Not so much as the barking of a dog suggested human habitation. The black bodies of the great trees formed a straight wall on both sides, terminating on the horizon in a point, like a diagram in a lesson in perspective. Overhead, as he looked up through this rift in the wood, shone great golden stars looking unfamiliar and grouped in strange constellations. He was sure they were arranged in some order which had a secret and malign significance. The wood on either side was full of singular noises, among which — once, twice, and again — he distinctly heard whispers in an unknown tongue.

His neck was in pain, and, lifting his hand to it, he found it horribly swollen. He knew that it had a circle of black where the rope had bruised it.

His eyes felt congested; he could no longer close them. His tongue was swollen with thirst; he relieved its fever by thrusting it forward from between his teeth into the cool air. How softly the turf had carpeted the untravelled avenue! He could no longer feel the roadway beneath his feet!

Doubtless, despite his suffering, he fell asleep while walking, for now he sees another scene — perhaps he has merely recovered from a delirium. He stands at the gate of his own home. All is as he left it, and all bright and beautiful in the morning sunshine. He must have travelled the entire night. As he pushes open the gate and passes up the wide white walk, he sees a flutter of female garments; his wife, looking fresh and cool and sweet, steps down from the verandah to meet him. At the bottom of the steps she stands waiting, with a smile of ineffable joy, an attitude of matchless grace and dignity. Ah, how beautiful she is! He springs forward with extended arms. As he is about to clasp her, he feels a stunning blow upon the back of the neck; a blinding white light blazes all about him, with a sound like a shock of a cannon — then all is darkness and silence!

Peyton Farquhar was dead; his body, with a broken neck, swung gently from side to side beneath the timbers of the Owl Creek bridge.

[1891]

HENRY JAMES (1843–1916) was born in New York City. His father was a religious philosopher, and his brother, William James, was a noted physician, philosopher, and psychologist. Educated mostly by tutors in the United States and Europe, Henry James published his first story at the age of twenty-one. In 1875 he chose to live permanently in England. He formed friendships with several European writers, including Turgenev, Flaubert, and Guy de Maupassant. During the first phase of James's long career, he explored personal relationships, most notably in the novel The Portrait of a Lady (1881). Then he turned to themes of social reform, as in The Bostonians (1886). He constantly experimented with ways to refine his writing, and commented on his "Art of Fiction" in many essays, prefaces, letters, and notebooks. The dense, symbolic style of his later work, whose fundamental theme was the innocence and exuberance of the New World clashing with the corruption and wisdom of the Old, can be seen in his three last novels, The Wings of the Dove (1902), The Ambassadors (1903), and The Golden Bowl (1904).

In his lifetime James wrote more than seventy stories. He began as a mediocre imitator of Hawthorne and ended as a great creative writer of fiction and literary criticism; the progression was the result of his professionalism, his constant self-examination, his self-knowledge, and his self-control. He felt that experience assumes meaning only when the proper form for its expression is found. One of his favorite words was "awareness," and he tried to make his own awareness encompass everything he could observe, relate, weigh, and judge. Thus his world was a world of connections, continually subjected to a controlled and harmonious ordering. In the essay "The Art of Fiction," he says that the source of fiction is not mere raw experience but "the power to guess the unseen from the seen, to trace the implication of things, to judge the whole piece by the pattern, the condition of feeling life in general so completely that you are well on your way to knowing any particular corner of it."

James's stories lack the characteristic compression and dramatic action typical of this literary form. Instead, through the device he called a "central intelligence," he revealed the world through one of his characters' silent thought, proceeding at a stately pace in the flow of his leisurely narrative. Yet in 1891, when James wrote in his notebook the idea that was the genesis of the story "The Real Thing," he apparently had in mind something else, a compressed short story in the manner of Maupassant, which he hoped would be easier to sell to a magazine than a longer work. He regarded this story as a great challenge: "To look at a thing hard and straight and seriously — to fix it."

214

Henry James

ಬಬ

THE REAL THING

I

When the porter's wife, who used to answer the house-bell, announced "A gentleman and a lady, sir," I had, as I often had in those days — the wish being father to the thought — an immediate vision of sitters. Sitters my visitors in this case proved to be; but not in the sense I should have preferred. There was nothing at first however to indicate that they mightn't have come for a portrait. The gentleman, a man of fifty, very high and very straight, with a moustache slightly grizzled and a dark grey walking-coat admirably fitted, both of which I noted professionally — I don't mean as a barber or yet as a tailor — would have struck me as a celebrity if celebrities often were striking. It was a truth of which I had for some time been conscious that a figure with a good deal of frontage was, as one might say, almost never a public institution. A glance at the lady helped to remind me of this paradoxical law: she also looked too distinguished to be a "personality." Moreover one would scarcely come across two variations together.

Neither of the pair immediately spoke — they only prolonged the preliminary gaze suggesting that each wished to give the other a chance. They were visibly shy; they stood there letting me take them in — which, as I afterwards perceived, was the most practical thing they could have done. In this way their embarrassment served their cause. I had seen people painfully reluctant to mention that they desired anything so gross as to be represented on canvas; but the scruples of my new friends appeared almost insurmountable. Yet the gentleman might have said "I should like a portrait of my wife," and the lady might have said "I should like a portrait of my husband." Perhaps they weren't husband and wife — this naturally would make the matter more delicate. Perhaps they wished to be done together — in which case they ought to have brought a third person to break the news.

"We come from Mr. Rivet," the lady finally said with a dim smile that had the effect of a moist sponge passed over a "sunk" piece of painting, as well as of a vague allusion to vanished beauty. She was as tall and straight, in her degree, as her companion, and with ten years less to carry. She looked as sad as a woman could look whose face was not charged with expression; that is her tinted oval mask showed waste as an exposed surface shows friction. The hand of time had played over her freely, but to an effect of elimination. She was slim and stiff, and so well-dressed, in dark blue cloth, with lappets and pockets and buttons, that it was clear she employed the same tailor as her husband. The couple had an indefinable air of prosperous thrift — they evidently got a good deal of luxury for their money. If I was to be one of their luxuries it would behoove me to consider my terms.

"Ah Claude Rivet recommended me?" I echoed; and I added that it was very kind of him, though I could reflect that, as he only painted landscape, this wasn't a sacrifice.

The lady looked very hard at the gentleman, and the gentleman looked round the room. Then staring at the floor a moment and stroking his moustache, he rested his pleasant eyes on me with the remark: "He said you were the right one."

"I try to be, when people want to sit."

"Yes, we should like to," said the lady anxiously.

"Do you mean together?"

My visitors exchanged a glance. "If you could do anything with *me* I suppose it would be double," the gentleman stammered.

"Oh yes, there's naturally a higher charge for two figures than for one."

"We should like to make it pay," the husband confessed.

"That's very good of you," I returned, appreciating so unwonted a sympathy — for I supposed he meant pay the artist.

A sense of strangeness seemed to dawn on the lady. "We mean for the illustrations — Mr. Rivet said you might put one in."

"Put in — an illustration?" I was equally confused.

"Sketch her off, you know," said the gentleman, coloring.

It was only then that I understood the service Claude Rivet had rendered me; he had told them how I worked in black-and-white, for magazines, for storybooks, for sketches of contemporary life, and consequently had copious employment for models. These things were true, but it was not less true — I may confess it now; whether because the aspiration was to lead to everything or to nothing I leave the reader to guess — that I couldn't get the honors, to say nothing of the emoluments, of a great painter of portraits out of my head. My "illustrations" were my pot-boilers; I looked to a different branch of art — far and away the most interesting it had always seemed to me — to perpetuate my fame. There was no shame in looking to it also to make my fortune; but that fortune was by so much further from being made from the moment my visitors wished to be "done" for nothing. I was disappointed; for in the pictorial sense I had immediately *seen* them. I had seized their type — I had already settled what I would do with it. Something that wouldn't absolutely have pleased them, I afterwards reflected.

"Ah you're — you're — a?" I began as soon as I had mastered my surprise. I couldn't bring out the dingy word "models": it seemed so little to fit the case.

"We haven't had much practice," said the lady.

"We've got to *do* something, and we've thought that an artist in your line might perhaps make something of us," her husband threw off. He further mentioned that they didn't know many artists and that they had gone first, on the off-chance — he painted views of course, but sometimes put in figures; perhaps I remembered — to Mr. Rivet, whom they had met a few years before at a place in Norfolk where he was sketching.

"We used to sketch a little ourselves," the lady hinted.

"It's very awkward, but we absolutely *must* do something," her husband went on.

"Of course we're not so *very* young," she admitted with a wan smile.

With the remark that I might as well know something more about them the husband had handed me a card extracted from a neat new pocket-book — their appurtenances were all of the freshest — and inscribed with the words "Major Monarch." Impressive as these words were they didn't carry my knowledge much further; but my visitor presently added: "I've left the army and we've had the misfortune to lose our money. In fact our means are dreadfully small."

"It's awfully trying — a regular strain," said Mrs. Monarch.

They evidently wished to be discreet — to take care not to swagger because they were gentlefolk. I felt them willing to recognize this as something of a drawback, at the same time that I guessed at an underlying sense — their consolation in adversity — that they *had* their points. They certainly had; but these advantages struck me as preponderantly social; such for instance as would help to make a drawing-room look well. However, a drawing-room was always, or ought to be, a picture.

In consequence of his wife's allusion to their age Major Monarch observed: "Naturally, it's more for the figure that we thought of going in. We can still hold ourselves up." On the instant I saw that the figure was indeed their strong point. His "naturally" didn't sound vain, but it lighted up the question. "*She* has got the best," he continued, nodding at his wife, with a pleasant after-dinner absence of circumlocution. I could only reply, as if we were in fact sitting over our wine, that this didn't prevent his own from being very good; which led him in turn to rejoin: "We thought that if you ever have to do people like us, we might be something like it. *She*, particularly — for a lady in a book, you know."

I was so amused by them that, to get more of it, I did my best to take their point of view; and though it was an embarrassment to find myself appraising physically, as if they were animals on hire or useful blacks, a pair whom I should have expected to meet only in one of the relations in which criticism is tacit, I looked at Mrs. Monarch judicially enough to be able to exclaim, after a moment, with conviction: "Oh yes, a lady in a book!" She was singularly like a bad illustration.

"We'll stand up, if you like," said the Major; and he raised himself before me with a really grand air.

I could take his measure at a glance — he was six feet two and a perfect gentleman. It would have paid any club in process of formation and in want of a stamp to engage him at a salary to stand in the principal window. What struck me immediately was that in coming to me they had rather missed their vocation; they could surely have been turned to better account for advertising purposes. I couldn't of course see the thing in detail, but I could see them make someone's fortune — I don't mean their own. There was something in them for a waistcoat-maker, an hotel-keeper or a soap-vendor. I could imagine "We always use it" pinned on their bosoms with the greatest effect; I had a vision of the promptitude with which they would launch a table d'hôte.

Mrs. Monarch sat still, not from pride but from shyness, and presently her husband said to her: "Get up my dear and show how smart you are." She obeyed, but she had no need to get up to show it. She walked to the end of the studio, and then she came back blushing, with her fluttered eyes on her husband. I was reminded of an incident I had accidentally had a glimpse of in Paris — being with a friend there, a dramatist about to produce a play — when an actress came to him to ask to be intrusted with a part. She went through her paces before him, walked up and down as Mrs. Monarch was doing. Mrs. Monarch did it quite as well, but I abstained from applauding. It was very odd to see such people apply for such poor pay. She looked as if she had ten thousand a year. Her husband had used the word that described her: she was in the London current jargon essentially and typically "smart." Her figure was, in the same order of ideas, conspicuously and irreproachably "good." For a woman of her age her waist was surprisingly small; her elbow moreover had the orthodox crook. She held her head at the conventional angle, but why did she come to *me?* She ought to have tried on jackets at a big shop. I feared my visitors were not only destitute but "artistic" — which would be a great complication. When she sat down again I thanked her, observing that what a draughtsman most valued in his model was the faculty of keeping quiet.

"Oh *she* can keep quiet," said Major Monarch. Then he added jocosely: "I've always kept her quiet."

"I'm not a nasty fidget, am I?" It was going to wring tears from me, I felt, the way she hid her head, ostrich-like, in the other broad bosom.

The owner of this expanse addressed his answer to me. "Perhaps it isn't out of place to mention — because we ought to be quite businesslike, oughtn't we? — that when I married her she was known as the Beautiful Statue."

"Oh dear!" said Mrs. Monarch ruefully.

"Of course I should want a certain amount of expression," I rejoined.

"Of *course!*" — and I had never heard such unanimity.

"And then I suppose you know that you'll get awfully tired."

"Oh, we *never* get tired!" they eagerly cried.

"Have you had any kind of practice?"

They hesitated — they looked at each other. "We've been photographed — *immensely*," said Mrs. Monarch.

"She means the fellows have asked us themselves," added the Major.

"I see — because you're so good-looking."

"I don't know what they thought, but they were always after us."

"We always got our photographs for nothing," smiled Mrs. Monarch.

"We might have brought some, my dear," her husband remarked.

"I'm not sure we have any left. We've given quantities away," she explained to me.

"With our autographs and that sort of thing," said the Major.

"Are they to be got in the shops?" I enquired as a harmless pleasantry.

"Oh yes, *hers* — they used to be."

"Not now," said Mrs. Monarch, with her eyes on the floor.

II

I could fancy the "sort of thing" they put on the presentation copies of their photographs, and I was sure they wrote a beautiful hand. It was odd how quickly I was sure of everything that concerned them. If they were now so poor as to have to earn shillings and pence they could never have had much of a margin. Their good looks had been their capital, and they had good-humoredly made the most of the career that this resource marked out for them. It was in their faces, the blankness, the deep intellectual repose of the twenty years of country-house visiting that had given them pleasant intonations. I could see the sunny drawing-rooms, sprinkled with periodicals she didn't read, in which Mrs. Monarch had continually sat; I could see the wet shrubberies in which she had walked, equipped to admiration for either exercise. I could see the rich covers the Major had helped to shoot and the wonderful garments in which, late at night, he repaired to the smoking-room to talk about them. I could imagine their leggings and waterproofs, their knowing tweeds and rugs, their rolls of sticks and cases of tackle and neat umbrellas; and I could evoke the exact appearance of their servants and the compact variety of their luggage on the platforms of country stations.

They gave small tips, but they were liked; they didn't do anything themselves, but they were welcome. They looked so well everywhere; they gratified the general relish for stature, complexion and "form." They knew it without fatuity or vulgarity, and they respected themselves in consequence. They weren't superficial; they were thorough and kept themselves up — it had been their line. People with such a taste for activity had to have some line. I could feel how even in a dull house they could have been counted on for the joy of life. At present something had happened — it didn't matter what, their little income had grown less, it had grown least — and they had to do something for pocket-money. Their friends could like them, I made out, without liking to support them. There was something about them that represented credit — their clothes, their manners, their type; but if credit is a large empty pocket in which an occasional chink reverberates, the chink at least must be audible. What they wanted of me was to help to make it so. Fortunately they had no children — I soon divined that. They would also perhaps wish our relations to be kept secret: this was why it was "for the figure" — the reproduction of the face would betray them.

I liked them — I felt, quite as their friends must have done — they were so simple; and I had no objection to them if they would suit. But somehow with all their perfections I didn't easily believe in them. After all they were amateurs, and the ruling passion of my life was the detestation of the amateur. Combined with this was another perversity — an innate preference for the represented subject over the real one: the defect of the real one was so apt to be a lack of representation. I like things that appeared; then one was sure. Whether they *were* or not was a subordinate and almost always a profitless question. There were other considerations, the first of which was that I already had two or three recruits in use, notably a young person with big feet, in alpaca, from Kilburn, who for a couple of years had come to me regularly for my illustrations and with whom I was still — perhaps ignobly — satisfied. I frankly explained to my visitors how the case stood, but they had taken more precautions than I supposed. They had reasoned out their opportunity, for Claude Rivet had told them of the projected *édition de luxe* of one of the writers of our day — the rarest of the novelists — who, long neglected by the multitudinous vulgar and dearly prized by the attentive (need I mention Philip Vincent?), had had the happy fortune of seeing, late in life, the dawn and then the full light of a higher criticism; an estimate in which on the part of the public there was something really of expiation. The edition preparing, planned by a publisher of taste, was practically an act of high reparation; the wood-cuts with which it was to be enriched were the homage of English art to one of the most independent representatives of English letters. Major and Mrs. Monarch confessed to me they had hoped I might be able to work *them* into my branch of the enterprise. They knew I was to do the first of the books, "Rutland Ramsay," but I had to make clear to them that my participation in the rest of the affair — this first book was to be a test — must depend on the satisfaction I should give. If this should be limited my employers would drop me with scarce common forms. It was therefore a crisis for me, and naturally I was making special preparations, looking about for new people, should they be necessary, and securing the best types. I admitted however that I should like to settle down to two or three good models who would do for everything.

"Should we have often to — a — put on special clothes?" Mrs. Monarch timidly demanded.

"Dear yes — that's half the business."

"And should we be expected to supply our own costumes?"

"Oh no; I've got a lot of things. A painter's models put on — or put off — anything he likes."

"And you mean — a — the same?"

"The same?"

Mrs. Monarch looked at her husband again.

"Oh she was just wondering," he explained, "if the costumes are in *general* use." I had to confess that they were, and I mentioned further that some of them — I had a lot of genuine greasy last-century things — had served their time, a hundred years ago, on living world-stained men and women; on figures not perhaps so far removed, in that vanished world, from *their* type, the Monarchs', *quoi!* of a breeched and bewigged age. "We'll put on anything that *fits*," said the Major.

"Oh I arrange that — they fit in the pictures."

"I'm afraid I should do better for the modern books. I'd come as you like," said Mrs. Monarch.

"She has got a lot of clothes at home: they might do for contemporary life," her husband continued.

"Oh I can fancy scenes in which you'd be quite natural." And indeed I could see the slipshod rearrangements of stale properties — the stories I tried to produce pictures for without the exasperation of reading them — whose sandy tracts the good lady might help to people. But I had to return to the fact that for this sort of work — the daily mechanical grind — I was already equipped: the people I was working with were fully adequate.

"We only thought we might be more like *some* characters," said Mrs. Monarch mildly, getting up.

Her husband also rose; he stood looking at me with a dim wistfulness that was touching in so fine a man. "Wouldn't it be rather a pull sometimes to have — a — to have — ?" He hung fire; he wanted me to help him by phrasing what he meant. But I couldn't — I didn't know. So he brought it out awkwardly: "The *real* thing; a gentleman, you know, or a lady." I was quite ready to give a general assent — I admitted that there was a great deal in that. This encouraged Major Monarch to say, following up his appeal with an unacted gulp: "It's awfully hard — we've tried everything." The gulp was communicative; it proved too much for his wife. Before I knew it Mrs. Monarch had dropped again upon a divan and burst into tears. Her husband sat down beside her, holding one of her hands; whereupon she quickly dried her eyes with the other, while I felt embarrassed as she looked up at me. "There isn't a confounded job I haven't applied for — waited for — prayed for. You can fancy we'd be pretty bad first. Secretaryships and that sort of thing? You might as well ask for a peerage. I'd be *anything* — I'm strong; a messenger or a coalheaver. I'd put on a gold-laced cap and open carriage-doors in front of the haberdasher's; I'd hang about a station to carry portmanteaux; I'd be a postman. But they won't *look* at you; there are thousands as good as yourself already on the ground. *Gentlemen,* poor beggars, who've drunk their wine, who've kept their hunters!"

I was as reassuring as I knew how to be, and my visitors were presently on their feet again while, for the experiment, we agreed on an hour. We were discussing it when the door opened and Miss Churm came in with a wet umbrella. Miss Churm had to take the omnibus to Maida Vale and then walk half a mile. She looked a trifle blowsy and slightly splashed. I scarcely ever saw her come in without thinking afresh how odd it was that, being so little in herself, she should yet be so much in others. She was a meagre little Miss Churm, but was such an ample heroine of romance. She was only a freckled cockney, but she could represent everything, from a fine lady to a shepherdess; she had the faculty as she might have had a fine voice or long hair. She couldn't spell and she loved beer, but she had two or three "points," and practice, and a knack, and mother-wit, and a whimsical sensibility, and a love of the theatre, and seven sisters, and not an ounce of respect, especially for the *h.* The first thing my visitors saw was that her umbrella was wet, and in their spotless perfection they visibly winced at it. The rain had come on since their arrival.

"I'm all in a soak; there *was* a mess of people in the 'bus. I wish you lived near a stytion," said Miss Churm. I requested her to get ready as quickly as possible, and she passed into the room in which she always changed her dress. But before going out she asked me what she was to get into this time.

"It's the Russian princess, don't you know?" I answered; "the one with the 'golden eyes,' in black velvet, for the long thing in the *Cheapside.*"

"Golden eyes? I *say!*" cried Miss Churm, while my companions watched her with intensity as she withdrew. She always arranged herself, when she was late, before I could turn round; and I kept my visitors a little on purpose, so that they might get an idea, from seeing her, what would be expected of themselves. I mentioned that she was quite my notion of an excellent model — she was really very clever.

"Do you think she looks like a Russian princess?" Major Monarch asked with lurking alarm.

"When I make her, yes."

"Oh if you have to *make* her — !" he reasoned, not without point.

"That's the most you can ask. There are so many who are not makeable."

"Well now, *here's* a lady" — and with a persuasive smile he passed his arm into his wife's — "who's already made!"

"Oh I'm not a Russian princess," Mrs. Monarch protested a little coldly. I could see she had known some and didn't like them. There at once was a complication of a kind I never had to fear with Miss Churm.

This young lady came back in black velvet — the gown was rather rusty and very low on her lean shoulders — and with a Japanese fan in her red hands. I reminded her that in the scene I was doing she had to look over some one's head. "I forget whose it is; but it doesn't matter. Just look over a head."

"I'd rather look over a stove," said Miss Churm; and she took her station near the fire. She fell into position, settled herself into a tall attitude, gave a certain backward inclination to her head and a certain forward droop to her fan, and looked, at least to my prejudiced sense, distinguished and charming, foreign and dangerous. We left her looking so while I went downstairs with Major and Mrs. Monarch.

"I believe I could come about as near it as that," said Mrs. Monarch.

"Oh you think she's shabby, but you must allow for the alchemy of art."

However, they went off with an evident increase of comfort founded on their demonstrable advantage in being the real thing. I could fancy them shuddering over Miss Churm. She was very droll about them when I went back, for I told her what they wanted.

"Well, if *she* can sit I'll tyke to book-keeping," said my model.

"She's very ladylike," I replied as an innocent form of aggravation.

"So much the worse for *you*. That means she can't turn round."

"She'll do for the fashionable novels."

"Oh yes, she'll *do* for them!" my model humorously declared. "Ain't they bad enough without her?" I had often sociably denounced them to Miss Churm.

III

It was for the elucidation of a mystery in one of these works that I first tried Mrs. Monarch. Her husband came with her, to be useful if necessary — it was sufficiently clear that as a general thing he would prefer to come with her. At first I wondered if this were for "propriety's" sake — if he were going to be jealous and meddling. The idea was too tiresome, and if it had been confirmed it would speedily have brought our acquaintance to a close. But I soon saw there was nothing in it and that if he accompanied Mrs. Monarch it was — in addition to the chance of being wanted — simply because he had nothing else to do. When they were separate his occupation was gone and they never *had* been separate. I judged rightly that in their awkward situation their close union was their main comfort and that this union had no weak spot. It was a real marriage, an encouragement to the hesitating, a nut for pessimists to crack. Their address was humble — I remember afterwards thinking it had been the only thing about them that was really professional — and I could fancy the lamentable lodgings in which the Major would have been left alone. He could sit there more or less grimly with his wife — he couldn't sit there anyhow without her.

He had too much tact to try and make himself agreeable when he couldn't be useful; so when I was too absorbed in my work to talk he simply sat and waited. But I liked to hear him talk — it made my work, when not interrupting it, less mechanical, less special. To listen to him was to combine the excitement of going out with the economy of staying at home. There was only one hindrance — that I seemed not to know any of the people this brilliant couple had known. I think he wondered extremely, during the term of our intercourse, whom the deuce I *did* know. He hadn't a stray sixpence of an idea to fumble for, so we didn't spin it very fine; we confined ourselves to questions of leather and even of liquor — saddlers and breeches-makers and how to get excellent claret cheap — and matters like "good trains" and the habits of small game. His lore on these last subjects was astonishing — he managed to interweave the station-master with the ornithologist. When he couldn't talk about greater things he could talk cheerfully about smaller, and since I couldn't accompany him into reminiscences of the fashionable world he could lower the conversation without a visible effort to my level.

So earnest a desire to please was touching in a man who could so easily have knocked one down. He looked after the fire and had an opinion on the draught of the stove without my asking him, and I could see that he thought many of my arrangements not half knowing. I remember telling him that if I were only rich I'd offer him a salary to come and teach me how to live. Sometimes he gave a random sigh of which the essence might have been: "Give me even such a bare old barrack as *this*, and I'd do something with it!" When I wanted to use him he came alone; which was an illustration of the superior courage of women. His wife could bear her solitary second floor, and she was in general more discreet; showing by various small reserves that she was alive to the propriety of keeping our relations markedly professional — not letting them slide into sociability. She wished it to remain clear that she and the Major were employed, not cultivated, and if she approved of me as a superior, who could be kept in his place, she never thought me quite good enough for an equal.

She sat with great intensity, giving the whole of her mind to it, and was capable of remaining for an hour almost as motionless as before a photographer's lens. I could see she had been photographed often, but somehow the very habit that made her good for that purpose unfitted her for mine. At first I was extremely pleased with her ladylike air, and it was a satisfaction, on coming to follow her lines, to see how good they were and how far they could lead the pencil. But after a little skirmishing I began to find her too insurmountably stiff; do what I would with it my drawing looked like a photograph or a copy of a photograph. Her figure had no variety of expression — she herself had no sense of variety. You may say that this was my business and was only a question of placing her. Yet I placed her in every conceivable position and she managed to obliterate their differences. She was always a lady certainly, and into the bargain was always the same lady. She was the real thing, but always the same thing. There were moments when I rather writhed under the serenity of her confidence that she *was* the real thing. All her dealings with me and all her husband's were an implication that this was lucky for *me*. Meanwhile I found myself trying to invent types that approached her own, instead of making her own transform itself — in the clever way that was not impossible for instance to poor Miss Churm. Arrange as I would and take the precautions I would, she always came out, in my pictures, too tall — landing me in the dilemma of having represented a fascinating woman as seven feet high, which (out of respect perhaps to my own very much scantier inches) was far from my idea of such a personage.

The case was worse with the Major — nothing I could do would keep *him* down, so that he became useful only for the representation of brawny giants. I adored variety and range, I cherished human accidents, the illustrative note; I wanted to characterize closely, and the thing in the world I most hated was the danger of being ridden by a type. I had quarreled with some of my friends about it; I had parted company with them for maintaining that one *had* to be, and that if the type was beautiful — witness Raphael and Leonardo — the servitude was only a gain. I was neither Leonardo nor Raphael — I might only be a presumptuous young modern searcher; but I held that everything was to be sacrificed sooner than character. When they claimed that the obsessional form could easily *be* character I retorted, perhaps superficially, "Whose?" It couldn't be everybody's — it might end in being nobody's.

After I had drawn Mrs. Monarch a dozen times I felt surer even than before that the value of such a model as Miss Churm resided precisely in the fact that she had no positive stamp, combined of course with the other fact that what she did have was a curious and inexplicable talent for imitation. Her usual appearance was like a curtain which she could draw up at request for a capital performance. This performance was simply suggestive; but it was a word to the wise — it was vivid and pretty. Sometimes even I thought it, though she was plain herself, too insipidly pretty; I made it a reproach to her that the figures drawn from her were monotonously (*bêtement*, as we used to say) graceful. Nothing made her more angry; it was so much her pride to feel she could sit for characters that had nothing in common with each other. She would accuse me at such moments of taking away her "reputytion."

It suffered a certain shrinkage, this queer quantity, from the repeated visits of my new friends. Miss Churm was greatly in demand, never in want of employment, so I had no scruple in putting her off occasionally, to try them more at my ease. It was certainly amusing at first to do the real thing — it was amusing to do Major Monarch's trousers. They *were* the real thing, even if he did come out colossal. It was amusing to do his wife's back hair — it was so mathematically neat — and the particular "smart" tension of her tight stays. She lent herself especially to positions in which the face was somewhat averted or blurred; she abounded in ladylike back views and *profils perdus.*[1] When she stood erect she took naturally one of the attitudes in which court-painters represent queens and princesses; so that I found myself wondering whether, to draw out this accomplishment, I couldn't get the editor of the *Cheapside* to publish a really royal romance, "A Tale of Buckingham Palace." Sometimes however the real thing and the make-believe came into contact; by which I mean that Miss Churm, keeping an appointment or coming to make one on days when I had much work in hand, encountered her invidious rivals. The encounter was not on their part, for they noticed her no more than if she had been the housemaid; not from intentional loftiness, but simply because as yet, professionally, they didn't know how to fraternize, as I could imagine they would have liked — or at least that the Major would. They couldn't talk about the omnibus — they always walked; and they didn't know what else to try — she wasn't interested in good trains or cheap claret. Besides, they must have felt — in the air — that she was amused at them, secretly derisive of their ever knowing how. She wasn't a person to conceal the limits of her faith if she had had a chance to show them. On the other hand Mrs. Monarch didn't think her tidy; for why else did she take pains to say to me — it was going out of the way, for Mrs. Monarch — that she didn't like dirty women?

One day when my young lady happened to be present with my other sitters — she even dropped in, when it was convenient, for a chat — I asked her to be so good as to lend a hand in getting tea, a service with which she was familiar and which was one of a class that, living as I did in a small way, with slender domestic resources, I often appealed to my models to render. They liked to lay hands on my property, to break the sitting, and sometimes the china — it made them feel Bohemian. The next time I saw Miss Churm after this incident she surprised me greatly by making a scene about it — she accused me of having wished to humiliate her. She hadn't resented the outrage at the time, but had seemed obliging and amused, enjoying the comedy of asking Mrs. Monarch, who sat vague and silent, whether she would have cream and sugar, and putting an exaggerated simper into the question. She had tried intonations — as if she too wished to pass for the real thing — till I was afraid my other visitors would take offense.

Oh they were determined not to do this, and their touching patience was the measure of their great need. They would sit by the hour, uncomplaining, till I was ready to use them; they would come back on the chance of being wanted and would walk away cheerfully if it failed. I used to go to the door with them to see in what magnificent order they retreated. I tried to find other employment for them — I introduced them to several artists.

[1] profiles in which the face is averted and its features remain unseen.

But they didn't "take," for reasons I could appreciate, and I became rather anxiously aware that after such disappointments they fell back upon me with a heavier weight. They did me the honor to think me most *their* form. They weren't romantic enough for the painters, and in those days there were few serious workers in black-and-white. Besides, they had an eye to the great job I had mentioned to them — they had secretly set their hearts on supplying the right essence for my pictorial vindication of our fine novelist. They knew that for this undertaking I should want no costume-effects, none of the frippery of past ages — that it was a case in which everything would be contemporary and satirical and presumably genteel. If I could work them into it their future would be assured, for the labor would of course be long and the occupation steady.

One day Mrs. Monarch came without her husband — she explained his absence by his having had to go to the City. While she sat there in her usual relaxed majesty there came at the door a knock which I immediately recognized as the subdued appeal of a model out of work. It was followed by the entrance of a young man whom I at once saw to be a foreigner and who proved in fact an Italian acquainted with no English word but my name, which he uttered in a way that made it seem to include all others. I hadn't then visited his country, nor was I proficient in his tongue; but as he was not so meanly constituted — what Italian is? — as to depend only on that member for expression he conveyed to me, in familiar but graceful mimicry, that he was in search of exactly the employment in which the lady before me was engaged. I was not struck with him at first, and while I continued to draw I dropped few signs of interest or encouragement. He stood his ground however — not importunately, but with a dumb dog-like fidelity in his eyes that amounted to innocent impudence, the manner of a devoted servant — he might have been in the house for years — unjustly suspected. Suddenly it struck me that this very attitude and expression made a picture; whereupon I told him to sit down and wait till I should be free. There was another picture in the way he obeyed me, and I observed as I worked that there were others still in the way he looked wonderingly, with his head thrown back, about the high studio. He might have been crossing himself in Saint Peter's. Before I finished I said to myself "The fellow's a bankrupt orange-monger, but a treasure."

When Mrs. Monarch withdrew he passed across the room like a flash to open the door for her, standing there with the rapt pure gaze of the young Dante spellbound by the young Beatrice. As I never insisted, in such situations, on the blankness of the British domestic, I reflected that he had the making of a servant — and I needed one, but couldn't pay him to be only that — as well as of a model; in short I resolved to adopt my bright adventurer if he would agree to officiate in the double capacity. He jumped at my offer, and in the event my rashness — for I had really known nothing about him — wasn't brought home to me. He proved a sympathetic though a desultory ministrant, and had in a wonderful degree the *sentiment de la pose.* It was uncultivated, instinctive, a part of the happy instinct that had guided him to my door and helped him to spell out my name on the card nailed to it. He had had no other introduction to me than a guess, from the shape of my high north window, seen outside, that my place was a studio and that as a studio it would contain an artist. He had wandered to England in search of fortune, like other itinerants, and had embarked, with a partner and a small green hand-cart, on the sale of penny ices. The ices had melted away and the partner had dissolved in their train. My young man wore tight yellow trousers with reddish stripes and his name was Oronte. He was sallow but fair, and when I put him into some old clothes of my own he looked like an Englishman. He was as good as Miss Churm, who could look, when requested, like an Italian.

IV

I thought Mrs. Monarch's face slightly convulsed when, on her coming back with her husband, she found Oronte installed. It was strange to have to recognize in a scrap of a lazzarone[2] a competitor to her magnificent Major. It was she who scented danger first, for the Major was anecdotically unconscious. But Oronte gave us tea, with a hundred eager confusions — he had never been concerned in so queer a process — and I think she thought better of me for having at last an "establishment." They saw a couple of drawings that I had made of the establishment, and Mrs. Monarch hinted that it never would have struck her he had sat for them. "Now the drawings you make from *us,* they look exactly like us," she reminded me, smiling in triumph; and I recognized that this was indeed just their defect. When I drew the Monarchs I couldn't anyhow get away from them — get into the character I wanted to represent; and I hadn't the least desire my model should be discoverable in my picture. Miss Churm never was, and Mrs. Monarch thought I hid her, very properly, because she was vulgar; whereas if she was lost it was only as the dead who got to heaven are lost — in the gain of an angel the more.

By this time I had got a certain start with "Rutland Ramsay," the first novel in the great projected series; that is I had produced a dozen drawings, several with the help of the Major and his wife, and I had sent them in for approval. My understanding with the publishers, as I have already hinted, had been that I was to be left to do my work, in this particular case, as I liked, with the whole book committed to me; but my connection with the rest of the series was only contingent. There were moments when, frankly, it *was* a comfort to have the real thing under one's hand; for there were characters in "Rutland Ramsay" that were very much like it. There were people presumably as erect as the Major and women of as good a fashion as Mrs. Monarch. There was a great deal of country-house life — treated, it is

---

[2] the name given to homeless beggars in Naples.

true, in a fine fanciful ironical generalized way — and there was a considerable implication of knickerbockers and kilts. There were certain things I had to settle at the outset; such things for instance as the exact appearance of the hero and the particular bloom and figure of the heroine. The author of course gave me a lead, but there was a margin for interpretation. I took the Monarchs into my confidence, I told them frankly what I was about, I mentioned my embarrassments and alternatives. "Oh take *him!*" Mrs. Monarch murmured sweetly, looking at her husband; and "What could you want better than my wife?" the Major enquired with the comfortable candor that now prevailed between us.

I wasn't obliged to answer these remarks — I was only obliged to place my sitters. I wasn't easy in mind, and I postponed a little timidly perhaps the solving of my question. The book was a large canvas, the other figures were numerous, and I worked off at first some of the episodes in which the hero and the heroine were not concerned. When once I had set *them* up I should have to stick to them — I couldn't make my young man seven feet high in one place and five feet nine in another. I inclined on the whole to the latter measurement, though the Major more than once reminded me that *he* looked about as young as any one. It was indeed quite possible to arrange him, for the figure, so that it would have been difficult to detect his age. After the spontaneous Oronte had been with me a month, and after I had given him to understand several times over that his native exuberance would presently constitute an insurmountable barrier to our further intercourse, I waked to a sense of his heroic capacity. He was only five feet seven, but the remaining inches were latent. I tried him almost secretly at first, for I was really rather afraid of the judgment my other models would pass on such a choice. If they regarded Miss Churm as little better than a snare what would they think of the representation by a person so little the real thing as an Italian street-vendor of a protagonist formed by a public school?

If I went a little in fear of them it wasn't because they bullied me, because they had got an oppressive foothold, but because in their really pathetic decorum and mysteriously permanent newness they counted on me so intensely. I was therefore very glad when Jack Hawley came home: he was always of such good counsel. He painted badly himself, but there was no one like him for putting his finger on the place. He had been absent from England for a year; he had been somewhere — I don't remember where — to get a fresh eye. I was in a good deal of dread of any such organ, but we were old friends; he had been away for months and a sense of emptiness was creeping into my life. I hadn't dodged a missile for a year.

He came back with a fresh eye, but with the same old black velvet blouse, and the first evening he spent in my studio we smoked cigarettes till the small hours. He had done no work himself, he had only got the eye; so the field was clear for the production of my little things. He wanted to see what I had produced for the *Cheapside,* but he was disappointed in the exhibition. That at least seemed the meaning of two or three comprehensive groans which, as he lounged on my big divan, his leg folded under him, looking at my latest drawings, issued from his lips with the smoke of the cigarette.

"What's the matter with you?" I asked.

"What's the matter with *you?*"

"Nothing save that I'm mystified."

"You are indeed. You're quite off the hinge. What's the meaning of this new fad?" And he tossed me, with visible irreverence, a drawing in which I happened to have depicted both my elegant models. I asked if he didn't think it good, and he replied that it struck him as execrable, given the sort of thing I had always represented myself to him as wishing to arrive at; but I let that pass — I was so anxious to see exactly what he meant. The two figures in the picture looked colossal, but I supposed this was *not* what he meant, inasmuch as, for aught he knew to the contrary, I might have been trying for some such effect. I maintained that I was working exactly in the same way as when he last had done me the honor to tell me I might do something some day. "Well, there's a screw loose somewhere," he answered; "wait a bit and I'll discover it." I depended upon him to do so: where else was the fresh eye? But he produced at last nothing more luminous than "I don't know — I don't like your types." This was lame for a critic who had never consented to discuss with me anything but the question of execution, the direction of strokes and the mystery of values.

"In the drawings you've been looking at I think my types are very handsome."

"Oh they won't do!"

"I've been working with new models."

"I see you have. *They* won't do."

"Are you very sure of that?"

"Absolutely — they're stupid."

"You mean *I* am — for I ought to get round that."

"You *can't* — with such people. Who are they?"

I told him, so far as was necessary, and he concluded heartlessly: "*Ce sont des gens qu'il faut mettre à la porte.*"[3]

"You're never seen them; they're awfully good" — I flew to their defense.

"Not seen them? Why all this recent work of yours drops to pieces with them. It's all I want to see of them."

"No one else has said anything against it — the *Cheapside* people are pleased."

"Every one else is an ass, and the *Cheapside* people the biggest asses of all. Come, don't pretend at this time of day to have pretty illusions about the public, especially about publishers and editors. It's not for *such* animals

---

[3] "You'll have to throw them out" (French).

you work — it's for those you know, *coloro che sanno;*[4] so keep straight for *me* if you can't keep straight for yourself. There was a certain sort of thing you used to try for — and a very good thing it was. But this twaddle isn't *in* it." When I talked with Hawley later about "Rutland Ramsay" and its possible successors he declared that I must get back into my boat again or I should go to the bottom. His voice in short was the voice of warning.

I noted the warning, but I didn't turn my friends out of doors. They bored me a good deal; but the very fact that they bored me admonished me not to sacrifice them — if there was anything to be done with them — simply to irritation. As I look back at this phase they seem to me to have pervaded my life not a little. I have a vision of them as most of the time in my studio, seated against the wall on an old velvet bench to be out of the way, and resembling the while a pair of patient courtiers in a royal ante-chamber. I'm convinced that during the coldest weeks of the winter they held their ground because it saved them fire. Their newness was losing its gloss, and it was impossible not to feel them objects of charity. Whenever Miss Churm arrived they went away, and after I was fairly launched in "Rutland Ramsay" Miss Churm arrived pretty often. They managed to express to me tacitly that they supposed I wanted her for the low life of the book, and I let them suppose it, since they had attempted to study the work — it was lying about the studio — without discovering that it dealt only with the highest circles. They had dipped into the most brilliant of our novelists without deciphering many passages. I still took an hour from them, now and again, in spite of Jack Hawley's warning: it would be time enough to dismiss them, if dismissal should be necessary, when the rigor of the season was over. Hawley had made their acquaintance — he had met them at my fireside — and thought them a ridiculous pair. Learning that he was a painter they tried to approach him, to show him too that they were the real thing; but he looked at them, across the big room, as if they were miles away: they were a compendium of everything he most objected to in the social system of his country. Such people as that, all convention and patent-leather, with ejaculations that stopped conversation, had no business in a studio. A studio was a place to learn to see, and how could you see through a pair of feather-beds?

The main inconvenience I suffered at their hands was that at first I was shy of letting it break upon them that my artful little servant had begun to sit to me for "Rutland Ramsay." They knew I had been odd enough — they were prepared by this time to allow oddity to artists — to pick a foreign vagabond out of the streets when I might have had a person with whiskers and credentials; but it was some time before they learned how high I rated his accomplishments. They found him in an attitude more than once, but they never doubted I was doing him as an organ-grinder. There were several things they never guessed, and one of them was that for a

---

[4] "the ones who understand" (Italian).

striking scene in the novel, in which a footman briefly figured, it occurred to me to make use of Major Monarch as the menial. I kept putting this off, I didn't like to ask him to don the livery — besides the difficulty of finding a livery to fit him. At last, one day late in the winter, when I was at work on the despised Oronte, who caught one's idea on the wing, and was in the glow of feeling myself go very straight, they came in, the Major and his wife, with their society laugh about nothing (there was less and less to laugh at); came in like country-callers — they always reminded me of that — who have walked across the park after church and are presently persuaded to stay to luncheon. Luncheon was over, but they could stay to tea — I knew they wanted it. The fit was on me, however, and I couldn't let my ardor cool and my work wait, with the fading daylight, while my model prepared it. So I asked Mrs. Monarch if she would mind laying it out — a request which for an instant brought all the blood to her face. Her eyes were on her husband's for a second, and some mute telegraphy passed between them. Their folly was over the next instant; his cheerful shrewdness put an end to it. So far from pitying their wounded pride, I must add, I was moved to give it as complete a lesson as I could. They bustled about together and got out the cups and saucers and made the kettle boil. I know they felt as if they were waiting on my servant, and when the tea was prepared I said: "He'll have a cup, please — he's tired." Mrs. Monarch brought him one where he stood, and he took it from her as if he had been a gentleman at a party squeezing a crush-hat with an elbow.

Then it came over me that she had made a great effort for me — made it with a kind of nobleness — and that I owed her a compensation. Each time I saw her after this I wondered what the compensation could be. I couldn't go on doing the wrong thing to oblige them. Oh it *was* the wrong thing, the stamp of the work for which they sat — Hawley was not the only person to say it now. I sent in a large number of the drawings I had made for "Rutland Ramsay," and I received a warning that was more to the point than Hawley's. The artistic adviser of the house for which I was working was of opinion that many of my illustrations were not what had been looked for. Most of these illustrations were the subjects in which the Monarchs had figured. Without going into the question of what *had* been looked for, I had to face the fact that at this rate I shouldn't get the other books to do. I hurled myself in despair on Miss Churm — I put her through all her paces. I not only adopted Oronte publicly as my hero, but one morning when the Major looked in to see if I didn't require him to finish a *Cheapside* figure for which he had begun to sit the week before, I told him I had changed my mind — I'd do the drawing from my man. At this my visitor turned pale and stood looking at me. "Is *he* your idea of an English gentleman?" he asked.

I was disappointed, I was nervous, I wanted to get on with my work; so I replied with irritation: "Oh my dear Major — I can't be ruined for *you!*"

It was a horrid speech, but he stood another moment — after which, without a word, he quitted the studio. I drew a long breath, for I said to myself that I shouldn't see him again. I hadn't told him definitely that I was in danger of having my work rejected, but I was vexed at his not having felt the catastrophe in the air, read with me the moral of our fruitless collaboration, the lesson that in the deceptive atmosphere of art even the highest respectability may fail of being plastic.

I didn't owe my friends money, but I did see them again. They reappeared together three days later; and, given all the other facts, there was something tragic in that one. It was a clear proof they could find nothing else in life to do. They had threshed the matter out in a dismal conference — they had digested the bad news that they were not in for the series. If they weren't useful to me for the *Cheapside* their function seemed difficult to determine, and I could only judge at first that they had come, forgivingly, decorously, to take a last leave. This made me rejoice in secret that I had little leisure for a scene; for I had placed both my other models in position together and I was pegging away at a drawing from which I hoped to derive glory. It had been suggested by the passage in which Rutland Ramsay, drawing up a chair to Artemisia's piano-stool, says extraordinary things to her while she ostensibly fingers out a difficult piece of music. I had done Miss Churm at the piano before — it was an attitude in which she knew how to take on an absolutely poetic grace. I wished the two figures to "compose" together with intensity, and my little Italian had entered perfectly into my conception. The pair were vividly before me, the piano had been pulled out; it was a charming show of blended youth and murmured love, which I had only to catch and keep. My visitors stood and looked at it, and I was friendly to them over my shoulder.

They made no response, but I was used to silent company and went on with my work, only a little disconcerted — even though exhilarated by the sense that *this* was at least the ideal thing — at not having got rid of them after all. Presently I heard Mrs. Monarch's sweet voice beside or rather above me: "I wish her hair were a little better done." I looked up and she was staring with a strange fixedness at Miss Churm, whose back was turned to her. "Do you mind my just touching it?" she went on — a question which made me spring up for an instant as with the instinctive fear that she might do the young lady a harm. But she quieted me with a glance I shall never forget — I confess I should like to have been able to paint *that* — and went for a moment to my model. She spoke to her softly, laying a hand on her shoulder and bending over her; and as the girl, understanding, gratefully assented, she disposed her rough curls, with a few quick passes, in such a way as to make Miss Churm's head twice as charming. It was one of the most heroic personal services I've ever seen rendered. Then Mrs. Monarch turned away with a low sigh and, looking about her as if for something to do, stooped to the floor with a noble humility and picked up a dirty rag that had dropped out of my paint-box.

The Major meanwhile had also been looking for something to do, and, wandering to the other end of the studio, saw before him my breakfast-things neglected, unremoved. "I say, can't I be useful *here?*" he called out to me with an irrepressible quaver. I assented with a laugh that I fear was awkward, and for the next ten minutes, while I worked, I heard the light clatter of china and the tinkle of spoons and glass. Mrs. Monarch assisted her husband — they washed up my crockery, they put it away. They wandered off into my little scullery, and I afterwards found that they had cleaned my knives and that my slender stock of plate had an unprecedented surface. When it came over me, the latent eloquence of what they were doing, I confess that my drawing was blurred for a moment — the picture swam. They had accepted their failure, but they couldn't accept their fate. They had bowed their heads in bewilderment to the perverse and cruel law in virtue of which the real thing could be so much less precious than the unreal; but they didn't want to starve. If my servants were my models, then my models might be my servants. They would reverse the parts — the others would sit for the ladies and gentlemen and *they* would do the work. They would still be in the studio — it was an intense dumb appeal to me not to turn them out. "Take us on," they wanted to say — "we'll do *any-thing.*"

My pencil dropped from my hand; my sitting was spoiled and I got rid of my sitters, who were also evidently rather mystified and awestruck. Then, alone with the Major and his wife I had a most uncomfortable moment. He put their prayer into a single sentence: "I say, you know — just let *us* do for you, can't you?" I couldn't — it was dreadful to see them emptying my slops; but I pretended I could, to oblige them, for about a week. Then I gave them a sum of money to go away, and I never saw them again. I obtained the remaining books, but my friend Hawley repeats that Major and Mrs. Monarch did me a permanent harm, got me into false ways. If it be true I'm content to have paid the price — for the memory.

[1891]

SARAH ORNE JEWETT (1849–1909) was born in South Berwick, Maine. Her father was a country doctor, and she often accompanied him on his horse-and-buggy rounds among sick people on the local farms. She later said that she got her real education from these trips, rather than from her classes at Miss Rayne's School and the Berwick Academy in Maine. She had a fine ear for local speech and the native idiom, which she used to good effect in her stories. Impressed as a girl by the sympathetic depiction of local color (the people and life of a particular geographical setting) in the fiction of Harriet Beecher Stowe, she began to write stories herself, publishing her earliest one, "Jenny Garrow's Lovers," in a Boston weekly when she was eighteen years old. Shortly after her twentieth birthday her work was accepted by the prestigious Atlantic Monthly, and her career was launched. Jewett published her first collection of stories, Deephaven, in 1877. She read Flaubert, Émile Zola, Tolstoy, and Henry James, and her style gradually matured, as is evident in the stories that make up the 1886 volume, The White Heron and Other Stories. Her masterpiece, The Country of the Pointed Firs (1896), was a book of short sketches linked by the narrator's account of her stay in a Maine seacoast village and her growing involvement in the quiet lives of the people there.

Many stories were written about New England in Jewett's time, but hers have a unique quality, stemming from her deep sympathy not just for the landscape but for the native characters. She was able to suggest a mysterious depth in her characters, and she insisted that the personal point of view was essential to writers of fiction. Once she laughingly told the younger writer Willa Cather that her head was full of dear old houses and dear old women, and when an old house and an old woman came together in her brain with a click, she knew a story was underway.

While it is true that Jewett's realism heightened the attractive aspects of the rural New England character at the same time that it diminished the harsher qualities, her literary technique is so candid and true to the larger aspects of human nature that the darker undercurrents of deprivation, both physical and psychological, are also evident beneath the surface of her descriptions. Henry James recognized that Jewett was "surpassed only by Hawthorne as producer of the most finished and penetrating of the numerous 'short stories' that have the domestic life of New England for their general and their doubtless somewhat lean subject." In her time she was lauded for possessing an exquisitely simple, natural, and graceful style. More recently, readers have responded to the serenity and honesty in stories like "The White Heron," with its hint of tragedy in the young girl's conflict between her admiration for the ornithologist and her love for the wild bird.

Sarah Orne Jewett

ගුනු

A WHITE HERON

I

The woods were already filled with shadows one June evening, just before eight o'clock, though a bright sunset still glimmered faintly among the trunks of the trees. A little girl was driving home her cow, a plodding, dilatory, provoking creature in her behavior, but a valued companion for all that. They were going away from the western light, and striking deep into the dark woods, but their feet were familiar with the path, and it was no matter whether their eyes could see it or not.

There was hardly a night the summer through when the old cow could be found waiting at the pasture bars; on the contrary, it was her greatest pleasure to hide herself away among the high huckleberry bushes, and though she wore a loud bell she had made the discovery that if one stood perfectly still it would not ring. So Sylvia had to hunt for her until she found her, and call Co'! Co'! with never an answering Moo, until her childish patience was quite spent. If the creature had not given good milk and plenty of it, the case would have seemed very different to her owners. Besides, Sylvia had all the time there was, and very little use to make of it. Sometimes in pleasant weather it was a consolation to look upon the cow's pranks as an intelligent attempt to play hide and seek, and as the child had no playmates she lent herself to this amusement with a good deal of zest. Though this chase had been so long that the wary animal herself had given an unusual signal of her whereabouts, Sylvia had only laughed when she came upon Mistress Moolly at the swamp-side, and urged her affectionately homeward with a twig of birch leaves. The old cow was not inclined to wander farther, she even turned in the right direction for once as they left the pasture, and stepped along the road at a good pace. She was quite ready to be milked now, and seldom stopped to browse. Sylvia wondered what her grandmother would say because they were so late. It was a great while since she had left home at half past five o'clock, but everybody knew the difficulty of making this errand a short one. Mrs. Tilley had chased the horned torment too many summer evenings herself to blame any one else for lingering, and was only thankful as she waited that she had Sylvia, nowadays, to give such valuable assistance. The good woman suspected that Sylvia loitered occasionally on her own account; there never was such a child for straying about out-of-doors since the world was made! Everybody said that it was a good change for a little maid who had tried to grow for eight years in a crowded manufacturing town, but, as for Sylvia herself, it seemed as if she never had been alive at all before she came to live at the farm. She thought often with wistful compassion of a wretched dry geranium that belonged to a town neighbor.

" 'Afraid of folks,' " old Mrs. Tilley said to herself, with a smile, after she had made the unlikely choice of Sylvia from her daughter's houseful of children, and was returning to the farm. " 'Afraid of folks,' they said! I guess she won't be troubled no great with 'em up to the old place!" When they reached the door of the lonely house and stopped to unlock it, and the cat came to purr loudly, and rub against them, a deserted pussy, indeed, but fat with young robins, Sylvia whispered that this was a beautiful place to live in, and she never should wish to go home.

The companions followed the shady wood-road, the cow taking slow steps, and the child very fast ones. The cow stopped long at the brook to drink, as if the pasture were not half a swamp, and Sylvia stood still and waited, letting her bare feet cool themselves in the shoal water, while the great twilight moths struck softly against her. She waded on through the brook as the cow moved away, and listened to the thrushes with a heart that beat fast with pleasure. There was a stirring in the great boughs overhead. They were full of little birds and beasts that seemed to be wide-awake, and going about their world, or else saying good-night to each other in sleepy twitters. Sylvia herself felt sleepy as she walked along. However, it was not much farther to the house, and the air was soft and sweet. She was not often in the woods so late as this, and it made her feel as if she were a part of the gray shadows and the moving leaves. She was just thinking how long it seemed since she first came to the farm a year ago, and wondering if everything went on in the noisy town just the same as when she was there; the thought of the great red-faced boy who used to chase and frighten her made her hurry along the path to escape from the shadow of the trees.

Suddenly this little woods-girl is horror-stricken to hear a clear whistle not very far away. Not a bird's whistle, which would have a sort of friendliness, but a boy's whistle, determined, and somewhat aggressive. Sylvia left the cow to whatever sad fate might await her, and stepped discreetly aside into the bushes, but she was just too late. The enemy had discovered her, and called out in a very cheerful and persuasive tone, "Halloa, little girl, how far is it to the road?" and trembling Sylvia answered almost inaudibly, "A good ways."

She did not dare to look boldly at the tall young man, who carried a gun over his shoulder, but she came out of her bush and again followed the cow, while he walked alongside.

"I have been hunting for some birds," the stranger said kindly, "and I have lost my way, and need a friend very much. Don't be afraid," he added gallantly. "Speak up and tell me what your name is, and whether you think I can spend the night at your house, and go out gunning early in the morning."

Sylvia was more alarmed than before. Would not her grandmother consider her much to blame? But who could have foreseen such an accident as this? It did not appear to be her fault, and she hung her head as if the stem of it were broken, but managed to answer, "Sylvy," with much effort when her companion again asked her name.

Mrs. Tilley was standing in the doorway when the trio came into view. The cow gave a loud moo by way of explanation.

"Yes, you'd better speak up for yourself, you old trial! Where'd she tucked herself away this time, Sylvy?" Sylvia kept an awed silence; she knew by instinct that her grandmother did not comprehend the gravity of the situation. She must be mistaking the stranger for one of the farmer-lads of the region.

The young man stood his gun beside the door, and dropped a heavy game-bag beside it; then he bade Mrs. Tilley good-evening, and repeated his wayfarer's story, and asked if he could have a night's lodging.

"Put me anywhere you like," he said. "I must be off early in the morning, before day; but I am very hungry, indeed. You can give me some milk at any rate, that's plain."

"Dear sakes, yes," responded the hostess, whose long slumbering hospitality seemed to be easily awakened. "You might fare better if you went out on the main road a mile or so, but you're welcome to what we've got. I'll milk right off, and you make yourself at home. You can sleep on husks or feathers," she proffered graciously. "I raised them all myself. There's good pasturing for geese just below here towards the ma'sh. Now step round and set a plate for the gentleman, Sylvy!" And Sylvia promptly stepped. She was glad to have something to do, and she was hungry herself.

It was a surprise to find so clean and comfortable a little dwelling in this New England wilderness. The young man had known the horrors of its most primitive housekeeping, and the dreary squalor of that level of society which does not rebel at the companionship of hens. This was the best thrift of an old-fashioned farmstead, though on such a small scale that it seemed like a hermitage. He listened eagerly to the old woman's quaint talk, he watched Sylvia's pale face and shining gray eyes with ever growing enthusiasm, and insisted that this was the best supper he had eaten for a month; then, afterward, the new-made friends sat down in the doorway together while the moon came up.

Soon it would be berry-time, and Sylvia was a great help at picking. The cow was a good milker, though a plaguy thing to keep track of, the hostess gossiped frankly, adding presently that she had buried four children, so that Sylvia's mother, and a son (who might be dead) in California were all the children she had left. "Dan, my boy, was a great hand to go gunning," she explained sadly. "I never wanted for pa'tridges or gray squer'ls while he was to home. He's been a great wand'rer, I expect, and he's no hand to write letters. There, I don't blame him, I'd ha' seen the world myself if it had been so I could.

"Sylvia takes after him," the grandmother continued affectionately, after a minute's pause. "There ain't a foot o' ground she don't know her way over, and the wild creatur's counts her one o' themselves. Squer'ls she'll tame to come an' feed right out o' her hands, and all sorts o' birds. Last winter she got the jay-birds to bangeing here, and I believe she'd 'a' scanted herself of her own meals to have plenty to throw out amongst 'em, if I hadn't kep' watch. Anything but crows, I tell her, I'm willin' to help support, — though Dan he went an' tamed one o' them that did seem to have reason same as folks. It was round here a good spell after he went away. Dan an' his father they didn't hitch, — but he never held up his head ag'in after Dan had dared him an' gone off."

The guest did not notice this hint of family sorrows in his eager interest in something else.

"So Sylvy knows all about birds, does she?" he exclaimed, as he looked round at the little girl who sat, very demure but increasingly sleepy, in the moonlight. "I am making a collection of birds myself. I have been at it ever since I was a boy." (Mrs. Tilley smiled.) "There are two or three very rare ones I have been hunting for these five years. I mean to get them on my own ground if they can be found."

"Do you cage 'em up?" asked Mrs. Tilley doubtfully, in response to this enthusiastic announcement.

"Oh, no, they're stuffed and preserved, dozens and dozens of them," said the ornithologist, "and I have shot or snared every one myself. I caught a glimpse of a white heron three miles from here on Saturday, and I have followed it in this direction. They have never been found in this district at all. The little white heron, it is," and he turned again to look at Sylvia with the hope of discovering that the rare bird was one of her acquaintances.

But Sylvia was watching a hop-toad in the narrow footpath.

"You would know the heron if you saw it," the stranger continued eagerly. "A queer tall white bird with soft feathers and long thin legs. And it would have a nest perhaps in the top of a high tree, made of sticks, something like a hawk's nest."

Sylvia's heart gave a wild beat; she knew that strange white bird, and had once stolen softly near where it stood in some bright green swamp grass, away over at the other side of the woods. There was an open place where the sunshine always seemed strangely yellow and hot, where tall, nodding rushes grew, and her grandmother had warned her that she might sink in the soft black mud underneath and never be heard of more. Not far beyond were the salt marshes and beyond those was the sea, the sea which

Sylvia wondered and dreamed about, but never had looked upon, though its great voice could often be heard above the noise of the woods on stormy nights.

"I can't think of anything I should like so much as to find that heron's nest," the handsome stranger was saying. "I would give ten dollars to anybody who could show it to me," he added desperately, "and I mean to spend my whole vacation hunting for it if need be. Perhaps it was only migrating, or had been chased out of its own region by some bird of prey."

Mrs. Tilley gave amazed attention to all this, but Sylvia still watched the toad, not divining, as she might have done at some calmer time, that the creature wished to get to its hole under the doorstep, and was much hindered by the unusual spectators at that hour of the evening. No amount of thought, that night, could decide how many wished-for treasures the ten dollars, so lightly spoken of, would buy.

The next day the young sportsman hovered about the woods, and Sylvia kept him company, having lost her first fear of the friendly lad, who proved to be most kind and sympathetic. He told her many things about the birds and what they knew and where they lived and what they did with themselves. And he gave her a jack-knife, which she thought as great a treasure as if she were a desert-islander. All day long he did not once make her troubled or afraid except when he brought down some unsuspecting singing creature from its bough. Sylvia would have liked him vastly better without his gun; she could not understand why he killed the very birds he seemed to like so much. But as the day waned, Sylvia still watched the young man with loving admiration. She had never seen anybody so charming and delightful; the woman's heart, asleep in the child, was vaguely thrilled by a dream of love. Some premonition of that great power stirred and swayed these young foresters who traversed the solemn woodlands with soft-footed silent care. They stopped to listen to a bird's song; they pressed forward again eagerly, parting the branches — speaking to each other rarely and in whispers; the young man going first and Sylvia following, fascinated, a few steps behind, with her gray eyes dark with excitement.

She grieved because the longed-for white heron was elusive, but she did not lead the guest, she only followed, and there was no such thing as speaking first. The sound of her own unquestioned voice would have terrified her — it was hard enough to answer yes or no when there was need of that. At last evening began to fall, and they drove the cow home together, and Sylvia smiled with pleasure when they came to the place where she heard the whistle and was afraid only the night before.

II

Half a mile from home, at the farther edge of the woods, where the land was highest, a great pine-tree stood, the last of its generation. Whether it was left for a boundary mark, or for what reason, no one could say; the woodchoppers who had felled its mates were dead and gone long ago, and a whole forest of sturdy trees, pines and oaks and maples, had grown again. But the stately head of this old pine towered above them all and made a landmark for sea and shore miles and miles away. Sylvia knew it well. She had always believed that whoever climbed to the top of it could see the ocean; and the little girl had often laid her hand on the great rough trunk and looked up wistfully at those dark boughs that the wind always stirred, no matter how hot and still the air might be below. Now she thought of the tree with a new excitement, for why, if one climbed it at break of day, could not one see all the world, and easily discover whence the white heron flew, and mark the place, and find the hidden nest?

What a spirit of adventure, what wild ambition! What fancied triumph and delight and glory for the later morning when she could make known the secret! It was almost too real and too great for the childish heart to bear.

All night the door of the little house stood open, and the whippoorwills came and sang upon the very step. The young sportsman and his old hostess were sound asleep, but Sylvia's great design kept her broad awake and watching. She forgot to think of sleep. The short summer night seemed as long as the winter darkness, and at last when the whippoorwills ceased, and she was afraid the morning would after all come too soon, she stole out of the house and followed the pasture path through the woods, hastening toward the open ground beyond, listening with a sense of comfort and companionship to the drowsy twitter of a half-awakened bird, whose perch she had jarred in passing. Alas, if the great wave of human interest which flooded for the first time this dull little life should sweep away the satifactions of an existence heart to heart with nature and the dumb life of the forest!

There was the huge tree asleep yet in the paling moonlight, and small and hopeful Sylvia began with utmost bravery to mount to the top of it, with tingling, eager blood coursing the channels of her whole frame, with her bare feet and fingers, that pinched and held like bird's claws to the monstrous ladder reaching up, up, almost to the sky itself. First she must mount the white oak tree that grew alongside, where she was almost lost among the dark branches and the green leaves heavy and wet with dew; a bird fluttered off its nest, and a red squirrel ran to and fro and scolded pettishly at the harmless housebreaker. Sylvia felt her way easily. She had often climbed there, and knew that higher still one of the oak's upper branches chafed against the pine trunk, just where its lower boughs were set close together. There, when she made the dangerous pass from one tree to the other, the great enterprise would really begin.

She crept out along the swaying oak limb at last, and took the daring step across into the old pine-tree. The way was harder than she thought; she must reach far and hold fast, the sharp dry twigs caught and held her and scratched her like angry talons, the pitch made her thin little fingers clumsy and stiff as she went round and round the tree's great stem, higher and higher upward. The sparrows and robins in the woods below were beginning to wake and twitter to the dawn, yet it seemed much lighter there aloft in the pine-tree, and the child knew that she must hurry if her project were to be of any use.

The tree seemed to lengthen itself out as she went up, and to reach farther and farther upward. It was like a great main-mast to the voyaging earth; it must truly have been amazed that morning through all its ponderous frame as it felt this determined spark of human spirit creeping and climbing from higher branch to branch. Who knows how steadily the least twigs held themselves to advantage this light, weak creature on her way! The old pine must have loved his new dependent. More than all the hawks, and bats, and moths, and even the sweet-voiced thrushes, was the brave, beating heart of the solitary gray-eyed child. And the tree stood still and held away the winds that June morning while the dawn grew bright in the east.

Sylvia's face was like a pale star, if one had seen it from the ground, when the last thorny bough was past, and she stood trembling and tired but wholly triumphant, high in the tree-top. Yes, there was the sea with the dawning sun making a golden dazzle over it, and toward that glorious east flew two hawks with slow-moving pinions. How low they looked in the air from that height when before one had only seen them far up, and dark against the blue sky. Their gray feathers were as soft as moths; they seemed only a little way from the tree, and Sylvia felt as if she too could go flying away among the clouds. Westward, the woodlands and farms reached miles and miles into the distance; here and there were church steeples, and white villages; truly it was a vast and awesome world.

The birds sang louder and louder. At last the sun came up bewilderingly bright. Sylvia could see the white sails of ships out at sea, and the clouds that were purple and rose-colored and yellow at first began to fade away. Where was the white heron's nest in the sea of green branches, and was this wonderful sight and pageant of the world the only reward for having climbed to such a giddy height? Now look down again, Sylvia, where the green marsh is set among the shining birches and dark hemlocks; there where you saw the white heron once you will see him again; look, look! a white spot of him like a single floating feather comes up from the dead hemlock and grows larger, and rises, and comes close at last, and goes by the landmark pine with steady sweep of wing and outstretched slender neck and crested head. And wait! wait! do not move a foot or a finger, little girl, do not send an arrow of light and consciousness from your two eager eyes, for the heron has perched on a pine bough not far beyond yours, and cries back to his mate on the nest, and plumes his feathers for the new day!

The child gives a long sigh a minute later when a company of shouting cat-birds comes also to the tree, and vexed by their fluttering and lawlessness the solemn heron goes away. She knows his secret now, the wild, light, slender bird that floats and wavers, and goes back like an arrow presently to his home in the green world beneath. Then Sylvia, well satisfied, makes her perilous way down again, not daring to look far below the branch she stands on, ready to cry sometimes because her fingers ache and her lamed feet slip. Wondering over and over again what the stranger would say to her, and what he would think when she told him how to find his way straight to the heron's nest.

"Sylvy, Sylvy!" called the busy old grandmother again and again, but nobody answered, and the small husk bed was empty, and Sylvia had disappeared.

The guest waked from a dream, and remembering his day's pleasure hurried to dress himself that it might sooner begin. He was sure from the way the shy little girl looked once or twice yesterday that she had at least seen the white heron, and now she must really be persuaded to tell. Here she comes now, paler than ever, and her worn old frock is torn and tattered, and smeared with pine pitch. The grandmother and the sportsman stand in the door together and question her, and the splendid moment has come to speak of the dead hemlock-tree by the green marsh.

But Sylvia does not speak after all, though the old grandmother fretfully rebukes her, and the young man's kind appealing eyes are looking straight in her own. He can make them rich with money; he has promised it, and they are poor now. He is so well worth making happy, and he waits to hear the story she can tell.

No, she must keep silence! What is it that suddenly forbids her and makes her dumb? Has she been nine years growing, and now, when the great world for the first time puts out a hand to her, must she thrust it aside for a bird's sake? The murmur of the pine's green branches is in her ears, she remembers how the white heron came flying through the golden air and how they watched the sea and the morning together, and Sylvia cannot speak; she cannot tell the heron's secret and give its life away.

Dear loyalty, that suffered a sharp pang as the guest went away disappointed later in the day, that could have served and followed him and loved him as a dog loves! Many a night Sylvia heard the echo of his whistle haunting the pasture path as she came home with the loitering cow. She forgot even her sorrow at the sharp report of his gun and the piteous sight of thrushes and sparrows dropping silent to the ground, their songs hushed and their pretty feathers stained and wet with blood. Were the birds better friends than their hunter might have been, — who can tell? Whatever treasures were lost to her, woodlands and summer-time, remember! Bring your gifts and graces and tell your secrets to this lonely country child!

[1886]

GUY DE MAUPASSANT (1850–1893) *was one of the reasons the English short story writer A. E. Coppard used to say that if he ever compiled an anthology of short stories, he would have an easy job. Half the book would be by Maupassant, Coppard said, and the other half by Chekhov.*

Maupassant was born in Normandy, the son of a wealthy stockbroker. Maupassant was rebellious in school, but he learned to accept army discipline during the Franco-Prussian war of 1870–1871. Then for seven years he apprenticed himself to Gustave Flaubert, a distant relative, who attempted to teach his young disciple how to write. Maupassant remembered, "I wrote verses, short stories, longer stories, even a wretched play. Nothing survived. The master read everything. Then, the following Sunday at lunch, he developed his criticisms." Flaubert taught Maupassant that talent "is nothing other than a long patience. Work."

The essence of Flaubert's now famous teaching was exactness of observation. The writer must look at everything to find some aspect of the object that no one has yet seen or expressed. As Maupassant wrote in his preface to Pierre and Jean *in 1888, "Everything contains some element of the unexplored because we are accustomed to use our eyes only with the memory of what other people before us have thought about the object we are looking at. The least thing has a bit of the unknown about it. Let us find this. In order to describe a fire burning or a tree in a field, let us stand in front of that fire and that tree until they no longer look to us like any other fire or any other tree." Flaubert taught Maupassant that "When you pass a grocer sitting at his door, or a concierge smoking his pipe, or a cab-stand, you must show me that grocer and that concierge, their attitude, their whole physical appearance, including as well — indicated by the aptness of your image — their entire moral nature, in such a way that I shan't confuse them with any other grocer or any other concierge; and you must make me see, with a single word, in what way one cab-horse is totally unlike fifty others that go before and after it."*

In 1880 Maupassant's career was launched with the publication of a single story, "Boule de Suif" ("Ball of Fat"), an uncompromising picture of bourgeois hypocrisy. During the next decade, before his gradual incapacitation and death from syphilis, he published nearly three hundred stories characterized by a compact and dramatic narrative line, unlike the long explanations and digressions of many earlier writers. Along with his younger contemporary Anton Chekhov, Maupassant is responsible for technical advances that moved the short story toward an increased austerity. They influenced nearly every writer of the short story who came after them. As Joseph Conrad wrote about "The String," "Facts, and again facts, are his

[Maupassant's] unique concern. That is why he is not always properly understood." Maupassant's lack of sentimentality toward his characters laid him open to charges of cynicism and hardness. In a story like "Miss Harriet," he looks at the Englishwoman's sexual frustration honestly, without romanticizing her situation. Both Maupassant and Chekhov wrote with compassion about a wide spectrum of characters and situations. If Maupassant's stories display a greater distance from his characters and a less sympathetic irony than Chekhov's, both writers are the most accomplished of narrators, equal in their powers of observation and in their supple, exact knowledge of their craft.

Guy de Maupassant

ღღ

THE STRING

– translated by Ernest Boyd

Along all the roads around Goderville the peasants and their wives were coming toward the little town, for it was market-day. The men walked with slow steps, their whole bodies bent forward at each movement of their long twisted legs, deformed by their hard work, by the weight on the plough which, at the same time, raises the left shoulder and distorts the figure, by the reaping of the wheat which forces the knees apart to get a firm stand, by all the slow and painful labors of the country. Their blouses, blue, starched, shining as if varnished, ornamented with a little design in white at the neck and wrists, puffed about their bony bodies, seemed like balloons ready to carry them off. From each of them a head, two arms, and two feet protruded.

Some led a cow or a calf at the end of a rope, and their wives, walking behind the animal, whipped its haunches with a leafy branch to hasten its progress. They carried on their arms large wicker-baskets, out of which a chicken here, a duck there, thrust out its head. And they walked with a quicker, livelier step than their husbands. Their spare, straight figures were wrapped in a scanty little shawl, pinned over their flat bosoms, and their heads were enveloped in a piece of white linen tightly pressed on the hair and surmounted by a cap.

Then a wagon passed, its nag's jerky trot shaking up and down two men seated side by side and a woman in the bottom of the vehicle, the latter holding on to the sides to lessen the hard jolts.

In the square of Goderville there was a crowd, a throng of human beings and animals mixed together. The horns of the cattle, the rough-napped top-hats of the rich peasants, and the head-gear of the peasant women rose above the surface of the crowd. And the clamorous, shrill, screaming voices made a continuous and savage din which sometimes was dominated by the robust lungs of some countryman's laugh, of the long lowing of a cow tied to the wall of a house.

It all smacked of the stable, the dairy, and the dung-heap, of hay and sweat, giving forth that sharp, unpleasant odor, human and animal, peculiar to the people of the fields.

Maître Hauchecorne, of Bréauté, had just arrived at Goderville, and was directing his steps toward the square, when he perceived upon the ground a little piece of string. Maître Hauchecorne, economical like a true Norman, thought that everything useful ought to be picked up, and he stooped painfully, for he suffered from rheumatism. He took the bit of thin cord from the ground and was beginning to roll it carefully when he noticed Maître Malandain, the harness-maker, on the threshold of his door, looking at him. They had once had a quarrel together on the subject of a halter, and they had remained on bad terms, being both good haters. Maître Hauche-corne was seized with a sort of shame to be seen thus by his enemy, picking a bit of string out of the dirt. He concealed his find quickly under his blouse, then in his trousers pocket; then he pretended to be still looking on the ground for something which he did not find, and he went towards the market, his head thrust forward, bent double by his pains.

He was soon lost in the noisy and slowly moving crowd, which was busy with interminable bargainings. The peasants looked at cows, went away, came back, perplexed, always in fear of being cheated, not daring to decide, watching the vendor's eye, ever trying to find the trick in the man and the flaw in the beast.

The women, having placed their great baskets at their feet, had taken out the poultry, which lay upon the ground, tied together by the feet, with terrified eyes and scarlet crests.

They heard offers, stated their prices with a dry air and impassive face, or perhaps, suddenly deciding on some proposed reduction, shouted to the customer who was slowly going away: "All right, Maître Anthime, I'll give it to you for that."

Then little by little the square was deserted, the Angelus rang for noon, and those who lived too far away went to the different inns.

At Jourdain's the great room was full of people eating, as the big yard was full of vehicles of all kinds, carts, gigs, wagons, nondescript carts, yellow with dirt, mended and patched, raising their shafts to the sky like two arms, or perhaps with their shafts on the ground and their backs in the air.

Right against the diners seated at the table, the immense fireplace, filled with bright flames, cast a lively heat on the backs of the row on the right. Three spits were turning on which were chickens, pigeons, and legs of mutton; and an appetizing odor of roast meat and gravy dripping over the nicely browned skin rose from the hearth, lightened hearts and made mouths water.

All the aristocracy of the plough ate there, at Maître Jourdain's, tavern keeper and horse dealer, a clever fellow who had money.

The dishes were passed and emptied, as were the jugs of yellow cider. Every one told his affairs, his purchases, and sales. They discussed the crops. The weather was favorable for the greens but rather damp for the wheat.

Suddenly the drum began to beat in the yard, before the house. Everybody rose, except a few indifferent persons, and ran to the door, or to the windows, their mouths still full, their napkins in their hands.

After the public crier had stopped beating his drum, he called out in a jerky voice, speaking his phrases irregularly:

"It is hereby made known to the inhabitants of Goderville, and in general to all persons present at the market, that there was lost this morning, on the road to Benzeville, between nine and ten o'clock, a black leather pocket-book containing five hundred francs and some business papers. The finder is requested to return same to the Mayor's office or to Maître Fortuné Houlbrèque of Manneville. There will be twenty francs reward."

Then the man went away. The heavy roll of the drum and the crier's voice were again heard at a distance.

Then they began to talk of this event discussing the chances that Maître Houlbrèque had of finding or not finding his pocket-book.

And the meal concluded. They were finishing their coffee when the chief of the gendarmes appeared upon the threshold.

He inquired:

"Is Maître Hauchecorne, of Bréauté, here?"

Maître Hauchecorne, seated at the other end of the table, replied:

"Here I am."

And the officer resumed:

"Maître Hauchecorne, will you have the goodness to accompany me to the Mayor's office? The Mayor would like to talk to you."

The peasant, surprised and disturbed, swallowed at a draught his tiny glass of brandy, rose, even more bent than in the morning, for the first steps after each rest were specially difficult, and set out, repeating: "Here I am, here I am."

The Mayor was awaiting him, seated in an armchair. He was the local lawyer, a stout, serious man, fond of pompous phrases.

"Maître Hauchecorne," said he, "you were seen this morning picking up, on the road to Benzeville, the pocket-book lost by Maître Houlbrèque, of Manneville."

The countryman looked at the Mayor in astonishment, already terrified by this suspicion resting on him without his knowing why.

"Me? Me? I picked up the pocket-book?"

"Yes, you, yourself."

"On my word of honor, I never heard of it."

"But you were seen."

"I was seen, me? Who says he saw me?"

"Monsieur Malandain, the harness-maker."

The old man remembered, understood, and flushed with anger.

"Ah, he saw me, the clodhopper, he saw me pick up this string, here, Mayor." And rummaging in his pocket he drew out the little piece of string.

But the Mayor, incredulous, shook his head.

"You will not make me believe, Maître Hauchecorne, that Monsieur Malandain, who is a man we can believe, mistook this cord for a pocket-book."

The peasant, furious, lifted his hand, spat at one side to attest his honor, repeating:

"It is nevertheless God's own truth, the sacred truth. I repeat it on my soul and my salvation."

The Mayor resumed:

"After picking up the object, you stood like a stilt, looking a long while in the mud to see if any piece of money had fallen out."

The old fellow choked with indignation and fear.

"How anyone can tell — how anyone can tell — such lies to take away an honest man's reputation! How can anyone —— "

There was no use in his protesting, nobody believed him. He was confronted with Monsieur Malandain, who repeated and maintained his affirmation. They abused each other for an hour. At his own request, Maître Hauchecorne was searched. Nothing was found on him.

Finally the Mayor, very much perplexed, discharged him with the warning that he would consult the Public Prosecutor and ask for further orders.

The news had spread. As he left the Mayor's office, the old man was surrounded and questioned with a serious or bantering curiosity, in which there was no indignation. He began to tell the story of the string. No one believed him. They laughed at him.

He went along, stopping his friends, beginning endlessly his statement and his protestations, showing his pockets turned inside out, to prove that he had nothing.

They said:

"Ah, you old devil!"

And he grew angry, becoming exasperated, hot, and distressed at not being believed, not knowing what to do and always repeating himself.

Night came. He had to leave. He started on his way with three neighbors to whom he pointed out the place where he had picked up the bit of string; and all along the road he spoke of his adventure.

In the evening he took a turn in the village of Bréauté, in order to tell it to everybody. He only met with incredulity.

It made him ill all night.

The next day about one o'clock in the afternoon, Marius Paumelle, a hired man in the employ of Maître Breton, husbandman at Ymauville, returned the pocket-book and its contents to Maître Houlbrèque of Manneville.

This man claimed to have found the object in the road; but not knowing how to read, he had carried it to the house and given it to his employer.

The news spread through the neighborhood. Maître Hauchecorne was informed of it. He immediately went the circuit and began to recount his story completed by the happy climax. He triumphed.

"What grieved me so much was not the thing itself, as the lying. There is nothing so shameful as to be placed under a cloud on account of a lie."

He talked of his adventure all day long, he told it on the highway to people who were passing by, in the inn to people who were drinking there, and to persons coming out of church the following Sunday. He stopped strangers to tell them about it. He was calm now, and yet something disturbed him without his knowing exactly what it was. People had the air of joking while they listened. They did not seem convinced. He seemed to feel that remarks were being made behind his back.

On Tuesday of the next week he went to the market at Goderville, urged solely by the necessity he felt of discussing the case.

Malandain, standing at his door, began to laugh on seeing him pass. Why?

He approached a farmer from Criquetot, who did not let him finish, and giving him a thump in the stomach said to his face:

"You clever rogue."

Then he turned his back on him.

Maître Hauchecorne was confused, why was he called a clever rogue?

When he was seated at the table, in Jourdain's tavern he commenced to explain "the affair."

A horse dealer from Monvilliers called to him:

"Come, come, old sharper, that's an old trick; I know all about your piece of string!"

Hauchecorne stammered:

"But the pocket-book was found."

But the other man replied:

"Shut up, papa, there is one that finds, and there is one that brings back. No one is any the wiser, so you get out of it."

The peasant stood choking. He understood. They accused him of having had the pocket-book returned by a confederate, by an accomplice.

He tried to protest. All the table began to laugh.

He could not finish his dinner and went away, in the midst of jeers.

He went home ashamed and indignant, choking with anger and confusion, the more dejected that he was capable with his Norman cunning of doing what they had accused him of, and even of boasting of it as a good trick. His innocence seemed to him, in a confused way, impossible to prove, as his sharpness was known. And he was stricken to the heart by the injustice of the suspicion.

Then he began to recount the adventure again, enlarging his story every day, adding each time new reasons, more energetic protestations, more solemn oaths which he imagined and prepared in his hours of solitude, his whole mind given up to the story of the string. He was believed so much the less as his defense was more complicated and his arguing more subtle.

"Those are lying excuses," they said behind his back.

He felt it, consumed his heart over it, and wore himself out with useless efforts. He was visibly wasting away.

The wags now made him tell about the string to amuse them, as they make a soldier who has been on a campaign tell about his battles. His mind, seriously affected, began to weaken.

Towards the end of December he took to his bed.

He died in the first days of January, and in the delirium of his death struggles he kept claiming his innocence, reiterating.

"A piece of string, a piece of string — look — here it is."

[1884]

Guy de Maupassant

ଓଓ

MISS HARRIET

– translated by Ernest Boyd

There were seven of us in the drag, four women, and three men, one of whom was on the box-seat beside the coachman. We were following, at a walking pace, the winding coast road up the hill.

Having set out from Étretat at daybreak to visit the ruins of Tancarville, we were still half asleep, benumbed by the fresh air of the morning. The women, especially, who were little accustomed to early rising, let their eyelids fall every moment, nodding their heads or yawning, quite insensible to the glory of the dawn.

It was autumn. On both sides of the road the bare fields stretched out, yellowed by the stubble of oats and wheat which covered the soil like a badly shaved beard. The misty earth looked as if it were steaming. Larks were singing in the air, while other birds piped in the bushes.

At length the sun rose in front of us, a bright red on the edge of the horizon; and as it ascended, growing clearer from minute to minute, the country seemed to awake, to smile, to stretch itself, to slip off its night-gown of white mist, like a young girl leaving her bed. The Comte d'Etraille, who was seated on the box, cried:

"Look! look! a hare!" and he stretched out his arm to the left, pointing to a patch of clover. The animal scurried along, almost concealed by the field, only its large ears visible. Then it swerved across a deep furrow, stopped, started off again at top speed, changed its course, stopped anew, uneasy, spying out every danger, and undecided as to the route it should take. Suddenly it began to run, with great bounds of its hind legs, disappearing finally in a large patch of beetroot. All the men had wakened up to watch the animal's movements.

René Lemanoir then exclaimed:

"We are not at all gallant this morning," and looking at his neighbor, the little Baroness de Sérennes, who was struggling with drowsiness, he said to her in a subdued voice: "You are thinking of your husband, Baroness. Reassure yourself; he will not return before Saturday, so you still have four days."

She replied, with a sleepy smile:

"How silly you are." Then, shaking off her torpor, she added: "Now, let somebody say something that will make us all laugh. You, Monsieur Chenal, who have the reputation of having more successes than the Duc de Richelieu, tell us a love-story in which you have been involved, anything you like."

Léon Chenal, an old painter, who had once been very handsome, very strong, very proud of his physique, and very popular, took his long white beard in his hand and smiled; then, after a few moments' reflection, he became suddenly grave.

"Ladies, it will not be an amusing tale; for I am going to relate to you the most lamentable love-affair of my life, and I sincerely hope that none of my friends may ever inspire a similar passion."

I

"At that time I was twenty-five years old, and I was daubing along the coast of Normandy. I mean by 'daubing' wandering about, with a knapsack on one's back, from inn to inn, under the pretext of making studies and sketches from nature. I know nothing more enjoyable than that happy-go-lucky wandering life, in which you are perfectly free, without shackles of any kind, without a care, without a single preoccupation, without even a thought of tomorrow. You go in any direction you please, without any guide save your fancy, without any counsellor save what pleases your eyes. You pull up, because a running brook seduces you, or because you are attracted, in front of an inn, by the smell of fried potatoes. Sometimes it is the perfume of clematis which decides you in your choice, or the glance of the servant at an inn. Do not despise these rustic affections. These girls have souls as well as bodies, firm cheeks and fresh lips; their vigorous kisses are strong and fragrant, like wild fruits. Love is always worth while, come whence it may. A heart that beats when you make your appearance, an eye that weeps when you go away, these are things so rare, so sweet, so precious, that they must never be despised.

"I have had rendezvous in ditches full of primroses, behind the stable in which the cattle slept, and among the straw in garrets still warm from the heat of the day. I have memories of coarse grey linen on supple, strong bodies, and of hearty, fresh, free kisses, more delicate, in their sincere brutality, than the subtle joys accorded by charming and distinguished women.

"But what one chiefly loves in these pilgrimages of adventure is the country, the woods, the sunrises, the twilights, the light of the moon. For the painter these are honeymoon trips with Nature. You are alone with her in a long, quiet rendezvous. You go to bed in the fields amid marguerites and wild poppies, and, with eyes wide open, under the bright sunlight, you regard far away some little village, with pointed clock-tower which sounds the hour of noon.

"You sit down by the side of a spring which gushes out from the foot of an oak, amid a covering of tall, fragile weeds, glistening with life. You go down on your knees, bend forward, and drink the cold and pellucid water, wetting your moustache and nose; you drink it with a physical pleasure, as though you were kissing the spring, lip to lip. Sometimes, when you find a deep hole along the course of these tiny brooks, you plunge into it, quite naked, and on your skin, from head to foot, like an icy and delicious caress, you feel the swift and gentle quivering of the current.

"You are gay on the hills, melancholy on the shores of the lagoons, exalted when the sun is drowned in an ocean of blood-red clouds and wakes red reflections in the rivers. And at night, under the moon, as she passes across the roof of heaven, you think of things, singular things, which would never have occurred to your mind under the brilliant light of day.

"So, in wandering through this same country where we are this year, I came one day to the little village of Bénouville, on the rocky coast between Yport and Étretat. I came from Fécamp, following the cliff, the tall cliff, perpendicular as a wall, with its bastions of chalk falling sheer down into the sea. I had walked since morning on the close-clipped grass, as smooth and yielding as a carpet, which grows along the edge of the cliff, fanned by the salt breezes of the ocean. Singing lustily, I walked with long strides, looking sometimes at the slow, curving flight of a gull, with its sweep of white wings sailing over the blue heavens, sometimes at the green sea, or at the brown sails of a fishing bark. In short, I had passed a happy day, a day of liberty and freedom from care.

"I was told there was a little farmhouse where travellers were put up, a kind of inn kept by a peasant, which stood in a Normandy courtyard, surrounded by a double row of beeches.

"Leaving the cliff, I reached the hamlet, which was shut in by great trees, and I presented myself at the house of Mother Lecacheur.

"She was an old country woman, wrinkled and austere, who always seemed to receive customers reluctantly, with a kind of contempt.

"It was the month of May: the flowering apple-trees covered the court with a roof of perfumed flowers, with a whirling shower of pink blossoms which rained unceasingly upon the people and upon the grass.

"I said:

" 'Well, Madame Lecacheur, have you a room for me?'

"Astonished to find that I knew her name, she answered:

" 'That depends; everything is let; but all the same, there will be no harm in looking.'

"In five minutes we had come to an agreement, and I deposited my bag upon the earthen floor of a rustic room, furnished with a bed, two chairs, a table, and a wash-stand. The room opened into the large, smoky kitchen, where the lodgers took their meals with the people of the farm and with the woman herself, who was a widow.

"I washed my hands, after which I went out. The old woman was making a chicken fricassee for dinner in a large fireplace, in which hung the stew-pot, black with smoke.

" 'You have visitors, then, at the present time?' I said to her.

"She answered in an offended tone of voice:

" 'I have a lady, an English lady, of a certain age. She is occupying the other room.'

"For an extra five sous a day, I obtained the privilege of dining out in the court when the weather was fine.

"My place was accordingly set in front of the door, and I began to champ the lean limbs of the Normandy chicken, to drink the clear cider, and to munch the hunk of white bread, which, though four days old, was excellent.

"Suddenly the wooden gate which opened on to the highway was opened, and a strange person walked toward the house. She was very thin, very tall, enveloped in a Scotch shawl with red cheeks. You would have believed that she had no arms, if you had not seen a long hand appear just above the hips, holding a white tourist's umbrella. The face of a mummy, surrounded with sausage-rolls of plaited grey hair, which shook at every step she took, made me think, I know not why, of a pickled herring adorned with curling-papers. Lowering her eyes, she passed quickly in front of me, and entered the house.

"This singular apparition amused me. She undoubtedly was my neighbor, the 'English lady of a certain age' of whom our hostess had spoken.

"I did not see her again that day. The next day, when I had begun to paint at the end of the beautiful valley which you know, which extends as far as Étretat, lifting my eyes suddenly, I perceived something singularly attired standing on the crest of the declivity; it looked like a pole decked out with flags. It was she. On seeing me, she disappeared.

"I returned to the house at midday for lunch, and took my seat at the common table, so as to make the acquaintance of this eccentric old creature. But she did not respond to my polite advances, was insensible even to my little attentions. I perseveringly poured water out for her, I passed her the dishes with an air. A slight, almost imperceptible movement of the head, and an English word, murmured so low that I did not understand it, were her only acknowledgments.

"I ceased taking any notice of her, although she had disturbed my thoughts. At the end of three days, I knew as much about her as Madame Lecacheur did herself.

"She was called Miss Harriet. Seeking a secluded village in which to pass the summer, she had stopped at Bénouville, some six weeks before, and did not seem disposed to leave it. She never spoke at table, ate rapidly, reading all the while a small book of Protestant propaganda. She gave a copy of this book to everybody. The curé himself had received no less than four copies, at the hands of an urchin to whom she had paid two sous' commission. She said sometimes to our hostess, abruptly, without the slightest preliminary leading up to this declaration:

" 'I love the Savior above all; I worship Him in all creation; I adore Him in all nature; I carry Him always in my heart.'

"And she would immediately present the old woman with one of her brochures destined to convert the universe.

"In the village she was not liked. In fact, the schoolmaster had declared that she was an atheist, and a kind of stigma attached to her. The curé, who had been consulted by Madame Lecacheur, responded:

" 'She is a heretic, but God does not wish the death of the sinner, and I believe her to be a person of pure morals.'

"These words, 'atheist,' 'heretic,' words which no one could precisely define, threw doubts into some minds. It was asserted further, that this Englishwoman was rich, and that she had passed her life in travelling through every country in the world, because her family had thrown her off. Why had her family thrown her off? Because of her impiety, of course.

"She was, in reality, one of those people of exalted principles, one of those obstinate puritans of whom England produces so many, one of those good and insupportable old women who haunt the tables d'hôte of every hotel in Europe, who spoil Italy, poison Switzerland, render the charming cities of the Mediterranean uninhabitable, carry everywhere their fantastic manias, their petrified vestal morals, their indescribable toilettes, and a certain odor of india-rubber, which makes one believe that at night they slip themselves into a case of that material. When I met one of these people in a hotel, I used to flee like the birds when they see a scarecrow in a field.

"This woman, however, appeared so singular that she did not displease me.

"Madame Lecacheur, hostile by instinct to everything that was not peasant, felt in her narrow soul a kind of hatred for the ecstatic extravagances of the old maid. She had found a phrase by which to describe her, a phrase assuredly contemptuous, which had sprung to her lips I know not how, invented probably by some confused and mysterious travail of soul. She said: 'That woman is a demoniac.' This phrase, applied to the austere and sentimental creature, seemed to me irresistibly comic. I, myself, never called her now anything else but 'the demoniac,' feeling a singular pleasure in pronouncing this word aloud on seeing her.

"I would ask Mother Lecacheur: 'Well, what is our demoniac doing today?' To which the peasant would respond with a scandalized air:

" 'What do you think, sir? She picked up a toad with a crushed paw, carried it to her room, put it in her wash-stand, and dressed its wound as if it were a human. If that is not profanation, I should like to know what is!'

"On another occasion, when walking along the shore, she had bought a large fish which had just been caught, simply to throw it back into the sea again. The sailor, from whom she had bought it, though paid handsomely, was greatly provoked at this act — more exasperated, indeed, than if she had put her hand into his pocket and taken his money. For a whole month he could not speak of the circumstance without getting into a fury and denouncing it as an outrage. Oh yes! She was indeed a demoniac, this Miss Harriet, and Mother Lecacheur must have had an inspiration of genius in thus christening her.

"The stable-boy, who was called Sapeur, because he had served in Africa in his youth, entertained other opinions. He said, with a knowing air: 'She is an old hag who has had her day.' If the poor woman had but known.

"Céleste, the little servant, did not like waiting on her, but I was never able to understand why. Probably her only reason was that she was a stranger, of another race, of a different tongue, and of another religion. She was a demoniac, in brief!

"She passed her time wandering about the country, adoring and searching for God in nature. I found her one evening on her knees in a cluster of bushes. Having discovered something red through the leaves, I brushed aside the branches, and Miss Harriet at once rose to her feet, confused at having been found thus, looking at me with eyes as frightened as those of an owl surprised in open day.

"Sometimes, when I was working among the rocks, I would suddenly see her on the edge of the cliff, standing like a semaphore signal. She gazed passionately at the vast sea, glittering in the sunlight, and the boundless sky empurpled with fire. Sometimes I would distinguish her at the bottom of a valley, walking quickly, with her elastic English step; and I would go toward her, mysteriously attracted, simply to see her visionary expression, her dried-up, ineffable features, full of an inward and profound happiness.

"Often I would encounter her in the corner of a field sitting on the grass, under the shadow of an apple-tree, with her little Bible lying open on her knee, while she looked meditatively into the distance.

"I could no longer tear myself away from that quiet country neighborhood, bound to it as I was by a thousand links of love for its soft and sweeping landscapes. I was happy at this farm, which was out of the world, far removed from everything, but in close proximity to the soil, the good, healthy, beautiful green soil, which we ourselves shall fertilize with our bodies some day. And, I must confess, there was perhaps a certain amount of curiosity which kept me at Mother Lecacheur's. I wished to become acquainted a little with this strange Miss Harriet, and to learn what passes in the solitary souls of those wandering old English dames."

II

"We became acquainted in a rather singular manner. I had just finished a study which I thought good, and so it was. It was sold for ten thousand francs, fifteen years later. It was as simple as twice two make four, and had nothing to do with academic rules. The whole of the right side of my canvas represented a rock, an enormous jagged rock, covered with seawrack, brown, yellow, and red, across which the sun poured like a stream of oil. The light fell upon the stone, and gilded it as if with fire, but the sun itself was behind me and could not be seen. That was all. A foreground dazzling with light, blazing, superb.

"On the left was the sea, not the blue sea, the slate-colored sea, but a sea of jade, greenish, milky, and hard under the deep sky.

"I was so pleased with my work that I danced as I carried it back to the inn. I wished that the whole world could have seen it at one and the same moment. I can remember that I showed it to a cow which was browsing by the wayside, exclaiming, at the same time: 'Look at that, my old beauty; you will not often see its like again.'

"When I had reached the front of the house, I immediately called out to Mother Lecacheur, bawling with all my might:

" 'Look at this! You won't see anything like it in a hurry.'

"The woman came and looked at my work with stupid eyes, which distinguished nothing, and did not even recognize whether the picture represented an ox or a house.

"Miss Harriet was coming into the house, and she passed behind me just at the moment when, holding out my canvas at arm's length, I was exhibiting it to the old innkeeper. The 'demoniac' could not help but see it, for I took care to exhibit the thing in such a way that it could not escape her notice. She stopped abruptly and stood motionless, stupefied. It was her rock which was depicted, the one which she usually climbed to dream away her time undisturbed.

"She uttered a British 'Oh,' which was at once so accentuated and so flattering, that I turned round to her, smiling, and said:

" 'This is my latest study, Mademoiselle.'

"She murmured ecstatically, comically, and tenderly:

" 'Oh! Monsieur, you understand nature in a most thrilling way!'

"I colored up, indeed I did, and was more excited by that compliment than if it had come from a queen. I was seduced, conquered, vanquished. I could have embraced her — upon my honor.

"I took my seat at the table beside her, as I had always done. For the first time, she spoke, following out her thought aloud:

" 'Oh! I love nature so much.'

"I offered her bread, water, wine. She now accepted these with a slight, dry smile. I then began to converse with her about the scenery.

"After the meal, we rose from the table together and walked leisurely across the court; then, attracted by the fiery glow which the setting sun cast over the surface of the sea, I opened the outside gate which faced in the direction of the cliff, and we walked on side by side, happy as two persons are who have just learned to understand and penetrate each other's motives and feelings.

"It was a misty, relaxing evening, one of those enjoyable evenings which impart happiness to mind and body alike. All is joy, all is charm. The luscious and balmy air, loaded with the perfume of grass, with the tang of seaweed, with the odor of the wild flowers, caresses the nostrils with its wild perfume, the palate with its salty savor, the soul with a penetrating sweetness. We were walking as on the brink of the abyss which overlooked the vast sea, which rolled its little waves a hundred yards below our feet.

"We drank, with open mouth and expanded chest, that fresh breeze from the ocean which glides slowly over the skin, salted by long contact with the waves.

"Wrapped in her plaid shawl, with a look of inspiration as she faced the breeze, the Englishwoman gazed fixedly at the great sun ball as it descended toward the horizon. Far off in the distance a three-master in full sail was outlined on the blood-red sky and a steamship, somewhat nearer, passed along, leaving behind it a trail of smoke on the horizon. The red sun-globe sank slowly lower and lower and presently touched the water just behind the motionless vessel, which, in its dazzling effulgence, looked as though framed in a flame of fire. We saw it plunge, grow smaller and disappear, swallowed up by the ocean.

"Miss Harriet gazed in rapture at the last gleams of the dying day. She seemed longing passionately to embrace the sky, the sea, the whole landscape.

"She murmured: 'Ah! I love — I love ——— ' I saw a tear in her eye.

She went on: 'I wish I were a little bird, so that I could mount up into the firmament.'

"She remained standing as I had often before seen her, perched on the cliff, her face as red as her shawl. I should have liked to have sketched her in my album. It would have been a caricature of ecstasy.

"I turned away so as not to laugh.

"I then spoke to her of painting as I would have done to a fellow-artist, using the technical terms common among the devotees of the profession. She listened attentively, eagerly seeking to divine the meaning of the terms, so as to understand my thoughts. From time to time she would exclaim: 'Oh! I understand, I understand. It is very interesting.'

"We returned home.

"The next day, on seeing me, she approached me, cordially holding out her hand; and we at once became firm friends.

"She was a good creature who had a kind of soul on springs, which became enthusiastic at a bound. She lacked equilibrium, like all women who are spinsters at the age of fifty. She seemed to be preserved in vinegary innocence, but her heart still retained something of youth and of girlish effervescence. She loved both nature and animals with a fervent ardor, a love like old wine, mellow through age, a sensual love that she had never bestowed on men.

"One thing is certain: a bitch feeding her pups, a mare roaming in a meadow with a foal at its side, a bird's nest full of young ones, squeaking, with their open mouths and enormous heads, and no feathers, made her quiver with the most violent emotion.

"Poor solitary beings! Sad wanderers from table d'hôte to table d'hôte, poor beings, ridiculous and lamentable, I love you ever since I became acquainted with Miss Harriet!

"I soon discovered that she had something she would like to tell me, but dared not, and I was amused at her timidity. When I started out in the morning with my box on my back, she would accompany me to the end of the village, silent, but evidently struggling inwardly to find words with which to begin a conversation. Then she would leave me abruptly, and walk away quickly with her jaunty step.

"One day, however, she plucked up courage:

"'I would like to see how you paint pictures. Will you show me? I have been very curious.'

"And she colored up as though she had given utterance to words of extreme audacity.

"I conducted her to the bottom of the Petit-Val, where I had commenced a large picture.

"She remained standing near me, following all my gestures with concentrated attention. Then, suddenly, fearing, perhaps, that she was disturbing me, she said to me: 'Thank you,' and walked away.

"But in a short time she became more familiar, and accompanied me every day, with visible pleasure. She carried her folding-stool under her arm, would not consent to my carrying it, and she sat by my side. She would remain there for hours immovable and mute, following with her eye the point of my brush in its every movement. When I would obtain, by a large splotch of color spread on with a knife, a striking and unexpected effect, she would, in spite of herself, give vent to a half-suppressed 'Oh!' of astonishment, of joy, of admiration. She had the most tender respect for my canvases, an almost religious respect for that human reproduction of a part of Nature's divine work. My studies appeared to her as a species of holy pictures, and sometimes she spoke to me of God, with the idea of converting me.

"Oh! He was a queer creature, this God of hers. He was a sort of village philosopher without any great resources, and without great power; for she always pictured him to herself as being in despair over injustices committed under his eyes, as if he were helpless to prevent them.

"She was, however, on excellent terms with him, affecting even to be the confidante of his secrets and of his whims. She said: 'God wills,' or 'God does not will,' just like a sergeant announcing to a recruit: 'The colonel has commanded.'

"At the bottom of her heart she deplored my ignorance of the intentions of the Eternal, which she strove to impart to me.

"Every day I found in my pockets, in my hat when I lifted it from the ground, in my box of colors, in my polished shoes, standing in the mornings in front of my door, those little pious brochures, which she, no doubt, received directly from Paradise.

"I treated her as one would an old friend, with unaffected cordiality. But I soon perceived that she had changed somewhat in her manner, though, for a while, I paid little attention to it.

"When I was painting, whether in my valley or in some country lane, I would see her suddenly appear with her rapid, springy walk. She would then sit down abruptly, out of breath, as though she had been running or were overcome by some profound emotion. Her face would be red, that English red which is denied to the people of all other countries; then, without any reason, she would turn ashy pale and seem about to faint away. Gradually, however, her natural color would return and she would begin to speak.

"Then, without warning, she would break off in the middle of a sentence, spring up from her seat and walk away so rapidly and so strangely that I was at my wits' ends to discover whether I had done or said anything to displease or wound her.

"I finally came to the conclusion that those were her normal manners, somewhat modified no doubt in my honor during the first days of our acquaintance.

"When she returned to the farm, after walking for hours on the windy coast, her long curls often hung straight down, as if their springs had been broken. This had hitherto seldom given her any concern, and she would come to dinner without embarrassment, all dishevelled by her sister, the breeze.

"But now she would go up to her room in order to adjust what I called her lamp-glasses. When I would say to her, with familiar gallantry, which, however, always offended her: 'You are as beautiful as a star today, Miss Harriet,' a little blood would immediately mount into her cheeks, the blood of a young maiden, the blood of sweet fifteen.

"Then she became very shy, and ceased coming to watch me paint. I thought:

" 'This is only a fit of temper. It will pass.'

"But it did not pass away. When I spoke to her now, she would answer me, either with an air of affected indifference, or in a sullen anger; and she became by turns rude, impatient, and nervous. I never saw her except at meals, and we spoke but little. I concluded, at length, that I must have offended her in something: and, accordingly, I said to her one evening:

" 'Miss Harriet, why have you changed towards me? What have I done to displease you? You are causing me much pain!'

"She responded in an angry tone, which was very funny: 'I have not changed towards you. It is not true, not true,' and she ran upstairs and shut herself up in her room.

"At times she would look upon me with strange eyes. Since that time I have often said to myself that those condemned to death must look thus when informed that their last day has come. In her eye there lurked a species of madness, an insanity at once mystical and violent — something more, a fever, an exasperated desire, impatient and impotent, for the unrealized and unrealizable!

"It seemed to me that there was also going on within her a combat, in which her heart struggled against an unknown force that she wished to overcome — perhaps, even, something else. But what could I know? What could I know?"

III

"It was indeed a singular revelation.

"For some time I had been working as soon as it got light on a picture the subject of which was as follows:

"A deep ravine, enclosed, surmounted by two thickets of rushes and trees, extended into the distance and was lost, submerged in that milky vapor, in that cloud-like cotton-down that sometimes floats over valleys at daybreak. And at the extreme end of that heavy, transparent fog one saw, or rather guessed, two human figures, a youth and a maiden, their arms interlaced, embracing, she with her head raised towards him, he bending over her, their lips joined.

"A first ray of the sun, glistening through the branches, pierced that fog of the dawn, illuminated it with a rosy reflection just behind the rustic lovers, framing their vague shadows in a silvery background. It was good; really good.

"I was working on the declivity which led to the valley of Étretat. On this particular morning I had, by chance, the sort of floating vapor which I needed.

"Suddenly something rose up in front of me like a phantom; it was Miss Harriet. On seeing me she was about to flee. But I called after her, saying: 'Come here, come here, Mademoiselle. I have a nice little picture for you.'

"She came forward, though with seeming reluctance. I handed her my sketch. She said nothing, but stood for a long time motionless, looking at it. Suddenly she burst into tears. She wept spasmodically, like men who have been struggling hard against shedding tears, but who can do so no longer, and abandon themselves to grief, resisting still. I got up, trembling, moved myself by the sight of a sorrow I did not understand, and I took her by the hand with a gesture of brusque affection, a real French impulse, in which action outruns thought.

"She let her hands rest in mine for a few seconds, and I felt them quiver, as if her whole nervous system were on the rack. Then she withdrew her hands abruptly, or, rather, tore them out of mine.

"I recognized that shiver as soon as I had felt it; I knew it perfectly. Ah! the love-thrill of a woman, whether she is fifteen or fifty years of age, whether she is of the people or in society, goes so straight to my heart that I never have any difficulty in understanding it!

"Her whole frail being trembled, vibrated, swooned. I knew it. She walked away before I had time to say a word, leaving me as surprised as if I had witnessed a miracle, and as troubled as if I had committed a crime.

"I did not go in to breakfast. I took a walk on the edge of the cliff, feeling that I could just as soon weep as laugh, looking on the adventure as both comic and deplorable, and my position as ridiculous, believing her unhappy enough to go mad.

"I asked myself what I ought to do. I decided that my only course was to leave the place, and at once made up my mind to do so.

"Somewhat sad and perplexed, I wandered about until dinner-time, and entered the farmhouse just when the soup had been served.

"I sat down at the table as usual. Miss Harriet was there, eating away solemnly, without speaking to anyone, without even lifting her eyes. Her manner and expression were the same as usual.

"I waited patiently till the meal had been finished, then, turning toward the landlady, I said: 'Well, Madame Lecacheur, it will not be long now before I shall have to take my leave of you.'

"The good woman, surprised and troubled, replied in her drawling voice: 'My dear sir, what's this? You are going to leave us after I have become so accustomed to you?'

"I glanced at Miss Harriet out of the corner of my eye. Her countenance did not change in the least. But Céleste, the little servant, looked up at me. She was a fat girl of about eighteen, rosy, fresh, as strong as a horse, and possessing the rare attribute of cleanliness. I had kissed her at odd times in out-of-the-way corners, after the manner of travellers — nothing more.

"The dinner being at length over, I went to smoke my pipe under the apple-trees, walking up and down from one end of the enclosure to the other. All the reflections which I had made during the day, the strange discovery of the morning, that passionate and grotesque attachment for me, the recollections which that revelation had suddenly called up, recollections at once charming and perplexing, perhaps also that look which the servant had cast on me at the announcement of my departure — all these things, mixed up and combined, put me now in a reckless humor, gave me a tickling sensation of kisses on the lips, and in my veins a something which urged me on to commit some folly.

"Night was coming on, casting its dark shadows under the trees, when I descried Céleste, who had gone to fasten up the poultry-yard at the other end of the enclosure. I darted towards her, running so noiselessly that she heard nothing, and as she got up from closing the small trap-door by which the chickens got in and out, I clasped her in my arms and rained on her coarse, fat face a shower of kisses. She struggled, laughing all the same, as she was accustomed to do in such circumstances. Why did I suddenly loose my grip of her? Why did I at once experience a shock? What was it that I heard behind me?

"It was Miss Harriet, who had come upon us, who had seen us and who stood in front of us motionless as a specter. Then she disappeared in the darkness.

"I was ashamed, embarrassed, more sorry at having been thus surprised by her than if she had caught me committing some criminal act.

"I slept badly that night. I was completely unnerved and haunted by sad thoughts. I seemed to hear loud weeping, but in this I was no doubt deceived. Moreover, I thought several times that I heard someone walking up and down in the house and opening the hall-door.

"Toward morning I was overcome by fatigue and fell asleep. I got up late and did not go downstairs until the late breakfast, being still in a bewildered state, not knowing what kind of expression to put on.

"No one had seen Miss Harriet. We waited for her at table, but she did not appear. At length, Mother Lecacheur went to her room. The Englishwoman had gone out. She must have set out at break of day, as she often did to see the sun rise.

"Nobody seemed surprised at this and we began to eat in silence.

"The weather was hot, very hot, one of those still, sultry days when not a leaf stirs. The table had been placed out of doors, under an apple-tree; and we drank so much that Sapeur had to go constantly to the cellar to replenish the cider-jug. Céleste brought the dishes from the kitchen, a ragout of mutton with potatoes, a cold rabbit, and a salad. Afterwards she placed before us a dish of cherries, the first of the season.

"As I wanted to wash and freshen these, I begged the servant to go and bring a pitcher of cold water.

"In about five minutes she returned, declaring that the well was dry. She had lowered the pitcher to the full extent of the cord, and had touched the bottom, but on drawing the pitcher up again, it was empty. Mother Lecacheur, anxious to examine the thing for herself, went and looked down the hole. She returned announcing that there must be something in the well, something altogether unusual. Doubtless a neighbor had thrown some bundles of straw down, out of spite.

"I wanted to look down the well, too, thinking I could better make out what it was. I leaned over the brink. I perceived, indistinctly, a white object. What could it be? I then conceived the idea of lowering a lantern at the end of a cord. The yellow flame danced on the stone walls, and gradually sank deeper. All four of us were leaning over the opening, Sapeur and Céleste having now joined us. The lantern rested on a black and white, indistinct mass, singular, incomprehensible. Sapeur exclaimed:

" 'It is a horse. I see the hoofs. It must have escaped from the meadow during the night, and fallen in.'

"But suddenly a cold shiver attacked my spine, I first recognized a foot, then a leg which protruded; the whole body and the other leg were submerged.

"I groaned and trembled so violently that the light of the lamp danced hither and thither over the object.

" 'It is a woman, who — who — is down there! It is Miss Harriet.'

"Sapeur alone did not flinch. He had witnessed worse things in Africa.

"Mother Lecacheur and Céleste began to scream piercingly, and ran away.

"But the corpse had to be recovered. I attached the boy securely by the loins, then I lowered him slowly, by means of the pulley, and watched him disappear in the darkness. In his hands he had a lantern, and another rope. Soon his voice, seeming to come from the center of the earth, cried:

" 'Stop.'

"I then saw him fish something out of the water. It was the other leg. He bound the two feet together and shouted anew:

" 'Haul up.'

"I commenced to wind him up, but I felt as if my arms were broken, my muscles relaxed, and I was in terror lest I should let the boy fall to the bottom. When his head appeared over the brink, I asked:

" 'Well,' as if I expected he had a message from the woman lying at the bottom.

"We both got on to the stone slab at the edge of the well, and, face to face, leaning over the aperture, hoisted the body.

"Mother Lecacheur and Céleste watched us from a distance, hidden behind the wall of the house. When they saw the black slippers and white stockings of the corpse emerge from the hole, they disappeared.

"Sapeur seized the ankles, and we pulled up that poor, chaste woman in the most immodest posture. The head was in a shocking state, bruised and black; and the long, grey hair, hanging down, out of curl for ever, was muddy and dripping with water.

" 'Good Lord, how thin she is!' exclaimed Sapeur, in a contemptuous tone.

"We carried her into the room, and as the women did not put in an appearance, I, with the assistance of the lad, dressed the corpse for burial.

"I washed her sad, disfigured face. By the touch of my hand an eye was slightly opened; it fixed me with that pale stare, with that cold, that terrible look which corpses have, a look which seems to come from the beyond. I plaited up, as well as I could, her dishevelled hair, and I arranged on her forehead a novel and singular coiffure. Then I took off her dripping wet garments, baring, not without a feeling of shame, as though I had been guilty of some profanation, her shoulders and her chest, and her long arms, slim as the twigs of branches.

"Then I went to fetch some flowers, poppies, corn-flowers, marguerites, and fresh, sweet-smelling grass, with which to strew her funeral couch.

"Being the only person near her, it was necessary for me to fulfil the usual formalities. In a letter found in her pocket written at the last moment, she asked that her body be buried in the village in which she had passed the last days of her life. A frightful thought then oppressed my heart. Was it not on my account that she wished to be laid at rest in this place?

"Toward evening, all the female gossips of the locality came to view the remains of the deceased; but I would not allow a single person to enter; I wanted to be alone; and I watched by the corpse the whole night.

"By the light of the candles, I looked at the body of this miserable woman, wholly unknown, who had died so lamentably and so far away from home. Had she left no friends, no relatives behind her? What had her infancy been? What had been her life? Whence had she come, all alone, a wanderer, like a dog driven from home? What secrets of suffering and of despair were sealed up in that uncouth body, like a shameful defect, concealed all her life beneath that ridiculous exterior, which had driven away from her all affection and all love?

"What unhappy beings there are! I felt that upon that human creature weighed the eternal injustice of implacable nature! Life was over with her, without her ever having experienced, perhaps, that which sustains the most miserable of us all — the hope of being once loved! Otherwise, why should she thus have concealed herself, have fled from others? Why did she love everything so tenderly and so passionately, everything living that was not a man?

"I understood, also, why she believed in a God, and hoped for compensation from him for the miseries she had endured. She had now begun to decompose, and to become, in turn, a plant. She would blossom in the sun, and be eaten up by the cattle, carried away in seed by the birds, and as flesh by the beasts, again to become human flesh. But that which is called the soul had been extinguished at the bottom of the dark well. She suffered no longer. She had changed her life for that of others yet to be born.

"Hours passed away in this silent and sinister communion with the dead. A pale light announced the dawn of a new day, and a bright ray glistened on the bed, casting a line of fire on the bed-clothes and on her hands. This was the hour she had so much loved, when the waking birds began to sing in the trees.

"I opened the window wide, I drew back the curtains, so that the whole heavens might look in upon us. Then bending toward the glassy corpse, I took in my hands the mutilated head, and slowly, without terror or disgust, imprinted a long, long kiss upon those lips, which had never before received the salute of love."

Léon Chenal was silent. The women wept. We heard the Comte d'Etraille on the box-seat blow his nose several times in succession. Only the coachman nodded. The horses, no longer feeling the sting of the whip, had slackened their pace and were dragging us slowly along. And the brake hardly moved at all, having become suddenly heavy, as if laden with sorrow.

[1884]

KATE CHOPIN (1851–1904) *was born in St. Louis, the daughter of an Irish immigrant father who died when she was four. She was raised by her Creole mother's family and educated at a convent. In 1870 she married Oscar Chopin, a cotton broker. They lived in Louisiana, first in New Orleans and then on a large plantation her husband's family owned on the Crane River among the French speaking Acadians, in a section of the country that later gave her the physical locale and the Creole, Cajun, and Negro characters portrayed in many of her short stories. When her husband died in 1882, Chopin moved back to St. Louis with her six children. Friends encouraged her to write, and when she was nearly forty years old she published her first novel,* At Fault *(1890). Her stories began to appear in* Century *and* Harper's, *and two collections followed:* Bayou Folk *(1894) and* A Night in Arcadie *(1897). Her last work, the novel* The Awakening *(1899), is her masterpiece, but its sympathetic treatment of adultery shocked reviewers and readers throughout America. In St. Louis the novel was taken out of circulation in the libraries, and she was denied membership in the St. Louis Fine Arts Club. When her third collection of stories was rejected by her publisher at the end of 1899, Chopin felt herself a literary outcast; she wrote very little in the last years of her life.*

What affronted the genteel readers of the 1890s in Kate Chopin's fiction was her attempt to write frankly about women's emotions in their relations with men, children, and their own sexuality. After her mother's death in 1885 she stopped being a practicing Catholic, believing that no author could be true to life who did not accept the Darwinian view of human evolution. Seeking God in nature rather than through the church, Chopin expressed herself freely on the subjects of sex and love, but she learned to her sorrow that for American authors "the limitations imposed upon their art by their environment hamper a full and spontaneous expression." She dealt in her fiction with such problems as adultery, slavery, miscegenation, and integration, but she was more interested in the psychology of the individual than in social issues. Magazine editors turned down her stories if they appeared to lack ethical value, as in the case of "The Story of an Hour," a remarkable account of a woman who exclaims, "Free! free! free!" when she hears of her husband's sudden death.

Chopin took her writing seriously, adopting Maupassant for a model after translating his stories from the French. She felt, "Here was life, not fiction; for where were the plots, the old fashioned mechanism and stage trapping that in a vague, unthinking way I had fancied were essential to the art of story telling?" Since she didn't need to depend on writing for her income, she wrote as she pleased and rarely revised, claiming she was guard-

ing her literary integrity in both subject and form. The result is that her stories are sometimes marred by stilted language or improbable coincidences. At her best she wrote with control and objectivity, usually emphasizing character rather than plot. In the story "Regret" she centers on a small event, taking the reader right into the story, and developing it logically toward its conclusion, where she dramatically reveals the emotional cost of her heroine's apparent freedom in choosing an independent life as her destiny.

Kate Chopin

REGRET

Mamzelle Aurélie possessed a good strong figure, ruddy cheeks, hair that was changing from brown to gray, and a determined eye. She wore a man's hat about the farm, and an old blue army overcoat when it was cold, and sometimes topboots.

Mamzelle Aurélie had never thought of marrying. She had never been in love. At the age of twenty she had received a proposal, which she had promptly declined, and at the age of fifty she had not yet lived to regret it.

So she was quite alone in the world, except for her dog Ponto, and the negroes who lived in her cabins and worked her crops, and the fowls, a few cows, a couple of mules, her gun (with which she shot chicken-hawks), and her religion.

One morning Mamzelle Aurélie stood upon her gallery, contemplating, with arms akimbo, a small band of very small children who, to all intents and purposes, might have fallen from the clouds, so unexpected and bewildering was their coming, and so unwelcome. They were the children of her nearest neighbor, Odile, who was not such a near neighbor, after all.

The young woman had appeared but five minutes before, accompanied by these four children. In her arms she carried little Elodie; she dragged Ti Nomme by an unwilling hand; while Marcéline and Marcélette followed with irresolute steps.

Her face was red and disfigured from tears and excitement. She had been summoned to a neighboring parish by the dangerous illness of her mother; her husband was away in Texas — it seemed to her a million miles away; and Valsin was waiting with the mule-cart to drive her to the station.

"It's no question, Mamzelle Aurélie; you jus' got to keep those youngsters fo' me tell I come back. Dieu sait,[1] I would n' botha you with 'em if it was any otha way to do! Make 'em mine you, Mamzelle Aurélie; don' spare 'em. Me, there, I'm half crazy between the chil'ren, an' Léon not home, an' maybe not even to fine po' maman alive encore!" — a harrowing possibility which drove Odile to take a final hasty and convulsive leave of her disconsolate family.

She left them crowded into the narrow strip of shade on the porch of the long, low house; the white sunlight was beating in on the white old boards; some chickens were scratching in the grass at the foot of the steps, and one had boldly mounted, and was stepping heavily, solemnly, and aimlessly across the gallery. There was a pleasant odor of pinks in the air, and the sound of negroes' laughter was coming across the flowering cotton-field.

Mamzelle Aurélie stood contemplating the children. She looked with a critical eye upon Marcéline, who had been left staggering beneath the weight of the chubby Elodie. She surveyed with the same calculating air Marcélette mingling her silent tears with the audible grief and rebellion of Ti Nomme. During those few contemplative moments she was collecting herself, determining upon a line of action which should be identical with a line of duty. She began by feeding them.

If Mamzelle Aurélie's responsibilities might have begun and ended there, they could easily have been dismissed; for her larder was amply provided against an emergency of this nature. But little children are not little pigs; they require and demand attentions which were wholly unexpected by Mamzelle Aurélie, and which she was ill prepared to give.

She was, indeed, very inapt in her management of Odile's children during the first few days. How could she know that Marcélette always wept when spoken to in a loud and commanding tone of voice? It was a peculiarity of Marcélette's. She became acquainted with Ti Nomme's passion for flowers only when he had plucked all the choicest gardenias and pinks for the apparent purpose of critically studying their botanical construction.

" 'Tain't enough to tell 'im, Mamzelle Aurélie," Marcéline instructed her; "you got to tie 'im in a chair. It's w'at maman all time do w'en he's bad: she tie 'im in a chair." The chair in which Mamzelle Aurélie tied Ti Nomme was roomy and comfortable, and he seized the opportunity to take a nap in it, the afternoon being warm.

At night, when she ordered them one and all to bed as she would have shooed the chickens into the hen-house, they stayed uncomprehending before her. What about the little white nightgowns that had to be taken from the pillow-slip in which they were brought over, and shaken by some strong hand till they snapped like ox-whips? What about the tub of water which had to be brought and set in the middle of the floor, in which the little tired, dusty, sunbrowned feet had every one to be washed sweet and clean? And it made Marcéline and Marcélette laugh merrily — the idea that

---

[1] "God knows."

Mamzelle Aurélie should for a moment have believed that Ti Nomme could fall asleep without being told the story of *Croque-mitaine*[2] or *Loup-garou*,[3] or both; or that Elodie could fall asleep at all without being rocked and sung to.

"I tell you, Aunt Ruby," Mamzelle Aurélie informed her cook in confidence; "me, I'd rather manage a dozen plantation' than fo' chil'ren. It's terrassent! Bonté! Don't talk to me about chil'ren!"

" 'Tain' ispected sich as you would know airy thing 'bout 'em, Mamzelle Aurélie. I see dat plainly yistiddy w'en I spy dat li'le chile playin' wid yo' baskit o' keys. You don' know dat makes chillun grow up hard-headed, to play wid keys? Des like it make 'em teeth hard to look in a lookin'-glass. Them's the things you got to know in the raisin' an' manigement o' chillun."

Mamzelle Aurélie certainly did not pretend or aspire to such subtle and far-reaching knowledge on the subject as Aunt Ruby possessed, who had "raised five an' bared (buried) six" in her day. She was glad enough to learn a few little mother-tricks to serve the moment's need.

Ti Nomme's sticky fingers compelled her to unearth white aprons that she had not worn for years, and she had to accustom herself to his moist kisses — the expressions of an affectionate and exuberant nature. She got down her sewing-basket, which she seldom used, from the top shelf of the armoire, and placed it within the ready and easy reach which torn slips and buttonless waists demanded. It took her some days to become accustomed to the laughing, the crying, the chattering that echoed through the house and around it all day long. And it was not the first or the second night that she could sleep comfortably with little Elodie's hot, plump body pressed close against her, and the little one's warm breath beating her cheek like the fanning of a bird's wing.

But at the end of two weeks Mamzelle Aurélie had grown quite used to these things, and she no longer complained.

It was also at the end of two weeks that Mamzelle Aurélie, one evening, looking away toward the crib where the cattle were being fed, saw Valsin's blue cart turning the bend of the road. Odile sat beside the mulatto, upright and alert. As they drew near, the young woman's beaming face indicated that her homecoming was a happy one.

But this coming, unannounced and unexpected, threw Mamzelle Aurélie into a flutter that was almost agitation. The children had to be gathered. Where was Ti Nomme? Yonder in the shed, putting an edge on his knife at the grindstone. And Marcéline and Marcélette? Cutting and fashioning doll-rags in the corner of the gallery. As for Elodie, she was safe enough in Mamzelle Aurélie's arms; and she had screamed with delight at sight of the familiar blue cart which was bringing her mother back to her.

---

[2] the bogey-man.
[3] the werewolf.

The excitement was all over, and they were gone. How still it was when they were gone! Mamzelle Aurélie stood upon the gallery, looking and listening. She could no longer see the cart; the red sunset and the blue-gray twilight had together flung a purple mist across the fields and road that hid it from her view. She could no longer hear the wheezing and creaking of its wheels. But she could still faintly hear the shrill, glad voices of the children.

She turned into the house. There was much work awaiting her, for the children had left a sad disorder behind them; but she did not at once set about the task of righting it. Mamzelle Aurélie seated herself beside the table. She gave one slow glance through the room, into which the evening shadows were creeping and deepening around her solitary figure. She let her head fall down upon her bended arm, and began to cry. Oh, but she cried! Not softly, as women often do. She cried like a man, with sobs that seemed to tear her very soul. She did not notice Ponto licking her hand.

[1894]

JOSEPH CONRAD (1857–1924) was born Jozef Teodore Konrad Nalecz Korzeniowski near Kiev, in what was then Russian Poland. His parents died when he was young, and he was raised by a strict, aristocratic uncle. At the age of seventeen he persuaded his uncle to let him go to sea, and for many years he sailed in the French and British navies. He then accepted a post as steamboat captain on the Congo River, an experience that later gave him material for some of his best fiction, including the stories "An Outpost of Progress" (1898) and "Heart of Darkness" (1902). He began to write adventure stories while he was still a seaman, but after his trip to the Congo he left his wandering life and settled in England to become a professional writer. Although Conrad did not learn English until after he was twenty (Polish was his native tongue and French his second language), he is considered one of the supreme English stylists. In 1895 he published his first novel, Almayer's Folly, followed in quick succession by the great books of his early period, An Outcast of the Islands (1896), The Nigger of the "Narcissus" (1897), Lord Jim (1902), and Nostromo (1904). His later novels include The Secret Agent (1907), Chance (1913), and Victory (1915).

Conrad believed that a freely ranging imagination was his most precious possession as a writer, and he did not consider himself bound by the "fettering dogmas of some romantic, realistic, or naturalistic creed." The avowed aim of his fiction was "to make you hear, to make you feel, above all to make you see." His tales are never simple adventure stories, although they contain a great deal of adventure. His epic descriptions of vast natural forces and limited human fortitude were recognized in his own time as reminiscent of the work of the Russian masters Turgenev and Tolstoy, but Conrad added his special poetic sense of the scene as a whole, with the human drama played against the surrounding, often menacing forces of nature. If the foreground of his stories is usually a somber narrative, the background is his poetic sense of nature as a ceaselessly flowing river of life in which an individual's existence emerges briefly, plays its small part, and then is lost again in the infinite succession of events in "the general aspect of things."

"An Outpost of Progress" was included with four other stories in Conrad's early collection, Tales of Unrest (1898). In his preface he stated that this story is "the lightest part of the loot I carried off from Central Africa. . . . Other men have found a lot of quite different things there and I have the comfortable conviction that what I took would not have been of much use to anybody else. And it must be said that it was but a very small amount of plunder. All of it could go into one's breast pocket when folded neatly. As for the story itself, it is true enough in its essentials. The sus-

tained invention of a really telling lie demands a talent which I do not possess."

"Heart of Darkness" *was begun a year after Conrad completed writing the five stories in* Tales of Unrest. *These earlier narratives were primarily objective and descriptive, but with* "Heart of Darkness" *he attempted to experiment artistically with a new approach to fiction, tending toward a more subjective, suggestive, and psychological interpretation of his material. At one point he doubted that he had succeeded:* "What I distinctly admit is the fault of having made Kurtz too symbolic or rather symbolic at all. But the story being mainly a vehicle for conveying a batch of personal impressions, I gave rein to my mental laziness and took the line of least resistance." *Conrad felt that the story* "pushed a little (and only very little)" *beyond the actual facts of his experience in the Congo, but his exaggeration of the events was justified by the meaning he found in them.*

Joseph Conrad

ༀ

AN OUTPOST OF PROGRESS

I

There were two white men in charge of the trading station. Kayerts, the chief, was short and fat; Carlier, the assistant, was tall, with a large head and a very broad trunk perched upon a long pair of thin legs. The third man on the staff was a Sierra Leone nigger, who maintained that his name was Henry Price. However, for some reason or other, the natives down the river had given him the name of Makola, and it stuck to him through all his wanderings about the country. He spoke English and French with a warbling accent, wrote a beautiful hand, understood bookkeeping, and cherished in his innermost heart the worship of evil spirits. His wife was a negress from Loanda, very large and very noisy. Three children rolled about in sunshine before the door of his low, shed-like dwelling. Makola, taciturn and impenetrable, despised the two white men. He had charge of a small clay storehouse with a dried-grass roof, and pretended to keep a correct amount of beads, cotton cloth, red kerchiefs, brass wire, and other trade goods it contained. Besides the storehouse and Makola's hut, there was only one large building in the cleared ground of the station. It was built neatly of reeds, with a verandah on all the four sides. There were three rooms in it. The one in the middle was the living-room, and had two rough tables and a few stools in it. The other two were the bedrooms for the white men. Each had a bedstead and a mosquito net for all furniture. The plank floor was littered with the belongings of the white men; open half-empty boxes, torn wearing apparel, old boots; all the things dirty, and all the things broken, that accumulate mysteriously round untidy men. There was also another dwelling-place some distance away from the buildings. In it, under a tall cross much out of the perpendicular, slept the man who had seen the beginning of all this; who had planned and had watched the construction of this outpost of progress. He had been, at home, an unsuccessful painter who, weary of pursuing fame on an empty stomach, had gone out there through high protections. He had been the first chief of that station. Makola had watched the energetic artist die of fever in the just finished house with his usual kind of "I told you so" indifference. Then, for a time, he dwelt alone with his family, his account books, and the Evil Spirit that rules the lands under the equator. He got on very well with his god. Perhaps he had propitiated him by a promise of more white men to play with, by and by. At any rate the director of the Great Trading Company, coming up in a steamer that resembled an enormous sardine box with a flat-roofed shed erected on it, found the station in good order, and Makola as usual quietly diligent. The director had the cross put up over the first agent's grave, and appointed Kayerts to the post. Carlier was told off as second in charge. The director was a man ruthless and efficient, who at times, but very imperceptibly, indulged in grim humor. He made a speech to Kayerts and Carlier, pointing out to them the promising aspect of their station. The nearest trading-post was about three hundred miles away. It was an exceptional opportunity for them to distinguish themselves and to earn percentages on the trade. This appointment was a favor done to beginners. Kayerts was moved almost to tears by his director's kindness. He would, he said, by doing his best, try to justify the flattering confidence, &c., &c. Kayerts had been in the Administration of the Telegraphs, and knew how to express himself correctly. Carlier, an ex-noncommissioned officer of cavalry in an army guaranteed from harm by several European Powers, was less impressed. If there were commissions to get, so much the better; and, trailing a sulky glance over the river, the forests, the impenetrable bush that seemed to cut off the station from the rest of the world, he muttered between his teeth, "We shall see, very soon."

Next day, some bales of cotton goods and a few cases of provisions having been thrown on shore, the sardine-box steamer went off, not to return for another six months. On the deck the director touched his cap to the two agents, who stood on the bank waving their hats, and turning to an old servant of the Company on his passage to headquarters, said, "Look at those two imbeciles. They must be mad at home to send me such specimens. I told those fellows to plant a vegetable garden, build new storehouses and fences, and construct a landing-stage. I bet nothing will be done! They won't know how to begin. I always thought the station on this river useless, and they just fit the station!"

"They will form themselves there," said the old stager with a quiet smile.

"At any rate, I am rid of them for six months," retorted the director.

The two men watched the steamer round the bend, then, ascending arm in arm the slope of the bank, returned to the station. They had been in this vast and dark country only a very short time, and as yet always in the midst of other white men, under the eye and guidance of their superiors. And now, dull as they were to the subtle influences of surroundings, they felt themselves very much alone, when suddenly left unassisted to face the wilderness; a wilderness rendered more strange, more incomprehensible by the mysterious glimpses of the vigorous life it contained. They were two perfectly insignificant and incapable individuals, whose existence is only rendered possible through the high organization of civilized crowds. Few men realize that their life, the very essence of their character, their capabilities and their audacities, are only the expression of their belief in the safety of their surroundings. The courage, the composure, the confidence; the emotions and principles; every great and every insignificant thought belongs not to the individual but to the crowd: to the crowd that believes blindly in the irresistible force of its institutions and of its morals, in the power of its police and of its opinion. But the contact with pure unmitigated savagery, with primitive nature and primitive man, brings sudden and profound trouble into the heart. To the sentiment of being alone of one's kind, to the clear perception of the loneliness of one's thoughts, of one's sensations — to the negation of the habitual, which is safe, there is added the affirmation of the unusual, which is dangerous; a suggestion of things vague, uncontrollable, and repulsive, whose discomposing intrusion excites the imagination and tries the civilized nerves of the foolish and the wise alike.

Kayerts and Carlier walked arm in arm, drawing close to one another as children do in the dark; and they had the same, not altogether unpleasant, sense of danger which one half suspects to be imaginary. They chatted persistently in familiar tones. "Our station is prettily situated," said one. The other assented with enthusiasm, enlarging volubly on the beauties of the situation. Then they passed near the grave. "Poor devil!" said Kayerts. "He died of fever, didn't he?" muttered Carlier, stopping short. "Why," retorted Kayerts, with indignation, "I've been told that the fellow exposed himself recklessly to the sun. The climate here, everybody says, is not at all worse than at home, as long as you keep out of the sun. Do you hear that, Carlier? I am chief here, and my orders are that you should not expose yourself to the sun!" He assumed his superiority jocularly, but his meaning was serious. The idea that he would, perhaps, have to bury Carlier and remain alone, gave him an inward shiver. He felt suddenly that this Carlier was more precious to him here, in the center of Africa, than a brother could be anywhere else. Carlier, entering into the spirit of the thing, made a military salute and answered in a brisk tone, "Your orders shall be attended to, chief!" Then he burst out laughing, slapped Kayerts on the back and shouted, "We shall let life run easily here! Just sit still and gather in the ivory those savages will bring. This country has its good points, after all!" They both laughed loudly while Carlier thought: "That poor Kayerts; he is so fat and unhealthy. It would be awful if I had to bury him here. He is a man I respect." . . . Before they reached the verandah of their house they called one another "my dear fellow."

The first day they were very active, pottering about with hammers and nails and red calico, to put up curtains, make their house habitable and pretty; resolved to settle down comfortably to their new life. For them an impossible task. To grapple effectually with even purely material problems requires more serenity of mind and more lofty courage than people generally imagine. No two beings could have been more unfitted for such a struggle. Society, not from any tenderness, but because of its strange needs, had taken care of those two men, forbidding them all independent thought, all initiative, all departure from routine; and forbidding it under pain of death. They could only live on condition of being machines. And now, released from the fostering care of men with pens behind the ears, or of men with gold lace on the sleeves, they were like those lifelong prisoners who, liberated after many years, do not know what use to make of their freedom. They did not know what use to make of their faculties, being both, through want of practice, incapable of independent thought.

At the end of two months Kayerts often would say, "If it was not for my Melie, you wouldn't catch me here." Melie was his daughter. He had thrown up his post in the Administration of the Telegraphs, though he had been for seventeen years perfectly happy there, to earn a dowry for his girl. His wife was dead, and the child was being brought up by his sisters. He regretted the streets, the pavements, the cafés, his friends of many years; all the things he used to see, day after day; all the thoughts suggested by familiar things — the thoughts effortless, monotonous, and soothing of a Government clerk; he regretted all the gossip, the small enmities, the mild venom, and the little jokes of Government offices. "If I had had a decent brother-in-law," Carlier would remark, "a fellow with a heart, I would not be here." He had left the army and had made himself so obnoxious to his family by his laziness and impudence, that an exasperated brother-in-law had made superhuman efforts to procure him an appointment in the Company as a second-class agent. Having not a penny in the world he was compelled to accept this means of livelihood as soon as it became quite clear to him that there was nothing more to squeeze out of his relations. He, like Kayerts, regretted his old life. He regretted the clink of sabre and spurs on a fine afternoon, the barrack-room witticisms, the girls of garrison towns; but, besides, he had also a sense of grievance. He was evidently a much ill-used man. This made him moody, at times. But the two men got on well together in the fellowship of their stupidity and laziness. Together they did nothing, absolutely nothing, and enjoyed the sense of the idleness for which they were paid. And in time they came to feel something resembling affection for one another.

They lived like blind men in a large room, aware only of what came in contact with them (and of that only imperfectly), but unable to see the general aspect of things. The river, the forest, all the great land throbbing with life, were like a great emptiness. Even the brilliant sunshine disclosed nothing intelligible. Things appeared and disappeared before their eyes in an unconnected and aimless kind of way. The river seemed to come from nowhere and flow nowhither. It flowed through a void. Out of that void, at times, came canoes, and men with spears in their hands would suddenly crowd the yard of the station. They were naked, glossy black, ornamented with snowy shells and glistening brass wire, perfect of limb. They made an uncouth babbling noise when they spoke, moved in a stately manner, and sent quick, wild glances out of their startled, never-resting eyes. Those warriors would squat in long rows, four or more deep, before the verandah, while their chiefs bargained for hours with Makola over an elephant tusk. Kayerts sat on his chair and looked down on the proceedings, understanding nothing. He stared at them with his round blue eyes, called out to Carlier, "Here, look! Look at that fellow there — and that other one, to the left. Did you ever see such a face? Oh, the funny brute!"

Carlier, smoking native tobacco in a short wooden pipe, would swagger up twirling his moustaches, and surveying the warriors with haughty indulgence, would say —

"Fine animals. Brought any bone? Yes? It's not any too soon. Look at the muscles of that fellow — third from the end. I wouldn't care to get a punch on the nose from him. Fine arms, but legs no good below the knee. Couldn't make cavalry men of them." And after glancing down complacently at his own shanks, he always concluded: "Pah! Don't they stink! You, Makola! Take that herd over to the fetish" (the storehouse was in every station called the fetish, perhaps because of the spirit of civilization it contained) "and give them up some of the rubbish you keep there. I'd rather see it full of bone than full of rags."

Kayerts approved.

"Yes, yes! Go and finish that palaver over there, Mr. Makola. I will come round when you are ready, to weigh the tusk. We must be careful." Then turning to his companion: "This is the tribe that lives down the river; they are rather aromatic. I remember, they had been once before here. D'ye hear that row? What a fellow has got to put up with in this dog of a country! My head is split."

Such profitable visits were rare. For days the two pioneers of trade and progress would look on their empty courtyard in the vibrating brilliance of vertical sunshine. Below the high bank, the silent river flowed on glittering and steady. On the sands in the middle of the stream, hippos and alligators sunned themselves side by side. And stretching away in all directions, surrounding the insignificant cleared spot of the trading post, immense forests, hiding fateful complications of fantastic life, lay in the eloquent silence of mute greatness. The two men understood nothing, cared for nothing but for the passage of days that separated them from the steamer's return. Their predecessor had left some torn books. They took up these wrecks of novels, and, as they had never read anything of the kind before, they were surprised and amused. Then during long days there were interminable and silly discussions about plots and personages. In the center of Africa they made acquaintance of Richelieu and of d'Artagnan, of Hawk's Eye and of Father Goriot, and of many other people. All these imaginary personages became subjects for gossip as if they had been living friends. They discounted their virtues, suspected their motives, decried their successes; were scandalized at their duplicity or were doubtful about their courage. The accounts of crimes filled them with indignation, while tender or pathetic passages moved them deeply. Carlier cleared his throat and said in a soldierly voice, "What nonsense!" Kayerts, his round eyes suffused with tears, his fat cheeks quivering, rubbed his bald head, and declared, "This is a splendid book. I had no idea there were such clever fellows in the world." They also found some old copies of a home paper. That print discussed what it was pleased to call "Our Colonial Expansion" in high-flown language. It spoke much of the rights and duties of civilization, of the sacredness of the civilizing work, and extolled the merits of those who went about bringing light, and faith and commerce to the dark places of the earth. Carlier and Kayerts read, wondered, and began to think better of themselves. Carlier said one evening, waving his hand about, "In a hundred years, there will be perhaps a town here. Quays, and warehouses, and barracks, and — and — billiard-rooms. Civilization, my boy, and virtue — and all. And then, chaps will read that two good fellows, Kayerts and Carlier, were the first civilized men to live in this very spot!" Kayerts nodded, "Yes, it is a consolation to think of that." They seemed to forget their dead predecessor; but, early one day, Carlier went out and replanted the cross firmly. "It used to make me squint whenever I walked that way," he explained to Kayerts over the morning coffee. "It made me squint, leaning over so much. So I just planted it upright. And solid, I promise you! I suspended myself with both hands to the cross-piece. Not a move. Oh, I did that properly."

At times Gobila came to see them. Gobila was the chief of the neighboring villages. He was a gray-headed savage, thin and black, with a white cloth round his loins and a mangy panther skin hanging over his back. He came up with long strides of his skeleton legs, swinging a staff as tall as himself, and, entering the common room of the station, would squat on his heels to the left of the door. There he sat, watching Kayerts, and now and then making a speech which the other did not understand. Kayerts, without interrupting his occupation, would from time to time say in a friendly manner: "How goes it, you old image?" and they would smile at one another. The two whites had a liking for that old and incomprehensible creature, and called him Father Gobila. Gobila's manner was paternal, and he seemed really to love all white men. They all appeared to him very young, indistinguishably alike (except for stature), and he knew that they were all brothers, and also immortal. The death of the artist, who was the first white man whom he knew intimately, did not disturb this belief, because he was firmly convinced that the white stranger had pretended to die and got himself buried for some mysterious purpose of his own, into which it was useless to inquire. Perhaps it was his way of going home to his own country? At any rate, these were his brothers, and he transferred his absurd affection to them. They returned it in a way. Carlier slapped him on the back, and recklessly struck off matches for his amusement. Kayerts was always ready to let him have a sniff at the ammonia bottle. In short, they behaved just like that other white creature that had hidden itself in a hole in the ground. Gobila considered them attentively. Perhaps they were the same being with the other — or one of them was. He couldn't decide — clear up that mystery; but he remained always very friendly. In consequence of that friendship the women of Gobila's village walked in single file through the reedy grass, bringing every morning to the station, fowls, and sweet potatoes, and palm wine, and sometimes a goat. The Company never provisions the stations fully, and the agents required those local supplies to live. They had them through the good-will of Gobila, and lived well. Now and then one of them had a bout of fever, and the other nursed him with gentle devotion. They did not think much of it. It left them weaker, and their appearance changed for the worse. Carlier was hollow-eyed and irritable. Kayerts showed a drawn, flabby face above the rotundity of his stomach, which gave him a weird aspect. But being constantly together, they did not notice the change that took place gradually in their appearance, and also in their dispositions.

Five months passed in that way.

Then, one morning, as Kayerts and Carlier, lounging in their chairs under the verandah, talked about the approaching visit of the steamer, a knot of armed men came out of the forest and advanced towards the station. They were strangers to that part of the country. They were tall, slight, draped classically from neck to heel in blue fringed cloths, and carried percussion muskets over their bare right shoulders. Makola showed signs of excitement, and ran out of the storehouse (where he spent all his days) to meet these visitors. They came into the courtyard and looked about them with steady, scornful glances. Their leader, a powerful and determined-looking negro with bloodshot eyes, stood in front of the verandah and made a long speech. He gesticulated much, and ceased very suddenly.

There was something in his intonation, in the sounds of the long sentences he used, that startled the two whites. It was like a reminiscence of something not exactly familiar, and yet resembling the speech of civilized men. It sounded like one of those impossible languages which sometimes we hear in our dreams.

"What lingo is that?" said the amazed Carlier. "In the first moment I fancied the fellow was going to speak French. Anyway, it is a different kind of gibberish to what we ever heard."

"Yes," replied Kayerts. "Hey, Makola, what does he say? Where do they come from? Who are they?"

But Makola, who seemed to be standing on hot bricks, answered hurriedly, "I don't know. They come from very far. Perhaps Mrs. Price will understand. They are perhaps bad men."

The leader, after waiting for a while, said something sharply to Makola, who shook his head. Then the man, after looking round, noticed Makola's hut and walked over there. The next moment Mrs. Makola was heard speaking with great volubility. The other strangers — they were six in all — strolled about with an air of ease, put their heads through the door of the storeroom, congregated round the grave, pointed understandingly at the cross, and generally made themselves at home.

"I don't like those chaps — and, I say, Kayerts, they must be from the coast; they've got firearms," observed the sagacious Carlier.

Kayerts also did not like those chaps. They both, for the first time, became aware that they lived in conditions where the unusual may be dangerous, and that there was no power on earth outside of themselves to stand between them and the unusual. They became uneasy, went in and loaded their revolvers. Kayerts said, "We must order Makola to tell them to go away before dark."

The strangers left in the afternoon, after eating a meal prepared for them by Mrs. Makola. The immense woman was excited, and talked much with the visitors. She rattled away shrilly, pointing here and there at the forests and at the river. Makola sat apart and watched. At times he got up and whispered to his wife. He accompanied the strangers across the ravine at the back of the station-ground, and returned slowly looking very thoughtful. When questioned by the white men he was very strange, seemed not to understand, seemed to have forgotten French — seemed to have forgotten how to speak altogether. Kayerts and Carlier agreed that the nigger had had too much palm wine.

There was some talk about keeping a watch in turn, but in the evening everything seemed so quiet and peaceful that they retired as usual. All night they were disturbed by a lot of drumming in the villages. A deep, rapid roll near by would be followed by another far off — then all ceased. Soon short appeals would rattle out here and there, then all mingle together, increase, become vigorous and sustained, would spread out over the forest, roll through the night, unbroken and ceaseless, near and far, as if the whole land had been one immense drum booming out steadily an appeal to heaven. And through the deep and tremendous noise sudden yells that resembled snatches of songs from a madhouse darted shrill and high in discordant jets of sound which seemed to rush far above the earth and drive all peace from under the stars.

Carlier and Kayerts slept badly. They both thought they had heard shots fired during the night — but they could not agree as to the direction. In the morning Makola was gone somewhere. He returned about noon with one of yesterday's strangers, and eluded all Kayerts' attempts to close with him: had become deaf apparently. Kayerts wondered. Carlier, who had been fishing off the bank, came back and remarked while he showed his catch, "The niggers seem to be in a deuce of a stir; I wonder what's up. I saw about fifteen canoes cross the river during the two hours I was there fishing." Kayerts, worried, said, "Isn't this Makola very queer today?" Carlier advised, "Keep all our men together in case of some trouble."

II

There were ten station men who had been left by the Director. Those fellows, having engaged themselves to the Company for six months (without having any idea of a month in particular and only a very faint notion of time in general), had been serving the cause of progress for upwards of two years. Belonging to a tribe from a very distant part of the land of darkness and sorrow, they did not run away, naturally supposing that as wandering strangers they would be killed by the inhabitants of the country; in which they were right. They lived in straw huts on the slope of a ravine overgrown with reedy grass, just behind the station buildings. They were not happy, regretting the festive incantations, the sorceries, the human sacrifices of their own land; where they also had parents, brothers, sisters, admired chiefs, respected magicians, loved friends, and other ties supposed generally to be human. Besides, the rice rations served out by the Company did not agree with them, being a food unknown to their land, and to which they could not get used. Consequently they were unhealthy and miserable. Had they been of any other tribe they would have made up their minds to die — for nothing is easier to certain savages than suicide — and so have escaped from the puzzling difficulties of existence. But belonging, as they did, to a warlike tribe with filed teeth, they had more grit, and went on stupidly living through disease and sorrow. They did very little work, and had lost their splendid physique. Carlier and Kayerts doctored them assiduously without being able to bring them back into condition again. They were mustered every morning and told off to different tasks — grass-cutting, fence-building, tree-felling, &c., &c., which no power on earth could induce them to execute efficiently. The two whites had practically very little control over them.

In the afternoon Makola came over to the big house and found Kayerts watching three heavy columns of smoke rising above the forests. "What is that?" asked Kayerts. "Some villages burn," answered Makola, who seemed to have regained his wits. Then he said abruptly: "We have got very little ivory; bad six months' trading. Do you like get a little more ivory?"

"Yes," said Kayerts, eagerly. He thought of percentages which were low.

"Those men who came yesterday are traders from Loanda who have got more ivory than they can carry home. Shall I buy? I know their camp."

"Certainly," said Kayerts. "What are those traders?"

"Bad fellows," said Makola, indifferently. "They fight with people, and catch women and children. They are bad men, and got guns. There is a great disturbance in the country. Do you want ivory?"

"Yes," said Kayerts. Makola said nothing for a while. Then: "Those workmen of ours are no good at all," he muttered, looking round. "Station in very bad order, sir. Director will growl. Better get a fine lot of ivory, then he say nothing."

"I can't help it; the men won't work," said Kayerts. "When will you get that ivory?"

"Very soon," said Makola. "Perhaps tonight. You leave it to me, and keep indoors, sir. I think you had better give some palm wine to our men to make a dance this evening. Enjoy themselves. Work better tomorrow. There's plenty palm wine — gone a little sour."

Kayerts said "yes," and Makola, with his own hands, carried big calabashes to the door of his hut. They stood there till the evening, and Mrs. Makola looked into every one. The men got them at sunset. When Kayerts and Carlier retired, a big bonfire was flaring before the men's huts. They could hear their shouts and drumming. Some men from Gobila's village had joined the station hands, and the entertainment was a great success.

In the middle of the night, Carlier waking suddenly, heard a man shout loudly; then a shot was fired. Only one. Carlier ran out and met Kayerts on the verandah. They were both startled. As they went across the yard to call Makola, they saw shadows moving in the night. One of them cried, "Don't shoot! It's me, Price." Then Makola appeared close to them. "Go back, go back, please," he urged, "you spoil all." "There are strange men about," said Carlier. "Never mind; I know," said Makola. Then he whispered, "All right. Bring ivory. Say nothing! I know my business." The two white men reluctantly went back to the house, but did not sleep. They heard footsteps, whispers, some groans. It seemed as if a lot of men came in, dumped heavy things on the ground, squabbled a long time, then went away. They lay on their hard beds and thought: "This Makola is invaluable." In the morning Carlier came out, very sleepy, and pulled at the cord of the big bell. The station hands mustered every morning to the sound of the bell. That morning nobody came. Kayerts turned out also, yawning. Across the yard they saw Makola come out of his hut, a tin basin of soapy water in his hand. Makola, a civilized nigger, was very neat in his person. He threw the soapsuds skillfully over a wretched little yellow cur he had, then turning his face to the agent's house, he shouted from the distance, "All the men gone last night!"

They heard him plainly, but in their surprise they both yelled out together: "What!" Then they stared at one another. "We are in a proper fix now," growled Carlier. "It's incredible!" muttered Kayerts. "I will go to the huts and see," said Carlier, striding off. Makola coming up found Kayerts standing alone.

"I can hardly believe it," said Kayerts, tearfully. "We took care of them as if they had been our children."

"They went with the coast people," said Makola after a moment of hesitation.

"What do I care with whom they went — the ungrateful brutes!" exclaimed the other. Then with sudden suspicion, and looking hard at Makola, he added: "What do you know about it?"

Makola moved his shoulders, looking down on the ground. "What do I know? I think only. Will you come and look at the ivory I've got there? It is a fine lot. You never saw such."

He moved towards the store. Kayerts followed him mechanically, thinking about the incredible desertion of the men. On the ground before the door of the fetish lay six splendid tusks.

"What did you give for it?" asked Kayerts, after surveying the lot with satisfaction.

"No regular trade," said Makola. "They brought the ivory and gave it to me. I told them to take what they most wanted in the station. It is a beautiful lot. No station can show such tusks. Those traders wanted carriers badly, and our men were no good here. No trade, no entry in books; all correct."

Kayerts nearly burst with indignation. "Why!" he shouted, "I believe you have sold our men for these tusks!" Makola stood impassive and silent. "I — I — will — I," stuttered Kayerts. "You fiend!" he yelled out.

"I did the best for you and the Company," said Makola, imperturbably. "Why you shout so much? Look at this tusk."

"I dismiss you! I will report you — I won't look at the tusk. I forbid you to touch them. I order you to throw them into the river. You — you!"

"You very red, Mr. Kayerts. If you are so irritable in the sun, you will get fever and die — like the first chief!" pronounced Makola impressively.

They stood still, contemplating one another with intense eyes, as if they had been looking with effort across immense distances. Kayerts shivered. Makola had meant no more than he said, but his words seemed to Kayerts full of ominous menace! He turned sharply and went away to the house. Makola retired into the bosom of his family; and the tusks, left lying before the store, looked very large and valuable in the sunshine.

Carlier came back on the verandah. "They're all gone, hey?" asked Kayerts from the far end of the common room in a muffled voice. "You did not find anybody?"

"Oh, yes," said Carlier, "I found one of Gobila's people lying dead before the huts — shot through the body. We heard that shot last night."

Kayerts came out quickly. He found his companion staring grimly over the yard at the tusks, away by the store. They both sat in silence for a while. Then Kayerts related his conversation with Makola. Carlier said nothing. At the midday meal they ate very little. They hardly exchanged a word that day. A great silence seemed to lie heavily over the station and press on their lips, Makola did not open the store; he spent the day playing with his children. He lay full-length on a mat outside his door, and the youngsters sat on his chest and clambered all over him. It was a touching picture. Mrs. Makola was busy cooking all day as usual. The white men made a somewhat better meal in the evening. Afterwards, Carlier smoking his pipe strolled over to the store; he stood for a long time over the tusks, touched one or two with his foot, even tried to lift the largest one by its small end. He came back to his chief, who had not stirred from the verandah, threw himself in the chair and said —

"I can see it! They were pounced upon while they slept heavily after drinking all that palm wine you've allowed Makola to give them. A put-up job! See? The worst is, some of Gobila's people were there, and got carried off too, no doubt. The least drunk woke up, and got shot for his sobriety. This is a funny country. What will you do now?"

"We can't touch it, of course," said Kayerts.

"Of course not," assented Carlier.

"Slavery is an awful thing," stammered out Kayerts in an unsteady voice.

"Frightful — the sufferings," grunted Carlier with conviction.

They believed their words. Everybody shows a respectful deference to certain sounds that he and his fellows can make. But about feelings people really know nothing. We talk with indignation or enthusiasm; we talk about oppression, cruelty, crime, devotion, self-sacrifice, virtue, and we know nothing real beyond the words. Nobody knows what suffering or sacrifice mean — except, perhaps the victims of the mysterious purpose of these illusions.

Next morning they saw Makola very busy setting up in the yard the big scales used for weighing ivory. By and by Carlier said: "What's that filthy scoundrel up to?" and lounged out into the yard. Kayerts followed. They stood watching. Makola took no notice. When the balance was swung true, he tried to lift a tusk into the scale. It was too heavy. He looked up helplessly without a word, and for a minute they stood round that balance as mute and still as three statues. Suddenly Carlier said: "Catch hold of the other end, Makola — you beast!" and together they swung the tusk up. Kayerts trembled in every limb. He muttered, "I say! O! I say!" and putting his hand in his pocket found there a dirty bit of paper and the stump of a pencil. He turned his back on the others, as if about to do something tricky, and noted stealthily the weights which Carlier shouted out to him with unnecessary loudness. When all was over Makola whispered to himself: "The sun's very strong here for the tusks." Carlier said to Kayerts in a careless tone: "I say, chief, I might just as well give him a lift with this lot into the store."

As they were going back to the house Kayerts observed with a sigh: "It had to be done." And Carlier said: "It's deplorable, but, the men being Company's men the ivory is Company's ivory. We must look after it." "I will report to the Director, of course," said Kayerts, "Of course; let him decide," approved Carlier.

At midday they made a hearty meal. Kayerts sighed from time to time. Whenever they mentioned Makola's name they always added to it an opprobrious epithet. It eased their conscience. Makola gave himself a half-holiday, and bathed his children in the river. No one from Gobila's villages came near the station that day. No one came the next day, and the next, nor for a whole week. Gobila's people might have been dead and buried for any sign of life they gave. But they were only mourning for those they had lost by the witchcraft of white men, who had brought wicked people into their country. The wicked people were gone, but fear remained. Fear always remains. A man may destroy everything within himself, love and hate and belief, and even doubt; but as long as he clings to life he cannot destroy fear: the fear, subtle, indestructible, and terrible, that pervades his being; that tinges his thoughts; that lurks in his heart; that watches on his lips the struggle of his last breath. In his fear, the mild old Gobila offered extra human sacrifices to all the Evil Spirits that had taken possession of his white friends. His heart was heavy. Some warriors spoke about burning and killing, but the cautious old savage dissuaded them. Who could foresee the woe those mysterious creatures, if irritated, might bring? They should be left alone. Perhaps in time they would disappear into the earth as the first one had disappeared. His people must keep away from them, and hope for the best.

Kayerts and Carlier did not disappear, but remained above on this earth, that, somehow, they fancied had become bigger and very empty. It was not the absolute and dumb solitude of the post that impressed them so much as an inarticulate feeling that something from within them was gone, something that worked for their safety, and had kept the wilderness from interfering with their hearts. The images of home; the memory of people like them, of men that thought and felt as they used to think and feel, receded into distances made indistinct by the glare of unclouded sunshine. And out of the great silence of the surrounding wilderness, its very hopelessness and savagery seemed to approach them nearer, to draw them gently, to look upon them, to envelop them with a solicitude irresistible, familiar, and disgusting.

Days lengthened into weeks, then into months. Gobila's people drummed and yelled to every new moon, as of yore, but kept away from the station. Makola and Carlier tried once in a canoe to open communications, but were received with a shower of arrows, and had to fly back to the station for dear life. That attempt set the country up and down the river into an uproar that could be very distinctly heard for days. The steamer was late. At first they spoke of delay jauntily, then anxiously, then gloomily. The matter was becoming serious. Stores were running short. Carlier cast his lines off the bank, but the river was low, and the fish kept out in the stream. They dared not stroll far away from the station to shoot. Moreover, there was no game in the impenetrable forest. Once Carlier shot a hippo in the river. They had no boat to secure it, and it sank. When it floated up it drifted away, and Gobila's people secured the carcase. It was the occasion for a national holiday, but Carlier had a fit of rage over it and talked about the necessity of exterminating all the niggers before the country could be made habitable. Kayerts mooned about silently; spent hours looking at the portrait of his Melie. It represented a little girl with long bleached tresses and a rather sour face. His legs were much swollen, and he could hardly walk. Carlier, undermined by fever, could not swagger any more, but kept tottering about, still with a devil-may-care air, as became a man who remembered his crack regiment. He had become hoarse, sarcastic, and inclined to say unpleasant things. He called it "being frank with you." They had long ago reckoned their percentages on trade, including in them that last deal of "this infamous Makola." They had also concluded not to say anything about it. Kayerts hesitated at first — was afraid of the Director.

"He has seen worse things done on the quiet," maintained Carlier, with a hoarse laugh. "Trust him! He won't thank you if you blab. He is no better than you or me. Who will talk if we hold our tongues? There is nobody here."

That was the root of the trouble! There was nobody there; and being left there alone with their weakness, they became daily more like a pair of accomplices than like a couple of devoted friends. They had heard nothing from home for eight months. Every evening they said, "Tomorrow we shall see the steamer." But one of the Company's steamers had been wrecked, and the Director was busy with the other, relieving very distant and important stations on the main river. He thought that the useless station, and the useless men, could wait. Meantime Kayerts and Carlier lived on rice boiled without salt, and cursed the Company, all Africa, and the day they were born. One must have lived on such diet to discover what ghastly trouble the necessity of swallowing one's food may become. There was literally nothing else in the station but rice and coffee; they drank the coffee without sugar. The last fifteen lumps Kayerts had solemnly locked away in his box, together with a half-bottle of Cognâc, "in case of sickness," he explained. Carlier approved. "When one is sick," he said, "any little extra like that is cheering."

They waited. Rank grass began to sprout over the courtyard. The bell never rang now. Days passed, silent, exasperating, and slow. When the two men spoke, they snarled; and their silences were bitter, as if tinged by the bitterness of their thoughts.

One day after a lunch of boiled rice, Carlier put down his cup un-tasted, and said: "Hang it all! Let's have a decent cup of coffee for once. Bring out that sugar, Kayerts!"

"For the sick," muttered Kayerts, without looking up.

"For the sick," mocked Carlier. "Bosh . . . Well! I am sick."

"You are no more sick than I am, and I go without," said Kayerts in a peaceful tone.

"Come! Out with that sugar, you stingy old slave-dealer."

Kayerts looked up quickly. Carlier was smiling with marked insolence. And suddenly it seemed to Kayerts that he had never seen that man before. Who was he? He knew nothing about him. What was he capable of? There was a surprising flash of violent emotion within him, as if in the presence of something undreamt-of, dangerous, and final. But he managed to pro-nounce with composure —

"That joke is in very bad taste. Don't repeat it."

"Joke!" said Carlier, hitching himself forward on his seat. "I am hun-gry — I am sick — I don't joke! I hate hypocrites. You are a hypocrite. You are a slave-dealer. I am a slave-dealer. There's nothing but slave-dealers in this cursed country. I mean to have sugar in my coffee today, anyhow!"

"I forbid you to speak to me in that way," said Kayerts with a fair show of resolution.

"You — What?" shouted Carlier, jumping up.

Kayerts stood up also. "I am your chief," he began, trying to master the shakiness of his voice.

"What?" yelled the other. "Who's chief? There's no chief here. There's nothing here: there's nothing but you and I. Fetch the sugar — you pot-bellied ass."

"Hold your tongue. Go out of this room," screamed Kayerts. "I dis-miss you — you scoundrel!"

Carlier swung a stool. All at once he looked dangerously in earnest. "You flabby, good-for-nothing civilian — take that!" he howled.

Kayerts dropped under the table, and the stool struck the grass inner wall of the room. Then, as Carlier was trying to upset the table, Kayerts in desperation made a blind rush, head low, like a cornered pig would do, and overturning his friend, bolted along the verandah, and into his room. He locked the door, snatched his revolver, and stood panting. In less than a minute Carlier was kicking at the door furiously, howling, "If you don't bring out that sugar, I will shoot you at sight, like a dog. Now then — one — two — three. You won't? I will show you who's the master."

Kayerts thought the door would fall in, and scrambled through the square hole that served for a window in his room. There was then the whole breadth of the house between them. But the other was apparently not strong enough to break in the door, and Kayerts heard him running round. Then he also began to run laboriously on his swollen legs. He ran as quickly as he could, grasping the revolver, and unable yet to understand what was happening to him. He saw in succession Makola's house, the store, the river, the ravine, and the low bushes; and he saw all those things again as he ran for the second time round the house. Then again they flashed past him. That morning he could not have walked a yard without a groan.

And now he ran. He ran fast enough to keep out of sight of the other man.

Then as, weak and desperate, he thought, "Before I finish the next round I shall die," he heard the other man stumble heavily, then stop. He stopped also. He had the back and Carlier the front of the house, as before. He heard him drop into a chair cursing, and suddenly his own legs gave way, and he slid down into a sitting posture with his back to the wall. His mouth was as dry as a cinder, and his face was wet with perspiration — and tears. What was it all about? He thought it must be a horrible illusion; he thought he was dreaming; he thought he was going mad! After a while he collected his senses. What did they quarrel about? That sugar! How absurd! He would give it to him — didn't want it himself. And he began scrambling to his feet with a sudden feeling of security. But before he had fairly stood upright, a common-sense reflection occurred to him and drove him back into despair. He thought: "If I give way now to that brute of a soldier, he will begin this horror again tomorrow — and the day after — every day — raise other pretensions, trample on me, torture me, make me his slave — and I will be lost! Lost! The steamer may not come for days — may never come." He shook so that he had to sit down on the floor again. He shivered forlornly. He felt he could not, would not move any more. He was completely distracted by the sudden perception that the position was without issue — that death and life had in a moment become equally difficult and terrible.

All at once he heard the other push his chair back; and he leaped to his feet with extreme facility. He listened and got confused. Must run again! Right or left? He heard footsteps. He darted to the left, grasping his revolver, and at the very same instant, as it seemed to him, they came into violent collision. Both shouted with surprise. A loud explosion took place between them; a roar of red fire, thick smoke; and Kayerts, deafened and blinded, rushed back thinking: "I am hit — it's all over." He expected the other to come round — to gloat over his agony. He caught hold of an upright of the roof — "All over!" Then he heard a crashing fall on the other side of the house, as if somebody had tumbled headlong over a chair — then silence. Nothing more happened. He did not die. Only his shoulder felt as if it had been badly wrenched, and he had lost his revolver. He was disarmed and helpless! He waited for his fate. The other man made no sound. It was a stratagem. He was stalking him now! Along what side? Perhaps he was taking aim this very minute!

After a few moments of an agony frightful and absurd, he decided to go and meet his doom. He was prepared for every surrender. He turned the corner, steadying himself with one hand on the wall; made a few paces, and nearly swooned. He had seen on the floor, protruding past the other corner, a pair of turned-up feet. A pair of white naked feet in red slippers. He felt deadly sick, and stood for a time in profound darkness. Then Makola appeared before him, saying quietly: "Come along, Mr. Kayerts. He is dead." He burst into tears of gratitude; a loud, sobbing fit of crying. After a time he found himself sitting in a chair and looking at Carlier, who lay stretched on his back. Makola was kneeling over the body.

"Is this your revolver?" asked Makola, getting up.

"Yes," said Kayerts; then he added very quickly, "He ran after me to shoot me — you saw!"

"Yes, I saw," said Makola. "There is only one revolver; where's his?"

"Don't know," whispered Kayerts in a voice that had become suddenly very faint.

"I will go and look for it," said the other, gently. He made the round along the verandah, while Kayerts sat still and looked at the corpse. Makola came back empty-handed, stood in deep thought, then stepped quietly into the dead man's room, and came out directly with a revolver, which he held up before Kayerts. Kayerts shut his eyes. Everything was going round. He found life more terrible and difficult than death. He had shot an unarmed man.

After meditating for a while, Makola said softly, pointing at the dead man who lay there with his right eye blown out —

"He died of fever." Kayerts looked at him with a stony stare. "Yes," repeated Makola, thoughtfully, stepping over the corpse, "I think he died of fever. Bury him tomorrow."

And he went away slowly to his expectant wife, leaving the two white men alone on the verandah.

Night came, and Kayerts sat unmoving on his chair. He sat quiet as if he had taken a dose of opium. The violence of the emotions he had passed through produced a feeling of exhausted serenity. He had plumbed in one short afternoon the depths of horror and despair, and now found repose in the conviction that life had no more secrets for him: neither had death! He sat by the corpse thinking; thinking very actively, thinking very new thoughts. He seemed to have broken loose from himself altogether. His old thoughts, convictions, likes and dislikes, things he respected and things he abhorred, appeared in their true light at last! Appeared contemptible and childish, false and ridiculous. He revelled in his new wisdom while he sat by the man he had killed. He argued with himself about all things under heaven with that kind of wrong-headed lucidity which may be observed in some lunatics. Incidentally he reflected that the fellow dead there had been a noxious beast anyway; that men died every day in thousands; perhaps in hundreds of thousands — who could tell? — and that in the number, that one death could not possibly make any difference; couldn't have any importance, at least to a thinking creature. He, Kayerts, was a thinking creature. He had been all his life, till that moment, a believer in a lot of nonsense like the rest of mankind — who are fools; but now he thought! He knew! He was at peace; he was familiar with the highest wisdom! Then he tried to imagine himself dead, and Carlier sitting in his chair watching him; and his attempt met with such unexpected success, that in a very few moments he became not at all sure who was dead and who was alive. This extraordinary achievement of his fancy startled him, however, and by a clever and timely effort of mind he saved himself just in time from becoming Carlier. His heart thumped, and he felt hot all over at the thought of that danger. Carlier! What a beastly thing! To compose his now disturbed nerves — and no wonder! — he tried to whistle a little. Then, suddenly, he fell asleep, or thought he had slept; but at any rate there was a fog, and somebody had whistled in the fog.

He stood up. The day had come, and a heavy mist had descended upon the land: the mist penetrating, enveloping, and silent; the morning mist of tropical lands; the mist that clings and kills; the mist white and deadly, immaculate and poisonous. He stood up, saw the body, and threw his arms above his head with a cry like that of a man who, waking from a trance, finds himself immured forever in a tomb. *"Help! . . . My God!"*

A shriek inhuman, vibrating and sudden, pierced like a sharp dart the white shroud of that land of sorrow. Three short, impatient screeches followed, and then, for a time, the fog-wreaths rolled on, undisturbed, through a formidable silence. Then many more shrieks, rapid and piercing, like the yells of some exasperated and ruthless creature, rent the air. Progress was calling to Kayerts from the river. Progress and civilization and all the virtues. Society was calling to its accomplished child to come, to be taken care of, to be instructed, to be judged, to be condemned; it called him to return to that rubbish heap from which he had wandered away, so that justice could be done.

Kayerts heard and understood. He stumbled out of the verandah, leaving the other man quite alone for the first time since they had been thrown there together. He groped his way through the fog, calling in his ignorance upon the invisible heaven to undo its work. Makola flitted by in the mist, shouting as he ran —

"Steamer! Steamer! They can't see. They whistle for the station. I go ring the bell. Go down to the landing, sir. I ring."

He disappeared. Kayerts stood still. He looked upwards; the fog rolled low over his head. He looked round like a man who has lost his way; and he saw a dark smudge, a cross-shaped stain, upon the shifting purity of the mist. As he began to stumble towards it, the station bell rang in a tumultuous peal its answer to the impatient clamor of the steamer.

The Managing Director of the Great Civilizing Company (since we know that civilization follows trade) landed first, and incontinently lost sight of the steamer. The fog down by the river was exceedingly dense; above, at the station, the bell rang unceasing and brazen.

The Director shouted loudly to the steamer:

"There is nobody down to meet us; there may be something wrong, though they are ringing. You had better come, too!"

And he began to toil up the steep bank. The captain and the engine-driver of the boat followed behind. As they scrambled up the fog thinned, and they could see their Director a good way ahead. Suddenly they saw him start forward, calling to them over his shoulder: — "Run! Run to the house! I've found one of them. Run, look for the other!"

He had found one of them! And even he, the man of varied and startling experience, was somewhat discomposed by the manner of this finding. He stood and fumbled in his pockets (for a knife) while he faced Kayerts, who was hanging by a leather strap from the cross. He had evidently climbed the grave, which was high and narrow, and after tying the end of the strap to the arm, had swung himself off. His toes were only a couple of inches above the ground; his arms hung stiffly down; he seemed to be standing rigidly at attention, but with one purple cheek playfully posed on the shoulder. And, irreverently, he was putting out a swollen tongue at his Managing Director.

[1898]

Joseph Conrad

ನಾ

HEART OF DARKNESS

I

The *Nellie*, a cruising yawl, swung to her anchor without a flutter of the sails, and was at rest. The flood had made, the wind was nearly calm, and being bound down the river, the only thing for it was to come to and wait for the turn of the tide.

The sea-reach of the Thames stretched before us like the beginning of an interminable waterway. In the offing the sea and the sky were welded together without a joint, and in the luminous space the tanned sails of the barges drifting up with the tide seemed to stand still in red clusters of canvas sharply peaked, with gleams of varnished sprits. A haze rested on the low shores that ran out to sea in vanishing flatness. The air was dark above Gravesend, and farther back still seemed condensed into a mournful gloom, brooding motionless over the biggest, and the greatest, town on earth.

The Director of Companies was our captain and our host. We four affectionately watched his back as he stood in the bows looking to seaward. On the whole river there was nothing that looked half so nautical. He resembled a pilot, which to a seaman is trustworthiness personified. It was difficult to realize his work was not out there in the luminous estuary, but behind him, within the brooding gloom.

Between us there was, as I have already said somewhere, the bond of the sea. Besides holding our hearts together through long periods of separation, it had the effect of making us tolerant of each other's yarns — and even convictions. The Lawyer — the best of old fellows — had, because of his many years and many virtues, the only cushion on deck, and was lying on the only rug. The accountant had brought out already a box of dominoes, and was toying architecturally with the bones. Marlow sat crosslegged right aft, leaning against the mizzen-mast. He had sunken cheeks, a yellow complexion, a straight back, and ascetic aspect, and, with his arms dropped, the palms of hands outwards, resembled an idol. The director, satisfied the anchor had good hold, made his way aft and sat down amongst us. We exchanged a few words lazily. Afterwards there was silence on board the yacht. For some reason or other we did not begin that game of dominoes. We felt meditative, and fit for nothing but placid staring. The day was ending in a serenity of still and exquisite brilliance. The water shone pacifically; the sky, without a speck, was a benign immensity of unstained light; the very mist on the Essex marshes was like a gauzy and radiant fabric, hung from the wooded rises inland, and draping the low shores in diaphanous folds. Only the gloom to the west, brooding over the upper reaches, became more somber every minute, as if angered by the approach of the sun.

And at last, in its curved and imperceptible fall, the sun sank low, and from glowing white changed to a dull red without rays and without heat, as if about to go out suddenly, stricken to death by the touch of that gloom brooding over a crowd of men.

Forthwith a change came over the water, and the serenity became less brilliant but more profound. The old river in its broad reach rested unruffled at the decline of day, after ages of good service done to the race that peopled its banks, spread out in the tranquil dignity of a waterway leading to the uttermost ends of the earth. We looked at the venerable stream not in the vivid flush of a short day that comes and departs forever, but in the august light of abiding memories. And indeed nothing is easier for a man who has, as the phrase goes, "followed the sea" with reverence and affection, than to evoke the great spirit of the past upon the lower reaches of the Thames. The tidal current runs to and fro in its unceasing service, crowded with memories of men and ships it had borne to the rest of home or to the battles of the sea. It had known and served all the men of whom the nation is proud, from Sir Francis Drake[1] to Sir John Franklin,[2] knights all, titled

---

[1] Sir Francis Drake (1540–1596), English navigator and pirate, sailed around the world (1577–1580) and led the fleet that defeated the Spanish Armada in 1588. The *Golden Hind* was his ship.

[2] Sir John Franklin (1786–1847), English explorer of the Arctic. His ships the *Erebus*

and untitled — the knights-errant of the sea. It had borne all the ships whose names are like jewels flashing in the night of time, from the *Golden Hind* returning with her round flanks full of treasure, to be visited by the Queen's Highness and thus pass out of the gigantic tale, to the *Erebus* and *Terror*, bound on other conquests — and that never returned. It had known the ships and the men. They had sailed from Deptford, from Greenwich, from Erith — the adventurers and the settlers; kings' ships and the ships of men on 'Change;[3] captains, admirals, the dark "interlopers" of the Eastern trade, and the commissioned "Generals" of East India fleets. Hunters for gold or pursuers of fame, they all had gone out on that stream, bearing the sword, and often the torch, messengers of the might within the land, bearers of a spark from the sacred fire. What greatness had not floated on the ebb of that river into the mystery of an unknown earth! . . . The dreams of men, the seed of commonwealths, the germs of empires.

The sun set; the dusk fell on the stream, and lights began to appear along the shore. The Chapman lighthouse, a three-legged thing erect on a mud-flat, shone strongly. Lights of ships moved in the fairway — a great stir of lights going up and going down. And farther west on the upper reaches the place of the monstrous town was still marked ominously on the sky, a brooding gloom in sunshine, a lurid glare under the stars.

"And this also," said Marlow suddenly, "has been one of the dark places on the earth."

He was the only man of us who still "followed the sea." The worst that could be said of him was that he did not represent his class. He was a seaman, but he was a wanderer, too, while most seamen lead, if one may so express it, a sedentary life. Their minds are of the stay-at-home order, and their home is always with them — the ship; and so is their country — the sea. One ship is very much like another, and the sea is always the same. In the immutability of their surroundings the foreign shores, the foreign faces, the changing immensity of life, glide past, veiled not by a sense of mystery but by a slightly disdainful ignorance; for there is nothing mysterious to a seaman unless it be the sea itself, which is the mistress of his existence and as inscrutable as Destiny. For the rest, after his hours of work, a casual stroll or a casual spree on shore suffices to unfold for him the secret of a whole continent, and generally he finds the secret not worth knowing. The yarns of seamen have a direct simplicity, the whole meaning of which lies within the shell of a cracked nut. But Marlow was not typical (if his propensity to spin yarns be excepted), and to him the meaning of an episode was not inside like a kernal but outside, enveloping the tale which brought it out only as a glow brings out a haze, in the likeness of one of these misty halos that sometimes are made visible by the special illumination of moonshine.

---

and the *Terror* were lost in an expedition to find the Northwest Passage from the Atlantic to the Pacific.
[3] investors at the London Stock Exchange.

His remark did not seem at all surprising. It was just like Marlow. It was accepted in silence. No one took the trouble to grunt even; and presently he said, very slow —

"I was thinking of very old times, when the Romans first came here, nineteen hundred years ago — the other day. . . . Light came out of this river since — you say Knights? Yes; but it is like a running blaze on a plain, like a flash of lightning in the clouds. We live in the flicker — may it last as long as the old earth keeps rolling! But darkness was here yesterday. Imagine the feelings of a commander of a fine — what d'ye call 'em? — trireme in the Mediterranean, ordered suddenly to the north; run overland across the Gauls in a hurry; put in charge of one of these craft the legionaries — a wonderful lot of handy men they must have been, too — used to build, apparently by the hundred, in a month or two, if we may believe what we read. Imagine him here — the very end of the world, a sea the color of lead, a sky the color of smoke, a kind of ship about as rigid as a concertina — and going up this river with stores, or orders, or what you like. Sand-banks, marshes, forests, savages — precious little to eat fit for a civilized man, nothing but Thames water to drink. No Falernian wine[4] here, no going ashore. Here and there a military camp lost in a wilderness, like a needle in a bundle of hay — cold, fog, tempests, disease, exile, and death — death skulking in the air, in the water, in the bush. They must have been dying like flies here. Oh, yes — he did it. Did it very well, too, no doubt, and without thinking much about it either, except afterwards to brag of what he had gone through in his time, perhaps. They were men enough to face the darkness. And perhaps he was cheered by keeping his eye on a chance of promotion to the fleet at Ravenna by and by, if he had good friends in Rome and survived the awful climate. Or think of a decent young citizen in a toga — perhaps too much dice, you know — coming out here in the train of some prefect, or taxgatherer, or trader even, to mend his fortunes. Land in a swamp, march through the woods, and in some inland post feel the savagery, the utter savagery, had closed round him — all that mysterious life of the wilderness that stirs in the forest, in the jungles, in the hearts of wild men. There's no initiation either into such mysteries. He has to live in the midst of the incomprehensible, which is also detestable. And it has a fascination, too, that goes to work upon him. The fascination of the abomination — you know, imagine the growing regrets, the longing to escape, the powerless digust, the surrender, the hate."

He paused.

"Mind," he began again, lifting one arm from the elbow, the palm of the hand outwards, so that, with his legs folded before him, he had the pose of a Buddha preaching in European clothes and without a lotus-flower — "Mind, none of us would feel exactly like this. What saves us is efficiency — the devotion to efficiency. But these chaps were not much ac-

---

[4] legendary Roman wine.

count, really. They were no colonists; their administration was merely a squeeze, and nothing more, I suspect. They were conquerors, and for that you want only brute force — nothing to boast of, when you have it, since your strength is just an accident arising from the weakness of others. They grabbed what they could get for the sake of what was to be got. It was just robbery with violence, aggravated murder on a great scale, and men going at it blind — as is very proper for those who tackle a darkness. The conquest of the earth, which mostly means the taking it away from those who have a different complexion or slightly flatter noses than ourselves, is not a pretty thing when you look into it too much. What redeems it is the idea only. An idea at the back of it; not a sentimental pretense but an idea; and an unselfish belief in the idea — something you can set up, and bow down before, and offer a sacrifice to. . . ."

He broke off. Flames glided in the river, small green flames, red flames, white flames, pursuing, overtaking, joining, crossing each other — then separating slowly or hastily. The traffic of the great city went on in the deepening night upon the sleepless river. We looked on, waiting patiently — there was nothing else to do till the end of the flood; but it was more after a long silence, when he said, in a hesitating voice, "I suppose you fellows remember I did once turn fresh-water sailor for a bit," that we knew we were fated, before the ebb began to run, to hear one of Marlow's inconclusive experiences.

"I don't want to bother you much with what happened to me personally," he began, showing in this remark the weakness of many tellers of tales who seem so often unaware of what their audience would best like to hear; "yet to understand the effect of it on me you ought to know how I got out there, what I saw, how I went up that river to the place where I first met the poor chap. It was the farthest point of navigation and the culminating point of my experience. It seemed somehow to throw a kind of light on everything about me — and into my thoughts. It was somber enough, too — and pitiful — not extraordinary in any way — not very clear either. No, not very clear. And yet it seemed to throw a kind of light.

"I had then, as you remember, just returned to London after a lot of Indian Ocean, Pacific, China Seas — a regular dose of the East — six years or so, and I was loafing about, hindering you fellows in your work and invading your homes, just as though I had got a heavenly mission to civilize you. It was very fine for a time, but after a bit I did get tired of resting. Then I began to look for a ship — I should think the hardest work on earth. But the ships wouldn't even look at me. And I got tired of that game, too.

"Now when I was a little chap I had a passion for maps. I would look for hours at South America, or Africa, or Australia, and lose myself in all the glories of exploration. At that time there were many blank spaces on the earth, and when I saw one that looked particularly inviting on a map (but they all look that) I would put my finger on it and say, When I grow up I will go there. The North Pole was one of these places, I remember. Well, I haven't been there yet, and shall not try now. The glamour's off. Other places were scattered about the Equator, and in every sort of latitude all over the two hemispheres. I have been in some of them, and . . . well, we won't talk about that. But there was one yet — the biggest, the most blank, so to speak — that I had a hankering after.

"True, by this time it was not a blank space any more. It had got filled since my childhood with rivers and lakes and names. It had ceased to be a blank space of delightful mystery—a white patch for a boy to dream gloriously over. It had become a place of darkness. But there was in it one river especially, a mighty big river, that you could see on the map, resembling an immense snake uncoiled, with its head in the sea, its body at rest curving afar over a vast country, and its tail lost in the depths of the land. And as I looked at the map of it in a shop-window, it fascinated me as a snake would a bird — a silly little bird. Then I remembered there was a big concern, a Company for trade on that river. Dash it all! I thought to myself, they can't trade without using some kind of craft on that lot of fresh water — steamboats! Why shouldn't I try to get charge of one? I went on along Fleet Street, but could not shake off the idea. The snake had charmed me.

"You understand it was a Continental concern, that Trading society; but I have a lot of relations living on the Continent, because it's cheap and not so nasty as it looks, they say.

"I am sorry to own I began to worry them. This was already a fresh departure for me. I was not used to getting things that way, you know. I always went my own road and on my own legs where I had a mind to go. I wouldn't have believed it of myself; but, then — you see — I felt somehow I must get there by hook or by crook. So I worried them. The men said 'My dear fellow,' and did nothing. Then — would you believe it? — I tried the women. I, Charlie Marlow, set the women to work — to get a job. Heavens! Well, you see, the notion drove me. I had an aunt, a dear enthusiastic soul. She wrote: "It will be delightful. I am ready to do anything, anything for you. It is a glorious idea. I know the wife of a very high personage in the Administration, and also a man who has lots of influence with,' etc., etc. She was determined to make no end of fuss to get me appointed skipper of a river steamboat, if such was my fancy.

"I got my appointment — of course; and I got it very quick. It appears the Company had received news that one of their captains had been killed in a scuffle with the natives. This was my chance, and it made me the more anxious to go. It was only months and months afterwards, when I made the attempt to recover what was left of the body, that I heard the original quarrel arose from a misunderstanding about some hens. Yes, two black hens. Fresleven — that was the fellow's name, a Dane — thought himself wronged somehow in the bargain, so he went ashore and started to hammer the chief of the village with a stick. Oh, it didn't surprise me in the least to hear this, and at the same time to be told that Fresleven was the gentlest, quietest creature that ever walked on two legs. No doubt he was; but he had been a couple of years already out there engaged in the noble cause, you know, and he probably felt the need at last of asserting his self-respect in some way. Therefore he whacked the old nigger mercilessly, while a big crowd of his people watched him, thunderstruck, till some man — I was told the chief's son — in desperation at hearing the old chap yell, made a tentative jab with a spear at the white man — and of course it went quite easy between the shoulder blades. Then the whole population cleared into the forest, expecting all kinds of calamities to happen, while, on the other hand, the steamer Fresleven commanded left also in a bad panic, in charge of the engineer, I believe. Afterwards nobody seemed to trouble much about Fresleven's remains, till I got out and stepped into his shoes. I couldn't let it rest, though; but when an opportunity offered at last to meet my predecessor, the grass growing through his ribs was tall enough to hide his bones. They were all there. The supernatural being had not been touched after he fell. And the village was deserted, the huts gaped black, rotting, all askew within the fallen enclosures. A calamity had come to it, sure enough. The people had vanished. Mad terror had scattered them, men, women, and children, through the bush, and they had never returned. What became of the hens I don't know either. I should think the cause of progress got them, anyhow. However, through this glorious affair I got my appointment, before I had fairly begun to hope for it.

"I flew around like mad to get ready, and before forty-eight hours I was crossing the Channel to show myself to my employers, and sign the contract. In a very few hours I arrived in a city that always makes me think of a whited sepulcher. Prejudice no doubt. I had no difficulty in finding the Company's offices. It was the biggest thing in the town, and everybody I met was full of it. They were going to run an over-sea empire, and make no end of coin by trade.

"A narrow and deserted street in deep shadow, high houses, innumerable windows with venetian blinds, a dead silence, grass sprouting between the stones, imposing carriage archways right and left, immense double doors standing ponderously ajar. I slipped through one of these cracks, went up a swept and ungarnished staircase, as arid as a desert, and opened the first door I came to. Two women, one fat and the other slim, sat on straw-bottomed chairs, knitting black wool. The slim one got up and walked straight at me — still knitting with downcast eyes — and only just as I began to think of getting out of her way, as you would for a somnambulist, stood still, and looked up. Her dress was as plain as an umbrella-cover, and she turned round without a word and preceded me into a waiting-room. I gave my name, and looked about. Deal table in the middle, plain chairs all around the walls, on one end a large shining map, marked with all the colors of a rainbow. There was a vast amount of red — good to see at any time, because one knows that some real work is done in there, a deuce of a lot of blue, a little green, smears of orange, and, on the East Coast, a purple patch, to show where the jolly pioneers of progress drink the jolly lagerbeer. However, I wasn't going into any of these. I was going into the yellow. Dead in the center. And the river was there — fascinating — deadly — like a snake. Ough! A door opened, a white-haired secretarial head, but wearing a compassionate expression, appeared, and a skinny forefinger beckoned me into the sanctuary. Its light was dim, and a heavy writing-desk squatted in the middle. From behind that structure came out an impression of pale plumpness in a frock-coat. The great man himself. He was five feet six, I should judge, and had his grip on the handle-end of ever so many millions. He shook hands, I fancy, murmured vaguely, was satisfied with my French. *Bon voyage.*

"In about forty-five seconds I found myself again in the waiting-room with the compassionate secretary, who, full of desolation and sympathy, made me sign some document. I believe I undertook amongst other things not to disclose any trade secrets. Well, I am not going to.

"I began to feel slightly uneasy. You know I am not used to such cere-monies, and there was something ominous in the atmosphere. It was just as though I had been let into some conspiracy — I don't know — something not quite right; and I was glad to get out. In the outer room the two women knitted black wool feverishly. People were arriving, and the younger one was walking back and forth introducing them. The old one sat on her chair. Her flat cloth slippers were propped up on a footwarmer, and a cat reposed on her lap. She wore a starched white affair on her head, had a wart on one cheek, and silver-rimmed spectacles hung on the tip of her nose. She glanced at me above the glasses. The swift and indifferent placidity of that look troubled me. Two youths with foolish and cheery countenances were being piloted over, and she threw at them the same quick glance of uncon-cerned wisdom. She seemed to know all about them and about me, too. An eerie feeling came over me. She seemed uncanny and fateful. Often far away there I thought of these two, guarding the door of Darkness, knitting black wool as for a warm pall, one introducing, introducing continuously to the unknown, the other scrutinizing the cheery and foolish faces with un-concerned old eyes. *Ave!* Old knitter of black wool. *Morituri te salutant.*[5] Not many of those she looked at ever saw her again — not half, by a long way.

"There was yet a visit to the doctor. 'A simple formality,' assured me the secretary, with an air of taking an immense part in all my sorrows. Ac-cordingly a young chap wearing his hat over the left eyebrow, some clerk I suppose — there must have been clerks in the business, though the house was as still as a house in a city of the dead — came from somewhere up-stairs, and led me forth. He was shabby and careless, with inkstains on the sleeves of his jacket, and his cravat was large and billowy, under a chin shaped like the toe of an old boot. It was a little too early for the doctor, so I

---

[5] "Those who are about to die salute you." (Latin)

proposed a drink, and thereupon he developed a vein of joviality. As we sat over our vermouths he glorified the Company's business, and by and by I expressed casually my surprise at him not going out there. He became very cool and collected all at once. 'I am not such a fool as I look, quoth Plato to his disciples,' he said sententiously, emptied his glass with great resolution, and we rose.

"The old doctor felt my pulse, evidently thinking of something else the while. 'Good, good for there,' he mumbled, and then with a certain eagerness asked me whether I would let him measure my head. Rather surprised, I said Yes, when he produced a thing like calipers and got the dimensions back and front and every way, taking notes carefully. He was an unshaven little man in a threadbare coat like a gaberdine, with his feet in slippers, and I thought him a harmless fool. 'I always ask leave, in the interests of science, to measure the crania of those going out there,' he said. 'And when they come back, too?' I asked, 'Oh, I never see them,' he remarked; 'and, moreover, the changes take place inside, you know.' He smiled, as if at some quiet joke. 'So you are going out there. Famous. Interesting, too.' He gave me a searching glance, and made another note. 'Ever any madness in your family?' he asked, in a matter-of-fact tone. I felt very annoyed. 'Is that question in the interests of science, too?' 'It would be,' he said, without taking notice of my irritation, 'interesting for science to watch the mental changes of individuals, on the spot, but. . . .' 'Are you an alienist?' I interrupted. 'Every doctor should be — a little,' answered that original, imperturbably. 'I have a little theory which you Messieurs who go out there must help me to prove. This is my share in the advantages my country shall reap from the possession of such a magnificent dependency. The mere wealth I leave to others. Pardon my questions, but you are the first Englishman coming under my observation. . . .' I hastened to assure him I was not in the least typical. 'If I were,' said I 'I wouldn't be talking like this with you.' 'What you say is rather profound, and probably erroneous,' he said, with a laugh. 'Avoid irritation more than exposure to the sun. Adieu. How do you English say, eh? Good-by. Ah! Good-by. Adieu. In the tropics one must before everything keep calm.' . . . He lifted a warning forefinger. . . . '*Du calme, du calme. Adieu.*'

"One thing more remained to do — say good-by to my excellent aunt. I found her triumphant. I had a cup of tea — the last decent cup of tea for many days — and in a room that most soothingly looked just as you would expect a lady's drawing-room to look, we had a long quiet chat by the fireside. In the course of these confidences it became quite plain to me I had been represented to the wife of the high dignitary, and goodness knows to how many more people besides, as an exceptional and gifted creature — a piece of good fortune for the Company — a man you don't get hold of every day. Good heavens! and I was going to take charge of a two-penny-half-penny river-steamboat with a penny whistle attached! It appeared, however, I was also one of the Workers, with a capital — you know. Something like an emissary of light, something like a lower sort of apostle. There had been a lot of such rot let loose in print and talk just about that time, and the excellent woman, living right in the rush of all that humbug, got carried off her feet. She talked about 'weaning those ignorant millions from their horrid ways,' till, upon my word, she made me quite uncomfortable. I ventured to hint that the Company was run for profit.

" 'You forget, dear Charlie, that the laborer is worthy of his hire,' she said, brightly. It's queer how out of touch with truth women are. They live in a world of their own, and there has never been anything like it, and never can be. It is too beautiful altogether, and if they were to set it up it would go to pieces before the first sunset. Some confounded fact we men have been living contentedly with ever since the day of creation would start up and knock the whole thing over.

"After this I got embraced, told to wear flannel, be sure to write often, and so on — and I left. In the street — I don't know why — a queer feeling came to me that I was an impostor. Odd thing that I, who used to clear out for any part of the world at twenty-four hours' notice, with less thought than most men give to the crossing of a street, had a moment — I won't say of hesitation, but of startled pause, before this commonplace affair. The best way I can explain it to you is by saying that, for a second or two, I felt as though, instead of going to the center of a continent, I were about to set off for the center of the earth.

"I left in a French steamer, and she called in every blamed port they have out there, for, as far as I could see, the sole purpose of landing soldiers and custom-house officers. I watched the coast. Watching a coast as it slips by the ship is like thinking about an enigma. There it is before you — smiling, frowning, inviting, grand, mean, insipid or savage, and always mute with an air of whispering, Come and find out. This one was almost featureless, as if still in the making, with an aspect of monotonous grimness. The edge of a colossal jungle, so dark-green as to be almost black, fringed with white surf, ran straight, like a ruled line, far, far away along a blue sea whose glitter was blurred by a creeping mist. The sun was fierce, the land seemed to glisten and drip with steam. Here and there grayish-whitish specks showed up clustered inside the white surf, with a flag flying above them perhaps. Settlements some centuries old, and still no bigger than pinheads on the untouched expanse of their background. We pounded along, stopped, landed soldiers; went on, landed custom-house clerks to levy toll in what looked like a God-forsaken wilderness, with a tin shed and a flag-pole lost in it; landed more soldiers — to take care of the custom-house clerks, presumably. Some, I heard, got drowned in the surf; but whether they did or not, nobody seemed particularly to care. They were just flung out there, and on we went. Every day the coast looked the same, as though we had not moved; but we passed various places — trading places — with names like Gran' Bassam, Little Popo; names that seemed to belong to some sordid farce acted in front of a sinister backcloth. The idleness of a passenger, my isolation amongst all these men with whom I had no point of contact, the oily and languid sea, the uniform somberness of the coast, seemed to keep me away from the truth of things, within the toil of a mournful and senseless delusion. The voice of the surf heard now and then was a positive pleasure, like the speech of a brother. It was something natural, that had its reason, that had a meaning. Now and then a boat from the shore gave one a momentary contact with reality. It was paddled by black fellows. You could see from afar the white of their eyeballs glistening. They shouted, sang; their bodies streamed with perspiration; they had faces like grotesque masks — these chaps; but they had bone, muscle, a wild vitality, an intense energy of movement, that was as natural and true as the surf along their coast. They wanted no excuse for being there. They were a great comfort to look at. For a time I would feel I belonged still to a world of straightforward facts; but the feeling would not last long. Something would turn up to scare it away. Once, I remember, we came upon a man-of-war anchored off the coast. There wasn't even a shed there, and she was shelling the bush. It appears the French had one of their wars going on thereabouts. Her ensign dropped limp like a rag; the muzzles of the long six-inch guns stuck out all over the low hull; the greasy, slimy swell swung her up lazily and let her down, swaying her thin masts. In the empty immensity of earth, sky, and water, there she was, incomprehensible, firing into a continent. Pop, would go one of the six-inch guns; a small flame would dart and vanish, a little white smoke would disappear, a tiny projectile would give a feeble screech — and nothing happened. Nothing could happen. There was a touch of insanity in the proceeding, a sense of lugubrious drollery in the sight; and it was not dissipated by somebody on board assuring me earnestly there was a camp of natives — he called them enemies! — hidden out of sight somewhere.

"We gave her her letters (I heard the men in that lonely ship were dying of fever at the rate of three a day) and went on. We called at some more places with farcical names, where the merry dance of death and trade goes on in a still and earthy atmosphere as of an overheated catacomb; all along the formless coast bordered by dangerous surf, as if Nature herself had tried to ward off intruders; in and out of rivers, streams of death in life, whose banks were rotting into mud, whose waters, thickened into slime, invaded the contorted mangroves, that seemed to writhe at us in the extremity of an impotent despair. Nowhere did we stop long enough to get a particularized impression, but the general sense of vague and oppressive wonder grew upon me. It was like a weary pilgrimage amongst hints for nightmares.

"It was upward of thirty days before I saw the mouth of the big river. We anchored off the seat of the government. But my work would not begin till some two hundred miles farther on. So as soon as I could I made a start for a place thirty miles higher up.

"I had my passage on a little sea-going steamer. Her captain was a

Swede, and knowing me for a seaman, invited me on the bridge. He was a young man, lean, fair, and morose, with lanky hair and a shuffling gait. As we left the miserable little wharf, he tossed his head contemptuously at the shore. 'Been living there?' he asked. I said, 'Yes,' 'Fine lot these government chaps — are they not?' he went on, speaking English with great precision and considerable bitterness. 'It is funny what some people will do for a few francs a month. I wonder what becomes of that kind when it goes upcountry?' I said to him I expected to see that soon. 'So-o-o!' he exclaimed. He shuffled athwart, keeping one eye ahead vigilantly. 'Don't be too sure,' he continued. 'The other day I took up a man who hanged himself on the road. He was a Swede, too.' 'Hanged himself! Why, in God's name?' I cried. I kept on looking out watchfully. 'Who knows? The sun was too much for him, or the country perhaps.'

"At last we opened a reach. A rocky cliff appeared, mounds of turned-up earth by the shore, houses on a hill, others with iron roofs, amongst a waste of excavations, or hanging to the declivity. A continuous noise of the rapids above hovered over this scene of inhabited devastation. A lot of people, mostly black and naked, moved about like ants. A jetty projected into the river. A blinding sunlight drowned all this at times in a sudden recrudescence of glare. 'There's your Company's station,' said the Swede, pointing to three wooden barrack-like structures on the rocky slope. 'I will send your things up. Four boxes did you say? So. Farewell.'

"I came upon a boiler wallowing in the grass, then found a path leading up the hill. It turned aside for the boulders, and also for an undersized railway-truck lying there on its back with its wheels in the air. One was off. The thing looked as dead as the carcass of some animal. I came upon more pieces of decaying machinery, a stack of rusty rails. To the left a clump of trees made a shady spot, where dark things seemed to stir feebly. I blinked, the path was steep. A horn tooted to the right, and I saw the black people run. A heavy and dull detonation shook the ground, a puff of smoke came out of the cliff, and that was all. No change appeared on the face of the rock. They were building a railway. The cliff was not in the way of anything; but the objectless blasting was all the work going on.

"A slight clinking behind me made me turn my head. Six black men advanced in a file, toiling up the path. They walked erect and slow, balancing small baskets full of earth on their heads, and the clink kept time with their footsteps. Black rags were wound round their loins, and the short ends behind waggled to and fro like tails. I could see every rib, the joints of their limbs were like knots in a rope; each had an iron collar on his neck, and all were connected together with a chain whose bights[6] swung between them, rhythmically clinking. Another report from the cliff made me think suddenly of that ship of war I had seen firing into a continent. It was the same kind of ominous voice; but these men could by no stretch of imagination be

---

[6] loops.

called enemies. They were called criminals, and the outraged law, like the bursting shells, had come to them, an insoluble mystery from the sea. All their meager breasts panted together, the violently dilated nostrils quivered, the eyes stared stonily up-hill. They passed me within six inches, without a glance, with that complete, deathlike indifference of unhappy savages. Behind this raw matter one of the reclaimed, the product of the new forces at work, strolled despondently, carrying a rifle by its middle. He had a uniform jacket with one button off, and seeing a white man on the path, hoisted his weapon to his shoulder with alacrity. This was simple prudence, white men being so much alike at a distance that he could not tell who I might be. He was speedily reassured, and with a large, white, rascally grin, and a glance at his charge, seemed to take me into partnership in his exalted trust. After that, I also was a part of the great cause of these high and just proceedings.

"Instead of going up, I turned and descended to the left. My idea was to let that chain-gang get out of sight before I climbed the hill. You know I am not particularly tender, I've had to strike and to fend off. I've had to resist and to attack sometimes — that's only one way of resisting — without counting the exact cost, according to the demands of such sort of life as I had blundered into. I've seen the devil of violence, and the devil of greed, and the devil of hot desire; but, by all the stars! these were strong, lusty, red-eyed devils, that swayed and drove men — men, I tell you. But as I stood on this hillside, I foresaw that in the blinding sunshine of that land I would become acquainted with a flabby, pretending, weak-eyed devil of a rapacious and pitiless folly. How insidious he could be, too, I was only to find out several months later and a thousand miles farther. For a moment I stood appalled, as though by a warning. Finally I descended the hill, obliquely, towards the trees I had seen.

"I avoided a vast artificial hole somebody had been digging on the slope, the purpose of which I found it impossible to divine. It wasn't a quarry or a sandpit, anyhow. It was just a hole. It might have been connected with the philanthropic desire of giving the criminals something to do. I don't know. Then I nearly fell into a very narrow ravine, almost no more than a scar in the hillside. I discovered that a lot of imported drainage-pipes for the settlement had been tumbled in there. There wasn't one that was not broken. It was a wanton smashup. At last I got under the trees. My purpose was to stroll into the shade for a moment; but no sooner within than it seemed to me I had stepped into the gloomy circle of some Inferno. The rapids were near, and an uninterrupted, uniform, headlong, rushing noise filled the mournful stillness of the grove, where not a breath stirred, not a leaf moved, with a mysterious sound — as though the tearing pace of the launched earth had suddenly become audible.

"Black shapes crouched, lay, sat between the trees leaning against the trunks, clinging to the earth, half coming out, half effaced within the dim light, in all the attitudes of pain, abandonment, and despair. Another mine on the cliff went off, followed by a slight shudder of the soil under my feet.

The work was going on. The work! and this was the place where some of the helpers had withdrawn to die.

"They were dying slowly — it was very clear. They were not enemies, they were not criminals, they were nothing earthly now — nothing but black shadows of disease and starvation, lying confusedly in the greenish gloom. Brought from all the recesses of the coast in all the legality of time contracts, lost in uncongenial surroundings, fed on unfamiliar food, they sickened, became inefficient, and were then allowed to crawl away and rest. These moribund shapes were free as air — and nearly as thin. I began to distinguish the gleam of the eyes under the trees. Then, glancing down, I saw a face near my hand. The black bones reclined at full length with one shoulder against the tree, and slowly the eyelids rose and the sunken eyes looked up at me, enormous and vacant, a kind of blind, white flicker in the depths of the orbs, which died out slowly. The man seemed young — almost a boy — but you know with them it's hard to tell. I found nothing else to do but to offer him one of my good Swede's ship's biscuits I had in my pocket. The fingers closed slowly on it and held — there was no other movement and no other glance. He had tied a bit of white worsted round his neck — Why? Where did he get it? Was it a badge — an ornament — a charm — a propitiatory act? Was there any idea at all connected with it? It looked startling round his black neck, this bit of white thread from beyond the seas.

"Near the same tree two more bundles of acute angles sat with their legs drawn up. One, with his chin propped on his knees, stared at nothing, in an intolerable and appalling manner: his brother phantom rested its forehead, as if overcome with a great weariness; and all about others were scattered in every pose of contorted collapse, as in some picture of a massacre or a pestilence. While I stood horror-struck, one of these creatures rose to his hands and knees, and went off on all-fours towards the river to drink. He lapped out of his hand, then sat up in the sunlight, crossing his shins in front of him, and after a time let his woolly head fall on his breastbone.

"I didn't want any more loitering in the shade, and I made haste towards the station. When near the buildings I met a white man, in such an unexpected elegance of get-up that in the first moment I took him for a sort of vision. I saw a high starched collar, white cuffs, a light alpaca jacket, snowy trousers, a clean necktie, and varnished boots. No hat. Hair parted, brushed, oiled, under a green-lined parasol held in a big white hand. He was amazing, and had a penholder behind his ear.

"I shook hands with this miracle, and I learned he was the Company's chief accountant, and that all the bookkeeping was done at this station. He had come out for a moment, he said, 'to get a breath of fresh air.' The expression sounded wonderfully odd, with its suggestion of sedentary desk-life. I wouldn't have mentioned the fellow to you at all, only it was from his lips that I first heard the name of the man who is so indissolubly connected with the memories of that time. Moreover, I respected the fellow. Yes; I respected his collars, his vast cuffs, his brushed hair. His appearance was certainly that of a hairdresser's dummy; but in the great demoralization of the land he kept up his appearance. That's backbone. His starched collars and got-up shirt-fronts were achievements of character. He had been out nearly three years; and, later, I could not help asking him how he managed to sport such linen. He had just the faintest blush, and said modestly, 'I've been teaching one of the native women about the station. It was difficult. She had a distaste for the work.' Thus this man had verily accomplished something. And he was devoted to his books, which were in apple-pie order.

"Everything else in the station was in a muddle — heads, things, buildings. Strings of dusty niggers with splay feet arrived and departed; a stream of manufactured goods, rubbishy cottons, beads, and brass-wire set into the depths of darkness, and in return came a precious trickle of ivory.

"I had to wait in the station for ten days — an eternity. I lived in a hut in the yard, but to be out of the chaos I would sometimes get into the accountant's office. It was built of horizontal planks, and so badly put together that, as he bent over his high desk, he was barred from neck to heels with narrow strips of sunlight. There was no need to open the big shutter to see. It was hot there, too; big flies buzzed fiendishly, and did not sting, but stabbed. I sat generally on the floor, while, of faultless appearance (and even slightly scented), perching on a high stool, he wrote, he wrote. Sometimes he stood up for exercise. When a trucklebed with a sick man (some invalid agent from up-country) was put in there, he exhibited a gentle annoyance. 'The groans of this sick person,' he said, 'distract my attention. And without that it is extremely difficult to guard against clerical errors in this climate.'

"One day he remarked, without lifting his head, 'In the interior you will no doubt meet Mr. Kurtz.' On my asking who Mr. Kurtz was, he said he was a first-class agent; and seeing my disappointment at this information, he added slowly, laying down his pen, 'He is a very remarkable person.' Further questions elicited from him that Mr. Kurtz was at present in charge of a trading post, a very important one, in the true ivory-country, at 'the very bottom of there. Sends in as much ivory as all the others put together. . . .' He began to write again. The sick man was too ill to groan. The flies buzzed in a great peace.

"Suddenly there was a growing murmur of voices and a great tramping of feet. A caravan had come in. A violent babble of uncouth sounds burst out on the other side of the planks. All the carriers were speaking together, and in the midst of the uproar the lamentable voice of the chief agent was heard 'giving it up' tearfully for the twentieth time that day. . . . He rose slowly. 'What a frightful row,' he said. He crossed the room gently to look at the sick man, and returning, said to me, 'He does not hear.' 'What! Dead?' I asked, startled. 'No, not yet,' he answered, with great composure. Then, alluding with a toss of the head to the tumult in the station-yard,

'When one has got to make correct entries, one comes to hate those savages — hate them to the death.' He remained thoughtful for a moment. 'When you see Mr. Kurtz,' he went on, 'tell him for me that everything here' — he glanced at the desk — 'is very satisfactory. I don't like to write to him — with those messengers of ours you never know who may get hold of your letter — at that Central Station.' He stared at me for a moment with his mild, bulging eyes. 'Oh, he will go far, very far,' he began again. 'He will be a somebody in the Administration before long. They, above — the Council in Europe, you know — mean him to be.'

"He turned to his work. The noise outside had ceased, and presently in going out I stopped at the door. In the steady buzz of flies the homeward-bound agent was lying flushed and insensible; the other, bent over his books, was making correct entries of perfectly correct transactions; and fifty feet below the doorstep I could see the still tree-tops of the grove of death.

"Next day I left the station at last, with a caravan of sixty men, for a two-hundred-mile tramp.

"No use telling you much about that. Paths, paths, everywhere; a stamped-in network of paths spreading over the empty land, through long grass, through burnt grass, through thickets, down and up chilly ravines, up and down stony hills ablaze with heat; and a solitude, a solitude, nobody, not a hut. The population had cleared out a long time ago. Well, if a lot of mysterious niggers armed with all kinds of fearful weapons suddenly took to traveling on the road between Deal and Gravesend, catching the yokels right and left to carry heavy loads for them, I fancy every farm and cottage thereabouts would get empty very soon. Only here the dwellings were gone, too. Still I passed through several abandoned villages. There's something pathetically childish in the ruins of grass walls. Day after day, with the stamp and shuffle of sixty pair of bare feet behind me, each pair under a sixty-pound load. Camp, cook, sleep, strike camp, march. Now and then a carrier dead in harness, at rest in the long grass near the path, with an empty water-gourd and his long staff lying by his side. A great silence around and above. Perhaps on some quiet night the tremor of far-off drums, sinking, swelling, a tremor vast, faint; a sound weird, appealing, suggestive, and wild — and perhaps with as profound a meaning as the sound of bells in a Christian country. Once a white man in an unbuttoned uniform, camping on the path with an armed escort of lank Zanzibaris, very hospitable and festive — not to say drunk. Was looking after the upkeep of the road, he declared. Can't say I saw any road or any upkeep, unless the body of a middle-aged Negro, with a bullet-hole in the forehead, upon which I absolutely stumbled three miles farther on, may be considered as a permanent improvement. I had a white companion, too, not a bad chap, but rather too fleshy and with the exasperating habit of fainting on the hot hillsides, miles away from the least bit of shade and water. Annoying, you know, to hold your own coat like a parasol over a man's head while he is coming to. I couldn't help asking him once what he meant by coming there at all. 'To make money, of course. What do you think?' he said, scornfully. Then he got fever, and had to be carried in a hammock slung under a pole. As he weighed sixteen stone[7] I had no end of rows with the carriers. They jibbed, ran away, sneaked off with their loads in the night — quite a mutiny. So, one evening, I made a speech in English with gestures, not one of which was lost to the sixty pairs of eyes before me, and the next morning I started the hammock off in front all right. An hour afterwards I came upon the whole concern wrecked in a bush — man, hammock, groans, blankets, horrors. The heavy pole had skinned his poor nose. He was very anxious for me to kill somebody, but there wasn't the shadow of a carrier near. I remember the old doctor—'It would be interesting for science to watch the mental changes of individuals, on the spot.' I felt I was becoming scientifically interesting. However, all that is to no purpose. On the fifteenth day I came in sight of the big river again, and hobbled into the Central Station. It was a backwater surrounded by scrub and forest, with a pretty border of smelly mud on one side, and on the three others enclosed by a crazy fence of rushes. A neglected gap was all the gate it had, and the first glance at the place was enough to let you see the flabby devil was running that show. White men with long staves in their hands appeared languidly from amongst the buildings, strolling up to take a look at me, and then retired out of sight somewhere. One of them, a stout, excitable chap with black mustaches, informed me with great volubility and many digressions, as soon as I told him who I was, that my steamer was at the bottom of the river. I was thunderstruck. What, how, why? Oh, it was 'all right.' The 'manager himself' was there. All quite correct. 'Everybody had behaved splendidly! splendidly!' — 'you must,' he said in agitation, 'go and see the general manager at once. He is waiting!'

"I did not see the real significance of that wreck at once. I fancy I see it now, but I am not sure — not at all. Certainly the affair was too stupid — when I think of it — to be altogether natural. Still. . . . But at the moment it presented itself simply as a confounded nuisance. The steamer was sunk. They had started two days before in a sudden hurry up the river with the manager on board, in charge of some volunteer skipper, and before they had been out three hours they tore the bottom out of her on stones, and she sank near the south bank. I asked myself what I was to do there, now my boat was lost. As a matter of fact, I had plenty to do in fishing my command out of the river. I had to set about it the very next day. That, and the repairs when I brought the pieces to the station, took some months.

"My first interview with the manager was curious. He did not ask me to sit down after my twenty-mile walk that morning. He was commonplace in complexion, in feature, in manners, and in voice. He was of middle size and of ordinary build. His eyes, of the usual blue, were perhaps remarkably cold, and he certainly could make his glance fall on one as trenchant and

---

[7] 224 pounds (a *stone* is the equivalent of fourteen pounds).

heavy as an ax. But even at these times the rest of his person seemed to disclaim the intention. Otherwise there was only an indefinable, faint expression of his lips, something stealthy — a smile — not a smile — I remember it, but I can't explain. It was unconscious, this smile was, though just after he had said something it got intensified for an instant. It came at the end of his speeches like a seal applied on the words to make the meaning of the commonest phrase appear absolutely inscrutable. He was a common trader, from his youth up employed in these parts — nothing more. He was obeyed, yet he inspired neither love nor fear, nor even respect. He inspired uneasiness. That was it! Uneasiness. Not a definite mistrust — just uneasiness — nothing more. You have no idea how effective such a . . . a . . . faculty can be. He had no genius for organizing, for initiative, or for order even. That was evident in such things as the deplorable state of the station. He had no learning, and no intelligence. His position had come to him — why? Perhaps because he was never ill. . . . He had served three terms of three years out there. . . . Because triumphant health in the general rout of constitutions is a kind of power in itself. When he went home on leave he rioted on a large scale — pompously. Jack ashore — with a difference — in externals only. This one could gather from his casual talk. He originated nothing, he could keep the routine going — that's all. But he was great. He was great by this little thing that it was impossible to tell what could control such a man. He never gave the secret away. Perhaps there was nothing within him. Such a suspicion made one pause — for out there there were no external checks. Once when various tropical diseases had laid low almost every 'agent' in the station, he was heard to say, 'Men who come out here should have no entrails.' He sealed the utterance with that smile of his, as though it had been a door opening into a darkness he had in his keeping. You fancied you had seen things — but the seal was on. When annoyed at meal-times by the constant quarrels of the white men about precedence, he ordered an immense round table to be made, for which a special house had to be built. This was the station's messroom. Where he sat was the first place — the rest were nowhere. One felt this to be his unalterable conviction. He was neither civil nor uncivil. He was quiet. He allowed his 'boy' — an overfed young Negro from the coast — to treat the white men, under his very eyes, with provoking insolence.

"He began to speak as soon as he saw me. I had been very long on the road. He could not wait. Had to start without me. The upriver stations had to be relieved. There had been so many delays already that he did not know who was dead and who was alive, and how they got on — and so on, and so on. He paid no attention to my explanations, and, playing with a stick of sealing-wax, repeated several times that the situation was 'very grave, very grave.' There were rumors that a very important station was in jeopardy, and its chief, Mr. Kurtz, was ill. Hoped it was not true. Mr. Kurtz was. . . . I felt weary and irritable. Hang Kurtz, I thought. I interrupted him by saying I had heard of Mr. Kurtz on the coast. 'Ah! So they talk of him down there,' he murmured to himself. Then he began again, assuring me Mr. Kurtz was the best agent he had, an exceptional man, of the greatest importance to the Company; therefore I could understand his anxiety. He was, he said, 'very, very uneasy.' Certainly he fidgeted on his chair a good deal, exclaimed, 'Ah, Mr. Kurtz!' broke the stick of sealing-wax and seemed dumfounded by the accident. Next thing he wanted to know 'how long it would take to. . . .' I interrupted him again. Being hungry, you know, and kept on my feet too, I was getting savage. 'How can I tell?' I said. 'I haven't even seen the wreck yet — some months, no doubt.' All this talk seemed to me so futile. 'Some months,' he said. 'Well, let us say three months before we can make a start. Yes. That ought to do the affair.' I flung out of his hut (he lived all alone in a clay hut with a sort of veranda) muttering to myself my opinion of him. He was a chattering idiot. Afterwards I took it back when it was borne in upon me startlingly with what extreme nicety he had estimated the time requisite for the 'affair.'

"I went to work the next day, turning, so to speak, my back on that station. In that way only it seemed to me I could keep my hold on the redeeming facts of life. Still, one must look about sometimes; and then I saw this station, these men strolling aimlessly about in the sunshine of the yard. I asked myself sometimes what it all meant. They wandered here and there with their absurd long staves in their hands, like a lot of faithless pilgrims bewitched inside a rotten fence. The word 'ivory' rang in the air, was whispered, was sighed. You would think they were praying to it. A taint of imbecile rapacity blew through it all, like a whiff from some corpse. By Jove! I've never seen anything so unreal in my life. And outside, the silent wilderness surrounding this cleared speck on the earth struck me as something great and invincible, like evil or truth, waiting patiently for the passing away of this fantastic invasion.

"Oh, these months! Well, never mind. Various things happened. One evening a grass shed full of calico, cotton prints, beads, and I don't know what else, burst into a blaze so suddenly that you would have thought the earth had opened to let an avenging fire consume all the trash. I was smoking my pipe quietly by my dismantled steamer, and saw them all cutting capers in the light, with their arms lifted high, when the stout man with mustaches came tearing down to the river, a tin pail in his hand, assured me that everybody was 'behaving splendidly, splendidly,' dipped about a quart of water and tore back again. I noticed there was a hole in the bottom of his pail.

"I strolled up. There was no hurry. You see the thing had gone off like a box of matches. It had been hopeless from the very first. The flame had leaped high, driven everybody back, lighted up everything — and collapsed. The shed was already a heap of embers glowing fiercely. A nigger was being beaten near by. They said he had caused the fire in some way; be that as it may, he was screeching most horribly. I saw him, later, for several days, sitting in a bit of shade looking very sick and trying to recover himself:

afterwards he arose and went out — and the wilderness without a sound
took him into its bosom again. As I approached the glow from the dark I
found myself at the back of two men, talking. I heard the name of Kurtz
pronounced, then the words, 'take advantage of this unfortunate accident.'
One of the men was the manager. I wished him a good evening. 'Did you
ever see anything like it — eh? it is incredible,' he said, and walked off. The
other man remained. He was a first-class agent, young, gentlemanly, a bit
reserved, with a forked little beard and a hooked nose. He was standoffish
with the other agents, and they on their side said he was the manager's spy
among them. As to me, I had hardly ever spoken to him before. We got
into talk, and by and by we strolled away from the hissing ruins. Then he
asked me to his room, which was in the main building of the station. He
struck a match, and I perceived that this young aristocrat had not only a
silver-mounted dressing-case but also a whole candle all to himself. Just at
that time the manager was the only man supposed to have any right to candles. Native mats covered the clay walls; a collection of spears, assegais,
shields, knives was hung up in trophies. The business intrusted to this fellow was the making of bricks — so I had been informed; but there wasn't a
fragment of a brick anywhere in the station, and he had been there more
than a year — waiting. It seems he could not make bricks without something, I don't know what — straw, maybe. Anyways, it could not be found
there, and as it was not likely to be sent from Europe, it did not appear clear
to me what he was waiting for. An act of special creation perhaps. However,
they were all waiting — all the sixteen or twenty pilgrims of them — for
something; and upon my word it did not seem an uncongenial occupation,
from the way they took it, though the only thing that ever came to them
was disease — as far as I could see. They beguiled the time by backbiting
and intriguing against each other in a foolish kind of way. There was an air
of plotting about that station, but nothing came of it, of course. It was as
unreal as everything else — as the philanthropic pretense of the whole concern, as their talk, as their government, as their show of work. The only real
feeling was a desire to get appointed to a trading-post where ivory was to be
had, so that they could earn percentages. They intrigued and slandered and
hated each other only on that account — but as to effectually lifting a little
finger — oh, no. By heavens! there is something after all in the world allowing one man to steal a horse while another must not look at the halter.
Steal a horse straight out. Very well. He has done it. Perhaps he can ride.
But there is a way of looking at a halter that would provoke the most charitable of saints into a kick.

"I had no idea why he wanted to be sociable, but as we chatted in
there it suddenly occurred to me the fellow was trying to get at something — in fact, pumping me. He alluded constantly to Europe, to the people I was supposed to know there — putting leading questions as to my
acquaintances in the sepulchral city, and so on. His little eyes glittered like
mica discs — with curiosity — though he tried to keep up a bit of supercil-

iousness. At first I was astonished, but very soon I became awfully curious to see what he would find out from me. I couldn't possibly imagine what I had in me to make it worth his while. It was very pretty to see how he baffled himself, for in truth my body was full only of chills, and my head had nothing in it but that wretched steamboat business. It was evident he took me for a perfectly shameless prevaricator. At last he got angry, and, to conceal a movement of furious annoyance, he yawned. I rose. Then I noticed a small sketch in oils, on a panel, representing a woman, draped and blindfolded, carrying a lighted torch. The background was somber — almost black. The movement of the woman was stately, and the effect of the torchlight on the face was sinister.

"It arrested me, and he stood by civilly, holding an empty half-pint champagne bottle (medical comforts) with the candle stuck in it. To my question he said Mr. Kurtz had painted this — in this very station more than a year ago — while waiting for means to go to his trading-post. 'Tell me, pray,' said I, 'who is this Mr. Kurtz?'

" 'The chief of the Inner Station,' he answered in a short tone, looking away. 'Much obliged,' I said, laughing. 'And you are the brickmaker of the Central Station. Everyone knows that.' He was silent for a while. 'He is a prodigy,' he said at last. 'He is an emissary of pity, and science, and progress, and devil knows what else. We want,' he began to declaim suddenly, 'for the guidance of the cause intrusted to us by Europe, so to speak, higher intelligence, wide sympathies, a singleness of purpose.' 'Who says that?' I asked. 'Lots of them,' he replied. 'Some even write that; and so *he* comes here, a special being, as you ought to know.' 'Why ought I to know?' I interrupted, really surprised. He paid no attention. 'Yes. Today he is chief of the best station, next year he will be assistant-manager, two years more and . . . but I daresay you know what he will be in two years' time. You are of the new gang — the gang of virtue. The same people who sent him specially also recommended you. Oh, don't say no. I've my own eyes to trust.' Light dawned upon me. My dear aunt's influential acquaintances were producing an unexpected effect upon that young man. I nearly burst into a laugh. 'Do you read the Company's confidential correspondence?' I asked. He hadn't a word to say. It was great fun. 'When Mr. Kurtz,' I continued, severely, 'is General Manager, you won't have the opportunity.'

"He blew the candle out suddenly, and we went outside. The moon had risen. Black figures strolled about listlessly, pouring water on the glow, whence proceeded a sound of hissing; steam ascended in the moonlight, the beaten nigger groaned somewhere. 'What a row the brute makes!' said the indefatigable man with the mustaches, appearing near us. 'Serves him right. Transgression — punishment — bang! Pitiless, pitiless. That's the only way. This will prevent all conflagrations for the future. I was just telling the manager. . . .' He noticed my companion, and became crestfallen all at once. 'Not in bed yet,' he said, with a kind of servile heartiness; 'it's so natural. Ha! Danger — agitation.' He vanished. I went on to the river-side, and the other followed me. I heard a scathing murmur at my ear, 'Heap of muffs — go to.' The pilgrims could be seen in knots gesticulating, discussing. Several had still their staves in their hands. I verily believe they took these sticks to bed with them. Beyond the fence the forest stood up spectrally in the moonlight, and through the dim stir, through the faint sounds of that lamentable courtyard, the silence of the land went home to one's very heart — its mystery, its greatness, the amazing reality of its concealed life. The hurt nigger moaned feebly somewhere near by, and then fetched a deep sigh that made me mend my pace away from there. I felt a hand introducing itself under my arm. 'My dear sir,' said the fellow, 'I don't want to be misunderstood, and especially by you, who will see Mr. Kurtz long before I can have that pleasure. I wouldn't like him to get a false idea of my disposition. . . .'

"I let him run on, this papier-mâché Mephistopheles, and it seemed to me that if I tried I could poke my forefinger through him, and would find nothing inside but a little loose dirt, maybe. He, don't you see, had been planning to be assistant-manager by and by under the present man, and I could see that the coming of that Kurtz had upset them both not a little. He talked precipitately, and I did not try to stop him. I had my shoulders against the wreck of my steamer, hauled up on the slope like a carcass of some big river animal. The smell of mud, of primeval mud, by Jove! was in my nostrils, the high stillness of primeval forest was before my eyes; there were shiny patches on the black creek. The moon had spread over everything a thin layer of silver — over the rank grass, over the mud, upon the wall of matted vegetation standing higher than the wall of a temple, over the great river I could see through a somber gap glittering, glittering, as it flowed broadly by without a murmur. All this was great, expectant, mute, while the man jabbered about himself. I wondered whether the stillness on the face of the immensity looking at us two were meant as an appeal or as a menace. What were we who had strayed in here? Could we handle that dumb thing, or would it handle us? I felt how big, how confoundedly big, was that thing that couldn't talk, and perhaps was deaf as well. What was in there? I could see a little ivory coming out from there, and I had heard Mr. Kurtz was in there. I had heard enough about it, too — God knows! Yet somehow it didn't bring any image with it — no more than if I had been told an angel or a fiend was in there. I believed it in the same way one of you might believe there are inhabitants in the planet Mars. I knew once a Scotch sailmaker who was certain, dead sure, there were people in Mars. If you asked him for some idea how they looked and behaved, he would get shy and mutter something about 'walking on all-fours.' If you as much as smiled, he would — though a man of sixty — offer to fight you. I would not have gone so far as to fight for Kurtz, but I went for him near enough to a lie. You know I hate, detest, and can't bear a lie, not because I am straighter than the rest of us, but simply because it appalls me. There is a taint of death, a flavor of mortality in lies — which is exactly what I hate and detest in the

world — what I want to forget. It makes me miserable and sick, like biting
something rotten would do. Temperament, I suppose. Well, I went near
enough to it by letting the young fool there believe anything he liked to
imagine as to my influence in Europe. I became in an instant as much of a
pretense as the rest of the bewitched pilgrims. This simply because I had a
notion it somehow would be of help to that Kurtz whom at the time I did
not see — you understand. He was just a word for me. I did not see the man
in the name any more than you do. Do you see him? Do you see the story?
Do you see anything? It seems to me I am trying to tell you a dream —
making a vain attempt, because no relation of a dream can convey the
dream-sensation, that commingling of absurdity, surprise, and bewilderment in a tremor of struggling revolt, that notion of being captured by the
incredible which is of the very essence of dreams. . . ."

He was silent for a while.

". . . No, it is impossible; it is impossible to convey the life-sensation of
any given epoch of one's existence — that which makes its truth, its meaning — its subtle and penetrating essence. It is impossible. We live, as we
dream — alone. . . ."

He paused again as if reflecting, then added —

"Of course in this you fellows see more than I could then. You see me,
whom you know. . . ."

It had become so pitch dark that we listeners could hardly see one another. For a long time already he, sitting apart, had been no more to us than
a voice. There was not a word from anybody. The others might have been
asleep, but I was awake. I listened, I listened on the watch for the sentence,
for the word, that would give me the clew of the faint uneasiness inspired
by this narrative that seemed to shape itself without human lips in the
heavy night-air of the river.

". . . Yes — I let him run on," Marlow began again, "and think what
he pleased about the powers that were behind me. I did! And there was
nothing behind me! There was nothing but that wretched, old, mangled
steamboat I was leaning against, while he talked fluently about 'the necessity for every man to get on.' 'And when one comes out here, you conceive,
it is not to gaze at the moon.' Mr. Kurtz was a 'universal genius,' but even a
genius would find it easier to work with 'adequate tools — intelligent men.'
He did not make bricks — why, there was a physical impossibility in the
way — as I was well aware; and if he did secretarial work for the manager, it
was because 'no sensible man rejects wantonly the confidence of his superiors.' Did I see it? I saw it. What more did I want? What I really wanted was
rivets, by heavens! Rivets. To get on with the work — to stop the hole.
Rivets I wanted. There were cases of them down at the coast — cases —
piled up — burst — split! You kicked a loose rivet at every second step in
that station yard on the hillside. Rivets had rolled into the grove of death.
You could fill your pockets with rivets for the trouble of stooping down —
and there wasn't one rivet to be found where it was wanted. We had plates

that would do, but nothing to fasten them with. And every week the messenger, a lone Negro, letter-bag on shoulder and staff in hand, left our station for the coast. And several times a week a coast caravan came in with trade goods — ghastly glazed calico that made you shudder only to look at it; glass beads, valued about a penny a quart, confounded spotted cotton handkerchiefs. And no rivets. Three carriers could have brought all that was wanted to set that steamboat afloat.

"He was becoming confidential now, but I fancy my unresponsive attitude must have exasperated him at last, for he judged it necessary to inform me he feared neither God nor devil, let alone any mere man. I said I could see that very well, but what I wanted was a certain quantity of rivets — and rivets were what really Mr. Kurtz wanted, if he had only known it. Now letters went to the coast every week. . . . 'My dear sir,' he cried, 'I write from dictation.' I demanded rivets. There was a way — for an intelligent man. He changed his manner; became very cold, and suddenly began to talk about a hippopotamus; wondered whether sleeping on board the steamer (I stuck to my salvage night and day) I wasn't disturbed. There was an old hippo that had the bad habit of getting out on the bank and roaming at night over the station grounds. The pilgrims used to turn out in a body and empty every rifle they could lay hands on at him. Some even had sat up o' nights for him. All this energy was wasted, though. 'That animal had a charmed life,' he said; 'but you can say this only of brutes in this country. No man — you apprehend me? — no man here bears a charmed life.' He stood there for a moment in the moonlight with his delicate hooked nose set a little askew, and his mica eyes glittering without a wink, then, with a curt good night, he strode off. I could see he was disturbed and considerably puzzled, which made me feel more hopeful than I had been for days. It was a great comfort to turn from that chap to my influential friend, the battered, twisted, ruined, tin-pot steamboat. I clambered on board. She rang under my feet like an empty Huntley & Palmer biscuit-tin kicked along a gutter; she was nothing so solid in make, and rather less pretty in shape, but I had expended enough hard work on her to make me love her. No influential friend would have served me better. She had given me a chance to come out a bit — to find out what I could do. No, I don't like work. I had rather laze about and think of all the fine things that can be done. I don't like work — no man does — but I like what is in the work — the chance to find yourself. Your own reality — for yourself, not for others — what no other man can ever know. They can only see the mere show, and never tell me what it really means.

"I was not surprised to see somebody sitting aft, on the deck, with his legs dangling over the mud. You see I rather chummed with the few mechanics there were in that station, whom the other pilgrims naturally despised — on account of their imperfect manners, I suppose. This was the foreman — a boiler-maker by trade — a good worker. He was a lank, bony, yellow-faced man, with big intense eyes. His aspect was worried, and his head was as bald as the palm of my hand; but his hair in falling seemed to have stuck to his chin, and had prospered in the new locality, for his beard hung down to his waist. He was a widower with six young children (he had left them in charge of a sister of his to come out there), and the passion of his life was pigeon-flying. He was an enthusiast and a connoiseur. He would rave about pigeons. After work hours he used sometimes to come over from his hut for a talk about his children and his pigeons; at work, when he had to crawl in the mud under the bottom of the steamboat, he would tie up that beard of his in a kind of white serviette he brought for the purpose. It had loops to go over his ears. In the evening he could be seen squatted on the bank rinsing that wrapper in the creek with great care, then spreading it solemnly on a bush to dry.

"I slapped him on the back and shouted, 'We shall have rivets!' He scrambled to his feet exclaiming, 'No! Rivets!' as though he couldn't believe his ears. Then in a low voice, 'You . . . eh?' I don't know why we behaved like lunatics. I put my finger to the side of my nose and nodded mysteriously. 'Good for you!' he cried, snapped his fingers above his head, lifting one foot. I tried a jig. We capered on the iron deck. A frightful clatter came out of that hulk, and the virgin forest on the other bank of the creek sent it back in a thundering roll upon the sleeping station. It must have made some of the pilgrims sit up in their hovels. A dark figure obscured the lighted doorway of the manager's hut, vanished, then, a second or so after, the doorway itself vanished, too. We stopped, and the silence driven away by the stamping of our feet flowed back again from the recesses of the land. The great wall of vegetation, an exuberant and entangled mass of trunks, branches, leaves, boughs, festoons, motionless in the moonlight, was like a rioting invasion of soundless life, a rolling wave of plants, piled up, crested, ready to topple over the creek, to sweep every little man of us out of his little existence. And it moved not. A deadened burst of mighty splashes and snorts reached us from afar as though an ichthyosaurus[8] had been taking a bath of glitter in the great river. 'After all,' said the boilermaker in a reasonable tone, 'why shouldn't we get the rivets?' Why not, indeed! I did not know of any reason why we shouldn't. 'They'll come in three weeks,' I said confidently.

"But they didn't. Instead of rivets there came an invasion, an infliction, a visitation. It came in sections during the next three weeks, each section headed by a donkey carrying a white man in new clothes and tan shoes, bowing from that elevation right and left to the impressed pilgrims. A quarrelsome band of footsore sulky niggers trod on the heels of the donkeys; a lot of tents, campstools, tin boxes, white cases, brown bales would be shot down in the courtyard, and the air of mystery would deepen a little over the muddle of the station. Five such installments came, with their absurd air of disorderly flight with the loot of innumerable outfit shops and provision

---

[8] water-dwelling dinosaur.

stores, that, one would think, they were lugging, after a raid, into the wilderness for equitable division. It was an extricable mess of things decent in themselves but that human folly made look like the spoils of thieving.

"This devoted band called itself the Eldorado Exploring Expedition, and I believe they were sworn to secrecy. Their talk, however, was the talk of sordid buccaneers: it was reckless without hardihood, greedy without audacity, and cruel without courage; there was not an atom of foresight or of serious intention in the whole batch of them, and they did not seem aware these things are wanted for the work of the world. To tear treasure out of the bowels of the land was their desire, with no more moral purpose at the back of it than there is in burglars breaking into a safe. Who paid the expenses of the noble enterprise I don't know; but the uncle of our manager was leader of that lot.

"In exterior he resembled a butcher in a poor neighborhood, and his eyes had a look of sleepy cunning. He carried his fat paunch with ostentation on his short legs, and during the time his gang infested the station spoke to no one but his nephew. You could see these two roaming about all day long with their heads close together in an everlasting confab.

"I had given up worrying myself about the rivets. One's capacity for that kind of folly is more limited than you would suppose. I said Hang! — and let things slide. I had plenty of time for meditation, and now and then I would give some thought to Kurtz. I wasn't very interested in him. No. Still, I was curious to see whether this man, who had come out equipped with moral ideas of some sort, would climb to the top after all and how he would set about his work when there."

II

"One evening as I was lying flat on the deck of my steamboat, I heard voices approaching — and there were the nephew and the uncle strolling along the bank. I laid my head on my arm again, and had nearly lost myself in a doze, when somebody said in my ear, as it were: 'I am as harmless as a little child, but I don't like to be dictated to. Am I the manager — or am I not? I was ordered to send him there. It's incredible.' . . . I became aware that the two were standing on the shore alongside the forepart of the steamboat, just below my head. I did not move; it did not occur to me to move: I was sleepy. 'It *is* unpleasant,' grunted the uncle. 'He has asked the Administration to be sent there,' said the other, 'with the idea of showing what he could do; and I was instructed accordingly. Look at the influence that man must have. Is it not frightful?' They both agreed it was frightful, then made several bizarre remarks: 'Make rain and fine weather — one man — the Council — by the nose' — bits of absurd sentences that got the better of my drowsiness, so that I had pretty near the whole of my wits about me when the uncle said, 'The climate may do away with this difficulty for you. Is he alone there?' 'Yes,' answered the manager; 'he sent his assistant down the river with a note to me in these terms: "Clear this poor devil out of the country, and don't bother sending more of that sort. I had rather be alone than have the kind of men you can dispose of with me." It was more than a year ago. Can you imagine such impudence!' 'Anything since then?' asked the other, hoarsely. 'Ivory,' jerked the nephew; 'lots of it — prime sort — lots — most annoying, from him.' 'And with that?' questioned the heavy rumble. 'Invoice,' was the reply fired out, so to speak. Then silence. They had been talking about Kurtz.

"I was broad awake by this time, but, lying perfectly at ease, remained still, having no inducement to change my position. 'How did that ivory come all this way?' growled the elder man, who seemed very vexed. The other explained that it had come with a fleet of canoes in charge of an English half-caste clerk Kurtz had with him; that Kurtz had apparently intended to return himself, the station being by that time bare of goods and stores, but after coming three hundred miles, had suddenly decided to go back, which he started to do alone in a small dugout with four paddlers, leaving the half-caste to continue down the river with the ivory. The two fellows there seemed astounded at anybody attempting such a thing. They were at a loss for an adequate motive. As to me, I seemed to see Kurtz for the first time. It was a distinct glimpse: the dugout, four paddling savages, and the lone white man turning his back suddenly on the headquarters, on relief, on thoughts of home — perhaps; setting his face towards the depths of the wilderness, towards his empty and desolate station. I did not know the motive. Perhaps he was just simply a fine fellow who stuck to his work for its own sake. His name, you understand, had not been pronounced once. He was 'that man.' The half-caste, who, as far as I could see, had conducted a difficult trip with great prudence and pluck, was invariably alluded to as 'that scoundrel.' The 'scoundrel' had reported that the 'man' had been very ill — had recovered imperfectly. . . . The two below me moved away then a few paces, and strolled back and forth at some little distance. I heard: 'Military post — doctor — two hundred miles — quite alone now — unavoidable delays — nine months — no news — strange rumors.' They approached again, just as the manager was saying, 'No one, as far as I know, unless a species of wandering trader — a pestilential fellow, snapping ivory from the natives.' Who was it they were talking about now? I gathered in snatches that this was some man supposed to be in Kurtz's district, and of whom the manager did not approve. 'We will not be free from unfair competition till one of these fellows is hanged for an example,' he said. 'Certainly,' grunted the other; 'get him hanged! Why not? Anything — anything can be done in this country. That's what I say; nobody here, you understand, *here*, can endanger your position. And why? You stand the climate — you outlast them all. The danger is in Europe; but there before I left I took care to — ' They moved off and whispered, then their voices rose again. 'The extraordinary series of delays is not my fault. I did my best.' The fat man sighed. 'Very sad.' 'And the pestiferous absurdity of his talk,' continued the other; 'he bothered me enough when he was here. "Each station should be like a beacon on the road towards better things, a center for trade, of course, but also for humanizing, improving, instructing." Conceive you — that ass! And he wants to be manager! No it's — ' Here he got choked by excessive indignation, and I lifted my head the least bit. I was surprised to see how near they were — right under me. I could have spat upon their hats. They were looking on the ground, absorbed in thought. The manager was switching his leg with a slender twig: his sagacious relative lifted his head. 'You have been well since you came out this time?' he asked. The other gave a start. 'Who? I? Oh! Like a charm — like a charm. But the rest — oh, my goodness! All sick. They die so quick, too, that I haven't the time to send them out of the country—it's incredible!' 'H'm. Just so,' grunted the uncle. 'Ah! my boy, trust to this — I say, trust to this.' I saw him extend his short flipper of an arm for a gesture that took in the forest, the creek, the mud, the river — seemed to beckon with a dishonoring flourish before the sunlit face of the land a treacherous appeal to the lurking death, to the hidden evil, to the profound darkness of its heart. It was so startling that I leaped to my feet and looked back at the edge of the forest, as though I had expected an answer of some sort to that black display of confidence. You know the foolish notions that come to one sometimes. The high stillness confronted these two figures with its ominous patience, waiting for the passing away of a fantastic invasion.

"They swore aloud together — out of sheer fright, I believe — then pretending not to know anything of my existence, turned back to the station. The sun was low; and leaning forward side by side, they seemed to be tugging painfully uphill their two ridiculous shadows of unequal length, that trailed behind them slowly over the tall grass without bending a single blade.

"In a few days the Eldorado Expedition went into the patient wilderness, that closed upon it as the sea closes over a diver. Long afterwards the news came that all the donkeys were dead. I know nothing as to the fate of the less valuable animals. They, no doubt, like the rest of us, found what they deserved. I did not inquire. I was then rather excited at the prospect of meeting Kurtz very soon. When I say very soon I mean it comparatively. It was just two months from the day we left the creek when we came to the bank below Kurtz's station.

"Going up that river was like traveling back to the earliest beginnings of the world, when vegetation rioted on the earth and the big trees were kings. An empty stream, a great silence, an impenetrable forest. The air was warm, thick, heavy, sluggish. There was no joy in the brilliance of sunshine. The long stretches of the waterway ran on, deserted, into the gloom of overshadowed distances. On silvery sandbanks hippos and alligators sunned themselves side by side. The broadening waters flowed through a mob of wooded islands; you lost your way on that river as you would in a desert, and butted all day long against shoals, trying to find the channel, till you thought yourself bewitched and cut off forever from everything you had known once — somewhere — far away — in another existence perhaps. There were moments when one's past came back to one, as it will sometimes when you have not a moment to spare to yourself; but it came in the shape of an unrestful and noisy dream, remembered with wonder amongst the overwhelming realities of this strange world of plants, and water, and silence. And this stillness of life did not in the least resemble a peace. It was the stillness of an implacable force brooding over an inscrutable intention. It looked at you with a vengeful aspect. I got used to it afterwards; I did not see it any more; I had no time. I had to keep guessing at the channel; I had to discern, mostly by inspiration, the signs of hidden banks; I watched for sunken stones; I was learning to clap my teeth smartly before my heart flew out, when I shaved by a fluke some infernal sly old snag that would have ripped the life out of the tin-pot steamboat and drowned all the pilgrims; I had to keep a lookout for the signs of dead wood we could cut up in the night for next day's steaming. When you have to attend to things of that sort, to the mere incidents of the surface, the reality — the reality, I tell you — fades. The inner truth is hidden — luckily, luckily. But I felt it all the same; I felt often its mysterious stillness watching me at my monkey tricks, just as it watches you fellows performing on your respective tight-ropes for — what is it? half-a-crown a tumble — "

"Try to be civil, Marlow," growled a voice, and I knew there was at least one listener awake besides myself.

"I beg your pardon. I forgot the heartache which makes up the rest of the price. And indeed what does the price matter, if the trick be well done? You do your tricks very well. And I didn't do badly either, since I managed not to sink that steamboat on my first trip. It's a wonder to me yet. Imagine a blindfolded man set to drive a van over a bad road. I sweated and shivered over the business considerably, I can tell you. After all, for a seaman, to scrape the bottom of the thing that's supposed to float all the time under his care is the unpardonable sin. No one may know of it, but you never forget the thump — eh? A blow on the very heart. You remember it, you dream of it, you wake up at night and think of it — years after — and go hot and cold all over. I don't pretend to say that steamboat floated all the time. More than once she had to wade for a bit, with twenty cannibals splashing around and pushing. We had enlisted some of these chaps on the way for a crew. Fine fellows — cannibals — in their place. They were men one could work with, and I am grateful to them. And, after all, they did not eat each other before my face: they had brought along a provision of hippo-meat which went rotten, and made the mystery of the wilderness stink in my nostrils. Phoo! I can sniff it now. I had the manager on board and three or four pilgrims with their staves — all complete. Sometimes we came upon a station close by the bank, clinging to the skirts of the unknown, and the white men rushing out of a tumble-down hovel, with great gestures of joy and surprise and welcome, seemed very strange — had the appearance of being held there captive by a spell. The word ivory would ring in the air for a while — and on we went again into the silence, along empty reaches, round the still bends, between the high walls of our winding way, reverberating in hollow claps the ponderous beat of the stern-wheel. Trees, trees, millions of trees, massive, immense, running up high; and at their foot, hugging the bank against the stream, crept the little begrimed steamboat, like a sluggish beetle crawling on the floor of a lofty portico. It made you feel very small, very lost, and yet it was not altogether depressing, that feeling. After all, if you were small, the grimy beetle crawled on — which was just what you wanted it to do. Where the pilgrims imagined it crawled to I don't know. To some place where they expected to get something, I bet! For me it crawled towards Kurtz — exclusively; but when the steam-pipes started leaking we crawled very slow. The reaches opened before us and closed behind, as if the forest had stepped leisurely across the water to bar the way for our return. We penetrated deeper and deeper into the heart of darkness. It was very quiet there. At night sometimes the roll of drums behind the curtain of trees would run up the river and remain sustained faintly, as if hovering in the air high over our heads, till the first break of day. Whether it meant war, peace, or prayer we could not tell. The dawns were heralded by the descent of a chill stillness; the wood-cutters slept, their fires burned low; the snapping of a twig would make you start. We were wanderers on a prehistoric earth, on an earth that wore the aspect of an unknown planet. We could have fancied ourselves the first men taking possession of an accursed inheritance, to be subdued at the cost of profound anguish and of excessive toil. But suddenly, as we struggled round a bend, there would be a glimpse of rush walls, of peaked grass-roofs, a burst of yells, a whirl of black limbs, a mass of hands clapping, of feet stamping, of bodies swaying, of eyes rolling, under the droop of heavy and motionless foliage. The steamer toiled along slowly on the edge of a black and incomprehensible frenzy. The prehistoric man was cursing us, praying to us, welcoming us — who could tell? We were cut off from the comprehension of our surroundings; we glided past like phantoms, wondering and secretly appalled, as sane men would be before an enthusiastic outbreak in a madhouse. We could not understand because we were too far and could not remember, because we were traveling in the night of first ages, of those ages that are gone, leaving hardly a sign — and no memories.

"The earth seemed unearthly. We are accustomed to look upon the shackled form of a conquered monster, but there — there you could look at a thing monstrous and free. It was unearthly, and the men were — No, they were not inhuman. Well, you know, that was the worst of it — this suspicion of their not being inhuman. It would come slowly to one. They howled and leaped, and spun, and made horrid faces; but what thrilled you was just the thought of their humanity — like yours — the thought of your remote kinship with this wild and passionate uproar. Ugly. Yes, it was ugly enough; but if you were man enough you would admit to yourself that there was in

you just the faintest trace of a response to the terrible frankness of that
noise, a dim suspicion of there being a meaning in it which you — you so
remote from the night of first ages — could comprehend. And why not?
The mind of man is capable of anything — because everything is in it, all
the past as well as all the future. What was there after all? Joy, fear, sorrow,
devotion, valor, rage — who can tell? — but truth — truth stripped of its
cloak of time. Let the fool gape and shudder — the man knows, and can
look on without a wink. But he must at least be as much of a man as these
on the shore. He must meet the truth with his own true stuff — with his
own inborn strength. Principles won't do. Acquisitions, clothes, pretty
rags — rags that would fly off at the first good shake. No; you want a deliberate belief. An appeal to me in this fiendish row — is there? Very well; I
hear; I admit, but I have a voice, too, and for good or evil mine is the speech
that cannot be silenced. Of course, a fool, what with sheer fright and fine
sentiments, is always safe. Who's that grunting? You wonder I didn't go
ashore for a howl and a dance? Well, no — I didn't. Fine sentiments, you
say? Fine sentiments, be hanged! I had no time. I had to mess about with
white-lead and strips of woolen blanket helping to put bandages on those
leaky steam-pipes — I tell you. I had to watch the steering, and circumvent
those snags, and get the tin-pot along by hook or by crook. There was
surface-truth enough in these things to save a wiser man. And between
whiles I had to look after the savage who was fireman. He was an improved
specimen; he could fire up a vertical boiler. He was there below me, and,
upon my word, to look at him was as edifying as seeing a dog in a parody of
breeches and a feather hat, walking on his hindlegs. A few months of training had done for that really fine chap. He squinted at the steam-gauge and
at the water-gauge with an evident effort of intrepidity — and he had filed
teeth, too, the poor devil, and the wool of his pate shaved into queer patterns, and three ornamental scars on each of his cheeks. He ought to have
been clapping his hands and stamping his feet on the bank, instead of
which he was hard at work, a thrall to strange witchcraft, full of improving
knowledge. He was useful because he had been instructed; and what he
knew was this — that should the water in that transparent thing disappear,
the evil spirit inside the boiler would get angry through the greatness of his
thirst, and take a terrible vengeance. So he sweated and fired up and
watched the glass fearfully (with an impromptu charm, made of rags, tied
to his arm, and a piece of polished bone, as big as a watch, stuck flatways
through his lower lip), while the wooden banks slipped past us slowly, the
short noise was left behind, the interminable miles of silence — and we
crept on, towards Kurtz. But the snags were thick, the water was treacherous and shallow, the boiler seemed indeed to have a sulky devil in it, and
thus neither that fireman nor I had any time to peer into our creepy
thoughts.

"Some fifty miles below the Inner Station we came upon a hut of
reeds, an inclined and melancholy pole, with the unrecognizable tatters of

what had been a flag of some sort flying from it, and a neatly stacked wood-pile. This was unexpected. We came to the bank, and on the stack of fire-wood found a flat piece of board with some faded pencil-writing on it. When deciphered it said: 'Wood for you. Hurry up. Approach cautiously.' There was a signature, but it was illegible — not Kurtz — a much longer word. 'Hurry up.' Where? Up the river? 'Approach cautiously.' We had not done so. But the warning could not have been meant for the place where it could be only found after approach. Something was wrong above. But what — and how much? That was the question. We commented adversely upon the imbecility of that telegraphic style. The bush around said nothing, and would not let us look very far, either. A torn curtain of red twill hung in the doorway of the hut, and flapped sadly in our faces. The dwelling was dismantled; but we could see a white man had lived there not very long ago. There remained a rude table — a plank on two posts; a heap of rubbish re-posed in a dark corner, and by the door I picked up a book. It had lost its covers, and the pages had been thumbed into a state of extremely dirty softness; but the back had been lovingly stitched afresh with white cotton thread, which looked clean yet. It was an extraordinary find. Its title was, *An Inquiry into Some Points of Seamanship*, by a man Towser, Towson — some such name — Master in his Majesty's Navy. The matter looked dreary reading enough, with illustrative diagrams and repulsive tables of fig-ures, and the copy was sixty years old. I handled this amazing antiquity with the greatest possible tenderness, lest it should dissolve in my hands. Within, Towson or Towser was inquiring earnestly into the breaking strain of ships' chains and tackle, and other such matters. Not a very enthralling book; but at the first glance you could see there a singleness of intention, an honest concern for the right way of going to work, which made these humble pages, thought out so many years ago, luminous with another than a pro-fessional light. The simple old sailor, with his talk of chains and purchases, made me forget the jungle and the pilgrims in a delicious sensation of hav-ing come upon something unmistakably real. Such a book being there was wonderful enough; but still more astounding were the notes penciled in the margin, and plainly referring to the text. I couldn't believe my eyes! They were in cipher! Yes, it looked like cipher. Fancy a man lugging with him a book of that description into this nowhere and studying it — and making notes — in cipher at that! It was an extravagant mystery.

"I had been dimly aware for some time of a worrying noise, and when I lifted my eyes I saw the woodpile was gone, and the manager, aided by all the pilgrims, was shouting at me from the riverside. I slipped the book into my pocket. I assure you to leave off reading was like tearing myself away from the shelter of an old and solid friendship.

"I started the lame engine ahead. 'It must be this miserable trader — this intruder,' exclaimed the manager, looking back malevolently at the place we had left. 'He must be English,' I said. 'It will not save him from getting into trouble if he is not careful,' muttered the manager darkly. I observed with assumed innocence that no man was safe from trouble in this world.

"The current was more rapid now, the steamer seemed at her last gasp, the stern-wheel flopped languidly, and I caught myself listening on tiptoe for the next beat of the float, for in sober truth I expected the wretched thing to give up every moment. It was like watching the last flickers of a life. But still we crawled. Sometimes I would pick out a tree a little way ahead to measure our progress towards Kurtz by, but I lost it invariably before we got abreast. To keep the eyes so long on one thing was too much for human patience. The manager displayed a beautiful resignation. I fretted and fumed and took to arguing with myself whether or not I would talk openly with Kurtz; but before I could come to any conclusion it occurred to me that my speech or my silence, indeed any action of mine, would be a mere futility. What did it matter what anyone knew or ignored? What did it matter who was manager? One gets sometimes such a flash of insight. The essentials of this affair lay deep under the surface, beyond my reach, and beyond my power of meddling.

"Towards the evening of the second day we judged ourselves about eight miles from Kurtz's station. I wanted to push on; but the manager looked grave, and told me the navigation up there was so dangerous that it would be advisable, the sun being very low already, to wait where we were till next morning. Moreover, he pointed out that if the warning to approach cautiously were to be followed, we must approach in daylight — not at dusk, or in the dark. This was sensible enough. Eight miles meant nearly three hours' steaming for us, and I could also see suspicious ripples at the upper end of the reach. Nevertheless, I was annoyed beyond expression at the delay, and most unreasonably, too, since one night more could not matter much after so many months. As we had plenty of wood, and caution was the word, I brought up in the middle of the stream. The reach was narrow, straight, with high sides like a railway cutting. The dusk came gliding into it long before the sun had set. The current ran smooth and swift, but a dumb immobility sat on the banks. The living trees, lashed together by the creepers and every living bush of the undergrowth, might have been changed into stone, even to the slenderest twig, to the lightest leaf. It was not sleep — it seemed unnatural, like a state of trance. Not the faintest sound of any kind could be heard. You looked on amazed, and began to suspect yourself of being deaf — then the night came suddenly, and struck you blind as well. About three in the morning some large fish leaped, and the loud splash made me jump as though a gun had been fired. When the sun rose there was a white fog, very warm and clammy, and more blinding than the night. It did not shift or drive; it was just there, standing all around you like something solid. At eight or nine, perhaps, it lifted as a shutter lifts. We had a glimpse of the towering multitude of trees, of the immense matted jungle, with the blazing little ball of the sun hanging over it — all perfectly still — and then the white shutter came down again, smoothly, as if sliding in greased grooves. I ordered the chain, which we had begun to heave in, to be paid out again. Before it stopped running with a muffled rattle, a cry, a very loud cry, as of infinite desolation, soared slowly in the opaque air. It ceased. A complaining clamor, modulated in savage discords, filled our ears. The sheer unexpectedness of it made my hair stir under my cap. I don't know how it struck the others: to me it seemed as though the mist itself had screamed, so suddenly, and apparently from all sides at once, did this tumultuous and mournful uproar arise. It culminated in a hurried outbreak of almost intolerably excessive shrieking, which stopped short, leaving us stiffened in a variety of silly attitudes, and obstinately listening to the nearly as appalling and excessive silence. 'Good God! What is the meaning — ' stammered at my elbow one of the pilgrims — a little fat man, with sandy hair and red whiskers, who wore side-spring boots, and pink pajamas tucked into his socks. Two others remained open-mouthed a whole minute, then dashed into the little cabin, to rush out incontinently and stand darting scared glances, with Winchesters at 'ready' in their hands. What we could see was just the steamer we were on, her outlines blurred as though she had been on the point if dissolving, and a misty strip of water, perhaps two feet broad, around her — and that was all. The rest of the world was nowhere, as far as our eyes and ears were concerned. Just nowhere. Gone, disappeared; swept off without leaving a whisper or a shadow behind.

"I went forward, and ordered the chain to be hauled in short, so as to be ready to trip the anchor and move the steamboat at once if necessary. 'Will they attack?' whispered an awed voice. 'We will be all butchered in this fog,' murmured another. The faces twitched with the strain, the hands trembling slightly, the eyes forgot to wink. It was very curious to see the contrast of expressions of the white men and of the black fellows of our crew, who were as much strangers to that part of the river as we, though their homes were only eight hundred miles away. The whites, of course, greatly discomposed, had besides a curious look of being painfully shocked by such an outrageous row. The others had an alert, naturally interested expression; but their faces were essentially quiet, even those of the one or two who grinned as they hauled at the chain. Several exchanged short, grunting phrases, which seemed to settle the matter to their satisfaction. Their headman, a young, broad-chested black, severely draped in dark-blue fringed cloths, with fierce nostrils and his hair all done up artfully in oily ringlets, stood near me. 'Aha!' I said, just for good fellowship's sake. 'Catch 'em,' he snapped, with a bloodshot widening of his eyes and a flash of sharp teeth — 'catch 'im. Give 'im to us.' 'To you, eh?' I asked; 'what would you do with them?' 'Eat 'em!' he said, curtly, and, leaning his elbow on the rail, looked out into the fog in a dignified and profoundly pensive attitude. I would no doubt have been properly horrified, had it not occurred to me that he and his chaps must be very hungry: that they must have been growing increasingly hungry for at least this month past. They had been engaged for six months (I don't think a single one of them had any clear idea of time, as we at the end of countless ages have. They still belonged to the beginnings of time — had no inherited experience to teach them as it were), and of course, as long as there was a piece of paper written over in accordance with some farcical law or other made down the river, it didn't enter anybody's head to trouble how they would live. Certainly they had brought with them some rotten hippo-meat, which couldn't have lasted very long, anyway, even if the pilgrims hadn't, in the midst of a shocking hullabaloo, thrown a considerable quantity of it overboard. It looked like a high-handed proceeding; but it was really a case of legitimate self-defense. You can't breathe dead hippo waking, sleeping, and eating, and at the same time keep your precarious grip on existence. Besides that, they had given them every week three pieces of brass wire, each about nine inches long; and the theory was they were to buy their provisions with that currency in riverside villages. You can see how *that* worked. There were either no villages, or the people were hostile, or the director, who like the rest of us fed out of tins, with an occasional old he-goat thrown in, didn't want to stop the steamer for some more or less recondite reason. So, unless they swallowed the wire itself, or made loops of it to snare the fishes with, I don't see what good their extravagant salary could be to them. I must say it was paid with a regularity worthy of a large and honorable trading company. For the rest, the only thing to eat — though it didn't look eatable in the least — I saw in their possession was a few lumps of some stuff like half-cooked dough, of a dirty lavender color, they kept wrapped in leaves, and now and then swallowed a piece of, but so small that it seemed done more for the looks of the thing than for any serious purpose of sustenance. Why in the name of all the gnawing devils of hunger they didn't go for us — they were thirty to five — and have a good tuck-in for once, amazes me now when I think of it. They were big powerful men, with not much capacity to weigh the consequences, with courage, with strength, even yet, though their skins were no longer glossy and their muscles no longer hard. And I saw that something restraining, one of those human secrets that baffle probability, had come into play there. I looked at them with a swift quickening of interest — not because it occurred to me I might be eaten by them before very long, though I own to you that just then I perceived — in a new light, as it were — how unwholesome the pilgrims looked, and I hoped, yes, I positively hoped, that my aspect was not so — what shall I say? — so — unappetizing: a touch of fantastic vanity which fitted well with the dream-sensation that pervaded all my days at that time. Perhaps I had a little fever, too. One can't live with one's finger everlastingly on one's pulse. I had often 'a little fever,' or a little touch of other things — the playful paw-strokes of the wilderness, the preliminary trifling before the more serious onslaught which came in due course. Yes; I looked at them as you would on any human being, with a curiosity of their impulses, motives, capacities, weaknesses, when brought to the test of an inexorable physical necessity. Restraint! What possible restraint? Was it superstition, disgust, patience, fear — or some kind of primitive honor? No fear can stand up to hunger, no patience can wear it out, disgust simply does not exist where hunger is; and as to superstition, beliefs, and what you may call principles, they are less than chaff in a breeze. Don't you know the devilry of lingering starvation, its exasperating torment, its black thoughts, its somber and brooding ferocity? Well, I do. It takes a man all his inborn strength to fight hunger properly. It's really easier to face bereavement, dishonor, and the perdition of one's soul — than this kind of prolonged hunger. Sad, but true. And these chaps, too, had no earthly reason for any kind of scruple. Restraint! I would just as soon have expected restraint from a hyena prowling amongst the corpses of a battlefield. But there was the fact facing me — the fact dazzling, to be seen, like the foam on the depths of the sea, like a ripple on an unfathomable enigma, a mystery greater — when I thought of it — than the curious, inexplicable note of desperate grief in this savage clamor that had swept by us on the riverbank, behind the blind whiteness of the fog.

"Two pilgrims were quarreling in hurried whispers as to which bank. 'Left.' 'No, no; how can you? Right, right, of course.' 'It is very serious,' said the manager's voice behind me; 'I would be desolated if anything should happen to Mr. Kurtz before we came up.' I looked at him, and had not the slightest doubt he was sincere. He was just the kind of man who would wish to preserve appearances. That was his restraint. But when he muttered something about going on at once, I did not even take the trouble to answer him. I knew, and he knew, that it was impossible. Were we to let go our hold of the bottom, we would be absolutely in the air — in space. We wouldn't be able to tell where we were going to — whether up or down stream, or across — till we fetched against one bank or the other — and then we wouldn't know at first which it was. Of course I made no move. I had no mind for a smash-up. You couldn't imagine a more deadly place for a shipwreck. Whether drowned at once or not, we were sure to perish speedily in one way or another. 'I authorize you to take all the risks,' he said, after a short silence. 'I refuse to take any,' I said, shortly; which was just the answer he expected, though its tone might have surprised him. 'Well, I must defer to your judgment. You are captain,' he said, with marked civility. I turned my shoulder to him in sign of my appreciation, and looked into the fog. How long would it last? It was the most hopeless lookout. The approach to this Kurtz grubbing for ivory in the wretched bush was beset by as many dangers as though he had been an enchanted princess sleeping in a fabulous castle. 'Will they attack, do you think?' asked the manager, in a confidential tone.

"I did not think they would attack, for several obvious reasons. The thick fog was one. If they left the bank in their canoes they would get lost in it, as we would be if we attempted to move. Still, I had also judged the jungle of both banks quite impenetrable — and yet eyes were in it, eyes that had seen us. The river-side bushes were certainly very thick; but the undergrowth behind was evidently penetrable. However, during the short lift I had seen no canoes anywhere in the reach — certainly not abreast of the steamer. But what made the idea of attack inconceivable to me was the nature of the noise — of the cries we had heard. They had not the fierce character boding immediate hostile intention. Unexpected, wild, and violent as they had been, they had given me an irresistible impression of sorrow. The glimpse of the steamboat had for some reason filled those savages with unrestrained grief. The danger, if any, I expounded, was from our proximity to a great human passion let loose. Even extreme grief may ultimately vent itself in violence — but more generally takes the form of apathy. . . .

"You should have seen the pilgrims stare! They had no heart to grin, or even to revile me: but I believe they thought me gone mad — with fright, maybe. I delivered a regular lecture. My dear boys, it was no good bothering. Keep a look-out? Well, you may guess I watched the fog for the signs of lifting as a cat watches a mouse; but for anything else our eyes were of no more use to us than if we had been buried miles deep in a heap of cotton-wool. It felt like it, too — choking, warm, stifling. Besides, all I said, though it sounded extravagant, was absolutely true to fact. What we afterwards alluded to as an attack was really an attempt at repulse. The action was very far from being aggressive — it was not even defensive, in the usual sense: it was undertaken under the stress of desperation, and in its essence was purely protective.

"It developed itself, I should say, two hours after the fog lifted, and its commencement was at a spot, roughly speaking, about a mile and a half below Kurtz's station. We had just floundered and flopped round a bend, when I saw an islet, a mere grassy hummock of bright green, in the middle of the stream. It was the only thing of the kind; but as we opened the reach more, I perceived it was the head of a long sandbank, or rather of a chain of shallow patches stretching down the middle of the river. They were discolored, just awash, and the whole lot was seen just under the water, exactly as a man's backbone is seen running down the middle of his back under the skin. Now, as far as I did see, I could go to the right or to the left of this. I didn't know either channel, of course. The banks looked pretty well alike, the depth appeared the same; but as I had been informed the station was on the west side, I naturally headed for the western passage.

"No sooner had we fairly entered it than I became aware it was much narrower than I had supposed. To the left of us there was the long uninterrupted shoal, and to the right a high, steep bank heavily overgrown with bushes. Above the bush the trees stood in serried ranks. The twigs overhung the current thickly, and from distance to distance a large limb of some tree projected rigidly over the stream. It was then well on in the afternoon, the face of the forest was gloomy, and a broad strip of shadow had already fallen on the water. In this shadow we steamed up — very slowly, as you may imagine. I sheered her well inshore — the water being deepest near the bank, as the sounding-pole informed me.

"One of my hungry and forbearing friends was sounding in the bows just below me. This steamboat was exactly like a decked scow. On the deck, there were two little teak-wood houses, with doors and windows. The boiler was in the fore-end, and the machinery right astern. Over the whole there was a light roof, supported on stanchions. The funnel projected through that roof, and in front of the funnel a small cabin built of light planks served for a pilot-house. It contained a couch, two campstools, a loaded Martini-Henry[9] leaning in one corner, a tiny table, and the steering-wheel. It had a wide door in front and a broad shutter at each side. All these were always thrown open, of course. I spent my days perched up there on the extreme fore-end of that roof, before the door. At night I slept, or tried to, on the couch. An athletic black belonging to some coast tribe, and educated by my poor predecessor, was the helmsman. He sported a pair of brass earrings, wore a blue cloth wrapper from the waist to the ankles, and thought all the world of himself. He was the most unstable kind of fool I had ever seen. He steered with no end to a swagger while you were by; but if he lost sight of you, he became instantly the prey of an abject funk, and would let that cripple of a steamboat get the upper hand of him in a minute.

"I was looking down at the sounding-pole, and feeling much annoyed to see at each try a little more of it stick out that river, when I saw my poleman give up the business suddenly, and stretch himself flat on the deck, without even taking the trouble to haul his pole in. He kept hold on it though, and it trailed in the water. At the same time the fireman, whom I could also see below me, sat down abruptly before his furnace and ducked his head. I was amazed. Then I had to look at the river mighty quick, because there was a snag in the fairway. Sticks, little sticks, were flying about — thick: they were whizzing before my nose, dropping below me, striking behind me against my pilot-house. All this time the river, the shore, the woods, were very quiet — perfectly quiet. I could only hear the heavy splashing thump of the stern-wheel and the patter of these things. We cleared the snag clumsily. Arrows, by Jove! We were being shot at! I stepped in quickly to close the shutter on the land-side. That fool-helmsman, his hands on the spokes, was lifting his knees high, stamping his feet, champing his mouth, like a reined-in horse. Confound him! And we were staggering within ten feet of the bank. I had to lean right out to swing the heavy shutter, and I saw a face amongst the leaves on the level with my own, looking at me very fierce and steady; and then suddenly, as though a veil had been removed from my eyes, I made out, deep in the tangled gloom, naked breasts, arms, legs, glaring eyes — the bush was swarming with human limbs in movement, glistening, of bronze color. The twigs shook, swayed, and rustled, the arrows flew out of them, and then the shutter came to. 'Steer her straight,' I said to the helmsman. He held his head rigid, face forward; but his eyes rolled, he kept on lifting and setting down his feet gently, his mouth foamed a little. 'Keep quiet!' I said in a fury. I

---

[9] a heavy military rifle.

might just as well have ordered a tree not to sway in the wind. I darted out.
Below me there was a great scuffle of feet on the iron deck; confused exclamations; a voice screamed, 'Can you turn back?' I caught sight of a
V-shaped ripple on the water ahead. What? Another snag! A fusillade burst
out under my feet. The pilgrims had opened with their Winchesters, and
were simply squirting lead into that bush. A deuce of a lot of smoke came
up and drove slowly forward. I swore at it. Now I couldn't see the ripple or
the snag either. I stood in the doorway, peering, and the arrows came in
swarms. They might have been poisoned, but they looked as though they
wouldn't kill a cat. The bush began to howl. Our wood-cutters raised a war-
like whoop; the report of a rifle just at my back deafened me. I glanced over
my shoulder, and the pilot-house was yet full of noise and smoke when I
made a dash at the wheel. The fool-nigger had dropped everything to throw
the shutter open and let off that Martini-Henry. He stood before the wide
opening, glaring, and I yelled at him to come back, while I straightened the
sudden twist out of that steamboat. There was no room to turn even if I had
wanted to, the snag was somewhere very near ahead in that confounded
smoke, there was no time to lose, so I just crowded her into the bank —
right into the bank, where I knew the water was deep.

"We tore slowly along the overhanging bushes in a whirl of broken
twigs and flying leaves. The fusillade below stopped short, as I had foreseen
it would when the squirts got empty. I threw my head back to a glinting
whizz that traversed the pilot-house, in at one shutter-hole and out at the
other. Looking past that mad helmsman, who was shaking the empty rifle
and yelling at the shore, I saw vague forms of men running bent double,
leaping, gliding, distinct, incomplete, evanescent. Something big appeared
in the air before the shutter, the rifle went overboard, and the man stepped
back swiftly, looked at me over his shoulder in an extraordinary, profound,
familiar manner, and fell upon my feet. The side of his head hit the wheel
twice, and the end of what appeared a long cane clattered round and
knocked over a little campstool. It looked as though after wrenching that
thing from somebody ashore he had lost his balance in the effort. The thin
smoke had blown away, we were clear of the snag, and looking ahead I
could see that in another hundred yards or so I would be free to sheer off,
away from the bank; but my feet felt so very warm and wet that I had to
look down. The man had rolled on his back and stared straight up at me;
both his hands clutched that cane. It was the shaft of a spear that, either
thrown or lunged through the opening, had caught him in the side just
below the ribs; the blade had gone in out of sight, after making a frightful
gash; my shoes were full; a pool of blood lay very still, gleaming dark-red
under the wheel; his eyes shone with an amazing luster. The fusillade burst
out again. He looked at me anxiously, gripping the spear like something
precious, with an air of being afraid I would try to take it away from him. I
had to make an effort to free my eyes from his gaze and attend to steering.
With one hand I felt above my head for the line of the steam-whistle, and

jerked out screech after screech hurriedly. The tumult of angry and warlike yells was checked instantly, and then from the depths of the woods went out such a tremulous and prolonged wail of mournful fear and utter despair as may be imagined to follow the flight of the last hope from the earth. There was a great commotion in the bush; the shower of arrows stopped, a few dropping shots rang out sharply — then silence, in which the languid beat of the stern-wheel came plainly to my ears. I put the helm hard a-starboard at the moment when the pilgrim in pink pajamas, very hot and agitated, appeared in the doorway. 'The manager sends me — ' he began in an official tone, and stopped short. 'Good God!' he said, glaring at the wounded man.

"We two whites stood over him, and his lustrous and inquiring glance enveloped us both. I declare it looked as though he would presently put to us some question in an understandable language; but he died without uttering a sound, without moving a limb, without twitching a muscle. Only in the very last moment, as though in response to some sign we could not see, to some whisper we could not hear, he frowned heavily, and that frown gave to his black death-mask an inconceivably somber, brooding, and menacing expression. The luster of inquiring glance faded swiftly into vacant glassiness. 'Can you steer?' I asked the agent eagerly. He looked very dubious; but I made a grab at his arm, and he understood at once I meant him to steer whether or no. To tell you the truth, I was morbidly anxious to change my shoes and socks. 'He is dead,' murmured the fellow, immensely impressed. 'No doubt about it,' said I tugging like mad at the shoe-laces. 'And by the way, I suppose Mr. Kurtz is dead as well by this time.'

"For the moment that was the dominant thought. There was a sense of extreme disappointment, as though I had found out I had been striving after something altogether without a substance. I couldn't have been more disgusted if I had traveled all this way for the sole purpose of talking with Mr. Kurtz. Talking with. . . . I flung one shoe overboard, and became aware that that was exactly what I had been looking forward to — a talk with Kurtz. I made the strange discovery that I had never imagined him as doing, you know, but as discoursing. I didn't say to myself, 'Now I will never see him,' or 'Now I will never shake him by the hand,' but, 'Now I will never hear him.' The man presented himself as a voice. Not of course that I did not connect him with some sort of action. Hadn't I been told in all the tones of jealousy and admiration that he had collected, bartered, swindled, or stolen more ivory than all the other agents together? That was not the point. The point was in his being a gifted creature, and that of all his gifts the one that stood out preeminently, that carried with it a sense of real presence, was his ability to talk, his words — the gift of expression, the bewildering, the illuminating, the most exalted and the most contemptible, the pulsating stream of light, or the deceitful flow from the heart of an impenetrable darkness.

"The other shoe went flying unto the devil-god of that river. I thought, by Jove! it's all over. We are too late; he has vanished — the gift has vanished, by means of some spear, arrow, or club. I will never hear that chap speak after all — and my sorrow had a startling extravagance of emotion, even such as I had noticed in the howling sorrow of these savages in the bush. I couldn't have felt more lonely desolation somehow, had I been robbed of a belief or had missed my destiny in life. . . . Why do you sigh in this beastly way, somebody? Absurd? Well, absurd. Good Lord! mustn't a man ever — Here, give me some tobacco." . . .

There was a pause of profound stillness, then a match flared, and Marlow's lean face appeared, worn, hollow, with downward folds and drooped eyelids, with an aspect of concentrated attention; and as he took vigorous draws at his pipe, it seemed to retreat and advance out of the night in the regular flicker of the tiny flame. The match went out.

"Absurd!" he cried. "This is the worst of trying to tell. . . . Here you all are, each moored with two good addresses, like a hulk with two anchors, a butcher round one corner, a policeman round another, excellent appetites, and temperature normal — you hear — normal from year's end to year's end. And you say, Absurd! Absurd be — exploded! Absurd! My dear boys, what can you expect from a man who out of sheer nervousness had just flung overboard a pair of new shoes! Now I think of it, it is amazing I did not shed tears. I am, upon the whole, proud of my fortitude. I was cut to the quick at the idea of having lost the inestimable privilege of listening to the gifted Kurtz. Of course I was wrong. The privilege was waiting for me. Oh, yes, I heard more than enough. And I was right, too. A voice. He was very little more than a voice. And I heard — him — it — this voice — other voices — all of them were so little more than voices — and the memory of that time itself lingers around me, impalpable, like a dying vibration of one immense jabber, silly, atrocious, sordid, savage, or simply mean, without any kind of sense. Voices, voices — even the girl herself — now —"

He was silent for a long time.

"I laid the ghost of his gifts at last with a lie," he began, suddenly. "Girl! What? Did I mention a girl? Oh, she is out of it — completely. They — the women I mean — are out of it — should be out of it. We must help them to stay in that beautiful world of their own, lest ours gets worse. Oh, she had to be out of it. You should have heard the disinterred body of Mr. Kurtz saying, 'My Intended.' You would have perceived directly then how completely she was out of it. And the lofty frontal bone of Mr. Kurtz! They say the hair goes on growing sometimes, but this — ah — specimen, was impressively bald. The wilderness had patted him on the head, and, behold, it was like a ball — an ivory ball; it had caressed him, and — lo! — he had withered; it had taken him, loved him, embraced him, got into his veins, consumed his flesh, and sealed his soul to its own by the inconceivable ceremonies of some devilish initiation. He was its spoiled and pampered favorite. Ivory? I should think so. Heaps of it, stacks of it. The old

mud shanty was bursting with it. You would think here was not a single
tusk left either above or below the ground in the whole country. 'Mostly
fossil,' the manager had remarked, disparagingly. It was no more fossil than
I am; but they call it fossil when it is dug up. It appears these niggers do
bury the tusks sometimes — but evidently they couldn't bury this parcel
deep enough to save the gifted Mr. Kurtz from his fate. We filled the
steamboat with it, and had to pile a lot on the deck. Thus he could see and
enjoy as long as he could see, because the appreciation of this favor had remained with him to the last. You should have heard him say, 'My ivory.'
Oh, yes, I heard him. 'My Intended, my ivory, my station, my river, my — '
everything belonged to him. It made me hold my breath in expectation of
hearing the wilderness burst into a prodigious peal of laughter that would
shake the fixed stars in their places. Everything belonged to him — but that
was a trifle. The thing was to know what he belonged to, how many powers
of darkness claimed him for their own. That was the reflection that made
you creepy all over. It was impossible — it was not good for one either —
trying to imagine. He had taken a high seat amongst the devils of the
land — I mean literally. You can't understand. How could you? — with
solid pavement under your feet, surrounded by kind neighbors ready to
cheer you or to fall on you, stepping delicately between the butcher and the
policeman, in the holy terror of scandal and gallows and lunatic asylums —
how can you imagine what particular region of the first ages a man's untrammeled feet may take him into by the way of solitude — utter solitude
without a policeman — by the way of silence — utter silence, where no
warning voice of a kind neighbor can be heard whispering of public opinion? These little things make all the great difference. When they are gone
you must fall back upon your own innate strength, upon your own capacity
for faithfulness. Of course you may be too much of a fool to go wrong —
too dull even to know you are being assaulted by the powers of darkness. I
take it, no fool ever made a bargain for his soul with the devil: the fool is too
much of a fool, or the devil too much of a devil — I don't know which. Or
you may be such a thunderingly exalted creature as to be altogether deaf
and blind to anything but heavenly sights and sounds. Then the earth for
you is only a standing place — and whether to be like this is your loss or
your gain I won't pretend to say. But most of us are neither one nor the
other. The earth for us is a place to live in, where we must put up with
sights, with sounds, with smells, too, by Jove! — breathe dead hippo, so to
speak and not be contaminated. And there, don't you see? your strength
comes in, the faith in your ability for the digging of unostentatious holes to
bury the stuff in — your power of devotion, not to yourself, but to an obscure, back-breaking business. And that's difficult enough. Mind, I am not
trying to excuse or even explain — I am trying to account to myself for —
for — Mr. Kurtz — for the shade of Mr. Kurtz. This initiated wraith from
the back of Nowhere honored me with its amazing confidence before it
vanished altogether. This was because it could speak English to me. The

original Kurtz had been educated partly in England, and — as he was good enough to say himself — his sympathies were in the right place. His mother was half-English, his father was half-French. All Europe contributed to the making of Kurtz; and by and by I learned that, most appropriately, the International Society for the Suppression of Savage Customs had intrusted him with the making of a report, for its future guidance. And he had written it, too. I've seen it. I've read it. It was eloquent, vibrating with eloquence, but too high-strung, I think. Seventeen pages of close writing he had found time for! But this must have been before his — let us say — nerves, went wrong, and caused him to preside at certain midnight dances ending with unspeakable rites, which — as far as I reluctantly gathered from what I heard at various times — were offered up to him — do you understand? — to Mr. Kurtz himself. But it was a beautiful piece of writing. The opening paragraph, however, in the light of later information, strikes me now as ominous. He began with the argument that we whites, from the point of development we had arrived at, 'must necessarily appear to them [savages] in the nature of supernatural beings — we approach them with the might as of a deity,' and so on, and so on. 'By the simple exercise of our will we can exert a power for good practically unbounded,' etc., etc. From that point he soared and took me with him. The peroration was magnificent, though difficult to remember, you know. It gave me the notion of an exotic Immensity ruled by an august Benevolence. It made me tingle with enthusiasm. This was the unbounded power of eloquence — of words — of burning noble words. There were no practical hints to interrupt the magic current of phrases, unless a kind of note at the foot of the last page, scrawled evidently much later, in an unsteady hand, may be regarded as the exposition of a method. It was very simple, and at the end of that moving appeal to every altruistic sentiment it blazed at you, luminous and terrifying, like a flash of lightning in a serene sky: 'Exterminate all the brutes!' The curious part was that he had apparently forgotten all about that valuable postscriptum, because, later on, when he in a sense came to himself, he repeatedly entreated me to take good care of 'my pamphlet' (he called it), as it was sure to have in the future a good influence upon his career. I had full information about all these things, and, besides, as it turned out, I was to have the care of his memory. I've done enough for it to give me the indisputable right to lay it, if I choose, for an everlasting rest in the dust-bin of progress, amongst all the sweepings and, figuratively speaking, all the dead cats of civilization. But then, you see, I can't choose. He won't be forgotten. Whatever he was, he was not common. He had the power to charm or frighten rudimentary souls into an aggravated witch-dance in his honor; he could also fill the small souls of the pilgrims with bitter misgivings: he had one devoted friend at least, and he had conquered one soul in the world that was neither rudimentary nor tainted with self-seeking. No; I can't forget him, though I am not prepared to affirm the fellow was exactly worth the life we lost in getting to him. I missed my late helmsman awfully — I missed him even while his body was still lying in the pilot-house. Perhaps you will think it passing strange this regret for a savage who was no more account than a grain of sand in a black Sahara. Well, don't you see, he had done something, he had steered; for months I had him at my back — a help — an instrument. It was a kind of partnership. He steered for me — I had to look after him, I worried about his deficiencies, and thus a subtle bond had been created, of which I only became aware when it was suddenly broken. And the intimate profundity of that look he gave me when he received his hurt remains to this day in my memory — like a claim of distant kinship affirmed in a supreme moment.

"Poor fool! If he had only left that shutter alone. He had no restraint, no restraint — just like Kurtz — a tree swayed by the wind. As soon as I had put on a dry pair of slippers, I dragged him out, after first jerking the spear out of his side, which operation I confess I performed with my eyes shut tight. His heels leaped together over the little door-step; his shoulders were pressed to my breast; I hugged him from behind desperately. Oh! he was heavy, heavy; heavier than any man on earth, I should imagine. Then without more ado I tipped him overboard. The current snatched him as though he had been a wisp of grass, and I saw the body roll over twice before I lost sight of it forever. All the pilgrims and the manager were then congregated on the awning-deck about the pilot-house, chattering at each other like a flock of excited magpies, and there was a scandalized murmur at my heartless promptitude. What they wanted to keep that body hanging about for I can't guess. Embalm it, maybe. But I had also heard another, and a very ominous, murmur on the deck below. My friends the wood-cutters were likewise scandalized, and with a better show of reason — though I admit that the reason itself was quite inadmissible. Oh, quite! I had made up my mind that if my late helmsman was to be eaten, the fishes alone should have him. He had been a very second-rate helmsman while alive, but now he was dead he might have become a first-class temptation, and possibly cause some startling trouble. Besides, I was anxious to take the wheel, the man in pink pajamas showing himself a hopeless duffer at the business.

"This I did directly the simple funeral was over. We were going half-speed, keeping right in the middle of the stream, and I listened to the talk about me. They had given up Kurtz, they had given up the station; Kurtz was dead, and the station had been burnt — and so on — and so on. The red-haired pilgrim was beside himself with the thought that at least this poor Kurtz had been properly avenged. 'Say! We must have made a glorious slaughter of them in the bush. Eh? What do you think? Say?' He positively danced, the blood-thirsty little gingery beggar. And he had nearly fainted when he saw the wounded man! I could not help saying, 'You made a glorious lot of smoke, anyhow.' I had seen, from the way the tops of the bushes rustled and flew, that almost all the shots had gone too high. You can't hit anything unless you take aim and fire from the shoulder; but these chaps fired from the hip with their eyes shut. The retreat, I maintained — and I was right — was caused by the screeching of the steam-whistle. Upon this they forgot Kurtz, and began to howl at me with indignant protests.

"The manager stood by the wheel murmuring confidentially about the necessity of getting well away down the river before dark at all events, when I saw in the distance a clearing on the riverside and the outlines of some sort of building. 'What's this?' I asked. He clapped his hands in wonder. 'The station!' he cried. I edged in at once, still going half-speed.

Through my glasses I saw the slope of a hill interspersed with rare trees and perfectly free from undergrowth. A long decaying building on the summit was half buried in the high grass; the large holes in the peaked roof gaped black from afar; the jungle and the woods made a background. There was no enclosure or fence of any kind; but there had been one apparently, for near the house half-a-dozen slim posts remained in a row, roughly trimmed, and with their upper ends ornamented with round carved balls. The rails, or whatever there had been between, had disappeared. Of course the forest surrounded all that. The river-bank was clear, and on the waterside I saw a white man under a hat like a cart-wheel beckoning persistently with his whole arm. Examining the edge of the forest above and below, I was almost certain I could see movements — human forms gliding here and there. I steamed past prudently, then stopped the engines and let her drift down. The man on the shore began to shout, urging us to land. 'We have been attacked,' screamed the manager. 'I know — I know. It's all right,' yelled back the other, as cheerful as you please. 'Come along. It's all right, I am glad.'

"His aspect reminded me of something I had seen — something funny I had seen somewhere. As I maneuvered to get alongside, I was asking myself, 'What does this fellow look like?' Suddenly I got it. He looked like a harlequin. His clothes had been made of some stuff that was brown holland probably, but it was covered with patches all over, with bright patches, blue, red, and yellow — patches on the back, patches on the front, patches on elbows, on knees; colored binding around his jacket, scarlet edging at the bottom of his trousers; and the sunshine made him look extremely gay and wonderfully neat withal, because you could see how beautifully all this patching had been done. A beardless, boyish face, very fair, no features to speak of, nose peeling, little blue eyes, smiles and frowns chasing each other over that open countenance like sunshine and shadow on a windswept plain. 'Look out, captain!' he cried; 'there's a snag lodged in here last night.' What! Another snag? I confess I swore shamefully. I had nearly holed my cripple, to finish off that charming trip. The harlequin on the bank turned his little pug-nose up to me. 'You English?' he asked, all smiles. 'Are you?' I shouted from the wheel. The smiles vanished, and he shook his head as if sorry for my disappointment. Then he brightened up. 'Never mind!' he cried, encouragingly. 'Are we in time?' I asked. 'He is up there,' he replied with a toss of the head up the hill, and becoming gloomy all of a sudden. His face was like the autumn sky, overcast one moment and bright the next.

"When the manager, escorted by the pilgrims, all of them armed to the teeth, had gone to the house this chap came on board. 'I say, I don't like this. These natives are in the bush,' I said. He assured me earnestly it was all right. 'They are simple people,' he added; 'well, I am glad you came. It took me all my time to keep them off.' 'But you said it was all right,' I cried. 'Oh, they meant no harm,' he said; and as I stared he corrected himself, 'Not exactly.' Then vivaciously, 'My faith, your pilot-house wants a clean-up!' In the next breath he advised me to keep enough steam on the boiler to blow the whistle in case of any trouble. 'One good screech will do more for you than all your rifles. They are simple people,' he repeated. He rattled away at such a rate he quite overwhelmed me. He seemed to be trying to make up for lots of silence, and actually hinted, laughing, that such was the case. 'Don't you talk with Mr. Kurtz?' I said. 'You don't talk with that man — you listen to him,' he exclaimed with severe exaltation. 'But now — ' He waved his arm, and in the twinkling of an eye was in the utter-most depths of despondency. In a moment he came up again with a jump, possessed himself of both my hands, and shook them continuously, while he gabbled: 'Brother sailor . . . honor . . . pleasure . . . delight . . . introduce myself . . . Russian . . . son of an arch-priest . . . Government of Tam-bov. . . . What? Tobacco! English tobacco; the excellent English tobacco! Now, that's brotherly. Smoke? Where's a sailor that does not smoke?'

"The pipe soothed him, and gradually I made out he had run away from school, had gone to sea in a Russian ship; ran away again; served some time in English ships; was now reconciled with the arch-priest. He made a point of that. 'But when one is young one must see things, gather experi-ence, ideas; enlarge the mind.' 'Here!' I interrupted. 'You can never tell! Here I met Mr. Kurtz,' he said, youthfully solemn and reproachful. I held my tongue after that. It appears he had persuaded a Dutch trading-house on the coast to fit him out with stores and goods, and had started for the interior with a light heart, and no more idea of what would happen to him than a baby. He had been wandering about that river for nearly two years alone, cut off from everybody and everything. 'I am not so young as I look. I am twenty-five,' he said. 'At first old Van Shuyten would tell me to go to the devil,' he narrated with keen enjoyment; 'but I stuck to him, and talked and talked, till at last he got afraid I would talk the hind-leg off his favorite dog, so he gave me some cheap things and a few guns, and told me he hoped he would never see my face again. Good old Dutchman, Van Shuyten. I've sent him one small lot of ivory a year ago, so that he can't call me a little thief when I get back. I hope he got it. And for the rest I don't care. I had some wood stacked for you. That was my old house. Did you see?'

I gave him Towson's book. He made as though he would kiss me, but restrained himself. 'The only book I had left, and I thought I had lost it,' he said, looking at it ecstatically. 'So many accidents happen to a man going about alone, you know. Canoes get upset sometimes — and sometimes you've got to clear out so quick when the people get angry.' He thumbed the pages. 'You made notes in Russian?' I asked. He nodded. 'I thought they were written in cipher,' I said. He laughed, then became serious. 'I had lots of trouble to keep these people off,' he said. 'Did they want to kill you?' I asked. 'Oh, no!' he cried, and checked himself. 'Why did they attack us?' I pursued. He hesitated, then said shamefacedly, 'They don't want him to go.' 'Don't they?' I said, curiously. He nodded a nod full of mystery and wisdom. 'I tell you,' he cried, 'this man has enlarged my mind.' He opened his arms wide, staring at me with his little blue eyes that were perfectly round."

III

"I looked at him, lost in astonishment. There he was before me, in motley, as though he had absconded from a troupe of mimes, enthusiastic, fabulous. His very existence was improbable, inexplicable, and altogether bewildering. He was an insoluble problem. It was inconceivable how he had existed, how he had succeeded in getting so far, how he had managed to remain — why he did not instantly disappear. 'I went a little farther,' he said, 'then still a little farther — till I had gone so far that I don't know how I'll ever get back. Never mind. Plenty time. I can manage. You take Kurtz away quick — quick — I tell you.' The glamour of youth enveloped his parti-colored rags, his destitution, his loneliness, the essential desolation of his futile wanderings. For months — for years — his life hadn't been worth a day's purchase; and there he was gallantly, thoughtlessly alive, to all appearance indestructible solely by the virtue of his few years and of his unreflecting audacity. I was seduced into something like admiration — like envy. Glamour urged him on, glamour kept him unscathed. He surely wanted nothing from the wilderness but space to breathe in and to push on through. His need was to exist, and to move onwards at the greatest possible risk, and with a maximum of privation. If the absolutely pure, uncalculating, unpractical spirit of adventure had ever ruled a human being, it ruled this be-patched youth. I almost envied him the possession of this modest and clear flame. It seemed to have consumed all thought of self so completely, that even while he was talking to you, you forgot that it was he — the man before your eyes — who had gone through these things. I did not envy him his devotion to Kurtz, though. He had not meditated over it. It came to him and he accepted it with a sort of eager fatalism. I must say that to me it appeared about the most dangerous thing in every way he had come upon so far.

"They had come together unavoidably, like two ships becalmed near each other, and lay rubbing sides at last. I suppose Kurtz wanted an audience, because on a certain occasion, when encamped in the forest, they had talked all night, or more probably Kurtz had talked. 'We talked of every-thing,' he said, quite transported at the recollection. 'I forgot there was such a thing as sleep. The night did not seem to last an hour. Everything! Every-thing! . . . Of love, too.' 'Ah, he talked to you of love!' I said, much amused. 'It isn't what you think,' he cried, almost passionately. 'It was in general. He made me see things — things.'

"He threw his arms up. We were on deck at the time, and the head-man of my wood-cutters, lounging near by, turned upon him his heavy and glittering eyes. I looked around, and I don't know why, but I assure you that never, never before, did this land, this river, this jungle, the very arch of this blazing sky, appear to me so hopeless and so dark, so impenetrable to human thought, so pitiless to human weakness. 'And, ever since, you have been with him, of course?' I said.

"On the contrary. It appears their intercourse had been very much broken by various causes. He had, as he informed me proudly, managed to nurse Kurtz through two illnesses (he alluded to it as you would to some risky feat), but as a rule Kurtz wandered alone far in the depths of the for-est. 'Very often coming to this station, I had to wait days and days before he would turn up,' he said. 'Ah, it was worth waiting for! — sometimes.' 'What was he doing? exploring or what?' I asked. 'Oh, yes, of course'; he had discovered lots of villages, a lake, too — he did not know exactly in what direction; it was dangerous to inquire too much — but mostly his ex-peditions had been for ivory. 'But he had no goods to trade with by that time,' I objected. 'There's a good lot of cartridges left even yet,' he an-swered, looking away. 'To speak plainly, he raided the country,' I said. He nodded. 'Not alone, surely!' He muttered something about the villages round that lake. 'Kurtz got the tribe to follow him, did he?' I suggested. He fidgeted a little. 'They adored him,' he said. The tone of these words was so extraordinary that I looked at him searchingly. It was curious to see his mingled eagerness and reluctance to speak of Kurtz. The man filled his life, occupied his thoughts, swayed his emotions. 'What can you expect?' he burst out; 'he came to them with thunder and lightning, you know — and they had never seen anything like it — and very terrible. He could be very terrible. You can't judge Mr. Kurtz as you would an ordinary man. No, no, no! Now — just to give you an idea — I don't mind telling you, he wanted to shoot me, too, one day — but I don't judge him.' 'Shoot you!' I cried. 'What for?' 'Well, I had a small lot of ivory the chief of that village near my house gave me. You see I used to shoot game for them. Well, he wanted it, and wouldn't hear reason. He declared he would shoot me unless I gave him the ivory and then cleared out of the country, because he could do so, and had a fancy for it, and there was nothing on earth to prevent him killing whom he jolly well pleased. And it was true, too. I gave him the ivory. What did I care! But I didn't clear out. No, no. I couldn't leave him. I had to be careful, of course, till we got friendly again for a time. He had his sec-ond illness then. Afterwards I had to keep out of the way; but I didn't mind.

He was living for the most part in those villages on the lake. When he came down to the river, sometimes he would take to me, and sometimes it was better for me to be careful. This man suffered too much. He hated all this, and somehow he couldn't get away. When I had a chance I begged him to try and leave while there was time; I offered to go back with him. And he would say yes, and then he would remain; go off on another ivory hunt; disappear for weeks; forget himself amongst these people — forget himself — you know.' 'Why! he's mad,' I said. He protested indignantly. Mr. Kurtz couldn't be mad. If I had heard him talk, only two days ago, I wouldn't dare hint at such a thing. . . . I had taken up my binoculars while we talked, and was looking at the shore, sweeping the limit of the forest at each side and at the back of the house. The consciousness of there being people in that bush, so silent, so quiet — as silent and quiet as the ruined house on the hill — made me uneasy. There was no sign on the face of nature of this amazing tale that was not so much told as suggested to me in desolate exclamations, completed by shrugs, in interrupted phrases, in hints ending in deep sighs. The woods were unmoved, like a mask — heavy, like the closed door of a prison — they looked with their air of hidden knowledge, of patient expectation, of unapproachable silence. The Russian was explaining to me that it was only lately that Mr. Kurtz had come down to the river, bringing along with him all the fighting men of that lake tribe. He had been absent for several months — getting himself adored, I suppose — and had come down unexpectedly, with the intention to all appearance of making a raid either across the river or down stream. Evidently the appetite for more ivory had got the better of the — what shall I say? — less material aspirations. However he had got much worse suddenly. 'I heard he was lying helpless, and so I came up — took my chance,' said the Russian. 'Oh, he is bad, very bad.' I directed my glass to the house. There were no signs of life, but there was the ruined roof, the long mud wall peeping above the grass, with three little square window-holes, no two of the same size; all this brought within reach of my hand, as it were. And then I made a brusque movement, and one of the remaining posts of that vanished fence leaped up in the field of my glass. You remember I told you I had been struck at the distance by certain attempts at ornamentation, rather remarkable in the ruinous aspect of the place. Now I had suddenly a nearer view, and its first result was to make me throw my head back as if before a blow. Then I went carefully from post to post with my glass, and I saw my mistake. These round knobs were not ornamental but symbolic; they were expressive and puzzling, striking and disturbing — food for thought and also for vultures if there had been any looking down from the sky; but at all events for such ants as were industrious enough to ascend the pole. They would have been even more impressive, those heads on the stakes, if their faces had not been turned to the house. Only one, the first I had made out, was facing my way. I was not so shocked as you may think. The start back I had given was really nothing but a movement of surprise. I had expected to see a knob of wood there, you know. I returned deliberately to the first I had seen — and there it was, black, dried, sunken, with closed eyelids — a head that seemed to sleep at the top of that pole, and with the shrunken dry lips showing a narrow white line of the teeth, was smiling, too, smiling continuously at some endless and jocose dream of that eternal slumber.

"I am not disclosing any trade secrets. In fact, the manager said afterwards that Mr. Kurtz's methods had ruined the district. I have no opinion on that point, but I want you clearly to understand that there was nothing exactly profitable in these heads being there. They only showed that Mr. Kurtz lacked restraint in the gratification of his various lusts, that there was something wanting in him — some small matter which, when the pressing need arose, could not be found under his magnificent eloquence. Whether he knew of this deficiency himself I can't say. I think the knowledge came to him at last — only at the very last. But the wilderness had found him out early, and had taken on him a terrible vengeance for the fantastic invasion. I think it had whispered to him things about himself which he did not know, things of which he had no conception till he took counsel with this great solitude — and the whisper had proved irresistibly fascinating. It echoed loudly within him because he was hollow at the core. . . . I put down the glass, and the head that had appeared near enough to be spoken to seemed at once to have leaped away from me into inaccessible distance.

"The admirer of Mr. Kurtz was a bit crestfallen. In a hurried indistinct voice he began to assure me he had not dared to take these — say, symbols — down. He was not afraid of the natives; they would not stir till Mr. Kurtz gave the word. His ascendancy was extraordinary. The camps of these people surrounded the place, and the chiefs came every day to see him. They would crawl. . . . 'I don't want to know anything of the ceremonies used when approaching Mr. Kurtz,' I shouted. Curious, this feeling that came over me that such details would be more intolerable than those heads drying on the stakes under Mr. Kurtz's windows. After all, that was only a savage sight, while I seemed at one bound to have been transported into some lightless region of subtle horrors, where pure, uncomplicated savagery was a positive relief, being something that had a right to exist — obviously — in the sunshine. The young man looked at me with surprise. I suppose it did not occur to him that Mr. Kurtz was no idol of mine. He forgot I hadn't heard any of these splendid monologues on, what was it? on love, justice, conduct of life — or what not. If it had come to crawling before Mr. Kurtz, he crawled as much as the veriest savage of them all. I had no idea of the conditions, he said: these heads were the heads of rebels. I shocked him excessively by laughing. Rebels! What would be the next definition I was to hear? There had been enemies, criminals, workers — and these were rebels. Those rebellious heads looked very subdued to me on their sticks. 'You don't know how such a life tries a man like Kurtz,' cried Kurtz's last disciple. 'Well, and you?' I said. 'I! I! I am a simple man. I have no great thoughts. I want nothing from anybody. How can you compare me to. . . ?' His feelings were too much for speech, and suddenly he broke down. 'I don't understand,' he groaned. 'I've been doing my best to keep him alive, and that's enough. I had no hand in all this. I have no abilities. There hasn't been a drop of medicine or a mouthful of invalid food for months here. He was shamefully abandoned. A man like this, with such ideas. Shamefully! Shamefully! I — I — haven't slept for the last ten nights. . . .'

"His voice lost itself in the calm of the evening. The long shadows of the forest had slipped downhill while we talked, had gone far beyond the ruined hovel, beyond the symbolic row of stakes. All this was in the gloom, while we down there were yet in the sunshine, and the stretch of the river abreast of the clearing glittered in a still and dazzling splendor, with a murky and overshadowed bend above and below. Not a living soul was seen on the shore. The bushes did not rustle.

"Suddenly round the corner of the house a group of men appeared, as though they had come up from the ground. They waded waist-deep in the grass, in a compact body, bearing an improvised stretcher in their midst. Instantly, in the emptiness of the landscape, a cry arose whose shrillness pierced the still air like a sharp arrow flying straight to the very heart of the land; and, as if by enchantment, streams of human beings — of naked human beings — with spears in their hands, with bows, with shields, with wild glances and savage movements, were poured into the clearing by the dark-faced and pensive forest. The bushes shook, the grass swayed for a time, and then everything stood still in attentive immobility.

" 'Now, if he does not say the right thing to them we are all done for,' said the Russian at my elbow. The knot of men with the stretcher had stopped, too, halfway to the steamer, as if petrified. I saw the man on the stretcher sit up, lank and with an uplifted arm, above the shoulders of the bearers. 'Let us hope that the man who can talk so well of love in general will find some particular reason to spare us this time,' I said. I resented bitterly the absurd danger of our situation, as if to be at the mercy of that atrocious phantom had been a dishonoring necessity. I could not hear a sound, but through my glasses I saw the thin arm extended commandingly, the lower jaw moving, the eyes of that apparition shining darkly far in its bony head that nodded with grotesque jerks. Kurtz — Kurtz — that means short in Germany — don't it? Well, the name was as true as everything else in his life — and death. He looked at least seven feet long. His covering had fallen off, and his body emerged from it pitiful and appalling as from a winding-sheet. I could see the cage of his ribs all astir, the bones of his arm waving. It was as though an animated image of death carved out of old ivory had been shaking its hand with menaces at a motionless crowd of men made of dark and glittering bronze. I saw him open his mouth wide — it gave him a weirdly voracious aspect, as though he had wanted to swallow all the air, all the earth, all the men before him. A deep voice reached me faintly. He must have been shouting. He fell back suddenly. The stretcher shook as the bearers staggered forward again, and almost at the same time I noticed that the crowd of savages was vanishing without any perceptible movement of retreat, as if the forest that had ejected these beings so suddenly had drawn them in again as the breath is drawn in a long aspiration.

"Some of the pilgrims behind the stretcher carried his arms — two shotguns, a heavy rifle, and a light revolver-carbine — the thunderbolts of that pitiful Jupiter. The manager bent over him murmuring as he walked beside his head. They laid him down in one of the little cabins — just a room for a bedplace and a campstool or two, you know. We had brought his belated correspondence, and a lot of torn envelopes and open letters littered his bed. His hand roamed feebly amongst these papers. I was struck by the fire in his eyes and the composed languor of his expression. It was not so much the exhaustion of disease. He did not seem in pain. This shadow looked satiated and calm, as though for the moment it had had its fill of all the emotions.

"He rustled one of the letters, and looking straight in my face said, 'I am glad.' Somebody had been writing to him about me. These special recommendations were turning up again. The volume of tone he emitted without effort, almost without the trouble of moving his lips, amazed me. A voice! a voice! It was grave, profound, vibrating, while the man did not seem capable of a whisper. However, he had enough strength in him — factitious no doubt — to very nearly make an end of us, as you shall hear directly.

"The manager appeared silently in the doorway; I stepped out at once and he drew the curtain after me. The Russian, eyed curiously by the pilgrims, was staring at the shore. I followed the direction of his glance.

"Dark human shapes could be made out in the distance, flitting indistinctly against the gloomy border of the forest, and near the river two bronze figures, leaning on tall spears, stood in the sunlight under fantastic headdresses of spotted skins, war-like and still in statuesque repose. And from right to left along the lighted shore moved a wild and gorgeous apparition of a woman.

"She walked with measured steps, draped in striped and fringed cloths, treading the earth proudly, with a slight jingle and flash of barbarous ornaments. She carried her head high; her hair was done in the shape of a helmet; she had brass leggings to the knee, brass wire gauntlets to the elbow, a crimson spot on her tawny cheek, innumerable necklaces of glass beads on her neck; bizarre things, charms, gifts of witch-men, that hung about her, glittered and trembled at every step. She must have had the value of several elephant tusks upon her. She was savage and superb, wild-eyed and magnificent; there was something ominous and stately in her deliberate progress. And in the hush that had fallen suddenly upon the whole sorrowful land, the immense wilderness, the colossal body of the fecund and mysterious life seemed to look at her, pensive, as though it had been looking at the image of its own tenebrous and passionate soul.

"She came abreast of the steamer, stood still, and faced us. Her long shadow fell to the water's edge. Her face had a tragic and fierce aspect of wild sorrow and of dumb pain mingled with the fear of some struggling, half-shaped resolve. She stood looking at us without a stir, and like the wilderness itself, with an air of brooding over an inscrutable purpose. A whole minute passed, and then she made a step forward. There was a low jingle, a glint of yellow metal, a sway of fringed draperies, and she stopped as if her heart had failed her. The young fellow by my side growled. The pilgrims murmured at my back. She looked at us all as if her life had depended upon the unswerving steadiness of her glance. Suddenly she opened her bared arms and threw them up rigid above her head, as though in an uncontrollable desire to touch the sky, and at the same time the swift shadows darted out on the earth, swept around on the river, gathering the steamer into a shadowy embrace. A formidable silence hung over the scene.

"She turned away slowly, walked on, following the bank, and passed into the bushes to the left. Once only her eyes gleamed back at us in the dusk of the thickets before she disappeared.

" 'If she had offered to come aboard I really think I would have tried to shoot her,' said the man of patches, nervously. 'I have been risking my life every day for the last fortnight to keep her out of the house. She got in one day and kicked up a row about those miserable rags I picked up in the storeroom to mend my clothes with. I wasn't decent. At least it must have been that, for she talked like a fury to Kurtz for an hour, pointing at me now and then. I don't understand the dialect of this tribe. Luckily for me, I fancy Kurtz felt too ill that day to care, or there would have been mischief. I don't understand. . . . No — it's too much for me. Ah, well, it's all over now.'

"At this moment I heard Kurtz's deep voice behind the curtain: 'Save me! — save the ivory, you mean. Don't tell me. Save *me!* Why, I've had to save you. You are interrupting my plans now. Sick! Sick! Not so sick as you would like to believe. Never mind. I'll carry my ideas out yet — I will return. I'll show you what can be done. You with your little peddling notions — you are interfering with me. I will return. I. . . .'

"The manager came out. He did me the honor to take me under the arm and lead me aside. 'He is very low, very low,' he said. He considered it necessary to sigh, but neglected to be consistently sorrowful. 'We have done all we could for him — haven't we? But there is no disguising the fact, Mr. Kurtz has done more harm than good to the Company. He did not see the time was not ripe for vigorous action. Cautiously, cautiously — that's my principle. We must be cautious yet. The district is closed to us for a time. Deplorable! Upon the whole, the trade will suffer. I don't deny there is a remarkable quantity of ivory — mostly fossil. We must save it, at all events — but look how precarious the position is — and why? Because the method is unsound.' 'Do you,' said I, looking at the shore, 'call it "unsound method"?' 'Without doubt,' he exclaimed, hotly. 'Don't you?' . . . 'No

method at all,' I murmured after a while. 'Exactly,' he exulted. 'I anticipated this. Shows a complete want of judgment. It is my duty to point it out
in the proper quarter.' 'Oh,' said I, 'that fellow — what's his name? — the
brick-maker, will make a readable report for you.' He appeared confounded
for a moment. It seemed to me I had never breathed an atmosphere so vile,
and I turned mentally to Kurtz for relief — positively for relief. 'Nevertheless I think Mr. Kurtz is a remarkable man,' I said with emphasis. He
started, dropped on me a cold heavy glance, said very quietly, 'he *was*,' and
turned his back on me. My hour of favor was over; I found myself lumped
along with Kurtz as a partisan of methods for which the time was not ripe: I
was unsound! Ah! but it was something to have at least a choice of nightmares.

"I had turned to the wilderness really, not to Mr. Kurtz, who, I was
ready to admit, was as good as buried. And for a moment it seemed to me as
if I also were buried in a vast grave full of unspeakable secrets. I felt an intolerable weight oppressing my breast, the smell of the damp earth, the unseen presence of victorious corruption, the darkness of an impenetrable
night. . . . The Russian tapped me on the shoulder. I heard him mumbling
and stammering something about 'brother seaman — couldn't conceal —
knowledge of matters that would affect Mr. Kurtz's reputation.' I waited.
For him evidently Mr. Kurtz was not in his grave; I suspect that for him
Mr. Kurtz was one of the immortals. 'Well!' said I at last, 'speak out. As it
happens, I am Mr. Kurtz's friend — in a way.'

'He stated with a good deal of formality that had we not been 'of the
same profession,' he would have kept the matter to himself without regard
to consequences. 'He suspected there was an active ill will towards him on
the part of these white men that — ' 'You are right,' I said, remembering a
certain conversation I had overheard. 'The manager thinks you ought to be
hanged.' He showed a concern at this intelligence which amused me at
first. 'I had better get out of the way quietly,' he said, earnestly. 'I can do no
more for Kurtz now, and they would soon find some excuse. What's to stop
them? There's a military post three hundred miles from here.' 'Well, upon
my word,' said I, 'perhaps you had better go if you have any friends
amongst the savages near by.' 'Plenty,' he said. 'They are simple people —
and I want nothing, you know.' He stood biting his lip, then: 'I don't want
any harm to happen to these whites here, but of course I was thinking of
Mr. Kurtz's reputation — but you are a brother seaman and — ' 'All right,'
said I, after a time. 'Mr. Kurtz's reputation is safe with me.' I did not know
how truly I spoke.

"He informed me, lowering his voice, that it was Kurtz who had ordered the attack to be made on the steamer. 'He hated sometimes the idea
of being taken away — and then again. . . . But I don't understand these
matters. I am a simple man. He thought it would scare you away — that
you would give it up, thinking him dead. I could not stop him. Oh, I had an
awful time of it this last month.' 'Very well,' I said. 'He is all right now.'

'Ye-e-es,' he muttered, not very convinced apparently. 'Thanks,' said I; 'I shall keep my eyes open.' 'But quiet — eh?' he urged, anxiously. 'It would be awful for his reputation if anybody here — ' I promised a complete discretion with great gravity. 'I have a canoe and three black fellows waiting not very far. I am off. Could you give me a few Martini-Henry cartridges?' I could, and did, with proper secrecy. He helped himself, with a wink at me, to a handful of my tobacco. 'Between sailors — you know — good English tobacco.' At the door of the pilothouse he turned round — 'I say, haven't you a pair of shoes you could spare?' He raised one leg. 'Look.' The soles were tied with knotted strings sandal-wise under his bare feet. I rooted out an old pair, at which he looked with admiration before tucking them under his left arm. One of his pockets (bright red) was bulging with cartridges, from the other (dark blue) peeped 'Towson's Inquiry,' etc., etc. He seemed to think himself excellently well equipped for a renewed encounter with the wilderness. 'Ah! I'll never, never meet such a man again. You ought to have heard him recite poetry — his own, too, it was, he told me. Poetry!' He rolled his eyes at the recollection of these delights. 'Oh, he enlarged my mind!' 'Good-by,' said I. He shook hands and vanished in the night. Sometimes I ask myself whether I had ever really seen him — whether it was possible to meet such a phenomenon! . . .

"When I woke up shortly after midnight his warning came to my mind with its hint of danger that seemed, in the starred darkness, real enough to make me get up for the purpose of having a look round. On the hill a big fire burned, illuminating fitfully a crooked corner of the station-house. One of the agents with a picket of a few of our blacks, armed for the purpose, was keeping guard over the ivory; but deep within the forest, red gleams that wavered, that seemed to sink and rise from the ground amongst confused columnar shapes of intense blackness, showed the exact position of the camp where Mr. Kurtz's adorers were keeping their uneasy vigil. The monotonous beating of a big drum filled the air with muffled shocks and a lingering vibration. A steady droning sound of many men chanting each to himself some weird incantation came out from the black, flat wall of the wood as the humming of bees comes out of a hive, and had a strange narcotic effect upon my half-awake senses. I believe I dozed off leaning over the rail, till an abrupt burst of yells, an overwhelming outbreak of a pent-up and mysterious frenzy, woke me up in a bewildered wonder. It was cut short all at once, and the low droning went on with an effect of audible and soothing silence. I glanced casually into the little cabin. A light was burning within, but Mr. Kurtz was not there.

"I think I would have raised an outcry if I had believed my eyes. But I didn't believe them at first — the thing seemed so impossible. The fact is I was completely unnerved by a sheer blank fright, pure abstract terror, unconnected with any distinct shape of physical danger. What made this emotion so overpowering as — how shall I define it? — the moral shock I received, as if something altogether monstrous, intolerable to thought and odious to the soul, had been thrust upon me unexpectedly. This lasted of course the merest fraction of a second, and then the usual sense of commonplace, deadly danger, the possibility of a sudden onslaught and massacre, or something of the kind, which I saw impending, was positively welcome and composing. It pacified me, in fact, so much, that I did not raise an alarm.

"There was an agent buttoned up inside an ulster and sleeping on a chair on deck within three feet of me. The yells had not awakened him; he snored very slightly; I left him to his slumbers and leaped ashore. I did not betray Mr. Kurtz — it was ordered I should never betray him — it was written I should be loyal to the nightmare of my choice. I was anxious to deal with this shadow by myself alone — and to this day I don't know why I was so jealous of sharing with anyone the peculiar blackness of that experience.

"As soon as I got on the bank I saw a trail — a broad trail through the grass. I remember the exultation with which I said to myself, 'He can't walk — he is crawling on all-fours — I've got him.' The grass was wet with dew. I strode rapidly with clenched fists. I fancy I had some vague notion of falling upon him and giving him a drubbing. I don't know. I had some imbecile thoughts. The knitting old woman with the cat obtruded herself upon my memory as a most improper person to be sitting at the other end of such an affair. I saw a row of pilgrims squirting lead in the air out of Winchesters held to the hip. I thought I would never get back to the steamer, and imagined myself living alone and unarmed in the woods to an advanced age. Such silly things — you know. And I remember I confounded the beat of the drum with the beating of my heart, and was pleased at its calm regularity.

"I kept to the track though — then stopped to listen. The night was very clear; a dark blue space, sparkling with dew and starlight, in which black things stood very still. I thought I could see a kind of motion ahead of me. I was strangely cocksure of everything that night. I actually left the track and ran in a wide semicircle (I verily believe chuckling to myself) so as to get in front of that stir, of that motion I had seen — if indeed I had seen anything. I was circumventing Kurtz as though it had been a boyish game.

"I came upon him, and, if he had not heard me coming, I would have fallen over him, too, but he got up in time. He rose, unsteady, long, pale, indistinct, like a vapor exhaled by the earth, and swayed slightly, misty and silent before me; while at my back the fires loomed between the trees, and the murmur of many voices issued from the forest. I had cut him off cleverly; but when actually confronting him I seemed to come to my senses, I saw the danger in its right proportion. It was by no means over yet. Suppose he began to shout? Though he could hardly stand, there was still plenty of vigor in his voice. 'Go away — hide yourself,' he said, in that profound tone. It was very awful. I glanced back. We were within thirty yards from the nearest fire. A black figure stood up, strode on long black legs, waving long black arms, across the glow. It had horns — antelope horns, I think — on its head. Some sorcerer, some witchman, no doubt: it looked fiend-like enough. 'Do you know what you are doing?' I whispered. 'Perfectly,' he answered, raising his voice for that single word: it sounded to me far off and yet loud, like a hail through a speaking-trumpet. If he makes a row we are lost, I thought to myself. This clearly was not a case for fisticuffs, even apart from the very natural aversion I had to beat that Shadow — this wandering and tormented thing. 'You will be lost,' I said — 'utterly lost.' One gets sometimes such a flash of inspiration, you know. I did say the right thing, though indeed he could not have been more irretrievably lost than he was at this very moment, when the foundations of our intimacy were being laid — to endure — to endure — even to the end — even beyond.

" 'I had immense plans,' he muttered irresolutely. 'Yes,' said I; 'but if you try to shout I'll smash your head with — ' There was not a stick or a stone near. 'I will throttle you for good,' I corrected myself. 'I was on the threshold of great things,' he pleaded, in a voice of longing, with a wistfulness of tone that made my blood run cold. 'And now for this stupid scoundrel — ' 'Your success in Europe is assured in any case,' I affirmed, steadily. I did not want to have the throttling of him, you understand — and indeed it would have been very little use for any practical purpose. I tried to break the spell — the heavy, mute spell of the wilderness — that seemed to draw him to its pitiless breast by the awakening of forgotten and brutal instincts, by the memory of gratified and monstrous passions. This alone, I was convinced, had driven him out to the edge of the forest, to the bush, towards the gleam of fires, the throb of drums, the drone of weird incantations; this alone had beguiled his unlawful soul beyond the bounds of permitted aspirations. And, don't you see, the terror of the position was not in being knocked on the head — though I had a very lively sense of that danger, too — but in this, that I had to deal with a being to whom I could not appeal in the name of anything high or low. I had, even like the niggers, to invoke him — himself — his own exalted and incredible degradation. There was nothing either above or below him, and I knew it. He had kicked himself loose of the earth. Confound the man! he had kicked the very earth to pieces. He was alone, and I before him did not know whether I stood on the ground or floated in the air. I've been telling you what we said — repeating the phrases we pronounced — but what's the good? They were common everyday words — the familiar, vague sounds exchanged on every waking day of life. But what of that? They had behind them, to my mind, the terrific suggestiveness of words heard in dreams, of phrases spoken in nightmares. Soul! If anybody had ever struggled with a soul, I am the man. And I wasn't arguing with a lunatic either. Believe me or not, his intelligence was perfectly clear — concentrated, it is true, upon himself with horrible intensity, yet clear; and therein was my only chance — barring, of course, the killing him there and then, which wasn't so good, on account of unavoidable noise. But his soul was mad. Being alone in the wilderness, it had looked within itself, and, by heavens! I tell you, it had gone mad. I had — for my sins, I suppose — to go through the ordeal of looking into it myself. No eloquence could have been so withering to one's belief in mankind as his final burst of sincerity. He struggled with himself, too. I saw it — I heard it. I saw the inconceivable mystery of a soul that knew no restraint, no faith, and no fear, yet struggling blindly with itself. I kept my head pretty well; but when I had him at last stretched on the couch, I wiped my forehead, while my legs shook under me as though I had carried half a ton on my back down that hill. And yet I had only supported him, his bony arm clasped round my neck — and he was not much heavier than a child.

"When next day we left at noon, the crowd, of whose presence behind the curtain of trees I had been acutely conscious all the time, flowed out of the woods again, filled the clearing, covered the slope with a mass of naked, breathing, quivering, bronze bodies. I steamed up a bit, then swung downstream, and two thousand eyes followed the evolutions of the splashing, thumping, fierce river-demon beating the water with its terrible tail and breathing black smoke into the air. In front of the first rank, along the river, three men, plastered with bright red earth from head to foot, strutted to and fro restlessly. When we came abreast again, they faced the river, stamped their feet, nodded their horned heads, swayed their scarlet bodies; they shook towards the fierce river-demon a bunch of black feathers, a mangy skin with a pendent tail — something that looked like a dried gourd; they shouted periodically together strings of amazing words that resembled no sounds of human language; and the deep murmurs of the crowd, interrupted suddenly, were like the responses of some satanic litany.

"We had carried Kurtz into the pilot-house: there was more air there. Lying on the couch, he stared through the open shutter. There was an eddy in the mass of human bodies, and the woman with helmeted head and tawny cheeks rushed out to the very brink of the stream. She put out her hands, shouted something, and all that wild mob took up the shout in a roaring chorus of articulated, rapid, breathless utterance.

" 'Do you understand this?' I asked.

"He kept on looking out past me with fiery, longing eyes, with a mingled expression of wistfulness and hate. He made no answer, but I saw a smile, a smile of indefinable meaning, appear on his colorless lips that a moment after twitched convulsively. 'Do I not?' he said slowly, gasping, as if the words had been torn out of him by a supernatural power.

"I pulled the string of the whistle, and I did this because I saw the pilgrims on deck getting out their rifles with an air of anticipating a jolly lark. At the sudden screech there was a movement of abject terror through that wedged mass of bodies. 'Don't! don't you frighten them away,' cried someone on deck disconsolately. I pulled the string time after time. They broke and ran, they leaped, they crouched, they swerved, they dodged the flying terror of the sound. The three red chaps had fallen flat, face down on the shore, as though they had been shot dead. Only the barbarous and superb woman did not so much as flinch, and stretched tragically her bare arms after us over the somber and glittering river.

"And then that imbecile crowd down on the deck started their little fun, and I could see nothing more for smoke.

"The brown current ran swiftly out of the heart of darkness, bearing us down towards the sea with twice the speed of our upward progress; and Kurtz's life was running swiftly, too, ebbing, ebbing out of his heart into the sea of inexorable time. The manager was very placid, he had no vital anxieties now, he took us both in with a comprehensive and satisfied glance: the 'affair' had come off as well as could be wished. I saw the time approaching when I would be left alone of the party of 'unsound method.' The pilgrims looked upon me with disfavor. I was, so to speak, numbered with the dead. It is strange how I accepted this unforeseen partnership, this choice of nightmares forced upon me in the tenebrous land invaded by these mean and greedy phantoms.

"Kurtz discoursed. A voice! a voice! It rang deep to the very last. It survived his strength to hide in the magnificent folds of eloquence the barren darkness of his heart. Oh, he struggled! he struggled! The wastes of his weary brain were haunted by shadowy images now — images of wealth and fame revolving obsequiously round his unextinguishable gift of noble and lofty expression. My Intended, my station, my career, my ideas — these were the objects for the occasional utterances of elevated sentiments. The shade of the original Kurtz frequented the bedside of the hollow sham, whose fate it was to be buried presently in the mold of primeval earth. But both the diabolic love and the unearthly hate of the mysteries it had penetrated fought for the possession of that soul satiated with primitive emotions, avid of lying fame, of sham distinction, of all the appearances of success and power.

"Sometimes he was contemptibly childish. He desired to have kings meet him at railway stations on his return from some ghastly Nowhere, where he intended to accomplish great things. 'You show them you have in you something that is really profitable, and then there will be no limits to the recognition of your ability,' he would say. 'Of course you must take care of the motives — right motives — always.' The long reaches that were like one and the same reach, monotonous bends that were exactly alike, slipped past the steamer with their multitude of secular trees looking patiently after this grimy fragment of another world, the forerunner of change, of conquest, of trade, of massacres, of blessings. I looked ahead — piloting. 'Close the shutter,' said Kurtz suddenly one day; 'I can't bear to look at this.' I did so. There was a silence. 'Oh, but I will wring your heart yet!' he cried at the invisible wilderness.

"We broke down — as I had expected — and had to lie up for repairs at the head of an island. This delay was the first thing that shook Kurtz's

confidence. One morning he gave me a packet of papers and a photograph — the lot tied together with a shoestring. 'Keep this for me,' he said.
'This noxious fool' (meaning the manager) 'is capable of prying into my
boxes when I am not looking.' In the afternoon I saw him. He was lying on
his back with closed eyes, and I withdrew quietly, but I heard him mutter,
'Live rightly, die, die. . . .' I listened. There was nothing more. Was he rehearsing some speech in his sleep, or was it a fragment of a phrase from
some newspaper article? He had been writing for the papers and meant to
do so again, 'for the furthering of my ideas. It's a duty.'

"His was an impenetrable darkness. I looked at him as you peer down
at a man who is lying at the bottom of a precipice where the sun never
shines. But I had not much time to give him, because I was helping the engine-driver to take to pieces the leaky cylinders, to straighten a bent con-
necting-rod, and in other such matters. I lived in an infernal mess of rust,
filings, nuts, bolts, spanners, hammers, ratchet-drills — things I abominate,
because I don't get on with them. I tended the little forge we fortunately
had aboard; I toiled wearily in a wretched scrap-heap — unless I had the
shakes too bad to stand.

"One evening coming in with a candle I was startled to hear him say a
little tremulously, 'I am lying here in the dark waiting for death.' The light
was within a foot of his eyes. I forced myself to murmur, 'Oh, nonsense!'
and stood over him as if transfixed.

"Anything approaching the change that came over his features I have
never seen before, and hope never to see again. Oh, I wasn't touched. I was
fascinated. It was as though a veil had been rent. I saw on that ivory face the
expression of somber pride, of ruthless power, of craven terror — of an intense and hopeless despair. Did he live his life again in every detail of desire, temptation, and surrender during that supreme moment of complete
knowledge? He cried in a whisper at some image, at some vision — he cried
out twice, a cry that was no more than a breath —

" 'The horror! The horror!'

"I blew the candle out and left the cabin. The pilgrims were dining in
the mess-room, and I took my place opposite the manager, who lifted his
eyes to give me a questioning glance, which I successfully ignored. He
leaned back, serene, with that peculiar smile of his sealing the unexpressed
depths of his meanness. A continuous shower of small flies streamed upon
the lamp, upon the cloth, upon our hands and faces. Suddenly the manager's boy put his insolent black head in the doorway, and said in a tone of
scathing contempt —

" 'Mistah Kurtz — he dead.'

"All the pilgrims rushed out to see. I remained, and went on with my
dinner. I believe I was considered brutally callous. However, I did not eat
much. There was a lamp in there — light, don't you know — and outside it
was so beastly, beastly dark. I went no more near the remarkable man who
had pronounced a judgment upon the adventures of his soul on this earth.

The voice was gone. What else had been there? But I am of course aware that next day the pilgrims buried something in a muddy hole.

"And then they very nearly buried me.

"However, as you see, I did not go to join Kurtz there and then. I did not. I remained to dream the nightmare out to the end, and to show my loyalty to Kurtz once more. Destiny. My destiny! Droll thing life is — that mysterious arrangement of merciless logic for a futile purpose. The most you can hope from it is some knowledge of yourself — that comes too late — a crop of unextinguishable regrets. I have wrestled with death. It is the most unexciting contest you can imagine. It takes place in an impalpable grayness, with nothing underfoot, with nothing around, without spectators, without clamor, without glory, without the great desire of victory, without the great fear of defeat, in a sickly atmosphere of tepid skepticism, without much belief in your own right, and still less in that of your adversary. If such is the form of ultimate wisdom, then life is a greater riddle than some of us think it to be. I was within a hair's breadth of the last opportunity for pronouncement, and I found with humiliation that probably I would have nothing to say. This is the reason why I affirm that Kurtz was a remarkable man. He had something to say. He said it. Since I had peeped over the edge myself, I understand better the meaning of his stare, that could not see the flame of the candle, but was wide enough to embrace the whole universe, piercing enough to penetrate all the hearts that beat in the darkness. He had summed up — he had judged. 'The horror!' He was a remarkable man. After all, this was the expression of some sort of belief; it had candor, it had conviction, it had a vibrating note of revolt in its whisper, it had the appalling face of a glimpsed truth — the strange commingling of desire and hate. And it is not my own extremity I remember best — a vision of grayness without form filled with physical pain, and a careless contempt for the evanescence of all things — even of this pain itself. No! It is his extremity that I seem to have lived through. True, he had made that last stride, he had stepped over the edge, while I had been permitted to draw back my hesitating foot. And perhaps in this is the whole difference; perhaps all the wisdom, and all truth, and all sincerity, are just compressed into that inappreciable moment of time in which we step over the threshold of the invisible. Perhaps! I like to think my summing-up would not have been a word of careless contempt. Better his cry — much better. It was an affirmation, a moral victory paid for by innumerable defeats, by abominable terrors, by abominable satisfactions. But it was a victory! That is why I have remained loyal to Kurtz to the last, and even beyond, when a long time after I heard once more, not his own choice, but the echo of his magnificent eloquence thrown to me from a soul as translucently pure as a cliff of crystal.

"No, they did not bury me, though there is a period of time which I remember mistily, with a shuddering wonder, like a passage through some inconceivable world that had no hope in it and no desire. I found myself

back in the sepulchral city resenting the sight of people hurrying through
the streets to filch a little money from each other, to devour their infamous
cookery, to gulp their unwholesome beer, to dream their insignificant and
silly dreams. They trespassed upon my thoughts. They were intruders
whose knowledge of life was to me an irritating pretense, because I felt so
sure they could not possibly know the things I knew. Their bearing, which
was simply the bearing of commonplace individuals going about their business in the assurance of perfect safety, was offensive to me like the outrageous flauntings of folly in the face of a danger it is unable to comprehend.
I had no particular desire to enlighten them, but I had some difficulty in
restraining myself from laughing in their faces, so full of stupid importance.
I daresay I was not very well at that time. I tottered about the streets —
there were various affairs to settle — grinning bitterly at perfectly respectable persons. I admit my behavior was inexcusable, but then my temperature was seldom normal in these days. My dear aunt's endeavors to 'nurse
up my strength' seemed altogether beside the mark. It was not my strength
that wanted nursing, it was my imagination that wanted soothing. I kept
the bundle of papers given me by Kurtz, not knowing exactly what to do
with it. His mother had died lately, watched over, as I was told, by his
Intended. A clean-shaven man, with an official manner and wearing
gold-rimmed spectacles, called on me one day and made inquiries, at first
circuitous, afterwards suavely pressing, about what he was pleased to de-
nominate certain 'documents.' I was not surprised, because I had had two
rows with the manager on the subject out there. I had refused to give up the
smallest scrap out of that package, and I took the same attitude with the
spectacled man. He became darkly menacing at last, and with much heat
argued that the Company had the right to every bit of information about its
'territories.' And said he, 'Mr. Kurtz's knowledge of unexplored regions
must have been necessarily extensive and peculiar — owing to his great
abilities and to the deplorable circumstances in which he had been placed:
therefore — ' I assured him Mr. Kurtz's knowledge, however extensive, did
not bear upon the problems of commerce or administration. He invoked
then the name of science. 'It would be an incalculable loss if,' etc., etc. I
offered him the report on the 'Suppression of Savage Customs,' with the
postscriptum torn off. He took it up eagerly, but ended by sniffing at it with
an air of contempt. 'This is not what we had a right to expect,' he remarked.
'Expect nothing else,' I said. 'There are only private letters.' He withdrew
upon some threat of legal proceedings, and I saw him no more; but another
fellow, calling himself Kurtz's cousin, appeared two days later, and was
anxious to hear all the details about his dear relative's last moments. Incidentally he gave me to understand that Kurtz had been essentially a great
musician. 'There was the making of an immense success,' said the man,
who was an organist, I believe, with lank gray hair flowing over a greasy
coat-collar. I had no reason to doubt his statement; and to this day I am
unable to say what was Kurtz's profession, whether he ever had any —

which was the greatest of his talents. I had taken him for a painter who wrote for the papers, or else for a journalist who could paint — but even the cousin (who took snuff during the interview) could not tell me what he had been — exactly. He was a universal genius — on that point I agreed with the old chap, who thereupon blew his nose noisily into a large cotton handkerchief and withdrew in senile agitation, bearing off some family letters and memoranda without importance. Ultimately a journalist anxious to know something of the fate of his 'dear colleague' turned up. This visitor informed me Kurtz's proper sphere ought to have been politics 'on the popular side.' He had furry straight eyebrows, bristly hair cropped short, an eye-glass on a broad ribbon, and, becoming expansive, confessed his opinion that Kurtz really couldn't write a bit — 'But heavens! how that man could talk. He electrified large meetings. He had faith — don't you see? — he had the faith. He could get himself to believe anything — anything. He would have been a splendid leader of an extreme party.' 'What party?' I asked. 'Any party,' answered the other. 'He was an — an — extremist.' Did I not think so? I assented. Did I know, he asked, with a sudden flash of curiosity, 'what it was that had induced him to go out there?' 'Yes,' said I, and forthwith handed him the famous Report for publication, if he thought fit. He glanced through it hurriedly, mumbling all the time, judged 'it would do,' and took himself off with this plunder.

"Thus I was left at last with a slim packet of letters and the girl's portrait. She struck me as beautiful — I mean she had a beautiful expression. I know that the sunlight can be made to lie, too, yet one felt that no manipulation of light and pose could have conveyed the delicate shade of truthfulness upon those features. She seemed ready to listen without mental reservation, without suspicion, without a thought for herself. I concluded I would go and give her back her portrait and those letters myself. Curiosity? Yes; and also some other feeling perhaps. All that had been Kurtz's had passed out of my hands: his soul, his body, his station, his plans, his ivory, his career. There remained only this memory and his Intended — and I wanted to give that up, too, to the past, in a way — to surrender personally all that remained of him with me to that oblivion which is the last word of our common fate. I don't defend myself. I had no clear perception of what it was I really wanted. Perhaps it was an impulse of unconscious loyalty, or the fulfillment of one of those ironic necessities that lurk in the facts of human existence. I don't know. I can't tell. But I went.

"I thought his memory was like the other memories of the dead that accumulate in every man's life — a vague impress on the brain of shadows that had fallen on it in their swift and final passage; but before the high and ponderous door, between the tall houses of a street as still and decorous as a well-kept alley in a cemetery, I had a vision of him on the stretcher, opening his mouth voraciously, as if to devour all the earth with all its mankind. He lived then before me; he lived as much as he had ever lived — a shadow insatiable of splendid appearances, of frightful realities; a shadow darker than the shadow of the night, and draped nobly in the folds of a gorgeous eloquence. The vision seemed to enter the house with me — the stretcher, the phantom-bearers, the wild crowd of obedient worshipers, the gloom of the forests, the glitter of the reach between the murky bends, the beat of the drum, regular and muffled like the beating of a heart—the heart of a conquering darkness. It was a moment of triumph for the wilderness, an invading and vengeful rush which, it seemed to me, I would have to keep back alone for the salvation of another soul. And the memory of what I had heard him say afar there, with the honored shapes stirring at my back, in the glow of fires, within the patient woods, those broken phrases came back to me, were heard again in their ominous and terrifying simplicity. I remembered his abject pleading, his abject threats, the colossal scale of his vile desires, the meanness, the torment, the tempestuous anguish of his soul. And later on I seem to see his collected languid manner, when he said one day, 'This lot of ivory now is really mine. The Company did not pay for it. I collected it myself at a very great personal risk. I am afraid they will try to claim it as theirs though. H'm. It is a difficult case. What do you think I ought to do — resist? Eh? I want no more than justice.'. . . He wanted no more than justice—no more than justice. I rang the bell before a mahogany door on the first floor, and while I waited he seemed to stare at me out of the glassy panel — stare with that wide and immense stare embracing, condemning, loathing all the universe. I seemed to hear the whispered cry, 'The horror! The horror!'

"The dusk was falling. I had to wait in a lofty drawing-room with three long windows from floor to ceiling that were like three luminous and bedraped columns. The bent gilt legs and backs of the furniture shone in indistinct curves. The tall marble fireplace had a cold and monumental whiteness. A grand piano stood massively in a corner; with dark gleams on the flat surfaces like a somber and polished sarcophagus. A high door opened — closed. I rose.

"She came forward, all in black, with a pale head, floating towards me in the dusk. She was in mourning. It was more than a year since his death, more than a year since the news came; she seemed as though she would remember and mourn forever. She took both my hands in hers and murmured, 'I had heard you were coming.' I noticed she was not very young — I mean not girlish. She had a mature capacity for fidelity, for belief, for suffering. The room seemed to have grown darker, as if all the sad light of the cloudy evening had taken refuge on her forehead. This fair hair, this pale visage, this pure brow, seemed surrounded by an ashy halo from which the dark eyes looked out at me. Their glance was guileless, profound, confident, and trustful. She carried her sorrowful head as though she were proud of that sorrow, as though she would say, I — I alone know how to mourn him as he deserves. But while we were still shaking hands, such a look of awful desolation came upon her face that I perceived she was one of those creatures that are not the playthings of Time. For her he had died only yesterday. And, by Jove! the impression was so powerful that for me, too, he seemed to have died only yesterday — nay, this very minute. I saw her and him in the same instant of time — his death and her sorrow — I saw her sorrow in the very moment of his death. Do you understand? I saw them together—I heard them together. She had said, with a deep catch of the breath, 'I have survived' while my strained ears seemed to hear distinctly, mingled with her tone of despairing regret, the summing up whisper of his eternal condemnation. I asked myself what I was doing there, with a sensation of panic in my heart as though I had blundered into a place of cruel and absurd mysteries not fit for a human being to behold. She motioned me to a chair. We sat down. I laid the packet gently on the little table, and she put her hand over it. . . . 'You knew him well,' she murmured, after a moment of mourning silence.

" 'Intimacy grows quickly out there,' I said. 'I knew him as well as it is possible for one man to know another.'

" 'And you admired him,' she said. 'It was impossible to know him and not to admire him. Was it?'

" 'He was a remarkable man,' I said, unsteadily. Then before the appealing fixity of her gaze, that seemed to watch for more words on my lips, I went on, 'It was impossible not to — '

" 'Love him,' she finished eagerly, silencing me into an appalled dumbness. 'How true! how true! But when you think that no one knew him so well as I! I had all his noble confidence. I knew him best.'

" 'You knew him best,' I repeated. And perhaps she did. But with every word spoken the room was growing darker, and only her forehead, smooth and white, remained illumined by the unextinguishable light of belief and love.

" 'You were his friend,' she went on. 'His friend,' she repeated, a little louder. 'You must have been, if he had given you this, and sent you to me. I feel I can speak to you — and oh! I must speak. I want you — you have heard his last words — to know I have been worthy of him. . . . It is not pride. . . . Yes! I am proud to know I understood him better than anyone on earth — he told me so himself. And since his mother died I have had no one — no one — to — to — '

"I listened. The darkness deepened. I was not even sure he had given me the right bundle. I rather suspect he wanted me to take care of another batch of his papers which, after his death, I saw the manager examining under the lamp. And the girl talked, easing her pain in the certitude of my sympathy; she talked as thirsty men drink. I had heard that her engagement with Kurtz had been disapproved by her people. He wasn't rich enough or something. And indeed I don't know whether he had not been a pauper all his life. He had given me some reason to infer that it was his impatience of comparative poverty that drove him out there.

" ' . . . Who was not his friend who had heard him speak once?' she was saying. 'He drew men towards him by what was best in them.' She looked at me with intensity. 'It is the gift of the great,' she went on, and the sound of her low voice seemed to have the accompaniment of all the other sounds, full of mystery, desolation, and sorrow, I had ever heard — the ripple of the river, the soughing of the trees swayed by the wind, the murmurs of the crowds, the faint ring of incomprehensible words cried from afar, the whisper of a voice speaking from beyond the threshold of an eternal darkness. 'But you have heard him! You know!' she cried.

" 'Yes, I know,' I said with something like despair in my heart, but bowing my head before the faith that was in her, before that great and saving illusion that shone with an unearthly glow in the darkness, in the triumphant darkness from which I could not have defended her — from which I could not even defend myself.

" 'What a loss to me — to us!' — she corrected herself with beautiful generosity; then added in a murmur, 'To the world.' By the last gleams of twilight I could see the glitter of her eyes, full of tears — of tears that would not fall.

" 'I have been very happy — very fortunate — very proud,' she went on. 'Too fortunate. Too happy for a little while. And now I am unhappy for — for life.'

"She stood up; her fair hair seemed to catch all the remaining light in a glimmer of gold. I rose, too.

" 'And of all this,' she went on, mournfully, 'of all his promise, and of all his greatness, of his generous mind, of his noble heart, nothing remains — nothing but a memory. You and I — '

" 'We shall always remember him,' I said, hastily.

" 'No!' she cried. "It is impossible that all this should be lost — that such a life should be sacrificed to leave nothing — but sorrow. You know what vast plans he had. I knew of them, too — I could not perhaps understand — but others knew of them. Something must remain. His words, at least, have not died.'

" 'His words will remain,' I said.

" 'And his example,' she whispered to herself. 'Men looked up to him — his goodness shone in every act. His example — '

" 'True,' I said; 'his example, too. Yes, his example. I forgot that.'

" 'But I do not. I cannot — I cannot believe — not yet. I cannot believe that I shall never see him again, that nobody will see him again, never, never, never."

"She put out her arms as if after a retreating figure, stretching them black and with clasped pale hands across the fading and narrow sheen of the window. Never see him! I saw him clearly enough then. I shall see this eloquent phantom as long as I live, and I shall see her, too, a tragic and familiar Shade, resembling in this gesture another one, tragic also, and bedecked with powerless charms, stretching bare brown arms over the glitter of the infernal stream, the stream of darkness. She said suddenly very low, 'He died as he lived.'

" 'His end,' said I, with dull anger stirring in me, 'was in every way worthy of his life."

" 'And I was not with him,' she murmured. My anger subsided before a feeling of infinite pity.

" 'Everything that could be done — ' I mumbled.

" 'Ah, but I believed in him more than anyone on earth — more than his own mother, more than — himself. He needed me! Me! I would have treasured every sigh, every word, every sign, every glance.'

"I felt like a chill grip on my chest. 'Don't,' I said, in a muffled voice.

" 'Forgive me. I — I have mourned so long in silence — in silence. . . . You were with him — to the last? I think of his loneliness. Nobody near to understand him as I would have understood. Perhaps no one to hear. . . .'

" 'To the very end,' I said shakily. 'I heard his very last words. . . .' I stopped in a fright.

" 'Repeat them, she murmured in a heart-broken tone. 'I want — I want — something — something — to — live with.'

"I was on the point of crying at her, 'Don't you hear them?' The dusk was repeating them in a persistent whisper all around us, in a whisper that seemed to swell menacingly like the first whisper of a rising wind. 'The horror! The horror!"

" 'His last word — to live with,' she insisted. 'Don't you understand I loved him — I loved him — I loved him!'

"I pulled myself together and spoke slowly.

" 'The last word he pronounced was — your name.'

"I heard a light sigh and then my heart stood still, stopped dead short by an exulting and terrible cry, by the cry of inconceivable triumph and of unspeakable pain. 'I knew it — I was sure!' . . . She knew. She was sure. I heard her weeping, she had hidden her face in her hands. It seemed to me that the house would collapse before I could escape, that the heavens would fall upon my head. But nothing happened. The heavens do not fall for such a trifle. Would they have fallen, I wonder, if I had rendered Kurtz that justice which was his due? Hadn't he said he wanted only justice? But I couldn't. I could not tell her. It would have been too dark — too dark altogether. . . ."

Marlow ceased, and sat apart, indistinct and silent, in the pose of a meditating Buddha. Nobody moved for a time. "We have lost the first of the ebb," said the Director, suddenly. I raised my head. The offing was barred by a black bank of clouds, and the tranquil waterway leading to the uttermost ends of the earth flowed somber under an overcast sky — seemed to lead into the heart of an immense darkness.

[1902]

ANTON CHEKHOV (1860–1904) *wrote his first stories while he was a medical student at Moscow University, to raise money for his family. His grandfather had been a serf who had bought his freedom. His father was an unsuccessful grocer in Tagarrog, in southeastern Russia. After completing his medical training, Chekhov became an assistant to the district doctor in a small provincial town, where he began to accumulate his vast store of observations of the peasants and provincial characters who came to the hospital. His early sketches were mostly humorous stories that he first published in newspapers under different pen names, keeping his true signature for his medical articles. But the popularity of these sketches made him determined to become a serious artist.*

Chekhov's first two collections of short stories, published in 1886 and 1887, were acclaimed by readers, and from that time on he was able to abandon his medical career and give all his time to writing. He bought a small estate near Moscow where he lived with his family and treated sick peasants in his home at no charge. Chekhov's kindness and good works were not a matter of any political program or religious philosophy, but rather "the natural coloration of his talent," as Vladimir Nabokov put it. Once Chekhov told a visitor, "Do you know how I write my stories? Here's how!" And he glanced at his table, took up the first object that met his eye — it was an ashtray — and said, "If you want it, you'll have a story tomorrow. It will be called 'The Ashtray.'" And it seemed to the visitor that a magical transformation of that ashtray was taking place: "Certain indefinite situations, adventures which had not yet found concrete form, were already beginning to crystallize about the ashtray."

In his short stories, Chekhov conveys an impression of beauty with a disarmingly simple technique, as in "A Trifle from Real Life." The variety of his moods, the flicker of his wit, and the spareness of his characterizations are enhanced because they are suffused with a faintly irridescent verbal haziness. Virginia Woolf said that "As we read these little stories about nothing at all, the horizon widens; the soul gains an astonishing sense of freedom." Chekhov's hard-won artistic control can be seen in a masterpiece like "The Lady with the Dog," with its great compassion for the adulterous couple. He once wrote a self-portrait for the editor who first encouraged him, in which he gave a sense of the depth of his self-knowledge and the extent of his remarkable human decency:

> *Write a story, do, about a young man, the son of a serf, a former grocery boy, a choir singer, a high school pupil and university student, brought up to respect rank, to kiss the hands of priests, to truckle to the ideas of*

others — a young man who expressed thanks for every piece of bread, who was whipped many times, who went without galoshes to do his tutoring, who used his fists, tortured animals, was fond of dining with rich relatives, was a hypocrite in his dealings with God and men, needlessly, solely out of a realization of his own insignificance — write how this young man squeezes the slave out of himself, drop by drop, and how, on awaking one fine morning, he feels that the blood coursing through his veins is no longer that of a slave but that of a real human being.

In his last years, Chekhov — already established as a great writer of short fiction — wrote plays for the Moscow Art Theater, which was then remaking the whole idea of theater in Russia under the direction of Konstantin Stanislavsky. These plays — including The Seagull (1896), Uncle Vanya (1898), The Three Sisters (1901), and The Cherry Orchard (1904) — established him as a great dramatist as well. In 1901 he married Olga Knipper, one of the leading actresses of the Moscow Art Theater. But he was already dying of tuberculosis, and he lived his last three years as an invalid.

Chekhov's hundreds of stories have immensely influenced the art of fiction. He was never concerned with giving a social or ethical message in his writing, but the complete integrity and harmony that his work conveys will live in the world, according to Nabokov, "as long as there are birchwoods and sunsets and the urge to write."

Anton Chekhov

ふひ

A TRIFLE FROM REAL LIFE

– translated by Marian Fell

Nikolai Ilitch Belayeff was a young gentleman of St. Petersburg, aged thirty-two, rosy, well fed, and a patron of the race-tracks. Once, toward evening, he went to pay a call on Olga Ivanovna with whom, to use his own expression, he was dragging through a long and tedious love-affair. And the truth was that the first thrilling, inspiring pages of this romance had long since been read, and that the story was now dragging wearily on, presenting nothing that was either interesting or novel.

Not finding Olga at home, my hero threw himself upon a couch and prepared to await her return.

"Good evening, Nikolai Ilitch!" he heard a child's voice say. "Mamma will soon be home. She has gone to the dressmaker's with Sonia."

On the divan in the same room lay Aliosha, Olga's son, a small boy of eight, immaculately and picturesquely dressed in a little velvet suit and long black stockings. He had been lying on a satin pillow, mimicking the antics of an acrobat he had seen at the circus. First he stretched up one pretty leg, then another; then, when they were tired, he brought his arms into play, and at last jumped up galvanically, throwing himself on all fours in an effort to stand on his head. He went through all these motions with the most serious face in the world, puffing like a martyr, as if he himself regretted that God had given him such a restless little body.

"Ah, good evening, my boy!" said Belayeff. "Is that you? I did not know you were here. Is mamma well?"

Aliosha seized the toe of his left shoe in his right hand, assumed the most unnatural position in the world, rolled over, jumped up, and peeped out at Belayeff from under the heavy fringes of the lampshade.

"Not very," he said shrugging his shoulders. "Mamma is never really well. She is a woman, you see, and women always have something the matter with them."

From lack of anything better to do, Belayeff began scrutinizing Aliosha's face. During all his acquaintance with Olga he had never bestowed any consideration upon the boy or noticed his existence at all. He had seen the child about, but what he was doing there Belayeff, somehow, had never cared to think.

Now, in the dusk of evening, Aliosha's pale face and fixed, dark eyes unexpectedly reminded Belayeff of Olga as she had appeared in the first pages of their romance. He wanted to pet the boy.

"Come here, little monkey," he said, "and let me look at you!"

The boy jumped down from the sofa and ran to Belayeff.

"Well," the latter began, laying his hand on the boy's thin shoulder. "And how are you? Is everything all right with you?"

"No, not very. It used to be much better."

"In what way?"

"That's easy to answer. Sonia and I used to learn only music and reading before, but now we have French verses, too. You have cut your beard!"

"Yes."

"So I noticed. It is shorter than it was. Please let me touch it — does that hurt?"

"No, not a bit."

"Why does it hurt if you pull one hair at a time, and not a bit if you pull lots? Ha! Ha! I'll tell you something. You ought to wear whiskers! You could shave here on the sides, here, and here you could let the hair grow —— "

The boy nestled close to Belayeff and began to play with his watch-chain.

"Mamma is going to give me a watch when I go to school, and I am going to ask her to give me a chain just like yours —— Oh, what a lovely locket! Papa has a locket just like that; only yours has little stripes on it, and papa's has letters. He has a portrait of mamma in his locket. Papa wears another watch-chain now made of ribbon."

"How do you know? Do you ever see your papa?"

"I — n-no — I —— "

Aliosha blushed deeply at being caught telling a fib and began to scratch the locket furiously with his nail. Belayeff looked searchingly into his face and repeated:

"Do you ever see your papa?"

"N-no!"

"Come, tell me honestly! I can see by your face that you are not telling the truth. It's no use quibbling now that the cat is out of the bag. Tell me, do you see him? Now then, as between friends!"

Aliosha reflected.

"You won't tell mamma?" he said.

"What an idea!"

"Honor bright?"

"Honor bright!"

"Promise!"

"Oh, you insufferable child! What do you take me for?"

Aliosha glanced around, opened his eyes wide, and said:

"For heaven's sake don't tell mamma! Don't tell a soul, because it's a secret. I don't know what would happen to Sonia and Pelagia and me if mamma should find out. Now, listen. Sonia and I see papa every Thursday and every Friday. When Pelagia takes us out walking before dinner we go to Anfel's confectionery and there we find papa already waiting for us. He is always sitting in the little private room with the marble table and the ashtray that's made like a goose without a back."

"What do you do in there?"

"We don't do anything. First we say how do you do, and then papa orders coffee and pasties for us. Sonia likes pasties with meat, you know, but I can't abide them with meat. I like mine with cabbage or eggs. We eat so much that we have a hard time eating our dinner afterward so that mamma won't guess anything."

"What do you talk about?"

"With papa? Oh, about everything. He kisses us and hugs us and tells us the funniest jokes. Do you know what? He says that when we grow bigger he is going to take us to live with him. Sonia doesn't want to go, but I wouldn't mind. Of course it would be lonely without mamma, but I could write letters to her. Isn't it funny, we might go and see her then on Sundays, mightn't we? Papa says too, he is going to buy me a pony. He is such a nice man! I don't know why mamma doesn't ask him to live with her and why she won't let us see him. He loves mamma very much. He always asks how she is and what she has been doing. When she was ill he took hold of his head just like this — and ran about the room. He always asks us whether we are obedient and respectful to her. Tell me, is it true that we are unfortunate?"

"H'm — why do you ask?"

"Because papa says we are. He says we are unfortunate children, and that he is unfortunate, and that mamma is unfortunate. He tells us to pray to God for her and for ourselves."

Aliosha fixed his eyes on the figure of a stuffed bird, and became lost in thought.

"Well, I declare —— " muttered Belayeff. "So, that's what you do, you hold meetings at a confectioner's? And your mamma doesn't know it?"

"N-no. How could she? Pelagia wouldn't tell her for the world. Day before yesterday papa gave us pears. They were as sweet as sugar. I ate two!"

"H'm. But — listen to me, does papa ever say anything about me?"

"About you? What shall I say?" Aliosha looked searchingly into Belayeff's face and shrugged his shoulders. "Nothing special," he answered.

"Well, what does he say, for instance?"

"You won't be angry if I tell you?"

"What an idea! Does he abuse me?"

"No, he doesn't abuse you, but, you know, he is angry with you. He says that it is your fault that mamma is unhappy, and that you have ruined mamma. He is such a funny man! I tell him that you are kind and that you never scold mamma, but he only shakes his head."

"So he says I have ruined her?"

"Yes — don't be angry, Nikolai Ilitch!"

Belayeff rose and began pacing up and down the room.

"How strange this is — and how ridiculous!" he muttered shrugging his shoulders and smiling sarcastically. "It is all *his* fault and yet he says *I* have ruined her! What an innocent baby this is! And so he told you I had ruined your mother?"

"Yes, but — you promised not to be angry!"

"I'm not angry and — and it is none of your business anyway. Yes, this is — this is really ridiculous! Here I have been caught like a mouse in a trap, and now it seems it is all my fault!"

The door-bell rang. The boy tore himself from Belayeff's arms and ran out of the room. A moment later a lady entered with a little girl. It was Aliosha's mother, Olga Ivanovna. Aliosha skipped into the room behind her, singing loudly and clapping his hands. Belayeff nodded and continued to walk up and down.

"Of course!" he muttered. "Whom should he blame but me? He has right on his side! He is the injured husband."

"What is that you are saying?" asked Olga Ivanovna.

"What am I saying? Just listen to what your young hopeful here has been preaching. It appears that I am a wicked scoundrel and that I have ruined you and your children. You are all unhappy, and I alone am frightfully happy. Frightfully, frightfully happy!"

"I don't understand you, Nikolai. What is the matter?"

"Just listen to what this young gentleman here has to say!" cried Belayeff pointing to Aliosha.

Aliosha flushed and then grew suddenly pale and his face became distorted with fear.

"Nikolai Ilitch!" he whispered loudly. "Hush!"

Olga Ivanovna looked at Aliosha in surprise, and then at Belayeff, and then back again at Aliosha.

"Ask him!" Belayeff continued. "That idiot of yours, Pelagia, takes them to a confectioner's and arranges meetings there between them and their papa. But that isn't the point. The point is that papa is the victim, and that I am an abandoned scoundrel who has wrecked the lives of both of you!"

"Nikolai Ilitch!" groaned Aliosha. "You gave me your word of honor!"

"Leave me alone!" Belayeff motioned to him impatiently. "This is more important than words of honor. This hypocrisy, these lies are intolerable!"

"I don't understand!" cried Olga Ivanovna, the tears glistening in her eyes. "Listen, Aliosha," she asked, turning to her son. "Do you really see your father?"

But Aliosha did not hear her, his eyes were fixed with horror on Belayeff.

"It cannot be possible!" his mother exclaimed, "I must go and ask Pelagia."

Olga Ivanovna left the room.

"But Nikolai Ilitch, you gave me your word of honor!" cried Aliosha trembling all over.

Belayeff made an impatient gesture and went on pacing the floor. He was absorbed in thoughts of the wrong that had been done him, and, as before, was unconscious of the boy's presence: a serious, grown-up person like him could not be bothered with little boys. But Aliosha crept into a corner and told Sonia with horror how he had been deceived. He trembled and hiccoughed and cried. This was the first time in his life that he had come roughly face to face with deceit; he had never imagined till now that there were things in this world besides pasties and watches and sweet pears, things for which no name could be found in the vocabulary of childhood.

[1888]

Anton Chekhov

ಬಿ

THE LADY WITH THE DOG

– translated by Avrahm Yarmolinsky

I

A new person, it was said, had appeared on the esplanade: a lady with a pet dog. Dmitry Dmitrich Gurov, who had spent a fortnight at Yalta and had got used to the place, had also begun to take an interest in new arrivals. As he sat in Vernet's confectionery shop, he saw, walking on the esplanade, a fair-haired young woman of medium height, wearing a beret; a white Pomeranian was trotting behind her.

And afterwards he met her in the public garden and in the square several times a day. She walked alone, always wearing the same beret and always with the white dog; no one knew who she was and everyone called her simply "the lady with the pet dog."

"If she is here alone without husband or friends," Gurov reflected, "it wouldn't be a bad thing to make her acquaintance."

He was under forty, but he already had a daughter twelve years old, and two sons at school. They had found a wife for him when he was very young, a student in his second year, and by now she seemed half as old again as he. She was a tall, erect woman with dark eyebrows, stately and dignified and, as she said of herself, intellectual. She read a great deal, used simplified spelling in her letters, called her husband, not Dmitry, but Dimitry, while he privately considered her of limited intelligence, narrow-minded, dowdy, was afraid of her, and did not like to be at home. He had begun being unfaithful to her long ago — had been unfaithful to her often and, probably for that reason, almost always spoke ill of women, and when they were talked of in his presence used to call them "the inferior race."

It seemed to him that he had been sufficiently tutored by bitter experience to call them what he pleased, and yet he could not have lived without "the inferior race" for two days together. In the company of men he was bored and ill at ease, he was chilly and uncommunicative with them; but when he was among women he felt free, and knew what to speak to them about and how to comport himself; and even to be silent with them was no strain on him. In his appearance, in his character, in his whole make-up there was something attractive and elusive that disposed women in his favor and allured them. He knew that, and some force seemed to draw him to them, too.

Oft-repeated and really bitter experience had taught him long ago that with decent people — particularly Moscow people — who are irresolute and slow to move, every affair which at first seems a light and charming adventure inevitably grows into a whole problem of extreme complexity, and in the end a painful situation is created. But at every new meeting with an interesting woman this lesson of experience seemed to slip from his memory, and he was eager for life, and everything seemed so simple and diverting.

One evening while he was dining in the public garden the lady in the beret walked up without haste to take the next table. Her expression, her gait, her dress, and the way she did her hair told him that she belonged to the upper class, that she was married, that she was in Yalta for the first time and alone, and that she was bored there. The stories told of the immorality in Yalta are to a great extent untrue; he despised them, and knew that such stories were made up for the most part by persons who would have been glad to sin themselves if they had had the chance; but when the lady sat down at the next table three paces from him, he recalled these stories of easy conquests, of trips to the mountains, and the tempting thought of a swift, fleeting liaison, a romance with an unknown woman of whose very name he was ignorant suddenly took hold of him.

He beckoned invitingly to the Pomeranian, and when the dog approached him, shook his finger at it. The Pomeranian growled; Gurov threatened it again.

The lady glanced at him and at once dropped her eyes.

"He doesn't bite," she said and blushed.

"May I give him a bone?" he asked; and when she nodded he inquired affably, "Have you been in Yalta long?"

"About five days."

"And I am dragging out the second week here."

There was a short silence.

"Time passes quickly, and yet it is so dull here!" she said, not looking at him.

"It's only the fashion to say it's dull here. A provincial will live in Belyov or Zhizdra and not be bored, but when he comes here it's 'Oh, the dullness! Oh, the dust!' One would think he came from Granada."

She laughed. Then both continued eating in silence, like strangers, but after dinner they walked together and there sprang up between them the light banter of people who are free and contented, to whom it does not matter where they go or what they talk about. They walked and talked of the strange light on the sea: the water was a soft, warm, lilac color, and there was a golden band of moonlight upon it. They talked of how sultry it was after a hot day. Gurov told her that he was a native of Moscow, that he had studied languages and literature at the university, but had a post in a bank; that at one time he had trained to become an opera singer but had given it up, that he owned two houses in Moscow. And he learned from her that she had grown up in Petersburg, but had lived in S — since her marriage two years previously, that she was going to stay in Yalta for about another month, and that her husband, who needed a rest, too, might perhaps come to fetch her. She was not certain whether her husband was a member of a Government Board or served on a Zemstvo Council,[1] and this amused her. And Gurov learned too that her name was Anna Sergeyevna.

Afterwards in his room at the hotel he thought about her — and was certain that he would meet her the next day. It was bound to happen. Getting into bed he recalled that she had been a schoolgirl only recently, doing lessons like his own daughter; he thought how much timidity and angularity there was still in her laugh and her manner of talking with a stranger. It must have been the first time in her life that she was alone in a setting in which she was followed, looked at, and spoken to for one secret purpose alone, which she could hardly fail to guess. He thought of her slim, delicate throat, her lovely gray eyes.

"There's something pathetic about her, though," he thought, and dropped off.

II

A week had passed since they had struck up an acquaintance. It was a holiday. It was close indoors, while in the street the wind whirled the dust about and blew people's hats off. One was thirsty all day, and Gurov often went into the restaurant and offered Anna Sergeyevna a soft drink or ice cream. One did not know what to do with oneself. *the problem with Dream World*

In the evening when the wind had abated they went out on the pier to watch the steamer come in. There were a great many people walking about the dock; they had come to welcome someone and they were carrying bunches of flowers. And two peculiarities of a festive Yalta crowd stood out: the elderly ladies were dressed like young ones and there were many generals.

Owing to the choppy sea, the steamer arrived late, after sunset, and it was a long time tacking about before it put in at the pier. Anna Sergeyevna peered at the steamer and the passengers through her lorgnette as though looking for acquaintances, and whenever she turned to Gurov her eyes were shining. She talked a great deal and asked questions jerkily, forgetting the next moment what she had asked; then she lost her lorgnette in the crush.

The festive crowd began to disperse; it was now too dark to see people's faces; there was no wind any more, but Gurov and Anna Sergeyevna still stood as though waiting to see someone else come off the steamer.

---

[1] county council.

Anna Sergeyevna was silent now, and sniffed her flowers without looking at Gurov.

"The weather has improved this evening," he said. "Where shall we go now? Shall we drive somewhere?"

She did not reply.

Then he looked at her intently, and suddenly embraced her and kissed her on the lips, and the moist fragrance of her flowers enveloped him; and at once he looked round him anxiously, wondering if anyone had seen them.

"Let us go to your place," he said softly. And they walked off together rapidly.

The air in her room was close and there was the smell of the perfume she had bought at the Japanese shop. Looking at her, Gurov thought: "What encounters life offers!" From the past he preserved the memory of carefree, good-natured women whom love made gay and who were grateful to him for the happiness he gave them, however brief it might be; and of women like his wife who loved without sincerity, with too many words, affectedly, hysterically, with an expression that it was not love or passion that engaged them but something more significant; and of two or three others, very beautiful, frigid women, across whose faces would suddenly flit a rapacious expression — an obstinate desire to take from life more than it could give, and these were women no longer young, capricious, unreflecting, domineering, unintelligent, and when Gurov grew cold to them their beauty aroused his hatred, and the lace on their lingerie seemed to him to resemble scales.

But here there was the timidity, the angularity of inexperienced youth, a feeling of awkwardness; and there was a sense of embarrassment, as though someone had suddenly knocked at the door. Anna Sergeyevna, "the lady with the pet dog," treated what had happened in a peculiar way, very seriously, as though it were her fall — so it seemed, and this was odd and inappropriate. Her features drooped and faded, and her long hair hung down sadly on either side of her face; she grew pensive and her dejected pose was that of a Magdalene in a picture by an old master.

"It's not right," she said. "You don't respect me now, you first of all."

There was a watermelon on the table. Gurov cut himself a slice and began eating it without haste. They were silent for at least half an hour.

There was something touching about Anna Sergeyevna; she had the purity of a well-bred, naive woman who has seen little of life. The single candle burning on the table barely illumined her face, yet it was clear that she was unhappy.

"Why should I stop respecting you, darling?" asked Gurov. "You don't know what you're saying."

"God forgive me," she said, and her eyes filled with tears. "It's terrible."

"It's as though you were trying to exonerate yourself."

"How can I exonerate myself? No. I am a bad, low woman; I despise myself and I have no thought of exonerating myself. It's not my husband but myself I have deceived. And not only just now; I have been deceiving myself for a long time. My husband may be a good, honest man, but he is a flunkey! I don't know what he does, what his work is, but I know he is a flunkey! I was twenty when I married him. I was tormented by curiosity; I wanted something better. 'There must be a different sort of life,' I said to myself. I wanted to live! To live, to live! Curiosity kept eating at me — you don't understand it, but I swear to God I could no longer control myself; something was going on in me; I could not be held back. I told my husband I was ill, and came here. And here I have been walking about as though in a daze, as though I were mad; and now I have become a vulgar, vile woman whom anyone may despise."

Gurov was already bored with her; he was irritated by her naive tone, by her repentance, so unexpected and so out of place, but for the tears in her eyes he might have thought she was joking or play-acting.

"I don't understand, my dear," he said softly. "What do you want?"

She hid her face on his breast and pressed close to him.

"Believe me, believe me, I beg you," she said, "I love honesty and purity, and sin is loathsome to me; I don't know what I'm doing. Simple people say, 'The Evil One has led me astray.' And I may say of myself now that the Evil One has led me astray."

"Quiet, quiet," he murmured.

He looked into her fixed, frightened eyes, kissed her, spoke to her softly and affectionately, and by degrees she calmed down, and her gaiety returned; both began laughing.

Afterwards when they went out there was not a soul on the esplanade. The town with its cypresses looked quite dead, but the sea was still sounding as it broke upon the beach; a single launch was rocking on the waves and on it a lantern was blinking sleepily.

They found a cab and drove to Oreanda.

"I found out your surname in the hall just now: it was written on the board — von Dideritz," said Gurov. "Is your husband German?"

"No; I believe his grandfather was German, but he is Greek Orthodox himself."

At Oreanda they sat on a bench not far from the church, looked down at the sea, and were silent. Yalta was barely visible through the morning mist; white clouds rested motionlessly on the mountaintops. The leaves did not stir on the trees, cicadas twanged, and the monotonous muffled sound of the sea that rose from below spoke of the peace, the eternal sleep awaiting us. So it rumbled below when there was no Yalta, no Oreanda here; so it rumbles now, and it will rumble as indifferently and as hollowly when we are no more. And in this constancy, in this complete indifference to the life and death of each of us, there lies, perhaps, a pledge of our eternal salvation, of the unceasing advance of life upon earth, of unceasing movement towards perfection. Sitting beside a young woman who in the dawn seemed so lovely, Gurov, soothed and spellbound by these magical surroundings — the sea, the mountains, the clouds, the wide sky — thought how everything is really beautiful in this world when one reflects: everything except what we think or do ourselves when we forget the higher aims of life and our own human dignity.

A man strolled up to them — probably a guard — looked at them and walked away. And this detail, too, seemed so mysterious and beautiful. They saw a steamer arrive from Feodosia, its lights extinguished in the glow of dawn.

"There is dew on the grass," said Anna Sergeyevna, after a silence.

"Yes, it's time to go home."

They returned to the city.

Then they met every day at twelve o'clock on the esplanade, lunched and dined together, took walks, admired the sea. She complained that she slept badly, that she had palpitations, asked the same questions, troubled now by jealousy and now by the fear that he did not respect her sufficiently. And often in the square or the public garden, when there was no one near them, he suddenly drew her to him and kissed her passionately. Complete idleness, these kisses in broad daylight exchanged furtively in dread of someone's seeing them, the heat, the smell of the sea, and the continual flitting before his eyes of idle, well-dressed, well-fed people, worked a complete change in him; he kept telling Anna Sergeyevna how beautiful she was, how seductive, was urgently passionate; he would not move a step away from her, while she was often pensive and continually pressed him to confess that he did not respect her, did not love her in the least, and saw in her nothing but a common woman. Almost every evening rather late they drove somewhere out of town, to Oreanda or to the waterfall; and the excursion was always a success, the scenery invariably impressed them as beautiful and magnificent.

They were expecting her husband, but a letter came from him saying that he had eye-trouble, and begging his wife to return home as soon as possible. Anna Sergeyevna made haste to go.

"It's a good thing I am leaving," she said to Gurov. "It's the hand of Fate!"

She took a carriage to the railway station, and he went with her. They were driving the whole day. When she had taken her place in the express, and when the second bell had rung, she said, "Let me look at you once more — let me look at you again. Like this."

She was not crying but was so sad that she seemed ill and her face was quivering.

"I shall be thinking of you — remembering you," she said. "God bless you; be happy. Don't remember evil against me. We are parting forever — it has to be, for we ought never to have met. Well, God bless you."

The train moved off rapidly, its lights soon vanished, and a minute later there was no sound of it, as though everything had conspired to end as quickly as possible that sweet trance, that madness. Left alone on the platform, and gazing into the dark distance, Gurov listened to the twang of the grasshoppers and the hum of the telegraph wires, feeling as though he had just waked up. And he reflected, musing, that there had now been another episode or adventure in his life, and it, too, was at an end, and nothing was left of it but a memory. He was moved, sad, and slightly remorseful: this young woman whom he would never meet again had not been happy with him; he had been warm and affectionate with her, but yet in his manner, his tone, and his caresses there had been a shade of light irony, the slightly coarse arrogance of a happy male who was, besides, almost twice her age. She had constantly called him kind, exceptional, high-minded; obviously he had seemed to her different from what he really was, so he had involuntarily deceived her.

Here at the station there was already a scent of autumn in the air; it was a chilly evening.

"It is time for me to go north, too," thought Gurov as he left the platform. "High time!"

III

At home in Moscow the winter routine was already established; the stoves were heated, and in the morning it was still dark when the children were having breakfast and getting ready for school, and the nurse would light the lamp for a short time. There were frosts already. When the first snow falls, on the first day the sleighs are out, it is pleasant to see the white earth, the white roofs; one draws easy, delicious breaths, and the season brings back the days of one's youth. The old limes and birches, white with hoar-frost, have a good-natured look; they are closer to one's heart than cypresses and palms, and near them one no longer wants to think of mountains and the sea.

Gurov, a native of Moscow, arrived there on a fine frosty day, and when he put on his fur coat and warm gloves and took a walk along Petrovka, and when on Saturday night he heard the bells ringing, his recent trip and the places he had visited lost all charm for him. Little by little he became immersed in Moscow life, greedily read three newspapers a day, and declared that he did not read the Moscow papers on principle. He already felt a longing for restaurants, clubs, formal dinners, anniversary celebrations, and it flattered him to entertain distinguished lawyers and actors, and to play cards with a professor at the physicians' club. He could eat a whole portion of meat stewed with pickled cabbage and served in a pan, Moscow style.

A month or so would pass and the image of Anna Sergeyevna, it seemed to him, would become misty in his memory, and only from time to time he would dream of her with her touching smile as he dreamed of others. But more than a month went by, winter came into its own, and everything was still clear in his memory as though he had parted from Anna Sergeyevna only yesterday. And his memories glowed more and more vividly. When in the evening stillness the voices of his children preparing their lessons reached his study, or when he listened to a song or to an organ playing in a restaurant, or when the storm howled in the chimney, suddenly everything would rise up in his memory; what had happened on the pier and the early morning with the mist on the mountains, and the steamer coming from Feodosia, and the kisses. He would pace about his room a long time, remembering and smiling; then his memories passed into reveries, and in his imagination the past would mingle with what was to come. He did not dream of Anna Sergeyevna, but she followed him about everywhere and watched him. When he shut his eyes he saw her before him as though she were there in the flesh, and she seemed to him lovelier, younger, tenderer than she had been, and he imagined himself a finer man than he had been in Yalta. Of evenings she peered out at him from the bookcase, from the fireplace, from the corner — he heard her breathing, the caressing rustle of her clothes. In the street he followed the women with his eyes, looking for someone who resembled her.

Already he was tormented by a strong desire to share his memories with someone. But in his home it was impossible to talk of his love, and he had no one to talk to outside; certainly he could not confide in his tenants or in anyone at the bank. And what was there to talk about? He hadn't loved her then, had he? Had there been anything beautiful, poetical, edifying, or simply interesting in his relations with Anna Sergeyevna? And he was forced to talk vaguely of love, of women, and no one guessed what he meant; only his wife would twitch her black eyebrows and say, "The part of a philanderer does not suit you at all, Dimitry."

One evening, coming out of the physicians' club with an official with whom he had been playing cards, he could not resist saying:

"If you only knew what a fascinating woman I became acquainted with at Yalta!"

The official got into his sledge and was driving away, but turned suddenly and shouted:

"Dmitry Dmitrich!"

"What is it?"

"You were right this evening: the sturgeon was a bit high."

These words, so commonplace, for some reason moved Gurov to indignation, and struck him as degrading and unclean. What savage manners, what mugs! What stupid nights, what dull, humdrum days! Frenzied gambling, gluttony, drunkenness, continual talk always about the same thing! Futile pursuits and conversations always about the same topics take up the better part of one's time, the better part of one's strength, and in the end there is left a life clipped and wingless, an absurd mess, and there is no escaping or getting away from it — just as though one were in a madhouse or a prison.

Gurov, boiling with indignation, did not sleep all night. And he had a headache all the next day. And the following nights too he slept badly; he sat up in bed, thinking, or paced up and down his room. He was fed up with his children, fed up with the bank; he had no desire to go anywhere or to talk of anything.

In December during the holidays he prepared to take a trip and told his wife he was going to Petersburg to do what he could for a young friend — and he set off for S — . What for? He did not know, himself. He wanted to see Anna Sergeyevna and talk with her, to arrange a rendezvous if possible.

He arrived at S — in the morning, and at the hotel took the best room, in which the floor was covered with gray army cloth, and on the table there was an inkstand, gray with dust and topped by a figure on horseback, its hat in its raised hand and its head broken off. The porter gave him the necessary information: von Dideritz lived in a house of his own on Staro-Goncharnaya Street, not far from the hotel: he was rich and lived well and kept his own horses; everyone in the town knew him. The porter pronounced the name: "Dridiritz."

Without haste Gurov made his way to Staro-Goncharnaya Street and found the house. Directly opposite the house stretched a long gray fence studded with nails.

"A fence like that would make one run away," thought Gurov, looking now at the fence, now at the windows of the house.

He reflected: this was a holiday, and the husband was apt to be at home. And in any case, it would be tactless to go into the house and disturb her. If he were to send her a note, it might fall into her husband's hands, and that might spoil everything. The best thing was to rely on chance. And he kept walking up and down the street and along the fence, waiting for the chance. He saw a beggar go in at the gate and heard the dogs attack him; then an hour later he heard a piano, and the sound came to him faintly and indistinctly. Probably it was Anna Sergeyevna playing. The front door opened suddenly, and an old woman came out, followed by the familiar white Pomeranian. Gurov was on the point of calling to the dog, but his heart began beating violently, and in his excitement he could not remember the Pomeranian's name.

He kept walking up and down, and hated the gray fence more and more, and by now he thought irritably that Anna Sergeyevna had forgotten him, and was perhaps already diverting herself with another man, and that that was very natural in a young woman who from morning till night had to look at that damn fence. He went back to his hotel room and sat on the couch for a long while, not knowing what to do, then he had dinner and a long nap.

"How stupid and annoying all this is!" he thought when he woke and looked at the dark windows: it was already evening. "Here I've had a good sleep for some reason. What am I going to do at night?"

He sat on the bed, which was covered with a cheap gray blanket of the kind seen in hospitals, and he twitted himself in his vexation:

"So there's your lady with the pet dog. There's your adventure. A nice place to cool your heels in."

That morning at the station a playbill in large letters had caught his eye. *The Geisha* was to be given for the first time. He thought of this and drove to the theater.

"It's quite possible that she goes to first nights," he thought.

The theater was full. As in all provincial theaters, there was a haze above the chandelier, the gallery was noisy and restless; in the front row, before the beginning of the performance the local dandies were standing with their hands clasped behind their backs; in the Governor's box the Governor's daughter, wearing a boa, occupied the front seat, while the Governor himself hid modestly behind the portiere and only his hands were visible; the curtain swayed; the orchestra was a long time tuning up. While the audience was coming in and taking their seats, Gurov scanned the faces eagerly.

Anna Sergeyevna, too, came in. She sat down in the third row, and when Gurov looked at her his heart contracted, and he understood clearly that in the whole world there was no human being so near, so precious, and so important to him; she, this little, undistinguished woman, lost in a provincial crowd, with a vulgar lorgnette in her hand, filled his whole life now, was his sorrow and his joy, the only happiness that he now desired for himself, and to the sounds of the bad orchestra, of the miserable local violins, he thought how lovely she was. He thought and dreamed.

A young man with small side-whiskers, very tall and stooped, came in with Anna Sergeyevna and sat down beside her; he nodded his head at every step and seemed to be bowing continually. Probably this was the husband whom at Yalta, in an access of bitter feeling, she had called a flunkey. And there really was in his lanky figure, his side-whiskers, his small bald patch, something of a flunkey's retiring manner; his smile was mawkish, and in his buttonhole there was an academic badge like a waiter's number.

During the first intermission the husband went out to have a smoke; she remained in her seat. Gurov, who was also sitting in the orchestra, went up to her and said in a shaky voice, with a forced smile:

"Good evening!"

She glanced at him and turned pale, then looked at him again in horror, unable to believe her eyes, and gripped the fan and the lorgnette tightly together in her hands, evidently trying to keep herself from fainting. Both were silent. She was sitting, he was standing, frightened by her distress and not daring to take a seat beside her. The violins and the flute that were being tuned up sang out. He suddenly felt frightened: it seemed as if all the people in the boxes were looking at them. She got up and went hurriedly to the exit; he followed her, and both of them walked blindly along the corridors and up and down stairs, and figures in the uniforms prescribed for magistrates, teachers, and officials of the Department of Crown Lands, all wearing badges, flitted before their eyes, as did also ladies, and fur coats on hangers; they were conscious of drafts and the smell of stale tobacco. And Gurov, whose heart was beating violently, thought:

"Oh, Lord! Why are these people here and this orchestra!"

And at that instant he suddenly recalled how when he had seen Anna Sergeyevna off at the station he had said to himself that all was over between them and that they would never meet again. But how distant the end still was!

On the narrow, gloomy staircase over which it said "To the Amphitheatre," she stopped.

"How you frightened me!" she said, breathing hard, still pale and stunned. "Oh, how you frightened me! I am barely alive. Why did you come? Why?"

"But do understand, Anna, do understand —" he said hurriedly, under his breath. "I implore you, do understand —"

She looked at him with fear, with entreaty, with love; she looked at him intently, to keep his features more distinctly in her memory.

"I suffer so," she went on, not listening to him. "All this time I have been thinking of nothing but you; I live only by the thought of you. And I wanted to forget, to forget; but why, oh, why have you come?"

On the landing above them two high school boys were looking down and smoking, but it was all the same to Gurov; he drew Anna Sergeyevna to him and began kissing her face and hands.

"What are you doing, what are you doing!" she was saying in horror, pushing him away. "We have lost our senses. Go away today; go away at once — I conjure you by all that is sacred, I implore you — People are coming this way!"

Someone was walking up the stairs.

"You must leave," Anna Sergeyevna went on in a whisper. "Do you hear, Dmitry Dmitrich? I will come and see you in Moscow. I have never been happy; I am unhappy now, and I never, never shall be happy, never! So don't make me suffer still more! I swear I'll come to Moscow. But now let us part. My dear, good, precious one, let us part!"

She pressed his hand and walked rapidly downstairs, turning to look round at him, and from her eyes he could see that she really was unhappy. Gurov stood for a while, listening, then when all grew quiet, he found his coat and left the theater.

IV

And Anna Sergeyevna began coming to see him in Moscow. Once every two or three months she left S — telling her husband that she was going to consult a doctor about a woman's ailment from which she was suffering — and her husband did and did not believe her. When she arrived in Moscow she would stop at the Slavyansky Bazar Hotel, and at once send a man in a red cap to Gurov. Gurov came to see her, and no one in Moscow knew of it.

Once he was going to see her in this way on a winter morning (the messenger had come the evening before and not found him in). With him walked his daughter, whom he wanted to take to school; it was on the way. Snow was coming down in big wet flakes.

"It's three degrees above zero,[2] and yet it's snowing," Gurov was saying to his daughter. "But this temperature prevails only on the surface of the earth; in the upper layers of the atmosphere there is quite a different temperature."

"And why doesn't it thunder in winter, papa?"

He explained that, too. He talked, thinking all the while that he was on his way to a rendezvous, and no living soul knew of it, and probably no one would ever know. He had two lives, an open one, seen and known by all who needed to know it, full of conventional truth and conventional falsehood, exactly like the lives of his friends and acquaintances; and another life that went on in secret. And through some strange, perhaps accidental, combination of circumstances, everything that was of interest and importance to him, everything that was essential to him, everything about which he felt sincerely and did not deceive himself, everything that constituted the core of his life, was going on concealed from others; while all that was false, the shell in which he hid to cover the truth — his work at the bank, for instance, his discussions at the club, his references to the "inferior race," his appearances at anniversary celebrations with his wife — all that went on in the open. Judging others by himself, he did not believe what he saw, and always fancied that every man led his real, most interesting life under cover of secrecy as under cover of night. The personal life of every individual is based on secrecy, and perhaps it is partly for that reason that civilized man is so nervously anxious that personal privacy should be respected.

Having taken his daughter to school, Gurov went on to the Slavyansky Bazar Hotel. He took off his fur coat in the lobby, went upstairs, and knocked gently at the door. Anna Sergeyevna, wearing his favorite gray dress, exhausted by the journey and by waiting, had been expecting him since the previous evening. She was pale, and looked at him without a smile, and he had hardly entered when she flung herself on his breast. That

---

[2] on the Celsius scale — about thirty-seven degrees Fahrenheit.

kiss was a long, lingering one, as though they had not seen one another for two years.

"Well, darling, how are you getting on there?" he asked. "What news?"

"Wait; I'll tell you in a moment — I can't speak."

She could not speak; she was crying. She turned away from him, and pressed her handkerchief to her eyes.

"Let her have her cry; meanwhile I'll sit down," he thought, and he seated himself in an armchair.

Then he rang and ordered tea, and while he was having his tea she remained standing at the window with her back to him. She was crying out of sheer agitation, in the sorrowful consciousness that their life was so sad; that they could only see each other in secret and had to hide from people like thieves! Was it not a broken life?

"Come, stop now, dear!" he said.

It was plain to him that this love of theirs would not be over soon, that the end of it was not in sight. Anna Sergeyevna was growing more and more attached to him. She adored him, and it was unthinkable to tell her that their love was bound to come to an end some day; besides, she would not have believed it!

He went up to her and took her by the shoulders, to fondle her and say something diverting, and at that moment he caught sight of himself in the mirror.

His hair was already beginning to turn gray. And it seemed odd to him that he had grown so much older in the last few years, and lost his looks. The shoulders on which his hands rested were warm and heaving. He felt compassion for this life, still so warm and lovely, but probably already about to begin to fade and wither like his own. Why did she love him so much? He always seemed to women different from what he was, and they loved in him not himself, but the man whom their imagination created and whom they had been eagerly seeking all their lives; and afterwards, when they saw their mistake, they loved him nevertheless. And not one of them had been happy with him. In the past he had met women, come together with them, parted from them, but he had never once loved; it was anything you please, but not love. And only now when his head was gray he had fallen in love, really, truly — for the first time in his life.

Anna Sergeyevna and he loved each other as people do who are very close and intimate, like man and wife, like tender friends; it seemed to them that Fate itself had meant them for one another, and they could not understand why he had a wife and she a husband; and it was as though they were a pair of migratory birds, male and female, caught and forced to live in different cages. They forgave each other what they were ashamed of in their past, they forgave everything in the present, and felt that this love of theirs had altered them both.

Formerly in moments of sadness he had soothed himself with what-ever logical arguments came into his head, but now he no longer cared for logic; he felt profound compassion, he wanted to be sincere and tender.

"Give it up now, my darling," he said. "You've had your cry; that's enough. Let us have a talk now, we'll think up something."

Then they spent a long time taking counsel together, they talked of how to avoid the necessity for secrecy, for deception, for living in different cities, and not seeing one another for long stretches of time. How could they free themselves from these intolerable fetters?

"How? How?" he asked, clutching his head. "How?"

And it seemed as though in a little while the solution would be found, and then a new and glorious life would begin; and it was clear to both of them that the end was still far off, and that what was to be most compli-cated and difficult for them was only just beginning.

[1899]

Thinking about the next goal / dream

EDITH WHARTON (1862–1937) *was born into a wealthy family in New York City. She later wrote, "My little-girl life, safe, guarded, monotonous, was cradled in the only world about which, according to Goethe, it is impossible to write poetry. The small society into which I was born was 'good' in the most prosaic sense of the term, and its only interest, for the generality of readers, lies in the fact of its sudden and total extinction." She was raised by governesses and tutors in the family homes in Paris, New York City, and Newport, Rhode Island. At an early age she decided to become a writer, and when she was only thirteen she published, at her own expense, a collection of verse. Later she found her chief literary task in adapting the conventional novel of manners, depicting the customs of a definite social class, to reveal the deeper human significance of her seemingly shallow characters. Her family persisted in viewing her literary work as an eccentricity best disregarded and left undiscussed.*

After her marriage to Edward Wharton of Boston in 1885, Wharton began to write stories for popular magazines. She was a prolific author, and her first collection of stories, The Greater Inclination (1899), *was followed by books of fiction almost every year for more than a quarter of a century. All told, she published eleven collections of stories and sixteen novels. She lived most of her life in Paris, but her photographic memory and her periodic visits to her country estate in the Berkshires, near Lenox, Massachusetts, helped her recall scenes of American life for her fiction. Her best works include the early novel* The House of Mirth (1905), Ethan Frome (1911), *a laconically powerful New England tragedy, and* The Age of Innocence (1920), *a novel about Newport society. Wharton's novels tend to be tragic and to concentrate on the presentation of characters, while her short stories, more satiric, emphasize plots. In both forms her point of view is usually poised and distant, and this is reflected in the elegance and clarity of her prose style.*

One of Wharton's good friends was another expatriate, Henry James, who also visited her in the Berkshires. James had a profound influence on her writing, as a guiding spirit encouraging her to set a high standard for herself. Both writers are important social historians of their era, keen observers of the society they knew so well. Unlike James, Wharton did not write experimentally, but, like him, she enjoyed defining her artistic methods as a storyteller. In 1925 she published The Writing of Fiction, *and in analyzing the French and Russian contributions to the short story form, she recognized that "instead of a loose web spread over the surface of life they have made it, at its best, a shaft driven straight into the heart of human experience." Her carefully crafted story "Roman Fever" has an ending that may strike the reader as "a shaft driven straight into the heart," but every* phrase in the realistic depiction of the characters and the situation is a sign-post that can be trusted for its relevance to the moral drama suddenly re-vealed in the last line.

Edith Wharton

ಜಲ

ROMAN FEVER

I

From the table at which they had been lunching two American ladies of ripe but well-cared-for middle age moved across the lofty terrace of the Roman restaurant and, leaning on its parapet, looked first at each other, and then down on the outspread glories of the Palatine and the Forum, with the same expression of vague but benevolent approval.

As they leaned there a girlish voice echoed up gaily from the stairs leading to the court below. "Well, come along, then," it cried, not to them but to an invisible companion, "and let's leave the young things to their knitting" and a voice as fresh laughed back: "Oh, look here, Babs, not ac-tually *knitting* — " "Well, I mean figuratively," rejoined the first. "After all, we haven't left our poor parents much else to do . . . " and at that point the turn of the stairs engulfed the dialogue.

The two ladies looked at each other again, this time with a tinge of smiling embarrassment, and the smaller and paler one shook her head and colored slightly.

"Barbara!" she murmured, sending an unheard rebuke after the mocking voice in the stairway.

The other lady, who was fuller, and higher in color, with a small de-termined nose supported by vigorous black eyebrows, gave a good-humored laugh. "That's what our daughters think of us!"

Her companion replied by a deprecating gesture. "Not of us individu-ally. We must remember that. It's just the collective modern idea of Moth-ers. And you see — " Half guiltily she drew from her handsomely mounted black hand-bag a twist of crimson silk run through by two fine knitting nee-dles. "One never knows," she murmured. "The new system has certainly given us a good deal of time to kill; and sometimes I get tired just look-ing — even at this." Her gesture was now addressed to the stupendous scene at their feet.

The dark lady laughed again, and they both relapsed upon the view, contemplating it in silence, with a sort of diffused serenity which might have been borrowed from the spring effulgence of the Roman skies. The luncheon-hour was long past, and the two had their end of the vast terrace to themselves. At its opposite extremity a few groups, detained by a lingering look at the outspread city, were gathering up guide-books and fumbling for tips. The last of them scattered, and the two ladies were alone on the air-washed height.

"Well, I don't see why we shouldn't just stay here," said Mrs. Slade, the lady of the high color and energetic brows. Two derelict basket-chairs stood near, and she pushed them into the angle of the parapet, and settled herself in one, her gaze upon the Palatine. "After all, it's still the most beautiful view in the world."

"It always will be, to me," assented her friend Mrs. Ansley, with so slight a stress on the "me" that Mrs. Slade, though she noticed it, wondered if it were not merely accidental, like the random underlinings of old-fashioned letter-writers.

"Grace Ansley was always old-fashioned," she thought; and added aloud, with a retrospective smile: "It's a view we've both been familiar with for a good many years. When we first met here we were younger than our girls are now. You remember?"

"Oh, yes, I remember," murmured Mrs. Ansley, with the same undefinable stress — "There's that head-waiter wondering," she interpolated. She was evidently far less sure than her companion of herself and of her rights in the world.

"I'll cure him of wondering," said Mrs. Slade, stretching her hand toward a bag as discreetly opulent-looking as Mrs. Ansley's. Signing to the head-waiter, she explained that she and her friend were old lovers of Rome, and would like to spend the end of the afternoon looking down on the view — that is, if it did not disturb the service? The head-waiter, bowing over her gratuity, assured her that the ladies were most welcome, and would be still more so if they would condescend to remain for dinner. A full moon night, they would remember. . . .

Mrs. Slade's black brows drew together, as though references to the moon were out-of-place and even unwelcome. But she smiled away her frown as the head-waiter retreated. "Well, why not? We might do worse. There's no knowing, I suppose, when the girls will be back. Do you even know back from *where*? I don't!"

Mrs. Ansley again colored slightly. "I think those young Italian aviators we met at the Embassy invited them to fly to Tarquinia for tea. I suppose they'll want to wait and fly back by moonlight."

"Moonlight — moonlight! What a part it still plays. Do you suppose they're as sentimental as we were?"

"I've come to the conclusion that I don't in the least know what they are," said Mrs. Ansley. "And perhaps we didn't know much more about each other."

"No; perhaps we didn't."

Her friend gave her a shy glance. "I never should have supposed you were sentimental, Alida."

"Well, perhaps I wasn't." Mrs. Slade drew her lids together in retrospect; and for a few moments the two ladies, who had been intimate since childhood, reflected how little they knew each other. Each one, of course, had a label ready to attach to the other's name; Mrs. Delphin Slade, for instance, would have told herself, or any one who asked her, that Mrs. Horace Ansley, twenty-five years ago, had been exquisitely lovely — no, you wouldn't believe it, would you? . . . though, of course, still charming, distinguished. . . . Well, as a girl she had been exquisite; far more beautiful than her daughter Barbara, though certainly Babs, according to the new standards at any rate, was more effective—had more *edge*, as they say. Funny where she got it, with those two nullities as parents. Yes; Horace Ansley was — well, just the duplicate of his wife. Museum specimens of old New York. Good-looking, irreproachable, exemplary. Mrs. Slade and Mrs. Ansley had lived opposite each other — actually as well as figuratively — for years. When the drawing-room curtains in No. 20 East 73rd Street were renewed, No. 23, across the way, was always aware of it. And of all the movings, buyings, travels, anniversaries, illnesses — the tame chronicle of an estimable pair. Little of it escaped Mrs. Slade. But she had grown bored with it by the time her husband made his big *coup* in Wall Street, and when they bought in upper Park Avenue had already begun to think: "I'd rather live opposite a speak-easy for a change; at least one might see it raided." The idea of seeing Grace raided was so amusing that (before the move) she launched it at a woman's lunch. It made a hit, and went the rounds — she sometimes wondered if it had crossed the street, and reached Mrs. Ansley. She hoped not, but didn't much mind. Those were the days when respectability was at a discount, and it did the irreproachable no harm to laugh at them a little.

A few years later, and not many months apart, both ladies lost their husbands. There was an appropriate exchange of wreaths and condolences, and a brief renewal of intimacy in the half-shadow of their mourning; and now, after another interval, they had run across each other in Rome, at the same hotel, each of them the modest appendage of a salient daughter. The similarity of their lot had again drawn them together, lending itself to mild jokes, and the mutual confession that, if in old days it must have been tiring to "keep up" with daughters, it was now, at times, a little dull not to.

No doubt, Mrs. Slade reflected, she felt her unemployment more than poor Grace ever would. It was a big drop from being the wife of Delphin Slade to being his widow. She had always regarded herself (with a certain conjugal pride) as his equal in social gifts, as contributing her full share to the making of the exceptional couple they were: but the difference after his death was irremediable. As the wife of the famous corporation lawyer, always with an international case or two on hand, every day brought its exciting and unexpected obligation: the impromptu entertaining of eminent colleagues from abroad, the hurried dashes on legal business to London, Paris or Rome, where the entertaining was so handsomely reciprocated; the amusement of hearing in her wake: "What, that handsome woman with the good clothes and the eyes is Mrs. Slade — *the* Slade's wife? Really? Generally the wives of celebrities are such frumps."

Yes; being *the* Slade's widow was a dullish business after that. In living up to such a husband all her faculties had been engaged; now she had only her daughter to live up to, for the son who seemed to have inherited his father's gifts had died suddenly in boyhood. She had fought through that agony because her husband was there, to be helped and to help; now, after the father's death, the thought of the boy had become unbearable. There was nothing left but to mother her daughter; and dear Jenny was such a perfect daughter that she needed no excessive mothering. "Now with Babs Ansley I don't know that I *should* be so quiet," Mrs. Slade sometimes half-enviously reflected; but Jenny, who was younger than her brilliant friend, was that rare accident, an extremely pretty girl who somehow made youth and prettiness seem as safe as their absence. It was all perplexing — and to Mrs. Slade a little boring. She wished that Jenny would fall in love — with the wrong man, even; that she might have to be watched, out-manœuvred, rescued. And instead, it was Jenny who watched her mother, kept her out of draughts, made sure that she had taken her tonic. . . .

Mrs. Ansley was much less articulate than her friend, and her mental portrait of Mrs. Slade was slighter, and drawn with fainter touches. "Alida Slade's awfully brilliant; but not as brilliant as she thinks," would have summed it up; though she would have added, for the enlightenment of strangers, that Mrs. Slade had been an extremely dashing girl; much more so than her daughter, who was pretty, of course, and clever in a way, but had none of her mother's — well, "vividness," some one had once called it. Mrs. Ansley would take up current words like this, and cite them in quotation marks, as unheard-of audacities. No; Jenny was not like her mother. Sometimes Mrs. Ansley thought Alida Slade was disappointed; on the whole she had had a sad life. Full of failures and mistakes; Mrs. Ansley had always been rather sorry for her. . . .

So these two ladies visualized each other, each through the wrong end of her little telescope.

II

For a long time they continued to sit side by side without speaking. It seemed as though, to both, there was a relief in laying down their somewhat futile activities in the presence of the vast Memento Mori which faced them. Mrs. Slade sat quite still, her eyes fixed on the golden slope of the Palace of the Caesars, and after a while Mrs. Ansley ceased to fidget with her bag, and she too sank into meditation. Like many intimate friends, the two ladies had never before had occasion to be silent together, and Mrs. Ansley was slightly embarrassed by what seemed, after so many years, a new stage in their intimacy, and one with which she did not yet know how to deal.

Suddenly the air was full of that deep clangor of bells which periodically covers Rome with a roof of silver. Mrs. Slade glanced at her wristwatch. "Five o'clock already," she said, as though surprised.

Mrs. Ansley suggested interrogatively: "There's bridge at the Embassy at five." For a long time Mrs. Slade did not answer. She appeared to be lost in contemplation, and Mrs. Ansley thought the remark had escaped her. But after a while she said, as if speaking out of a dream: "Bridge, did you say? Not unless you want to. . . . But I don't think I will, you know."

"Oh, no," Mrs. Ansley hastened to assure her. "I don't care to at all. It's so lovely here; and so full of old memories, as you say." She settled herself in her chair, and almost furtively drew forth her knitting. Mrs. Slade took sideway note of this activity, but her own beautifully cared-for hands remained motionless on her knee.

"I was just thinking," she said slowly, "what different things Rome stands for to each generation of travelers. To our grandmothers, Roman fever; to our mothers, sentimental danger — how we used to be guarded! — to our daughters, no more dangers than the middle of Main Street. They don't know it — but how much they're missing!"

The long golden light was beginning to pale, and Mrs. Ansley lifted her knitting a little closer to her eyes. "Yes; how we were guarded!"

"I always used to think," Mrs. Slade continued, "that our mothers had a much more difficult job than our grandmothers. When Roman fever stalked the streets it must have been comparatively easy to gather in the girls at the danger hour; but when you and I were young, with such beauty calling us, and the spice of disobedience thrown in, and no worse risk than catching cold during the cool hour after sunset, the mothers used to be put to it to keep us in — didn't they?"

She turned again toward Mrs. Ansley, but the latter had reached a delicate point in her knitting. "One, two, three — slip two; yes, they must have been," she assented, without looking up.

Mrs. Slade's eyes rested on her with a deepened attention. "She can knit — in the face of *this!* How like her. . . ."

Mrs. Slade leaned back, brooding, her eyes ranging from the ruins which faced her to the long green hollow of the Forum, the fading glow of the church fronts beyond it, and the outlying immensity of the Colosseum. Suddenly she thought: "It's all very well to say that our girls have done away with sentiment and moonlight. But if Babs Ansley isn't out to catch that young aviator — the one who's a Marchese — then I don't know anything. And Jenny has no chance beside her. I know that too. I wonder if that's why Grace Ansley likes the two girls to go everywhere together? My poor Jenny as a foil — !" Mrs. Slade gave a hardly audible laugh, and at the sound Mrs. Ansley dropped her knitting.

"Yes — ?"

"I — oh, nothing. I was only thinking how your Babs carries everything before her. That Campolieri boy is one of the best matches in Rome. Don't look so innocent, my dear — you know he is. And I was wondering, ever so respectfully, you understand . . . wondering how two such exemplary characters as you and Horace had managed to produce anything quite so dynamic." Mrs. Slade laughed again, with a touch of asperity.

Mrs. Ansley's hands lay inert across her needles. She looked straight out at the great accumulated wreckage of passion and splendor at her feet. But her small profile was almost expressionless. At length she said: "I think you overrate Babs, my dear."

Mrs. Slade's tone grew easier. "No; I don't. I appreciate her. And perhaps envy you. Oh, my girl's perfect; if I were a chronic invalid I'd — well, I think I'd rather be in Jenny's hands. There must be times . . . but there! I always wanted a brilliant daughter . . . and never quite understood why I got an angel instead."

Mrs. Ansley echoed her laugh in a faint murmur. "Babs is an angel too."

"Of course — of course! But she's got rainbow wings. Well, they're wandering by the sea with their young men; and here we sit . . . and it all brings back the past a little too acutely."

Mrs. Ansley had resumed her knitting. One might almost have imagined (if one had known her less well, Mrs. Slade reflected) that, for her also, too many memories rose from the lengthening shadows of those august ruins. But no; she was simply absorbed in her work. What was there for her to worry about? She knew that Babs would almost certainly come back engaged to the extremely eligible Campolieri. "And she'll sell the New York house, and settle down near them in Rome, and never be in their way . . . she's much too tactful. But she'll have an excellent cook, and just the right people in for bridge and cocktails . . . and a perfectly peaceful old age among her grandchildren."

Mrs. Slade broke off this prophetic flight with a recoil of self-disgust. There was no one of whom she had less right to think unkindly than of Grace Ansley. Would she never cure herself of envying her? Perhaps she had begun too long ago.

She stood up and leaned against the parapet, filling her troubled eyes with the tranquilizing magic of the hour. But instead of tranquilizing her the sight seemed to increase her exasperation. Her gaze turned toward the Colosseum. Already its golden flank was drowned in purple shadow, and above it the sky curved crystal clear, without light or color. It was the moment when afternoon and evening hang balanced in mid-heaven.

Mrs. Slade turned back and laid her hand on her friend's arm. The gesture was so abrupt that Mrs. Ansley looked up, startled.

"The sun's set. You're not afraid, my dear?"

"Afraid — ?"

"Of Roman fever or pneumonia? I remember how ill you were that winter. As a girl you had a very delicate throat, hadn't you?"

"Oh, we're all right up here. Down below, in the Forum, it does get deathly cold, all of a sudden . . . but not here."

"Ah, of course you know because you had to be so careful." Mrs. Slade turned back to the parapet. She thought: "I must make one more effort not to hate her." Aloud she said: "Whenever I look at the Forum from up here I remember that story about a great-aunt of yours, wasn't she? A dreadfully wicked great-aunt?"

"Oh yes; Great-aunt Harriet. The one who was supposed to have sent her young sister out to the Forum after sunset to gather a night-blooming flower for her album. All our great-aunts and grandmothers used to have albums of dried flowers."

Mrs. Slade nodded. "But she really sent her because they were in love with the same man — "

"Well, that was the family tradition. They said Aunt Harriet confessed it years afterward. At any rate, the poor little sister caught the fever and died. Mother used to frighten us with the story when we were children."

"And you frightened *me* with it, that winter when you and I were here as girls. The winter I was engaged to Delphin."

Mrs. Ansley gave a faint laugh. "Oh, did I? Really frightened you? I don't believe you're easily frightened."

"Not often; but I was then. I was easily frightened because I was too happy. I wonder if you know what that means?"

"I — yes. . . ." Mrs. Ansley faltered.

"Well, I suppose that was why the story of your wicked aunt made such an impression on me. And I thought: 'There's no more Roman fever, but the Forum is deathly cold after sunset — especially after a hot day. And the Colosseum's even colder and damper'."

"The Colosseum — ?"

"Yes. It wasn't easy to get in, after the gates were locked for the night. Far from easy. Still, in those days it could be managed; it was managed, often. Lovers met there who couldn't meet elsewhere. You knew that?"

"I — I daresay. I don't remember."

"You don't remember? You don't remember going to visit some ruins or other one evening, just after dark, and catching a bad chill? You were supposed to have gone to see the moon rise. People always said that expedition was what caused your illness."

There was a moment's silence; then Mrs. Ansley rejoined: "Did they? It was all so long ago."

"Yes. And you got well again — so it didn't matter. But I suppose it struck your friend — the reason given for your illness, I mean — because everybody knew you were so prudent on account of your throat, and your mother took such care of you. . . . You *had* been out late sight-seeing, hadn't you, that night?"

"Perhaps I had. The most prudent girls aren't always prudent. What made you think of it now?"

Mrs. Slade seemed to have no answer ready. But after a moment she broke out: "Because I simply can't bear it any longer — !"

Mrs. Ansley lifted her head quickly. Her eyes were wide and very pale. "Can't bear what?"

"Why — your not knowing that I've always known why you went."

"Why I went — ?"

"Yes. You think I'm bluffing, don't you? Well, you went to meet the man I was engaged to — and I can repeat every word of the letter that took you there."

While Mrs. Slade spoke Mrs. Ansley had risen unsteadily to her feet. Her bag, her knitting and gloves, slid in a panic-stricken heap to the ground. She looked at Mrs. Slade as though she were looking at a ghost.

"No, no — don't," she faltered out.

"Why not? Listen, if you don't believe me. 'My one darling, things can't go on like this. I must see you alone. Come to the Colosseum immediately after dark tomorrow. There will be somebody to let you in. No one whom you need fear will suspect' — but perhaps you've forgotten what the letter said?"

Mrs. Ansley met the challenge with an unexpected composure. Steadying herself against the chair she looked at her friend, and replied: "No; I know it by heart too."

"And the signature? 'Only *your* D. S.' Was that it? I'm right, am I? That was the letter that took you out that evening after dark?"

Mrs. Ansley was still looking at her. It seemed to Mrs. Slade that a slow struggle was going on behind the voluntarily controlled mask of her small quiet face. "I shouldn't have thought she had herself so well in hand," Mrs. Slade reflected, almost resentfully. But at this moment Mrs. Ansley spoke, "I don't know how you knew. I burnt that letter at once."

"Yes; you would, naturally — you're so prudent!" The sneer was open now. "And if you burnt the letter you're wondering how on earth I know what was in it. That's it, isn't it?"

Mrs. Slade waited, but Mrs. Ansley did not speak.

"Well, my dear, I know what was in that letter because I wrote it!"

"You wrote it?"

"Yes."

The two women stood for a minute staring at each other in the last golden light. Then Mrs. Ansley dropped back into her chair. "Oh," she murmured, and covered her face with her hands.

Mrs. Slade waited nervously for another word or movement. None came, and at length she broke out: "I horrify you."

Mrs. Ansley's hands dropped to her knee. The face they uncovered was streaked with tears. "I wasn't thinking of you. I was thinking — it was the only letter I ever had from him!"

"And I wrote it. Yes; I wrote it! But I was the girl he was engaged to. Did you happen to remember that?"

Mrs. Ansley's head drooped again. "I'm not trying to excuse myself. . . . I remembered. . . ."

"And still you went?"

"Still I went."

Mrs. Slade stood looking down on the small bowed figure at her side. The flame of her wrath had already sunk, and she wondered why she had ever thought there would be any satisfaction in inflicting so purposeless a wound on her friend. But she had to justify herself.

"You do understand? I'd found out — and I hated you, hated you. I knew you were in love with Delphin — and I was afraid; afraid of you, of your quiet ways, your sweetness . . . your . . . well, I wanted you out of the way, that's all. Just for a few weeks; just till I was sure of him. So in a blind fury I wrote that letter. . . . I don't know why I'm telling you now."

"I suppose," said Mrs. Ansley slowly, "it's because you've always gone on hating me."

"Perhaps. Or because I wanted to get the whole thing off my mind." She paused. "I'm glad you destroyed the letter. Of course I never thought you'd die."

Mrs. Ansley relapsed into silence, and Mrs. Slade, leaning above her, was conscious of a strange sense of isolation, of being cut off from the warm current of human communion. "You think me a monster!"

"I don't know. . . . It was the only letter I had, and you say he didn't write it?"

"Ah, how you care for him still!"

"I cared for that memory," said Mrs. Ansley.

Mrs. Slade continued to look down on her. She seemed physically reduced by the blow — as if, when she got up, the wind might scatter her like a puff of dust. Mrs. Slade's jealousy suddenly leapt up again at the sight. All these years the woman had been living on that letter. How she must have loved him, to treasure the mere memory of its ashes! The letter of the man her friend was engaged to. Wasn't it she who was the monster?

"You tried your best to get him away from me, didn't you? But you failed; and I kept him. That's all."

"Yes. That's all."

"I wish now I hadn't told you. I'd no idea you'd feel about it as you do; I thought you'd be amused. It all happened so long ago, as you say; and you must do me the justice to remember that I had no reason to think you'd ever taken it seriously. How could I, when you were married to Horace Ansley two months afterward? As soon as you could get out of bed your mother rushed you off to Florence and married you. People were rather surprised — they wondered at its being done so quickly; but I thought I knew. I had an idea you did it out of *pique* — to be able to say you'd got ahead of Delphin and me. Girls have such silly reasons for doing the most serious things. And your marrying so soon convinced me that you'd never really cared."

"Yes. I suppose it would," Mrs. Ansley assented.

The clear heaven overhead was emptied of all its gold. Dusk spread over it, abruptly darkening the Seven Hills. Here and there lights began to twinkle through the foliage at their feet. Steps were coming and going on the deserted terrace — waiters looking out of the doorway at the head of the stairs, then reappearing with trays and napkins and flasks of wine. Tables were moved, chairs straightened. A feeble string of electric lights flickered out. Some vases of faded flowers were carried away, and brought back replenished. A stout lady in a dust-coat suddenly appeared, asking in broken Italian if any one had seen the elastic band which held together her tattered Baedeker. She poked with her stick under the table at which she had lunched, the waiters assisting.

The corner where Mrs. Slade and Mrs. Ansley sat was still shadowy and deserted. For a long time neither of them spoke. At length Mrs. Slade began again: "I suppose I did it as a sort of joke — "

"A joke?"

"Well, girls are ferocious sometimes, you know. Girls in love especially. And I remember laughing to myself all that evening at the idea that you were waiting around there in the dark, dodging out of sight, listening for every sound, trying to get in — Of course I was upset when I heard you were so ill afterward."

Mrs. Ansley had not moved for a long time. But now she turned slowly toward her companion. "But I didn't wait. He'd arranged everything. He was there. We were let in at once," she said.

Mrs. Slade sprang up from her leaning position. "Delphin there? They let you in? — Ah, now you're lying!" she burst out with violence.

Mrs. Ansley's voice grew clearer, and full of surprise. "But of course he was there. Naturally he came — "

"Came? How did he know he'd find you there? You must be raving!"

Mrs. Ansley hesitated, as though reflecting. "But I answered the letter. I told him I'd be there. So he came."

Mrs. Slade flung her hands up to her face. "Oh, God — you answered! I never thought of your answering. . . . "

"It's odd you never thought of it, if you wrote the letter."

"Yes. I was blind with rage."

Mrs. Ansley rose, and drew her fur scarf about her. "It is cold here. We'd better go. . . . I'm sorry for you," she said as she clasped the fur about her throat.

The unexpected words sent a pang through Mrs. Slade. "Yes; we'd better go." She gathered up her bag and cloak. "I don't know why you should be sorry for me," she muttered.

Mrs. Ansley stood looking away from her toward the dusky secret mass of the Colosseum. "Well — because I didn't have to wait that night."

Mrs. Slade gave an unquiet laugh. "Yes; I was beaten there. But I oughtn't to begrudge it to you, I suppose. At the end of all these years. After all, I had everything; I had him for twenty-five years. And you had nothing but that one letter that he didn't write."

Mrs. Ansley was again silent. At length she turned toward the door of the terrace. She took a step, and turned back, facing her companion.

"I had Barbara," she said, and began to move ahead of Mrs. Slade toward the stairway.

[1936]

RUDYARD KIPLING *(1865–1936) was born in Bombay, India. His father was an English pottery designer and connoisseur of Indian art, and his mother was the daughter of a Methodist minister. A delicate child, he was sent back to England at the age of six to board with the family of a woman who was such a tyrant that he suffered a nervous breakdown; and when his mother arrived to visit and bent over to kiss him, he instinctively raised his arm as if to ward off a blow. When he was twelve he went to an English boarding school, but he decided not to go on to a university, returning instead to India to begin work as a journalist for the Lahore* Civil and Military Gazette. *There he wrote his first short stories, later collected in* Plain Tales from the Hills *(1888). Kipling was a prolific author throughout his long life, and he earned the Nobel Prize for Literature in 1907. Today he is probably best known for the whimsy of his short fiction about animals and children, collected in* The Jungle Book *(1894) and* Just So Stories *(1902), and for his picture of Indian life in the novel* Kim *(1901).*

At the turn of the century, when Kipling's popularity was at its height, he stood for the qualities of British imperialism, championing discipline, bravery, and self-sufficiency in patriotic songs and poems like "Gunga Din" and "The Road to Mandalay." Sing-song lines like these:

> *Take up the White Man's Burden —*
> *Send forth the best ye breed —*
> *Go bind your sons to exile*
> *To serve your captive's need . . .*

made Kipling's name synonymous with jingoism and racism. But in more recent years literary critics have called attention to other qualities in his writing, especially to the variety of form in his poetry and to the larger vision of life revealed in the short stories he wrote after he settled down in middle age to live in Sussex, England.

Perhaps his most remarkable story from this period is "The Wish House" (1924), which he wrote in the local English dialect spoken by the two old women who are his main characters. Here he presents what the poet T. S. Eliot regards as a "pagan vision" of the harmony with nature possessed by a selfless, dying country woman who believes superstitiously that she can take on herself "everythin' bad that's in store for my man." Kipling felt that the highest human virtue was the ability to endure the hardships and vicissitudes of life without self-pity. In this story he blends reality and fantasy to suggest the power of love's selflessness and ultimate triumph.

Rudyard Kipling

ౠ

The Wish House

The new church visitor had just left after a twenty minutes' call. During that time, Mrs. Ashcroft had used such English as an elderly, experienced, and pensioned cook should, who had seen life in London. She was the readier, therefore, to slip back into easy, ancient Sussex, (*t*'s softening to '*d*'s as one warmed) when the 'bus brought Mrs. Fettley from thirty miles away for a visit, that pleasant March Saturday. The two had been friends since childhood, but, of late, destiny had separated their meetings by long intervals.

Much was to be said, and many ends, loose since last time, to be ravelled up on both sides, before Mrs. Fettley, with her bag of quilt-patches, took the couch beneath the window commanding the garden, and the football-ground in the valley below.

"Most folk got out at Bush Tye for the match there," she explained, "so there weren't no one for me to cushion agin, the last five mile. An' she *do* justabout bounce ye."

"You've took no hurt," said her hostess. "You don't brittle by agein', Liz."

Mrs. Fettley chuckled and made to match a couple of patches to her liking. "No, or I'd ha' broke twenty year back. You can't ever mind when I was so's to be called round, can ye?"

Mrs. Ashcroft shook her head slowly — she never hurried — and went on stitching a sack-cloth lining into a list-bound rush tool-basket. Mrs. Fettley laid out more patches in the spring light through the geraniums on the window-sill, and they were silent awhile.

"What like's this new Visitor o' yourn?" Mrs. Fettley inquired, with a nod toward the door. Being very short-sighted, she had, on her entrance, almost bumped into the lady.

Mrs. Ashcroft suspended the big packing-needle judicially on high, ere she stabbed home. "Settin' aside she don't bring much news with her yet, I dunno as I've anythin' special agin her."

"Ourn, at Keyneslade," said Mrs. Fettley, "she's full o' words an' pity, but she don't stay for answers. Ye can get on with your thoughts while she clacks."

"This 'un don't clack. She's aimin' to be one o' those High Church nuns, like."

"Ourn's married, but, by what they say, she've made no great gains of it. . . ." Mrs. Fettley threw up her sharp chin. "Lord! How they dam' cherubim do shake the very bones o' the place!"

The tile-sided cottage trembled at the passage of two specially chartered forty-seat charabancs[1] on their way to the Bush Tye match; a regular Saturday "shopping" 'bus, for the county's capital, fumed behind them; while, from one of the crowded inns, a fourth car backed out to join the procession, and held up the stream of through pleasure-traffic.

"You're as free-tongued as ever, Liz," Mrs. Ashcroft observed.

"Only when I'm with you. Otherwhiles, I'm Granny — three times over. I lay that basket's for one o' your gran'-chiller — ain't it?"

" 'Tis for Arthur — my Jane's eldest."

"But he ain't workin' nowheres, is he?"

"No. 'Tis a picnic-basket."

"You're let off light. My Willie, he's allus at me for money for them aireated wash-poles folk puts up in their gardens to draw the music from Lunnon, like. An' I give it 'im — pore fool me!"

"An' he forgets to give you the promise-kiss after, don't he?" Mrs. Ashcroft's heavy smile seemed to strike inwards.

"He do. No odds 'twixt boys now an' forty year back. Take all an' give naught — an we to put up with it! Pore fool we! Three shillin' at a time Willie'll ask me for!"

"They don't make nothin' o' money these days," Mrs. Ashcroft said.

"An' on'y last week," the other went on, "me daughter she ordered a quarter-pound suet at the butchers's; an' she sent it back to 'im to be chopped. She said she couldn't bother with choppin' it."

"I lay he charged her, then."

"I lay he did. She told me there was a whisk-drive that afternoon at the Institute, an' she couldn't bother to do the choppin'."

"Tck!"

Mrs. Ashcroft put the last firm touches to the basket-lining. She had scarcely finished when her sixteen-year-old grandson, a maiden of the moment in attendance, hurried up the garden-path shouting to know if the thing were ready, snatched it, and made off without acknowledgment. Mrs. Fettley peered at him closely.

"They're goin' picnickin' somewheres," Mrs. Ashcroft explained.

"Ah," said the other, with narrowed eyes. "I lay he won't show much mercy to any he comes across, either. Now 'oo the dooce do he remind me of, all of a sudden?"

---

[1] sightseeing buses.

"They must look arter theirselves — same as we did." Mrs. Ashcroft began to set out the tea.

"No denyin' *you* could, Gracie," said Mrs. Fettley.

"What's in your head now?"

"Dunno. . . . But it come over me, sudden-like — about dat woman from Rye — I've slipped the name — Barnsley, wadn't it?"

"Batten — Polly Batten, you're thinkin' of."

"That's it — Polly Batten. That day she had it in for you with a hay-fork — time we was all hayin' at Smalldene — for stealin' her man."

"But you heered me tell her she had my leave to keep him?" Mrs. Ashcroft's voice and smile were smoother than ever.

"I did — an' we was all looking that she'd prod the fork spang through your breastës when you said it."

"No-oo. She'd never go beyond bounds — Polly. She shruck too much for reel doin's."

"Allus seems to *me*," Mrs. Fettley said after a pause, "that a man 'twixt two fightin' women is the foolishest thing on earth. Like a dog bein' called two ways."

"Mebbe. But what set ye off on those times, Liz?"

"That boy's fashion o' carryin' his head an' arms. I haven't rightly looked at him since he's growed. Your Jane never showed it, but — *him!* Why, 'tis Jim Batten and his tricks come to life again! . . . Eh?"

"Mebbe. There's some that would ha' made it out so — bein' barren-like, themselves."

"Oho! Ah well! Dearie, dearie me, now! . . . An' Jim Batten's been dead this —— "

"Seven-and-twenty year," Mrs. Ashcroft answered briefly. "Won't ye draw up, Liz?"

Mrs. Fettley drew up to buttered toast, currant bread, stewed tea, bitter as leather, some home-preserved pears, and a cold boiled pig's tail to help down the muffins. She paid all the proper compliments.

"Yes. I dunno as I've ever owed me belly much," said Mrs. Ashcroft thoughtfully. "We only go through this world once."

"But don't it lay heavy on ye, sometimes?" her guest suggested.

"Nurse says I'm a sight liker to die o' me indigestion than me leg." For Mrs. Ashcroft had a long-standing ulcer on her shin, which needed regular care from the Village Nurse, who boasted (or others did, for her) that she had dressed it one hundred and three times already during her term of office.

"An' you that *was* so able, too! It's all come on ye before your full time, like. *I've* watched ye goin'." Mrs. Fettley spoke with real affection.

"Somethin's bound to find ye sometime. I've me 'eart left me still," Mrs. Ashcroft returned.

"You was always big-hearted enough for three. That's somethin' to look back on at the day's eend."

"I reckon you've *your* back-lookin's, too," was Mrs. Ashcroft's answer.

"You know it. But I don't think much regardin' such matters excep' when I'm along with you, Gra'. Takes two sticks to make a fire."

Mrs. Fettley stared, with jaw half-dropped, at the grocer's bright calendar on the wall. The cottage shook again to the roar of the motor-traffic, and the crowded football-ground below the garden roared almost as loudly; for the village was well set to its Saturday leisure.

Mrs. Fettley had spoken very precisely for some time without interruption, before she wiped her eyes. "And," she concluded, "they read 'is death-notice to me, out o' the paper last month. O' course it wasn't any o' *my* becomin' concerns — let be I 'adn't set eyes on him for so long. O' course *I* couldn't say nor show nothin'. Nor I've no rightful call to go to Eastbourne to see 'is grave, either. I've been schemin' to slip over there by the 'bus some day; but they'd ask questions at 'ome past endurance. So I 'aven't even *that* to stay me."

"But you've 'ad your satisfactions?"

"Godd! Yess! Those four years 'e was workin' on the rail near us. An' the other drivers they gave him a brave funeral, too."

"Then you've naught to cast-up about. 'Nother cup o' tea?"

The light and air had changed a little with the sun's descent, and the two elderly ladies closed the kitchen-door against chill. A couple of jays squealed and skirmished through the undraped apple-trees in the garden. This time, the word was with Mrs. Ashcroft, her elbows on the tea-table, and her sick leg propped on a stool. . . .

"Well, I never! But what did your 'usband say to that?" Mrs. Fettley asked, when the deep-toned recital halted.

" 'E said I might go where I pleased for all of 'im. But seein' 'e was bedrid, I said I'd 'tend 'im out. 'E knowed I wouldn't take no advantage of 'im in that state. 'E lasted eight or nine week. Then he was took with a seizure-like; an' laid stone-still for days. Then 'e propped 'imself up abed an' says: 'You pray, no man'll ever deal with you like you've dealt with some.' 'An' you?' I says, for *you* know, Liz, what a rover 'e was. 'It cuts both ways,' says 'e, 'but I'm death-wise, an' I can see what's comin' to you.' He died a-Sunday an' was buried a-Thursday . . . An' yet I'd set a heap by him — one time, or — did I ever?"

"You never told me that before," Mrs. Fettley ventured.

"I'm payin' ye for what ye told me just now. Him bein' dead, I wrote up, sayin' I was free for good, to that Mrs. Marshall in Lunnon — which gave me my first place as kitchen-maid — Lord, how long ago! She was well pleased, for they two was both gettin' on, an' I knowed their ways. You remember, Liz, I used to go to 'em in service between whiles, for years — when we wanted money, or — or my 'usband was away — on occasion."

" 'E *did* get that six months at Chichester, didn't 'e?" Mrs. Fettley whispered. "We never rightly won to the bottom of it."

" 'E'd ha' got more, but the man didn't die."

"None o' your doin's, was it, Gra'?"

"No! 'Twas the woman's 'usband this time. An' so, my man bein' dead, I went back to them Marshalls, as cook, to get me legs under a gentleman's table again, and be called with a handle to me name. That was the year you shifted to Portsmouth."

"Cosham," Mrs. Fettley corrected. "There was a middlin' lot o' new buildin' bein' done there. My man went first, an' got the room, an' I follered."

"Well, then, I was a year-abouts in Lunnon, all at a breath, like, four meals a day an' livin' easy. Then, 'long towards autumn, they two went travellin', like, to France; keepin' me on, for they couldn't do without me. I put the house to rights for the caretaker, an' then I slipped down 'ere to me sister Bessie — me wages in me pockets, an' all 'ands glad to be'old of me."

"That would be when I was at Cosham," said Mrs. Fettley.

"*You* know, Liz, there wasn't no cheap-dog pride to folk, those days, no more than there was cinemas nor whisk-drives. Man or woman 'ud lay hold o' any job that promised a shillin' to the backside of it, didn't they? I was all peaked up after Lunnon, an' I thought the fresh airs 'ud serve me. So I took on at Smalldene, obligin' with a hand at the early potato-liftin', stubbin' hens, an' such-like. They'd ha' mocked me sore in my kitchen in Lunnon, to see me in men's boots, an' me petticoats all shorted."

"Did it bring ye any good?" Mrs. Fettley asked.

"Twadn't for that I went. You know, 's well's me, that na'un happens to ye till it '*as* 'appened. Your mind don't warn ye before'and of the road ye've took, till you're at the far eend of it. We've only a backwent view of our proceedin's."

" 'Oo was it?"

" 'Arry Mockler." Mrs. Ashcroft's face puckered to the pain of her sick leg.

Mrs. Fettley gasped. " 'Arry? Bert Mockler's son! An' *I* never guessed!"

Mrs. Ashcroft nodded. "An' I told myself — *an'* I beleft it — that I wanted field-work."

"What did ye get out of it?"

"The usuals. Everythin' at first — worse than naught after. I had signs an' warnings a-plenty, but I took no heed of 'em. For we was burnin' rubbish one day, just when we'd come to know how 'twas with — with both of us. 'Twas early in the year for burnin', an' I said so. 'No!' says he. 'The sooner dat old stuff's off an' done with,' 'e says, 'the better.' 'Is face was harder'n rocks when he spoke. Then it come over me that I'd found me master, which I 'adn't ever before. I'd allus owned 'em, like."

"Yes! Yes! They're yourn or you're theirn," the other sighed. "I like the right way best."

"I didn't. But 'Arry did . . . 'Long then, it come time for me to go back to Lunnon. I couldn't. I clean couldn't! So I took an' tipped a dollop o' scaldin' water out o' the copper one Monday mornin' over me left 'and and arm. Dat stayed me where I was for another fortnight."

"Was it worth it?" said Mrs. Fettley, looking at the silvery scar on the wrinkled forearm.

Mrs. Ashcroft nodded. "An' after that, we two made it up 'twixt us so's 'e could come to Lunnon for a job in a liv'ry-stable not far from me. 'E got it. I 'tended to that. There wadn't no talk nowhere. His own mother never suspicioned how 'twas. He just slipped up to Lunnon, an' there we abode that winter, not 'alf a mile 'tother from each."

"Ye paid 'is fare an' all, though." Mrs. Fettley spoke convincedly.

Again Mrs. Ashcroft nodded. "Dere wadn't much I didn't do for him. 'E was me master, an' — O God, help us! — we'd laugh over it walkin' together after dark in them paved streets, an' me corns fair wrenchin' in me boots! I'd never been like that before. Ner he! Ner he!"

Mrs. Fettley clucked sympathetically.

"An' when did ye come to the eend?" she asked.

"When 'e paid it all back again, every penny. Then I knowed, but I wouldn't *suffer* meself to know. 'You've been mortal kind to me,' he says. 'Kind!' I said. ' 'Twixt *us*?' But 'e kep' all on tellin' me 'ow kind I'd been an' 'e'd never forget it all his days. I held it from off o' me for three evenin's, because I would *not* believe. Then 'e talked about not bein' satisfied with 'is job in the stables, an' the men there puttin' tricks on 'im, an' all they lies which a man tells when 'e's leavin' ye. I heard 'im out, neither 'elpin' nor 'inderin'. At the last, I took off a liddle brooch, which he'd give me an' I says: 'Dat'll do. I ain't askin' na'un.' An' I turned me round an' walked off to me own sufferin's. 'E didn't make 'em worse. 'E didn't come nor write after that. 'E slipped off 'ere back 'ome to 'is mother again."

"An' 'ow often did ye look for 'en to come back?" Mrs. Fettley demanded mercilessly.

"More'n once — more'n once! Goin' over the streets we'd used, I thought de very pave-stones 'ud shruck out under me feet."

"Yes," said Mrs. Fettley. "I dunno but dat don't 'urt as much as aught else. An' dat was all ye got?"

"No. 'Twadn't. That's the curious part, if you'll believe it, Liz."

"I do. I lay you're further off lyin' now than in all your life, Gra'."

"I am. . . . An' I suffered, like I'd not wish my most arrantest enemies to. God's Own Name! I went through the hoop that spring! One part of it was 'eddicks which I'd never known all me days before. Think o' *me* with an 'eddick! But I come to be grateful for 'em. They kep' me from thinkin'. . . ."

" 'Tis like a tooth," Mrs. Fettley commented. "It must rage an' rugg till it tortures itself quiet on ye; an' then — then there's na'un left."

"*I* got enough lef' to last me all *my* days on earth. It come about through our charwoman's liddle girl — Sophy Ellis was 'er name — all eyes an' elbers an' hunger. I used to give 'er vittles. Otherwhiles, I took no special notice of 'er, an' a sight less, o' course, when me trouble about 'Arry was on me. But — you know how liddle maids first feel it sometimes — she come to be crazy-fond o' me, pawin' an' cuddlin' all whiles; an' I 'adn't the 'eart to beat 'er off. . . . One afternoon, early in spring 'twas, 'er mother 'ad sent 'er round to scutchel up what vittles she could off of us. I was settin' by the fire, me apern over me head, half-mad with the 'eddick, when she slips in. I reckon I was middlin' short with 'er. 'Lor'!' she says. 'Is *that* all? I'll take it off you in two-twos!' I told her not to lay a finger on me, for I thought she'd want to stroke my forehead; an' — I ain't that make. '*I* won't tech ye,' she says, an' slips out again. She 'adn't been gone ten minutes 'fore me old 'eddick took off quick as bein' kicked. So I went about my work. Prasin'ly, Sophy comes back, an' creeps into my chair quiet as a mouse. 'Er eyes was deep in 'er 'ead an' 'er face all drawed. I asked 'er what 'ad 'appened. 'Nothin',' she says. 'On'y *I've* got it now.' 'Got what?' I says. 'Your 'eddick,' she says, all hoarse an' sticky-lipped. 'I've took it on me.' 'Nonsense,' I says, 'it went of itself when you was out. Lay still an' I'll make ye a cup o' tea.' ' 'Twon't do no good,' she says, 'til your time's up. 'Ow long do *your* 'eddicks last?' 'Don't talk silly,' I says, 'or I'll send for the Doctor.' It looked to me like she might be hatchin' de measles. 'Oh, Mrs. Ashcroft,' she says, stretchin' out 'er liddle thin arms. 'I *do* love ye.' There wasn't any holdin' agin that. I took 'er into me lap an' made much of 'er. 'Is it truly gone?' she says. 'Yes,' I says, 'an' if 'twas you took it away, I'm truly grateful.' ' '*Twas* me,' she says, layin' 'er cheek to mine. 'No one but me knows how.' An' then she said she'd changed me 'eddick for me at a Wish 'Ouse."

"Whatt?" Mrs. Fettley spoke sharply.

"A Wish House. No! *I* 'adn't 'eard o' such things, either. I couldn't get it straight at first, but, puttin' all together, I made out that a Wish 'Ouse 'ad to be a house which 'ad stood unlet an' empty long enough for Some One, like, to come an' in'abit there. She said a liddle girl that she'd played with in the livery-stables where 'Arry worked 'ad told 'er so. She said the girl 'ad belonged in a caravan that laid up, o' winters, in Lunnon. Gipsy, I judge."

"Oh! There's no sayin' what Gippos know, but *I've* never 'eard of a Wish 'Ouse, an' I know — some things," said Mrs. Fettley.

"Sophy said there was a Wish 'Ouse in Wadloes Road — just a few streets off, on the way to our greengrocer's. All you 'ad to do, she said, was to ring the bell an' wish your wish through the slit o' the letter-box. I asked 'er if the fairies give it 'er. 'Don't ye know,' she says, 'there's no fairies in a Wish 'Ouse? There's on'y a Token.' "

"Goo' Lord A'mighty! Where did she come by *that* word?" cried Mrs. Fettley; for a Token is a wraith of the dead or, worse still, of the living.

"The caravan-girl 'ad told 'er, she said. Well, Liz, it troubled me to 'ear 'er, an' lyin' in me arms she must ha' felt it. 'That's very kind o' you, ' I says, holdin' 'er tight, 'to wish me 'eddick away. But why didn't ye ask somethin' nice for yourself?' 'You can't do that,' she says. 'All you'll get at a Wish 'Ouse is leave to take some one else's trouble. I've took Ma's 'eddicks, when she's been kind to me; but this is the first time I've been able to do aught for you. Oh, Mrs. Ashcroft, I *do* justabout love you.' An' she goes on all like that. Liz, I tell you my 'air e'en a'most stood on end to 'ear 'er. I asked 'er what like a Token was. 'I dunno,' she says, 'but after you've ringed the bell, you'll 'ear it run up from the basement, to the front door. Then say your wish,' she says, 'an' go away.' 'The Token don't open de door to ye, then?' I says. 'Oh no,' she says. 'You on'y 'ear gigglin', like, be'ind the front door. Then you say you'll take the trouble off of 'ooever 'tis you've chose for your love; an' ye'll get it,' she says. I didn't ask no more — she was too 'ot an' fevered. I made much of 'er till it come time to light de gas, an' a liddle after that 'er 'eddick — mine, I suppose — took off, an' she got down an' played with the cat."

"Well, I never!" said Mrs. Fettley. "Did — did ye foller it up, anyways?"

"She askt me to, but I wouldn't 'ave no such dealin's with a child."

"What *did* ye do, then?"

"Sat in me own room 'stid o' the kitchen when me 'eddicks come on. But it lay at de back o' me mind."

" 'Twould. Did she tell ye more, ever?"

"No. Besides what the Gippo girl 'ad told 'er, she knew naught, 'cept that the charm worked. An', next after that — in May 'twas — I suffered the summer out in Lunnon. 'Twas hot an' windy for weeks, an' the streets stinkin' o' dried 'orse-dung blowin' from side to side an' lyin' level with the kerb. We don't get that nowadays. I 'ad my 'ol'day just before hoppin', an' come down 'ere to stay with Bessie again. She noticed I'd lost flesh, an' was all poochy under the eyes."

"Did ye see 'Arry?"

Mrs. Ashcroft nodded. "The fourth — no, the fifth day. Wednesday 'twas. I knowed 'e was workin' at Smalldene again. I asked 'is mother in the street, bold as brass. She 'adn't room to say much, for Bessie — you know 'er tongue — was talkin' full-clack. But that Wednesday, I was walkin' with one o' Bessie's chillern hangin' on me skirts, at de back o' Chanter's Tot. Prasin'ly, I felt 'e was be'ind me on the footpath, an' I knowed by 'is tread 'e'd changed 'is nature. I slowed, an' I heard 'im slow. Then I fussed a piece with the child, to force him past me, like. So 'e 'ad to come past. 'E just says 'Good-evenin',' and goes on, tryin' to pull 'isself together."

"Drunk, was he?" Mrs. Fettley asked.

"Never! S'runk an' wizen; 'is clothes 'angin' on 'im like bags, an' the back of 'is neck whiter'n chalk. 'Twas all I could do not to oppen my arms an' cry after him. But I swallered me spittle till I was back 'ome again an' the chillern abed. Then I says to Bessie, after supper, 'What in de world's come to 'Arry Mockler?' Bessie told me 'e'd been a-Hospital for two months, 'long o' cuttin' 'is foot wid a spade, muckin' out de old pond at Smalldene. There was poison in de dirt, an' it rooshed up 'is leg, like, an' come out all over him. 'E 'adn't been back to 'is job — carterin' at Small-dene — more'n a fortnight. She told me the Doctor said he'd go off, likely, with the November frostës; an' 'is mother 'ad told 'er that 'e didn't rightly eat nor sleep, an' sweated 'imself into pools, no odds 'ow chill 'e lay. *An'* spit terrible o' mornin's. 'Dearie me,' I says. 'But, mebbe, hoppin' 'll set 'im right again,' an' I licked me thread-point, an' I fetched me needle's eye up to it an' I threads me needle under de lamp, steady as rocks. An' dat night (me bed was in de wash-house) I cried an' I cried. An' *you* know, Liz — for you've been with me in me throes — it takes summat to make me cry."

"Yes; but chile-bearin' is on'y just pain," said Mrs. Fettley.

"I come round by cock-crow, an' dabbed cold tea on me eyes to take away the signs. Long towards nex' evenin' — I was settin' out to lay some flowers on me 'usband's grave, for the look o' the thing — I met 'Arry over against where the War Memorial is now. 'E was comin' back from 'is 'orses, so 'e couldn't *not* see me. I looked 'im all over, an' ''Arry,' I says 'twix' me teeth, 'come back an' rest-up in Lunnon.' 'I won't take it,' he says, 'for I can give ye naught.' 'I don't ask it,' I says. 'By God's Own Name, I don't ask na'un! On'y come up an' see a Lunnon doctor.' 'E lifts 'is two 'eavy eyes at me: ' 'Tis past that, Gra',' 'e says. 'I've but a few months left.' ''Arry!' I says. '*My* man!' I says. I couldn't say no more. 'Twas all up in me throat. 'Thank ye kindly, Gra',' 'e says (but 'e never says 'my woman'), an' 'e went on up-street, an' 'is mother — Oh, damn 'er! — she was watchin' for 'im, an' she shut de door be'ind 'im."

Mrs. Fettley stretched an arm across the table, and made to finger Mrs. Ashcroft's sleeve at the wrist, but the other moved it out of reach.

"So I went on the churchyard with me flowers, an' I remembered me 'usband's warnin' that night he spoke. 'E *was* death-wise, an' it 'ad 'appened as 'e said. But as I was settin' down de jam-pot on the grave-mound, it come over me there was one thing I *could* do for 'Arry. Doctor or no Doctor, I thought I'd make a trial of it. So I did. Nex' mornin', a bill came down from our Lunnon greengrocer. Mrs. Marshall she'd lef' me petty cash for suchlike — o' course — but I tole Bess 'twas for me to come an' open the 'ouse. So I went up, afternoon train."

"An' — but I know you 'adn't — 'adn't you no fear?"

"What for? There was nothin' front o' me but me own shame an' God's croolty. I couldn't ever get 'Arry — 'ow *could* I? I knowed it must go on burnin' till it burned me out."

"Aie!" said Mrs. Fettley, reaching for the wrist again, and this time Mrs. Ashcroft permitted it.

"Yit 'twas a comfort to know I could try *this* for 'im. So I went an' I paid the greengrocer's bill, an' put 'is receipt in me hand-bag, an' then I stepped round to Mrs. Ellis — our char — an' got the 'ouse-keys an' opened the 'ouse. First, I made me bed to come back to (God's Own Name! Me bed to lie upon!). Nex' I made me a cup o' tea an' sat down in the kitchen thinkin', till 'long towards dusk. Terrible close, 'twas. Then I dressed me an' went out with the receipt in me 'and-bag, feignin' to study it for an address, like. Fourteen, Wadloes Road, was the place — a liddle basement-kitchen 'ouse, in a row of twenty-thirty such, an' tiddy strips o' walled garden in front — the paint off the front doors, an' na'un done to na'un since ever so long. There wasn't 'ardly no one in the streets 'cept the cats. *'Twas* 'ot, too! I turned into the gate bold as brass; up de steps I went an' I ringed the front-door bell. She pealed loud, like it do in an empty house. When she'd all ceased, I 'eard a cheer, like, pushed back on de floor o' the kitchen. Then I 'eard feet on de kitchen-stairs, like it might ha' been a heavy woman in slippers. Dey come up to de stair-head, acrost the hall — I 'eard the bare boards creak under 'em — an' at de front door dey stopped. I stooped me to the letter-box slit, an' I says: 'Let me take everythin' bad that's in store for my man, 'Arry Mockler, for love's sake.' Then, whatever it was 'tother side the door let its breath out, like, as if it 'ad been holdin' it for to 'ear better."

"Nothin' was *said* to ye?" Mrs. Fettley demanded.

"Na'un. She just breathed out — a sort of *A-ah*, like. Then the steps went back an' downstairs to the kitchen — all draggy — an' I heard the cheer drawed up again."

"An' you abode on de doorstep, throughout all, Gra'?"

Mrs. Ashcroft nodded.

"Then I went away, an' a man passin' says to me: 'Didn't you know that house was empty?' 'No,' I says. 'I must ha' been give the wrong number.' An' I went back to our 'ouse, an' I went to bed; for I was fair flogged out. 'Twas too 'ot to sleep more'n snatches, so I walked me about, lying down betweens, till crack o' dawn. Then I went to the kitchen to make me a cup o' tea, an' I hitted meself just above the ankle on an old roastin'-jack o' mine that Mrs. Ellis had moved out from the corner, her last cleanin'. An' so — nex' after that — I waited till the Marshalls come back o' their holiday."

"Alone there? I'd ha' thought you'd 'ad enough of empty houses," said Mrs. Fettley, horrified.

"Oh, Mrs. Ellis an' Sophy was runnin' in an' out soon's I was back, an' 'twixt us we cleaned de house again top-to-bottom. There's allus a hand's turn more to do in every house. An' that's 'ow 'twas with me that autumn an' winter, in Lunnon."

"Then na'un hap — overtook ye for your doin's?"

Mrs. Ashcroft smiled. "No. Not then. 'Long in November I sent Bessie ten shillin's."

"You was allus free-'anded," Mrs. Fettley interrupted.

"An' I got what I paid for, with the rest o' the news. She said the hoppin' 'ad set 'im up wonderful. 'E'd 'ad six weeks of it, and now 'e was back again carterin' at Smalldene. No odds to me *'ow* it 'ad 'appened — 's long's it *'ad*. But I dunno as my ten shillin's eased me much. 'Arry bein' *dead*, like, 'e'd ha' been mine, till Judgment. 'Arry bein' alive, 'e'd like as not pick up with some woman middlin' quick. I raged over that. Come spring, I 'ad somethin' else to rage for. I'd growed a nasty little weepin' boil, like, on me shin, just above the boot-top, that wouldn't heal no shape. It made me sick to look at it, for I'm clean-fleshed by nature. Chop me all over with a spade, an' I'd heal like turf. Then Mrs. Marshall she set 'er own doctor at me. 'E said I ought to ha' come to him at first go-off, 'stead o' drawin' all manner o' dyed stockin's over it for months. 'E said I'd stood up too much to me work, for it was settin' very close atop of a big swelled vein, like, behither the small o' me ankle. 'Slow come, slow go,' 'e says. 'Lay your leg up on high an' rest it,' he says, 'an' 'twill ease off. Don't let it close up too soon. You've got a very fine leg, Mrs. Ashcroft,' 'e says. An' he put wet dressin's on it."

" 'E done right." Mrs. Fettley spoke firmly. "Wet dressin's to wet wounds. They draw de humors, same's a lamp-wick draws de oil."

"That's true. An' Mrs. Marshall was allus at me to make me set down more, an' dat nigh healed it up. An' then after a while they packed me off down to Bessie's to finish the cure; for I ain't the sort to sit down when I ought to stand up. You was back in the village then, Liz."

"I was. I was, but — never did I guess!"

"I didn't desire ye to." Mrs. Ashcroft smiled. "I saw 'Arry once or twice in de street, wonnerful fleshed up an' restored back. Then, one day I didn't see 'im, an' 'is mother told me one of 'is 'orses 'ad lashed out an' caught 'im on the 'ip. So 'e was abed an' middlin' painful. An' Bessie, she says to his mother, 'twas a pity 'Arry 'adn't a woman of 'is own to take the nursin' off 'er. And the old lady *was* mad! She told us that 'Arry 'ad never looked after any woman in 'is born days, an' as long as she was atop the mowlds, she'd contrive for 'im till 'er two 'ands dropped off. So I knowed she'd do watch-dog for me, 'thout askin' for bones."

Mrs. Fettley rocked with small laughter.

"That day," Mrs. Ashcroft went on, "I'd stood on me feet nigh all the time, watchin' the doctor go in an' out; for they thought it might be 'is ribs, too. That made my boil break again, issuin' an' weepin'. But it turned out 'twadn't ribs at all, an' 'Arry 'ad a good night. When I heard that, nex' mornin', I says to meself, 'I won't lay two an' two together *yit*. I'll keep me leg down a week, an' see what comes of it.' It didn't hurt me that day, to speak of — seemed more to draw the strength out o' me like — an' 'Arry 'ad another good night. That made me persevere; but I didn't dare lay two an' two together till the week-end, an' then, 'Arry come forth e'en a'most 'imself again — na'un hurt outside ner in of him. I nigh fell on me knees in de wash-house when Bessie was up-street. 'I've got ye now, my man,' I says. 'You'll take your good from me 'thout knowin' it till my life's end. O God, send me long to live for 'Arry's sake!' I says. An' I dunno that didn't still me ragin's."

"For good?" Mrs. Fettley asked.

"They come back, plenty times, but, let be how 'twould, I knowed I was doin' for 'im. I *knowed* it. I took an' worked me pains on an' off, like regulatin' me own range, till I learned to 'ave 'em at my commandments. An' that was funny, too. There was times, Liz, when my trouble 'ud all s'rink an' dry up, like. First, I used to try an' fetch it on again; bein' fearful to leave 'Arry alone too long for anythin' to lay 'old of. Prasin'ly I come to see that was a sign he'd do all right awhile, an' so I saved myself."

" 'Ow long for?" Mrs. Fettley asked, with deepest interest.

"I've gone de better part of a year onct or twice with na'un more to show than the liddle weepin' core of it, like. *All* s'rinked up an' dried off. Then he'd inflame up — for a warnin' — an' I'd suffer it. When I couldn't no more — an' I 'ad to keep on goin' with my Lunnon work — I'd lay me leg high on a cheer till it eased. Not too quick. I knowed by the feel of it, those times, dat 'Arry was in need. Then I'd send another five shillin's to Bess, or somethin' for the chillern, to find out if, mebbe, 'e'd took any hurt through my neglects. 'Twas *so!* Year in, year out, I worked in dat way, Liz, an' 'e got 'is good from me 'thout knowin' — for years and years."

"But what did *you* get out of it, Gra'?" Mrs. Fettley almost wailed. "Did ye see 'im reg'lar?"

"Times — when I was 'ere on me 'ol'days. An' more, now that I'm 'ere for good. But 'e's never looked at me, ner any other woman 'cept 'is mother. 'Ow I used to watch an' listen! So did she."

"Years an' years!" Mrs. Fettley repeated. "An' where's 'e workin' at now?"

"Oh, 'e's give up carterin' quite a while. He's workin' for one o' them big tractorisin' firms — plowin' sometimes, an' sometimes off with lorries — fur as Wales, I've 'eard. He comes 'ome to 'is mother 'tween whiles; but I don't set eyes on him now, fer weeks on end. No odds! 'Is job keeps 'im from continuin' in one stay anywheres."

"But — just for de sake o' sayin' somethin' — s'pose 'Arry *did* get married?" said Mrs. Fettley.

Mrs. Ashcroft drew her breath sharply between her still even and natural teeth. "*Dat* ain't been required of me," she answered. "I reckon my pains 'ull be counted agin that. Don't *you*, Liz?"

"It ought to be, dearie. It ought to be."

"It *do* 'urt sometimes. You shall see it when Nurse comes. She thinks I don't know it's turned."

Mrs. Fettley understood. Human nature seldom walks up to the word "cancer."

"Be ye certain sure, Gra'?" she asked.

"I was sure of it when old Mr. Marshall 'ad me up to 'is study an' spoke a long piece about my faithful service. I've obliged 'em on an' off for a goodish time, but not enough for a pension. But they give me a weekly 'lowance for life. I knew what *that* sinnified — as long as three years ago."

"Dat don't *prove* it, Gra'."

"To give fifteen bob a week to a woman 'oo'd live twenty year in the course o' nature? It *do!*"

"You're mistook! You're mistook!" Mrs. Fettley insisted.

"Liz, there's *no* mistakin' when the edges are all heaped up, like — same as a collar. You'll see it. An' I laid out Dora Wickwood, too. *She* 'ad it under the arm-pit, like."

Mrs. Fettley considered awhile, and bowed her head in finality.

" 'Ow long d'you reckon 'twill allow ye, countin' from now, dearie?"

"Slow come, slow go. But if I don't set eyes on ye 'fore next hoppin', this'll be good-bye, Liz."

"Dunno as I'll be able to manage by then — not 'thout I have a liddle dog to lead me. For de chillern, dey won't be troubled, an' — O Gra'! — I'm blindin' up — I'm blindin' up!"

"Oh, *dat* was why you didn't more'n finger with your quilt-patches all this while! I was wonderin'. . . . But the pain *do* count, don't ye think, Liz? The pain *do* count to keep 'Arry — where I want 'im. Say it can't be wasted, like."

"I'm sure of it — sure of it, dearie. You'll 'ave your reward."

"I don't want no more'n this — *if* de pain is taken into de reckonin'."

" 'Twill be — 'twill be, Gra'."

There was a knock on the door.

"That's Nurse. She's before 'er time," said Mrs. Ashcroft. "Open to 'er."

The young lady entered briskly, all the bottles in her bag clicking. "Evenin', Mrs. Ashcroft," she began. "I've come raound a little earlier than usual because of the Institute dance to-na-ite. You won't ma-ind, will you?"

"Oh no. Me dancin' days are over." Mrs. Ashcroft was the self-contained domestic at once. "My old friend, Mrs. Fettley 'ere, has been settin' talkin' with me a while."

"I hope she 'asn't been fatiguing you," said the Nurse a little frostily.

"Quite the contrary. It 'as been a pleasure. Only — only — just at the end I felt a bit — a bit flogged out, like."

"Yes, yes." The Nurse was on her knees already, with the washes to hand. "When old ladies get together they talk a deal too much, I've noticed."

"Mebbe we do," said Mrs. Fettley, rising. "So now I'll make myself scarce."

"Look at it first, though," said Mrs. Ashcroft feebly. "I'd like ye to look at it."

Mrs. Fettley looked, and shivered. Then she leaned over, and kissed Mrs. Ashcroft once on the waxy yellow forehead, and again on the faded grey eyes.

"It *do* count, don't it — de pain?" The lips that still kept trace of their original moulding hardly more than breathed the words.

Mrs. Fettley kissed them and moved toward the door.

[1924]

STEPHEN CRANE (1871–1900), *in his short stories and novels, forecast a new direction in American literature. As the literary critics Carl and Mark Van Doren wrote, "Modern fiction may be said to begin with Stephen Crane." Although he lived only twenty-nine years — a shorter lifetime than Poe's — Crane wrote some of the most memorable fiction and poetry ever created by an American. He published fourteen books in his energetic lifetime, even while striking his contemporaries as a typically irresponsible genius who acted out the legend of the writer as soldier of fortune. The poet John Berryman, who wrote a biography of Crane, observed the essential truth about him, however: "Crane was a writer and nothing else: a man alone in a room with the English language, trying to get human feelings right." Crane's style in his short stories is as intensely personal as Poe's and Hawthorne's, but he does not make use of the techniques of fantasy and allegory. "His eyes remained wide open on his world. He was almost illusionless, whether about his subjects or himself. Perhaps his sole illusion was the heroic one; and not even this, especially if he was concerned in it himself as a man, escaped his irony."*

Stephen Crane was born in Newark, New Jersey, the youngest of fourteen children. His father, a Methodist minister, died when Crane was just a boy, and his mother supported the family by writing articles for Methodist papers and reporting for the New York Tribune and the Philadelphia Press. Crane briefly attended Lafayette College and Syracuse University before going to work in New York City as a freelance journalist. He became deeply interested in life along the Bowery, one of the worst slums in New York, and he used this setting for his novel Maggie: A Girl of the Streets. *Maggie was so grimly naturalistic in its portrayal of slum life and so frank in its treatment of sex that Crane had to publish it at his own expense in 1893. Two years later he sold a long story about the Civil War to a syndicate for less than $100. That work,* The Red Badge of Courage, *was such a vivid, imaginatively rendered account of wartime experience — even though Crane had never been in a battle himself — that it established his literary reputation. It remains his most famous work. In the last five years of his life, before he died of tuberculosis in Germany, Crane traveled extensively as a reporter, first to the American West, then to Florida. He was en route to Florida on the steamship* Commodore *when that ship was wrecked on New Year's Day, 1897, and Crane recreated the ordeal after the disaster in one of his finest short stories, "The Open Boat." Next he went to Greece to report the Greco-Turkish war, and finally — after he had moved to England — to Cuba to cover the Spanish-American war. Like Ernest Hemingway after him, Crane couldn't keep away from war or revolution, believing that "the nearer a writer gets to life, the greater he becomes as an artist."*

Crane's chief literary importance is as a unique stylist. His short fiction has an affinity with Chekhov's stories, where the plots often build up to a crucial moment of impasse and then collapse. In the final confrontation in "The Bride Comes to Yellow Sky," for example, contrary to the reader's expectations, no violent action occurs. Crane also uses language poetically. His patterning of words has been termed "prose pointillism," composed of disconnected images which coalesce like the points of color in a French Impressionist painting, every word-group making a cross-reference, every seemingly disconnected detail being interrelated to the whole. To be as honest as possible was Crane's supreme ambition; toward the end of his life he told a younger writer, "An artist, I think, is nothing but a powerful memory that can move itself at will through certain experiences sideways, and every artist must be in some things powerless as a dead snake."

Stephen Crane

ಌಌ

THE OPEN BOAT

A Tale Intended to Be after the Fact, Being the Experience of Four Men from the Sunk Steamer Commodore

I

None of them knew the color of the sky. Their eyes glanced level, and were fastened upon the waves that swept toward them. These waves were of the hue of slate, save for the tops, which were of foaming white, and all of the men knew the colors of the sea. The horizon narrowed and widened, and dipped and rose, and at all times its edge was jagged with waves that seemed thrust up in points like rocks.

Many a man ought to have a bath-tub larger than the boat which here rode upon the sea. These waves were most wrongfully and barbarously abrupt and tall, and each froth-top was a problem in small boat navigation.

The cook squatted in the bottom and looked with both eyes at the six inches of gunwale which separated him from the ocean. His sleeves were rolled over his fat forearms, and the two flaps of his unbuttoned vest dangled as he bent to bail out the boat. Often he said: "Gawd! That was a narrow clip." As he remarked it he invariably gazed eastward over the broken sea.

The oiler, steering with one of the two oars in the boat sometimes raised himself suddenly to keep clear of water that swirled in over the stern. It was a thin little oar and it seemed often ready to snap.

The correspondent, pulling at the other oar, watched the waves and wondered why he was there.

The injured captain, lying in the bow, was at this time buried in that profound dejection and indifference which comes, temporarily at least, to even the bravest and most enduring when, willy nilly, the firm fails, the army loses, the ship goes down. The mind of the master of a vessel is rooted deep in the timbers of her, though he command for a day or a decade, and this captain had on him the stern impression of a scene in the grays of dawn of seven turned faces, and later a stump of a top-mast with a white ball on it that slashed to and fro at the waves, went low and lower, and down. Thereafter there was something strange in his voice. Although steady, it was deep with mourning, and of a quality beyond oration or tears.

"Keep 'er a little more south, Billie," said he.

" 'A little more south,' sir," said the oiler in the stern.

A seat in this boat was not unlike a seat upon a bucking broncho, and, by the same token, a broncho is not much smaller. The craft pranced and reared, and plunged like an animal. As each wave came, and she rose for it, she seemed like a horse making at a fence outrageously high. The manner of her scramble over these walls of water is a mystic thing, and, moreover, at the top of them were ordinarily these problems in white water, the foam racing down from the summit of each wave, requiring a new leap, and a leap from the air. Then, after scornfully bumping a crest, she would slide, and race, and splash down a long incline and arrive bobbing and nodding in front of the next menace.

A singular disadvantage of the sea lies in the fact that after successfully surmounting one wave you discover that there is another behind it just as important and just as nervously anxious to do something effective in the way of swamping boats. In a ten-foot dingey one can get an idea of the resources of the sea in the line of waves that is not probable to the average experience, which is never at sea in a dingey. As each slaty wall of water approached, it shut all else from the view of the men in the boat, and it was not difficult to imagine that this particular wave was the final outburst of the ocean, the last effort of the grim water. There was a terrible grace in the move of the waves, and they came in silence, save for the snarling of the crests.

In the wan light, the faces of the men must have been gray. Their eyes must have glinted in strange ways as they gazed steadily astern. Viewed from a balcony, the whole thing would doubtlessly have been weirdly picturesque. But the men in the boat had no time to see it, and if they had had leisure there were other things to occupy their minds. The sun swung steadily up the sky, and they knew it was broad day because the color of the sea changed from slate to emerald-green, streaked with amber lights, and the

foam was like tumbling snow. The process of the breaking day was unknown to them. They were aware only of this effect upon the color of the
waves that rolled toward them.

In disjointed sentences the cook and the correspondent argued as
to the difference between a life-saving station and a house of refuge. The
cook had said: "There's a house of refuge just north of the Mosquito Inlet
Light, and as soon as they see us, they'll come off in their boat and pick
us up."

"As soon as who see us?" said the correspondent.

"The crew," said the cook.

"Houses of refuge don't have crews," said the correspondent. "As I
understand them, they are only places where clothes and grub are stored for
the benefit of shipwrecked people. They don't carry crews."

"Oh, yes, they do," said the cook.

"No, they don't," said the correspondent.

"Well, we're not there yet, anyhow," said the oiler, in the stern.

"Well," said the cook, "perhaps it's not a house of refuge that I'm
thinking of as being near Mosquito Inlet Light. Perhaps it's a life-saving
station."

"We're not there yet," said the oiler, in the stern.

II

As the boat bounced from the top of each wave, the wind tore through
the hair of the hatless men, and as the craft plopped her stern down again
the spray slashed past them. The crest of each of these waves was a hill,
from the top of which the men surveyed, for a moment, a broad tumultuous
expanse, shining and wind-riven. It was probably splendid. It was probably
glorious, this play of the free sea, wild with lights of emerald and white and
amber.

"Bully good thing it's an on-shore wind," said the cook. "If not where
would we be? Wouldn't have a show."

"That's right," said the correspondent.

The busy oiler nodded his assent.

Then the captain, in the bow, chuckled in a way that expressed
humor, contempt, tragedy, all in one. "Do you think we've got a show,
now, boys?" said he.

Whereupon the three went silent, save for a trifle of hemming and
hawing. To express any particular optimism at this time they felt to be childish and stupid, but they all doubtless possessed this sense of the situation
in their mind. A young man thinks doggedly at such times. On the other
hand, the ethics of their condition was decidedly against any open suggestion of hopelessness. So they were silent.

"Oh, well," said the captain, soothing his children, "we'll get ashore
all right."

But there was that in his tone which made them think, so the oiler quoth: "Yes! If this wind holds!"

The cook was bailing. "Yes! If we don't catch hell in the surf."

Canton flannel gulls flew near and far. Sometimes they sat down on the sea, near patches of brown sea-weed that rolled over the waves with a movement like carpets on a line in a gale. The birds sat comfortably in groups, and they were envied by some in the dingey, for the wrath of the sea was no more to them than it was to a covey of prairie chickens a thousand miles inland. Often they came very close and stared at the men with black bead-like eyes. At these times they were uncanny and sinister in their unblinking scrutiny, and the men hooted angrily at them, telling them to be gone. One came, and evidently decided to alight on the top of the captain's head. The bird flew parallel to the boat and did not circle, but made short sidelong jumps in the air in chicken-fashion. His black eyes were wistfully fixed upon the captain's head. "Ugly brute," said the oiler to the bird. "You look as if you were made with a jack-knife." The cook and the correspondent swore darkly at the creature. The captain naturally wished to knock it away with the end of the heavy painter, but he did not dare do it, because anything resembling an emphatic gesture would have capsized this freighted boat, and so with his open hand, the captain gently and carefully waved the gull away. After it had been discouraged from the pursuit the captain breathed easier on account of his hair, and others breathed easier because the bird struck their minds at this time as being somehow gruesome and ominous.

In the meantime the oiler and the correspondent rowed. And also they rowed.

They sat together in the same seat, and each rowed an oar. Then the oiler took both oars; then the correspondent took both oars; then the oiler; then the correspondent. They rowed and they rowed. The very ticklish part of the business was when the time came for the reclining one in the stern to take his turn at the oars. By the very last star of truth, it is easier to steal eggs from under a hen than it was to change seats in the dingey. First the man in the stern slid his hand along the thwart and moved with care, as if he were of Sèvres.[1] Then the man in the rowing seat slid his hand along the other thwart. It was all done with the most extraordinary care. As the two sidled past each other, the whole party kept watchful eyes on the coming wave, and the captain cried: "Look out now! Steady there!"

The brown mats of sea-weed that appeared from time to time were like islands, bits of earth. They were travelling, apparently, neither one way nor the other. They were, to all intents, stationary. They informed the men in the boat that it was making progress slowly toward the land.

The captain, rearing cautiously in the bow, after the dingey soared on a great swell, said that he had seen the light-house at Mosquito Inlet. Pres-

---

[1] a delicate French porcelain.

ently the cook remarked that he had seen it. The correspondent was at the oars, then, and for some reason he too wished to look at the light-house, but his back was toward the far shore and the waves were important, and for some time he could not seize an opportunity to turn his head. But at last there came a wave more gentle than the others, and when at the crest of it he swiftly scoured the western horizon.

"See it?" said the captain.

"No," said the correspondent, slowly, "I didn't see anything."

"Look again," said the captain. He pointed. "It's exactly in that direction."

At the top of another wave, the correspondent did as he was bid, and this time his eyes chanced on a small still thing on the edge of the swaying horizon. It was precisely like the point of a pin. It took an anxious eye to find a light-house so tiny.

"Think we'll make it, Captain?"

"If this wind holds and the boat don't swamp, we can't do much else," said the captain.

The little boat, lifted by each towering sea, and splashed viciously by the crests, made progress that in the absence of sea-weed was not apparent to those in her. She seemed just a wee thing wallowing, miraculously, top-up, at the mercy of five oceans. Occasionally, a great spread of water, like white flames, swarmed into her.

"Bail her, cook," said the captain, serenely.

"All right, Captain," said the cheerful cook.

III

It would be difficult to describe the subtle brotherhood of men that was here established on the seas. No one said that it was so. No one mentioned it. But it dwelt in the boat, and each man felt it warm him. They were a captain, an oiler, a cook, and a correspondent, and they were friends, friends in a more curiously iron-bound degree than may be common. The hurt captain, lying against the water-jar in the bow, spoke always in a low voice and calmly, but he could never command a more ready and swiftly obedient crew than the motely three of the dingey. It was more than a mere recognition of what was best for the common safety. There was surely in it a quality that was personal and heartfelt. And after this devotion to the commander of the boat there was this comradeship that the correspondent, for instance, who had been taught to be cynical of men, knew even at the time was the best experience of his life. But no one said that it was so. No one mentioned it.

"I wish we had a sail," remarked the captain. "We might try my overcoat on the end of an oar and give you two boys a chance to rest." So the cook and the correspondent held the mast and spread wide the overcoat. The oiler steered, and the little boat made good way with her new rig.

Sometimes the oiler had to scull sharply to keep a sea from breaking into the boat, but otherwise sailing was a success.

Meanwhile the light-house had been growing slowly larger. It had now almost assumed color, and appeared like a little gray shadow on the sky. The man at the oars could not be prevented from turning his head rather often to try for a glimpse of this little gray shadow.

At last, from the top of each wave the men in the tossing boat could see land. Even as the light-house was an upright shadow on the sky, this land seemed but a long black shadow on the sea. It certainly was thinner than paper. "We must be about opposite New Smyrna," said the cook, who had coasted this shore often in schooners. "Captain, by the way, I believe they abandoned that life-saving station there about a year ago."

"Did they?" said the captain.

The wind slowly died away. The cook and the correspondent were not now obliged to slave in order to hold high the oar. But the waves continued their old impetuous swooping at the dingey, and the little craft, no longer under way, struggled woundily over them. The oiler or the correspondent took the oars again.

Shipwrecks are *apropos* of nothing. If men could only train for them and have them occur when the men had reached pink condition, there would be less drowning at sea. Of the four in the dingey none had slept any time worth mentioning for two days and two nights previous to embarking in the dingey, and in the excitement of clambering about the deck of a foundering ship they had also forgotten to eat heartily.

For these reasons, and for others, neither the oiler nor the correspondent was fond of rowing at this time. The correspondent wondered ingenuously how in the name of all that was sane could there be people who thought it amusing to row a boat. It was not an amusement; it was a diabolical punishment, and even a genius of mental aberrations could never conclude that it was anything but a horror to the muscles and a crime against the back. He mentioned to the boat in general how the amusement of rowing struck him, and the weary-faced oiler smiled in full sympathy. Previously to the foundering, by the way, the oiler had worked double-watch in the engine-room of the ship.

"Take her easy, now, boys," said the captain. "Don't spend yourselves. If we have to run a surf you'll need all your strength, because we'll sure have to swim for it. Take your time."

Slowly the land arose from the sea. From a black line it became a line of black and a line of white — trees and sand. Finally, the captain said that he could make out a house on the shore. "That's the house of refuge, sure," said the cook. "They'll see us before long, and come out after us."

The distant light-house reared high. "The keeper ought to be able to make us out now, if he's looking through a glass," said the captain. "He'll notify the life-saving people."

"None of those other boats could have got ashore to give word of the wreck," said the oiler, in a low voice. "Else the life-boat would be out hunting us."

Slowly and beautifully the land loomed out of the sea. The wind came again. It had veered from the northeast to the southeast. Finally, a new sound struck the ears of the men in the boat. It was the low thunder of the surf on the shore. "We'll never be able to make the light-house now," said the captain. "Swing her head a little more north, Billie."

" 'A little more north,' sir," said the oiler.

Whereupon the little boat turned her nose once more down the wind, and all but the oarsman watched the shore grow. Under the influence of this expansion doubt and direful apprehension was leaving the minds of the men. The management of the boat was still most absorbing, but it could not prevent a quiet cheerfulness. In an hour, perhaps, they would be ashore.

Their back-bones had become thoroughly used to balancing in the boat and they now rode this wild colt of a dingey like circus men. The correspondent thought that he had been drenched to the skin, but happening to feel in the top pocket of his coat, he found therein eight cigars. Four of them were soaked with seawater; four were perfectly scatheless. After a search, somebody produced three dry matches, and thereupon the four waifs rode impudently in their little boat, and with an assurance of an impending rescue shining in their eyes, puffed at the big cigars and judged well and ill of all men. Everybody took a drink of water.

IV

"Cook," remarked the captain, "there don't seem to be any signs of life about your house of refuge."

"No," replied the cook. "Funny they don't see us!"

A broad stretch of lowly coast lay before the eyes of the men. It was of dunes topped with dark vegetation. The roar of the surf was plain, and sometimes they could see the white lip of a wave as it spun up the beach. A tiny house was blocked out black upon the sky. Southward, the slim light-house lifted its little gray length.

Tide, wind, and waves were swinging the dingey northward. "Funny they don't see us," said the men.

The surf's roar was here dulled, but its tone was, nevertheless, thunderous and mighty. As the boat swam over the great rollers, the men sat listening to this roar. "We'll swamp sure," said everybody.

It is fair to say here that there was not a life-saving station within twenty miles in either direction, but the men did not know this fact and in consequence they made dark and opprobrious remarks concerning the eyesight of the nation's life-savers. Four scowling men sat in the dingey and surpassed records in the invention of epithets.

"Funny they don't see us."

The light-heartedness of a former time had completely faded. To their sharpened minds it was easy to conjure pictures of all kinds of incompetency and blindness and, indeed, cowardice. There was the shore of the populous land, and it was bitter and bitter to them that from it came no sign.

"Well," said the captain, ultimately, "I suppose we'll have to make a try for ourselves. If we stay out here too long, we'll none of us have strength left to swim after the boat swamps."

And so the oiler, who was at the oars, turned the boat straight for the shore. There was a sudden tightening of muscles. There was some thinking.

"If we don't all get ashore — " said the captain. "If we don't all get ashore, I suppose you fellows know where to send news of my finish?"

They then briefly exchanged some addresses and admonitions. As for the reflections of the men, there was a great deal of rage in them. Perchance they might be formulated thus: "If I am going to be drowned — if I am going to be drowned — if I am going to be drowned, why, in the name of the seven mad gods who rule the sea, was I allowed to come thus far and contemplate sand and trees? Was I brought here merely to have my nose dragged away as I was about to nibble the sacred cheese of life? It is preposterous. If this old ninny-woman, Fate, cannot do better than this, she should be deprived of the management of men's fortunes. She is an old hen who knows not her intention. If she has decided to drown me, why did she not do it in the beginning and save me all this trouble. The whole affair is absurd. . . . But, no, she cannot mean to drown me. She dare not drown me. She cannot drown me. Not after all this work." Afterward the man might have had an impulse to shake his fist at the clouds. "Just you drown me, now, and then hear what I call you!"

The billows that came at this time were more formidable. They seemed always just about to break and roll over the little boat in a turmoil of foam. There was a preparatory and long growl in the speech of them. No mind unused to the sea would have concluded that the dingey could ascend these sheer heights in time. The shore was still afar. The oiler was a wily surfman. "Boys," he said, swiftly, "she won't live three minutes more and we're too far out to swim. Shall I take her to sea again, Captain?"

"Yes! Go ahead!" said the captain.

This oiler, by a series of quick miracles, and fast and steady oarsmanship, turned the boat in the middle of the surf and took her safely to sea again.

There was a considerable silence as the boat bumped over the furrowed sea to deeper water. Then somebody in gloom spoke. "Well, anyhow, they must have seen us from the shore by now."

The gulls went in slanting flight up the wind toward the gray desolate east. A squall, marked by dingy clouds, and clouds brick-red, like smoke from a burning building, appeared from the southeast.

"What do you think of those life-saving people? Ain't they peaches?"

"Funny they haven't seen us."

"Maybe they think we're out here for sport! Maybe they think we're fishin'. Maybe they think we're damned fools."

It was a long afternoon. A changed tide tried to force them southward, but wind and wave said northward. Far ahead, where coast-line, sea, and sky formed their mighty angle, there were little dots which seemed to indicate a city on the shore.

"St. Augustine?"

The captain shook his head. "Too near Mosquito Inlet."

And the oiler rowed, and then the correspondent rowed. Then the oiler rowed. It was a weary business. The human back can become the seat of more aches and pains than are registered in books for the composite anatomy of a regiment. It is a limited area, but it can become the theatre of innumerable muscular conflicts, tangles, wrenches, knots, and other comforts.

"Did you ever like to row, Billie?" asked the correspondent.

"No," said the oiler, "Hang it."

When one exchanged the rowing-seat for a place in the bottom of the boat, he suffered a bodily depression that caused him to be careless of everything save an obligation to wiggle one finger. There was cold sea-water swashing to and fro in the boat, and he lay in it. His head, pillowed on a thwart, was within an inch of the swirl of a wave crest, and sometimes a particularly obstreperous sea came in-board and drenched him once more. But these matters did not annoy him. It is almost certain that if the boat had capsized he would have tumbled comfortably out upon the ocean as if he felt sure that it was a great soft mattress.

"Look! There's a man on the shore!"

"Where?"

"There! See 'im? See 'im?"

"Yes, sure! He's walking along."

"Now he's stopped. Look! He's facing us!"

"He's waving at us!"

"So he is! By thunder!"

"Ah, now, we're all right! There'll be a boat out here for us in half an hour."

"He's going on. He's running. He's going up to that house there."

The remote beach seemed lower than the sea, and it required a searching glance to discern the little black figure. The captain saw a floating stick and they rowed to it. A bath-towel was by some weird chance in the boat, and, tying this on the stick, the captain waved it. The oarsman did not dare turn his head, so he was obliged to ask questions.

"What's he doing now?"

"He's standing still again. He's looking, I think. . . . There he goes again. Toward the house. . . . Now he's stopped again."

"Is he waving at us?"

"No, not now! He was, though."

"Look! There comes another man!"

"He's running."

"Look at him go, would you."

"Why, he's on a bicycle. Now he's met the other man. They're both waving at us. Look!"

"There comes something up the beach."

"What the devil is that thing?"

"Why, it looks like a boat."

"Why, certainly it's a boat."

"No, it's on wheels."

"Yes, so it is. Well, that must be the life-boat. They drag them along shore on a wagon."

"That's the life-boat, sure."

"No, by, it's — it's an omnibus."

"I tell you it's a life-boat."

"It is not! It's an omnibus. I can see it plain. See? One of those big hotel omnibuses."

"By thunder, you're right. It's an omnibus, sure as fate. What do you suppose they are doing with an omnibus? Maybe they are going around collecting the life-crew, hey?"

"That's it, likely. Look! There's a fellow waving a little black flag. He's standing on the steps of the omnibus. There come those other two fellows. Now they're all talking together. Look at the fellow with the flag. Maybe he ain't waving it!"

"That ain't a flag, is it? That's his coat. Why, certainly, that's his coat."

"So it is. It's his coat. He's taken it off and is waving it around his head. But would you look at him swing it!"

"Oh, say, there isn't any life-saving station there. That's just a winter resort hotel omnibus that has brought over some of the boarders to see us drown."

"What's that idiot with the coat mean? What's he signaling, anyhow?"

"It looks as if he were trying to tell us to go north. There must be a life-saving station up there."

"No! He thinks we're fishing. Just giving us a merry hand. See? Ah, there, Willie."

"Well, I wish I could make something out of those signals. What do you suppose he means?"

"He don't mean anything. He's just playing."

"Well, if he'd just signal us to try the surf again, or to go to sea and wait, or go north, or go south, or go to hell — there would be some reason in it. But look at him. He just stands there and keeps his coat revolving like a wheel. The ass!"

"There come more people."

"Now there's quite a mob. Look! Isn't that a boat?"

"Where? Oh, I see where you mean. No, that's no boat."

"That fellow is still waving his coat."

"He must think we like to see him do that. Why don't he quit it. It don't mean anything."

"I don't know. I think he is trying to make us go north. It must be that there's a life-saving station there somewhere."

"Say, he ain't tired yet. Look at 'im wave."

"Wonder how long he can keep that up. He's been revolving his coat ever since he caught sight of us. He's an idiot. Why aren't they getting men to bring a boat out. A fishing boat — one of those big yawls — could come out here all right. Why don't he do something?"

"Oh, it's all right, now."

"They'll have a boat out here for us in less than no time, now that they've seen us."

A faint yellow tone came into the sky over the low land. The shadows on the sea slowly deepened. The wind bore coldness with it, and the men began to shiver.

"Holy smoke!" said one, allowing his voice to express his impious mood, "if we keep on monkeying out here! If we've got to flounder out here all night!"

"Oh, we'll never have to stay here all night! Don't you worry. They've seen us now, and it won't be long before they'll come chasing out after us."

The shore grew dusky. The man waving a coat blended gradually into this gloom, and it swallowed in the same manner the omnibus and the group of people. The spray, when it dashed uproariously over the side, made the voyagers shrink and swear like men who were being branded.

"I'd like to catch the chump who waved the coat. I feel like soaking him one, just for luck."

"Why? What did he do?"

"Oh, nothing, but then he seemed so damned cheerful."

In the meantime the oiler rowed, and then the correspondent rowed, and then the oiler rowed. Gray-faced and bowed forward, they mechanically, turn by turn, plied the leaden oars. The form of the light-house had vanished from the southern horizon, but finally a pale star appeared, just lifting from the sea. The streaked saffron in the west passed before the all-merging darkness, and the sea to the east was black. The land had vanished, and was expressed only by the low and drear thunder of the surf.

"If I am going to be drowned — if I am going to be drowned — if I am going to be drowned, why, in the name of the seven mad gods who rule the sea, was I allowed to come thus far and contemplate sand and trees? Was I brought here merely to have my nose dragged away as I was about to nibble the sacred cheese of life?"

The patient captain, drooped over the water-jar, was sometimes obliged to speak to the oarsman.

"Keep her head up! Keep her head up!"

" 'Keep her head up,' sir." The voices were weary and low.

This was surely a quiet evening. All save the oarsman lay heavily and listlessly in the boat's bottom. As for him, his eyes were just capable of noting the tall black waves that swept forward in a most sinister silence, save for an occasional subdued growl of a crest.

The cook's head was on a thwart, and he looked without interest at the water under his nose. He was deep in other scenes. Finally he spoke. "Billie," he murmured, dreamfully, "what kind of pie do you like best?"

V

"Pie," said the oiler and the correspondent, agitatedly. "Don't talk about those things, blast you!"

"Well," said the cook, "I was just thinking about ham sandwiches, and ―― "

A night on the sea in an open boat is a long night. As darkness settled finally, the shine of the light, lifting from the sea in the south, changed to full gold. On the northern horizon a new light appeared, a small bluish gleam on the edge of the waters. These two lights were the furniture of the world. Otherwise there was nothing but waves.

Two men huddled in the stern, and distances were so magnificent in the dingey that the rower was enabled to keep his feet partly warmed by thrusting them under his companions. Their legs indeed extended far under the rowing-seat until they touched the feet of the captain forward. Sometimes, despite the efforts of the tired oarsman, a wave came piling into the boat, an icy wave of the night, and the chilling water soaked them anew. They would twist their bodies for a moment and groan, and sleep the dead sleep once more, while the water in the boat gurgled about them as the craft rocked.

The plan of the oiler and the correspondent was for one to row until he lost the ability, and then arouse the other from his sea-water couch in the bottom of the boat.

The oiler plied the oars until his head drooped forward, and the overpowering sleep blinded him. And he rowed yet afterward. Then he touched a man in the bottom of the boat, and called his name. "Will you spell me for a little while?" he said, meekly.

"Sure, Billie," said the correspondent, awakening and dragging himself to a sitting position. They exchanged places carefully, and the oiler, cuddling down in the sea-water at the cook's side, seemed to go to sleep instantly.

The particular violence of the sea had ceased. The waves came without snarling. The obligation of the man at the oars was to keep the boat headed so that the tilt of the rollers would not capsize her, and to preserve her from filling when the crests rushed past. The black waves were silent and hard to be seen in the darkness. Often one was almost upon the boat before the oarsman was aware.

In a low voice the correspondent addressed the captain. He was not sure that the captain was awake, although this iron man seemed to be always awake. "Captain, shall I keep her making for that light north, sir?"

The same steady voice answered him. "Yes. Keep it about two points off the port bow."

The cook had tied a life-belt around himself in order to get even the warmth which this clumsy cork contrivance could donate, and he seemed almost stove-like when a rower, whose teeth invariably chattered wildly as soon as he ceased his labor, dropped down to sleep.

The correspondent, as he rowed, looked down at the two men sleeping under foot. The cook's arm was around the oiler's shoulders, and, with their fragmentary clothing and haggard faces, they were the babes of the sea, a grotesque rendering of the old babes in the wood.

Later he must have grown stupid at his work, for suddenly there was a growling of water, and a crest came with a roar and a swash into the boat, and it was a wonder that it did not set the cook afloat in his life-belt. The cook continued to sleep, but the oiler sat up, blinking his eyes and shaking with the new cold.

"Oh, I'm awful sorry, Billie," said the correspondent, contritely.

"That's all right, old boy," said the oiler, and lay down again and was asleep.

Presently it seemed that even the captain dozed, and the correspondent thought that he was the one man afloat on all the oceans. The wind had a voice as it came over the waves, and it was sadder than the end.

There was a long, loud swishing astern of the boat, and a gleaming trail of phosphorescence, like blue flame, was furrowed on the black waters. It might have been made by a monstrous knife.

Then there came a stillness, while the correspondent breathed with the open mouth and looked at the sea.

Suddenly there was another swish and another long flash of bluish light, and this time it was alongside the boat, and might almost have been reached with an oar. The correspondent saw an enormous fin speed like a shadow through the water, hurling the crystalline spray and leaving the long glowing trail.

The correspondent looked over his shoulder at the captain. His face was hidden, and he seemed to be asleep. He looked at the babes of the sea. They certainly were asleep. So, being bereft of sympathy, he leaned a little way to one side and swore softly into the sea.

But the thing did not then leave the vicinity of the boat. Ahead or astern, on one side or the other, at intervals long or short, fled the long sparkling streak, and there was to be heard the whiroo of the dark fin. The speed and power of the thing was greatly to be admired. It cut the water like a gigantic and keen projectile.

The presence of this biding thing did not affect the man with the same horror that it would if he had been a picnicker. He simply looked at the sea dully and swore in an undertone.

Nevertheless, it is true that he did not wish to be alone with the thing. He wished one of his companions to awaken by chance and keep him company with it. But the captain hung motionless over the water-jar and the oiler and the cook in the bottom of the boat were plunged in slumber.

VI

"If I am going to be drowned — if I am going to be drowned — if I am going to be drowned, why, in the name of the seven mad gods who rule the sea, was I allowed to come thus far and contemplate sand and trees?"

During this dismal night, it may be remarked that a man would conclude that it was really the intention of the seven mad gods to drown him, despite the abominable injustice of it. For it was certainly an abominable injustice to drown a man who had worked so hard, so hard. The man felt it would be a crime most unnatural. Other people had drowned at sea since galleys swarmed with painted sails, but still —

When it occurs to a man that nature does not regard him as important, and that she feels she would not maim the universe by disposing of him, he at first wishes to throw bricks at the temple, and he hates deeply the fact that there are no bricks and no temples. Any visible expression of nature would surely be pelleted with his jeers.

Then, if there be no tangible thing to hoot he feels, perhaps, the desire to confront a personification and indulge in pleas, bowed to one knee, and with hands supplicant, saying: "Yes, but I love myself."

A high cold star on a winter's night is the word he feels that she says to him. Thereafter he knows the pathos of his situation.

The men in the dingey had not discussed these matters, but each had, no doubt, reflected upon them in silence and according to his mind. There was seldom any expression upon their faces save the general one of complete weariness. Speech was devoted to the business of the boat.

To chime the notes of his emotion, a verse mysteriously entered the correspondent's head. He had even forgotten that he had forgotten this verse, but it suddenly was in his mind.

> A soldier of the Legion lay dying in Algiers,
> There was lack of woman's nursing, there was dearth of woman's tears;
> But a comrade stood beside him, and he took that comrade's hand,
> And he said: "I never more shall see my own, my native land."

In his childhood, the correspondent had been made acquainted with the fact that a soldier of the Legion lay dying in Algiers, but he had never regarded it as important. Myriads of his school-fellows had informed him of the soldier's plight, but the dinning had naturally ended by making him perfectly indifferent. He had never considered it his affair that a soldier of the Legion lay dying in Algiers, nor had it appeared to him as a matter for sorrow. It was less to him than the breaking of a pencil's point.

Now, however, it quaintly came to him as a human, living thing. It was no longer merely a picture of a few throes in the breast of a poet, meanwhile drinking tea and warming his feet at the grate; it was an actuality — stern, mournful, and fine.

The correspondent plainly saw the soldier. He lay on the sand with his feet out straight and still. While his pale left hand was upon his chest in an attempt to thwart the going of his life, the blood came between his fingers. In the far Algerian distance, a city of low square forms was set against a sky that was faint with the last sunset hues. The correspondent, plying the oars and dreaming of the slow and slower movements of the lips of the soldier, was moved by a profound and perfectly impersonal comprehension. He was sorry for the soldier of the Legion who lay dying in Algiers.

The thing which had followed the boat and waited had evidently grown bored at the delay. There was no longer to be heard the slash of the cut-water, and there was no longer the flame of the long trail. The light in the north still glimmered, but it was apparently no nearer to the boat. Sometimes the boom of the surf rang in the correspondent's ears, and he turned the craft seaward then and rowed harder. Southward, some one had evidently built a watch-fire on the beach. It was too low and too far to be seen, but it made a shimmering, roseate reflection upon the bluff back of it, and this could be discerned from the boat. The wind came stronger, and sometimes a wave suddenly raged out like a mountain-cat and there was to be seen the sheen and sparkle of a broken crest.

The captain, in the bow, moved on his water-jar and sat erect. "Pretty long night," he observed to the correspondent. He looked at the shore. "Those life-saving people take their time."

"Did you see that shark playing around?"

"Yes, I saw him. He was a big fellow, all right."

"Wish I had known you were awake."

Later the correspondent spoke into the bottom of the boat.

"Billie!" There was a slow and gradual disentanglement. "Billie, will you spell me?"

"Sure," said the oiler.

As soon as the correspondent touched the cold comfortable sea-water in the bottom of the boat, and had huddled close to the cook's life-belt he was deep in sleep, despite the fact that his teeth played all the popular airs. This sleep was so good to him that it was but a moment before he heard a voice call his name in a tone that demonstrated the last stages of exhaustion. "Will you spell me?"

"Sure, Billie."

The light in the north had mysteriously vanished, but the correspondent took his course from the wide-awake captain.

Later in the night they took the boat farther out to sea, and the captain directed the cook to take one oar at the stern and keep the boat facing the seas. He was to call out if he should hear the thunder of the surf. This plan enabled the oiler and the correspondent to get respite together. "We'll give those boys a chance to get into shape again," said the captain. They curled down and, after a few preliminary chatterings and trembles, slept once more the dead sleep. Neither knew they had bequeathed to the cook the company of another shark, or perhaps the same shark.

As the boat caroused on the waves, spray occasionally bumped over the side and gave them a fresh soaking, but this had no power to break their repose. The ominous slash of the wind and the water affected them as it would have affected mummies.

"Boys," said the cook, with the notes of every reluctance in his voice, "she's drifted in pretty close. I guess one of you had better take her to sea again." The correspondent, aroused, heard the crash of the toppled crests.

As he was rowing, the captain gave him some whiskey and water, and this steadied the chills out of him. "If I ever get ashore and anybody shows me even a photograph of an oar — "

At last there was a short conversation.

"Billie. . . . Billie, will you spell me?"

"Sure," said the oiler.

VII

When the correspondent again opened his eyes, the sea and the sky were each of the gray hue of the dawning. Later, carmine and gold was painted upon the waters. The morning appeared finally, in its splendor, with a sky of pure blue, and the sunlight flamed on the tips of the waves.

On the distant dunes were set many little black cottages, and a tall white wind-mill reared above them. No man, nor dog, nor bicycle appeared on the beach. The cottages might have formed a deserted village.

The voyagers scanned the shore. A conference was held in the boat. "Well," said the captain, "if no help is coming, we might better try a run through the surf right away. If we stay out here much longer we will be too weak to do anything for ourselves at all." The others silently acquiesced in this reasoning. The boat was headed for the beach. The correspondent wondered if none ever ascended the tall wind-tower, and if then they never looked seaward. This tower was a giant, standing with its back to the plight of the ants. It represented in a degree, to the correspondent, the serenity of nature amid the struggles of the individual — nature in the wind, and nature in the vision of men. She did not seem cruel to him then, nor beneficent, nor treacherous, nor wise. But she was indifferent, flatly indifferent. It is, perhaps, plausible that a man in this situation, impressed with the unconcern of the universe, should see the innumerable flaws of his life and have them taste wickedly in his mind and wish for another chance. A distinction between right and wrong seems absurdly clear to him, then, in this new ignorance of the grave-edge, and he understands that if he were given another opportunity he would mend his conduct and his words, and be better and brighter during an introduction, or at a tea.

"Now, boys," said the captain, "she is going to swamp sure. All we can do is to work her in as far as possible, and then when she swamps, pile out and scramble for the beach. Keep cool now, and don't jump until she swamps sure."

The oiler took the oars. Over his shoulders he scanned the surf. "Captain," he said, "I think I'd better bring her about, and keep her head-on to the seas and back her in."

"All right, Billie," said the captain. "Back her in." The oiler swung the boat then and, seated in the stern, the cook and the correspondent were obliged to look over their shoulders to contemplate the lonely and indifferent shore.

The monstrous inshore rollers heaved the boat high until the men were again enabled to see the white sheets of water scudding up the slanted beach. "We won't get in very close," said the captain. Each time a man could wrest his attention from the rollers, he turned his glance toward the shore, and in the expression of the eyes during this contemplation there was a singular quality. The correspondent, observing the others, knew that they were not afraid, but the full meaning of their glances was shrouded.

As for himself, he was too tired to grapple fundamentally with the fact. He tried to coerce his mind into thinking of it, but the mind was dominated at this time by the muscles, and the muscles said they did not care. It merely occurred to him that if he should drown it would be a shame.

There were no hurried words, no pallor, no plain agitation. The men simply looked at the shore. "Now, remember to get well clear of the boat when you jump," said the captain.

Seaward the crest of a roller suddenly fell with a thunderous crash, and the long white comber came roaring down upon the boat.

"Steady now," said the captain. The men were silent. They turned their eyes from the shore to the comber and waited. The boat slid up the incline, leaped at the furious top, bounced over it, and swung down the long back of the wave. Some water had been shipped and the cook bailed it out.

But the next crest crashed also. The tumbling boiling flood of white water caught the boat and whirled it almost perpendicular. Water swarmed in from all sides. The correspondent had his hands on the gunwale at this time, and when the water entered at that place he swiftly withdrew his fingers, as if he objected to wetting them.

The little boat, drunken with this weight of water, reeled and snuggled deeper into the sea.

"Bail her out, cook! Bail her out," said the captain.

"All right, Captain," said the cook.

"Now boys, the next one will do for us, sure," said the oiler. "Mind to jump clear of the boat."

The third wave moved forward, huge, furious, implacable. It fairly swallowed the dingey, and almost simultaneously the men tumbled into the sea. A piece of life-belt had lain in the bottom of the boat, and as the correspondent went overboard he held this to his chest with his left hand.

The January water was icy, and he reflected immediately that it was colder than he had expected to find it off the coast of Florida. This appeared to his dazed mind as a fact important enough to be noted at the time. The coldness of the water was sad; it was tragic. This fact was somehow so mixed and confused with his opinion of his own situation that it seemed almost a proper reason for tears. The water was cold.

When he came to the surface he was conscious of little but the noisy water. Afterward he saw his companions in the sea. The oiler was ahead in the race. He was swimming strongly and rapidly. Off to the correspondent's left, the cook's great white and corked back bulged out of the water, and in the rear the captain was hanging with his one good hand to the keel of the overturned dingey.

There is a certain immovable quality to a shore, and the correspondent wondered at it amid the confusion of the sea.

It seemed also very attractive, but the correspondent knew that it was a long journey, and he paddled leisurely. The piece of life-preserver lay under him, and sometimes he whirled down the incline of a wave as if he were on a hand-sled.

But finally he arrived at a place in the sea where travel was beset with difficulty. He did not pause swimming to inquire what manner of current had caught him, but there his progress ceased. The shore was set before him like a bit of scenery on a stage, and he looked at it and understood with his eyes each detail of it.

As the cook passed, much farther to the left, the captain was calling to him, "Turn over on you back, cook! Turn over on your back and use the oar."

"All right, sir." The cook turned on his back, and, paddling with an oar, went ahead as if he were a canoe.

Presently the boat also passed to the left of the correspondent with the captain clinging with one hand to the keel. He would have appeared like a man raising himself to look over a board fence, if it were not for the extraordinary gymnastics of the boat. The correspondent marvelled that the captain could still hold to it.

They passed on, nearer to shore — the oiler, the cook, the captain — and following them went the water-jar, bouncing gayly over the seas.

The correspondent remained in the grip of this strange new enemy — a current. The shore, with its white slope of sand and its green bluff, topped with little silent cottages, was spread like a picture before him. It was very near to him then, but he was impressed as one who in a gallery looks at a scene from Brittany or Holland.

He thought: "I am going to drown? Can it be possible? Can it be possible? Can it be possible?" Perhaps an individual must consider his own death to be the final phenomenon of nature.

But later a wave perhaps whirled him out of his small deadly current, for he found suddenly that he could again make progress toward the shore. Later still, he was aware that the captain, clinging with one hand to the keel of the dingey, had his face turned away from the shore and toward him, and was calling his name. "Come to the boat! Come to the boat!"

In his struggle to reach the captain and the boat, he reflected that when one gets properly wearied, drowning must really be a comfortable arrangement, a cessation of hostilities accompanied by a large degree of relief, and he was glad of it, for the main thing in his mind for some moments had been the horror of the temporary agony. He did not wish to be hurt.

Presently he saw a man running along the shore. He was undressing with most remarkable speed. Coat, trousers, shirt, everything flew magically off him.

"Come to the boat," called the captain.

"All right, Captain." As the correspondent paddled, he saw the captain let himself down to bottom and leave the boat. Then the correspondent performed his one little marvel of the voyage. A large wave caught him and flung him with ease and supreme speed completely over the boat and far beyond it. It struck him even then as an event in gymnastics, and a true miracle of the sea. An overturned boat in the surf is not a plaything to a swimming man.

The correspondent arrived in water that reached only to his waist, but his condition did not enable him to stand for more than a moment. Each wave knocked him into a heap, and the under-tow pulled at him.

Then he saw the man who had been running and undressing, and undressing and running, come bounding into the water. He dragged ashore the cook, and then waded toward the captain, but the captain waved him away, and sent him to the correspondent. He was naked, naked as a tree in winter, but a halo was about his head, and he shone like a saint. He gave a strong pull, and a long drag, and a bully heave at the correspondent's hand. The correspondent, schooled in the minor formulae, said: "Thanks, old man." But suddenly the man cried: "What's that?" He pointed a swift finger. The correspondent said: "Go."

In the shallows, face downward, lay the oiler. His forehead touched sand that was periodically, between each wave, clear of the sea.

The correspondent did not know all that transpired afterward. When he achieved safe ground he fell, striking the sand with each particular part of his body. It was as if he had dropped from a roof, but the thud was grateful to him.

It seems that instantly the beach was populated with men with blankets, clothes, and flasks, and women with coffee-pots and all the remedies sacred to their minds. The welcome of the land to the men from the sea was warm and generous, but a still and dripping shape was carried slowly up the beach, and the land's welcome for it could only be the different and sinister hospitality of the grave.

When it came night, the white waves paced to and fro in the moonlight, and the wind brought the sound of the great sea's voice to the men on shore, and they felt that they could then be interpreters.

[1897]

Stephen Crane

ເວ

THE BRIDE COMES TO YELLOW SKY

I

The great Pullman was whirling onward with such dignity of motion that a glance from the window seemed simply to prove that the plains of Texas were pouring eastward. Vast flats of green grass, dull-hued spaces of mesquit and cactus, little groups of frame houses, woods of light and tender trees, all were sweeping into the east, sweeping over the horizon, a precipice.

A newly married pair had boarded this coach at San Antonio. The man's face was reddened from many days in the wind and sun, and a direct result of his new black clothes was that his brick-colored hands were constantly performing in a most conscious fashion. From time to time he looked down respectfully at his attire. He sat with a hand on each knee, like a man waiting in a barber's shop. The glances he devoted to other passengers were furtive and shy.

The bride was not pretty, nor was she very young. She wore a dress of blue cashmere, with small reservations of velvet here and there, and with steel buttons abounding. She continually twisted her head to regard her puff sleeves, very stiff, straight, and high. They embarrassed her. It was quite apparent that she had cooked, and that she expected to cook, dutifully. The blushes caused by the careless scrutiny of some passengers as she had entered the car were strange to see upon this plain, under-class countenance, which was drawn in placid, almost emotionless lines.

They were evidently very happy. "Ever been in a parlor-car before?" he asked, smiling with delight.

"No," she answered; "I never was. It's fine, ain't it?"

"Great! And then after a while we'll go forward to the diner, and get a big lay-out. Finest meal in the world. Charge a dollar."

"Oh, do they?" cried the bride. "Charge a dollar? Why, that's too much — for us — ain't it, Jack?"

"Not this trip, anyhow," he answered bravely. "We're going to go the whole thing."

Later he explained to her about the trains. "You see, it's a thousand miles from one end of Texas to the other; and this train runs right across it, and never stops but four times." He had the pride of an owner. He pointed out to her the dazzling fittings of the coach; and in truth her eyes opened wider as she contemplated the sea-green figured velvet, the shining brass, silver, and glass, the wood that gleamed as darkly brilliant as the surface of a pool of oil. At one end a bronze figure sturdily held a support for a separated chamber, and at convenient places on the ceiling were frescos in olive and silver.

To the minds of the pair, their surroundings reflected the glory of their marriage that morning in San Antonio; this was the environment of their new estate; and the man's face in particular beamed with an elation that made him appear ridiculous to the negro porter. This individual at times surveyed them from afar with an amused and superior grin. On other occasions he bullied them with skill in ways that did not make it exactly plain to them that they were being bullied. He subtly used all the manners of the most unconquerable kind of snobbery. He oppressed them; but of this oppression they had small knowledge, and they speedily forgot that infrequently a number of travellers covered them with stares of derisive enjoyment. Historically there was supposed to be something infinitely humorous in their situation.

"We are due in Yellow Sky at 3:42," he said, looking tenderly into her eyes.

"Oh, are we?" she said, as if she had not been aware of it. To evince surprise at her husband's statement was part of her wifely amiability. She took from a pocket a little silver watch; and as she held it before her, and stared at it with a frown of attention, the new husband's face shone.

"I bought it in San Anton' from a friend of mine," he told her gleefully.

"It's seventeen minutes past twelve," she said, looking up at him with a kind of shy and clumsy coquetry. A passenger, noting this play, grew excessively sardonic, and winked at himself in one of the numerous mirrors.

At last they went to the dining-car. Two rows of negro waiters, in glowing white suits, surveyed their entrance with the interest, and also the equanimity, of men who had been forewarned. The pair fell to the lot of a waiter who happened to feel pleasure in steering them through their meal. He viewed them with the manner of a fatherly pilot, his countenance radiant with benevolence. The patronage, entwined with the ordinary deference, was not plain to them. And yet, as they returned to their coach, they showed in their faces a sense of escape.

To the left, miles down a long purple slope, was a little ribbon of mist where moved the keening Rio Grande. The train was approaching it at an angle, and the apex was Yellow Sky. Presently it was apparent that, as the distance from Yellow Sky grew shorter, the husband became commensurately restless. His brick-red hands were more insistent in their prominence. Occasionally he was even rather absent-minded and far-away when the bride leaned forward and addressed him.

As a matter of truth, Jack Potter was beginning to find the shadow of a deed weigh upon him like a leaden slab. He, the town marshal of Yellow Sky, a man known, liked, and feared in his corner, a prominent person, had gone to San Antonio to meet a girl he believed he loved, and there, after the usual prayers, had actually induced her to marry him, without consulting Yellow Sky for any part of the transaction. He was now bringing his bride before an innocent and unsuspecting community.

Of course people in Yellow Sky married as it pleased them in accordance with a general custom; but such was Potter's thought of his duty to his friends, or of their idea of his duty, or of an unspoken form which does not control men in these matters, that he felt he was heinous. He had committed an extraordinary crime. Face to face with this girl in San Antonio, and spurred by his sharp impulse, he had gone headlong over all the social hedges. At San Antonio he was like a man hidden in the dark. A knife to sever any friendly duty, any form, was easy to his hand in that remote city. But the hour of Yellow Sky — the hour of daylight — was approaching.

He knew full well that his marriage was an important thing to his town. It could only be exceeded by the burning of the new hotel. His friends could not forgive him. Frequently he had reflected on the advisability of telling them by telegraph, but a new cowardice had been upon him. He feared to do it. And now the train was hurrying him toward a scene of amazement, glee, and reproach. He glanced out of the window at the line of haze swinging slowly in toward the train.

Yellow Sky had a kind of brass band, which played painfully, to the delight of the populace. He laughed without heart as he thought of it. If the citizens could dream of his prospective arrival with his bride, they would parade the band at the station and escort them, amid cheers and laughing congratulations, to his adobe home.

He resolved that he would use all the devices of speed and plainscraft in making the journey from the station to his house. Once within that safe citadel, he could issue some sort of vocal bulletin, and then not go among the citizens until they had time to wear off a little of their enthusiasm.

The bride looked anxiously at him. "What's worrying you, Jack?"

He laughed again. "I'm not worrying, girl; I'm only thinking of Yellow Sky."

She flushed in comprehension.

A sense of mutual guilt invaded their minds and developed a finer tenderness. They looked at each other with eyes softly aglow. But Potter often laughed the same nervous laugh; the flush upon the bride's face seemed quite permanent.

The traitor to the feelings of Yellow Sky narrowly watched the speeding landscape. "We're nearly there," he said.

Presently the porter came and announced the proximity of Potter's home. He held a brush in his hand, and, with all his airy superiority gone, he brushed Potter's new clothes as the latter slowly turned this way and that way. Potter fumbled out a coin and gave it to the porter, as he had seen others do. It was a heavy and muscle-bound business, as that of a man shoeing his first horse.

The porter took their bag, and as the train began to slow they moved forward to the hooded platform of the car. Presently the two engines and their long string of coaches rushed into the station of Yellow Sky.

"They have to take water here," said Potter, from a constricted throat and in mournful cadence, as one announcing death. Before the train stopped his eye had swept the length of the platform, and he was glad and astonished to see there was none upon it but the station-agent, who, with a slightly hurried and anxious air, was walking toward the water-tanks. When the train had halted, the porter alighted first, and placed in position a little temporary step.

"Come on, girl," said Potter, hoarsely. As he helped her down they each laughed on a false note. He took the bag from the negro, and bade his wife cling to his arm. As they slunk rapidly away, his hang-dog glance perceived that they were unloading the two trunks, and also that the station-agent, far ahead near the baggage-car, had turned and was running toward him, making gestures. He laughed, and groaned as he laughed, when he noted the first effect of his marital bliss upon Yellow Sky. He gripped his wife's arm firmly to his side, and they fled. Behind them the porter stood, chuckling fatuously.

II

The California express on the Southern Railway was due at Yellow Sky in twenty-one minutes. There were six men at the bar of the Weary Gentleman saloon. One was a drummer who talked a great deal and rapidly; three were Texans who did not care to talk at that time; and two were Mexican sheep-herders, who did not talk as a general practice in the Weary Gentleman saloon. The barkeeper's dog lay on the board walk that crossed in front of the door. His head was on his paws, and he glanced drowsily here and there with the constant vigilance of a dog that is kicked on occasion.

Across the sandy street were some vivid green grass-plots, so wonderful in appearance, amid the sands that burned near them in a blazing sun, that they caused a doubt in the mind. They exactly resembled the grass mats used to represent lawns on the stage. At the cooler end of the railway station, a man without a coat sat in a tilted chair and smoked his pipe. The fresh-cut bank of the Rio Grande circled near the town, and there could be seen beyond it a great plum-colored plain of mesquit.

Save for the busy drummer and his companions in the saloon, Yellow Sky was dozing. The new-comer leaned gracefully upon the bar, and recited many tales with the confidence of a bard who has come upon a new field.

"— and at the moment that the old man fell downstairs with the bureau in his arms, the old woman was coming up with two scuttles of coal, and of course —"

The drummer's tale was interrupted by a young man who suddenly appeared in the open door. He cried: "Scratchy Wilson's drunk, and has turned loose with both hands." The two Mexicans at once set down their glasses and faded out of the rear entrance of the saloon.

The drummer, innocent and jocular, answered: "All right, old man. S'pose he has? Come in and have a drink, anyhow."

But the information had made such an obvious cleft in every skull in the room that the drummer was obliged to see its importance. All had become instantly solemn. "Say," said he, mystified, "what is this?" His three companions made the introductory gesture of eloquent speech; but the young man at the door forestalled them.

"It means, my friend," he answered, as he came into the saloon, "that for the next two hours this town won't be a health resort."

The barkeeper went to the door, and locked and barred it; reaching out of the window, he pulled in heavy wooden shutters, and barred them. Immediately a solemn, chapel-like gloom was upon the place. The drummer was looking from one to another.

"But, say," he cried, "what is this, anyhow? You don't mean there is going to be a gun-fight?"

"Don't know whether there'll be a fight or not," answered one man, grimly; "but there'll be some shootin' — some good shootin'."

The young man who had warned them waved his hand. "Oh, there'll be a fight fast enough, if any one wants it. Anybody can get a fight out there in the street. There's a fight just waiting."

The drummer seemed to be swayed between the interest of a foreigner and a perception of personal danger.

"What did you say his name was?" he asked.

"Scratchy Wilson," they answered in chorus.

"And will he kill anybody? What are you going to do? Does this happen often? Does he rampage around like this once a week or so? Can he break in that door?"

"No; he can't break down that door," replied the barkeeper. "He's tried it three times. But when he comes you'd better lay down on the floor, stranger. He's dead sure to shoot at it, and a bullet may come through."

Thereafter the drummer kept a strict eye upon the door. The time had not yet called for him to hug the floor, but, as a minor precaution, he sidled near the wall. "Will he kill anybody?" he said again.

The men laughed low and scornfully at the question.

"He's out to shoot, and he's out for trouble. Don't see any good in experimentin' with him."

"But what do you do in a case like this? What do you do?"

A man responded: "Why, he and Jack Potter —"

"But," in chorus the other men interrupted, "Jack Potter's in San Anton'."

"Well, who is he? What's he got to do with it?"

"Oh, he's the town marshal. He goes out and fights Scratchy when he gets on one of these tears."

"Wow!" said the drummer, mopping his brow. "Nice job he's got."

The voices had toned away to mere whisperings. The drummer wished to ask further questions, which were born of an increasing anxiety and bewilderment; but when he attempted them, the men merely looked at him in irritation and motioned him to remain silent. A tense waiting hush was upon them. In the deep shadows of the room their eyes shone as they listened for sounds from the street. One man made three gestures at the barkeeper; and the latter, moving like a ghost, handed him a glass and a bottle. The man poured a full glass of whisky, and set down the bottle noiselessly. He gulped the whisky in a swallow, and turned again toward the door in immovable silence. The drummer saw that the barkeeper, without a sound, had taken a Winchester from beneath the bar. Later he saw this individual beckoning to him, so he tiptoed across the room.

"You better come with me back of the bar."

"No, thanks," said the drummer, perspiring; "I'd rather be where I can make a break for the back door."

Whereupon the man of bottles made a kindly but peremptory gesture. The drummer obeyed it, and, finding himself seated on a box with his head below the level of the bar, balm was laid upon his soul at sight of various zinc and copper fittings that bore a resemblance to armor-plate. The barkeeper took a seat comfortably upon an adjacent box.

"You see," he whispered, "this here Scratchy Wilson is a wonder with a gun — a perfect wonder; and when he goes on the war-trail, we hunt our holes — naturally. He's about the last one of the old gang that used to hang out along the river here. He's a terror when he's drunk. When he's sober he's all right — kind of simple — wouldn't hurt a fly — nicest fellow in town. But when he's drunk — whoo!"

There were periods of stillness. "I wish Jack Potter was back from San

Anton'," said the barkeeper. "He shot Wilson up once — in the leg — and he would sail in and pull out the kinks in this thing."

Presently they heard from a distance the sound of a shot, followed by three wild yowls. It instantly removed a bond from the men in the darkened saloon. There was a shuffling of feet. They looked at each other. "Here he comes," they said.

III

A man in a maroon-colored flannel shirt, which had been purchased for purposes of decoration, and made principally by some Jewish women on the East Side of New York, rounded a corner and walked into the middle of the main street of Yellow Sky. In either hand the man held a long, heavy, blue-black revolver. Often he yelled, and these cries rang through a semblance of a deserted village, shrilly flying over the roofs in a volume that seemed to have no relation to the ordinary vocal strength of a man. It was as if the surrounding stillness formed the arch of a tomb over him. These cries of ferocious challenge rang against walls of silence. And his boots had red tops with gilded imprints, of the kind beloved in winter by little sledding boys on the hillsides of New England.

The man's face flamed in a rage begot of whisky. His eyes, rolling, and yet keen for ambush, hunted the still doorways and windows. He walked with the creeping movement of the midnight cat. As it occurred to him, he roared menacing information. The long revolvers in his hands were as easy as straws; they were removed with an electric swiftness. The little fingers of each hand played sometimes in a musician's way. Plain from the low collar of the shirt, the cords of his neck straightened and sank, straightened and sank, as passion moved him. The only sounds were his terrible invitations. The calm adobes preserved their demeanor at the passing of this small thing in the middle of the street.

There was no offer of fight — no offer of fight. The man called to the sky. There were no attractions. He bellowed and fumed and swayed his revolvers here and everywhere.

The dog of the barkeeper of the Weary Gentleman saloon had not appreciated the advance of events. He yet lay dozing in front of his master's door. At sight of the dog, the man paused and raised his revolver humorously. At sight of the man, the dog sprang up and walked diagonally away, with a sullen head, and growling. The man yelled, and the dog broke into a gallop. As it was about to enter the alley, there was a loud noise, a whistling, and something spat the ground directly before it. The dog screamed, and, wheeling in terror, galloped headlong in a new direction. Again there was a noise, a whistling, and sand was kicked viciously before it. Fear-stricken, the dog turned and flurried like an animal in a pen. The man stood laughing, his weapons at his hips.

Ultimately the man was attracted by the closed door of the Weary

Gentleman saloon. He went to it and, hammering with a revolver, demanded drink.

The door remaining imperturbable, he picked a bit of paper from the walk, and nailed it to the framework with a knife. He then turned his back contemptuously upon this popular resort and, walking to the opposite side of the street and spinning there on his heel quickly and lithely, fired at the bit of paper. He missed it by a half inch. He swore at himself, and went away. Later he comfortably fusilladed the windows of his most intimate friend. The man was playing with this town; it was a toy for him.

But still there was no offer of fight. The name of Jack Potter, his ancient antagonist, entered his mind, and he concluded that it would be a glad thing if he should go to Potter's house, and by bombardment induce him to come out and fight. He moved in the direction of his desire, chanting Apache scalp-music.

When he arrived at it, Potter's house presented the same still front as had the other adobes. Taking up a strategic position, the man howled a challenge. But this house regarded him as might a great stone god. It gave no sign. After a decent wait, the man howled further challenges, mingling with them wonderful epithets.

Presently there came the spectacle of a man churning himself into deepest rage over the immobility of a house. He fumed at it as the winter wind attacks a prairie cabin in the North. To the distance there should have gone the sound of a tumult like the fighting of two hundred Mexicans. As necessity bade him, he paused for breath or to reload his revolvers.

IV

Potter and his bride walked sheepishly and with speed. Sometimes they laughed together shamefacedly and low.

"Next corner, dear," he said finally.

They put forth the efforts of a pair walking bowed against a strong wind. Potter was about to raise a finger to point the first appearance of the new home when, as they circled the corner, they came face to face with a man in a maroon-colored shirt, who was feverishly pushing cartridges into a large revolver. Upon the instant the man dropped his revolver to the ground and, like lightning, whipped another from its holster. The second weapon was aimed at the bridegroom's chest.

There was a silence. Potter's mouth seemed to be merely a grave for his tongue. He exhibited an instinct to at once loosen his arm from the woman's grip, and he dropped the bag to the sand. As for the bride, her face had gone as yellow as old cloth. She was a slave to hideous rites, gazing at the apparitional snake.

The two men faced each other at a distance of three paces. He of the revolver smiled with a new and quiet ferocity.

"Tried to sneak up on me," he said. "Tried to sneak up on me!" His eyes grew more baleful. As Potter made a slight movement, the man thrust his revolver venomously forward. "No; don't you do it, Jack Potter. Don't you move a finger toward a gun just yet. Don't you move an eyelash. The time has come for me to settle with you and I'm goin' to do it my own way, and loaf along with no interferin'. So if you don't want a gun bent on you, just mind what I tell you."

Potter looked at his enemy. "I ain't got a gun on me Scratchy," he said. "Honest, I ain't." He was stiffening and steadying, but yet somewhere at the back of his mind a vision of the Pullman floated: the sea-green figured velvet, the shining brass, silver, and glass, the wood that gleamed as darkly brilliant as the surface of a pool of oil — all the glory of marriage, the environment of the new estate. "You know I fight when it comes to fighting, Scratchy Wilson; but I ain't got a gun on me. You'll have to do all the shootin' yourself."

His enemy's face went livid. He stepped forward, and lashed his weapon to and fro before Potter's chest. "Don't you tell me you ain't got no gun on you, you whelp. Don't tell me no lie like that. There ain't a man in Texas ever seen you without no gun. Don't take me for no kid." His eyes blazed with light, and his throat worked like a pump.

"I ain't takin' you for no kid," answered Potter. His heels had not moved an inch backward. "I'm takin' you for a damn fool. I tell you I ain't got a gun, and I ain't. If you're goin' to shoot me up, you better begin now; you'll never get a chance like this again."

So much enforced reasoning had told on Wilson's rage; he was calmer. "If you ain't got a gun, why ain't you got a gun?" he sneered. "Been to Sunday-school?"

"I ain't got a gun because I've just come from San Anton' with my wife. I'm married," said Potter. "And if I'd thought there was going to be any galoots like you prowling around when I brought my wife home, I'd had a gun, and don't you forget it."

"Married!" said Scratchy, not at all comprehending.

"Yes, married. I'm married," said Potter, distinctly.

"Married?" said Scratchy. Seemingly for the first time, he saw the drooping, drowning woman at the other man's side. "No!" he said. He was like a creature allowed a glimpse of another world. He moved a pace backward, and his arm, with the revolver, dropped to his side. "Is this the lady?" he asked.

"Yes; this is the lady," answered Potter.

There was another period of silence.

"Well," said Wilson at last, slowly, "I s'pose it's all off now."

"It's all off if you say so, Scratchy. You know I didn't make the trouble." Potter lifted his valise.

"Well, I 'low it's off, Jack," said Wilson. He was looking at the ground. "Married!" He was not a student of chivalry; it was merely that in the presence of this foreign condition he was a simple child of the earlier plains. He picked up his starboard revolver, and, placing both weapons in their holsters, he went away. His feet made funnel-shaped tracks in the heavy sand.

[1898]

WILLA CATHER (1873–1947) *once wrote that "a creative writer can do his best only with what lies within the range and character of his deepest sympathies." She herself was thirty-nine before her true subject came into focus for her. Born in rural Virginia, she moved to Nebraska with her family nine years later. The oldest of seven children, she was raised in a loving home, but her strongest response to the frontier prairie village of Red Cloud, Nebraska, where her family finally settled, was the urge to escape. She went to a preparatory school in Lincoln, where she also continued at the University of Nebraska, studying classics. After her graduation in 1895 she went to Pittsburgh, working as a journalist for seven years, and then for another three years teaching English and Latin in high schools. At this time her stories and poems began to appear in popular magazines. Her first book was a volume of poetry,* April Twilights *(1903), followed in 1905 by* The Troll Gardens, *the first of four collections of short stories. In 1906 she joined the staff of McClure's magazine in New York City, assuming the position of managing editor before she left to devote full time to her writing.*

As a university student Cather had read Flaubert, whose restraint as a stylist she admired, but the most important influence on her work was Sarah Orne Jewett, who taught her that beautiful writing was a consequence of steady concentration on a thoroughly understood scene. Cather met Jewett in Boston, and Jewett urged her to develop her talents as a writer, advising her to "find your own quiet center of life and write to the human heart, the great consciousness that all humanity goes to make up." It was not until 1912 that Cather found her subject, after a trip home to Red Cloud: She no longer saw her adolescence on the prairie as deprived and stifling, and she was able to feel that her own experience was significant enough to write about. O Pioneers! *(1913), the first of three novels about immigrant life on the western frontier, was followed in 1915 by* The Song of the Lark *and in 1918 by* My Ántonia, *a portrait of a pioneer woman that is generally regarded as her masterpiece.*

Cather went on to publish a total of twelve novels and several collections of stories, many about artists, but she did not value her forty-four stories as highly as her novels, including only three of them in the definitive "Library Edition" that represents her final judgment of her work. Many critics have commented on the purity of her prose style, and her early study of classical languages helped form her attitudes toward rigorous control in her fiction. Her own kind of realism embodied her conviction that "We like a writer much as we like individuals. Oftener than we realize, it is for some moral quality, some ideal which he himself cherishes. . . . It is this very personal quality of perception, a vivid and intensely personal experience of life, which makes 'style.' " Cather wrote "Paul's Case," a story about a sensitive boy who hungers for art and feels stifled by everyday life, in 1904, while she was still a high school teacher in Pittsburgh.

Willa Cather

ಬಬ

PAUL'S CASE

It was Paul's afternoon to appear before the faculty of the Pittsburgh High School to account for his various misdemeanors. He had been suspended a week ago, and his father had called at the Principal's office and confessed his perplexity about his son. Paul entered the faculty room suave and smiling. His clothes were a trifle outgrown and the tan velvet on the collar of his open overcoat was frayed and worn; but for all that there was something of the dandy about him, and he wore an opal pin in his neatly knotted black four-in-hand, and a red carnation in his buttonhole. This latter adornment the faculty somehow felt was not properly significant of the contrite spirit befitting a boy under the ban of suspension.

Paul was tall for his age and very thin, with high, cramped shoulders and a narrow chest. His eyes were remarkable for a certain hysterical brilliancy and he continually used them in a conscious, theatrical sort of way, peculiarly offensive in a boy. The pupils were abnormally large, as though he were addicted to belladonna, but there was a glassy glitter about them which that drug does not produce.

When questioned by the Principal as to why he was there, Paul stated, politely enough, that he wanted to come back to school. This was a lie, but Paul was quite accustomed to lying; found it, indeed, indispensable for overcoming friction. His teachers were asked to state their respective charges against him, which they did with such a rancor and aggrievedness as evinced that this was not a usual case. Disorder and impertinence were among the offenses named, yet each of his instructors felt that it was scarcely possible to put into words the real cause of the trouble, which lay in a sort of hysterically defiant manner of the boy's; in the contempt which they all knew he felt for them, and which he seemingly made not the least effort to conceal. Once, when he had been making a synopsis of a paragraph at the blackboard, his English teacher had stepped to his side and attempted to guide his hand. Paul had started back with a shudder and thrust his hands violently behind him. The astonished woman could scarcely have been more hurt and embarrassed had he struck at her. The insult was so in-

voluntary and definitely personal as to be unforgettable. In one way and another, he had made all his teachers, men and women alike, conscious of the
same feeling of physical aversion. In one class he habitually sat with his
hand shading his eyes; in another he always looked out of the window during the recitation; in another he made a running commentary on the lecture, with humorous intention.

His teachers felt this afternoon that his whole attitude was symbolized
by his shrug and his flippantly red carnation flower, and they fell upon him
without mercy, his English teacher leading the pack. He stood through it
smiling, his pale lips parted over his white teeth. (His lips were continually
twitching, and he had a habit of raising his eyebrows that was contemptuous and irritating to the last degree.) Older boys than Paul had broken
down and shed tears under that baptism of fire, but his set smile did not
once desert him, and his only sign of discomfort was the nervous trembling
of the fingers that toyed with the buttons of his overcoat, and an occasional
jerking of the other hand that held his hat. Paul was always smiling, always
glancing about him, seeming to feel that people might be watching him and
trying to detect something. This conscious expression, since it was as far as
possible from boyish mirthfulness, was usually attributed to insolence or
"smartness."

As the inquisition proceeded, one of his instructors repeated an imper-
tinent remark of the boy's, and the Principal asked him whether he thought
that a courteous speech to have made a woman. Paul shrugged his shoulders slightly and his eyebrows twitched.

"I don't know," he replied. "I didn't mean to be polite or impolite,
either. I guess it's a sort of way I have of saying things regardless."

The Principal, who was a sympathetic man, asked him whether he
didn't think that a way it would be well to get rid of. Paul grinned and said
he guessed so. When he was told that he could go, he bowed gracefully and
went out. His bow was but a repetition of the scandalous red carnation.

His teachers were in despair, and his drawing master voiced the feeling
of them all when he declared there was something about the boy which
none of them understood. He added: "I don't really believe that smile of his
comes altogether from insolence; there's something sort of haunted about
it. The boy is not strong, for one thing. I happen to know that he was born
in Colorado, only a few months before his mother died out there of a long
illness. There is something wrong about the fellow."

The drawing master had come to realize that, in looking at Paul, one
saw only his white teeth and the forced animation of his eyes. One warm
afternoon the boy had gone to sleep at his drawing-board, and his master
had noted with amazement what a white, blue-veined face it was; drawn
and wrinkled like an old man's about the eyes, the lips twitching even in his
sleep, and stiff with a nervous tension that drew them back from his teeth.

His teachers left the building dissatisfied and unhappy; humiliated to
have felt so vindictive toward a mere boy, to have uttered this feeling in

cutting terms, and to have set each other on, as it were, in the gruesome game of intemperate reproach. Some of them remembered having seen a miserable street cat set at bay by a ring of tormentors.

As for Paul, he ran down the hill whistling the Soldiers' Chorus from *Faust* looking wildly behind him now and then to see whether some of his teachers were not there to writhe under this light-heartedness. As it was now late in the afternoon and Paul was on duty that evening as usher at Carnegie Hall, he decided that he would not go home to supper. When he reached the concert hall the doors were not yet open and, as it was chilly outside, he decided to go up into the picture gallery — always deserted at this hour — where there were some of Raffelli's gay studies of Paris streets and an airy blue Venetian scene or two that always exhilarated him. He was delighted to find no one in the gallery but the old guard, who sat in one corner, a newspaper on his knee, a black patch over one eye and the other closed. Paul possessed himself of the place and walked confidently up and down, whistling under his breath. After a while he sat down before a blue Rico and lost himself. When he bethought him to look at his watch, it was after seven o'clock, and he rose with a start and ran downstairs, making a face at Augustus, peering out from the cast-room, and an evil gesture at the Venus of Milo as he passed her on the stairway.

When Paul reached the ushers' dressing-room half-a-dozen boys were there already, and he began excitedly to tumble into his uniform. It was one of the few that at all approached fitting, and Paul thought it very becoming — though he knew that the tight, straight coat accentuated his narrow chest, about which he was exceedingly sensitive. He was always considerably excited while he dressed, twanging all over to the tuning of the strings and the preliminary flourishes of the horns in the music-room; but to-night he seemed quite beside himself, and he teased and plagued the boys until, telling him that he was crazy, they put him down on the floor and sat on him.

Somewhat calmed by his suppression, Paul dashed out to the front of the house to seat the early comers. He was a model usher; gracious and smiling he ran up and down the aisles; nothing was too much trouble for him; he carried messages and brought programmes as though it were his greatest pleasure in life, and all the people in his section thought him a charming boy, feeling that he remembered and admired them. As the house filled, he grew more and more vivacious and animated, and the color came to his cheeks and lips. It was very much as though this were a great reception and Paul were the host. Just as the musicians came out to take their places, his English teacher arrived with checks for the seats which a prominent manufacturer had taken for the season. She betrayed some embarrassment when she handed Paul the tickets, and a *hauteur* which subsequently made her feel very foolish. Paul was startled for a moment, and had the feeling of wanting to put her out; what business had she here among all these fine people and gay colors? He looked her over and decided that she was not appropriately dressed and must be a fool to sit downstairs in such togs. The tickets had probably been sent her out of kindness, he reflected as he put down a seat for her, and she had about as much right to sit there as he had.

When the symphony began Paul sank into one of the rear seats with a long sigh of relief, and lost himself as he had done before the Rico. It was not that symphonies, as such, meant anything in particular to Paul, but the first sigh of the instruments seemed to free some hilarious and potent spirit within him; something that struggled there like the Genius in the bottle found by the Arab fisherman. He felt a sudden zest of life; the lights danced before his eyes and the concert hall blazed into unimaginable splendor. When the soprano soloist came on, Paul forgot even the nastiness of his teacher's being there and gave himself up to the peculiar stimulus such personages always had for him. The soloist chanced to be a German woman, by no means in her first youth, and the mother of many children; but she wore an elaborate gown and a tiara, and above all she had that indefinable air of achievement, that world-shine upon her, which, in Paul's eyes, made her a veritable queen of Romance.

After a concert was over Paul was always irritable and wretched until he got to sleep, and tonight he was even more than usually restless. He had the feeling of not being able to let down, of its being impossible to give up this delicious excitement which was the only thing that could be called living at all. During the last number he withdrew and, after hastily changing his clothes in the dressing-room, slipped out to the side door where the soprano's carriage stood. Here he began pacing rapidly up and down the walk, waiting to see her come out.

Over yonder the Schenley, in its vacant stretch, loomed big and square through the fine rain, the windows of its twelve stories glowing like those of a lighted cardboard house under a Christmas tree. All the actors and singers of the better class stayed there when they were in the city, and a number of the big manufacturers of the place lived there in the winter. Paul had often hung about the hotel, watching the people go in and out, longing to enter and leave school-masters and dull care behind him forever.

At last the singer came out, accompanied by the conductor, who helped her into her carriage and closed the door with a cordial *auf wiedersehen* which set Paul to wondering whether she were not an old sweetheart of his. Paul followed the carriage over to the hotel, walking so rapidly as not to be far from the entrance when the singer alighted and disappeared behind the swinging glass doors that were opened by a negro in a tall hat and a long coat. In the moment that the door was ajar it seemed to Paul that he, too, entered. He seemed to feel himself go after her up the steps, into the warm, lighted building, into an exotic, a tropical world of shiny, glistening surfaces and basking ease. He reflected upon the mysterious dishes that were brought into the dining-room, the green bottles in buckets of ice, as he had seen them in the supper party pictures of the *Sunday World* supplement. A quick gust of wind brought the rain down with sudden vehemence, and Paul was startled to find that he was still outside in the slush of the gravel driveway; that his boots were letting in the water and his scanty overcoat was clinging wet about him; that the lights in front of the concert hall were out, and that the rain was driving in sheets between him and the orange glow of the windows above him. There it was, what he wanted — tangibly before him, like the fairy world of a Christmas pantomime, but mocking spirits stood guard at the doors, and, as the rain beat in his face, Paul wondered whether he were destined always to shiver in the black night outside, looking up at it.

He turned and walked reluctantly toward the car tracks. The end had to come sometime; his father in his night-clothes at the top of the stairs, explanations that did not explain, hastily improvised fictions that were forever tripping him up, his upstairs room and its horrible yellow wall-paper, the creaking bureau with the greasy plush collar-box, and over his painted wooden bed the pictures of George Washington and John Calvin, and the framed motto, "Feed my Lambs," which had been worked in red worsted by his mother.

Half an hour later, Paul alighted from his car and went slowly down one of the side streets off the main thoroughfare. It was a highly respectable street, where all the houses were exactly alike, and where businessmen of moderate means begot and reared large families of children, all of whom went to Sabbath-school and learned the shorter catechism, and were interested in arithmetic; all of whom were as exactly alike as their homes, and of a piece with the monotony in which they lived. Paul never went up Cordelia Street without a shudder of loathing. His home was next to the house of the Cumberland minister. He approached it tonight with the nerveless sense of defeat, the hopeless feeling of sinking back forever into ugliness and commonness that he had always had when he came home. The moment he turned into Cordelia Street he felt the waters close above his head. After each of these orgies of living, he experienced all the physical depression which follows a debauch; the loathing of respectable beds, of common food, of a house penetrated by kitchen odors; a shuddering repulsion for the flavorless, colorless mass of every-day existence; a morbid desire for cool things and soft lights and fresh flowers.

The nearer he approached the house, the more absolutely unequal Paul felt to the sight of it all; his ugly sleeping chamber; the cold bathroom with the grimy zinc tub, the cracked mirror, the dripping spiggots; his father, at the top of the stairs, his hairy legs sticking out from his night-shirt, his feet thrust into carpet slippers. He was so much later than usual that there would certainly be inquiries and reproaches. Paul stopped short before the door. He felt that he could not be accosted by his father tonight;

that he could not toss again on that miserable bed. He would not go in. He would tell his father that he had no car fare, and it was raining so hard he had gone home with one of the boys and stayed all night.

Meanwhile, he was wet and cold. He went around to the back of the house and tried one of the basement windows, found it open, raised it cautiously, and scrambled down the cellar wall to the floor. There he stood, holding his breath, terrified by the noise he had made, but the floor above him was silent, and there was no creak on the stairs. He found a soap-box, and carried it over to the soft ring of light that streamed from the furnace door, and sat down. He was horribly afraid of rats, so he did not try to sleep, but sat looking distrustfully at the dark, still terrified lest he might have awakened his father. In such reactions, after one of the experiences which made days and nights out of the dreary blanks of the calendar, when his senses were deadened, Paul's head was always singularly clear. Suppose his father had heard him getting in at the window and had come down and shot him for a burglar? Then, again, suppose his father had come down, pistol in hand, and he had cried out in time to save himself, and his father had been horrified to think how nearly he had killed him? Then, again, suppose a day should come when his father would remember that night, and wish there had been no warning cry to stay his hand? With this last supposition Paul entertained himself until daybreak.

The following Sunday was fine; the sodden November chill was broken by the last flash of autumnal summer. In the morning Paul had to go to church and Sabbath-school, as always. On seasonable Sunday afternoons the burghers of Cordelia Street always sat out on their front "stoops," and talked to their neighbors on the next stoop, or called to those across the street in neighborly fashion. The men usually sat on gay cushions placed upon the steps that led down to the sidewalk, while the women, in their Sunday "waists," sat in rockers on the cramped porches, pretending to be greatly at their ease. The children played in the streets; there were so many of them that the place resembled the recreation grounds of a kindergarten. The men on the steps — all in their shirt sleeves, their vests unbuttoned — sat with their legs well apart, their stomachs comfortably protruding, and talked of the prices of things, or told anecdotes of the sagacity of their various chiefs and overlords. They occasionally looked over the multitude of squabbling children, listened affectionately to their high-pitched, nasal voices, smiling to see their own proclivities reproduced in their offspring, and interspersed their legends of the iron kings with remarks about their sons' progress at school, their grades in arithmetic, and the amounts they had saved in their toy banks.

On this last Sunday of November, Paul sat all the afternoon on the lowest step of his "stoop," staring into the street, while his sisters, in their rockers, were talking to the minister's daughters next door about how many shirt-waists they had made in the last week, and how many waffles some one had eaten at the last church supper. When the weather was warm, and his father was in a particularly jovial frame of mind, the girls made lemonade, which was always brought out in a red-glass pitcher, ornamented with forget-me-nots in blue enamel. This the girls thought very fine, and the neighbors always joked about the suspicious color of the pitcher.

Today Paul's father sat on the top step, talking to a young man who shifted a restless baby from knee to knee. He happened to be the young man who was daily held up to Paul as a model, and after whom it was his father's dearest hope that he would pattern. This young man was of a ruddy complexion, with a compressed, red mouth, and faded, near-sighted eyes, over which he wore thick spectacles, with gold bows that curved about his ears. He was clerk to one of the magnates of a great steel corporation, and was looked upon in Cordelia Street as a young man with a future. There was a story that, some five years ago — he was now barely twenty-six — he had been a trifle dissipated but in order to curb his appetites and save the loss of time and strength that a sowing of wild oats might have entailed, he had taken his chief's advice, oft reiterated to his employees, and at twenty-one had married the first woman whom he could persuade to share his fortunes. She happened to be an angular school-mistress, much older than he, who also wore thick glasses, and who had now borne him four children, all near-sighted, like herself.

The young man was relating how his chief, now cruising in the Mediterranean, kept in touch with all the details of the business, arranging his office hours on his yacht just as though he were at home, and "knocking off work enough to keep two stenographers busy." His father told, in turn, the plan his corporation was considering, of putting in an electric railway plant at Cairo. Paul snapped his teeth; he had an awful apprehension that they might spoil it all before he got there. Yet he rather liked to hear these legends of the iron kings, that were told and retold on Sundays and holidays; these stories of palaces in Venice, yachts on the Mediterranean, and high play at Monte Carlo appealed to his fancy, and he was interested in the triumphs of these cash boys who had become famous, though he had no mind for the cash-boy stage.

After supper was over, and he had helped to dry the dishes, Paul nervously asked his father whether he could go to George's to get some help in his geometry, and still more nervously asked for car fare. This latter request he had to repeat, as his father, on principle, did not like to hear requests for money, whether much or little. He asked Paul whether he could not go to some boy who lived nearer, and told him that he ought not to leave his school work until Sunday; but he gave him the dime. He was not a poor man, but he had a worthy ambition to come up in the world. His only reason for allowing Paul to usher was, that he thought a boy ought to be earning a little.

Paul bounded upstairs, scrubbed the greasy odor of the dish-water from his hands with the ill-smelling soap he hated, and then shook over his fingers a few drops of violet water from the bottle he kept hidden in his drawer. He left the house with his geometry conspicuously under his arm, and the moment he got out of Cordelia Street and boarded a downtown car, he shook off the lethargy of two deadening days, and began to live again.

The leading juvenile of the permanent stock company which played at one of the downtown theatres was an acquaintance of Paul's, and the boy had been invited to drop in at the Sunday-night rehearsals whenever he could. For more than a year Paul had spent every available moment loitering about Charley Edwards's dressing-room. He had won a place among Edwards's following not only because the young actor, who could not afford to employ a dresser, often found him useful, but because he recognized in Paul something akin to what churchmen term "vocation."

It was at the theatre and at Carnegie Hall that Paul really lived; the rest was but a sleep and a forgetting. This was Paul's fairy tale, and it had for him all the allurement of a secret love. The moment he inhaled the gassy, painty, dusty odor behind the scenes, he breathed like a prisoner set free, and felt within him the possibility of doing or saying splendid, brilliant, poetic things. The moment the cracked orchestra beat out the overture from *Martha*, or jerked at the serenade from *Rigoletto*, all stupid and ugly things slid from him, and his senses were deliciously, yet delicately fired.

Perhaps it was because, in Paul's world, the natural nearly always wore the guise of ugliness, that a certain element of artificiality seemed to him necessary in beauty. Perhaps it was because his experience of life elsewhere was so full of Sabbath-school picnics, petty economies, wholesome advice as to how to succeed in life, and the unescapable odors of cooking, that he found this existence so alluring, these smartly-clad men and women so attractive, that he was so moved by these starry apple orchards that bloomed perennially under the lime-light.

It would be difficult to put it strongly enough how convincingly the stage entrance of that theatre was for Paul the actual portal of Romance. Certainly none of the company ever suspected it, least of all Charley Edwards. It was very like the old stories that used to float about London of fabulously rich Jews, who had subterranean halls there, with palms, and fountains, and soft lamps and richly apparelled women who never saw the disenchanting light of London day. So, in the midst of that smoke-palled city, enamored of figures and grimy toil, Paul had his secret temple, his wishing carpet, his bit of blue-and-white Mediterranean shore bathed in perpetual sunshine.

Several of Paul's teachers had a theory that his imagination had been perverted by garish fiction, but the truth was that he scarcely ever read at all. The books at home were not such as would either tempt or corrupt a youthful mind, and as for reading the novels that some of his friends urged upon him — well, he got what he wanted much more quickly from music; any sort of music, from an orchestra to a barrel organ. He needed only the spark, the indescribable thrill that made his imagination master of his senses, and he could make plots and pictures enough of his own. It was equally true that he was not stage struck — not, at any rate, in the usual acceptation of that expression. He had no desire to become an actor, any more than he had to become a musician. He felt no necessity to do any of these things; what he wanted was to see, to be in the atmosphere, float on the wave of it, to be carried out, blue league after blue league, away from everything.

After a night behind the scenes, Paul found the school-room more than ever repulsive; the bare floors and naked walls; the prosy men who never wore frock coats, or violets in their buttonholes; the women with their dull gowns, shrill voices, and pitiful seriousness about prepositions that govern the dative. He could not bear to have the other pupils think, for a moment, that he took these people seriously; he must convey to them that he considered it all trivial, and was there only by way of a jest, anyway. He had autographed pictures of all the members of the stock company which he showed his classmates, telling them the most incredible stories of his familiarity with these people, of his acquaintance with the soloists who came to Carnegie Hall, his suppers with them and the flowers he sent them. When these stories lost their effect, and his audience grew listless, he became desperate and would bid all the boys good-bye, announcing that he was going to travel for a while; going to Naples, to Venice, to Egypt. Then, next Monday, he would slip back, conscious and nervously smiling; his sister was ill, and he should have to defer his voyage until spring.

Matters went steadily worse with Paul at school. In the itch to let his instructors know how heartily he despised them and their homilies, and how thoroughly he was appreciated elsewhere, he mentioned once or twice that he had no time to fool with theorems; adding — with a twitch of the eyebrows and a touch of that nervous bravado which so perplexed them — that he was helping the people down at the stock company; they were old friends of his.

The upshot of the matter was that the Principal went to Paul's father, and Paul was taken out of school and put to work. The manager at Carnegie Hall was told to get another usher in his stead; the door-keeper at the theatre was warned not to admit him to the house; and Charley Edwards remorsefully promised the boy's father not to see him again.

The members of the stock company were vastly amused when some of Paul's stories reached them — especially the women. They were hardworking women, most of them supporting indigent husbands or brothers, and they laughed rather bitterly at having stirred the boy to such fervid and florid inventions. They agreed with the faculty and with his father that Paul's was a bad case.

The east-bound train was ploughing through a January snow-storm; the dull dawn was beginning to show grey when the engine whistled a mile out of Newark. Paul started up from the seat where he had lain curled in uneasy slumber, rubbed the breath-misted window glass with his hand, and peered out. The snow was whirling in curling eddies above the white bottom lands, and the drifts lay already deep in the fields and along the fences, while here and there the long dead grass and dried weed stalks protruded black above it. Lights shone from the scattered houses, and a gang of laborers who stood beside the track waved their lanterns.

Paul had slept very little, and he felt grimy and uncomfortable. He had made the all-night journey in a day coach, partly because he was ashamed, dressed as he was, to go into a Pullman, and partly because he was afraid of being seen there by some Pittsburgh businessman, who might have noticed him in Denny & Carson's office. When the whistle awoke him, he clutched quickly at his breast pocket, glancing about him with an uncertain smile. But the little, clay-bespattered Italians were still sleeping, the slatternly women across the aisle were in open-mouthed oblivion, and even the crumby, crying babies were for the nonce stilled. Paul settled back to struggle with his impatience as best he could.

When he arrived at the Jersey City station, he hurried through his breakfast, manifestly ill at ease and keeping a sharp eye about him. After he reached the Twenty-third Street station, he consulted a cabman, and had himself driven to a men's furnishing establishment that was just opening for the day. He spent upward of two hours there, buying with endless reconsidering and great care. His new street suit he put on in the fitting-room; the frock coat and dress clothes he had bundled into the cab with his linen. Then he drove to a hatter's and a shoe house. His next errand was at Tiffany's, where he selected his silver and a new scarf-pin. He would not wait to have his silver marked, he said. Lastly, he stopped at a trunk shop on Broadway, and had his purchases packed into various travelling bags.

It was a little after one o'clock when he drove up to the Waldorf, and after settling with the cabman, went into the office. He registered from Washington; said his mother and father had been abroad, and that he had come down to await the arrival of their steamer. He told his story plausibly and had no trouble, since he volunteered to pay for them in advance, in engaging his rooms; a sleeping-room, sitting-room and bath.

Not once, but a hundred times Paul had planned this entry into New York. He had gone over every detail of it with Charley Edwards, and in his scrap book at home there were pages of description about New York hotels, cut from the Sunday papers. When he was shown to his sitting-room on the eighth floor, he saw at a glance that everything was as it should be; there was but one detail in his mental picture that the place did not realize, so he rang for the bell boy and sent him down for flowers. He moved about nervously until the boy returned, putting away his new linen and fingering it delightedly as he did so. When the flowers came, he put them hastily into water, and then tumbled into a hot bath. Presently he came out of his white bath-room, resplendent in his new silk underwear, and playing with the tassels of his red robe. The snow was whirling so fiercely outside his windows that he could scarcely see across the street, but within the air was deliciously soft and fragrant. He put the violets and jonquils on the taboret beside the couch, and threw himself down, with a long sigh, covering himself with a Roman blanket. He was thoroughly tired; he had been in such haste, he had stood up to such a strain, covered so much ground in the last twenty-four hours, that he wanted to think how it had all come about. Lulled by the sound of the wind, the warm air, and the cool fragrance of the flowers, he sank into deep, drowsy retrospection.

It had been wonderfully simple; when they had shut him out of the theatre and concert hall, when they had taken away his bone, the whole thing was virtually determined. The rest was a mere matter of opportunity. The only thing that at all surprised him was his own courage — for he realized well enough that he had always been tormented by fear, a sort of apprehensive dread that, of late years, as the meshes of the lies he had told closed about him, had been pulling the muscles of his body tighter and tighter. Until now, he could not remember the time when he had not been dreading something. Even when he was a little boy, it was always there — behind him, or before, or on either side. There had always been the shadowed corner, the dark place into which he dared not look, but from which something seemed always to be watching him — and Paul had done things that were not pretty to watch, he knew.

But now he had a curious sense of relief, as though he had at last thrown down the gauntlet to the thing in the corner.

Yet it was but a day since he had been sulking in the traces; but yesterday afternoon that he had been sent to the bank with Denny & Carson's deposit, as usual — but this time he was instructed to leave the book to be balanced. There was above two thousand dollars in checks, and nearly a thousand in the bank notes which he had taken from the book and quietly transferred to his pocket. At the bank he had made out a new deposit slip. His nerves had been steady enough to permit of his returning to the office, where he had finished his work and asked for a full day's holiday tomorrow, Saturday, giving a perfectly reasonable pretext. The bank book, he knew, would not be returned before Monday or Tuesday, and his father would be out of town for the next week. From the time he slipped the bank notes into his pocket until he boarded the night train for New York, he had not known a moment's hesitation. It was not the first time Paul had steered through treacherous waters.

How astonishingly easy it had all been; here he was, the thing done; and this time there would be no awakening, no figure at the top of the stairs. He watched the snow flakes whirling by his window until he fell asleep.

When he awoke, it was three o'clock in the afternoon. He bounded up with a start; half of one of his precious days gone already! He spent more than an hour in dressing, watching every stage of his toilet carefully in the mirror. Everything was quite perfect; he was exactly the kind of boy he had always wanted to be.

When he went downstairs, Paul took a carriage and drove up Fifth Avenue toward the Park. The snow had somewhat abated; carriages and tradesmen's wagons were hurrying soundlessly to and fro in the winter twilight; boys in woollen mufflers were shovelling off the doorsteps; the avenue stages made fine spots of color against the white street. Here and there on the corners were stands, with whole flower gardens blooming under glass cases, against the sides of which the snow flakes stuck and melted; violets, roses, carnations, lilies of the valley — somewhat vastly more lovely and alluring that they blossomed thus unnaturally in the snow. The Park itself was a wonderful stage winterpiece.

When he returned, the pause of the twilight had ceased, and the tune of the streets had changed. The snow was falling faster, lights streamed from the hotels that reared their dozen stories fearlessly up into the storm, defying the raging Atlantic winds. A long, black stream of carriages poured down the avenue, intersected here and there by other streams, tending horizontally. There were a score of cabs about the entrance of his hotel, and his driver had to wait. Boys in livery were running in and out of the awning stretched across the sidewalk, up and down the red velvet carpet laid from the door to the street. Above, about, within it all was the rumble and roar, the hurry and toss of thousands of human beings as hot for pleasure as himself, and on every side of him towered the glaring affirmation of the omnipotence of wealth.

The boy set his teeth and drew his shoulders together in a spasm of realization: the plot of all dramas, the text of all romances, the nerve-stuff of all sensations was whirling about him like the snow flakes. He burnt like a faggot in a tempest.

When Paul went down to dinner, the music of the orchestra came floating up the elevator shaft to greet him. His head whirled as he stepped into the thronged corridor, and he sank back into one of the chairs against the wall to get his breath. The lights, the chatter, the perfumes, the bewildering medley of color — he had, for a moment, the feeling of not being able to stand it. But only for a moment; these were his own people, he told himself. He went slowly about the corridors, through the writing-rooms, smoking-rooms, reception-rooms, as though he were exploring the chambers of an enchanted palace, built and peopled for him alone.

When he reached the dining-room he sat down at a table near a window. The flowers, the white linen, the many-colored wine glasses, the gay toilettes of the women, the low popping of corks, the undulating repetitions of the *Blue Danube* from the orchestra, all flooded Paul's dream with bewildering radiance. When the roseate tinge of his champagne was added — that cold, precious, bubbling stuff that creamed and foamed in his glass — Paul wondered that there were honest men in the world at all. This was what all the world was fighting for, he reflected; this was what all the struggle was about. He doubted the reality of his past. Had he ever known a place called Cordelia Street, a place where fagged-looking businessmen got on the early car; mere rivets in a machine they seemed to Paul — sickening men, with combings of children's hair always hanging to their coats, and the smell of cooking in their clothes. Cordelia Street — Ah! that belonged to another time and country; had he not always been thus, had he not sat here night after night, from as far back as he could remember, looking pensively over just such shimmering textures, and slowly twirling the stem of a glass like this one between his thumb and middle finger? He rather thought he had.

He was not in the least abashed or lonely. He had no especial desire to meet or to know any of these people; all he demanded was the right to look on and conjecture, to watch the pageant. The mere stage properties were all he contended for. Nor was he lonely later in the evening, in his loge at the Metropolitan. He was now entirely rid of his nervous misgivings, of his forced aggressiveness, of the imperative desire to show himself different from his surroundings. He felt now that his surroundings explained him. Nobody questioned the purple; he had only to wear it passively. He had only to glance down at his attire to reassure himself that here it would be impossible for anyone to humiliate him.

He found it hard to leave his beautiful sitting-room to go to bed that night, and sat long watching the raging storm from his turret window. When he went to sleep it was with the lights turned on in his bedroom; partly because of his old timidity, and partly so that, if he should wake in the night, there would be no wretched moment of doubt, no horrible suspicion of yellow wall-paper, or of Washington and Calvin above his bed.

Sunday morning the city was practically snow-bound. Paul breakfasted late, and in the afternoon he fell in with a wild San Francisco boy, a freshman at Yale, who said he had run down for a "little flyer" over Sunday. The young man offered to show Paul the night side of the town, and the two boys went out together after dinner, not returning to the hotel until seven o'clock the next morning. They had started out in the confiding warmth of a champagne friendship, but their parting in the elevator was singularly cool. The freshman pulled himself together to make his train, and Paul went to bed. He awoke at two o'clock in the afternoon, very thirsty and dizzy, and rang for ice-water, coffee, and the Pittsburgh papers.

On the part of the hotel management, Paul excited no suspicion. There was this to be said for him, that he wore his spoils with dignity and in no way made himself conspicuous. Even under the glow of his wine he was never boisterous, though he found the stuff like a magician's wand for wonder-building. His chief greediness lay in his ears and eyes, and his excesses were not offensive ones. His dearest pleasures were the grey winter twilights in his sitting-room; his quiet enjoyment of his flowers, his clothes, his wide divan, his cigarette, and his sense of power. He could not remember a time when he had felt so at peace with himself. The mere release from the necessity of petty lying, lying every day and every day, restored his self-respect. He had never lied for pleasure, even at school; but to be noticed and admired, to assert his difference from other Cordelia Street boys; and he felt a good deal more manly, more honest, even, now that he had no need for boastful pretensions, now that he could, as his actor friends used to say, "dress the part." It was characteristic that remorse did not occur to him. His golden days went by without a shadow, and he made each as perfect as he could.

On the eighth day after his arrival in New York, he found the whole affair exploited in the Pittsburgh papers, exploited with a wealth of detail which indicated that local news of a sensational nature was at a low ebb. The firm of Denny & Carson announced that the boy's father had refunded the full amount of the theft, and that they had no intention of prosecuting. The Cumberland minister had been interviewed, and expressed his hope of yet reclaiming the motherless lad, and his Sabbath-school teacher declared that she would spare no effort to that end. The rumor had reached Pittsburgh that the boy had been seen in a New York hotel, and his father had gone East to find him and bring him home.

Paul had just come in to dress for dinner; he sank into a chair, weak to the knees, and clasped his head in his hands. It was to be worse than jail, even; the tepid waters of Cordelia Street were to close over him finally and forever. The grey monotony stretched before him in hopeless, unrelieved years; Sabbath-school, Young People's Meeting, the yellow-papered room, the damp dish-towels; it all rushed back upon him with a sickening vividness. He had the old feeling that the orchestra had suddenly stopped, the sinking sensation that the play was over. The sweat broke out on his face, and he sprang to his feet, looked about him with his white, conscious smile, and winked at himself in the mirror. With something of the old childish belief in miracles with which he had so often gone to class, all his lessons unlearned, Paul dressed and dashed whistling down the corridor to the elevator.

He had no sooner entered the dining-room and caught the measure of the music than his remembrance was lightened by his old elastic power of claiming the moment, mounting with it, and finding it all sufficient. The glare and glitter about him, the mere scenic accessories had again, and for the last time, their old potency. He would show himself that he was game, he would finish the thing splendidly. He doubted, more than ever, the existence of Cordelia Street, and for the first time he drank his wine recklessly. Was he not, after all, one of those fortunate beings born to the purple, was he not still himself and in his own place? He drummed a nervous accompaniment to the Pagliacci music and looked about him, telling himself over and over that it had paid.

He reflected drowsily, to the swell of the music and the chill sweetness of his wine, that he might have done it more wisely. He might have caught an outboard steamer and been well out of their clutches before now. But the other side of the world had seemed too far away and too uncertain then; he could not have waited for it; his need had been too sharp. If he had to choose over again, he would do the same thing tomorrow. He looked affectionately about the dining-room, now gilded with a soft mist. Ah, it had paid indeed!

Paul was awakened next morning by a painful throbbing in his head and feet. He had thrown himself across the bed without undressing, and had slept with his shoes on. His limbs and hands were lead heavy, and his tongue and throat were parched and burnt. There came upon him one of those fateful attacks of clear-headedness that never occurred except when he was physically exhausted and his nerves hung loose. He lay still and closed his eyes and let the tide of things wash over him.

His father was in New York; "stopping at some joint or other," he told himself. The memory of successive summers on the front stoop fell upon him like a weight of black water. He had not a hundred dollars left; and he knew now, more than ever, that money was everything, the wall that stood between all he loathed and all he wanted. The thing was winding itself up; he had thought of that on his first glorious day in New York, and had even provided a way to snap the thread. It lay on his dressing-table now; he had got it out last night when he came blindly up from dinner, but the shiny metal hurt his eyes, and he disliked the looks of it.

He rose and moved about with a painful effort, succumbing now and again to attacks of nausea. It was the old depression exaggerated; all the world had become Cordelia Street. Yet somehow he was not afraid of anything, was absolutely calm; perhaps because he had looked into the dark corner at last and knew. It was bad enough, what he saw there, but somehow not so bad as his long fear of it had been. He saw everything clearly now. He had a feeling that he had made the best of it, that he had lived the sort of life he was meant to live, and for half an hour he sat staring at the revolver. But he told himself that was not the way, so he went downstairs and took a cab to the ferry.

When Paul arrived at Newark, he got off the train and took another cab, directing the driver to follow the Pennsylvania tracks out of the town. The snow lay heavy on the roadways and had drifted deep in the open fields. Only here and there the dead grass or dried weed stalks projected, singularly black, above it. Once well into the country, Paul dismissed the carriage and walked, floundering along the tracks, his mind a medley of irrelevant things. He seemed to hold in his brain an actual picture of everything he had seen that morning. He remembered every feature of both his drivers, of the toothless old woman from whom he had bought the red flowers in his coat, the agent from whom he had got his ticket, and all of his fellow-passengers on the ferry. His mind, unable to cope with vital matters near at hand, worked feverishly and deftly at sorting and grouping these images. They made for him a part of the ugliness of the world, of the ache in his head, and the bitter burning on his tongue. He stooped and put a handful of snow into his mouth as he walked, but that, too, seemed hot. When he reached a little hillside, where the tracks ran through a cut some twenty feet below him, he stopped and sat down.

The carnations in his coat were drooping with the cold, he noticed; their red glory all over. It occurred to him that all the flowers he had seen in the glass cases that first night must have gone the same way, long before this. It was only one splendid breath they had, in spite of their brave mockery at the winter outside the glass; and it was a losing game in the end, it seemed, this revolt against the homilies by which the world is run. Paul took one of the blossoms carefully from his coat and scooped a little hole in the snow, where he covered it up. Then he dozed a while, from his weak condition, seemingly insensible to the cold.

The sound of an approaching train awoke him, and he started to his feet, remembering only his resolution, and afraid lest he should be too late. He stood watching the approaching locomotive, his teeth chattering, his lips drawn away from them in a frightened smile; once or twice he glanced nervously sidewise, as though he were being watched. When the right moment came, he jumped. As he fell, the folly of his haste occurred to him with merciless clearness, the vastness of what he had left undone. There flashed through his brain, clearer than ever before, the blue of Adriatic water, the yellow of Algerian sands.

He felt something strike his chest, and that his body was being thrown swiftly through the air, on and on, immeasurably far and fast, while his limbs were gently relaxed. Then, because the picture making mechanism was crushed, the disturbing visions flashed into black, and Paul dropped back into the immense design of things.

[1905]

GERTRUDE STEIN (1874–1946) was born in Allegheny, Pennsylvania. When she was a girl she moved with her family to Oakland, California, where her father, a German immigrant, invested so wisely in San Francisco street railways that he was able to leave a comfortable fortune to each of his children when he died in 1891. In 1897 she graduated from Radcliffe College, where she had studied psychology under William James and published a paper on her experiments with spontaneous automatic writing. She went on to study medicine at Johns Hopkins Medical School but, tiring of scientific work before she finished her degree, she joined her brother Leo in Paris and settled with him there in 1903, living on their inherited income. That same year she began to write, starting with a short novel based on her own lesbian experience, Q.E.D., which she then rewrote as the "Melanctha" section of her first published book, Three Lives (1909). This work was modeled on Flaubert's stories in Three Tales.

After posing for a portrait by Pablo Picasso, Stein abandoned realistic narrative to develop her own prose style, attempting to use words to create the Cubist effects of avant-garde painters like Picasso, Henri Matisse, and Georges Braque, whose canvases she and her brother had begun to collect. Tender Buttons (1914), a collection of sketches departing from traditional syntax and grammar, and The Making of Americans (1925), her most ambitious book, running 925 closely printed pages, exhibit her celebrated abstract Cubist style after she abandoned conventional plot and character development. Stein produced nearly 600 works, but most of them remained unpublished until after her death. Except for Three Lives and The Autobiography of Alice B. Toklas (1933), her work is largely unread today; yet she was an acknowledged influence on a number of important writers, including Sherwood Anderson, Ernest Hemingway, and Richard Wright. She is without question a major figure in the Modernist movement of the first part of this century, which attempted radical innovations in all the arts.

In 1935, following the success of The Autobiography of Alice B. Toklas, Stein made her only trip back to the United States, with her lifelong companion, Alice B. Toklas. She gave lectures on her philosophy of composition, explaining that she was not telling stories with words, but making Cubist portraits of what she called the "actual present." Comparing her technique to motion pictures, in which no two frames are exactly alike and yet the sequence presents a flowing continuity to the viewer, Stein used repetitive statements to attempt to grasp a living moment in words. Writing about herself in the third person, she said that "Gertrude Stein in her work has always been possessed by the intellectual passion for exactitude in the description of inner and outer reality. She has produced a simplification by *this concentration, and as a result the destruction of the associational emotion in poetry and prose." Stein was apparently never troubled by the thought that it might not be wise for a writer to try to destroy the connotative resources of language.*

Indebted to the philosophy of William James and Henri Bergson, Stein felt that the essence of telling stories was solving the problem of time, because "if time exists, your writing is ephemeral." In her opinion, Anderson and Hemingway never freed themselves from the influence of traditional nineteenth-century narrative, writing fiction that had plots based on consecutive events. Stein wanted her writing to depart from the traditional role of fiction as a mirror of the temporal and spatial relations of people, places, and things in the "real world." She felt that literature should have a self-contained existence, and that her prose should create a world with its own sense of internal coherence on the page. "As a Wife Has a Cow," subtitled "A Love Story," was first published in a limited edition in Paris in 1926, with original lithographs by Juan Gris. It is an example of Stein's abstract style, where the words cease to convey conventional meaning and become objects to be manipulated, just as Cubist painters used form and color, in obedience to the artist's expressive will. You may find that the sense of the story is clarified somewhat if you read the words aloud.

Gertrude Stein

ʑʑ

AS A WIFE HAS A COW

A Love Story

Nearly all of it to be as a wife has a cow, a love story. All of it to be as a wife has a cow, all of it to be as a wife has a cow, a love story.

As to be all of it as to be a wife as a wife has a cow, a love story, all of it as to be all of it as a wife all of it as to be as a wife has a cow a love story, all of it as a wife has a cow as a wife has a cow a love story.

Has made, as it has made as it has made, has made has to be as a wife has a cow, a love story. Has made as to be as a wife has a cow a love story. As a wife has a cow, as a wife has a cow, a love story. Has to be as a wife has a cow a love story. Has made as to be as a wife has a cow a love story.

When he can, and for that when he can, for that. When he can and for that when he can. For that. When he can. For that when he can. For that. And when he can and for that. Or that, and when he can. For that and when he can.

And to in six and another. And to and in and six and another. And to and in and six and another. And to in six and and to and in and six and another. And to and in and six and another. And to and six and in and another and and to and six and another and and to and in and six and and to and six and in and another.

In came in there, came in there come out of there. In came in come out of there. Come out there in came in there. Come out of there and in and come out of there. Came in there, come out of there.

Feeling or for it, as feeling or for it, came in or come in, or come out of there or feeling as feeling or feeling as for it.

As a wife has a cow.

Came in and come out.

As a wife has a cow a love story.

As a love story, as a wife has a cow, a love story.

Not and now, now and not, not and now, by and by not and now, as not, as soon as not not and now, now as soon now now as soon, now as soon as soon as now. Just as soon just now just now just as soon just as soon as now. Just as soon as now.

And in that, as and in that, in that and and in that, so that, so that and in that, and in that and so that and as for that and as for that and that. In that. In that and and for that as for that and in that. Just as soon and in that. In that as that and just as soon. Just as soon as that.

Even now, now and even now and now and even now. Not as even now, therefor, even now and therefor, therefor and even now and even now and therefor even now. So not to and moreover and even now and therefor and moreover and even now and so and even now and therefor even now.

Do they as they do so. And do they do so.

We feel we feel. We feel or if we feel if we feel or if we feel. We feel or if we feel. As it is made made a day made a day or two made a day, as it is made a day or two, as it is made a day. Made a day. Made a day. Not away a day. By day. As it is made a day.

On the fifteenth of October as they say, said anyway, what is it as they expect, as they expect it or as they expected it, as they expect it and as they expected it, expect it or for it, expected it and it is expected of it. As they say said anyway. What is it as they expect for it, what is it and it is as they expect of it. What is it. What is it the fifteenth of October as they say as they expect or as they expected as they expect for it. What is it as they say the fifteenth of October as they say and as expected of it, the fifteenth of October as they say, what is it as expected of it. What is it and the fifteenth of October as they say and expected of it.

And prepare and prepare so prepare to prepare and prepare to prepare and prepare so as to prepare, so to prepare and prepare to prepare to prepare for and to prepare for it to prepare, to prepare for it, in preparation, as preparation in preparation by preparation. They will be too busy afterwards to prepare. As preparation prepare, to prepare, as to preparation and to prepare. Out there.

Have it as having having it as happening, happening to have it as having, having to have it as happening. Happening and have it as happening and having it happen as happening and having to have it happen as happening, and my wife has a cow as now, my wife having a cow as now, my wife having a cow as now and having a cow as now and having a cow and having a cow now, my wife has a cow and now. My wife has a cow.

[1926]

JACK LONDON (1876–1916), unlike Bret Harte, Mark Twain, and most of the early American writers who wrote stories about the American West, was born in that region — in San Francisco. He had a hard childhood, forced to earn his own living by manual labor in a canning factory starting at age fifteen. Later he worked in a laundry, and still later he was a sailor. Descriptive writing came naturally to him, and two years before he graduated from Oakland High School he won first prize in a local newspaper's article contest for "Story of a Typhoon off the Coast of Japan." He attended the University of California at Berkeley for one semester, but he regarded himself as self-taught, reading Karl Marx and Friedrich Engels, Herbert Spencer, and Friedrich Nietzsche as a young man. He joined the Socialist Labor Party after he had become convinced that it was impossible for workers to secure better conditions without organizing to take over the means of production. In 1897 he joined the Klondike gold rush and spent the winter in the Yukon. Two years later, after his return from Alaska on a 2,000-mile boat trip down the Yukon River, he published his first professional story, "To the Man on the Trail," in the Overland Monthly, and began to write for his living. London's first collection of fiction, Son of the Wolf, appeared in 1900. His novel The Call of the Wild (1903) was his biggest success, selling 1.5 million copies, and he became the highest-paid author of his time. He regarded his adventure stories as inferior to his political writing, however; they were merely a means of making money to meet his expanding interests in social reform as a Socialist speaker and political candidate. He covered the Russian-Japanese war as a correspondent, and wrote articles on the San Francisco earthquake of 1906 and the Mexican revolution of 1914. Shortly before his death at the age of forty, he resigned from the Socialist Party "because of its lack of fire and fight, and its loss of emphasis on the class struggle." London's death, possibly by his own hand, strangely echoed the events of his semiautobiographical novel Martin Eden (1909), in which a writer achieves success, but after rejecting Socialist aims finds his life meaningless and commits suicide.

London produced almost fifty volumes of prose, including several collections of short stories such as Son of the Wolf, South Sea Tales (1911), and The House of Pride and Other Tales of Hawaii (1912). He learned to tell stories, he claimed, when he was bumming across the United States and had to decide exactly the right line to pitch between the moment the housewife opened the door and the moment she asked him what he wanted. He felt that poverty had made him hustle, but that only his good luck had prevented it from destroying him. Claiming "no mentor but myself" as a writer, he placed the highest value on original experience; the stamp of self on a writer's work was "a trademark of far greater value than copyright."

London's reputation as a storyteller has declined in the United States in recent times, but he remains one of our most translated authors. His literary style is simple, often journalistic, and his stories are known to countless readers around the world as embodying the theme of social protest and dramatizing this country's rugged pioneer experience. As Jorge Luis Borges has observed, the vitality which permeated London's life is apparent in his best work. "To Build a Fire" (1907) tells a story of man's struggle against nature, trying to survive against impossible odds in a universe indifferent to his individual fate.

Jack London

ΩΩ

TO BUILD A FIRE

Day had broken cold and grey, exceedingly cold and grey, when the man turned aside from the main Yukon trail and climbed the high earth-bank, where a dim and little-travelled trail led eastward through the fat spruce timberland. It was a steep bank, and he paused for breath at the top, excusing the act to himself by looking at his watch. It was nine o'clock. There was no sun nor hint of sun, though there was not a cloud in the sky. It was a clear day, and yet there seemed an intangible pall over the face of things, a subtle gloom that made the day dark, and that was due to the absence of sun. This fact did not worry the man. He was used to the lack of sun. It had been days since he had seen the sun, and he knew that a few more days must pass before that cheerful orb, due south, would just peep above the skyline and dip immediately from view.

The man flung a look back along the way he had come. The Yukon lay a mile wide and hidden under three feet of ice. On top of this ice were as many feet of snow. It was all pure white, rolling in gentle undulations where the ice jams of the freeze-up had formed. North and south, as far as his eye could see, it was unbroken white, save for a dark hairline that curved and twisted from around the spruce-covered island to the south, and that curved and twisted away into the north, where it disappeared behind another spruce-covered island. This dark hairline was the trail — the main trail — that led south five hundred miles to the Chilcoot Pass, Dyea, and salt water; and that led north seventy miles to Dawson, and still on to the north a thousand miles to Nulato, and finally to St. Michael, on Bering Sea, a thousand miles and half a thousand more.

But all this — the mysterious, far-reaching hairline trail, the absence of sun from the sky, the tremendous cold, and the strangeness and weirdness of it all — made no impression on the man. It was not because he was long used to it. He was a newcomer in the land, a *chechaquo*, and this was his first winter. The trouble with him was that he was without imagination. He was quick and alert in the things of life, but only in the things, and not in the significances. Fifty degrees below zero meant eighty-odd degrees of frost. Such fact impressed him as being cold and uncomfortable, and that was all. It did not lead him to meditate upon his frailty as a creature of temperature, and upon man's frailty in general, able only to live within certain narrow limits of heat and cold; and from there on it did not lead him to the conjectural field of immortality and man's place in the universe. Fifty degrees below zero stood for a bite of frost that hurt and that must be guarded against by the use of mittens, ear flaps, warm moccasins, and thick socks. Fifty degrees below zero. That there should be anything more to it than that was a thought that never entered his head.

As he turned to go on, he spat speculatively. There was a sharp explosive crackle that startled him. He spat again. And again, in the air, before it could fall to the snow, the spittle crackled. He knew that at fifty below spittle crackled on the snow, but this spittle had crackled in the air. Undoubtedly it was colder than fifty below — how much colder he did not know. But the temperature did not matter. He was bound for the old claim on the left fork of Henderson Creek, where the boys were already. They had come over across the divide from the Indian Creek country, while he had come the roundabout way to take a look at the possibilities of getting out logs in the spring from the islands in the Yukon. He would be in to camp by six o'clock; a bit after dark, it was true, but the boys would be there, a fire would be going, and a hot supper would be ready. As for lunch, he pressed his hand against the protruding bundle under his jacket. It was also under his shirt, wrapped up in a handkerchief and lying against the naked skin. It was the only way to keep the biscuits from freezing. He smiled agreeably to himself as he thought of those biscuits, each cut open and sopped in bacon grease, and each enclosing a generous slice of fried bacon.

He plunged in among the big spruce trees. The trail was faint. A foot of snow had fallen since the last sled had passed over, and he was glad he was without a sled, travelling light. In fact, he carried nothing but the lunch wrapped in the handkerchief. He was surprised, however, at the cold. It certainly was cold, he concluded, as he rubbed his numb nose and cheekbones with his mittened hand. He was a warm-whiskered man, but the hair on his face did not protect the high cheekbones and the eager nose that thrust itself aggressively into the frosty air.

At the man's heels trotted a dog, a big native husky, the proper wolf-dog, grey-coated and without any visible or temperamental difference from its brother, the wild wolf. The animal was depressed by the tremendous cold. It knew that it was no time for travelling. Its instinct told it a truer tale than was told to the man by the man's judgment. In reality, it was not merely colder than fifty below zero; it was colder than sixty below, than seventy below. It was seventy-five below zero. Since the freezing point is thirty-two above zero, it meant that one hundred and seven degrees of frost obtained. The dog did not know anything about thermometers. Possibly in its brain there was no sharp consciousness of a condition of very cold such as was in the man's brain. But the brute had its instinct. It experienced a vague but menacing apprehension that subdued it and made it slink along at the man's heels, and that made it question eagerly every unwonted movement of the man as if expecting him to go into camp or to seek shelter somewhere and build a fire. The dog had learned fire, and it wanted fire, or else to burrow under the snow and cuddle its warmth away from the air.

The frozen moisture of its breathing had settled on its fur in a fine powder of frost, and especially were its jowls, muzzle, and eyelashes whitened by its crystal breath. The man's red beard and moustache were likewise frosted, but more solidly, the deposit taking the form of ice and increasing with every warm, moist breath he exhaled. Also, the man was chewing tobacco, and the muzzle of ice held his lips so rigidly that he was unable to clear his chin when he expelled the juice. The result was a crystal beard of the color and solidity of amber that was increasing its length on his chin. If he fell down it would shatter itself, like glass, into brittle fragments. But he did not mind the appendage. It was the penalty all tobacco chewers paid in that country, and he had been out before in two cold snaps. They had not been so cold as this, he knew, but by the spirit thermometer at Sixty Mile he knew they had been registered at fifty below and at fifty-five.

He held on through the level stretch of woods for several miles, crossed a wide flat of nigger heads, and dropped down a bank to the frozen bed of a small stream. This was Henderson Creek, and he knew he was ten miles from the forks. He looked at his watch. It was ten o'clock. He was making four miles an hour, and he calculated that he would arrive at the forks at half-past twelve. He decided to celebrate that event by eating his lunch there.

The dog dropped in again at his heels, with a tail drooping discouragement, as the man swung along the creek bed. The furrow of the old sled trail was plainly visible, but a dozen inches of snow covered up the marks of the last runners. In a month no man had come up or down that silent creek. The man held steadily on. He was not much given to thinking, and just then particularly he had nothing to think about save that he would eat lunch at the forks and that at six o'clock he would be in camp with the boys. There was nobody to talk to; and, had there been, speech would have been impossible because of the ice muzzle on his mouth. So he continued monotonously to chew tobacco and to increase the length of his amber beard.

Once in a while the thought reiterated itself that it was very cold and that he had never experienced such cold. As he walked along he rubbed his cheekbones and nose with the back of his mittened hand. He did this automatically, now and again changing hands. But, rub as he would, the instant he stopped his cheekbones went numb, and the following instant the end of his nose went numb. He was sure to frost his cheeks; he knew that, and experienced a pang of regret that he had not devised a nose strap of the sort Bud wore in cold snaps. Such a strap passed across the cheeks, as well, and saved them. But it didn't matter much, after all. What were frosted cheeks? A bit painful, that was all; they were never serious.

Empty as the man's mind was of thoughts, he was keenly observant, and he noticed the changes in the creeks, the curves and bends and timber jams, and always he sharply noted where he placed his feet. Once, coming round a bend, he shied abruptly, like a startled horse, curved away from the place where he had been walking, and retreated several paces back along the trail. The creek he knew was frozen clear to the bottom — no creek could contain water in that arctic winter — but he knew also that there were springs that bubbled out from the hillsides and ran along under the snow and on top of the ice of the creek. He knew that the coldest snaps never froze these springs, and he knew likewise their danger. They were traps. They hid pools of water under the snow that might be three inches deep, or three feet. Sometimes a skin of ice half an inch thick covered them, and in turn was covered by the snow. Sometimes there were alternate layers of water and ice skin, so that when one broke through he kept on breaking through for a while, sometimes wetting himself to the waist.

That was why he had shied in such a panic. He had felt the give under his feet and heard the crackle of a snow-hidden ice skin. And to get his feet wet in such a temperature meant trouble and danger. At the very least it meant delay, for he would be forced to stop and build a fire, and under its protection to bare his feet while he dried his socks and moccasins. He stood and studied the creek bed and its banks, and decided that the flow of water came from the right. He reflected awhile, rubbing his nose and cheeks, then skirted to the left, stepping gingerly and testing the footing for each step. Once clear of the danger, he took a fresh chew of tobacco and swung along at his four-mile gait.

In the course of the next two hours he came upon several similar traps. Usually the snow above the hidden pools had a sunken, candied appearance that advertised the danger. Once again, however, he had a close call; and once, suspecting danger, he compelled the dog to go on in front. The dog did not want to go. It hung back until the man shoved it forward, and then it went quickly across the white, unbroken surface. Suddenly it broke through, floundered to one side, and got away to firmer footing. It had wet its forefeet and legs, and almost immediately the water that clung to it turned to ice. It made quick efforts to lick the ice off its legs, then dropped down in the snow and began to bite out the ice that had formed between the toes. This was a matter of instinct. To permit the ice to remain would mean sore feet. It did not know this. It merely obeyed the mysterious prompting that arose from the deep crypts of its being. But the man knew, having achieved a judgment on the subject, and he removed the mitten from his right hand and helped to tear out the ice particles. He did not expose his fingers more than a minute, and was astonished at the swift numbness that smote them. It certainly was cold. He pulled on the mitten hastily, and beat the hand savagely across his chest.

At twelve o'clock the day was at its brightest. Yet the sun was too far south on its winter journey to clear the horizon. The bulge of the earth intervened between it and Henderson Creek, where the man walked under a clear sky at noon and cast no shadow. At half-past twelve, to the minute, he arrived at the forks of the creek. He was pleased at the speed he had made. If he kept it up, he would certainly be with the boys by six. He unbuttoned his jacket and shirt and drew forth his lunch. The action consumed no more than a quarter of a minute, yet in that brief moment the numbness laid hold of the exposed fingers. He did not put the mitten on, but, instead, struck the fingers a dozen sharp smashes against his leg. Then he sat down on a snow-covered log to eat. The sting that followed upon the striking of his fingers against his leg ceased so quickly that he was startled. He had had no chance to take a bite of biscuit. He struck the fingers repeatedly and returned them to the mitten, baring the other hand for the purpose of eating. He tried to take a mouthful, but the ice muzzle prevented. He had forgotten to build a fire and thaw out. He chuckled at his foolishness, and as he chuckled he noted the numbness creeping into the exposed fingers. Also, he noted that the stinging which had first come to his toes when he sat down was already passing away. He wondered whether the toes were warm or numb. He moved them inside the moccasins and decided that they were numb.

He pulled the mitten on hurriedly and stood up. He was a bit frightened. He stamped up and down until the stinging returned into the feet. It certainly was cold, was his thought. That man from Sulphur Creek had spoken the truth when telling how cold it sometimes got in the country. And he had laughed at him at the time! That showed one must not be too sure of things. There was no mistake about it, it *was* cold. He strode up and down, stamping his feet and threshing his arms, until reassured by the returning warmth. Then he got out matches and proceeded to make a fire. From the undergrowth, where high water of the previous spring had lodged a supply of seasoned twigs, he got his firewood. Working carefully from a small beginning, he soon had a roaring fire, over which he thawed the ice from his face and in the protection of which he ate his biscuits. For the moment the cold of space was outwitted. The dog took satisfaction in the fire, stretching out close enough for warmth and far enough away to escape being singed.

When the man had finished, he filled his pipe and took his comfortable time over a smoke. Then he pulled on his mittens, settled the ear flaps of his cap firmly about his ears, and took the creek trail up the left fork. The dog was disappointed and yearned back towards the fire. This man did not know cold. Possibly all the generations of his ancestry had been ignorant of cold, of real cold, of cold one hundred and seven degrees below freezing point. But the dog knew; all its ancestry knew, and it had inherited the knowledge. And it knew that it was not good to walk abroad in such fearful cold. It was the time to lie snug in a hole in the snow and wait for a curtain of cloud to be drawn across the face of outer space whence this cold came. On the other hand, there was no keen intimacy between the dog and the man. The one was the toil slave of the other, and the only caresses it had ever received were the caresses of the whip lash and of harsh and menacing throat sounds that threatened the whip lash. So the dog made no effort to communicate its apprehension to the man. It was not concerned in the welfare of the man; it was for its own sake that it yearned back towards the fire. But the man whistled, and spoke to it with the sound of whip lashes, and the dog swung in at the man's heels and followed after.

The man took a chew of tobacco and proceeded to start a new amber beard. Also, his moist breath quickly powdered with white his moustache, eyebrows, and lashes. There did not seem to be so many springs on the left fork of the Henderson, and for half an hour the man saw no signs of any. And then it happened. At a place where there were no signs, where the soft, unbroken snow seemed to advertise solidity beneath, the man broke through. It was not deep. He wet himself half-way to the knees before he floundered out of the firm crust.

He was angry, and cursed his luck aloud. He had hoped to get into camp with the boys at six o'clock, and this would delay him an hour, for he would have to build a fire and dry out his footgear. This was imperative at that low temperature — he knew that much; and he turned aside to the bank, which he climbed. On top, tangled in the underbrush about the trunks of several small spruce trees, was a high-water deposit of dry firewood—sticks and twigs, principally, but also larger portions of seasoned branches and fine, dry, last year's grasses. He threw down several large pieces on top of the snow. This served for a foundation and prevented the young flame from drowning itself in the snow it otherwise would melt. The flame he got by touching a match to a small shred of birch bark that he took from his pocket. This burned even more readily than paper. Placing it on the foundation, he fed the young flame with wisps of dry grass and with the tiniest dry twigs.

He worked slowly and carefully, keenly aware of his danger. Gradually, as the flame grew stronger, he increased the size of the twigs with which he fed it. He squatted in the snow pulling the twigs out from their entanglement in the brush and feeding directly to the flame. He knew there must be no failure. When it is seventy-five below zero, a man must not fail in his first attempt to build a fire — that is, if his feet are wet. If his feet are dry, and he fails, he can run along the trail for half a mile and restore his circulation. But the circulation of wet and freezing feet cannot be restored by running when it is seventy-five below. No matter how fast he runs, the wet feet will freeze the harder.

All this the man knew. The old-timer on Sulphur Creek had told him about it the previous fall, and now he was appreciating the advice. Already all sensation had gone out of his feet. To build the fire he had been forced to remove his mittens, and the fingers had quickly gone numb. His pace of four miles an hour had kept his heart pumping blood to the surface of his body and to all the extremities. But the instant he stopped, the action of the pump eased down. The cold of space smote the unprotected tip of the planet, and he, being on that unprotected tip, received the full force of the blow. The blood of his body recoiled before it. The blood was alive, like the dog, and like the dog it wanted to hide away and cover itself up from the fearful cold. So long as he walked four miles an hour, he pumped that blood, willy-nilly, to the surfaces; but now it ebbed away and sank down into the recesses of his body. The extremities were the first to feel its absence. His wet feet froze the faster, and his exposed fingers numbed the faster, though they had not yet begun to freeze. Nose and cheeks were already freezing, while the skin of all his body chilled as it lost its blood.

But he was safe. Toes and nose and cheeks would be only touched by the frost, for the fire was beginning to burn with strength. He was feeding it with twigs the size of his finger. In another minute he would be able to feed it with branches the size of his wrist, and then he could remove his wet footgear, and, while it dried, he could keep his naked feet warm by the fire, rubbing them at first, of course, with snow. The fire was a success. He was safe. He remembered the advice of the old-timer on Sulphur Creek, and smiled. The old-timer had been very serious in laying down the law that no man must travel alone in the Klondike after fifty below. Well, here he was; he had had the accident; he was alone; and he had saved himself. Those old-timers were rather womanish, some of them, he thought. All a man had to do was to keep his head, and he was all right. Any man who was a man could travel alone. But it was surprising, the rapidity with which his cheeks and nose were freezing. And he had not thought his fingers could go lifeless in so short a time. Lifeless they were, for he could scarcely make them move together to grip a twig, and they seemed remote from his body and from him. When he touched a twig, he had to look and see whether or not he had hold of it. The wires were pretty well down between him and his finger ends.

All of which counted for little. There was the fire, snapping and crackling and promising life with every dancing flame. He started to untie his moccasins. They were coated with ice; the thick German socks were like sheaths of iron halfway to the knees; and the moccasin strings were like rods of steel all twisted and knotted as by some conflagration. For a moment he tugged with his numb fingers, then, realizing the folly of it, he drew his sheath knife.

But before he could cut the strings, it happened. It was his own fault or, rather, his mistake. He should not have built the fire under the spruce tree. He should have built it in the open. But it had been easier to pull the twigs from the brush and drop them directly on the fire. Now the tree under which he had done this carried a weight of snow on its boughs. No wind had blown for weeks, and each bough was fully freighted. Each time he had pulled a twig he had communicated a slight agitation to the tree — an imperceptible agitation, so far as he was concerned, but an agitation sufficient to bring about the disaster. High up in the tree one bough capsized its load of snow. This fell on the boughs beneath, capsizing them. This process continued, spreading out and involving the whole tree. It grew like an avalanche, and it descended without warning upon the man and the fire, and the fire was blotted out! Where it had burned was a mantle of fresh and disordered snow.

The man was shocked. It was as though he had just heard his own sentence of death. For a moment he sat and stared at the spot where the fire had been. Then he grew very calm. Perhaps the old-timer on Sulphur Creek was right. If he had only had a trail mate he would have been in no danger now. The trail mate could have built the fire. Well, it was up to him to build the fire over again, and this second time there must be no failure. Even if he succeeded, he would most likely lose some toes. His feet must be badly frozen by now, and there would be some time before the second fire was ready.

Such were his thoughts, but he did not sit and think them. He was busy all the time they were passing through his mind. He made a new foundation for a fire, this time in the open, where no treacherous tree could blot it out. Next he gathered dry grasses and tiny twigs from the high-water flotsam. He could not bring his fingers together to pull them out, but he was able to gather them by the handful. In this way he got many rotten twigs and bits of green moss that were undesirable, but it was the best he could do. He worked methodically, even collecting an armful of the larger branches to be used later when the fire gathered strength. And all the while the dog sat and watched him, a certain yearning wistfulness in its eyes, for it looked upon him as the fire provider, and the fire was slow in coming.

When all was ready, the man reached in his pocket for a second piece of birch bark. He knew the bark was there, and, though he could not feel it with his fingers, he could hear its crisp rustling as he fumbled for it. Try as he would, he could not clutch hold of it. And all the time, in his consciousness, was the knowledge that each instant his feet were freezing. This thought tended to put him in a panic, but he fought against it and kept calm. He pulled on his mittens with his teeth, and threshed his arms back and forth, beating his hands with all his might against his sides. He did this sitting down, and he stood up to do it; and all the while the dog sat in the snow, its wolf brush of a tail curled around warmly over its forefront, its sharp wolf ears pricked forward intently as it watched the man. And the man, as he beat and threshed with his arms and hands, felt a great surge of envy as he regarded the creature that was warm and secure in its natural covering.

After a time he was aware of the first faraway signals of sensation in his beaten fingers. The faint tingling grew stronger till it evolved into a stinging ache that was excruciating, but which the man hailed with satisfaction. He stripped the mitten from his right hand and fetched forth the birch bark. The exposed fingers were quickly going numb again. Next he brought out his bunch of sulphur matches. But the tremendous cold had already driven the life out of his fingers. In his effort to separate one match from the others, the whole bunch fell in the snow. He tried to pick it out of the snow, but failed. The dead fingers could neither touch nor clutch. He was very careful. He drove the thought of his freezing feet, and nose, and cheeks, out of his mind, devoting his whole soul to the matches. He watched, using the sense of vision in place of that touch, and when he saw his fingers on each side the bunch, he closed them — that is, he willed to close them, for the wires were down, and the fingers did not obey. He pulled the mitten on the right hand, and beat it fiercely against his knee. Then with both mittened hands, he scooped the bunch of matches, along with much snow, into his lap. Yet he was no better off.

After some manipulation he managed to get the bunch between the heels of his mittened hands. In this fashion he carried it to his mouth. The ice crackled and snapped when by a violent effort he opened his mouth. He drew the lower jaw in, curled the upper lip out of the way, and scraped the bunch with his upper teeth in order to separate a match. He succeeded in getting one, which he dropped on his lap. He was no better off. He could not pick it up. Then he devised a way. He picked it up in his teeth and scratched it on his leg. Twenty times he scratched before he succeeded in lighting it. As it flamed he held it with his teeth to the birch bark. But the burning brimstone went up his nostrils and into his lungs, causing him to cough spasmodically. The match fell into the snow and went out.

The old-timer on Sulphur Creek was right, he thought in the moment of controlled despair that ensued: after fifty below, a man should travel with a partner. He beat his hands, but failed in exciting any sensation. Suddenly he bared both hands, removing the mittens with his teeth. He caught the whole bunch between the heels of his hands. His arm muscles not being frozen enabled him to press the hand heels tightly against the matches. Then he scratched the bunch along his leg. It flared into flame, seventy sulphur matches at once! There was no wind to blow them out. He kept his head to one side to escape the strangling fumes, and held the blazing bunch to the birch bark. As he so held it, he became aware of sensation in his hand. His flesh was burning. He could smell it. Deep down below the surface he could feel it. The sensation developed into pain that grew acute. And still he endured it, holding the flame of the matches clumsily to the bark that would not light readily because his own burning hands were in the way, absorbing most of the flame.

At last, when he could endure no more, he jerked his hands apart. The blazing matches fell sizzling into the snow, but the birch bark was alight. He began laying dry grasses and the tiniest twigs on the flame. He could not pick and choose, for he had to lift the fuel between the heels of his hands. Small pieces of rotten wood and green moss clung to the twigs, and he bit them off as well as he could with his teeth. He cherished the flame carefully and awkwardly. It meant life, and it must not perish. The withdrawal of blood from the surface of his body now made him begin to shiver, and he grew more awkward. A large piece of green moss fell squarely on the little fire. He tried to poke it out with his fingers, but his shivering frame made him poke too far, and he disrupted the nucleus of the little fire, the burning grasses and tiny twigs separating and scattering. He tried to poke them together again, but in spite of the tenseness of the effort, his shivering got away with him, and the twigs were hopelessly scattered. Each twig gushed a puff of smoke and went out. The fire provider had failed. As he looked apathetically about him, his eyes chanced on the dog, sitting across the ruins of the fire from him, in the snow, making restless, hunching movements, slightly lifting one forefoot and then the other, shifting its weight back and forth on them with wistful eagerness.

The sight of the dog put a wild idea into his head. He remembered the tale of the man, caught in a blizzard, who killed a steer and crawled inside the carcass, and so was saved. He would kill the dog and bury his hands in the warm body until the numbness went out of them. Then he could build another fire. He spoke to the dog, calling it to him; but in his voice was a strange note of fear that frightened the animal, who had never known the man to speak in such a way before. Something was the matter, and its suspicious nature sensed danger — it knew not what danger, but somewhere, somehow, in its brain arose an apprehension of the man. It flattened its ears down at the sound of the man's voice, and its restless, hunching movements and the liftings and shiftings of its forefeet became more pronounced; but it would not come to the man. He got on his hands and knees and crawled towards the dog. This unusual posture again excited suspicion, and the animal sidled mincingly away.

The man sat up in the snow for a moment and struggled for calmness. Then he pulled on his mittens, by means of his teeth, and got upon his feet. He glanced down at first in order to assure himself that he was really standing up, for the absence of sensation in his feet left him unrelated to the earth. His erect position in itself started to drive the webs of suspicion from the dog's mind; and when he spoke peremptorily, with the sound of whip lashes in his voice, the dog rendered its customary allegiance and came to him. As it came within reaching distance, the man lost his control. His arms flashed out to the dog, and he experienced genuine surprise when he discovered that his hands could not clutch, that there was neither bend nor feeling in the fingers. He had forgotten for the moment that they were frozen and that they were freezing more and more. All this happened quickly, and before the animal could get away, he encircled its body with his arms. He sat down in the snow, and in this fashion held the dog, while it snarled and whined and struggled.

But it was all he could do, hold its body encircled in his arms and sit there. He realized he could not kill the dog. There was no way to do it. With his helpless hands he could neither draw nor hold his sheath knife nor throttle the animal. He released it, and it plunged wildly away, with tail between its legs, and still snarling. It halted forty feet away and surveyed him curiously, with ears sharply pricked forward.

The man looked down at his hands in order to locate them, and found them hanging on the ends of his arms. It struck him as curious that one should have to use his eyes in order to find out where his hands were. He began threshing his arms back and forth, beating the mittened hands against his sides. He did this for five minutes, violently, and his heart pumped enough blood up to the surface to put a stop to his shivering. But no sensation was aroused in the hands. He had an impression that they hung like weights on the ends of his arms, but when he tried to run the impression down, he could not find it.

A certain fear of death, dull and oppressive, came to him. This fear quickly became poignant as he realized that it was no longer a mere matter of freezing his fingers and toes, or of losing his hands and feet, but that it was a matter of life and death with the chances against him. This threw him into a panic, and he turned and ran up the creek bed along the old, dim trail. The dog joined in behind him and kept up with him. He ran blindly, without intention, in fear such as he had never known in his life. Slowly, as he ploughed and floundered through the snow, he began to see things again — the banks of the creek, the old timber jams, the leafless aspens, and the sky. The running made him feel better. He did not shiver. Maybe, if he ran on, his feet would thaw out; and, anyway, if he ran far enough, he would reach camp and the boys. Without doubt he would lose some fingers and toes and some of his face; but the boys would take care of him, and save the rest of him when he got there. And at the same time there was another thought in his mind that said he would never get to the camp and the boys; that it was too many miles away, that the freezing had too great a start on him, and that he would soon be stiff and dead. This thought he kept in the background and refused to consider. Sometimes it pushed itself forward and demanded to be heard, but he thrust it back and strove to think of other things.

It struck him as curious that he could run at all on feet so frozen that he could not feel them when they struck the earth and took the weight of his body. He seemed to himself to skim along above the surface, and to have no connection with the earth. Somewhere he had once seen a winged Mercury, and he wondered if Mercury felt as he felt when skimming over the earth.

His theory of running until he reached camp and the boys had one flaw in it: he lacked the endurance. Several times he stumbled, and finally he tottered, crumpled up, and fell. When he tried to rise, he failed. He must sit and rest, he decided, and next time he would merely walk and keep on going. As he sat and regained his breath, he noted that he was feeling quite warm and comfortable. He was not shivering, and it even seemed that a warm glow had come to his chest and trunk. And yet, when he touched his nose or cheeks, there was no sensation. Running would not thaw them out. Nor would it thaw out his hands and feet. Then the thought came to him that the frozen portions of his body must be extending. He tried to keep this thought down, to forget it, to think of something else; he was aware of the panicky feeling that it caused, and he was afraid of the panic. But the thought asserted itself, and persisted, until it produced a vision of his body totally frozen. This was too much, and he made another wild run along the trail. Once he slowed down to a walk, but the thought of the freezing extending itself made him run again.

And all the time the dog ran with him, at his heels. When he fell down a second time, it curled its tail over its forefeet and sat in front of him, facing him, curiously eager and intent. The warmth and security of the animal angered him, and he cursed it till it flattened down its ears appeasingly. This time the shivering came more quickly upon the man. He was losing in his battle with the frost. It was creeping into his body from all sides. The thought of it drove him on, but he ran no more than a hundred feet, when he staggered and pitched headlong. It was his last panic. When he had recovered his breath and control, he sat up and entertained in his mind the conception of meeting death with dignity. However, the conception did not come to him in such terms. His idea of it was that he had been making a fool of himself, running around like a chicken with its head cut off — such was the simile that occurred to him. Well, he was bound to freeze anyway, and he might as well take it decently. With this new-found peace of mind came the first glimmerings of drowsiness. A good idea, he thought, to sleep off to death. It was like taking an anaesthetic. Freezing was not so bad as people thought. There were lots worse ways to die.

He pictured the boys finding his body next day. Suddenly he found himself with them, coming along the trail looking for himself. And, still with them, he came around a turn in the trail and found himself lying in the snow. He did not belong with himself any more, for even then he was out of himself, standing with the boys and looking at himself in the snow. It certainly was cold, was his thought. When he got back to the States he could tell the folks what real cold was. He drifted on from this to a vision of the old-timer on Sulphur Creek. He could see him quite clearly, warm and comfortable, and smoking a pipe.

"You were right, old hoss; you were right," the man mumbled to the old-timer of Sulphur Creek.

Then the man drowsed off into what seemed to him the most comfortable and satisfying sleep he had ever known. The dog sat facing him and waiting. The brief day drew to a close in a long, slow twilight. There were no signs of a fire to be made, and, besides, never in the dog's experience had it known a man to sit like that in the snow and make no fire. As the twilight drew on, its eager yearning for the fire mastered it, and with a great lifting and shifting of forefeet, it whined softly, then flattened its ears down in anticipation of being chidden by the man. But the man remained silent. Later the dog whined loudly. And still later it crept close to the man and caught the scent of death. This made the animal bristle and back away. A little longer it delayed, howling under the stars that leaped and danced and shone brightly in the cold sky. Then it turned and trotted up the trail in the direction of the camp it knew, where were the other food providers and fire providers.

[1908]

SHERWOOD ANDERSON (1876–1941), *born the son of a jack-of-all-trades father in Camden, Ohio, spent his youth drifting with his family from town to town in midwestern America. He did not publish his first book until he was over forty years old. Later, when he analyzed the impulse toward writing fiction that he had experienced after working for many years as a newsboy, farm laborer, stable boy, factory hand, and advertising copywriter, Anderson recalled that he said to himself, "I'll take some fellow, a little like myself, something of the same circumstances, same experiences in life. I'll put him down on paper, his life, his relations with others, the story of the things that happen to him, how he feels — all this on sheets of paper. It seemed to me, when I began to do it, that I could, by writing, push myself, as self, far off. I could get myself, as self, in the unimportant position I deserved. I became, for the nonce, to myself, just a passing thing, just one of a long, long procession of men . . . any one other figure in the procession certainly as important as myself . . . a kind of new gladness inside."*

Dissatisfied with the commercial spirit of the advertising business, Anderson made friends with writers in Chicago and began to publish his own poetry and fiction. The poet Carl Sandburg encouraged him, but Anderson's literary style was most influenced by Three Lives, *an early book of the expatriate American writer Gertrude Stein, which he felt revolutionized the language of narrative. In 1916 he published his first novel,* Windy McPherson's Son. *He followed it with another novel and a volume of poetry, but he did not receive wide recognition until 1919, with the book* Winesburg, Ohio. *This was a collection of related stories about life in a small town, including "Hands," that developed the theme of youth in revolt against the repressive conventions of a materialistic society. It was followed by other important collections of stories:* The Triumph of the Egg *(1921),* Horses and Men *(1923), and* Death in the Woods and Other Stories *(1933). In Anderson's time he was a strong influence on Ernest Hemingway, William Saroyan, and John Steinbeck, and the best of his stories, like "Hands," "The Egg," "I'm a Fool," and "Death in the Woods," have an enduring vitality and are important contributions to the achievement of the American short story.*

The characteristic tone of Anderson's short fiction is melancholy reminiscence. His stories are largely autobiographical, often recalling the tales told by his father or other members of his family. In an understated fashion, Anderson weaves carefully selected realistic details into a narrative that moves by apparently formless associations of thought and feeling, but is actually a controlled progression of fully dramatized situations. At the heart of "Death in the Woods," as of all his best work, is Anderson's obsession with the theme of love denied and life destroyed by an uncaring, hostile environ-

*ment. His importance in literary history is accurately summed up in Wil-
liam Faulkner's statement that Anderson was "the father of my generation
of American writers and the tradition of American writing which our successors will carry on."*

Sherwood Anderson

∾

HANDS

Upon the half decayed veranda of a small frame house that stood near
the edge of a ravine near the town of Winesburg, Ohio, a fat little old man
walked nervously up and down. Across a long field that had been seeded for
clover but that had produced only a dense crop of yellow mustard weeds, he
could see the public highway along which went a wagon filled with berry
pickers returning from the fields. The berry pickers, youths and maidens,
laughed and shouted boisterously. A boy clad in a blue shirt leaped from
the wagon and attempted to drag after him one of the maidens who
screamed and protested shrilly. The feet of the boy in the road kicked up a
cloud of dust that floated across the face of the departing sun. Over the long
field came a thin girlish voice. "Oh, you Wing Biddlebaum, comb your
hair, it's falling into your eyes," commanded the voice to the man, who was
bald and whose nervous little hands fiddled about the bare white forehead
as though arranging a mass of tangled locks.

Wing Biddlebaum, forever frightened and beset by a ghostly band of
doubts, did not think of himself as in any way a part of the life of the town
where he had lived for twenty years. Among all the people of Winesburg
but one had come close to him. With George Willard, son of Tom Willard,
the proprietor of the new Willard House, he had formed something like a
friendship. George Willard was the reporter on the *Winesburg Eagle* and
sometimes in the evenings he walked out along the highway to Wing Biddlebaum's house. Now as the old man walked up and down on the veranda,
his hands moving nervously about, he was hoping that George Willard
would come and spend the evening with him. After the wagon containing
the berry pickers had passed, he went across the field through the tall mustard weeds and climbing a rail fence peered anxiously along the road to the
town. For a moment he stood thus, rubbing his hands together and looking
up and down the road, and then, fear overcoming him, ran back to walk
again upon the porch on his own house.

In the presence of George Willard, Wing Biddlebaum, who for twenty years had been the town mystery, lost something of his timidity, and his shadowy personality, submerged in a sea of doubts, came forth to look at the world. With the young reporter at his side, he ventured in the light of day into Main Street or strode up and down on the rickety front porch of his own house, talking excitedly. The voice that had been low and trembling became shrill and loud. The bent figure straightened. With a kind of wriggle, like a fish returned to the brook by the fisherman, Biddlebaum the silent began to talk, striving to put into words the ideas that had been accumulated by his mind during long years of silence.

Wing Biddlebaum talked much with his hands. The slender expressive fingers, forever active, forever striving to conceal themselves in his pockets or behind his back, came forth and became the piston rods of his machinery of expression.

The story of Wing Biddlebaum is a story of hands. Their restless activity, like unto the beating of the wings of an imprisoned bird, had given him his name. Some obscure poet of the town had thought of it. The hands alarmed their owner. He wanted to keep them hidden away and looked with amazement at the quiet inexpressive hands of other men who worked beside him in the fields, or passed, driving sleepy teams on country roads.

When he talked to George Willard, Wing Biddlebaum closed his fists and beat with them upon a table or on the walls of his house. The action made him more comfortable. If the desire to talk came to him when the two were walking in the fields, he sought out a stump or the top board of a fence and with his hands pounding busily talked with renewed ease.

The story of Wing Biddlebaum's hands is worth a book itself. Sympathetically set forth it would tap many strange, beautiful qualities in obscure men. It is a job for a poet. In Winesburg the hands had attracted attention merely because of their activity. With them Wing Biddlebaum had picked as high as a hundred and forty quarts of strawberries in a day. They became his distinguishing feature, the source of his fame. Also they made more grotesque an already grotesque and elusive individuality. Winesburg was proud of the hands of Wing Biddlebaum in the same spirit in which it was proud of Banker White's new stone house and Wesley Moyer's bay stallion, Tony Tip, that had won the two-fifteen trot at the fall races in Cleveland.

As for George Willard, he had many times wanted to ask about the hands. At times an almost overwhelming curiosity had taken hold of him. He felt that there must be a reason for their strange activity and their inclination to keep hidden away and only a growing respect for Wing Biddlebaum kept him from blurting out the questions that were often in his mind.

Once he had been on the point of asking. The two were walking in the fields on a summer afternoon and had stopped to sit upon a grassy bank. All afternoon Wing Biddlebaum had talked as one inspired. By a fence he had stopped and beating like a giant woodpecker upon the top board had shouted at George Willard, condemning his tendency to be too much influenced by the people about him. "You are destroying yourself," he cried.

"You have the inclination to be alone and to dream and you are afraid of dreams. You want to be like others in town here. You hear them talk and you try to imitate them."

On the grassy bank Wing Biddlebaum had tried again to drive his point home. His voice became soft and reminiscent, and with a sigh of contentment he launched into a long rambling talk, speaking as one lost in a dream.

Out of the dream Wing Biddlebaum made a picture for George Willard. In the picture men lived again in a kind of pastoral golden age. Across a green open country came clean-limbed young men, some afoot, some mounted upon horses. In crowds the young men came to gather about the feet of an old man who sat beneath a tree in a tiny garden and who talked to them.

Wing Biddlebaum became wholly inspired. For once he forgot the hands. Slowly they stole forth and lay upon George Willard's shoulders. Something new and bold came into the voice that talked. "You must try to forget all you have learned," said the old man. "You must begin to dream. From this time on you must shut your ears to the roaring of the voices."

Pausing in his speech, Wing Biddlebaum looked long and earnestly at George Willard. His eyes glowed. Again he raised the hands to caress the boy and then a look of horror swept over his face.

With a convulsive movement of his body, Wing Biddlebaum sprang to his feet and thrust his hands deep into his trousers pockets. Tears came to his eyes. "I must be getting along home. I can talk no more with you," he said nervously.

Without looking back, the old man had hurried down the hillside and across a meadow, leaving George Willard perplexed and frightened upon the grassy slope. With a shiver of dread the boy arose and went along the road toward town. "I'll not ask him about his hands," he thought, touched by the memory of the terror he had seen in the man's eyes. "There's something wrong, but I don't want to know what it is. His hands have something to do with his fear of me and of everyone."

And George Willard was right. Let us look briefly into the story of the hands. Perhaps our talking of them will arouse the poet who will tell the hidden wonder story of the influence for which the hands were but fluttering pennants of promise.

In his youth Wing Biddlebaum had been a school teacher in a town in Pennsylvania. He was not then known as Wing Biddlebaum, but went by the less euphonic name of Adolph Myers. As Adolph Myers he was much loved by the boys of his school.

Adolph Myers was meant by nature to be a rare teacher of youth. He was one of those rare, little-understood men who rule by a power so gentle that it passes as a lovable weakness. In their feeling for the boys under their charge such men are not unlike the finer sort of women in their love of men.

And yet that is but crudely stated. It needs the poet there. With the boys of his school, Adolph Myers had walked in the evening or had sat talking until dusk upon the schoolhouse steps lost in a kind of dream. Here and there went his hands, caressing the shoulders of the boys, playing about the tousled heads. As he talked his voice became soft and musical. There was a caress in that also. In a way the voice and the hands, the stroking of the shoulders and the touching of the hair was a part of the schoolmaster's effort to carry a dream into the young minds. By the caress that was in his fingers he expressed himself. He was one of those men in whom the force that creates life is diffused, not centralized. Under the caress of his hands doubt and disbelief went out of the minds of the boys and they began also to dream.

And then the tragedy. A half-witted boy of the school became enamored of the young master. In his bed at night he imagined unspeakable things and in the morning went forth to tell his dreams as facts. Strange, hideous accusations fell from his loose-hung lips. Through the Pennsylvania town went a shiver. Hidden, shadowy doubts that had been in men's minds concerning Adolph Myers were galvanized into beliefs.

The tragedy did not linger. Trembling lads were jerked out of bed and questioned. "He put his arms about me," said one. "His fingers were always playing in my hair," said another.

One afternoon a man of the town, Henry Bradford, who kept a saloon, came to the schoolhouse door. Calling Adolph Myers into the school yard he began to beat him with his fists. As his hard knuckles beat down into the frightened face of the schoolmaster, his wrath became more and more terrible. Screaming with dismay, the children ran here and there like disturbed insects. "I'll teach you to put your hands on my boy, you beast," roared the saloon keeper, who, tired of beating the master, had begun to kick him about the yard.

Adolph Myers was driven from the Pennsylvania town in the night. With lanterns in their hands a dozen men came to the door of the house where he lived alone and commanded that he dress and come forth. It was raining and one of the men had a rope in his hands. They had intended to hang the schoolmaster, but something in his figure, so small, white, and pitiful, touched their hearts and they let him escape. As he ran away into the darkness they repented of their weakness and ran after him, swearing and throwing sticks and great balls of soft mud at the figure that screamed and ran faster and faster into the darkness.

For twenty years Adolph Myers had lived along in Winesburg. He was but forty but looked sixty-five. The name of Biddlebaum he got from a box of goods seen at a freight station as he hurried through an eastern Ohio town. He had an aunt in Winesburg, a black-toothed old woman who raised chickens, and with her he lived until she died. He had been ill for a year after the experience in Pennsylvania, and after his recovery worked as a day laborer in the fields, going timidly about and striving to conceal his hands. Although he did not understand what had happened he felt that the hands must be to blame. Again and again the fathers of the boys had talked of the hands. "Keep your hands to yourself," the saloon keeper had roared, dancing with fury in the schoolhouse yard.

Upon the veranda of his house by the ravine, Wing Biddlebaum continued to walk up and down until the sun had disappeared and the road beyond the field was lost in the grey shadows. Going into his house he cut slices of bread and spread honey upon them. When the rumble of the evening train that took away the express cars loaded with the day's harvest of berries had passed and restored the silence of the summer night, he went again to walk upon the veranda. In the darkness he could not see the hands and they became quiet. Although he still hungered for the presence of the boy, who was the medium through which he expressed his love of man, the hunger became again a part of his loneliness and his waiting. Lighting a lamp, Wing Biddlebaum washed the few dishes soiled by his simple meal and, setting up a folding cot by the screen door that led to the porch, prepared to undress for the night. A few stray white bread crumbs lay on the cleanly washed floor by the table; putting the lamp upon a low stool he began to pick up the crumbs, carrying them to his mouth one by one with unbelievable rapidity. In the dense blotch of light beneath the table, the kneeling figure looked like a priest engaged in some service of his church. The nervous expressive fingers, flashing in and out of the light, might well have been mistaken for the fingers of the devotee going swiftly through decade after decade of his rosary.

[1919]

Sherwood Anderson

ひひ

DEATH IN THE WOODS

I

She was an old woman and lived on a farm near the town in which I lived. All country and small-town people have seen such old women, but no one knows much about them. Such an old woman comes into town driving an old worn-out horse or she comes afoot carrying a basket. She may own a few hens and have eggs to sell. She brings them in a basket and takes them to a grocer. There she trades them in. She gets some salt pork and some beans. Then she gets a pound or two of sugar and some flour.

Afterwards she goes to the butcher's and asks for some dog-meat. She may spend ten or fifteen cents, but when she does she asks for something. Formerly the butchers gave liver to any one who wanted to carry it away. In our family we were always having it. Once one of my brothers got a whole cow's liver at the slaughter-house near the fairgrounds in our town. We had it until we were sick of it. It never cost a cent. I have hated the thought of it ever since.

The old farm woman got some liver and a soup-bone. She never visited with any one, and as soon as she got what she wanted she lit out for home. It made quite a load for such an old body. No one gave her a lift. People drive right down a road and never notice an old woman like that.

There was such an old woman who used to come into town past our house one Summer and Fall when I was a young boy and was sick with what was called inflammatory rheumatism. She went home later carrying a heavy pack on her back. Two or three large gaunt-looking dogs followed at her heels.

The old woman was nothing special. She was one of the nameless ones that hardly anyone knows, but she got into my thoughts. I have just suddenly now, after all these years, remembered her and what happened. It is a story. Her name was Grimes, and she lived with her husband and son in a small unpainted house on the bank of a small creek four miles from town.

The husband and son were a tough lot. Although the son was but twenty-one, he had already served a term in jail. It was whispered about that the woman's husband stole horses and ran them off to some other county. Now and then, when a horse turned up missing, the man had also disappeared. No one ever caught him. Once, when I was loafing at Tom Whitehead's livery-barn, the man came there and sat on the bench in front. Two or three other men were there, but no one spoke to him. He sat for a few minutes and then got up and went away. When he was leaving he turned around and stared at the men. There was a look of defiance in his eyes. "Well, I have tried to be friendly. You don't want to talk to me. It has been so wherever I have gone in this town. If, some day, one of your fine horses turns up missing, well, then what?" He did not say anything actually. "I'd like to bust one of you on the jaw," was about what his eyes said. I remember how the look in his eyes made me shiver.

The old man belonged to a family that had had money once. His name was Jake Grimes. It all comes back clearly now. His father, John Grimes, had owned a sawmill when the country was new, and had made money. Then he got to drinking and running after women. When he died there wasn't much left.

Jake blew in the rest. Pretty soon there wasn't any more lumber to cut and his land was nearly all gone.

He got his wife off a German farmer, for whom he went to work one June day in the wheat harvest. She was a young thing then and scared to death. You see, the farmer was up to something with the girl — she was, I think, a bound girl and his wife had her suspicions. She took it out on the girl when the man wasn't around. Then, when the wife had to go off to town for supplies, the farmer got after her. She told young Jake that nothing really ever happened, but he didn't know whether to believe it or not.

He got her pretty easy himself, the first time he was out with her. He wouldn't have married her if the German farmer hadn't tried to tell him where to get off. He got her to go riding with him in his buggy one night when he was threshing on the place, and then he came for her the next Sunday night.

She managed to get out of the house without her employer's seeing, but when she was getting into the buggy he showed up. It was almost dark, and he just popped up suddenly at the horse's head. He grabbed the horse by the bridle and Jake got out his buggy-whip.

They had it out all right! The German was a tough one. Maybe he didn't care whether his wife knew or not. Jake hit him over the face and shoulders with the buggy-whip, but the horse got to acting up and he had to get out.

Then the two men went for it. The girl didn't see it. The horse started to run away and went nearly a mile down the road before the girl got him stopped. Then she managed to tie him to a tree beside the road. (I wonder how I know all this. It must have stuck in my mind from small-town tales when I was a boy.) Jake found her there after he got through with the German. She was huddled up in the buggy seat, crying, scared to death. She told Jake a lot of stuff, how the German had tried to get her, how he chased her once into the barn, how another time, when they happened to be alone in the house together, he tore her dress open clear down the front. The German, she said, might have got her that time if he hadn't heard his old woman drive in at the gate. She had been off to town for supplies. Well, she would be putting the horse in the barn. The German managed to sneak off to the fields without his wife seeing. He told the girl he would kill her if she told. What could she do? She told a lie about ripping her dress in the barn when she was feeding the stock. I remember now that she was a bound girl and did not know where her father and mother were. Maybe she did not have any father. You know what I mean.

Such bound children were often enough cruelly treated. They were children who had no parents, slaves really. There were very few orphan homes then. They were legally bound into some home. It was a matter of pure luck how it came out.

II

She married Jake and had a son and daughter, but the daughter died.

Then she settled down to feed stock. That was her job. At the German's place she had cooked the food for the German and his wife. The wife was a strong woman with big hips and worked most of the time in the fields with her husband. She fed them and fed the cows in the barn, fed the pigs, the horses and the chickens. Every moment of every day, as a young girl, was spent feeding something.

Then she married Jake Grimes and he had to be fed. She was a slight thing, and when she had been married for three or four years, and after the two children were born, her slender shoulders became stooped.

Jake always had a lot of big dogs around the house, that stood near the unused sawmill near the creek. He was always trading horses when he wasn't stealing something and had a lot of poor bony ones about. Also he kept three or four pigs and a cow. They were all pastured in the few acres left of the Grimes place and Jake did little enough work.

He went into debt for a threshing outfit and ran it for several years, but it did not pay. People did not trust him. There were afraid he would steal the grain at night. He had to go a long way off to get work and it cost too much to get there. In the Winter he hunted and cut a little firewood, to be sold in some nearby town. When the son grew up he was just like the father. They got drunk together. If there wasn't anything to eat in the house when they came home the old man gave his old woman a cut over the head. She had a few chickens of her own and had to kill one of them in a hurry. When they were all killed she wouldn't have any eggs to sell when she went to town, and then what would she do?

She had to scheme all her life about getting things fed, getting the pigs fed so they would grow fat and could be butchered in the Fall. When they were butchered her husband took most of the meat off to town and sold it. If he did not do it first the boy did. They fought sometimes and when they fought the old woman stood aside trembling.

She had got the habit of silence anyway — that was fixed. Sometimes, when she began to look old — she wasn't forty yet — and when the husband and son were both off, trading horses or drinking or hunting or stealing, she went around the house and the barnyard muttering to herself.

How was she going to get everything fed? — that was her problem. The dogs had to be fed. There wasn't enough hay in the barn for the horses and the cow. If she didn't feed the chickens how could they lay eggs? Without eggs to sell how could she get things in town, things she had to have to keep the life of the farm going? Thank heaven, she did not have to feed her husband — in a certain way. That hadn't lasted long after their marriage and after the babies came. Where he went on his long trips she did not know. Sometimes he was gone from home for weeks, and after the boy grew up they went off together.

They left everything at home for her to manage and she had no money. She knew no one. No one ever talked to her in town. When it was Winter she had to gather sticks of wood for her fire, had to try to keep the stock fed with very little grain.

The stock in the barn cried to her hungrily, the dogs followed her about. In the Winter the hens laid few enough eggs. They huddled in the corners of the barn and she kept watching them. If a hen lays an egg in the barn in the Winter and you do not find it, it freezes and breaks.

One day in Winter the old woman went off to town with a few eggs and the dogs followed her. She did not get started until nearly three o'clock and the snow was heavy. She hadn't been feeling very well for several days and so she went muttering along, scantily clad, her shoulders stooped. She had an old grain bag in which she carried her eggs, tucked away down in the bottom. There weren't many of them, but in Winter the price of eggs is up. She would get a little meat in exchange for the eggs, some salt pork, a little sugar, and some coffee perhaps. It might be the butcher would give her a piece of liver.

When she had got to town and was trading in her eggs the dogs lay by the door outside. She did pretty well, got the things she needed, more than she had hoped. Then she went to the butcher and he gave her some liver and some dog-meat.

It was the first time any one had spoken to her in a friendly way for a long time. The butcher was alone in his shop when she came in and was annoyed by the thought of such a sick-looking old woman out on such a day. It was bitter cold and the snow, that had let up during the afternoon, was falling again. The butcher said something about her husband and her son, swore at them, and the old woman stared at him, a look of mild surprise in her eyes as he talked. He said that if either the husband or the son were going to get any of the liver or the heavy bones with scraps of meat hanging to them that he had put into the grain bag, he'd see him starve first.

Starve, eh? Well, things had to be fed. Men had to be fed, and horses that weren't any good but maybe could be traded off, and the poor thin cow that hadn't given any milk for three months.

Horses, cows, pigs, dogs, men.

III

The old woman had to get back before darkness came if she could. The dogs followed at her heels, sniffing at the heavy grain bag she had fastened on her back. When she got to the edge of town she stopped by a fence and tied the bag on her back with a piece of rope she had carried in her dress-pocket for just that purpose. It was hard when she had to crawl over fences and once she fell over and landed in the snow. The dogs went frisking about. She had to struggle to get to her feet again, but she made it. The point of climbing over the fences was that there was a short cut over a hill and through a woods. She might have gone around by the road, but it was a mile farther that way. She was afraid she couldn't make it. And then, besides, the stock had to be fed. There was a little hay left and a little corn. Perhaps her husband and son would bring some home when they came.

They had driven off in the only buggy the Grimes family had, a rickety thing, a rickety horse hitched to the buggy, two other rickety horses led by halters. They were going to trade horses, get a little money if they could. They might come home drunk. It would be well to have something in the house when they came back.

The son had an affair on with a woman at the county seat, fifteen miles away. She was a rough enough woman, a tough one. Once, in the Summer, the son had brought her to the house. Both she and the son had been drinking. Jake Grimes was away and the son and his woman ordered the old woman about like a servant. She didn't mind much; she was used to it. Whatever happened she never said anything. That was her way of getting along. She had managed that way when she was a young girl at the German's and ever since she had married Jake. That time her son brought his woman to the house they stayed all night, sleeping together just as though they were married. It hadn't shocked the old woman, not much. She had got past being shocked early in life.

With the pack on her back she went painfully along across an open field, wading in the deep snow, and got into the woods.

There was a path, but it was hard to follow. Just beyond the top of the hill, where the woods was thickest, there was a small clearing. Had some one once thought of building a house there? The clearing was as large as a building lot in town, large enough for a house and a garden. The path ran along the side of the clearing, and when she got there the old woman sat down to rest at the foot of a tree.

It was a foolish thing to do. When she got herself placed, the pack against the tree's trunk, it was nice, but what about getting up again? She worried about that for a moment and then quietly closed her eyes.

She must have slept for a time. When you are about so cold you can't get any colder. The afternoon grew a little warmer and the snow came thicker than ever. Then after a time the weather cleared. The moon even came out.

There were four Grimes dogs that had followed Mrs. Grimes into town, all tall gaunt fellows. Such men as Jake Grimes and his son always keep just such dogs. They kick and abuse them, but they stay. The Grimes dogs, in order to keep from starving, had to do a lot of foraging for themselves, and they had been at it while the old woman slept with her back to the tree at the side of the clearing. They had been chasing rabbits in the woods and in adjoining fields and in their ranging had picked up three other farm dogs.

After a time all the dogs came back to the clearing. They were excited about something. Such nights, cold and clear and with a moon, do things to dogs. It may be that some old instinct, come down from the time when they were wolves, and ranged the woods in packs on Winter nights, comes back to them.

The dogs in the clearing, before the old woman, had caught two or three rabbits and their immediate hunger had been satisfied. They began to play, running in circles in the clearing. Round and round they ran, each dog's nose at the tail of the next dog. In the clearing, under the snow-laden trees and under the wintry moon they made a strange picture, running thus silently, in a circle their running had beaten in the soft snow. The dogs made no sound. They ran around and around in the circle.

It may have been that the old woman saw them doing that before she died. She may have awakened once or twice and looked at the strange sight with dim old eyes.

She wouldn't be very cold now, just drowsy. Life hangs on a long time. Perhaps the old woman was out of her head. She may have dreamed of her girlhood at the German's, and before that, when she was a child and before her mother lit out and left her.

Her dreams couldn't have been very pleasant. Not many pleasant things had happened to her. Now and then one of the Grimes dogs left the running circle and came to stand before her. The dog thrust his face to her face. His red tongue was hanging out.

The running of the dogs may have been a kind of death ceremony. It may have been that the primitive instinct of the wolf, having been aroused in the dogs by the night and the running, made them somehow, afraid.

"Now we are no longer wolves. We are dogs, the servants of men. Keep alive, man! When man dies we become wolves again." When one of the dogs came to where the old woman sat with her back against the tree and thrust his nose close to her face he seemed satisfied and went back to run with the pack. All the Grimes dogs did it at some time during the evening, before she died. I knew all about it afterward, when I grew to be a man, because once in a woods in Illinois, on another Winter night, I saw a pack of dogs act just like that. The dogs were waiting for me to die as they had waited for the old woman that night when I was a child, but when it happened to me I was a young man and had no intention whatever of dying.

The old woman died softly and quietly. When she was dead and when one of the Grimes dogs had come to her and had found her dead all the dogs stopped running.

They gathered about her.

Well, she was dead now. She had fed the Grimes dogs when she was alive, what about now?

There was the pack on her back, the grain bag containing the piece of salt pork, the liver the butcher had given her, the dog-meat, the soup bones. The butcher in town, having been suddenly overcome with a feeling of pity, had loaded her grain bag heavily. It had been a big haul for the old woman.

It was a big haul for the dogs now.

IV

One of the Grimes dogs sprang suddenly out from among the others and began worrying the pack on the old woman's back. Had the dogs really been wolves that one would have been the leader of the pack. What he did, all the others did.

All of them sank their teeth into the grain bag the old woman had fastened with ropes to her back.

They dragged the old woman's body out into the open clearing. The worn-out dress was quickly torn from her shoulders. When she was found, a day or two later, the dress had been torn from her body clear to the hips, but the dogs had not touched her body. They had got the meat out of the grain bag, that was all. Her body was frozen stiff when it was found, and the shoulders were so narrow and the body so slight that in death it looked like the body of some charming young girl.

Such things happened in towns of the Middle West, on farms near town, when I was a boy. A hunter out after rabbits found the old woman's body and did not touch it. Something, the beaten round path in the little snow-covered clearing, the silence of the place, the place where the dogs had worried the body trying to pull the grain bag away or tear it open — something startled the man and he hurried off to town.

I was in Main Street with one of my brothers who was town newsboy and who was taking the afternoon papers to the stores. It was almost night.

The hunter came into a grocery and told his story. Then he went into a hardware-shop and into a drugstore. Men began to gather on the sidewalks. Then they started out along the road to the place in the woods.

My brother should have gone on about his business of distributing papers but he didn't. Every one was going to the woods. The undertaker went and the town marshal. Several men got on a dray and rode out to where the path left the road and went into the woods, but the horses weren't very sharply shod and slid about on the slippery roads. They made no better time than those of us who walked.

The town marshal was a large man whose leg had been injured in the Civil War. He carried a heavy cane and limped rapidly along the road. My brother and I followed at his heels, and as we went other men and boys joined the crowd.

It had grown dark by the time we got to where the old woman had left the road but the moon had come out. The marshal was thinking there might have been a murder. He kept asking the hunter questions. The hunter went along with his gun across his shoulders, a dog following at his heels. It isn't often a rabbit hunter has a chance to be so conspicuous. He was taking full advantage of it, leading the procession with the town marshal. "I didn't see any wounds. She was a beautiful young girl. Her face was buried in the snow. No, I didn't know her." As a matter of fact, the hunter had not looked closely at the body. He had been frightened. She might have

been murdered and some one might spring out from behind a tree and murder him. In a woods, in the late afternoon, when the trees are all bare and
there is white snow on the ground, when all is silent, something creepy
steals over the mind and body. If something strange or uncanny has happened in the neighborhood all you think about is getting away from there as
fast as you can.

The crowd of men and boys had got to where the old woman had
crossed the field and went, following the marshal and the hunter, up the
slight incline and into the woods.

My brother and I were silent. He had his bundle of papers in a bag
slung across his shoulder. When he got back to town he would have to go
on distributing his papers before he went home to supper. If I went along,
as he had no doubt already determined I should, we would both be late.
Either mother or our older sister would have to warm our supper.

Well, we would have something to tell. A boy did not get such a
chance very often. It was lucky we just happened to go into the grocery
when the hunter came in. The hunter was a country fellow. Neither of us
had ever seen him before.

Now the crowd of men and boys had got to the clearing. Darkness
comes quickly on such Winter nights, but the full moon made everything
clear. My brother and I stood near the tree, beneath which the old woman
had died.

She did not look old, lying there in that light, frozen and still. One of
the men turned her over in the snow and I saw everything. My body trembled with some strange mystical feeling and so did my brother's. It might
have been the cold.

Neither of us had ever seen a woman's body before. It may have been
the snow, clinging to the frozen flesh, that made it look so white and lovely,
so like marble. No woman had come with the party from town; but one of
the men, he was the town blacksmith, took off his overcoat and spread it
over her. Then he gathered her into his arms and started off to town, all the
others following silently. At that time no one knew who she was.

V

I had seen everything, had seen the oval in the snow, like a miniature
race-track, where the dogs had run, had seen how the men were mystified,
had seen the white bare young-looking shoulders, had heard the whispered
comments of the men.

The men were simply mystified. They took the body to the undertaker's, and when the blacksmith, the hunter, the marshal and several
others had got inside they closed the door. If father had been there perhaps
he could have got in, but we boys couldn't.

I went with my brother to distribute the rest of his papers and when
we got home it was my brother who told the story.

I kept silent and went to bed early. It may have been I was not satisfied with the way he told it.

Later, in the town, I must have heard other fragments of the old woman's story. She was recognized the next day and there was an investigation.

The husband and son were found somewhere and brought to town and there was an attempt to connect them with the woman's death, but it did not work. They had perfect enough alibis.

However, the town was against them. They had to get out. Where they went I never heard.

I remember only the picture there in the forest, the men standing about, the naked girlish-looking figure, face down in the snow, the tracks made by the running dogs and the clear cold Winter sky above. White fragments of clouds were drifting across the sky. They went racing across the little open space among the trees.

The scene in the forest had become for me, without my knowing it, the foundation for the real story I am now trying to tell. The fragments, you see, had to be picked up slowly, long afterwards.

Things happened. When I was a young man I worked on the farm of a German. The hired-girl was afraid of her employer. The farmer's wife hated her.

I saw things at that place. Once later, I had a half-uncanny, mystical adventure with dogs in an Illinois forest on a clear, moon-lit Winter night. When I was a schoolboy, and on a Summer day, I went with a boy friend out along a creek some miles from town and came to the house where the old woman had lived. No one had lived in the house since her death. The doors were broken from the hinges; the window lights were all broken. As the boy and I stood in the road outside, two dogs, just roving farm dogs no doubt, came running around the corner of the house. The dogs were tall, gaunt fellows and came down to the fence and glared through at us, standing in the road.

The whole thing, the story of the old woman's death, was to me as I grew older like music heard from far off. The notes had to be picked up slowly one at a time. Something had to be understood.

The woman who died was one destined to feed animal life. Anyway, that is all she ever did. She was feeding animal life before she was born, as a child, as a young woman working on the farm of the German, after she married, when she grew old and when she died. She fed animal life in cows, in chickens, in pigs, in horses, in dogs, in men. Her daughter had died in childhood and with her one son she had no articulate relations. On the night when she died she was hurrying homeward, bearing on her body food for animal life.

She died in the clearing in the woods and even after her death continued feeding animal life.

You see it is likely that, when my brother told the story, that night when we got home and my mother and sister sat listening, I did not think he got the point. He was too young and so was I. A thing so complete has its own beauty.

I shall not try to emphasize the point. I am only explaining why I was dissatisfied then and have been ever since. I speak of that only that you may understand why I have been impelled to try to tell the simple story over again.

[1933]

A. E. COPPARD (1878–1957) *was born at Folkestone, Kent, the son of a tailor and a housemaid. When he was nine years old his father died, and he was forced to leave school and begin work as a vendor of paraffin, shouting "Oil! Oil!" from street to street. During his early years he worked mostly as an errand boy for a succession of auctioneers, cheesemongers, soap-sellers, and carriers. "From the age of sixteen to twenty-six my life now appears to me to be a sort of kaleidoscope of running, reading, falling in love, and trying to write verse." Coppard educated himself by reading the English poets, and although his own verse was not very good, some of it was printed. After he went to live in Oxford in 1907 as an accountant for an engineering firm, he met other people interested in books and writing, and began to write short stories. The turning point in his life came in 1919, when he had saved 50 pounds and rented a tiny cottage in the middle of a field near Oxford, living frugally and writing short stories of remarkable poetic quality. In 1921 his first collection of stories,* Adam and Eve and Pinch Me, *established his reputation. From then on he sold his stories steadily to magazines and published collections at nearly yearly intervals. His autobiography,* It's Me, O Lord!, *was published in 1957, the year of his death.*

Doris Lessing observed of Coppard that his stories belong in the "steadily flowing stream in English writing that is quiet, low in key"; his is "a sparrow's-eye view, sharp, wry, surviving." From Chekhov, Coppard learned how to present his characters with psychological exactitude, but the pace of his unfolding characterizations is more leisurely than Chekhov's. His tales unwind through various curves and twists of fate like a narrow English country lane. They are filled with vivid, meticulously observed details of the English pastoral landscape, where the seasonal rhythms of nature and the habits of small birds and animals often seem to harmonize with the characters' emotional situations.

At the center of Coppard's best work, like "The Higgler," is a sense of solitude. He described in his autobiography his own "desire to go most of my way alone, as though I was instinctively seeking after something still a way out of my reach. What this was, or what it might have been, I didn't know, I didn't care, I didn't bother, I went after it. I still don't know if I ever found it, it may have been sheer idiotic mysticism. Whatever it was, it had no objectivity beyond a craving to shun the familiarities, the nonsense of consciousness and awareness, and simply be; to commune with something — with whom or what but myself!" A religious skeptic, Coppard found his greatest sense of freedom and beauty in the "imperturbability of unhuman nature everywhere manifested in flowers, fields, birds, beasts, trees, hills, and rivers."

A. E. Coppard

 space

THE HIGGLER

I

On a cold April afternoon a higgler was driving across Shag Moor in a two-wheeled cart.

H. WITLOW

DEALER IN POULTRY

DINNOP

was painted on the hood; the horse was of mean appearance but notorious ancestry. A high upland common was this moor, two miles from end to end, and full of furze and bracken. There were no trees and not a house, nothing but a line of telegraph poles following the road, sweeping with rigidity from north to south; nailed upon one of them a small scarlet notice to stone-throwers was prominent as a wound. On so high and wide a region as Shag Moor the wind always blew, or if it did not quite blow there was a cool activity in the air. The furze was always green and growing, and, taking no account of seasons, often golden. Here in summer solitude lounged and snoozed; at other times, as now, it shivered and looked sinister.

Higglers in general are ugly and shrewd, old and hard, crafty and callous, but Harvey Witlow though shrewd was not ugly; he was hard but not old, crafty but not at all unkind. If you had eggs to sell he would buy them, by the score he would, or by the long hundred. Other odds and ends he would buy or do, paying good bright silver, bartering a bag of apples, carrying your little pig to market, or fetching a tree from the nurseries. But the season was backward, eggs were scarce, trade was bad — by crumps, it was indeed! — and as he crossed the moor Harvey could not help discussing the situation with himself.

"If things don't change, and change for the better, and change soon, I can't last and I can't endure it; I'll be damned and done, and I'll have to sell," he said, prodding the animal with the butt of his whip, "this cob. And," he said, as if in afterthought, prodding the footboard, "this cart, and go back to the land. And I'll have lost my fifty pounds. Well, that's what war does for you. It does it for you, sir," he announced sharply to the vacant moor, "and it does it for me. Fifty pounds! I was better off in the war. I was

486

better off working for farmers; much; but it's no good chattering about it, it's the trick of life; when you get so far, then you can go and order your funeral. Get along, Dodger!"

The horse responded briskly for a few moments.

"I tell ye," said Harvey adjuring the ambient air, "you can go and order your funeral. Get along, Dodger!"

Again Dodger got along.

"Then there's Sophy, what about Sophy and me?"

He was not engaged to Sophy Daws, not exactly, but he was keeping company with her. He was not pledged or affianced, he was just keeping company with her. But Sophy, as he knew, not only desired a marriage with Mr. Witlow, she expected it, and expected it soon. So did her parents, her friends, and everybody in the village, including the postman, who didn't live in it but wished he did, and the parson, who did live in it but wished he didn't.

"Well, that's damned and done, fair damned and done now, unless things take a turn, and soon, so it's no good chattering about it."

And just then and there things did take a turn. He had never been across the moor before; he was prospecting for trade. At the end of Shag Moor he saw standing back in the common, fifty yards from the road, a neat square house set in a little farm. Twenty acres, perhaps. The house was girded by some white palings; beside it was a snug orchard in a hedge covered with blackthorn bloom. It was very green and pleasant in front of the house. The turf was cleared and closely cropped, some ewes were grazing and under the blackthorn, out of the wind, lay half a dozen lambs, but what chiefly moved the imagination of Harvey Witlow was a field on the far side of the house. It had a small rickyard with a few small stacks in it; everything here seemed on the small scale, but snug, very snug; and in that field and yard were hundreds of fowls, hundreds of good breed, and mostly white. Leaving his horse to sniff the greensward, the higgler entered a white wicket gateway and passed to the back of the house, noting as he did so a yellow wagon inscribed

ELIZABETH SADGROVE
PRATTLE CORNER

At the kitchen door he was confronted by a tall gaunt woman of middle age with a teapot in her hands.

"Afternoon, ma'am. Have you anything to sell?" began Harvey Witlow, tilting his hat with a confident affable air. The tall woman was cleanly dressed, a superior person; her hair was grey. She gazed at him.

"It's cold," he continued. She looked at him as uncomprehendingly as a mouse might look at a gravestone.

"I'll buy any mottal thing, ma'am. Except trouble; I'm full up wi' that already. Eggs? Fowls?"

"I've not seen you before," commented Mrs. Sadgrove a little bleakly, in a deep husky voice.

"No, 'tis the first time as ever I drove in this part. To tell you the truth, ma'am, I'm new to the business. Six months. I was in the war a year ago. Now I'm trying to knock up a connection. Difficult work. Things are very quiet."

Mrs. Sadgrove silently removed the lid of the teapot, inspected the interior of the pot with an intense glance, and then replaced the lid as if she had seen a black-beetle there.

"Ah, well," sighed the higgler. "You've a neat little farm here, ma'am."

"It's quiet enough," said she.

"Sure it is, ma'am. Very lonely."

"And it's difficult work, too." Mrs. Sadgrove almost smiled.

"Sure it is, ma'am; but you does it well, I can see. Oh, you've some nice little ricks of corn, ah! I does well enough at the dealing now and again, but it's teasy work, and mostly I don't earn enough to keep my horse in shoe leather."

"I've a few eggs, perhaps," said she.

"I could do with a score or two, ma'am, if you could let me have 'em."

"You'll have to come all my way if I do."

"Name your own price, ma'am, if you don't mind trading with me."

"Mind! Your money's as good as my own, isn't it?"

"It must be, ma'am. That's meaning no disrespects to you," the young higgler assured her hastily, and was thereupon invited to enter the kitchen.

A stone floor with two or three mats; open hearth with burning logs; a big dresser painted brown, carrying a row of white cups on brass hooks, and shelves of plates overlapping each other like scales of fish. A dark settle half-hid a flight of stairs with a small gate at the top. Under the window a black sofa, deeply indented, invited you a little repellingly, and in the middle of the room stood a large table, exquisitely scrubbed, with one end of it laid for tea. Evidently a living-room as well as kitchen. A girl, making toast at the fire, turned as the higgler entered. Beautiful she was: red hair, a complexion like the inside of a nut, blue eyes, and the hands of a lady. He saw it all at once, jacket of bright green wool, black dress, grey stockings and shoes, and forgot his errand, her mother, his fifty pounds, Sophy — momentarily he forgot everything. The girl stared strangely at him. He was tall, clean-shaven, with a loop of black hair curling handsomely over one side of his brow.

"Good afternoon," said Harvey Witlow, as softly as if he had entered a church.

"Some eggs, Mary," Mrs. Sadgrove explained. The girl laid down her toasting-fork. She was less tall than her mother, whom she resembled only enough for the relationship to be noted. Silently she crossed the kitchen and opened a door that led into a dairy. Two pans of milk were creaming on a bench there, and on the flags were two great baskets filled with eggs.

"How many are there?" asked Mrs. Sadgrove, and the girl replied: "Fifteen score, I think."

"Take the lot, higgler?"

"Yes, ma'am," he cried eagerly, and ran out to his cart and fetched a number of trays. In them he packed the eggs as the girl handed them to him from the baskets. Mrs. Sadgrove left them together. For a time the higgler was silent.

"No," at length he murmured, "I've never been this road before."

There was no reply from Mary. Sometimes their fingers touched, and often, as they bent over the eggs, her bright hair almost brushed his face.

"It is a loneish spot," he ventured again.

"Yes," said Mary Sadgrove.

When the eggs were all transferred her mother came in again.

"Would you buy a few pullets, higgler?"

"Any number, ma'am," he declared quickly. Any number; by crumps, the tide was turning. He followed the mother into the yard, and there again she left him, waiting. He mused about the girl and wondered about the trade. If they offered him ten thousand chickens, he'd buy them, somehow, he would. She had stopped in the kitchen. Just in there she was, just behind him, a few feet away. Over the low wall of the yard a fat black pony was strolling in a field of bright greensward. In the yard, watching him, was a young gander, and on a stone staddle beside it lay a dead thrush on its back, its legs stiff in the air. The girl stayed in the kitchen; she was moving about, though, he could hear her; perhaps she was spying at him through the window. Twenty million eggs he would buy if Mrs. Sadgrove had got them. She was gone a long time. It was very quiet. The gander began to comb its white breast with its beak. Its three-toed feet were a most tender pink, shaped like wide diamonds, and at each of the three forward points here was a toe like a small blanched nut. It lifted one foot, folding the webs, and hid it under its wing and sank into a resigned meditation on one leg. It had a blue eye that was meek — it had two, but you could only see one at a time — a meek blue eye, set in a pink rim that gave it a dissolute air, and its beak had raw red nostrils as though it suffered from the damp. Altogether a beautiful bird. And in some absurd way it resembled Mrs. Sadgrove.

"Would you sell that young gollan, ma'am?" Harvey inquired when the mother returned.

Yes, she would sell him, and she also sold him two dozen pullets. Harvey packed the fowls in a crate.

"Come on," he cried cuddling the squalling gander in his arms, "you needn't be afeared of me, I never kills anything afore Saturdays."

He roped it by its leg to a hook inside his cart. Then he took out his bag of money, paid Mrs. Sadgrove her dues, said: "Good day, ma'am, good day" and drove off without seeing another sign or stitch of that fine young girl.

"Get along, Dodger, get along wi' you." They went bowling along for nearly an hour, and then he could see the landmark on Dan'el Green's Hill, a windmill that never turned though it looked a fine competent piece of architecture, just beyond Dinnop.

Soon he reached his cottage and was chaffing his mother, a hearty buxom dame, who stayed at home and higgled with any chance callers. At this business she was perhaps more enlightened than her son. It was almost a misfortune to get into her clutches.

"How much you give for this?" he cried, eyeing with humorous contempt an object in a coop that was neither flesh nor rude red herring.

"Oh crumps," he declared when she told him, "I am damned and done!"

"Go on with you, that's a good bird, I tell you, with a full heart, as will lay in a month."

"I doubt it's a hen at all," he protested. "Oh what a ravenous beak! Damned and done I am."

Mrs. Witlow's voice began indignantly to rise.

"Oh well," mused her son, "it's thrifty perhaps. It ain't quite right, but it's not so wrong as to make a fuss about, especially as I be pretty sharp set. And if it's hens you want," he continued triumphantly, dropping the crate of huddled fowls before her, "there's hens for you; and a gander! There's a gander for you, if it's a gander you want."

Leaving them all in his cottage yard he went and stalled the horse and cart at the inn, for he had no stable of his own. After supper he told his mother about the Sadgroves of Prattle Corner. "Prettiest girl you ever seen, but the shyest mottal alive. Hair like a squirrel, lovely."

"An't you got to go over and see Sophy tonight," inquired his mother, lighting the lamp.

"Oh lord, if I an't clean forgot that. Well, I'm tired, shan't go tonight. See her tomorrow."

II

Mrs. Sadgrove had been a widow for ten years — and she was glad of it. Prattle Corner was her property, she owned it and farmed it with the aid of a little old man and a large lad. The older this old man grew, and the less wages he received (for Elizabeth Sadgrove was reputed a "grinder"), the more ardently he worked; the older the lad grew, the less he laboured and the more he swore. She was thriving. She was worth money, was Mrs. Sadgrove. Ah! And her daughter Mary, it was clear, had received an education fit for a lord's lady; she had been at a seminary for gentlefolk's females until she was seventeen. Well, whether or no, a clock must run as you time it; but it wronged her for the work of a farm, it spoiled her, it completely deranged her for the work of a farm; and this was a pity and foolish, because some day the farm was coming to her as didn't know hay from a bull's foot.

All this, and more, the young higgler quickly learned, and plenty more he soon divined. Business began to flourish with him now; his despair was gone, he was established, he could look forward, to whatever it was he wanted to look forward, with equanimity and such pleasurable anticipation as the chances and charges of life might engender. Every week, and twice a week, he would call at the farm, and though these occasions had their superior business inducements they often borrowed a less formal tone and intention.

"Take a cup of tea, higgler?" Mrs. Sadgrove would abruptly invite him; and he would drink tea and discourse with her for half an hour on barndoor ornithology, on harness, and markets, the treatment of swine, the wear and tear of gear. Mary, always present, was always silent, seldom uttering a word to the higgler; yet a certain grace emanated from her to him, an interest, a light, a favour, circumscribed indeed by some modesty, shyness, some inhibition, that neither had the wit or the opportunity to overcome.

One evening he pulled up at the white palings of Prattle Corner. It was a calm evening in May, the sun was on its down-going, chaffinches and wrens sung ceaselessly. Mary in the orchard was heavily veiled; he could see her over the hedge, holding a brush in her gloved hands, and a bee skep. A swarm was clustered like a great gnarl on the limb of an apple tree. Bloom was thickly covering the twigs. She made several timid attempts to brush the bees into the skep but they resented this.

"They knows if you be afraid of 'em," bawled Harvey. "I better come and give you a hand."

When he took the skep and brush from her she stood like one helpless, released by fate from a task ill-understood and gracelessly waived. But he liked her shyness, her almost uncouth immobility.

"Never mind about that," said Harvey, as she unfastened her veil, scattering the white petals that had collected upon it; "when they kicks they hurts; but I've been stung so often that I'm 'noculated against 'em. They knows if you be afraid of 'em."

Wearing neither veil nor gloves he went confidently to the tree and collected the swarm without mishap.

"Don't want to show no fear of them," said Harvey. "Nor of anything else, come to that," he added with a guffaw, "nor anybody."

At that she blushed and thanked him very softly, and she did look straight and clearly at him.

Never anything beyond a blush and a thank-you. When in the kitchen, or the parlour, Mrs. Sadgrove sometimes left them alone together Harvey would try a lot of talk, blarneying talk or sensible talk, or talk about events in the world that was neither the one nor the other. No good. The girl's responses were ever brief and confused. Why was this? Again and again he asked himself that question. Was there anything the matter with her? Nothing that you could see; she was a bright and beautiful being. And it was not contempt, either, for despite her fright, her voicelessness, her timid eyes, he divined her friendly feeling for himself; and he would discourse to his own mother about her and her mother:

"They are well-up people, you know, well off, plenty of money and nothing to do with it. The farm's their own, freehold. A whole row of cottages she's got, too, in Smoorton Comfrey, so I heard; good cottages, well let. She's worth a few thousands, I warrant. Mary's beautiful. I took a fancy to that girl the first moment I see her. But she's very highly cultivated — and, of course, there's Sophy."

To this enigmatic statement Mrs. Witlow offered no response; but mothers are inscrutable beings to their sons, always.

Once he bought some trees of cherries from Mrs. Sadgrove, and went on a July morning to pick the fruit. Under the trees Mary was walking slowly to and fro, twirling a clapper to scare away the birds. He stood watching her from the gateway. Among the bejewelled trees she passed, turning the rattle with a listless air, as if beating time to a sad music that only she could hear. The man knew that he was deeply fond of her. He passed into the orchard, bade her good morning, and lifting his ladder into one of the trees nearest the hedge began to pluck cherries. Mary moved slimly in her white frock up and down a shady avenue in the orchard, waving the clapper. The brightness of sun and sky was almost harsh; there was a little wind that feebly lifted the despondent leaves. He had doffed his coat; his shirt was white and clean. The lock of dark hair drooped over one side of his forehead; his face was brown and pleasant, his bare arms were brown and powerful. From his high perch among the leaves Witlow watched for the girl to draw near to him in her perambulation. Knavish birds would scatter at her approach, only to drop again into the trees she had passed. His soul had an immensity of longing for her, but she never spoke a word to him. She would come from the shade of the little avenue, through the dumb trees that could only bend to greet her, into the sunlight whose dazzle gilded her own triumphant bloom. Fine! Fine! And always as she passed his mind refused to register a single thought he could offer her, or else his tongue would refuse to utter it. But his glance never left her face until she had passed out of sight again, and then he would lean against the ladder in the tree, staring down at the ground, seeing nothing or less than nothing, except a field mouse climbing to the top of a coventry bush in the hedge below him, nipping off one thick leaf and descending with the leaf in its mouth. Sometimes Mary rested at the other end of the avenue; the clapper would be silent and she would not appear for — oh, hours! She never rested near the trees Witlow was denuding. The mouse went on ascending and descending, and Witlow filled his basket, and shifted his stand, and wondered.

At noon he got down and sat on the hedge bank to eat a snack of lunch. Mary had gone indoors for hers, and he was alone for a while. Capriciously enough, his thoughts dwelt upon Sophy Daws. Sophy was a fine girl too; not such a lady as Mary Sadgrove — oh lord, no! her father was a gamekeeper! — but she was jolly and ample. She had been a little captious lately, said he was neglecting her. That wasn't true; hadn't he been busy? Besides, he wasn't bound to her in any sort of way, and of course he couldn't afford any marriage yet awhile. Sophy hadn't got any money, never had any. What she did with her wages — she was a parlour-maid — was a teaser! Harvey grunted a little, and said "Well!" And that is all he said, and all he thought about Sophy Daws then, for he could hear Mary's clapper begin again in a corner of the orchard. He went back to his work. There at the foot of the tree were the baskets full of cherries, and those yet to be filled.

"Phew, but that's hot!" commented the man, "I'm as dry as a rattle."

A few cherries had spilled from one basket and lay on the ground. The little furry mouse had found them and was industriously nibbling at one. The higgler nonchalantly stamped his foot upon it, and kept it so for a moment or two. Then he looked at the dead mouse. A tangle of entrails had gushed from its whiskered muzzle.

He resumed his work and the clapper rattled on throughout the afternoon, for there were other cherry trees that other buyers would come to strip in a day or two. At four o'clock he was finished. Never a word had he spoken with Mary, or she with him. When he went over to the house to pay Mrs. Sadgrove Mary stopped in the orchard scaring the birds.

"Take a cup of tea, Mr. Witlow," said Mrs. Sadgrove; and then she surprisingly added: "Where's Mary?"

"Still a-frightening the birds, and pretty well tired of that, I should think, ma'am."

The mother had poured out three cups of tea.

"Shall I go and call her in?" he asked, rising.

"You might," said she.

In the orchard the clappering had ceased. He walked all round, and in among the trees, but saw no sign of Mary; nor on the common, nor in the yard. But when he went back to the house Mary was there already, chatting at the table with her mother. She did not greet him, though she ceased talking to her mother as he sat down. After drinking his tea he went off briskly to load the baskets into the cart. As he climbed up to drive off, Mrs. Sadgrove came out and stood beside the horse.

"You're off now?" said she.

"Yes, ma'am; all loaded, and thank you."

She glanced vaguely along the road he had to travel. The afternoon was as clear as wine, the greensward itself dazzled him; lonely Shag Moor stretched away, humped with sweet yellow furze and pilastered with its telegraph poles. No life there, no life at all. Harvey sat on his driving board, musingly brushing the flank of his horse with the trailing whip.

"Ever round this way on Sundays?" inquired the woman, peering up at him.

"Well, not in a manner of speaking, I'm not, ma'am," he answered her.

The widow laid her hand on the horse's back, patting vaguely. The horse pricked up its ears, as if it were listening.

"If you are, at all, ever, you must look in and have a bit of dinner with us."

"I will, ma'am, I will."

"Next Sunday?" she went on.

"I will, ma'am, yes, I will," he repeated, "and thank you."

"One o'clock?" The widow smiled up at him.

"At one o'clock, ma'am; next Sunday; I will, and thank you," he said.

She stood away from the horse and waved her hand. The first tangible thought that floated mutely out of the higgler's mind as he drove away was: "I'm damned if I ain't a-going it, Sophy!"

He told his mother of Mrs. Sadgrove's invitation with an air of curbed triumph. "Come round — she says. Yes — I says — I 'ull. That's right — she says — so do."

III

On the Sunday morn he dressed himself gallantly. It was again a sweet unclouded day. The church bell at Dinnop had begun to ring. From his window, as he fastened his most ornate tie, Harvey could observe his neighbour's two small children in the next garden, a boy and girl clad for church-going and each carrying a clerical book. The tiny boy placed his sister in front of a hen-roost and, opening his book, began to pace to and fro before her, shrilly intoning: "Jesus is the shepherd, ring the bell. Oh lord, ring the bell, am I a good boy? Amen. Oh lord, ring the bell." The little girl bowed her head piously over her book. The lad then picked up from the ground a dish that had contained the dog's food, and presented it momentarily before the lilac bush, the rabbit in a hutch, the axe fixed in a chopping block, and then before his sister. Without lifting her peering gaze from her book she meekly dropped two pebbles in the plate, and the boy passed on, lightly moaning, to the clothes-line post and a cock scooping in some dust.

"Ah, the little impets!" cried Harvey Witlow, "Here, Toby! Here, Margaret!" He took two pennies from his pocket and lobbed them from the window to the astonished children. As they stooped to pick up the coins Harvey heard the hoarse voice of neighbour Nathan, their father, bawl from his kitchen: "Come on in, and shut that bloody door, d'y'ear!"

Harnessing his moody horse to the gig Harvey was soon bowling away to Shag Moor, and as he drove along he sung loudly. He had a pink rose in his buttonhole. Mrs. Sadgrove received him almost affably, and though Mary was more shy than ever before, Harvey had determined to make an impression. During the dinner he fired off his bucolic jokes, and pleasant tattle of a more respectful and sober nature; but after dinner Mary sat like

Patience, not upon a monument but as if upon a rocking-horse, shy and fearful, and her mother made no effort to inspire her as the higgler did, unsuccessful though he was. They went to the pens to look at the pigs, and as they leaned against the low walls and poked the maudlin inhabitants, Harvey began: "Reminds me, when I was in the war. . . ."

"Were you in the war!" interrupted Mrs. Sadgrove.

"Oh yes, I was in that war, ah, and there was a pig. . . . Danger? Oh lord bless me it was a bit dangerous, but you never knew where it was or what it 'ud be at next; it was like the sword of Damockels. There was a bullet once come 'ithin a foot of my head, and it went through a board an inch thick, slap through that board." Both women gazed at him apprehendingly. "Why, I might 'a' been killed, you know," said Harvey, cocking his eye musingly at the weather-vane on the barn. "We was in billets[1] at St. Gratien, and one day a chasseur came up — a French yoossar, you know — and he began talking to our sergeant. That was Hubert Luxter, the butcher: died a month or two ago of measles. But this yoossar couldn't speak English at all, and none of us chaps could make sense of him. I never could understand that lingo somehow, never; and though there was half a dozen of us chaps there, none of us were man enough for it neither. 'Nil compree,' we says, 'non compos.' I told him straight: 'You ought to learn English,' I said, 'it's much easier than your kind of bally chatter.' So he kept shaping up as if he was holding a rifle, and then he'd say 'Fusee — bang!' and then he'd say 'cushion' — kept on saying 'cushion.' Then he gets a bit of chalk and draws on the wall something that looks like a horrible dog, and says 'cushion' again."

"Pig," interjected Mary Sadgrove, softly.

"Yes, yes!" ejaculated Harvey, "so 'twas! Do you know any French lingo?"

"Oh yes," declared her mother, "Mary knows it very well."

"Ah," sighed the higgler, "I don't, although I been to France. And I couldn't do it now, not for luck nor love. You learnt it, I suppose. Well, this yoossar wants to borrow my rifle, but of course I can't lend him. So he taps on this horrible pig he'd drawn, and then he taps on his own head, and rolls his eyes about dreadful! 'Mad?' I says. And that was it, that was it. He'd got a pig on his little farm there what had gone mad, and he wanted us to come and shoot it; he was on leave and he hadn't got any ammunition. So Hubert Luxter he says: 'Come on, some of you,' and we all goes with the yoossar and shot the pig for him. Ah, that was a pig! And when it died it jumped a somersault just like a rabbit. It had got the mange, and was mad as anything I ever see in my life; it was full of madness. Couldn't hit him at all at first, and it kicked up bobs-a-dying. 'Ready, present, fire!' Hubert Luxter says, and bang goes the six of us, and every time we missed him he spotted us and we had to run for our lives."

---

[1] quartered in private homes.

As Harvey looked up he caught a glance of the girl fixed on him. She dropped her gaze at once and, turning away, walked off to the house.

"Come and take a look at the meadow," said Mrs. Sadgrove to him, and they went into the soft smooth meadow where the black pony was grazing. Very bright and green it was, and very blue the sky. He sniffed at the pink rose in his buttonhole, and determined that come what may he would give it to Mary if he could get a nice quiet chance to offer it. And just then, while he and Mrs. Sadgrove were strolling alone in the soft smooth meadow, quite alone, she suddenly, startlingly, asked him: "Are you courting anybody?"

"Beg pardon, ma'am?" he exclaimed.

"You haven't got a sweetheart, have you?" she asked, most deliberately.

Harvey grinned sheepishly: "Ha ha ha," and then he said: "No."

"I want to see my daughter married," the widow went on significantly.

"Miss Mary!" he cried.

"Yes," said she; and something in the higgler's veins began to pound rapidly. His breast might have been a revolving cage and his heart a demon squirrel. "I can't live for ever," said Mrs. Sadgrove, almost with levity, "in fact, not for long, and so I'd like to see her settled soon with some decent understanding young man, one that could carry on here, and not make a mess of things."

"But, but," stuttered the understanding young man, "I'm no scholar, and she's a lady. I'm a poor chap, rough, and no scholar, ma'am. But mind you. . . ."

"That doesn't matter at all," the widow interrupted, "not as things are. You want a scholar for learning, but for the land. . . ."

"Ah, that's right, Mrs. Sadgrove, but. . . ."

"I want to see her settled. This farm, you know, with the stock and things are worth nigh upon three thousand pounds."

"You want a farmer for farming, that's true, Mrs. Sadgrove, but when you come to marriage, well, with her learning and French and all that. . . ."

"A sensible woman will take a man rather than a box of tricks any day of the week," the widow retorted. "Education may be a fine thing, but it often costs a lot of foolish money."

"It do, it do. You want to see her settled?"

"I want to see her settled and secure. When she is twenty-five she comes into five hundred pounds of her own right."

The distracted higgler hummed and haa-ed in his bewilderment as if he had just been offered the purchase of a dubious duck. "How old is she, ma'am?" he at last huskily inquired.

"Two and twenty nearly. She's a good healthy girl for I've never spent a pound on a doctor for her, and very quiet she is, and very sensible; but she's got a strong will of her own, though you might not think it or believe it."

"She's a fine creature, Mrs. Sadgrove, and I'm very fond of her, I don't mind owning up to that, very fond of her I am."

"Well, think it over, take your time, and see what you think. There's no hurry I hope, please God."

"I shan't want much time," he declared with a laugh, "but I doubt I'm the fair right sort for her."

"Oh, fair days, fair doings!" said she inscrutably, "I'm not a long liver, I'm afraid."

"God forbid, ma'am!" His ejaculation was intoned with deep gravity.

"No, I'm not a long-living woman." She surveyed him with her calm eyes, and he returned her gaze. Hers was a long sallow face, with heavy lips. Sometimes she would stretch her features (as if to keep them from petrifying) in an elastic grin, and display her dazzling teeth; the lips would curl thickly, no longer crimson but blue. He wondered if there was any sign of a doom registered upon her gaunt face. She might die, and die soon.

"You couldn't do better than think it over, then, eh?" She had a queer frown as she regarded him.

"I couldn't do worse than not, Mrs. Sadgrove," he said gaily.

They left it at that. He had no reason for hurrying away, and he couldn't have explained his desire to do so, but he hurried away. Driving along past the end of the moor, and peering back at the lonely farm where they dwelled amid the thick furze snoozing in the heat, he remembered that he had not asked if Mary was willing to marry him! Perhaps the widow took her agreement for granted. That would be good fortune, for otherwise how the devil was he to get round a girl who had never spoken half a dozen words to him! And never would! She was a lady, a girl of fortune, knew her French; but there it was, the girl's own mother was asking him to wed her. Strange, very strange! He dimly feared something, but he did not know what it was he feared. He had still got the pink rose in his buttonhole.

IV

At first his mother was incredulous; when he told her of the astonishing proposal she declared he was a joker; but she was soon as convinced of his sincerity as she was amazed at his hesitation. And even vexed: "Was there anything the matter with this Mary?"

"No, no, no! She's quiet, very quiet indeed, I tell you, but a fine young woman, and a beautiful young woman. Oh, she's all right, right as rain, right as a trivet, right as ninepence. But there's a catch in it somewheres, I fear. I can't see through it yet, but I shall afore long, or I'd have the girl, like a shot I would. 'Tain't the girl, mother, it's the money, if you understand me."

"Well, I don't understand you, certainly I don't. What about Sophy?"

"Oh lord!" He scratched his head ruefully.

"You wouldn't think of giving this the go-by for Sophy, Harvey, would you? A girl as you ain't even engaged to, Harvey, would you?"

"We don't want to chatter about that," declared her son. "I got to think it over, and it's going to tie my wool, I can tell you, for there's a bit of craft somewheres, I'll take my oath. If there ain't, there ought to be!"

Over the alluring project his decision wavered for days, until his mother became mortified at his inexplicable vacillation.

"I tell you," he cried, "I can't make tops or bottoms of it all. I like the girl well enough, but I like Sophy, too, and it's no good beating about the bush. I like Sophy, she's the girl I love; but Mary's a fine creature, and money like that wants looking at before you throw it away, love or no love. Three thousand pounds! I'd be a made man."

And as if in sheer spite to his mother; as if a bushel of money lay on the doorstep for him to kick over whenever the fancy seized him; in short (as Mrs. Witlow very clearly intimated) as if in contempt of Providence, he began to pursue Sophy Daws with a new fervour, and walked with that young girl more than he was accustomed to, more than ever before; in fact, as his mother bemoaned, more than he had need to. It was unreasonable, it was a shame, a foolishness; it wasn't decent and it wasn't safe.

On his weekly visits to the farm his mind still wavered. Mrs. Sadgrove let him alone; she was very good, she did not pester him with questions and entreaties. There was Mary with her white dress and her red hair and her silence; a girl with a great fortune, walking about the yard, or sitting in the room, and casting not a glance upon him. Not that he would have known it if she did, for now he was just as shy of her. Mrs. Sadgrove often left them alone, but when they were alone he could not dish up a word for the pretty maid; he was dumb as a statue. If either she or her mother had lifted so much as a finger, then there would have been an end to his hesitations or suspicions, for in Mary's presence the fine glory of the girl seized him incontinently; he was again full of a longing to press her lips, to lay down his doubts, to touch her bosom — though he could not think she would ever allow that! Not an atom of doubt about *her* ever visited him; she was unaware of her mother's queer project. Rather, if she became aware he was sure it would be the end of him. Too beautiful she was, too learned, and too rich. Decidedly it was his native cunning, and no want of love, that inhibited him. Folks with property did not often come along and bid you help yourself. Not very often! And throw in a grand bright girl, just for good measure as you might say. Not very often!

For weeks the higgler made his customary calls, and each time the outcome was the same; no more, no less. "Some dodge," he mused, "something the girl don't know and the mother does." Were they going bankrupt, or were they mortgaged up to the neck, or was there anything the matter with the girl, or was it just the mother wanted to get hold of him? He knew his own value if he didn't know his own mind, and his value couldn't match that girl any more than his mind could. So what *did* they want him for?

Whatever it was, Harvey Witlow was ready for it whenever he was in Mary's presence, but once away from her his own craftiness asserted itself; it was a snare, they were trying to make a mock of him!

But nothing could prevent his own mother mocking him, and her treatment of Sophy was so unbearable that if the heart of that dusky beauty had not been proof against all impediments, Harvey might have had to whistle for her favour. But whenever he was with Sophy he had only one heart, undivided and true, and certain as time itself.

"I love Sophy best. It's true enough I love Mary, too, but I love Sophy better. I know it; Sophy's the girl I must wed. It might not be so if I weren't all dashed and doddered about the money; I don't know. But I do know that Mary's innocent of all this craftiness; it's her mother trying to mogue me into it."

Later he would be wishing he could only forget Sophy and do it. Without the hindrance of conscience he could do it, catch or no catch.

He went on calling at the farm, with nothing said or settled, until October. Then Harvey made up his mind, and without a word to the Sadgroves he went and married Sophy Daws and gave up calling at the farm altogether. This gave him some feeling of dishonesty, some qualm and a vague unhappiness; likewise he feared the cold hostility of Mrs. Sadgrove. She would be terribly vexed. As for Mary, he was nothing to her, poor girl; it was a shame. The last time he drove that way he did not call at the farm. Autumn was advancing, and the apples were down, the bracken dying, the furze out of bloom, and the farm on the moor looked more and more lonely, and most cold, though it lodged a flame-haired silent woman, fit for a nobleman, whom they wanted to mate with a common higgler. Crafty, you know, too crafty!

V

The marriage was a gay little occasion, but they did not go away for a honeymoon. Sophy's grandmother from a distant village, Cassandra Fundy, who had a deafness and a speckled skin, brought her third husband, Amos, whom the family had never seen before. Not a very wise man, indeed he was a common man, stooping like a decayed tree, he was so old. But he shaved every day and his hairless skull was yellow. Cassandra, who was yellow too, had long since turned into a fool; she did not shave, though she ought to have done. She was like to die soon, but everybody said old Amos would live to be a hundred; it was expected of him, and he, too, was determined.

The guests declared that a storm was threatening; but Amos Fundy denied it and scorned it.

"Thunder p'raps, but 'twill clear; 'tis only de pride o' der morning."

"Don't you be a fool," remarked his wife, enigmatically, "you'll die soon enough."

"You must behold der moon," continued the octogenarian; "de closer it is to der wheel, de closer der rain; de furder away it is, de furder der rain."

"You could pour that man's brains into a thimble," declared Cassandra of her spouse, "and they wouldn't fill it — he's deaf."

Fundy was right; the day did clear. The marriage was made and the guests returned with the man and his bride to their home. But Fundy was also wrong, for storm came soon after and rain set in. The guests stayed on for tea, and then, as it was no better, they feasted and stayed till night. And Harvey began to think they never would go, but of course they couldn't and so there they were. Sophy was looking wonderful in white stockings and shiny shoes and a red frock with a tiny white apron. A big girl she seemed, with her shaken dark hair and flushed face. Grandmother Fundy spoke seriously, but not secretly to her.

"I've had my fourteen touch of children," said Grandmother Fundy. "Yes, they were flung on the mercy of God — poor little devils. I've followed most of 'em to the churchyard. You go slow, Sophia."

"Yes, granny."

"Why," continued Cassandra, embracing the whole company, as it were, with her disclosure, "my mother had me by some gentleman!"

The announcement aroused no response except sympathetic, and perhaps encouraging, nods from the women.

"She had me by some gentleman — she ought to ha' had a twal' month, she did!"

"Wasn't she ever married?" Sophy inquired of her grandmother.

"Married? Yes, course she was," replied the old dame, "of course. But marriage ain't everything. Twice she was, but not to he, she wasn't."

"Not to the gentleman?"

"No! Oh no! He'd got money — bushels! Marriage ain't much, not with these gentry."

"Ho, ho, that's a tidy come-up!" laughed Harvey.

"Who was the gentleman?" Sophia's interest was deeply engaged. But Cassandra Fundy was silent, pondering like a china image. Her gaze was towards the mantelpiece, where there were four lamps — but only one usable — and two clocks — but only one going — and a coloured greeting card a foot long with large letters KEEP SMILING adorned with lithographic honeysuckle.

"She's hard of hearing," interpolated Grandfather Amos, "very hard, gets worse. She've a horn at home, big as that. . . ." His eyes roved the room for an object of comparison, and he seized upon the fire shovel that lay in the fender. "Big as that shovel. Crown silver it is, and solid, a beautiful horn, but" — he brandished the shovel before them — "her won't use 'en."

"Granny, who was that gentleman?" shouted Sophy. "Did you know him?"

"No! No!" declared the indignant dame. "I dunno ever his name, nor

I don't want to. He took hisself off to Ameriky, and now he's in the land of heaven. I never seen him. If I had, I'd 'a' given it to him properly; oh, my dear, not blay-guarding him, you know, but just plain language! Where's your seven commandments?"

At last the rain abated. Peeping into the dark garden you could see the fugitive moonlight hung in a million raindrops in the black twigs of all sorts of bushes and trees, while along the cantle of the porch a line of raindrops hung, even and regular, as if they were nailheads made of glass. So all the guests departed, in one long staggering, struggling, giggling, guffawing body, into the village street. The bride and her man stood in the porch, watching, and waving hands. Sophy was momentarily grieving: what a lot of trouble and fuss when you announced that henceforward you were going to sleep with a man because you loved him true! She had said good-bye to her Grandmother Cassandra, to her father and her little sister. She had hung on her mother's breast, sighing an almost intolerable farewell to innocence — never treasured until it is gone — and thenceforward a pretty sorrow cherished more deeply than wilder joys.

Into Harvey's mind, as they stood there at last alone, momentarily stole an image of a bright-haired girl, lovely, silent, sad, whom he felt he had deeply wronged. And he was sorry. He had escaped the snare, but if there had been no snare he might this night have been sleeping with a different bride. And it would have been just as well. Sophy looked but a girl with her blown hair and wet face. She was wiping her tears on the tiny apron. But she had the breasts of a woman and decoying eyes.

"Sophy, Sophy!" breathed Harvey, wooing her in the darkness.

"It blows and it rains, and it rains and it blows," chattered the crumpled bride, "and I'm all so bescambled I can't tell wet from windy."

"Come, my love," whispered the bridegroom, "come in, to home."

VI

Four or five months later the higgler's affairs had again taken a rude turn. Marriage, alas, was not all it might be; his wife and his mother quarrelled unendingly. Sometimes he sided with the one, sometimes with the other. He could not yet afford to install his mother in a separate cottage, and therefore even Sophy had to admit that her mother-in-law had a right to be living there with them, the home being hers. Harvey hadn't bought much of it; and though he was welcome to it all now, and it would be exclusively his as soon as she died, still, it was her furniture and you couldn't drive any woman (even your mother) off her own property. Sophy, who wanted a home of her own, was vexed and moody, and antagonistic to her man. Business, too, had gone down sadly of late. He had thrown up the Shag Moor round months ago; he could not bring himself to go there again, and he had not been able to square up the loss by any substantial new connections. On top of it all his horse died. It stumbled on a hill one day and fell, and it couldn't get up, or it wouldn't — at any rate, it didn't. Harvey thrashed it and coaxed it, then he cursed it and kicked it; after that he sent for a veterinary man, and the veterinary man ordered it to be shot. And it was shot. A great blow to Harvey Witlow was that. He had no money to buy another horse; money was tight with him, very tight; and so he had to hire at fabulous cost a decrepit nag that ate like a good one. It ate — well, it would have astonished you to see what that creature disposed of, with hay the price it was, and corn gone up to heaven nearly. In fact Harvey found that he couldn't stand the racket much longer, and as he could not possibly buy another it looked very much as if he was in queer street once more, unless he could borrow the money from some friendly person. Of course there were plenty of friendly persons but they had no money, just as there were many persons who had the money but were not what you might call friendly; and so the higgler began to reiterate twenty times a day, and forty times a day, that he was entirely and absolutely damned and done. Things were thus very bad with him, they were at their worst — for he had a wife to keep now, as well as a mother, and a horse that ate like Satan, and worked like a gnat — when it suddenly came into his mind that Mrs. Sadgrove was reputed to have a lot of money, and had no call to be unfriendly to him. He had his grave doubts about the size of her purse, but there could be no harm in trying so long as you approached her in a right reasonable manner.

For a week or two he held off from this appeal, but the grim spectre of destitution gave him no rest, and so, near the close of a wild March day he took his desperate courage and his cart and the decrepit nag to Shag Moor. Wild it was, though dry, and the wind against them, a vast turmoil of icy air strident and baffling. The nag threw up its head and declined to trot. Evening was but an hour away, the fury of the wind did not retard it, nor the clouds hasten it. Low down the sun was quitting the wrack of storm, exposing a jolly orb of magnifying fire that shone flush under eaves and through the casements of cottages, casting a pattern of lattice and tossing boughs under the interior walls, lovelier than dreamed-of pictures. The heads of mothers and old dames were also imaged there, recognizable in their black shadows; and little children held up their hands between window and wall to make five-fingered shapes upon the golden screen. To drive on the moor then was to drive into blasts more dire. Darkness began to fall, and bitter cold it was. No birds to be seen, neither beast nor man; empty of everything it was, except sound and a marvel of dying light, and Harvey Witlow of Dinnop with a sour old nag driving from end to end of it. At Prattle Corner dusk was already abroad: there was just one shaft of light that broached a sharp-angled stack in the rickyard, an ark of darkness, along whose top the gads and wooden pins and tilted straws were miraculously fringed in the last glare. Hitching his nag to the palings he knocked at the door, and knew in the gloom that it was Mary who opened it and stood peering forth at him.

"Good evening," he said, touching his hat.

"Oh!" the girl uttered a cry, "higgler! What do you come for?" It was the longest sentence she had ever spoken to him; a sad frightened voice.

"I thought," he began, "I'd call — and see Mrs. Sadgrove. I wondered. . . ."

"Mother's dead," said the girl. She drew the door farther back, as if inviting him, and he entered. The door was shut behind him, and they were alone in darkness, together. The girl was deeply grieving. Trembling, he asked the question: "What is it you tell me, Mary?"

"Mother's dead," repeated the girl, "all day, all day, all day." They were close to each other, but he could not see her. All round the house the wind roved lamentingly, shuddering at doors and windows. "She died in the night. The doctor was to have come, but he has not come all day," Mary whispered, "all day, all day. I don't understand; I have waited for him, and he has not come. She died, she was dead in her bed this morning, and I've been alone all day, all day, and I don't know what is to be done."

"I'll go for the doctor," he said hastily, but she took him by the hand and drew him into the kitchen. There was no candle lit; a fire was burning there, richly glowing embers, that laid a gaunt shadow of the table across a corner of the ceiling. Every dish on the dresser gleamed, the stone floor was rosy, and each smooth curve on the dark settle was shining like ice. Without invitation he sat down.

"No," said the girl, in a tremulous voice, "you must help me." She lit a candle: her face was white as the moon, her lips were sharply red, and her eyes were wild. "Come," she said, and he followed her behind the settle and up the stairs to a room where there was a disordered bed, and what might be a body lying under the quilt. The higgler stood still, staring at the form under the quilt. The girl, too, was still and staring. Wind dashed upon the ivy at the window and hallooed like a grieving multitude. A crumpled gown hid the body's head, but thrust from under it, almost as if to greet him, was her naked lean arm, the palm of the hand lying uppermost. At the foot of the bed was a large washing-bowl, with sponge and towels.

"You've been laying her out! Yourself!" exclaimed Witlow. The pale girl set down the candle on a chest of drawers. "Help me now," she said, and moving to the bed she lifted the crumpled gown from off the face of the dead woman, at the same time smoothing the quilt closely up to the body's chin. "I cannot put the gown on, because of her arm, it has gone stiff." She shuddered, and stood holding the gown as if offering it to the man. He lifted that dead naked arm and tried to place it down at the body's side, but it resisted and he let go his hold. The arm swung back to its former outstretched position, as if it still lived and resented that pressure. The girl retreated from the bed with a timorous cry.

"Get me a bandage," he said, "or something we can tear up."

She gave him some pieces of linen.

"I'll finish this for you," he brusquely whispered, "you get along downstairs and take a swig of brandy. Got any brandy?"

She did not move. He put his arm around her and gently urged her to the door.

"Brandy," he repeated, "and light your candles."

He watched her go heavily down the stairs before he shut the door. Returning to the bed he lifted the quilt. The dead body was naked and smelt of soap. Dropping the quilt he lifted the outstretched arm again, like cold wax to the touch and unpliant as a sturdy sapling, and tried once more to bend it to the body's side. As he did so the bedroom door blew open with a crash. It was only a draught of the wind, and a loose latch — Mary had opened a door downstairs, perhaps — but it awed him, as if some invisible looker were there resenting his presence. He went and closed the door, the latch had a loose hasp, and tiptoeing nervously back, he seized the dreadful arm with a sudden brutal energy, and bent it by thrusting his knee violently into the hollow of the elbow. Hurriedly he slipped the gown over the head and inserted the arm in the sleeve. A strange impulse of modesty stayed him for a moment: should he call the girl and let her complete the robing of the naked body under the quilt? That preposterous pause seemed to add a new anger to the wind, and again the door sprang open. He delayed no longer, but letting it remain open, he uncovered the dead woman. As he lifted the chill body the long outstretched arm moved and tilted like the boom of a sail, but crushing it to its side he bound the limb fast with the strips of linen. So Mrs. Sadgrove was made ready for her coffin. Drawing the quilt back to her neck, with a gush of relief he glanced about the room. It was a very ordinary bedroom, bed, washstand, chest of drawers, chair, and two pictures — one of deeply religious import, and the other a little pink print, in a gilded frame, of a bouncing nude nymph recumbent upon a cloud. It was queer: a lot of people, people whom you wouldn't think it of, had that sort of picture in their bedrooms.

Mary was now coming up the stairs again, with a glass half full of liquid. She brought it to him.

"No, you drink it," he urged, and Mary sipped the brandy.

"I've finished — I've finished," he said as he watched her, "she's quite comfortable now."

The girl looked her silent thanks at him, again holding out the glass. "No, sup it yourself," he said; but as she stood in the dim light, regarding him with her strange gaze, and still offering the drink, he took it from her, drained it at a gulp, and put the glass upon the chest, beside the candle. "She's quite comfortable now. I'm very grieved, Mary," he said with awkward kindness, "about all this trouble that's come on you."

She was motionless as a wax image, as if she had died in her steps, her hand still extended as when he took the glass from it. So piercing was her gaze that his own drifted from her face and took in again the objects in the room, the washstand, the candle on the chest, the little pink picture. The wind beat upon the ivy outside the window as if a monstrous whip were lashing its slaves.

"You must notify the registrar," he began again, "but you must see the doctor first."

"I've waited for him all day," Mary whispered, "all day. The nurse will come again soon. She went home to rest in the night." She turned towards the bed. "She has only been ill a week."

"Yes?" he lamely said. "Dear me, it is sudden."

"I must see the doctor," she continued.

"I'll drive you over to him in my gig." He was eager to do that.

"I don't know," said Mary slowly.

"Yes, I'll do that, soon's you're ready. Mary," he fumbled with his speech, "I'm not wanting to pry into your affairs, or anything as don't concern me, but how are you going to get along now? Have you got any relations?"

"No," the girl shook her head, "no."

"That's bad. What was you thinking of doing? How has she left you — things were in a baddish way, weren't they?"

"Oh no." Mary looked up quickly. "She has left me very well off. I shall go on with the farm; there's the old man and the boy — they've gone to a wedding today; I shall go on with it. She was so thoughtful for me, and I would not care to leave all this, I love it."

"But you can't do it by yourself, alone?"

"No. I'm to get a man to superintend, a working bailiff," she said.

"Oh!" And again they were silent. The girl went to the bed and lifted the covering. She saw the bound arm and then drew the quilt tenderly over the dead face. Witlow picked up his hat and found himself staring again at the pink picture. Mary took the candle preparatory to descending the stairs. Suddenly the higgler turned to her and ventured: "Did you know as she once asked me to marry you?" he blurted.

Her eye turned from him, but he guessed — he could feel that she *had* known.

"I've often wondered why," he murmured, "why she wanted that."

"She didn't," said the girl.

That gave pause to the man; he felt stupid at once, and roved his fingers in a silly way along the roughened nap of his hat.

"Well, she asked me to," he bluntly protested.

"She knew," Mary's voice was no louder than a sigh, "that you were courting another girl, the one you married."

"But, but," stuttered the honest higgler, "if she knew that, why did she want for me to marry you?"

"She didn't," said Mary again; and again, in the pause, he did silly things to his hat. How shy this girl was, how lovely in her modesty and grief!

"I can't make tops or bottoms of it," he said, "but she asked me, as sure as God's my maker."

"I know. It was me, I wanted it."

"You!" he cried, "you wanted to marry me!"

The girl bowed her head, lovely in her grief and modesty. "She was against it, but I made her ask you."

"And I hadn't an idea that you cast a thought on me," he murmured. "I feared it was a sort of trick she was playing on me. I didn't understand, I had no idea that you knew about it even. And so I didn't ever ask you."

"Oh, why not, why not? I was fond of you then," whispered she. "Mother tried to persuade me against it, but I was fond of you — then."

He was in a queer distress and confusion: "Oh, if you'd only tipped me a word, or given me a sort of look," he sighed. "Oh, Mary!"

She said no more but went downstairs. He followed her and immediately fetched the lamps from his gig. As he lit the candles: "How strange," Mary said, "that you should come back just as I most needed help! I am very grateful."

"Mary, I'll drive you to the doctor's now."

She shook her head; she was smiling.

"Then I'll stay till the nurse comes."

"No, you must go. Go at once."

He picked up the two lamps and, turning at the door, said: "I'll come again tomorrow." Then the wind rushed into the room. "Good-bye," she cried, shutting the door quickly behind him.

He drove away in deep darkness, the wind howling, his thoughts strange and bitter. He had thrown away a love, a love that was dumb and hid itself. By God, he had thrown away a fortune, too! And he had forgotten all about his real errand until now, forgotten all about the loan! Well; let it go; give it up. He would give up higgling; he would take some other job; a bailiff, a working bailiff, that was the job as would suit him, a working bailiff. Of course, there was Sophy; but still — Sophy!

[1925]

JAMES JOYCE *(1882–1941) was born James Augustine Aloysius Joyce in Rathgar, a suburb of Dublin, during a turbulent era of political change in Ireland. His parents sent him at the age of six to the best Jesuit school, Clongowes Wood College, where he spent three years; but in 1891 his father was no longer able to afford the tuition, and he was withdrawn from the school. During the period of his parents' financial decline, Joyce — a brilliant student — was educated at home and then given free tuition at Belvedere College, where he won prizes for his essays. Shortly after taking his bachelor's degree in 1902 from University College, Dublin, he left Ireland for Paris, where he attended one class at the Collège de Médecine but dropped out because he could not afford the fees. Nearly starving, he remained in Paris and wrote some plotless sketches he called "Epiphanies." These were notebook jottings of overheard conversations or passing observations that he later incorporated into his fiction, thinking that they illuminated in a flash the meaning of a group of apparently unrelated phenomena.*

In April 1903 Joyce returned to Dublin because his mother was dying. He remained in Ireland a short time as a teacher, but the following year he went to live abroad again, disillusioned by his home country's political corruption and religious hypocrisy.

Dubliners (1916), a group of short stories begun in 1904, was Joyce's attempt to "write a chapter of the moral history" of Ireland. He chose Dublin for the setting because that city seemed to him "the center of paralysis," but he also thought of following the book with another entitled "Provincials." As if to prove his perception of the extent of stifling moral repression in his country, he had great difficulties getting the book published — a struggle lasting nine years. This so angered and frustrated Joyce that he never again lived in Ireland, settling in Trieste, Zurich, and Paris and writing the novels that established him as one of the greatest writers of modern times: A Portrait of the Artist as a Young Man (1916), Ulysses (1922), and Finnegan's Wake (1939).

When Joyce wrote his brother Stanislaus about the Dubliner stories in 1905, he described his struggle against social conventions with a characteristic blend of arrogance and insight: "Maupassant writes very well, of course, but I am afraid that his moral sense is rather obtuse. . . . The struggle against conventions in which I am at present involved was not entered into by me so much as a protest against these conventions as with the intention of living in conformity with my moral nature." Joyce's stories about the lives of young people, servants, politicians, and the complacent middle class were intended to represent a broad spectrum of Dublin life, not "a collection of tourist impressions" but rather a penetrating account of the spiritual waste of his times. Today's reader finds it difficult to believe that the fifteen stories in Dubliners *could have appeared so scandalous to Joyce's publishers that at one stage in the book's tortuous journey toward publication the plates were destroyed at the printers. "An Encounter," the second story in the collection, was one that the publisher objected to as immoral. Joyce's technique was based on a rare blend of sympathy for his subject combined with a "scrupulous meanness" of observed detail. The language of the stories goes beyond pictorial exactness to exhibit a concern for the sound and cadence of the words as well as the specific details of description. As Frank O'Connor realized, Joyce was not only "insisting that we shall see the scene exactly as he saw it by his use of Flaubert's 'proper word,' " but also "he is insisting that we shall feel it as he felt it by a deliberate though carefully concealed juxtaposition of key words." The "key words" in "The Dead," the final story in* Dubliners, *cluster in the often repeated images of light and fire, cold and snow that appear throughout the story, embodying its meaning. In "The Dead," Joyce gave his first major statement of the themes that obsessed him in his later, longer works — the conflict of pride with love, and of the private ego with the soul of humanity.*

James Joyce

ဢ

AN ENCOUNTER

It was Joe Dillon who introduced the Wild West to us. He had a little library made up of old numbers of *The Union Jack, Pluck* and *The Halfpenny Marvel.* Every evening after school we met in his back garden and arranged Indian battles. He and his fat young brother Leo the idler held the loft of the stable while we tried to carry it by storm; or we fought a pitched battle on the grass. But, however well we fought, we never won siege or battle and all our bouts ended with Joe Dillon's war dance of victory. His parents went to eight-o'clock mass every morning in Gardiner Street and the peaceful odour of Mrs. Dillon was prevalent in the hall of the house. But he played too fiercely for us who were younger and more timid. He looked like some kind of an Indian when he capered round the garden, an old tea-cosy on his head, beating a tin with his fist and yelling:

— Ya! yaka, yaka, yaka!

Everyone was incredulous when it was reported that he had a vocation for the priesthood. Nevertheless it was true.

A spirit of unruliness diffused itself among us and, under its influence, differences of culture and constitution were waived. We banded ourselves together, some boldly, some in jest and some almost in fear: and of the number of these latter, the reluctant Indians who were afraid to seem studious or lacking in robustness, I was one. The adventures related in the literature of the Wild West were remote from my nature but, at least, they opened doors of escape. I like better some American detective stories which were traversed from time to time by unkempt fierce and beautiful girls. Though there was nothing wrong in these stories and though their intention was sometimes literary they were circulated secretly at school. One day when Father Butler was hearing the four pages of Roman History clumsy Leo Dillon was discovered with a copy of *The Halfpenny Marvel.*

— This page or this page? This page? Now, Dillon, up! *Hardly had the day . . .* Go on! What day? *Hardly had the day dawned . . .* Have you studied it? What have you there in your pocket?

Everyone's heart palpitated as Leo Dillon handed up the paper and everyone assumed an innocent face. Father Butler turned over the pages, frowning.

— What is this rubbish? he said. *The Apache Chief!* Is this what you read instead of studying your Roman History? Let me not find any more of this wretched stuff in this college. The man who wrote it, I suppose, was some wretched scribbler that writes these things for a drink. I'm surprised at boys like you, educated, reading such stuff. I could understand it if you were . . . National School boys. Now, Dillon, I advise you strongly, get at your work or . . .

This rebuke during the sober hours of school paled much of the glory of the Wild West for me and the confused puffy face of Leo Dillon awakened one of my consciences. But when the restraining influence of the school was at a distance I began to hunger again for wild sensations, for the escape which those chronicles of disorder alone seemed to offer me. The mimic warfare of the evening became at last as wearisome to me as the routine of school in the morning because I wanted real adventures to happen to myself. But real adventures, I reflected, do not happen to people who remain at home: they must be sought abroad.

The summer holidays were near at hand when I made up my mind to break out of the weariness of school-life for one day at least. With Leo Dillon and a boy named Mahony I planned a day's miching. Each of us saved up sixpence. We were to meet at ten in the morning on the Canal Bridge. Mahony's big sister was to write an excuse for him and Leo Dillon was to tell his brother to say he was sick. We arranged to go along the Wharf Road until we came to the ships, then to cross in the ferryboat and walk out to see the Pigeon House. Leo Dillon was afraid we might meet Father Butler or someone out of the college; but Mahony asked, very sensibly, what would Father Butler be doing out at the Pigeon House. We were reassured: and I brought the first stage of the plot to an end by collecting sixpence from the other two, at the same time showing them my own sixpence. When we were making the last arrangements on the eve we were all vaguely excited. We shook hands, laughing, and Mahony said:

— Till to-morrow, mates.

That night I slept badly. In the morning I was firstcomer to the bridge as I lived nearest. I hid my books in the long grass near the ashpit at the end of the garden where nobody ever came and hurried along the canal bank. It was a mild sunny morning in the first week of June. I sat up on the coping of the bridge admiring my frail canvas shoes which I had diligently pipe-clayed overnight and watching the docile horses pulling a tramload of business people up the hill. All the branches of the tall trees which lined the mall were gay with little light green leaves and the sunlight slanted through them on to the water. The granite stone of the bridge was beginning to be warm and I began to pat it with my hands in time to an air in my head. I was very happy.

When I had been sitting there for five or ten minutes I saw Mahony's grey suit approaching. He came up the hill, smiling, and clambered up beside me on the bridge. While we were waiting he brought out the catapult which bulged from his inner pocket and explained some improvements which he had made in it. I asked him why he had brought it and he told me he had brought it to have some gas with the birds. Mahony used slang freely, and spoke of Father Butler as Bunsen Burner. We waited on for a quarter of an hour more but still there was no sign of Leo Dillon. Mahony, at last, jumped down and said:

— Come along. I knew Fatty'd funk it.

— And his sixpence. . . ? I said.

— That's forfeit, said Mahony. And so much the better for us — a bob and a tanner instead of a bob.

We walked along the North Strand Road till we came to the Vitriol Works and then turned to the right along the Wharf Road. Mahony began to play the Indian as soon as we were out of public sight. He chased a crowd of ragged girls, brandishing his unloaded catapult and, when two ragged boys began, out of chivalry, to fling stones at us, he proposed that we should charge them. I objected that the boys were too small, and so we walked on, the ragged troop screaming after us: *Swaddlers! Swaddlers!* thinking that we were Protestants because Mahony, who was dark-complexioned, wore the silver badge of a cricket club in his cap. When we came to the Smoothing Iron we arranged a siege; but it was a failure because you must have at least three. We revenged ourselves on Leo Dillon by saying what a funk he was and guessing how many he would get at three o'clock from Mr. Ryan.

We came then near the river. We spent a long time walking about the noisy streets flanked by high stone walls, watching the working of cranes and engines and often being shouted at for our immobility by the drivers of groaning carts. It was noon when we reached the quays and, as all the labourers seemed to be eating their lunches, we bought two big currant buns and sat down to eat them on some metal piping beside the river. We pleased ourselves with the spectacle of Dublin's commerce — the barges signalled from far away by their curls of woolly smoke, the brown fishing fleet beyond Ringsend, the big white sailing-vessel which was being discharged on the opposite quay. Mahony said it would be right skit to run away to sea on one of those big ships and even I, looking at the high masts, saw, or imagined, the geography which had been scantily dosed to me at school gradually taking substance under my eyes. School and home seemed to recede from us and their influences upon us seemed to wane.

We crossed the Liffey in the ferryboat, paying our toll to be transported in the company of two labourers and a little Jew with a bag. We were serious to the point of solemnity, but once during the short voyage our eyes met and we laughed. When we landed we watched the discharging of the graceful three-master which we had observed from the other quay. Some bystander said that she was a Norwegian vessel. I went to the stern and tried to decipher the legend upon it but, failing to do so, I came back and examined the foreign sailors to see had any of them green eyes for I had some confused notion. . . . The sailors' eyes were blue and grey and even black. The only sailor whose eyes could have been called green was a tall man who amused the crowd on the quay by calling out cheerfully every time the planks fell:

— All right! All right!

When we were tired of this sight we wandered slowly into Ringsend. The day had grown sultry, and in the windows of the grocers' shops musty biscuits lay bleaching. We bought some biscuits and chocolate which we ate sedulously as we wandered through the squalid streets where the families of the fishermen live. We could find no dairy and so we went into a huckster's shop and bought a bottle of raspberry lemonade each. Refreshed by this, Mahony chased a cat down a lane, but the cat escaped into a wide field. We both felt rather tired and when we reached the field we made at once for a sloping bank over the ridge of which we could see the Dodder.

It was too late and we were too tired to carry out our project of visiting the Pigeon House. We had to be home before four o'clock lest our adventure should be discovered. Mahony looked regretfully at his catapult and I had to suggest going home by train before he regained any cheerfulness. The sun went in behind some clouds and left us to our jaded thoughts and the crumbs of our provisions.

There was nobody but ourselves in the field. When we had lain on the bank for some time without speaking I saw a man approaching from the far end of the field. I watched him lazily as I chewed one of those green stems on which girls tell fortunes. He came along by the bank slowly. He walked with one hand upon his hip and in the other hand he held a stick with which he tapped the turf lightly. He was shabbily dressed in a suit of greenish-black and wore what we used to call a jerry hat with a high crown. He seemed to be fairly old for his moustache was ashen-grey. When he passed at our feet he glanced up at us quickly and then continued his way.

We followed him with our eyes and saw that when he had gone on for perhaps fifty paces he turned about and began to retrace his steps. He walked towards us very slowly, always tapping the ground with his stick, so slowly that I thought he was looking for something in the grass.

He stopped when he came level with us and bade us good-day. We answered him and he sat down beside us on the slope slowly and with great care. He began to talk of the weather, saying that it would be a very hot summer and adding that the seasons had changed greatly since he was a boy — a long time ago. He said that the happiest time of one's life was undoubtedly one's schoolboy days and that he would give anything to be young again. While he expressed these sentiments which bored us a little we kept silent. Then he began to talk of school and of books. He asked us whether we had read the poetry of Thomas Moore or the works of Sir Walter Scott and Lord Lytton. I pretended that I had read every book he mentioned so that in the end he said:

— Ah, I can see you are a bookworm like myself. Now, he added, pointing to Mahony who was regarding us with open eyes, he is different; he goes in for games.

He said he had all Sir Walter Scott's works and all Lord Lytton's works at home and never tired of reading them. Of course, he said, there were some of Lord Lytton's works which boys couldn't read. Mahony asked why couldn't boys read them — a question which agitated and pained me because I was afraid the man would think I was as stupid as Mahony. The man, however, only smiled. I saw that he had great gaps in his mouth between his yellow teeth. Then he asked us which of us had the most sweethearts. Mahony mentioned lightly that he had three totties. The man asked me how many I had. I answered that I had none. He did not believe me and said he was sure I must have one. I was silent.

— Tell us, said Mahony pertly to the man, how many have you yourself?

The man smiled as before and said that when he was our age he had lots of sweethearts.

— Every boy, he said, has a little sweetheart.

His attitude on this point struck me as strangely liberal in a man of his age. In my heart I thought that what he said about boys and sweethearts was reasonable. But I disliked the words in his mouth and I wondered why he shivered once or twice as if he feared something or felt a sudden chill. As he proceeded I noticed that his accent was good. He began to speak to us about girls, saying what nice soft hair they had and how soft their hands were and how all girls were not so good as they seemed to be if one only knew. There was nothing he liked, he said, so much as looking at a nice young girl, at her nice white hands and her beautiful soft hair. He gave me the impression that he was repeating something which he had learned by heart or that, magnetised by some words of his own speech, his mind was slowly circling round and round in the same orbit. At times he spoke as if he were simply alluding to some fact that everybody knew, and at times he lowered his voice and spoke mysteriously as if he were telling us something secret which he did not wish others to overhear. He repeated his phrases over and over again, varying them and surrounding them with his monotonous voice. I continued to gaze towards the foot of the slope, listening to him.

After a long while his monologue paused. He stood up slowly, saying that he had to leave us for a minute or so, a few minutes, and, without changing the direction of my gaze, I saw him walking slowly away from us towards the near end of the field. We remained silent when he had gone. After a silence of a few minutes I heard Mahony exclaim:

— I say! Look what he's doing!

As I neither answered nor raised my eyes Mahony exclaimed again:

— I say . . . He's a queer old josser!

— In case he asks us for our names, I said, let you be Murphy and I'll be Smith.

We said nothing further to each other. I was still considering whether I would go away or not when the man came back and sat down beside us again. Hardly had he sat down when Mahony, catching sight of the cat which had escaped him, sprang up and pursued her across the field. The man and I watched the chase. The cat escaped once more and Mahony began to throw stones at the wall she had escaladed. Desisting from this, he began to wander about the far end of the field, aimlessly.

After an interval the man spoke to me. He said that my friend was a very rough boy and asked did he get whipped often at school. I was going to reply indignantly that we were not National School boys to be *whipped*, as he called it; but I remained silent. He began to speak on the subject of chastising boys. His mind, as if magnetised again by his speech, seemed to circle slowly round and round its new centre. He said that when boys were that kind they ought to be whipped and well whipped. When a boy was rough and unruly there was nothing would do him any good but a good sound whipping. A slap on the hand or a box on the ear was no good: what he wanted was to get a nice warm whipping. I was surprised at this sentiment and involuntarily glanced up at his face. As I did so I met the gaze of a pair of bottle-green eyes peering at me from under a twitching forehead. I turned my eyes away again.

The man continued his monologue. He seemed to have forgotten his recent liberalism. He said that if ever he found a boy talking to girls or having a girl for a sweetheart he would whip him and whip him; and that would teach him not to be talking to girls. And if a boy had a girl for a sweetheart and told lies about it then he would give him such a whipping as no boy ever got in this world. He said that there was nothing in this world he would like so well as that. He described to me how he would whip such a boy as if he were unfolding some elaborate mystery. He would love that, he said, better than anything in this world; and his voice, as he led me monotonously through the mystery, grew almost affectionate and seemed to plead with me that I should understand him.

I waited till his monologue paused again. Then I stood up abruptly. Lest I should betray my agitation I delayed a few moments pretending to fix my shoe properly and then, saying that I was obliged to go, I bade him a good-day. I went up the slope calmly but my heart was beating quickly with fear that he would seize me by the ankles. When I reached the top of the slope I turned round and, without looking at him, called loudly across the field:

— Murphy!

My voice had an accent of forced bravery in it and I was ashamed of my paltry stratagem. I had to call the name again before Mahony saw me and hallooed in answer. How my heart beat as he came running across the field to me! He ran as if to bring me aid. And I was penitent; for in my heart I had always despised him a little.

[1916]

James Joyce

tʊʊ

THE DEAD

Lily, the caretaker's daughter, was literally run off her feet. Hardly had she brought one gentleman into the little pantry behind the office on the ground floor and helped him off with his overcoat than the wheezy hall-door bell clanged again and she had to scamper along the bare hallway to let in another guest. It was well for her she had not to attend to the ladies also. But Miss Kate and Miss Julia had thought of that and had converted the bathroom upstairs into a ladies' dressing-room. Miss Kate and Miss Julia were there, gossiping and laughing and fussing, walking after each other to the head of the stairs, peering down over the banisters and calling down to Lily to ask her who had come.

It was always a great affair, the Misses Morkan's annual dance. Everybody who knew them came to it, members of the family, old friends of the family, the members of Julia's choir, any of Kate's pupils that were grown up enough and even some of Mary Jane's pupils too. Never once had it fallen flat. For years and years it had gone off in splendid style as long as anyone could remember; ever since Kate and Julia, after the death of their brother Pat, had left the house in Stoney Batter and taken Mary Jane, their only niece, to live with them in the dark gaunt house on Usher's Island, the upper part of which they had rented from Mr Fulham, the corn-factor on the ground floor. That was a good thirty years ago if it was a day. Mary Jane, who was then a little girl in short clothes, was now the main prop of the household for she had the organ in Haddington Road. She had been through the Academy and gave a pupils' concert every year in the upper room of the Antient Concert Rooms. Many of her pupils belonged to better-class families on the Kingstown and Dalkey line. Old as they were, her aunts also did their share. Julia, though she was quite grey, was still the leading soprano in Adam and Eve's, and Kate, being too feeble to go about much, gave music lessons to beginners on the old square piano in the back room. Lily, the caretaker's daughter, did house-maid's work for them. Though their life was modest they believed in eating well; the best of everything: diamond-bone sirloins, three-shilling tea and the best bottled stout. But Lily seldom made a mistake in the orders so that she got on well with her three mistresses. They were fussy, that was all. But the only thing they would not stand was back answers.

Of course they had good reason to be fussy on such a night. And then it was long after ten o'clock and yet there was no sign of Gabriel and his wife. Besides they were dreadfully afraid that Freddy Malins might turn up screwed. They would not wish for worlds that any of Mary Jane's pupils should see him under the influence; and when he was like that it was some-times very hard to manage him. Freddy Malins always came late but they wondered what could be keeping Gabriel: and that was what brought them every two minutes to the banisters to ask Lily had Gabriel or Freddy come.

— O, Mr Conroy, said Lily to Gabriel when she opened the door for him, Miss Kate and Miss Julia thought you were never coming. Good-night, Mrs Conroy.

— I'll engage they did, said Gabriel, but they forget that my wife here takes three mortal hours to dress herself.

He stood on the mat, scraping the snow from his goloshes, while Lily led his wife to the foot of the stairs and called out:

— Miss Kate, here's Mrs Conroy.

Kate and Julia came toddling down the dark stairs at once. Both of them kissed Gabriel's wife, said she must be perished alive and asked was Gabriel with her.

— Here I am as right as the mail, Aunt Kate! Go on up. I'll follow, called out Gabriel from the dark.

He continued scraping his feet vigorously while the three women went upstairs, laughing, to the ladies' dressing-room. A light fringe of snow lay like a cape on the shoulders of his overcoat and like toecaps on the toes of his goloshes; and, as the buttons of his overcoat slipped with a squeaking noise through the snow-stiffened frieze, a cold fragrant air from out-of-doors escaped from crevices and folds.

—Is it snowing again, Mr Conroy? asked Lily.

She had preceded him into the pantry to help him off with his overcoat. Gabriel smiled at the three syllables she had given his surname and glanced at her. She was a slim, growing girl, pale in complexion and with hay-coloured hair. The gas in the pantry made her look still paler. Gabriel had known her when she was a child and used to sit on the lowest step nursing a rag doll.

— Yes, Lily, he answered, and I think we're in for a night of it.

He looked up at the pantry ceiling, which was shaking with the stamping and shuffling of feet on the floor above, listened for a moment to the piano and then glanced at the girl, who was folding his overcoat carefully at the end of a shelf.

— Tell me, Lily, he said in a friendly tone, do you still go to school?

— O no, sir, she answered. I'm done schooling this year and more.

— O, then, said Gabriel gaily, I suppose we'll be going to your wedding one of these fine days with your young man, eh?

The girl glanced back at him over her shoulder and said with great bitterness:

— The men that is now is only all palaver and what they can get out of you.

Gabriel coloured as if he felt he had made a mistake and, without looking at her, kicked off his goloshes and flicked actively with his muffler at his patent-leather shoes.

He was a stout tallish young man. The high colour of his cheeks pushed upwards even to his forehead where it scattered itself in a few formless patches of pale red; and on his hairless face there scintillated restlessly the polished lenses and the bright gilt rims of the glasses which screened his delicate and restless eyes. His glossy black hair was parted in the middle and brushed in a long curve behind his ears where it curled slightly beneath the groove left by his hat.

When he had flicked lustre into his shoes he stood up and pulled his waistcoat down more tightly on his plump body. Then he took a coin rapidly from his pocket.

— O Lily, he said, thrusting it into her hands, it's Christmas-time, isn't it? Just . . . here's a little. . . .

He walked rapidly towards the door.

— O no, sir! cried the girl, following him. Really, sir, I wouldn't take it.

— Christmas-time! Christmas-time! said Gabriel, almost trotting to the stairs and waving his hand to her in deprecation.

The girl, seeing that he had gained the stairs, called out after him:

— Well, thank you, sir.

He waited outside the drawing-room door until the waltz should finish, listening to the skirts that swept against it and to the shuffling of feet. He was still discomposed by the girl's bitter and sudden retort. It had cast a gloom over him which he tried to dispel by arranging his cuffs and the bows of his tie. Then he took from his waistcoat pocket a little paper and glanced at the headings he had made for his speech. He was undecided about the lines from Robert Browning for he feared they would be above the heads of his hearers. Some quotation that they could recognise from Shakespeare or from the Melodies would be better. The indelicate clacking of the men's heels and the shuffling of their soles reminded him that their grade of culture differed from his. He would only make himself ridiculous by quoting poetry to them which they could not understand. They would think that he was airing his superior education. He would fail with them just as he had failed with the girl in the pantry. He had taken up a wrong tone. His whole speech was a mistake from first to last, an utter failure.

Just then his aunts and his wife came out of the ladies' dressing-room. His aunts were two small plainly dressed old women. Aunt Julia was an inch or so the taller. Her hair, drawn low over the tops of her ears, was grey; and grey also, with darker shadows, was her large flaccid face. Though she was stout in build and stood erect her slow eyes and parted lips gave her the appearance of a woman who did not know where she was or where she was going. Aunt Kate was more vivacious. Her face, healthier than her sister's, was all puckers and creases, like a shrivelled red apple, and her hair, braided in the same old-fashioned way, had not lost its ripe nut colour.

They both kissed Gabriel frankly. He was their favourite nephew, the son of their dead elder sister, Ellen, who had married T. J. Conroy of the Port and Docks.

— Gretta tells me you're not going to take a cab back to Monkstown to-night, Gabriel, said Aunt Kate.

— No, said Gabriel, turning to his wife, we had quite enough of that last year, hadn't we? Don't you remember, Aunt Kate, what a cold Gretta got out of it? Cab windows rattling all the way, and the east wind blowing in after we passed Merrion. Very jolly it was. Gretta caught a dreadful cold.

Aunt Kate frowned severely and nodded her head at every word.

— Quite right, Gabriel, quite right, she said. You can't be too careful.

— But as for Gretta there, said Gabriel, she'd walk home in the snow if she were let.

Mrs Conroy laughed.

— Don't mind him, Aunt Kate, she said. He's really an awful bother, what with green shades for Tom's eyes at night and making him do the dumb-bells, and forcing Eva to eat the stirabout. The poor child! And she simply hates the sight of it! . . . O, but you'll never guess what he makes me wear now!

She broke out into a peal of laughter and glanced at her husband, whose admiring and happy eyes had been wandering from her dress to her face and hair. The two aunts laughed heartily too, for Gabriel's solicitude was a standing joke with them.

— Goloshes! said Mrs Conroy. That's the latest. Whenever it's wet underfoot I must put on my goloshes. To-night even he wanted me to put them on, but I wouldn't. The next thing he'll buy me will be a diving suit.

Gabriel laughed nervously and patted his tie reassuringly while Aunt Kate nearly doubled herself, so heartily did she enjoy the joke. The smile soon faded from Aunt Julia's face and her mirthless eyes were directed towards her nephew's face. After a pause she asked:

— And what are goloshes, Gabriel?

— Goloshes, Julia! exclaimed her sister. Goodness me, don't you know what goloshes are? You wear them over your . . . over your boots, Gretta, isn't it?

— Yes, said Mrs Conroy. Guttapercha things. We both have a pair now. Gabriel says everyone wears them on the continent.

— O, on the continent, murmured Aunt Julia, nodding her head slowly.

Gabriel knitted his brows and said, as if he were slightly angered:

— It's nothing very wonderful but Gretta thinks it very funny because she says the word reminds her of Christy Minstrels.

— But tell me, Gabriel, said Aunt Kate, with brisk tact. Of course, you've seen about the room. Gretta was saying . . .

— O, the room is all right, replied Gabriel. I've taken one in the Gresham.

— To be sure, said Aunt Kate, by far the best thing to do. And the children, Gretta, you're not anxious about them?

— O, for one night, said Mrs Conroy. Besides, Bessie will look after them.

— To be sure, said Aunt Kate again. What a comfort it is to have a girl like that, one you can depend on! There's that Lily, I'm sure I don't know what has come over her lately. She's not the girl she was at all.

Gabriel was about to ask his aunt some questions on this point but she broke off suddenly to gaze after her sister who had wandered down the stairs and was craning her neck over the banisters.

— Now, I ask you, she said, almost testily, where is Julia going? Julia! Julia! Where are you going?

Julia, who had gone halfway down one flight, came back and announced blandly:

— Here's Freddy.

At the same moment a clapping of hands and a final flourish of the pianist told that the waltz had ended. The drawing-room door was opened from within and some couples came out. Aunt Kate drew Gabriel aside hurriedly and whispered into his ear:

— Slip down, Gabriel, like a good fellow and see if he's all right, and don't let him up if he's screwed. I'm sure he's screwed. I'm sure he is.

Gabriel went to the stairs and listened over the banisters. He could

hear two persons talking in the pantry. Then he recognised Freddy Malins'
laugh. He went down the stairs noisily.

— It's such a relief, such Aunt Kate to Mrs Conroy, that Gabriel is
here. I always feel easier in my mind when he's here. . . . Julia, there's Miss
Daly and Miss Power will take some refreshment. Thanks for your beautiful
waltz, Miss Daly. It made lovely time.

A tall wizen-faced man, with a stiff grizzled moustache and swarthy
skin, who was passing out with his partner said:

— And may we have some refreshment, too, Miss Morkan?

— Julia, said Aunt Kate summarily, and here's Mr Browne and Miss
Furlong. Take them in, Julia, with Miss Daly and Miss Power.

— I'm the man for the ladies, said Mr Browne, pursing his lips until
his moustache bristled and smiling in all his wrinkles. You know, Miss
Morkan, the reason they are so fond of me is —

He did not finish his sentence, but, seeing that Aunt Kate was out of
earshot, at once led the three young ladies into the back room. The middle
of the room was occupied by two square tables placed end to end, and on
these Aunt Julia and the caretaker were straightening and smoothing a large
cloth. On the sideboard were arrayed dishes and plates, and glasses and
bundles of knives and forks and spoons. The top of the closed square piano
served also as a sideboard for viands and sweets. At a smaller sideboard in
one corner two young men were standing, drinking hop-bitters.

Mr Browne led his charges thither and invited them all, in jest, to
some ladies' punch, hot, strong and sweet. As they said they never took anything strong he opened three bottles of lemonade for them. Then he asked
one of the young men to move aside, and, taking hold of the decanter, filled
out for himself a goodly measure of whisky. The young men eyed him respectfully while he took a trial sip.

— God help me, he said, smiling, it's the doctor's orders.

His wizened face broke into a broader smile, and the three young
ladies laughed in musical echo to his pleasantry, swaying their bodies to and
fro, with nervous jerks of their shoulders. The boldest said:

— O, now, Mr Browne, I'm sure the doctor never ordered anything of
the kind.

Mr Browne took another sip of his whisky and said, with sidling mimicry:

— Well, you see, I'm like the famous Mrs Cassidy, who is reported to
have said: Now, Mary Grimes, if I don't take it, make me take it, for I feel I
want it.

His hot face had leaned forward a little too confidentially and he had
assumed a very low Dublin accent so that the young ladies, with one instinct, received his speech in silence. Miss Furlong, who was one of Mary
Jane's pupils, asked Miss Daly what was the name of the pretty waltz she
had played; and Mr Browne, seeing that he was ignored, turned promptly to
the two young men who were more appreciative.

A red-faced young woman, dressed in pansy, came into the room, excitedly clapping her hands and crying:

— Quadrilles! Quadrilles!

Close on her heels came Aunt Kate, crying:

— Two gentlemen and three ladies, Mary Jane!

— O, here's Mr Bergin and Mr Kerrigan, said Mary Jane. Mr Kerrigan, will you take Miss Power? Miss Furlong, may I get you a partner, Mr Bergin. O, that'll just do now.

— Three ladies, Mary Jane, said Aunt Kate.

The two young gentlemen asked the ladies if they might have the pleasure, and Mary Jane turned to Miss Daly.

— O, Miss Daly, you're really awfully good, after playing for the last two dances, but really we're so short of ladies to-night.

— I don't mind in the least, Miss Morkan.

— But I've a nice partner for you, Mr Bartell D'Arcy, the tenor. I'll get him to sing later on. All Dublin is raving about him.

— Lovely voice, lovely voice! said Aunt Kate.

As the piano had twice begun the prelude to the first figure Mary Jane led her recruits quickly from the room. They had hardly gone when Aunt Julia wandered slowly into the room, looking behind her at something.

— What is the matter, Julia? asked Aunt Kate anxiously. Who is it?

Julia, who was carrying in a column of table-napkins, turned to her sister and said, simply, as if the question had surprised her:

— It's only Freddy, Kate, and Gabriel with him.

In fact right behind her Gabriel could be seen piloting Freddy Malins across the landing. The latter, a young man of about forty, was of Gabriel's size and build, with very round shoulders. His face was fleshy and pallid, touched with colour only at the thick hanging lobes of his ears and at the wide wings of his nose. He had coarse features, a blunt nose, a convex and receding brow, tumid and protruded lips. His heavy-lidded eyes and the disorder of his scanty hair made him look sleepy. He was laughing heartily in a high key at a story which he had been telling Gabriel on the stairs and at the same time rubbing the knuckles of his left fist backwards and forwards into his left eye.

— Good-evening, Freddy, said Aunt Julia.

Freddy Malins bade the Misses Morkan good-evening in what seemed an offhand fashion by reason of the habitual catch in his voice and then, seeing that Mr Browne was grinning at him from the sideboard, crossed the room on rather shaky legs and began to repeat in an undertone the story he had just told to Gabriel.

— He's not so bad, is he? said Aunt Kate to Gabriel.

Gabriel's brows were dark but he raised them quickly and answered:

— O no, hardly noticeable.

— Now, isn't he a terrible fellow! she said. And his poor mother made

him take the pledge on New Year's Eve. But come on, Gabriel, into the
drawing-room.

Before leaving the room with Gabriel she signalled to Mr Browne by
frowning and shaking her forefinger in warning to and fro. Mr Browne nodded in answer and, when she had gone, said to Freddy Malins:

— Now, then, Teddy, I'm going to fill you out a good glass of lemonade just to buck you up.

Freddy Malins, who was nearing the climax of his story, waved the
offer aside impatiently but Mr Browne, having first called Freddy Malins'
attention to a disarray in his dress, filled out and handed him a full glass of
lemonade. Freddy Malins' left hand accepted the glass mechanically, his
right hand being engaged in the mechanical readjustment of his dress. Mr
Browne, whose face was once more wrinkling with mirth, poured out for
himself a glass of whisky while Freddy Malins exploded, before he had well
reached the climax of his story, in a kink of high-pitched bronchitic laughter
and, setting down his untasted and overflowing glass, began to rub the
knuckles of his left fist backwards and forwards into his left eye, repeating
words of his last phrase as well as his fit of laughter would allow him.

Gabriel could not listen while Mary Jane was playing her Academy
piece, full of runs and difficult passages, to the hushed drawing-room. He
liked music but the piece she was playing had no melody for him and he
doubted whether it had any melody for the other listeners, though they had
begged Mary Jane to play something. Four young men, who had come from
the refreshment-room to stand in the doorway at the sound of the piano,
had gone away quietly in couples after a few minutes. The only persons who
seemed to follow the music were Mary Jane herself, her hands racing along
the key-board or lifted from it at the pauses like those of a priestess in momentary imprecation, and Aunt Kate standing at her elbow to turn the
page.

Gabriel's eyes, irritated by the floor, which glittered with beeswax
under the heavy chandelier, wandered to the wall above the piano. A picture of the balcony scene in *Romeo and Juliet* hung there and beside it was
a picture of the two murdered princes in the Tower which Aunt Julia had
worked in red, blue and brown wools when she was a girl. Probably in the
school they had gone to as girls that kind of work had been taught, for one
year his mother had worked for him as a birthday present a waistcoat of
purple tabinet, with little foxes' heads upon it, lined with brown satin and
having round mulberry buttons. It was strange that his mother had had no
musical talent though Aunt Kate used to call her the brains carrier of the
Morkan family. Both she and Julia had always seemed a little proud of their
serious and matronly sister. Her photograph stood before the pierglass. She
held an open book on her knees and was pointing out something in it to
Constantine who, dressed in a man-o'-war suit, lay at her feet. It was she

who had chosen the names for her sons for she was very sensible of the dignity of family life. Thanks to her, Constantine was now senior curate in Balbriggan and, thanks to her, Gabriel himself had taken his degree in the Royal University. A shadow passed over his face as he remembered her sullen opposition to his marriage. Some slighting phrases she had used still rankled in his memory; she had once spoken of Gretta as being country cute and that was not true of Gretta at all. It was Gretta who had nursed her during all her last long illness in their house at Monkstown.

He knew that Mary Jane must be near the end of her piece for she was playing again the opening melody with runs of scales after every bar and while he waited for the end the resentment died down in his heart. The piece ended with a trill of octaves in the treble and a final deep octave in the bass. Great applause greeted Mary Jane as, blushing and rolling up her music nervously, she escaped from the room. The most vigorous clapping came from the four young men in the doorway who had gone away to the refreshment-room at the beginning of the piece but had come back when the piano had stopped.

Lancers were arranged. Gabriel found himself partnered with Miss Ivors. She was a frank-mannered talkative young lady, with a freckled face and prominent brown eyes. She did not wear a low-cut bodice and the large brooch which was fixed in the front of her collar bore on it an Irish device.

When they had taken their places she said abruptly:

— I have a crow to pluck with you.

— With me? said Gabriel.

She nodded her head gravely.

— What is it? asked Gabriel, smiling at her solemn manner.

— Who is G. C.? answered Miss Ivors, turning her eyes upon him.

Gabriel coloured and was about to knit his brows, as if he did not understand, when she said bluntly:

— O, innocent Amy! I have found out that you write for *The Daily Express*. Now, aren't you ashamed of yourself?

— Why should I be ashamed of myself? asked Gabriel, blinking his eyes and trying to smile.

— Well, I'm ashamed of you, said Miss Ivors frankly. To say you'd write for a rag like that. I didn't think you were a West Briton.

A look of perplexity appeared on Gabriel's face. It was true that he wrote a literary column every Wednesday in *The Daily Express*, for which he was paid fifteen shillings. But that did not make him a West Briton surely. The books he received for review were almost more welcome than the paltry cheque. He loved to feel the covers and turn over the pages of newly printed books. Nearly every day when his teaching in the college was ended he used to wander down the quays to the second-hand booksellers, to Hickey's on Bachelor's Walk, to Webb's or Massey's on Aston's Quay, or to O'Clohissey's in the by-street. He did not know how to meet her charge. He wanted to say that literature was above politics. But they were friends of many years' standing and their careers had been parallel, first at the University and then as teachers: he could not risk a grandiose phrase with her. He continued blinking his eyes and trying to smile and murmured lamely that he saw nothing political in writing reviews of books.

When their turn to cross had come he was still perplexed and inattentive. Miss Ivors promptly took his hand in a warm grasp and said in a soft friendly tone:

— Of course, I was only joking. Come, we cross now.

When they were together again she spoke of the University question and Gabriel felt more at ease. A friend of hers had shown her his review of Browning's poems. That was how she had found out the secret: but she liked the review immensely. Then she said suddenly:

— O, Mr Conroy, will you come for an excursion to the Aran Isles this summer? We're going to stay there a whole month. It will be splendid out in the Atlantic. You ought to come. Mr Clancy is coming, and Mr Kilkelly and Kathleen Kearney. It would be splendid for Gretta too if she'd come. She's from Connacht, isn't she?

— Her people are, said Gabriel shortly.

— But you will come, won't you? said Miss Ivors, laying her warm hand eagerly on his arm.

— The fact is, said Gabriel, I have already arranged to go —

— Go where? asked Miss Ivors.

— Well, you know, every year I go for a cycling tour with some fellows and so —

— But where? asked Miss Ivors.

— Well, we usually go to France or Belgium or perhaps Germany, said Gabriel awkwardly.

— And why do you go to France and Belgium, said Miss Ivors, instead of visiting your own land?

— Well, said Gabriel, it's partly to keep in touch with the languages and partly for a change.

— And haven't you your own language to keep in touch with — Irish? asked Miss Ivors.

— Well, said Gabriel, if it comes to that, you know, Irish is not my language.

Their neighbours had turned to listen to the cross-examination. Gabriel glanced right and left nervously and tried to keep his good humour under the ordeal which was making a blush invade his forehead.

— And haven't you your own land to visit, continued Miss Ivors, that you know nothing of, your own people, and your own country?

— O, to tell you the truth, retorted Gabriel suddenly, I'm sick of my own country, sick of it!

— Why? asked Miss Ivors.

Gabriel did not answer for his retort had heated him.

— Why? repeated Miss Ivors.

They had to go visiting together and, as he had not answered her, Miss Ivors said warmly:

— Of course, you've no answer.

Gabriel tried to cover his agitation by taking part in the dance with great energy. He avoided her eyes for he had seen a sour expression on her face. But when they met in the long chain he was surprised to feel his hand firmly pressed. She looked at him from under her brows for a moment quizzically until he smiled. Then, just as the chain was about to start again, she stood on tiptoe and whispered into his ear:

— West Briton!

When the lancers were over Gabriel went away to a remote corner of the room where Freddy Malins' mother was sitting. She was a stout feeble old woman with white hair. Her voice had a catch in it like her son's and she stuttered slightly. She had been told that Freddy had come and that he was nearly all right. Gabriel asked her whether she had had a good crossing. She lived with her married daughter in Glasgow and came to Dublin on a visit once a year. She answered placidly that she had had a beautiful crossing and that the captain had been most attentive to her. She spoke also of the beautiful house her daughter kept in Glasgow, and of all the nice friends they had there. While her tongue rambled on Gabriel tried to banish from his mind all memory of the unpleasant incident with Miss Ivors. Of course the girl or woman, or whatever she was, was an enthusiast but there was a time for all things. Perhaps he ought not to have answered her like that. But she had no right to call him a West Briton before people, even in joke. She had tried to make him ridiculous before people, heckling him and staring at him with her rabbit's eyes.

He saw his wife making her way towards him through the waltzing couples. When she reached him she said into his ear:

— Gabriel, Aunt Kate wants to know won't you carve the goose as usual. Miss Daly will carve the ham and I'll do the pudding.

— All right, said Gabriel.

— She's sending in the younger ones first as soon as this waltz is over so that we'll have the tables to ourselves.

— Were you dancing? asked Gabriel.

— Of course I was. Didn't you see me? What words had you with Molly Ivors?

— No words. Why? Did she say so?

— Something like that. I'm trying to get that Mr D'Arcy to sing. He's full of conceit, I think.

— There were no words, said Gabriel moodily, only she wanted me to go for a trip to the west of Ireland and I said I wouldn't.

His wife clasped her hands excitedly and gave a little jump.

— O, do go, Gabriel, she cried. I'd love to see Galway again.

— You can go if you like, said Gabriel coldly.

She looked at him for a moment, then turned to Mrs Malins and said:

— There's a nice husband for you, Mrs Malins.

While she was threading her way back across the room Mrs Malins, without adverting to the interruption, went on to tell Gabriel what beautiful places there were in Scotland and beautiful scenery. Her son-in-law brought them every year to the lakes and they used to go fishing. Her son-in-law was a splendid fisher. One day he caught a fish, a beautiful big big fish, and the man in the hotel boiled it for their dinner.

Gabriel hardly heard what she said. Now that supper was coming near he began to think again about his speech and about the quotation. When he saw Freddy Malins coming across the room to visit his mother Gabriel left the chair free for him and retired into the embrasure of the window. The room had already cleared and from the back room came the clatter of plates and knives. Those who still remained in the drawing-room seemed tired of dancing and were conversing quietly in little groups. Gabriel's warm trembling fingers tapped the cold pane of the window. How cool it must be outside! How pleasant it would be to walk out alone, first along by the river and then through the park! The snow would be lying on the branches of the trees and forming a bright cap on the top of the Wellington Monument. How much more pleasant it would be there than at the supper-table!

He ran over the headings of his speech: Irish hospitality, sad memories, the Three Graces, Paris, the quotation from Browning. He repeated to himself a phrase he had written in his review: *One feels that one is listening to a thought-tormented music.* Miss Ivors had praised the review. Was she sincere? Had she really any life of her own behind all her propagandism? There had never been any ill-feeling between them until that night. It unnerved him to think that she would be at the supper-table, looking up at him while he spoke with her critical quizzing eyes. Perhaps she would not be sorry to see him fail in his speech. An idea came into his mind and gave him courage. He would say, alluding to Aunt Kate and Aunt Julia: *Ladies and Gentlemen, the generation which is now on the wane among us may have had its faults but for my part I think it had certain qualities of hospitality, of humour, of humanity, which the new and very serious and hypereducated generation that is growing up around us seems to me to lack.* Very good: that was one for Miss Ivors. What did he care that his aunts were only two ignorant old women?

A murmur in the room attracted his attention. Mr Browne was advancing from the door, gallantly escorting Aunt Julia, who leaned upon his arm, smiling and hanging her head. An irregular musketry of applause escorted her also as far as the piano and then, as Mary Jane seated herself on the stool, and Aunt Julia, no longer smiling, half turned so as to pitch her voice fairly into the room, gradually ceased. Gabriel recognised the prelude. It was that of an old song of Aunt Julia's — *Arrayed for the Bridal.* Her voice, strong and clear in tone, attacked with great spirit the runs which embellish the air and though she sang very rapidly she did not miss even the smallest of the grace notes. To follow the voice, without looking at the singer's face, was to feel and share the excitement of swift and secure flight. Gabriel applauded loudly with all the others at the close of the song and loud applause was borne in from the invisible supper-table. It sounded so genuine that a little colour struggled into Aunt Julia's face as she bent to replace in the music-stand the old leather-bound song-book that had her initials on the cover. Freddy Malins, who had listened with his head perched sideways to hear her better, was still applauding when everyone else had ceased and talking animatedly to his mother who nodded her head gravely and slowly in acquiescence. At last, when he could clap no more, he stood up suddenly and hurried across the room to Aunt Julia whose hand he seized and held in both his hands, shaking it when words failed him or the catch in his voice proved too much for him.

— I was just telling my mother, he said, I never heard you sing so well, never. No, I never heard your voice so good as it is to-night. Now! Would you believe that now? That's the truth. Upon my word and honour that's the truth. I never heard your voice sound so fresh and so . . . so clear and fresh, never.

Aunt Julia smiled broadly and murmured something about compliments as she released her hand from his grasp. Mr Browne extended his open hand towards her and said to those who were near him in the manner of a showman introducing a prodigy to an audience:

— Miss Julia Morkan, my latest discovery!

He was laughing very heartily at this himself when Freddy Malins turned to him and said:

— Well, Browne, if you're serious you might make a worse discovery. All I can say is I never heard her sing half so well as long as I am coming here. And that's the honest truth.

— Neither did I, said Mr Browne. I think her voice has greatly improved.

Aunt Julia shrugged her shoulders and said with meek pride:

— Thirty years ago I hadn't a bad voice as voices go.

— I often told Julia, said Aunt Kate emphatically, that she was simply thrown away in that choir. But she never would be said by me.

She turned as if to appeal to the good sense of the others against a refractory child while Aunt Julia gazed in front of her, a vague smile of reminiscence playing on her face.

— No, continued Aunt Kate, she wouldn't be said or led by anyone, slaving there in that choir night and day, night and day. Six o'clock on Christmas morning! And all for what?

— Well, isn't it for the honour of God, Aunt Kate? asked Mary Jane, twisting round on the piano-stool and smiling.

Aunt Kate turned fiercely on her niece and said:

— I know all about the honour of God, Mary Jane, but I think it's not at all honourable for the pope to turn out the women out of the choirs that have slaved there all their lives and put little whipper-snappers of boys over their heads. I suppose it is for the good of the Church if the pope does it. But it's not just, Mary Jane, and it's not right.

She had worked herself into a passion and would have continued in defence of her sister for it was a sore subject with her but Mary Jane, seeing that all the dancers had come back, intervened pacifically:

— Now, Aunt Kate, you're giving scandal to Mr Browne who is of the other persuasion.

Aunt Kate turned to Mr Browne, who was grinning at this allusion to his religion, and said hastily:

— O, I don't question the pope's being right. I'm only a stupid old woman and I wouldn't presume to do such a thing. But there's such a thing as common everyday politeness and gratitude. And if I were in Julia's place I'd tell that Father Healy straight up to his face. . . .

— And besides, Aunt Kate, said Mary Jane, we really are all hungry and when we are hungry we are all very quarrelsome.

— And when we are thirsty we are also quarrelsome, added Mr Browne.

— So that we had better go to supper, said Mary Jane, and finish the discussion afterwards.

On the landing outside the drawing-room Gabriel found his wife and Mary Jane trying to persuade Miss Ivors to stay for supper. But Miss Ivors, who had put on her hat and was buttoning her cloak, would not stay. She did not feel in the least hungry and she had already overstayed her time.

— But only for ten minutes, Molly, said Mrs Conroy. That won't delay you.

— To take a pick itself, said Mary Jane, after all your dancing.

— I really couldn't, said Miss Ivors.

— I am afraid you didn't enjoy yourself at all, said Mary Jane hopelessly.

— Ever so much, I assure you, said Miss Ivors, but you really must let me run off now.

— But how can you get home? asked Mrs Conroy.

— O, it's only two steps up the quay.

Gabriel hesitated a moment and said:

— If you will allow me, Miss Ivors, I'll see you home if you really are obliged to go.

But Miss Ivors broke away from them.

— I won't hear of it, she cried. For goodness sake go in to your suppers and don't mind me. I'm quite well able to take care of myself.

— Well, you're the comical girl, Molly, said Mrs Conroy frankly.

— *Beannacht libh*,[1] cried Miss Ivors, with a laugh, as she ran down the staircase.

[1] "A blessing on you" (Irish — traditional way of saying "farewell").

Mary Jane gazed after her, a moody puzzled expression on her face, while Mrs Conroy leaned over the banisters to listen for the hall-door. Gabriel asked himself was he the cause of her abrupt departure. But she did not seem to be in ill humour: she had gone away laughing. He stared blankly down the staircase.

At that moment Aunt Kate came toddling out of the supper-room, almost wringing her hands in despair.

— Where is Gabriel? she cried. Where on earth is Gabriel? There's everyone waiting in there, stage to let, and nobody to carve the goose!

— Here I am, Aunt Kate! cried Gabriel, with sudden animation, ready to carve a flock of geese, if necessary.

A fat brown goose lay at one end of the table and at the other end, on a bed of creased paper strewn with sprigs of parsley, lay a great ham, stripped of its outer skin and peppered over with crust crumbs, a neat paper frill round its shin and beside this was a round of spiced beef. Between these rival ends ran parallel lines of side-dishes: two little minsters of jelly, red and yellow; a shallow dish full of blocks of blancmange and red jam, a large green leaf-shaped dish with a stalk-shaped handle, on which lay bunches of purple raisins and peeled almonds, a companion dish on which lay a solid rectangle of Smyrna figs, a dish of custard topped with grated nutmeg, a small bowl full of chocolates and sweets wrapped in gold and silver papers and a glass vase in which stood some tall celery stalks. In the centre of the table there stood, as sentries to a fruit-stand which upheld a pyramid of oranges and American apples, two squat old-fashioned decanters of cut glass, one containing port and the other dark sherry. On the closed square piano a pudding in a huge yellow dish lay in waiting and behind it were three squads of bottles of stout and ale and minerals, drawn up according to the colours of their uniforms, the first two black, with brown and red labels, the third and smallest squad white, with transverse green sashes.

Gabriel took his seat boldly at the head of the table and, having looked to the edge of the carver, plunged his fork firmly into the goose. He felt quite at ease now for he was an expert carver and liked nothing better than to find himself at the head of a well-laden table.

— Miss Furlong, what shall I send you? he asked. A wing or a slice of the breast?

— Just a small slice of the breast.

— Miss Higgins, what for you?

— O, anything at all, Mr Conroy.

While Gabriel and Miss Daly exchanged plates of goose and plates of ham and spiced beef Lily went from guest to guest with a dish of hot floury potatoes wrapped in a white napkin. This was Mary Jane's idea and she had also suggested apple sauce for the goose but Aunt Kate had said that plain roast goose without apple sauce had always been good enough for her and she hoped she might never eat worse. Mary Jane waited on her pupils and saw that they got the best slices and Aunt Kate and Aunt Julia opened and carried across from the piano bottles of stout and ale for the gentlemen and bottles of minerals for the ladies. There was a great deal of confusion and laughter and noise, the noise of orders and counter-orders, of knives and forks, of corks and glass-stoppers. Gabriel began to carve second helpings as soon as he had finished the first round without serving himself. Everyone protested loudly so that he compromised by taking a long draught of stout for he had found the carving hot work. Mary Jane settled down quietly to her supper but Aunt Kate and Aunt Julia were still toddling round the table, walking on each other's heels, getting in each other's way and giving each other unheeded orders. Mr Browne begged of them to sit down and eat their suppers and so did Gabriel but they said there was time enough so that, at last, Freddy Malins stood up and, capturing Aunt Kate, plumped her down on her chair amid general laughter.

When everyone had been well served Gabriel said, smiling:

— Now, if anyone wants a little more of what vulgar people call stuffing let him or her speak.

A chorus of voices invited him to begin his own supper and Lily came forward with three potatoes which she had reserved for him.

— Very well, said Gabriel amiably, as he took another preparatory draught, kindly forget my existence, ladies and gentlemen, for a few minutes.

He set to his supper and took no part in the conversation with which the table covered Lily's removal of the plates. The subject of talk was the opera company which was then at the Theatre Royal. Mr Bartell D'Arcy, the tenor, a dark-complexioned young man with a smart moustache, praised very highly the leading contralto of the company but Miss Furlong thought she had a rather vulgar style of production. Freddy Malins said there was a negro chieftain singing in the second part of the Gaiety pantomime who had one of the finest tenor voices he had ever heard.

— Have you heard him? he asked Mr Bartell D'Arcy across the table.

— No, answered Mr Bartell D'Arcy carelessly.

— Because, Freddy Malins explained, now I'd be curious to hear your opinion of him. I think he has a grand voice.

— It takes Teddy to find out the really good things, said Mr Browne familiarly to the table.

— And why couldn't he have a voice too? asked Freddy Malins sharply. Is it because he's only a black?

Nobody answered this question and Mary Jane led the table back to the legitimate opera. One of her pupils had given her a pass for *Mignon*. Of course it was very fine, she said, but it made her think of poor Georgina Burns. Mr Browne could go back farther still, to the old Italian companies that used to come to Dublin — Tietjens, Ilma de Murzka, Campanini, the great Trebelli, Giuglini, Ravelli, Aramburo. Those were the days, he said, when there was something like singing to be heard in Dublin. He told too of how the top gallery of the old Royal used to be packed night after night, of how one night an Italian tenor had sung five encores to *Let Me Like a Soldier Fall,* introducing a high C every time, and of how the gallery boys would sometimes in their enthusiasm unyoke the horses from the carriage of some great *prima donna* and pull her themselves through the streets to her hotel. Why did they never play the grand old operas now, he asked, *Dinorah, Lucrezia Borgia?* Because they could not get the voices to sing them: that was why.

— O, well, said Mr Bartell D'Arcy, I presume there are as good singers to-day as there were then.

— Where are they? asked Mr Browne defiantly.

— In London, Paris, Milan, said Mr Bartell D'Arcy warmly. I suppose Caruso, for example, is quite as good, if not better than any of the men you have mentioned.

— Maybe so, said Mr Browne. But I may tell you I doubt it strongly.

— O, I'd give anything to hear Caruso sing, said Mary Jane.

— For me, said Aunt Kate, who had been picking a bone, there was only one tenor. To please me, I mean. But I suppose none of you ever heard of him.

— Who was he, Miss Morkan? asked Mr Bartell D'Arcy politely.

— His name, said Aunt Kate, was Parkinson. I heard him when he was in his prime and I think he had then the purest tenor voice that was ever put into a man's throat.

— Strange, said Mr Bartell D'Arcy. I never even heard of him.

— Yes, yes, Miss Morkan is right, said Mr. Browne. I remember hearing of old Parkinson but he's too far back for me.

— A beautiful pure sweet mellow English tenor, said Aunt Kate with enthusiasm. ·

Gabriel having finished, the huge pudding was transferred to the table. The clatter of forks and spoons began again. Gabriel's wife served out spoonfuls of the pudding and passed the plates down the table. Midway down they were held up by Mary Jane, who replenished them with raspberry or orange jelly or with blancmange and jam. The pudding was of Aunt Julia's making and she received praises for it from all quarters. She herself said that it was not quite brown enough.

— Well, I hope, Miss Morkan, said Mr Browne, that I'm brown enough for you because, you know, I'm all brown.

All the gentlemen, except Gabriel, ate some of the pudding out of compliment to Aunt Julia. As Gabriel never ate sweets the celery had been left for him. Freddy Malins also took a stalk of celery and ate it with his pudding. He had been told that celery was a capital thing for the blood and he was just then under the doctor's care. Mrs Malins, who had been silent all through the supper, said that her son was going down to Mount Melleray in a week or so. The table then spoke of Mount Melleray, how bracing the air was down there, how hospitable the monks were and how they never asked for a penny-piece from their guests.

— And do you mean to say, asked Mr Browne incredulously, that a chap can go down there and put up there as if it were a hotel and live on the fat of the land and then come away without paying a farthing?

— O, most people give some donation to the monastery when they leave, said Mary Jane.

— I wish we had an institution like that in our Church, said Mr Browne candidly.

He was astonished to hear that the monks never spoke, got up at two in the morning and slept in their coffins. He asked what they did it for.

— That's the rule of the order, said Aunt Kate firmly.

— Yes, but why? asked Mr Browne.

Aunt Kate repeated that it was the rule, that was all. Mr Browne still seemed not to understand. Freddy Malins explained to him, as best he could, that the monks were trying to make up for the sins committed by all the sinners in the outside world. The explanation was not very clear for Mr Browne grinned and said:

— I like that idea very much but wouldn't a comfortable spring bed do them as well as a coffin?

— The coffin, said Mary Jane, is to remind them of their last end.

As the subject had grown lugubrious it was buried in a silence of the table during which Mrs Malins could be heard saying to her neighbour in an indistinct undertone:

— They are very good men, the monks, very pious men.

The raisins and almonds and figs and apples and oranges and chocolates and sweets were now passed about the table and Aunt Julia invited all the guests to have either port or sherry. At first Mr Bartell D'Arcy refused to take either but one of his neighbours nudged him and whispered something to him upon which he allowed his glass to be filled. Gradually as the last glasses were being filled the conversation ceased. A pause followed, broken only by the noise of the wine and by unsettlings of chairs. The Misses Morkan, all three, looked down at the tablecloth. Someone coughed once or twice and then a few gentlemen patted the table gently as a signal for silence. The silence came and Gabriel pushed back his chair and stood up.

The patting at once grew louder in encouragement and then ceased altogether. Gabriel leaned his ten trembling fingers on the tablecloth and smiled nervously at the company. Meeting a row of upturned faces he raised his eyes to the chandelier. The piano was playing a waltz tune and he could hear the skirts sweeping against the drawing-room door. People, perhaps, were standing in the snow on the quay outside, gazing up at the lighted windows and listening to the waltz music. The air was pure there. In the distance lay the park where the trees were weighted with snow. The Wellington Monument wore a gleaming cap of snow that flashed westward over the white field of Fifteen Acres.

He began:

— Ladies and Gentlemen.

— It has fallen to my lot this evening, as in years past, to perform a very pleasing task but a task for which I am afraid my poor powers as a speaker are all too inadequate.

— No, no! said Mr Browne.

— But, however that may be, I can only ask you to-night to take the will for the deed and to lend me your attention for a few moments while I endeavour to express to you in words what my feelings are on this occasion.

— Ladies and Gentlemen. It is not the first time that we have gathered together under this hospitable roof, around this hospitable board. It is not the first time that we have been the recipients — or perhaps, I had better say, the victims — of the hospitality of certain good ladies.

He made a circle in the air with his arm and paused. Everyone laughed or smiled at Aunt Kate and Aunt Julia and Mary Jane who all turned crimson with pleasure. Gabriel went on more boldly:

— I feel more strongly with every recurring year that our country has no tradition which does it so much honour and which it should guard so jealously as that of its hospitality. It is a tradition that is unique as far as my experience goes (and I have visited not a few places abroad) among the modern nations. Some would say, perhaps, that with us it is rather a failing than anything to be boasted of. But granted even that, it is, to my mind, a princely failing, and one that I trust will long be cultivated among us. Of one thing, at least, I am sure. As long as this one roof shelters the good ladies aforesaid — and I wish from my heart it may do so for many and many a long year to come — the tradition of genuine warm-hearted courteous Irish hospitality, which our forefathers have handed down to us and which we in turn must hand down to our descendants, is still alive among us.

A hearty murmur of assent ran round the table. It shot through Gabriel's mind that Miss Ivors was not there and that she had gone away discourteously: and he said with confidence in himself:

— Ladies and Gentlemen.

— A new generation is growing up in our midst, a generation actuated by new ideas and new principles. It is serious and enthusiastic for these new ideas and its enthusiasm, even when it is misdirected, is, I believe, in the main sincere. But we are living in a sceptical and, if I may use the phrase, a thought-tormented age: and sometimes I fear that this new generation, educated or hypereducated as it is, will lack those qualities of humanity, of hospitality, of kindly humour which belonged to an older day. Listening to-night to the names of all those great singers of the past it seemed to me, I must confess, that we were living in a less spacious age. Those days might, without exaggeration, be called spacious days: and if they are gone beyond recall let us hope, at least, that in gatherings such as this we shall still speak of them with pride and affection, still cherish in our hearts the memory of those dead and gone great ones whose fame the world will not willingly let die.

— Hear, hear! said Mr Browne loudly.

— But yet, continued Gabriel, his voice falling into a softer inflection, there are always in gatherings such as this sadder thoughts that will recur to our minds: thoughts of the past, of youth, of changes, of absent faces that we miss here to-night. Our path through life is strewn with many such sad memories: and were we to brood upon them always we could not find the heart to go on bravely with our work among the living. We have all of us living duties and living affections which claim, and rightly claim, our strenuous endeavours.

— Therefore, I will not linger on the past. I will not let any gloomy moralising intrude upon us here to-night. Here we are gathered together for a brief moment from the bustle and rush of our everyday routine. We are met here as friends, in the spirit of good-fellowship, as colleagues, also to a certain extent, in the true spirit of *camaraderie*, and as the guests of — what shall I call them? — the Three Graces of the Dublin musical world.

The table burst into applause and laughter at this sally. Aunt Julia vainly asked each of her neighbours in turn to tell her what Gabriel had said.

— He says we are the Three Graces, Aunt Julia, said Mary Jane.

Aunt Julia did not understand but she looked up, smiling, at Gabriel, who continued in the same vein:

— Ladies and Gentlemen.

— I will not attempt to play to-night the part that Paris played on another occasion. I will not attempt to choose between them. The task would be an invidious one and one beyond my poor powers. For when I view them in turn, whether it be our chief hostess herself, whose good heart, whose too good heart, has become a byword with all who know her, or her sister, who seems to be gifted with perennial youth and whose singing must have been a surprise and a revelation to us all to-night, or, last but not least, when I consider our youngest hostess, talented, cheerful, hard-working and the best of nieces, I confess, Ladies and Gentlemen, that I do not know to which of them I should award the prize.

Gabriel glanced down at his aunts and, seeing the large smile on Aunt Julia's face and the tears which had risen to Aunt Kate's eyes, hastened to close. He raised his glass of port gallantly, while every member of the company fingered a glass expectantly, and said loudly:

— Let us toast them all three together. Let us drink to their health, wealth, long life, happiness and prosperity and may they long continue to hold the proud and self-won position which they hold in their profession and the position of honour and affection which they hold in our hearts.

All the guests stood up, glass in hand, and, turning towards the three seated ladies, sang in unison, with Mr Browne as leader:

> *For they are jolly gay fellows,*
> *For they are jolly gay fellows,*
> *For they are jolly gay fellows,*
> *Which nobody can deny.*

Aunt Kate was making frank use of her handkerchief and even Aunt Julia seemed moved. Freddy Malins beat time with his pudding-fork and the singers turned towards one another, as if in melodious conference, while they sang, with emphasis:

> *Unless he tells a lie,*
> *Unless he tells a lie.*

Then, turning once more towards their hostesses, they sang:

> *For they are jolly gay fellows,*
> *For they are jolly gay fellows,*
> *For they are jolly gay fellows,*
> *Which nobody can deny.*

The acclamation which followed was taken up beyond the door of the supper-room by many of the other guests and renewed time after time, Freddy Malins acting as officer with his fork on high.

The piercing morning air came into the hall where they were standing so that Aunt Kate said:

— Close the door, somebody. Mrs Malins will get her death of cold.

— Browne is out there, Aunt Kate, said Mary Jane.

— Browne is everywhere, said Aunt Kate, lowering her voice.

Mary Jane laughed at her tone.

— Really, she said archly, he is very attentive.

— He has been laid on here like the gas, said Aunt Kate in the same tone, all during the Christmas.

She laughed herself this time good-humouredly and then added quickly:

— But tell him to come in, Mary Jane, and close the door. I hope to goodness he didn't hear me.

At that moment the hall-door was opened and Mr Browne came in from the doorstep, laughing as if his heart would break. He was dressed in a long green overcoat with mock astrakhan cuffs and collar and wore on his head an oval fur cap. He pointed down the snow-covered quay from where the sound of shrill prolonged whistling was borne in.

— Teddy will have all the cabs in Dublin out, he said.

Gabriel advanced from the little pantry behind the office, struggling into his overcoat and, looking round the hall, said:

— Gretta not down yet?

— She's getting on her things, Gabriel, said Aunt Kate.

— Who's playing up there? asked Gabriel.

— Nobody. They're all gone.

— O no, Aunt Kate, said Mary Jane. Bartell D'Arcy and Miss O'Callaghan aren't gone yet.

— Someone is strumming at the piano, anyhow, said Gabriel.

Mary Jane glanced at Gabriel and Mr Browne and said with a shiver:

— It makes me feel cold to look at you two gentlemen muffled up like that. I wouldn't like to face your journey home at this hour.

— I'd like nothing better this minute, said Mr Browne stoutly, than a rattling fine walk in the country or a fast drive with a good spanking goer between the shafts.

— We used to have a very good horse and trap at home, said Aunt Julia sadly.

— The never-to-be-forgotten Johnny, said Mary Jane, laughing.

Aunt Kate and Gabriel laughed too.

— Why, what was wonderful about Johnny? asked Mr Browne.

— The late lamented Patrick Morkan, our grandfather, that is, explained Gabriel, commonly known in his later years as the old gentleman, was a glue-boiler.

— O, now, Gabriel, said Aunt Kate, laughing, he had a starch mill.

— Well, glue or starch, said Gabriel, the old gentleman had a horse by the name of Johnny. And Johnny used to work in the old gentleman's mill, walking round and round in order to drive the mill. That was all very well; but now comes the tragic part about Johnny. One fine day the old gentleman thought he'd like to drive out with the quality to a military review in the park.

— The Lord have mercy on his soul, said Aunt Kate compassionately.

— Amen, said Gabriel. So the old gentleman, as I said, harnessed Johnny and put on his very best tall hat and his very best stock collar and drove out in grand style from his ancestral mansion somewhere near Back Lane, I think.

Everyone laughed, even Mrs Malins, at Gabriel's manner and Aunt Kate said:

— O now, Gabriel, he didn't live in Back Lane, really. Only the mill was there.

— Out from the mansion of his forefathers, continued Gabriel, he drove with Johnny. And everything went on beautifully until Johnny came in sight of King Billy's statue: and whether he fell in love with the horse King Billy sits on or whether he thought he was back again in the mill, anyhow he began to walk round the statue.

Gabriel paced in a circle round the hall in his goloshes amid the laughter of the others.

— Round and round he went, said Gabriel, and the old gentleman, who was a very pompous old gentleman, was highly indignant. *Go on, sir! What do you mean, sir? Johnny! Johnny! Most extraordinary conduct! Can't understand the horse!*

The peals of laughter which followed Gabriel's imitation of the incident were interrupted by a resounding knock at the hall-door. Mary Jane
ran to open it and let in Freddy Malins. Freddy Malins, with his hat well
back on his head and his shoulders humped with cold, was puffing and
steaming after his exertions.

— I could only get one cab, he said.

— O, we'll find another along the quay, said Gabriel.

— Yes, said Aunt Kate. Better not keep Mrs Malins standing in the
draught.

Mrs Malins was helped down the front steps by her son and Mr
Browne and, after many manœuvres, hoisted into the cab. Freddy Malins
clambered in after her and spent a long time settling her on the seat, Mr
Browne helping him with advice. At last she was settled comfortably and
Freddy Malins invited Mr Browne into the cab. There was a good deal of
confused talk, and then Mr Browne got into the cab. The cabman settled
his rug over his knees, and bent down for the address. The confusion grew
greater and the cabman was directed differently by Freddy Malins and Mr
Browne, each of whom had his head out through a window of the cab. The
difficulty was to know where to drop Mr Browne along the route and Aunt
Kate, Aunt Julia and Mary Jane helped the discussion from the doorstep
with cross-directions and contradictions and abundance of laughter. As for
Freddy Malins he was speechless with laughter. He popped his head in and
out of the window every moment, to the great danger of his hat, and told
his mother how the discussion was progressing till at last Mr Browne
shouted to the bewildered cabman above the din of everybody's laughter:

— Do you know Trinity College?

— Yes, sir, said the cabman.

— Well, drive bang up against Trinity College gates, said Mr Browne,
and then we'll tell you where to go. You understand now?

— Yes, sir, said the cabman.

— Make like a bird for Trinity College.

— Right, sir, cried the cabman.

The horse was whipped up and the cab rattled off along the quay amid
a chorus of laughter and adieus.

Gabriel had not gone to the door with the others. He was in a dark
part of the hall gazing up the staircase. A woman was standing near the top
of the first flight, in the shadow also. He could not see her face but he could
see the terracotta and salmonpink panels of her skirt which the shadow
made appear black and white. It was his wife. She was leaning on the banisters, listening to something. Gabriel was surprised at her stillness and
strained his ear to listen also. But he could hear little save the noise of
laughter and dispute on the front steps, a few chords struck on the piano
and a few notes of a man's voice singing.

He stood still in the gloom of the hall, trying to catch the air that the
voice was singing and gazing up at his wife. There was grace and mystery in

her attitude as if she were a symbol of something. He asked himself what is a woman standing on the stairs in the shadow, listening to distant music, a symbol of. If he were a painter he would paint her in that attitude. Her blue felt hat would show off the bronze of her hair against the darkness and the dark panels of her skirt would show off the light ones. *Distant Music* he would call the picture if he were a painter.

The hall-door closed; and Aunt Kate, Aunt Julia and Mary Jane came down the hall, still laughing.

— Well, isn't Freddy terrible? said Mary Jane. He's really terrible.

Gabriel said nothing but pointed up the stairs towards where his wife was standing. Now that the hall-door was closed the voice and the piano could be heard more clearly. Gabriel held up his hand for them to be silent. The song seemed to be in the old Irish tonality and the singer seemed uncertain both of his words and of his voice. The voice, made plaintive by distance and by the singer's hoarseness, faintly illuminated the cadence of the air with words expressing grief:

> *O, the rain falls on my heavy locks*
> *And the dew wets my skin,*
> *My babe lies cold . . .*

— O, exclaimed Mary Jane. It's Bartell D'Arcy singing and he wouldn't sing all the night. O, I'll get him to sing a song before he goes.

— O do, Mary Jane, said Aunt Kate.

Mary Jane brushed past the others and ran to the staircase but before she reached it the singing stopped and the piano was closed abruptly.

— O, what a pity! she cried. Is he coming down, Gretta?

Gabriel heard his wife answer yes and saw her come down towards them. A few steps behind her were Mr Bartell D'Arcy and Miss O'Callaghan.

— O, Mr D'Arcy, cried Mary Jane, it's downright mean of you to break off like that when we were all in raptures listening to you.

— I have been at him all the evening, said Miss O'Callaghan, and Mrs Conroy too and he told us he had a dreadful cold and couldn't sing.

— O, Mr D'Arcy, said Aunt Kate, now that was a great fib to tell.

— Can't you see that I'm as hoarse as a crow? said Mr D'Arcy roughly.

He went into the pantry hastily and put on his overcoat. The others, taken aback by his rude speech, could find nothing to say. Aunt Kate wrinkled her brows and made signs to the others to drop the subject. Mr D'Arcy stood swathing his neck carefully and frowning.

— It's the weather, said Aunt Julia, after a pause.

— Yes, everybody has colds, said Aunt Kate readily, everybody.

— They say, said Mary Jane, we haven't had snow like it for thirty years; and I read this morning in the newspapers that the snow is general all over Ireland.

— I love the look of snow, said Aunt Julia sadly.

— So do I, said Miss O'Callaghan. I think Christmas is never really Christmas unless we have the snow on the ground.

— But poor Mr D'Arcy doesn't like the snow, said Aunt Kate, smiling.

Mr D'Arcy came from the pantry, fully swathed and buttoned, and in a repentant tone told them the history of the cold. Everyone gave him advice and said it was a great pity and urged him to be very careful of his throat in the night air. Gabriel watched his wife who did not join in the conversation. She was standing right under the dusty fanlight and the flame of the gas lit up the rich bronze of her hair which he had seen her drying at the fire a few days before. She was in the same attitude and seemed unaware of the talk about her. At last she turned towards them and Gabriel saw that there was colour on her cheeks and that her eyes were shining. A sudden tide of joy went leaping out of his heart.

— Mr D'Arcy, she said, what is the name of that song you were singing?

— It's called *The Lass of Aughrim*, said Mr D'Arcy, but I couldn't remember it properly. Why? Do you know it?

— *The Lass of Aughrim*, she repeated. I couldn't think of the name.

— It's a very nice air, said Mary Jane. I'm sorry you were not in voice to-night.

— Now, Mary Jane, said Aunt Kate, don't annoy Mr D'Arcy. I won't have him annoyed.

Seeing that all were ready to start she shepherded them to the door where good-night was said:

— Well, good-night, Aunt Kate, and thanks for the pleasant evening.

— Good-night, Gabriel. Good-night, Gretta!

— Good-night, Aunt Kate, and thanks ever so much. Good-night, Aunt Julia.

— O, good-night, Gretta, I didn't see you.

— Good-night, Mr D'Arcy. Good-night, Miss O'Callaghan.

— Good-night, Miss Morkan.

— Good-night, again.

— Good-night, all. Safe home.

— Good-night. Good-night.

The morning was still dark. A dull yellow light brooded over the houses and the river; and the sky seemed to be descending. It was slushy underfoot; and only streaks and patches of snow lay on the roofs, on the parapets of the quay and on the area railings. The lamps were still burning redly in the murky air and, across the river, the palace of the Four Courts stood out menacingly against the heavy sky.

She was walking on before him with Mr Bartell D'Arcy, her shoes in a brown parcel tucked under one arm and her hands holding her skirt up from the slush. She had no longer any grace of attitude but Gabriel's eyes were still bright with happiness. The blood went bounding along his veins; and the thoughts were rioting through his brain, proud, joyful, tender, valorous.

She was walking on before him so lightly and so erect that he longed to run after her noiselessly, catch her by the shoulders and say something foolish and affectionate into her ear. She seemed to him so frail that he longed to defend her against something and then to be alone with her. Moments of their secret life together burst like stars upon his memory. A heliotrope envelope was lying beside his breakfast-cup and he was caressing it with his hand. Birds were twittering in the ivy and the sunny web of the curtain was shimmering along the floor: he could not eat for happiness. They were standing on the crowded platform and he was placing a ticket inside the warm palm of her glove. He was standing with her in the cold, looking in through a grated window at a man making bottles in a roaring furnace. It was very cold. Her face, fragrant in the cold air, was quite close to his; and suddenly she called out to the man at the furnace.

— Is the fire hot, sir?

But the man could not hear her with the noise of the furnace. It was just as well. He might have answered rudely.

A wave of yet more tender joy escaped from his heart and went coursing in warm flood along his arteries. Like the tender fires of stars moments of their life together, that no one knew of or would ever know of, broke upon and illumined his memory. He longed to recall to her those moments, to make her forget the years of their dull existence together and remember only their moments of ecstasy. For the years, he felt, had not quenched his soul or hers. Their children, his writing, her household cares had not quenched all their souls' tender fire. In one letter that he had written to her then he had said: *Why is it that words like these seem to me so dull and cold? Is it because there is no word tender enough to be your name?*

Like distant music these words that he had written years before were borne towards him from the past. He longed to be alone with her. When the others had gone away, when he and she were in their room in the hotel, then they would be alone together. He would call her softly:

— Gretta!

Perhaps she would not hear at once: she would be undressing. Then something in his voice would strike her. She would turn and look at him. . . .

At the corner of Winetavern Street they met a cab. He was glad of its rattling noise as it saved him from conversation. She was looking out of the window and seemed tired. The others spoke only a few words, pointing out some building or street. The horse galloped along wearily under the murky morning sky, dragging his old rattling box after his heels, and Gabriel was again in a cab with her, galloping to catch the boat, galloping to their honeymoon.

As the cab drove across O'Connell Bridge Miss O'Callaghan said:

— They say you never cross O'Connell Bridge without seeing a white horse.

— I see a white man this time, said Gabriel.

— Where? asked Mr Bartell D'Arcy.

Gabriel pointed to the statue, on which lay patches of snow. Then he nodded familiarly to it and waved his hand.

— Good-night, Dan, he said gaily.

When the cab drew up before the hotel Gabriel jumped out and, in spite of Mr Bartell D'Arcy's protest, paid the driver. He gave the man a shilling over his fare. The man saluted and said:

— A prosperous New Year to you, sir.

— The same to you, said Gabriel cordially.

She leaned for a moment on his arm in getting out of the cab and while standing at the curbstone, bidding the others good-night. She leaned lightly on his arm, as lightly as when she had danced with him a few hours before. He had felt proud and happy then, happy that she was his, proud of her grace and wifely carriage. But now, after the kindling again of so many memories, the first touch of her body, musical and strange and perfumed, sent through him a keen pang of lust. Under cover of her silence he pressed her arm closely to his side; and, as they stood at the hotel door, he felt that they had escaped from their lives and duties, escaped from home and friends and run away together with wild and radiant hearts to a new adventure.

An old man was dozing in a great hooded chair in the hall. He lit a candle in the office and went before them to the stairs. They followed him in silence, their feet falling in soft thuds on the thickly carpeted stairs. She mounted the stairs behind the porter, her head bowed in the ascent, her frail shoulders curved as with a burden, her skirt girt tightly about her. He could have flung his arms about her hips and held her still for his arms were trembling with desire to seize her and only the stress of his nails against the palms of his hands held the wild impulse of his body in check. The porter halted on the stairs to settle his guttering candle. They halted too on the steps below him. In the silence Gabriel could hear the falling of the molten wax into the tray and the thumping of his own heart against his ribs.

The porter led them along a corridor and opened a door. Then he set his unstable candle down on a toilet-table and asked at what hour they were to be called in the morning.

— Eight, said Gabriel.

The porter pointed to the tap of the electric-light and began a muttered apology but Gabriel cut him short.

— We don't want any light. We have enough light from the street. And I say, he added, pointing to the candle, you might remove that handsome article, like a good man.

The porter took up his candle again, but slowly for he was surprised by such a novel idea. Then he mumbled good-night and went out. Gabriel shot the lock to.

A ghostly light from the street lamp lay in a long shaft from one window to the door. Gabriel threw his overcoat and hat on a couch and crossed the room towards the window. He looked down into the street in order that his emotion might calm a little. Then he turned and leaned against a chest of drawers with his back to the light. She had taken off her hat and cloak and was standing before a large swinging mirror, unhooking her waist. Gabriel paused for a few moments, watching her, and then said:

— Gretta!

She turned away from the mirror slowly and walked along the shaft of light towards him. Her face looked so serious and weary that the words would not pass Gabriel's lips. No, it was not the moment yet.

— You look tired, he said.

— I am a little, she answered.

— You don't feel ill or weak?

— No, tired: that's all.

She went on to the window and stood there, looking out. Gabriel waited again and then, fearing that diffidence was about to conquer him, he said abruptly:

— By the way, Gretta!

— What is it?

— You know that poor fellow Malins? he said quickly.

— Yes. What about him?

— Well, poor fellow, he's a decent sort of chap after all, continued Gabriel in a false voice. He gave me back that sovereign I lent him and I didn't expect it really. It's a pity he wouldn't keep away from that Browne, because he's not a bad fellow at heart.

He was trembling now with annoyance. Why did she seem so abstracted? He did not know how he could begin. Was she annoyed, too, about something? If she would only turn to him or come to him of her own accord! To take her as she was would be brutal. No, he must see some ardour in her eyes first. He longed to be master of her strange mood.

— When did you lend him the pound? she asked, after a pause.

Gabriel strove to restrain himself from breaking out into brutal language about the sottish Malins and his pound. He longed to cry to her from his soul, to crush her body against his, to overmaster her. But he said:

— O, at Christmas, when he opened that little Christmas-card shop in Henry Street.

He was in such a fever of rage and desire that he did not hear her come from the window. She stood before him for an instant, looking at him strangely. Then, suddenly raising herself on tiptoe and resting her hands lightly on his shoulders, she kissed him.

— You are a very generous person, Gabriel, she said.

Gabriel, trembling with delight at her sudden kiss and at the quaintness of her phrase, put his hands on her hair and began smoothing it back, scarcely touching it with his fingers. The washing had made it fine and brilliant. His heart was brimming over with happiness. Just when he was wishing for it she had come to him of her own accord. Perhaps her thoughts had been running with his. Perhaps she had felt the impetuous desire that was in him and then the yielding mood had come upon her. Now that she had fallen to him so easily he wondered why he had been so diffident.

He stood, holding her head between his hands. Then, slipping one arm swiftly about her body and drawing her towards him, he said softly:

— Gretta dear, what are you thinking about?

She did not answer nor yield wholly to his arm. He said again, softly:

— Tell me what it is, Gretta. I think I know what is the matter. Do I know?

She did not answer at once. Then she said in an outburst of tears:

— O, I am thinking about that song, *The Lass of Aughrim.*

She broke loose from him and ran to the bed and, throwing her arms across the bed-rail, hid her face. Gabriel stood stock-still for a moment in astonishment and then followed her. As he passed in the way of the cheval-glass he caught sight of himself in full length, his broad, well-filled shirt-front, the face whose expression always puzzled him when he saw it in a mirror and his glimmering gilt-rimmed eyeglasses. He halted a few paces from her and said:

— What about the song? Why does that make you cry?

She raised her head from her arms and dried her eyes with the back of her hand like a child. A kinder note than he had intended went into his voice.

— Why, Gretta? he asked.

— I am thinking about a person long ago who used to sing that song.

— And who was the person long ago? asked Gabriel, smiling.

— It was a person I used to know in Galway when I was living with my grandmother, she said.

The smile passed away from Gabriel's face. A dull anger began to gather again at the back of his mind and the dull fires of his lust began to glow angrily in his veins.

— Someone you were in love with? he asked ironically.

— It was a young boy I used to know, she answered, named Michael Furey. He used to sing that song, *The Lass of Aughrim.* He was very delicate.

Gabriel was silent. He did not wish her to think that he was interested in this delicate boy.

— I can see him so plainly, she said after a moment. Such eyes as he had: big dark eyes! And such an expression in them — an expression!

— O then, you were in love with him? said Gabriel.

— I used to go out walking with him, she said, when I was in Galway.

A thought flew across Gabriel's mind.

— Perhaps that was why you wanted to go to Galway with that Ivors girl? he said coldly.

She looked at him and asked in surprise:

— What for?

Her eyes made Gabriel feel awkward. He shrugged his shoulders and said:

— How do I know? To see him perhaps.

She looked away from him along the shaft of light towards the window in silence.

— He is dead, she said at length. He died when he was only seventeen. Isn't that a terrible thing to die so young as that?

— What was he? asked Gabriel, still ironically.

— He was in the gasworks, she said.

Gabriel felt humiliated by the failure of his irony and by the evocation of this figure from the dead, a boy in the gasworks. While he had been full of memories of their secret life together, full of tenderness and joy and desire, she had been comparing him in her mind with another. A shameful consciousness of his own person assailed him. He saw himself as a ludicrous figure, acting as a pennyboy for his aunts, a nervous well-meaning sentimentalist, orating to vulgarians and idealising his own clownish lusts, the pitiable fatuous fellow he had caught a glimpse of in the mirror. Instinctively he turned his back more to the light lest she might see the shame that burned upon his forehead.

He tried to keep up his tone of cold interrogation but his voice when he spoke was humble and indifferent.

— I suppose you were in love with this Michael Furey, Gretta, he said.

— I was great with him at that time, she said.

Her voice was veiled and sad. Gabriel, feeling now how vain it would be to try to lead her whither he had purposed, caressed one of her hands and said, also sadly:

— And what did he die of so young, Gretta? Consumption, was it?

— I think he died for me, she answered.

A vague terror seized Gabriel at this answer as if, at that hour when he had hoped to triumph, some impalpable and vindictive being was coming against him, gathering forces against him in its vague world. But he shook himself free of it with an effort of reason and continued to caress her hand. He did not question her again for he felt that she would tell him of herself. Her hand was warm and moist: it did not respond to his touch but he continued to caress it just as he had caressed her first letter to him that spring morning.

— It was in the winter, she said, about the beginning of the winter when I was going to leave my grandmother's and come up here to the convent. And he was ill at the time in his lodgings in Galway and wouldn't be let out and his people in Oughterard were written to. He was in decline, they said, or something like that. I never knew rightly.

She paused for a moment and sighed.

— Poor fellow, she said. He was very fond of me and he was such a gentle boy. We used to go out together, walking, you know, Gabriel, like the way they do in the country. He was going to study singing only for his health. He had a very good voice, poor Michael Furey.

— Well; and then? asked Gabriel.

— And then when it came to the time for me to leave Galway and come up to the convent he was much worse and I wouldn't be let see him so I wrote a letter saying I was going up to Dublin and would be back in the summer and hoping he would be better then.

She paused for a moment to get her voice under control and then went on:

— Then the night before I left I was in my grandmother's house in Nuns' Island, packing up, and I heard gravel thrown up against the window. The window was so wet I couldn't see so I ran downstairs as I was and slipped out the back into the garden and there was the poor fellow at the end of the garden, shivering.

— And did you not tell him to go back? asked Gabriel.

— I implored of him to go home at once and told him he would get his death in the rain. But he said he did not want to live. I can see his eyes as well as well! He was standing at the end of the wall where there was a tree.

— And did he go home? asked Gabriel.

— Yes, he went home. And when I was only a week in the convent he died and he was buried in Oughterard where his people came from. O, the day I heard that, that he was dead!

She stopped, choking with sobs, and, overcome by emotion, flung herself face downward on the bed, sobbing in the quilt. Gabriel held her hand for a moment longer, irresolutely, and then, shy of intruding on her grief, let it fall gently and walked quietly to the window.

She was fast asleep.

Gabriel, leaning on his elbow, looked for a few moments unresentfully on her tangled hair and half-open mouth, listening to her deep-drawn breath. So she had had that romance in her life: a man had died for her sake. It hardly pained him now to think how poor a part he, her husband, had played in her life. He watched her while she slept as though he and she had never lived together as man and wife. His curious eyes rested long upon her face and on her hair: and, as he thought of what she must have been then, in that time of her first girlish beauty, a strange friendly pity for her entered his soul. He did not like to say even to himself that her face was no longer beautiful but he knew that it was no longer the face for which Michael Furey had braved death.

Perhaps she had not told him all the story. His eyes moved to the chair over which she had thrown some of her clothes. A petticoat string dangled to the floor. One boot stood upright, its limp upper fallen down: the fellow of it lay upon its side. He wondered at his riot of emotions of an hour before. From what had it proceeded? From his aunt's supper, from his own foolish speech, from the wine and dancing, the merry-making when saying good-night in the hall, the pleasure of the walk along the river in the snow. Poor Aunt Julia! She, too, would soon be a shade with the shade of Patrick Morkan and his horse. He had caught that haggard look upon her face for a moment when she was singing *Arrayed for the Bridal.* Soon, perhaps, he would be sitting in that same drawing-room, dressed in black, his silk hat on his knees. The blinds would be drawn down and Aunt Kate would be sitting beside him, crying and blowing her nose and telling him how Julia had died. He would cast about his mind for some words that might console her, and would find only lame and useless ones. Yes, yes: that would happen very soon.

The air of the room chilled his shoulders. He stretched himself cautiously along under the sheets and lay down beside his wife. One by one they were all becoming shades. Better pass boldly into that other world, in the full glory of some passion, than fade and wither dismally with age. He thought of how she who lay beside him had locked in her heart for so many years that image of her lover's eyes when he had told her that he did not wish to live.

Generous tears filled Gabriel's eyes. He had never felt like that himself towards any woman but he knew that such a feeling must be love. The tears gathered more thickly in his eyes and in the partial darkness he imagined he saw the form of a young man standing under a dripping tree. Other forms were near. His soul had approached that region where dwell the vast hosts of the dead. He was conscious of, but could not apprehend, their wayward and flickering existence. His own identity was fading out into a grey impalpable world: the solid world itself which these dead had one time reared and lived in was dissolving and dwindling.

A few light taps upon the pane made him turn to the window. It had begun to snow again. He watched sleepily the flakes, silver and dark, falling obliquely against the lamplight. The time had come for him to set out on his journey westward. Yes, the newspapers were right: snow was general all over Ireland. It was falling on every part of the dark central plain, on the treeless hills, falling softly upon the Bog of Allen and, farther westward, softly falling into the dark mutinous Shannon waves. It was falling, too, upon every part of the lonely churchyard on the hill where Michael Furey lay buried. It lay thickly drifted on the crooked crosses and headstones, on the spears of the little gate, on the barren thorns. His soul swooned slowly as he heard the snow falling faintly through the universe and faintly falling, like the descent of their last end, upon all the living and the dead.

[1916]

VIRGINIA WOOLF *(1882–1941) is best known as a novelist, critic, and essayist; she published only one book of short stories, early in her career. The daughter of Sir Leslie Stephens, a scholar and editor of the monumental* Dictionary of Literary Biography, *she was educated at her home in her father's library, keenly aware that if she had been born a boy she would have gone on to Cambridge or Oxford. Later, guided by this sense of injustice, she wrote two enduring feminist works,* A Room of One's Own *(1929) and* Three Guineas *(1938). In frail health all her life, she married the journalist and political philosopher Leonard Woolf in 1912, and they lived in Bloomsbury, the fashionably bohemian section of London. Her first novel,* The Voyage Out, *was published in 1915. Two years later the Woolfs set two stories by "L. and V. Woolf" on an old handpress and published them under the imprint of the Hogarth Press. The little pamphlet was so successful that their press became a thriving enterprise, publishing such authors as Katherine Mansfield and T. S. Eliot. In 1921 the Hogarth Press published* Monday or Tuesday, *Woolf's collection of short stories, and the following year — influenced by the writing of Sigmund Freud, James Joyce, and Marcel Proust — she began to publish the unconventional novels that made her reputation:* Jacob's Room *(1922)* Mrs. Dalloway *(1925),* To the Lighthouse *(1927), and* The Waves *(1931). Dissatisfied with realistic fiction, Woolf explained in her* Writer's Diary *her ambition to eliminate "all waste, deadness, superfluity" in her novels in order "to give the moment whole, whatever it includes."*

In most of Woolf's fiction she explores the psychological nature of consciousness, depicting her characters' moods and personal attitudes. Her characters pose the questions, "What is life? What is love? What is reality? Who are you? Who am I?" She believed that beneath the appearance of change and disorder that marks daily life was a timeless reality that becomes apparent only during pure "moments of being," when the self is transcended and the individual consciousness becomes an undifferentiated part of a greater whole. For Woolf, the description of the immediate flow of her characters' thoughts and feelings was more important than the realistic depiction of their physical behavior. Some readers, like her good friend and critic E. M. Forster, wondered whether she hadn't gone too far: "She does not tell a story or weave a plot — can she create character?"

Throughout her life, Woolf wrote short stories as a way to relax between the arduous bouts of work on her novels, usually sketching her stories out in rough form before putting the draft away in a drawer. She felt that by putting experiences into words, she revealed "some order" about the world, "a token of some real thing behind appearances; and I make it real by putting it into words. It is only by putting it into words that I make it whole. . . ." Then, if an editor asked her for a short story, she would take out a sketch and rewrite it several times. She discussed with her husband the possibility of republishing Monday or Tuesday *together with her later stories, and after her suicide in 1941 Leonard Woolf saw this book through to publication as* A Haunted House and Other Stories *(1953). "Moments of Being" was included in it as one of the few stories "finally revised by her."*

Virginia Woolf

ༀ

MOMENTS OF BEING

"Slater's Pins Have No Points"

"Slater's pins have no points — don't you always find that?" said Miss Craye, turning round as the rose fell out of Fanny Wilmot's dress, and Fanny stooped, with her ears full of the music, to look for the pin on the floor.

The words gave her an extraordinary shock, as Miss Craye struck the last chord of the Bach fugue. Did Miss Craye actually go to Slater's and buy pins then, Fanny Wilmot asked herself, transfixed for a moment. Did she stand at the counter waiting like anybody else, and was she given a bill with coppers wrapped in it, and did she slip them into her purse and then, an hour later, stand by her dressing table and take out the pins? What need had she of pins? For she was not so much dressed as cased, like a beetle compactly in its sheath, blue in winter, green in summer. What need had she of pins — Julia Craye — who lived, it seemed in the cool glassy world of Bach fugues, playing to herself what she liked, and only consenting to take one or two pupils at the Archer Street College of Music (so the Principal, Miss Kingston, said) as a special favor to herself, who had "the greatest admiration for her in every way." Miss Craye was left badly off, Miss Kingston was afraid, at her brother's death. Oh, they used to have such lovely things, when they lived at Salisbury, and her brother Julius was, of course, a very well-known man: a famous archaeologist. It was a great privilege to stay with them, Miss Kingston said ("My family had always known them — they were regular Canterbury people," Miss Kingston said), but a little frightening for a child; one had to be careful not to slam the door or bounce into the room unexpectedly. Miss Kingston, who gave little character sketches like this on the first day of term while she received cheques and wrote out receipts for them, smiled here. Yes, she had been rather a tomboy; she had bounced in and set all those green Roman glasses and things jumping in their case. The Crayes were not used to children. The Crayes were none of them married. They kept cats; the cats, one used to feel, knew as much about the Roman urns and things as anybody.

"Far more than I did!" said Miss Kingston brightly, writing her name across the stamp in her dashing, cheerful, full-bodied hand, for she had always been practical. That was how she made her living, after all.

Perhaps then, Fanny Wilmot thought, looking for the pin, Miss Craye said that about "Slater's pins having no points," at a venture. None of the Crayes had ever married. She knew nothing about pins — nothing whatever. But she wanted to break the spell that had fallen on the house; to break the pane of glass which separated them from other people. When Polly Kingston, that merry little girl, had slammed the door and made the Roman vases jump, Julius, seeing that no harm was done (that would be his first instinct) looked, for the case was stood in the window, at Polly skipping home across the fields; looked with the look his sister often had, that lingering, driving look.

"Stars, sun, moon," it seemed to say, "the daisy in the grass, fires, frost on the window pane, my heart goes out to you. But," it always seemed to add, "you break, you pass, you go." And simultaneously it covered the intensity of both these states of mind with "I can't reach you — I can't get at you," spoken wistfully, frustratedly. And the stars faded, and the child went. That was the kind of spell that was the glassy surface, that Miss Craye wanted to break by showing, when she had played Bach beautifully as a reward to a favorite pupil (Fanny Wilmot knew that she was Miss Craye's favorite pupil), that she, too, knew, like other people, about pins. Slater's pins had no points.

Yes, the "famous archaeologist" had looked like that too. "The famous archaeologist" — as she said that, endorsing cheques, ascertaining the day of the month, speaking so brightly and frankly, there was in Miss Kingston's voice an indescribable tone which hinted at something odd; something queer in Julius Craye; it was the very same thing that was odd perhaps in Julia too. One could have sworn, thought Fanny Wilmot, as she looked for the pin, that at parties, meetings (Miss Kingston's father was a clergyman), she had picked up some piece of gossip, or it might only have been a smile, or a tone when his name was mentioned, which had given her "a feeling" about Julius Craye. Needless to say, she had never spoken about it to anybody. Probably she scarcely knew what she meant by it. But whenever she spoke of Julius, or heard him mentioned, that was the first thing that came to mind; and it was a seductive thought; there was something odd about Julius Craye.

It was so that Julia looked too, as she sat half turned on the music stool, smiling. It's on the field, it's on the pane, it's in the sky — beauty;

and I can't get at it; I can't have it — I, she seemed to add, with that little clutch of the hand which was so characteristic, who adore it so passionately, would give the whole world to possess it! And she picked up the carnation which had fallen on the floor, while Fanny searched for the pin. She crushed it, Fanny felt, voluptuously in her smooth veined hands stuck about with water-colored rings set in pearls. The pressure of her fingers seemed to increase all that was most brilliant in the flower; to set it off; to make it more frilled, fresh, immaculate. What was odd in her, and perhaps in her brother, too, was that this crush and grasp of the finger was combined with a perpetual frustration. So it was even now with the carnation. She had her hands on it; she pressed it; but she did not possess it, enjoy it, not entirely and altogether.

None of the Crayes had married, Fanny Wilmot remembered. She had in mind how one evening when the lesson had lasted longer than usual and it was dark, Julia Craye had said "it's the use of men, surely, to protect us," smiling at her that same odd smile, as she stood fastening her cloak, which made her, like the flower, conscious to her finger tips of youth and brilliance, but, like the flower, too, Fanny suspected, made her feel awkward.

"Oh, but I don't want protection," Fanny had laughed, and when Julia Craye, fixing on her that extraordinary look, had said she was not so sure of that, Fanny positively blushed under the admiration in her eyes.

It was the only use of men, she had said. Was it for that reason then, Fanny wondered, with her eyes on the floor, that she had never married? After all, she had not lived all her life in Salisbury. "Much the nicest part of London," she had said once, "(but I'm speaking of fifteen or twenty years ago) is Kensington. One was in the Gardens in ten minutes — it was like the heart of the country. One could dine out in one's slippers without catching cold. Kensington — it was like a village then, you know," she had said.

Here she broke off, to denounce acridly the draughts in the Tubes.

"It was the use of men," she had said, with a queer wry acerbity. Did that throw any light on the problem why she had not married? One could imagine every sort of scene in her youth, when with her good blue eyes, her straight firm nose, her air of cool distinction, her piano playing, her rose flowering with chaste passion in the bosom of her muslin dress, she had attracted first the young men to whom such things, the china tea cups and the silver candlesticks and the inlaid table, for the Crayes had such nice things, were wonderful; young men not sufficiently distinguished; young men of the cathedral town with ambitions. She had attracted them first, and then her brother's friends from Oxford or Cambridge. They would come down in the summer; row her on the river; continue the argument about Browning by letter; and arrange perhaps, on the rare occasions when she stayed in London, to show her — Kensington Gardens?

"Much the nicest part of London — Kensington (I'm speaking of fifteen or twenty years ago)," she had said once. One was in the gardens in ten minutes — in the heart of the country. One could make that yield what one liked, Fanny Wilmot thought, single out, for instance, Mr. Sherman, the painter, an old friend of hers; make him call for her, by appointment, one sunny day in June; take her to have tea under the trees. (They had met, too, at those parties to which one tripped in slippers without fear of catching cold.) The aunt or other elderly relative was to wait there while they looked at the Serpentine. They looked at the Serpentine. He may have rowed her across. They compared it with the Avon. She would have considered the comparison very furiously. Views of rivers were important to her. She sat hunched a little, a little angular, though she was graceful then, steering. At the critical moment, for he had determined that he must speak now — it was his only chance of getting her alone — he was speaking with his head turned at an absurd angle, in his great nervousness, over his shoulder — at that very moment she interrupted fiercely. He would have them into the Bridge, she cried. It was a moment of horror, of disillusionment, of revelation, for both of them. I can't have it, I can't possess it, she thought. He could not see why she had come then. With a great splash of his oar he pulled the boat round. Merely to snub him? He rowed her back and said good-bye to her.

The setting of that scene could be varied as one chose, Fanny Wilmot reflected. (Where had that pin fallen?) It might be Ravenna; or Edinburgh, where she had kept house for her brother. The scene could be changed; and the young man and the exact manner of it all, but one thing was constant — her refusal, and her frown, and her anger with herself afterwards, and her argument, and her relief — yes, certainly her immense relief. The very next day, perhaps, she would get up at six, put on her cloak, and walk all the way from Kensington to the river. She was so thankful that she had not sacrificed her right to go and look at things when they are at their best — before people are up, that is to say she could have her breakfast in bed if she liked. She had not sacrificed her independence.

Yes, Fanny Wilmot smiled, Julia had not endangered her habits. They remained safe; and her habits would have suffered if she had married. "They're ogres," she had said one evening, half laughing, when another pupil, a girl lately married, suddenly bethinking her that she would miss her husband, had rushed off in haste.

"They're ogres," she had said, laughing grimly. An ogre would have interfered perhaps with breakfast in bed; with walks at dawn down to the river. What would have happened (but one could hardly conceive this) had she had children? She took astonishing precautions against chills, fatigue, rich food, the wrong food, draughts, heated rooms, journeys in the Tube, for she could never determine which of these it was exactly that brought on those terrible headaches that gave her life the semblance of a battlefield. She was always engaged in outwitting the enemy, until it seemed as if the pursuit had its interest; could she have beaten the enemy finally she would have found life a little dull. As it was, the tug-of-war was perpetual — on the one side the nightingale or the view which she loved with passion — yes, for views and birds she felt nothing less than passion; on the other the damp path or the horrid long drag up a steep hill which would certainly make her good for nothing next day and bring on one of her headaches. When, therefore, from time to time, she managed her forces adroitly and brought off a visit to Hampton Court the week the crocuses — those glossy bright flowers were her favorite — were at their best, it was a victory. It was something that lasted; something that mattered forever. She strung the afternoon on the necklace of memorable days, which was not too long for her to be able to recall this one or that one; this view, that city; to finger it, to feel it, to savor, sighing, the quality that made it unique.

"It was so beautiful last Friday," she said, "that I determined I must go there." So she had gone off to Waterloo on her great undertaking — to visit Hampton Court — alone. Naturally, but perhaps foolishly, one pitied her for the thing she never asked pity for (indeed she was reticent habitually, speaking of her health only as a warrior might speak of her foe) — one pitied her for always doing everything alone. Her brother was dead. Her sister was asthmatic. She found the climate of Edinburgh good for her. It was too bleak for Julia. Perhaps, too, she found the associations painful, for her brother, the famous archaeologist, had died there; and she had loved her brother. She lived in a little house off the Brompton Road entirely alone.

Fanny Wilmot saw the pin; she picked it up. She looked at Miss Craye. Was Miss Craye so lonely? No, Miss Craye was steadily, blissfully, if only for that moment, a happy woman. Fanny had surprised her in a moment of ecstasy. She sat there, half turned away from the piano, with her hands clasped in her lap holding the carnation upright, while behind her was the sharp square of the window, uncurtained, purple in the evening, intensely purple after the brilliant electric lights which burnt unshaded in the bare music room. Julia Craye, sitting hunched and compact holding her flower, seemed to emerge out of the London night, seemed to fling it like a cloak behind her, it seemed, in its bareness and intensity, the effluence of her spirit, something she had made which surrounded her. Fanny stared.

All seemed transparent, for a moment, to the gaze of Fanny Wilmot, as if looking through Miss Craye, she saw the very fountain of her being spurting its pure silver drops. She saw back and back into the past behind her. She saw the green Roman vases stood in their case; heard the choristers playing cricket; saw Julia quietly descend the curving steps on to the lawn; then saw her pour out tea beneath the cedar tree; softly enclosed the old man's hand in hers; saw her going round and about the corridors of that ancient Cathedral dwelling place with towels in her hand to mark them; lamenting, as she went, the pettiness of daily life; and slowly aging, and putting away clothes when summer came, because at her age they were too bright to wear; and tending her father's sickness; and cleaving her way ever more definitely as her will stiffened toward her solitary goal; travelling frugally; counting the cost and measuring out of her tight shut purse the sum needed for this journey or for that old mirror; obstinately adhering, whatever people might say, in choosing her pleasures for herself. She saw Julia ——

Julia blazed. Julia kindled. Out of the night she burnt like a dead white star. Julia opened her arms. Julia kissed her on the lips. Julia possessed it.

"Slater's pins have no points," Miss Craye said, laughing queerly and relaxing her arms, as Fanny Wilmot pinned the flower to her breast with trembling fingers.

[1921]

FRANZ KAFKA (1883–1924) *led a life whose facts are simple and sad. He was born into a Jewish family in the city of Prague, and from youth onward he feared his authoritarian father so much that he stuttered in his presence, although he spoke easily with others. In 1906 he received a doctorate in jurisprudence, and for many years he worked a tedious job as a civil service lawyer investigating claims at the state Worker's Accident Insurance Institute. He never married and lived for the most part at home, where he wrote fiction at night (he was an insomniac), publishing only a few slim volumes of stories during his lifetime. Meditation, a collection of sketches, appeared in 1912; The Stoker: A Fragment in 1913; The Metamorphosis in 1915; The Judgment in 1916; In the Penal Colony in 1919; and A Country Doctor in 1920. Only a few of his friends knew that he was also at work on the great novels that were published after his death from tuberculosis: Amerika, The Trial, and The Castle. (He asked his literary executor, Max Brod, to burn these novels in manuscript, but Brod refused.) Kafka's despair with his writing, with his job, with his father, and with his life was complete, and like Flaubert — whom he admired — he used his fiction as a "rock" to which he clung in order not to be drowned in the waves of the world around him. With typical irony, however, he saw the effort as futile: "By scribbling I run ahead of myself in order to catch myself up at the finishing post. I cannot run away from myself."*

In his diaries, Kafka recorded his obsession with literature. "What will be my fate as a writer is very simple. My talent for portraying my dreamlike inner life has thrust all other matters into the background...." The "dreamlike" quality of his imagination is apparent in all his work. He is perhaps best known as the author of the waking nightmare "The Metamorphosis," whose remarkable first sentence is one of the most famous in short story literature. The hero of the story, Gregor Samsa (pronounced Zamza), is the son of philistine, middle-class parents in Prague, as was Kafka, and the tendency of literary critics has been to interpret the story as an autobiographical fiction, using the "monstrous insect" as a Freudian symbol that characterizes Kafka's sense of inadequacy before his demanding father. Kafka himself considered psychoanalysis "a helpless error," regarding Freud's theories as very rough pictures which did not do justice to either the details or the essence of life. The greatest literary influence upon Kafka was Flaubert; both writers used language with similar ironic precision and with no intrusion of their own private sentiments.

At the center of "The Metamorphosis" is Kafka's portrayal of the cruelty of the family and Gregor Samsa's feelings of isolation and sacrifice that result from the conflict. The visionary, nightmarish quality of the story is in

striking contrast to its precise and formal style, the clarity of which intensi-
fies the dark richness of the fantasy. In 1922 Kafka wrote Max Brod that to
be a writer meant for him a "descent to the dark powers" of the night, when
anxiety kept him from sleeping. "And what is devilish in it seems to me
quite clear. It is the vanity and the craving for enjoyment, which is forever
whirring around oneself. . . . The wish that a naive person sometimes has: 'I
would like to die and watch the others crying over me' is what such a writer
constantly experiences: he dies (or he does not live) and continually cries
over himself."

Franz Kafka

ನಿಲ್

THE METAMORPHOSIS

– translated by Willa and Edwin Muir

I

As Gregor Samsa awoke one morning from uneasy dreams he found himself transformed in his bed into a gigantic insect. He was lying on his hard, as it were armor-plated, back and when he lifted his head a little he could see his dome-like brown belly divided into stiff arched segments on top of which the bed quilt could hardly keep in position and was about to slide off completely. His numerous legs, which were pitifully thin compared to the rest of his bulk, waved helplessly before his eyes.

What has happened to me? he thought. It was no dream. His room, a regular human bedroom, only rather too small, lay quiet between the four familiar walls. Above the table on which a collection of cloth samples was unpacked and spread out — Samsa was a commercial traveler — hung the picture which he had recently cut out of an illustrated magazine and put into a pretty gilt frame. It showed a lady, with a fur cap on and a fur stole, sitting upright and holding out to the spectator a huge fur muff into which the whole of her forearm had vanished!

Gregor's eyes turned next to the window, and the overcast sky — one could hear rain drops beating on the window gutter — made him quite melancholy. What about sleeping a little longer and forgetting all this nonsense, he thought, but it could not be done, for he was accustomed to sleep on his right side and in his present condition he could not turn himself over. However violently he forced himself towards his right side he always rolled on to his back again. He tried it at least a hundred times, shutting his eyes to keep from seeing his struggling legs, and only desisted when he began to feel in his side a faint dull ache he had never experienced before.

Oh God, he thought, what an exhausting job I've picked on! Traveling about day in, day out. It's much more irritating work than doing the actual business in the office, and on top of that there's the trouble of constant traveling, of worrying about train connections, the bed and irregular meals, casual acquaintances that are always new and never become intimate friends. The devil take it all! He felt a slight itching up on his belly; slowly pushed himself on his back nearer to the top of the bed so that he could lift his head more easily; identified the itching place which was surrounded by many small white spots the nature of which he could not understand and made to touch it with a leg, but drew the leg back immediately, for the contact made a cold shiver run through him.

He slid down again into his former position. This getting up early, he thought, makes one quite stupid. A man needs his sleep. Other commercials live like harem women. For instance, when I come back to the hotel of a morning to write up the orders I've got, these others are only sitting down to breakfast. Let me just try that with my chief; I'd be sacked on the spot. Anyhow, that might be quite a good thing for me, who can tell? If I didn't have to hold my hand because of my parents I'd have given notice long ago, I'd have gone to the chief and told him exactly what I think of him. That would knock him endways from his desk! It's a queer way of doing, too, this sitting on high at a desk and talking down to employees, especially when they have to come quite near because the chief is hard of hearing. Well, there's still hope; once I've saved enough money to pay back my parents' debts to him — that should take another five or six years — I'll do it without fail. I'll cut myself completely loose then. For the moment, though, I'd better get up, since my train goes at five.

He looked at the alarm clock ticking on the chest. Heavenly Father! he thought. It was half-past six o'clock and the hands were quietly moving on, it was even past the half-hour, it was getting on toward a quarter to seven. Had the alarm clock not gone off? From the bed one could see that it had been properly set for four o'clock; of course it must have gone off. Yes, but was it possible to sleep quietly through that ear-splitting noise? Well, he had not slept quietly, yet apparently all the more soundly for that. But what was he to do now? The next train went at seven o'clock; to catch that he would need to hurry like mad and his samples weren't even packed up, and he himself wasn't feeling particularly fresh and active. And even if he did catch the train he wouldn't avoid a row with the chief, since the firm's porter would have been waiting for the five o'clock train and would have long since reported his failure to turn up. The porter was a creature of the chief's, spineless and stupid. Well, supposing he were to say he was sick? But that would be most unpleasant and would look suspicious, since during his five years' employment he had not been ill once. The chief himself would be sure to come with the sick-insurance doctor, would reproach his parents with their son's laziness and would cut all excuses short by referring to the insurance doctor, who of course regarded all mankind as perfectly healthy malingerers. And would he be so far wrong on this occasion? Gregor really felt quite well, apart from a drowsiness that was utterly superfluous after such a long sleep, and he was even unusually hungry.

As all this was running through his mind at top speed without his being able to decide to leave his bed — the alarm clock had just struck a quarter to seven — there came a cautious tap at the door behind the head of his bed. "Gregor," said a voice — it was his mother's — "it's a quarter to seven. Hadn't you a train to catch?" That gentle voice! Gregor had a shock as he heard his own voice answering hers, unmistakably his own voice, it was true, but with a persistent horrible twittering squeak behind it like an undertone, that left the words in their clear shape only for the first moment and then rose up reverberating round them to destroy their sense, so that one could not be sure one had heard them rightly. Gregor wanted to answer at length and explain everything, but in the circumstances he confined himself to saying: "Yes, yes, thank you, Mother, I'm getting up now." The wooden door between them must have kept the change in his voice from being noticeable outside, for his mother contented herself with this statement and shuffled away. Yet this brief exchange of words had made the other members of the family aware that Gregor was still in the house, as they had not expected, and at one of the side doors his father was already knocking, gently, yet with his fist. "Gregor, Gregor," he called, "what's the matter with you?" And after a little while he called again in a deeper voice: "Gregor! Gregor!" At the other side door his sister was saying in a low, plaintive tone: "Gregor? Aren't you well? Are you needing anything?" He answered them both at once: "I'm just ready," and did his best to make his voice sound as normal as possible by enunciating the words very clearly and leaving long pauses between them. So his father went back to his breakfast, but his sister whispered: "Gregor, open the door, do." However, he was not thinking of opening the door, and felt thankful for the prudent habit he had acquired in traveling of locking all doors during the night, even at home.

His immediate intention was to get up quietly without being disturbed, to put on his clothes and above all eat his breakfast, and only then to consider what else was to be done, since in bed, he was well aware, his meditations would come to no sensible conclusion. He remembered that often enough in bed he had felt small aches and pains, probably caused by awkward postures, which had proved purely imaginary once he got up, and he looked forward eagerly to seeing this morning's delusions gradually fall away. That the change in his voice was nothing but the precursor of a severe chill, a standing ailment of commercial travelers, he had not the least possible doubt.

To get rid of the quilt was quite easy; he had only to inflate himself a little and it fell off by itself. But the next move was difficult, especially because he was so uncommonly broad. He would have needed arms and hands to hoist himself up; instead he had only the numerous little legs which never stopped waving in all directions and which he could not control in the least. When he tried to bend one of them it was the first to stretch itself straight; and did he succeed at last in making it do what he wanted, all the other legs meanwhile waved the more wildly in a high degree of unpleasant agitation. "But what's the use of lying idle in bed," said Gregor to himself.

He thought that he might get out of bed with the lower part of his body first, but this lower part, which he had not yet seen and of which he could form no clear conception, proved too difficult to move; it shifted so slowly; and when finally, almost wild with annoyance, he gathered his forces together and thrust out recklessly, he had miscalculated the direction and bumped heavily against the lower end of the bed, and the stinging pain he felt informed him that precisely this lower part of his body was at the moment probably the most sensitive.

So he tried to get the top part of himself out first, and cautiously moved his head towards the edge of the bed. That proved easy enough, and despite its breadth and mass the bulk of his body at last slowly followed the movement of his head. Still, when he finally got his head free over the edge of the bed he felt too scared to go on advancing, for after all if he let himself fall in this way it would take a miracle to keep his head from being injured. And at all costs he must not lose consciousness now, precisely now; he would rather stay in bed.

But when after a repetition of the same efforts he lay in his former position again, sighing, and watched his little legs struggling against each other more wildly than ever, if that were possible, and saw no way of bringing any order into this arbitrary confusion, he told himself again that it was impossible to stay in bed and that the most sensible course was to risk everything for the smallest hope of getting away from it. At the same time he did not forget meanwhile to remind himself that cool reflection, the coolest possible, was much better than desperate resolves. In such moments he focused his eyes as sharply as possible on the window, but, unfortunately, the prospect of the morning fog, which muffled even the other side of the narrow street, brought him little encouragement and comfort. "Seven o'clock already," he said to himself when the alarm clock chimed again, "seven o'clock already and still such a thick fog." And for a little while he lay quiet, breathing lightly, as if perhaps expecting such complete repose to restore all things to their real and normal condition.

But then he said to himself: "Before it strikes a quarter past seven I must be quite out of this bed, without fail. Anyhow, by that time someone will have come from the office to ask for me, since it opens before seven." And he set himself to rocking his whole body at once in a regular rhythm, with the idea of swinging it out of the bed. If he tipped himself out in that way he could keep his head from injury by lifting it at an acute angle when he fell. His back seemed to be hard and was not likely to suffer from a fall on the carpet. His biggest worry was the loud crash he would not be able to help making, which would probably cause anxiety, if not terror, behind all the doors. Still, he must take the risk.

When he was already half out of the bed — the new method was more a game than an effort, for he needed only to hitch himself across by rocking to and fro — it struck him how simple it would be if he could get help. Two strong people — he thought of his father and the servant girl — would be amply sufficient; they would only have to thrust their arms under his convex back, lever him out of the bed, bend down with their burden and then be patient enough to let him turn himself right over on to the floor, where it was to be hoped his legs would then find their proper function. Well, ignoring the fact that the doors were all locked, ought he really to call for help? In spite of his misery he could not suppress a smile at the very idea of it.

He had got so far that he could barely keep his equilibrium when he rocked himself strongly, and he would have to nerve himself very soon for the final decision since in five minutes' time it would be a quarter past seven — when the front doorbell rang. "That's someone from the office," he said to himself, and grew almost rigid, while his little legs only jigged about all the faster. For a moment everything stayed quiet. "They're not going to open the door," said Gregor to himself, catching at some kind of irrational hope. But then of course the servant girl went as usual to the door with her heavy tread and opened it. Gregor needed only to hear the first good morning of the visitor to know immediately who it was — the chief clerk himself. What a fate, to be condemned to work for a firm where the smallest omission at once gave rise to the gravest suspicion! Were all employees in a body nothing but scoundrels, was there not among them one single loyal devoted man who, had he wasted only an hour or so of the firm's time in a morning, was so tormented by conscience as to be driven out of his mind and actually incapable of leaving his bed? Wouldn't it really have been sufficient to send an apprentice to inquire — if any inquiry were necessary at all — did the chief clerk himself have to come and thus indicate to the entire family, an innocent family, that this suspicious circumstance could be investigated by no one less versed in affairs than himself? And more through the agitation caused by these reflections than through any act of will Gregor swung himself out of bed with all his strength. There was a loud thump, but it was not really a crash. His fall was broken to some extent by the carpet, his back, too, was less stiff then he thought, and so there was merely a dull thud, not so very startling. Only he had not lifted his head carefully enough and had hit it; he turned it and rubbed it on the carpet in pain and irritation.

"That was something falling down in there," said the chief clerk in the next room to the left. Gregor tried to suppose to himself that something like what had happened to him today might some day happen to the chief clerk; one really could not deny that it was possible. But as if in brusque reply to this supposition the chief clerk took a couple of firm steps in the next-door room and his patent leather boots creaked. From the right-hand room his sister was whispering to inform him of the situation: "Gregor, the chief clerk's here." "I know," muttered Gregor to himself; but he didn't dare to make his voice loud enough for his sister to hear it.

"Gregor," said his father now from the left-hand room, "the chief clerk has come and wants to know why you didn't catch the early train. We don't know what to say to him. Besides, he wants to talk to you in person. So open the door, please. He will be good enough to excuse the untidiness of your room." "Good morning, Mr. Samsa," the chief clerk was calling amiably meanwhile. "He's not well," said his mother to the visitor, while his father was still speaking through the door, "he's not well, sir, believe me. What else would make him miss a train! The boy thinks about nothing but his work. It makes me almost cross the way he never goes out in the evenings; he's been here the last eight days and has stayed at home every single evening. He just sits there quietly at the table reading a newspaper or looking through railway timetables. The only amusement he gets is doing fretwork. For instance, he spent two or three evenings cutting out a little picture frame; you would be surprised to see how pretty it is; it's hanging in his room; you'll see it in a minute when Gregor opens the door. I must say I'm glad you've come, sir; we should never have got him to unlock the door by ourselves; he's so obstinate; and I'm sure he's unwell, though he wouldn't have it to be so this morning." "I'm just coming," said Gregor slowly and carefully, not moving an inch for fear of losing one word of the conversation. "I can't think of any other explanation, madam," said the chief clerk, "I hope it's nothing serious. Although on the other hand I must say that we men of business — fortunately or unfortunately — very often simply have to ignore any slight indisposition, since business must be attended to." "Well, can the chief clerk come in now?" asked Gregor's father impatiently, again knocking on the door. "No," said Gregor. In the left-hand room a painful silence followed this refusal, in the right-hand room his sister began to sob.

Why didn't his sister join the others? She was probably newly out of bed and hadn't even begun to put on her clothes yet. Well, why was she crying? Because he wouldn't get up and let the chief clerk in, because he was in danger of losing his job, and because the chief would begin dunning his parents again for the old debts? Surely these were things one didn't need to worry about for the present. Gregor was still at home and not in the least thinking of deserting the family. At the moment, true, he was lying on the carpet and no one who knew the condition he was in could seriously expect him to admit the chief clerk. But for such a small discourtesy, which could plausibly be explained away somehow later on, Gregor could hardly be dismissed on the spot. And it seemed to Gregor that it would be much more sensible to leave him in peace for the present than to trouble him with tears and entreaties. Still, of course, their uncertainty bewildered them all and excused their behavior.

"Mr. Samsa," the chief clerk called now in a louder voice, "what's the matter with you? Here you are, barricading yourself in your room, giving only 'yes' and 'no' for answers, causing your parents a lot of unnecessary trouble and neglecting — I mention this only in passing — neglecting your business duties in an incredible fashion. I am speaking here in the name of your parents and of your chief, and I beg you quite seriously to give me an immediate and precise explanation. You amaze me, you amaze me. I thought you were a quiet, dependable person, and now all at once you seem bent on making a disgraceful exhibition of yourself. The chief did hint to me early this morning a possible explanation for your disappearance — with reference to the cash payments that were entrusted to you recently — but I almost pledged my solemn word of honor that this could not be so. But now that I see how incredibly obstinate you are, I no longer have the slightest desire to take your part at all. And your position in the firm is not so unassailable. I came with the intention of telling you all this in private, but since you are wasting my time so needlessly I don't see why your parents shouldn't hear it too. For some time past your work has been most unsatisfactory; this is not the season of the year for a business boom, of course, we admit that, but a season of the year for doing no business at all, that does not exist, Mr. Samsa, must not exist."

"But, sir," cried Gregor, beside himself and in his agitation forgetting everything else, "I'm just going to open the door this very minute. A slight illness, an attack of giddiness, has kept me from getting up. I'm still lying in bed. But I feel all right again. I'm getting out of bed now. Just give me a moment or two longer! I'm not quite so well as I thought. But I'm all right, really. How a thing like that can suddenly strike one down! Only last night I was quite well, my parents can tell you, or rather I did have a slight presentiment. I must have showed some sign of it. Why didn't I report it at the office! But one always thinks that an indisposition can be got over without staying in the house. Oh sir, do spare my parents! All that you're reproaching me with now has no foundation; no one has ever said a word to me about it. Perhaps you haven't looked at the last orders I sent in. Anyhow, I can still catch the eight o'clock train, I'm much the better for my few hours' rest. Don't let me detain you here, sir; I'll be attending to business very soon, and do be good enough to tell the chief so and to make my excuses to him!"

And while all this was tumbling out pell-mell and Gregor hardly knew what he was saying, he had reached the chest quite easily, perhaps because of the practice he had had in bed, and was now trying to lever himself upright by means of it. He meant actually to open the door, actually to show himself and speak to the chief clerk; he was eager to find out what the others, after all their insistence, would say at the sight of him. If they were horrified then the responsibility was no longer his and he could stay quiet.

[handwritten notes at bottom of page:] Until this point its almost humorous that this bug still thinks he can go to work. View changes when reader realizes that he really is a bug since humans can't understand him & he hurts his mouth opening door.

But if they took it calmly, then he had no reason either to be upset, and could really get to the station for the eight o'clock train if he hurried. At first he slipped down a few times from the polished surface of the chest, but at length with a last heave he stood upright; he paid no more attention to the pains in the lower part of his body, however they smarted. Then he let himself fall against the back of a near-by chair, and clung with his little legs to the edges of it. That brought him into control of himself again and he stopped speaking, for now he could listen to what the chief clerk was saying.

"Did you understand a word of it?" the chief clerk was asking; "surely he can't be trying to make fools of us?" "Oh dear," cried his mother, in tears, "perhaps he's terribly ill and we're tormenting him. Grete! Grete!" she called out then. "Yes Mother?" called his sister from the other side. They were calling to each other across Gregor's room. "You must go this minute for the doctor. Gregor is ill. Go for the doctor, quick. Did you hear how he was speaking?" "That was no human voice," said the chief clerk in a voice noticeably low beside the shrillness of the mother's. "Anna! Anna!" his father was calling through the hall to the kitchen, clapping his hands, "get a locksmith at once!" And the two girls were already running through the hall with a swish of skirts — how could his sister have got dressed so quickly? — and were tearing the front door open. There was no sound of its closing again; they had evidently left it open, as one does in houses where some great misfortune has happened.

But Gregor was now much calmer. The words he uttered were no longer understandable, apparently, although they seemed clear enough to him, even clearer than before, perhaps because his ear had grown accustomed to the sound of them. Yet at any rate people now believed that something was wrong with him, and were ready to help him. The positive certainty with which these first measures had been taken comforted him. He felt himself drawn once more into the human circle and hoped for great and remarkable results from both the doctor and the locksmith, without really distinguishing precisely between them. To make his voice as clear as possible for the decisive conversation that was now imminent he coughed a little, as quietly as he could, of course, since this noise too might not sound like a human cough for all he was able to judge. In the next room meanwhile there was complete silence. Perhaps his parents were sitting at the table with the chief clerk, whispering, perhaps they were all leaning against the door and listening.

Slowly Gregor pushed the chair towards the door, then let go of it, caught hold of the door for support — the soles at the end of his little legs were somewhat sticky — and rested against it for a moment after his efforts. Then he set himself to turning the key in the lock with his mouth. It seemed, unhappily, that he hadn't really any teeth — what could he grip the key with? — but on the other hand his jaws were certainly very strong; with their help he did manage to set the key in motion, heedless of the fact that he was undoubtedly damaging them somewhere, since a brown fluid issued from his mouth, flowed over the key and dripped on the floor. "Just listen to that," said the chief clerk next door; "he's turning the key." That was a great encouragement to Gregor; but they should all have shouted encouragement to him, his father and mother too: "Go on, Gregor," they should have called out, "keep going, hold on to that key!" And in the belief that they were all following his efforts intently, he clenched his jaws recklessly on the key with all the force at his command. As the turning of the key progressed he circled round the lock, holding on now only with his mouth, pushing on the key, as required, or pulling it down again with all the weight of his body. The louder click of the finally yielding lock literally quickened Gregor. With a deep breath of relief he said to himself: "So I didn't need the locksmith," and laid his head on the handle to open the door wide.

Since he had to pull the door towards him, he was still invisible when it was really wide open. He had to edge himself slowly round the near half of the double door, and to do it very carefully if he was not to fall plump upon his back just on the threshold. He was still carrying out this difficult manoeuvre, with no time to observe anything else, when he heard the chief clerk utter a loud "Oh!" — it sounded like a gust of wind — and now he could see the man, standing as he was nearest to the door, clapping one hand before his open mouth and slowly backing away as if driven by some invisible steady pressure. His mother — in spite of the chief clerk's being there her hair was still undone and sticking up in all directions — first clasped her hands and looked at his father, then took two steps towards Gregor and fell on the floor among her outspread skirts, her face hidden on her breast. His father knotted his fist with a fierce expression on his face as if he meant to knock Gregor back into his room, then looked uncertainly round the living room, covered his eyes with his hands and wept till his great chest heaved.

Gregor did not go now into the living room, but leaned against the inside of the firmly shut wing of the door, so that only half his body was visible and his head above it bending sideways to look at the others. The light had meanwhile strengthened; on the other side of the street one could see clearly a section of the endlessly long, dark gray building opposite — it was a hospital — abruptly punctuated by its row of regular windows; the rain was still falling, but only in large singly discernible and literally singly splashing drops. The breakfast dishes were set out on the table lavishly, for breakfast was the most important meal of the day to Gregor's father, who lingered it out for hours over various newspapers. Right opposite Gregor on the wall hung a photograph of himself on military service, as a lieutenant, hand on sword, a carefree smile on his face, inviting one to respect his uniform and military bearing. The door leading to the hall was open, and one could see that the front door stood open too, showing the landing beyond and the beginning of the stairs going down.

"Well," said Gregor, knowing perfectly that he was the only one who had retained any composure, "I'll put my clothes on at once, pack up my samples and start off. Will you only let me go? You see, sir, I'm not obstinate, and I'm willing to work; traveling is a hard life, but I couldn't live without it. Where are you going, sir? To the office? Yes? Will you give a true account of all this? One can be temporarily incapacitated, but that's just the moment for remembering former services and bearing in mind that later on, when the incapacity has been got over, one will certainly work with all the more industry and concentration. I'm loyally bound to serve the chief, you know that very well. Besides, I have to provide for my parents and my sister. I'm in great difficulties, but I'll get out of them again. Don't make things any worse for me than they are. Stand up for me in the firm. Travelers are not popular there, I know. People think they earn sacks of money and just have a good time. A prejudice there's no particular reason for revising. But you, sir, have a more comprehensive view of affairs than the rest of the staff, yes, let me tell you in confidence, a more comprehensive view than the chief himself, who, being the owner, lets his judgment easily be swayed against one of his employees. And you know very well that the traveler, who is never seen in the office almost the whole year round, can so easily fall a victim to gossip and ill luck and unfounded complaints, which he mostly knows nothing about, except when he comes back exhausted from his rounds, and only then suffers in person from their evil consequences, which he can no longer trace back to the original causes. Sir, sir, don't go away without a word to me to show that you think me in the right at least to some extent!"

But at Gregor's very first words the chief clerk had already backed away and only stared at him with parted lips over one twitching shoulder. And while Gregor was speaking he did not stand still one moment but stole away towards the door, without taking his eyes off Gregor, yet only an inch at a time, as if obeying some secret injunction to leave the room. He was already at the hall, and the suddenness with which he took his last step out of the living room would have made one believe he had burned the sole of his foot. Once in the hall he stretched his right arm before him towards the staircase, as if some supernatural power were waiting there to deliver him.

Gregor perceived that the chief clerk must on no account be allowed to go away in this frame of mind if his position in the firm were not to be endangered to the utmost. His parents did not understand this so well; they had convinced themselves in the course of years that Gregor was settled for life in this firm, and besides they were so occupied with their immediate troubles that all foresight had forsaken them. Yet Gregor had this foresight. The chief clerk must be detained, soothed, persuaded and finally won over; the whole future of Gregor and his family depended on it! If only his sister had been there! She was intelligent; she had begun to cry while Gregor was still lying quietly on his back. And no doubt the chief clerk, so partial to ladies, would have been guided by her; she would have shut the door of the flat and in the hall talked him out of his horror. But she was not there, and

Gregor would have to handle the situation himself. And without remembering that he was still unaware what powers of movement he possessed, without even remembering that his words in all possibility, indeed in all likelihood, would again be unintelligible, he let go the wing of the door, pushed himself through the opening, started to walk towards the chief clerk, who was already ridiculously clinging with both hands to the railing on the landing; but immediately, as he was feeling for a support, he fell down with a little cry upon all his numerous legs. Hardly was he down when he experienced for the first time this morning a sense of physical comfort; his legs had firm ground under them; they were completely obedient, as he noted with joy; they even strove to carry him forward in whatever direction he chose; and he was inclined to believe that a final relief from all his sufferings was at hand. But in the same moment as he found himself on the floor, rocking with suppressed eagerness to move, not far from his mother, indeed just in front of her, she, who had seemed so completely crushed, sprang all at once to her feet, her arms and fingers outspread, cried: "Help, for God's sake, help!" bent her head down as if to see Gregor better, yet on the contrary kept backing senselessly away; had quite forgotten that the laden table stood behind her; sat upon it hastily, as if in absence of mind, when she bumped into it; and seemed altogether unaware that the big coffee pot beside her was upset and pouring coffee in a flood over the carpet.

"Mother, Mother," said Gregor in a low voice, and looked up at her. The chief clerk, for the moment, had quite slipped from his mind; instead, he could not resist snapping his jaws together at the sight of the streaming coffee. That made his mother scream again, she fled from the table and fell into the arms of his father, who hastened to catch her. But Gregor had now no time to spare for his parents; the chief clerk was already on the stairs; with his chin on the banisters he was taking one last backward look. Gregor made a spring, to be as sure as possible of overtaking him; the chief clerk must have divined his intention, for he leaped down several steps and vanished; he was still yelling "Ugh!" and it echoed through the whole staircase.

Unfortunately, the flight of the chief clerk seemed completely to upset Gregor's father, who had remained relatively calm until now, for instead of running after the man himself, or at least not hindering Gregor in his pursuit, he seized in his right hand the walking stick which the chief clerk had left behind on a chair, together with a hat and greatcoat, snatched in his left hand a large newspaper from the table and began stamping his feet and flourishing the stick and the newspaper to drive Gregor back into his room. No entreaty of Gregor's availed, indeed no entreaty was even understood, however humbly he bent his head his father only stamped on the floor the more loudly. Behind his father his mother had torn open a window, despite the cold weather, and was leaning far out of it with her face in her hands. A strong draught set in from the street to the staircase, the window curtains blew in, the newspapers on the table fluttered, stray pages whisked over the floor. Pitilessly Gregor's father drove him back, hissing and crying "Shoo!" like a savage. But Gregor was quite unpracticed in walking backwards, it really was a slow business. If he only had a chance to turn round he could get back to his room at once, but he was afraid of exasperating his father by the slowness of such a rotation and at any moment the stick in his father's hand might hit him a fatal blow on the back or on the head. In the end, however, nothing else was left for him to do since to his horror he observed that in moving backwards he could not even control the direction he took; and so, keeping an anxious eye on his father all the time over his shoulder, he began to turn round as quickly as he could, which was in reality very slowly. Perhaps his father noted his good intentions, for he did not interfere except every now and then to help him in the manoeuvre from a distance with the point of the stick. If only he would have stopped making that unbearable hissing noise! It made Gregor quite lose his head. He had turned almost completely round when the hissing noise so distracted him that he even turned a little the wrong way again. But when at last his head was fortunately right in front of the doorway, it appeared that his body was too broad simply to get through the opening. His father, of course, in his present mood was far from thinking of such a thing as opening the other half of the door, to let Gregor have enough space. He had merely the fixed idea of driving Gregor back into his room as quickly as possible. He would never have suffered Gregor to make the circumstantial preparations for standing up on end and perhaps slipping his way through the door. Maybe he was now making more noise than ever to urge Gregor forward, as if no obstacle impeded him; to Gregor, anyhow, the noise in his rear sounded no longer like the voice of one single father; this was really no joke, and Gregor thrust himself — come what might — into the doorway. One side of his body rose up, he was tilted at an angle in the doorway, his flank was quite bruised, horrid blotches stained the white door, soon he was stuck fast and, left to himself, could not have moved at all, his legs on one side fluttered trembling to the air, those on the other were crushed painfully to the floor — when from behind his father gave him a strong push which was literally a deliverance and he flew far into the room, bleeding freely. The door was slammed behind him with the stick, and then at last there was silence.

II

Not until it was twilight did Gregor awake out of a deep sleep, more like a swoon than a sleep. He would certainly have waked up of his own accord not much later, for he felt himself sufficiently rested and well-slept, but it seemed to him as if a fleeting step and a cautious shutting of the door leading into the hall had aroused him. The electric lights in the street cast a pale sheen here and there on the ceiling and the upper surfaces of the furniture, but down below, where he lay, it was dark. Slowly, awkwardly trying out his feelers, which he now first learned to appreciate, he pushed his way to the door to see what had been happening there. His left side felt like one single long, unpleasant tense scar, and he had actually to limp on his two rows of legs. One little leg, moreover, had been severely damaged in the course of that morning's events — it was almost a miracle that only one had been damaged — and trailed uselessly behind him.

He had reached the door before he discovered what had really drawn him to it: the smell of food. For there stood a basin filled with fresh milk in which floated little sops of white bread. He could almost have laughed with joy, since he was now still hungrier than in the morning, and he dipped his head almost over the eyes straight into the milk. But soon in disappointment he withdrew it again; not only did he find it difficult to feed because of his tender left side — and he could only feed with the palpitating collaboration of his whole body — he did not like the milk either, although milk had been his favorite drink and that was certainly why his sister had set it there for him, indeed it was almost with repulsion that he turned away from the basin and crawled back to the middle of the room.

He could see through the crack of the door that the gas was turned on in the living room, but while usually at this time his father made a habit of reading the afternoon newspaper in a loud voice to his mother and occasionally to his sister as well, not a sound was now to be heard. Well, perhaps his father had recently given up this habit of reading aloud, which his sister had mentioned so often in conversation and in her letters. But there was the same silence all around, although the flat was certainly not empty of occupants. "What a quiet life our family has been leading," said Gregor to himself, and as he sat there motionless staring into the darkness he felt great pride in the fact that he had been able to provide such a life for his parents and sister in such a fine flat. But what if all the quiet, the comfort, the contentment were now to end in horror? To keep himself from being lost in such thoughts Gregor took refuge in movement and crawled up and down the room.

Once during the long evening one of the side doors was opened a little and quickly shut again, later the other side door too; someone had apparently wanted to come in and then thought better of it. Gregor now stationed himself immediately before the living room door, determined to persuade any hesitating visitor to come in or at least to discover who it might be; but the door was not opened again and he waited in vain. In the early morning, when the doors were locked, they had all wanted to come in, now that he had opened one door and the other had apparently been opened during the day, no one came in and even the keys were on the other side of the doors.

It was late at night before the gas went out in the living room, and Gregor could easily tell that his parents and his sister had all stayed awake until then, for he could clearly hear the three of them stealing away on tiptoe. No one was likely to visit him, not until the morning, that was certain;

so he had plenty of time to meditate at his leisure on how he was to arrange his life afresh. But the lofty, empty room in which he had to lie flat on the floor filled him with an apprehension he could not account for, since it had been his very own room for the past five years — and with a half-unconscious action, not without a slight feeling of shame, he scuttled under the sofa, where he felt comfortable at once, although his back was a little cramped and he could not lift his head up, and his only regret was that his body was too broad to get the whole of it under the sofa.

He stayed there all night, spending the time partly in a light slumber, from which his hunger kept waking him up with a start, and partly in worrying and sketching vague hopes, which all led to the same conclusion, that he must lie low for the present and, by exercising patience, and the utmost consideration, help the family to bear the inconvenience he was bound to cause them in his present condition.

Very early in the morning, it was still almost night, Gregor had the chance to test the strength of his new resolutions, for his sister, nearly fully dressed, opened the door from the hall and peered in. She did not see him at once, yet when she caught sight of him under the sofa — well, he had to be somewhere, he couldn't have flown away, could he? — she was so startled that without being able to help it she slammed the door shut again. But as if regretting her behavior she opened the door again immediately and came in on tiptoe, as if she were visiting an invalid or even a stranger. Gregor had pushed his head forward to the very edge of the sofa and watched her. Would she notice that he had left the milk standing, and not for lack of hunger, and would she bring in some other kind of food more to his taste? If she did not do it of her own accord, he would rather starve than draw her attention to the fact, although he felt a wild impulse to dart out from under the sofa, throw himself at her feet and beg her for something to eat. But his sister at once noticed, with surprise, that the basin was still full, except for a little milk that had been spilt all around it, she lifted it immediately, not with her bare hands, true, but with a cloth and carried it away. Gregor was wildly curious to know what she would bring instead, and made various speculations about it. Yet what she actually did next, in the goodness of her heart, he could never have guessed at. To find out what he liked she brought him a whole selection of food, all set out on an old newspaper. There were old, half-decayed vegetables, bones from last night's supper covered with a white sauce that had thickened; some raisins and almonds; a piece of cheese that Gregor would have called uneatable two days ago; a dry roll of bread, a buttered roll, and a roll both buttered and salted. Besides all that, she set down again the same basin, into which she had poured some water, and which was apparently to be reserved for his exclusive use. And with fine tact, knowing that Gregor would not eat in her presence, she withdrew quickly and even turned the key, to let him understand that he could take his ease as much as he liked. Gregor's legs all whizzed towards the food. His wounds must have healed completely, moreover, for he felt no disability, which amazed him and made him reflect how more than a month ago he had cut one finger a little with a knife and had still suffered pain from the wound only the day before yesterday. Am I less sensitive now? he thought, and sucked greedily at the cheese, which above all the other edibles attracted him at once and strongly. One after another and with tears of satisfaction in his eyes he quickly devoured the cheese, the vegetables and the sauce; the fresh food, on the other hand, had no charms for him, he could not even stand the smell of it and actually dragged away to some little distance the things he could eat. He had long finished his meal and was only lying lazily on the same spot when his sister turned the key slowly as a sign for him to retreat. That roused him at once, although he was nearly asleep, and he hurried under the sofa again. But it took considerable self-control for him to stay under the sofa, even for the short time his sister was in the room, since the large meal had swollen his body somewhat and he was so cramped he could hardly breathe. Slight attacks of breathlessness afflicted him and his eyes were starting a little out of his head as he watched his unsuspecting sister sweeping together with a broom not only the remains of what he had eaten but even the things he had not touched, as if these were now of no use to anyone, and hastily shoveling it all into a bucket, which she covered with a wooden lid and carried away. Hardly had she turned her back when Gregor came from under the sofa and stretched and puffed himself out.

In this manner Gregor was fed, once in the early morning while his parents and the servant girl were still asleep, and a second time after they had all had their midday dinner, for then his parents took a short nap and the servant girl could be sent out on some errand or other by his sister. Not that they would have wanted him to starve, of course, but perhaps they could not have borne to know more about his feeding than from hearsay, perhaps too his sister wanted to spare them such little anxieties wherever possible, since they had quite enough to bear as it was.

Under what pretext the doctor and the locksmith had been got rid of on that first morning Gregor could not discover, for since what he had said was not understood by the others it never struck any of them, not even his sister, that he could understand what they said, and so whenever his sister came into his room he had to content himself with hearing her utter only a sigh now and then and an occasional appeal to the saints. Later on, when she had got a little used to the situation — of course she could never get completely used to it — she sometimes threw out a remark which was kindly meant or could be so interpreted. "Well, he liked his dinner today," she would say when Gregor had made a good clearance of his food; and when he had not eaten, which gradually happened more and more often, she would say almost sadly: "Everything's been left standing again."

But although Gregor could get no news directly, he overheard a lot from the neighboring rooms, and as soon as voices were audible, he would run to the door of the room concerned and press his whole body against it.

In the first few days especially there was no conversation that did not refer to him somehow, even if only indirectly. For two whole days there were family consultations at every mealtime about what should be done; but also between meals the same subject was discussed, for there were always at least two members of the family at home, since no one wanted to be alone in the flat and to leave it quite empty was unthinkable. And on the very first of these days the household cook — it was not quite clear what and how much she knew of the situation — went down on her knees to his mother and begged leave to go, and when she departed, a quarter of an hour later, gave thanks for her dismissal with tears in her eyes as if for the greatest benefit that could have been conferred on her, and without any prompting swore a solemn oath that she would never say a single word to anyone about what had happened.

Now Gregor's sister had to cook too, helping her mother; true, the cooking did not amount to much, for they ate scarcely anything. Gregor was always hearing one of the family vainly urging another to eat and getting no answer but: "Thanks, I've had all I want," or something similar. Perhaps they drank nothing either. Time and again his sister kept asking his father if he wouldn't like some beer and offered kindly to go and fetch it herself, and when he made no answer suggested that she could ask the concierge to fetch it, so that he need feel no sense of obligation, but then a round "No" came from his father and no more was said about it.

In the course of that very first day Gregor's father explained the family's financial position and prospects to both his mother and his sister. Now and then he rose from the table to get some voucher or memorandum out of the small safe he had rescued from the collapse of his business five years earlier. One could hear him opening the complicated lock and rustling papers out and shutting it again. This statement made by his father was the first cheerful information Gregor had heard since his imprisonment. He had been of the opinion that nothing at all was left over from his father's business, at least his father had never said anything to the contrary, and of course he had not asked him directly. At the time Gregor's sole desire was to do his utmost to help the family to forget as soon as possible the catastrophe which had overwhelmed the business and thrown them all into a state of complete despair. And so he had set to work with unusual ardor and almost overnight had become a commercial traveler instead of a little clerk, with of course much greater chances of earning money, and his success was immediately translated into good round coin which he could lay on the table for his amazed and happy family. These had been fine times, and they had never recurred, at least not with the same sense of glory, although later on Gregor had earned so much money that he was able to meet the expenses of the whole household and did so. They had simply got used to it, both the family and Gregor; the money was gratefully accepted and gladly given, but there was no special uprush of warm feeling. With his sister alone had he remained intimate, and it was a secret plan of his that she, who loved music, unlike himself, and could play movingly on the violin, should be sent next year to study at the Conservatorium, despite the great expense that would entail, which must be made up in some other way. During his brief visits home the Conservatorium was often mentioned in the talks he had with his sister, but always merely as a beautiful dream which could never come true, and his parents discouraged even these innocent references to it; yet Gregor had made up his mind firmly about it and meant to announce the fact with due solemnity on Christmas Day.

Such were the thoughts, completely futile in his present condition, that went through his head as he stood clinging upright to the door and listening. Sometimes out of sheer weariness he had to give up listening and let his head fall negligently against the door, but he always had to pull himself together again at once, for even the slight sound his head made was audible next door and brought all conversation to a stop. "What can he be doing now?" his father would say after a while, obviously turning towards the door, and only then would the interrupted conversation gradually be set going again.

Gregor was now informed as amply as he could wish — for his father tended to repeat himself in his explanations, partly because it was a long time since he had handled such matters and partly because his mother could not always grasp things at once — that a certain amount of investments, a very small amount it was true, had survived the wreck of their fortunes and had even increased a little because the dividends had not been touched meanwhile. And besides that, the money Gregor brought home every month — he had kept only a few dollars for himself — had never been quite used up and now amounted to a small capital sum. Behind the door Gregor nodded his head eagerly, rejoiced at this evidence of unexpected thrift and foresight. True, he could really have paid off some more of his father's debts to the chief with his extra money, and so brought much nearer the day on which he could quit his job, but doubtless it was better the way his father had arranged it.

Yet this capital was by no means sufficient to let the family live on the interest of it; for one year, perhaps, or at the most two, they could live on the principal, that was all. It was simply a sum that ought not to be touched and should be kept for a rainy day; money for living expenses would have to be earned. Now his father was still hale enough but an old man, and he had done no work for the past five years and could not be expected to do much; during these five years, the first years of leisure in his laborious though unsuccessful life, he had grown rather fat and become sluggish. And Gregor's old mother, how was she to earn a living with her asthma, which troubled her even when she walked through the flat and kept her lying on a sofa every other day panting for breath beside an open window? And was his sister to earn her bread, she who was still a child of seventeen and whose life hitherto had been so pleasant, consisting as it did in dressing herself nicely, sleeping long, helping in the housekeeping, going out to a few modest en-

tertainments and above all playing the violin? At first whenever the need for
earning money was mentioned Gregor let go his hold on the door and threw
himself down on the cool leather sofa beside it, he felt so hot with shame
and grief.

Often he just lay there the long nights through without sleeping at all,
scrabbling for hours on the leather. Or he nerved himself to the great effort
of pushing an armchair to the window, then crawled up over the window
sill and, braced against the chair, leaned against the window panes, obviously in some recollection of the sense of freedom that looking out of a
window always used to give him. For in reality day by day things that were
even a little way off were growing dimmer to his sight; the hospital across
the street, which he used to execrate for being all too often before his eyes,
was now quite beyond his range of vision, and if he had not known that he
lived in Charlotte Street, a quiet street but still a city street, he might have
believed that his window gave on a desert waste where gray sky and gray
land blended indistinguishably into each other. His quick-witted sister only
needed to observe twice that the armchair stood by the window; after that
whenever she had tidied the room she always pushed the chair back to the
same place at the window and even left the inner casements open.

If he could have spoken to her and thanked her for all she had to do
for him, he could have borne her ministrations better; as it was, they oppressed him. She certainly tried to make as light as possible of whatever was
disagreeable in her task, and as time went on she succeeded, of course, more
and more, but time brought more enlightenment to Gregor too. The very
way she came in distressed him. Hardly was she in the room when she
rushed to the window, without even taking time to shut the door, careful as
she was usually to shield the sight of Gregor's room from the others, and as
if she were almost suffocating tore the casements open with hasty fingers,
standing then in the open draught for a while even in the bitterest cold and
drawing deep breaths. This noisy scurry of hers upset Gregor twice a day; he
would crouch trembling under the sofa all the time, knowing quite well that
she would certainly have spared him such a disturbance had she found it at
all possible to stay in his presence without opening a window.

On one occasion, about a month after Gregor's metamorphosis, when
there was surely no reason for her to be still startled at his appearance, she
came a little earlier than usual and found him gazing out of the window,
quite motionless, and thus well placed to look like a bogey. Gregor would
not have been surprised had she not come in at all, for she could not immediately open the window while he was there, but not only did she retreat,
she jumped back as if in alarm and banged the door shut; a stranger might
well have thought that he had been lying in wait for her there meaning to
bite her. Of course he hid himself under the sofa at once, but he had to wait
until midday before she came again, and she seemed more ill at ease than
usual. This made him realize how repulsive the sight of him still was to her,
and that it was bound to go on being repulsive, and what an effort it must

cost her not to run away even from the sight of the small portion of his body that stuck out from under the sofa. In order to spare her that, therefore, one day he carried a sheet on his back to the sofa — it cost him four hours' labor — and arranged it there in such a way as to hide him completely, so that even if she were to bend down she could not see him. Had she considered the sheet unnecessary, she would certainly have stripped it off the sofa again, for it was clear enough that this curtaining and confining of himself was not likely to conduce Gregor's comfort, but she left it where it was, and Gregor even fancied that he caught a thankful glance from her eye when he lifted the sheet carefully a very little with his head to see how she was taking the new arrangement.

For the first fortnight his parents could not bring themselves to the point of entering his room, and he often heard them expressing their appreciation of his sister's activities, whereas formerly they had frequently scolded her for being as they thought a somewhat useless daughter. But now, both of them often waited outside the door, his father and his mother, while his sister tidied his room, and as soon as she came out she had to tell them exactly how things were in the room, what Gregor had eaten, how he had conducted himself this time and whether there was not perhaps some slight improvement in his condition. His mother, moreover, began relatively soon to want to visit him, but his father and sister dissuaded her at first with arguments which Gregor listened to very attentively and altogether approved. Later, however, she had to be held back by main force, and when she cried out: "Do let me in to Gregor, he is my unfortunate son! Can't you understand that I must go to him?" Gregor thought that it might be well to have her come in, not every day, of course, but perhaps once a week; she understood things, after all, much better than his sister, who was only a child despite the efforts she was making and had perhaps taken on so difficult a task merely out of childish thoughtlessness.

Gregor's desire to see his mother was soon fulfilled. During the daytime he did not want to show himself at the window, out of consideration for his parents, but he could not crawl very far around the few square yards of floor space he had, nor could he bear lying quietly at rest all during the night, while he was fast losing any interest he had ever taken in food, so that for mere recreation he had formed the habit of crawling crisscross over the walls and ceiling. He especially enjoyed hanging suspended from the ceiling; it was much better than lying on the floor; one could breathe more freely; one's body swung and rocked lightly; and in the almost blissful absorption induced by this suspension it could happen to his own surprise that he let go and fell plump on the floor. Yet he now had his body much better under control than formerly, and even such a big fall did him no harm. His sister at once remarked the new distraction Gregor had found for himself — he left traces behind him of the sticky stuff on his soles wherever he crawled — and she got the idea in her head of giving him as wide a field as possible to crawl in and of removing the pieces of furniture that hindered him, above all the chest of drawers and the writing desk. But that was more than she could manage all by herself; she did not dare ask her father to help her; and as for the servant girl, a young creature of sixteen who had had the courage to stay on after the cook's departure, she could not be asked to help, for she had begged as an especial favor that she might keep the kitchen door locked and open it only on a definite summons; so there was nothing left but to apply to her mother at an hour when her father was out. And the old lady did come, with exclamations of joyful eagerness, which, however, died away at the door of Gregor's room. Gregor's sister, of course, went in first, to see that everything was in order before letting his mother enter. In great haste Gregor pulled the sheet lower and rucked it more in folds so that it really looked as if it had been thrown accidentally over the sofa. And this time he did not peer out from under it; he renounced the pleasure of seeing his mother on this occasion and was only glad that she had come at all. "Come in, he's out of sight," said his sister, obviously leading her mother in by the hand. Gregor could now hear the two women struggling to shift the heavy old chest from its place, and his sister claiming the greater part of the labor for herself, without listening to the admonitions of her mother who feared she might overstrain herself. It took a long time. After at least a quarter of an hour's tugging his mother objected that the chest had better be left where it was, for in the first place it was too heavy and could never be got out before his father came home, and standing in the middle of the room like that it would only hamper Gregor's movements, while in the second place it was not at all certain that removing the furniture would be doing a service to Gregor. She was inclined to think to the contrary; the sight of the naked walls made her own heart heavy, and why shouldn't Gregor have the same feeling, considering that he had been used to his furniture for so long and might feel forlorn without it. "And doesn't it look," she concluded in a low voice — in fact she had been almost whispering all the time as if to avoid letting Gregor, whose exact whereabouts she did not know, hear even the tones of her voice, for she was convinced that he could not understand her words — "doesn't it look as if we were showing him, by taking away his furniture, that we have given up hope of his ever getting better and are just leaving him coldly to himself? I think it would be best to keep his room exactly as it has always been, so that when he comes back to us he will find everything unchanged and be able all the more easily to forget what has happened in between."

On hearing these words from his mother Gregor realized that the lack of all direct human speech for the past two months together with the monotony of family life must have confused his mind, otherwise he could not account for the fact that he had quite earnestly looked forward to having his room emptied of furnishing. Did he really want his warm room, so comfortably fitted with old family furniture, to be turned into a naked den in which he would certainly be able to crawl unhampered in all directions but at the price of shedding simultaneously all recollection of his human background? He had indeed been so near the brink of forgetfulness that only the voice of his mother, which he had not heard for so long, had drawn him back from it. Nothing should be taken out of his room; everything must stay as it was; he could not dispense with the good influence of the furniture on his state of mind; and even if the furniture did hamper him in his sense-less crawling round and round, that was no drawback but a great advantage.

Unfortunately his sister was of the contrary opinion; she had grown accustomed, and not without reason, to consider herself an expert in Gre-gor's affairs as against her parents, and so her mother's advice was now enough to make her determined on the removal not only of the chest and the writing desk, which had been her first intention, but of all the furniture except the indispensable sofa. This determination was not, of course, merely the outcome of childish recalcitrance and of the self-confidence she had recently developed so unexpectedly and at such cost; she had in fact perceived that Gregor needed a lot of space to crawl about in, while on the other hand he never used the furniture at all, so far as could be seen. An-other factor might have been also the enthusiastic temperament of an ado-lescent girl, which seeks to indulge itself on every opportunity and which now tempted Grete to exaggerate the horror of her brother's circumstances in order that she might do all the more for him. In a room where Gregor lorded it all alone over empty walls no one save herself was likely ever to set foot.

And so she was not to be moved from her resolve by her mother who seemed moreover to be ill at ease in Gregor's room and therefore unsure of herself, was soon reduced to silence and helped her daughter as best she could to push the chest outside. Now, Gregor could do without the chest, if need be, but the writing desk he must retain. As soon as the two women had got the chest out of his room, groaning as they pushed it, Gregor stuck his head out from under the sofa to see how he might intervene as kindly and cautiously as possible. But as bad luck would have it, his mother was the first to return, leaving Grete clasping the chest in the room next door where she was trying to shift it all by herself, without of course moving it from the spot. His mother however was not accustomed to the sight of him, it might sicken her and so in alarm Gregor backed quickly to the other end of the sofa, yet could not prevent the sheet from swaying a little in front. That was enough to put her on the alert. She paused, stood still for a mo-ment and then went back to Grete.

Although Gregor kept reassuring himself that nothing out of the way was happening, but only a few bits of furniture were being changed round, he soon had to admit that all this trotting to and fro of the two women, their little ejaculations and the scraping of furniture along the floor affected him like a vast disturbance coming from all sides at once, and however much he tucked in his head and legs and cowered to the very floor he was bound to confess that he would not be able to stand it for long. They were clearing his room out; taking away everything he loved; the chest in which he kept his fret saw and other tools was already dragged off; they were now loosening the writing desk which had almost sunk into the floor, the desk at which he had done all his homework when he was at the commercial academy, at the grammar school before that, and, yes, even at the primary school — he had no more time to waste in weighing the good intentions of the two women, whose existence he had by now almost forgotten, for they were so exhausted that they were laboring in silence and nothing could be heard but the heavy scuffling of their feet.

And so he rushed out — the women were just leaning against the writing desk in the next room to give themselves a breather — and four times changed his direction, since he really did not know what to rescue first, then on the wall opposite, which was already otherwise cleared, he was struck by the picture of the lady muffled in so much fur and quickly crawled up to it and pressed himself to the glass, which was a good surface to hold on to and comforted his hot belly. This picture at least, which was entirely hidden beneath him, was going to be removed by nobody. He turned his head towards the door of the living room so as to observe the women when they came back.

They had not allowed themselves much of a rest and were already coming; Grete had twined her arm round her mother and was almost supporting her. "Well, what shall we take now?" said Grete, looking round. Her eyes met Gregor's from the wall. She kept her composure, presumably because of her mother, bent her head down to her mother, to keep her from looking up, and said, although in a fluttering, unpremeditated voice: "Come, hadn't we better go back to the living room for a moment?" Her intentions were clear enough to Gregor, she wanted to bestow her mother in safety and then chase him down from the wall. Well, just let her try it! He clung to his picture and would not give it up. He would rather fly in Grete's face.

But Grete's words had succeeded in disquieting her mother, who took a step to one side, caught sight of the huge brown mass on the flowered wallpaper, and before she was really conscious that what she saw was Gregor screamed in a loud, hoarse voice: "Oh God, oh God!" fell with outspread arms over the sofa as if giving up and did not move. "Gregor!" cried his sister, shaking her fist and glaring at him. This was the first time she had directly addressed him since his metamorphosis. She ran into the next room for some aromatic essence with which to rouse her mother from her fainting fit. Gregor wanted to help too — there was still time to rescue the picture — but he was stuck fast to the glass and had to tear himself loose; he then ran after his sister into the next room as if he could advise her, as he used to do; but then had to stand helplessly behind her; she meanwhile searched among various small bottles and when she turned round started in alarm at the sight of him; one bottle fell on the floor and broke; a splinter of glass cut Gregor's face and some kind of corrosive medicine splashed him; without pausing a moment longer Grete gathered up all the bottles she could carry and ran to her mother with them; she banged the door shut with her foot. Gregor was now cut off from his mother, who was perhaps nearly dying because of him; he dared not open the door for fear of frightening away his sister, who had to stay with her mother; there was nothing he could do but wait; and harassed by self-reproach and worry he began now to crawl to and fro, over everything, walls, furniture and ceiling, and finally in his despair, when the whole room seemed to be reeling round him, fell down on to the middle of the big table.

A little while elapsed, Gregor was still lying there feebly and all around was quiet, perhaps that was a good omen. Then the doorbell rang. The servant girl was of course locked in her kitchen, and Grete would have to open the door. It was his father. "What's been happening?" were his first words; Grete's face must have told him everything. Grete answered in a muffled voice, apparently hiding her head on his breast: "Mother has been fainting, but she's better now. Gregor's broken loose." "Just what I expected," said his father, "just what I've been telling you, but you women would never listen." It was clear to Gregor that his father had taken the worst interpretation of Grete's all too brief statement and was assuming that Gregor had been guilty of some violent act. Therefore Gregor must now try to propitiate his father, since he had neither time nor means for an explanation. And so he fled to the door of his own room and crouched against it, to let his father see as soon as he came in from the hall that his son had the good intention of getting back into his room immediately and that it was not necessary to drive him there, but that if only the door were opened he would disappear at once.

Yet his father was not in the mood to perceive such fine distinctions. "Ah!" he cried as soon as he appeared, in a tone which sounded at once angry and exultant. Gregor drew his head back from the door and lifted it to look at his father. Truly, this was not the father he had imagined to himself; admittedly he had been too absorbed of late in his new recreation of crawling over the ceiling to take the same interest as before in what was happening elsewhere in the flat, and he ought really to be prepared for some changes. And yet, and yet, could that be his father? The man who used to lie wearily sunk in bed whenever Gregor set out on a business journey; who welcomed him back of an evening lying in a long chair in a dressing gown; who could not really rise to his feet but only lifted his arms in greeting, and on the rare occasions when he did go out with his family, on one or two Sundays a year and on high holidays, walked between Gregor and his mother, who were slow walkers anyhow, even more slowly than they did, muffled in his old greatcoat, shuffling laboriously forward with the help of his crook-handled stick which he set down most cautiously at every step and, whenever he wanted to say anything, nearly always came to a full stop and gathered his escort around him? Now he was standing there in fine shape; dressed in a smart blue uniform with gold buttons, such as bank messengers wear; his strong double chin bulged over the stiff high collar of his jacket; from under his bushy eyebrows his black eyes darted fresh and penetrating glances; his onetime tangled white hair had been combed flat on either side of a shining and carefully exact parting. He pitched his cap, which bore a gold monogram, probably the badge of some bank, in a wide sweep across the whole room on to a sofa and with the tail-ends of his jacket thrown back, his hands in his trouser pockets, advanced with a grim visage towards Gregor. Likely enough he did not himself know what he meant to do; at any rate he lifted his feet uncommonly high, and Gregor was dumbfounded at the enormous size of his shoe soles. But Gregor could not risk standing up to him, aware as he had been from the very first day of his new life that his father believed only the severest measures suitable for dealing with him. And so he ran before his father, stopping when he stopped and scuttling forward again when his father made any kind of move. In this way they circled the room several times without anything decisive happening; indeed the whole operation did not even look like a pursuit because it was carried out so slowly. And so Gregor did not leave the floor, for he feared that his father might take as a piece of peculiar wickedness any excursion of his over the walls or the ceiling. All the same, he could not stay this course much longer, for while his father took one step he had to carry out a whole series of movements. He was already beginning to feel breathless, just as in his former life his lungs had not been very dependable. As he was staggering along, trying to concentrate his energy on running, hardly keeping his eyes open; in his dazed state never even thinking of any other escape than simply going forward; and having almost forgotten that the walls were free to him, which in this room were well provided with finely carved pieces of furniture full of knobs and crevices — suddenly something lightly flung landed close behind him and rolled before him. It was an apple; a second apple followed immediately; Gregor came to a stop in alarm; there was no point in running on, for his father was determined to bombard him. He had filled his pockets with fruit from the dish on the sideboard and was now shying apple after apple, without taking particularly good aim for the moment. The small red apples rolled about the floor as if magnetized and cannoned into each other. An apple thrown without much force grazed Gregor's back and glanced off harmlessly. But another following immediately landed right on his back and sank in; Gregor wanted to drag himself forward, as if this startling, incredible pain could be left behind him: but he felt as if nailed to the spot and flattened himself out in a complete derangement of all his senses. With his last conscious look he saw the door of his room being torn open and his mother rushing out ahead of his screaming sister, in her underbodice, for her daughter had loosened her clothing to let her breathe more freely and recover from her swoon, he saw his mother rushing towards his father, leaving one after another behind her on the floor her loosened petticoats, stumbling over her petticoats straight to his father and embracing him, in complete union with him — but here Gregor's sight began to fail — with her hands clasped round his father's neck as she begged for her son's life.

III

The serious injury done to Gregor, which disabled him for more than a month — the apple went on sticking in his body as a visible reminder, since no one ventured to remove it — seemed to have made even his father recollect that Gregor was a member of the family, despite his present unfortunate and repulsive shape, and ought not to be treated as an enemy, that, on the contrary, family duty required the suppression of disgust and the exercise of patience, nothing but patience.

And although his injury had impaired, probably for ever, his power of movement, and for the time being it took him long, long minutes to creep across his room like an old invalid — there was no question now of crawling up the wall — yet in his own opinion he was sufficiently compensated for this worsening of his condition by the fact that towards evening the living-room door, which he used to watch intently for an hour or two beforehand, was always thrown open, so that lying in the darkness of his room, invisible to the family, he could see them all at the lamp-lit table and listen to their talk, by general consent as it were, very different from his earlier eavesdropping.

True, their intercourse lacked the lively character of former times, which he had always called to mind with a certain wistfulness in the small hotel bedrooms where he had been wont to throw himself down, tired out, on damp bedding. They were now mostly very silent. Soon after supper his father would fall asleep in his armchair; his mother and sister would admonish each other to be silent; his mother, bending low over the lamp, stitched at fine sewing for an underwear firm; his sister, who had taken a job as a salesgirl, was learning shorthand and French in the evenings on the chance of bettering herself. Sometimes his father woke up, and as if quite unaware that he had been sleeping said to his mother: "What a lot of sewing you're doing today!" and at once fell asleep again, while the two women exchanged a tired smile.

With a kind of mulishness his father persisted in keeping his uniform on even in the house; his dressing gown hung uselessly on its peg and he slept fully dressed where he sat, as if he were ready for service at any moment and even here only at the beck and call of his superior. As a result, his uniform, which was not brand-new to start with, began to look dirty, despite all the loving care of the mother and sister to keep it clean, and Gregor often spent whole evenings gazing at the many greasy spots on the garment, gleaming with gold buttons always in a high state of polish, in which the old man sat sleeping in extreme discomfort and yet quite peacefully.

As soon as the clock struck ten his mother tried to rouse his father with gentle words and to persuade him after that to get into bed, for sitting there he could not have a proper sleep and that was what he needed most, since he had to go to duty at six. But with the mulishness that had obsessed him since he became a bank messenger he always insisted on staying longer at the table, although he regularly fell asleep again and in the end only with the greatest trouble could be got out of his armchair and into his bed. However insistently Gregor's mother and sister kept urging him with gentle reminders, he would go on slowly shaking his head for a quarter of an hour, keeping his eyes shut, and refuse to get to his feet. The mother plucked at his sleeve, whispering endearments in his ear, the sister left her lessons to come to her mother's help, but Gregor's father was not to be caught. He would only sink down deeper in his chair. Not until the two women hoisted him up by the armpits did he open his eyes and look at them both, one after the other, usually with the remark: "This is a life. This is the peace and quiet of my old age." And leaning on the two of them he would heave himself up, with difficulty, as if he were a great burden to himself, suffer them to lead him as far as the door and then wave them off and go on alone, while the mother abandoned her needlework and the sister her pen in order to run after him and help him farther.

Who could find time, in this overworked and tired-out family, to bother about Gregor more than was absolutely needful? The household was reduced more and more; the servant girl was turned off; a gigantic bony charwoman with white hair flying round her head came in morning and evening to do the rough work; everything else was done by Gregor's mother, as well as great piles of sewing. Even various family ornaments, which his mother and sister used to wear with pride at parties and celebrations, had to be sold, as Gregor discovered of an evening from hearing them all discuss the prices obtained. But what they lamented most was the fact that they could not leave the flat which was much too big for their present circumstances, because they could not think of any way to shift Gregor. Yet Gregor saw well enough that consideration for him was not the main difficulty preventing the removal, for they could have easily shifted him in some suitable box with a few air holes in it; what really kept them from moving into another flat was rather their own complete hopelessness and the belief that they had been singled out for a misfortune such as had never happened to any of their relations or acquaintances. They fulfilled to the uttermost all that the world demands of poor people, the father fetched breakfast for the small clerks in the bank, the mother devoted her energy to making underwear for strangers, the sister trotted to and fro behind the counter at the behest of customers, but more than this they had not the strength to do. And the wound in Gregor's back began to nag at him afresh when his mother and sister, after getting his father into bed, came back again, left their work lying, drew close to each other and sat cheek by cheek; when his mother, pointing towards his room, said: "Shut that door now, Grete," and he was left again in darkness, while next door the women mingled their tears or perhaps sat dry-eyed staring at the table.

Gregor hardly slept at all by night or by day. He was often haunted by the idea that next time the door opened he would take the family's affairs in hand again just as he used to do; once more, after this long interval, there appeared in his thoughts the figures of the chief and the chief clerk, the commercial travelers and the apprentices, the porter who was so dull-witted, two or three friends in other firms, a chambermaid in one of the rural hotels, a sweet and fleeting memory, a cashier in a milliner's shop, whom he had wooed earnestly but too slowly — they all appeared, together with strangers or people he had quite forgotten, but instead of helping him and his family they were one and all unapproachable and he was glad when they vanished. At other times he would not be in the mood to bother about his family, he was only filled with rage at the way they were neglecting him, and although he had no clear idea of what he might care to eat he would make plans for getting into the larder to take the food that was after all his due, even if he were not hungry. His sister no longer took thought to bring him what might especially please him, but in the morning and at noon before she went to business hurriedly pushed into his room with her foot any food that was available, and in the evening cleared it out again with one sweep of the broom, heedless of whether it had been merely tasted, or — as most frequently happened — left untouched. The cleaning of his room, which she now did always in the evenings, could not have been more hastily done. Streaks of dirt stretched along the walls, here and there lay balls of dust and filth. At first Gregor used to station himself in some particularly filthy corner when his sister arrived, in order to reproach her with it, so to speak. But he could have sat there for weeks without getting her to make any improvements; she could see the dirt as well as he did, but she had simply made up her mind to leave it alone. And yet, with a touchiness that was new to her, which seemed anyhow to have infected the whole family, she jealously guarded her claim to be the sole caretaker of Gregor's room. His mother once subjected his room to a thorough cleaning, which was achieved only by means of several buckets of water — all this dampness of course upset Gregor too and he lay widespread, sulky and motionless on the sofa — but she was well punished for it. Hardly had his sister noticed the changed aspect of his room than she rushed in high dudgeon into the living room and, despite the imploringly raised hands of her mother, burst into a storm of weeping, while her parents — her father had of course been startled out of his chair — looked on at first in helpless amazement; then they too began to go into action; the father reproached the mother on his right for not having left the cleaning of Gregor's room to his sister; shrieked at the sister on his left that never again was she to be allowed to clean Gregor's room; while the mother tried to pull the father into his bedroom, since he was beyond himself with agitation; the sister, shaken with sobs, then beat upon the table with her small fists; and Gregor hissed loudly with rage because not one of them thought of shutting the door to spare him such a spectacle and so much noise.

Still, even if the sister, exhausted by her daily work, had grown tired of looking after Gregor as she did formerly, there was no need for his mother's intervention or for Gregor's being neglected at all. The charwoman was there. This old widow, whose strong bony frame had enabled her to survive the worst a long life could offer, by no means recoiled from Gregor. Without being in the least curious she had once by chance opened the door of his room and at the sight of Gregor, who, taken by surprise, began to rush to and fro although no one was chasing him, merely stood there with her arms folded. From that time she never failed to open his door a little for a moment, morning and evening, to have a look at him. At first she even used to call him to her, with words which apparently she took to be friendly, such as: "Come along, then, you old dung beetle!" or "Look at the old dung beetle, then!" To such allocutions Gregor made no answer, but stayed motionless where he was, as if the door had never been opened. Instead of being allowed to disturb him so senselessly whenever the whim took her, she should rather have been ordered to clean out his room daily, that charwoman! Once, early in the morning — heavy rain was lashing on the windowpanes, perhaps a sign that spring was on the way — Gregor was so exasperated when she began addressing him again that he ran at her, as if to attack her, although slowly and feebly enough. But the charwoman instead of showing fright merely lifted high a chair that happened to be beside the door, and as she stood there with her mouth wide open it was clear that she meant to shut it only when she brought the chair down on Gregor's back. "So you're not coming any nearer?" she asked, as Gregor turned away again, and quietly put the chair back into the corner.

Gregor was now eating hardly anything. Only when he happened to pass the food laid out for him did he take a bit of something in his mouth as a pastime, kept it there for an hour at a time and usually spat it out again. At first he thought it was chagrin over the state of his room that prevented him from eating, yet he soon got used to the various changes in his room. It had become a habit in the family to push into his room things there was no room for elsewhere, and there were plenty of these now, since one of the rooms had been let to three lodgers. These serious gentlemen — all three of them with full beards, as Gregor once observed through a crack in the door — had a passion for order, not only in their own room but, since they were now members of the household, in all its arrangements, especially in the kitchen. Superfluous, not to say dirty, objects they could not bear. Besides, they had brought with them most of the furnishings they needed. For this reason many things could be dispensed with that it was no use trying to sell but that should not be thrown away either. All of them found their way into Gregor's room. The ash can likewise and the kitchen garbage can. Anything that was not needed for the moment was simply flung into Gregor's room by the charwoman, who did everything in a hurry; fortunately Gregor usually saw only the object, whatever it was, and the hand that held it. Perhaps she intended to take the things away again as time and opportunity offered, or to collect them until she could throw them all out in a heap, but in fact they just lay whenever she happened to throw them, except when Gregor pushed his way through the junk heap and shifted it somewhat, at first out of necessity, because he had not room enough to crawl, but later with increasing enjoyment, although after such excursions, being sad and weary to death, he would lie motionless for hours. And since the lodgers often ate their supper at home in the common living room, the living-room door stayed shut many an evening, yet Gregor reconciled himself quite easily to the shutting of the door, for often enough on evenings when it was opened he had disregarded it entirely and lain in the darkest corner of his room, quite unnoticed by the family. But on one occasion the charwoman left the door open a little and it stayed ajar even when the lodgers came in for supper and the lamp was lit. They set themselves at the top end of the table where formerly Gregor and his father and mother had eaten their meals, unfolded their napkins and took knife and fork in hand. At once his mother appeared in the other doorway with a dish of meat and close behind her his sister with a dish of potatoes piled high. The food steamed with a thick vapor. The lodgers bent over the food set before them as if to scrutinize it before eating, in fact the man in the middle, who seemed to pass for an authority with the other two, cut a piece of meat as it lay on the dish, obviously to discover if it were tender or should be sent back to the kitchen. He showed satisfaction, and Gregor's mother and sister, who had been watching anxiously, breathed freely and began to smile.

The family itself took its meals in the kitchen. Nonetheless, Gregor's father came into the living room before going into the kitchen and with one prolonged bow, cap in hand, made a round of the table. The lodgers all stood up and murmured something in their beards. When they were alone again they ate their food in almost complete silence. It seemed remarkable to Gregor that among the various noises coming from the table he could always distinguish the sound of their masticating teeth, as if this were a sign to Gregor that one needed teeth in order to eat, and that with toothless jaws even of the finest make one could do nothing. "I'm hungry enough," said Gregor sadly to himself, "But not for that kind of food. How these lodgers are stuffing themselves, and here am I dying of starvation!"

On that very evening — during the whole of his time there Gregor could not remember ever having heard the violin — the sound of violin-playing came from the kitchen. The lodgers had already finished their supper, the one in the middle had brought out a newspaper and given the other two a page apiece, and now they were leaning back at ease reading and smoking. When the violin began to play they pricked up their ears, got to their feet, and went on tiptoe to the hall door where they stood huddled together. Their movements must have been heard in the kitchen, for Gregor's father called out: "Is the violin-playing disturbing you, gentlemen? It can be stopped at once." "On the contrary," said the middle lodger, "could not Fräulein Samsa come and play in this room, beside us, where it is much more convenient and comfortable?" "Oh certainly," cried Gregor's father, as if he were the violin-player. The lodgers came back into the living room and waited. Presently Gregor's father arrived with the music stand, his mother carrying the music and his sister with the violin. His sister quietly made everything ready to start playing; his parents, who had never let rooms before and so had an exaggerated idea of the courtesy due to lodgers, did not venture to sit down on their own chairs; his father leaned against the door, the right hand thrust between two buttons of his livery coat, which was formally buttoned up; but his mother was offered a chair by one of the lodgers and, since she left the chair just where he had happened to put it, sat down in a corner to one side.

Gregor's sister began to play; the father and mother, from either side, intently watched the movements of her hands. Gregor, attracted by the playing, ventured to move forward a little until his head was actually inside the living room. He felt hardly any surprise at his growing lack of consideration for the others; there had been a time when he prided himself on being considerate. And yet just on this occasion he had more reason than ever to hide himself, since owing to the amount of dust which lay thick in his room and rose into the air at the slightest movement, he too was covered with dust; fluff and hair and remnants of food trailed with him, caught on his back and along his sides; his indifference to everything was much too great for him to turn on his back and scrape himself clean on the carpet, as once he had done several times a day. And in spite of his condition, no shame deterred him from advancing a little over the spotless floor of the living room.

To be sure, no one was aware of him. The family was entirely absorbed in the violin-playing; the lodgers, however, who first of all had stationed themselves, hands in pockets, much too close behind the music stand so that they could all have read the music, which must have bothered his sister, had soon retreated to the window, half-whispering with downbent heads, and stayed there while his father turned an anxious eye on them. Indeed, they were making it more than obvious that they had been disappointed in their expectation of hearing good or enjoyable violin-playing, that they had had more than enough of the performance and only out of courtesy suffered a continued disturbance of their peace. From the way they all kept blowing the smoke of their cigars high in the air through nose and mouth one could divine their irritation. And yet Gregor's sister was playing so beautifully. Her face leaned sideways, intently and sadly her eyes followed the notes of music. Gregor crawled a little farther forward and lowered his head to the ground so that it might be possible for his eyes to meet hers. Was he an animal, that music had such an effect upon him? He felt as if the way were opening before him to the unknown nourishment he craved. He was determined to push forward till he reached his sister, to pull at her skirt and so let her know that she was to come into his room with her violin, for no one here appreciated her playing as he would appreciate it. He would never let her out of his room, at least, not so long as he lived; his frightful appearance would become, for the first time, useful to him; he would watch all the doors of his room at once and spit at intruders; but his sister should need no constraint, she should stay with him of her own free will; she should sit beside him on the sofa, bend down her ear to him and hear him confide that he had had the firm intention of sending her to the Conservatorium, and that, but for his mishap, last Christmas — surely Christmas was long past? — he would have announced it to everybody without allowing a single objection. After this confession his sister would be so touched that she would burst into tears, and Gregor would then raise himself to her shoulder and kiss her on the neck, which, now that she went to business, she kept free of any ribbon or collar.

"Mr. Samsa!" cried the middle lodger, to Gregor's father, and pointed, without wasting any more words, at Gregor, now working himself slowly forwards. The violin fell silent, the middle lodger first smiled to his friends with a shake of the head and then looked at Gregor again. Instead of driving Gregor out, his father seemed to think it more needful to begin by soothing down the lodgers, although they were not at all agitated and ap- parently found Gregor more entertaining than the violin-playing. He hur- ried toward them and, spreading out his arms, tried to urge them back into their own room and at the same time to block their view of Gregor. They now began to be really a little angry, one could not tell whether because of the old man's behavior or because it had just dawned on them that all un- wittingly they had such a neighbor as Gregor next door. They demanded explanations of his father, they waved their arms like him, tugged uneasily at their beards, and only with reluctance backed towards their room. Mean- while Gregor's sister, who stood there as if lost when her playing was so abruptly broken off, came to life again, pulled herself together all at once after standing for a while holding violin and bow in nervelessly hanging hands and staring at her music, pushed her violin into the lap of her mother, who was still sitting in her chair fighting asthmatically for breath, and ran into the lodgers' room to which they were now being shepherded by her father rather more quickly than before. One could see the pillows and blankets on the beds flying under her accustomed fingers and being laid in order. Before the lodgers had actually reached their room she had finished making the beds and slipped out.

The old man seemed once more to be so possessed by his mulish self- assertiveness that he was forgetting all the respect he should show to his lodgers. He kept driving them on and driving them on until in the very door of the bedroom the middle lodger stamped his foot loudly on the floor and so brought him to a halt. "I beg to announce," said the lodger, lifting one hand and looking also at Gregor's mother and sister, "that because of the disgusting conditions prevailing in this household and family" — here he spat on the floor with emphatic brevity — "I give you notice on the spot. Naturally I won't pay you a penny for the days I have lived here, on the contrary I shall consider bringing an action for damages against you, based on claims — believe me — that will be easily susceptible of proof." He ceased and stared straight in front of him, as if he expected something. In fact his two friends at once rushed into the breach with these words: "And we too give notice on the spot." On that he seized the door-handle and shut the door with a slam.

Gregor's father, groping with his hands, staggered forward and fell into his chair; it looked as if he were stretching himself there for his ordinary evening nap, but the marked jerkings of his head, which was as if uncontrollable, showed that he was far from asleep. Gregor had simply stayed quietly all the time on the spot where the lodgers had espied him. Disappointment at the failure of his plan, perhaps also the weakness arising from extreme hunger, made it impossible for him to move. He feared, with a fair degree of certainty, that at any moment the general tension would discharge itself in a combined attack upon him, and he lay waiting. He did not react even to the noise made by the violin as it fell off his mother's lap from under her trembling fingers and gave out a resonant note.

"My dear parents," said his sister, slapping her hand on the table by way of introduction, "things can't go on like this. Perhaps you don't realize that, but I do. I won't utter my brother's name in the presence of this creature, and so all I say is: we must try to get rid of it. We've tried to look after it and to put up with it as far as is humanly possible, and I don't think anyone could reproach us in the slightest."

"She is more than right," said Gregor's father to himself. His mother, who was still choking for lack of breath, began to cough hollowly into her hand with a wild look in her eyes.

His sister rushed over to her and held her forehead. His father's thoughts seemed to have lost their vagueness at Grete's words, he sat more upright, fingering his service cap that lay among the plates still lying on the table from the lodgers' supper, and from time to time looked at the still form of Gregor.

"We must try to get rid of it," his sister now said explicitly to her father, since her mother was coughing too much to hear a word, "it will be the death of both of you, I can see that coming. When one has to work as hard as we do, all of us, one can't stand this continual torment at home on top of it. At least I can't stand it any longer." And she burst into such a passion of sobbing that her tears dropped on her mother's face, where she wiped them off mechanically.

"My dear," said the old man sympathetically, and with evident understanding, "but what can we do?"

Gregor's sister merely shrugged her shoulders to indicate the feeling of helplessness that had now overmastered her during her weeping fit, in contrast to her former confidence.

"If he could understand us," said her father, half questioningly; Grete, still sobbing, vehemently waved a hand to show how unthinkable that was.

"If he could understand us," repeated the old man, shutting his eyes to consider his daughter's conviction that understanding was impossible, "then perhaps we might come to some agreement with him. But as it is — "

"He must go," cried Gregor's sister, "That's the only solution, Father. You must just try to get rid of the idea that this is Gregor. The fact that we've believed it for so long is the root of all our trouble. But how can it be Gregor? If this were Gregor, he would have realized long ago that human beings can't live with such a creature, and he'd have gone away on his own accord. Then we wouldn't have any brother, but we'd be able to go on living and keep his memory in honor. As it is, this creature persecutes us, drives away our lodgers, obviously wants the whole apartment to himself and would have us all sleep in the gutter. Just look, Father," she shrieked all at once, "he's at it again!" And in an access of panic that was quite incomprehensible to Gregor she even quitted her mother, literally thrusting the chair from her as if she would rather sacrifice her mother than stay so near to Gregor, and rushed behind her father, who also rose up, being simply upset by her agitation, and half-spread his arms out as if to protect her.

Yet Gregor had not the slightest intention of frightening anyone, far less his sister. He had only begun to turn round in order to crawl back to his room, but it was certainly a startling operation to watch, since because of his disabled condition he could not execute the difficult turning movements except by lifting his head and then bracing it against the floor over and over again. He paused and looked round. His good intentions seemed to have been recognized; the alarm had only been momentary. Now they were all watching him in melancholy silence. His mother lay in her chair, her legs stiffly outstretched and pressed together, her eyes almost closing for sheer weariness; his father and his sister were sitting beside each other, his sister's arm around the old man's neck.

Perhaps I can go on turning round now, thought Gregor, and began his labors again. He could not stop himself from panting with the effort, and had to pause now and then to take breath. Nor did anyone harass him, he was left entirely to himself. When he had completed the turn-round he began at once to crawl straight back. He was amazed at the distance separating him from his room and could not understand how in his weak state he had managed to accomplish the same journey so recently, almost without remarking it. Intent on crawling as fast as possible, he barely noticed that not a single word, not an ejaculation from his family, interfered with his progress. Only when he was already in the doorway did he turn his head round, not completely, for his neck muscles were getting stiff, but enough to see that nothing had changed behind him except that his sister had risen to her feet. His last glance fell on his mother, who was not quite overcome by sleep.

Hardly was he well inside his room when the door was hastily pushed shut, bolted and locked. The sudden noise in his rear startled him so much that his little legs gave beneath him. It was his sister who had shown such haste. She had been standing ready waiting and had made a light spring forward, Gregor had not even heard her coming, and she cried "At last!" to her parents as she turned the key in the lock.

"And what now?" said Gregor to himself, looking round in the darkness. Soon he made the discovery that he was now unable to stir a limb. This did not surprise him, rather it seemed unnatural that he should ever actually have been able to move on these feeble little legs. Otherwise he felt relatively comfortable. True, his whole body was aching, but it seemed that the pain was gradually growing less and would finally pass away. The rotting apple in his back and the inflamed area around it, all covered with soft dust, already hardly troubled him. He thought of his family with tenderness and love. The decision that he must disappear was one that he held to even more strongly than his sister, if that were possible. In this state of vacant and peaceful meditation he remained until the tower clock struck three in the morning. The first broadening of light in the world outside the window entered his consciousness once more. Then his head sank to the floor of its own accord and from his nostrils came the last faint flicker of his breath.

When the charwoman arrived early in the morning — what between her strength and her impatience she slammed all the doors so loudly, never mind how often she had been begged not to do so, that no one in the whole apartment could enjoy any quiet sleep after her arrival — she noticed nothing unusual as she took her customary peep into Gregor's room. She thought he was lying motionless on purpose, pretending to be in the sulks; she credited him with every kind of intelligence. Since she happened to have the long-handled broom in her hand she tried to tickle him up with it from the doorway. When that too produced no reaction she felt provoked and poked at him a little harder, and only when she had pushed him along the floor without meeting any resistance was her attention aroused. It did not take her long to establish the truth of the matter, and her eyes widened, she let out a whistle, yet did not waste much time over it but tore open the door of the Samsas' bedroom and yelled into the darkness at the top of her voice: "Just look at this, it's dead; it's lying here dead and done for!"

Mr. and Mrs. Samsa started up in their double bed and before they realized the nature of the charwoman's announcement had some difficulty in overcoming the shock of it. But then they got out of bed quickly, one on either side, Mr. Samsa throwing a blanket over his shoulders, Mrs. Samsa in nothing but her nightgown; in this array they entered Gregor's room. Meanwhile the door of the living room opened, too, where Grete had been sleeping since the advent of the lodgers; she was completely dressed as if she had not been to bed, which seemed to be confirmed also by the paleness of her face. "Dead?" said Mrs. Samsa, looking questioningly at the charwoman, although she could have investigated for herself, and the fact was obvious enough without investigation. "I should say so," said the charwoman, proving her words by pushing Gregor's corpse a long way to one side with her broomstick. Mrs. Samsa made a movement as if to stop her, but checked it. "Well," said Mr. Samsa, "now thanks be to God." He crossed himself, and the three women followed his example. Grete, whose eyes never left the corpse, said: "Just see how thin he was. It's such a long time since he's eaten anything. The food came out again just as it went in." Indeed, Gregor's body was completely flat and dry, as could only now be seen when it was no longer supported by the legs and nothing prevented one from looking closely at it.

"Come in beside us, Grete, for a little while," said Mrs. Samsa with a tremulous smile, and Grete, not without looking back at the corpse, followed her parents into their bedroom. The charwoman shut the door and opened the window wide. Although it was so early in the morning a certain softness was perceptible in the fresh air. After all, it was already the end of March.

The three lodgers emerged from their room and were surprised to see no breakfast; they had been forgotten. "Where's our breakfast?" said the middle lodger peevishly to the charwoman. But she put her finger to her lips and hastily, without a word, indicated by gestures that they should go into Gregor's room. They did so and stood, their hands in the pockets of their somewhat shabby coats, around Gregor's corpse in the room where it was now fully light.

At that the door of the Samsas' bedroom opened and Mr. Samsa appeared in his uniform, his wife on one arm, his daughter on the other. They all looked a little as if they had been crying; from time to time Grete hid her face on her father's arm.

"Leave my house at once!" said Mr. Samsa, and pointed to the door without disengaging himself from the women. "What do you mean by that?" said the middle lodger, taken somewhat aback, with a feeble smile. The two others put their hands behind them and kept rubbing them together, as if in gleeful expectation of a fine set-to in which they were bound to come off the winners. "I mean just what I say," answered Mr. Samsa, and advanced in a straight line with his two companions towards the lodger. He stood his ground at first quietly, looking at the floor as if his thoughts were taking a new pattern in his head. "Then let us go, by all means," he said, and looked up at Mr. Samsa as if in a sudden access of humility he were expecting some renewed sanction for this decision. Mr. Samsa merely nodded briefly once or twice with meaning eyes. Upon that the lodger really did go with long strides into the hall, his two friends had been listening and had quite stopped rubbing their hands for some moments and now went scuttling after him as if afraid that Mr. Samsa might get into the hall before them and cut them off from their leader. In the hall they all three took their hats from the rack, their sticks from the umbrella stand, bowed in silence and quitted the apartment. With a suspiciousness which proved quite unfounded Mr. Samsa and the two women followed them out to the landing; leaning over the banister they watched the three figures slowly but surely going down the long stairs, vanishing from sight at a certain turn of the staircase on every floor and coming into view again after a moment or so; the more they dwindled, the more the Samsa family's interest in them dwindled, and when a butcher's boy met them and passed them on the stairs coming up proudly with a tray on his head, Mr. Samsa and the two women soon left the landing and as if a burden had been lifted from them went back into their apartment.

They decided to spend this day in resting and going for a stroll; they had not only deserved such a respite from work, but absolutely needed it. And so they sat down at the table and wrote three notes of excuse, Mr. Samsa to his board of management, Mrs. Samsa to her employer and Grete to the head of her firm. While they were writing, the charwoman came in to say that she was going now, since her morning's work was finished. At first they only nodded without looking up, but as she kept hovering there they eyed her irritably. "Well?" said Mr. Samsa. The charwoman stood grinning in the doorway as if she had good news to impart to the family but meant not to say a word unless properly questioned. The small ostrich feather standing upright on her hat, which had annoyed Mr. Samsa ever since she was engaged, was waving gaily in all directions. "Well, what is it then?" asked Mrs. Samsa, who obtained more respect from the charwoman than the others. "Oh," said the charwoman, giggling so amiably that she could not at once continue, "just this, you don't need to bother about how to get rid of the thing next door. It's been seen to already." Mrs. Samsa and Grete bent over their letters again, as if preoccupied; Mr. Samsa, who perceived that she was eager to begin describing it all in detail, stopped her with a decisive hand. But since she was not allowed to tell her story, she remembered the great hurry she was in, being obviously deeply huffed: "Bye, everybody," she said, whirling off violently, and departed with a frightful slamming of doors.

"She'll be given notice tonight," said Mr. Samsa, but neither from his wife nor his daughter did he get any answer, for the charwoman seemed to have shattered again the composure they had barely achieved. They rose, went to the window and stayed there, clasping each other tight. Mr. Samsa turned in his chair to look at them and quietly observed them for a little. Then he called out: "Come along, now, do. Let bygones be bygones. And you might have some consideration for me." The two of them complied at once, hastened to him, caressed him and quickly finished their letters.

Then they all three left the apartment together, which was more than they had done for months, and went by tram into the open country outside the town. The tram, in which they were the only passengers, was filled with warm sunshine. Leaning comfortably back in their seats they canvassed their prospects for the future, and it appeared on closer inspection that these were not at all bad, for the jobs they had got, which so far they had never really discussed with each other, were all three admirable and likely to lead to better things later on. The greatest immediate improvement in their condition would of course arise from moving to another house; they wanted to take a smaller and cheaper but also better situated and more easily run apartment than the one they had, which Gregor had selected. While they were thus conversing, it struck both Mr. and Mrs. Samsa, almost at the same moment, as they became aware of their daughter's increasing vivacity, that in spite of all the sorrow of recent times, which had made her cheeks pale, she had bloomed into a pretty girl with a good figure. They grew quieter and half unconsciously exchanged glances of complete agreement, having come to the conclusion that it would soon be time to find a good husband for her. And it was like a confirmation of their new dreams and excellent intentions that at the end of their journey their daughter sprang to her feet first and stretched her young body.

[1915]

Family Glad that Gregor died.
    Seemed to metamorphsize the family + rejuvenate. them.

Seems like Gregor wants pity from family.
Wants them to give to _him_. (not vice versa)

Seem's to show that people can do well (ok) if they really try.

Gregor was a block to family seeing its possibilities
both before and after meta.
    before: they didnt worky ... he took care of them
    after: they seemed to think that greyor kept
        them from living.

? gregor has Low self esteme
  gregor as a handicapped person?
  gregor felt like bug, insignificant to family
  anti family

DAVID HERBERT LAWRENCE *(1885–1930) was born the son of a miner in the industrial town of Eastwood, in Nottinghamshire, the coal-mining country of England. His mother had been a schoolteacher, and she was frustrated by the hard existence of a coal miner's wife. She harbored great ambitions for her son, whom she was determined to keep out of the mines. Through his mother's financial sacrifices, Lawrence was able to attend Nottingham High School; then he studied to become a teacher. He also wrote poetry and started a novel, and in 1909 — shortly after he began teaching in South London — his work was published for the first time; a group of his poems appeared in the* English Review. *His first novel,* The White Peacock, *appeared later that year, but he was not established as a major literary figure until the publication of the novel* Sons and Lovers *(1913), based on the tensions in his own family and his struggle to escape his mother's possessiveness. Much of his fiction, like the story "The Primrose Path," focuses on characters caught between an attempt to relate to others and a struggle to break free. Lawrence sought an ideal balance or, as he wrote in the novel* Women in Love *(1920), a "star equilibrium," where two beings are attracted to each other but never lose their individuality. As he wrote in his essay "Morality and the Novel," "No emotion is supreme, or exclusively worth living for. All emotions go to the achieving of a living relationship between a human being and the other human being or creature or thing he becomes purely related to." His stories deal primarily with the physical and emotional aspects of human relationships, so Lawrence carefully created realistic and convincing fictional characters.*

Lawrence, who was a prolific writer, suffered from tuberculosis, and most of his life was spent wandering in Italy, Australia, Mexico, New Mexico, and Southern France, seeking a warm, dry climate. He also fled to primitive societies to escape the industrialization and commercialism of Western life, which he despised. A virulent social critic, he was frequently harassed by censorship, because his short stories, novels, and poetry flouted conventional notions of correct behavior. He wrote stories all his life, publishing his first collection, The Prussian Officer, *in 1914, followed by* England, My England *in 1922,* The Ladybird *in 1923,* Glad Ghosts *in 1926, and* The Woman Who Rode Away *in 1928. In 1961, his stories were collected in a three-volume edition that has gone through more than ten reprintings. The style of the early stories was harshly realistic, but his depiction of his characters' emotional situations matured in his later work, in which he created fantasies that explored deeper strata of the unconscious. Among these are his famous story "The Rocking Horse Winner," which shows him in the role of moralist and preacher against materialist values.*

As a writer, Lawrence found the detachment of Flaubert antithetical.

591

As in Tolstoy's writing, the point of view in Lawrence's fiction is omniscient, giving the sense of an author with a clear moral outlook. Lawrence's
conception of art was that it must be concrete and true to life: "The business of art is to reveal the relation between man and his circumambient universe, at the living moment. As mankind is always struggling in the toils of
old relationships, art is always ahead of the 'times,' which themselves are
always far in the rear of the living moment." Literature, for Lawrence, was
always connected to life, because art had two great functions: It provided an
emotional experience, and then, if the reader had the courage of his or her
own feelings and could live imaginatively, it became "a mine of practical
truth."

D. H. Lawrence

ॐ

THE PRIMROSE PATH

A young man came out of the Victoria station, looking undecidedly at
the taxi-cabs, dark red and black, pressing against the kerb under the glass
roof. Several men in greatcoats and brass buttons jerked themselves erect to
catch his attention, at the same time keeping an eye on the other people as
they filtered through the open doorways of the station. Berry, however, was
occupied by one of the men, a big, burly fellow whose blue eyes glared back
and whose red-brown moustache bristled in defiance.

"Do you *want* a cab, sir?" the man asked, in a half-mocking, challeng-
ing voice.

Berry hesitated still.

"Are you Daniel Sutton?" he asked.

"Yes," replied the other defiantly, with uneasy conscience.

"Then you are my uncle," said Berry.

They were alike in coloring, and somewhat in features, but the taxi
driver was a powerful, well-fleshed man who glared at the world aggressively, being really on the defensive against his own heart. His nephew, of
the same height, was thin, well-dressed, quiet and indifferent in his manner.
And yet they were obviously kin.

"And who the devil are you?" asked the taxi driver.

"I'm Daniel Berry," replied the nephew.

"Well, I'm damned — never saw you since you were a kid."

Rather awkwardly at this late hour the two shook hands. "How are you, lad?"

"All right. I thought you were in Australia."

"Been back three months — bought a couple of these damned things" — he kicked the tire of his taxi-cab in affectionate disgust. There was a moment's silence.

"Oh, but I'm going back out there. I can't stand this cankering, rotten-hearted hell of a country any more; you want to come out to Sydney with me, lad. That's the place for you — beautiful place, oh, you could wish for nothing better. And money in it, too. How's your mother?"

"She died at Christmas," said the young man.

"Dead! What! — our Anna!" The big man's eyes stared, and he recoiled in fear. "God, lad," he said, "that's three of 'em gone!"

The two men looked away at the people passing along the pale grey pavements, under the wall of Trinity Church.

"Well, strike me lucky!" said the taxi driver at last, out of breath. "She wor th' best o' th' bunch of 'em. I see nowt nor hear nowt from any of 'em — they're not worth it, I'll be damned if they are — our sermon-lapping Adela and Maud," he looked scornfully at his nephew. "But she was the best of 'em, our Anna was, that's a fact."

He was talking because he was afraid.

"An' after a hard life like she'd had. How old was she, lad?"

"Fifty-five."

"Fifty-five. . . ." He hesitated. Then, in a rather hushed voice, he asked the question that frightened him: "And what was it, then?"

"Cancer."

"Cancer again, like Julia! I never knew there was cancer in our family. Oh, my good God, our poor Anna, after the life she'd had! What, lad, do you see any God at the back of that? I'm damned if I do."

He was glaring, very blue-eyed and fierce, at his nephew. Berry lifted his shoulders slightly.

"God?" went on the taxi driver, in a curious intense tone. "You've only to look at the folk in the street to know there's nothing keeps it going but gravitation. Look at 'em. Look at him!" A mongrel-looking man was nosing past. "Wouldn't *he* murder you for your watch-chain, but that he's afraid of society? He's got it *in* him. . . . Look at 'em."

Berry watched the townspeople go by, and, sensitively feeling his uncle's antipathy, it seemed he was watching a sort of *danse macabre* of ugly criminals.

"Did you ever see such a God-forsaken crew creeping about! It gives you the very horrors to look at 'em. I sit in this damned car and watch 'em till, I can tell you, I feel like running the cab amuck among 'em, and running myself to kingdom come —— "

Berry wondered at this outburst. He knew his uncle was the black sheep, the youngest, the darling of his mother's family. He knew him to be at outs with respectability, mixing with the looser, sporting type, all betting and drinking and showing dogs and birds, and racing. As a critic of life, however, he did not know him. But the young man felt curiously understanding. "He uses words like I do, he talks nearly as I talk, except that I shouldn't say those things. But I might feel like that, in myself, if I went a certain road."

"I've got to go to Watmore," he said. "Can you take me?"

"When d'you want to go?" asked the uncle fiercely.

"Now."

"Come on, then. What d'yer stand gassin' on th' causeway for?"

The nephew took his seat beside the driver. The cab began to quiver, then it started forward with a whirr. The uncle, his hands and feet acting mechanically, kept his blue eyes fixed on the high road into whose traffic the car was insinuating its way. Berry felt curiously as if he were sitting beside an older development of himself. His mind went back to his mother. She had been twenty years older than this brother of hers, whom she had loved so dearly. "He was one of the most affectionate little lads, and such a curly head! I could never have believed he would grow into the great, coarse bully he is — for he's nothing else. My father made a god of him — well, it's a good thing his father is dead. He got in with that sporting gang, that's what did it. Things were made too easy for him, and so he thought of no one but himself, and this is the result."

Not that "Joky" Sutton was so very black a sheep. He had lived idly till he was eighteen, then had suddenly married a young, beautiful girl with clear brows and dark-grey eyes, a factory girl. Having taken her to live with his parents he, lover of dogs and pigeons, went on to the staff of a sporting paper. But his wife was without uplift or warmth. Though they made money enough, their house was dark and cold and uninviting. He had two or three dogs, and the whole attic was turned into a great pigeon-house. He and his wife lived together roughly, with no warmth, no refinement, no touch of beauty anywhere, except that she was beautiful. He was a blustering, impetuous man, she was rather cold in her soul, did not care about anything very much, was rather capable and close with money. And she had a common accent in her speech. He outdid her a thousand times in coarse language, and yet that cold twang in her voice tortured him with shame that he stamped down in bullying and in becoming more violent in his own speech.

Only his dogs adored him, and to them, and to his pigeons, he talked with rough, yet curiously tender caresses while they leaped and fluttered for joy.

After he and his wife had been married for seven years a little girl was born to them, then later, another. But the husband and wife drew no nearer together. She had an affection for her children almost like a cool governess. He had an emotional man's fear of sentiment, which helped to nip his wife from putting out any shoots. He treated his children roughly, and pretended to think it a good job when one was adopted by a well-to-do maternal aunt. But in his soul he hated his wife that she could give away one of his children. For after her cool fashion, she loved him. With a chaos of a man such as he, she had no chance of being anything but cold and hard, poor thing. For she did love him.

In the end he fell absurdly and violently in love with a rather sentimental young woman who read Browning. He made his wife an allowance and established a new *ménage* with the young lady, shortly after emigrating with her to Australia. Meanwhile his wife had gone to live with a publican, a widower, with whom she had had one of those curious, tacit understandings of which quiet women are capable, something like an arrangement for provision in the future.

This was as much as the nephew knew. He sat beside his uncle, wondering how things stood at the present. They raced lightly out past the cemetery and along the boulevard, then turned into the rather grimy country. The mud flew out on either side, there was a fine mist of rain which blew in their faces. Berry covered himself up.

In the lanes the high hedges shone black with rain. The silvery-grey sky, faintly dappled, spread wide over the low, green land. The elder man glanced fiercely up the road, then turned his red face to his nephew.

"And how're you going on, lad?" he said loudly. Berry noticed that his uncle was slightly uneasy of him. It made him also uncomfortable. The elder man had evidently some thing pressing on his soul.

"Who are you living with in town?" asked the nephew. "Have you gone back to Aunt Maud?"

"No," barked the uncle. "She wouldn't have me. I offered to — I wanted to — but she wouldn't."

"You're alone, then?"

"No, I'm not alone."

He turned and glared with his fierce blue eyes at his nephew, but said no more for some time. The car ran on through the mud, under the wet wall of the park.

"That other devil tried to poison me," suddenly shouted the elder man. "The one I went to Australia with." At which, in spite of himself, the younger smiled in secret.

"How was that?" he asked.

"Wanted to get rid of me. She got in with another fellow on the ship. . . . By Jove, I was bad."

"Where — on the ship?"

"No," bellowed the other. "No. That was in Wellington, New Zealand. I was bad, and got lower an' lower — couldn't think what was up. I could hardly crawl about. As certain as I'm here, she was poisoning me, to get to th' other chap — I'm certain of it."

"And what did you do?"

"I cleared out — went to Sydney —— "

"And left her?"

"Yes, I thought begod I'd better clear out if I wanted to live."

"And you were all right in Sydney?"

"Better in no time — I *know* she was putting poison in my coffee."

"Hm!"

There was a glum silence. The driver stared at the road ahead, fixedly, managing the car as if it were a live thing. The nephew felt that his uncle was afraid, quite stupefied with fear, fear of life, of death, of himself.

"You're in rooms, then?" asked the nephew.

"No, I'm in a house of my own," said the uncle defiantly, "wi' th' best little woman in th' Midlands. She's a marvel. Why don't you come an see us?"

"I will. Who is she?"

"Oh, she's a good girl — a beautiful little thing. I was clean gone on her first time I saw her. An' she was on me. Her mother lives with us — respectable girl, none o' your. . . ."

"And how old is she?"

"How old is she? She's twenty-one."

"Poor thing."

"*She's* right enough."

"You'd marry her — getting a divorce —— ?"

"I shall marry her."

There was a little antagonism between the two men.

"Where's Aunt Maud?" asked the younger.

"She's at the 'Railway Arms' — we passed it, just against Rollin's Mill Crossing. . . . They sent me a note this morning to go an' see her when I can spare time. She's got consumption."

"Good Lord! Are you going?"

"Yes —— "

But again Berry felt that his uncle was afraid.

The young man got through his commission in the village, had a drink with his uncle at the inn, and the two were returning home. The elder man's subject of conversation was Australia. As they drew near the town they grew silent, thinking both of the public-house. At last they saw the gates of the railway crossing were closed before them.

"Shan't you call?" asked Berry, jerking his head in the direction of the inn, which stood at the corner between two roads, its sign hanging under a bare horse-chestnut tree in front.

"I might as well. Come in an' have a drink," said the uncle.

It had been raining all the morning, so shallow pools of water lay about. A brewer's wagon, with wet barrels and warm-smelling horses, stood near the door of the inn. Everywhere seemed silent, but for the rattle of trains at the crossing. The two men went uneasily up the steps and into the bar. The place was paddled with wet feet, empty. As the barman was heard approaching, the uncle asked, his usual bluster slightly hushed by fear:

"What yer goin' ta have, lad? Same as last time?"

A man entered, evidently the proprietor. He was good-looking, with a long, heavy face and quick, dark eyes. His glance at Sutton was swift, a start, a recognition, and a withdrawal, into heavy neutrality.

"How are yer, Dan?" he said, scarcely troubling to speak.

"Are yer, George?" replied Sutton, hanging back. "My nephew, Dan Berry. Give us Red Seal, George."

The publican nodded to the younger man, and set the glasses on the bar. He pushed forward the two glasses, then leaned back in the dark corner behind the door, his arms folded, evidently preferring to get back from the watchful eyes of the nephew.

" —— 's luck," said Sutton.

The publican nodded in acknowledgment. Sutton and his nephew drank.

"Why the hell don't you get that road mended in Cinder Hill —— " said Sutton fiercely, pushing back his driver's cap and showing his short-cut, bristling hair.

"They can't find it in their hearts to pull it up," replied the publican, laconically.

"Find in their hearts! They want settin' in barrows an' runnin' up an' down it till they cried for mercy."

Sutton put down his glass. The publican renewed it with a sure hand, at ease in whatsoever he did. Then he leaned back against the bar. He wore no coat. He stood with arms folded, his chin on his chest, his long moustache hanging. His back was round and slack, so that the lower part of his abdomen stuck forward, though he was not stout. His cheek was healthy, brown-red, and he was muscular. Yet there was about him this physical slackness, a reluctance in his slow, sure movements. His eyes were keen under his dark brows, but reluctant also, as if he were gloomily apathetic.

There was a halt. The publican evidently would say nothing. Berry looked at the mahogany bar-counter, slopped with beer, at the whisky-bottles on the shelves. Sutton, his cap pushed back, showing a white brow above a weather-reddened face, rubbed his cropped hair uneasily.

The publican glanced round suddenly. It seemed that only his dark eyes moved.

"Going up?" he asked.

And something, perhaps his eyes, indicated the unseen bed-chamber.

"Ay — that's what I came for," replied Sutton, shifting nervously from one foot to the other. "She's been asking for me?"

"This morning," replied the publican, neutral.

Then he put up a flap of the bar, and turned away through the dark doorway behind. Sutton, pulling off his cap, showing a round, short-cropped head which now was ducked forward, followed after him, the buttons holding the strap of his greatcoat behind glittering for a moment.

They climbed the dark stairs, the husband placing his feet carefully, because of his big boots. Then he followed down the passage, trying vaguely to keep a grip on his bowels, which seemed to be melting away, and definitely wishing for a neat brandy. The publican opened a door. Sutton, big and burly in his greatcoat, went past him.

The bedroom seemed light and warm after the passage. There was a red eiderdown on the bed. Then, making an effort, Sutton turned his eyes to see the sick woman. He met her eyes direct, dark, dilated. It was such a shock he almost started away. For a second he remained in torture, as if some invisible flame were playing on him to reduce his bones and fuse him down. Then he saw the sharp white edge of her jaw, and the black hair beside the hollow cheek. With a start he went towards the bed.

"Hello, Maud!" he said. "Why, what ye been doin'?"

The publican stood at the window with his back to the bed. The husband, like one condemned but on the point of starting away, stood by the bedside staring in horror at his wife, whose dilated grey eyes, nearly all black now, watched him wearily, as if she were looking at something a long way off.

Going exceedingly pale, he jerked up his head and stared at the wall over the pillows. There was a little colored picture of a bird perched on a bell, and a nest among ivy leaves beneath. It appealed to him, made him wonder, roused a feeling of childish magic in him. They were wonderfully fresh, green ivy leaves, and nobody had seen the nest among them save him.

Then suddenly he looked down again at the face on the bed, to try and recognize it. He knew the white brow and the beautiful clear eyebrows. That was his wife, with whom he had passed his youth, flesh of his flesh, his, himself. Then those tired eyes, which met his again from a long way off, disturbed him until he did not know where he was. Only the sunken cheeks and the mouth that seemed to protrude now were foreign to him, and filled him with horror. It seemed he lost his identity. He was the young husband of the woman with the clear brows; he was the married man fighting with her whose eyes watched him, a little indifferently, from a long way off; and he was a child in horror of that protruding mouth.

There came a crackling sound of her voice. He knew she had consumption of the throat, and braced himself hard to bear the noise.

"What was it, Maud?" he asked in panic.

Then the broken, crackling voice came again. He was too terrified of the sound of it to hear what was said. There was a pause.

"You'll take Winnie?" the publican's voice interpreted from the window.

"Don't you bother, Maud, I'll take her," he said, stupefying his mind so as not to understand.

He looked curiously round the room. It was not a bad bedroom, light and warm. There were many medicine bottles aggregated in a corner of the washstand — and a bottle of Three Star brandy, half full. And there were also photographs of strange people on the chest of drawers. It was not a bad room.

Again he started as if he were shot. She was speaking. He bent down, but did not look at her.

"Be good to her," she whispered.

When he realized her meaning, that he should be good to their child when the mother was gone, a blade went through his flesh.

"I'll be good to her, Maud, don't you bother," he said, beginning to feel shaky.

He looked again at the picture of the bird. It perched cheerfully under a blue sky, with robust, jolly ivy leaves near. He was gathering his courage to depart. He looked down, but struggled hard not to take in the sight of his wife's face.

"I s'll come again, Maud," he said. "I hope you'll go on all right. Is there anything as you want?"

There was an almost imperceptible shake of the head from the sick woman, making his heart melt swiftly again. Then, dragging his limbs, he got out of the room and down the stairs.

The landlord came after him.

"I'll let you know if anything happens," the publican said, still laconic, but with his eyes dark and swift.

"Ay, a' right," said Sutton blindly. He looked round for his cap, which he had all the time in his hand. Then he got out of doors.

In a moment the uncle and nephew were in the car jolting on the level crossing. The elder man seemed as if something tight in his brain made him open his eyes wide, and stare. He held the steering-wheel firmly. He knew he could steer accurately, to a hair's breadth. Glaring fixedly ahead, he let the car go, till it bounded over the uneven road. There were three coal-carts in a string. In an instant the car grazed past them, almost biting the kerb on the other side. Sutton aimed his car like a projectile, staring ahead. He did not want to know, to think, to realize, he wanted to be only the driver of that quick taxi.

The town drew near suddenly. There were allotment-gardens, with dark-purple twiggy fruit trees and wet alleys between the hedges. Then suddenly the streets of dwelling-houses whirled close, and the car was climbing the hill, with an angry whirr — up — up — till they rode out on to the crest and could see the tramcars, dark red and yellow, threading their way round the corner below, and all the traffic roaring between the shops.

"Got anywhere to go?" asked Sutton of his nephew.

"I was going to see one or two people."

"Come an' have a bit o' dinner with us," said the other.

Berry knew that his uncle wanted to be distracted, so that he should not think nor realize. The big man was running hard away from the horror of realization.

"All right," Berry agreed.

The car went quickly through the town. It ran up a long street nearly into the country again. Then it pulled up at a house that stood alone, below the road.

"I s'll be back in ten minutes," said the uncle.

The car went on to the garage. Berry stood curiously at the top of the stone stairs that led from the high-road down to the level of the house, an old stone place. The garden was dilapidated. Broken fruit trees leaned at a sharp angle down the steep bank. Right across the dim grey atmosphere, in a kind of valley on the edge of the town, new suburb-patches showed pink-ish on the dark earth. It was a kind of unresolved border-land.

Berry went down the steps. Through the broken black fence of the orchard, long grass showed yellow. The place seemed deserted. He knocked, then knocked again. An elderly woman appeared. She looked like a house-keeper. At first she said suspiciously that Mr. Sutton was not in.

"My uncle just put me down. He'll be in in ten minutes," replied the visitor.

"Oh, are you the Mr. Berry who is related to him?" exclaimed the elderly woman. "Come in — come in."

She was at once kindly and a little bit servile. The young man entered. It was an old house, rather dark, and sparsely furnished. The elderly woman sat nervously on the edge of one of the chairs in a drawing-room that looked as if it were furnished from dismal relics of dismal homes, and there was a little straggling attempt at conversation. Mrs. Greenwell was evidently a working-class woman unused to service or to any formality.

Presently she gathered up courage to invite her visitor into the dining-room. There from the table under the window rose a tall, slim girl with a cat in her arms. She was evidently a little more lady-like than was habitual to her, but she had a gentle, delicate, small nature. Her brown hair almost covered her ears, her dark lashes came down in shy awkwardness over her beautiful blue eyes. She shook hands in a frank way, yet she was shrinking. Evidently she was not sure how her position would affect her visitor. And yet she was assured in herself, shrinking and timid as she was.

"She must be a good deal in love with him," thought Berry.

Both women glanced shamefacedly at the roughly laid table. Evidently they ate in a rather rough and ready fashion.

Elaine — she had this poetic name — fingered her cat timidly, not knowing what to say or to do, unable even to ask her visitor to sit down. He noticed how her skirt hung almost flat on her hips. She was young, scarce developed, a long, slender thing. Her clothing was warm and exquisite.

The elder woman bustled out to the kitchen. Berry fondled the terrier dogs that had come curiously to his heels, and glanced out of the window at the wet, deserted orchard.

This room, too, was not well furnished, and rather dark. But there was a big red fire.

"He always has fox-terriers," he said.

"Yes," she answered, showing her teeth in a smile.

"Do you like them, too?"

"Yes" — she glanced down at the dogs. "I like Tam better than Sally ——"

Her speech always tailed off into an awkward silence.

"We've been to see Aunt Maud," said the nephew.

Her eyes, blue and scared and shrinking, met his.

"Dan had a letter," he explained. "She's very bad."

"Isn't it horrible!" she exclaimed, her face crumbling up with fear.

The old woman, evidently a hard-used, rather down-trodden workman's wife, came in with two soup-plates. She glanced anxiously to see how her daughter was progressing with the visitor.

"Mother, Dan's been to see Maud," said Elaine, in a quiet voice full of fear and trouble.

The old woman looked up anxiously, in question.

"I think she wanted him to take the child. She's very bad, I believe," explained Berry.

"Oh, we should take Winnie!" cried Elaine. But both women seemed uncertain, wavering in their position. Already Berry could see that his uncle had bullied them, as he bullied everybody. But they were used to unpleasant men, and seemed to keep at a distance.

"Will you have some soup?" asked the mother humbly.

She evidently did the work. The daughter was to be a lady, more or less, always dressed and nice for when Sutton came in.

They heard him heavily running down the steps outside. The dogs got up. Elaine seemed to forget the visitor. It was as if she came into life. Yet she was nervous and afraid. The mother stood as if ready to exculpate herself.

Sutton burst open the door. Big, blustering, wet in his immense grey coat, he came into the dining-room.

"Hello!" he said to his nephew, "making yourself at home?"

"Oh yes," replied Berry.

"Hello, Jack," he said to the girl. "Got owt to grizzle about?"

"What for?" she asked, in a clear, half-challenging voice, that had that peculiar twang, almost petulant, so female and so attractive. Yet she was defiant like a boy.

"It's a wonder if you haven't," growled Sutton. And, with a really intimate movement, he stooped down and fondled his dogs, though paying no attention to them. Then he stood up, and remained with feet apart on the hearth-rug, his head ducked forward, watching the girl. He seemed abstracted, as if he could only watch her. His greatcoat hung open, so that she could see his figure, simple and human in the great husk of cloth. She stood nervously with her hands behind her, glancing at him, unable to see anything else. And he was scarcely conscious but of her. His eyes were still strained and staring, and as they followed the girl, when, long-limbed and languid, she moved away, it was as if he saw in her something impersonal, the female, not the woman.

"Had your dinner?" he asked.

"We were just going to have it," she replied, with the same curious little vibration in her voice, like the twang of a string.

The mother entered, bringing a saucepan from which she ladled soup into three plates.

"Sit down, lad," said Sutton. "You sit down, Jack, an' give me mine here."

"Oh, aren't you coming to table?" she complained.

"No, I tell you," he snarled, almost pretending to be disagreeable. But she was slightly afraid even of the pretense, which pleased and relieved him. He stood on the hearth-rug eating his soup noisily.

"Aren't you going to take your coat off?" she said. "It's filling the place full of steam."

He did not answer, but, with his head bent forward over the plate, he ate his soup hastily, to get it done with. When he put down his empty plate, she rose and went to him.

"Do take your coat off, Dan," she said, and she took hold of the breast of his coat, trying to push it back over his shoulder. But she could not. Only the stare in his eyes changed to a glare as her hand moved over his shoulder. He looked down into her eyes. She became pale, rather frightened-looking, and she turned her face away, and it was drawn slightly with love and fear and misery. She tried again to put off his coat, her thin wrists pulling at it. He stood solidly planted, and did not look at her, but stared straight in front. She was playing with passion, afraid of it, and really wretched because it left her, the person, out of count. Yet she continued. And there came into his bearing, into his eyes, the curious smile of passion, pushing away even the death-horror. It was life stronger than death in him. She stood close to his breast. Their eyes met, and she was carried away.

"Take your coat off, Dan," she said coaxingly, in a low tone meant for no one but him. And she slid her hands on his shoulder, and he yielded, so that the coat was pushed back. She had flushed, and her eyes had grown very bright. She got hold of the cuff of his coat. Gently, he eased himself, so that she drew it off. Then he stood in a thin suit, which revealed his vigorous, almost mature form.

"What a weight!" she exclaimed, in a peculiar penetrating voice, as she went out hugging the overcoat. In a moment she came back.

He stood still in the same position, a frown over his fiercely staring eyes. The pain, the fear, the horror in his breast were all burning away in the new, fiercest flame of passion.

"Get your dinner," he said roughly to her.

"I've had all I want," she said. "You come an' have yours."

He looked at the table as if he found it difficult to see things.

"I want no more," he said.

She stood close to his chest. She wanted to touch him and to comfort him. There was something about him now that fascinated her. Berry felt slightly ashamed that she seemed to ignore the presence of others in the room.

The mother came in. She glanced at Sutton, standing planted on the hearth-rug, his head ducked, the heavy frown hiding his face. There was a peculiar braced intensity about him that made the elder woman afraid. Suddenly he jerked his head round to his nephew.

"Get on wi' your dinner, lad," he said, and he went to the door. The dogs, which had continually lain down and got up again, uneasy, now rose and watched. The girl went after him, saying, clearly:

"What did you want, Dan?"

Her slim, quick figure was gone, the door was closed behind her.

There was silence. The mother, still more slave-like in her movement, sat down in a low chair. Berry drank some beer.

"That girl will leave him," he said to himself. "She'll hate him like poison. And serve him right. Then she'll go off with somebody else."

And she did.

[1922]

D. H. Lawrence

ʔ⳽ʕ

THE ROCKING HORSE WINNER

There was a woman who was beautiful, who started with all the advantages, yet she had no luck. She married for love, and the love turned to dust. She had bonny children, yet she felt they had been thrust upon her, and she could not love them. They looked at her coldly, as if they were finding fault with her. And hurriedly she felt she must cover up some fault in herself. Yet what it was that she must cover up she never knew. Nevertheless, when her children were present, she always felt the center of her heart go hard. This troubled her, and in her manner she was all the more gentle and anxious for her children, as if she loved them very much. Only she herself knew that at the center of her heart was a hard little place that could not feel love, no, not for anybody. Everybody else said of her: "She is such a good mother. She adores her children." Only she herself, and her children themselves, knew it was not so. They read it in each other's eyes.

There were a boy and two little girls. They lived in a pleasant house, with a garden, and they had discreet servants, and felt themselves superior to anyone in the neighborhood.

Although they lived in style, they felt always an anxiety in the house. There was never enough money. The mother had a small income, and the father had a small income, but not nearly enough for the social position which they had to keep up. The father went into town to some office. But though he had good prospects, these prospects never materialized. There was always the grinding sense of the shortage of money, though the style was always kept up.

At last the mother said: "I will see if *I* can't make something." But she did not know where to begin. She racked her brains, and tried this thing and the other, but could not find anything successful. The failure made deep lines come into her face. Her children were growing up, they would have to go to school. There must be more money, there must be more money. The father, who was always very handsome and expensive in his tastes, seemed as if he never *would* be able to do anything worth doing. And the mother, who had a great belief in herself, did not succeed any better, and her tastes were just as expensive.

And so the house came to be haunted by the unspoken phrase: *There must be more money! There must be more money!* The children could hear it all the time, though nobody said it aloud. They heard it at Christmas, when the expensive and splendid toys filled the nursery. Behind the shining modern rocking horse, behind the smart doll's house, a voice would start whispering: "There *must* be more money! There *must* be more money!" And the children would stop playing, to listen for a moment. They would look into each other's eyes, to see if they had all heard. And each one saw in the eyes of the other two that they too had heard. "There *must* be more money! There *must* be more money!"

It came whispering from the springs of the still-swaying rocking horse, and even the horse, bending his wooden, champing head, heard it. The big doll, sitting so pink and smirking in her new pram, could hear it quite plainly, and seemed to be smirking all the more self-consciously because of it. The foolish puppy, too, that took the place of the teddy bear, he was looking so extraordinarily foolish for no other reason but that he heard the secret whisper all over the house: "There *must* be more money!"

Yet nobody ever said it aloud. The whisper was everywhere, and therefore no one spoke it. Just as no one ever says: "We are breathing!" in spite of the fact that breath is coming and going all the time.

"Mother," said the boy Paul one day, "why don't we keep a car of our own? Why do we always use Uncle's, or else a taxi?"

"Because we're the poor members of the family," said the mother.

"But why *are* we, Mother?"

"Well — I suppose," she said slowly and bitterly, "it's because your father has no luck."

The boy was silent for some time.

"Is luck money, Mother?" he asked rather timidly.

"No, Paul. Not quite. It's what causes you to have money."

"Oh!" said Paul vaguely. "I thought when Uncle Oscar said *filthy lucker*, it meant money."

"*Filthy lucre* does mean money," said the mother. "But it's lucre, not luck."

"Oh!" said the boy. "Then what *is* luck, Mother?"

"It's what causes you to have money. If you're lucky you have money. That's why it's better to be born lucky than rich. If you're rich, you may lose your money. But if you're lucky, you will always get more money."

"Oh! Will you? And is Father not lucky?"

"Very unlucky, I should say," she said bitterly.

The boy watched her with unsure eyes.

"Why?" he asked.

"I don't know. Nobody ever knows why one person is lucky and another unlucky."

"Don't they? Nobody at all? Does *nobody* know?"

"Perhaps God. But He never tells."

"He ought to, then. And aren't you lucky either, Mother?"

"I can't be, if I married an unlucky husband."

"But by yourself, aren't you?"

"I used to think I was, before I married. Now I think I am very unlucky indeed."

"Why?"

"Well — never mind! Perhaps I'm not really," she said.

The child looked at her, to see if she meant it. But he saw, by the lines of her mouth, that she was only trying to hide something from him.

"Well, anyhow," he said stoutly, "I'm a lucky person."

"Why?" said his mother, with a sudden laugh.

He stared at her. He didn't even know why he had said it.

"God told me," he asserted, brazening it out.

"I hope He did, dear!" she said, again with a laugh, but rather bitter.

"He did, Mother!"

"Excellent!" said the mother.

The boy saw she did not believe him; or, rather, that she paid no attention to his assertion. This angered him somewhat, and made him want to compel her attention.

He went off by himself, vaguely, in a childish way, seeking for the clue to "luck." Absorbed, taking no heed of other people, he went about with a sort of stealth, seeking inwardly for luck. He wanted luck, he wanted it, he wanted it. When the two girls were playing dolls in the nursery, he would sit on his big rocking horse, charging madly into space, with a frenzy that made the little girls peer at him uneasily. Wildly the horse careered, the waving dark hair of the boy tossed, his eyes had a strange glare in them. The little girls dared not speak to him.

When he had ridden to the end of his mad little journey, he climbed down and stood in front of his rocking horse, staring fixedly into its lowered face. Its red mouth was slightly open, its big eye was wide and glassy-bright.

Now! he would silently command the snorting steed. Now, take me to where there is luck! Now take me!

And he would slash the horse on the neck with the little whip he had asked Uncle Oscar for. He *knew* the horse could take him to where there was luck, if only he forced it. So he would mount again, and start on his furious ride, hoping at last to get there. He knew he could get there.

"You'll break your horse, Paul!" said the nurse.

"He's always riding like that! I wish he'd leave off!" said his elder sister Joan.

But he only glared down on them in silence. Nurse gave him up. She could make nothing of him. Anyhow he was growing beyond her.

One day his mother and his uncle Oscar came in when he was on one of his furious rides. He did not speak to them.

"Hallo, you young jockey! Riding a winner?" said his uncle.

"Aren't you growing too big for a rocking horse? You're not a very little boy any longer, you know," said his mother.

But Paul only gave a blue glare from his big, rather close-set eyes. He would speak to nobody when he was in full tilt. His mother watched him with an anxious expression on her face.

At last he suddenly stopped forcing his horse into the mechanical gallop, and slid down.

"Well, I got there!" he announced fiercely, his blue eyes still flaring, and his sturdy long legs straddling apart.

"Where did you get to?" asked his mother.

"Where I wanted to go," he flared back at her.

"That's right, son!" said Uncle Oscar. "Don't you stop till you get there. What's the horse's name?"

"He doesn't have a name," said the boy.

"Gets on without all right?" asked the uncle.

"Well, he has different names. He was called Sansovino last week."

"Sansovino, eh? Won the Ascot. How did you know his name?"

"He always talks about horse races with Bassett," said Joan.

The uncle was delighted to find that his small nephew was posted with all the racing news. Bassett, the young gardener, who had been wounded in the left foot in the war and had got his present job through Oscar Cresswell, whose batman he had been, was a perfect blade of the "turf." He lived in the racing events, and the small boy lived with him.

Oscar Cresswell got it all from Bassett.

"Master Paul comes and asks me, so I can't do more than tell him, sir," said Bassett, his face terribly serious, as if he were speaking of religious matters.

"And does he ever put anything on a horse he fancies?"

"Well — I don't want to give him away — he's a young sport, a fine sport, sir. Would you mind asking him himself? He sort of takes a pleasure in it, and perhaps he'd feel I was giving him away, sir, if you don't mind."

Bassett was serious as a church.

The uncle went back to his nephew and took him off for a ride in the car.

"Say, Paul, old man, do you ever put anything on a horse?" the uncle asked.

The boy watched the handsome man closely.

"Why, do you think I oughtn't to?" he parried.

"Not a bit of it! I thought perhaps you might give me a tip for the Lincoln."

The car sped on into the country, going down to Uncle Oscar's place in Hampshire.

"Honor bright?" said the nephew.

"Honor bright, son!" said the uncle.

"Well, then, Daffodil."

"Daffodil! I doubt it, sonny. What about Mirza?"

"I only know the winner," said the boy. "That's Daffodil."

"Daffodil, eh?"

There was a pause. Daffodil was an obscure horse comparatively.

"Uncle!"

"Yes, son?"

"You won't let it go any further, will you? I promised Bassett."

"Bassett be damned, old man! What's he got to do with it?"

"We're partners. We've been partners from the first. Uncle, he lent me my first five shillings, which I lost. I promised him, honor bright, it was only between me and him; only you gave me that ten-shilling note I started winning with, so I thought you were lucky. You won't let it go any further, will you?"

The boy gazed at his uncle from those big, hot, blue eyes, set rather close together. The uncle stirred and laughed uneasily.

"Right you are, son! I'll keep your tip private. Daffodil, eh? How much are you putting on him?"

"All except twenty pounds," said the boy. "I keep that in reserve."

The uncle thought it a good joke.

"You keep twenty pounds in reserve, do you, you young romancer? What are you betting, then?"

"I'm betting three hundred," said the boy gravely. "But it's between you and me, Uncle Oscar! Honor bright?"

The uncle burst into a roar of laughter.

"It's between you and me all right, you young Nat Gould," he said, laughing. "But where's your three hundred?"

"Bassett keeps it for me. We're partners."

"You are, are you! And what is Bassett putting on Daffodil?"

"He won't go quite as high as I do, I expect. Perhaps he'll go a hundred and fifty."

"What, pennies?" laughed the uncle.

"Pounds," said the child, with a surprised look at his uncle. "Bassett keeps a bigger reserve than I do."

Between wonder and amusement Uncle Oscar was silent. He pursued the matter no further, but he determined to take his nephew with him to the Lincoln races.

"Now, son," he said, "I'm putting twenty on Mirza, and I'll put five for you on any horse you fancy. What's your pick?"

"Daffodil, Uncle."

"No, not the fiver on Daffodil!"

"I should if it was my own fiver," said the child.

"Good! Good! Right you are! A fiver for me and a fiver for you on Daffodil."

The child had never been to a race meeting before, and his eyes were blue fire. He pursed his mouth tight, and watched. A Frenchman just in front had put his money on Lancelot. Wild with excitement, he flailed his arms up and down, yelling "*Lancelot! Lancelot!*" in his French accent.

Daffodil came in first, Lancelot second, Mirza third. The child, flushed and with eyes blazing, was curiously serene. His uncle brought him four five-pound notes, four to one.

"What am I to do with these?" he cried, waving them before the boy's eyes.

"I suppose we'll talk to Bassett," said the boy. "I expect I have fifteen hundred now; and twenty in reserve; and this twenty."

His uncle studied him for some moments.

"Look here, son!" he said. "You're not serious about Bassett and that fifteen hundred, are you?"

"Yes, I am. But it's between you and me, Uncle. Honor bright!"

"Honor bright all right, son! But I must talk to Bassett."

"If you'd like to be a partner, Uncle, with Bassett and me, we could all be partners. Only, you'd have to promise, honor bright, Uncle, not to let it go beyond us three. Bassett and I are lucky, and you must be lucky, because it was your ten shillings I started winning with. . . ."

Uncle Oscar took both Bassett and Paul into Richmond Park for an afternoon, and there they talked.

"It's like this, you see, sir," Bassett said. "Master Paul would get me talking about racing events, spinning yarns, you know, sir. And he was always keen on knowing if I'd made or if I'd lost. It's about a year since, now, that I put five shillings on Blush of Dawn for him — and we lost. Then the luck turned, with that ten shillings he had from you, that we put on Singhalese. And since then, it's been pretty steady, all things considering. What do you say, Master Paul?"

"We're all right when we're sure," said Paul. "It's when we're not quite sure that we go down."

"Oh, but we're careful then," said Bassett.

"But when are you *sure?*" Uncle Oscar smiled.

"It's Master Paul, sir," said Bassett, in a secret, religious voice. "It's as if he had it from heaven. Like Daffodil, now, for the Lincoln. That was as sure as eggs."

"Did you put anything on Daffodil?" asked Oscar Cresswell.

"Yes, sir. I made my bit."

"And my nephew?"

Bassett was obstinately silent, looking at Paul.

"I made twelve hundred, didn't I, Bassett? I told Uncle I was putting three hundred on Daffodil."

"That's right," said Bassett, nodding.

"But where's the money?" asked the uncle.

"I keep it safe locked up, sir. Master Paul he can have it any minute he likes to ask for it.

"What, fifteen hundred pounds?"

"And twenty! And *forty*, that is, with the twenty he made on the course."

"It's amazing!" said the uncle.

"If Master Paul offers you to be partners, sir, I would, if I were you; if you'll excuse me," said Bassett.

Oscar Cresswell thought about it.

"I'll see the money," he said.

They drove home again, and sure enough, Bassett came round to the garden house with fifteen hundred pounds in notes. The twenty pounds reserve was left with Joe Glee, in the Turf Commission deposit.

"You see, it's all right, Uncle, when I'm *sure!* Then we go strong, for all we're worth. Don't we, Bassett?"

"We do that, Master Paul."

"And when are you sure?" said the uncle, laughing.

"Oh, well, sometimes I'm *absolutely* sure, like about Daffodil," said the boy; "and sometimes I have an idea; and sometimes I haven't even an idea, have I, Bassett? Then we're careful, because we mostly go down."

"You do, do you! And when you're sure, like about Daffodil, what makes you sure, sonny?"

"Oh, well, I don't know," said the boy uneasily. "I'm sure, you know, Uncle; that's all."

"It's as if he had it from heaven, sir," Bassett reiterated.

"I should say so!" said the uncle.

But he became a partner. And when the Leger was coming on, Paul was "sure" about Lively Spark, which was a quite inconsiderable horse. The boy insisted on putting a thousand on the horse, Bassett went for five hundred, and Oscar Cresswell two hundred. Lively Spark came in first, and the betting had been ten to one against him. Paul had made ten thousand.

"You see," he said, "I was absolutely sure of him."

Even Oscar Cresswell had cleared two thousand.

"Look here, son," he said, "this sort of thing makes me nervous."

"It needn't, Uncle! Perhaps I shan't be sure again for a long time."

"But what are you going to do with your money?" asked the uncle.

"Of course," said the boy. "I started it for Mother. She said she had no luck, because Father is unlucky, so I thought if *I* was lucky, it might stop whispering."

"What might stop whispering?"

"Our house. I *hate* our house for whispering."

"What does it whisper?"

"Why — why" — the boy fidgeted — "why, I don't know. But it's always short of money, you know, Uncle."

"I know it, son, I know it."

"You know people send Mother writs, don't you, Uncle?"

"I'm afraid I do," said the uncle.

"And then the house whispers, like people laughing at you behind your back. It's awful, that is! I thought if I was lucky. . . ."

"You might stop it," added the uncle.

The boy watched him with big blue eyes, that had an uncanny cold fire in them, and he said never a word.

"Well, then!" said the uncle. "What are we doing?"

"I shouldn't like Mother to know I was lucky," said the boy.

"Why not, son?"

"She'd stop me."

"I don't think she would."

"Oh!" — and the boy writhed in an odd way — "I *don't* want her to know, Uncle."

"All right, son! We'll manage it without her knowing."

They managed it very easily. Paul, at the other's suggestion, handed over five thousand pounds to his uncle, who deposited it with the family lawyer, who was then to inform Paul's mother that a relative had put five thousand pounds into his hands, which sum was to be paid out a thousand pounds at a time, on the mother's birthday, for the next five years.

"So she'll have a birthday present of a thousand pounds for five successive years," said Uncle Oscar. "I hope it won't make it all the harder for her later."

Paul's mother had her birthday in November. The house had been "whispering" worse than ever lately, and, even in spite of his luck, Paul could not bear up against it. He was very anxious to see the effect of the birthday letter, telling his mother about the thousand pounds.

When there were no visitors, Paul now took his meals with his parents, as he was beyond the nursery control. His mother went into town nearly every day. She had discovered that she had an odd knack of sketching furs and dress materials, so she worked secretly in the studio of a friend who was the chief artist for the leading drapers. She drew the figures of ladies in furs and ladies in silk and sequins for the newspaper advertisements. This young woman artist earned several thousand pounds a year, but Paul's mother only made several hundreds, and she was again dissatisfied. She so wanted to be first in something, and she did not succeed, even in making sketches for drapery advertisements.

She was down to breakfast on the morning of her birthday. Paul watched her face as she read her letters. He knew the lawyer's letter. As his mother read it, her face hardened and became more expressionless. Then a cold, determined look came on her mouth. She hid the letter under the pile of others, and said not a word about it.

"Didn't you have anything nice in the post for your birthday, Mother?" said Paul.

"Quite moderately nice," she said, her voice cold and absent.

She went away to town without saying more.

But in the afternoon Uncle Oscar appeared. He said Paul's mother had had a long interview with the lawyer, asking if the whole five thousand could not be advanced at once, as she was in debt.

"What do you think, Uncle?" said the boy.

"I leave it to you, son."

"Oh, let her have it, then! We can get some more with the other," said the boy.

"A bird in the hand is worth two in the bush, laddie!" said Uncle Oscar.

"But I'm sure to *know* for the Grand National; or the Lincolnshire; or else the Derby. I'm sure to know for *one* of them," said Paul.

So Uncle Oscar signed the agreement, and Paul's mother touched the whole five thousand. Then something very curious happened. The voices in the house suddenly went mad, like a chorus of frogs on a spring evening. There were certain new furnishings, and Paul had a tutor. He was *really* going to Eton, his father's school, in the following autumn. There were flowers in the winter, and a blossoming of the luxury Paul's mother had been used to. And yet the voices in the house, behind the sprays of mimosa and almond blossom, and from under the piles of iridescent cushions, simply trilled and screamed in a sort of ecstasy: "There *must* be more money! Oh-h-h; there *must* be more money. Oh, now, now-w! Now-w-w — there *must* be more money! — more than ever! More than ever!"

It frightened Paul terribly. He studied away at his Latin and Greek.

But his intense hours were spent with Bassett. The Grand National had gone by; he had not "known," and had lost a hundred pounds. Summer was at hand. He was in agony for the Lincoln. But even for the Lincoln he didn't "know," and he lost fifty pounds. He became wild-eyed and strange, as if something were going to explode in him.

"Let it alone, son! Don't you bother about it!" urged Uncle Oscar. But it was as if the boy couldn't really hear what his uncle was saying.

"I've got to know for the Derby! I've got to know for the Derby!" the child reiterated, his big blue eyes blazing with a sort of madness.

His mother noticed how overwrought he was.

"You'd better go to the seaside. Wouldn't you like to go now to the seaside, instead of waiting? I think you'd better," she said, looking down at him anxiously, her heart curiously heavy because of him.

But the child lifted his uncanny blue eyes. "I couldn't possibly go before the Derby, Mother!" he said. "I couldn't possibly!"

"Why not?" she said, her voice becoming heavy when she was opposed. "Why not? You can still go from the seaside to see the Derby with your uncle Oscar, if that's what you wish. No need for you to wait here. Besides, I think you care too much about these races. It's a bad sign. My family has been a gambling family, and you won't know till you grow up how much damage it has done. But it has done damage. I shall have to send Bassett away, and ask Uncle Oscar not to talk racing to you, unless you promise to be reasonable about it; go away to the seaside and forget it. You're all nerves!"

"I'll do what you like, Mother, so long as you don't send me away till after the Derby," the boy said.

"Send you away from where? Just from this house?"

"Yes," he said, gazing at her.

"Why, you curious child, what makes you care about this house so much, suddenly? I never knew you loved it."

He gazed at her without speaking. He had a secret within a secret, something he had not divulged, even to Bassett or to his uncle Oscar.

But his mother, after standing undecided and a little bit sullen for some moments, said:

"Very well, then! Don't go to the seaside till after the Derby, if you don't wish it. But promise me you won't let your nerves go to pieces. Promise you won't think so much about horse racing and *events*, as you call them!"

"Oh, no," said the boy casually. "I won't think much about them, Mother. You needn't worry. I wouldn't worry, Mother, if I were you."

"If you were me and I were you," said his mother, "I wonder what we *should* do!"

"But you know you needn't worry, Mother, don't you?" the boy repeated.

"I should be awfully glad to know it," she said wearily.

"Oh, well, you *can,* you know. I mean, you *ought* to know you needn't worry," he insisted.

"Ought I? Then I'll see about it," she said.

Paul's secret of secrets was his wooden horse, that which had no name. Since he was emancipated from a nurse and a nursery governess, he had had his rocking horse removed to his own bedroom at the top of the house.

"Surely, you're too big for a rocking horse!" his mother had remonstrated.

"Well, you see, Mother, till I can have a *real* horse, I like to have *some* sort of animal about," had been his quaint answer.

"Do you feel he keeps you company?" She laughed.

"Oh, yes! He's very good, he always keeps me company, when I'm there," said Paul.

So the horse, rather shabby, stood in an arrested prance in the boy's bedroom.

The Derby was drawing near, and the boy grew more and more tense. He hardly heard what was spoken to him, he was very frail, and his eyes were really uncanny. His mother had sudden strange seizures of uneasiness about him. Sometimes, for half an hour, she would feel a sudden anxiety about him that was almost anguish. She wanted to rush to him at once, and know he was safe.

Two nights before the Derby, she was at a big party in town, when one of her rushes of anxiety about her boy, her firstborn, gripped her heart till she could hardly speak. She fought with the feeling, might and main, for she believed in common sense. But it was too strong. She had to leave the dance and go downstairs to telephone to the country. The children's nursery governess was terribly surprised and startled at being rung up in the night.

"Are the children all right, Miss Wilmot?"

"Oh, yes, they are quite all right."

"Master Paul? Is he all right?"

"He went to bed as right as a trivet. Shall I run up and look at him?"

"No," said Paul's mother reluctantly. "No! Don't trouble. It's all right. Don't sit up. We shall be home fairly soon." She did not want her son's privacy intruded upon.

"Very good," said the governess.

It was about one o'clock when Paul's mother and father drove up to their house. All was still. Paul's mother went to her room and slipped off her white fur cloak. She had told her maid not to wait up for her. She heard her husband downstairs, mixing a whisky and soda.

And then, because of the strange anxiety at her heart, she stole upstairs to her son's room. Noiselessly she went along the upper corridor. Was there a faint noise? What was it?

She stood, with arrested muscles, outside his door, listening. There was a strange, heavy, and yet not loud noise. Her heart stood still. It was a soundless noise, yet rushing and powerful. Something huge, in violent, hushed motion. What was it? What in God's name was it? She ought to know. She felt that she knew the noise. She knew what it was.

Yet she could not place it. She couldn't say what it was. And on and on it went, like a madness.

Softly, frozen with anxiety and fear, she turned the door handle.

The room was dark. Yet in the space near the window, she heard and saw something plunging to and fro. She gazed in fear and amazement.

Then suddenly she switched on the light, and saw her son, in his green pajamas, madly surging on the rocking horse. The blaze of light suddenly lit him up, as he urged the wooden horse, and lit her up, as she stood, blonde, in her dress of pale green and crystal, in the doorway.

"Paul!" she cried. "Whatever are you doing?"

"It's Malabar!" he screamed, in a powerful, strange voice. "It's Malabar!"

His eyes blazed at her for one strange and senseless second, as he ceased urging his wooden horse. Then he fell with a crash to the ground, and she, all her tormented motherhood flooding upon her, rushed to gather him up.

But he was unconscious, and unconscious he remained, with some brain fever. He talked and tossed, and his mother sat stonily by his side.

"Malabar! It's Malabar! Bassett, Bassett, I *know*! It's Malabar!"

So the child cried, trying to get up and urge the rocking horse that gave him his inspiration.

"What does he mean by Malabar?" asked the heart-frozen mother.

"I don't know," said the father stonily.

"What does he mean by Malabar?" she asked her brother Oscar.

"It's one of the horses running for the Derby," was the answer.

And, in spite of himself, Oscar Cresswell spoke to Bassett, and himself put a thousand on Malabar: at fourteen to one.

The third day of the illness was critical: they were waiting for a change. The boy, with his rather long, curly hair, was tossing ceaselessly on the pillow. He neither slept nor regained consciousness, and his eyes were like blue stones. His mother sat, feeling her heart had gone, turned actually into a stone.

In the evening, Oscar Cresswell did not come, but Bassett sent a message, saying could he come up for one moment, just one moment? Paul's mother was very angry at the intrusion, but on second thought she agreed. The boy was the same. Perhaps Bassett might bring him to consciousness.

The gardener, a shortish fellow with a little brown mustache, and sharp little brown eyes, tiptoed into the room, touched his imaginary cap to Paul's mother, and stole to the bedside, staring with glittering, smallish eyes at the tossing, dying child.

"Master Paul!" he whispered. "Master Paul! Malabar came in first all right, a clean win. I did as you told me. You've made over seventy thousand pounds, you have; you've got over eighty thousand. Malabar came in all right, Master Paul."

"Malabar! Malabar! Did I say Malabar, Mother? Did I say Malabar? Do you think I'm lucky, Mother? I knew Malabar, didn't I? Over eighty thousand pounds! I call that lucky, don't you, Mother? Over eighty thousand pounds! I knew, didn't I know I knew? Malabar came in all right. If I ride my horse till I'm sure, then I tell you, Bassett, you can go as high as you like. Did you go for all you were worth, Bassett?"

"I went a thousand on it, Master Paul."

"I never told you, Mother, that if I can ride my horse, and *get there,* then I'm absolutely sure — oh, absolutely! Mother, did I ever tell you? I *am* lucky!"

"No, you never did," said the mother.

But the boy died in the night.

And even as he lay dead, his mother heard her brother's voice saying to her: "My God, Hester, you're eighty-odd thousand to the good, and a poor devil of a son to the bad. But, poor devil, poor devil, he's best gone out of a life where he rides his rocking horse to find a winner."

[1933]

ISAK DINESEN *was the name under which the Danish Baroness Karen Blixen (1885–1962) published her writings. She was born Karen Christentze Dinesen near Elsinore, Denmark, and grew up in her family's ancestral home close to the sea. When she was a child her father committed suicide, and she felt that a part of herself had also died. Preferring her father's love of freedom to her mother's absorption in motherhood, Dinesen had such an "intuitive fear of being trapped" that she decided not to become a professional writer after publishing some short stories at the age of twenty. She felt that every profession invariably assigns a definite role in life, which would cut her off from the infinite possibilities of life itself. In 1914 she married her cousin, Baron Bror Blixen, and went with him to British East Africa (now Kenya) to manage a large coffee plantation. In 1921 she and her husband divorced and she took over the management of the plantation. When coffee prices dropped in 1931 she had to give it up—a severe blow, because the seventeen years she spent in Africa had been the happiest years of her life. She also lost her lover, the Englishman Denys Finch-Hatton, in a plane crash at this time. With a sense that her life was over, she returned to Denmark.*

Grief over having lost her farm and her lover in Africa made Karen Blixen a writer. She decided that the chief trap in life was not a single profession, as she had feared as a girl, but rather a single identity, so she created another one for herself as a writer. "Slowly the center of gravity of my being will shift over from the world of day . . . into the world of Imagination." She chose to write in English out of loyalty to her dead lover, and she took the male pseudonym Isak, meaning "the one who laughs," in the spirit of the saying "God loves a joke." In her first collection of short stories, Seven Gothic Tales — published in 1934 when she was nearly fifty years old — Dinesen's genius was so immediately apparent that she became world famous. That collection was followed by Out of Africa *(1937), a reminiscence of her years in Africa, and a second book of stories,* Winter's Tales *(1942). Both were best-sellers. Her imaginative brilliance as a teller of spellbinding tales prompted Ernest Hemingway to say in his acceptance speech for the Nobel Prize that it should have been given to "that beautiful writer Isak Dinesen." In the final years of her life she published* Last Tales *(1957) and* Anecdotes of Destiny *(1958).*

Dinesen's fiction does not fit any literary or ideological formula. She has said, "I am a storyteller and nothing else. What interests me is the story and the way to tell it." As Eudora Welty recognized, her tales are "glimpses out of, rather than into, an extraordinary mind." Dinesen spins her stories out of the impulse to bring to life a world of marvels and enchantments, a world filled with such an intensity of emotions that her fiction often takes on a legendary quality. "The Old Chevalier," from Seven Gothic Tales, is such a story, telling about a remarkable encounter between a despairing nobleman and a girl of the streets. The style of the story is the essence of delicacy. Discovering that "All sorrows can be borne if you put them into a story or tell a story about them," Dinesen showed that the storyteller could make meaning out of what otherwise would remain an unbearable sequence of events or sheer happenings. In the repetition and selection performed by the imagination, the happenings become part of a pattern, what she called a "destiny." Her creation of that destiny in a work of fiction revealed meaning in life without committing the error of defining it. For Dinesen, the answer to the question "Who are you?" is given in the reply, "Let me tell you a story."

Isak Dinesen

ಬ

THE OLD CHEVALIER

My father had a friend, old Baron von Brackel, who had in his day traveled much and known many cities and men. Otherwise he was not at all like Odysseus, and could least of all be called ingenious, for he had shown very little skill in managing his own affairs. Probably from a sense of failure in this respect he carefully kept from discussing practical matters with an efficient younger generation, keen on their careers and success in life. But on theology, the opera, moral right and wrong, and other unprofitable pursuits he was a pleasant talker.

He had been a singularly good-looking young man, a sort of ideally handsome youth, and although no trace of this past beauty could be found in his face, the history of it could be traced in a certain light-hearted dignity and self-reliance which are the product of a career of good looks, and which will be found, unaccountably, in the carriage of those shaking ruins who used to look into the mirrors of the last century with delight. In this way one should be able to point out, at a *danse macabre*, the skeletons of the real great beauties of their time.

One night he and I came to discuss an old theme, which has done its duty in the literature of the past: namely, whether one is ever likely to get any real benefit, any lasting moral satisfaction, out of forsaking an inclination for the sake of principle, and in the course of our talk he told me the following story:

On a rainy night in the winter of 1874, on an avenue in Paris, a drunken young girl came up and spoke to me. I was then, as you will understand, quite a young man. I was very upset and unhappy, and was sitting bareheaded in the rain on a seat along the avenue because I had just parted from a lady whom, as we said then, I did adore, and who had within this last hour tried to poison me.

This, though it has nothing to do with what I was going to tell you, was in itself a curious story. I had not thought of it for many years until, when I was last in Paris, I saw the lady in her box at the opera, now a very old woman, with two charming little girls in pink who were, I was told, her great-granddaughters. She was lovely no more, but I had never, in the time that I have known her, seen her look so contented. I was sorry afterward that I had not gone up and called on her in her box, for though there had been but little happiness for either of us in that old love affair of ours, I think that she would have been as pleased to be reminded of the beautiful young woman, who made men unhappy, as I had been to remember, vaguely as it was, the young man who had been so unhappy that long time ago.

Her great beauty, unless some rare artist has been able to preserve it in color or clay, now probably exists only within a few very old brains like mine. It was in its day something very wonderful. She was a blonde, the fairest, I think, that I have ever seen, but not one of your pink-and-white beauties. She was pale, colorless, all through, like an old pastel or the image of a woman in a dim mirror. Within that cool and frail form there was an unrivaled energy, and a distinction such as women have no more, or no more care to have.

I had met her and had fallen in love with her in the autumn, at the château of a friend where we were both staying together with a large party of other gay young people who are now, if they are alive, faded and crooked and deaf. We were there to hunt, and I think that I shall be able to remember to the last of my days how she used to look on a big bay horse that she had, and that autumn air, just touched with frost, when we came home in the evenings, warm in cold clothes, tired, riding side by side over an old stone bridge. My love was both humble and audacious, like that of a page for his lady, for she was so much admired, and her beauty had in itself a sort of disdain which might well give sad dreams to a boy of twenty, poor and a stranger in her set. So that every hour of our rides, dances and *tableaux vivants*[1] was exuberant with ecstasy and pain, the sort of thing you will know yourself: a whole orchestra in the heart. When she made me happy, as one says, I thought that I was happy indeed. I remembered smoking a cigar on the terrace one morning, looking out over the large view of low, wood-covered blue hills, and giving the Lord a sort of receipt for all the happiness

---

[1] a parlor game in which the players strike the poses of a famous sculpture, painting, or other artistic portrayal of a group of people.

that I should ever have any claim to in my life. Whatever would happen to me now, I had had my due, and declared myself satisfied.

Love, with very young people, is a heartless business. We drink at that age from thirst, or to get drunk; it is only later in life that we occupy ourselves with the individuality of our wine. A young man in love is essentially enraptured by the forces within himself. You may come back to that view again, in a second adolescence. I knew a very old Russian in Paris, enormously rich, who used to keep the most charming young dancers, and who when once asked whether he had, or needed to have, any illusions as to their feelings for him, thought the question over and said: "I do not think, if my chef succeeds in making me a good omelette, that I bother much whether he loves me or not." A young man could not have put his answer into those words, but he might say that he did not care whether his wine merchant was of his own religion or not, and imagine that he had got close to the truth of things. In middle age, though, you arrive at a deeper humility, and you come to consider it of importance that the person who sells or grows your wine shall be of the same religion as you yourself. In this case of my own, of which I am telling you, my youthful vanity, if I had too much of it, was to be taught a lesson very soon. For during the months of that winter, while we were both living in Paris, where her house was the meeting place of many *bel-esprits,* and she herself the admired dilettante in music and arts, I began to think that she was making use of me, or of her own love for me, if such can be said, to make her husband jealous. This has happened, I suppose, to many young men down through the ages, without the total sum of their experience being much use to the young man who finds himself in the same position today. I began to wonder what the relations between those two were really like, and what strange forces there might be in her or in him, to toss me about between them in this way, and I think that I began to be afraid. She was jealous of me, too, and would scold me with a sort of moral indignation, as if I had been a groom failing in his duties. I thought that I could not live without her, and also that she did not want to live without me, but exactly what she wanted me for I did not know. Her contact hurt me as one is hurt by touching iron on a winter day: you do not know whether the pain comes from heat or from cold.

Before I had ever met her I had read about her family, whose name ran down for centuries through the history of France, and learned that there used to be werewolves amongst them, and I sometimes thought that I should have been happier to see her really go down on all fours and snarl at me, for then I should have known where I was. And even up to the end we had hours together of a particular charm, for which I shall always be thankful to her. During my first year in Paris, before I knew any people there, I had taken up studying the history of the old hotels of the town, and this hobby of mine appealed to her, so that we used to dive into old quarters and ages of Paris, and dwell together in the age of Abélard or of Molière, and while we were playing in this way she was serious and gentle with me, like a little girl. But at other times I thought that I could stand it no longer, and would try to get away from her, and any suspicion of this was enough, I imagine, to make her lie awake at night thinking out new methods of punishing me. It was between us the old game of the cat and the mouse — probably the original model of all the games of the world. But because the cat has more passion in it, and the mouse only the plain interest of existence, the mouse is bound to become tired first. Toward the end I thought that she wished us to be found out, she was so careless in this *liaison* of ours; and in those days a love affair had to be managed with prudence.

I remember during this period coming to her hotel on the night of a ball to which she was going, while I had not been asked, disguised as a hairdresser. In the 'seventies ladies had large chignons and the work of a *coiffeur* took time. And through everything the thought of her husband would follow me, like, I thought, the gigantic shadow, upon the white backcurtain, of an absurd little punchinello. I began to feel so tired — not exactly of her, but really exhausted in myself — that I was making up my mind to have a scene and an explanation from her, even if I should lose her by it, when suddenly, on the night of which I am telling you, she herself produced both the scene and the explanation, such a hurricane as I have never again been out in; and all with exactly the same weapons as I had myself had ready: with the accusation that I thought more of her husband than I did of her. And when she said this to me, in that pale blue boudoir of hers that I knew so well — the silk-lined, upholstered and scented box, such as the ladies of that time liked to keep themselves in, with, I remember, some paintings of flowers on the walls, and very soft silk cushions everywhere, and a lot of lilacs in the corner behind me, with the lamp subdued by a large red shade — I had no reply, for I knew that she was right.

You would know his name if I told you, for he is still talked about, though he has been dead for many years. Or you would find it in any of the memoirs of that period, for he was the idol of our generation. Later on, great unhappiness came upon him, but at that moment — I believe that he was then thirty-three years old — he was walking quietly in the full splendor of his strange power. I once, about that time, heard two old men talk about his mother, who had been one of the beauties of the Restoration, and one of them said of her that she carried all her famous jewels as lightly and gracefully as other young ladies would wear garlands of field flowers. "Yes," the other said after he had thought it over for a moment, "and she scattered them about her, in the end, like flowers, *à la* Ophelia." Therefore, I think that this rare lightness of his must have been, together with the weakness, a family trait. Even in his wildest whims, and in a sort of mannerism which we then named *fin de siècle* and were rather proud of, he had something of *le grand siècle* about him: a straight nobility that belonged to the old France.

I have looked since at those great buildings of the seventeenth century which seem altogether inexpedient as dwellings for human beings, and have thought that they must have been built for him — and his mother, I suppose — to live in. He had a confidence in life, independent of the successes which we envied him, as if he knew that he could draw upon greater forces, unknown to us, if he wanted to. It gave me much to think about, on the fate of man, when many years later I was told how this young man had, toward the end of his tragic destiny, answered the friends who implored him in the name of God, in the words of Sophocles's Ajax: "You worry me too much, woman. Do you not know that I am no longer a debtor of the gods?"

I see that I ought not to have started talking about him, even after all these years; but an ideal of one's youth will always be a landmark amongst happenings and feelings long gone. He himself has nothing to do with this story.

I told you that I myself felt it to be true that my feelings for the lovely young woman, whom I adored, were really light of weight compared to my feelings for the young man. If he had been with her when we first met, or if I had known him before I met her, I do not think that I should ever have dreamed of falling in love with his wife.

But his wife's love for him, and her jealousy, were indeed of a strange nature. For that she was in love with him I knew from the moment that she began to speak of him. Probably I had known it a long time before. And she was jealous. She suffered, she cried — she was, as I have told you, ready to kill if nothing else would help her — and all the time that fight, which was very likely the only reality in her life, was not a struggle for possession, but a competition. She was jealous of him as if he had been another young woman of fashion, her rival, or as if she herself had been a young man who envied him his triumphs. I think that she was, in herself, always alone with him in a world that she despised. When she rode so madly, when she surrounded herself with admirers, she had her eye on him, as a competitor in a chariot race would have his eyes only on the driver just beside him. As for the rest of us, we only existed for her insofar as we were to belong to her or to him, and she took her lovers as she took her fences, to pile up more conquests than the man with whom she was in love.

I cannot, of course, know how this had begun between them. Afterward I tried to believe that it must have arisen from a desire for revenge, on her side, for something that he had done to her in the past. But I had the feeling that it was this barren passion which had burned all the color out of her.

Now you will know that all this happened in the early days of what we called then the "emancipation of woman." Many strange things took place then. I do not think that at the time the movement went very deep down in the social world, but here were the young women of the highest intelligence, and the most daring and ingenious of them, coming out of the chiaroscuro of a thousand years, blinking at the sun and wild with desire to try their wings. I believe that some of them put on the armor and the halo of St. Joan of Arc, who was herself an emancipated virgin, and became like white-hot angels. But most women, when they feel free to experiment with life, will go straight to the witches' Sabbath. I myself respect them for it, and do not think that I could ever really love a woman who had not, at some time or other, been up on a broomstick.

I have always thought it unfair to woman that she has never been alone in the world. Adam had a time, whether long or short, when he could wander about on a fresh and peaceful earth, among the beasts, in full possession of his soul, and most men are born with a memory of that period. But poor Eve found him there, with all his claims upon her, the moment she looked into the world. That is a grudge that woman has always had against the Creator: she feels that she is entitled to have that epoch of paradise back for herself. Only, worse luck, when chasing a time that has gone, one is bound to get hold of it by the tail, the wrong way around. Thus these young witches got everything they wanted as in a catoptric image.[2]

Old ladies of those days, patronesses of the church and of home, said that emancipation was turning the heads of the young women. Probably there were more young ladies than my mistress galloping high up above the ground, with their fair faces at the backs of their necks, after the manner of the wild huntsman in the tale. And in the air there was a theory, which caught hold of them there, that the jealousy of lovers was an ignoble affair, and that no woman should allow herself to be possessed by any male but the devil. On their way to him they were proud of being, according to Doctor Faust, always a hundred steps ahead of man. But the jealousy of competition was, as between Adam and Lilith, a noble striving. So there you would find, not only the old witches of Macbeth, of whom one might have expected it, but even young ladies with faces smooth as flowers, wild and mad with jealousy of their lovers' mustachios. All this they got from reading — in the orthodox witches' manner — the book of Genesis backwards. Left to themselves, they might have got a lot out of it. It was the poor, tame, male preachers of emancipation, cutting, as warlocks always will, a miserable figure at the Sabbath, who spoiled the style and flight of the whole thing by bringing it down to earth and under laws of earthly reason. I believe, though, that things have changed by now, and that at the present day, when males have likewise emancipated themselves, you may find the young lover on the hearth, following the track of the witch's shadow along the ground, and with infinitely less imagination, blending the deadly brew for his mistress, out of envy of her breasts.

The part which had been granted to me, in the story of my emancipated young witch, was not in itself flattering. Still I believe that she was desperately fond of me, probably with the kind of passion which a little girl has for her favorite doll. And as far as that goes I was really the central figure of our drama. If she would be Othello, it was I, and not her husband, who must take the part of Desdemona, and I can well imagine her sighing,

[2] a mirror image.

"Oh, the pity of it, the pity of it, Iago," over this unfortunate business, even wanting to give me a kiss and yet another before finishing it altogether. Only she did not want to kill me out of a feeling of justice or revenge. She wished to destroy me so that she should not have to lose me and to see a very dear possession belong to her rival, in the manner of a determined general, who will blow up a fortress which he can no longer hold, rather than see it in the hands of the enemy.

It was toward the end of our interview that she tried to poison me. I believe that this was really against her program, and that she had meant to tell me what she thought of me when I already had the poison in me, but had been unable to control herself for so long. There was, as you will understand, something unnatural in drinking coffee at that stage of our dialogue. The way in which she insisted upon it, and her sudden deadly silence as I raised the cup to my mouth, gave her away. I can still, although I only just touched it, recall the mortal, insipid taste of the opium, and had I emptied the cup, it could not have made my stomach rise and the marrow in my bones turn to water more than did the abrupt and fatal conviction that she wanted me to die. I let the cup drop, faint as a drowning man, and stood and stared at her, and she made one wild movement, as if she meant to throw herself at me still. Then we stood quite immovable for a minute, both knowing that all was lost. And after a little while she began to rock and whimper, with her hands at her mouth, suddenly changed into a very old woman. For my own part, I was not able to utter a sound, and I think that I just ran from the house as soon as I had strength enough to move. The air, the rain, and the street itself met me like old forgotten friends, faithful still in the hour of need.

And there I sat on a seat of the Avenue Montaigne, with the entire building of my pride and happiness lying around me in ruins, sick to death with horror and humiliation, when this girl, of whom I was telling you, came up to me.

I think that I must have been sitting there for some time, and that she must have stood and watched me before she could summon up her courage to approach. She probably felt herself in sympathy with me, thinking that I was drunk too, as sensible people do not sit without a hat in the rain, perhaps also because I was so near her own age. I did not hear what she said, neither the first nor the second time. I was not in a mood to enter into talk with a little girl of the streets. I think that it must have been from sheer instinct of self-preservation that I did in the end come to look at her and to listen. I had to get away from my own thoughts, and any human being was welcome to assist me. But there was at the same time something extraordinarily graceful and expressive about the girl, which may have attracted my attention. She stood there in the rain, highly rouged, with radiant eyes like stars, very erect though only just steady on her legs. When I kept on staring at her, she laughed at me, a low, clear laughter. She was very young. She was holding up her dress with one hand — in those days ladies wore long trains in the streets. On her head she had a black hat with ostrich feathers drooping sadly in the rain and overshadowing her forehead and eyes. The firm gentle curve of her chin, and her round neck shone in the light of the gas lamp. Thus I can see her still, though I have another picture of her as well.

What impressed me about her was that she seemed altogether so strangely moved, intoxicated by the situation. Hers was not the conventional advance. She looked like a person out on a great adventure, or someone keeping a secret. I think that on looking at her I began to smile, some sort of bitter and wild smile, known only to young people, and that this encouraged her. She came nearer. I fumbled in my pocket for some money to give her, but I had no money on me. I got up and started to walk, and she came on, walking beside me. There was, I remember, a certain comfort in having her near me, for I did not want to be alone. In this way it happened that I let her come with me.

I asked her what her name was. She told me that it was Nathalie.

At this time I had a job at the Legation, and I was living in an apartment on the Place François I, so we had not far to go. I was prepared to come back late, and in those days, when I would come home at all sorts of hours, I used to keep a fire and a cold supper waiting for me. When we came into the room it was lighted and warm, and the table was laid for me in front of the fire. There was a bottle of champagne on ice. I used to keep a bottle of champagne to drink when I returned from my shepherd's hours.

The young girl looked around the room with a contented face. Here in the light of my lamp I could see how she really looked. She had soft brown curls and blue eyes. Her face was round, with a broad forehead. She was wonderfully pretty and graceful. I think that I just wondered at her, as one would wonder at finding a fresh bunch of roses in a gutter, no more. If I had been normally balanced I suppose I should have tried to get from her some explanation of that sort of mystery that she seemed to be, but now I do not think that this occurred to me at all.

The truth was that we must both have been in quite a peculiar sort of mood, such as will hardly ever have repeated itself for either of us. I knew as little of what moved her as she could have known about my state of mind, but, highly excited and strained, we met in a special sort of sympathy. I, partly stunned and partly abnormally wide awake and sensitive, took her quite selfishly, without any thought of where she came from or where she would disappear to again, as if she were a gift to me, and her presence a kind and friendly act of fate at this moment when I could not be alone. She seemed to me to have come as a little wild spirit from the great town outside — Paris — which may at any moment bestow unexpected favors on one, and which had in the right moment sent her to me. What she thought of me or what she felt about me, of that I can say nothing. At the moment I did not think about it, but on looking back now I should say that I must also have symbolized something to her, and that I hardly existed for her as an individual.

I felt it as a great happiness, a warmth all through me, that she was so young and lovely. It made me laugh again after those weird and dismal hours. I pulled off her hat, lifted her face up, and kissed her. Then I felt how wet she was. She must have walked for a long time on the streets in the rain, for her clothes were like the feathers of a wet hen. I went over and opened the bottle on the table, poured her out a glass, and handed it to her. She took it, standing in front of the fire, her tumbled wet curls falling down over her forehead. With her red cheeks and shining eyes she looked like a child that has just awakened from sleep, or like a doll. She drank half the glass of wine quite slowly, with her eyes on my face, and, as if this half-glass of champagne had brought her to a point where she could no longer be silent, she started to sing, in a low, gentle voice, hardly moving her lips, the first lines of a song, a waltz, which was then sung in all the music halls. She broke it off, emptied her glass, and handed it back to me. A *votre santé*, she said.

Her voice was so merry, so pure, like the song of a bird in a bush, and of all things music at that time went most directly to my heart. Her song increased the feeling I had, that something special and more than natural had been sent to me. I filled her glass again, put my hand on her round white neck, and brushed the damp ringlets back from her face. "How on earth have you come to be so wet, Nathalie?" I said, as if I had been her grandmother. "You must take off your clothes and get warm." As I spoke my voice changed. I began to laugh again. She fixed her starlike eyes on me. Her face quivered for a moment. Then she started to unbutton her cloak, and let it fall onto the floor. Underneath this cloak of black lace, badly suited for the season and faded at the edges into a rusty brown, she had a black silk frock, tightly fitted over the bust, waist and hips, and pleated and draped below, with flounces and ruffles such as ladies wore at that time, in the early days of the bustle. Its folds shone in the light of my fire. I began to undress her, as I might have undressed a doll, very slowly and clumsily, and she stood up straight and let me do it. Her fresh face had a grave and child-like expression. Once or twice she colored under my hands, but as I undid her tight bodice and my hands touched her cool shoulders and bosom, her face broke into a gentle and wide smile, and she lifted up her hand and touched my fingers.

The old Baron von Brackel made a long pause. "I think that I must explain to you," he said, "so that you may be able to understand this tale aright, that to undress a woman was then a very different thing from what it must be now. What are the clothes that your ladies of these days are wearing? In themselves as little as possible — a few perpendicular lines, cut off again before they have had time to develop any sense. There is no plan about them. They exist for the sake of the body, and have no career of their own, or, if they have any mission at all, it is to reveal.

"But in those days a woman's body was a secret which her clothes did their utmost to keep. We would walk about in the streets in bad weather in order to catch a glimpse of an ankle, the sight of which must be as familiar to you young men of the present day as the stems of these wineglasses of ours. Clothes then had a being, an idea of their own. With a serenity that it was not easy to look through, they made it their object to transform the body which they encircled, and to create a silhouette so far from its real form as to make it a mystery which it was a divine privilege to solve. The long tight stays, the whalebones, skirts and petticoats, bustle and draperies, all that mass of material under which the women of my day were buried where they were not laced together as tightly as they could possibly stand it — all aimed at one thing: to disguise.

"Out of a tremendous froth of trains, pleatings, lace, and flounces which waved and undulated, *secundum artem,*[3] at every movement of the bearer, the waist would shoot up like the chalice of a flower, carrying the bust, high and rounded as a rose, but imprisoned in whalebone up to the shoulder. Imagine now how different life must have appeared and felt to creatures living in those tight corsets within which they could just manage to breathe, and in those fathoms of clothes which they dragged along with them wherever they walked or sat, and who never dreamed that it could be otherwise, compared to the existence of your young women, whose clothes hardly touch them and take up no room. A woman was then a work of art, the product of centuries of civilization, and you talked of her figure as you talked of her salon, with the admiration which one gives to the achievement of a skilled and untiring artist.

"And underneath all this Eve herself breathed and moved, to be indeed a revelation to us every time she stepped out of her disguise, with her waist still delicately marked by the stays, as with a girdle of rose petals.

"To you young people who laugh at the ideas, as at the bustles, of the 'seventies, and who will tell me that in spite of all our artificiality there can have been but little mystery left to any of us, may I be allowed to say that you do not, perhaps, quite understand the meaning of the word? Nothing is mysterious until it symbolizes something. The bread and wine of the church itself has to be baked and bottled, I suppose. The women of those days were more than a collection of individuals. They symbolized, or represented, Woman. I understand that the word itself, in that sense, has gone out of the language. Where we talked of woman — pretty cynically, we liked to think — you talk of women, and all the difference lies there.

"Do you remember the scholars of the middle ages who discussed the question of which had been created first: the idea of a dog, or the individual

[3] according to the accepted practice (Latin).

dogs? To you, who are taught statistics in your kindergartens, there is no doubt, I suppose. And it is but justice to say that your world does in reality look as if it had been made experimentally. But to us even the ideas of old Mr. Darwin were new and strange. We had our ideas from such undertakings as symphonies and ceremonials of court, and had been brought up with strong feelings about the distinction between legitimate and illegitimate birth. We had faith in purpose. The idea of Woman — of *das ewig weibliche*,[4] about which you yourself will not deny that there is some mystery — had to us been created in the beginning, and our women made it their mission to represent it worthily, as I suppose the mission of the individual dog must have been worthily to represent the Creator's idea of a dog.

"You could follow, then, the development of this idea in a little girl, as she was growing up and was gradually, no doubt in accordance with very ancient rules, inaugurated into the rites of the cult, and finally ordained. Slowly the center of gravity of her being would be shifted from individuality to symbol, and you would be met with that particular pride and modesty characteristic of the representative of the great powers — such as you may find again in a really great artist. Indeed, the haughtiness of the pretty young girl, or the old ladies' majesty, existed no more on account of personal vanity, or on any personal account whatever, than did the pride of Michelangelo himself, or the Spanish Ambassador to France. However much greeted at the banks of the Styx by the indignation of his individual victims with flowing hair and naked breasts, Don Giovanni would have been acquitted by a board of women of my day, sitting in judgment on him, for the sake of his great faith in the idea of Woman. But they would have agreed with the masters of Oxford in condemning Shelley as an atheist; and they managed to master Christ himself only by representing him forever as an infant in arms, dependent upon the Virgin.

"The multitude outside the temple of mystery is not very interesting. The real interest lies with the priest inside. The crowd waiting at the porch for the fulfillment of the miracle of the boiling blood of St. Pantaleone — that I have seen many times and in many places. But very rarely have I had admittance to the cool vaults behind, or the chance of seeing the priests, old and young, down to the choirboys, who feel themselves to be the most important persons at the ceremony, and are both scared and impudent, occupying themselves, in a measure of their own, with the preparations, guardians of a mystery that they know all about. What was the cynicism of Lord Byron, or of Baudelaire, whom we were just reading then with the *frisson nouveau*,[5] to the cynicism of these little priestesses, augurs all of them, performing with the utmost conscientiousness all the rites of a religion which they knew all about and did not believe in, upholding, I feel

---

[4] the eternal feminine (German).
[5] the thrill of novelty (French — literally, "new excitement").

sure, the doctrine of their mystery even amongst themselves. Our poets of those days would tell us how a party of young beauties, behind the curtains of the bathing-machine, would blush and giggle as they 'put lilies in water.'

"I do not know if you remember the tale of the girl who saves the ship under mutiny by sitting on the powder barrel with her lighted torch, threatening to put fire to it, and all the time knowing herself that it is empty? This has seemed to me a charming image of the woman of my time. There they were, keeping the world in order, and preserving the balance and rhythm of it, by sitting upon the mystery of life, and knowing themselves that there was no mystery. I have heard you young people saying that the women of old days had no sense of humor. Thinking of the face of my young girl upon the barrel, with severely downcast eyes, I have wondered if our famous male humor be not a little insipid compared to theirs. If we were more thankful to them for existing than you are to your women of the present day, I think that we had good reason for it.

"I trust that you will not mind," he said, "an old man lingering over these pictures of an age gone by. It will be, I suppose, like being detained a little in a museum, before a *montre*[6] showing its fashions. You may laugh at them, if you like."

The old chevalier then resumed his story:

As I then undressed this young girl, and the layers of clothes which so severely dominated and concealed her fell one by one there in front of my fire, in the light of my large lamp, itself swathed in layers of silk — all, my dear, was thus draped in those days, and my large chairs had, I remember, long silk fringes all around them and on the tops of those little velvet pompons. Otherwise they would not have been thought really pretty — until she stood naked, I had before me the greatest masterpiece of nature that my eyes have ever been privileged to rest upon, a sight to take away your breath. I know that there may be something very lovable in the little imperfections of the female form, and I have myself worshiped a knock-kneed Venus, but this young figure was pathetic, was heart-piercing, by reason of its pure faultlessness. She was so young that you felt, in the midst of your deep admiration, the anticipation of a still higher perfection, and that was all there was to be said.

All her body shone in the light, delicately rounded and smooth as marble. One straight line ran through it from neck to ankle, as though the heaven-aspiring column of a young tree. The same character was expressed in the high instep of the foot, as she pushed off her old shoes, as in the curve of the chin, as in the straight, gentle glance of her eyes, and the delicate and strong lines of her shoulder and wrist.

The comfort of the warmth of the fire on her skin, after the clinging of her wet and tumbled clothes, made her sigh with pleasure and turn a little,

[6] a display (French).

like a cat. She laughed softly, like a child who quits the doorstep of school for a holiday. She stood up erect before the fire; her wet curls fell down over her forehead and she did not try to push them back; her bright painted cheeks looked even more like a doll's above her fair naked body.

I think that all my soul was in my eyes. Reality had met me, such a short time ago, in such an ugly shape, that I had no wish to come into contact with it again. Somewhere in me a dark fear was still crouching, and I took refuge within the fantastic like a distressed child in his book of fairy tales. I did not want to look ahead, and not at all to look back. I felt the moment close over me, like a wave. I drank a large glass of wine to catch up with her, looking at her.

I was so young then that I could no more than other young people give up the deep faith in my own star, in a power that loved me and looked after me in preference to all other human beings. No miracle was incredible to me as long as it happened to myself. It is when this faith begins to wear out, and when you conceive the possibility of being in the same position as other people, that youth is really over. I was not surprised or suspicious of this act of favor on the part of the gods, but I think that my heart was filled with a very sweet gratitude toward them. I thought it after all only reasonable, only to be expected, that the great friendly power of the universe should manifest itself again, and send me, out of the night, as a help and consolation, this naked and drunk young girl, a miracle of gracefulness.

We sat down to supper, Nathalie and I, high up there in my warm and quiet room, with the great town below us and my heavy silk curtains drawn upon the wet night, like two owls in a ruined tower within the depth of the forest, and nobody in the world knew about us. She leaned one arm on the table and rested her head on it. I think that she was very hungry, under the influence of the food. We had some caviar, I remember, and a cold bird. She began to beam on me, to laugh, to talk to me, and to listen to what I said to her.

I do not remember what we talked about. I think we were very open-hearted, and that I told her, what I could not have mentioned to anybody else, of how I had come near to being poisoned just before I met her. I also think that I must have told her about my country, for I know that at a time afterwards the idea came to me that she would write to me there, or even come to look for me. I remember that she told me, rather sadly to begin with, a story of a very old monkey which could do tricks, and had belonged to an Armenian organ-grinder. Its master had died, and now it wanted to do its tricks and was always waiting for the catchword, but nobody knew it. In the course of this tale she imitated the monkey in the funniest and most gracefully inspired manner that one can imagine. But I remember most of her movements. Sometimes I have thought that the understanding of some pieces of music for violin and piano has come to me through the contemplation of the contrast, or the harmony, between her long slim hand and her short rounded chin as she held the glass to her mouth.

I have never in any other love affair — if this can be called a love affair — had the same feeling of freedom and security. In my last adventure I had all the time been worrying to find out what my mistress really thought of me, and what part I was playing in the eyes of the world. But no such doubts or fears could possibly penetrate into our little room here. I believe that this feeling of safety and perfect freedom must be what happily married people mean when they talk about the two being one. I wonder if that understanding can possibly, in marriage, be as harmonious as when you meet as strangers; but this, I suppose, is a matter of taste.

One thing did play in to both of us, though we were not conscious of it. The world outside was bad, was dreadful. Life had made a very nasty face at me, and must have made a worse at her. But this room and this night were ours, and were faithful to us. Although we did not think about it, ours was in reality a supper of the Girondists.

The wine helped us. I had not drunk much, but my head was fairly light before I began. Champagne is a very kind and friendly thing on a rainy night. I remember an old Danish bishop's saying to me that there are many ways to the recognition of truth, and that Burgundy is one of them. This is, I know, very well for an old man within his paneled study. But young people, who have seen the devil face to face, need a stronger helping hand. Over our softly hissing glasses we were brought back to seeing ourselves and this night of ours as a great artist might have seen us and it, worthy of the genius of a god.

I had a guitar lying on my sofa, for I was to serenade, in a *tableau vivant,* a romantic beauty — in real life an American woman from the Embassy who could not have given you an echo back from whatever angle you would have cried to her. Nathalie reached out for it, a little later in our supper. She shuddered slightly at the first sound, for I had not had time or thought for playing it, and crossing her knees, in my large low chair, she began to tune it. Then she sang two little songs to me. In my quiet room her low voice, a little hoarse, was clear as a bell, faintly giddy with happiness, like a bee's in a flower. She sang first a song from the music halls, a gay tune with a striking rhythm. Then she thought for a moment and changed over into a strange plaintive little song in a language that I did not understand. She had a great sense of music. That strong and delicate personality which showed itself in all her body came out again in her voice. The light metallic timbre, the straightness and ease of it, corresponded with her eyes, knees, and fingers. Only it was a little richer and fuller, as if it had grown up faster or had stolen a march somehow upon her body. Her voice knew more than she did herself, as did the bow of Mischa Elman when he played as a *Wunkerkind.*

All my balance, which I had kept somehow while looking at her, suddenly left me at the sound of her voice. These words that I did not understand seemed to me more directly meaningful than any I had ever understood. I sat in another low chair, opposite her. I remember the silence when her song was finished, and that I pushed the table away, and how I came slowly down on one knee before her. She looked at me with such a clear, severe, wild look as I think that a hawk's eyes must have when they lift off his hood. I went down on my other knee and put my arms around her legs. I do not know what there was in my face to convince her, but her own face changed and lighted up with a kind of heroic gentleness. Altogether there had been from the beginning something heroic about her. That was, I think, what had made her put up with the young fool that I was. For *du ridicule jusqu'au sublime,* surely, *il n'y a qu'un pas.*[7]

My friend, she was as innocent as she looked. She was the first young girl who had been mine. There is a theory that a very young man should not make love to a virgin, but ought to have a more experienced partner. That is not true; it is the only natural thing.

It must have been an hour or two later in the night that I woke up to the feeling that something was wrong, or dangerous. We say when we turn suddenly cold that someone is walking over our grave — the future brings itself into memory. And as *l'on meurt en plein bonheur de ses malheurs passés,*[8] so do we let go our hold of our present happiness on account of coming misfortune. It was not the *omne animal*[9] affair only; it was a distrust of the future as if I had heard myself asking it: "I am to pay for this; what am I to pay?" But at the time I may have believed that what I felt was only fear of her going away.

Once before she had sat up and moved as if to leave me, and I had dragged her back. Now she said: "I must go back," and got up. The lamp was still burning, the fire was smoldering. It seemed to me natural that she should be taken away by the same mysterious forces which had brought her, like Cinderella, or a little spirit out of the *Arabian Nights.* I was waiting for her to come up and let me know when she would come back to me, and what I was to do. All the same I was more silent now.

She dressed and got back into her black shabby disguise. She put on her hat and stood there just as I had seen her first in the rain on the avenue. Then she came up to me where I was sitting on the arm of my chair, and said: "And you will give me twenty francs, will you not?" As I did not answer, she repeated her question and said: "Marie said that — she said that I should get twenty francs."

I did not speak. I sat there looking at her. Her clear and light eyes met mine.

A great clearness came upon me then, as if all the illusions and arts with which we try to transform our world, coloring and music and dreams, had been drawn aside, and reality was shown to me, waste as a burnt house. This was the end of the play. There was no room for any superfluous word.

---

[7] "It is but a step from the ridiculous to the sublime" (French).

[8] "One dies full of happiness about one's past unhappiness" (French).

[9] *Omne animal post coitem triste est* — "Every animal becomes sad after intercourse" (Latin saying).

This was the first moment, I think, since I had met her those few hours ago, in which I saw her as a human being, within an existence of her own, and not as a gift to me. I believe that all thoughts of myself left me at the sight, but now it was too late.

We two had played. A rare jest had been offered me and I had accepted it; now it was up to me to keep the spirit of our game until the end. Her own demand was well within the spirit of the night. For the palace which he builds, for four hundred white and four hundred black slaves all loaded with jewels, the djinn asks for an old copper lamp; and the forest-witch who moves three towns and creates for the woodcutter's son an army of horse-soldiers demands for herself the heart of a hare. The girl asked me for her pay in the voice and manner of the djinn and the forest-witch, and if I were to give her twenty francs she might still be safe within the magic circle of her free and graceful and defiant spirit. It was I who was out of character, as I sat there in silence, with all the weight of the cold and real world upon me, knowing well that I should have to answer her or I might, even within these few seconds, pass it on to her.

Later on I reflected that I might have had it in me to invent something which would have kept her safe, and still have allowed me to keep her. I thought then that I should only have had to give her twenty francs and to have said: "And if you want another twenty, come back tomorrow night." If she had been less lovely to me, if she had not been so young and so innocent, I might perhaps have done it. But this young girl had called, during our few hours, on all the chivalrousness that I had in my nature. And chivalrousness, I think, means this: to love, or cherish, the pride of your partner, or of your adversary, as you will define it, as highly, or higher than, your own. Or if I had been as innocent of heart as she was, I might perhaps have thought of it, but I had kept company with this deadly world of reality. I was practiced in its laws and had the mortal bacilli of its ways in my blood. Now it did not enter my head any more than it ever has to alter my answers in church. When the priest says: "O God, make clean our hearts within us," I have never thought of telling him that it is not needed, or to answer anything whatever but, "And take not your holy spirit from us."

So, as if it were the only natural and reasonable thing to do, I took out twenty francs and gave them to her.

Before she went she did a thing that I have never forgotten. With my note in her left hand she stood close to me. She did not kiss me or take my hand to say good-by, but with the three fingers of her right hand she lifted my chin up a little and looked at me, gave me an encouraging, consoling glance, such as a sister might give her brother in farewell. Then she went away.

In the days that followed — not the first days, but later — I tried to construct for myself some theory and explanation of my adventure.

This happened only a short time after the fall of the Second Empire, that strange sham millennium, and the Commune of Paris.[10] The atmosphere had been filled with catastrophe. A world had fallen. The Empress herself, whom, on a visit to Paris as a child, I have envisaged as a female deity resting upon clouds, smilingly conducting the ways of humanity, had flown in the night, in a carriage with her American dentist, miserable for the lack of a handkerchief. The members of her court were crowded into lodgings in Brussels and London while their country houses served as stables for the Prussians' horses. The Commune had followed, and the massacres in Paris by the Versailles army. A whole world must have tumbled down within these months of disaster.

This was also the time of Nihilism[11] in Russia, when the revolutionaries had lost all and were fleeing into exile. I thought of them because of the little song that Nathalie had sung to me, of which I had not understood the words.

Whatever it was that had happened to her, it must have been a catastrophe of an extraordinary violent nature. She must have gone down with a unique swiftness, or she would have known something of the resignation, the dreadful reconciliation to fate which life works upon us when it gets time to impress us drop by drop.

Also, I thought, she must have been tied to, and dragged down with, somebody else, for if she had been alone it could not have happened. It would have been, I reflected, somebody who held her, and yet was unable to help her, someone either very old, helpless from shock and ruin, or very young, children or a child, a little brother or sister. Left to herself she would have floated, or she would have been picked up near the surface by someone who would have valued her rare beauty, grace, and charm and have congratulated himself upon acquiring them; or, lower down, by somebody who might not have understood them, but whom they would still have impressed. Or, near the bottom, by people who would have thought of turning them to their own advantage. But she must have gone straight down from the world of beauty and harmony in which she had learned that confidence and radiance of hers, where they had taught her to sing, and to move and laugh as she did, where they had loved her, to a world where beauty and grace are of no account, and where the facts of life look you in the face, quite straight to ruin, desolation and starvation. And there, on the last step of the ladder, had been Marie, whoever she was, a friend who out of her

---

[10] The Second Empire was the reign of Napoleon III in France (1852–1870), overthrown in a bloodless coup on September 4, 1870. The Commune of Paris, a leftist revolutionary council set up six months later to battle the new conservative, rural government, led its followers in a rebellion that was quashed in a bloody massacre from May 21 to May 28, 1871.

[11] a revolutionary reform movement whose adherents believed that the existing system was so bad as to require its total destruction, through acts of terrorism, assassinations, and the like.

narrow and dark knowledge of the world had given her advice, and lent her the miserable clothes, and poured some sort of spirit into her, to give her courage.

About all this I thought much, and for a long time; but of course I could not know.

As soon as she had gone and I was alone — so strange are the automatic movements which we make within the hands of fate — I had no thought but to go after her and get her back. I think that I went, in those minutes, through the exact experience, even to the sensation of suffocation, of a person who has been buried alive. But I had no clothes on. When I got into some clothes and came down to the street it was empty. I walked about in the streets for a long time. I came back, in the course of the early morning, to the seat on which I had been sitting when she first spoke to me, and to the hotel of my former mistress. I thought what a strange thing is a young man who runs about, within the selfsame night, driven by the mad passion and loss of two women. Mercutio's words to Romeo about it came into my mind, and, as if I had been shown a brilliant caricature of myself or of all young men, I laughed. When the day began to spring I walked back to my room, and there was the lamp, still burning, and the supper table.

This state of mine lasted for some time. During the first days it was not so bad, for I lived then in the thought of going down, at the same hour, to the same place where I had met her first. I thought that she might come there again. I attached much hope to this idea, which only slowly died away.

I tried many things to make it possible to live. One night I went to the opera, because I had heard other people talk about going there. It was clear that it was done, and there might be something in it. It happened to be a performance of *Orpheus*. Do you remember the music where he implores the shadows in Hades, and where Euridice is for such a short time given back to him? There I sat, in the brilliant light of the *entr'actes*, a young man in a white tie and lavender gloves, with bright people who smiled and talked all around, some of them nodding to me, closely covered and wrapped up in the huge black wings of the Eumenides.[12]

At this time I developed also another theory. I thought of the goddess Nemesis, and I believed that had I not had the moment of doubt and fear in the night, I might have felt, in the morning, the strength in me, and the right, to move her destiny and mine. It is said about the highwaymen who in the old days haunted the forests of Denmark that they used to have a wire stretched across the road with a bell attached. The coaches in passing would touch the wire and the bell would ring within their den and call out the robbers. I had touched the wire and a bell had rung somewhere. The girl had not been afraid, but I had been afraid. I had asked: "What am I to pay for this?" and the goddess herself had answered: "Twenty francs," and

---

[12] in Greek mythology, the Furies.

with her you cannot bargain. You think of many things, when you are young.

All this is now a long time ago. The Eumenides, if they will excuse me for saying so, are like fleas, by which I was also much worried as a child. They like young blood, and leave us alone later in life. I have had, however, the honor of having them on me once more, not very many years ago. I had sold a piece of my land to a neighbor, and when I saw it again, he had cut down the forest that had been on it. Where were now the green shades, the glades and the hidden footpaths? And when I then heard again the whistle of their wings in the air, it gave me, with the pain, also a strange feeling of hope and strength — it was, after all, music of my youth.

"And did you never see her again?" I asked him.

"No," he said, and then, after a little while, "but I had a fantasy about her, a *fantaisie macabre*, if you like.

"Fifteen years later, in 1889, I passed through Paris on my way to Rome, and stayed there for a few days to see the exhibition and the Eiffel Tower which they had just built. One afternoon I went to see a friend, a painter. He had been rather wild as a young artist, but later had turned about completely, and was at the time studying anatomy with great zeal, after the example of Leonardo. I stayed there over the evening, and after we had discussed his pictures, and art in general, he said that he would show me the prettiest thing that he had in his studio. It was a skull from which he was drawing. He was keen to explain its rare beauty to me. 'It is really,' he said, 'the skull of a young woman, but the skull of Antinoüs[13] must have looked like that, if one had been able to get hold of it.'

"I had it in my hand, and as I was looking at the broad, low brow, the clear and noble line of the chin, and the clean deep sockets of the eyes, it seemed suddenly familiar to me. The white polished bone shone in the light of the lamp, so pure. And safe. In those few seconds I was taken back to my room in the Place François I, with the silk fringes and the heavy curtains, on a rainy night of fifteen years before."

"Did you ask your friend anything about it?" I said.

"No," said the old man, "what would have been the use? He would not have known."

[1934]

---

[13] Youthful companion and lover of the Roman emperor Hadrian. After he drowned in the Nile on a visit to Egypt, Antinoüs was deified by Hadrian; his likeness was often sculpted or carved, and a new city was named after him.

KATHERINE MANSFIELD (1888–1923) *was born Kathleen Mansfield Beauchamp at Wellington, New Zealand. She persuaded her father, a banker and industrialist, to send her to London in 1903 to study the cello. After a brief return to New Zealand, which she hated for its provincialism and isolation, she went back to London with a small allowance from her family, deciding to become a writer instead of a musician after meeting such literary people as D. H. Lawrence. Her first book of short stories,* In a German Pension, *was published in 1911. In the same year she met the literary critic and journalist John Middleton Murray, who became her husband in 1918.* Bliss and Other Stories (1920) *established her reputation and was followed by* The Garden Party (1922). *Mansfield took Chekhov as her model as a writer of stories, but after she was stricken with tuberculosis in 1918 she found it difficult to continue to work. In her posthumously published* Journal (1927), *she often upbraided herself when her vitality waned and she felt too ill to write: "Look at the stories that wait and wait just at the threshold. Why don't I let them in? And their place would be taken by others who are lurking beyond just there — waiting for the chance." Finally she sought a cure for her illness at the Gurdjieff Institute in France, an establishment run by the noted Armenian mystic Georges Ivanovitch Gurdjieff, whose methods combined spiritual and physical healing. She died at the institute a few months after her thirty-fourth birthday.*

Although only eighty-eight of Mansfield's stories have been published (including fifteen left unfinished), they have had a great influence on the development of the literary form. Like Chekhov, she simplified her plot to intensify the story's emotional impact, dramatizing small moments to reveal the larger significance in the lives of people, or, as Willa Cather observed, approaching "the major forces of life through comparatively trivial incidents." Mansfield developed her own technique of prose narration: to present a decisive psychological moment when a character's life is illuminated in an unforgettable manner. Her stories affected later writers as powerfully as Chekhov's stories had affected her. "Bliss," in which she depicts the secret and passionate lives of individuals flowing treacherously beneath the seemingly smooth and harmonious surface of a marriage, shows the purity of her style.

The setting of most of Mansfield's stories is Europe, but the death of her beloved younger brother in World War I made her reconsider her memories of New Zealand and dedicate herself to recreating life as she remembered it there as a child. Mansfield was triumphant when she heard that the local printer who set the type for her first work based on her New Zealand memories exclaimed on reading the manuscript, "My! But these kids are real." "The Doll's House" is set in New Zealand, and its details about the village school where children from all the social classes mingled is true to the experience Mansfield herself had in a small township called Karori, a few miles from Wellington, where she lived as a young girl.

＊

Katherine Mansfield

ဢ

BLISS

Although Bertha Young was thirty she still had moments like this when she wanted to run instead of walk, to take dancing steps on and off the pavement, to bowl a hoop, to throw something up in the air and catch it again, or to stand still and laugh at — nothing — at nothing, simply.

What can you do if you are thirty and, turning the corner of your own street, you are overcome, suddenly, by a feeling of bliss — absolute bliss! — as though you'd suddenly swallowed a bright piece of that late afternoon sun and it burned in your bosom, sending out a little shower of sparks into every particle, into every finger and toe? . . .

Oh, is there no way you can express it without being "drunk and disorderly"? How idiotic civilization is! Why be given a body if you have to keep it shut up in a case like a rare, rare fiddle?

"No, that about the fiddle is not quite what I mean," she thought, running up the steps and feeling in her bag for the key — she's forgotten it, as usual — and rattling the letter-box. "It's not what I mean, because —— Thank you, Mary" — she went into the hall. "Is nurse back?"

"Yes, M'm."

"And has the fruit come?"

"Yes, M'm. Everything's come."

"Bring the fruit up to the dining-room, will you? I'll arrange it before I go upstairs."

It was dusky in the dining-room and quite chilly. But all the same Bertha threw off her coat; she could not bear the tight clasp of it another moment, and the cold air fell on her arms.

But in her bosom there was still that bright glowing place — that shower of little sparks coming from it. It was almost unbearable. She hardly dared to breathe for fear of fanning it higher, and yet she breathed deeply, deeply. She hardly dared to look into the cold mirror — but she did look, and it gave her back a woman, radiant, with smiling, trembling lips, with big, dark eyes and an air of listening, waiting for something . . . divine to happen . . . that she knew must happen . . . infallibly.

Mary brought in the fruit on a tray and with it a glass bowl, and a blue dish, very lovely, with a strange sheen on it as though it had been dipped in milk.

"Shall I turn on the light, M'm?"

"No, thank you. I can see quite well."

There were tangerines and apples stained with strawberry pink. Some yellow pears, smooth as silk, some white grapes covered with a silver bloom and a big cluster of purple ones. These last she had bought to tone in with the new dining-room carpet. Yes, that did sound rather far-fetched and absurd, but it was really why she had bought them. She had thought in the shop: "I must have some purple ones to bring the carpet up to the table." And it had seemed quite sense at the time.

When she had finished with them and had made two pyramids of these bright round shapes, she stood away from the table to get the effect — and it really was most curious. For the dark table seemed to melt into the dusky light and the glass dish and the blue bowl to float in the air. This, of course in her present mood, was so incredibly beautiful. . . . She began to laugh.

"No, no. I'm getting hysterical." And she seized her bag and coat and ran upstairs to the nursery.

Nurse sat at a low table giving Little B her supper after her bath. The baby had on a white flannel gown and a blue woollen jacket, and her dark, fine hair was brushed up into a funny little peak. She looked up when she saw her mother and began to jump.

"Now, my lovey, eat it up like a good girl," said Nurse, setting her lips in a way that Bertha knew, and that meant she had come into the nursery at another wrong moment.

"Has she been good, Nanny?"

"She's been a little sweet all the afternoon," whispered Nanny. "We went to the park and I sat down on a chair and took her out of the pram and a big dog came along and put his head on my knee and she clutched its ear, tugged it. Oh, you should have seen her."

Bertha wanted to ask if it wasn't rather dangerous to let her clutch at a strange dog's ear. But she did not dare to. She stood watching them, her hands by her side, like the poor little girl in front of the rich little girl with the doll.

The baby looked up at her again, stared, and then smiled so charmingly that Bertha couldn't help crying:

"Oh, Nanny, do let me finish giving her her supper while you put the bath things away."

"Well, M'm, she oughtn't to be changed hands while she's eating," said Nanny, still whispering. "It unsettles her; it's very likely to upset her."

How absurd it was. Why have a baby if it has to be kept — not in a case like a rare, rare fiddle — but in another woman's arms?

"Oh, I must!" said she.

Very offended, Nanny handed her over.

"Now, don't excite her after her supper. You know you do, M'm. And I have such a time with her after!"

Thank heaven! Nanny went out of the room with the bath towels.

"Now I've got you to myself, my little precious," said Bertha, as the baby leaned against her.

She ate delightfully, holding up her lips for the spoon and then waving her hands. Sometimes she wouldn't let the spoon go; and sometimes, just as Bertha had filled it, she waved it away to the four winds.

When the soup was finished Bertha turned round to the fire. "You're nice — you're very nice!" said she, kissing her warm baby. "I'm fond of you. I like you."

And, indeed, she loved Little B so much — her neck as she bent forward, her exquisite toes as they shone transparent in the firelight — that all her feeling of bliss came back again, and again she didn't know how to express it — what to do with it.

"You're wanted on the telephone," said Nanny, coming back in triumph and seizing *her* Little B.

Down she flew. It was Harry. "Oh, is that you, Ber? Look here. I'll be late. I'll take a taxi and come along as quickly as I can, but get dinner put back ten minutes — will you? All right?"

"Yes, perfectly. Oh, Harry!"

"Yes?"

What had she to say? She'd nothing to say. She only wanted to get in touch with him for a moment. She couldn't absurdly cry: "Hasn't it been a divine day!"

"What is it?" rapped out the little voice.

"Nothing. *Entendu*," said Bertha, and hung up the receiver, thinking how more than idiotic civilization was.

They had people coming to dinner. The Norman Knights — a very sound couple — he was about to start a theater, and she was awfully keen on interior decoration, a young man, Eddie Warren, who had just published a little book of poems and whom everybody was asking to dine, and a "find" of Bertha's called Pearl Fulton. What Miss Fulton did, Bertha didn't know. They had met at the club and Bertha had fallen in love with her, as she always did fall in love with beautiful women who had something strange about them.

The provoking thing was that, though they had been about together and met a number of times and really talked, Bertha couldn't yet make her out. Up to a certain point Miss Fulton was rarely, wonderfully frank, but the certain point was there, and beyond that she would not go.

Was there anything beyond it? Harry said "No." Voted her dullish, and "cold like all blond women, with a touch, perhaps, of anæmia of the brain." But Bertha wouldn't agree with him; not yet, at any rate.

"No, the way she has of sitting with her head a little on one side, and smiling, has something behind it, Harry, and I must find out what that something is."

"Most likely it's a good stomach," answered Harry.

He made a point of catching Bertha's heels with replies of that kind . . . "liver frozen, my dear girl," or "pure flatulence," or "kidney disease," . . . and so on. For some strange reason Bertha liked this, and almost admired it in him very much.

She went into the drawing-room and lighted the fire; then, picking up the cushions, one by one, that Mary had disposed so carefully, she threw them back on to the chairs and the couches. That made all the difference; the room came alive at once. As she was about to throw the last one she surprised herself by suddenly hugging it to her, passionately, passionately. But it did not put out the fire in her bosom. Oh, on the contrary!

The windows of the drawing-room opened on to a balcony overlooking the garden. At the far end, against the wall, there was a tall, slender pear tree in fullest, richest bloom; it stood perfect, as though becalmed against the jade-green sky. Bertha couldn't help feeling, even from this distance, that it had not a single bud or a faded petal. Down below, in the garden beds, the red and yellow tulips, heavy with flowers, seemed to lean upon the dusk. A grey cat, dragging its belly, crept across the lawn, and a black one, its shadow, trailed after. The sight of them, so intent and so quick, gave Bertha a curious shiver.

"What creepy things cats are!" she stammered, and she turned away from the window and began walking up and down. . . .

How strong the jonquils smelled in the warm room. Too strong? Oh, no. And yet, as though overcome, she flung down on a couch and pressed her hands to her eyes.

"I'm too happy — too happy!" she murmured.

And she seemed to see on her eyelids the lovely pear tree with its wide open blossoms as a symbol of her own life.

Really — really — she had everything. She was young. Harry and she were as much in love as ever, and they got on together splendidly and were really good pals. She had an adorable baby. They didn't have to worry about money. They had this absolutely satisfactory house and garden. And friends — modern, thrilling friends, writers and painters and poets or people keen on social questions — just the kind of friends they wanted. And then there were books, and there was music, and she had found a wonderful little dressmaker, and they were going abroad in the summer, and their new cook made the most superb omelettes. . . .

"I'm absurd! Absurd!" She sat up; but she felt quite dizzy, quite drunk. It must have been the spring.

Yes, it was the spring. Now she was so tired she could not drag herself upstairs to dress.

A white dress, a string of jade beads, green shoes and stockings. It wasn't intentional. She had thought of this scheme hours before she stood at the drawing-room window.

Her petals rushed softly into the hall, and she kissed Mrs. Norman Knight, who was taking off the most amusing orange coat with a procession of black monkeys round the hem and up the fronts.

". . . Why! Why! Why is the middle-class so stodgy — so utterly without a sense of humor! My dear, it's only a fluke that I am here at all — Norman being the protective fluke. For my darling monkeys so upset the train that it rose to a man and simply ate me with its eyes. Didn't laugh — wasn't amused — that I should have loved. No, just stared — and bored me through and through."

"But the cream of it was," said Norman, pressing a large tortoiseshell-rimmed monocle into his eye, "you don't mind me telling this, Face, do you?" (In their home and among their friends they called each other Face and Mug.) "The cream of it was when she, being full fed, turned to the woman beside her and said: 'Haven't you ever seen a monkey before?' "

"Oh, yes!" Mrs. Norman Knight joined in the laughter. "Wasn't that too absolutely creamy?"

And a funnier thing still was that now her coat was off she did look like a very intelligent monkey — who had even made that yellow silk dress out of scraped banana skins. And her amber earrings; they were like little dangling nuts.

"This is a sad, sad fall!" said Mug, pausing in front of Little B's perambulator. "When the perambulator comes into the hall —— " and he waved the rest of the quotation away.

The bell rang. It was lean, pale Eddie Warren (as usual) in a state of acute distress.

"It *is* the right house, *isn't* it?" he pleaded.

"Oh, I think so — I hope so," said Bertha brightly.

"I have had such a *dreadful* experience with a taxi-man; he was *most* sinister. I couldn't get him to *stop*. The *more* I knocked and called the *faster* he went. And *in* the moonlight this *bizarre* figure with the *flattened* head *crouching* over the *lit-tle* wheel. . . ."

He shuddered, taking off an immense white silk scarf. Bertha noticed that his socks were white, too — most charming.

"But how dreadful!" she cried.

"Yes, it really was," said Eddie, following her into the drawing-room. "I saw myself *driving* through Eternity in a *timeless* taxi."

He knew the Norman Knights. In fact, he was going to write a play for N. K. when the theater scheme came off.

"Well, Warren, how's the play?" said Norman Knight, dropping his monocle and giving his eye a moment in which to rise to the surface before it was screwed down again.

And Mrs. Norman Knight: "Oh, Mr. Warren, what happy socks!"

"I *am* so glad you like them," said he, staring at his feet. "They seem to have got so *much* whiter since the moon rose." And he turned his lean sorrowful young face to Bertha. "There *is* a moon, you know."

She wanted to cry: "I am sure there is — often — often!"

He really was a most attractive person. But so was Face, crouched before the fire in her banana skins, and so was Mug, smoking a cigarette and saying as he flicked the ash: "Why doth the bridegroom tarry?"

"There he is, now."

Bang went the front door open and shut. Harry shouted: "Hullo, you people. Down in five minutes." And they heard him swarm up the stairs. Bertha couldn't help smiling; she knew how he loved doing things at high pressure. What, after all, did an extra five minutes matter? But he would pretend to himself that they mattered beyond measure. And then he would make a great point of coming into the drawing-room, extravagantly cool and collected.

Harry had such a zest for life. Oh, how she appreciated it in him. And his passion for fighting — for seeking in everything that came up against him another test of his power and of his courage — that, too, she understood. Even when it made him just occasionally, to other people, who didn't know him well, a little ridiculous perhaps. . . . For there were moments when he rushed into battle where no battle was. . . . She talked and laughed and positively forgot until he had come in (just as she had imagined) that Pearl Fulton had not turned up.

"I wonder if Miss Fulton has forgotten?"

"I expect so," said Harry. "Is she on the 'phone?"

"Ah! There's a taxi, now." And Bertha smiled with that little air of proprietorship that she always assumed while her women finds were new and mysterious. "She lives in taxis."

"She'll run to fat if she does," said Harry coolly, ringing the bell for dinner. "Frightful danger for blond women."

"Harry — don't," warned Bertha, laughing up at him.

Came another tiny moment, while they waited, laughing and talking, just a trifle too much at their ease, a trifle too unaware. And then Miss Fulton, all in silver, with a silver fillet binding her pale blond hair, came in smiling, her head a little on one side.

"Am I late?"

"No, not at all," said Bertha. "Come along." And she took her arm and they moved into the dining-room.

What was there in the touch of that cool arm that could fan — fan — start blazing — blazing — the fire of bliss that Bertha did not know what to do with?

Miss Fulton did not look at her; but then she seldom did look at people directly. Her heavy eyelids lay upon her eyes and the strange half smile came and went upon her lips as though she lived by listening rather than seeing. But Bertha knew, suddenly, as if the longest, most intimate look had passed between them — as if they had said to each other: "You, too?" — that Pearl Fulton, stirring the beautiful red soup in the grey plate, was feeling just what she was feeling.

And the others? Face and Mug, Eddie and Harry, their spoons rising and falling — dabbing their lips with their napkins, crumbling bread, fiddling with the forks and glasses and talking.

"I met her at the Alpha shore — the weirdest little person. She'd not only cut off her hair, but she seemed to have taken a dreadfully good snip off her legs and arms and her neck and her poor little nose as well."

"Isn't she very *liée*[1] with Michael Oat?"

"The man who wrote *Love in False Teeth?*"

"He wants to write a play for me. One act. One man. Decides to commit suicide. Gives all the reasons why he should and why he shouldn't. And just as he has made up his mind either to do it or not to do it — curtain. Not half a bad idea."

"What's he going to call it — 'Stomach Trouble'?"

"I *think* I've come across the *same* idea in a lit-tle French review, *quite* unknown in England."

No, they didn't share it. They were dears — dears — and she loved having them there, at her table, and giving them delicious food and wine. In fact, she longed to tell them how delightful they were, and what a decorative group they made, how they seemed to set one another off and how they reminded her of a play by Tchekof!

Harry was enjoying his dinner. It was part of his — well, not his nature, exactly, and certainly not his pose — his — something or other — to talk about food and to glory in his "shameless passion for the white flesh of the lobster" and "the green of pistachio ices — green and cold like the eyelids of Egyptian dancers."

When he looked up at her and said: "Bertha, this is a very admirable *soufflée!*" she almost could have wept with child-like pleasure.

Oh, why did she feel so tender toward the whole world tonight? Everything was good — was right. All that happened seemed to fill again her brimming cup of bliss.

And still, in the back of her mind, there was the pear tree. It would be

---

[1] linked or connected with; friendly with (the implication being that they are more than just "friends").

silver now, in the light of poor dear Eddie's moon, silver as Miss Fulton, who sat there turning a tangerine in her slender fingers that were so pale a light seemed to come from them.

What she simply couldn't make out — what was miraculous — was how she should have guessed Miss Fulton's mood so exactly and so instantly. For she never doubted for a moment that she was right, and yet what had she to go on? Less than nothing.

"I believe this does happen very, very rarely between women. Never between men," thought Bertha. "But while I am making coffee in the drawing-room perhaps she will 'give a sign.' "

What she meant by that she did not know, and what would happen after that she could not imagine.

While she thought like this she saw herself talking and laughing. She had to talk because of her desire to laugh.

"I must laugh or die."

But when she noticed Face's funny little habit of tucking something down the front of her bodice — as if she kept a tiny, secret hoard of nuts there, too — Bertha had to dig her nails into her hands — so as not to laugh too much.

It was over at last. And: "Come and see my new coffee machine," said Bertha.

"We only have a new coffee machine once a fortnight," said Harry. Face took her arm this time; Miss Fulton bent her head and followed after.

The fire had died down in the drawing-room to a red, flickering "nest of baby phoenixes," said Face.

"Don't turn up the light for a moment. It is so lovely." And down she crouched by the fire again. She was always cold . . . "without her little red flannel jacket, of course," thought Bertha.

At that moment Miss Fulton "gave the sign."

"Have you a garden?" said the cool, sleepy voice.

This was so exquisite on her part that all Bertha could do was to obey. She crossed the room, pulled the curtains apart, and opened those long windows.

"There!" she breathed.

And the two women stood side by side looking at the slender, flowering tree. Although it was so still it seemed, like the flame of a candle, to stretch up, to point, to quiver in the bright air, to grow taller and taller as they gazed — almost to touch the rim of the round, silver moon.

How long did they stand there? Both, as it were, caught in that circle of unearthly light, understanding each other perfectly, creatures of another world, and wondering what they were to do in this one with all this blissful treasure that burned in their bosoms and dropped, in silver flowers, from their hair and hands?

Forever — for a moment? And did Miss Fulton murmur: "Yes. Just *that*." Or did Bertha dream it?

Then the light was snapped on and Face made the coffee and Harry said: "My dear Mrs. Knight, don't ask me about my baby. I never see her. I shan't feel the slightest interest in her until she has a lover," and Mug took his eye out of the conservatory for a moment and then put it under glass again and Eddie Warren drank his coffee and set down the cup with a face of anguish as though he had drunk and seen the spider.

"What I want to do is to give the young men a show. I believe London is simply teeming with first-chop, unwritten plays. What I want to say to 'em is: 'Here's the theater. Fire ahead.' "

"You know, my dear, I am going to decorate a room for the Jacob Nathans. Oh, I am so tempted to do a fried-fish scheme, with the backs of the chairs shaped like frying pans and lovely chip potatoes embroidered all over the curtains."

"The trouble with our young writing men is that they are still too romantic. You can't put out to sea without being seasick and wanting a basin. Well, why won't they have the courage of those basins?"

"A *dreadful* poem about a *girl* who was *violated* by a beggar *without* a nose in a lit-tle wood. . . ."

Miss Fulton sank into the lowest, deepest chair and Harry handed round the cigarettes.

From the way he stood in front of her shaking the silver box and saying abruptly: "Egyptian? Turkish? Virginian? They're all mixed up," Bertha realized that she not only bored him; he really disliked her. And she decided from the way Miss Fulton said: "No, thank you, I won't smoke," that she felt it, too, and was hurt.

"Oh, Harry, don't dislike her. You are quite wrong about her. She's wonderful, wonderful. And, besides, how can you feel so differently about someone who means so much to me? I shall try to tell you when we are in bed tonight what has been happening. What she and I have shared."

At those last words something strange and almost terrifying darted into Bertha's mind. And this something blind and smiling whispered to her: "Soon these people will go. The house will be quiet — quiet. The lights will be out. And you and he will be alone together in the dark room — the warm bed. . . ."

She jumped up from her chair and ran over to the piano.

"What a pity someone does not play!" she cried. "What a pity somebody does not play."

For the first time in her life Bertha Young desired her husband.

Oh, she loved him — she'd been in love with him, of course, in every other way, but just not in that way. And, equally, of course, she'd understood that he was different. They'd discussed it so often. It had worried her dreadfully at first to find that she was so cold, but after a time it had not seemed to matter. They were so frank with each other — such good pals. That was the best of being modern.

But now — ardently! ardently! The word ached in her ardent body! Was this what that feeling of bliss had been leading up to? But then — then ——

"My dear," said Mrs. Norman Knight, "you know our shame. We are the victims of time and train. We live in Hampstead. It's been so nice."

"I'll come with you into the hall," said Bertha. "I love having you. But you must not miss the last train. That's so awful, isn't it?"

"Have a whisky, Knight, before you go?" called Harry.

"No, thanks, old chap."

Bertha squeezed his hand for that as she shook it.

"Good night, good-bye," she cried from the top step, feeling that this self of hers was taking leave of them forever.

When she got back into the drawing-room the others were on the move.

". . . Then you can come part of the way in my taxi."

"I shall be *so* thankful *not* to have to face *another* drive *alone* after my *dreadful* experience."

"You can get a taxi at the rank just at the end of the street. You won't have to walk more than a few yards."

"That's comfort. I'll go and put on my coat."

Miss Fulton moved toward the hall and Bertha was following when Harry almost pushed past.

"Let me help you."

Bertha knew that he was repenting his rudeness — she let him go. What a boy he was in some ways — so impulsive — so — simple.

And Eddie and she were left by the fire.

"I *wonder* if you have seen Bilks' *new* poem called *Table d'Hôte*," said Eddie softly. "It's *so* wonderful. In the last Anthology. Have you got a copy? I'd *so* like to *show* it to you. It begins with an *incredibly* beautiful line: 'Why Must it Always be Tomato Soup?' "

"Yes," said Bertha. And she moved noiselessly to a table opposite the drawing-room door and Eddie glided noiselessly after her. She picked up the little book and gave it to him; they had not made a sound.

While he looked it up she turned her head toward the hall. And she saw . . . Harry with Miss Fulton's coat in his arms and Miss Fulton with her back turned to him and her head bent. He tossed the coat away, put his hands on her shoulders and turned her violently to him. His lips said: "I adore you," and Miss Fulton laid her moonbeam fingers on his cheeks and smiled her sleepy smile. Harry's nostrils quivered; his lips curled back in a hideous grin while he whispered: "Tomorrow," and with her eyelids Miss Fulton said: "Yes."

"Here it is," said Eddie. " 'Why Must it Always be Tomato Soup?' It's so *deeply* true, don't you feel? Tomato soup is so *dreadfully* eternal."

"If you prefer," said Harry's voice, very loud, from the hall, "I can 'phone you a cab to come to the door."

"Oh, no. It's not necessary," said Miss Fulton, and she came up to Bertha and gave her the slender fingers to hold.

"Good-bye. Thank you so much."

"Good-bye," said Bertha.

Miss Fulton held her hand a moment longer.

"Your lovely pear tree!" she murmured.

And then she was gone, with Eddie following, like the black cat following the grey cat.

"I'll shut up shop," said Harry, extravagantly cool and collected.

"Your lovely pear tree — pear tree — pear tree!"

Bertha simply ran over to the long windows.

"Oh, what is going to happen now?" she cried.

But the pear tree was as lovely as ever and as full of flower and as still.

[1920]

Katherine Mansfield

ଽେଽ

THE DOLL'S HOUSE

When dear old Mrs. Hay went back to town after staying with the Burnells she sent the children a doll's house. It was so big that the carter and Pat carried it into the courtyard, and there it stayed, propped up on two wooden boxes beside the feed-room door. No harm could come to it; it was summer. And perhaps the smell of paint would have gone off by the time it had to be taken in. For, really, the smell of paint coming from that doll's house ("Sweet of old Mrs. Hay, of course; most sweet and generous!") — but the smell of paint was quite enough to make anyone seriously ill, in Aunt Beryl's opinion. Even before the sacking was taken off. And when it was. . . .

There stood the doll's house, a dark, oily, spinach green, picked out with bright yellow. Its two solid little chimneys, glued on to the roof, were painted red and white, and the door, gleaming with yellow varnish, was like a little slab of toffee. Four windows, real windows, were divided into panes by a broad streak of green. There was actually a tiny porch, too, painted yellow, with big lumps of congealed paint hanging along the edge.

But perfect, perfect little house! Who could possibly mind the smell? It was part of the joy, part of the newness.

"Open it quickly, some one!"

The hook at the side was stuck fast. Pat pried it open with his pen-knife, and the whole house-front swung back, and — there you were, gazing at one and the same moment into the drawing-room and dining-room, the kitchen and two bedrooms. That is the way for a house to open! Why don't all houses open like that? How much more exciting than peering through the slit of a door into a mean little hall with a hatstand and two umbrellas! That is — isn't it? — what you long to know about a house when you put your hand on the knocker. Perhaps it is the way God opens houses at dead of night when He is taking a quiet turn with an angel. . . .

"O-oh!" The Burnell children sounded as though they were in despair. It was too marvelous; it was too much for them. They had never seen anything like it in their lives. All the rooms were papered. There were pictures on the walls, painted on the paper, with gold frames complete. Red carpet covered all the floors except the kitchen; red plush chairs in the drawing-room, green in the dining-room; tables, beds with real bedclothes, a cradle, a stove, a dresser with tiny plates and one big jug. But what Kezia liked more than anything, what she liked frightfully, was the lamp. It stood in the middle of the dining-room table, an exquisite little amber lamp with a white globe. It was even filled all ready for lighting, though, of course, you couldn't light it. But there was something inside that looked like oil, and that moved when you shook it.

The father and mother dolls, who sprawled very stiff as though they had fainted in the drawing-room, and their two little children asleep up-stairs, were really too big for the doll's house. They didn't look as though they belonged. But the lamp was perfect. It seemed to smile at Kezia, to say, "I live here." The lamp was real.

The Burnell children could hardly walk to school fast enough the next morning. They burned to tell everybody, to describe, to — well — to boast about their doll's house before the school-bell rang.

"I'm to tell," said Isabel, "because I'm the eldest. And you two can join in after. But I'm to tell first."

There was nothing to answer. Isabel was bossy, but she was always right, and Lottie and Kezia knew too well the powers that went with being eldest. They brushed through the thick buttercups at the road edge and said nothing.

"And I'm to choose who's to come and see it first. Mother said I might."

For it had been arranged that while the doll's house stood in the court-yard they might ask the girls at school, two at a time, to come and look. Not to stay to tea, of course, or to come traipsing through the house. But just to stand quietly in the courtyard while Isabel pointed out the beauties, and Lottie and Kezia look pleased. . . .

But hurry as they might, by the time they had reached the tarred pal-ings of the boys' playground the bell had begun to jangle. They only just had time to whip off their hats and fall into line before the roll was called. Never mind. Isabel tried to make up for it by looking very important and mysterious and by whispering behind her hand to the girls near her, "Got something to tell you at playtime."

Playtime came and Isabel was surrounded. The girls of her class nearly fought to put their arms round her, to walk away with her, to beam flatteringly, to be her special friend. She held quite a court under the huge pine trees at the side of the playground. Nudging, giggling together, the little girls pressed up close. And the only two who stayed outside the ring were the two who were always outside, the little Kelveys. They knew better than to come anywhere near the Burnells.

For the fact was, the school the Burnell children went to was not at all the kind of place their parents would have chosen if there had been any choice. But there was none. It was the only school for miles. And the consequence was all the children in the neighborhood, the Judge's little girls, the doctor's daughters, the storekeeper's children, the milkman's, were forced to mix together. Not to speak of there being an equal number of rude, rough little boys as well. But the line had to be drawn somewhere. It was drawn at the Kelveys. Many of the children, including the Burnells, were not allowed even to speak to them. They walked past the Kelveys with their heads in the air, and as they set the fashion in all matters of behavior, the Kelveys were shunned by everybody. Even the teacher had a special voice for them, and a special smile for the other children when Lil Kelvey came up to her desk with a bunch of dreadfully common-looking flowers.

They were the daughters of a spry, hardworking little washerwoman, who went about from house to house by the day. This was awful enough. But where was Mr. Kelvey? Nobody knew for certain. But everybody said he was in prison. So they were the daughters of a washerwoman and a gaolbird. Very nice company for other people's children! And they looked it. Why Mrs. Kelvey made them so conspicuous was hard to understand. The truth was they were dressed in "bits" given to her by the people for whom she worked. Lil, for instance, who was a stout, plain child, with big freckles, came to school in a dress made from a green art-serge table-cloth of the Burnells', with red plush sleeves from the Logans' curtains. Her hat, perched on top of her high forehead, was a grown-up woman's hat, once the property of Miss Lecky, the postmistress. It was turned up at the back and trimmed with a large scarlet quill. What a little guy she looked! It was impossible not to laugh. And her little sister, our Else, wore a long white dress, rather like a nightgown, and a pair of little boy's boots. But whatever our Else wore she would have looked strange. She was a tiny wishbone of a child, with cropped hair and enormous solemn eyes — a little white owl. Nobody had ever seen her smile; she scarcely ever spoke. She went through life holding on to Lil, with a piece of Lil's skirt screwed up in her hand. Where Lil went our Else followed. In the playground, on the road going to and from school, there was Lil marching in front and our Else holding on behind. Only when she wanted anything, or when she was out of breath, our Else gave Lil a tug, a twitch, and Lil stopped and turned around. The Kelveys never failed to understand each other.

Now they hovered at the edge; you couldn't stop them listening. When the little girls turned round and sneered, Lil, as usual, gave her silly, shamefaced smile, but our Else only looked.

And Isabel's voice, so very proud, went on telling. The carpet made a great sensation, but so did the beds with real bedclothes, and the stove with an oven door.

When she finished Kezia broke in. "You've forgotten the lamp, Isabel."

"Oh, yes," said Isabel, "and there's a teeny little lamp, all made of yellow glass, with a white globe that stands on the dining-room table. You couldn't tell it from a real one."

"The lamp's best of all," cried Kezia. She thought Isabel wasn't making half enough of the little lamp. But nobody paid any attention. Isabel was choosing the two who were to come back with them that afternoon and see it. She chose Emmie Cole and Lena Logan. But when the others knew they were all to have a chance, they couldn't be nice enough to Isabel. One by one they put their arms round Isabel's waist and walked her off. They had something to whisper to her, a secret. "Isabel's *my* friend."

Only the little Kelveys moved away forgotten; there was nothing more for them to hear.

Days passed, and as more children saw the doll's house, the fame of it spread. It became the one subject, the rage. The one question was, "Have you seen Burnells' doll's house? Oh, ain't it lovely!" "Haven't you seen it? Oh, I say!"

Even the dinner hour was given up to talking about it. The little girls sat under the pines eating their thick mutton sandwiches and big slabs of johnny cake spread with butter. While always, as near as they could get, sat the Kelveys, our Else holding on to Lil, listening too, while they chewed their jam sandwiches out of a newspaper soaked with large red blobs. . . .

"Mother," said Kezia, "can't I ask the Kelveys just once?"

"Certainly not, Kezia."

"But why not?"

"Run away, Kezia; you know quite well why not."

At last everybody had seen it except them. On that day the subject rather flagged. It was the dinner hour. The children stood together under the pine trees, and suddenly, as they looked at the Kelveys eating out of their paper, always by themselves, always listening, they wanted to be horrid to them. Emmie Cole started the whisper.

"Lil Kelvey's going to be a servant when she grows up."

"O-oh, how awful!" said Isabel Burnell, and she made eyes at Emmie.

Emmie swallowed in a very meaning way and nodded to Isabel as she'd seen her mother do on those occasions.

"It's true — it's true — it's true," she said.

Then Lena Logan's little eyes snapped. "Shall I ask her?" she whispered.

"Bet you don't," said Jessie May.

"Pooh, I'm not frightened," said Lena. Suddenly she gave a little squeal and danced in front of the other girls. "Watch! Watch me! Watch me now!" said Lena. And sliding, gliding, dragging one foot, giggling behind her hand, Lena went over to the Kelveys.

Lil looked up from her dinner. She wrapped the rest quickly away. Our Else stopped chewing. What was coming now?

"Is it true you're going to be a servant when you grow up, Lil Kelvey?" shrilled Lena.

Dead silence. But instead of answering, Lil only gave her silly, shamefaced smile. She didn't seem to mind the question at all. What a sell for Lena! The girls began to titter.

Lena couldn't stand that. She put her hands on her hips; she shot forward. "Yah, yer father's in prison!" she hissed, spitefully.

This was such a marvelous thing to have said that the little girls rushed away in a body, deeply, deeply excited, wild with joy. Some one found a long rope, and they began skipping. And never did they skip so high, run in and out so fast, or do such daring things as on that morning.

In the afternoon Pat called for the Burnell children with the buggy and they drove home. There were visitors. Isabel and Lottie, who liked visitors, went upstairs to change their pinafores. But Kezia thieved out at the back. Nobody was about; she began to swing on the big white gates of the courtyard. Presently, looking along the road, she saw two little dots. They grew bigger, they were coming toward her. Now she could see that one was in front and one close behind. Now she could see that they were the Kelveys. Kezia stopped swinging. She slipped off the gate as if she was going to run away. Then she hesitated. The Kelveys came nearer, and beside them walked their shadows, very long, stretching right across the road with their heads in the buttercups. Kezia clambered back on the gate; she had made up her mind; she swung out.

"Hullo," she said to the passing Kelveys.

They were so astounded that they stopped. Lil gave her silly smile. Our Else stared.

"You can come and see our doll's house if you want to," said Kezia, and she dragged one toe on the ground. But at that Lil turned red and shook her head quickly.

"Why not?" asked Kezia.

Lil gasped, then she said, "Your ma told our ma you wasn't to speak to us."

"Oh, well," said Kezia. She didn't know what to reply. "It doesn't matter. You can come and see our doll's house all the same. Come on. Nobody's looking."

But Lil shook her head still harder.

"Don't you want to?" asked Kezia.

Suddenly there was a twitch, a tug at Lil's skirt. She turned round. Our Else was looking at her with big, imploring eyes; she was frowning; she wanted to go. For a moment Lil looked at our Else very doubtfully. But then our Else twitched her skirt again. She started forward. Kezia led the way. Like two little stray cats they followed across the courtyard to where the doll's house stood.

"There it is," said Kezia.

There was a pause. Lil breathed loudly, almost snorted; our Else was still as a stone.

"I'll open it for you," said Kezia kindly. She undid the hook and they looked inside.

"There's the drawing-room and the dining-room, and that's the — "

"Kezia!"

Oh, what a start they gave!

"Kezia!"

It was Aunt Beryl's voice. They turned round. At the back door stood Aunt Beryl, staring as if she couldn't believe what she saw.

"How dare you ask the little Kelveys into the courtyard?" said her cold, furious voice. "You know as well as I do, you're not allowed to talk to them. Run away, children, run away at once. And don't come back again," said Aunt Beryl. And she stepped into the yard and shooed them out as if they were chickens.

"Off you go immediately!" she called, cold and proud.

They did not need telling twice. Burning with shame, shrinking together, Lil huddling along like her mother, our Else dazed, somehow they crossed the big courtyard and squeezed through the white gate.

"Wicked, disobedient little girl!" said Aunt Beryl bitterly to Kezia, and she slammed the doll's house to.

The afternoon had been awful. A letter had come from Willie Brent, a terrifying, threatening letter, saying if she did not meet him that evening in Pulman's Bush, he'd come to the front door and ask the reason why! But now that she had frightened those little rats of Kelveys and given Kezia a good scolding, her heart felt lighter. That ghastly pressure was gone. She went back to the house humming.

When the Kelveys were well out of sight of Burnells', they sat down to rest on a big red drainpipe by the side of the road. Lil's cheeks were still burning; she took off the hat with the quill and held it on her knee. Dreamily they looked over the hay paddocks, past the creek, to the group of wattles where Logan's cows stood waiting to be milked. What were their thoughts?

Presently our Else nudged up close to her sister. But now she had forgotten the cross lady. She put out a finger and stroked her sister's quill; she smiled her rare smile.

"I seen the little lamp," she said, softly.

Then both were silent once more.

[1923]

KATHERINE ANNE PORTER (1890–1980) was born Callie Russell Porter in Indian Creek, Texas. When she was only two years old her mother died, and then the family moved to Kyle, Texas, where they lived until her grandmother's death in 1901. Porter attended boarding schools and an Ursuline convent. She married for the first time in 1906, and after her divorce five years later she worked briefly as a reporter in Chicago and Denver. As a child she had wanted to be a writer, but it took fifteen years once she started writing seriously before she trusted herself enough as a stylist to approach a publisher. Most of her life during this time was a financial struggle; she spent only 10 percent of her energies on writing, and "the other 90 percent went to keeping my head above water." She nearly lost her life in the influenza epidemic that swept the United States at the end of World War I, and when she recovered she went to Mexico to study Aztec and Mayan art. There she found herself "smack into the Obregón revolution" of 1921, the setting of her story "Flowering Judas." She published her first story, "María Concepción," in Century magazine two years later, and achieved acclaim as a writer with her first collection of short stories, Flowering Judas and Other Stories, in 1930. Her most productive decade as a writer was the 1930s, when she published Noon Wine (1937) and Pale Horse, Pale Rider: Three Short Novels (1939). After World War II she supported herself by lecture tours and teaching jobs at various universities while she worked on her novel Ship of Fools (1962), which took more than two decades to complete. In 1965 her Collected Stories won both the Pulitzer Prize and the National Book Award.

Porter's style is not so recognizably "southern" as William Faulkner's or Flannery O'Connor's. She was a southerner by tradition and inheritance, but she had thought of herself since childhood as being "always restless, always a roving spirit." Her fiction often deals with the theme of loss and reconciliation, as in "María Concepción." She was very conscious of her own art as a storyteller, and of the art of fiction in general, writing personal essays on Willa Cather, Katherine Mansfield, Virginia Woolf, Gertrude Stein, Eudora Welty, and Flannery O'Connor, among others. Particularly indebted in her best stories to Katherine Mansfield, Porter attempted to dramatize a character's state of mind, rather than develop a complicated plot. The analysis Porter gave of Mansfield's literary practice in her essay "The Art of Katherine Mansfield" can also be applied to a story like "Flowering Judas": "With fine objectivity, she bares a moment of experience, real experience, in the life of some one human being; she states no belief, gives no motives, airs no theories, but simply presents to the reader a situation, a place, and a character, and there it is; and the emotional content is present as implicitly as the germ is in the grain of wheat."

Porter was a highly disciplined writer whose craftsmanship triumphed over the confusions of her personal life. She rewrote "María Concepción" fifteen or sixteen times before submitting it to a publisher, but other stories were written quickly after a long period of gestation. "Flowering Judas," a complex story about a girl who "was not able to face her own nature and who was afraid of everything," was based on a sudden intuition about an American girl living, like herself, in Mexico during the revolution. "I started 'Flowering Judas' at seven P.M. and at one-thirty I was standing on a snowy windy corner putting it in the mailbox."

Katherine Anne Porter

ဢ

MARÍA CONCEPCIÓN

María Concepción walked carefully, keeping to the middle of the white dusty road, where the maguey thorns and the treacherous curved spines of organ cactus had not gathered so profusely. She would have enjoyed resting for a moment in the dark shade by the roadside, but she had no time to waste drawing cactus needles from her feet. Juan and his chief would be waiting for their food in the damp trenches of the buried city.

She carried about a dozen living fowls slung over her right shoulder, their feet fastened together. Half of them fell upon the flat of her back, the balance dangled uneasily over her breast. They wriggled their benumbed and swollen legs against her neck, they twisted their stupefied eyes and peered into her face inquiringly. She did not see them or think of them. Her left arm was tired with the weight of the food basket, and she was hungry after her long morning's work.

Her straight back outlined itself strongly under her clean bright blue cotton rebozo. Instinctive serenity softened her black eyes, shaped like almonds, set far apart, and tilted a bit endwise. She walked with the free, natural, guarded ease of the primitive woman carrying an unborn child. The shape of her body was easy, the swelling life was not a distortion, but the right inevitable proportions of a woman. She was entirely contented. Her husband was at work and she was on her way to market to sell her fowls.

Her small house sat half-way up a shallow hill, under a clump of pepper-trees, a wall of organ cactus enclosing it on the side nearest to the road. Now she came down into the valley, divided by the narrow spring, and crossed a bridge of loose stones near the hut where María Rosa the beekeeper lived with her old godmother, Lupe the medicine woman. María Concepción had no faith in the charred owl bones, the singed rabbit fur, the cat entrails, the messes and ointments sold by Lupe to the ailing of the village. She was a good Christian, and drank simple herb teas for headache and stomach ache, or bought her remedies bottled, with printed directions that she could not read, at the drugstore near the city market, where she went almost daily. But she often bought a jar of honey from young María Rosa, a pretty, shy child only fifteen years old.

María Concepción and her husband, Juan Villegas, were each a little past their eighteenth year. She had a good reputation with the neighbors as an energetic religious woman who could drive a bargain to the end. It was commonly known that if she wished to buy a new rebozo for herself or a shirt for Juan, she could bring out a sack of hard silver coins for the purpose.

She had paid for the license, nearly a year ago, the potent bit of stamped paper which permits people to be married in the church. She had given money to the priest before she and Juan walked together up to the altar the Monday after Holy Week. It had been the adventure of the villagers to go, three Sundays one after another, to hear the banns called by the priest for Juan de Dios Villegas and María Concepción Manríquez, who were actually getting married in the church, instead of behind it, which was the usual custom, less expensive, and as binding as any other ceremony. But María Concepción was always as proud as if she owned a hacienda.

She paused on the bridge and dabbled her feet in the water, her eyes resting themselves from the sun-rays in a fixed gaze to the far-off mountains, deeply blue under their hanging drift of clouds. It came to her that she would like a fresh crust of honey. The delicious aroma of bees, their slow thrilling hum, awakened a pleasant desire for a flake of sweetness in her mouth.

"If I do not eat it now, I shall mark my child," she thought, peering through the crevices in the thick hedge of cactus that sheered up nakedly, like bared knife blades set protectingly around the small clearing. The place was so silent she doubted if María Rosa and Lupe were at home.

The leaning jacal[1] of dried rush-withes and corn sheaves, bound to tall saplings thrust into the earth, roofed with yellowed maguey leaves flattened and overlapping like shingles, hunched drowsy and fragrant in the warmth of noonday. The hives, similarly made, were scattered toward the back of the clearing, like small mounds of clean vegetable refuse. Over each mound there hung a dusty golden shimmer of bees.

A light gay scream of laughter rose from behind the hut; a man's

---

[1] hut.

short laugh joined in. "Ah, hahahaha!" went the voices together high and low, like a song.

"So María Rosa has a man!" María Concepción stopped short, smiling, shifted her burden slightly, and bent forward shading her eyes to see more clearly through the spaces of the hedge.

María Rosa ran, dodging between beehives, parting two stunted jasmine bushes as she came, lifting her knees in swift leaps, looking over her shoulder and laughing in a quivering, excited way. A heavy jar, swung to her wrist by the handle, knocked against her thighs as she ran. Her toes pushed up sudden spurts of dust, her half-raveled braids showered around her shoulders in long crinkled wisps.

Juan Villegas ran after her, also laughing strangely, his teeth set, both rows gleaming behind the small soft black beard growing sparsely on his lips, his chin, leaving his brown cheeks girl-smooth. When he seized her, he clenched so hard her chemise gave way and ripped from her shoulder. She stopped laughing at this, pushed him away and stood silent, trying to pull up the torn sleeve with one hand. Her pointed chin and dark red mouth moved in an uncertain way, as if she wished to laugh again; her long black lashes flickered with the quick-moving lights in her hidden eyes.

María Concepción did not stir nor breathe for some seconds. Her forehead was cold, and yet boiling water seemed to be pouring slowly along her spine. An unaccountable pain was in her knees, as if they were broken. She was afraid Juan and María Rosa would feel her eyes fixed upon them and would find her there, unable to move, spying upon them. But they did not pass beyond the enclosure, nor even glance towards the gap in the wall opening upon the road.

Juan lifted one of María Rosa's loosened braids and slapped her neck with it playfully. She smiled softly, consentingly. Together they moved back through the hives of honey-comb. María Rosa balanced her jar on one hip and swung her long full petticoats with every step. Juan flourished his wide hat back and forth, walking proudly as a game-cock.

María Concepción came out of the heavy cloud which enwrapped her head and bound her throat, and found herself walking onward, keeping the road without knowing it, feeling her way delicately, her ears strumming as if all María Rosa's bees had hived in them. Her careful sense of duty kept her moving toward the buried city where Juan's chief, the American archeologist, was taking his midday rest, waiting for his food.

Juan and María Rosa! She burned all over now, as if a layer of tiny fig-cactus bristles, as cruel as spun glass, had crawled under her skin. She wished to sit down quietly and wait for her death, but not until she had cut the throats of her man and that girl who were laughing and kissing under the cornstalks. Once when she was a young girl she had come back from market to find her jacal burned to a pile of ash and her few silver coins gone. A dark empty feeling had filled her; she kept moving about the place, not believing her eyes, expecting it all to take shape again before her. But it was gone, and though she knew an enemy had done it, she could not find out who it was, and could only curse and threaten the air. Now here was a worse thing, but she knew her enemy. María Rosa, that sinful girl, shameless! She heard herself saying a harsh, true word about María Rosa, saying it aloud as if she expected someone to agree with her: "Yes, she is a whore! She has no right to live."

At this moment the gray untidy head of Givens appeared over the edges of the newest trench he had caused to be dug in his field of excavations. The long deep crevasses, in which a man might stand without being seen, lay crisscrossed like orderly gashes of a giant scalpel. Nearly all of the men of the community worked for Givens, helping him to uncover the lost city of their ancestors. They worked all the year through and prospered, digging every day for those small clay heads and bits of pottery and fragments of painted walls for which there was no good use on earth, being all broken and encrusted with clay. They themselves could make better ones, perfectly stout and new, which they took to town and peddled to foreigners for real money. But the unearthly delight of the chief in finding these worn-out things was an endless puzzle. He would fairly roar for joy at times, waving a shattered pot or a human skull above his head, shouting for his photographer to come and make a picture of this!

Now he emerged, and his young enthusiast's eyes welcomed María Concepción from his old-man face, covered with hard wrinkles and burned to the color of red earth. "I hope you've brought me a nice fat one." He selected a fowl from the bunch dangling nearest him as María Concepción, wordless, leaned over the trench. "Dress it for me, there's a good girl. I'll broil it."

María Concepción took the fowl by the head, and silently, swiftly drew her knife across its throat, twisting the head off with the casual firmness she might use with the top of a beet.

"Good God, woman, you do have nerve," said Givens, watching her. "I can't do that. It gives me the creeps."

"My home country is Guadalajara," explained María Concepción, without bravado, as she picked and gutted the fowl.

She stood and regarded Givens condescendingly, that diverting white man who had no woman of his own to cook for him, and moreover appeared not to feel any loss of dignity in preparing his own food. He squatted now, eyes squinted, nose wrinkled to avoid the smoke, turning the roasting fowl busily on a stick. A mysterious man, undoubtedly rich, and Juan's chief, therefore to be respected, to be placated.

"The tortillas are fresh and hot, señor," she murmured gently. "With your permission I will now go to market."

"Yes, yes, run along; bring me another of these tomorrow." Givens turned his head to look at her again. Her grand manner sometimes reminded him of royalty in exile. He noticed her unnatural paleness. "The sun is too hot, eh?" he said.

"Yes, sir. Pardon me, but Juan will be here soon?"

"He ought to be here now. Leave his food. The others will eat it."

She moved away; the blue of her rebozo became a dancing spot in the heat waves that rose from the gray-red soil. Givens liked his Indians best when he could feel a fatherly indulgence for their primitive childish ways. He told comic stories of Juan's escapades, of how often he had saved him, in the past five years, from going to jail, and even from being shot, for his varied and always unexpected misdeeds.

"I am never a minute too soon to get him out of one pickle or another," he would say. "Well, he's a good worker, and I know how to manage him."

After Juan was married, he used to twit him, with exactly the right shade of condescension, on his many infidelities to María Concepción. "She'll catch you yet, and God help you!" he was fond of saying, and Juan would laugh with immense pleasure.

It did not occur to María Concepción to tell Juan she had found him out. During the day her anger against him died, and her anger against María Rosa grew. She kept saying to herself, "When I was a young girl like María Rosa, if a man had caught hold of me so, I would have broken my jar over his head." She forgot completely that she had not resisted even so much as María Rosa, on the day that Juan had first taken hold of her. Besides she had married him afterwards in the church, and that was a very different thing.

Juan did not come home that night, but went away to war and María Rosa went with him. Juan had a rifle at his shoulders and two pistols at his belt. María Rosa wore a rifle also, slung on her back along with the blankets and the cooking pots. They joined the nearest detachment of troops in the field, and María Rosa marched ahead with the battalion of experienced women of war, which went over the crops like locusts, gathering provisions for the army. She cooked with them, and ate with them what was left after the men had eaten. After battles she went out on the field with the others to salvage clothing and ammunition and guns from the slain before they should begin to swell in the heat. Sometimes they would encounter the women from the other army, and a second battle as grim as the first would take place.

There was no particular scandal in the village. People shrugged, grinned. It was far better that they were gone. The neighbors went around saying that María Rosa was safer in the army than she would be in the same village with María Concepción.

María Concepción did not weep when Juan left her; and when the baby was born, and died within four days, she did not weep. "She is mere stone," said old Lupe, who went over and offered charms to preserve the baby.

"May you rot in hell with your charms," said María Concepción.

If she had not gone so regularly to church, lighting candles before the saints, kneeling with her arms spread in the form of a cross for hours at a time, and receiving holy communion every month, there might have been talk of her being devil-possessed, her face was so changed and blind-looking. But this was impossible when, after all, she had been married by the priest. It must be, they reasoned, that she was being punished for her pride. They decided that this was the true cause for everything: she was altogether too proud. So they pitied her.

During the year that Juan and María Rosa were gone María Concepción sold her fowls and looked after her garden and her sack of hard coins grew. Lupe had no talent for bees, and the hives did not prosper. She began to blame María Rosa for running away, and to praise María Concepción for her behavior. She used to see María Concepción at the market or at church, and she always said that no one could tell by looking at her now that she was a woman who had such a heavy grief.

"I pray God everything goes well with María Concepción from this out," she would say, "for she has had her share of trouble."

When some idle person repeated this to the deserted woman, she went down to Lupe's house and stood within the clearing and called to the medicine woman, who sat in her doorway stirring a mess of her infallible cure for sores: "Keep your prayers to yourself, Lupe, or offer them for others who need them. I will ask God for what I want in this world."

"And will you get it, you think, María Concepción?" asked Lupe, tittering cruelly and smelling the wooden mixing spoon. "Did you pray for what you have now?"

Afterward everyone noticed that María Concepción went oftener to church, and even seldomer to the village to talk with the other women as they sat along the curb, nursing their babies and eating fruit, at the end of the market-day.

"She is wrong to take us for enemies," said old Soledad, who was a thinker and a peace-maker. "All women have these troubles. Well, we should suffer together."

But María Concepción lived alone. She was gaunt, as if something were gnawing her away inside, her eyes were sunken, and she would not speak a word if she could help it. She worked harder than ever, and her butchering knife was scarcely ever out of her hand.

Juan and María Rosa, disgusted with military life, came home one day without asking permission of anyone. The field of war had unrolled itself, a long scroll of vexations, until the end had frayed out within twenty miles of Juan's village. So he and María Rosa, now lean as a wolf, burdened with a child daily expected, set out with no farewells to the regiment and walked home.

They arrived one morning about daybreak. Juan was picked up on sight by a group of military police from the small barracks on the edge of town, and taken to prison, where the officer in charge told him with impersonal cheerfulness that he would add one to a catch of ten waiting to be shot as deserters the next morning.

María Rosa, screaming and falling on her face in the road, was taken under the armpits by two guards and helped briskly to her jacal, now sadly run down. She was received with professional importance by Lupe, who helped the baby to be born at once.

Limping with foot soreness, a layer of dust concealing his fine new clothes got mysteriously from somewhere, Juan appeared before the captain at the barracks. The captain recognized him as head digger for his good friend Givens, and dispatched a note to Givens saying: "I am holding the person of Juan Villegas awaiting your further disposition."

When Givens showed up Juan was delivered to him with the urgent request that nothing be made public about so humane and sensible an operation on the part of military authority.

Juan walked out of the rather stifling atmosphere of the drum-head court, a definite air of swagger about him. His hat, of unreasonable dimensions and embroidered with silver thread, hung over one eyebrow, secured at the back by a cord of silver dripping with bright blue tassels. His shirt was of a checkerboard pattern in green and black, his white cotton trousers were bound by a belt of yellow leather tooled in red. His feet were bare, full of stone bruises, and sadly ragged as to toenails. He removed his cigarette from the corner of his full-lipped wide mouth. He removed the splendid hat. His black dusty hair, pressed moistly to his forehead, sprang up suddenly in a cloudy thatch on his crown. He bowed to the officer, who appeared to be gazing at a vacuum. He swung his arm wide in a free circle upsoaring towards the prison window, where forlorn heads poked over the window sill, hot eyes following after the lucky departing one. Two or three of the heads nodded, and a half-dozen hands were flipped at him in an effort to imitate his own casual and heady manner.

Juan kept up this insufferable pantomime until they rounded the first clump of fig-cactus. Then he seized Givens' hand and burst into oratory. "Blessed be the day your servant Juan Villegas first came under your eyes. From this day my life is yours without condition, ten thousand thanks with all my heart!"

"For God's sake stop playing the fool," said Givens irritably. "Some day I'm going to be five minutes too late."

"Well, it is nothing much to be shot, my chief — certainly you know I was not afraid — but to be shot in a drove of deserters, against a cold wall, just in the moment of my home-coming, by order of that. . . ."

Glittering epithets tumbled over one another like explosions of a rocket. All the scandalous analogies from the animal and vegetable worlds were applied in a vivid, unique, and personal way to the life, loves, and family history of the officer who had just set him free. When he had quite cursed himself dry, and his nerves were soothed, he added: "With your permission, my chief!"

"What will María Concepción say to all this?" asked Givens. "You are very informal, Juan, for a man who was married in the church."

Juan put on his hat.

"Oh, María Concepción! That's nothing. Look, my chief, to be married in the church is a great misfortune for a man. After that he is not himself any more. How can that woman complain when I do not drink even at fiestas enough to be really drunk? I do not beat her; never, never. We are always at peace. I say to her, Come here, and she comes straight. I say, Go there, and she goes quickly. Yet sometimes I looked at her and thought, Now I am married to that woman in the church, and I felt a sinking inside, as if something were lying heavy on my stomach. With María Rosa it is all different. She is not silent; she talks. When she talks too much, I slap her and say, Silence, thou simpleton! and she weeps. She is just a girl with whom I do as I please. You know how she used to keep those clean little bees in their hives? She is like their honey to me. I swear it. I would not harm María Concepción because I am married to her in the church; but also, my chief, I will not leave María Rosa, because she pleases me more than any other woman."

"Let me tell you, Juan, things haven't been going as well as you think. You be careful. Some day María Concepción will just take your head off with that carving knife of hers. You keep that in mind."

Juan's expression was the proper blend of masculine triumph and sentimental melancholy. It was pleasant to see himself in the rôle of hero to two such desirable women. He had just escaped from the threat of a disagreeable end. His clothes were new and handsome, and they had cost him just nothing. María Rosa had collected them for him here and there after battles. He was walking in the early sunshine, smelling the good smells of ripening cactus-figs, peaches, and melons, of pungent berries dangling from the pepper-trees, and the smoke of his cigarette under his nose. He was on his way to civilian life with his patient chief. His situation was ineffably perfect, and he swallowed it whole.

"My chief," he addressed Givens handsomely, as one man of the world to another, "women are good things, but not at this moment. With your permission, I will now go to the village and eat. My God, *how* I shall eat! Tomorrow morning very early I will come to the buried city and work like seven men. Let us forget María Concepción and María Rosa. Each one in her place. I will manage them when the time comes."

News of Juan's adventure soon got abroad, and Juan found many friends about him during the morning. They frankly commended his way of leaving the army. It was in itself the act of a hero. The new hero ate a great deal and drank somewhat, the occasion being better than a feast-day. It was almost noon before he returned to visit María Rosa.

He found her sitting on a clean straw mat, rubbing fat on her three-hour-old son. Before this felicitous vision Juan's emotions so twisted him that he returned to the village and invited every man in the "Death and Resurrection" pulque[2] shop to drink with him.

Having thus taken leave of his balance, he started back to María Rosa, and found himself unaccountably in his own house, attempting to beat María Concepción by way of reestablishing himself in his legal household.

María Concepción, knowing all the events of that unhappy day, was not in a yielding mood, and refused to be beaten. She did not scream nor implore; she stood her ground and resisted; she even struck at him. Juan, amazed, hardly knowing what he did, stepped back and gazed at her inquiringly through a leisurely whirling film which seemed to have lodged behind his eyes. Certainly he had not even thought of touching her. Oh, well, no harm done. He gave up, turned away, half-asleep on his feet. He dropped amiably in a shadowed corner and began to snore.

María Concepción, seeing that he was quiet, began to bind the legs of her fowls. It was market-day and she was late. She fumbled and tangled the bits of cord in her haste, and set off across the plowed fields instead of taking the accustomed road. She ran with a crazy panic in her head, her stumbling legs. Now and then she would stop and look about her, trying to place herself, then go on a few steps, until she realized that she was not going toward the market.

At once she came to her senses completely, recognized the thing that troubled her so terribly, was certain of what she wanted. She sat down quietly under a sheltering thorny bush and gave herself over to her long devouring sorrow. The thing which had for so long squeezed her whole body into a tight dumb knot of suffering suddenly broke with shocking violence. She jerked with the involuntary recoil of one who receives a blow, and the sweat poured from her skin as if the wounds of her whole life were shedding their salt ichor. Drawing her rebozo over her head, she bowed her forehead on her updrawn knees, and sat there in deadly silence and immobility. From time to time she lifted her head where the sweat formed steadily and poured down her face, drenching the front of her chemise, and her mouth had the shape of crying, but there were no tears and no sound. All her being was a dark confused memory of grief burning in her at night, of deadly baffled anger eating at her by day, until her very tongue tasted bitter, and her feet were as heavy as if she were mired in the muddy roads during the time of rains.

After a great while she stood up and threw the rebozo off her face, and set out walking again.

Juan awakened slowly, with long yawns and grumblings, alternated with short relapses into sleep full of visions and clamors. A blur of orange

---

[2] liquor made from maguey leaves.

light seared his eyeballs when he tried to unseal his lids. There came from somewhere a low voice weeping without tears, saying meaningless phrases over and over. He began to listen. He tugged at the leash of his stupor, he strained to grasp those words which terrified him even though he could not quite hear them. Then he came awake with frightening suddenness, sitting up and staring at the long sharpened streak of light piercing the corn-husk walls from the level disappearing sun.

María Concepción stood in the doorway, looming colossally tall to his betrayed eyes. She was talking quickly, and calling his name. Then he saw her clearly.

"God's name!" said Juan, frozen to the marrow, "here I am facing my death!" for the long knife she wore habitually at her belt was in her hand. But instead, she threw it away, clear from her, and got down on her knees, crawling toward him as he had seen her crawl many times toward the shrine at Guadalupe Villa. He watched her approach with such horror that the hair of his head seemed to be lifting itself away from him. Falling forward upon her face, she huddled over him, lips moving in a ghostly whisper. Her words became clear, and Juan understood them all.

For a second he could not move nor speak. Then he took her head between both his hands, and supported her in this way, saying swiftly, anxiously reassuring, almost in a babble:

"Oh, thou poor creature! Oh, madwoman! Oh, my María Concepción, unfortunate! Listen. . . . Don't be afraid. Listen to me! I will hide thee away, I thy own man will protect thee! Quiet! Not a sound!"

Trying to collect himself, he held her and cursed under his breath for a few moments in the gathering darkness. María Concepción bent over, face almost on the ground, her feet folded under her, as if she would hide behind him. For the first time in his life Juan was aware of danger. This was danger. María Concepción would be dragged away between two gendarmes, with him following helpless and unarmed, to spend the rest of her days in Belén Prison, maybe. Danger! The night swarmed with threats. He stood up and dragged her up with him. She was silent and perfectly rigid, holding to him with resistless strength, her hands stiffened on his arms.

"Get me the knife," he told her in a whisper. She obeyed, her feet slipping along the hard earth floor, her shoulders straight, her arms close to her side. He lighted a candle. María Concepción held the knife out to him. It was stained and dark even to the handle with drying blood.

He frowned at her harshly, noting the same stains on her chemise and hands.

"Take off thy clothes and wash thy hands," he ordered. He washed the knife carefully, and threw the water wide of the doorway. She watched him and did likewise with the bowl in which she had bathed.

"Light the brasero and cook food for me," he told her in the same peremptory tone. He took her garments and went out. When he returned, she was wearing an old soiled dress, and was fanning the fire in the charcoal burner. Seating himself cross-legged near her, he stared at her as at a creature unknown to him, who bewildered him utterly, for whom there was no possible explanation. She did not turn her head, but kept silent and still, except for the movements of her strong hands fanning the blaze which cast sparks and small jets of white smoke, flaring and dying rhythmically with the motion of the fan, lighting her face and darkening it by turns.

Juan's voice barely disturbed the silence: "Listen to me carefully, and tell me the truth, and when the gendarmes come here for us, thou shalt have nothing to fear. But there will be something for us to settle between us afterward."

The light from the charcoal burner shone in her eyes; a yellow phosphorescence glimmered behind the dark iris.

"For me everything is settled now," she answered, in a tone so tender, so grave, so heavy with suffering, that Juan felt his vitals contract. He wished to repent openly, not as a man, but as a very small child. He could not fathom her, nor himself, nor the mysterious fortunes of life grown so instantly confused where all had seemed so gay and simple. He felt too that she had become invaluable, a woman without equal among a million women, and he could not tell why. He drew an enormous sigh that rattled in his chest.

"Yes, yes, it is all settled. I shall not go away again. We must stay here together."

Whispering, he questioned her and she answered whispering, and he instructed her over and over until she had her lesson by heart. The hostile darkness of the night encroached upon them, flowing over the narrow threshold, invading their hearts. It brought with it sighs and murmurs, the pad of secretive feet in the nearby road, the sharp staccato whimper of wind through the cactus leaves. All these familiar, once friendly cadences were now invested with sinister terrors; a dread, formless and uncontrollable, took hold of them both.

"Light another candle," said Juan, loudly, in too resolute, too sharp a tone. "Let us eat now."

They sat facing each other and ate from the same dish, after their old habit. Neither tasted what they ate. With food halfway to his mouth, Juan listened. The sound of voices rose, spread, widened at the turn of the road along the cactus wall. A spray of lantern light shot through the hedge, a single voice slashed the blackness, ripped the fragile layer of silence suspended above the hut.

"Juan Villegas!"

"Pass, friends!" Juan roared back cheerfully.

They stood in the doorway, simple cautious gendarmes from the village, mixed-bloods themselves with Indian sympathies, well known to all the community. They flashed their lanterns almost apologetically upon the pleasant, harmless scene of a man eating supper with his wife.

"Pardon, brother," said the leader. "Someone has killed the woman

María Rosa, and we must question her neighbors and friends." He paused, and added with an attempt at severity, "Naturally!"

"Naturally," agreed Juan. "You know that I was a good friend of María Rosa. This is bad news."

They all went away together, the men walking in a group, María Concepción following a few steps in the rear, near Juan. No one spoke.

The two points of candlelight at María Rosa's head fluttered uneasily; the shadows shifted and dodged on the stained darkened walls. To María Concepción everything in the smothering enclosing room shared an evil restlessness. The watchful faces of those called as witnesses, the faces of old friends, were made alien by the look of speculation in their eyes. The ridges of the rose-colored rebozo thrown over the body varied continually, as though the thing it covered was not perfectly in repose. Her eyes swerved over the body in the open painted coffin, from the candle tips at the head to the feet, jutting up thinly, the small scarred soles protruding, freshly washed, a mass of crooked, half-healed wounds, thorn-pricks and cuts of sharp stones. Her gaze went back to the candle flame, to Juan's eyes warning her, to the gendarmes talking among themselves. Her eyes would not be controlled.

With a leap that shook her her gaze settled upon the face of María Rosa. Instantly her blood ran smoothly again: there was nothing to fear. Even the restless light could not give a look of life to that fixed countenance. She was dead. María Concepción felt her muscles give way softly; her heart began beating steadily without effort. She knew no more rancor against that pitiable thing, lying indifferently in its blue coffin under the fine silk rebozo. The mouth drooped sharply at the corners in a grimace of weeping arrested half-way. The brows were distressed; the dead flesh could not cast off the shape of its last terror. It was all finished. María Rosa had eaten too much honey and had had too much love. Now she must sit in hell, crying over her sins and her hard death forever and ever.

Old Lupe's cackling voice arose. She had spent the morning helping María Rosa, and it had been hard work. The child had spat blood the moment it was born, a bad sign. She thought then that bad luck would come to the house. Well, about sunset she was in the yard at the back of the house grinding tomatoes and peppers. She had left mother and babe asleep. She heard a strange noise in the house, a choking and smothered calling, like someone wailing in sleep. Well, such a thing is only natural. But there followed a light, quick, thudding sound ——

"Like the blows of a fist?" interrupted an officer.

"No, not at all like such a thing."

"How do you know?"

"I am well acquainted with that sound, friends," retorted Lupe. "This was something else."

She was at a loss to describe it exactly. A moment later, there came the sound of pebbles rolling and slipping under feet; then she knew someone had been there and was running away.

"Why did you wait so long before going to see?"

"I am old and hard in the joints," said Lupe: "I cannot run after people. I walked as fast as I could to the cactus hedge, for it is only by this way that anyone can enter. There was no one in the road, sir, no one. Three cows, and a dog driving them; nothing else. When I got to María Rosa, she was lying all tangled up, and from her neck to her middle she was full of knife-holes. It was a sight to move the Blessed Image Himself! Her eyes were ——— "

"Never mind. Who came oftenest to her house before she went away? Did you know her enemies?"

Lupe's face congealed, closed. Her spongy skin drew into a network of secretive wrinkles. She turned withdrawn and expressionless eyes upon the gendarmes.

"I am an old woman. I do not see well. I cannot hurry on my feet. I know no enemy of María Rosa. I did not see anyone leave the clearing."

"You did not hear splashing in the spring near the bridge?"

"No, sir."

"Why, then, do our dogs follow a scent there and lose it?"

"God only knows, my friend. I am an old wo ——— "

"Yes. How did the footfalls sound?"

"Like the tread of an evil spirit!" Lupe broke forth in a swelling oracular tone that startled them. The Indians stirred uneasily, glanced at the dead, then at Lupe. They half expected her to produce the evil spirit among them at once.

The gendarme began to lose his temper.

"No, poor unfortunate; I mean, were they heavy or light? The footsteps of a man or of a woman? Was the person shod or barefoot?"

A glance at the listening circle assured Lupe of their thrilled attention. She enjoyed the dangerous importance of her situation. She could have ruined that María Concepción with a word, but it was even sweeter to make fools of these gendarmes who went about spying on honest people. She raised her voice again. What she had not seen she could not describe, thank God! No one could harm her because her knees were stiff and she could not run even to seize a murderer. As for knowing the difference between footfalls, shod or bare, man or woman, nay, between devil and human, who ever heard of such madness?

"My eyes are not ears, gentlemen," she ended grandly, "but upon my heart I swear those footsteps fell as the tread of the spirit of evil!"

"Imbecile!" yapped the leader in a shrill voice. "Take her away, one of you! Now, Juan Villegas, tell me ——— "

Juan told his story patiently, several times over. He had returned to his wife that day. She had gone to market as usual. He had helped her prepare her fowls. She had returned about mid-afternoon, they had talked, she had cooked, they had eaten, nothing was amiss. Then the gendarmes came with the news about María Rosa. That was all. Yes, María Rosa had run away with him, but there had been no bad blood between him and his wife on this account, nor between his wife and María Rosa. Everybody knew that his wife was a quiet woman.

María Concepción heard her own voice answering without a break. It was true at first she was troubled when her husband went away, but after that she had not worried about him. It was the way of men, she believed. She was a church-married woman and knew her place. Well, he had come home at last. She had gone to market, but had come back early, because now she had her man to cook for. That was all.

Other voices broke in. A toothless old man said: "She is a woman of good reputation among us, and María Rosa was not." A smiling young mother, Anita, baby at breast, said: "If no one thinks so, how can you accuse her? It was the loss of her child and not of her husband that changed her so." Another: "María Rosa had a strange life, apart from us. How do we know who might have come from another place to do her evil?" And old Soledad spoke up boldly: "When I saw María Concepción in the market today, I said, 'Good luck to you, María Concepción, this is a happy day for you!' " and she gave María Concepción a long easy stare, and the smile of a born wise-woman.

María Concepción suddenly felt herself guarded, surrounded, upborne by her faithful friends. They were around her, speaking for her, defending her, the forces of life were ranged invincibly with her against the beaten dead. María Rosa had thrown away her share of strength in them, she lay forfeited among them. María Concepción looked from one to the other of the circling, intent faces. Their eyes gave back reassurance, understanding, a secret and mighty sympathy.

The gendarmes were at a loss. They, too, felt that sheltering wall cast impenetrably around her. They were certain she had done it, and yet they could not accuse her. Nobody could be accused; there was not a shred of true evidence. They shrugged their shoulders and snapped their fingers and shuffled their feet. Well, then, good night to everybody. Many pardons for having intruded. Good health!

A small bundle lying against the wall at the head of the coffin squirmed like an eel. A wail, a mere sliver of sound, issued. María Concepción took the son of María Rosa in her arms.

"He is mine," she said clearly, "I will take him with me."

No one assented in words, but an approving nod, a bare breath of complete agreement, stirred among them as they made way for her.

María Concepción, carrying the child, followed Juan from the clearing. The hut was left with its lighted candles and a crowd of old women who would sit up all night, drinking coffee and smoking and telling ghost stories.

Juan's exaltation had burned out. There was not an ember of excitement left in him. He was tired. The perilous adventure was over. María Rosa had vanished, to come no more forever. Their days of marching, of eating, of quarreling and making love between battles, were all over. Tomorrow he would go back to dull and endless labor, he must descend into the trenches of the buried city as María Rosa must go into her grave. He felt his veins fill up with bitterness, with black unendurable melancholy. Oh, Jesus! what bad luck overtakes a man!

Well, there was no way out of it now. For the moment he craved only to sleep. He was so drowsy he could scarcely guide his feet. The occasional light touch of the woman at his elbow was as unreal, as ghostly as the brushing of a leaf against his face. He did not know why he had fought to save her, and now he forgot her. There was nothing in him except a vast blind hurt like a covered wound.

He entered the jacal, and without waiting to light a candle, threw off his clothing, sitting just within the door. He moved with lagging, half-awake hands, to strip his body of its heavy finery. With a long groaning sigh of relief he fell straight back on the floor, almost instantly asleep, his arms flung up and outward.

María Concepción, a small clay jar in her hand, approached the gentle little mother goat tethered to a sapling, which gave and yielded as she pulled at the rope's end after the farthest reaches of grass about her. The kid, tied up a few feet away, rose bleating, its feathery fleece shivering in the fresh wind. Sitting on her heels, holding his tether, she allowed him to suckle a few moments. Afterward — all her movements very deliberate and even — she drew a supply of milk for the child.

She sat against the wall of her house, near the doorway. The child, fed and asleep, was cradled in the hollow of her crossed legs. The silence over-filled the world, the skies flowed down evenly to the rim of the valley, the stealthy moon crept slantwise to the shelter of the mountains. She felt soft and warm all over; she dreamed that the newly born child was her own, and she was resting deliciously.

María Concepción could hear Juan's breathing. The sound vapored from the low doorway, calmly; the house seemed to be resting after a burdensome day. She breathed, too, very slowly and quietly, each inspiration saturating her with repose. The child's light, faint breath was a mere shadowy moth of sound in the silver air. The night, the earth under her, seemed to swell and recede together with a limitless, unhurried, benign breathing. She drooped and closed her eyes, feeling the slow rise and fall within her own body. She did not know what it was, but it eased her all through. Even as she was falling asleep, head bowed over the child, she was still aware of a strange, wakeful happiness.

[1930]

Katherine Anne Porter

ୠୠ

FLOWERING JUDAS

Braggioni sits heaped upon the edge of a straight-backed chair much too small for him, and sings to Laura in a furry, mournful voice. Laura has begun to find reasons for avoiding her own house until the latest possible moment, for Braggioni is there almost every night. No matter how late she is, he will be sitting there with a surly, waiting expression, pulling at his kinky yellow hair, thumbing the strings of his guitar, snarling a tune under his breath. Lupe the Indian maid meets Laura at the door, and says with a flicker of a glance towards the upper room, "He waits."

Laura wishes to lie down, she is tired of her hairpins and the feel of her long tight sleeves, but she says to him, "Have you a new song for me this evening?" If he says yes, she asks him to sing it. If he says no, she remembers his favorite one, and asks him to sing it again. Lupe brings her a cup of chocolate and a plate of rice, and Laura eats at the small table under the lamp, first inviting Braggioni, whose answer is always the same: "I have eaten, and besides, chocolate thickens the voice."

Laura says, "Sing, then," and Braggioni heaves himself into song. He scratches the guitar familiarly as though it were a pet animal, and sings passionately off key, taking the high notes in a prolonged painful squeal. Laura, who haunts the markets listening to the ballad singers, and stops every day to hear the blind boy playing his reed-flute in Sixteenth of September Street, listens to Braggioni with pitiless courtesy, because she dares not smile at his miserable performance. Nobody dares to smile at him. Braggioni is cruel to everyone, with a kind of specialized insolence, but he is so vain of his talents, and so sensitive to slights, it would require a cruelty and vanity greater than his own to lay a finger on the vast cureless wound of his self-esteem. It would require courage, too, for it is dangerous to offend him, and nobody has this courage.

Braggioni loves himself with such tenderness and amplitude and eternal charity that his followers — for he is a leader of men, a skilled revolutionist, and his skin has been punctured in honorable warfare — warm themselves in the reflected glow, and say to each other: "He has a real nobility, a love of humanity raised above mere personal affections." The excess of this self-love has flowed out, inconveniently for her, over Laura, who, with so many others, owes her comfortable situation and her salary to him. When he is in a very good humor, he tells her, "I am tempted to forgive you for being a *gringa, gringita!*" and Laura, burning, imagines herself leaning forward suddenly, and with a sound back-handed slap wiping the suety smile from his face. If he notices her eyes at these moments he gives no sign.

She knows what Braggioni would offer her, and she must resist tenaciously without appearing to resist, and if she could avoid it she would not admit even to herself the slow drift of his intention. During these long evenings which have spoiled a long month for her, she sits in her deep chair with an open book on her knees, resting her eyes on the consoling rigidity of the printed page when the sight and sound of Braggioni singing threaten to identify themselves with all her remembered afflictions and to add their weight to her uneasy premonitions of the future. The gluttonous bulk of Braggioni has become a symbol of her many disillusions, for a revolutionist should be lean, animated by heroic faith, a vessel of abstract virtues. This is nonsense, she knows it now and is ashamed of it. Revolution must have leaders, and leadership is a career for energetic men. She is, her comrades tell her, full of romantic error, for what she defines as cynicism in them is merely "a developed sense of reality." She is almost too willing to say, "I am wrong, I suppose I don't really understand the principles," and afterward she makes a secret truce with herself, determined not to surrender her will to such expedient logic. But she cannot help feeling that she has been betrayed irreparably by the disunion between her way of living and her feeling of what life should be, and at times she is almost contented to rest in this sense of grievance as a private store of consolation. Sometimes she wishes to run away, but she stays. Now she longs to fly out of this room, down the narrow stairs, and into the street where the houses lean together like conspirators under a single mottled lamp, and leave Braggioni singing to himself.

Instead she looks at Braggioni, frankly and clearly, like a good child who understands the rules of behavior. Her knees cling together under sound blue serge, and her round white collar is not purposely nun-like. She wears the uniform of an idea, and has renounced vanities. She was born Roman Catholic, and in spite of her fear of being seen by someone who might make a scandal of it, she slips now and again into some crumbling little church, kneels on the chilly stone, and says a Hail Mary on the gold rosary she bought in Tehuantepec. It is no good and she ends by examining the altar with its tinsel flowers and ragged brocades, and feels tender about the battered doll-shape of some male saint whose white, lace-trimmed drawers hang limply around his ankles below the hieratic dignity of his velvet robe. She has encased herself in a set of principles derived from her early training, leaving no detail of gesture or of personal taste untouched, and for this reason she will not wear lace made on machines. This is her private heresy, for in her special group the machine is sacred, and will be the salvation of the workers. She loves fine lace, and there is a tiny edge of fluted cobweb on this collar, which is one of twenty precisely alike, folded in blue tissue paper in the upper drawer of her clothes chest.

Braggioni catches her glance solidly as if he had been waiting for it, leans forward, balancing his paunch between his spread knees, and sings with tremendous emphasis, weighing his words. He has, the song relates, no father and no mother, nor even a friend to console him; lonely as a wave of the sea he comes and goes, lonely as a wave. His mouth opens round and yearns sideways, his balloon cheeks grow oily with the labor of song. He bulges marvelously in his expensive garments. Over his lavender collar, crushed upon a purple necktie, held by a diamond hoop: over his ammunition belt of tooled leather worked in silver, buckled cruelly around his gasping middle: over the tops of his glossy yellow shoes Braggioni swells with ominous ripeness, his mauve silk hose stretched taut, his ankles bound with the stout leather thongs of his shoes.

When he stretches his eyelids at Laura she notes again that his eyes are the true tawny yellow cat's eyes. He is rich, not in money, he tells her, but in power, and this power brings with it the blameless ownership of things, and the right to indulge his love of small luxuries. "I have a taste for the elegant refinements," he said once, flourishing a yellow silk handkerchief before her nose. "Smell that? It is Jockey Club, imported from New York." Nonetheless he is wounded by life. He will say so presently. "It is true everything turns to dust in the hand, to gall on the tongue." He sighs and his leather belt creaks like a saddle girth. "I am disappointed in everything as it comes. Everything." He shakes his head. "You, poor thing, you will be disappointed too. You are born for it. We are more alike than you realize in some things. Wait and see. Some day you will remember what I have told you, you will know that Braggioni was your friend."

Laura feels a slow chill, a purely physical sense of danger, a warning in her blood that violence, mutilation, a shocking death, wait for her with lessening patience. She has translated this fear into something homely, immediate, and sometimes hesitates before crossing the street. "My personal fate is nothing, except as the testimony of a mental attitude," she reminds herself, quoting from some forgotten philosophic primer, and is sensible enough to add, "Anyhow, I shall not be killed by an automobile if I can help it."

"It may be true I am as corrupt, in another way, as Braggioni," she thinks in spite of herself, "as callous, as incomplete," and if this is so, any kind of death seems preferable. Still she sits quietly, she does not run. Where could she go? Uninvited she has promised herself to this place; she can no longer imagine herself as living in another country, and there is no pleasure in remembering her life before she came here.

Precisely what is the nature of this devotion, its true motives, and what are its obligations? Laura cannot say. She spends part of her days in Xochimilco, near by, teaching Indian children to say in English, "The cat is on the mat." When she appears in the classroom they crowd about her with smiles on their wise, innocent, clay-colored faces, crying, "Good morning, my titcher!" in immaculate voices, and they make of her desk a fresh garden of flowers every day.

During her leisure she goes to union meetings and listens to busy important voices quarreling over tactics, methods, internal politics. She visits the prisoners of her own political faith in their cells, where they entertain themselves with counting cockroaches, repenting of their indiscretions, composing their memoirs, writing out manifestoes and plans for their comrades who are still walking about free, hands in pockets, sniffing fresh air. Laura brings them food and cigarettes and a little money, and she brings messages disguised in equivocal phrases from the men outside who dare not set foot in the prison for fear of disappearing into the cells kept empty for them. If the prisoners confuse night and day, and complain, "Dear little Laura, time doesn't pass in this infernal hole, and I won't know when it is time to sleep unless I have a reminder," she brings them their favorite narcotics, and says in a tone that does not wound them with pity, "Tonight will really be night for you," and though her Spanish amuses them they find her comforting, useful. If they lose patience and all faith, and curse the slowness of their friends in coming to their rescue with money and influence, they trust her not to repeat everything, and if she inquires, "Where do you think we can find money, or influence?" they are certain to answer, "Well, there is Braggioni, why doesn't he do something?"

She smuggles letters from headquarters to men hiding from firing squads in back streets in mildewed houses, where they sit in tumbled beds and talk bitterly as if all Mexico were at their heels, when Laura knows positively they might appear at the band concert in the Alameda[1] on Sunday morning, and no one would notice them. But Braggioni says, "Let them sweat a little. The next time they may be careful. It is very restful to have them out of the way for a while." She is not afraid to knock on any door in any street after midnight, and enter in the darkness, and say to one of these men who is really in danger: "They will be looking for you — seriously — tomorrow morning after six. Here is some money from Vicente. Go to Vera Cruz and wait."

She borrows money from the Rumanian agitator to give to his bitter enemy the Polish agitator. The favor of Braggioni is their disputed territory, and Braggioni holds the balance nicely, for he can use them both. The Polish agitator talks love to her over café tables, hoping to exploit what he believes is her secret sentimental preference for him, and he gives her misinformation which he begs her to repeat as the solemn truth to certain persons. The Rumanian is more adroit. He is generous with his money in all good causes, and lies to her with an air of ingenuous candor, as if he were her good friend and confidant. She never repeats anything they may say.

[1] a public square in Mexico City.

Braggioni never asks questions. He has other ways to discover all that he wishes to know about them.

Nobody touches her, but all praise her gray eyes, and the soft, round under lip which promises gaiety, yet is always grave, nearly always firmly closed: and they cannot understand why she is in Mexico. She walks back and forth on her errands, with puzzled eyebrows, carrying her little folder of drawings and music and school papers. No dancer dances more beautifully than Laura walks, and she inspires some amusing, unexpected ardors, which cause little gossip, because nothing comes of them. A young captain who had been a soldier in Zapata's[2] army attempted, during a horseback ride near Cuernavaca, to express his desire for her with the noble simplicity befitting a rude folk-hero; but gently, because he was gentle. This gentleness was his defeat, for when he alighted, and removed her foot from the stirrup, and essayed to draw her down into his arms, her horse, ordinarily a tame one, shied fiercely, reared and plunged away. The young hero's horse careened blindly after his stable-mate, and the hero did not return to the hotel until rather late that evening. At breakfast he came to her table in full charro dress, gray buckskin jacket and trousers with strings of silver buttons down the leg, and he was in a humorous, careless mood. "May I sit with you?" and "You are a wonderful rider. I was terrified that you might be thrown and dragged. I should never have forgiven myself. But I cannot admire you enough for your riding."

"I learned to ride in Arizona," said Laura.

"If you will ride with me again this morning, I promise you a horse that will not shy with you," he said. But Laura remembered that she must return to Mexico City at noon.

Next morning the children made a celebration and spent their playtime writing on the blackboard, "We lov ar titcher," and with tinted chalks they drew wreaths of flowers around the words. The young hero wrote her a letter: "I am a very foolish, wasteful, impulsive man. I should have first said I love you, and then you would not have run away. But you shall see me again." Laura thought, "I must sent him a box of colored crayons," but she was trying to forgive herself for having spurred her horse at the wrong moment.

A brown shock-haired youth came and stood in her patio one night and sang like a lost soul for two hours, but Laura could think of nothing to do about it. The moonlight spread a wash of gauzy silver over the clear spaces of the garden, and the shadows were cobalt blue. The scarlet blossoms of the Judas tree were dull purple, and the names of the colors repeated themselves automatically in her mind, while she watched not the boy, but his shadow, fallen like a dark garment across the fountain rim, trailing in the water. Lupe came silently and whispered expert counsel in

[2] Emiliano Zapata (1883–1919), rebel general who was a leader in the Mexican revolution of 1910–1917.

her ear: "If you will throw him one little flower, he will sing another song or two and go away." Laura threw the flower, and he sang a last song and went away with the flower tucked in the band of his hat. Lupe said, "He is one of the organizers of the Typographers Union, and before that he sold corridos[3] in the Merced market, and before that, he came from Guanajuato, where I was born. I would not trust any man, but I trust least those from Guanajuato."

She did not tell Laura that he would be back again the next day, and the next, nor that he would follow her at a certain fixed distance around the Merced market, through the Zocolo, up Francesco I. Madero Avenue, and so along the Paseo de la Reforma to Chapultepec Park, and into the Philosopher's Footpath, still with that flower withering in his hat, and an indivisible attention in his eyes.

Now Laura is accustomed to him, it means nothing except that he is nineteen years old and is observing a convention with all propriety, as though it were founded on a law of nature, which in the end it might very well prove to be. He is beginning to write poems which he prints on a wooden press, and he leaves them stuck like handbills in her door. She is pleasantly disturbed by the abstract, unhurried watchfulness of his black eyes which will in time turn easily toward another object. She tells herself that throwing the flower was a mistake, for she is twenty-two years old and knows better; but she refuses to regret it, and persuades herself that her negation of all external events as they occur is a sign that she is gradually perfecting herself in the stoicism she strives to cultivate against that disaster she fears, though she cannot name it.

She is not at home in the world. Every day she teaches children who remain strangers to her, though she loves their tender round hands and their charming opportunistic savagery. She knocks at unfamiliar doors not knowing whether a friend or a stranger shall answer, and even if a known face emerges from the sour gloom of that unknown interior, still it is the face of a stranger. No matter what this stranger says to her, nor what her message to him, the very cells of her flesh reject knowledge and kinship in one monotonous word. No. No. No. She draws her strength from this one holy talismanic word which does not suffer her to be led into evil. Denying everything, she may walk anywhere in safety, she looks at everything without amazement.

No, repeats this firm unchanging voice of her blood; and she looks at Braggioni without amazement. He is a great man, he wishes to impress this simple girl who covers her great round breasts with thick dark cloth, and who hides long, invaluably beautiful legs under a heavy skirt. She is almost thin except for the incomprehensible fullness of her breasts, like a nursing mother's, and Braggioni, who considers himself a judge of women, speculates again on the puzzle of her notorious virginity, and takes the liberty of

---

[3] tickets to bullfights.

speech which she permits without a sign of modesty, indeed, without any sort of sign, which is disconcerting.

"You think you are so cold, *gringita!* Wait and see. You will surprise yourself someday! May I be there to advise you!" He stretches his eyelids at her, and his ill-humored cat's eyes waver in a separate glance for the two points of light marking the opposite ends of a smoothly drawn path between the swollen curve of her breasts. He is not put off by that blue serge, nor by her resolutely fixed gaze. There is all the time in the world. His cheeks are bellying with the wind of song. "O girl with the dark eyes," he sings, and reconsiders. "But yours are not dark. I can change all that. O girl with the green eyes, you have stolen my heart away." Then his mind wanders to the song, and Laura feels the weight of his attention being shifted elsewhere. Singing thus, he seems harmless, he is quite harmless, there is nothing to do but sit patiently and say "No," when the moment comes. She draws a full breath, and her mind wanders also, but not far. She dares not wander too far.

Not for nothing has Braggioni taken pains to be a good revolutionist and a professional lover of humanity. He will never die of it. He has the malice, the cleverness, the wickedness, the sharpness of wit, the hardness of heart, stipulated for loving the world profitably. He *will never die of it.* He will live to see himself kicked out from his feeding trough by other hungry world-saviors. Traditionally he must sing in spite of his life which drives him to bloodshed, he tells Laura, for his father was a Tuscany peasant who drifted to Yucatan and married a Maya woman: a woman of race, an aristocrat. They gave him the love and knowledge of music, thus: and under the rip of his thumbnail, the strings of the instrument complain like exposed nerves.

Once he was called Delgadito[4] by all the girls and married women who ran after him; he was so scrawny all his bones showed under his thin cotton clothing, and he could squeeze his emptiness to the very backbone with his two hands. He was a poet and the revolution was only a dream then; too many women loved him and sapped away his youth, and he could never find enough to eat anywhere, anywhere! Now he is a leader of men, crafty men who whisper in his ear, hungry men who wait for hours outside his office for a word with him, emaciated men with wild faces who waylay him at the street gate with a timid, "Comrade, let me tell you . . ." and they blow the foul breath from their empty stomachs in his face.

He is always sympathetic. He gives them handfuls of small coins from his own pockets, he promises them work, there will be demonstrations, they must join the unions and attend the meetings, above all they must be on the watch for spies. They are closer to him than his own brothers, without them he can do nothing — until tomorrow, comrade!

[4] "the little skinny one" (Spanish).

Until tomorrow. "They are stupid, they are lazy, they are treacherous, they would cut my throat for nothing," he says to Laura. He has good food and abundant drink, he hires an automobile and drives in the Paseo on Sunday morning, and enjoys plenty of sleep in a soft bed beside a wife who dares not disturb him; and he sits pampering his bones in easy billows of fat, singing to Laura, who knows and thinks these things about him. When he was fifteen, he tried to drown himself because he loved a girl, his first love, and she laughed at him. "A thousand women have paid for that," and his tight little mouth turns down at the corners. Now he perfumes his hair with Jockey Club, and confides to Laura: "One woman is really as good as another for me in the dark. I prefer them all."

His wife organizes unions among the girls in the cigarette factories, and walks in picket lines, and even speaks at meetings in the evening. But she cannot be brought to acknowledge the benefits of true liberty. "I tell her I must have my freedom, net. She does not understand my point of view." Laura has heard this many times. Braggioni scratches the guitar and meditates. "She is an instinctively virtuous woman, pure gold, no doubt of that. If she were not, I should lock her up, and she knows it."

His wife, who works so hard for the good of the factory girls, employs part of her leisure lying on the floor weeping because there are so many women in the world, and only one husband for her, and she never knows where nor when to look for him. He told her: "Unless you can learn to cry when I am not here, I must go away for good." That day he went away and took a room at the Hotel Madrid.

It is this month of separation for the sake of higher principles that has been spoiled not only for Mrs. Braggioni, whose sense of reality is beyond criticism, but for Laura, who feels herself bogged in a nightmare. Tonight Laura envies Mrs. Braggioni, who is alone, and free to weep as much as she pleases about a concrete wrong. Laura has just come from a visit to the prison, and she is waiting for tomorrow with a bitter anxiety as if tomorrow may not come, but time may be caught immovably in this hour, with herself transfixed, Braggioni singing on forever, and Eugenio's body not yet discovered by the guard.

Braggioni says: "Are you going to sleep?" Almost before she can shake her head, he begins telling her about the May-day disturbances coming on in Morelia, for the Catholics hold a festival in honor of the Blessed Virgin, and the Socialists celebrate their martyrs on that day. "There will be two independent processions, starting from either end of town, and they will march until they meet, and the rest depends. . . ." He asks her to oil and load his pistols. Standing up, he unbuckles his ammunition belt, and spreads it laden across her knees. Laura sits with the shells slipping through the cleaning cloth dipped in oil, and he says again he cannot understand why she works so hard for the revolutionary idea unless she loves some man who is in it. "Are you not in love with someone?" "No," says Laura. "And no one is in love with you?" "No." "Then it is your own fault. No woman need go begging. Why, what is the matter with you? The legless beggar woman in the Alameda has a perfectly faithful lover. Did you know that?"

Laura peers down the pistol barrel and says nothing, but a long, slow faintness rises and subsides in her; Braggioni curves his swollen fingers around the throat of the guitar and softly smothers the music out of it, and when she hears him again he seems to have forgotten her, and is speaking in the hypnotic voice he uses when talking in small rooms to a listening, close-gathered crowd. Some day this world, now seemingly so composed and eternal, to the edges of every sea shall be merely a tangle of gaping trenches, of crashing walls and broken bodies. Everything must be torn from its accustomed place where it has rotted for centuries, hurled skyward and distributed, cast down again clean as rain, without separate identity. Nothing shall survive that the stiffened hands of poverty have created for the rich and no one shall be left alive except the elect spirits destined to procreate a new world cleansed of cruelty and injustice, ruled by benevolent anarchy: "Pistols are good, I love them, cannon are even better, but in the end I pin my faith to good dynamite," he concludes, and strokes the pistol lying in her hands. "Once I dreamed of destroying this city, in case it offered resistance to General Ortiz,[5] but it fell into his hands like an overripe pear."

He is made restless by his own words, rises and stands waiting. Laura holds up the belt to him: "Put that on, and go kill somebody in Morelia, and you will be happier," she says softly. The presence of death in the room makes her bold. "Today, I found Eugenio going into a stupor. He refused to allow me to call the prison doctor. He had taken all the tablets I brought him yesterday. He said he took them because he was bored."

"He is a fool, and his death is his own business," says Braggioni, fastening his belt carefully.

"I told him if he had waited only a little while longer, you would have got him set free," says Laura. "He said he did not want to wait."

"He is a fool and we are well rid of him," says Braggioni, reaching for his hat.

He goes away. Laura knows his mood has changed, she will not see him any more for a while. He will send word when he needs her to go on errands into strange streets, to speak to the strange faces that will appear, like clay masks with the power of human speech, to mutter their thanks to Braggioni for his help. Now she is free, and she thinks, I must run while there is time. But she does not go.

Braggioni enters his own house where for a month his wife has spent many hours every night weeping and tangling her hair upon her pillow. She is weeping now, and she weeps more at the sight of him, the cause of all her sorrows. He looks about the room. Nothing is changed, the smells are good

---

[5] Pascual Ortiz Rubio (1877–1963), a revolutionary general who later, from 1930 to 1932, served as president of Mexico.

and familiar, he is well acquainted with the woman who comes toward him with no reproach except grief on her face. He says to her tenderly: "You are so good, please don't cry any more, you dear good creature." She says, "Are you tired, my angel? Sit here and I will wash your feet." She brings a bowl of water, and kneeling, unlaces his shoes, and when from her knees she raises her sad eyes under her blackened lids, he is sorry for everything, and bursts into tears. "Ah, yes, I am hungry, I am tired, let us eat something together," he says, between sobs. His wife leans her head on his arm and says, "Forgive me!" and this time he is refreshed by the solemn, endless rain of her tears.

Laura takes off her serge dress and puts on a white linen nightgown and goes to bed. She turns her head a little to one side, and lying still, reminds herself that it is time to sleep. Numbers tick in her brain like little clocks, soundless doors close of themselves around her. If you would sleep, you must not remember anything, the children will say tomorrow, good morning, my teacher, the poor prisoners who come every day bringing flowers to their jailer. 1–2–3–4–5 — it is monstrous to confuse love with revolution, night with day, life with death — ah Eugenio!

The tolling of the midnight bell is a signal, but what does it mean? Get up, Laura, and follow me: come out of your sleep, out of your bed, out of this strange house. What are you doing in this house? Without a word, without fear she rose and reached for Eugenio's hand, but he eluded her with a sharp, sly smile and drifted away. This is not all, you shall see — Murderer, he said, follow me, I will show you a new country, but it is far away and we must hurry. No, said Laura, not unless you take my hand, no; and she clung first to the stair rail, and then to the topmost branch of the Judas tree that bent down slowly and set her upon the earth, and then to the rocky ledge of a cliff, and then to the jagged wave of a sea that was not water but a desert of crumbling stone. Where are you taking me? she asked in wonder but without fear. To death, and it is a long way off, and we must hurry, said Eugenio. No, said Laura, not unless you take my hand. Then eat these flowers, poor prisoner, said Eugenio in a voice of pity, take and eat: and from the Judas tree he stripped the warm bleeding flowers, and held them to her lips. She saw that his hand was fleshless, a cluster of small white petrified branches, and his eye sockets were without light, but she ate the flowers greedily for they satisfied both hunger and thirst. Murderer! said Eugenio, and Cannibal! This is my body and my blood. Laura cried No! and at the sound of her own voice, she awoke trembling, and was afraid to sleep again.

[1930]

*J*AMES THURBER (1894–1961), *the American humorist, was born in Columbus, Ohio. When he was only a boy he lost an eye, which kept him from military service in World War I. His eyesight failed him entirely later in life. After his graduation from Ohio State University, he worked as a newspaper reporter in Columbus and New York and lived in Paris. He came back to New York in 1926 to submit his humorous sketches to a new magazine* The New Yorker, *where he also served briefly as managing editor.* The New Yorker *printed his cartoons as well as his fables, stories, and essays for many years. In 1940 he wrote a successful play,* The Male Animal, *with Elliott Nugent. Among his many books of stories, fables, essays, and cartoons are* Fables for Our Time *(1940),* My World — And Welcome to It *(1942),* The Thurber Carnival *(1945), and* Thurber Country *(1953).*

In discussing how he wrote stories, Thurber once quoted a definition of the difference between English and American humor: "The English treat the commonplace as if it were remarkable and the Americans treat the remarkable as if it were commonplace." In his best work, as in "The Secret Life of Walter Mitty," his stories venture into fantasy while still treating the remarkable as commonplace. He felt at home in the genre of the short story, never wanting to write a longer work, yet he recognized that there could also be serious elements in his fiction. "In anything funny you write that isn't close to serious you've missed something along the line." To Thurber, humor was "emotional chaos remembered in tranquility," and although the chaos provoked the immediate comic response, the power of ordered remembering gave the incident its deeper meaning. Thurber resisted comparisons between his funny stories and Mark Twain's rambling, humorous sketches. Instead he said he began to write as a young man in "a rather curious style . . . tight journalese laced with heavy doses of Henry James," but his contact with E. B. White and Harold Ross at The New Yorker *taught him to value clarity above all else in a literary style. After he matured as a writer he reflected on why Henry James's way of writing no longer worked for him: "James is like — well, I had a bulldog once who used to drag rails around, enormous ones. . . . Once he brought home a chest of drawers — without the drawers in it. Found it on an ash-heap. Well, he'd start to get these things in the garden gate, everything finely balanced, you see, and then* crash, *he'd come up against the gate posts. He'd get it through finally, but I had that feeling in some of James's novels: that he was trying to get that rail through a gate not wide enough for it."*

Thurber wrote his stories very slowly, often revising them several times in an attempt to make the finished version seem smooth and effortless. It was only in his cartoons and drawing that he worked quickly, "sometimes so

quickly that the result is an accident, something I hadn't intended at all,"
but he felt that he did these for relaxation and they came too fast to be
called art. His best fiction and drawings are inspired by his comic view of
the perennial battle of the sexes, in which intimidating women try to keep
the upper hand over shy, trapped little men like the gentle Waterbury
shopper, Walter Mitty.

James Thurber

ಌಌ

THE SECRET LIFE OF WALTER MITTY

"We're going through!" The Commander's voice was like thin ice breaking. He wore his full-dress uniform, with the heavily braided white cap pulled down rakishly over one cold gray eye. "We can't make it, sir. It's spoiling for a hurricane, if you ask me." "I'm not asking you, Lieutenant Berg," said the Commander. "Throw on the power lights! Rev her up to 8,500! We're going through!" The pounding of the cylinders increased: ta-pocketa-pocketa-pocketa-*pocketa-pocketa.* The Commander stared at the ice forming on the pilot window. He walked over and twisted a row of complicated dials. "Switch on No. 8 auxiliary!" he shouted. "Switch on No. 8 auxiliary!" repeated Lieutenant Berg. "Full strength in No. 3 turret!" shouted the Commander. "Full strength in No. 3 turret!" The crew, bending to their various tasks in the huge, hurtling eight-engined Navy hydroplane, looked at each other and grinned. "The Old Man'll get us through," they said to one another. "The Old Man ain't afraid of Hell!" . . .

"Not so fast! You're driving too fast!" said Mrs. Mitty. "What are you driving so fast for?"

"Hmm?" said Walter Mitty. He looked at his wife, in the seat beside him, with shocked astonishment. She seemed grossly unfamiliar, like a strange woman who had yelled at him in a crowd. "You were up to fifty-five," she said. "You know I don't like to go more than forty. You were up to fifty-five." Walter Mitty drove on toward Waterbury in silence, the roaring of the SN202 through the worst storm in twenty years of Navy flying fading in the remote, intimate airways of his mind. "You're tensed up again," said Mrs. Mitty. "It's one of your days. I wish you'd let Dr. Renshaw look you over."

Walter Mitty stopped the car in front of the building where his wife went to have her hair done. "Remember to get those overshoes while I'm having my hair done," she said. "I don't need overshoes," said Mitty. She put her mirror back into her bag. "We've been all through that," she said, getting out of the car. "You're not a young man any longer." He raced the engine a little. "Why don't you wear your gloves? Have you lost your gloves?" Walter Mitty reached in a pocket and brought out the gloves. He put them on, but after she had turned and gone into the building and he had driven on to a red light, he took them off again. "Pick it up, brother!" snapped a cop as the light changed, and Mitty hastily pulled on his gloves and lurched ahead. He drove around the streets aimlessly for a time, and then he drove past the hospital on his way to the parking lot.

. . . "It's the millionaire banker, Wellington McMillan," said the pretty nurse. "Yes?" said Walter Mitty, removing his gloves slowly. "Who has the case?" "Dr. Renshaw and Dr. Benbow, but there are two specialists here, Dr. Remington from New York and Dr. Pritchard-Mitford from London. He flew over." A door opened down a long, cool corridor and Dr. Renshaw came out. He looked distraught and haggard. "Hello, Mitty," he said. "We're having the devil's own time with McMillan, the millionaire banker and close personal friend of Roosevelt. Obstreosis of the ductal tract. Tertiary. Wish you'd take a look at him." "Glad to," said Mitty.

In the operating room there were whispered introductions: "Dr. Remington, Dr. Mitty, Mr. Pritchard-Mitford, Dr. Mitty." "I've read your book on streptothricosis," said Pritchard-Mitford, shaking hands. "A brilliant performance, sir." "Thank you," said Walter Mitty. "Didn't know you were in the States, Mitty," grumbled Remington. "Coals to Newcastle, bringing Mitford and me up here for a tertiary." "You are very kind," said Mitty. A huge, complicated machine, connected to the operating table, with many tubes and wires, began at this moment to go pocketa-pocketa-pocketa. "The new anesthetizer is giving way!" shouted an interne. "There is no one in the East who knows how to fix it!" "Quiet, man!" said Mitty, in a low, cool voice. He sprang to the machine, which was now going pocketa-pocketa-queep-pocketa-queep. He began fingering delicately a row of glistening dials. "Give me a fountain pen!" he snapped. Someone handed him a fountain pen. He pulled a faulty piston out of the machine and inserted the pen in its place. "That will hold for ten minutes," he said. "Get on with the operation." A nurse hurried over and whispered to Renshaw, and Mitty saw the man turn pale. "Coreopsis has set in," said Renshaw nervously. "If you would take over, Mitty?" Mitty looked at him and at the craven figure of Benbow, who drank, and at the grave, uncertain faces of the two great specialists. "If you wish," he said. They slipped a white gown on him; he adjusted a mask and drew on thin gloves; nurses handed him shining. . . .

"Back it up, Mac! Look out for that Buick!" Walter Mitty jammed on the brakes. "Wrong lane, Mac," said the parking-lot attendant, looking at Mitty closely. "Gee. Yeh," muttered Mitty. He began cautiously to back out of the lane marked "Exit Only." "Leave her sit there," said the attendant. "I'll put her away." Mitty got out of the car. "Hey, better leave the key." "Oh," said Mitty, handing the man the ignition key. The attendant vaulted into the car, backed it up with insolent skill, and put it where it belonged.

They're so damn cocky, thought Walter Mitty, walking along Main Street; they think they know everything. Once he had tried to take his chains off, outside New Milford, and he had got them wound around the axles. A man had had to come out in a wrecking car and unwind them, a young, grinning garageman. Since then Mrs. Mitty always made him drive to the garage to have the chains taken off. The next time, he thought, I'll wear my right arm in a sling; they won't grin at me then. I'll have my right arm in a sling and they'll see I couldn't possibly take the chains off myself. He kicked at the slush on the sidewalk. "Overshoes," he said to himself, and he began looking for a shoe store.

When he came out into the street again, with the overshoes in a box under his arm, Walter Mitty began to wonder what the other thing was his wife had told him to get. She had told him, twice, before they set out from their house for Waterbury. In a way he hated these weekly trips to town — he was always getting something wrong. Kleenex, he thought, Squibb's, razor blades? No. Toothpaste, toothbrush, bicarbonate, carborundum, initiative and referendum? He gave it up. But she would remember it. "Where's the what's-its-name?" she would ask. "Don't tell me you forgot the what's-its-name." A newsboy went by shouting something about the Waterbury trial.

. . . "Perhaps this will refresh your memory." The District Attorney suddenly thrust a heavy automatic at the quiet figure on the witness stand. "Have you ever seen this before?" Walter Mitty took the gun and examined it expertly. "This is my Webley-Vickers 50.80," he said calmly. An excited buzz ran around the courtroom. The Judge rapped for order. "You are a crack shot with any sort of firearms, I believe?" said the District Attorney, insinuatingly. "Objection!" shouted Mitty's attorney. "We have shown that the defendant could not have fired the shot. We have shown that he wore his right arm in a sling on the night of the fourteenth of July." Walter Mitty raised his hand briefly and the bickering attorneys were stilled. "With any known make of gun," he said evenly, "I could have killed Gregory Fitzhurst at three hundred feet *with my left hand.*" Pandemonium broke loose in the courtroom. A woman's scream rose above the bedlam and suddenly a lovely, dark-haired girl was in Walter Mitty's arms. The District Attorney struck at her savagely. Without rising from his chair, Mitty let the man have it on the point of the chin. "You miserable cur!" . . .

"Puppy biscuit," said Walter Mitty. He stopped walking and the buildings of Waterbury rose up out of the misty courtroom and surrounded him again. A woman who was passing laughed. "He said 'Puppy biscuit,'" she said to her companion. "That man said 'Puppy biscuit' to himself." Walter Mitty hurried on. He went into an A. & P., not the first one he came to but a smaller one farther up the street. "I want some biscuit for small, young dogs," he said to the clerk. "Any special brand, sir?" The greatest pistol shot in the world thought a moment. "It says 'Puppies Bark for It' on the box," said Walter Mitty.

His wife would be through at the hairdresser's in fifteen minutes, Mitty saw in looking at his watch, unless they had trouble drying it; sometimes they had trouble drying it. She didn't like to get to the hotel first; she would want him to be there waiting for her as usual. He found a big leather chair in the lobby, facing a window, and he put the overshoes and the puppy biscuit on the floor beside it. He picked up an old copy of *Liberty* and sank down into the chair. "Can Germany Conquer the World through the Air?" Walter Mitty looked at the pictures of bombing planes and of ruined streets.

... "The cannonading has got the wind up in young Raleigh, sir," said the sergeant. Captain Mitty looked up at him through tousled hair. "Get him to bed," he said wearily. "With the others. I'll fly alone." "But you can't, sir," said the sergeant anxiously. "It takes two men to handle that bomber and the Archies are pounding hell out of the air. Von Richtman's circus is between here and Saulier." "Somebody's got to get that ammunition dump," said Mitty. "I'm going over. Spot of brandy?" He poured a drink for the sergeant and one for himself. War thundered and whined around the dugout and battered at the door. There was a rending of wood and splinters flew through the room. "A bit of a near thing," said Captain Mitty carelessly. "The box barrage is closing in," said the sergeant. "We only live once, Sergeant," said Mitty, with his faint, fleeting smile. "Or do we?" He poured another brandy and tossed it off. "I never see a man could hold his brandy like you, sir," said the sergeant. "Begging your pardon, sir." Captain Mitty stood up and strapped on his huge Webley-Vickers automatic. "It's forty kilometers through hell, sir," said the sergeant. Mitty finished one last brandy. "After all," he said softly, "what isn't?" The pounding of the cannon increased; there was the rat-tat-tatting of machine guns, and from somewhere came the menacing pocket-pocketa-pocketa of the new flame-throwers. Walter Mitty walked to the door of the dugout humming "Auprès de Ma Blonde." He turned and waved to the sergeant. "Cheerio!" he said. . . .

Something struck his shoulder. "I've been looking all over this hotel for you," said Mrs. Mitty. "Why do you have to hide in this old chair? How did you expect me to find you?" "Things close in," said Walter Mitty vaguely. "What?" Mrs. Mitty said. "Did you get the what's-its-name? The puppy biscuit? What's in that box?" "Overshoes," said Mitty. "Couldn't you have put them on in the store?" "I was thinking," said Walter Mitty. "Does it ever occur to you that I am sometimes thinking?" She looked at him. "I'm going to take your temperature when I get you home," she said.

They went out through the revolving doors that made a faintly derisive whistling sound when you pushed them. It was two blocks to the parking lot. At the drugstore on the corner she said, "Wait here for me. I forgot something. I won't be a minute." She was more than a minute. Walter Mitty lighted a cigarette. It began to rain, rain with sleet in it. He stood up against the wall of the drugstore, smoking. . . . He put his shoulders back and his heels together. "To hell with the handkerchief," said Walter Mitty scornfully. He took one last drag on his cigarette and snapped it away. Then, with that faint, fleeting smile playing about his lips, he faced the firing squad; erect and motionless, proud and disdainful, Walter Mitty the Undefeated, inscrutable to the last.

[1942]

*I*SAAC BABEL (1894–1939?) *was born in the Moldavanka district of Odessa, in Russia. His father, a Jewish businessman, made him study Yiddish, the Bible, and the Talmud, but his favorite subject was French, because the teacher was a native of Brittany who loved literature. By the time Babel was fifteen he began to write stories in French "à la Maupassant," and his later story, "Guy de Maupassant" (1932), is a tribute to the influence of this writer. In 1915 Babel moved to St. Petersburg and tried unsuccessfully to publish his stories. His only encouragement came from the Russian writer Maxim Gorky, who advised him to get more life experience: "Go to the people." For six years Babel took Gorky at his word. He became a soldier on the Romanian Front in World War I, worked as a press correspondent attached to the Soviet Cavalry, and found other jobs as a reporter and a printer during the chaotic period of civil war that followed the Russian Revolution of 1917. In 1923 Babel decided that he had learned enough to express his thoughts clearly and concisely. The following year he began to publish his stories in* Left, *a Soviet avant-garde literary magazine devoted to revolution in politics and the arts. A year later he published a collection of his tales,* The Story of My Dove-Cote, *and in 1925 his best work appeared — Red Cavalry, thirty-four sketches depicting scenes of bravery and suffering during the Polish campaign of 1920, when he was with the Soviet Cavalry.*

Babel's literary style has been called "as terse as algebra," but its lyricism is also unmistakable. His plots are often episodic or anecdotal. He juxtaposes poetic and natural details in his descriptions, often stressing the grotesque and sensual to assault the reader with a barrage of sights, sounds, and smells, as in "My First Goose." These tactics are Babel's way of catching us off guard and breaking down our defenses, so we will be more receptive to perceiving his main theme as a writer, the complex relationship between our illusions about life and truth of life. In "Guy de Maupassant," Babel's young narrator lives entirely in his illusions. He is constantly faced with reminders of his mortality, but he is oblivious to them, until the conclusion of the story.

Babel was an exacting critic of his own work and often revised his stories several times before he was satisfied: "No steel can pierce the human heart so chillingly as a period at the right moment." When his books of stories first appeared in the 1920s, he was hailed in the Soviet Union as a master prose stylist, but during Stalin's purges in the 1930s he was attacked for his ideological shortcomings. In 1937 he told his Soviet critics, who asked him why he wrote so little, that he could only manage short things, but not long ones. "Let me put it this way; the point is that Tolstoy was

686

able to describe what happened to him minute by minute, he remembered it all, whereas I, evidently, only have it in me to describe the most interesting five minutes I've experienced in twenty-four hours." The tone of Babel's reply was joking, but underneath is a sense of his bitterness and frustration. His brave affirmation of individuality was unacceptable to the Soviet authorities, however, and in May 1939 he was arrested and disappeared into a concentration camp.

Isaac Babel

ᚵᚲᚵ

MY FIRST GOOSE

– translated by Walter Morison

Savitsky, Commander of the VI Division, rose when he saw me, and I wondered at the beauty of his giant's body. He rose, the purple of his riding-breeches and the crimson of his little tilted cap and the decorations stuck on his chest cleaving the hut as a standard cleaves the sky. A smell of scent and sickly sweet freshness of soap emanated from him. His long legs were like girls sheathed to the neck in shining riding-boots.

He smiled at me, struck his riding-whip on the table, and drew toward him an order that the Chief of Staff had just finished dictating. It was an order for Ivan Chesnokov to advance on Chugunov-Dobryvodka with the regiment entrusted to him, to make contact with the enemy and destroy the same.

"For which destruction," the Commander began to write, smearing the whole sheet, "I make this same Chesnokov entirely responsible, up to and including the supreme penalty, and will if necessary strike him down on the spot; which you, Chesnokov, who have been working with me at the front for some months now, cannot doubt."

The Commander signed the order with a flourish, tossed it to his orderlies, and turned upon me grey eyes that danced with merriment.

I handed him a paper with my appointment to the Staff of the Division.

"Put it down in the Order of the Day," said the Commander. "Put him down for every satisfaction save the front one. Can you read and write?"

"Yes, I can read and write," I replied, envying the flower and iron of that youthfulness. "I graduated in law from St. Petersburg University."

"Oh, are you one of those grinds?" he laughed. "Specs on your nose, too! What a nasty little object! They've sent you along without making any inquiries; and this is a hot place for specs. Think you'll get on with us?"

"I'll get on all right," I answered, and went off to the village with the quartermaster to find a billet for the night.

The quartermaster carried my trunk on his shoulder. Before us stretched the village street. The dying sun, round and yellow as a pumpkin, was giving up its roseate ghost to the skies.

We went up to a hut painted over with garlands. The quartermaster stopped, and said suddenly, with a guilty smile:

"Nuisance with specs. Can't do anything to stop it, either. Not a life for the brainy type here. But you go and mess up a lady, and a good lady too, and you'll have the boys patting you on the back."

He hesitated, my little trunk on his shoulder; then he came quite close to me, only to dart away again despairingly and run to the nearest yard. Cossacks were sitting there, shaving one another.

"Here, you soldiers," said the quartermaster, setting my little trunk down on the ground. "Comrade Savitsky's orders are that you're to take this chap in your billets, so no nonsense about it, because the chap's been through a lot in the learning line."

The quartermaster, purple in the face, left us without looking back. I raised my hand to my cap and saluted the Cossacks. A lad with long straight flaxen hair and the handsome face of the Ryazan Cossacks went over to my little trunk and tossed it out at the gate. Then he turned his back on me and with remarkable skill emitted a series of shameful noises.

"To your guns — number double-zero!" an older Cossack shouted at him, and burst out laughing. "Running fire!"

His guileless art exhausted, the lad made off. Then, crawling over the ground, I began to gather together the manuscripts and tattered garments that had fallen out of the trunk. I gathered them up and carried them to the other end of the yard. Near the hut, on a brick stove, stood a cauldron in which pork was cooking. The steam that rose from it was like the far-off smoke of home in the village, and it mingled hunger with desperate loneliness in my head. Then I covered my little broken trunk with hay, turning it into a pillow, and lay down on the ground to read in *Pravda* Lenin's speech at the Second Congress of the Comintern. The sun fell upon me from behind the toothed hillocks, the Cossacks trod on my feet, the lad made fun of me untiringly, the beloved lines came toward me along a thorny path and could not reach me. Then I put aside the paper and went out to the landlady, who was spinning on the porch.

"Landlady," I said, "I've got to eat."

The old woman raised to me the diffused whites of her purblind eyes and lowered them again.

"Comrade," she said, after a pause, "what with all this going on, I want to go and hang myself."

"Christ!" I muttered, and pushed the old woman in the chest with my fist. "You don't suppose I'm going to go into explanations with you, do you?"

And turning around I saw somebody's sword lying within reach. A severe-looking goose was waddling about the yard, inoffensively preening its feathers. I overtook it and pressed it to the ground. Its head cracked beneath my boot, cracked and emptied itself. The white neck lay stretched out in the dung, the wings twitched.

"Christ!" I said, digging into the goose with my sword. "Go and cook it for me, landlady."

Her blind eyes and glasses glistening, the old woman picked up the slaughtered bird, wrapped it in her apron, and started to bear it off toward the kitchen.

"Comrade," she said to me, after a while. "I want to go and hang myself." And she closed the door behind her.

The Cossacks in the yard were already sitting around their cauldron. They sat motionless, stiff as heathen priests at a sacrifice, and had not looked at the goose.

"The lad's all right," one of them said, winking and scooping up the cabbage soup with his spoon.

The Cossacks commenced their supper with all the elegance and restraint of peasants who respect one another. And I wiped the sword with sand, went out at the gate, and came in again, depressed. Already the moon hung above the yard like a cheap earring.

"Hey, you," suddenly said Surovkov, an older Cossack. "Sit down and feed with us till your goose is done."

He produced a spare spoon from his boot and handed it to me. We supped up the cabbage soup they had made, and ate the pork.

"What's in the newspaper?" asked the flaxen-haired lad, making room for me.

"Lenin writes in the paper," I said, pulling out *Pravda.* "Lenin writes that there's a shortage of everything."

And loudly, like a triumphant man hard of hearing, I read Lenin's speech out to the Cossacks.

Evening wrapped about me the quickening moisture of its twilight sheets; evening laid a mother's hand upon my burning forehead. I read on and rejoiced, spying out exultingly the secret curve of Lenin's straight line.

"Truth tickles everyone's nostrils," said Surovkov, when I had come to the end. "The question is, how's it to be pulled from the heap. But he goes and strikes at it straight off like a hen pecking at a grain!"

This remark about Lenin was made by Surovkov, platoon commander of the Staff Squadron; after which we lay down to sleep in the hayloft. We slept, all six of us, beneath a wooden roof that let in the stars, warming one another, our legs intermingled. I dreamed: and in my dreams saw women. But my heart, stained with bloodshed, grated and brimmed over.

[1925]

Isaac Babel

ର୍ଷ

GUY DE MAUPASSANT

– *translated by Raymond Rosenthal and Waclaw Selski*

In the winter of 1916 I found myself in St. Petersburg with a forged passport and not a cent to my name. Alexey Kazantsev, a teacher of Russian literature, took me into his house.

He lived on a yellow, frozen, evil-smelling street in the Peski district. The miserable salary he received was padded out a bit by doing translations from the Spanish. Blasco-Ibáñez[1] was just becoming famous at that time. Kazantsev had never so much as passed through Spain, but his love for that country filled his whole being. He knew every castle, every garden, and every river in Spain. There were many other people huddling around Kazantsev, all of them, like myself, flung out of the round of ordinary life. We were half-starved. From time to time the yellow press would publish, in the smallest print, unimportant news-items we had written.

I spent my mornings hanging around the morgues and police stations.

Kazantsev was happier than any of us, for he had a country of his own — Spain.

In November I was given the chance to become a clerk at the Obukhov Mills. It was a rather good position, and would have exempted me from military service.

I refused to become a clerk.

Even in those days, when I was twenty years old, I had told myself: better starve, go to jail, or become a bum than spend ten hours every day behind a desk in an office.

There was nothing particularly laudable in my resolve, but I have never broken it and I never will. The wisdom of my ancestors was firmly lodged in my head: we are born to enjoy our work, our fights, and our love; we are born for that and for nothing else.

Listening to my bragging, Kazantsev ruffled the short yellow fluff on the top of his head. The horror in his stare was mixed with admiration.

At Christmastime we had luck. Bendersky the lawyer, who owned a

---

[1] Vicente Blasco-Ibáñez (1867–1928), Spanish novelist.

publishing house called "Halcyon," decided to publish a new edition of Maupassant's works. His wife Raïsa tried her hand at the translation, but nothing came of her lofty ambition.

Kazantsev, who was known as a translator of Spanish, had been asked whether he could recommend someone to assist Raïsa Mikhaylovna. He told them of me.

The next day, in someone else's coat, I made my way to the Benderskys'. They lived at the corner of the Nevsky and the Moyka, in a house of Finland granite adorned with pink columns, crenellations and coats-of-arms worked in stone.

Bankers without a history and catapulted out of nowhere, converted Jews who had grown rich selling materials to the army, they put up these pretentious mansions in St. Petersburg before the war.

There was a red carpet on the stairs. On the landings, upon their hindlegs, stood plush bears. Crystal lamps burned in their open mouths.

The Benderskys lived on the second floor. A high-breasted maid with a white cap on her head opened the door. She lead me into a drawing-room decorated in the old Slav style. Blue paintings by Roerich[2] depicting prehistoric stones and monsters hung on the walls. On stands in the corners stood ancestral icons.

The high-breasted maid moved smoothly and majestically. She had an excellent figure, was nearsighted and rather haughty. In her open gray eyes one saw a petrified lewdness. She moved slowly. I thought: when she makes love she must move with unheard-of agility. The brocade portiere over the doorway suddenly swayed, and a black-haired woman with pink eyes and a wide bosom entered the room. It was easy to recognize in Raïsa Bendersky one of those charming Jewesses who have come to us from Kiev and Poltava, from the opulent steppe-towns full of chestnut trees and acacias. The money made by their clever husbands is transformed by these women into a pink layer of fat on the belly, the back of the neck, and the well-rounded shoulders. Their subtle sleepy smiles drive officers from the local garrisons crazy.

"Maupassant," Raïsa said to me, "is the only passion of my life."

Trying to keep the swaying of her great hips under control, she left the room and returned with a translation of "Miss Harriet." In her translation not even a trace was left of Maupassant's free-flowing sentences with their fragrance of passion. Raïsa Bendersky took pains to write correctly and precisely, and all that resulted was something loose and lifeless, the way Jews wrote Russian in the old days.

I took the manuscript with me, and in Kazantsev's attic, among my sleeping friends, spent the night cutting my way through the tangled undergrowth of her prose. It was not such dull work as it might seem. A phrase is born into the world both good and bad at the same time. The secret lies

---

[2] Nicholas Konstantin Roerich (1874–1947), Russian painter.

in a slight, an almost invisible twist. The lever should rest in your hand, getting warm, and you can only turn it once not twice.

Next morning I took back the corrected manuscript. Raïsa wasn't lying when she told me that Maupassant was her sole passion. She sat motionless, her hands clasped, as I read it to her. Her satin hands drooped to the floor, her forehead paled, and the lace between her constricted breasts danced and heaved.

"How did you do it?"

I began to speak of style, of the army of words, of the army in which all kinds of weapons may come into play. No iron can stab the heart with such force as a period put just at the right place. She listened with her head down and her painted lips half open. In her hair, pressed smooth, divided by a parting and looking like patent leather, shone a dark gleam. Her legs in tight-fitting stockings, with their strong soft calves, were planted wide apart on the carpet.

The maid, glancing to the side with her petrified wanton eyes, brought in breakfast on a tray.

The glassy rays of the Petersburg sun lay on the pale and uneven carpet. Twenty-nine volumes of Maupassant stood on the shelf above the desk. The sun with its fingers of melting dissolution touched the morocco backs of the books — the magnificent grave of a human heart.

Coffee was served in blue cups, and we started translating "Idyl." Everyone remembers the story of the youthful, hungry carpenter who sucked the breast of the stout nursing-mother to relieve her of the milk with which she was overladen. It happened in a train going from Nice to Marseille, at noon on a very hot day, in the land of roses, the birthplace of roses, where beds of flowers flow down to the seashore.

I left the Banderskys with a twenty-five rouble advance. That night our crowd at Peski got as drunk as a flock of drugged geese. Between drinks we spooned up the best caviar, and then changed over to liver sausage. Half-soused, I began to berate Tolstoy.

"He turned yellow, your Count; he was afraid. His religion was all fear. He was frightened by the cold, by old age, by death; and he made himself a warm coat out of his faith."

"Go on, go on," Kazantsev urged, swaying his birdlike head.

We fell asleep on the floor beside our beds. I dreamed of Katya, a forty-year-old washerwoman who lived a floor below us. We went to her every morning for our hot water. I had never seen her face distinctly, but in my dream we did god-awful things together. We almost destroyed each other with kisses. The very next morning I couldn't restrain myself from going to her for hot water.

I saw a wan woman, a shawl across her chest, with ash-gray hair and labor-worn, withered hands.

From then on I took my breakfast at the Benderskys' every day. A new stove, herrings, and chocolate appeared in our attic. Twice Raïsa took me out in her carriage for drives to the islands. I couldn't prevent myself from telling her all about my childhood. To my amazement the story turned out to be very sordid. From under her moleskin cowl her gleaming, frightened eyes stared at me. The rusty fringe of her eyelashes quivered with pity.

I met Raïsa's husband, a yellow-faced Jew with a bald skull and a flat, powerful body that seemed always posed obliquely, ready for flight.

There were rumors about his being close to Rasputin. The enormous profits he made from war supplies drove him almost crazy, giving him the expression of a person with a fixed hallucination. His eyes never remained still: it seemed that reality was lost to him for ever. Raïsa was embarrassed whenever she had to introduce him to new acquaintances. Because of my youth I noticed this a full week later than I should have.

After the New Year Raïsa's two sisters arrived from Kiev. One day I took along the manuscript of "L'Aveu" and, not finding Raïsa at home, returned that evening. They were at dinner. Silvery, neighing laughter and excited male voices came from the dining-room. In rich houses without tradition dinners are always noisy. It was a Jewish noise, rolling and tripping and ending up on a melodious, singsong note. Raïsa came out to me in evening dress, her back bare. Her feet stepped awkwardly in wavering patent-leather slippers.

"I'm drunk, darling," she said, and held out her arms, loaded with chains of platinum and emerald stars.

Her body swayed like a snake's dancing to music. She tossed her marcelled hair about, and suddenly, with a tinkle of rings, slumped into a chair with ancient Russian carvings. Scars glowed on her powdered back.

Women's laughter again came from the dining-room. Raïsa's sisters, with delicate mustaches and as full-bosomed and round-bodied as Raïsa herself, entered the room. Their busts jutted out and their black hair fluttered. Both of them had their own Benderskys for husbands. The room was filled with disjointed, chaotic feminine merriment, the hilarity of ripe women. The husbands wrapped the sisters in their sealskins and Orenburg shawls and shod them in black boots. Beneath the snowy visors of their shawls only painted glowing cheeks, marble noses, and eyes with their myopic Jewish glitter could be seen. After making some more happy noise they left for the theater, where Chaliapin was singing *Judith*.

"I want to work," Raïsa lisped, stretching her bare arms to me, "we've skipped a whole week."

She brought a bottle and two glasses from the dining room. Her breasts swung free beneath the sacklike gown, the nipples rose beneath the clinging silk.

"It's very valuable," said Raïsa, pouring out the wine. "Muscatel '83. My husband will kill me when he finds out."

I had never drunk Muscatel '83, and tossed off three glasses one after the other without thinking. They carried me swiftly away into alleys where an orange flame danced and sounds of music could be heard.

"I'm drunk, darling. What are we doing today?"

"Today, it's *'L'Aveu.'* 'The Confession,' then. The sun is the hero of this story, *le soleil de France.* Molten drops of it pattering on the red-haired Céleste changed into freckles. The sun's direct rays and wine and apple-cider burnished the face of the coachman Polyte. Twice a week Céleste drove into town to sell cream, eggs and chickens. She gave Polyte ten sous for herself and four for her basket. And every time Polyte would wink at the red-haired Céleste and ask: 'When are we going to have some fun, *ma belle?'* — 'What do you mean, Monsieur Polyte?' Jogging up and down on the box, the coachman explained: 'To have some fun means . . . why, what the hell, to have some fun! A lad with a lass; no music necessary. . . .'

" 'I do not care for such jokes, Monsieur Polyte,' replied Céleste, moving further away the skirts that hung over her mighty calves in red stockings.

"But that devil Polyte kept right on guffawing and coughing: 'Ah, but one day we shall have our bit of fun, *ma belle,'* while tears of delight rolled down a face the color of brick-red wine and blood."

I downed another glass of the rare muscatel. Raïsa touched glasses with me. The maid with the stony eyes crossed the room and disappeared.

"Ce diable de Polyte[3]*. . . .* In the course of two years Céleste had paid him forty-eight francs; that is, two francs short of fifty! At the end of the second year, when they were alone in the carriage, Polyte, who had some cider before setting out, asked her his usual question: 'What about having some fun today, Mamselle Céleste?' And she replied, lowering her eyes: 'I am at your disposal, Monsieur Polyte.' "

Raïsa flung herself down on the table, laughing. *"Ce diable de Po-lyte. . . ."*

"A white spavined mare was harnessed to the carriage. The white hack, its lips pink with age, went forward at a walking pace. The gay sun of France poured down on the ancient coach, screened from the world by a weatherbeaten hood. A lad with a lass; no music necessary. . . . "

Raïsa held out a glass to me. It was the fifth.

"Mon vieux, to Maupassant."

"And what about having some fun today, *ma belle?"*

I reached over to Raïsa and kissed her on the lips. They quivered and swelled.

"You're funny," she mumbled through her teeth, recoiling.

She pressed herself against the wall, stretching out her bare arms. Spots began to glow on her arms and shoulders. Of all the gods ever put on a crucifix, this was the most ravishing.

"Be so kind as to sit down, Monsieur Polyte."

She pointed to an oblique blue armchair done in Slavonic style. Its

---

[3] "that devil Polyte" (French).

back was constructed of carved interlacing bands with colorful pendants. I groped my way to it, stumbling as I went.

Night had blocked the path of my famished youth with a bottle of Muscatel '83 and twenty-nine books, twenty-nine bombs stuffed with pity, genius, and passion. I sprang up, knocking over the chair and banging against the shelf. The twenty-nine volumes crashed to the floor, their pages flew open, they fell on their edges . . . and the white mare of my fate went on at a walking pace.

"You are funny," growled Raïsa.

I left the granite house on the Moyka between eleven and twelve, before the sisters and the husband returned from the theater. I was sober and could have walked a chalk line, but it was pleasanter to stagger, so I swayed from side to side, singing in a language I had just invented. Through the tunnels of the streets bounded by lines of street lights the steamy fog billowed. Monsters roared behind the boiling walls. The roads amputated the legs of those walking on them.

Kazantsev was asleep when I got home. He slept sitting up, his thin legs extended in their felt boots. The canary fluff rose on his head. He had fallen asleep by the stove bending over a volume of Don Quixote, the edition of 1624. On the title-page of the book was a dedication to the Duc de Broglie. I got into bed quietly, so as not to wake Kazantsev; moved the lamp close to me and began to read a book by Edouard Maynial on Guy de Maupassant's life and work.

Kazantsev's lips moved; his head kept keeling over.

That night I learned from Edouard Maynial that Maupassant was born in 1850, the child of a Normandy gentleman and Laure Lepoiteven, Flaubert's cousin. He was twenty-five when he was first attacked by congenital syphilis. His productivity and joie de vivre withstood the onsets of the disease. At first he suffered from headaches and fits of hypochondria. Then the specter of blindness arose before him. His sight weakened. He became suspicious of everyone, unsociable and pettily quarrelsome. He struggled furiously, dashed about the Mediterranean in a yacht, fled to Tunis, Morocco, Central Africa . . . and wrote ceaselessly. He attained fame, and at forty years of age cut his throat; lost a great deal of blood, yet lived through it. He was then put away in a madhouse. There he crawled about on his hands and knees, devouring his own excrement. The last line in his hospital report read: Monsieur de Maupassant va s'animaliser.[4] He died at the age of forty-two, his mother surviving him.

I read the book to the end and got out of bed. The fog came close to the window, the world was hidden from me. My heart contracted as the foreboding of some essential truth touched me with light fingers.

[1932]

---

[4] "M. Maupassant is becoming an animal."

$F.$ SCOTT FITZGERALD (1896–1940), *regarded as the literary spokesman for the "Lost Generation" of the 1920s in America, was born in St. Paul, Minnesota. His family had some social standing but little money, and it was only with help from a maiden aunt that he was able to go to an eastern preparatory school and then on to Princeton, where his family hoped that he would attend to his studies and stop "wasting his time scribbling." He withdrew from college before graduating to accept a commission as a second lieutenant in the Regular Army during World War I, but he spent most of his time in the service writing his first novel, which he revised several times before it was published in 1920 as* This Side of Paradise. *The novel was such a success that magazines were eager to print Fitzgerald's stories, and his first story collection,* Flappers and Philosophers, *was rushed into print later the same year to take advantage of the novel's popularity. Another story collection,* Tales of the Jazz Age, *followed in 1922. Years later Fitzgerald would say, writing in the third person, that he was grateful to the Jazz Age because "It bore him up, flattered him and gave him more money than he had dreamed of, simply for telling people that he felt as they did, that something had to be done with all the nervous energy stored up and unexpended in the War."*

In 1925, with the publication of his novel The Great Gatsby, *Fitzgerald reached the peak of his fame as a writer. His reputation declined rapidly in the harsher years of the 1930s. The Great Depression in the United States and around the world coincided with his own emotional and physical collapse, as his marriage and career floundered on his wife's mental illness and his alcoholism. Gertrude Stein had coined the term "Lost Generation" to describe the young men who had served in World War I and were forced to grow up "to find all Gods dead, all wars fought, all faiths in man shaken." But Fitzgerald's last years were truly lost, when he confronted the "waste and horror" of his dissipated talent, writing Hollywood screenplays and struggling unsuccessfully to finish his novel* The Last Tycoon.

At the time of his death Fitzgerald had written about 160 stories. As one of his editors, Malcolm Cowley, has said, the exact number is hard to set because some of his work was on the borderline between fiction and the informal essay or "magazine piece." Simple and clear in style, Fitzgerald's stories make up an informal history of his career, dating from before the publication of his first novel to after his final crack-up. "Babylon Revisited" (1931) is one of his later stories, perhaps one of the best he ever wrote. It is more complicated emotionally than his earlier short fiction, as Cowley realized, "with less regret for the past and more dignity in the face of real sorrow."

F. Scott Fitzgerald

ಬಲ

BABYLON REVISITED

I

"And where's Mr. Campbell?" Charlie asked.

"Gone to Switzerland. Mr. Campbell's a pretty sick man, Mr. Wales."

"I'm sorry to hear that. And George Hardt?" Charlie inquired.

"Back in America, gone to work."

"And where is the Snow Bird?"

"He was in here last week. Anyway, his friend, Mr. Schaeffer, is in Paris."

Two familiar names from the long list of a year and a half ago. Charlie scribbled an address in his notebook and tore out the page.

"If you see Mr. Schaeffer, give him this," he said. "It's my brother-in-law's address. I haven't settled on a hotel yet."

He was not really disappointed to find Paris was so empty. But the stillness in the Ritz bar was strange and portentous. It was not an American bar any more — he felt polite in it, and not as if he owned it. It had gone back into France. He felt the stillness from the moment he got out of the taxi and saw the doorman, usually in a frenzy of activity at this hour, gossiping with a *chasseur*[1] by the servants' entrance.

Passing through the corridor, he heard only a single, bored voice in the once-clamorous women's room. When he turned into the bar he traveled the twenty feet of green carpet with his eyes fixed straight ahead by old habit; and then, with his foot firmly on the rail, he turned and surveyed the room, encountering only a single pair of eyes that fluttered up from a newspaper in the corner. Charlie asked for the head barman, Paul, who in the latter days of the bull market had come to work in his own custom-built car — disembarking, however, with due nicety at the nearest corner. But Paul was at his country house today and Alix giving him information.

"No, no more," Charlie said, "I'm going slow these days."

Alix congratulated him: "You were going pretty strong a couple of years ago."

---

[1] bellhop.

"I'll stick to it all right," Charlie assured him. "I've stuck to it for over a year and a half now."

"How do you find conditions in America?"

"I haven't been to America for months. I'm in business in Prague, representing a couple of concerns there. They don't know about me down there."

Alix smiled.

"Remember the night of George Hardt's bachelor dinner here?" said Charlie. "By the way, what's become of Claude Fessenden?"

Alix lowered his voice confidentially: "He's in Paris, but he doesn't come here any more. Paul doesn't allow it. He ran up a bill of thirty thousand francs, charging all his drinks and his lunches, and usually his dinner, for more than a year. And when Paul finally told him he had to pay, he gave him a bad check."

Alix shook his head sadly.

"I don't understand it, such a dandy fellow. Now he's all bloated up — " He made a plump apple of his hands.

Charlie watched a group of strident queens installing themselves in a corner.

"Nothing affects them," he thought. "Stocks rise and fall, people loaf or work, but they go on forever." The place oppressed him. He called for the dice and shook with Alix for the drink.

"Here for long, Mr. Wales?"

"I'm here for four or five days to see my little girl."

"Oh-h! You have a little girl?"

Outside, the fire-red, gas-blue, ghost-green signs shone smokily through the tranquil rain. It was late afternoon and the streets were in movement; the *bistros* gleamed. At the corner of the Boulevard des Capucines he took a taxi. The Place de la Concorde moved by in pink majesty; they crossed the logical Seine, and Charlie felt the sudden provincial quality of the Left Bank.

Charlie directed his taxi to the Avenue de l'Opera, which was out of his way. But he wanted to see the blue hour spread over the magnificent façade, and imagine that the cab horns, playing endlessly the first few bars of *La Plus que Lente*,[2] were the trumpets of the Second Empire.[3] They were closing the iron grill in front of Brentano's Book-store, and people were already at dinner behind the trim little bourgeois hedge of Duval's. He had never eaten at a really cheap restaurant in Paris. Five-course dinner, four francs fifty, eighteen cents, wine included. For some odd reason he wished that he had.

As they rolled on to the Left Bank and he felt its sudden provincialism, he thought, "I spoiled this city for myself. I didn't realize it, but the

---

[2] "Slower than Slow," whimsical piano piece by Claude Debussy (1862–1918).
[3] the reign of Napoleon III, 1852–1870.

days came along one after another, and then two years were gone, and everything was gone, and I was gone."

He was thirty-five, and good to look at. The Irish mobility of his face was sobered by a deep wrinkle between his eyes. As he rang his brother-in-law's bell in the Rue Palatine, the wrinkle deepened till it pulled down his brows; he felt a cramping sensation in his belly. From behind the maid who opened the door darted a lovely little girl of nine who shrieked "Daddy!" and flew up, struggling like a fish, into his arms. She pulled his head around by one ear and set her cheek against his.

"My old pie," he said.

"Oh, daddy, daddy, daddy, daddy, dads, dads, dads!"

She drew him into the salon, where the family waited, a boy and a girl his daughter's age, his sister-in-law and her husband. He greeted Marion with his voice pitched carefully to avoid either feigned enthusiasm or dislike, but her response was more frankly tepid, though she minimized her expression of unalterable distrust by directing her regard toward his child. The two men clasped hands in a friendly way and Lincoln Peters rested his for a moment on Charlie's shoulder.

The room was warm and comfortably American. The three children moved intimately about, playing through the yellow oblongs that led to other rooms; the cheer of six o'clock spoke in the eager smacks of the fire and the sounds of French activity in the kitchen. But Charlie did not relax; his heart sat up rigidly in his body and he drew confidence from his daughter, who from time to time came close to him, holding in her arms the doll he had brought.

"Really extremely well," he declared in answer to Lincoln's question. "There's a lot of business there that isn't moving at all, but we're doing even better than ever. In fact, damn well. I'm bringing my sister over from America next month to keep house for me. My income last year was bigger than it was when I had money. You see, the Czechs —— "

His boasting was for a specific purpose; but after a moment, seeing a faint restiveness in Lincoln's eye, he changed the subject:

"Those are fine children of yours, well brought up, good manners."

"We think Honoria's a great little girl too."

Marion Peters came back from the kitchen. She was a tall woman with worried eyes, who had once possessed a fresh American loveliness. Charlie had never been sensitive to it and was always surprised when people spoke of how pretty she had been. From the first there had been an instinctive antipathy between them.

"Well, how do you find Honoria?" she asked.

"Wonderful. I was astonished how much she's grown in ten months. All the children are looking well."

"We haven't had a doctor for a year. How do you like being back in Paris?"

"It seems very funny to see so few Americans around."

"I'm delighted," Marion said vehemently. "Now at least you can go into a store without their assuming you're a millionaire. We've suffered like everybody, but on the whole it's a good deal pleasanter."

"But it was nice while it lasted," Charlie said. "We were a sort of royalty, almost infallible, with a sort of magic around us. In the bar this afternoon" — he stumbled, seeing his mistake — "there wasn't a man I knew."

She looked at him keenly. "I should think you'd have had enough of bars."

"I only stayed a minute. I take one drink every afternoon, and no more."

"Don't you want a cocktail before dinner?" Lincoln asked.

"I take only one drink every afternoon, and I've had that."

"I hope you keep to it," said Marion.

Her dislike was evident in the coldness with which she spoke, but Charlie only smiled; he had larger plans. Her very aggressiveness gave him an advantage, and he knew enough to wait. He wanted them to initiate the discussion of what they knew had brought him to Paris.

At dinner he couldn't decide whether Honoria was most like him or her mother. Fortunate if she didn't combine the traits of both that had brought them to disaster. A great wave of protectiveness went over him. He thought he knew what to do for her. He believed in character; he wanted to jump back a whole generation and trust in character again as the eternally valuable element. Everything else wore out.

He left soon after dinner, but not to go home. He was curious to see Paris by night with clearer and more judicious eyes than those of other days. He bought a *strapontin*[4] for the Casino and watched Josephine Baker go through her chocolate arabesques.

After an hour he left and strolled toward Montmartre, up the Rue Pigalle into the Place Blanche. The rain had stopped and there were a few people in evening clothes disembarking from taxis in front of cabarets, and *cocottes*[5] prowling singly or in pairs, and many Negroes. He passed a lighted door from which issued music, and stopped with the sense of familiarity; it was Bricktop's, where he had parted with so many hours and so much money. A few doors farther on he found another ancient rendezvous and incautiously put his head inside. Immediately an eager orchestra burst into sound, a pair of professional dancers leaped to their feet and a maître d'hôtel swooped toward him, crying, "Crowd just arriving, sir!" But he withdrew quickly.

"You have to be damn drunk," he thought.

Zelli's was closed, the bleak and sinister cheap hotels surrounding it were dark; up in the Rue Blanche there was more light and a local, colloquial French crowd. The Poet's Cave had disappeared, but the two great

---

[4] Cheap seat in the aisle. Josephine Baker was an American black entertainer who gained fame in Paris in the 1920s and 1930s.
[5] prostitutes.

mouths of the Café of Heaven and the Café of Hell still yawned — even devoured, as he watched, the meager contents of a tourist bus — a German, a Japanese, and an American couple who glanced at him with frightened eyes.

So much for the effort and ingenuity of Montmartre. All the catering to vice and waste was on an utterly childish scale, and he suddenly realized the meaning of the word "dissipate" — to dissipate into thin air; to make nothing out of something. In the little hours of the night every move from place to place was an enormous human jump, an increase of paying for the privilege of slower and slower motion.

He remembered thousand-franc notes given to an orchestra for playing a single number, hundred-franc notes tossed to a doorman for calling a cab.

But it hadn't been given for nothing.

It had been given, even the most wildly squandered sum, as an offering to destiny that he might not remember the things most worth remembering, the things that now he would always remember — his child taken from his control, his wife escaped to a grave in Vermont.

In the glare of a *brasserie*[6] a woman spoke to him. He bought her some eggs and coffee, and then, eluding her encouraging stare, gave her a twenty-franc note and took a taxi to his hotel.

II

He woke upon a fine fall day — football weather. The depression of yesterday was gone and he liked the people on the streets. At noon he sat opposite Honoria at Le Grand Vatel, the only restaurant he could think of not reminiscent of champagne dinners and long luncheons that began at two and ended in a blurred and vague twilight.

"Now, how about vegetables? Oughtn't you to have some vegetables?"

"Well, yes."

"Here's *épinards* and *chou-fleur* and carrots and *haricots*."[7]

"I'd like *chou-fleur*."

"Wouldn't you like to have two vegetables?"

"I usually only have one at lunch."

The waiter was pretending to be inordinately fond of children. "*Qu'elle est mignonne la petite! Elle parle exactement comme une Française.*"[8]

"How about dessert? Shall we wait and see?"

The waiter disappeared. Honoria looked at her father expectantly.

"What are we going to do?"

"First, we're going to that toy store in the Rue Saint-Honoré and buy

---

[6] small, informal restaurant.
[7] spinach, cauliflower, beans.
[8] "What a cute little girl! She speaks exactly like a French girl."

you anything you like. And then we're going to the vaudeville at the Empire."

She hesitated. "I like it about the vaudeville, but not the toy store."

"Why not?"

"Well, you brought me this doll." She had it with her. "And I've got lots of things. And we're not rich any more, are we?"

"We never were. But today you are to have anything you want."

"All right," she agreed resignedly.

When there had been her mother and a French nurse he had been inclined to be strict; now he extended himself, reached out for a new tolerance; he must be both parents to her and not shut any of her out of communication.

"I want to get to know you," he said gravely. "First let me introduce myself. My name is Charles J. Wales, of Prague."

"Oh, daddy!" her voice cracked with laughter.

"And who are you, please?" he persisted, and she accepted a rôle immediately: "Honoria Wales, Rue Palatine, Paris."

"Married or single?"

"No, not married. Single."

He indicated the doll. "But I see you have a child, madame."

Unwilling to disinherit it, she took it to her heart and thought quickly: "Yes, I've been married, but I'm not married now. My husband is dead."

He went on quickly, "And the child's name?"

"Simone. That's after my best friend at school."

"I'm very pleased that you're doing so well at school."

"I'm third this month," she boasted. "Elsie" — that was her cousin — "is only about eighteenth, and Richard is at the bottom."

"You like Richard and Elsie, don't you?"

"Oh, yes. I like Richard quite well and I like her all right."

Cautiously and casually he asked: "And Aunt Marion and Uncle Lincoln — which do you like best?"

"Oh, Uncle Lincoln, I guess."

He was increasingly aware of her presence. As they came in, a murmur of " . . . adorable" followed them, and now the people at the next table bent all their silences upon her, staring as if she were something no more conscious than a flower.

"Why don't I live with you?" she asked suddenly. "Because mamma's dead?"

"You must stay here and learn more French. It would have been hard for daddy to take care of you so well."

"I don't really need much taking care of any more. I do everything for myself."

Going out of the restaurant, a man and a woman unexpectedly hailed him.

"Well, the old Wales!"

"Hello there, Lorraine. . . . Dunc."

Sudden ghosts out of the past: Duncan Schaeffer, a friend from college. Lorraine Quarrles, a lovely, pale blonde of thirty; one of a crowd who had helped them make months into days in the lavish times of three years ago.

"My husband couldn't come this year," she said, in answer to his question. "We're poor as hell. So he gave me two hundred a month and told me I could do my worst on that. . . . This your little girl?"

"What about coming back and sitting down?" Duncan asked.

"Can't do it." He was glad for an excuse. As always, he felt Lorraine's passionate, provocative attraction, but his own rhythm was different now.

"Well, how about dinner?" she asked.

"I'm not free. Give me your address and let me call you."

"Charlie, I believe you're sober," she said judicially. "I honestly believe he's sober, Dunc. Pinch him and see if he's sober."

Charlie indicated Honoria with his head. They both laughed.

"What's your address?" said Duncan skeptically.

He hesitated, unwilling to give the name of his hotel.

"I'm not settled yet. I'd better call you. We're going to see the vaudeville at the Empire."

"There! That's what I want to do," Lorraine said. "I want to see some clowns and acrobats and jugglers. That's just what we'll do, Dunc."

"We've got to do an errand first," said Charlie. "Perhaps we'll see you there."

"All right, you snob. . . . Good-by, beautiful little girl."

"Good-by."

Honoria bobbed politely.

Somehow, an unwelcome encounter. They liked him because he was functioning, because he was serious; they wanted to see him, because he was stronger than they were now, because they wanted to draw a certain sustenance from his strength.

At the Empire, Honoria proudly refused to sit upon her father's folded coat. She was already an individual with a code of her own, and Charlie was more and more absorbed by the desire of putting a little of himself into her before she crystallized utterly. It was hopeless to try to know her in so short a time.

Between the acts they came upon Duncan and Lorraine in the lobby where the band was playing.

"Have a drink?"

"All right, but not up at the bar. We'll take a table."

"The perfect father."

Listening abstractedly to Lorraine, Charlie watched Honoria's eyes leave their table, and he followed them wistfully about the room, wondering what they saw. He met her glance and she smiled.

"I liked that lemonade," she said.

What had she said? What had he expected? Going home in a taxi afterward, he pulled her over until her head rested against his chest.

"Darling, do you ever think of your mother?"

"Yes, sometimes," she answered vaguely.

"I don't want you to forget her. Have you got a picture of her?"

"Yes, I think so. Anyhow, Aunt Marion has. Why don't you want me to forget her?"

"She loved you very much."

"I loved her too."

They were silent for a moment.

"Daddy, I want to come and live with you," she said suddenly.

His heart leaped; he had wanted it to come like this.

"Aren't you perfectly happy?"

"Yes, but I love you better than anybody. And you love me better than anybody, don't you, now that mummy's dead?"

"Of course I do. But you won't always like me best, honey. You'll grow up and meet somebody your own age and go marry him and forget you ever had a daddy."

"Yes, that's true," she agreed tranquilly.

He didn't go in. He was coming back at nine o'clock and he wanted to keep himself fresh and new for the thing he must say then.

"When you're safe inside, just show yourself in that window."

"All right. Good-by, dads, dads, dads, dads."

He waited in the dark street until she appeared, all warm and glowing, in the window above and kissed her fingers out into the night.

III

They were waiting. Marion sat behind the coffee service in a dignified black dinner dress that just faintly suggested mourning. Lincoln was walking up and down with the animation of one who had already been talking. They were as anxious as he was to get into the question. He opened it almost immediately:

"I suppose you know what I want to see you about — why I really came to Paris."

Marion played with the black stars on her necklace and frowned.

"I'm awfully anxious to have a home," he continued. "And I'm awfully anxious to have Honoria in it. I appreciate your taking in Honoria for her mother's sake, but things have changed now" — he hesitated and then continued more forcibly — "changed radically with me, and I want to ask you to reconsider the matter. It would be silly for me to deny that about three years ago I was acting badly —— "

Marion looked up at him with hard eyes.

" — but all that's over. As I told you, I haven't had more than a drink a day for over a year, and I take that drink deliberately, so that the idea of alcohol won't get too big in my imagination. You see the idea?"

"No," said Marion succinctly.

"It's a sort of stunt I set myself. It keeps the matter in proportion."

"I get you," said Lincoln. "You don't want to admit it's got any attraction for you."

"Something like that. Sometimes I forget and don't take it. But I try to take it. Anyhow, I couldn't afford to drink in my position. The people I represent are more than satisfied with what I've done, and I'm bringing my sister over from Burlington to keep house for me, and I want awfully to have Honoria too. You know that even when her mother and I weren't getting along well we never let anything that happened touch Honoria. I know she's fond of me and I know I'm able to take care of her and — well, there you are. How do you feel about it?"

He knew that now he would have to take a beating. It would last an hour or two hours, and it would be difficult, but if he modulated his inevitable resentment to the chastened attitude of the reformed sinner, he might win his point in the end.

Keep your temper, he told himself. You don't want to be justified. You want Honoria.

Lincoln spoke first: "We've been talking it over ever since we got your letter last month. We're happy to have Honoria here. She's a dear little thing, and we're glad to be able to help her, but of course that isn't the question —— "

Marion interrupted suddenly. "How long are you going to stay sober, Charlie?" she asked.

"Permanently, I hope."

"How can anybody count on that?"

"You know I never did drink heavily until I gave up business and came over here with nothing to do. Then Helen and I began to run around with —— "

"Please leave Helen out of it. I can't bear to hear you talk about her like that."

He stared at her grimly; he had never been certain how fond of each other the sisters were in life.

"My drinking only lasted about a year and a half — from the time we came over until I — collapsed."

"It was time enough."

"It was time enough," he agreed.

"My duty is entirely to Helen," she said. "I try to think what she would have wanted me to do. Frankly, from the night you did that terrible thing you haven't really existed for me. I can't help that. She was my sister."

"Yes."

"When she was dying she asked me to look out for Honoria. If you hadn't been in a sanitarium then, it might have helped matters."

He had no answer.

"I'll never in my life be able to forget the morning when Helen knocked at my door, soaked to the skin and shivering and said you'd locked her out."

Charlie gripped the sides of the chair. This was more difficult than he expected; he wanted to launch out into a long expostulation and explanation, but he only said: "The night I locked her out —" and she interrupted, "I don't feel up to going over that again."

After a moment's silence Lincoln said: "We're getting off the subject. You want Marion to set aside her legal guardianship and give you Honoria. I think the main point for her is whether she has confidence in you or not."

"I don't blame Marion," Charlie said slowly, "but I think she can have entire confidence in me. I had a good record up to three years ago. Of course, it's within human possibilities I might go wrong any time. But if we wait much longer I'll lose Honoria's childhood and my chance for a home." He shook his head, "I'll simply lose her, don't you see?"

"Yes, I see," said Lincoln.

"Why didn't you think of all this before?" Marion asked.

"I suppose I did, from time to time, but Helen and I were getting along badly. When I consented to the guardianship, I was flat on my back in a sanitarium and the market had cleaned me out. I knew I'd acted badly, and I thought if it would bring any peace to Helen, I'd agree to anything. But now it's different. I'm functioning, I'm behaving damn well, so far as ——"

"Please don't swear at me," Marion said.

He looked at her, startled. With each remark the force of her dislike became more and more apparent. She had built up all her fear of life into one wall and faced it toward him. This trivial reproof was possibly the result of some trouble with the cook several hours before. Charlie became increasingly alarmed at leaving Honoria in this atmosphere of hostility against himself; sooner or later it would come out, in a word here, a shake of the head there, and some of that distrust would be irrevocably implanted in Honoria. But he pulled his temper down out of his face and shut it up inside him; he had won a point, for Lincoln realized the absurdity of Marion's remark and asked her lightly since when she had objected to the word "damn."

"Another thing," Charlie said: "I'm able to give her certain advantages now. I'm going to take a French governess to Prague with me. I've got a lease on a new apartment ——"

He stopped, realizing that he was blundering. They couldn't be expected to accept with equanimity the fact that his income was again twice as large as their own.

"I suppose you can give her more luxuries than we can," said Marion.

"When you were throwing away money we were living along watching every ten francs. . . . I suppose you'll start doing it again."

"Oh, no," he said. "I've learned. I worked hard for ten years, you know — until I got lucky in the market, like so many people. Terribly lucky. It won't happen again."

There was a long silence. All of them felt their nerves straining, and for the first time in a year Charlie wanted a drink. He was sure now that Lincoln Peters wanted him to have his child.

Marion shuddered suddenly; part of her saw that Charlie's feet were planted on the earth now, and her own maternal feeling recognized the naturalness of his desire; but she had lived for a long time with a prejudice — a prejudice founded on a curious disbelief in her sister's happiness, and which, in the shock of one terrible night, had turned to hatred for him. It had all happened at a point in her life where the discouragement of ill health and adverse circumstances made it necessary for her to believe in tangible villainy and a tangible villain.

"I can't help what I think!" she cried out suddenly. "How much you were responsible for Helen's death, I don't know. It's something you'll have to square with your own conscience."

An electric current of agony surged through him; for a moment he was almost on his feet, an unuttered sound echoing in his throat. He hung on to himself for a moment, another moment.

"Hold on there," said Lincoln uncomfortably. "I never thought you were responsible for that."

"Helen died of heart trouble," Charlie said dully.

"Yes, heart trouble." Marion spoke as if the phrase had another meaning for her.

Then, in the flatness that followed her outburst, she saw him plainly and she knew he had somehow arrived at control over the situation. Glancing at her husband, she found no help from him, and as abruptly as if it were a matter of no importance, she threw up the sponge.

"Do what you like!" she cried, springing up from her chair. "She's your child. I'm not the person to stand in your way. I think if it were my child I'd rather see her — " She managed to check herself. "You two decide it. I can't stand this. I'm sick. I'm going to bed."

She hurried from the room; after a moment Lincoln said:

"This has been a hard day for her. You know how strongly she feels — " His voice was almost apologetic: "When a woman gets an idea in her head."

"Of course."

"It's going to be all right. I think she sees now that you — can provide for the child, and so we can't very well stand in your way or Honoria's way."

"Thank you, Lincoln."

"I'd better go along and see how she is."

"I'm going."

He was still trembling when he reached the street, but a walk down the Rue Bonaparte to the *quais* set him up, and as he crossed the Seine, fresh and new by the *quai* lamps, he felt exultant. But back in his room he couldn't sleep. The image of Helen haunted him. Helen whom he had loved so until they had senselessly begun to abuse each other's love, tear it into shreds. On that terrible February night that Marion remembered so vividly, a slow quarrel had gone on for hours. There was a scene at the Florida, and then he attempted to take her home, and then she kissed young Webb at a table; after that there was what she had hysterically said. When he arrived home alone he turned the key in the lock in wild anger. How could he know she would arrive an hour later alone, that there would be a snowstorm in which she wandered about in slippers, too confused to find a taxi? Then the aftermath, her escaping pneumonia by a miracle, and all the attendant horror. They were "reconciled," but that was the beginning of the end, and Marion, who had seen with her own eyes and who imagined it to be one of many scenes from her sister's martyrdom, never forgot.

Going over it again brought Helen nearer, and in the white, soft light that steals upon half sleep near morning he found himself talking to her again. She said that he was perfectly right about Honoria and that she wanted Honoria to be with him. She said she was glad he was being good and doing better. She said a lot of other things — very friendly things — but she was in a swing in a white dress, and swinging faster and faster all the time, so that at the end he could not hear clearly all that she said.

IV

He woke up feeling happy. The door of the world was open again. He made plans, vistas, futures for Honoria and himself, but suddenly he grew sad, remembering all the plans he and Helen had made. She had not planned to die. The present was the thing — work to do and someone to love. But not to love too much, for he knew the injury that a father can do to a daughter or a mother to a son by attaching them too closely: afterward, out in the world, the child would seek in the marriage partner the same blind tenderness and, failing probably to find it, turn against love and life.

It was another bright, crisp day. He called Lincoln Peters at the bank where he worked and asked if he could count on taking Honoria when he left for Prague. Lincoln agreed that there was no reason for delay. One thing — the legal guardianship. Marion wanted to retain that a while longer. She was upset by the whole matter, and it would oil things if she felt that the situation was still in her control for another year. Charlie agreed, wanting only the tangible, visible child.

Then the question of a governess. Charles sat in a gloomy agency and talked to a cross Béarnaise and to a buxom Breton peasant, neither of whom he could have endured. There were others whom he would see tomorrow.

He lunched with Lincoln Peters at Griffons, trying to keep down his exultation.

"There's nothing quite like your own child," Lincoln said. "But you understand how Marion feels too."

"She's forgotten how hard I worked for seven years there," Charlie said. "She just remembers one night."

"There's another thing." Lincoln hesitated. "While you and Helen were tearing around Europe throwing money away, we were just getting along. I didn't touch any of the prosperity because I never got ahead enough to carry anything but my insurance. I think Marion felt there was some kind of injustice in it — you not even working toward the end, and getting richer and richer."

"It went just as quick as it came," said Charlie.

"Yes, a lot of it stayed in the hands of *chasseurs* and saxophone players and maîtres d'hôtel — well, the big party's over now. I just said that to explain Marion's feeling about those crazy years. If you drop in about six o'clock tonight before Marion's too tired, we'll settle the details on the spot."

Back at his hotel, Charlie found a *pneumatique*[9] that had been redirected from the Ritz bar where Charlie had left his address for the purpose of finding a certain man.

> Dear Charlie: You were so strange when we saw you the other day that I wondered if I did something to offend you. If so, I'm not conscious of it. In fact, I have thought about you too much for the last year, and it's always been in the back of my mind that I might see you if I came over here. We *did* have such good times that crazy spring, like the night you and I stole the butcher's tricycle, and the time we tried to call on the president and you had the old derby rim and the wire cane. Everybody seems so old lately, but I don't feel old a bit. Couldn't we get together some time today for old time's sake? I've got a vile hang-over for the moment, but will be feeling better this afternoon and will look for you about five in the sweatshop at the Ritz.
>
> Always devotedly,
> Lorraine

His first feeling was one of awe that he had actually, in his mature years, stolen a tricycle and pedaled Lorraine all over the Étoile between the small hours and dawn. In retrospect it was a nightmare. Locking out Helen didn't fit in with any other act of his life, but the tricycle incident did — it was one of many. How many weeks or months of dissipation to arrive at that condition of utter irresponsibility?

He tried to picture how Lorraine had appeared to him then — very attractive; Helen was unhappy about it, though she said nothing. Yesterday,

---

[9] message delivered through a citywide system of pneumatic tubes.

in the restaurant, Lorraine had seemed trite, blurred, worn away. He emphatically did not want to see her, and he was glad Alix had not given away his hotel address. It was a relief to think, instead, of Honoria, to think of Sundays spent with her and of saying good morning to her and of knowing she was there in his house at night, drawing her breath in the darkness.

At five he took a taxi and bought presents for all the Peters — a piquant cloth doll, a box of Roman soldiers, flowers for Marion, big linen handkerchiefs for Lincoln.

He saw, when he arrived in the apartment, that Marion had accepted the inevitable. She greeted him now as though he were a recalcitrant member of the family, rather than a menacing outsider. Honoria had been told she was going; Charlie was glad to see that her tact made her conceal her excessive happiness. Only on his lap did she whisper her delight and the question "When?" before she slipped away with the other children.

He and Marion were alone for a minute in the room, and on an impulse he spoke out boldly:

"Family quarrels are bitter things. They don't go according to any rules. They're not like aches or wounds; they're more like splits in the skin that won't heal because there's not enough material. I wish you and I could be on better terms."

"Some things are hard to forget," she answered. "It's a question of confidence." There was no answer to this and presently she asked, "When do you propose to take her?"

"As soon as I can get a governess. I hoped the day after tomorrow."

"That's impossible. I've got to get her things in shape. Not before Saturday."

He yielded. Coming back into the room, Lincoln offered him a drink. "I'll take my daily whisky," he said.

It was warm here, it was a home, people together by a fire. The children felt very safe and important; the mother and father were serious, watchful. They had things to do for the children more important than his visit here. A spoonful of medicine was, after all, more important than the strained relations between Marion and himself. They were not dull people, but they were very much in the grip of life and circumstances. He wondered if he couldn't do something to get Lincoln out of his rut at the bank.

A long peal at the door-bell; the *bonne d tout faire*[10] passed through and went down the corridor. The door opened upon another long ring, and then voices, and the three in the salon looked up expectantly; Richard moved to bring the corridor within his range of vision, and Marion rose. Then the maid came back along the corridor, closely followed by the voices, which developed under the light into Duncan Schaeffer and Lorraine Quarrles.

They were gay, they were hilarious, they were roaring with laughter.

---

[10] maid.

For a moment Charlie was astounded; unable to understand how they ferreted out the Peters' address.

"Ah-h-h!" Duncan wagged his finger roguishly at Charlie. "Ah-h-h!"

They both slid down another cascade of laughter. Anxious and at a loss, Charlie shook hands with them quickly and presented them to Lincoln and Marion. Marion nodded, scarcely speaking. She had drawn back a step toward the fire; her little girl stood beside her, and Marion put an arm about her shoulder.

With growing annoyance at the intrusion, Charlie waited for them to explain themselves. After some concentration Duncan said:

"We came to invite you out to dinner. Lorraine and I insist that all this shishi, cagy business 'bout your address got to stop."

Charlie came closer to them, as if to force them backward down the corridor.

"Sorry, but I can't. Tell me where you'll be and I'll phone you in half an hour."

This made no impression. Lorraine sat down suddenly on the side of a chair, and focusing her eyes on Richard, cried, "Oh, what a nice little boy! Come here, little boy." Richard glanced at his mother, but did not move. With a perceptible shrug of her shoulders, Lorraine turned back to Charlie:

"Come and dine. Sure your cousins won' mine. See you so sel'om. Or solemn."

"I can't," said Charlie sharply. "You two have dinner and I'll phone you."

Her voice became suddenly unpleasant. "All right, we'll go. But I remember once when you hammered on my door at four A.M. I was enough of a good sport to give you a drink. Come on, Dunc."

Still in slow motion, with blurred, angry faces, with uncertain feet, they retired along the corridor.

"Good night," Charlie said.

"Good night!" responded Lorraine emphatically.

When he went back into the salon Marion had not moved, only now her son was standing in the circle of her other arm. Lincoln was still swinging Honoria back and forth like a pendulum from side to side.

"What an outrage!" Charlie broke out. "What an absolute outrage!"

Neither of them answered. Charlie dropped into an armchair, picked up his drink, set it down again and said:

"People I haven't seen for two years having the colossal nerve —— "

He broke off. Marion had made the sound "Oh!" in one swift, furious breath, turned her body from him with a jerk and left the room.

Lincoln set down Honoria carefully.

"You children go in and start your soup," he said, and when they obeyed, he said to Charlie:

"Marion's not well and she can't stand shocks. That kind of people make her really physically sick."

"I didn't tell them to come here. They wormed your name out of somebody. They deliberately ——— "

"Well, it's too bad. It doesn't help matters. Excuse me a minute."

Left alone, Charlie sat tense in his chair. In the next room he could hear the children eating, talking in monosyllables, already oblivious to the scene between their elders. He heard a murmur of conversation from a farther room and then the ticking bell of a telephone receiver picked up, and in a panic he moved to the other side of the room and out of earshot.

In a minute Lincoln came back. "Look here, Charlie. I think we'd better call off dinner for tonight. Marion's in bad shape."

"Is she angry with me?"

"Sort of," he said, almost roughly. "She's not strong and ——— "

"You mean she's changed her mind about Honoria?"

"She's pretty bitter right now. I don't know. You phone me at the bank tomorrow."

"I wish you'd explain to her I never dreamed these people would come here. I'm just as sore as you are."

"I couldn't explain anything to her now."

Charlie got up. He took his coat and hat and started down the corridor. Then he opened the door of the dining room and said in a strange voice, "Good night, children."

Honoria rose and ran around the table to hug him.

"Good night, sweetheart," he said vaguely, and then trying to make his voice more tender, trying to conciliate something, "Good night, dear children."

V

Charlie went directly to the Ritz bar with the furious idea of finding Lorraine and Duncan, but they were not there, and he realized that in any case there was nothing he could do. He had not touched his drink at the Peters, and now he ordered a whisky-and-soda. Paul came over to say hello.

"It's a great change," he said sadly. "We do about half the business we did. So many fellows I hear about back in the States lost everything, maybe not in the first crash, but then in the second. Your friend George Hardt lost every cent, I hear. Are you back in the States?"

"No, I'm in business in Prague."

"I heard that you lost a lot in the crash."

"I did," and he added grimly, "but I lost everything I wanted in the boom."

"Selling short."

"Something like that."

Again the memory of those days swept over him like a nightmare — the people they had met travelling; then people who couldn't add a row of figures or speak a coherent sentence. The little man Helen had consented to dance with at the ship's party, who had insulted her ten feet from the table; the women and girls carried screaming with drink or drugs out of public places ——

—— The men who locked their wives out in the snow, because the snow of twenty-nine wasn't real snow. If you didn't want it to be snow, you just paid some money.

He went to the phone and called the Peters' apartment; Lincoln answered.

"I called up because this thing is on my mind. Has Marion said anything definite?"

"Marion's sick," Lincoln answered shortly. "I know this thing isn't altogether your fault, but I can't have her go to pieces about it. I'm afraid we'll have to let it slide for six months; I can't take the chance of working her up to this state again."

"I see."

"I'm sorry, Charlie."

He went back to his table. His whisky glass was empty, but he shook his head when Alix looked at it questioningly. There wasn't much he could do now except send Honoria some things; he would send her a lot of things tomorrow. He thought rather angrily that this was just money — he had given so many people money. . . .

"No, no more," he said to the waiter. "What do I owe you?"

He would come back some day; they couldn't make him pay forever. But he wanted his child, and nothing was much good now, beside that fact. He wasn't young any more, with a lot of nice thoughts and dreams to have by himself. He was absolutely sure Helen wouldn't have wanted him to be so alone.

[1935]

WILLIAM FAULKNER (1897–1962) was born in New Albany, Mississippi, into an old southern family that had lost its fortune in the Civil War. When Faulkner was a child, his parents moved to the isolated county-seat town of Oxford, Mississippi, and except for his service in World War I and some time in New Orleans and Hollywood, he spent the rest of his life there. "I discovered my own little postage stamp of native soil was worth writing about and that I would never live long enough to exhaust it." Faulkner went to high school in Oxford and, after serving in the Royal Canadian Air Force during World War I, he attended the University of Mississippi from 1919 to 1921. His literary career began in New Orleans, where he lived for six months and wrote newspaper sketches and stories for the Times-Picayune. He met Sherwood Anderson in New Orleans, and Anderson helped him publish his first novel, Soldier's Pay, in 1926. Faulkner's major work was written in the late 1920s and the 1930s, when he created an imaginary county adjacent to Oxford, calling it Yoknapatawpha County and chronicling its history in a series of highly experimental novels, including The Sound and the Fury (1929), As I Lay Dying (1930), Sanctuary (1931), Light in August (1932), Absalom, Absalom! (1936) and The Hamlet (1940). In these works he showed himself to be a writer of genius, although "a willfully and perversely chaotic one," as Jorge Luis Borges has noted, whose "labyrinthine world" required a no less labyrinthine prose technique to describe in epic manner the disintegration of the South through many generations.

In his short stories, Faulkner wrote about the same themes that obsessed him in his novels. He said in his acceptance speech on receiving the Nobel Prize for Literature in 1950 that it was "the problems of the human heart in conflict with itself which alone can make good writing because only that is worth writing about, worth the agony and the sweat." His literary style was less experimental in his stories, rarely including poetic imagery or stream-of-consciousness narration to the extent he did in his longer fiction. Faulkner wrote nearly 100 stories, often revising them later to fit as a section into one of his novels. Four books of short stories were published in his lifetime: These Thirteen (1931), Doctor Martino and Other Stories (1934), Knight's Gambit (1949), and Collected Stories (1950). Faulkner thought of each as a collection that possessed a discernible internal organization of its own. He wrote his editor Malcolm Cowley that he believed the only worthwhile purpose of any book was to uplift men's hearts, "and so even to a collection of short stories, form, integration, is as important as to a novel — an entity of its own, single, set for one pitch, contrapuntal in integration, toward one end, one finale."

"A Rose for Emily" and "Dry September" were both included in

These Thirteen. *They appeared in the second section of that book, a section devoted to several stories about Yoknapatawpha County. Miss Emily Grierson and Miss Minnie Cooper are similar characters, yet Faulkner resisted having one story follow the other in his collection, intending a "contrapuntal" effect by placing three other stories between them. Although some readers found symbolism in "A Rose for Emily" that suggested Faulkner was implying a battle between the North (the character Homer Barron) and the South (Miss Emily herself), Faulkner denied a schematic interpretation. He said he had intended to write a ghost story, and "I think that the writer is too busy trying to create flesh-and-blood people that will stand up and cast a shadow to have time to be conscious of all the symbolism that he may put into what he does or what people may read into it."*

William Faulkner

১৩৫২

A ROSE FOR EMILY

I

When Miss Emily Grierson died, our whole town went to her funeral: the men through a sort of respectful affection for a fallen monument, the women mostly out of curiosity to see the inside of her house, which no one save an old manservant — a combined gardener and cook — had seen in at least ten years.

It was a big, squarish frame house that had once been white, decorated with cupolas and spires and scrolled balconies in the heavily lightsome style of the seventies, set on what had once been our most select street. But garages and cotton gins had encroached and obliterated even the august names of that neighborhood; only Miss Emily's house was left, lifting its stubborn and coquettish decay above the cotton wagons and the gasoline pumps — an eyesore among eyesores. And now Miss Emily had gone to join the representatives of those august names where they lay in the cedar-bemused cemetery among the ranked and anonymous graves of Union and Confederate soldiers who fell at the battle of Jefferson.

Alive, Miss Emily had been a tradition, a duty, and a care; a sort of hereditary obligation upon the town, dating from that day in 1894 when Colonel Sartoris, the mayor — he who fathered the edict that no Negro woman should appear on the streets without an apron — remitted her taxes, the dispensation dating from the death of her father on into perpetuity. Not that Miss Emily would have accepted charity. Colonel Sartoris invented an involved tale to the effect that Miss Emily's father had loaned money to the town, which the town, as a matter of business, preferred this way of repaying. Only a man of Colonel Sartoris' generation and thought could have invented it, and only a woman could have believed it.

When the next generation, with its more modern ideas, became mayors and aldermen, this arrangement created some little dissatisfaction. On the first of the year they mailed her a tax notice. February came, and there was no reply. They wrote her a formal letter, asking her to call at the sheriff's office at her convenience. A week later the mayor wrote her himself, offering to call or to send his car for her, and received in reply a note on paper of an archaic shape, in a thin, flowing calligraphy in faded ink, to the effect that she no longer went out at all. The tax notice was also enclosed, without comment.

They called a special meeting of the Board of Aldermen. A deputation waited upon her, knocked at the door through which no visitor had passed since she ceased giving china-painting lessons eight or ten years earlier. They were admitted by the old Negro into a dim hall from which a stairway mounted into still more shadow. It smelled of dust and disuse — a close, dank smell. The Negro led them into the parlor. It was furnished in heavy, leather-covered furniture. When the Negro opened the blinds of one window, they could see that the leather was cracked; and when they sat down, a faint dust rose sluggishly about their thighs, spinning with slow motes in the single sun-ray. On a tarnished gilt easel before the fireplace stood a crayon portrait of Miss Emily's father.

They rose when she entered — a small, fat woman in black, with a thin gold chain descending to her waist and vanishing into her belt, leaning on an ebony cane with a tarnished gold head. Her skeleton was small and spare; perhaps that was why what would have been merely plumpness in another was obesity in her. She looked bloated, like a body long submerged in motionless water, and of that pallid hue. Her eyes, lost in the fatty ridges of her face, looked like two small pieces of coal pressed into a lump of dough as they moved from one face to another while the visitors stated their errand.

She did not ask them to sit. She just stood in the door and listened quietly until the spokesman came to a stumbling halt. Then they could hear the invisible watch ticking at the end of the gold chain.

Her voice was dry and cold. "I have no taxes in Jefferson. Colonel Sartoris explained it to me. Perhaps one of you can gain access to the city records and satisfy yourselves."

"But we have. We are the city authorities, Miss Emily. Didn't you get a notice from the sheriff, signed by him?"

"I received a paper, yes," Miss Emily said. "Perhaps he considers himself the sheriff. . . . I have no taxes in Jefferson."

"But there is nothing on the books to show that, you see. We must go by the — "

"See Colonel Sartoris. I have no taxes in Jefferson."

"But, Miss Emily — "

"See Colonel Sartoris." (Colonel Sartoris had been dead almost ten years.) "I have no taxes in Jefferson. Tobe!" The Negro appeared. "Show these gentlemen out."

II

So she vanquished them, horse and foot, just as she had vanquished their fathers thirty years before about the smell. That was two years after her father's death and a short time after her sweetheart — the one we believed would marry her — had deserted her. After her father's death she went out very little; after her sweetheart went away, people hardly saw her at all. A few of the ladies had the temerity to call, but were not received, and the only sign of life about the place was the Negro man — a young man then — going in and out with a market basket.

"Just as if a man — any man — could keep a kitchen properly," the ladies said; so they were not surprised when the smell developed. It was another link between the gross, teeming world and the high and mighty Griersons.

A neighbor, a woman, complained to the mayor, Judge Stevens, eighty years old.

"But what will you have me do about it, madam?" he said.

"Why, send her word to stop it," the woman said. "Isn't there a law?"

"I'm sure that won't be necessary," Judge Stevens said. "It's probably just a snake or a rat that nigger of hers killed in the yard. I'll speak to him about it."

The next day he received two more complaints, one from a man who came in diffident deprecation. "We really must do something about it, Judge. I'd be the last one in the world to bother Miss Emily, but we've got to do something." That night the Board of Aldermen met — three graybeards and one younger man, a member of the rising generation.

"It's simple enough," he said. "Send her word to have her place cleaned up. Give her a certain time to do it in, and if she don't. . . ."

"Dammit, sir," Judge Stevens said, "will you accuse a lady to her face of smelling bad?"

So the next night, after midnight, four men crossed Miss Emily's lawn and slunk about the house like burglars, sniffing along the base of the brickwork and at the cellar openings while one of them performed a regular sowing motion with his hand out of a sack slung from his shoulder. They broke open the cellar door and sprinkled lime there, and in all the outbuildings. As they recrossed the lawn, a window that had been dark was lighted and

Miss Emily sat in it, the light behind her, and her upright torso motionless as that of an idol. They crept quietly across the lawn and into the shadow of the locusts that lined the street. After a week or two the smell went away.

That was when people had begun to feel really sorry for her. People in our town, remembering how old lady Wyatt, her great-aunt, had gone completely crazy at last, believed that the Griersons held themselves a little too high for what they really were. None of the young men were quite good enough for Miss Emily and such. We had long thought of them as a tableau, Miss Emily a slender figure in white in the background, her father a spraddled silhouette in the foreground, his back to her and clutching a horsewhip, the two of them framed by the backflung front door. So when she got to be thirty and was still single, we were not pleased exactly, but vindicated; even with insanity in the family she wouldn't have turned down all of her chances if they had really materialized.

When her father died, it got about that the house was all that was left to her; and in a way, people were glad. At last they could pity Miss Emily. Being left alone, and a pauper, she had become humanized. Now she too would know the old thrill and the old despair of a penny more or less.

The day after his death all the ladies prepared to call at the house and offer condolence and aid, as is our custom. Miss Emily met them at the door, dressed as usual and with no trace of grief on her face. She told them that her father was not dead. She did that for three days, with the ministers calling on her, and the doctors, trying to persuade her to let them dispose of the body. Just as they were about to resort to law and force, she broke down, and they buried her father quickly.

We did not say she was crazy then. We believed she had to do that. We remembered all the young men her father had driven away, and we knew that with nothing left, she would have to cling to that which had robbed her, as people will.

III

She was sick for a long time. When we saw her again, her hair was cut short, making her look like a girl, with a vague resemblance to those angels in colored church windows — sort of tragic and serene.

The town had just let the contracts for paving the sidewalks, and in the summer after her father's death they began the work. The construction company came with niggers and mules and machinery, and a foreman named Homer Barron, a Yankee — a big, dark, ready man, with a big voice and eyes lighter than his face. The little boys would follow in groups to hear him cuss the niggers, and the niggers singing in time to the rise and fall of picks. Pretty soon he knew everybody in town. Whenever you heard a lot of laughing anywhere about the square, Homer Barron would be in the center of the group. Presently, we began to see him and Miss Emily on Sunday afternoons driving in the yellow-wheeled buggy and the matched team of bays from the livery stable.

At first we were glad that Miss Emily would have an interest, because the ladies all said, "Of course a Grierson would not think seriously of a Northerner, a day laborer." But there were still others, older people, who said that even grief could not cause a real lady to forget *noblesse oblige* — without calling it *noblesse oblige*. They just said, "Poor Emily. Her kinsfolk should come to her." She had some kin in Alabama; but years ago her father had fallen out with them over the estate of old lady Wyatt, the crazy woman, and there was no communication between the two families. They had not even been represented at the funeral.

And as soon as the old people said, "Poor Emily," the whispering began. "Do you suppose it's really so?" they said to one another. "Of course it is. What else could. . . ." This behind their hands; rustling of craned silk and satin behind jalousies closed upon the sun of Sunday afternoon as the thin, swift clop-clop-clop of the matched team passed: "Poor Emily."

She carried her head high enough — even when we believed that she was fallen. It was as if she demanded more than ever the recognition of her dignity as the last Grierson; as if it had wanted that touch of earthiness to reaffirm her imperviousness. Like when she bought the rat poison, the arsenic. That was over a year after they had begun to say "Poor Emily," and while the two female cousins were visiting her.

"I want some poison," she said to the druggist. She was over thirty then, still a slight woman, though thinner than usual, with cold, haughty black eyes in a face the flesh of which was strained across the temples and about the eyesockets as you imagine a lighthouse-keeper's face ought to look. "I want some poison," she said.

"Yes, Miss Emily. What kind? For rats and such? I'd recom —— "

"I want the best you have. I don't care what kind."

The druggist named several. "They'll kill anything up to an elephant. But what you want is —— "

"Arsenic," Miss Emily said. "Is that a good one?"

"Is . . . arsenic? Yes, ma'am. But what you want —— "

"I want arsenic."

The druggist looked down at her. She looked back at him, erect, her face like a strained flag. "Why, of course," the druggist said. "If that's what you want. But the law requires you to tell what you are going to use it for."

Miss Emily just stared at him, her head tilted back in order to look him eye for eye, until he looked away and went and got the arsenic and wrapped it up. The Negro delivery boy brought her the package; the druggist didn't come back. When she opened the package at home there was written on the box, under the skull and bones: "For rats."

IV

So the next day we all said, "She will kill herself"; and we said it would be the best thing. When she had first begun to be seen with Homer Barron, we had said, "She will marry him." Then we said, "She will persuade him yet," because Homer himself had remarked — he liked men, and it was known that he drank with the younger men in the Elks' Club — that he was not a marrying man. Later we said, "Poor Emily" behind the jalousies as they passed on Sunday afternoon in the glittering buggy, Miss Emily with her head high and Homer Barron with his hat cocked and a cigar in his teeth, reins and whip in a yellow glove.

Then some of the ladies began to say that it was a disgrace to the town and a bad example to the young people. The men did not want to interfere, but at last the ladies forced the Baptist minister — Miss Emily's people were Episcopal — to call upon her. He would never divulge what happened during that interview, but he refused to go back again. The next Sunday they again drove about the streets, and the following day the minister's wife wrote to Miss Emily's relations in Alabama.

So she had blood-kin under her roof again and we sat back to watch developments. At first nothing happened. Then we were sure that they were to be married. We learned that Miss Emily had been to the jeweler's and ordered a man's toilet set in silver, with the letters H.B. on each piece. Two days later we learned that she had bought a complete outfit of men's clothing, including a nightshirt, and we said, "They are married." We were really glad. We were glad because the two female cousins were even more Grierson than Miss Emily had ever been.

So we were not surprised when Homer Barron — the streets had been finished some time since — was gone. We were a little disappointed that there was not a public blowing-off, but we believed that he had gone on to prepare for Miss Emily's coming, or to give her a chance to get rid of the cousins. (By that time it was a cabal, and we were all Miss Emily's allies to help circumvent the cousins.) Sure enough, after another week they departed. And, as we had expected all along, within three days Homer Barron was back in town. A neighbor saw the Negro man admit him at the kitchen door at dusk one evening.

And that was the last we saw of Homer Barron. And of Miss Emily for some time. The Negro man went in and out with the market basket, but the front door remained closed. Now and then we would see her at the window for a moment, as the men did that night when they sprinkled the lime, but for almost six months she did not appear on the streets. Then we knew that this was to be expected too; as if that quality of her father which had thwarted her woman's life so many times had been too virulent and too furious to die.

When we next saw Miss Emily, she had grown fat and her hair was turning gray. During the next few years it grew grayer and grayer until it attained an even pepper-and-salt iron-gray, when it ceased turning. Up to the day of her death at seventy-four it was still that vigorous iron-gray, like the hair of an active man.

From that time on her front door remained closed, save during a period of six or seven years, when she was about forty, during which she gave lessons in china-painting. She fitted up a studio in one of the downstairs rooms, where the daughters and granddaughters of Colonel Sartoris' contemporaries were sent to her with the same regularity and in the same spirit that they were sent to church on Sundays with a twenty-five-cent piece for the collection plate. Meanwhile her taxes had been remitted.

Then the newer generation became the backbone and the spirit of the town, and the painting pupils grew up and fell away and did not send their children to her with boxes of color and tedious brushes and pictures cut from the ladies' magazines. The front door closed upon the last one and remained closed for good. When the town got free postal delivery, Miss Emily alone refused to let them fasten the metal numbers above her door and attach a mailbox to it. She would not listen to them.

Daily, monthly, yearly we watched the Negro grow grayer and more stooped, going in and out with the market basket. Each December we sent her a tax notice, which would be returned by the post office a week later, unclaimed. Now and then we would see her in one of the downstairs windows — she had evidently shut up the top floor of the house — like the carven torso of an idol in a niche, looking or not looking at us, we could never tell which. Thus she passed from generation to generation — dear, inescapable, impervious, tranquil, and perverse.

And so she died. Fell ill in the house filled with dust and shadows, with only a doddering Negro man to wait on her. We did not even know she was sick; we had long since given up trying to get any information from the Negro. He talked to no one, probably not even to her, for his voice had grown harsh and rusty, as if from disuse.

She died in one of the downstairs rooms, in a heavy walnut bed with a curtain, her gray head propped on a pillow yellow and moldy with age and lack of sunlight.

V

The Negro met the first of the ladies at the front door and let them in, with their hushed, sibilant voices and their quick, curious glances, and then he disappeared. He walked right through the house and out the back and was not seen again.

The two female cousins came at once. They held the funeral on the second day, with the town coming to look at Miss Emily beneath a mass of bought flowers, with the crayon face of her father musing profoundly above the bier and the ladies sibilant and macabre; and the very old men — some in their brushed Confederate uniforms — on the porch and the lawn, talking of Miss Emily as if she had been a contemporary of theirs, believing that they had danced with her and courted her perhaps, confusing time with its mathematical progression, as the old do, to whom all the past is not a diminishing road but, instead, a huge meadow which no winter ever quite touches, divided from them now by the narrow bottleneck of the most recent decade of years.

Already we knew that there was one room in that region above stairs which no one had seen in forty years, and which would have to be forced. They waited until Miss Emily was decently in the ground before they opened it.

The violence of breaking down the door seemed to fill this room with pervading dust. A thin, acrid pall as of the tomb seemed to lie everywhere upon this room decked and furnished as for a bridal: upon the valance curtains of faded rose color, upon the rose-shaded lights, upon the dressing table, upon the delicate array of crystal and the man's toilet things backed with tarnished silver, silver so tarnished that the monogram was obscured. Among them lay a collar and tie, as if they had just been removed, which, lifted, left upon the surface a pale crescent in the dust. Upon a chair hung the suit, carefully folded; beneath it the two mute shoes and the discarded socks.

The man himself lay in the bed.

For a long while we just stood there, looking down at the profound and fleshless grin. The body had apparently once lain in the attitude of an embrace, but now the long sleep that outlasts love, that conquers even the grimace of love, had cuckolded him. What was left of him, rotted beneath what was left of the nightshirt, had become inextricable from the bed in which he lay; and upon him and upon the pillow beside him lay that even coating of the patient and biding dust.

Then we noticed that in the second pillow was the indentation of a head. One of us lifted something from it, and leaning forward, that faint and invisible dust dry and acrid in the nostrils, we saw a long strand of iron-gray hair.

[1931]

William Faulkner

ಬಬ

DRY SEPTEMBER

I

Through the bloody September twilight, aftermath of sixty-two rain-less days, it had gone like a fire in dry grass — the rumor, the story, what-ever it was. Something about Miss Minnie Cooper and a Negro. Attacked, insulted, frightened: none of them, gathered in the barber shop on that Sat-urday evening where the ceiling fan stirred, without freshening it, the vi-tiated air, sending back upon them, in recurrent surges of stale pomade and lotion, their own stale breath and odors, knew exactly what had happened.

"Except it wasn't Will Mayes," a barber said. He was a man of middle age; a thin, sand-colored man with a mild face, who was shaving a client. "I know Will Mayes. He's a good nigger. And I know Miss Minnie Cooper, too."

"What do you know about her?" a second barber said.

"Who is she?" the client said. "A young girl?"

"No," the barber said. "She's about forty, I reckon. She aint married. That's why I dont believe—"

"Believe, hell!" a hulking youth in a sweat-stained silk shirt said. "Wont you take a white woman's word before a nigger's?"

"I dont believe Will Mayes did it," the barber said. "I know Will Mayes."

"Maybe you know who did it, then. Maybe you already got him out of town, you damn niggerlover."

"I dont believe anybody did anything. I dont believe anything hap-pened. I leave it to you fellows if them ladies that get old without getting married dont have notions that a man cant — "

"Then you are a hell of a white man," the client said. He moved under the cloth. The youth had sprung to his feet.

"You dont?" he said. "Do you accuse a white woman of lying?"

The barber held the razor poised above the half-risen client. He did not look around.

"It's this durn weather," another said. "It's enough to make a man do anything. Even to her."

723

Nobody laughed. The barber said in his mild, stubborn tone: "I aint accusing nobody of nothing. I just know and you fellows know how a woman that never — "

"You damn niggerlover!" the youth said.

"Shut up, Butch," another said. "We'll get the facts in plenty of time to act."

"Who is? Who's getting them?" the youth said. "Facts, hell! I — "

"You're a fine white man," the client said. "Aint you?" In his frothy beard he looked like a desert rat in the moving pictures. "You tell them, Jack," he said to the youth. "If there aint any white men in this town, you can count on me, even if I aint only a drummer and a stranger."

"That's right, boys," the barber said. "Find out the truth first. I know Will Mayes."

"Well, by God!" the youth shouted. "To think that a white man in this town — "

"Shut up, Butch," the second speaker said. "We got plenty of time."

The client sat up. He looked at the speaker. "Do you claim that anything excuses a nigger attacking a white woman? Do you mean to tell me you are a white man and you'll stand for it? You better go back North where you came from. The South dont want your kind here."

"North what?" the second said. "I was born and raised in this town."

"Well, by God!" the youth said. He looked about with a strained, baffled gaze, as if he was trying to remember what it was he wanted to say or to do. He drew his sleeve across his sweating face. "Damn if I'm going to let a white woman — "

"You tell them, Jack," the drummer said. "By God, if they — "

The screen door crashed open. A man stood in the floor, his feet apart and his heavy-set body poised easily. His white shirt was open at the throat; he wore a felt hat. His hot, bold glance swept the group. His name was McLendon. He had commanded troops at the front in France and had been decorated for valor.

"Well," he said, "are you going to sit there and let a black son rape a white woman on the streets of Jefferson?"

Butch sprang up again. The silk of his shirt clung flat to his heavy shoulders. At each armpit was a dark halfmoon. "That's what I been telling them! That's what I — "

"Did it really happen?" a third said. "This aint the first man scare she ever had, like Hawkshaw says. Wasn't there something about a man on the kitchen roof, watching her undress, about a year ago?"

"What?" the client said. "What's that?" The barber had been slowly forcing him back into the chair; he arrested himself reclining, his head lifted, the barber still pressing him down.

McLendon whirled on the third speaker. "Happen? What the hell difference does it make? Are you going to let the black sons get away with it until one really does it?"

"That's what I'm telling them!" Butch shouted. He cursed, long and steady, pointless.

"Here, here," a fourth said. "Not so loud. Dont talk so loud."

"Sure," McLendon said; "no talking necessary at all. I've done my talking. Who's with me?" He poised on the balls of his feet, roving his gaze.

The barber held the drummer's face down, the razor poised. "Find the facts first, boys. I know Willy Mayes. It wasn't him. Let's get the sheriff and do this thing right."

McLendon whirled upon him his furious, rigid face. The barber did not look away. They looked like men of different races. The other barbers had ceased also above their prone clients. "You mean to tell me," McLendon said, "that you'd take a nigger's word before a white woman's? Why, you damn niggerloving — "

The third speaker rose and grasped McLendon's arm; he too had been a soldier. "Now, now. Let's figure this thing out. Who knows anything about what really happened?"

"Figure out hell!" McLendon jerked his arm free. "All that're with me get up from there. The ones that aint — " He roved his gaze, dragging his sleeve across his face.

Three men rose. The drummer in the chair sat up. "Here," he said, jerking at the cloth about his neck; "get this rag off me. I'm with him. I dont live here, but by God, if our mothers and wives and sisters — " He smeared the cloth over his face and flung it to the floor. McLendon stood in the floor and cursed the others. Another rose and moved toward him. The remainder sat uncomfortable, not looking at one another, then one by one they rose and joined him.

The barber picked the cloth from the floor. He began to fold it neatly. "Boys, dont do that. Will Mayes never done it. I know."

"Come on," McLendon said. He whirled. From his hip pocket protruded the butt of a heavy automatic pistol. They went out. The screen door crashed behind them reverberant in the dead air.

The barber wiped the razor carefully and swiftly, and put it away, and ran to the rear, and took his hat from the wall. "I'll be back as soon as I can," he said to the other barbers. "I cant let — " He went out, running. The two other barbers followed him to the door and caught it on the rebound, leaning out and looking up the street after him. The air was flat and dead. It had a metallic taste at the base of the tongue.

"What can he do?" the first said. The second one was saying "Jees Christ, Jees Christ" under his breath. "I'd just as lief be Will Mayes as Hawk, if he gets McLendon riled."

"Jees Christ, Jees Christ," the second whispered.

"You reckon he really done it to her?" the first said.

II

She was thirty-eight or thirty-nine. She lived in a small frame house with her invalid mother and a thin, sallow, unflagging aunt, where each morning between ten and eleven she would appear on the porch in a lace-trimmed boudoir cap, to sit swinging in the porch swing until noon. After dinner she lay down for a while, until the afternoon began to cool. Then, in one of the three or four new voile dresses which she had each summer, she would go downtown to spend the afternoon in the stores with the other ladies, where they would handle the goods and haggle over the prices in cold, immediate voices, without any intention of buying.

She was of comfortable people — not the best in Jefferson, but good people enough — and she was still on the slender side of ordinary looking, with a bright, faintly haggard manner and dress. When she was young she had had a slender, nervous body and a sort of hard vivacity which had enabled her for a time to ride upon the crest of the town's social life as exemplified by the high school party and church social period of her con-temporaries while still children enough to be unclassconscious.

She was the last to realize that she was losing ground; that those among whom she had been a little brighter and louder flame than any other were beginning to learn the pleasure of snobbery — male — and retalia-tion — female. That was when her face began to wear that bright, haggard look. She still carried it to parties on shadowy porticoes and summer lawns, like a mask or a flag, with that bafflement of furious repudiation of truth in her eyes. One evening at a party she heard a boy and two girls, all school-mates, talking. She never accepted another invitation.

She watched the girls with whom she had grown up as they married and got homes and children, but no man ever called on her steadily until the children of the other girls had been calling her "aunty" for several years, the while their mothers told them in bright voices about how popular Aunt Minnie had been as a girl. Then the town began to see her driving on Sun-day afternoons with the cashier in the bank. He was a widower of about forty — a high-colored man, smelling always faintly of the barber shop or of whisky. He owned the first automobile in town, a red runabout; Minnie had the first motoring bonnet and veil the town ever saw. Then the town began to say: "Poor Minnie." "But she is old enough to take care of herself," others said. That was when she began to ask her old schoolmates that their children call her "cousin" instead of "aunty."

It was twelve years now since she had been relegated into adultery by public opinion, and eight years since the cashier had gone to a Memphis bank, returning for one day each Christmas, which he spent at an annual bachelors' party at the hunting club on the river. From behind their cur-tains the neighbors would see the party pass, and during the over-the-way Christmas day visiting they would tell her about him, about how well he looked, and how they heard that he was prospering in the city, watching with bright, secret eyes her haggard, bright face. Usually by that hour there would be the scent of whisky on her breath. It was supplied her by a youth, a clerk at the soda fountain: "Sure; I buy it for the old gal. I reckon she's entitled to a little fun."

Her mother kept to her room altogether now; the gaunt aunt ran the house. Against that background Minnie's bright dresses, her idle and empty days, had a quality of furious unreality. She went out in the evenings only with women now, neighbors, to the moving pictures. Each afternoon she dressed in one of the new dresses and went downtown alone, where her young "cousins" were already strolling in the late afternoons with their delicate, silken heads and thin, awkward arms and conscious hips, clinging to one another or shrieking and giggling with paired boys in the soda fountain when she passed and went on along the serried store fronts, in the doors of which the sitting and lounging men did not even follow her with their eyes any more.

III

The barber went swiftly up the street where the sparse lights, insect-swirled, glared in rigid and violent suspension in the lifeless air. The day had died in a pall of dust; above the darkened square, shrouded by the spent dust, the sky was as clear as the inside of a brass bell. Below the east was a rumor of the twice-waxed moon.

When he overtook them McLendon and three others were getting into a car parked in an alley. McLendon stooped his thick head, peering out beneath the top. "Changed your mind, did you?" he said. "Damn good thing; by God, tomorrow when this town hears about how you talked to-night —"

"Now, now," the other ex-soldier said. "Hawkshaw's all right. Come on Hawk; jump in."

"Will Mayes never done it, boys," the barber said. "If anybody done it. Why, you all know well as I do there aint any town where they got better niggers than us. And you know how a lady will kind of think things about men when there aint any reason to, and Miss Minnie anyway —"

"Sure, sure," the soldier said. "We're just going to talk to him a little; that's all."

"Talk hell!" Butch said. "When we're through with the —"

"Shut up, for God's sake!" the soldier said. "Do you want everybody in town —"

"Tell them, by God!" McLendon said. "Tell every one of the sons that'll let a white woman —"

"Let's go; let's go: here's the other car." The second car slid squealing out of a cloud of dust at the alley mouth. McLendon started his car and took the lead. Dust lay like fog in the street. The street lights hung nimbused as in water. They drove on out of town.

A rutted lane turned at right angles. Dust hung above it too, and above all the land. The dark bulk of the ice plant, where the Negro Mayes was night watchman, rose against the sky. "Better stop here, hadn't we?" the soldier said. McLendon did not reply. He hurled the car up and slammed to a stop, the headlights glaring on the blank wall.

"Listen here, boys," the barber said; "if he's here, dont that prove he never done it? Dont it? If it was him, he would run. Dont you see he would?" The second car came up and stopped. McLendon got down; Butch sprang down beside him. "Listen, boys," the barber said.

"Cut the lights off!" McLendon said. The breathless dark rushed down. There was no sound in it save their lungs as they sought air in the parched dust in which for two months they had lived; then the diminishing crunch of McLendon's and Butch's feet, and a moment later McLendon's voice:

"Will! . . . Will!"

Below the east the wan hemorrhage of the moon increased. It heaved above the ridge, silvering the air, the dust, so that they seemed to breathe, live, in a bowl of molten lead. There was no sound of nightbird nor insect, no sound save their breathing and a faint ticking of contracting metal about the cars. Where their bodies touched one another they seemed to sweat dryly, for no more moisture came. "Christ!" a voice said; "let's get out of here."

But they didn't move until vague noises began to grow out of the darkness ahead; then they got out and waited tensely in the breathless dark. There was another sound: a blow, a hissing expulsion of breath and McLendon cursing in undertone. They stood a moment longer, then they ran forward. They ran in a stumbling clump, as though they were fleeing something. "Kill him, kill the son," a voice whispered. McLendon flung them back.

"Not here," he said. "Get him into the car." "Kill him, kill the black son!" the voice murmured. They dragged the Negro to the car. The barber had waited beside the car. He could feel himself sweating and he knew he was going to be sick at the stomach.

"What is it, captains?" the Negro said. "I aint done nothing. 'Fore god, Mr John." Someone produced handcuffs. They worked busily about the Negro as though he were a post, quiet, intent, getting in one another's way. He submitted to the handcuffs, looking swiftly and constantly from dim face to dim face. "Who's here, captains?" he said, leaning to peer into the faces until they could feel his breath and smell his sweaty reek. He spoke a name or two. "What you all say I done, Mr John?"

McLendon jerked the car door open. "Get in!" he said.

The Negro did not move. "What you all going to do with me, Mr John? I aint done nothing. White folks, captains, I aint done nothing: I swear 'fore God." He called another name.

"Get in!" McLendon said. He struck the Negro. The others expelled

their breath in a dry hissing and struck him with random blows and he
whirled and cursed them, and swept his manacled hands across their faces
and slashed the barber upon the mouth, and the barber struck him also.
"Get him in there," McLendon said. They pushed at him. He ceased
struggling and got in and sat quietly as the others took their places. He sat
between the barber and the soldier, drawing his limbs in so as not to touch
them, his eyes going swiftly and constantly from face to face. Butch clung
to the running board. The car moved on. The barber nursed his mouth with
his handkerchief.

"What's the matter, Hawk?" the soldier said.

"Nothing," the barber said. They regained the high road and turned
away from town. The second car dropped back out of the dust. They went
on, gaining speed; the final fringe of houses dropped behind.

"Goddamn, he stinks!" the soldier said.

"We'll fix that," the drummer in the front beside McLendon said. On
the running board Butch cursed into the hot rush of air. The barber leaned
suddenly forward and touched McLendon's arm.

"Let me out, John," he said.

"Jump out, niggerlover," McLendon said without turning his head.
He drove swiftly. Behind them the sourceless lights of the second car glared
in the dust. Presently McLendon turned into a narrow road. It was rutted
with disuse. It led back to an abandoned brick kiln — a series of reddish
mounds and weed- and vine-choked vats without bottom. It had been used
for pasture once, until one day the owner missed one of his mules. Although he prodded carefully in the vats with a long pole, he could not even
find the bottom of them.

"John," the barber said.

"Jump out, then," McLendon said, hurling the car along the ruts. Beside the barber the Negro spoke:

"Mr Henry."

The barber sat forward. The narrow tunnel of the road rushed up and
past. Their motion was like an extinct furnace blast; cooler, but utterly
dead. The car bounded from rut to rut.

"Mr Henry," the Negro said.

The barber began to tug furiously at the door. "Look out, there!" the
soldier said, but the barber had already kicked the door open and swung
onto the running board. The soldier leaned across the Negro and grasped at
him, but he had already jumped. The car went on without checking speed.

The impetus hurled him crashing through dust-sheathed weeds, into
the ditch. Dust puffed about him, and in a thin, vicious crackling of sapless
stems he lay choking and retching until the second car passed and died
away. Then he rose and limped on until he reached the high road and
turned toward town, brushing at his clothes with his hands. The moon was
higher, riding high and clear of the dust at last, and after a while the town
began to glare beneath the dust. He went on, limping. Presently he heard

cars and the glow of them grew in the dust behind him and he left the road and crouched again in the weeds until they passed. McLendon's car came last now. There were four people in it and Butch was not on the running board.

They went on; the dust swallowed them; the glare and the sound died away. The dust of them hung for a while, but soon the eternal dust absorbed it again. The barber climbed back onto the road and limped on toward town.

IV

As she dressed for supper on that Saturday evening, her own flesh felt like fever. Her hands trembled among the hooks and eyes and her eyes had a feverish look, and her hair swirled crisp and crackling under the comb. While she was still dressing the friends called for her and sat while she donned her sheerest underthings and stockings and a new voile dress. "Do you feel strong enough to go out?" they said, their eyes bright too, with a dark glitter. "When you have had time to get over the shock, you must tell us what happened. What he said and did; everything."

In the leafed darkness, as they walked toward the square, she began to breathe deeply, something like a swimmer preparing to dive, until she ceased trembling, the four of them walking slowly because of the terrible heat and out of solicitude for her. But as they neared the square she began to tremble again, walking with her head up, her hands clenched at her sides, their voices about her murmurous, also with that feverish, glittering quality of their eyes. They entered the square, she in the center of the group, fragile in her fresh dress. She was trembling worse. She walked slower and slower, as children eat ice cream, her head up and her eyes bright in the haggard banner of her face, passing the hotel and the coatless drummers in chairs along the curb looking around at her: "That's the one: see? The one in pink in the middle." "Is that her? What did they do with the nigger? Did they — ?" "Sure. He's all right." "All right, is he?" "Sure. He went on a little trip." Then the drug store, where even the young men lounging in the doorway tipped their hats and followed with their eyes the motion of her hips and legs when she passed.

They went on, passing the lifted hats of the gentlemen, the suddenly ceased voices, deferent, protective. "Do you see?" the friends said. Their voices sounded like long, hovering sighs of hissing exultation. "There's not a Negro on the square. Not one."

They reached the picture show. It was like a miniature fairyland with its lighted lobby and colored lithographs of life caught in its terrible and beautiful mutations. Her lips began to tingle. In the dark, when the picture began, it would be all right; she could hold back the laughing so it would not waste away so fast and so soon. So she hurried on before the turning faces, the undertones of low astonishment, and they took their accustomed places where she could see the aisle against the silver glare and the young men and girls coming in two and two against it.

The lights flicked away; the screen glowed silver, and soon life began to unfold, beautiful and passionate and sad, while still the young men and girls entered, scented and sibilant in the half dark, their paired backs in silhouette delicate and sleek, their slim, quick bodies awkward, divinely young, while beyond them the silver dream accumulated, inevitably on and on. She began to laugh. In trying to suppress it, it made more noise than ever; heads began to turn. Still laughing, her friends raised her and led her out, and she stood at the curb, laughing on a high, sustained note, until the taxi came up and they helped her in.

They removed the pink voile and the sheer underthings and the stockings, and put her to bed, and cracked ice for her temples, and sent for the doctor. He was hard to locate, so they ministered to her with hushed ejaculations, renewing the ice and fanning her. While the ice was fresh and cold she stopped laughing and lay still for a time, moaning only a little. But soon the laughing welled again and her voice rose screaming.

"Shhhhhhhhhhh! Shhhhhhhhhhhhhhh!" they said, freshening the ice-pack, smoothing her hair, examining it for gray; "poor girl!" Then to one another: "Do you suppose anything really happened?" their eyes darkly aglitter, secret and passionate. "Shhhhhhhhhh! Poor girl! Poor Minnie!"

V

It was midnight when McLendon drove up to his neat new house. it was trim and fresh as a birdcage and almost as small, with its clean, green-and-white paint. He locked the car and mounted the porch and entered. His wife rose from a chair beside the reading lamp. McLendon stopped in the floor and stared at her until she looked down.

"Look at that clock," he said, lifting his arm, pointing. She stood before him, her face lowered, a magazine in her hands. Her face was pale, strained, and weary-looking. "Haven't I told you about sitting up like this, waiting to see when I come in?"

"John," she said. She laid the magazine down. Poised on the balls of his feet, he glared at her with his hot eyes, his sweating face.

"Didn't I tell you?" He went toward her. She looked up then. He caught her shoulder. She stood passive, looking at him.

"Don't, John. I couldn't sleep. . . . The heat; something. Please, John. You're hurting me."

"Didn't I tell you?" He released her and half struck, half flung her across the chair, and she lay there and watched him quietly as he left the room.

He went on through the house, ripping off his shirt, and on the dark, screened porch at the rear he stood and mopped his head and shoulders with the shirt and flung it away. He took the pistol from his hip and laid it on the table beside the bed, and sat on the bed and removed his shoes, and rose and slipped his trousers off. He was sweating again already, and he stooped and hunted furiously for the shirt. At last he found it and wiped his body again, and, with his body pressed against the dusty screen, he stood panting. There was no movement, no sound, not even an insect. The dark world seemed to lie stricken beneath the cold moon and the lidless stars.

[1931]

ERNEST HEMINGWAY (1898–1961) *was born in Oak Park, Illinois, but he spent most of his boyhood in Michigan, where his father, a doctor, encouraged his enthusiasm for camping and hunting in order to teach him the rudiments of physical courage and endurance. Active as a reporter for his high school newspaper, Hemingway decided not to go on to college after graduating from high school. Instead he worked as a reporter on the Kansas City* Star *for a few months before volunteering to serve in an American ambulance unit in France during World War I. Then he went to Italy, served at the front, and was severely wounded in action just before his nineteenth birthday. After the war he was too restless to settle down in the United States, so, like many American writers of his time, he lived in Paris and supported himself and his young family as a newspaper correspondent. He worked hard at learning how to write fiction; as he later said, "I found the greatest difficulty, aside from knowing what you really felt, rather than what you were supposed to feel, or had been taught to feel, was to put down what really happened in action: what the actual things were which produced the emotion that you experienced." In America he had admired the work of Sherwood Anderson, especially the colloquial, "unliterary" tone of his stories, and in Paris he came under the influence of Gertrude Stein, telling Anderson in a letter of 1922 that "Gertrude Stein and me are just like brothers."*

Although Hemingway was unwilling to experiment so radically with his prose style as was Stein — he refused to abandon the narrative line in his fiction — her technique of the repetition of simple words and ideas for emphasis is evident in his first book, In Our Time *(1925), a collection of stories about his boyhood, and in his early novels,* The Sun Also Rises *(1926) and* A Farewell to Arms *(1929). With these works Hemingway was established as a master stylist, probably the most influential writer of English prose in the first half of the twentieth century. Yet he was as much identified with the spectacle of such blood sports as hunting and bullfighting, and with the experience of men at war, as he was with literature. He was a reporter sympathetic to the Loyalist side in the Spanish Civil War, writing one of his most acclaimed novels,* For Whom the Bell Tolls *(1940), about that struggle. He worked as a correspondent during World War II. In 1954, after the publication of* The Old Man and the Sea, *he was awarded the Nobel Prize for Literature. Seven years later, in poor health and haunted by the memory of the suicide of his father, who had shot himself with a Civil War pistol in 1929, Hemingway killed himself with a shotgun in his Idaho hunting lodge.*

Hemingway, unlike his American contemporaries Fitzgerald and Faulkner, achieved the same level of artistry in his short fiction that he did in his novels. His terse way of writing short stories attracted many imitators. He once explained how he achieved the effect of intense compression in his stories by comparing his method to the principle of the iceberg. "There is seven-eighths of it under water for every part that shows. Anything you know you can eliminate and it only strengthens your iceberg. It is the part that doesn't show. If a writer omits something because he does not know it then there is a hole in the story." Hemingway's stories often suggest complex meanings because beneath the surface of the apparently simple action and dialogue, like "The Snows of Kilimanjaro," he presents a skillfully contrived dramatization of his philosophy that the highest human goal is to defy death and preserve one's dignity by acts of courage and integrity. Hemingway's best stories were written before 1938, and he earned a great deal of money from them. Many were anthologized after their first appearance in magazines, or made into motion pictures; his income from "The Snows of Kilimanjaro" alone ran into six figures. He disliked analyzing his method of writing, but in the preface to his collection of forty-nine stories published in 1938, he justified the way he was living his life, even if it seemed to be at the cost of his fiction: "In going where you have to go, and doing what you have to do, and seeing what you have to see, you dull and blunt the instrument you write with. But I would rather have it bent and dull and know I had to put it on the grindstone again and hammer it into shape and put a whetstone to it, and know that I had something to write about, than to have it bright and shining and nothing to say, or smooth and well-oiled in the closet, but unused."

Ernest Hemingway

ဂ္ဂ

THE SNOWS OF KILIMANJARO

Kilimanjaro is a snow covered mountain 19,710 feet high, and is said to be the highest mountain in Africa. Its western summit is called the Masai "Ngàje Ngài," the House of God. Close to the western summit there is the dried and frozen carcass of a leopard. No one has explained what the leopard was seeking at that altitude.

"The marvellous thing is that it's painless," he said. "That's how you know when it starts."

"Is it really?"

"Absolutely. I'm awfully sorry about the odor though. That must bother you."

"Don't! Please don't."

"Look at them," he said. "Now is it sight or is it scent that brings them like that?"

The cot the man lay on was in the wide shade of a mimosa tree and as he looked out past the shade onto the glare of the plain there were three of the big birds squatted obscenely, while in the sky a dozen more sailed, making quick-moving shadows as they passed.

"They've been there since the day the truck broke down," he said. "Today's the first time any have lit on the ground. I watched the way they sailed very carefully at first in case I ever wanted to use them in a story. That's funny now."

"I wish you wouldn't," she said.

"I'm only talking," he said. "It's much easier if I talk. But I don't want to bother you."

"You know it doesn't bother me," she said. "It's that I've gotten so very nervous not being able to do anything. I think we might make it as easy as we can until the plane comes."

"Or until the plane doesn't come."

"Please tell me what I can do. There must be something I can do."

"You can take the leg off and that might stop it, though I doubt it. Or you can shoot me. You're a good shot now. I taught you to shoot didn't I?"

"Please don't talk that way. Couldn't I read to you?"

"Read what?"

"Anything in the book bag that we haven't read."

"I can't listen to it," he said. "Talking is the easiest. We quarrel and that makes the time pass."

"I don't quarrel. I never want to quarrel. Let's not quarrel any more. No matter how nervous we get. Maybe they will be back with another truck today. Maybe the plane will come."

"I don't want to move," the man said. "There is no sense in moving now except to make it easier for you."

"That's cowardly."

"Can't you let a man die as comfortably as he can without calling him names? What's the use of slanging me?"

"You're not going to die."

"Don't be silly. I'm dying now. Ask those bastards." He looked over to where the huge, filthy birds sat, their naked heads sunk in the hunched feathers. A fourth planed down, to run quick-legged and then waddle slowly toward the others.

"They are around every camp. You never notice them. You can't die if you don't give up."

"Where did you read that? You're such a bloody fool."

"You might think about some one else."

"For Christ's sake," he said, "That's been my trade."

He lay then and was quiet for a while and looked across the heat shimmer of the plain to the edge of the bush. There were a few Tommies that showed minute and white against the yellow and, far off, he saw a herd of zebra, white against the green of the bush. This was a pleasant camp under big trees against a hill, with good water, and close by, a nearly dry water hole where sand grouse flighted in the mornings.

"Wouldn't you like me to read?" she asked. She was sitting on a canvas chair beside his cot. "There's a breeze coming up."

"No thanks."

"Maybe the truck will come."

"I don't give a damn about the truck."

"I do."

"You give a damn about so many things that I don't."

"Not so many, Harry."

"What about a drink?"

"It's supposed to be bad for you. It said in Black's to avoid all alcohol. You shouldn't drink."

"Molo!" he shouted.

"Yes Bwana."

"Bring whiskey-soda."

"Yes Bwana."

"You shouldn't," she said. "That's what I mean by giving up. It says it's bad for you. I know it's bad for you."

"No," he said. "It's good for me."

So now it was all over, he thought. So now he would never have a chance to finish it. So this was the way it ended in a bickering over a drink. Since the gangrene started in his right leg he had no pain and with the pain the horror had gone and all he felt now was a great tiredness and anger that this was the end of it. For this, that now was coming, he had very little curiosity. For years it had obsessed him; but now it meant nothing in itself. It was strange how easy being tired enough made it.

Now he would never write the things that he had saved to write until he knew enough to write them well. Well, he would not have to fail at trying to write them either. Maybe you could never write them, and that was why you put them off and delayed the starting. Well he would never know, now.

"I wish we'd never come," the woman said. She was looking at him holding the glass and biting her lip. "You never would have gotten anything like this in Paris. You always said you loved Paris. We could have stayed in Paris or gone anywhere. I'd have gone anywhere. I said I'd go anywhere you wanted. If you wanted to shoot we could have gone shooting in Hungary and been comfortable."

"Your bloody money," he said.

"That's not fair," she said. "It was always yours as much as mine. I left everything and I went wherever you wanted to go and I've done what you wanted to do. But I wish we'd never come here."

"You said you loved it."

"I did when you were all right. But now I hate it. I don't see why that had to happen to your leg. What have we done to have that happen to us?"

"I suppose what I did was to forget to put iodine on it when I first scratched it. Then I didn't pay any attention to it because I never infect. Then, later, when it got bad, it was probably using that weak carbolic solution when the other antiseptics ran out that paralyzed the minute blood vessels and started the gangrene." He looked at her, "What else?"

"I don't mean that."

"If we would have hired a good mechanic instead of a half-baked kikuyu driver, he would have checked the oil and never burned out that bearing in the truck."

"I don't mean that."

"If you hadn't left your own people, your goddamned Old Westbury, Saratoga, Palm Beach people to take me on ―― "

"Why, I loved you. That's not fair. I love you now. I'll always love you. Don't you love me?"

"No," said the man. "I don't think so. I never have."

"Harry, what are you saying? You're out of your head."

"No. I haven't any head to go out of."

"Don't drink that," she said. "Darling, please don't drink that. We have to do everything we can."

"You do it," he said. "I'm tired."

Now in his mind he saw a railway station at Karagatch and he was standing with his pack and that was the headlight of the Simplon-Orient cutting the dark now and he was leaving Thrace then after the retreat. That was one of the things he had saved to write, with, in the morning at breakfast, looking out the window and seeing snow on the mountains in Bulgaria and Nansen's Secretary asking the old man if it were snow and the old man looking at it and saying, No, that's not snow. It's too early for snow. And the Secretary repeating to the other girls, No, you see. It's not snow and them all saying, It's not snow we were mistaken. But it was the snow all right and he sent them on into it when he evolved exchange of populations. And it was snow they tramped along in until they died that winter.

It was snow too that fell all Christmas week that year up in the Gauertal, that year they lived in the woodcutter's house with the big square porcelain stove that filled half the room, and they slept on mattresses filled with beech leaves, the time the deserter came with his feet bloody in the snow. He saw the police were right behind him and they gave him woolen socks and held the gendarmes talking until the tracks had drifted over.

In Schrunz, on Christmas day, the snow was so bright it hurt your eyes when you looked out from the weinstube and saw every one coming home from church. That was where they walked up the sleigh-smoothed urine-yellowed road along the river with the steep pine hills, skis heavy on the shoulder, and where they ran that great run down the glacier above the Madlener-haus, the snow as smooth to see as cake frosting and as light as powder and he remembered the noiseless rush the speed made as you dropped down like a bird.

They were snow-bound a week in the Madlener-haus that time in the blizzard playing cards in the smoke by the lantern light and the stakes were higher all the time as Herr Lent lost more. Finally he lost it all. Everything, the skischule money and all the season's profit and then his capital. He could see him with his long nose, picking up the cards and then opening, "Sans Voir." There was always gambling then. When there was no snow you gambled and when there was too much you gambled. He thought of all the time in his life he had spent gambling.

But he had never written a line of that, nor of that cold, bright Christmas day with the mountains showing across the plain that Barker had flown across the lines to bomb the Austrian officer's leave train, machine-gunning them as they scattered and ran. He remembered Barker afterwards coming into the mess and starting to tell about it. And how quiet it got and then somebody saying, "You bloody murderous bastard."

Those were the same Austrians they killed then that he skied with later. No not the same. Hans, that he skied with all that year, had been in the Kaiser-Jägers and when they went hunting hares together up the little valley above the saw-mill they had talked of the fighting on Pasubio and of the attack on Pertica and Asalone and he had never written a word of that. Nor of Monte Corno, nor the Siete Commum, nor of Arsiedo.

How many winters had he lived in the Voralberg and the Arlberg? It was four and then he remembered the man who had the fox to sell when they had walked into Bludenz, that time to buy presents, and the cherry-pit taste of good kirsch, the fast-slipping rush of running powder-snow on crust, singing "Hi! Ho! said Rolly!" as you ran down the last stretch to the steep drop, taking it straight, then running the orchard in three turns and out across the ditch and onto the icy road behind the inn. Knocking your bindings loose, kicking the skis free and leaning them up against the wooden wall of the inn, the lamplight coming from the window, where inside, in the smoky, new-wine smelling warmth, they were playing the accordion.

"Where did we stay in Paris?" he asked the woman who was sitting by him in a canvas chair, now, in Africa.

"At the Crillon. You know that."

"Why do I know that?"

"That's where we always stayed."

"No. Not always."

"There and at the Pavillion Henri-Quatre in St. Germain. You said you loved it there."

"Love is a dunghill," said Harry. "And I'm the cock that gets on it to crow."

"If you have to go away," she said, "is it absolutely necessary to kill off everything you leave behind? I mean do you have to take away everything? Do you have to kill your horse, and your wife and burn your saddle and your armour?"

"Yes," he said. "Your damned money was my armour. My Swift and my Armour."

"Don't."

"All right. I'll stop that. I don't want to hurt you."

"It's a little bit late now."

"All right then. I'll go on hurting you. It's more amusing. The only thing I ever really liked to do with you I can't do now."

"No, that's not true. You liked to do many things and everything you wanted to do I did."

"Oh, for Christ sake stop bragging, will you?"

He looked at her and saw her crying.

"Listen," he said. "Do you think that it is fun to do this? I don't know why I'm doing it. It's trying to kill to keep yourself alive, I imagine. I was all right when we started talking. I didn't mean to start this, and now I'm crazy as a coot and being as cruel to you as I can be. Don't pay any attention, darling, to what I say. I love you, really. You know I love you. I've never loved anyone else the way I love you."

He slipped into the familiar lie he made his bread and butter by.

"You're sweet to me."

"You bitch," he said. "You rich bitch. That's poetry. I'm full of poetry now. Rot and poetry. Rotten poetry."

"Stop it. Harry, why do you have to turn into a devil now?"

"I don't like to leave anything," the man said. "I don't like to leave things behind."

It was evening now and he had been asleep. The sun was gone behind the hill and there was a shadow all across the plain and the small animals were feeding close to camp; quick dropping heads and switching tails, he watched them keeping well out away from the bush now. The birds no longer waited on the ground. They were all perched heavily in a tree. There were many more of them. His personal boy was sitting by the bed.

"Memsahib's gone to shoot," the boy said. "Does Bwana want?"

"Nothing."

She had gone to kill a piece of meat and, knowing how he liked to watch the game, she had gone well away so she would not disturb this little pocket of the plain that he could see. She was always thoughtful, he thought. On anything she knew about, or had read, or that she had ever heard.

It was not her fault that when he went to her he was already over. How could a woman know that you meant nothing that you said; that you spoke only from habit and to be comfortable? After he no longer meant what he said, his lies were more successful with women than when he had told them the truth.

It was not so much that he lied as that there was no truth to tell. He had had his life and it was over and then he went on living it again with different people and more money, with the best of the same places, and some new ones.

You kept from thinking and it was all marvellous. You were equipped with good insides so that you did not go to pieces that way, the way most of them had, and you made an attitude that you cared nothing for the work you used to do, now that you could no longer do it. But, in yourself, you said that you would write about these people; about the very rich; that you were really not of them but a spy in their country; that you would leave it and write of it and for once it would be written by someone who knew what he was writing of. But he would never do it, because each day of not writing, of comfort, of being that which he despised, dulled his ability and softened his will to work so that, finally, he did no work at all. The people he knew now were all much more comfortable when he did not work. Africa was where he had been happiest in the good time of his life, so he had come out here to start again. They had made this safari with the minimum of comfort. There was no hardship; but there was no luxury and he had thought he could get back into training that way. That in some way he could work the fat off his soul the way a fighter went into the mountains to work and train in order to burn it out of his body.

She had liked it. She said she loved it. She loved anything that was exciting, that involved a change of scene, where there were new people and where things were pleasant. And he had felt the illusion of returning strength of will to work. Now if this was how it ended, and he knew it was, he must not turn like some snake biting itself because its back was broken. It wasn't this woman's fault. If it had not been she it would have been another. If he lived by a lie he should try to die by it. He heard a shot beyond the hill.

She shot very well this good, this rich bitch, this kindly caretaker and destroyer of his talent. Nonsense. He had destroyed his talent himself. Why should he blame this woman because she kept him well? He had destroyed his talent by not using it, by betrayals of himself and what he believed in, by drinking so much that he blunted the edge of his perceptions, by laziness, by sloth, and by snobbery, by pride and by prejudice, by hook and by crook. What was this? A catalogue of old books? What was his talent anyway? It was a talent all right but instead of using it, he had traded on it. It was never what he had done, but always what he could do. And he had chosen to make his living with something else instead of a pen or a pencil. It was strange, too, wasn't it, that when he fell in love with another woman, that woman should always have more money than the last one? But when he no longer was in love, when he was only lying, as to this woman, now, who had the most money of all, who had all the money there was, who had had a husband and children, who had taken lovers and been dissatisfied with them, and who loved him dearly as a writer, as a man, as a companion and as a proud possession; it was strange that when he did not love her at all and was lying, that he should be able to give her more for her money than when he had really loved.

We must all be cut out for what we do, he thought. However you make your living is where your talent lies. He had sold vitality, in one form or another, all his life and when your affections are not too involved you give much better value for the money. He had found that out but he would never write that, now, either. No, he would not write that, although it was well worth writing.

Now she came in sight, walking across the open toward the camp. She was wearing jodhpurs and carrying her rifle. The two boys had a Tommie slung and they were coming along behind her. She was still a good-looking woman, he thought, and she had a pleasant body. She had a great talent and appreciation for the bed, she was not pretty, but he liked her face, she read enormously, liked to ride and shoot and, certainly, she drank too much. Her husband had died when she was still a comparatively young woman and for a while she had devoted herself to her two just-grown children, who did not need her and were embarrassed at having her about, to her stable of horses, to books, and to bottles. She liked to read in the evening before dinner and she drank Scotch and soda while she read. By dinner she was fairly drunk and after a bottle of wine at dinner she was usually drunk enough to sleep.

That was before the lovers. After she had the lovers she did not drink so much because she did not have to be drunk to sleep. But the lovers bored her. She had been married to a man who had never bored her and these people bored her very much.

Then one of her two children was killed in a plane crash and after that was over she did not want the lovers, and drink being no anæsthetic she had to make another life. Suddenly, she had been acutely frightened of being alone. But she wanted someone that she respected with her.

It had begun very simply. She liked what he wrote and she had always envied the life he led. She thought he did exactly what he wanted to. The steps by which she had acquired him and the way in which she had finally fallen in love with him were all part of a regular progression in which she had built herself a new life and he had traded away what remained of his old life.

He had traded it for security, for comfort too, there was no denying that, and for what else? He did not know. She would have bought him anything he wanted. He knew that. She was a damned nice woman too. He would as soon be in bed with her as anyone; rather with her, because she was richer, because she was very pleasant and appreciative and because she

never made scenes. And now this life that she had built again was coming
to a term because he had not used iodine two weeks ago when a thorn had
scratched his knee as they moved forward trying to photograph a herd of
waterbuck standing, their heads up, peering while their nostrils searched
the air, their ears spread wide to hear the first noise that would send them
rushing into the bush. They had bolted, too, before he got the picture.

Here she came now.

He turned his head on the cot to look toward her. "Hello," he said.

"I shot a Tommy ram," she told him. "He'll make you good broth and
I'll have them mash some potatoes with the Klim. How do you feel?"

"Much better."

"Isn't that lovely? You know I thought perhaps you would. You were
sleeping when I left."

"I had a good sleep. Did you walk far?"

"No. Just around behind the hill. I made quite a good shot on the
Tommy."

"You shoot marvellously, you know."

"I love it. I've loved Africa. Really. If *you're* all right it's the most fun
that I've ever had. You don't know the fun it's been to shoot with you. I've
loved the country."

"I love it too."

"Darling, you don't know how marvellous it is to see you feeling better. I couldn't stand it when you felt that way. You won't talk to me like
that again, will you? Promise me?"

"No," he said. "I don't remember what I said."

"You don't have to destroy me. Do you? I'm only a middle-aged
woman who loves you and wants to do what you want to do. I've been destroyed two or three times already. You wouldn't want to destroy me again,
would you?"

"I'd like to destroy you a few times in bed," he said.

"Yes. That's the good destruction. That's the way we're made to be
destroyed. The plane will be here tomorrow."

"How do you know?"

"I'm sure. It's bound to come. The boys have the wood all ready and
the grass to make the smudge. I went down and looked at it again today.
There's plenty of room to land and we have the smudges ready at both
ends."

"What makes you think it will come tomorrow?"

"I'm sure it will. It's overdue now. Then, in town, they will fix up your
leg and then we will have some good destruction. Not that dreadful talking
kind."

"Should we have a drink? The sun is down."

"Do you think you should?"

"I'm having one."

"We'll have one together. *Molo, letti dui whiskey-soda!*" she called.

"You'd better put on your mosquito boots," he told her.

"I'll wait till I bathe. . . ."

While it grew dark they drank and just before it was dark and there was no longer enough light to shoot, a hyena crossed the open on his way around the hill.

"That bastard crosses there every night," the man said. "Every night for two weeks."

"He's the one makes the noise at night. I don't mind it. They're a filthy animal though."

Drinking together, with no pain now except the discomfort of lying in the one position, the boys lighting a fire, its shadow jumping on the tents, he could feel the return of acquiescence in this life of pleasant surrender. She *was* very good to him. He had been cruel and unjust in the afternoon. She was a fine woman, marvellous really. And just then it occurred to him that he was going to die.

It came with a rush; not as a rush of water nor of wind; but of a sudden evil-smelling emptiness and the odd thing was that the hyena slipped lightly along the edge of it.

"What is it, Harry?" she asked him.

"Nothing," he said. "You had better move over to the other side. To windward."

"Did Molo change the dressing?"

"Yes. I'm just using the boric now."

"How do you feel?"

"A little wobbly."

"I'm going in to bathe," she said. "I'll be right out. I'll eat with you and then we'll put the cot in."

So, he said to himself, we did well to stop the quarrelling. He had never quarrelled much with this woman, while with the women that he loved he had quarrelled so much they had finally, always, with the corrosion of the quarrelling, killed what they had together. He had loved too much, demanded too much, and he wore it all out.

He thought about alone in Constantinople that time, having quarrelled in Paris before he had gone out. He had whored the whole time and then, when that was over, and he had failed to kill his loneliness, but only made it worse, he had written her, the first one, the one who left him, a letter telling her how he had never been able to kill it. . . . How when he thought he saw her outside the Regence one time it made him go all faint and sick inside, and that he would follow a woman who looked like her in some way, along the Boulevard, afraid to see it was not she, afraid to lose the feeling it gave him. How every one he had slept with had only made him miss her more. How what she had done could never matter since he knew he could not cure himself of loving her. He wrote this letter at the Club, cold sober, and mailed it to New York asking her to write him at the office in Paris. That seemed safe. And that night missing her so much it made him feel hollow sick inside, he wandered up past Taxim's, picked a girl up and took her out to supper. He had gone to a place to dance with her afterward, she danced badly, and left her for a hot Armenian slut, that swung her belly against him so it almost scalded. He took her away from a British gunner subaltern after a row. The gunner asked him outside and they fought in the street on the cobbles in the dark. He'd hit him twice, hard, on the side of the jaw and when he didn't go down he knew he was in for a fight. The gunner hit him in the body, then beside his eye. He swung with his left again and landed and the gunner fell on him and grabbed his coat and tore the sleeve off and he clubbed him twice behind the ear and then smashed him with his right as he pushed him away. When the gunner went down his head hit first and he ran with the girl because they heard the M.P.'s coming. They got into a taxi and drove out to Rimmily Hissa along the Bosphorus, and around, and back in the cool night and went to bed and she felt as over-ripe as she looked but smooth, rose-petal, syrupy, smooth-bellied, big-breasted and needed no pillow under her buttocks, and he left her before she was awake looking blousy enough in the first daylight and turned up at the Pera Palace with a black eye, carrying his coat because one sleeve was missing.

That same night he left for Anatolia and he remembered, later on that trip, riding all day through fields of the poppies that they raised for opium and how strange it made you feel, finally, and all the distances seemed wrong, to where they had made the attack with the newly arrived Constantine officers, that did not know a god-damned thing, and the artillery had fired into the troops and the British observer had cried like a child.

That was the day he'd first seen dead men wearing white ballet skirts and upturned shoes with pompons on them. The Turks had come steadily and lumpily and he had seen the skirted men running and the officers shooting into them and running then themselves and he and the British observer had run too until his lungs ached and his mouth was full of the taste of pennies and they stopped behind some rocks and there were the Turks coming as lumpily as ever. Later he had seen the things that he could never think of and later still he had seen much worse. So when he got back to Paris that time he could not talk about it or stand to have it mentioned. And there in the café as he passed was that American poet with a pile of saucers in front of him and a stupid look on his potato face talking about the Dada movement[1] with a Rumanian who said his name was Tristan Tzara, who always wore a monocle and had a headache, and, back at the apartment with his wife that now he loved again, the quarrel all over, the madness all over, glad to be home, the office sent his mail up to the flat. So

---

[1] Artistic and literary movement of the 1920s, emphasizing deliberate irrationality and repudiation of earlier artistic values. Leading dadaists included French painter Marcel Duchamp, American painter Man Ray, and Rumanian writer Tristan Tzara, all of whom lived in Paris at the time. Tzara invented the name for the movement.

then the letter in answer to the one he'd written came in on a platter one morning and when he saw the handwriting he went cold all over and tried to slip the letter underneath another. But his wife said, "Who is that letter from, dear?" and that was the end of the beginning of that.

He remembered the good times with them all, and the quarrels. They always picked the finest places to have the quarrels. And why had they always quarrelled when he was feeling best? He had never written any of that because, at first, he never wanted to hurt anyone and then it seemed as though there was enough to write without it. But he had always thought that he would write it finally. There was so much to write. He had seen the world change; not just the events; although he had seen many of them and had watched the people, but he had seen the subtler change and he could remember how the people were at different times. He had been in it and he had watched it and it was his duty to write of it; but now he never would.

"How do you feel?" she said. She had come out from the tent now after her bath.

"All right."

"Could you eat now?" He saw Molo behind her with the folding table and the other boy with the dishes.

"I want to write," he said.

"You ought to take some broth to keep your strength up."

"I'm going to die tonight," he said. "I don't need my strength up."

"Don't be melodramatic, Harry, please," she said.

"Why don't you use your nose? I'm rotted half way up my thigh now. What the hell should I fool with broth for? Molo bring whiskey-soda."

"Please take the broth," she said gently.

"All right."

The broth was too hot. He had to hold it in the cup until it cooled enough to take it and then he just got it down without gagging.

"You're a fine woman," he said. "Don't pay any attention to me."

She looked at him with her well-known, well-loved face from *Spur* and *Town and Country*, only a little the worse for drink, only a little the worse for bed, but *Town and Country* never showed those good breasts and those useful thighs and those lightly small-of-back-caressing hands, and as he looked and saw her well-known pleasant smile, he felt death come again. This time there was no rush. It was a puff, as of a wind that makes a candle flicker and the flame go tall.

"They can bring my net out later and hang it from the tree and build the fire up. I'm not going in the tent tonight. It's not worth moving. It's a clear night. There won't be any rain."

So this was how you died, in whispers that you did not hear. Well, there would be no more quarrelling. He could promise that. The one experience that he had never had he was not going to spoil now. He probably would. You spoiled everything. But perhaps he wouldn't.

"You can't take dictation, can you?"

"I never learned," she told him.

"That's all right."

There wasn't time, of course, although it seemed as though it telescoped so that you might put it all into one paragraph if you could get it right.

There was a log house, chinked white with mortar, on a hill above the lake. There was a bell on a pole by the door to call the people in to meals. Behind the house were fields and behind the fields was the timber. A line of Lombardy poplars ran from the house to the dock. Other poplars ran along the point. A road went up to the hills along the edge of the timber and along that road he picked blackberries. Then that log house was burned down and all the guns that had been on deer foot racks above the open fire place were burned and afterwards their barrels, with the lead melted in the magazines, and the stocks burned away, lay out on the heap of ashes that were used to make lye for the big iron soap kettles, and you asked Grandfather if you could have them to play with, and he said, no. You see they were his guns still and he never bought any others. Nor did he hunt any more. The house was rebuilt in the same place out of lumber now and painted white and from its porch you saw the poplars and the lake beyond; but there were never any more guns. The barrels of the guns that had hung on the deer feet on the wall of the log house lay out there on the heap of ashes and no one ever touched them.

In the Black Forest, after the war, we rented a trout stream and there were two ways to walk to it. One was down the valley from Triberg and around the valley road in the shade of the trees that bordered the white road, and then up a side road that went up through the hills past many small farms, with the big Schwarzwald houses, until that road crossed the stream. That was where our fishing began.

The other way was to climb steeply up to the edge of the woods and then go across the top of the hills through the pine woods, and then out to the edge of a meadow and down across this meadow to the bridge. There were birches along the stream and it was not big, but narrow, clear and fast, with pools where it had cut under the roots of the birches. At the Hotel in Triberg the proprietor had a fine season. It was very pleasant and we were all great friends. The next year came the inflation and the money he had made the year before was not enough to buy supplies to open the hotel and he hanged himself.

You could dictate that, but you could not dictate the Place Contrescarpe where the flower sellers dyed their flowers in the street and the dye ran over the paving where the autobus started and the old men and the women, always drunk on wine and bad marc; and the children with their noses running in the cold; the smell of dirty sweat and poverty and drunkenness at the Café des Amateurs and the whores at the Bal Musette they

lived above. The Concierge who entertained the trooper of the Garde Re-
publicaine in her loge, his horse-hair-plumed helmet on a chair. The loca-
taire across the hall whose husband was a bicycle racer and her joy that
morning at the Cremerie when she had opened L'Auto and seen where he
placed third in Paris-Tours, his first big race. She had blushed and laughed
and then gone upstairs crying with the yellow sporting paper in her hand.
The husband of the woman who ran the Bal Musette drove a taxi and when
he, Harry, had to take an early plane the husband knocked upon the door to
wake him and they each drank a glass of white wine at the zinc of the bar
before they started. He knew his neighbors in that quarter then because
they all were poor.

Around that Place there were two kinds; the drunkards and the sportifs. The drunkards killed their poverty that way; the sportifs took it out in
exercise. They were the descendants of the Communards[2] and it was no
struggle for them to know their politics. They knew who had shot their fathers, their relatives, their brothers, and their friends when the Versailles
troops came in and took the town after the Commune and executed any
one they could catch with calloused hands, or who wore a cap, or carried
any other sign he was a working man. And in that poverty, and in that quarter across the street from a Boucherie Chevaline and a wine co-operative he
had written the start of all he was to do. There never was another part of
Paris that he loved like that, the sprawling trees, the old white plastered
houses painted brown below, the long green of the autobus in that round
square, the purple flower dye upon the paving, the sudden drop down the
hill of the rue Cardinal Lemoine to the River, and the other way the narrow
crowded world of the rue Mouffetard. The street that ran up toward the
Pantheon and the other that he always took with the bicycle, the only as-
phalted street in all that quarter, smooth under the tires, with the high narrow houses and the cheap tall hotel where Paul Verlaine had died. There
were only two rooms in the apartments where they lived and he had a room
on the top floor of that hotel that cost him sixty francs a month where he
did his writing, and from it he could see the roofs and chimney pots and all
the hills of Paris.

From the apartment you could only see the wood and coal man's
place. He sold wine too, bad wine. The golden horse's head outside the
Boucherie Chevaline where the carcasses hung yellow gold and red in the
open window, and the green painted co-operative where they bought their
wine; good wine and cheap. The rest was plaster walls and the windows of
the neighbors. The neighbors who, at night, when some one lay drunk in
the street, moaning and groaning in that typical French ivresse[3] that you
were propaganded to believe did not exist, would open their windows and
then the murmur of talk.

[2] members and supporters of the Commune of Paris, 1871 (see note 10 on page 633).
[3] drunkenness.

*"Where is the policeman? When you don't want him the bugger is al-
ways there. He's sleeping with some concierge. Get the Agent."* Till some
one threw a bucket of water from a window and the moaning stopped.
"What's that? Water. Ah, that's intelligent." And the windows shutting.
Marie, his femme de menage, protesting against the eight-hour day saying,
*"If a husband works until six he gets only a little drunk on the way home
and does not waste too much. If he works only until five he is drunk every
night and one has no money. It is the wife of the working man who suffers
from this shortening of hours."*

"Wouldn't you like some more broth?" the woman asked him now.

"No, thank you very much. It is awfully good."

"Try just a little."

"I would like a whiskey-soda."

"It's not good for you."

"No. It's bad for me. Cole Porter wrote the words and the music. This
knowledge that you're going mad for me."

"You know I like you to drink."

"Oh yes. Only it's bad for me."

When she goes, he thought. I'll have all I want. Not all I want but all
there is. Ayee he was tired. Too tired. He was going to sleep a little while.
He lay still and death was not there. It must have gone around another
street. It went in pairs, on bicycles, and moved absolutely silently on the
pavements.

No, he had never written about Paris. Not the Paris that he cared
about. But what about the rest that he had never written?

What about the ranch and the silvered gray of the sage brush, the
quick, clear water in the irrigation ditches, and the heavy green of the alfalfa. The trail went up into the hills and the cattle in the summer were shy
as deer. The bawling and the steady noise and slow moving mass raising a
dust as you brought them down in the fall. And behind the mountains, the
clear sharpness of the peak in the evening light and, riding down along the
trail in the moonlight, bright across the valley. Now he remembered coming down through the timber in the dark holding the horse's tail when you
could not see and all the stories that he meant to write.

About the half-wit chore boy who was left at the ranch that time and
told not to let anyone get any hay, and that old bastard from the Forks who
had beaten the boy when he had worked for him stopping to get some feed.
The boy refusing and the old man saying he would beat him again. The boy
got the rifle from the kitchen and shot him when he tried to come into the
barn and when they came back to the ranch he'd been dead a week, frozen
in the corral, and the dogs had eaten part of him. But what was left you
packed on a sled wrapped in a blanket and roped on and you got the boy to

help you haul it, and the two of you took it out over the road on skis, and sixty miles down to town to turn the boy over. He having no idea that he would be arrested. Thinking he had done his duty and that you were his friend and he would be rewarded. He'd helped to haul the old man in so everybody could know how bad the old man had been and how he'd tried to steal some feed that didn't belong to him, and when the sheriff put the handcuffs on the boy he couldn't believe it. Then he'd started to cry. That was one story he had saved to write. He knew at least twenty good stories from out there and he had never written one. Why?

"You tell them why," he said.

"Why what, dear?"

"Why nothing."

She didn't drink so much, now, since she had him. But if he lived he would never write about her, he knew that now. Nor about any of them. The rich were dull and they drank too much, or they played too much backgammon. They were dull and they were repetitious. He remembered poor Julian and his romantic awe of them and how he had started a story once that began, "The very rich are different from you and me." And how someone had said to Julian, Yes, they have more money.[4] But that was not humorous to Julian. He thought they were a special glamorous race and when he found they weren't it wrecked him just as much as any other thing that wrecked him.

He had been contemptuous of those who wrecked. You did not have to like it because you understood it. He could beat anything, he thought, because no thing could hurt him if he did not care.

All right. Now he would not care for death. One thing he had always dreaded was the pain. He could stand pain as well as any man, until it went on too long, and wore him out, but here he had something that had hurt frightfully and just when he had felt it breaking him, the pain had stopped.

He remembered long ago when Williamson, the bombing officer, had been hit by a stick bomb someone in a German patrol had thrown as he was coming in through the wire that night and, screaming, had begged every one to kill him. He was a fat man, very brave, and a good officer, although addicted to fantastic shows. But that night he was caught in the wire, with a flare lighting him up and his bowels spilled out into the wire, so when they brought him in, alive, they had to cut him loose. Shoot me, Harry. For Christ sake shoot me. They had had an argument one time about our Lord never sending you anything you could not bear and someone's theory had been that meant that at a certain time the pain passed you out automati-

---

[4] This exchange is alleged to have actually occurred between Hemingway and F. Scott Fitzgerald, with Fitzgerald speaking the line attributed to "Julian."

*cally. But he had always remembered Williamson, that night. Nothing
passed out Williamson until he gave him all his morphine tablets that he
had always saved to use himself and then they did not work right away.*

Still this now, that he had, was very easy; and if it was no worse as it
went on there was nothing to worry about. Except that he would rather be
in better company.

He thought a little about the company that he would like to have.

No, he thought, when everything you do, you do too long, and do too
late, you can't expect to find the people still there. The people all are gone.
The party's over and you are with your hostess now.

I'm getting as bored with dying as with everything else, he thought.

"It's a bore," he said out loud.

"What is, my dear?"

"Anything you do too bloody long."

He looked at her face between him and the fire. She was leaning back
in the chair and the firelight shone on her pleasantly lined face and he could
see that she was sleepy. He heard the hyena make a noise just outside the
range of the fire.

"I've been writing," he said. "But I got tired."

"Do you think you will be able to sleep?"

"Pretty sure. Why don't you turn in?"

"I like to sit here with you."

"Do you feel anything strange?" he asked her.

"No. Just a little sleepy."

"I do," he said.

He had just felt death come by again.

"You know the only thing I've never lost is curiosity," he said to her.

"You've never lost anything. You're the most complete man I've ever
known."

"Christ," he said. "How little a woman knows. What is that? Your intuition?"

Because, just then, death had come and rested its head on the foot of
the cot and he could smell its breath.

"Never believe any of that about a scythe and a skull," he told her. "It
can be two bicycle policemen as easily, or be a bird. Or it can have a wide
snout like a hyena."

It had moved up on him now, but it had no shape any more. It simply
occupied space.

"Tell it to go away."

It did not go away but moved a little closer.

"You've got a hell of a breath," he told it. "You stinking bastard."

It moved up closer to him still and now he could not speak to it, and
when it saw he could not speak it came a little closer, and now he tried to
send it away without speaking, but it moved in on him so its weight was all

upon his chest, and while it crouched there and he could not move, or speak, he heard the woman say, "Bwana is asleep now. Take the cot up very gently and carry it into the tent."

He could not speak to tell her to make it go away and it crouched now, heavier, so he could not breathe. And then, while they lifted the cot, suddenly it was all right and the weight went from his chest.

It was morning and had been morning for some time and he heard the plane. It showed very tiny and then made a wide circle and the boys ran out and lit the fires, using kerosene, and piled on grass so there were two big smudges at each end of the level place and the morning breeze blew them toward the camp and the plane circled twice more, low this time, and then glided down and levelled off and landed smoothly and, coming walking toward him, was old Compton in slacks, a tweed jacket and a brown felt hat.

"What's the matter, old cock?" Compton said.

"Bad leg," he told him. "Will you have some breakfast?"

"Thanks. I'll just have some tea. It's the Puss Moth you know. I won't be able to take the Memsahib. There's only room for one. Your lorry is on the way."

Helen had taken Compton aside and was speaking to him. Compton came back more cheery than ever.

"We'll get you right in," he said. "I'll be back for the Mem. Now I'm afraid I'll have to stop at Arusha to refuel. We'd better get going."

"What about the tea?"

"I don't really care about it you know."

The boys had picked up the cot and carried it around the green tents and down along the rock and out onto the plain and along past the smudges that were burning brightly now, the grass all consumed, and the wind fanning the fire, to the little plane. It was difficult getting him in, but once in he lay back in the leather seat, and the leg was stuck straight out to one side of the seat where Compton sat. Compton started the motor and got in. He waved to Helen and to the boys and, as the clatter moved into the old familiar roar, they swung around with Compie watching for wart-hog holes and roared, bumping, along the stretch between the fires and with the last bump rose and he saw them all standing below, waving, and the camp beside the hill, flattening now, and the plain spreading, clumps of trees, and the bush flattening, while the game trails ran now smoothly to the dry waterholes, and there was a new water that he had never known of. The zebra, small rounded backs now, and the wildebeeste, big-headed dots seeming to climb as they moved in long fingers across the plain, now scattering as the shadow came toward them, they were tiny now, and the movement had no gallop, and the plain as far as you could see, gray-yellow now and ahead old Compie's tweed back and the brown felt hat. Then they were over the first hills and the wildebeeste were trailing up them, and then they were over mountains with sudden depths of green-rising forest and the solid bamboo slopes, and then the heavy forest again, sculptured into peaks and hollows until they crossed, and hills sloped down and then another plain, hot now, and purple brown, bumpy with heat and Compie looking back to see how he was riding. Then there were other mountains dark ahead.

And then instead of going on to Arusha they turned left, he evidently figured that they had the gas, and looking down he saw a pink sifting cloud, moving over the ground, and in the air, like the first snow in a blizzard, that comes from nowhere, and he knew the locusts were coming up from the South. Then they began to climb and they were going to the East it seemed, and then it darkened and they were in a storm, the rain so thick it seemed like flying through a waterfall, and then they were out and Compie turned his head and grinned and pointed and there, ahead, all he could see, as wide as all the world, great, high, and unbelievably white in the sun, was the square top of Kilimanjaro. And then he knew that there was where he was going.

Just then the hyena stopped whimpering in the night and started to make a strange, human, almost crying sound. The woman heard it and stirred uneasily. She did not wake. In her dream she was at the house on Long Island and it was the night before her daughter's début. Somehow her father was there and he had been very rude. Then the noise the hyena made was so loud she woke and for a moment she did not know where she was and she was very afraid. Then she took the flashlight and shone it on the other cot that they had carried in after Harry had gone to sleep. She could see his bulk under the mosquito bar but somehow he had gotten his leg out and it hung down alongside the cot. The dressings had all come down and she could not look at it.

"Molo," she called, "Molo! Molo!"

Then she said, "Harry, Harry!" Then her voice rising, "Harry! Please, Oh Harry!"

There was no answer and she could not hear him breathing.

Outside the tent the hyena made the same strange noise that had awakened her. But she did not hear him for the beating of her heart.

[1938]

VLADIMIR NABOKOV (1899–1977), *claiming that "the nation-ality of a worthwhile writer is of secondary importance," resists classifica-tion as a Russian, American, or even Swiss writer. Born into an aristocratic and wealthy family in St. Petersburg (now Leningrad), he was educated at the Prince Tenishev School there. As a boy he was an avid reader and loved literature: "Between the ages of ten and fifteen in St. Petersburg, I must have read more fiction and poetry — English, Russian, and French — than in any other five-year period in my life." He published a collection of his own poems at the age of sixteen. When the Bolsheviks seized power after the Russian Revolution of 1917, Nabokov fled to Europe with his family. He took a degree in French and Russian literature at Cambridge University in 1922, the same year his father, who had been a liberal politician in Rus-sia, was assassinated in Berlin by right-wing Russians. Nabokov lived as an émigré in Germany and France until the outbreak of World War II forced him, his wife Vera, and their young son Dmitri to move to the United States. He had published many novels in Europe and had begun to write in English, but he made his living in the United States as a lecturer on Russian language and literature at Stanford, Wellesley, Harvard, and Cornell, as-cending "from lean lecturer to full professor." In his time away from teach-ing, he wrote fiction, selling occasional stories to* The Atlantic Monthly *and* The New Yorker *before the financial success of his novel* Lolita *(1955) a best-seller when it finally found an American publisher in 1958, enabled him to give up teaching and return to Europe. In 1961 he settled at the Pal-ace Hotel in Montreux, Switzerland, where he remained with his wife and continued to write until his death. The more than thirty volumes of his complete works include such novels as* The Real Life of Sebastian Knight *(1941),* Pnin *(1957),* Pale Fire *(1962), and* Ada, or Ardor: A Family Chronicle *(1969). His lectures at Cornell on European and Russian litera-ture, published in 1980 and 1981, show him teaching his students to be good readers of great literature by insisting that style and structure are the essence of a book; "caress the details," he would intone, rolling the* r — *"the divine details!"*

Nabokov once told an interviewer that "the writer's art is his real pass-port. His identity should be immediately recognized by a special pattern or unique coloration." His "special pattern" as a writer was a passionate inter-est in language and experience that led him to create works where memories of the past mingled with an ironic sense of the precariousness of the pre-sent. A meticulous craftsman, he revised his manuscripts to polish his wit and style to razor sharpness: "I think like a genius, I write like a distin-guished author, and I speak like a child. . . . At parties, if I attempt to en-tertain people with a good story, I have to go back to every other sentence

*for oral erasures and inserts. Even the dream I describe to my wife across
the breakfast table is only a first draft."*

A half-dozen books of Nabokov's short stories were published in his
lifetime, many of them translated from Russian into English by his son.
The early collections show him learning his craft in Berlin; perhaps the best
collection is Nabokov's Dozen (1958), thirteen stories written in Berlin in
the 1930s, Boston in the 1940s, and Ithaca in the 1950s. In "First Love," a
story from Nabokov's Dozen, he reminisces about a summer in France during his childhood, evoking memories of different times and places and
refashioning them into autobiographical fiction in which chronological
fidelity is less important than the emotional impressions made upon him by
the characters and events he remembers.*

Vladimir Nabokov

ଓଔ

FIRST LOVE

I

In the early years of this century, a travel agency on Nevski Avenue
displayed a three-foot-long model of an oak-brown international sleeping
car. In delicate verisimilitude it completely outranked the painted tin of my
clockwork trains. Unfortunately it was not for sale. One could make out the
blue upholstery inside, the embossed leather lining of the compartment
walls, their polished panels, inset mirrors, tulip-shaped reading lamps, and
other maddening details. Spacious windows alternated with narrower ones,
single or geminate, and some of these were of frosted glass. In a few of the
compartments, the beds had been made.

The then great and glamorous Nord Express (it was never the same
after World War I), consisting solely of such international cars and running
but twice a week, connected St. Petersburg with Paris. I would have said:
directly with Paris, had passengers not been obliged to change from one train
to a superficially similar one at the Russo-German frontier (Verzhbolovo-
Eydtkuhnen), where the ample and lazy Russian sixty-and-a-half-inch gauge
was replaced by the fifty-six-and-a-half-inch standard of Europe and coal
succeeded birch logs.

In the far end of my mind I can unravel, I think, at least five such
journeys to Paris, with the Riviera or Biarritz as their ultimate destination.
In 1909, the year I now single out, my two small sisters had been left at

home with nurses and aunts. Wearing gloves and a traveling cap, my father sat reading a book in the compartment he shared with our tutor. My brother and I were separated from them by a washroom. My mother and her maid occupied a compartment adjacent to ours. The odd one of our party, my father's valet, Osip (whom, a decade later, the pedantic Bolsheviks were to shoot, because he appropriated our bicycles instead of turning them over to the nation), had a stranger for companion.

In April of that year, Peary had reached the North Pole. In May, Chaliapin had sung in Paris. In June, bothered by rumors of new and better Zeppelins, the United States War Department had told reporters of plans for an aerial Navy. In July, Blériot had flown from Calais to Dover (with a little additional loop when he lost his bearings). It was late August now. The firs and marshes of northwestern Russia sped by, and on the following day gave way to German pine barrens and heather.

At a collapsible table, my mother and I played a card game called *durachki*. Although it was still broad daylight, our cards, a glass, and on a different plane the locks of a suitcase were reflected in the window. Through forest and field, and in sudden ravines, and among scuttling cottages, those discarnate gamblers kept steadily playing on for steadily sparkling stakes.

"*Ne budet-li, ti ved' ustal* [Haven't you had enough, aren't you tired]?" my mother would ask, and then would be lost in thought as she slowly shuffled the cards. The door of the compartment was open and I could see the corridor window, where the wires — six thin black wires — were doing their best to slant up, to ascend skywards, despite the lightning blows dealt them by one telegraph pole after another; but just as all six, in a triumphant swoop of pathetic elation, were about to reach the top of the window, a particularly vicious blow would bring them down, as low as they had ever been, and they would have to start all over again.

When, on such journeys as these, the train changed its pace to a dignified amble and all but grazed house fronts and shop signs, as we passed through some big German town, I used to feel a twofold excitement, which terminal stations could not provide. I saw a city with its toylike trams, linden trees, and brick walls enter the compartment, hobnob with the mirrors, and fill to the brim the windows on the corridor side. This informal contact between train and city was one part of the thrill. The other was putting myself in the place of some passer-by who, I imagined, was moved as I would be moved myself to see the long, romantic, auburn cars, with their intervestibular connecting curtains as black as bat wings and their metal lettering copper-bright in the low sun, unhurriedly negotiate an iron bridge across an everyday thoroughfare and then turn, with all windows suddenly ablaze, around a last block of houses.

There were drawbacks to those optical amalgamations. The wide-windowed dining car, a vista of chaste bottles of mineral water, miter-folded napkins, and dummy chocolate bars (whose wrappers — Cailler, Kohler, and so forth — enclosed nothing but wood) would be perceived at first as a cool haven beyond a consecution of reeling blue corridors; but as the meal progressed toward its fatal last course, one would keep catching the car in the act of being recklessly sheathed, lurching waiters and all, in the landscape, while the landscape itself went through a complex system of motion, the daytime moon stubbornly keeping abreast of one's plate, the distant meadows opening fanwise, the near trees sweeping up on invisible swings toward the track, a parallel rail line all at once committing suicide by anastomosis, a bank of nictitating grass rising, rising, rising, until the little witness of mixed velocities was made to disgorge his portion of *omelette aux confitures de fraises.*

It was at night, however, that the *Compagnie Internationale des Wagons-Lits et des Grands Express Européens* lived up to the magic of its name. From my bed under my brother's bunk (Was he asleep? Was he there at all?), in the semidarkness of our compartment, I watched things, and parts of things, and shadows, and sections of shadows cautiously moving about and getting nowhere. The woodwork gently creaked and crackled. Near the door that led to the toilet, a dim garment on a peg and, higher up, the tassel of the blue, bivalved night light swung rhythmically. It was hard to correlate those halting approaches, that hooded stealth, with the headlong rush of the outside night, which I knew *was* rushing by, spark-streaked, illegible.

I would put myself to sleep by the simple act of identifying myself with the engine driver. A sense of drowsy well-being invaded my veins as soon as I had everything nicely arranged — the carefree passengers in their rooms enjoying the ride I was giving them, smoking, exchanging knowing smiles, nodding, dozing; the waiters and cooks and train guards (whom I had to place somewhere) carousing in the diner; and myself, goggled and begrimed, peering out of the engine cab at the tapering track, at the ruby or emerald point in the black distance. And then, in my sleep, I would see something totally different — a glass marble rolling under a grand piano or a toy engine lying on its side with its wheels still working gamely.

A change in the speed of the train sometimes interrupted the current of my sleep. Slow lights were stalking by; each, in passing, investigated the same chink, and then a luminous compass measured the shadows. Presently, the train stopped with a long-drawn Westinghousian sigh. Something (my brother's spectacles, as it proved next day) fell from above. It was marvelously exciting to move to the foot of one's bed, with part of the bedclothes following, in order to undo cautiously the catch of the window shade, which could be made to slide only halfway up, impeded as it was by the edge of the upper berth.

Like moons around Jupiter, pale moths revolved about a lone lamp. A dismembered newspaper stirred on a bench. Somewhere on the train one could hear muffled voices, somebody's comfortable cough. There was noth-

ing particularly interesting in the portion of station platform before me, and
still I could not tear myself away from it until it departed of its own accord.

Next morning, wet fields with misshapen willows along the radius of a
ditch or a row of poplars afar, traversed by a horizontal band of milky-white
mist, told one that the train was spinning through Belgium. It reached Paris
at 4 P.M.; and even if the stay was only an overnight one, I had always time
to purchase something — say, a little brass *Tour Eiffel*, rather roughly
coated with silver paint — before we boarded at noon on the following day
the Sud Express, which, on its way to Madrid, dropped us around 10 P.M. at
the La Négresse station of Biarritz, a few miles from the Spanish frontier.

II

Biarritz still retained its quiddity in those days. Dusty blackberry
bushes and weedy *terrains à vendre* bordered the road that led to our villa.
The Carlton was still being built. Some thirty-six years had to elapse before
Brigadier General Samuel McCroskey would occupy the royal suite of the
Hotel du Palais, which stands on the site of a former palace, where, in the
sixties, that incredibly agile medium, Daniel Home, is said to have been
caught stroking with his bare foot (in imitation of a ghost hand) the kind,
trustful face of Empress Eugénie. On the promenade near the Casino, an
elderly flower girl, with carbon eyebrows and a painted smile, nimbly
slipped the plump torus of a carnation into the buttonhole of an intercepted stroller whose left jowl accentuated its royal fold as he glanced down
sideways at the coy insertion of the flower.

Along the back line of the *plage*, various seaside chairs and stools supported the parents of straw-hatted children who were playing in front on the
sand. I could be seen on my knees trying to set a found comb aflame by
means of a magnifying glass. Men sported white trousers that to the eye of
today would look as if they had comically shrunk in the washing; ladies
wore, that particular season, light coats with silk-faced lapels, hats with big
crowns and wide brims, dense embroidered white veils, frill-fronted blouses,
frills at their wrists, frills on their parasols. The breeze salted one's lips. At a
tremendous pace a stray golden-orange butterfly came dashing across the
palpitating *plage*.

Additional movement and sound were provided by vendors hawking
cacahuètes, sugared violets, pistachio ice cream of a heavenly green, cachou
pellets, and huge convex pieces of dry, gritty, waferlike stuff that came from
a red barrel. With a distinctness that no later superpositions have dimmed,
I see that waffleman stomp along through deep mealy sand, with the heavy
cask on his bent back. When called, he would sling it off his shoulder by a
twist of its strap, bang it down on the sand in a Tower of Pisa position, wipe
his face with his sleeve, and proceed to manipulate a kind of arrow-and-dial
arrangement with numbers on the lid of the cask. The arrow rasped and

whirred around. Luck was supposed to fix the size of a sou's worth of wafer. The bigger the piece, the more I was sorry for him.

The process of bathing took place on another part of the beach. Professional bathers, burly Basques in black bathing suits, were there to help ladies and children enjoy the terrors of the surf. Such a *baigneur* would place you with your back to the incoming wave and hold you by the hand as the rising, rotating mass of foamy, green water violently descended upon you from behind, knocking you off your feet with one mighty wallop. After a dozen of these tumbles, the *baigneur*, glistening like a seal, would lead his panting, shivering, moistly snuffling charge landward, to the flat foreshore, where an unforgettable old woman with gray hairs on her chin promptly chose a bathing robe from several hanging on a clothesline. In the security of a little cabin, one would be helped by yet another attendant to peel off one's soggy, sand-heavy bathing suit. It would plop onto the boards, and, still shivering, one would step out of it and trample on its bluish, diffuse stripes. The cabin smelt of pine. The attendant, a hunchback with beaming wrinkles, brought a basin of steaming-hot water, in which one immersed one's feet. From him I learned, and have preserved ever since in a glass cell of my memory, that "butterfly" in the Basque language is *misericoletea* — or at least it sounded so (among the seven words I have found in dictionaries the closest approach is *micheletea*).

III

On the browner and wetter part of the *plage*, that part which at low tide yielded the best mud for castles, I found myself digging, one day, side by side with a little French girl called Colette.

She would be ten in November, I had been ten in April. Attention was drawn to a jagged bit of violent mussel shell upon which she had stepped with the bare sole of her narrow long-toed foot. No, I was not English. Her greenish eyes seemed flecked with the overflow of the freckles that covered her sharp-featured face. She wore what might now be termed a playsuit, consisting of a blue jersey with rolled-up sleeves and blue knitted shorts. I had taken her at first for a boy and then had been puzzled by the bracelet on her thin wrist and the corkscrew brown curls dangling from under her sailor cap.

She spoke in birdlike bursts of rapid twitter, mixing governess English and Parisian French. Two years before, on the same *plage*, I had been much attached to the lovely, sun-tanned little daughter of a Serbian physician; but when I met Colette, I knew at once that this was the real thing. Colette seemed to me so much stranger than all my other chance playmates at Biarritz! I somehow acquired the feeling that she was less happy than I, less loved. A bruise on her delicate, downy forearm gave rise to awful conjectures. "He pinches as bad as my mummy," she said, speaking of a crab. I evolved various schemes to save her from her parents, who were "*des bour-*

geois de Paris" as I heard somebody tell my mother with a slight shrug. I interpreted the disdain in my own fashion, as I knew that those people had come all the way from Paris in their blue-and-yellow limousine (a fashionable adventure in those days) but had drably sent Colette with her dog and governess by an ordinary coach train. The dog was a female fox terrier with bells on her collar and a most waggly behind. From sheer exuberance, she would lap up salt water out of Colette's toy pail. I remember the sail, the sunset, and the lighthouse pictured on that pail, but I cannot recall the dog's name, and this bothers me.

During the two months of our stay at Biarritz, my passion for Colette all but surpassed my passion for butterflies. Since my parents were not keen to meet hers, I saw her only on the beach; but I thought of her constantly. If I noticed she had been crying, I felt a surge of helpless anguish that brought tears to my own eyes. I could not destroy the mosquitoes that had left their bites on her frail neck, but I could, and did, have a successful fist fight with a red-haired boy who had been rude to her. She used to give me warm handfuls of hard candy. One day, as we were bending together over a starfish, and Colette's ringlets were tickling my ear, she suddenly turned toward me and kissed me on the cheek. So great was my emotion that all I could think of saying was, "You little monkey."

I had a gold coin that I assumed would pay for our elopement. Where did I want to take her? Spain? America? The mountains above Pau? "*Là-bas, là-bas, dans la montagne,*" as I had heard Carmen sing at the opera. One strange night, I lay awake, listening to the recurrent thud of the ocean and planning our flight. The ocean seemed to rise and grope in the darkness and then heavily fall on its face.

Of our actual getaway, I have little to report. My memory retains a glimpse of her obediently putting on rope-soled canvas shoes, on the lee side of a flapping tent, while I stuffed a folding butterfly net into a brown paper bag. The next glimpse is of our evading pursuit by entering a pitch-dark *cinéma* near the Casino (which, of course, was absolutely out of bounds). There we sat, holding hands across the dog, which now and then gently jingled in Colette's lap, and were shown a jerky, drizzly, but highly exciting bullfight at St. Sebástian. My final glimpse is of myself being led along the promenade by my tutor. His long legs move with a kind of ominous briskness and I can see the muscles of his grimly set jaw working under the tight skin. My bespectacled brother, aged nine, whom he happens to hold with his other hand, keeps trotting out forward to peer at me with awed curiosity, like a little owl.

Among the trivial souvenirs acquired at Biarritz before leaving, my favorite was not the small bull of black stone and not the sororous sea shell but something which now seems almost symbolic — a meerschaum penholder with a tiny peephole of crystal in its ornamental part. One held it quite close to one's eye, screwing up the other, and when one had got rid of the shimmer of one's own lashes, a miraculous photographic view of the bay and of the line of cliffs ending in a lighthouse could be seen inside.

And now a delightful thing happens. The process of recreating that penholder and the microcosm in its eyelet stimulates my memory to a last effort. I try again to recall the name of Colette's dog — and, sure enough, along those remote beaches, over the glossy evening sands of the past, where each footprint slowly fills up with sunset water, here it comes, here it comes, echoing and vibrating: Floss, Floss, Floss!

Colette was back in Paris by the time we stopped there for a day before continuing our homeward journey; and there, in a fawn park under a cold blue sky, I saw her (by arrangement between our mentors, I believe) for the last time. She carried a hoop and a short stick to drive it with, and everything about her was extremely proper and stylish in an autumnal, Parisian, *tenue-de-ville-pour-fillettes* way. She took from her governess and slipped into my brother's hand a farewell present, a box of sugar-coated almonds, meant, I knew, solely for me; and instantly she was off, tap-tapping her glinting hoop through light and shade, around and around a fountain choked with dead leaves near which I stood. The leaves mingle in my memory with the leather of her shoes and gloves, and there was, I remember, some detail in her attire (perhaps a ribbon on her Scottish cap, or the pattern of her stockings) that reminded me then of the rainbow spiral in a glass marble. I still seem to be holding that wisp of iridescence, not knowing exactly where to fit it, while she runs with her hoop ever faster around me and finally dissolves among the slender shadows cast on the graveled path by the interlaced arches of its low looped fence.

[1958]

JORGE LUIS BORGES (b. 1899), the Argentinean writer of fiction, poetry, and criticism, was born in Buenos Aires. His father, a professor of psychology, amused him in childhood with various philosophical puzzles which continued to intrigue Borges when he grew up and became a writer. Educated in Europe, he began to write as a member of a Spanish avant-garde literary movement called Ultráisme, a development of Expressionism in which image and metaphor were exaggerated to become more important than plot, character, or theme. Borges rejected this extreme view when he matured as an artist, but he remained an antirealist. After his return to Buenos Aires in 1921, he worked in the National Library, rising to the position of its director before the dictator Juan Perón hounded him out of the job for political reasons. Borges published his first book in 1923, but in the 1930s he was most active as an essayist and editor, and also wrote detective stories under other names. Then came Fictions (1944), a collection of short, often playful prose assertions in which Borges examined various ideas to show that every human effort is a "fiction." Labyrinths (1962), The Aleph and Other Stories (1970), and Doctor Brodie's Report (1972) were more collections of sketches and stories. Borges on Writing (1973) contained his views on fiction, poetry, and translation. Borges still lives in Buenos Aires, where his progressive blindness has circumscribed his life. He continues to write, and he lectured and taught in the United States until recently.

Borges has said that he writes stories for the "sheer fun of it. . . . I'm fond of short stories, but I'm far too lazy for novel writing. I'd get tired of the whole thing after writing ten or fifteen pages." He wrote his first short story, "Streetcorner Man," as a literary experiment after seeing a gangster film by Josef von Sternberg. He wanted to write a vivid, visual story, not a realistic one: "I knew quite well it was all unreal, but as I wasn't striving after reality I didn't mind." An erudite man, Borges often bases his stories on anecdotes that he thinks are interesting, as in "The End of the Duel," but the creative process of its reappearance in the form of a short story is a slow one: "If you tell me an anecdote today, it wouldn't find its way into print until some four or five years from now. . . . I have to sit back and wait, and then, when the moment comes, I have to be very receptive and try not to tamper or tinker with it."

One of the central images that appears in Borges's short fiction is the labyrinth, representing the central paradox that "the rich symmetries" of the mind, and of history and the world, end only in confusion or mystery. The sketch "Borges and I" is a reflection on the question of his own identity. Less concerned with character than with plot or situation in his fiction, Borges works into every story the idea that he, as author, is not sure of all

things, "because that's the way reality is." He is equally undogmatic when
he speculates on his practices as a writer. From Ralph Waldo Emerson he
got the idea that all literary works are one work and that all writers are one
impersonal writer, one single all-knowing "gentleman." Wondering if he
has ever created a single original line in his writing, Borges has said that if
the reader looked long enough, a source might be found for everything he
has written. Invention is just "mixing up memories. I don't think we're capable of creation in the way that God created the world."

Jorge Luis Borges

ଽଔ

THE END OF THE DUEL

– translated by Anthony Kerrigan

It's a good many years ago now that Carlos Reyles, the son of the Uru-
guayan novelist, told me the story one summer evening out in Adrogué. In
my memory, after all this time, the long chronicle of a feud and its grim
ending are mixed up with the medicinal smell of the eucalyptus trees and
the babbling voices of birds.

We sat talking, as usual, of the tangled history of our two countries,
Uruguay and the Argentine. Reyles said that probably I'd heard of Juan
Patricio Nolan, who had won quite a reputation as a brave man, a practical
joker, and a rogue. Lying, I answered yes. Though Nolan had died back in
the nineties, people still thought of him as a friend. As always happens,
however, he had his enemies as well. Reyles gave me an account of one of
Nolan's many pranks. The thing had happened a short time before the battle of Manantiales; two gauchos from Cerro Largo, Manuel Cardoso and
Carmen Silveira, were the leading characters.

How and why did they begin hating each other? How, after a century,
can one unearth the long-forgotten story of two men whose only claim to
being remembered is their last duel? A foreman of Reyles' father, whose
name was Laderecha and "who had the whiskers of a tiger," had collected
from oral accounts certain details that I transcribe now with a good deal of
misgiving, since both forgetfulness and memory are apt to be inventive.

Manuel Cardoso and Carmen Silveira had a few acres of land that
bordered each other. Like the roots of other passions, those of hatred are
mysterious, but there was talk of a quarrel over some unbranded cattle or a
free-for-all horse race in which Silveira, who was the stronger of the two,
had run Cardoso's horse off the edge of the course. Months afterward, a

long two-handed game of *truco*[1] of thirty points was to take place in the local saloon. Following almost every hand, Silveira congratulated his opponent on his skill, but in the end left him without a cent. When he tucked his winnings away in his money belt, Silveira thanked Cardoso for the lesson he had been given. It was then, I believe, that they were at the point of having it out. The game had had its ups and downs. In those rough places and in that day, man squared off against man and steel against steel. But the onlookers, who were quite a few, separated them. A peculiar twist of the story is that Manuel Cardoso and Carmen Silveira must have run across each other out in the hills on more than one occasion at sundown or at dawn, but they never actually faced each other until the very end. Maybe their poor and monotonous lives held nothing else for them than their hatred, and that was why they nursed it. In the long run, without suspecting it, each of the two became a slave to the other.

I no longer know whether the events I am about to relate are effects or causes. Cardoso, less out of love than out of boredom, took up with a neighbor girl, La Serviliana. That was all Silveira had to find out, and, after his manner, he began courting her and brought her to his shack. A few months later, finding her in the way, he threw her out. Full of spite, the woman tried to seek shelter at Cardoso's. Cardoso spent one night with her, and by the next noon packed her off. He did not want the other man's leavings.

It was around that same time, just before or just after La Serviliana, that the incident of Silveira's sheepdog took place. Silveira was very fond of the animal, and had named him Treinta y Tres, after Uruguay's thirty-three founding fathers. When the dog was found dead in a ditch, Silveira was quick to suspect who had given it poison.

Sometime during the winter of 1870, a civil war broke out between the Colorados, or Reds, who were in power, and Aparicio's Blancos, or Whites. The revolution found Silveira and Cardoso in the same crossroads saloon where they had played their game of cards. A Brazilian half-breed, at the head of a detachment of gaucho militiamen, harangued all those present, telling them that the country needed them and that the government oppression was unbearable. He handed around white badges to mark them as Blancos, and at the end of his speech, which nobody understood, everyone in the place was rounded up. They were not allowed even to say goodbye to their families.

Manuel Cardoso and Carmen Silveira accepted their fate; a soldier's life was no harder than a gaucho's. Sleeping in the open on their sheepskin saddle blankets was something to which they were already hardened, and as for killing men, that held no difficulty for hands already in the habit of killing cattle. The clinking of stirrups and weapons is one of the things always heard when cavalry enter into action. The man who is not wounded at the

---

[1] a South American card game.

outset thinks himself invulnerable. A lack of imagination freed Cardoso and Silveira from fear and from pity, although once in a while, heading a charge, fear brushed them. They were never homesick. The idea of patriotism was alien to them, and, in spite of the badges they wore on their hats, one party was to them the same as the other. During the course of marches and countermarches, they learned what a man could do with a spear, and they found out that being companions allowed them to go on being enemies. They fought shoulder to shoulder and, for all we know, did not exchange a single word.

It was in the sultry fall of 1871 that their end was to come. The fight, which would not last an hour, happened in a place whose name they never knew. (Such places are later named by historians.) On the eve of battle, Cardoso crept on all fours into his officer's tent and asked him sheepishly would he save him one of the Reds if the Whites won the next day, because up till then he had not cut anyone's throat and he wanted to know what it was like. His superior promised him that if he handled himself like a man he would be granted that favor.

The Whites outnumbered the enemy, but the Reds were better equipped and cut them down from the crown of a hill. After two unsuccessful charges that never reached the summit, the Whites' commanding officer, badly wounded, surrendered. On the very spot, at his own request, he was put to death by the knife.

The men laid down their arms. Captain Juan Patricio Nolan, who commanded the Reds, arranged the expected execution of the prisoners down to the last detail. He was from Cerro Largo himself, and knew all about the old rivalry between Silveira and Cardoso. He sent for the pair and told them, "I already know you two can't stand the sight of each other, and that for some time now you've been looking for a chance to have it out. I have good news for you. Before sundown, the two of you are going to have that chance to show who's the better man. I'm going to stand you up and have your throats cut, and then you'll run a race. God knows who'll win." The soldier who had brought them took them away.

It was not long before the news spread throughout the camp. Nolan had made up his mind that the race would close the proceedings, but the prisoners sent him a representative to tell him that they, too, wanted to be spectators and to place wagers on the outcome. Nolan, who was an understanding man, let himself be convinced. The bets were laid down — money, riding gear, spears, sabers, and horses. In due time they would be handed over to the widows and next of kin. The heat was unusual. So that no one would miss his siesta, things were delayed until four o'clock. Nolan, in the South American style, kept them waiting another hour. He was probably discussing the campaign with his officers, his aide shuttling in and out with the maté kettle.

Both sides of the dirt road in front of the tents were lined with prisoners, who, to make things easier, squatted on the ground with their hands tied behind their backs. A few of them relieved their feelings in a torrent of swearwords, one went over and over the beginning of the Lord's Prayer, almost all were stunned. Of course, they would not smoke. They no longer cared about the race now, but they all watched.

"They'll be cutting my throat on me, too," one of them said, showing his envy.

"Sure, but along with the mob," said his neighbor.

"Same as you," the first man snapped back.

With his saber, a sergeant drew a line in the dust across the road. Silveira's and Cardoso's wrists had been untied so that they could run freely. A space of some five yards was between them. Each man toed the mark. A couple of the officers asked the two not to let them down because everyone had placed great faith in them, and the sums they had bet on them came to quite a pile.

It fell to Silveira's lot to draw as executioner the mulatto Nolan, whose forefathers had no doubt been slaves of the captain's family and therefore bore his name. Cardoso drew the Red's official cutthroat, a man from Corrientes well along in years, who, to comfort a condemned man, would pat him on the shoulder and tell him, "Take heart, friend. Women go through far worse when they give birth."

Their torsos bent forward, the two eager men did not look at each other. Nolan gave the signal.

The mulatto, swelling with pride to be at the center of attention, overdid his job and opened a showy slash that ran from ear to ear; the man from Corrientes did his with a narrow slit. Spurts of blood gushed from the men's throats. They dashed forward a number of steps before tumbling face down. Cardoso, as he fell, stretched out his arms. Perhaps never aware of it, he had won.

[1973]

Jorge Luis Borges

༞

BORGES AND I

– translated by Anthony Kerrigan

Things happen to him, the other one, to Borges. I stroll about Buenos Aires and stop, almost mechanically now perhaps, to look at the arch of an entranceway and the ironwork gate; news of Borges reaches me in the mail and I see his name on an academic ballot or in a biographical dictionary. I like hourglasses, maps, eighteenth-century typography, etymologies, the taste of coffee, and Robert Louis Stevenson's prose; he shares these preferences, but with a vanity that turns them into the attributes of an actor. It would be an exaggeration to say that our relationship is a hostile one; I live, I go on living, so that Borges may contrive his literature; and that literature justifies me. I do not find it hard to admit that he has achieved some valid pages, but these pages can not save me, perhaps because what is good no longer belongs to anyone, not even to him, the other one, but to the language or to tradition. In any case, I am destined to perish, definitively, and only some instant of me may live on in him. Little by little, I yield him ground, the whole terrain, though I am quite aware of his perverse habit of magnifying and falsifying. Spinoza realized that all things strive to persist in their own nature: the stone eternally wishes to be stone and the tiger a tiger. I shall subsist in Borges, not in myself (assuming I am someone), and yet I recognize myself less in his books than in many another, or than in the intricate flourishes played on a guitar. Years ago I tried to free myself from him, and I went from the mythologies of the city suburbs to games with time and infinity, but now those games belong to Borges, and I will have to think up something else. Thus is my life a flight, and I lose everything, and everything belongs to oblivion, or to him.

I don't know which one of the two of us is writing this page.

[1961]

SEAN O'FAOLAIN (b. 1900), the Irish short story writer, was born Sean Whelan in county Cork. An ardent nationalist, he adopted the Gaelic variant of his name as part of a personal campaign to support the values of the Irish past. While still a teenager he fought in the Irish Revolution (1918–1921), and later served as director of publicity for the Irish Republican Army. Then he returned to school. He earned two M.A. degrees, one from the National University of Ireland and another from Harvard University, but he says that his education has been "mainly by good conversation." A teacher of Gaelic and Anglo-Irish literature in the United States and England, he returned to Ireland after the success of his first book of short stories, Midsummer Night Madness and Other Stories (1932), and his novel, A Nest of Simple Folk (1933), made it possible for him to devote himself to writing full time. He writes travel books and biographies as well as fiction, and in the 1950s his critical studies in The Short Story (1951) and his essays on modern novelists in The Vanishing Hero (1957) further strengthened his reputation. In recent years collections of his finely crafted short stories, like The Heat of the Sun (1966) and Selected Stories (1978), continue to appear regularly in America, establishing him as a contemporary master of the genre.

In O'Faolain's early short stories, he wrote about his experience as a revolutionary, taking as his subject Irish life from the time of the Easter Uprising in 1916 to the establishment of the Irish Free State five years later. These stories had a romantic view of the world, and he was praised by Malcolm Cowley for his "power of suggestion and vague evocation" of the atmosphere of those times. In his second collection, A Purse of Coppers (1938), his fiction had a more pessimistic viewpoint, depicting the plight of the individual in a stagnant, postrevolutionary society. His compassion grew as he developed as a writer, and in more recent years O'Faolain has often humorously described the contradictory nature of the modern Irishman, not particularly concerned with social or moral issues. In "How to Write a Short Story," from his collection Foreign Affairs and Other Stories (1976), O'Faolain makes fun of the earnest efforts of an aspiring writer of fiction to apply the "rules" of constructing short stories to real-life experience.

Sean O'Faolain

How to Write a Short Story

One wet January night, some six months after they had met, young Morgan Myles, our county librarian, was seated in the doctor's pet armchair, on one side of the doctor's fire, digesting the pleasant memory of a lavish dinner, while leafing the pages of a heavy photographic album and savoring a warm brandy. From across the hearth the doctor was looking admiringly at his long, ballooning Gaelic head when, suddenly, Morgan let out a cry of delight.

"Good Lord, Frank! There's a beautiful boy! One of Raphael's little angels." He held up the open book for Frank to see. "Who was he?"

The doctor looked across at it and smiled.

"Me. Aged twelve. At school in Mount Saint Bernard."

"That's in England. I didn't know you went to school in England."

"Alas!"

Morgan glanced down at twelve, and up at sixty.

"It's not possible, Frank!"

The doctor raised one palm six inches from the arm of his chair and let it fall again.

"It so happened that I was a ridiculously beautiful child."

"Your mother must have been gone about you. And," with a smile, "the girls too."

"I had no interest in girls. Nor in boys either, though by your smile you seem to say so.[1] But there was one boy who took a considerable interest in me."

Morgan at once lifted his nose like a pointer. At this period of his life he had rested from writing poetry and was trying to write short stories. For weeks he had read nothing but Maupassant. He was going to out-Maupassant Maupassant. He was going to write stories that would make poor old Maupassant turn as green as the grass on his grave.

[1] The doctor is paraphrasing Hamlet's line to Rosencrantz and Guildenstern: "Man delights not me; no, nor woman neither, though by your smiling you seem to say so" (*Hamlet* II.ii. 300–301).

"Tell me about it," he ordered. "Tell me every single detail."

"There is nothing to it. Or at any rate, as I now know, nothing abnormal. But, at that age!" — pointing with his pipestem. "I was as innocent as . . . well, as innocent as a child of twelve! Funny that you should say that about Raphael's angels. At my preparatory school here — it was a French order — Sister Angélique used to call me her *petit ange*, because, she said, I had '*une tête d'ange et une voix d'ange.*'[2] She used to make me sing solo for them at Benediction, dressed in a red soutane, a white lacy surplice and a purple bow tie.

"After that heavenly place Mount Saint Bernard was ghastly. Mobs of howling boys. Having to play games; rain, hail or snow. I was a funk at games. When I'd see a fellow charging me at rugger I'd at once pass the ball or kick for touch. I remember the coach cursing me. 'Breen, you're a bloody little coward, there are boys half your weight on this field who wouldn't do a thing like that.' And the constant discipline. The constant priestly distrust. Watching us like jail warders."

"Can you give me an example of that?" Morgan begged. "Mind you, you could have had that, too, in Ireland. Think of Clongowes. It turns up in Joyce. And he admired the Jesuits!"

"Yes, I can give you an example. It will show you how innocent I was. A month after I entered Mount Saint Bernard I was so miserable that I decided to write to my mother to take me away. I knew that every letter had to pass under the eyes of the Prefect of Discipline, so I wrote instead to Sister Angélique asking her to pass on the word to my mother. The next day old Father George Lee — he's long since dead — summoned me to his study. 'Breen!' he said darkly, holding up my unfortunate letter, 'you have tried to do a very underhand thing, something for which I could punish you severely. Why did you write this letter *in French?*'" The doctor sighed. "I was a very truthful little boy. My mother had brought me up to be truthful simply by never punishing me for anything I honestly owned up to. I said, 'I wrote it in French, sir, because I hoped you wouldn't be able to understand it.' He turned his face away from me but I could tell from his shoulders that he was laughing. He did not cane me, he just tore up the letter, told me never to try to deceive him again, and sent me packing with my tail between my legs."

"The old bastard!" Morgan said sympathetically, thinking of the lonely little boy.

"No, no! He was a nice old man. And a good classical scholar, I later discovered. But that day as I walked down the long corridor, with all its photographs of old boys who had made good, I felt the chill of the prison walls!"

"But this other boy?" Morgan insinuated. "Didn't his friendship help at all?"

---

[2] "an angel's head and an angel's voice."

The doctor rose and stood with his back to the fire staring fixedly in front of him.

(He rises, Morgan thought, his noble eyes shadowed. No! God damn it, no! Not noble. Shadowed? Literary word. Pensive? Blast it, that's worse. 'Pensive eye!' Romantic fudge. His eyes are dark as a rabbit's droppings. That's got it! In his soul. . . . Oh, Jase!)

"Since I was so lonely I suppose he *must* have helped. But he was away beyond me. Miles above me. He was a senior. He was the captain of the school."

"His name," Morgan suggested, "was, perhaps, Cyril?"

"We called him Bruiser. I would rather not tell you his real name."

"Because he is still alive," Morgan explained, "and remembers you vividly to this day."

"He was killed at the age of twenty."

"In the war! In the heat of the battle."

"By a truck in Oxford. Two years after he went up there from Mount Saint Bernard. I wish I knew what happened to him in those two years. I can only hope that before he died he found a girl."

"A girl? I don't follow. Oh yes! Of course, yes, I take your point."

(He remembers with tenderness? No. With loving kindness! No! With benevolence? Dammit, no! With his wonted chivalry to women? But he remembered irritably that the old man sitting opposite to him was a bachelor. And a virgin?)

"What happened between the pair of ye? 'Brothers and companions in tribulation on the isle that is called Patmos?' "

The doctor snorted.

"Brothers? I have told you I was twelve. Bruiser was eighteen. The captain of the school. Captain of the rugby team. Captain of the tennis team. First in every exam. Tops. Almost a man. I looked up to him as a shining hero. I never understood what he saw in me. I have often thought since that he may have been amused by my innocence. Like the day he said to me, 'I suppose, Rosy,' that was my nickname, I had such rosy cheeks, 'suppose you think you are the best-looking fellow in the school?' I said, 'No, I don't, Bruiser. I thing there's one fellow better-looking than me, Jimmy Simcox.' "

"Which he, of course, loyally refused to believe!"

The old doctor laughed heartily.

"He laughed heartily."

"A queer sense of humor!"

"I must confess I did not at the time see the joke. Another day he said, 'Would you like, Rosy, to sleep with me?' "

Morgan's eyes opened wide. Now they were getting down to it.

"I said, 'Oh, Bruiser, I don't think you would like that at all. I'm an awful chatterbox in bed. Whenever I sleep with my Uncle Tom he's always saying to me, "Will you for God's sake, stop your bloody gabble and let me sleep." ' He laughed for five minutes at that."

"I don't see much to laugh at. He should have sighed. I will make him sigh. Your way makes him sound a queer hawk. And nothing else happened between ye but this sort of innocent gabble? Or are you keeping something back? Hang it, Frank, there's no story at all in this!"

"Oh, he used sometimes take me on his lap. Stroke my bare knee. Ruffle my hair. Kiss me."

"How did you like that?"

"I made nothing of it. I was used to being kissed by my elders — my mother, my bachelor uncles, Sister Angélique, heaps of people." The doctor laughed. "I laugh at it now. But his first kiss! A few days before, a fellow named Calvert said to me, 'Hello, pretty boy, would you give me a smuck?' I didn't know what a smuck was. I said, 'I'm sorry, Calvert, but I haven't got one.' The story must have gone around the whole school. The next time I was alone with Bruiser he taunted me. I can hear his angry, toploftical English voice. 'You are an innocent mug, Rosy! A smuck is a kiss. Would you let *me* kiss you?' I said, 'Why not?' He put his arm around my neck in a vice and squashed his mouth to my mouth, hard, sticky. I thought I'd choke. 'O Lord,' I thought, 'this is what he gets from playing rugger. This is a rugger kiss.' And, I was thinking, 'His poor mother! Having to put up with this from him every morning and every night.' When he let me go, he said, 'Did you like that?' Not wanting to hurt his feelings I said, imitating his English voice, 'It was all right, Bruiser! A bit like ruggah, isn't it?' He laughed again and said, 'All right? Well, never mind. I shan't rush you.' "

Morgan waved impatiently.

"Look here, Frank! I want to get the background to all this. The telling detail, you know. 'The little actual facts' as Stendhal called them. You said the priests watched you all like hawks. The constant discipline, you said. The constant priestly distrust. How did ye ever manage to meet alone?"

"It was very simple. He was the captain of the school. The apple of their eye. He could fool them. He knew the ropes. After all, he had been there for five years. I remember old Father Lee saying to me once, 'You are a very lucky boy, Breen, it's not every junior that the captain of the school would take an interest in. You ought to feel very proud of his friendship.' We used to have a secret sign about our meetings. Every Wednesday morning when he would be walking out of chapel, leading the procession, if that day was all right for us he used to put his right hand in his pocket. If for any reason it was not all right he would put his left hand in his pocket. I was always on the aisle of the very last row. Less than the dust. Watching for the sign like a hawk. We had a double check. I'd then find a note in my overcoat in the cloakroom. All it ever said was, 'The same place.' He was very careful. He only took calculated risks. If he had lived he would have made a marvelous politician, soldier, or diplomat."

"And where would ye meet? I know! By the river. Or in the woods? 'Enter these enchanted woods ye who dare!' "

"No river. No woods. There was a sort of dirty old trunk room upstairs, under the roof, never used. A rather dark place with only one dormer window. It had double doors. He used to lock the outside one. There was a big cupboard there — for cricket bats or something. 'If anyone comes,' he told me, 'you will have time to pop in there.' He had it all worked out. Cautious man! I had to be even more cautious, stealing up there alone. One thing that made it easier for us was that I was so much of a junior and he was so very much of a senior, because, you see, those innocent guardians of ours had the idea that the real danger lay between the seniors and the middles, or the middles and the juniors, but never between the seniors and the juniors. They kept the seniors and the middles separated by iron bars and stone walks. Any doctor could have told them that in cold climates like ours the really dangerous years are not from fifteen up but from eighteen to anything, up or down. It simply never occurred to them that any senior could possibly be interested in any way in a junior. I, of course, had no idea of what he was up to. I had not even reached the age of puberty. In fact I honestly don't believe he quite knew himself what he was up to."

"But, dammit, you must have had some idea! The secrecy, the kissing, alone, up there in that dim, dusty box room, not a sound but the wind in the slates."

"Straight from the nuns? *Un petit ange?* I thought it was all just pally fun."

Morgan clapped his hands.

"I've got it! An idyll! Looking out dreamily over the fields from that dusty dormer window? That's it, that's the ticket. Did you ever read that wonderful story by Maupassant — it's called *An Idyll* — about two young peasants meeting in a train, a poor, hungry young fellow who has just left home, and a girl with her first baby. He looked so famished that she took pity on him like a mother, opened her blouse and gave him her breast. When he finished he said, 'That was my first meal in three days.' Frank! You are telling the most beautiful story I ever heard in my whole life."

"You think so?" the doctor said morosely. "I think he was going through hell all that year. At eighteen? On the threshold of manhood? In love with a child of twelve? That is, if you will allow that a youth of eighteen may suffer as much from love as a man twenty years older. To me the astonishing thing is that he did so well all that year at his studies and at sports. Killing the pain of it, I suppose? Or trying to? But the in between? What went on in the poor devil in between?"

Morgan sank back dejectedly.

"I'm afraid this view of the course doesn't appeal to me at all. All I can see is the idyll idea. After all, I mean, nothing happened!"

Chafing, he watched his friend return to his armchair, take another pipe from the rack, fill it slowly and ceremoniously from a black tobacco jar and light it with care. Peering through the nascent smoke, Morgan leaned slowly forward.

"Or did something happen?"

"Yes," the doctor resumed quietly. "Every year, at the end of the last term, the departing captain was given a farewell dinner. I felt sad that morning because we had not met for a whole week. And now, in a couple of days we would be scattered and I would never see him again."

"Ha, ha! You see, you too were in love!"

"Of course I was, I was hooked," the doctor said with more than a flicker of impatience. "However. . . . That Wednesday as he passed me in the chapel aisle he put his right hand in his pocket. I belted off at once to my coat hanging in the cloakroom and found his note. It said, 'At five behind the senior tennis court.' I used always chew up his *billet doux* immediately I read it. He had ordered me to. When I read this one my mouth went so dry with fear that I could hardly swallow it. He had put me in an awful fix. To meet alone in the box room was risky enough, but for anybody to climb over the wall into the seniors' grounds was unheard of. If I was caught I would certainly be flogged. I might very well be expelled. And what would my mother and father think of me then? On top of all I was in duty bound to be with all the other juniors at prep at five o'clock, and to be absent from studies without permission was another crime of the first order. After lunch I went to the Prefect of Studies and asked him to excuse me from prep because I had an awful headache. He wasn't taken in one bit. He just ordered me to be at my place in prep as usual. The law! Orders! Tyranny! There was only one thing for it, to dodge prep, knowing well that whatever else happened later I would pay dearly for it."

"And what about him? He knew all this. And he knew that if *he* was caught they couldn't do anything to him. The captain of the school? Leaving in a few days? It was very unmanly of him to put you to such a risk. His character begins to emerge, and not very pleasantly. Go on!"

The doctor did not need the encouragement. He looked like a small boy sucking a man's pipe.

"I waited until the whole school was at study and then I crept out into the empty grounds. At that hour the school, the grounds, everywhere, was as silent as the grave. Games over. The priests at their afternoon tea. Their charges safely under control. I don't know how I managed to get over that high wall, but when I fell scrambling down on the other side, there he was. 'You're bloody late,' he said crossly. 'How did you get out of prep? What excuse did you give?' When I told him he flew into a rage. 'You little fool!' he growled. 'You've balloxed it all up. They'll know you dodged. They'll give you at least ten on the backside for this.' He was carrying a cane. Seniors at Saint Bernard's did carry walking sticks. I'd risked so much for him, and now he was so angry with me that I burst into tears. He put his arms around me — I thought, to comfort me — but after that all I remember from that side of the wall was him pulling down my short pants, holding me tight, I felt something hard, like his cane, and the next thing I knew I was wet. I thought I was bleeding. I thought he was gone mad. When I smelled whiskey I thought, 'He is trying to kill me.' 'Now run,' he ordered me, 'and get back to prep as fast as you can.' "

Morgan covered his eyes with his hand.

"He shoved me up to the top of the wall. As I peered around I heard his footsteps running away. I fell down into the shrubs on the other side and I immediately began to vomit and vomit. There was a path beside the shrubs. As I lay there puking I saw a black-soutaned priest approaching slowly along the path. He was an old, old priest named Constable. I did not stir. Now, I felt, I'm for it. This is the end. I am certain he saw me but he passed by as if he had not seen me. I got back to the study hall, walked up to the Prefect's desk and told him I was late because I had been sick. I must have looked it because he at once sent me to the matron in the infirmary. She took my temperature and put me to bed. It was summer. I was the only inmate of the ward. One of those evenings of prolonged daylight."

"You poor little bugger!" Morgan groaned in sympathy.

"A detail comes back to me. It was the privilege of seniors attending the captain's dinner to send down gifts to the juniors' table — sweets, fruit, a cake, for a younger brother or some special protégé. Bruiser ordered a whole white blancmange with a rosy cherry on top of it to be sent to me. He did not know I was not in the dining hall so the blancmange was brought up to me in the infirmary. I vomited again when I saw it. The matron, with my more than ready permission, took some of it for herself and sent the rest back to the juniors' table, 'with Master Breen's compliments.' I am sure it was gobbled greedily. In the morning the doctor saw me and had me sent home to Ireland immediately."

"Passing the buck," said Morgan sourly, and they both looked at a coal that tinkled from the fire into the fender.

The doctor peered quizzically at the hissing coal.

"Well?" he slurred around his pipestem. "There is your lovely idyll."

Morgan did not lift his eyes from the fire. Under a downdraft from the chimney a few specks of gray ashes moved clockwise on the worn hearth. He heard a car hissing past the house on the wet macadam. His eyebrows had gone up over his spectacles in two Gothic arches.

"I am afraid," he said at last, "it is no go. Not even a Maupassant could have made a story out of it. And Chekhov wouldn't have wanted to try. Unless the two boys lived on, and on, and met years afterward in Moscow or Yalta or somewhere, each with a wife and a squad of kids, and talked of everything except their schooldays. You are sure you never did hear of him, or from him, again?"

"Never! Apart from the letter he sent with the blancmange and the cherry."

Morgan at once leaped alive.

"A letter? Now we are on to something! What did he say to you in it? Recite every word of it to me! Every syllable. I'm sure you have not forgotten one word of it. No!" he cried excitedly. "You have kept it. Hidden away somewhere all these years. Friendship surviving everything. Fond memories of. . . ."

The doctor sniffed.

"I tore it into bits unread and flushed it down the W.C."

"Oh, God blast you, Frank!" Morgan roared. "That was the climax of the whole thing. The last testament. The final revelation. The summing up. The *document humain*. And you 'just tore it up!' Let's reconstruct it. 'Dearest Rosy, As long as I live I will never forget your innocence, your sweetness, your. . . .' "

"My dear boy!" the doctor protested mildly. "I am sure he wrote nothing of the sort. He was much too cautious, and even the captain was not immune from censorship. Besides, sitting in public glory at the head of the table? It was probably a place-card with something on the lines of, 'All my sympathy, sorry, better luck next term.' A few words, discreet, that I could translate any way I liked."

Morgan raised two despairing arms.

"If that was all the damned fellow could say to you after that appalling experience, he was a character of no human significance whatever, a shallow creature, a mere agent, a catalyst, a cad. The story becomes your story."

"I must admit I have always looked on it in that way. After all it did happen to me. . . . Especially in view of the sequel."

"Sequel? What sequel? I can't have sequels. In a story you always have to observe unity of time, place, and action. Everything happening at the one time, in the same place, between the same people. *The Necklace. Boule de Suif. The Maison Tellier.* The examples are endless. What was this bloody sequel?"

The doctor puffed thoughtfully.

"In fact there were two sequels. Even three sequels. And all of them equally important."

"In what way were they important?"

"It was rather important to me that after I was sent home I was in the hospital for four months. I could not sleep. I had constant nightmares, always the same one — me running through a wood and him running after me with his cane. I could not keep down my food. Sweating hot. Shivering cold. The vomiting was recurrent. I lost weight. My mother was beside herself with worry. She brought doctor after doctor to me, and only one of them spotted it, an old, blind man from Dublin named Whiteside. He said, 'That boy has had some kind of shock,' and in private he asked me if some boy, or man, had interfered with me. Of course, I denied it hotly."

"I wish I was a doctor," Morgan grumbled. "So many writers were doctors. Chekhov. William Carlos Williams. Somerset Maugham. A. J. Cronin."

The doctor ignored the interruption.

"The second sequel was that when I at last went back to Mount Saint Bernard my whole nature changed. Before that I had been dreamy and idle. During my last four years at school I became their top student. I suppose psychologists would say nowadays that I compensated by becoming extroverted. I became a crack cricket player. In my final year I was the college champion at billiards. I never became much good at rugger but I no longer minded playing it and I wasn't all that bad. If I'd been really tops at it, or at boxing, or swimming I might very well have ended up as captain of the school. Like him."

He paused for so long that Morgan became alerted again.

"And the third sequel?" he prompted.

"I really don't know why I am telling you all this. I have never told a soul about it before. Even still I find it embarrassing to think about, let alone to talk about. When I left Mount Saint Bernard and had taken my final at the College of Surgeons I went on to Austria to continue my medical studies. In Vienna I fell in with a young woman. The typical blonde fräulein, handsome, full of life, outgoing, wonderful physique, what you might call an outdoor girl, free as the wind, frank as the daylight. She taught me skiing. We used to go mountain climbing together. I don't believe she knew the meaning of the word fear. She was great fun and the best of company. Her name was Brigitte. At twenty-six she was already a woman of the world. I was twenty-four, and as innocent of women as . . . as. . . ."

To put him at his ease Morgan conceded his own embarrassing confession.

"As I am, at twenty-four."

"You might think that what I am going to mention could not happen to a doctor, however young but, on our first night in bed, immediately she touched my body I vomited. I pretended to her that I had eaten something that upset me. You can imagine how nervous I felt all through the next day wondering what was going to happen that night. Exactly the same thing happened that night. I was left with no option. I told her the whole miserable story of myself and Bruiser twelve years before. As I started to tell her I had no idea how she was going to take it. Would she leave me in disgust? Be coldly sympathetic? Make a mock of me? Instead, she became wild with what I can only call gleeful curiosity. 'Tell me more, *mein Schätzerl*,' she begged. 'Tell me everything! What exactly did he do to you? I want to know it all. This is *wunderbar*. Tell me! Oh do tell me!' I did tell her, and on the spot everything became perfect between us. We made love like Trojans. That girl saved my sanity."

In a silence Morgan gazed at him. Then coldly —

"Well, of course, this is another story altogether. I mean I don't see how I can possibly blend these two themes together. I mean no writer worth his salt can say things like, 'Twelve long years passed over his head. Now read on.' I'd have to leave her out of it. She is obviously irrelevant to the main theme. Whatever the hell the main theme is." Checked by an ironical glance he poured the balm. "Poor Frank! I foresee it all. You adored her. You wanted madly to marry her. Her parents objected. You were star-crossed lovers. You had to part."

"I never thought of marrying the bitch. She had the devil's temper. We had terrible rows. Once we threw plates at one another. We would have parted anyway. She was a lovely girl but quite impossible. Anyway, toward the end of that year my father fell seriously ill. Then my mother fell ill. Chamberlain was in Munich that year. Everybody knew the war was coming. I came back to Ireland that autumn. For keeps."

"But you tried again and again to find out what happened to her. And failed. She was swallowed up in the fire and smoke of war. I don't care what you say, Frank, you *must* have been heartbroken."

The doctor lifted a disinterested shoulder.

"A student's love affair? Of thirty and more years ago?"

No! He had never enquired. Anyway if she was alive now what would she be but a fat, blowsy old baggage of sixty-three? Morgan, though shocked, guffawed dutifully. There was the real Maupassant touch. In his next story a touch like that! The clock on the mantelpiece whirred and began to tinkle the hour. Morgan opened the album for a last look at the beautiful child. Dejectedly he slammed it shut, and rose.

"There is too much in it," he declared. "Too many strands. Your innocence. His ignorance. Her worldliness. Your forgetting her. Remembering him. Confusion and bewilderment. The ache of loss? Loss? *Lost Innocence?* Would that be a theme? But nothing rounds itself off. You are absolutely certain you never heard of him again after that day behind the tennis courts?"

They were both standing now. The rain brightly spotted the midnight window.

"In my first year in Surgeons, about three years after Bruiser was killed, I lunched one day with his mother and my mother at the Shelbourne Hotel in Dublin. By chance they had been educated at the same convent in England. They talked about him. My mother said, 'Frank here knew him in Mount Saint Bernard.' His mother smiled condescendingly at me. 'No, Frank. You were too young to have met him.' 'Well,' I said, 'I did actually speak to him a couple of times, and he was always very kind to me.' She said sadly, 'He was kind to everybody. Even to perfect strangers.' "

Morgan thrust out an arm and a wildly wagging finger.

"Now, *there* is a possible shape! Strangers to begin. Strangers to end! What a title! *Perfect Strangers.*" He blew out a long, impatient breath and shook his head. "But that is a fourth sequel! I'll think about it," as if he were bestowing a great favor. "But it isn't a story as it stands. I would have to fake it up a lot. Leave out things. Simplify. Mind you, I could still see it as an idyll. Or I could if only you hadn't torn up his last, farewell letter, which I still don't believe at all said what you said it said. If only we had that letter I bet you any money we could haul in the line and land our fish."

The doctor knocked out the dottle of his pipe against the fireguard, and throating a yawn looked at the fading fire.

"I am afraid I have been boring you with my reminiscences."

"Not at all, Frank! By no means! I was most interested in your story. And I do honestly mean what I said. I really will think about it. I promise. Who was it," he asked in the hall as he shuffled into his overcoat and his muffler and moved out to the wet porch, the tail of his raincoat rattling in the wind, "said that the two barbs of childhood are its innocence and its ignorance?" He failed to remember. He threw up his hand. "Ach, to hell with it for a story! It's all too bloody convoluted for me. And to hell with Maupassant, too! That vulgarian oversimplified everything. And he's full of melodrama. A besotted Romantic at heart! Like all the bloody French."

The doctor peeped out at him through three inches of door. Morgan, standing with his back to the arrowy night, suddenly lit up as if a spotlight had shone on his face.

"I know what I'll do with it!" he cried. "I'll turn it into a poem about a seashell!"

"About a seashell?"

"Don't you remember?" In his splendid voice Morgan chanted above the rain and wind: — 'A curious child holding to his ear/ The convolutions of a smoothlipped seashell/ To which, in silence hushed . . . ' How the hell does it go? ' . . . his very soul listened to the murmurings of his native sea.' It's as clear as daylight, man! You! Me! Everyone! Always wanting to launch a boat in search of some far-off golden sands. And something or somebody always holding us back. 'The Curious Child.' *There's* a title!"

"Ah, well!" the doctor said, peering at him blankly. "There it is! As your friend Maupassant might have said, 'C'est la vie!' "

"*La vie!*" Morgan roared, now on the gravel beyond the porch, indifferent to the rain pelting on his bare head. "That trollop? She's the one who always bitches up everything. No, Frank! For me there is only one fountain of truth, one beauty, one perfection. Art, Frank! Art! And bugger *la vie!*"

At the untimely verb the doctor's drooping eyelids shot wide open.

"It is a view," he said courteously and let his hand be shaken fervently a dozen times.

"I can never repay you, Frank. A splendid dinner. A wonderful story. Marvelous inspiration. I must fly. I'll be writing it all night!" — and vanished head down through the lamplit rain, one arm uplifted triumphantly behind him.

The doctor slowly closed his door, carefully locked it, bolted it, tested it, and prudently put its chain in place. He returned to his sitting room, picked up the cinder that had fallen into the hearth and tossed it back into the remains of his fire, then stood, hand on mantelpiece, looking down at it.

What a marvelous young fellow! He would be tumbling and tossing all night over that story. Then he would be around in the morning apologizing, and sympathizing, saying, "Of course, Frank, I do realize that it was a terribly sad experience for both of you."

Gazing at the ashes his whole being filled with memory after memory like that empty vase in his garden being slowly filled by drops of rain.

[1976]

LANGSTON HUGHES (1902–1967) *was born in Joplin, Missouri. He spent most of his childhood living with his grandmother in Lawrence, Kansas, and his first contact with a large number of other blacks came when he attended high school in Cleveland in 1916. In his high school English classes he read the poetry of Carl Sandburg and Edgar Lee Masters, and he published several poems in the literary magazine. Hughes's father was a college graduate who persuaded him to study engineering at Columbia University in 1921, but after only one year Hughes abandoned his studies and signed on as a mess boy on a ship that took him to Africa and Europe. He was determined to be a writer. He had begun to publish his poetry in the NAACP magazine* The Crisis, *including what was to become one of his best-known poems, "The Negro Speaks of Rivers" (which he had written as a teenager). His career as a poet was launched a few years later with his book* The Weary Blues *(1926), poems about a Harlem musician who plays the piano all night and then goes home to sleep. After five years of writing and travel, Hughes took a bachelor's degree from Lincoln University in Pennsylvania, and then settled in New York. He became an important member of the literary coterie including Countee Cullen, Zora Hurston, Nella Larsen, Claude McKay, and Jean Toomer, that helped form the Harlem Renaissance of the late 1920s, a group of writers who emphasized Negro topics — the African heritage, the slave era, and life in Harlem. Hughes wrote plays as well as poetry, and was active in the organization of black theater companies in New York, Los Angeles, and Chicago. His most famous play,* Tambourines to Glory, *was adapted from his novel of the same name in 1963. Exhibiting an impressive versatility and productivity in his career, Hughes also wrote newspaper columns for the Chicago* Defender *and the New York* Post, *and edited twenty-eight collections of African and Negro poetry and folklore in addition to writing his own plays, translations, poetry, and fiction.*

Hughes's interest in fiction developed later than his talent for poetry. As he described it in his autobiography I Wonder As I Wander *(1956), he was traveling in the Soviet Union when he picked up a paperback copy of a collection of short stories he had never read before by D. H. Lawrence. He was so impressed with them — especially with "The Rocking Horse Winner" — that a night or two later he sat down at his well-traveled portable typewriter to try to write stories of his own. "If D. H. Lawrence can write such psychologically powerful accounts of folks in England, that send shivers up and down my spine," he reasoned, "maybe I could write stories like his about folks in America." Hughes sent his first three stories from Russia to his literary agent in New York, and by the time he returned to the*

United States all three had been sold to popular magazines. "The money came in handy. And once started, I wrote almost nothing but short stories."

Hughes found it easy to write conventional short stories — his early stories were published as The Ways of White Folks *in 1934 — but his most original work in this literary form can be seen in his stories about Jesse B. Simple, a character he created in 1942 when he wrote columns for the Chicago* Defender. *Jesse is a black working man living in Harlem, whose conversations with the middle-class, intellectual narrator are occasions for exhibiting his down-home blend of urban cynicism and genial mother wit on a wide variety of timely topics, such as unemployment, war, divorce, women's rights, and education for blacks.* Simple Speaks His Mind *(1950),* Simple Takes a Wife *(1952),* Simple Stakes a Claim *(1957), and* The Best of Simple *(1961) were the collections of stories about this popular character published in Hughes's lifetime, written in a supple blend of Simple's colloquial speech and the narrator's standard English.*

Langston Hughes

♋

CONVERSATION ON THE CORNER

It was the summer the young men in Harlem stopped wearing their hair straightened, oiled or conked, and started having it cut short, leaving it natural, standing up about an inch or two in front in a kind of brush. When Simple took off his hat to fan his brow, I saw by the light of the neon sign outside the Wishing Well Bar that he had gotten a new haircut.

"What happened to your head?" I asked.

"Cut short," said Simple. "My baby likes to run her fingers through it. This gives her a better chance."

"As much as you hang out on this corner," I said, "I don't see when she has much of a chance."

"You know Joyce is a working woman," said Simple, "also decent. She won't come to see me, so I goes to see her early. I already paid my nightly call."

"I understand that you work also and it's midnight now. When do you sleep?"

"In between times," Simple answered, lighting a butt and taking a long draw. "Sleep don't worry me. I just hate to go back to my little old furnished room alone. How about you? What're you doing up so late?"

"Observing life for literary purposes. Gathering material, contemplating how people play so desperately when the stakes are so little."

"What do you mean by all that language?" asked Simple.

"I mean there are very few people of substance out late at night — mostly hustlers. And all the hustlers around here hustle for such *small* change."

"They will not hustle off of me," said Simple. "No, sir! Somebody is always trying to take disadvantage of me. The other night I went to a poker game and lost Twelve Bucks. They was playing partners, dealing seconds, stripping the deck and palming, so all I could do was lose. I could not win — so I prefer to drink it up."

"At least you'll have it *in* you," I said. "But why do you imbibe practically every night?"

"Because I like it. I also drink because I don't have anything better to do."

"Why don't you read a book," I asked, "go to a show or a dance?"

"I do not read a book because I don't understand books, daddy-o. I do not go to the show because you see nothing but white folks on the screen. And I do not go to a dance because if I do, I get in trouble with Joyce, who is one girl friend I respect."

"Trouble with Joyce?"

"Yes," said Simple, leaning on the mailbox so no one could mail a letter. "Joyce thinks every time I put my arms around a woman to dance with her, I am hugging the woman! Now, how can you dance with a woman without hugging her? I see Joyce enough as it is. I drink because I am lonesome."

"Lonesome? How can you be lonesome when you've got plenty of friends, also girl friends?"

"I'm lonesome inside myself."

"How do you explain that?"

"I do not know," said Simple, "but that is why I drink. I don't do nobody no harm, do I? You don't see me out here hustling off nobody, do you? I am not mugging and cheating and robbing, am I?"

"You're not."

"So I don't see why I shouldn't take a beer now and then."

"*When* did you say?"

"Now," said Simple.

"You said 'now and then,' which is putting it mildly."

"I meant *now*," said Simple, "*right now* since I have met up with you, old buddy, and I know you will buy a beer."

"I saw Zarita in that bar," I said, "and if we go in there, you will have to buy her more than a beer."

"No, I won't! I'm off that dame. She talks too loud — come near getting me put out of my room. Besides, she will drink you up coming and going and not try to pay you back in no way. She is one of them hustlers you was talking about always out in the street at blip-A.M."

"Most of these people where you hang out are hustlers."

"All but you and me. I came out here hoping to run across you to borrow a fin until payday."

"I regret to say that I don't have anything to lend."

"Too bad — because I was going to buy you a drink."

"Then lose the rest in a game?"

"I was not," said Simple. "You see that cat inside the bar with that long fingernail, don't you? Well, he uses that nail to mark cards with. Every time I get in a game, there is somebody dealing with a *long* fingernail. It ain't safe! I am tired of trickeration. Also I have had too many hypes laid down on me. Now I am hep."

"I'm glad to hear that," I said. "It's about time you settled down anyhow and married Joyce."

"Right. I would marry her," said Simple, "except that that girl insists that I get a divorce first. But my wife won't pay for it. And looks like I can't get that much dough ahead myself — in my line of work, I can't grow no long fingernails because they would break off before night."

"Oh, so you would like to be a hustler, too."

"Only until I pay for my divorce from Isabel," said Simple.

"If you hadn't quit your wife, you wouldn't need a divorce," I said. "If I had a wife, *I* would stay with her."

"You have never been married, pal, so you do not know how hard it is sometimes to stay with a wife."

"Elucidate," I said, "while we go in the bar and have a beer."

"A wife you have to take with a grain of salt," Simple explained. "But sometimes the salt runs out."

"What do you mean by that parable?"

"Don't take serious everything a wife says. I did. For instant, I believed her when my wife said, 'Baby, I don't mind you going out. I know a man has to get out sometimes and he don't want his wife running with him everywhere he goes.'

"So I went out. I didn't take her. She got mad. I should have taken that with a grain of salt. Also take money. My wife said, 'A man is due to have his own spending change.' So every week I kept Five Dollars out of my salary. When that ran out 'long toward the end of the week, and I would ask Isabel for a quarter or so, she'd say, 'What did you do with that Five Dollars?'

"I'd say, 'I spent it.'

" 'Spent it on what?' she'd say.

" 'I drunk it up.'

" 'What did you do that for?' she'd yell. 'Why didn't you have your clothes pressed, or spend it on some good books?'

" 'I didn't want any good books.'

" 'Why didn't you send some of it to your old aunt?'

" 'Next time I will *tell* you that I sent it *all* to my old aunt.'

" 'Then you intend to lie to me?' says my wife.

" 'Anything to keep down an argument,' I says.

" 'You do not trust me,' Isabel hollers. Then she starts to quarrel. So you see how it is. A woman will get you going and coming. You can't out-argue a woman. She even had the nerve to tell me, 'Why don't you buy your beer by the case and set up home here and drink it with me?'

"I said, 'Baby, I cannot set up here at home and look into your face each and every night.'

"She said, 'You took me for better or worse. Do I look worse to you now?'

"I said, 'You do not look any worse, baby, but neither does you look any better as time goes on.'

"She said, 'If you would buy me some clothes, maybe I could look like something.'

"I said, 'Honey, we ain't got our furniture paid for yet.'

"She said, 'So you care more for an old kitchen stove than you does for me?'

"I said, 'A man has to eat, and a woman can't cook on the floor.'

" 'All you got me for is to cook,' Isabel said. 'If I had knowed that, I could of stayed home with my mother.'

" 'I must admit,' I said, 'your mother cooks better than you.'

" 'Huh! I can't do nothing with them stringy old round steaks you bring home for us to eat,' she says.

" 'My money won't stretch to no T-bones,' I says. 'Anyhow, baby, no matter how tough the steak may be, you can always stick a fork in the gravy.'

"I just said that for a joke, but somehow it made her mad. She flew off the handle. I flew off the handle, too, and we had one of the biggest quarrels you ever saw. Our first battle royal — but it were not our last. Every time night fell from then on we quarreled — and night falls every night in Baltimore."

"Night does," I said.

"The first of the month falls every month, too, North or South. And them white folks who sends bills never forgets to send them — the phone bill, the furniture bill, the water bill, the gas bill, insurance, house rent. They also never forget you got their furniture in the house — and they will come and take it out if you do not pay the bill. Not only was my nose kept to the grindstone when I was married, but my bohunkus also. It were de-pression, too. They cut my wages down once at the foundry. They cut my wages down again. Then they cut my wages *out*, also the job. My old lady had to go cook for some rich white folks. *And don't you know Isabel wouldn't bring me home a thing to eat!* Neither would she open a can when she got home.

"I said, 'Baby, what is the matter with you? Don't you know I have to eat, too?'

"She said, 'You know what is the matter with me. Ever since I have been with you, I have been treated like a dog for convenience. Who is paying for this furniture? Me! Who keeps up the house rent? Me! Who pays that little dime insurance of yourn? Me! And if you was to die, I would not benefit but Three Hundred Dollars. It looks like you can't even get on WPA. But you better get on something, Jess. In fact, take over or take off.'

"Then it were that I took off," said Simple.

"And ever since you've been a free man."

"Free?" said Simple. "I would have been free if I hadn't run into some old Baltimore friend boy here in Harlem who wrote and told my wife where I was at. So for the last year now she's been writing me that if I wasn't going to even give her a divorce, to at least buy her a fur coat this winter."

"Why didn't you give her a divorce when you left?" I asked.

"You can't buy no divorce on WPA. And when the war came, she was working in a war plant making just as much money as me," said Simple. "She could get her own divorce. But no! She still wanted me to pay for it. I told her to send me the money then and I would pay for it. But she wrote back and said I would never spend none of her money on Joyce. Baltimore womens is evil."

"Evidently she does not trust you."

"I would not trust myself with Three Hundrd Dollars," said Simple.

"So you are just going to keep on being married then. You can't get loose if neither one of you is willing to pay for the divorce."

"I've been trying to get Joyce to pay for it," explained Simple. "Only thing is, Joyce says I will have to marry her *first*. She says she will not pay for no divorce for another woman unless I am hers beforehand."

"That would be bigamy," I said, "married to two women at once."

"It would be worse than that," said Simple. "Married to one woman is bad enough. But if I am married to two, it would be hell!"

"Legally it would be bigamy."

"Is bigamy worse than hell?"

"I have had no experience with either," I said. "But if you go in for bigamy, you will end up in the arms of justice."

"Any old arms are better than none," said Simple.

[1950]

FRANK O'CONNOR was the pseudonym for Michael Francis O'Donovan (1903–1966), who was born in Cork, Ireland. His parents were so poor that he only attended school through the fourth grade, at the Christian Brothers School in Cork. There was no money for further education. During the Irish struggle for independence from England (1918–1921) he was briefly a member of the Irish Republican Army. For several years thereafter he worked as a librarian in Cork and Dublin; it was at this time that he changed his name so he could publish under a pseudonym and not jeopardize his job as a public official. He had begun to write stories as a boy, and for a while he could not decide whether to be a painter or a writer. "I discovered by the time I was sixteen or seventeen that paints cost too much money, so I became a writer because you could be a writer with a pencil and a penny notebook."

When O'Connor was twenty-eight years old, The Atlantic Monthly published his story "Guests of the Nation," which he later said was an imitation of Isaac Babel's stories in Red Cavalry. His first collection of stories appeared that same year (1931), also called Guests of the Nation. From then on he made his living as a writer. During the 1950s he lived in the United States, teaching at Harvard and Northwestern and publishing two excellent critical works about fiction, The Mirror in the Roadway (1956), a study of the modern novel, and The Lonely Voice (1963), a book about the history of the short story. O'Connor was a prolific writer, editor, critic, and translator, with almost fifty books to his credit, including fourteen volumes of short stories. He often rewrote his stories several times, even after they were published, so many of them appear in different versions in his various volumes.

O'Connor was productive in many literary forms, but his greatest achievement was in the short story. Primarily indebted to Chekhov as his model, he declared himself to be an old-fashioned storyteller, believing that a story should have the sound of a person speaking. This gives his fiction an engaging tone, confirming — as do Chekhov's stories — the author's basically sympathetic attitude toward his characters. In praising O'Connor's stories, the noted Irish poet William Butler Yeats said that he was "doing for Ireland what Chekhov did for Russia." O'Connor felt that a good short story had the same qualities of intensity and compression as a good lyric poem. Two recurrent themes in his best stories are loneliness and the difficult search for personal independence, both humorously suggested in his semiautobiographical story about his childhood, "My Oedipus Complex."

Frank O'Connor

ဢ

GUESTS OF THE NATION

I

At dusk the big Englishman, Belcher, would shift his long legs out of the ashes and say "Well, chums, what about it?" and Noble or me would say "All right, chum" (for we had picked up some of their curious expressions), and the little Englishman, Hawkins, would light the lamp and bring out the cards. Sometimes Jeremiah Donovan would come up and supervise the game and get excited over Hawkins's cards, which he always played badly, and shout at him as if he was one of our own "Ah, you divil, you, why didn't you play the tray?"

But ordinarily Jeremiah was a sober and contented poor devil like the big Englishman, Belcher, and was looked up to only because he was a fair hand at documents, though he was slow enough even with them. He wore a small cloth hat and big gaiters over his long pants, and you seldom saw him with his hands out of his pockets. He reddened when you talked to him, tilting from toe to heel and back, and looking down all the time at his big farmer's feet. Noble and me used to make fun of his broad accent, because we were from the town.

I couldn't at the time see the point of me and Noble guarding Belcher and Hawkins at all, for it was my belief that you could have planted that pair down anywhere from this to Claregalway and they'd have taken root there like a native weed. I never in my short experience seen two men to take to the country as they did.

They were handed on to us by the Second Battalion when the search for them became too hot, and Noble and myself, being young, took over with a natural feeling of responsibility, but Hawkins made us look like fools when he showed that he knew the country better than we did.

"You're the bloke they calls Bonaparte," he says to me. "Mary Brigid O'Connell told me to ask you what you done with the pair of her brother's socks you borrowed."

For it seemed, as they explained it, that the Second used to have little evenings, and some of the girls of the neighbourhood turned in, and, seeing they were such decent chaps, our fellows couldn't leave the two Englishmen out of them. Hawkins learned to dance "The Walls of Limerick," "The Siege of Ennis," and "The Waves of Tory" as well as any of them, though, naturally, he couldn't return the compliment, because our lads at that time did not dance foreign dances on principle.

So whatever privileges Belcher and Hawkins had with the Second they just naturally took with us, and after the first day or two we gave up all pretense of keeping a close eye on them. Not that they could have got far, for they had accents you could cut with a knife and wore khaki tunics and overcoats with civilian pants and boots. But it's my belief that they never had any idea of escaping and were quite content to be where they were.

It was a treat to see how Belcher got off with the old woman of the house where we were staying. She was a great warrant to scold, and cranky even with us, but before ever she had a chance of giving our guests, as I may call them, a lick of her tongue, Belcher had made her his friend for life. She was breaking sticks, and Belcher, who hadn't been more than ten minutes in the house, jumped up from his seat and went over to her.

"Allow me, madam," he says, smiling his queer little smile, "please allow me"; and he takes the bloody hatchet. She was struck too paralytic to speak, and after that, Belcher would be at her heels, carrying a bucket, a basket, or a load of turf, as the case might be. As Noble said, he got into looking before she leapt, and hot water, or any little thing she wanted, Belcher would have it ready for her. For such a huge man (and though I am five foot ten myself I had to look up at him) he had an uncommon shortness — or should I say lack? — of speech. It took us some time to get used to him, walking in and out, like a ghost, without a word. Especially because Hawkins talked enough for a platoon, it was strange to hear big Belcher with his toes in the ashes come out with a solitary "Excuse me, chum," or "That's right, chum." His one and only passion was cards, and I will say for him that he was a good card-player. He could have fleeced myself and Noble, but whatever we lost to him Hawkins lost to us, and Hawkins played with the money Belcher gave him.

Hawkins lost to us because he had too much old gab, and we probably lost to Belcher for the same reason. Hawkins and Noble would spit at one another about religion into the early hours of the morning, and Hawkins worried the soul out of Noble, whose brother was a priest, with a string of questions that would puzzle a cardinal. To make it worse even in treating of holy subjects, Hawkins had a deplorable tongue. I never in all my career met a man who could mix such a variety of cursing and bad language into an argument. He was a terrible man, and a fright to argue. He never did a stroke of work, and when he had no one else to talk to, he got stuck in the old woman.

He met his match in her, for one day when he tried to get her to complain profanely of the drought, she gave him a great come-down by blaming it entirely on Jupiter Pluvius (a deity neither Hawkins nor I have ever heard of, though Noble said that among the pagans it was believed that he had something to do with the rain). Another day he was swearing at the capitalists for starting the German war when the old lady laid down her iron, puckered up her little crab's mouth, and said: "Mr. Hawkins, you can say what you like about the war, and think you'll deceive me because I'm only a simple poor countrywoman, but I know what started the war. It was the Italian Count that stole the heathen divinity out of the temple in Japan. Believe me, Mr. Hawkins, nothing but sorrow and want can follow the people that disturb the hidden powers."

A queer old girl, all right.

II

We had our tea one evening, and Hawkins lit the lamp and we all sat into cards. Jeremiah Donovan came in too, and sat down and watched us for a while, and it suddenly struck me that he had no great love for the two Englishmen. It came as a great surprise to me, because I hadn't noticed anything about him before.

Late in the evening a really terrible argument blew up between Hawkins and Noble, about capitalists and priests and love of your country.

"The capitalists," says Hawkins with an angry gulp, "pays the priests to tell you about the next world so as you won't notice what the bastards are up to in this."

"Nonsense, man!" says Noble, losing his temper. "Before ever a capitalist was thought of, people believed in the next world."

Hawkins stood up as though he was preaching a sermon.

"Oh, they did, did they?" he says with a sneer. "They believed all the things you believe, isn't that what you mean? And you believe that God created Adam, and Adam created Shem, and Shem created Jehoshophat. You believe all that silly old fairytale about Eve and Eden and the apple. Well, listen to me, chum. If you're entitled to hold a silly belief like that, I'm entitled to hold my silly belief — which is that the first thing your God created was a bleeding capitalist, with morality and Rolls-Royce complete. Am I right, chum?" he says to Belcher.

"You're right, chum," says Belcher with his amused smile, and got up from the table to stretch his long legs into the fire and stroke his moustache. So, seeing that Jeremiah Donovan was going, and that there was no knowing when the argument about religion would be over, I went out with him. We strolled down to the village together, and then he stopped and started blushing and mumbling and saying I ought to be behind, keeping guard on the prisoners. I didn't like the tone he took with me, and anyway I was bored with life in the cottage, so I replied by asking him what the hell we wanted guarding them at all for. I told him I'd talked it over with Noble, and that we'd both rather be out with a fighting column.

"What use are those fellows to us?" says I.

He looked at me in surprise and said: "I thought you knew we were keeping them as hostages."

"Hostages?" I said.

"The enemy have prisoners belonging to us," he says, "and now they're talking of shooting them. If they shoot our prisoners, we'll shoot theirs."

"Shoot them?" I said.

"What else did you think we were keeping them for?" he says.

"Wasn't it very unforeseen of you not to warn Noble and myself of that in the beginning?" I said.

"How was it?" says he. "You might have known it."

"We couldn't know it, Jeremiah Donovan," says I. "How could we when they were on our hands so long?"

"The enemy have our prisoners as long and longer," says he.

"That's not the same thing at all," says I.

"What difference is there?" says he.

I couldn't tell him, because I knew he wouldn't understand. If it was only an old dog that was going to the vet's, you'd try and not get too fond of him, but Jeremiah Donovan wasn't a man that would ever be in danger of that.

"And when is this thing going to be decided?" says I.

"We might hear tonight," he says. "Or tomorrow or the next day at latest. So if it's only hanging round here that's a trouble to you, you'll be free soon enough."

It wasn't the hanging round that was a trouble to me at all by this time. I had worse things to worry about. When I got back to the cottage the argument was still on. Hawkins was holding forth in his best style, maintaining that there was no next world, and Noble was maintaining that there was; but I could see that Hawkins had had the best of it.

"Do you know what, chum?" he was saying with a saucy smile. "I think you're just as big a bleeding unbeliever as I am. You say you believe in the next world, and you know just as much about the next world as I do, which is sweet damn-all. What's heaven? You don't know. Where's heaven? You don't know. You know sweet damn-all! I ask you again, do they wear wings?"

"Very well, then," says Noble, "they do. Is that enough for you? They do wear wings."

"Where do they get them, then? Who makes them? Have they a factory for wings? Have they a sort of store where you hands in your chit and takes your bleeding wings?"

"You're an impossible man to argue with," says Noble. "Now, listen to me — " And they were off again.

It was long after midnight when we locked up and went to bed. As I blew out the candle I told Noble what Jeremiah Donovan was after telling me. Noble took it very quietly. When we'd been in bed about an hour he asked me did I think we ought to tell the Englishmen. I didn't think we should, because it was more than likely that the English wouldn't shoot our men, and even if they did, the brigade officers, who were always up and down with the Second Battalion and knew the Englishmen well, wouldn't be likely to want them plugged. "I think so too," says Noble. "It would be great cruelty to put the wind up them now."

"It was very unforeseen of Jeremiah Donovan anyhow," says I.

It was next morning that we found it so hard to face Belcher and Hawkins. We went about the house all day scarcely saying a word. Belcher didn't seem to notice; he was stretched into the ashes as usual, with his usual look of waiting in quietness for something unforeseen to happen, but Hawkins noticed and put it down to Noble's being beaten in the argument of the night before.

"Why can't you take a discussion in the proper spirit?" he says severely. "You and your Adam and Eve! I'm a Communist, that's what I am. Communist or anarchist, it all comes to much the same thing." And for hours he went round the house, muttering when the fit took him. "Adam and Eve! Adam and Eve! Nothing better to do with their time than picking bleeding apples!"

III

I don't know how we got through that day, but I was very glad when it was over, the tea things were cleared away, and Belcher said in his peaceable way: "Well, chums, what about it?" We sat round the table and Hawkins took out the cards, and just then I heard Jeremiah Donovan's footstep on the path and a dark presentiment crossed my mind. I rose from the table and caught him before he reached the door.

"What do you want?" I asked.

"I want those two soldier friends of yours," he says, getting red.

"Is that the way, Jeremiah Donovan?" I asked.

"That's the way. There were four of our lads shot this morning, one of them a boy of sixteen."

"That's bad," I said.

At that moment Noble followed me out, and the three of us walked down the path together, talking in whispers. Feeney, the local intelligence officer, was standing by the gate.

"What are you going to do about it?" I asked Jeremiah Donovan.

"I want you and Noble to get them out; tell them they're being shifted again; that'll be the quietest way."

"Leave me out of that," says Noble under his breath.

Jeremiah Donovan looks at him hard.

"All right," he says. "You and Feeney get a few tools from the shed

and dig a hole by the far end of the bog. Bonaparte and myself will be after
you. Don't let anyone see you with the tools. I wouldn't like it to go beyond
ourselves."

We saw Feeney and Noble go round to the shed and went in ourselves. I left Jeremiah Donovan to do the explanations. He told them that
he had orders to send them back to the Second Battalion. Hawkins let out a
mouthful of curses, and you could see that though Belcher didn't say anything, he was a bit upset too. The old woman was for having them stay in
spite of us, and she didn't stop advising them until Jeremiah Donovan lost
his temper and turned on her. He had a nasty temper, I noticed. It was
pitch-dark in the cottage by this time, but no one thought of lighting the
lamp, and in the darkness the two Englishmen fetched their topcoats and
said good-bye to the old woman.

"Just as a man makes a home of a bleeding place, some bastard at
headquarters thinks you're too cushy and shunts you off," says Hawkins,
shaking her hand.

"A thousand thanks, madam," says Belcher. "A thousand thanks for
everything" — as though he'd made it up.

We went round to the back of the house and down towards the bog. It
was only then that Jeremiah Donovan told them. He was shaking with excitement.

"There were four of our fellows shot in Cork this morning and now
you're to be shot as a reprisal."

"What are you talking about?" snaps Hawkins. "It's bad enough being
mucked about as we are without having to put up with your funny jokes."

"It isn't a joke," says Donovan. "I'm sorry, Hawkins, but it's true,"
and begins on the usual rigmarole about duty and how unpleasant it is.

I never noticed that people who talk a lot about duty find it much of a
trouble to them.

"Oh, cut it out!" says Hawkins.

"Ask Bonaparte," says Donovan, seeing that Hawkins isn't taking him
seriously. "Isn't it true, Bonaparte?"

"It is," I say, and Hawkins stops.

"Ah, for Christ's sake, chum!"

"I mean it, chum," I say.

"You don't sound as if you mean it."

"If he doesn't mean it, I do," says Donovan, working himself up.

"What have you against me, Jeremiah Donovan?"

"I never said I had anything against you. But why did your people take
out four of our prisoners and shoot them in cold blood?"

He took Hawkins by the arm and dragged him on, but it was impossible to make him understand that we were in earnest. I had the Smith and
Wesson in my pocket and I kept fingering it and wondering what I'd do if
they put up a fight for it or ran, and wishing to God they'd do one or the
other. I knew if they did run for it, that I'd never fire on them. Hawkins

wanted to know was Noble in it, and when we said yes, he asked us why Noble wanted to plug him. Why did any of us want to plug him? What had he done to us? Weren't we all chums? Didn't we understand him and didn't he understand us? Did we imagine for an instant that he'd shoot us for all the so-and-so officers in the so-and-so British Army?

By this time we'd reached the bog, and I was so sick I couldn't even answer him. We walked along the edge of it in the darkness, and every now and then Hawkins would call a halt and begin all over again, as if he was wound up, about our being chums, and I knew that nothing but the sight of the grave would convince him that we had to do it. And all the time I was hoping that something would happen; that they'd run for it or that Noble would take over the responsibility from me. I had the feeling that it was worse on Noble than on me.

IV

At last we saw the lantern in the distance and made towards it. Noble was carrying it, and Feeney was standing somewhere in the darkness behind him, and the picture of them so still and silent in the bogland brought it home to me that we were in earnest, and banished the last bit of hope I had.

Belcher, on recognizing Noble, said: "Hallo, chum," in his quiet way, but Hawkins flew at him at once, and the argument began all over again, only this time Noble had nothing to say for himself and stood with his head down, holding the lantern between his legs.

It was Jeremiah Donovan who did the answering. For the twentieth time, as though it was haunting his mind, Hawkins asked if anybody thought he'd shoot Noble.

"Yes, you would," says Jeremiah Donovan.

"No, I wouldn't, damn you!"

"You would, because you'd know you'd be shot for not doing it."

"I wouldn't, not if I was to be shot twenty times over. I wouldn't shoot a pal. And Belcher wouldn't — isn't that right, Belcher?"

"That's right, chum," Belcher said, but more by way of answering the question than of joining in the argument. Belcher sounded as though whatever unforeseen thing he'd always been waiting for had come at last.

"Anyway, who says Noble would be shot if I wasn't? What do you think I'd do if I was in his place, out in the middle of a blasted bog?"

"What would you do?" asks Donovan.

"I'd go with him wherever he was going, of course. Share my last bob with him and stick by him through thick and thin. No one can ever say of me that I let down a pal."

"We had enough of this," says Jeremiah Donovan, cocking his revolver. "Is there any message you want to send?"

"No, there isn't."

"Do you want to say your prayers?"

Hawkins came out with a cold-blooded remark that even shocked me and turned on Noble again.

"Listen to me, Noble," he says. "You and me are chums. You can't come over to my side, so I'll come over to your side. That show you I mean what I say? Give me a rifle and I'll go along with you and the other lads."

Nobody answered him. We knew that was no way out.

"Hear what I'm saying?" he says. "I'm through with it. I'm a deserter or anything else you like. I don't believe in your stuff, but it's no worse than mine. That satisfy you?"

Noble raised his head, but Donovan began to speak and he lowered it again without replying.

"For the last time, have you any messages to send?" says Donovan in a cool, excited sort of voice.

"Shut up, Donovan! You don't understand me, but these lads do. They're not the sort to make a pal and kill a pal. They're not the tools of any capitalist."

I alone of the crowd saw Donovan raise his Webley to the back of Hawkins's neck, and as he did so I shut my eyes and tried to pray. Hawkins had begun to say something else when Donovan fired, and as I opened my eyes at the bang, I saw Hawkins stagger at the knees and lie out flat at Noble's feet, slowly and as quiet as a kid falling asleep, with the lantern-light on his lean legs and bright farmer's boots. We all stood very still, watching him settle out in the last agony.

Then Belcher took out a handkerchief and began to tie it about his own eyes (in our excitement we'd forgotten to do the same for Hawkins), and, seeing it wasn't big enough, turned and asked for the loan of mine. I gave it to him and he knotted the two together and pointed with his foot at Hawkins.

"He's not quite dead," he says. "Better give him another."

Sure enough, Hawkins's left knee is beginning to rise. I bend down and put my gun to his head; then, recollecting myself, I get up again. Belcher understands what's in my mind.

"Give him his first," he says. "I don't mind. Poor bastard, we don't know what's happening to him now."

I knelt and fired. By this time I didn't seem to know what I was doing. Belcher, who was fumbling a bit awkwardly with the handkerchiefs, came out with a laugh as he heard the shot. It was the first time I heard him laugh and it sent a shudder down my back; it sounded so unnatural.

"Poor bugger!" he said quietly. "And last night he was so curious about it all. It's very queer, chums, I always think. Now he knows as much about it as they'll ever let him know, and last night he was all in the dark."

Donovan helped him to tie the handkerchiefs about his eyes. "Thanks, chum," he said. Donovan asked if there were any messages he wanted sent.

"No, chum," he says. "Not for me. If any of you would like to write to Hawkins's mother, you'll find a letter from her in his pocket. He and his mother were great chums. But my missus left me eight years ago. Went away with another fellow and took the kid with her. I like the feeling of a home, as you may have noticed, but I couldn't start again after that."

It was an extraordinary thing, but in those few minutes Belcher said more than in all the weeks before. It was just as if the sound of the shot had started a flood of talk in him and he could go on the whole night like that, quite happily, talking about himself. We stood round like fools now that he couldn't see us any longer. Donovan looked at Noble, and Noble shook his head. Then Donovan raised his Webley, and at that moment Belcher gives his queer laugh again. He may have thought we were talking about him, or perhaps he noticed the same thing I'd noticed and couldn't understand it.

"Excuse me, chums," he says. "I feel I'm talking the hell of a lot, and so silly, about my being so handy about a house and things like that. But this thing came on me suddenly. You'll forgive me, I'm sure."

"You don't want to say a prayer?" asks Donovan.

"No, chum," he says. "I don't think it would help. I'm ready, and you boys want to get it over."

"You understand that we're only doing our duty?" says Donovan.

Belcher's head was raised like a blind man's, so that you could only see his chin and the tip of his nose in the lantern-light.

"I never could make out what duty was myself," he said. "I think you're all good lads, if that's what you mean. I'm not complaining."

Noble, just as if he couldn't bear any more of it, raised his fist at Donovan, and in a flash Donovan raised his gun and fired. The big man went over like a sack of meal, and this time there was no need of a second shot.

I don't remember much about the burying, but that it was worse than all the rest because we had to carry them to the grave. It was all mad lonely with nothing but a patch of lantern-light between ourselves and the dark, and birds hooting and screeching all round, disturbed by the guns. Noble went through Hawkins's belongings to find the letter from his mother, and then joined his hands together. He did the same with Belcher. Then, when we'd filled the grave, we separated from Jeremiah Donovan and Feeney and took our tools back to the shed. All the way we didn't speak a word. The kitchen was dark and cold as we'd left it, and the old woman was sitting over the hearth, saying her beads. We walked past her into the room, and Noble struck a match to light the lamp. She rose quietly and came to the doorway with all her cantankerousness gone.

"What did ye do with them?" she asked in a whisper, and Noble started so that the match went out in his hand.

"What's that?" he asked without turning round.

"I heard ye," she said.

"What did you hear?" asked Noble.

"I heard ye. Do ye think I didn't hear ye, putting the spade back in the houseen?"

Noble struck another match and this time the lamp lit for him.

"Was that what ye did to them?" she asked.

Then, by God, in the very doorway, she fell on her knees and began praying, and after looking at her for a minute or two Noble did the same by the fireplace. I pushed my way out past her and left them at it. I stood at the door, watching the stars and listening to the shrieking of the birds dying out over the bogs. It is so strange what you feel at times like that that you can't describe it. Noble says he saw everything ten times the size, as though there were nothing in the whole world but that little patch of bog with the two Englishmen stiffening into it, but with me it was as if the patch of bog where the Englishmen were was a million miles away, and even Noble and the old woman, mumbling behind me, and the birds and the bloody stars were all far away, and I was somehow very small and very lost and lonely like a child astray in the snow. And anything that happened to me afterwards, I never felt the same about again.

[1931]

Frank O'Connor

ᖩᘉ

MY OEDIPUS COMPLEX

Father was in the army all through the war — the first war, I mean — so, up to the age of five, I never saw much of him, and what I saw did not worry me. Sometimes I woke and there was a big figure in khaki peering down at me in the candlelight. Sometimes in the early morning I heard the slamming of the front door and the clatter of nailed boots down the cobbles of the lane. These were Father's entrances and exits. Like Santa Claus he came and went mysteriously.

In fact, I rather liked his visits, though it was an uncomfortable squeeze between Mother and him when I got into the big bed in the early morning. He smoked, which gave him a pleasant musty smell, and shaved, an operation of astounding interest. Each time he left a trail of souvenirs — model tanks and Gurkha knives with handles made of bullet cases, and German helmets and cap badges and button sticks, and all sorts of military equipment — carefully stowed away in a long box on top of the wardrobe, in case they ever came in handy. There was a bit of the magpie about Father; he expected everything to come in handy. When his back was turned, Mother let me get a chair and rummage through his treasures. She didn't seem to think so highly of them as he did.

The war was the most peaceful period of my life. The window of my attic faced southeast. My mother had curtained it, but that had small effect. I always woke with the first light and, with all the responsibilities of the previous day melted, feeling myself rather like the sun, ready to illumine and rejoice. Life never seemed so simple and clear and full of possibilities as then. I put my feet out from under the clothes — I called them Mrs. Left and Mrs. Right — and invented dramatic situations for them in which they discussed the problems of the day. At least Mrs. Right did; she was very demonstrative, but I hadn't the same control of Mrs. Left, so she mostly contented herself with nodding agreement.

They discussed what Mother and I should do during the day, what Santa Claus should give a fellow for Christmas, and what steps should be taken to brighten the home. There was that little matter of the baby, for instance. Mother and I could never agree about that. Ours was the only house in the terrace without a new baby, and Mother said we couldn't afford one till Father came back from the war because they cost seventeen and six.

That showed how simple she was. The Geneys up the road had a baby, and everyone knew they couldn't afford seventeen and six. It was probably a cheap baby, and Mother wanted something really good, but I felt she was too exclusive. The Geneys' baby would have done us fine.

Having settled my plans for the day, I got up, put a chair under the attic window, and lifted the frame high enough to stick out my head. The window overlooked the front gardens of the terrace behind ours, and beyond these it looked over a deep valley to the tall, red brick houses terraced up the opposite hillside, which were all still in shadow, while those at our side of the valley were all lit up, though with long strange shadows that made them seem unfamiliar; rigid and painted.

After that I went into Mother's room and climbed into the big bed. She woke and I began to tell her of my schemes. By this time, though I never seemed to have noticed it, I was petrified in my nightshirt, and I thawed as I talked until, the last frost melted, I fell asleep beside her and woke again only when I heard her below in the kitchen, making the breakfast.

After breakfast we went into town; heard Mass at St. Augustine's and said a prayer for Father, and did the shopping. If the afternoon was fine we either went for a walk in the country or a visit to Mother's great friend in the convent, Mother Saint Dominic. Mother had them all praying for Father, and every night, going to bed, I asked God to send him back safe from the war to us. Little, indeed, did I know what I was praying for!

One morning, I got into the big bed, and there, sure enough, was Father in his usual Santa Claus manner, but later, instead of uniform, he put on his best blue suit, and Mother was as pleased as anything. I saw nothing to be pleased about, because, out of uniform, Father was altogether less interesting, but she only beamed, and explained that our prayers had been answered, and off we went to Mass to thank God for having brought Father safely home.

The irony of it! That very day when he came in to dinner he took off his boots and put on his slippers, donned the dirty old cap he wore about the house to save him from colds, crossed his legs, and began to talk gravely to Mother, who looked anxious. Naturally, I disliked her looking anxious, because it destroyed her good looks, so I interrupted him.

"Just a moment, Larry!" she said gently.

This was only what she said when we had boring visitors, so I attached no importance to it and went on talking.

"Do be quiet, Larry!" she said impatiently. "Don't you hear me talking to Daddy?"

This was the first time I heard those ominous words, "talking to Daddy," and I couldn't help feeling that if this was how God answered prayers, he couldn't listen to them very attentively.

"Why are you talking to Daddy?" I asked with as great a show of indifference as I could muster.

"Because Daddy and I have business to discuss. Now, don't interrupt again!"

In the afternoon, at Mother's request, Father took me for a walk. This time we went into town instead of out in the country, and I thought at first, in my usual optimistic way, that it might be an improvement. It was nothing of the sort. Father and I had quite different notions of a walk in town. He had no proper interest in trams, ships, and horses, and the only thing that seemed to divert him was talking to fellows as old as himself. When I wanted to stop he simply went on, dragging me behind him by the hand; when he wanted to stop I had no alternative but to do the same. I noticed that it seemed to be a sign that he wanted to stop for a long time whenever he leaned against a wall. The second time I saw him do it I got wild. He seemed to be settling himself forever. I pulled him by the coat and trousers, but, unlike Mother who, if you were too persistent, got into a wax and said: "Larry, if you don't behave yourself, I'll give you a good slap," Father had an extraordinary capacity for amiable inattention. I sized him up and wondered would I cry, but he seemed to be too remote to be annoyed even by that. Really, it was like going for a walk with a mountain! He either ignored the wrenching and pummeling entirely, or else glanced down with a grin of amusement from his peak. I had never met anyone so absorbed in himself as he seemed.

At teatime, "talking to Daddy" began again, complicated this time by the fact that he had an evening paper, and every few minutes he put it down and told Mother something new out of it. I felt this was foul play. Man for man, I was prepared to compete with him any time for Mother's attention, but when he had it all made up for him by other people it left me no chance. Several times I tried to change the subject without success.

"You must be quiet while Daddy is reading, Larry," Mother said impatiently.

It was clear that she either genuinely liked talking to Father better than talking to me, or else that he had some terrible hold on her which made her afraid to admit the truth.

"Mummy," I said that night when she was tucking me up, "do you think if I prayed hard God would send Daddy back to the war?"

She seemed to think about that for a moment.

"No, dear," she said with a smile. "I don't think He would."

"Why wouldn't He, Mummy?"

"Because there isn't a war any longer, dear."

"But, Mummy, couldn't God make another war, if He liked?"

"He wouldn't like to, dear. It's not God who makes wars, but bad people."

"Oh!" I said.

I was disappointed about that. I began to think that God wasn't quite what He was cracked up to be.

Next morning I woke at my usual hour, feeling like a bottle of champagne. I put out my feet and invented a long conversation in which Mrs. Right talked of the trouble she had with her own father till she put him in the Home. I didn't quite know what the Home was but it sounded the right place for Father. Then I got my chair and stuck my head out of the attic window. Dawn was just breaking, with a guilty air that made me feel I had caught it in the act. My head bursting with stories and schemes, I stumbled in next door, and in the half-darkness scrambled into the big bed. There was no room at Mother's side so I had to get between her and Father. For the time being I had forgotten about him, and for several minutes I sat bolt upright, racking my brains to know what I could do with him. He was taking up more than his fair share of the bed, and I couldn't get comfortable, so I gave him several kicks that made him grunt and stretch. He made room all right, though. Mother waked and felt for me. I settled back comfortably in the warmth of the bed with my thumb in my mouth.

"Mummy!" I hummed, loudly and contentedly.

"Sssh! dear," she whispered. "Don't wake Daddy!"

This was a new development, which threatened to be even more serious than "talking to Daddy." Life without my early-morning conferences was unthinkable.

"Why?" I asked severely.

"Because poor Daddy is tired."

This seemed to me a quite inadequate reason, and I was sickened by the sentimentality of her "poor Daddy." I never liked that sort of gush; it always struck me as insincere.

"Oh!" I said lightly. Then in my most winning tone: "Do you know where I want to go with you today, Mummy?"

"No, dear," she sighed.

"I want to go down the Glen and fish for thornybacks with my new net, and then I want to go out to the Fox and Hounds, and—"

"Don't-wake-Daddy!" she hissed angrily, clapping her hand across my mouth.

But it was too late. He was awake, or nearly so. He grunted and reached for the matches. Then he stared incredulously at his watch.

"Like a cup of tea, dear?" asked Mother in a meek, hushed voice I had never heard her use before. It sounded almost as though she were afraid.

"Tea?" he exclaimed indignantly. "Do you know what the time is?"

"And after that I want to go up the Rathcooney Road," I said loudly, afraid I'd forget something in all those interruptions.

"Go to sleep at once, Larry!" she said sharply.

I began to snivel. I couldn't concentrate, the way that pair went on, and smothering my early-morning schemes was like burying a family from the cradle.

Father said nothing, but lit his pipe and sucked it, looking out into the shadows without minding Mother or me. I knew he was mad. Every time I made a remark Mother hushed me irritably. I was mortified. I felt it wasn't fair; there was even something sinister in it. Every time I had pointed out to her the waste of making two beds when we could both sleep in one, she had told me it was healthier like that, and now here was this man, this stranger, sleeping with her without the least regard for her health!

He got up early and made tea, but though he brought Mother a cup he brought none for me.

"Mummy," I shouted, "I want a cup of tea, too."

"Yes, dear," she said patiently. "You can drink from Mummy's saucer."

That settled it. Either Father or I would have to leave the house. I didn't want to drink from Mother's saucer; I wanted to be treated as an equal in my own home, so, just to spite her, I drank it all and left none for her. She took that quietly, too.

But that night when she was putting me to bed she said gently: "Larry, I want you to promise me something."

"What is it?" I asked.

"Not to come in and disturb poor Daddy in the morning. Promise?"

"Poor Daddy" again! I was becoming suspicious of everything involving that quite impossible man.

"Why?" I asked.

"Because poor Daddy is worried and tired and he doesn't sleep well."

"Why doesn't he, Mummy?"

"Well, you know, don't you, that while he was at the war Mummy got the pennies from the post office?"

"From Miss MacCarthy?"

"That's right. But now, you see, Miss MacCarthy hasn't any more pennies, so Daddy must go out and find us some. You know what would happen if he couldn't?"

"No," I said, "tell us."

"Well, I think we might have to go out and beg for them like the poor old woman on Fridays. We wouldn't like that, would we?"

"No," I agreed. "We wouldn't."

"So you'll promise not to come in and wake him?"

"Promise."

Mind you, I meant that. I knew pennies were a serious matter, and I was all against having to go out and beg like the old woman on Fridays. Mother laid out all my toys in a complete ring round the bed so that, whatever way I got out, I was bound to fall over one of them.

When I woke I remembered my promise all right. I got up and sat on the floor and played — for hours, it seemed to me. Then I got my chair and looked out the attic window for more hours. I wished it was time for Father to wake; I wished someone would make me a cup of tea. I didn't feel in the least like the sun; instead, I was bored and so very, very cold! I simply longed for the warmth and depth of the big feather bed.

At last I could stand it no longer. I went into the next room. As there was still no room at Mother's side I climbed over her and she woke with a start.

"Larry," she whispered, gripping my arm very tightly, "what did you promise?"

"But I did, Mummy," I wailed, caught in the very act. "I was quiet for ever so long."

"Oh, dear, and you're perished!" she said sadly, feeling me all over. "Now, if I let you stay will you promise not to talk?"

"But I want to talk, Mummy," I wailed.

"That has nothing to do with it," she said with a firmness that was new to me. "Daddy wants to sleep. Now, do you understand that?"

I understood it only too well. I wanted to talk, he wanted to sleep — whose house was it, anyway?

"Mummy," I said with equal firmness, "I think it would be healthier for Daddy to sleep in his own bed."

That seemed to stagger her, because she said nothing for a while.

"Now, once for all," she went on, "you're to be perfectly quiet or go back to your own bed. Which is it to be?"

The injustice of it got me down. I had convicted her out of her own mouth of inconsistency and unreasonableness, and she hadn't even attempted to reply. Full of spite, I gave Father a kick, which she didn't notice but which made him grunt and open his eyes in alarm.

"What time is it?" he asked in a panic-stricken voice, not looking at mother but at the door, as if he saw someone there.

"It's early yet," she replied soothingly. "It's only the child. Go to sleep again. . . . Now, Larry," she added, getting out of bed, "you've wakened Daddy and you must go back."

This time, for all her quiet air, I knew she meant it, and knew that my principal rights and privileges were as good as lost unless I asserted them at once. As she lifted me, I gave a screech, enough to wake the dead, not to mind Father. He groaned.

"That damn child! Doesn't he ever sleep?"

"It's only a habit, dear," she said quietly, though I could see she was vexed.

"Well, it's time he got out of it," shouted Father, beginning to heave in the bed. He suddenly gathered all the bedclothes about him, turned to the wall, and then looked back over his shoulder with nothing showing only two small, spiteful, dark eyes. The man looked very wicked.

To open the bedroom door, Mother had to let me down, and I broke free and dashed for the farthest corner, screeching. Father sat bolt upright in bed.

"Shut up, you little puppy!" he said in a choking voice.

I was so astonished that I stopped screeching. Never, never had anyone spoken to me in that tone before. I looked at him incredulously and saw his face convulsed with rage. It was only then that I fully realized how God had codded me, listening to my prayers for the safe return of this monster.

"Shut up, you!" I bawled, beside myself.

"What's that you said?" shouted Father, making a wild leap out of the bed.

"Mick, Mick!" cried Mother. "Don't you see the child isn't used to you?"

"I see he's better fed than taught," snarled Father, waving his arms wildly. "He wants his bottom smacked."

All his previous shouting was as nothing to these obscene words referring to my person. They really made my blood boil.

"Smack your own!" I screamed hysterically. "Smack your own! Shut up! Shut up!"

At this he lost his patience and let fly at me. He did it with the lack of conviction you'd expect of a man under Mother's horrified eyes, and it ended up as a mere tap, but the sheer indignity of being struck at all by a stranger, a total stranger who had cajoled his way back from the war into our big bed as a result of my innocent intercession, made me completely dotty. I shrieked and shrieked, and danced in my bare feet, and Father, looking awkward and hairy in nothing but a short gray army shirt, glared down at me like a mountain out for murder. I think it must have been then that I realized he was jealous too. And there stood Mother in her night-dress, looking as if her heart was broken between us. I hoped she felt as she looked. It seemed to me that she deserved it all.

From that morning out my life was a hell. Father and I were enemies, open and avowed. We conducted a series of skirmishes against one another, he trying to steal my time with Mother and I his. When she was sitting on my bed, telling me a story, he took to looking for some pair of old boots which he alleged he had left behind him at the beginning of the war. While he talked to Mother I played loudly with my toys to show my total lack of concern. He created a terrible scene one evening when he came in from work and found me at his box, playing with his regimental badges, Gurkha knives and button sticks. Mother got up and took the box from me.

"You mustn't play with Daddy's toys unless he lets you, Larry," she said severely. "Daddy doesn't play with yours."

For some reason Father looked at her as if she had struck him and then turned away with a scowl.

"Those are not toys," he growled, taking down the box again to see had I lifted anything. "Some of those curios are very rare and valuable."

But as time went on I saw more and more how he managed to alienate Mother and me. What made it worse was that I couldn't grasp his method or see what attraction he had for Mother. In every possible way he was less winning than I. He had a common accent and made noises at his tea. I thought for a while that it might be the newspapers she was interested in, so I made up bits of news of my own to read to her. Then I thought it might be the smoking, which I personally thought attractive, and took his pipes and went round the house dribbling into them till he caught me. I even made noises at my tea, but Mother only told me I was disgusting. It all seemed to hinge round that unhealthy habit of sleeping together, so I made a point of dropping into their bedroom and nosing round, talking to myself, so that they wouldn't know I was watching them, but they were never up to anything that I could see. In the end it beat me. It seemed to depend on being grown-up and giving people rings, and I realized I'd have to wait.

But at the same time I wanted him to see that I was only waiting, not giving up the fight. One evening when he was being particularly obnoxious, chattering away well above my head, I let him have it. "Mummy," I said, "do you know what I'm going to do when I grow up?"

"No, dear," she replied. "What?"

"I'm going to marry you," I said quietly.

Father gave a great guffaw out of him, but he didn't take me in. I knew it must only be pretense. And Mother, in spite of everything, was pleased. I felt she was probably relieved to know that one day Father's hold on her would be broken. "Won't that be nice?" she said with a smile.

"It'll be very nice," I said confidently. "Because we're going to have lots and lots of babies."

"That's right, dear," she said placidly. "I think we'll have one soon, and then you'll have plenty of company."

I was no end pleased about that because it showed that in spite of the way she gave in to Father she still considered my wishes. Besides, it would put the Geneys in their place.

It didn't turn out like that, though. To begin with, she was very preoccupied — I supposed about where she would get the seventeen and six — and though Father took to staying out late in the evenings it did me no particular good. She stopped taking me for walks, became as touchy as blazes, and smacked me for nothing at all. Sometimes I wished I'd never mentioned the confounded baby — I seemed to have a genius for bringing calamity on myself.

And calamity it was! Sonny arrived in the most appalling hullabaloo — even that much he couldn't do without a fuss — and from the first moment I disliked him. He was a difficult child — so far as I was concerned he was always difficult — and demanded far too much attention.

Mother was simply silly about him, and couldn't see when he was only showing off. As company he was worse than useless. He slept all day, and I had to go round the house on tiptoe to avoid waking him. It wasn't any longer a question of not waking Father. The slogan now was "Don't-wake-Sonny!" I couldn't understand why the child wouldn't sleep at the proper time, so whenever Mother's back was turned I woke him. Sometimes to keep him awake I pinched him as well. Mother caught me at it one day and gave me a most unmerciful flaking.

One evening, when Father was coming in from work, I was playing trains in the front garden.

I let on not to notice him; instead, I pretended to be talking to myself, and said in a loud voice: "If another bloody baby comes into this house, I'm going out."

Father stopped dead and looked at me over his shoulder.

"What's that you said?" he asked sternly.

"I was only talking to myself," I replied, trying to conceal my panic. "It's private."

He turned and went in without a word. Mind you, I intended it as a solemn warning, but its effect was quite different. Father started being quite nice to me. I could understand that, of course. Mother was quite sickening about Sonny. Even at mealtimes she'd get up and gawk at him in the cradle with an idiotic smile, and tell Father to do the same. He was always polite about it, but he looked so puzzled you could see he didn't know what she was talking about. He complained of the way Sonny cried at night, but she only got cross and said that Sonny never cried except when there was something up with him — which was a flaming lie, because Sonny never had anything up with him, and only cried for attention. It was really painful to see how simpleminded she was. Father wasn't attractive, but he had a fine intelligence. He saw through Sonny, and now he knew that I saw through him as well.

One night I woke with a start. There was someone beside me in the bed. For one wild moment I felt sure it must be Mother, having come to her senses and left Father for good, but then I heard Sonny in convulsions in the next room, and Mother saying: "There! There! There!" and I knew it wasn't she. It was Father. He was lying beside me, wide-awake, breathing hard and apparently as mad as hell.

After a while it came to me what he was mad about. It was his turn now. After turning me out of the big bed, he had been turned out himself. Mother had no consideration now for anyone but that poisonous pup, Sonny. I couldn't help feeling sorry for Father. I had been through it all myself, and even at that age I was magnanimous. I began to stroke him down and say: "There! There!" He wasn't exactly responsive.

"Aren't you asleep either?" he snarled.

"Ah, come on and put your arm around us, can't you?" I said, and he did, in a sort of way. Gingerly, I suppose, is how you'd describe it. He was very bony but better than nothing.

At Christmas he went out of his way to buy me a really nice model railway.

[1944]

ISAAC BASHEVIS SINGER (b. 1904) *was born in Radzymin, Po-*
land. After his education at the Tachkemoni Rabbinical Seminary in War-
saw, he worked as a proofreader and translator before emigrating to the
United States in 1935. Settling in New York City, he made his living as a
journalist for the Jewish Daily Forward, *a Yiddish-language paper. He also*
wrote autobiographical sketches, short stories, and novels in Yiddish for
many years. In 1950 his writing became available to a wider audience for
the first time when he began to publish his work in English translations,
starting with the realistic historical chronicle, The Family Moskat. *Singer's*
first collection of short stories, Gimpel the Fool and Other Stories (*trans-*
lated by noted American novelist Saul Bellow and others), appeared in
1957, and during the 1960s and 1970s he alternated novels with books of
short fiction, including such popular collections of stories as The Spinoza of
Market Street and Other Stories (1961), A Friend of Kafka and Other
Stories (1970), A Crown of Feathers and Other Stories (1973), Passions
and Other Stories (1975), *and* Old Love and Other Stories (1979). *In these*
books, Singer collected stories from different periods in his life without or-
ganizing them around a central theme. A prolific writer, he has also pub-
lished three volumes of autobiographical reminiscences. In 1978 he was
awarded the Nobel Prize for Literature. His Collected Stories *appeared in*
1981.

In all of his work, Singer explores the traditions of Jewish life, past and
present, expressing his fascination with the history of his people: "I was
born with the feeling that I am part of an unlikely adventure, something
that couldn't have happened, but happened all the same." In the best of his
short stories, as in "A Crown of Feathers," he dramatizes a complex mysti-
cism in his treatment of Jewish characters, suggesting multiple levels of
human existence, both physical and spiritual, and the ambiguous nature of
life itself, capable as it is of both natural and supernatural interpretation.
Singer's vision of humanity is modern in its treatment of sexuality and in-
sanity, but his interest in mysticism extends back to his roots as the son of a
rabbi studying the medieval kaballah, *the tradition of Jewish mystical lore.*
Singer refuses to interpret the mysticism in his stories. He believes that the
writer must produce fiction that creates a coherent and self-sustaining illu-
sion of reality on the page, including paradox to give a true picture of the
existence of things in the world. "Everything to me, everything is a paradox.
The very existence of things is a paradox."

Singer has said that in his short stories he is interested in writing about
people who are "obsessed by some mania or fixed idea, and everything turns
around this idea. . . . Since we don't know really what reality is, whatever
we are obsessed with becomes our reality." He believes in demons and the

supernatural: "Powers which we don't know take a great part in our life. . . . The supernatural for me is not really supernatural; it's powers which we don't know." His own stories are always based on a realistically observed setting, however, since "a miracle must be invented among realism, because, if it's one miracle after the other and there's no realism, the miracle itself becomes nothing." All great literature begins in realism, according to Singer, who with great clear-sightedness puts the events of our everyday existence in the category of the marvelous too. "Once a man brought me a story which began with a cut-off head which spoke. And I said to the man, 'Isn't it miracle enough that a head which is not chopped off can talk?' "

Isaac Bashevis Singer

ဘာ

A Crown of Feathers

– translated by the author and Laurie Colwin

Reb Naftali Holishitzer, the community leader in Krasnobród, was left in his old age with no children. One daughter had died in childbirth and the other in a cholera epidemic. A son had drowned when he tried to cross the San River on horseback. Reb Naftali had only one grandchild — a girl, Akhsa, an orphan. It was not the custom for a female to study at a yeshiva, because "the King's daughter is all glorious within" and Jewish daughters are all the daughters of kings. But Akhsa studied at home. She dazzled everyone with her beauty, wisdom, and diligence. She had white skin and black hair; her eyes were blue.

Reb Naftali managed an estate that had belonged to the Prince Czartoryski. Since he owed Reb Naftali twenty thousand guldens, the prince's property was a permanent pawn, and Reb Naftali had built for himself a water mill and a brewery and had sown hundreds of acres with hops. His wife, Nesha, came from a wealthy family in Prague. They could afford to hire the finest tutors for Akhsa. One taught her the Bible, another French, still another the pianoforte, and a fourth dancing. She learned everything quickly. At eight, she was playing chess with her grandfather. Reb Naftali didn't need to offer a dowry for her marriage, since she was heir to his entire fortune.

Matches were sought for her early, but her grandmother was hard to please. She would look at a boy proposed by the marriage brokers and say, "He has the shoulders of a fool," or, "He has the narrow forehead of an ignoramus."

One day Nesha died unexpectedly. Reb Naftali was in his late seventies and it was unthinkable that he remarry. Half his day he devoted to religion, the other half to business. He rose at daybreak and pored over the Talmud and the Commentaries and wrote letters to community elders. When a man was sick, Reb Naftali went to comfort him. Twice a week he visited the poorhouse with Akhsa, who carried a contribution of soup and groats herself. More than once, Akhsa, the pampered and scholarly, rolled up her sleeves and made beds there.

In the summer, after midday sleep, Reb Naftali ordered his britska harnessed and he rode around the fields and village with Akhsa. While they rode, he discussed business, and it was known that he listened to her advice just as he had listened to her grandmother's.

But there was one thing that Akhsa didn't have — a friend. Her grandmother had tried to find friends for her; she even lowered her standards and invited girls from Krasnobród. But Akhsa had no patience with their chatter about clothes and household matters. Since the tutors were all men, Akhsa was kept away from them, except for lessons. Now her grandfather became her only companion. Reb Naftali had met famous noblemen in his lifetime. He had been to fairs in Warsaw, Kraków, Danzig, and Koenigsberg. He would sit for hours with Akhsa and tell her about rabbis and miracle workers, about the disciples of the false messiah Sabbatai Zevi, quarrels in the Sejm, the caprices of the Zamojskis, the Radziwills, and the Czartoryskis — their wives, lovers, courtiers. Sometimes Akhsa would cry out, "I wish you were my fiancé, not my grandfather!" and kiss his eyes and his white beard.

Reb Naftali would answer, "I'm not the only man in Poland. There are plenty like me, and young to boot."

"Where, Grandfather? Where?"

After her grandmother's death, Akhsa refused to rely on anyone else's judgment in the choice of a husband — not even her grandfather's. Just as her grandmother saw only bad, Reb Naftali saw only good. Akhsa demanded that the matchmakers allow her to meet her suitor, and Reb Naftali finally consented. The young pair would be brought together in a room, the door would be left open, and a deaf old woman servant would stand at the threshold to watch that the meeting be brief and without frivolity. As a rule, Akhsa stayed with the young man not more than a few minutes. Most of the suitors seemed dull and silly. Others tried to be clever and made undignified jokes. Akhsa dismissed them abruptly. How strange, but her grandmother still expressed her opinion. Once, Akhsa heard her say clearly, "He has the snout of a pig." Another time, she said, "He talks like the standard letter book."

Akhsa knew quite well that it was not her grandmother speaking. The dead don't return from the other world to comment on prospective fiancés. Just the same, it was her grandmother's voice, her style. Akhsa wanted to talk to her grandfather about it, but she was afraid he would think her crazy. Besides, her grandfather longed for his wife, and Akhsa didn't want to stir up his grief.

When Reb Naftali Holishitzer realized that his granddaughter was driving away the matchmakers, he was troubled. Akhsa was now past her eighteenth year. The people in Krasnobród had begun to gossip — she was demanding a knight on a white horse or the moon in heaven; she would stay a spinster. Reb Naftali decided not to give in to her whims any more but to marry her off. He went to a yeshiva and brought back with him a young man named Zemach, an orphan and a devout scholar. He was dark as a gypsy, small, with broad shoulders. His sidelocks were thick. He was nearsighted and studied eighteen hours a day. The moment he reached Krasno-bród, he went to the study house and began to sway in front of an open volume of the Talmud. His sidelocks swayed, too. Students came to talk with him, and he spoke without lifting his gaze from the book. He seemed to know the Talmud by heart, since he caught everyone misquoting.

Akhsa demanded a meeting, but Reb Naftali replied that this was conduct befitting tailors and shoemakers, not a girl of good breeding. He warned Akhsa that if she drove Zemach away he would disinherit her. Since men and women were in separate rooms during the engagement party, Akhsa had no chance of seeing Zemach until the marriage contract was to be signed. She looked at him and heard her grandmother say, "They've sold you shoddy goods."

Her words were so clear it seemed to Akhsa that everyone should have heard them, but no one had. The girls and women crowded around her, congratulating her and praising her beauty, her dress, her jewelry. Her grandfather passed her the contract and a quill, and her grandmother cried out, "Don't sign!" She grabbed Akhsa's elbow and a blot formed on the paper.

Reb Naftali shouted, "What have you done!"

Akhsa tried to sign, but the pen fell from her hand. She burst into tears. "Grandfather, I can't."

"Akhsa, you shame me."

"Grandfather, forgive me." Akhsa covered her face with her hands. There was an outcry. Men hissed and women laughed and wept. Akhsa cried silently. They half led, half carried her to her room and put her on her bed.

Zemach exclaimed, "I don't want to be married to this shrew!"

He pushed through the crowd and ran to get a wagon back to the yeshiva. Reb Naftali went after him, trying to pacify him with words and money, but Zemach threw Reb Naftali's banknotes to the ground. Someone brought his wicker trunk from the inn where he had stayed. Before the wagon pulled away, Zemach cried out, "I don't forgive her, and God won't, either."

For days after that, Akhsa was ill. Reb Naftali Holishitzer, who had been successful all his life, was not accustomed to failure. He became sick;

his face took on a yellow pallor. Women and girls tried to comfort Akhsa. Rabbis and elders came to visit Reb Naftali, but he got weaker as the days passed. After a while, Akhsa gained back her strength and left her sickbed. She went to her grandfather's room, bolting the door behind her. The maid who listened and spied through the keyhole reported that she had heard him say, "You are mad!"

Akhsa nursed her grandfather, brought him his medicine and bathed him with a sponge, but the old man developed an inflammation of the lungs. Blood ran from his nose. His urine stopped. Soon he died. He had written his will years before and left one-third of his estate to charity and the rest to Akhsa.

According to the law, one does not sit shivah in mourning after the death of a grandfather, but Akhsa went through the ceremony anyway. She sat on a low stool and read the book of Job. She ordered that no one be let in. She had shamed an orphan — a scholar — and caused the death of her grandfather. She became melancholy. Since she had read the story of Job before, she began search in her grandfather's library for another book to read. To her amazement, she found a Bible translated into Polish — the New Testament as well as the Old. Akhsa knew it was a forbidden book, but she turned the pages anyway. Had her grandfather read it, Akhsa wondered. No, it couldn't be. She remembered that on the Gentile feast days, when holy icons and pictures were carried in processions near the house, she was not allowed to look out of the window. Her grandfather told her it was idolatry. She wondered if her grandmother had read this Bible. Among the pages she found some pressed cornflowers — a flower her grandmother had often picked. Grandmother came from Bohemia; it was said that her father had belonged to the Sabbatai Zevi sect. Akhsa recalled that Prince Czartoryski used to spend time with her grandmother when he visited the estate, and praised the way she spoke Polish. If she hadn't been a Jewish girl, he said, he would have married her — a great compliment.

That night Akhsa read the New Testament to the last page. It was difficult for her to accept that Jesus was God's only begotten son and that He rose from the grave, but she found this book more comforting to her tortured spirit than the castigating words of the prophets, who never mentioned the Kingdom of Heaven or the resurrection of the dead. All they promised was a good harvest for good deeds and starvation and plague for bad ones.

On the seventh night of shivah, Akhsa went to bed. The light was out and she was dozing when she heard footsteps that she recognized as her grandfather's. In the darkness, her grandfather's figure emerged: the light face, the white beard, the mild features, even the skullcap on his high forehead. He said in a quiet voice, "Akhsa, you have committed an injustice."

Akhsa began to cry. "Grandfather, what should I do?"

"Everything can be corrected."

"How?"

"Apologize to Zemach. Become his wife."

"Grandfather, I hate him."

"He is your destined one."

He lingered for a moment, and Akhsa could smell his snuff, which he used to mix with cloves and smelling salts. Then he vanished and an empty space remained in the darkness. She was too amazed to be frightened. She leaned against the headboard, and after some time she slept.

She woke with a start. She heard her grandmother's voice. This was not a murmuring like Grandfather's but the strong voice of a living person. "Akhsa, my daughter."

Akhsa burst into tears. "Grandmother, where are you?"

"I'm here."

"What should I do?"

"Whatever your heart desires."

"What, Grandmother?"

"Go to the priest. He will advise you."

Akhsa became numb. Fear constricted her throat. She managed to say, "You're not my grandmother. You're a demon."

"I am your grandmother. Do you remember how we went wading in the pond that summer night near the flat hill and you found a gulden in the water?"

"Yes, Grandmother."

"I could give you other proof. Be it known that the Gentiles are right. Jesus of Nazareth is the Son of God. He was born of the Holy Spirit as prophesied. The rebellious Jews refused to accept the truth and therefore they are punished. The Messiah will not come to them because He is here already."

"Grandmother, I'm afraid."

"Akhsa, don't listen!" her grandfather suddenly shouted into her right ear. "This isn't your grandmother. It's an evil spirit disguised to trick you. Don't give in to his blasphemies. He will drag you into perdition."

"Akhsa, that is not your grandfather but a goblin from behind the bathhouse," Grandmother interrupted. "Zemach is a ne'er-do-well, and vengeful to boot. He will torment you, and the children he begets will be vermin like him. Save yourself while there is time. God is with the Gentiles."

"Lilith! She-demon! Daughter of Ketev M'riri!" Grandfather growled. "Liar!"

Grandfather became silent, but Grandmother continued to talk, although her voice faded. She said, "Your real grandfather learned the truth in Heaven and converted. They baptized him with heavenly water and he rests in Paradise. The saints are all bishops and cardinals. Those who remain stubborn are roasted in the fires of Gehenna. If you don't believe me, ask for a sign."

"What sign?"

"Unbutton your pillowcase, rip open the seams of the pillow, and there you will find a crown of feathers. No human hand could make a crown like this."

Her grandmother disappeared, and Akhsa fell into a heavy sleep. At dawn, she awoke and lit a candle. She remembered her grandmother's words, unbuttoned the pillowcase, and ripped open the pillow. What she saw was so extraordinary she could scarcely believe her eyes: down and feathers entwined into a crown, with little ornaments and complex designs no worldly master could have duplicated. On the top of the crown was a tiny cross. It was all so airy that Akhsa's breath made it flutter. Akhsa gasped. Whoever had made this crown — an angel or a demon — had done his work in darkness, in the inside of a pillow. She was beholding a miracle. She extinguished the candle and stretched out on the bed. For a long time she lay without any thoughts. Then she went back to sleep.

In the morning when she awoke, Akhsa thought she had had a dream, but on the night table she saw the crown of feathers. The sun made it sparkle with the colors of the rainbow. It looked as if it were set with the smallest of gems. She sat and contemplated the wonder. Then she put on a black dress and a black shawl and asked that the carriage be brought round for her. She rode to the house where Koscik, the priest, resided. The housekeeper answered her knock. The priest was nearing seventy and he knew Akhsa. He had often come to the estate to bless the peasants' bread at Easter time and to give rites to the dying and conduct weddings and funerals. One of Akhsa's teachers had borrowed a Latin-Polish dictionary from him. Whenever the priest visited, Akhsa's grandmother invited him to her parlor and they conversed over cake and vishniak.

The priest offered Akhsa a chair. She sat down and told him everything. He said, "Don't go back to the Jews. Come to us. We will see to it that your fortune remains intact."

"I forgot to take the crown. I want to have it with me."

"Yes, my daughter, go and bring it."

Akhsa went home, but a maid had cleaned her bedroom and dusted the night table; the crown had vanished. Akhsa searched in the garbage ditch, in the slops, but not a trace could she find.

Soon after that, the terrible news was abroad in Krasnobród that Akhsa had converted.

Six years passed. Akhsa married and became the Squiress Maria Malkowska. The old squire, Wladyslaw Malkowski, had died without direct heir and had left his estate to his nephew Ludwik. Ludwik had remained a bachelor until he was forty-five, and it seemed he would never marry. He lived in his uncle's castle with his spinster sister, Gloria. His love affairs were with peasant girls, and he had sired a number of bastards. He was small and light, with a blond goatee. Ludwik kept to himself, reading old books of history, religion, and genealogy. He smoked a porcelain pipe, drank alone, hunted by himself, and avoided the noblemen's dances. The business of the estate he handled with a strong hand, and he made sure his bailiff never stole from him. His neighbors thought he was a pedant, and some considered him half mad. When Akhsa accepted the Christian faith, he asked her — now Maria — to marry him. Gossips said that Ludwik, the miser, had fallen in love with Maria's inheritance. The priests and others persuaded Akhsa to accept Ludwik's proposal. He was a descendant of the Polish king Leszczynski. Gloria, who was ten years older than Ludwik, opposed the match, but Ludwik for once did not listen to her.

The Jews of Krasnobród were afraid that Akhsa would become their enemy and instigate Ludwik against them, as happened with so many converts, but Ludwik continued to trade with the Jews, selling them fish, grain, and cattle. Zelig Frampoler, a court Jew, delivered all kinds of merchandise to the estate. Gloria remained the lady of the castle.

In the first weeks of the marriage, Akhsa and Ludwik took trips together in a surrey. Ludwik even began to pay visits to neighboring squires, and he talked of giving a ball. He confessed all his past adventures with women to Maria and promised to behave like a God-fearing Christian. But before long he fell back into his old ways; he withdrew from his neighbors, started up his affairs with peasant girls, and began to drink again. An angry silence hung between man and wife. Ludwik ceased coming to Maria's bedroom, and she did not conceive. In time, they stopped dining at the same table, and when Ludwik needed to tell Maria something he sent a note with a servant. Gloria, who managed the finances, allowed her sister-in-law a gulden a week; Maria's fortune now belonged to her husband. It became clear to Akhsa that God was punishing her and that nothing remained but to wait for death. But what would happen to her after she died? Would she be roasted on a bed of needles and be thrown into the waste of the netherworld? Would she be reincarnated as a dog, a mouse, a millstone?

Because she had nothing to occupy her time with, Akhsa spent all day and part of the night in her husband's library. Ludwik had not added to it, and the books were old, bound in leather, in wood, or in moth-eaten velvet and silk. The pages were yellow and foxed. Akhsa read stories of ancient kings, faraway countries, of all sorts of battles and intrigues among princes, cardinals, dukes. She pored over tales of the Crusades and the Black Plague. The world crawled with wickedness, but it was also full of wonders. Stars in the sky warred and swallowed one another. Comets foretold catastrophes. A child was born with a tail; a woman grew scales and fins. In India, fakirs stepped barefooted on red-hot coals without being burned. Others let themselves be buried alive, and then rose from their graves.

It was strange, but after the night Akhsa found the crown of feathers in her pillow she was not given another sign from the powers that rule the universe. She never heard from her grandfather or grandmother. There were times when Akhsa desired to call out to her grandfather, but she did not dare mention his name with her unclean lips. She had betrayed the Jewish God and she no longer believed in the Gentile one, so she refrained from praying. Often when Zelig Frampoler came to the estate and Akhsa saw him from the window, she wanted to ask him about the Jewish community, but she was afraid that he might hold it a sin to speak to her, and that Gloria would denounce her for associating with Jews.

Years rolled by. Gloria's hair turned white and her head shook. Ludwik's goatee became gray. The servants grew old, deaf, and half blind. Akhsa, or Maria, was in her thirties, but she often imagined herself an old woman. With the years she became more and more convinced that it was the Devil who had persuaded her to convert and that it was he who had fashioned the crown of feathers. But the road back was blocked. The Russian law forbade a convert to return to his faith. The bit of information that reached her about the Jews was bad: the synagogue in Krasnobród had burned down, as well as the stores in the marketplace. Dignified householders and community elders hung bags on their shoulders and went begging. Every few months there was an epidemic. There was nowhere to return to. She often contemplated suicide, but how? She lacked the courage to hang herself or cut her veins; she had no poison.

Slowly, Akhsa came to the conclusion that the universe was ruled by the black powers. It was not God holding dominion but Satan. She found a thick book about witchcraft that contained detailed descriptions of spells and incantations, talismans, the conjuring up of demons and goblins, the sacrifices to Asmodeus, Lucifer, and Beelzebub. There were accounts of the Black Mass; and of how the witches anointed their bodies, gathered in the forest, partook of human flesh, and flew in the air riding on brooms, shovels, and hoops, accompanied by bevies of devils and other creatures of the night that had horns and tails, bat's wings, and the snouts of pigs. Often these monsters lay with the witches, who gave birth to freaks.

Akhsa reminded herself of the Yiddish proverb "If you cannot go over, go under." She had lost the world to come; therefore, she decided to enjoy some revelry while she had this life. At night she began to call the Devil, prepared to make a covenant with him as many neglected women had done before.

Once in the middle of the night, after Akhsa had swallowed a potion of mead, spittle, human blood, crow's egg spiced with galbanum and mandrake, she felt a cold kiss on her lips. In the shine of the late-night moon she saw a naked male figure — tall and black, with long elflocks, the horns of a buck, and two protruding teeth, like a boar's. He bent down over her, whispering, "What is your command, my mistress? You may ask for half my kingdom."

His body was as translucent as a spider web. He stank of pitch. Akhsa had been able to reply, "You, my slave, come and have me." Instead, she murmured, "My grandparents."

The Devil burst into laughter. "They are dust!"

"Did you braid the crown of feathers?" Akhsa asked.

"Who else?"

"You deceived me?"

"I am a deceiver," the Devil answered with a giggle.

"Where is the truth?" Akhsa asked.

"The truth is that there is no truth."

The Devil lingered for a while and then disappeared. For the remainder of the night, Akhsa was neither asleep nor awake. Voices spoke to her. Her breasts because swollen, her nipples hard, her belly distended. Pain bored into her skull. Her teeth were on edge, and her tongue enlarged so that she feared it would split her palate. Her eyes bulged from their sockets. There was a knocking in her ears as loud as a hammer on an anvil. Then she felt as if she were in the throes of labor. "I'm giving birth to a demon!" Akhsa cried out. She began to pray to the God she had forsaken. Finally she fell asleep, and when she awoke in the pre-dawn darkness all her pains had ceased. She saw her grandfather standing at the foot of her bed. He wore a white robe and cowl, such as he used to wear on the eve of Yom Kippur when he blessed Akhsa before going to the Kol Nidre prayer. A light shone from his eyes and lit up Akhsa's quilt. "Grandfather," Akhsa murmured.

"Yes, Akhsa. I am here."

"Grandfather, what shall I do?"

"Run away. Repent."

"I'm lost."

"It is never too late. Find the man you shamed. Become a Jewish daughter."

Later, Akhsa did not remember whether her grandfather had actually spoken to her or she had understood him without words. The night was over. Daybreak reddened the window. Birds were twittering. Akhsa examined her sheet. There was no blood. She had not given birth to a demon. For the first time in years, she recited the Hebrew prayer of thanksgiving.

She got out of bed, washed at the basin, and covered her hair with a shawl. Ludwik and Gloria had robbed her of her inheritance, but she still possessed her grandmother's jewelry. She wrapped it in a handkerchief and put it in a basket, together with a shirt and underwear. Ludwik had either stayed the night with one of his mistresses or he had left at dawn to hunt. Gloria lay sick in her boudoir. The maid brought Akhsa her breakfast, but she ate little. Then she left the estate. Dogs barked at her as if she were a stranger. The old servants looked in amazement as the squiress passed through the gates with a basket on her arm and a kerchief on her head like a peasant woman.

Although Malkowski's property was not far from Krasnobród, Akhsa spent most of the day on the road. She sat down to rest and washed her hands in a stream. She recited grace and ate the slice of bread she had brought with her.

Near the Krasnobród cemetery stood the hut of Eber, the gravedigger. Outside, his wife was washing linen in a tub. Akhsa asked her, "Is this the way to Krasnobród?"

"Yes, straight ahead."

"What's the news from the village?"

"Who are you?"

"I'm a relative of Reb Naftali Holishitzer."

The woman wiped her hands on her apron. "Not a soul is left of that family."

"Where is Akhsa?"

The old woman trembled. "She should have been buried head first, Father in Heaven." And she told about Akhsa's conversion. "She's had her punishment already in this world."

"What became of the yeshiva boy she was betrothed to?"

"Who knows? He isn't from around here."

Akhsa asked about the graves of her grandparents, and the old woman pointed to two headstones bent one toward the other, overgrown with moss and weeds. Akhsa prostrated herself in front of them and lay there until nightfall.

For three months, Akhsa wandered from yeshiva to yeshiva, but she did not find Zemach. She searched in community record books, questioned elders and rabbis — without result. Since not every town had an inn, she often slept in the poorhouse. She lay on a pallet of straw, covered with a mat, praying silently that her grandfather would appear and tell her where to find Zemach. He gave no sign. In the darkness, the old and the sick coughed and muttered. Children cried. Mothers cursed. Although Akhsa accepted this as part of her punishment, she could not overcome her sense of indignity. Community leaders scolded her. They made her wait for days to see them. Women were suspicious of her — why was she looking for a man who no doubt had a wife and children, or might even be in his grave? "Grandfather, why did you drive me to this?" Akhsa cried. "Either show me the way or send death to take me."

On a wintry afternoon, while Akhsa was sitting in an inn in Lublin, she asked the innkeeper if he had ever heard of a man called Zemach — small in stature, swarthy, a former yeshiva boy and scholar. One of the other guests said, "You mean Zemach, the teacher from Izbica?"

He described Zemach, and Akhsa knew she had found the one she was looking for. "He was engaged to marry a girl in Krasnobród," she said.

"I know. The convert. Who are you?"

"A relative."

"What do you want with him?" the guest asked. "He's poor, and stubborn to boot. All his pupils have been taken away from him. He's a wild and contrary man."

"Does he have a wife?"

"He's had two already. One he tortured to death and the other left him."

"Does he have children?"

"No, he's sterile."

The guest was about to say more, but a servant came to call for him.

Akhsa's eyes filled with tears. Her grandfather had not forsaken her. He had led her in the right direction. She went to arrange conveyance to Izbica, and in front of the inn stood a covered wagon ready to leave. "No, I am not alone," she said to herself. "Every step is known in Heaven."

In the beginning, the roads were paved, but soon they became dirt trails full of holes and ditches. The night was wet and dark. Often the passengers had to climb down and help the coachman push the wagon out of the mud. The others scolded him, but Akhsa accepted her discomfort with grace. Wet snow was falling and a cold wind blew. Every time she got out of the wagon she sank over her ankles in mud. They arrived in Izbica late in the evening. The whole village was a swamp. The huts were dilapidated. Someone showed Akhsa the way to Zemach the Teacher's house — it was on a hill near the butcher shops. Even though it was winter, there was a stench of decay in the air. Butcher-shop dogs were slinking around.

Akhsa looked into the window of Zemach's hut and saw peeling walls, a dirt floor, and shelves of worn books. A wick in a dish of oil gave the only light. At the table sat a little man with a black beard, bushy brows, a yellow face, and a pointed nose. He was bending myopically over a large volume. He wore the lining of a skullcap and a quilted jacket that showed the dirty batting. As Akhsa stood watching, a mouse came out of its hole and scurried over to the bed, which had a pallet of rotting straw, a pillow without a case, and a moth-eaten sheepskin for a blanket. Even though Zemach had aged, Akhsa recognized him. He scratched himself. He spat on his fingertips and wiped them on his forehead. Yes, that was he. Akhsa wanted to laugh and cry at the same time. In a moment she turned her face toward the darkness. For the first time in years, she heard her grandmother's voice. "Akhsa, run away."

"Where to?"

"Back to Esau."

Then she heard her grandfather's voice. "Akhsa, he will save you from the abyss."

Akhsa had never heard her grandfather speak with such fervor. She felt the emptiness that comes before fainting. She leaned against the door and it opened.

Zemach lifted one bushy brow. His eyes were bulging and jaundiced. "What do you want?" he rasped.

"Are you Reb Zemach?"

"Yes, who are you?"

"Akhsa, from Krasnobród. Once your fiancée. . . ."

Zemach was silent. He opened his crooked mouth, revealing a single tooth, black as a hook. "The convert?"

"I have come back to Jewishness."

Zemach jumped up. A terrible cry tore from him. "Get out of my house! Blotted be your name!"

"Reb Zemach, please hear me!"

He ran toward her with clenched fists. The dish of oil fell and the light was extinguished. "Filth!"

The study house in Holishitz was packed. It was the day before the new moon, and a crowd had gathered to recite the supplications. From the women's section came the sound of pious recitation. Suddenly the door opened, and a black-bearded man wearing tattered clothes strode in. A bag was slung over his shoulder. He was leading a woman on a rope as if she were a cow. She wore a black kerchief on her head, a dress made of sackcloth, and rags on her feet. Around her neck hung a wreath of garlic. The worshippers stopped their prayers. The stranger gave a sign to the woman and she prostrated herself on the threshold. "Jews, step on me!" she called. "Jews, spit on me!"

Turmoil rose in the study house. The stranger went up to the reading table, tapped for silence, and intoned, "This woman's family comes from your town. Her grandfather was Reb Naftali Holishitzer. She is the Akhsa who converted and married a squire. She has seen the truth now and wants to atone for her abominations."

Though Holishitz was in the part of Poland that belonged to Austria, the story of Akhsa had been heard there. Some of the worshippers protested that this was not the way of repentance; a human being should not be dragged by a rope, like cattle. Others threatened the stranger with their fists. It was true that in Austria a convert could return to Jewishness according to the law of the land. But if the Gentiles were to learn that one who went over to their faith had been humiliated in such a fashion, harsh edicts and recriminations might result. The old rabbi, Reb Bezalel, approached Akhsa with quick little steps. "Get up, my daughter. Since you have repented, you are one of us."

Akhsa rose. "Rabbi, I have disgraced my people."

"Since you repent, the Almighty will forgive you."

When the worshippers in the women's section heard what was going on, they rushed into the room with the men, the rabbi's wife among them. Reb Bezalel said to her, "Take her home and dress her in decent clothing. Man was created in God's image."

"Rabbi," Akhsa said, "I want to atone for my iniquities."

"I will prescribe a penance for you. Don't torture yourself."

Some of the women began to cry. The rabbi's wife took off her shawl and hung it over Akhsa's shoulders. Another matron offered Akhsa a cape. They led her into the chamber where in olden times they had kept captive those who sinned against the community — it still contained a block and chain. The women dressed Akhsa there. Someone brought her a skirt and shoes. As they busied themselves about her, Akhsa beat her breast with her fist and recounted her sins: she had spited God, served idols, copulated with a Gentile. She sobbed, "I practiced witchcraft. I conjured up Satan. He braided me a crown of feathers." When Akhsa was dressed, the rabbi's wife took her home.

After prayers, the men began to question the stranger as to who he was and how he was connected with Reb Naftali's granddaughter.

He replied, "My name is Zemach. I was supposed to become her husband, but she refused me. Now she has come to ask my forgiveness."

"A Jew should forgive."

"I forgive her, but the Almighty is a God of vengeance."

"He is also a God of mercy."

Zemach began a debate with the scholars, and his erudition was obvious at once. He quoted the Talmud, the Commentaries, and the Responsa. He even corrected the rabbi when he misquoted.

Reb Bezalel asked him, "Do you have a family?"

"I am divorced."

"In that case, everything can be set right."

The rabbi invited Zemach to go home with him. The women sat with Akhsa out in the kitchen. They urged her to eat bread with chicory. She had been fasting for three days. In the rabbi's study the men looked after Zemach. They brought him trousers, shoes, a coat, and a hat. Since he was infested with lice, they took him to the baths.

In the evening, the seven outstanding citizens of the town and all the important elders gathered. The wives brought Akhsa. The rabbi pronounced that, according to the law, Akhsa was not married. Her union with the squire was nothing but an act of lechery. The rabbi asked, "Zemach, do you desire Akhsa for your wife?"

"I do."

"Akhsa, will you take Zemach for a husband?"

"Yes, Rabbi, but I am not worthy."

The rabbi outlined Akhsa's penance. She must fast each Monday and Thursday, abstain from meat and fish on the weekdays, recite psalms, and rise at dawn for prayers. The rabbi said to her, "The chief thing is not the punishment but the remorse. 'And he will return and be healed,' the prophet says."

"Rabbi, excuse," Zemach interrupted. "This kind of penance is for common sins, not for conversion."

"What do you want her to do?"

"There are more severe forms of contrition."

"What, for example?"

"Wearing pebbles in the shoes. Rolling naked in the snow in winter — in nettles in summer. Fasting from Sabbath to Sabbath."

"Nowadays, people do not have the strength for such rigors," the rabbi said after some hesitation.

"If they have the strength to sin, they should have the strength to expiate."

"Holy Rabbi," said Akhsa, "do not let me off lightly. Let the rabbi give me a harsh penance."

"I have said what is right."

All kept silent. Then Akhsa said, "Zemach, give me my bundle." Zemach had put her bag in a corner. He brought it to the table and she took out a little sack. A sigh could be heard from the group as she poured out settings of pearls, diamonds, and rubies. "Rabbi, this is my jewelry," Akhsa said. "I do not deserve to own it. Let the rabbi dispose of it as he wishes."

"Is it yours or the squire's?"

"Mine, Rabbi, inherited from my sacred grandmother."

"It is written that even the most charitable should never give up more than a fifth part."

Zemach shook his head. "Again I am in disagreement. She disgraced her grandmother in Paradise. She should not be permitted to inherit her jewels."

The rabbi clutched his beard. "If you know better, you become the rabbi." He rose from his chair and then sat down again. "How will you sustain yourselves?"

"I will be a water carrier," Zemach said.

"Rabbi, I can knead dough and wash linen," Akhsa said.

"Well, do as you choose. I believe in the mercy, not in the rigor, of the law."

In the middle of the night Akhsa opened her eyes. Husband and wife lived in a hut with a dirt floor, not far from the cemetery. All day long Zemach carried water. Akhsa washed linen. Except for Saturday and holidays, both fasted every day and ate only in the evening. Akhsa had put sand and pebbles into her shoes and wore a rough woolen skirt next to her skin. At night they slept separately on the floor — he on a mat by the window, she on a straw pallet by the oven. On a rope that stretched from wall to wall hung shrouds she had made for them.

They had been married for three years, but Zemach still had not approached her. He had confessed that he, too, was dipped in sin. While he had a wife, he had lusted for Akhsa. He had spilled his seed like Onan. He had craved revenge upon her, had railed against the Almighty, and had taken out his wrath on his wives, one of whom died. How could he be more defiled?

Even though the hut was near a forest and they could get wood for nothing, Zemach would not allow the stove to be heated at night. They slept in their clothes, covered with sacks and rags. The people of Holishitz maintained that Zemach was a madman; the rabbi had called for man and wife and explained that it is as cruel to torture oneself as it is to torture others, but Zemach quoted from *The Beginning of Wisdom* that repentance without mortification is meaningless.

Akhsa made a confession every night before sleep, and still her dreams were not pure. Satan came to her in the image of her grandmother and described dazzling cities, elegant balls, passionate squires, lusty women. Her grandfather had become silent again.

In Akhsa's dreams, Grandmother was young and beautiful. She sang bawdy songs, drank wine, and danced with charlatans. Some nights she led Akhsa into temples where priests chanted and idolators kneeled before golden statues. Naked courtesans drank wine from horns and gave themselves over to licentiousness.

One night Akhsa dreamed that she stood naked in a round hole. Midgets danced around her in circles. They sang obscene dirges. There was a blast of trumpets and the drumming of drums. When she awoke, the black singing still rang in her ears. "I am lost forever," she said to herself.

Zemach had also wakened. For a time he looked out through the one windowpane he had not boarded up. Then he asked, "Akhsa, are you awake? A new snow has fallen."

Akhsa knew too well what he meant. She said, "I have no strength."

"You had strength to give yourself to the wicked."

"My bones ache."

"Tell that to the Avenging Angel."

The snow and the late-night moon cast a bright glare into the room. Zemach had let his hair grow long, like an ancient ascetic. His beard was wild and his eyes glowed in the night. Akhsa could never understand how he had the power to carry water all day long and still study half the night. He scarcely partook of the evening meal. To keep himself from enjoying the food, he swallowed his bread without chewing it, he oversalted and peppered the soup she cooked for him. Akhsa herself had become emaciated. Often she looked at her reflection in the slops and saw a thin face, sunken cheeks, a sickly pallor. She coughed frequently and spat phlegm with blood. Now she said, "Forgive me, Zemach, I can't get up."

"Get up, adulteress. This may be your last night."

"I wish it were."

"Confess! Tell the truth."

"I have told everything."

"Did you enjoy the lechery?"

"No, Zemach, no."

"Last time you admitted that you did."

Akhsa was silent for a long time. "Very rarely. Perhaps for a second."

"And you forgot God?"

"Not altogether."

"You knew God's law, but you defied Him willfully."

"I thought the truth was with the Gentiles."

"All because Satan braided you a crown of feathers?"

"I thought it was a miracle."

"Harlot, don't defend yourself!"

"I do not defend myself. He spoke with Grandmother's voice."

"Why did you listen to your grandmother and not to your grandfather?"

"I was foolish."

"Foolish? For years you wallowed in utter desecration."

After a while man and wife went out barefoot into the night. Zemach threw himself into the snow first. He rolled over and over with great speed. His skullcap fell off. His body was covered with black hair, like fur. Akhsa waited a minute, and then she too threw herself down. She turned in the snow slowly and in silence while Zemach recited, "We have sinned, we have betrayed, we have robbed, we have lied, we have mocked, we have rebelled." And then he added, "Let it be Thy will that my death shall be the redemption for all my iniquities."

Akhsa had heard this lamentation often, but it made her tremble every time. This was the way the peasants had wailed when her husband, Squire Malkowski, whipped them. She was more afraid of Zemach's wailing than of the cold in winter and the nettles in summer. Occasionally, when he was in a gentler temper, Zemach promised that he would come to her as husband to wife. He even said that he would like to be the father of her children. But when? He kept on searching for new misdeeds in both of them. Akhsa grew weaker from day to day. The shrouds on the rope and the headstones in the graveyard seemed to beckon her. She made Zemach vow that he would recite the Kaddish over her grave.

On a hot day in the month of Tammuz, Akhsa went to gather sorrel leaves from the pasture that bordered the river. She had fasted all day long and she wanted to cook schav for herself and Zemach for their evening meal. In the middle of her gathering she was overcome by exhaustion. She stretched out on the grass and dozed off, intending to rest only a quarter of an hour. But her mind went blank and her legs turned to stone. She fell into a deep sleep. When she opened her eyes, night had fallen. The sky was overcast, the air heavy with humidity. There was a storm coming. The earth steamed with the scent of grass and herbs, and it made Akhsa's head reel. In the darkness she found her basket, but it was empty. A goat or cow had eaten her sorrel. Suddenly she remembered her childhood, when she was pampered by her grandparents, dressed in velvet and silk, and served by maids and butlers. Now coughing choked her, her forehead was hot, and chills flashed through her spine. Since the moon did not shine and the stars were obscured, she scarcely knew her way. Her bare feet stepped on thorns and cow pats. "What a trap I have fallen into!" something cried out in her. She came to a tree and stopped to rest. At that moment she saw her grandfather. His white beard glowed in the darkness. She recognized his high forehead, his benign smile, and the loving kindness of his gaze. She called out, "Grandfather!" And in a second her face was washed with tears.

"I know everything," her grandfather said. "Your tribulations and your grief."

"Grandfather, what shall I do?"

"My daughter, your ordeal is over. We are waiting for you — I, Grandmother, all who love you. Holy angels will come to meet you."

"When, Grandfather?"

In that instant the image dissolved. Only the darkness remained. Akhsa felt her way home like someone blind. Finally, she reached her hut. As she opened the door she could feel that Zemach was there. He sat on the floor and his eyes were like two coals. He called out, "It's you?"

"Yes, Zemach."

"Why were you so long? Because of you I couldn't say my evening prayers in peace. You confused my thoughts."

"Forgive me, Zemach. I was tired and I fell asleep in the pasture."

"Liar! Convert! Scum!" Zemach screeched. "I searched for you in the pasture. You were whoring with a shepherd."

"What are you saying? God forbid!"

"Tell me the truth!" He jumped up and began to shake her. "Bitch! Demon! Lilith!"

Zemach had never acted so wildly. Akhsa said to him, "Zemach, my husband, I am faithful to you. I fell asleep on the grass. On the way home I saw my grandfather. My time is up." She was seized with such weakness that she sank to the floor.

Zemach's wrath vanished immediately. A mournful wail broke from him. "Sacred soul, where will I be without you? You are a saint. Forgive me my harshness. It was because of my love. I wanted to cleanse you so that you could sit in Paradise with the Holy Mothers."

"As I deserve, so shall I sit."

"Why should this happen to you? Is there no justice in Heaven?" And Zemach wailed in the voice that terrified her. He beat his head against the wall.

The next morning Akhsa did not rise from her bed. Zemach brought porridge he had cooked for her on the tripod. When he fed it to her, it spilled out of her mouth. Zemach fetched the town healer, but the healer did not know what to do. The women of the Burial Society came. Akhsa lay in a state of utter weakness. Her life was draining away. In the middle of the day Zemach went on foot to the town of Jaroslaw to bring a doctor. Evening came and he had not returned. That morning the rabbi's wife had sent a pillow to Akhsa. It was the first time in years she had slept on a pillow. Toward evening, the Burial Society women went home to their families and Akhsa remained alone. A wick burned in a dish of oil. A tepid breeze came through the open window. The moon did not shine, but the stars glittered. Crickets chirped, and frogs croaked with human voices. Once in a while a shadow passed the wall across from her bed. Akhsa knew that her end was near, but she had no fear of death. She took stock of her soul. She had been born rich and beautiful, with more gifts than all the others around her. Bad luck had made everything turn to the opposite. Did she suffer for her own sins or was she a reincarnation of someone who had sinned in a former generation? Akhsa knew that she should be spending her last hours in repentance and prayer. But such was her fate that doubt did not leave her even now. Her grandfather had told her one thing, her grandmother another. Akhsa had read in an old book about the Apostates who denied God, considering the world a random combination of atoms. She had now one desire — that a sign should be given, the pure truth revealed. She lay and prayed for a miracle. She fell into a light sleep and dreamed she was falling into depths that were tight and dark. Each time it seemed that she had reached the bottom, the foundation collapsed under her and she began to sink again with greater speed. The dark became heavier and the abyss even deeper.

She opened her eyes and knew what to do. With her last strength she got up and found a knife. She took off the pillowcase and with numb fingers ripped open the seams of the pillow. From the down stuffing she pulled out a crown of feathers. A hidden hand had braided in its top the four letters of God's name.

Akhsa put the crown beside her bed. In the wavering light of the wick, she could see each letter clearly; the *Yud*, the *Hai*, the *Vov*, and the other *Hai*. But, she wondered, in what way was this crown more a revelation of truth than the other? Was it possible that there were different faiths in Heaven? Akhsa began to pray for a new miracle. In her dismay she remembered the Devil's words: "The truth is that there is no truth."

Late at night, one of the Burial Society women returned. Akhsa wanted to implore her not to step on the crown, but she was too weak. The woman stepped on the crown, and its delicate structure dissolved. Akhsa closed her eyes and never opened them again. At dawn she sighed and gave up her soul.

One of the women lifted a feather and put it to her nostrils, but it did not flutter.

Later in the day, the Burial Society women cleansed Akhsa and dressed her in the shroud that she had sewn for herself. Zemach still had not returned from Jaroslaw and he was never heard of again. There was talk in Holishitz that he had been killed on the road. Some surmised that Zemach was not a man but a demon. Akhsa was buried near the chapel of a holy man, and the rabbi spoke a eulogy for her.

One thing remained a riddle. In her last hours Akhsa had ripped open the pillow that the rabbi's wife had sent her. The women who washed her body found bits of down between her fingers. How could a dying woman have the strength to do this? And what had she been searching for? No matter how much the townspeople pondered and how many explanations they tried to find, they never discovered the truth.

Because if there is such a thing as truth it is as intricate and hidden as a crown of feathers.

[1973]

RICHARD WRIGHT (1908–1960) *was born on a plantation near Natchez, Mississippi, the son of a farmhand and a country schoolteacher. His home life was disrupted after his father deserted the family; after that he lived off and on with his grandmother, a Seventh Day Adventist whose repressive religious code curbed his early attempts to write fiction, which she labeled "lies" and "the Devil's work." Wright was stubborn, however, and continued to write stories at the Smith-Robinson secondary school in Jackson, Mississippi. After his graduation, he moved North, first to Memphis, then to Chicago, and then to New York City, where he became involved in radical politics. He was a member of the Communist Party from 1932 to 1942. In the 1930s he worked as a reporter for* New Masses, *a correspondent for the Harlem bureau of the* Daily Worker, *and an editor for* New Challenge, *a left-wing magazine.* New Challenge *published his* "Blueprint for Negro Writing," *an effort to bridge the gap between Marxism and black nationalism, in 1938. He was also writing the stories that appeared in* Uncle Tom's Children, *a book that won first prize in a contest for writers on the Federal Writers Project sponsored by* Story *magazine during the Depression. Wright's early fiction was strongly influenced by Gertrude Stein's "insistent and original" use of informal American speech in* Three Lives, *and Ernest Hemingway's "simple, direct way" of writing stories, but he also set himself the problem of how to use their Modernist style to write about social issues:*

> Practically all of us, young writers, were influenced by Ernest Hemingway. We liked the simple, direct way in which he wrote, but a great many of us wanted to write about social problems. The question came up: How could we write about social problems and use a simple style? Hemingway's style is so concentrated on naturalistic detail that there is no room for social comment. One boy said that one way was to dig deeper into the character and try to get something that will live. I decided to try it.

The result was the five stories published in Uncle Tom's Children *in 1938. Next Wright turned to his first novel,* Native Son (1940), *an American classic dramatizing a story of racial conflict. This was followed by* Black Boy (1945), *a brilliant autobiography written when he was not yet forty. The next year he left the United States to live the last fourteen years of his life in Paris, feeling himself alienated from the capitalistic goals of American society and looking beyond the scope of racial and political commitment for answers to social problems. In France he wrote the novels* The Outsider (1953), Savage Holiday (1954), *and* The Long Dream (1958). *This last was conceived as the first volume of a trilogy depicting the gradual liberation of a black American from the ways of thinking imposed on him* by racial oppression. In 1960, the year Wright died, he gathered for publication his second book of short stories, Eight Men, made up of fiction that had appeared over the years in magazines and anthologies, including "The Man Who Was Almost a Man," written in the 1930s.

Telling stories from a realistic view of black experience, Wright was an artist who experimented with literary techniques in all his fiction. His short stories dramatize the same themes as his novels and are equally experimental. The early story "The Man Who Was Almost a Man" weaves illiterate Southern black dialect so skillfully with standard English narration that most readers are unaware of the effect of the deliberate juxtaposition, but the technique brings us closer to the simple farm boy's world while making an implicit social comment about his world's distance from the exploitative white society engulfing him.

Richard Wright

ოიე

THE MAN WHO WAS ALMOST A MAN

Dave struck out across the fields, looking homeward through paling light. Whut's the use talkin wid em niggers in the field? Anyhow, his mother was putting supper on the table. Them niggers can't understan nothing. One of these days he was going to get a gun and practice shooting, then they couldn't talk to him as though he were a little boy. He slowed, looking at the ground. Shucks, Ah ain scareda them even ef they are biggern me! Aw, Ah know whut Ahma do. Ahm going by ol Joe's sto n git that Sears Roebuck catlog n look at them guns. Mebbe Ma will lemme buy one when she gits mah pay from ol man Hawkins. Ahma beg her t gimme some money. Ahm ol ernough to hava gun. Ahm seventeen. Almost a man. He strode, feeling his long loose-jointed limbs. Shucks, a man oughta hava little gun aftah he done worked hard all day.

He came in sight of Joe's store. A yellow lantern glowed on the front porch. He mounted steps and went through the screen door, hearing it bang behind him. There was a strong smell of coal oil and mackerel fish. He felt very confident until he saw fat Joe walk in through the rear door, then his courage began to ooze.

"Howdy, Dave! Whutcha want?"

"How yuh, Mistah Joe? Aw, Ah don wanna buy nothing. Ah jus wanted t see ef yuhd lemme look at tha catlog erwhile."

"Sure! You wanna see it here?"

"Nawsuh. Ah wants t take it home wid me. Ah'll bring it back ter-morrow when Ah come in from the fiels."

"You plannin on buying something?"

"Yessuh."

"Your ma lettin you have your own money now?"

"Shucks. Mistah Joe, Ahm gittin t be a man like anybody else!"

Joe laughed and wiped his greasy white face with a red bandanna.

"Whut you plannin on buyin?"

Dave looked at the floor, scratched his head, scratched his thigh, and smiled. Then he looked up shyly.

"Ah'll tell yuh, Mistah Joe, ef yuh promise yuh won't tell."

"I promise."

"Waal, Ahma buy a gun."

"A gun? What you want with a gun?"

"Ah wanna keep it."

"You ain't nothing but a boy. You don't need a gun."

"Aw, lemme have the catlog, Mistah Joe. Ah'll bring it back."

Joe walked through the rear door. Dave was elated. He looked around at barrels of sugar and flour. He heard Joe coming back. He craned his neck to see if he were bringing the book. Yeah, he's got it. Gawddog, he's got it!

"Here, but be sure you bring it back. It's the only one I got."

"Sho, Mistah Joe."

"Say, if you wanna buy a gun, why don't you buy one from me? I gotta gun to sell."

"Will it shoot?"

"Sure it'll shoot."

"Whut kind is it?"

"Oh, it's kinda old . . . a left-hand Wheeler. A pistol. A big one."

"Is it got bullets in it?"

"It's loaded."

"Kin Ah see it?"

"Where's your money?"

"What yuh wan fer it?"

"I'll let you have it for two dollars."

"Just two dollahs? Shucks, Ah could buy tha when Ah git mah pay."

"I'll have it here when you want it."

"Awright, suh. Ah be in fer it."

He went through the door, hearing it slam again behind him. Ahma git some money from Ma n buy me a gun! Only two dollahs! He tucked the thick catalogue under his arm and hurried.

"Where yuh been, boy?" His mother held a steaming dish of black-eyed peas.

"Aw, Ma, Ah jus stopped down the road t talk wid the boys."

"Yuh know bettah t keep suppah waitin."

He sat down, resting the catalogue on the edge of the table.

"Yuh git up from there and git to the well n wash yosef! Ah ain feedin no hogs in mah house!"

She grabbed his shoulder and pushed him. He stumbled out of the room, then came back to get the catalogue.

"Whut this?"

"Aw, Ma, it's jusa catlog."

"Who yuh git it from?"

"From Joe, down at the sto."

"Waal, thas good. We kin use it in the outhouse."

"Naw, Ma." He grabbed for it. "Gimme ma catlog, Ma."

She held onto it and glared at him

"Quit hollerin at me! Whut's wrong wid yuh? Yuh crazy?"

"But Ma, please. It ain mine! It's Joe's! He tol me t bring it back t im termorrow."

She gave up the book. He stumbled down the back steps, hugging the thick book under his arm. When he had splashed water on his face and hands, he groped back to the kitchen and fumbled in a corner for the towel. He bumped into a chair; it clattered to the floor. The catalogue sprawled at his feet. When he had dried his eyes he snatched up the book and held it again under his arm. His mother stood watching him.

"Now, ef yuh gonna act a fool over that ol book, Ah'll take it n burn it up."

"Naw, Ma, please."

"Waal, set down n be still!"

He sat down and drew the oil lamp close. He thumbed page after page, unaware of the food his mother set on the table. His father came in. Then his small brother.

"Whutcha got there, Dave?" his father asked.

"Jusa catlog," he answered, not looking up.

"Yeah, here they is!" His eyes glowed at blue-and-black revolvers. He glanced up, feeling sudden guilt. His father was watching him. He eased the book under the table and rested it on his knees. After the blessing was asked, he ate. He scooped up peas and swallowed fat meat without chewing. Buttermilk helped to wash it down. He did not want to mention money before his father. He would do much better by cornering his mother when she was alone. He looked at his father uneasily out of the edge of his eye.

"Boy, how come yuh don quit foolin wid tha book n eat yo suppah?"

"Yessuh."

"How you n ol man Hawkins gitten erlong?"

"Suh?"

"Can't yuh hear? Why don yuh lissen? Ah ast yu how wuz yuh n ol man Hawkins gittin erlong?"

"Oh, swell, Pa. Ah plows mo lan than anybody over there."

"Waal, yuh oughta keep you mind on whut yuh doin."

"Yessuh."

He poured his plate full of molasses and sopped it up slowly with a chunk of cornbread. When his father and brother had left the kitchen, he still sat and looked again at the guns in the catalogue, longing to muster courage enough to present his case to his mother. Lawd, ef Ah only had tha pretty one! He could almost feel the slickness of the weapon with his fingers. If he had a gun like that he would polish it and keep it shining so it would never rust. N Ah'd keep it loaded, by Gawd!

"Ma?" His voice was hesitant.

"Hunh?"

"Ol man Hawkins give yuh mah money yit?"

"Yeah, but ain no usa yuh thinking bout throwin nona it erway. Ahm keeping tha money sos yuh kin have cloes t go to school this winter."

He rose and went to her side with the open catalogue in his palms. She was washing dishes, her head bent low over a pan. Shyly he raised the book. When he spoke, his voice was husky, faint.

"Ma, Gawd knows Ah wans one of these."

"One of whut?" she asked, not raising her eyes.

"One of these," he said again, not daring even to point. She glanced up at the page, then at him with wide eyes.

"Nigger, is yuh gone plumb crazy?"

"Aw, Ma — "

"Git outta here! Don yuh talk t me bout no gun! Yuh a fool!"

"Ma, Ah kin buy one fer two dollahs."

"Not ef Ah knows it, yuh ain!"

"But yuh promised me one — "

"Ah don care what Ah promised! Yuh ain nothing but a boy yit!"

"Ma, ef yuh lemme buy one Ah'll *never* ast yuh fer nothing no mo."

"Ah tol yuh t git outta here! Yuh ain gonna toucha penny of tha money fer no gun! Thas how come Ah has Mistah Hawkins t pay yo wages t me, cause Ah knows yuh ain got no sense."

"But, Ma, we needa gun. Pa ain got no gun. We needa gun in the house. Yuh kin never tell whut might happen."

"Now don yuh try to maka fool outta me, boy! Ef we did hava gun, yuh wouldn't have it!"

He laid the catalogue down and slipped his arm around her waist.

"Aw, Ma, Ah done worked hard alla summer n ain ast yuh fer nothing, is Ah, now?"

"Thas whut yuh spose t do!"

"But Ma, Ah wans a gun. Yuh kin lemme have two dollahs outta mah money. Please, Ma. I kin give it to Pa. . . . Please, Ma! Ah loves yuh, Ma."

When she spoke her voice came soft and low.

"What yu wan wida gun, Dave? Yuh don need no gun. Yuh'll git in trouble. N ef yo pa jus thought Ah let yuh have money t buy a gun he'd hava fit."

"Ah'll hide it, Ma. It ain but two dollahs."

"Lawd, chil, whut's wrong wid yuh?"

"Ain nothin wrong. Ma. Ahm almos a man now. Ah wans a gun."

"Who gonna sell yuh a gun?"

"Ol Joe at the sto."

"N it don cos but two dollahs?"

"Thas all, Ma. Jus two dollahs. Please, Ma."

She was stacking the plates away; her hands moved slowly, reflectively. Dave kept an anxious silence. Finally, she turned to him.

"Ah'll let yuh git tha gun ef yuh promise me one thing."

"What's tha, Ma?"

"Yuh bring it straight back t me, yuh hear? It be fer Pa."

"Yessum! Lemme go now, Ma."

She stooped, turned slightly to one side, raised the hem of her dress, rolled down the top of her stocking, and came up with a slender wad of bills.

"Here," she said. "Lawd knows yuh don need no gun. But yer pa does. Yuh bring it right back t me, yuh hear? Ahma put it up. Now ef yuh don, Ahma have yuh pa lick yuh so hard yuh won fergit it."

"Yessum."

He took the money, ran down the steps, and across the yard.

"Dave! Yuuuuuh Daaaaave!"

He heard, but he was not going to stop now. "Naw, Lawd!"

The first movement he made the following morning was to reach under his pillow for the gun. In the gray light of dawn he held it loosely, feeling a sense of power. Could kill a man with a gun like this. Kill anybody, black or white. And if he were holding his gun in his hand, nobody could run over him; they would have to respect him. It was a big gun, with a long barrel and a heavy handle. He raised and lowered it in his hand, marveling at its weight.

He had not come straight home with it as his mother had asked; instead he had stayed out in the fields, holding the weapon in his hand, aiming it now and then at some imaginary foe. But he had not fired it; he had been afraid that his father might hear. Also he was not sure he knew how to fire it.

To avoid surrendering the pistol he had not come into the house until he knew that they were all asleep. When his mother had tiptoed to his bedside late that night and demanded the gun, he had first played possum; then he had told her that the gun was hidden outdoors, that he would bring it to her in the morning. Now he lay turning it slowly in his hands.

He broke it, took out the cartridges, felt them, and then put them back.

He slid out of bed, got a long strip of old flannel from a trunk, wrapped the gun in it, and tied it to his naked thigh while it was still loaded. He did not go in to breakfast. Even though it was not yet daylight, he started for Jim Hawkins' plantation. Just as the sun was rising he reached the barns where the mules and plows were kept.

"Hey! That you, Dave?"

He turned. Jim Hawkins stood eying him suspiciously.

"What're yuh doing here so early?"

"Ah didn't know Ah wuz gittin up so early, Mistah Hawkins. Ah was fixin t hitch up ol Jenny n take her t the fiels."

"Good. Since you're so early, how about plowing that stretch down by the woods?"

"Suits me, Mistah Hawkins."

"O.K. Go to it!"

He hitched Jenny to a plow and started across the fields. Hot dog! This was just what he wanted. If he could get down by the woods, he could shoot his gun and nobody would hear. He walked behind the plow, hearing the traces creaking, feeling the gun tied tight to his thigh.

When he reached the woods, he plowed two whole rows before he decided to take out the gun. Finally, he stopped, looked in all directions, then untied the gun and held it in his hand. He turned to the mule and smiled.

"Know whut this is, Jenny? Naw, yuh wouldn know! Yuhs jusa ol mule! Anyhow, this is a gun, n it kin shoot, by Gawd!"

He held the gun at arm's length. Whut t hell, Ahma shoot this thing! He looked at Jenny again.

"Lissen here, Jenny! When Ah pull this ol trigger, Ah don wan yuh t run n acka fool now!"

Jenny stood with head down, her short ears pricked straight. Dave walked off about twenty feet, held the gun far out from him at arm's length, and turned his head. Hell, he told himself, Ah ain afraid. The gun felt loose in his fingers; he waved it wildly for a moment. Then he shut his eyes and tightened his forefinger. Bloom! A report half deafened him and he thought his right hand was torn from his arm. He heard Jenny whinnying and galloping over the field, and he found himself on his knees, squeezing his fingers hard between his legs. His hand was numb; he jammed it into his mouth, trying to warm it, trying to stop the pain. The gun lay at his feet. He did not quite know what had happened. He stood up and stared at the gun as though it were a living thing. He gritted his teeth and kicked the gun. Yuh almos broke mah arm! He turned to look for Jenny; she was far over the fields, tossing her head and kicking wildly.

"Hol on there, ol mule!"

When he caught up with her she stood trembling, walling her big white eyes at him. The plow was far away; the traces had broken. Then

Dave stopped short, looking, not believing. Jenny was bleeding. Her left side was red and wet with blood. He went closer. Lawd, have mercy! Wondah did Ah shoot this mule? He grabbed for Jenny's mane. She flinched, snorted, whirled, tossing her head.

"Hol on now! Hol on."

Then he saw the hole in Jenny's side, right between the ribs. It was round, wet, red. A crimson stream streaked down the front leg, flowing fast. Good Gawd! Ah wuzn't shootin at tha mule. He felt panic. He knew he had to stop that blood, or Jenny would bleed to death. He had never seen so much blood in all his life. He chased the mule for half a mile, trying to catch her. Finally she stopped, breathing hard, stumpy tail half arched. He caught her mane and led her back to where the plow and gun lay. Then he stopped and grabbed handfuls of damp black earth and tried to plug the bullet hole. Jenny shuddered, whinnied, and broke from him.

"Hol on! Hol on now!"

He tried to plug it again, but blood came anyhow. His fingers were hot and sticky. He rubbed dirt into his palms, trying to dry them. Then again he attempted to plug the bullet hole, but Jenny shied away, kicking her heels high. He stood helpless. He had to do something. He ran at Jenny; she dodged him. He watched a red stream of blood flow down Jenny's leg and form a bright pool at her feet.

"Jenny . . . Jenny," he called weakly.

His lips trembled. She's bleeding t death! He looked in the direction of home, wanting to go back, wanting to get help. But he saw the pistol lying in the damp black clay. He had a queer feeling that if he only did something, this would not be; Jenny would not be there bleeding to death.

When he went to her this time, she did not move. She stood with sleepy, dreamy eyes; and when he touched her she gave a low-pitched whinny and knelt to the ground, her front knees slopping in blood.

"Jenny . . . Jenny . . . " he whispered.

For a long time she held her neck erect; then her head sank, slowly. Her ribs swelled with a mighty heave and she went over.

Dave's stomach felt empty, very empty. He picked up the gun and held it gingerly between his thumb and forefinger. He buried it at the foot of a tree. He took a stick and tried to cover the pool of blood with dirt — but what was the use? There was Jenny lying with her mouth open and her eyes walled and glassy. He could not tell Jim Hawkins he had shot his mule. But he had to tell something. Yeah, Ah'll tell em Jenny started gittin wil n fell on the joint of the plow. . . . But that would hardly happen to a mule. He walked across the field slowly, head down.

It was sunset. Two of Jim Hawkins' men were over near the edge of the woods digging a hole in which to bury Jenny. Dave was surrounded by a knot of people, all of whom were looking down at the dead mule.

"I don't see how in the world it happened," said Jim Hawkins for the tenth time.

The crowd parted and Dave's mother, father, and small brother pushed into the center.

"Where Dave?" his mother called.

"There he is," said Jim Hawkins.

His mother grabbed him.

"Whut happened, Dave? Whut yuh done?"

"Nothin."

"C mon, boy, talk," his father said.

Dave took a deep breath and told the story he knew nobody believed.

"Waal," he drawled. "Ah brung ol Jenny down here sos Ah could do mah plowin. Ah plowed bout two rows, just like yuh see." He stopped and pointed at the long rows of upturned earth. "Then somethin musta been wrong wid ol Jenny. She wouldn ack right a-tall. She started snortin n kickin her heels. Ah tried t hol her, but she pulled erway, rearin n goin in. Then when the point of the plow was stickin up in the air, she swung erroun n twisted herself back on it. . . . She stuck herself n started t bleed. N fo Ah could do anything, she wuz dead."

"Did you ever hear of anything like that in all your life?" asked Jim Hawkins.

There were white and black standing in the crowd. They murmured. Dave's mother came close to him and looked hard into his face. "Tell the truth, Dave," she said.

"Looks like a bullet hole to me," said one man.

"Dave, whut yuh do wid the gun?" his mother asked.

The crowd surged in, looking at him. He jammed his hands into his pockets, shook his head slowly from left to right, and backed away. His eyes were wide and painful.

"Did he hava gun?" asked Jim Hawkins.

"By Gawd, Ah tol yuh tha wuz a gun wound," said a man, slapping his thigh.

His father caught his shoulders and shook him till his teeth rattled.

"Tell whut happened, yuh rascal! Tell whut. . . . "

Dave looked at Jenny's stiff legs and began to cry.

"Whut yuh do wid tha gun?" his mother asked.

"What wuz he doin wida gun?" his father asked.

"Come on and tell the truth," said Hawkins. "Ain't nobody going to hurt you. . . . "

His mother crowded close to him.

"Did yuh shoot tha mule, Dave?"

Dave cried, seeing blurred white and black faces.

"Ahh ddinn gggo tt sshooot hher. . . . Ah ssswear ffo Gawd Ahh ddin. . . . Ah wuz a-tryin t sssee ef the old gggun would sshoot — "

"Where yuh git the gun from?" his father asked.

"Ah got it from Joe, at the sto."

"Where yuh git the money?"

"Ma give it t me."

"He kept worryin me, Bob. Ah had t. Ah tol im t bring the gun right back t me. . . . It was fer yuh, the gun."

"But how yuh happen to shoot that mule?" asked Jim Hawkins.

"Ah wuzn shootin at the mule, Mistah Hawkins. The gun jumped when Ah pulled the trigger. . . . N fo Ah knowed anythin Jenny was there a-bleedin."

Somebody in the crowd laughed. Jim Hawkins walked close to Dave and looked into his face.

"Well, looks like you have bought you a mule, Dave."

"Ah swear fo Gawd, Ah didn go t kill the mule, Mistah Hawkins!"

"But you killed her!"

All the crowd was laughing now. They stood on tiptoe and poked heads over one another's shoulders.

"Well, boy, looks like yuh done bought a dead mule! Hahaha!"

"Ain tha ershame."

"Hohohohoho."

Dave stood, head down, twisting his feet in the dirt.

"Well, you needn't worry about it, Bob," said Jim Hawkins to Dave's father. "Just let the boy keep on working and pay me two dollars a month."

"Whut yuh wan fer yo mule, Mistah Hawkins?"

Jim Hawkins screwed up his eyes.

"Fifty dollars."

"Whut yuh do wid tha gun?" Dave's father demanded.

Dave said nothing.

"Yuh wan me t take a tree n beat yuh till yuh talk!"

"Nawsuh!"

"Whut yuh do wid it?"

"Ah throwed it erway."

"Where?"

"Ah . . . Ah throwed it in the creek."

"Waal, c mon home. N firs thing in the mawnin git to tha creek n fin tha gun."

"Yessuh."

"Whut yuh pay fer it?"

"Two dollahs."

"Take tha gun n git yo money back n carry it to Mistah Hawkins, yuh hear? N don fergit Ahma lam you black bottom good fer this! Now march yosef on home, suh!"

Dave turned and walked slowly. He heard people laughing. Dave glared, his eyes welling with tears. Hot anger bubbled in him. Then he swallowed and stumbled on.

That night Dave did not sleep. He was glad that he had gotten out of killing the mule so easily, but he was hurt. Something hot seemed to turn over inside him each time he remembered how they had laughed. He tossed on his bed, feeling his hard pillow. N Pa says he's gonna beat me. . . . He remembered other beatings, and his back quivered. Naw, naw, Ah sho don wan im t beat me tha way no mo. Dam em all! Nobody ever gave him anything. All he did was work. They treat me like a mule, n then they beat me. He gritted his teeth. N Ma had t tell on me.

Well, if he had to, he would take old man Hawkins that two dollars. But that meant selling the gun. And he wanted to keep that gun. Fifty dollars for a dead mule.

He turned over, thinking how he had fired the gun. He had an itch to fire it again. Ef other men kin shoota gun, by Gawd, Ah kin! He was still, listening. Mebbe they all sleepin now. The house was still. He heard the soft breathing of his brother. Yes, now! He would go down and get that gun and see if he could fire it! He eased out of bed and slipped into overalls.

The moon was bright. He ran almost all the way to the edge of the woods. He stumbled over the ground, looking for the spot where he had buried the gun. Yeah, here it is. Like a hungry dog scratching for a bone, he pawed it up. He puffed his black cheeks and blew dirt from the trigger and barrel. He broke it and found four cartridges unshot. He looked around; the fields were filled with silence and moonlight. He clutched the gun stiff and hard in his fingers. But, as soon as he wanted to pull the trigger, he shut his eyes and turned his head. Naw, Ah can't shoot wid mah eyes closed n mah head turned. With effort he held his eyes open; then he squeezed. *Blooooom!* He was stiff, not breathing. The gun was still in his hands. Dammit, he'd done it! He fired again. *Blooooom!* He smiled. *Blooooom! Blooooom! Click, click.* There! It was empty. If anybody could shoot a gun, he could. He put the gun into his hip pocket and started across the fields.

When he reached the top of a ridge he stood straight and proud in the moonlight, looking at Jim Hawkins' big white house, feeling the gun sagging in his pocket. Lawd, ef Ah had just one mo bullet Ah'd taka shot at tha house. Ah'd like t scare ol man Hawkins jusa little. . . . Jusa enough t let im know Dave Saunders is a man.

To his left the road curved, running to the tracks of the Illinois Central. He jerked his head, listening. From far off came a faint *hoooof-hoooof; hoooof-hoooof.* . . . He stood rigid. Two dollahs a mont. Les see now. . . . Tha means it'll take bout two years. Shucks! Ah'll be dam!

He started down the road, toward the tracks. Yeah, here she comes! He stood beside the track and held himself stiffly. Here she comes, erroun the ben. . . . C mon, yuh slow poke! C mon! He had his hand on his gun; something quivered in his stomach. Then the train thundered past, the gray and brown box cars rumbling and clinking. He gripped the gun tightly; then he jerked his hand out of his pocket. Ah betcha Bill wouldn't do it! Ah betcha. . . . The cars slid past, steel grinding upon steel. Ahm ridin yuh ter-night, so hep me Gawd! He was hot all over. He hesitated just a moment; then he grabbed, pulled atop of a car, and lay flat. He felt his pocket; the gun was still there. Ahead the long rails were glinting in the moonlight, stretching away, away to somewhere, somewhere where he could be a man. . . .

[1961]

EUDORA WELTY (b. 1909) *was born in Jackson, Mississippi, where she has spent nearly her whole life. She has a predominately tranquil view of the South, so her stories and novels provide a strong contrast to the turbulent fiction of William Faulkner and Richard Wright, whose geographical terrain somewhat overlaps hers. Welty grew up as one of three children in a close-knit family living two blocks away from the Mississippi state capitol. Her father was the president of an insurance company, and her mother was a thrifty housewife who kept a Jersey cow in a little pasture behind the backyard. Welty regards her personal history as hardly worth mentioning. An insatiable reader as a child, she was also a born writer. She began writing spontaneously and continued, without any particular encouragement or any plan for a profession as a writer, during her years at the Mississippi State College for Women, the University of Wisconsin, and the Columbia University School of Business. In her mid-twenties she began to publish stories in* The Southern Review, *but she credits the persistence of her New York agent Diarmuid Russell with helping her get a story published in a general-circulation magazine,* The Atlantic Monthly, *in 1941. This event led directly to the publication of her first book of stories,* A Curtain of Green, *the same year, when she was a writer "hardly known, true, but in print." During World War II she was a staff member of* The New York Times Book Review *while she lived at home with her mother and continued to write short fiction. Another collection was published in 1943 as* The Wide Net and Other Stories. *After leaving her newspaper work, she turned a short story into her first novel,* Delta Wedding *(1946), on the advice of her agent. She has produced other story collections over the years:* The Golden Apples *(1949),* The Bride of the Innisfallen and Other Stories *(1955), and* Thirteen Stories *(1965). Her novel* The Optimist's Daughter *won the Pulitzer Prize in 1972. In 1980* The Collected Stories of Eudora Welty *appeared, forty-one stories in all. Welty is also a fine critic of the short story. Her essays and reviews of the work of writers like Chekhov, Cather, Porter, Woolf, and Dinesen, as well as some comments on her own work, were collected in* The Eye of the Story *(1977).*

In the preface to her collected stories, Welty stated, "I have been told, both in approval and in accusation, that I seem to love all my characters. What I do in writing of any character is to try to enter into the mind, heart, and skin of a human being who is not myself. Whether this happens to be a man or a woman, old or young, with skin black or white, the primary challenge lies in making the jump itself. It is the act of a writer's imagination that I set most high." Although her fiction contains occasional sharp glances at southern society, as in "Petrified Man," her usual manner is a calm celebration of the minor victories of her characters, in narratives that

have some of the willed simplicity of folk tales, catching the accent, intona-
tion, and rhythms of southern speech with apparent effortlessness.

As Katherine Anne Porter recognized in her introduction to A Curtain
of Green, *"A Worn Path" is a story "where external act and the internal*
voiceless life of the human imagination almost meet and mingle on the
mysterious threshold between dream and waking, one reality refusing to
admit or confirm the existence of the other, yet both conspiring toward the
same end." Welty's own interpretation of this story, presented in her essay
"Is Phoenix Jackson's Grandson Really Dead?" in Part II of this anthology
(p. 1187), is considerably more down-to-earth.

Eudora Welty

ฌ

PETRIFIED MAN

"Reach in my purse and git me a cigarette without no powder in it if
you kin, Mrs. Fletcher, honey," said Leota to her ten o'clock shampoo-and-
set customer. "I don't like no perfumed cigarettes."

Mrs. Fletcher gladly reached over to the lavender shelf under the
lavender-framed mirror, shook a hair net loose from the clasp of the patent-
leather bag, and slapped her hand down quickly on a powder puff which
burst out when the purse was opened.

"Why, look at the peanuts, Leota!" said Mrs. Fletcher in her marvel-
ling voice.

"Honey, them goobers has been in my purse a week if they's been in it
a day. Mrs. Pike bought them peanuts."

"Who's Mrs. Pike?" asked Mrs. Fletcher, settling back. Hidden in this
den of curling fluid and henna packs, separated by a lavender swing-door
from the other customers, who were being gratified in other booths, she
could give her curiosity its freedom. She looked expectantly at the black
part in Leota's yellow curls as she bent to light the cigarette.

"Mrs. Pike is this lady from New Orleans," said Leota, puffing, and
pressing into Mrs. Fletcher's scalp with strong red-nailed fingers. "A friend,
not a customer. You see, like maybe I told you last time, me and Fred and
Sal and Joe all had us a fuss, so Sal and Joe up and moved out, so we didn't
do a thing but rent out their room. So we rented it to Mrs. Pike. And Mr.
Pike." She flicked an ash into the basket of dirty towels. "Mrs. Pike is a very
decided blonde. *She* bought me the peanuts."

"She must be cute," said Mrs. Fletcher.

"Honey, 'cute' ain't the word for what she is. I'm tellin' you, Mrs. Pike is attractive. She has her a good time. She's got a sharp eye out, Mrs. Pike has."

She dashed the comb through the air, and paused dramatically as a cloud of Mrs. Fletcher's hennaed hair floated out of the lavender teeth like a small storm-cloud.

"Hair fallin'."

"Aw, Leota."

"Uh-huh, commencin' to fall out," said Leota, combing again, and letting fall another cloud.

"Is it any dandruff in it?" Mrs. Fletcher was frowning, her hair-line eyebrows diving down toward her nose, and her wrinkled, beady-lashed eyelids batting with concentration.

"Nope." She combed again. "Just fallin' out."

"Bet it was that last perm'nent you gave me that did it," Mrs. Fletcher said cruelly. "Remember you cooked me fourteen minutes."

"You had fourteen minutes comin' to you," said Leota with finality.

"Bound to be somethin'," persisted Mrs. Fletcher. "Dandruff, dandruff. I couldn't of caught a thing like that from Mr. Fletcher, could I?"

"Well," Leota answered at last, "you know what I heard in here yestiddy, one of Thelma's ladies was settin' over yonder in Thelma's booth gittin' a machineless, and I don't mean to insist or insinuate or anything, Mrs. Fletcher, but Thelma's lady just happ'med to throw out — I forgotten what she was talkin' about at the time — that you was p-r-e-g., and lots of times that'll make your hair do awful funny, fall out and God knows what all. It just ain't our fault, is the way I look at it."

There was a pause. The women stared at each other in the mirror.

"Who was it?" demanded Mrs. Fletcher.

"Honey, I really couldn't say," said Leota. "Not that you look it."

"Where's Thelma? I'll get it out of her," said Mrs. Fletcher.

"Now, honey, I wouldn't go and git mad over a little thing like that," Leota said, combing hastily, as though to hold Mrs. Fletcher down by the hair. "I'm sure it was somebody didn't mean no harm in the world. How far gone are you?"

"Just wait," said Mrs. Fletcher, and shrieked for Thelma, who came in and took a drag from Leota's cigarette.

"Thelma, honey, throw your mind back to yestiddy if you kin," said Leota, drenching Mrs. Fletcher's hair with a thick fluid and catching the overflow in a cold wet towel at her neck.

"Well, I got my lady half wound for a spiral," said Thelma doubtfully.

"This won't take but a minute," said Leota. "Who is it you got in there, old Horse Face? Just cast your mind back and try to remember who your lady was yestiddy who happ'm to mention that my customer was pregnant, that's all. She's dead to know."

Thelma drooped her blood-red lips and looked over Mrs. Fletcher's head into the mirror. "Why, honey, I ain't got the faintest," she breathed. "I really don't recollect the faintest. But I'm sure she meant no harm. I declare, I forgot my hair finally got combed and thought it was a stranger behind me."

"Was it that Mrs. Hutchinson?" Mrs. Fletcher was tensely polite.

"Mrs. Hutchinson? Oh, Mrs. Hutchinson." Thelma batted her eyes. "Naw, precious, she come on Thursday and didn't ev'm mention your name. I doubt if she ev'm knows you're on the way."

"Thelma!" cried Leota staunchly.

"All I know is, whoever it is 'll be sorry some day. Why, I just barely knew it myself!" cried Mrs. Fletcher. "Just let her wait!"

"Why? What're you gonna do to her?"

It was a child's voice, and the women looked down. A little boy was making tents with aluminum wave pinchers on the floor under the sink.

"Billy Boy, hon, mustn't bother nice ladies," Leota smiled. She slapped him brightly and behind her back waved Thelma out of the booth. "Ain't Billy Boy a sight? Only three years old and already just nuts about the beauty-parlor business."

"I never saw him here before," said Mrs. Fletcher, still unmollified.

"He ain't been here before, that's how come," said Leota. "He belongs to Mrs. Pike. She got her a job but it was Fay's Millinery. He oughtn't to try on those ladies' hats, they come down over his eyes like I don't know what. They just git to look ridiculous, that's what, an' of course he's gonna put 'em on: hats. They tole Mrs. Pike they didn't appreciate him hangin' around there. Here, he couldn't hurt a thing."

"Well! I don't like children that much," said Mrs. Fletcher.

"Well!" said Leota moodily.

"Well! I'm almost tempted not to have this one," said Mrs. Fletcher. "That Mrs. Hutchinson! Just looks straight through you when she sees you on the street and then spits at you behind your back."

"Mr. Fletcher would beat you on the head if you didn't have it now," said Leota reasonably. "After going this far."

Mrs. Fletcher sat up straight. "Mr. Fletcher can't do a thing with me."

"He can't!" Leota winked at herself in the mirror.

"No, siree, he can't. If he so much as raises his voice against me, he knows good and well I'll have one of my sick headaches, and then I'm just not fit to live with. And if I really look pregnant already — "

"Well, now, honey, I just want you to know — I habm't told any of my ladies and I ain't goin' to tell 'em — even that you're losin' your hair. You just get you one of those Stork-a-Lure dresses and stop worryin'. What people don't know don't hurt nobody, as Mrs. Pike says."

"Did you tell Mrs. Pike?" asked Mrs. Fletcher sulkily.

"Well, Mrs. Fletcher, look, you ain't ever goin' to lay eyes on Mrs. Pike or her lay eyes on you, so what diffunce does it make in the long run?"

"I knew it!" Mrs. Fletcher deliberately nodded her head so as to destroy a ringlet Leota was working on behind her ear. "Mrs. Pike!"

Leota sighed. "I reckon I might as well tell you. It wasn't any more Thelma's lady tole me you was pregnant than a bat."

"Not Mrs. Hutchinson?"

"Naw, Lord! It was Mrs. Pike."

"Mrs. Pike!" Mrs. Fletcher could only sputter and let curling fluid roll into her ear. "How could Mrs. Pike possibly know I was pregnant or otherwise, when she doesn't even know me? The nerve of some people!"

"Well, here's how it was. Remember Sunday?"

"Yes," said Mrs. Fletcher.

"Sunday, Mrs. Pike an' me was all by ourself. Mr. Pike and Fred had gone over to Eagle Lake, sayin' they was goin' to catch 'em some fish, but they didn't a course. So we was settin' in Mrs. Pike's car, it's a 1939 Dodge — "

"1939, eh," said Mrs. Fletcher.

" — An' we was gettin' us a Jax beer apiece — that's the beer that Mrs. Pike says is made right in N.O., so she won't drink no other kind. So I seen you drive up to the drugstore an' run in for just a secont, leavin' I reckon Mr. Fletcher in the car, an' come runnin' out with looked like a perscription. So I says to Mrs. Pike, just to be makin' talk, 'Right yonder's Mrs. Fletcher, and I reckon that's Mr. Fletcher — she's one of my regular customers,' I says."

"I had on a figured print," said Mrs. Fletcher tentatively.

"You sure did," agreed Leota. "So Mrs. Pike, she give you a good look — she's very observant, a good judge of character, cute as a minute, you know — and she says, 'I bet you another Jax that lady's three months on the way.' "

"What gall!" said Mrs. Fletcher. "Mrs. Pike!"

"Mrs. Pike ain't goin' to bite you," said Leota. "Mrs. Pike is a lovely girl, you'd be crazy about her, Mrs. Fletcher. But she can't sit still a minute. We went to the travellin' freak show yestiddy after work. I got through early — nine o'clock. In the vacant store next door. What, you ain't been?"

"No, I despise freaks," declared Mrs. Fletcher.

"Aw. Well, honey, talkin' about bein' pregnant an' all, you ought to see those twins in a bottle, you really owe it to yourself."

"What twins?" asked Mrs. Fletcher out of the side of her mouth.

"Well, honey, they got these two twins in a bottle, see? Born joined plumb together — dead a course." Leota dropped her voice into a soft lyrical hum. "They was about this long — pardon — must of been full time, all right, wouldn't you say? — an' they had these two heads an' two faces an' four arms an' four legs, all kind of joined *here*. See, this face looked this-a-way, and the other face looked that-a-way, over their shoulder, see. Kinda pathetic."

"Glah!" said Mrs. Fletcher disapprovingly.

"Well, ugly? Honey, I mean to tell you — their parents was first cousins and all like that. Billy Boy, git me a fresh towel from off Teeny's stack — this 'n's wringin' wet — an' quit ticklin' my ankles with that curler. I declare! He don't miss nothin'."

"Me and Mr. Fletcher aren't one speck of kin, or he could never of had me," said Mrs. Fletcher placidly.

"Of course not!" protested Leota. "Neither is me an' Fred, not that we know of. Well, honey, what Mrs. Pike liked was the pygmies. They've got these pygmies down there, too, an' Mrs. Pike was just wild about 'em. You know, the teeniniest men in the universe? Well, honey, they can just rest back on their little bohunkus an' roll around an' you can't hardly tell if they're sittin' or standin'. That'll give you some idea. They're about forty-two years old. Just suppose it was your husband!"

"Well, Mr. Fletcher is five foot nine and one-half," said Mrs. Fletcher quickly.

"Fred's five foot ten," said Leota, "but I tell him he's still a shrimp account of I'm so tall." She made a deep wave over Mrs. Fletcher's other temple with the comb. "Well, these pygmies are a kind of a dark brown, Mrs. Fletcher. Not bad lookin' for what they are, you know."

"I wouldn't care for them," said Mrs. Fletcher. "What does that Mrs. Pike see in them?"

"Aw, I don't know," said Leota. "She's just cute, that's all. But they got this man, this petrified man, that ever'thing ever since he was nine years old, when it goes through his digestion, see, somehow Mrs. Pike says it goes to his joints and has been turning to stone."

"How awful!" said Mrs. Fletcher.

"He's forty-two too. That looks like a bad age."

"Who said so, that Mrs. Pike? I bet she's forty-two," said Mrs. Fletcher.

"Naw," said Leota, "Mrs. Pike's thirty-three, born in January, an Aquarian. He could move his head — like this. A course his head and mind ain't a joint, so to speak, and I guess his stomach ain't, either — not yet, anyways. But see — his food, he eats it, and it goes down, see, and then he digests it" — Leota rose on her toes for an instant — "and it goes out to his joints and before you can say 'Jack Robinson,' it's stone — pure stone. He's turning to stone. How'd you like to be married to a guy like that? All he can do, he can move his head just a quarter of an inch. A course he *looks* just *terrible*."

"I should think he would," said Mrs. Fletcher frostily. "Mr. Fletcher takes bending exercises every night of the world. I make him."

"All Fred does is lay around the house like a rug. I wouldn't be surprised if he woke up some day and couldn't move. The petrified man just sat there moving his quarter of an inch though," said Leota reminiscently.

"Did Mrs. Pike like the petrified man?" asked Mrs. Fletcher.

"Not as much as she did the others," said Leota deprecatingly. "And then she likes a man to be a good dresser, and all that."

"Is Mr. Pike a good dresser?" asked Mrs. Fletcher sceptically.

"Oh, well, yeah," said Leota, "but he's twelve or fourteen years older'n her. She ast Lady Evangeline about him."

"Who's Lady Evangeline?" asked Mrs. Fletcher.

"Well, it's this mind reader they got in the freak show," said Leota. "Was real good. Lady Evangeline is her name, and if I had another dollar I wouldn't do a thing but have my other palm read. She had what Mrs. Pike said was the 'sixth mind' but she had the worst manicure I ever saw on a living person."

"What did she tell Mrs. Pike?" asked Mrs. Fletcher.

"She told her Mr. Pike was as true to her as he could be and besides, would come into some money."

"Humph!" said Mrs. Fletcher. "What does he do?"

"I can't tell," said Leota, "because he don't work. Lady Evangeline didn't tell me enough about my nature or anything. And I would like to go back and find out some more about this boy. Used to go with this boy until he got married to this girl. Oh, shoot, that was about three and a half years ago, when you was still goin' to the Robert E. Lee Beauty Shop in Jackson. He married her for her money. Another fortune-teller tole me that at the time. So I'm not in love with him any more, anyway, besides being married to Fred, but Mrs. Pike thought, just for the hell of it, see, to ask Lady Evangeline was he happy."

"Does Mrs. Pike know everything about you already?" asked Mrs. Fletcher unbelievingly. "Mercy!"

"Oh, yeah, I tole her ever'thing about ever'thing, from now on back to I don't know when — to when I first started goin' out," said Leota. "So I ast Lady Evangeline for one of my questions, was he happily married, and she says, just like she was glad I ask her, 'Honey,' she says, 'naw, he idn't. You write down this day, March 8, 1941,' she says, 'and mock it down: three years from today him and her won't be occupyin' the same bed.' There it is, up on the wall with them other dates — see, Mrs. Fletcher? And she says, 'Child, you ought to be glad you didn't git him, because he's so mercenary.' So I'm glad I married Fred. He sure ain't mercenary, money don't mean a thing to him. But I sure would like to go back and have my other palm read."

"Did Mrs. Pike believe in what the fortune-teller said?" asked Mrs. Fletcher in a superior tone of voice.

"Lord, yes, she's from New Orleans. Ever'body in New Orleans believes ever'thing spooky. One of 'em in New Orleans before it was raided says to Mrs. Pike one summer she was goin' to go from State to State and meet some grey-headed men, and, sure enough, she says she went on a beautician convention up to Chicago. . . ."

"Oh!" said Mrs. Fletcher. "Oh, is Mrs. Pike a beautician too?"

"Sure she is," protested Leota. "She's a beautician. I'm goin' to git her in here if I can. Before she married. But it don't leave you. She says sure enough, there was three men who was a very large part of making her trip what it was, and they all three had grey in their hair and they went in six States. Got Christmas cards from 'em. Billy Boy, go see if Thelma's got any dry cotton. Look how Mrs. Fletcher's a-drippin'."

"Where did Mrs. Pike meet Mr. Pike?" asked Mrs. Fletcher primly.

"On another train," said Leota.

"I met Mr. Fletcher, or rather he met me, in a rental library," said Mrs. Fletcher with dignity, as she watched the net come down over her head.

"Honey, me an' Fred, we met in a rumble seat eight months ago and we was practically on what you might call the way to the altar inside of half an hour," said Leota in a guttural voice, and bit a bobby pin open. "Course it don't last. Mrs. Pike says nothin' like that ever lasts."

"Mr. Fletcher and myself are as much in love as the day we married," said Mrs. Fletcher belligerently as Leota stuffed cotton into her ears.

"Mrs. Pike says it don't last," repeated Leota in a louder voice. "Now go git under the dryer. You can turn yourself on, can't you? I'll be back to comb you out. Durin' lunch I promised to give Mrs. Pike a facial. You know — free. Her bein' in the business, so to speak."

"I bet she needs one," said Mrs. Fletcher, letting the swing-door fly back against Leota. "Oh, pardon me."

A week later, on time for her appointment, Mrs. Fletcher sank heavily into Leota's chair after first removing a drugstore rental book, called *Life Is Like That*, from the seat. She stared in a discouraged way into the mirror.

"You can tell it when I'm sitting down, all right," she said.

Leota seemed preoccupied and stood shaking out a lavender cloth. She began to pin it around Mrs. Fletcher's neck in silence.

"I said you sure can tell it when I'm sitting straight on and coming at you this way," Mrs. Fletcher said.

"Why, honey, naw you can't," said Leota gloomily. "Why, I'd never know. If somebody was to come up to me on the street and say, 'Mrs. Fletcher is pregnant!' I'd say, 'Heck, she don't look it to me.' "

"If a certain party hadn't found it out and spread it around, it wouldn't be too late even now," said Mrs. Fletcher frostily, but Leota was almost choking her with the cloth, pinning it so tight, and she couldn't speak clearly. She paddled her hands in the air until Leota wearily loosened her.

"Listen, honey, you're just a virgin compared to Mrs. Montjoy," Leota was going on, still absent-minded. She bent Mrs. Fletcher back in the chair and, sighing, tossed liquid from a teacup onto her head and dug both hands into her scalp. "You know Mrs. Montjoy — her husband's that premature-grey-headed fella?"

"She's in the Trojan Garden Club, is all I know," said Mrs. Fletcher.

"Well, honey," said Leota, but in a weary voice, "she come in here not the week before and not the day before she had her baby — she come in here the very selfsame day, I mean to tell you. Child, we was all plumb scared to death. There she was! Come for her shampoo an' set. Why, Mrs. Fletcher, in an hour an' twenty minutes she was layin' up there in the Babtist Hospital with a seb'm-pound son. It was that close a shave. I declare, if I hadn't been so tired I would of drank up a bottle of gin that night."

"What gall," said Mrs. Fletcher. "I never knew her at all well."

"See, her husband was waitin' outside in the car, and her bags was all packed an' in the back seat, an' she was all ready, 'cept she wanted her shampoo an' set. An' havin' one pain right after another. Her husband kep' comin' in here, scared-like, but couldn't do nothin' with her a course. She yelled bloody murder, too, but she always yelled her head off when I give her a perm'nent."

"She must of been crazy," said Mrs. Fletcher. "How did she look?"

"Shoot!" said Leota.

"Well, I can guess," said Mrs. Fletcher. "Awful."

"Just wanted to look pretty while she was havin' her baby, is all," said Leota airily. "Course, we was glad to give the lady what she was after — that's our motto — but I bet a hour later she wasn't payin' no mind to them little end curls. I bet she wasn't thinkin' about she ought to have on a net. It wouldn't of done her no good if she had."

"No, I don't suppose it would," said Mrs. Fletcher.

"Yeah man! She was a-yellin'. Just like when I give her perm'nent."

"Her husband ought to make her behave. Don't it seem that way to you?" asked Mrs. Fletcher. "He ought to put his foot down."

"Ha," said Leota. "A lot he could do. Maybe some women is soft."

"Oh, you mistake me, I don't mean for her to get soft — far from it! Women have to stand up for themselves, or there's just no telling. But now you take me — I ask Mr. Fletcher's advice now and then, and he appreciates it, especially on something important, like is it time for a permanent — not that I've told him about the baby. He says, 'Why, dear, go ahead!' Just ask their *advice*."

"Huh! If I ever ast Fred's advice we'd be floatin' down the Yazoo River on a houseboat or somethin' by this time," said Leota. "I'm sick of Fred. I told him to go over to Vicksburg."

"Is he going?" demanded Mrs. Fletcher.

"Sure. See, the fortune-teller — I went back and had my other palm read, since we've got to rent the room agin — said my lover was goin' to work in Vicksburg, so I don't know who she could mean, unless she meant Fred. And Fred ain't workin' here — that much is so."

"Is he going to work in Vicksburg?" asked Mrs. Fletcher. "And — "

"Sure. Lady Evangeline said so. Said the future is going to be brighter than the present. He don't want to go, but I ain't gonna put up with nothin' like that. Lays around the house an' bulls — did bull — with that good-for-nothin' Mr. Pike. He says if he goes who'll cook, but I says I never get to eat anyway — not meals. Billy Boy, take Mrs. Grover that *Screen Secrets* and leg it."

Mrs. Fletcher heard stamping feet go out the door.

"Is that that Mrs. Pike's little boy here again?" she asked, sitting up gingerly.

"Yeah, that's still him." Leota stuck out her tongue.

Mrs. Fletcher could hardly believe her eyes. "Well! How's Mrs. Pike, your attractive new friend with the sharp eyes who spreads it around town that perfect strangers are pregnant?" she asked in a sweetened tone.

"Oh, Mizriz Pike." Leota combed Mrs. Fletcher's hair with heavy strokes.

"You act like you're tired," said Mrs. Fletcher.

"Tired? Feel like it's four o'clock in the afternoon already," said Leota. "I ain't told you the awful luck we had, me and Fred? It's the worst thing you ever heard of. Maybe *you* think Mrs. Pike's got sharp eyes. Shoot, there's a limit! Well, you know, we rented out our room to this Mr. and Mrs. Pike from New Orleans when Sal an' Joe Fentress got mad at us 'cause they drank up some home-brew we had in the closet — Sal an' Joe did. So, a week ago Sat'day Mr. and Mrs. Pike moved in. Well, I kinda fixed up the room, you know — put a sofa pillow on the couch and picked some ragged robbins and put in a vase, but they never did say they appreciated it. Anyway, then I put some old magazines on the table."

"I think that was lovely," said Mrs. Fletcher.

"Wait. So, come night 'fore last, Fred and this Mr. Pike, who Fred just took up with, was back from they said they was fishin', bein' as neither one of 'em has got a job to his name, and we was all settin' around in their room. So Mrs. Pike was settin' there, readin' a old *Startling G-Man Tales* that was mine, mind you, I'd bought it myself, and all of a sudden she jumps! — into the air—you'd 'a' thought she'd set on a spider — an' says, 'Canfield' — ain't that silly, that's Mr. Pike — 'Canfield, my God A'mighty,' she says, 'honey,' she says, 'we're rich, and you won't have to work.' Not that he turned one hand anyway. Well, me and Fred rushes over to her, and Mr. Pike, too, and there she sets, pointin' her finger at a photo in my copy of *Startling G-Man.* 'See that man?' yells Mrs. Pike. 'Remember him, Canfield?' 'Never forget a face,' says Mr. Pike. 'It's Mr. Petrie, that we stayed with him in the apartment next to ours in Toulouse Street in N.O. for six weeks. Mr. Petrie.' 'Well,' says Mrs. Pike, like she can't hold out one secont longer, 'Mr. Petrie is wanted for five hundred dollars cash, for rapin' four women in California, and I know where he is.' "

"Mercy!" said Mrs. Fletcher. "Where was he?"

At some time Leota had washed her hair and now she yanked her up by the back locks and sat her up.

"Know where he was?"

"I certainly don't," Mrs. Fletcher said. Her scalp hurt all over.

Leota flung a towel around the top of her customer's head. "Nowhere else but in that freak show! I saw him just as plain as Mrs. Pike. *He* was the petrified man!"

"Who would ever have thought that!" cried Mrs. Fletcher sympathetically.

"So Mr. Pike says, 'Well whatta you know about that,' an' he looks real hard at the photo and whistles. And she starts dancin' and singin' about their good luck. She meant our bad luck! I made a point of tellin' that fortune-teller the next time I saw her. I said, 'Listen, that magazine was layin' around the house for a month, and there was the freak show runnin' night an' day, not two steps away from my beauty parlor, with Mr. Petrie just settin' there waitin'. An' it had to be Mr. and Mrs. Pike, almost perfect strangers.'"

"What gall," said Mrs. Fletcher. She was only sitting there, wrapped in a turban, but she did not mind.

"Fortune-tellers don't care. And Mrs. Pike, she goes around actin' like she thinks she was Mrs. God," said Leota. "So they're goin' to leave tomorrow, Mr. and Mrs. Pike. And in the meantime I got to keep that mean, bad little ole kid here, gettin' under my feet ever' minute of the day an' talkin' back too."

"Have they gotten the five hundred dollars' reward already?" asked Mrs. Fletcher.

"Well," said Leota, "at first Mr. Pike didn't want to do anything about it. Can you feature that? Said he kinda liked that ole bird and said he was real nice to 'em, lent 'em money or somethin'. But Mrs. Pike simply tole him he could just go to hell, and I can see her point. She says, 'You ain't worked a lick in six months, and here I make five hundred dollars in two seconts, and what thanks do I get for it? You go to hell, Canfield,' she says. So," Leota went on in a despondent voice, "they called up the cops and they caught the ole bird, all right, right there in the freak show where I saw him with my own eyes, thinkin' he was petrified. He's the one. Did it under his real name — Mr. Petrie. Four women in California, all in the month of August. So Mrs. Pike gits five hundred dollars. And my magazine, and right next door to my beauty parlor. I cried all night, but Fred said it wasn't a bit of use and to go to sleep, because the whole thing was just a sort of coincidence — you know: can't do nothin' about it. He says it put him clean out of the notion of goin' to Vicksburg for a few days till we rent out the room agin — no tellin' who we'll git this time."

"But can you imagine anybody knowing this old man, that's raped four women?" persisted Mrs. Fletcher, and she shuddered audibly. "Did Mrs. Pike *speak* to him when she met him in the freak show?"

Leota had begun to comb Mrs. Fletcher's hair. "I says to her, I says, 'I didn't notice you fallin' on his neck when he was the petrified man — don't tell me you didn't recognize your fine friend?' And she says, 'I didn't recognize him with that white powder all over his face. He just looked familiar,' Mrs. Pike says, 'and lots of people look familiar.' But she says that ole petrified man did put her in mind of somebody. She wondered who it was! Kep' her awake, which man she'd ever knew it reminded her of. So when she seen the photo, it all come to her. Like a flash. Mr. Petrie. The way he'd turn his head and look at her when she took him in his breakfast."

"Took him in his breakfast!" shrieked Mrs. Fletcher. "Listen — don't tell me. I'd 'a' felt something."

"Four women. I guess those women didn't have the faintest notion at the time they'd be worth a hundred an' twenty-five bucks apiece some day to Mrs. Pike. We ast her how old the fella was then, an' she says he musta had one foot in the grave, at least. Can you beat it?"

"Not really petrified at all, of course," said Mrs. Fletcher meditatively. She drew herself up. "I'd 'a' felt something," she said proudly.

"Shoot! I did feel somethin'," said Leota. "I tole Fred when I got home I felt so funny. I said, 'Fred, that ole petrified man sure did leave me with a funny feelin'.' He says, 'Funny-haha or funny-peculiar?' and I says, 'Funny-peculiar.' " She pointed her comb into the air emphatically.

"I'll bet you did," said Mrs. Fletcher.

They both heard a crackling noise.

Leota screamed, "Billy Boy! What you doin' in my purse?"

"Aw, I'm just eatin' these ole stale peanuts up," said Billy Boy.

"You come here to me!" screamed Leota, recklessly flinging down the comb, which scattered a whole ashtray full of bobby pins and knocked down a row of Coca-Cola bottles. "This is the last straw!"

"I caught him! I caught him!" giggled Mrs. Fletcher. "I'll hold him on my lap. You bad, bad boy, you! I guess I better learn how to spank little old bad boys," she said.

Leota's eleven o'clock customer pushed open the swing-door upon Leota paddling him heartily with the brush, while he gave angry but belittling screams which penetrated beyond the booth and filled the whole curious beauty parlor. From everywhere ladies began to gather round to watch the paddling. Billy Boy kicked both Leota and Mrs. Fletcher as hard as he could, Mrs. Fletcher with her new fixed smile.

Billy Boy stomped through the group of wild-haired ladies and went out the door, but flung back the words, "If you're so smart, why ain't you rich?"

[1941]

Eudora Welty

తు

A WORN PATH

It was December — a bright frozen day in the early morning. Far out in the country there was an old Negro woman with her head tied in a red rag, coming along a path through the pinewoods. Her name was Phoenix Jackson. She was very old and small and she walked slowly in the dark pine shadows, moving a little from side to side in her steps, with the balanced heaviness and lightness of a pendulum in a grandfather clock. She carried a thin, small cane made from an umbrella, and with this she kept tapping the frozen earth in front of her. This made a grave and persistent noise in the still air, that seemed meditative like the chirping of a solitary little bird.

She wore a dark striped dress reaching down to her shoe tops, and an equally long apron of bleached sugar sacks, with a full pocket: all neat and tidy, but every time she took a step she might have fallen over her shoelaces, which dragged from her unlaced shoes. She looked straight ahead. Her eyes were blue with age. Her skin had a pattern all its own of numberless branching wrinkles and as though a whole little tree stood in the middle of her forehead, but a golden color ran underneath, and the two knobs of her cheeks were illumined by a yellow burning under the dark. Under the red rag her hair came down on her neck in the frailest of ringlets, still black, and with an odor like copper.

Now and then there was a quivering in the thicket. Old Phoenix said, "Out of my way, all you foxes, owls, beetles, jack rabbits, coons and wild animals! . . . Keep out from under these feet, little bobwhites. . . . Keep the big wild hogs out of my path. Don't let none of those come running my direction. I got a long way." Under her small black-freckled hand her cane, limber as a buggy whip, would switch at the brush as if to rouse up any hiding things.

On she went. The woods were deep and still. The sun made the pine needles almost too bright to look at, up where the wind rocked. The cones dropped as light as feathers. Down in the hollow was the mourning dove — it was not too late for him.

The path ran up a hill. "Seem like there is chains about my feet, time I get this far," she said, in the voice of argument old people keep to use with themselves. "Something always take a hold of me on this hill — pleads I should stay."

After she got to the top she turned and gave a full, severe look behind her where she had come. "Up through pines," she said at length. "Now down through oaks."

Her eyes opened their widest, and she started down gently. But before she got to the bottom of the hill a bush caught her dress.

Her fingers were busy and intent, but her skirts were full and long, so that before she could pull them free in one place they were caught in another. It was not possible to allow the dress to tear. "I in the thorny bush," she said. "Thorns, you doing your appointed work. Never want to let folks pass, no sir. Old eyes thought you was a pretty little *green* bush."

Finally, trembling all over, she stood free, and after a moment dared to stoop for her cane.

"Sun so high!" she cried, leaning back and looking, while the thick tears went over her eyes. "The time getting all gone here."

At the foot of this hill was a place where a log was laid across the creek.

"Now comes the trial," said Phoenix.

Putting her right foot out, she mounted the log and shut her eyes. Lifting her skirt, leveling her cane fiercely before her, like a festival figure in some parade, she began to march across. Then she opened her eyes and she was safe on the other side.

"I wasn't as old as I thought," she said.

But she sat down to rest. She spread her skirts on the bank around her and folded her hands over her knees. Up above her was a tree in a pearly cloud of mistletoe. She did not dare to close her eyes, and when a little boy brought her a plate with a slice of marble-cake on it she spoke to him. "That would be acceptable," she said. But when she went to take it there was just her own hand in the air.

So she left that tree, and had to go through a barbed-wire fence. There she had to creep and crawl, spreading her knees and stretching her fingers like a baby trying to climb the steps. But she talked loudly to herself: she could not let her dress be torn now, so late in the day, and she could not pay for having her arm or her leg sawed off if she got caught fast where she was.

At last she was safe through the fence and risen up out in the clearing. Big dead trees, like black men with one arm, were standing in the purple stalks of the withered cotton field. There sat a buzzard.

"Who you watching?"

In the furrow she made her way along.

"Glad this not the season for bulls," she said, looking sideways, "and the good Lord made his snakes to curl up and sleep in the winter. A pleasure I don't see no two-headed snake coming around that tree, where it come once. It took a while to get by him, back in the summer."

She passed through the old cotton and went into a field of dead corn.

It whispered and shook and was taller than her head. "Through the maze now," she said, for there was no path.

Then there was something tall, black, and skinny there, moving before her.

At first she took it for a man. It could have been a man dancing in the field. But she stood still and listened, and it did not make a sound. It was as silent as a ghost.

"Ghost," she said sharply, "who be you the ghost of? For I have heard of nary death close by."

But there was no answer — only the ragged dancing in the wind.

She shut her eyes, reached out her hand, and touched a sleeve. She found a coat and inside that an emptiness, cold as ice.

"You scarecrow," she said. Her face lighted. "I ought to be shut up for good," she said with laughter. "My senses is gone. I too old. I the oldest people I ever know. Dance, old scarecrow," she said, "while I dancing with you."

She kicked her foot over the furrow, and with mouth drawn down, shook her head once or twice in a little strutting way. Some husks blew down and whirled in streamers about her skirts.

Then she went on, parting her way from side to side with the cane, through the whispering field. At last she came to the end, to a wagon track where the silver grass blew between the red ruts. The quail were walking around like pullets, seeming all dainty and unseen.

"Walk pretty," she said. "This the easy place. This the easy going."

She followed the track, swaying through the quiet bare fields, through the little strings of trees silver in their dead leaves, past cabins silver from weather, with the doors and windows boarded shut, all like old women under a spell sitting there. "I walking in their sleep," she said, nodding her head vigorously.

In a ravine she went where a spring was silently flowing through a hollow log. Old Phoenix bent and drank. "Sweet-gum makes the water sweet," she said, and drank more. "Nobody know who made this well, for it was here when I was born."

The track crossed a swampy part where the moss hung as white as lace from every limb. "Sleep on, alligators, and blow your bubbles." Then the track went into the road.

Deep, deep the road went down between the high green-colored banks. Overhead the live-oaks met, and it was as dark as a cave.

A black dog with a lolling tongue came up out of the weeds by the ditch. She was meditating, and not ready, and when he came at her she only hit him a little with her cane. Over she went in the ditch, like a little puff of milkweed.

Down there, her senses drifted away. A dream visited her, and she reached her hand up, but nothing reached down and gave her a pull. So she lay there and presently went to talking. "Old woman," she said to herself, "that black dog come up out of the weeds to stall you off, and now there he sitting on his fine tail, smiling at you."

A white man finally came along and found her — a hunter, a young man, with his dog on a chain.

"Well, Granny!" he laughed. "What are you doing there?"

"Lying on my back like a June-bug waiting to be turned over, mister," she said, reaching up her hand.

He lifted her up, gave her a swing in the air, and set her down. "Anything broken, Granny?"

"No sir, them old dead weeds is springy enough," said Phoenix, when she had got her breath. "I thank you for your trouble."

"Where do you live, Granny?" he asked, while the two dogs were growling at each other.

"Away back yonder, sir, behind the ridge. You can't even see it from here."

"On your way home?"

"No sir, I going to town."

"Why, that's too far! That's as far as I walk when I come out myself, and I get something for my trouble." He patted the stuffed bag he carried, and there hung down a little closed claw. It was one of the bobwhites, with its beak hooked bitterly to show it was dead. "Now you go on home, Granny!"

"I bound to go to town, mister," said Phoenix. "The time come around."

He gave another laugh, filling the whole landscape. "I know you old colored people! Wouldn't miss going to town to see Santa Claus!"

But something held old Phoenix very still. The deep lines in her face went into a fierce and different radiation. Without warning, she had seen with her own eyes a flashing nickel fall out of the man's pocket onto the ground.

"How old are you, Granny?" he was saying.

"There is no telling, mister," she said, "no telling."

Then she gave a little cry and clapped her hands and said, "Git on away from here, dog! Look! Look at that dog!" She laughed as if in admiration. "He ain't scared of nobody. He a big black dog." She whispered, "Sic him!"

"Watch me get rid of that cur," said the man. "Sic him, Pete! Sic him!"

Phoenix heard the dogs fighting, and heard the man running and throwing sticks. She even heard a gunshot. But she was slowly bending forward by that time, further and further forward, the lid stretched down over her eyes, as if she were doing this in her sleep. Her chin was lowered almost to her knees. The yellow palm of her hand came out from the fold of her apron. Her fingers slid down and along the ground under the piece of money with the grace and care they would have in lifting an egg from under a setting hen. Then she slowly straightened up, she stood erect, and the nickel was in her apron pocket. A bird flew by. Her lips moved. "God watching me the whole time. I come to stealing."

The man came back, and his own dog panted about them. "Well, I scared him off that time," he said, and then he laughed and lifted his gun and pointed it at Phoenix.

She stood straight and faced him.

"Doesn't the gun scare you?" he said, still pointing it.

"No, sir, I seen plenty go off closer by, in my day, and for less than what I done," she said, holding utterly still.

He smiled, and shouldered the gun. "Well, Granny," he said, "you must be a hundred years old, and scared of nothing. I'd give you a dime if I had any money with me. But you take my advice and stay home, and nothing will happen to you."

"I bound to go on my way, mister," said Phoenix. She inclined her head in the red rag. Then they went in different directions, but she could hear the gun shooting again and again over the hill.

She walked on. The shadows hung from the oak trees to the road like curtains. Then she smelled wood-smoke, and smelled the river, and she saw a steeple and the cabins on their steep steps. Dozens of little black children whirled around her. There ahead was Natchez shining. Bells were ringing. She walked on.

In the paved city it was Christmas time. There were red and green electric lights strung and crisscrossed everywhere, and all turned on in the daytime. Old Phoenix would have been lost if she had not distrusted her eyesight and depended on her feet to know where to take her.

She paused quietly on the sidewalk where people were passing by. A lady came along in the crowd, carrying an armful of red-, green-, and silver-wrapped presents; she gave off perfume like the red roses in hot summer, and Phoenix stopped her.

"Please, missy, will you lace up my shoe?" She held up her foot.

"What do you want, Grandma?"

"See my shoe," said Phoenix. "Do all right for out in the country, but wouldn't look right to go in a big building."

"Stand still then, Grandma," said the lady. She put her packages down on the sidewalk beside her and laced and tied both shoes tightly.

"Can't lace 'em with a cane," said Phoenix. "Thank you, missy. I doesn't mind asking a nice lady to tie up my shoe, when I gets out on the street."

Moving slowly and from side to side, she went into the big building, and into a tower of steps, where she walked up and around and around until her feet knew to stop.

She entered a door, and there she saw nailed up on the wall the document that had been stamped with the gold seal and framed in the gold frame, which matched the dream that was hung up in her head.

"Here I be," she said. There was a fixed and ceremonial stiffness over her body.

"A charity case, I suppose," said an attendant who sat at the desk before her.

But Phoenix only looked above her head. There was sweat on her face, the wrinkles in her skin shone like a bright net.

"Speak up, Grandma," the woman said. "What's your name? We must have your history, you know. Have you been here before? What seems to be the trouble with you?"

Old Phoenix only gave a twitch to her face as if a fly were bothering her.

"Are you deaf?" cried the attendant.

But then the nurse came in.

"Oh, that's just old Aunt Phoenix," she said. "She doesn't come for herself — she has a little grandson. She makes these trips just as regular as clockwork. She lives away back off the Old Natchez Trace." She bent down. "Well, Aunt Phoenix, why don't you just take a seat? We won't keep you standing after your long trip." She pointed.

The old woman sat down, bolt upright in the chair.

"Now, how is the boy?" asked the nurse.

Old Phoenix did not speak.

"I said, how is the boy?"

But Phoenix only waited and stared straight ahead, her face very solemn and withdrawn into rigidity.

"Is his throat any better?" asked the nurse. "Aunt Phoenix, don't you hear me? Is your grandson's throat any better since the last time you came for the medicine?"

With her hands on her knees, the old woman waited, silent, erect and motionless, just as if she were in armor.

"You mustn't take up our time this way, Aunt Phoenix," the nurse said. "Tell us quickly about your grandson, and get it over. He isn't dead, is he?"

At last there came a flicker and then a flame of comprehension across her face, and she spoke.

"My grandson. It was my memory had left me. There I sat and forgot why I made my long trip."

"Forgot?" The nurse frowned. "After you came so far?"

Then Phoenix was like an old woman begging a dignified forgiveness for waking up frightened in the night. "I never did go to school, I was too old at the Surrender," she said in a soft voice. "I'm an old woman without an education. It was my memory fail me. My little grandson, he is just the same, and I forgot it in the coming."

"Throat never heals, does it?" said the nurse, speaking in a loud, sure voice to old Phoenix. By now she had a card with something written on it, a little list. "Yes. Swallowed lye. When was it? — January — two, three years ago — "

Phoenix spoke unasked now. "No, missy, he not dead, he just the same. Every little while his throat begin to close up again, and he not able to swallow. He not get his breath. He not able to help himself. So the time come around, and I go on another trip for the soothing medicine."

"All right. The doctor said as long as you came to get it, you could have it," said the nurse. "But it's an obstinate case."

"My little grandson, he sit up there in the house all wrapped up, wait-ing by himself," Phoenix went on. "We is the only two left in the world. He suffer and it don't seem to put him back at all. He got a sweet look. He going to last. He wear a little patch quilt and peep out holding his mouth open like a little bird. I remembers so plain now. I not going to forget him again, no, the whole enduring time. I could tell him from all the others in creation."

"All right." The nurse was trying to hush her now. She brought her a bottle of medicine. "Charity," she said, making a check mark in a book.

Old Phoenix held the bottle close to her eyes, and then carefully put it into her pocket.

"I thank you," she said.

"It's Christmas time, Grandma," said the attendant. "Could I give you a few pennies out of my purse?"

"Five pennies is a nickel," said Phoenix stiffly.

"Here's a nickel," said the attendant.

Phoenix rose carefully and held out her hand. She received the nickel and then fished the other nickel out of her pocket and laid it beside the new one. She stared at her palm closely, with her head on one side.

Then she gave a tap with her cane on the floor.

"This is what come to me to do," she said. "I going to the store and buy my child a little windmill they sells, made out of paper. He going to find it hard to believe there such a thing in the world. I'll march myself back where he waiting, holding it straight up in this hand."

She lifted her free hand, gave a little nod, turned around, and walked out of the doctor's office. Then her slow step began on the stairs, going down.

[1941]

JOHN CHEEVER (1912–1982), *the leading exponent of the kind of carefully fashioned story of modern urban and suburban manners that* The New Yorker *popularized, has been called by the reviewer John Leonard "the Chekhov of the suburbs." Cheever spent most of his life in New York City and in small towns similar to the ones he describes in much of his fiction. Born in Quincy, Massachusetts, he was raised by parents who owned a prosperous business that failed after the 1929 stock market crash. His mother then opened a seaside curio shop to support the family. His parents enjoyed reading literature to him, so at an early age he was acquainted with the fiction of Charles Dickens, Jack London, and Robert Louis Stevenson. (Poe was forbidden, but Cheever read him on the sly.) Cheever began to write when he was about ten years old, and when he was twelve, he said, he was given his parents' permission to write for a living only after he had promised that he had "no idea of becoming famous or wealthy." He started his career at an unusually young age. Expelled from Thayer Academy at seventeen for being, by his own account, a "quarrelsome, intractable, . . . and lousy student," he moved to New York City, lived in a cell of a room on a bread-and-buttermilk diet, and wrote stories. When his first one, "Expelled," was accepted for publication by Malcolm Cowley, then editor of* The New Republic, *Cheever was launched as a teenager into a career as a writer of fiction. Earlier Cowley had told him that his stories were too long to get published by magazines that paid, so he made Cheever write a story of not more than a thousand words every day for four days to encourage discipline. As Cowley remembered, "One of them was a sketch, so I printed it in* The New Republic. *I sent the other three to Katharine White at* The New Yorker, *and she bought two. No one but John could have written those stories in four days."*

In the 1930s Cheever published short fiction in the The New Republic, Collier's, Story, The Atlantic Monthly, *and* The New Yorker. *His first collection of stories,* The Way Some People Live, *appeared in 1942, while he was completing a four-year stint of army duty during World War II. After the war he wrote television scripts, but his main interest was writing stories. In 1953 he strengthened his literary reputation with the book* The Enormous Radio and Other Stories, *a collection of fourteen of his New Yorker pieces. Six years later appeared another story collection,* The Housebreaker of Shady Hill. *His first novel,* The Wapshot Chronicle, *had been published in 1957, and its sequel,* The Wapshot Scandal, *appeared in 1964. In the 1960s and 1970s he published three more books of short stories and two widely acclaimed novels,* Bullet Park *(1969) and* Falconer *(1977).* The Stories of John Cheever, *published in 1978, won both the Pulitzer Prize and the National Book Critics Circle award and became one of the few* books of short stories ever to make the New York Times *best-seller list.* *Shortly before his death he published a last short novel and saw a final tele-* *vision play produced on PBS. In more than fifty years, Cheever published* *over 200 magazine stories; he figured that he earned "enough money to* *feed the family and buy a new suit every other year."*

Usually a rapid writer, Cheever said he liked best the stories that he *wrote in less than a week, although he spent months working on "The* *Swimmer," a story included in his 1964 collection,* The Brigadier and the Golf Widow. *He originally wrote a draft of the plot as "a perfectly good"* *novel, but then he burned it. "I could very easily have sold the book," he* *said, "but the trick was to get the winter constellations in the midsummer* *sky without anyone knowing about it, and it didn't take 250 pages to do* *that." Cheever is a moralist, and most of his stories present a precise dis-* *section of the values of the ascending American middle class in the years* *after World War II. The stylistic elegance of stories like "The Enormous* *Radio" is an ironic contrast to the tensions of contemporary urban life dra-* *matized in the narrative.*

John Cheever

ฌ

THE ENORMOUS RADIO

Jim and Irene Westcott were the kind of people who seem to strike that satisfactory average of income, endeavor, and respectability that is reached by the statistical reports in college alumni bulletins. They were the parents of two young children, they had been married nine years, they lived on the twelfth floor of an apartment house near Sutton Place, they went to the theatre on an average of 10.3 times a year, and they hoped someday to live in Westchester. Irene Westcott was a pleasant, rather plain girl with soft brown hair and a wide, fine forehead upon which nothing at all had been written, and in the cold weather she wore a coat of fitch skins dyed to resemble mink. You could not say that Jim Westcott looked younger than he was, but you could at least say of him that he seemed to feel younger. He wore his graying hair cut very short, he dressed in the kind of clothes his class had worn at Andover, and his manner was earnest, vehement, and intentionally naïve. The Westcotts differed from their friends, their class-mates, and their neighbors only in an interest they shared in serious music. They went to a great many concerts — although they seldom mentioned this to anyone — and they spent a good deal of time listening to music on the radio.

Their radio was an old instrument, sensitive, unpredictable, and beyond repair. Neither of them understood the mechanics of radio — or of any of the other appliances that surrounded them — and when the instrument faltered, Jim would strike the side of the cabinet with his hand. This sometimes helped. One Sunday afternoon, in the middle of a Schubert quartet, the music faded away altogether. Jim struck the cabinet repeatedly, but there was no response; the Schubert was lost to them forever. He promised to buy Irene a new radio, and on Monday when he came home from work he told her that he had got one. He refused to describe it, and said it would be a surprise for her when it came.

The radio was delivered at the kitchen door the following afternoon, and with the assistance of her maid and the handyman Irene uncrated it and brought it into the living room. She was struck at once with the physical ugliness of the large gumwood cabinet. Irene was proud of her living room, she had chosen its furnishings and colors as carefully as she chose her clothes, and now it seemed to her that the new radio stood among her intimate possessions like an aggressive intruder. She was confounded by the number of dials and switches on the instrument panel, and she studied them thoroughly before she put the plug into a wall socket and turned the radio on. The dials flooded with a malevolent green light, and in the distance she heard the music of a piano quintet. The quintet was in the distance for only an instant; it bore down upon her with a speed greater than light and filled the apartment with the noise of music amplified so mightily that it knocked a china ornament from a table to the floor. She rushed to the instrument and reduced the volume. The violent forces that were snared in the ugly gumwood cabinet made her uneasy. Her children came home from school then, and she took them to the Park. It was not until later in the afternoon that she was able to return to the radio.

The maid had given the children their suppers and was supervising their baths when Irene turned on the radio, reduced the volume, and sat down to listen to a Mozart quintet that she knew and enjoyed. The music came through clearly. The new instrument had a much purer tone, she thought, than the old one. She decided that tone was most important and that she could conceal the cabinet behind a sofa. But as soon as she had made her peace with the radio, the interference began. A crackling sound like the noise of a burning powder fuse began to accompany the singing of the strings. Beyond the music, there was a rustling that reminded Irene unpleasantly of the sea, and as the quintet progressed, these noises were joined by many others. She tried all the dials and switches but nothing dimmed the interference, and she sat down, disappointed and bewildered, and tried to trace the flight of the melody. The elevator shaft in her building ran beside the living-room wall, and it was the noise of the elevator that gave her a clue to the character of the static. The rattling of the elevator cables and the opening and closing of the elevator doors were reproduced in her loudspeaker, and, realizing that the radio was sensitive to electrical currents of all sorts, she began to discern through the Mozart the ringing of telephone bells, the dialing of phones, and the lamentation of a vacuum cleaner. By listening more carefully, she was able to distinguish doorbells, elevator bells, electric razors, and Waring mixers, whose sounds had been picked up from the apartments that surrounded hers and transmitted through her loudspeaker. The powerful and ugly instrument, with its mistaken sensitivity to discord, was more than she could hope to master, so she turned the thing off and went into the nursery to see her children.

When Jim Westcott came home that night, he went to the radio confidently and worked the controls. He had the same sort of experience Irene had had. A man was speaking on the station Jim had chosen, and his voice swung instantly from the distance into a force so powerful that it shook the apartment. Jim turned the volume control and reduced the voice. Then, a minute or two later, the interference began. The ringing of telephones and doorbells set in, joined by the rasp of the elevator doors and the whir of cooking appliances. The character of the noise had changed since Irene had tried the radio earlier; the last of the electric razors was being unplugged, the vacuum cleaners had all been returned to their closets, and the static reflected that change in pace that overtakes the city after the sun goes down. He fiddled with the knobs but couldn't get rid of the noises, so he turned the radio off and told Irene that in the morning he'd call the people who had sold it to him and give them hell.

The following afternoon, when Irene returned to the apartment from a luncheon date, the maid told her that a man had come and fixed the radio. Irene went into the living room before she took off her hat or her furs and tried the instrument. From the loudspeaker came a recording of the "Missouri Waltz." It reminded her of the thin, scratchy music from an old-fashioned phonograph that she sometimes heard across the lake where she spent her summers. She waited until the waltz had finished, expecting an explanation of the recording, but there was none. The music was followed by silence, and then the plaintive and scratchy record was repeated. She turned the dial and got a satisfactory burst of Caucasian music — the thump of bare feet in the dust and the rattle of coin jewelry — but in the background she could hear the ringing of bells and a confusion of voices. Her children came home from school then, and she turned off the radio and went to the nursery.

When Jim came home that night, he was tired, and he took a bath and changed his clothes. Then he joined Irene in the living room. He had just turned on the radio when the maid announced dinner, so he left it on, and he and Irene went to the table.

Jim was too tired to make even pretense of sociability, and there was nothing about the dinner to hold Irene's interest, so her attention wandered from the food to the deposits of silver polish on the candlesticks and from there to the music in the other room. She listened for a few minutes to a Chopin prelude and then was surprised to hear a man's voice break in. "For Christ's sake, Kathy," he said, "do you always have to play the piano when I get home?" The music stopped abruptly. "It's the only chance I have," a woman said. "I'm at the office all day." "So am I," the man said. He added something obscene about an upright piano, and slammed a door. The passionate and melancholy music began again.

"Did you hear that?" Irene asked.

"What?" Jim was eating his dessert.

"The radio. A man said something while the music was still going on — something dirty."

"It's probably a play."

"I don't think it *is* a play," Irene said.

They left the table and took their coffee into the living room. Irene asked Jim to try another station. He turned the knob. "Have you seen my garters?" a man asked. "Button me up," a woman said. "Have you seen my garters?" the man said again. "Just button me up and I'll find your garters," the woman said. Jim shifted to another station. "I wish you wouldn't leave apple cores in the ashtrays," a man said. "I hate the smell."

"This is strange," Jim said.

"Isn't it?" Irene said.

Jim turned the knob again. " 'On the coast of Coromandel where the early pumpkins blow,' " a woman with a pronounced English accent said, " 'in the middle of the woods lived the Yonghy-Bonghy-Bò. Two old chairs, and half a candle, one old jug without a handle. . . .' "[1]

"My God!" Irene cried. "That's the Sweeneys' nurse."

" 'These were all his worldly goods,' " the British voice continued.

"Turn that thing off," Irene said. "Maybe they can hear *us*." Jim switched the radio off. "That was Miss Armstrong, the Sweeneys' nurse," Irene said. "She must be reading to the little girl. They live in 17-B. I've talked with Miss Armstrong in the Park. I know her voice very well. We must be getting other people's apartments."

"That's impossible," Jim said.

"Well, that was the Sweeneys' nurse," Irene said hotly. "I know her voice. I know it very well. I'm wondering if they can hear us."

Jim turned the switch. First from a distance and then nearer, nearer, as if borne on the wind, came the pure accents of the Sweeneys' nurse again: " *'Lady Jingly! Lady Jingly!'* " she said, " '*sitting where the pumpkins blow, will you come and be my wife? said the Yonghy-Bonghy-Bò. . . .*' "

Jim went over to the radio and said "Hello" loudly into the speaker.

" '*I am tired of living singly,*' " the nurse went on, " '*on this coast so*

---

[1] lines from "The Courtship of the Yonghy-Bonghy-Bò," nonsense poem by Edward Lear (1812–1888).

wild and shingly, I'm a-weary of my life; if you'll come and be my wife, quite serene would be my life. . . . ' "

"I guess she can't hear us," Irene said. "Try something else."

Jim turned to another station, and the living room was filled with the uproar of a cocktail party that had overshot its mark. Someone was playing the piano and singing the "Whiffenpoof Song," and the voices that surrounded the piano were vehement and happy. "Eat some more sandwiches," a woman shrieked. There were screams of laughter and a dish of some sort crashed to the floor.

"Those must be the Fullers, in 11-E," Irene said. "I knew they were giving a party this afternoon. I saw her in the liquor store. Isn't this too divine? Try something else. See if you can get those people in 18-C."

The Westcotts overheard that evening a monologue on salmon fishing in Canada, a bridge game, running comments on home movies of what had apparently been a fortnight at Sea Island, and a bitter family quarrel about an overdraft at the bank. They turned off their radio at midnight and went to bed, weak with laughter. Sometime in the night, their son began to call for a glass of water and Irene got one and took it to his room. It was very early. All the lights in the neighborhood were extinguished, and from the boy's window she could see the empty street. She went into the living room and tried the radio. There was some faint coughing, a moan, and then a man spoke. "Are you all right, darling?" he asked. "Yes," a woman said wearily. "Yes, I'm all right, I guess," and then she added with great feeling, "But, you know, Charlie, I don't feel like myself any more. Sometimes there are about fifteen or twenty minutes in the week when I feel like myself. I don't like to go to another doctor, because the doctor's bills are so awful already, but I just don't feel like myself, Charlie. I just never feel like myself." They were not young, Irene thought. She guessed from the timbre of their voices that they were middle-aged. The restrained melancholy of the dialogue and the draft from the bedroom window made her shiver, and she went back to bed.

The following morning, Irene cooked breakfast for the family — the maid didn't come up from her room in the basement until ten — braided her daughter's hair, and waited at the door until her children and her husband had been carried away in the elevator. Then she went into the living room and tried the radio. "I don't want to go to school," a child screamed. "I hate school. I won't go to school. I hate school." "You will go to school," an enraged woman said. "We paid eight hundred dollars to get you into that school and you'll go if it kills you." The next number on the dial produced the worn record of the "Missouri Waltz." Irene shifted the control and invaded the privacy of several breakfast tables. She overheard demonstrations of indigestion, carnal love, abysmal vanity, faith, and despair. Irene's life was nearly as simple and sheltered as it appeared to be, and the forthright and sometimes brutal language that came from the loudspeaker that morning astonished and troubled her. She continued to listen until her maid came in. Then she turned off the radio quickly, since this insight, she realized, was a furtive one.

Irene had a luncheon date with a friend that day, and she left her apartment at a little after twelve. There were a number of women in the elevator when it stopped at her floor. She stared at their handsome and impassive faces, their furs, and the cloth flowers in their hats. Which one of them had been to Sea Island? she wondered. Which one had overdrawn her bank account? The elevator stopped at the tenth floor and a woman with a pair of Skye terriers joined them. Her hair was rigged high on her head and she wore a mink cape. She was humming the "Missouri Waltz."

Irene had two Martinis at lunch, and she looked searchingly at her friend and wondered what her secrets were. They had intended to go shopping after lunch, but Irene excused herself and went home. She told the maid that she was not to be disturbed; then she went into the living room, closed the doors, and switched on the radio. She heard, in the course of the afternoon, the halting conversation of a woman entertaining her aunt, the hysterical conclusion of a luncheon party, and a hostess briefing her maid about some cocktail guests. "Don't give the best Scotch to anyone who hasn't white hair," the hostess said. "See if you can get rid of that liver paste before you pass those hot things, and could you lend me five dollars? I want to tip the elevator man."

As the afternoon waned, the conversations increased in intensity. From where Irene sat, she could see the open sky above the East River. There were hundreds of clouds in the sky, as though the south wind had broken the winter into pieces and were blowing it north, and on her radio she could hear the arrival of cocktail guests and the return of children and businessmen from their schools and offices. "I found a good-sized diamond on the bathroom floor this morning," a woman said. "It must have fallen out of that bracelet Mrs. Dunston was wearing last night." "We'll sell it," a man said. "Take it down to the jeweler on Madison Avenue and sell it. Mrs. Dunston won't know the difference, and we could use a couple of hundred bucks. . . ." " 'Oranges and lemons, say the bells of St. Clement's,' " the Sweeneys' nurse sang. " 'Halfpence and farthings, say the bells of St. Martin's. When will you pay me? say the bells at old Bailey. . . .' " "It's not a hat," a woman cried, and at her back roared a cocktail party. "It's not a hat, it's a love affair. That's what Walter Florell said. He said it's not a hat, it's a love affair," and then, in a lower voice, the same woman added, "Talk to somebody, for Christ's sake, honey, talk to somebody. If she catches you standing here not talking to anybody, she'll take us off her invitation list, and I love these parties."

The Westcotts were going out for dinner that night, and when Jim came home, Irene was dressing. She seemed sad and vague, and he brought her a drink. They were dining with friends in the neighborhood, and they walked to where they were going. The sky was broad and filled with light. It was one of those splendid spring evenings that excite memory and desire, and the air that touched their hands and faces felt very soft. A Salvation Army band was on the corner playing "Jesus Is Sweeter." Irene drew on her husband's arm and held him there for a minute, to hear the music. "They're really such nice people, aren't they?" she said. "They have such nice faces. Actually, they're so much nicer than a lot of the people we know." She took a bill from her purse and walked over and dropped it into the tambourine. There was in her face, when she returned to her husband, a look of radiant melancholy that he was not familiar with. And her conduct at the dinner party that night seemed strange to him, too. She interrupted her hostess rudely and stared at the people across the table from her with an intensity for which she would have punished her children.

It was still mild when they walked home from the party, and Irene looked up at the spring stars. " 'How far that little candle throws its beams,' " she exclaimed. " 'So shines a good deed in a naughty world.' "[2] She waited that night until Jim had fallen asleep, and then went into the living room and turned on the radio.

Jim came home at about six the next night. Emma, the maid, let him in, and he had taken off his hat and was taking off his coat when Irene ran into the hall. Her face was shining with tears and her hair was disordered. "Go up to 16-C, Jim!" she screamed. "Don't take off your coat. Go up to 16-C. Mr. Osborn's beating his wife. They've been quarreling since four o'clock, and now he's hitting her. Go up there and stop him."

From the radio in the living room, Jim heard screams, obscenities, and thuds. "You know you don't have to listen to this sort of thing," he said. He strode into the living room and turned the switch. "It's indecent," he said. "It's like looking in windows. You know you don't have to listen to this sort of thing. You can turn it off."

"Oh, it's so horrible, it's so dreadful," Irene was sobbing. "I've been listening all day, and it's so depressing."

"Well, if it's so depressing, why do you listen to it? I bought this damned radio to give you pleasure," he said. "I paid a great deal of money for it. I thought it might make you happy. I wanted to make you happy."

"Don't, don't, don't, don't quarrel with me," she moaned, and laid her head on his shoulder. "All the others have been quarreling all day. Everybody's been quarreling. They're all worried about money. Mrs. Hutchinson's mother is dying of cancer in Florida and they don't have enough money to send her to the Mayo Clinic. At least, Mr. Hutchinson says they don't have enough money. And some woman in this building is having an affair with the handyman — with that hideous handyman. It's too disgusting. And Mrs. Melville has heart trouble and Mr. Hendricks is going to lose his job in April and Mrs. Hendricks is horrid about the whole thing and

[2] Irene is quoting from Shakespeare's *The Merchant of Venice*, V.i. 101–102.

that girl who plays the 'Missouri Waltz' is a whore, a common whore, and the elevator man has tuberculosis and Mr. Osborn has been beating Mrs. Osborn." She wailed, she trembled with grief and checked the stream of tears down her face with the heel of her palm.

"Well, why do you have to listen?" Jim asked again. "Why do you have to listen to this stuff if it makes you so miserable?"

"Oh, don't, don't, don't," she cried. "Life is too terrible, too sordid and awful. But we've never been like that, have we, darling? Have we? I mean, we've always been good and decent and loving to one another, haven't we? And we have two children, two beautiful children. Our lives aren't sordid, are they, darling? Are they?" She flung her arms around his neck and drew his face down to hers. "We're happy, aren't we, darling? We are happy, aren't we?"

"Of course we're happy," he said tiredly. He began to surrender his resentment. "Of course we're happy. I'll have that damned radio fixed or taken away tomorrow." He stroked her soft hair. "My poor girl," he said.

"You love me, don't you?" she asked. "And we're not hypercritical or worried about money or dishonest, are we?"

"No, darling," he said.

A man came in the morning and fixed the radio. Irene turned it on cautiously and was happy to hear a California-wine commercial and a recording of Beethoven's Ninth Symphony, including Schiller's "Ode to Joy." She kept the radio on all day and nothing untoward came from the speaker.

A Spanish suite was being played when Jim came home. "Is everything all right?" he asked. His face was pale, she thought. They had some cocktails and went in to dinner to the "Anvil Chorus" from *Il Trovatore*. This was followed by Debussy's "La Mer."

"I paid the bill for the radio today," Jim said. "It cost four hundred dollars. I hope you'll get some enjoyment out of it."

"Oh, I'm sure I will," Irene said.

"Four hundred dollars is a good deal more than I can afford," he went on. "I wanted to get something that you'd enjoy. It's the last extravagance we'll be able to indulge in this year. I see that you haven't paid your clothing bills yet. I saw them on your dressing table." He looked directly at her. "Why did you tell me you'd paid them? Why did you lie to me?"

"I just didn't want you to worry, Jim," she said. She drank some water. "I'll be able to pay my bills out of this month's allowance. There were the slipcovers last month, and that party."

"You've got to learn to handle the money I give you a little more intelligently, Irene," he said. "You've got to understand that we don't have as much money this year as we had last. I had a very sobering talk with Mitchell today. No one is buying anything. We're spending all our time promoting new issues, and you know how long that takes. I'm not getting any younger, you know. I'm thirty-seven. My hair will be gray next year. I haven't done as well as I'd hoped to do. And I don't suppose things will get any better."

"Yes, dear," she said.

"We've got to start cutting down," Jim said. "We've got to think of the children. To be perfectly frank with you, I worry about money a great deal. I'm not at all sure of the future. No one is. If anything should happen to me, there's the insurance, but that wouldn't go very far today. I've worked awfully hard to give you and the children a comfortable life," he said bitterly. "I don't like to see all my energies, all of my youth, wasted in fur coats and radios and slipcovers and — "

"Please, Jim," she said. "Please. They'll hear us."

"*Who'll hear us?* Emma can't hear us."

"The radio."

"Oh, I'm sick!" he shouted. "I'm sick to death of your apprehensiveness. The radio can't hear us. Nobody can hear us. And what if they can hear us? Who cares?"

Irene got up from the table and went into the living room. Jim went to the door and shouted at her from there. "Why are you so Christly all of a sudden? What's turned you overnight into a convent girl? You stole your mother's jewelry before they probated her will. You never gave your sister a cent of that money that was intended for her — not even when she needed it. You made Grace Howland's life miserable, and where was all your piety and your virtue when you went to that abortionist? I'll never forget how cool you were. You packed your bag and went off to have that child murdered as if you were going to Nassau. If you'd had any reasons, if you'd had any good reasons — "

Irene stood for a minute before the hideous cabinet, disgraced and sickened, but she held her hand on the switch before she extinguished the music and the voices, hoping that the instrument might speak to her kindly, that she might hear the Sweeneys' nurse. Jim continued to shout at her from the door. The voice on the radio was suave and noncommital. "An early-morning railroad disaster in Tokyo," the loudspeaker said, "killed twenty-nine people. A fire in a Catholic hospital near Buffalo for the care of blind children was extinguished early this morning by nuns. The temperature is forty-seven. The humidity is eighty-nine."

[1953]

John Cheever

ဘာ

THE SWIMMER

It was one of those midsummer Sundays when everyone sits around saying, "I *drank* too much last night." You might have heard it whispered by the parishioners leaving church, heard it from the lips of the priest himself, struggling with his cassock in the *vestiarium*, heard it from the golf links and the tennis courts, heard it from the wild-life preserve where the leader of the Audubon group was suffering from a terrible hangover. "I *drank* too much," said Donald Westerhazy. "We all *drank* too much," said Lucinda Merrill. "It must have been the wine," said Helen Westerhazy. "I *drank* too much of that claret."

This was the edge of the Westerhazys' pool. The pool, fed by an artesian well with a high iron content, was a pale shade of green. It was a fine day. In the west there was a massive stand of cumulus cloud so like a city seen from a distance — from the bow of an approaching ship — that it might have had a name. Lisbon. Hackensack. The sun was hot. Neddy Merrill sat by the green water, one hand in it, one around a glass of gin. He was a slender man — he seemed to have the especial slenderness of youth — and while he was far from young he had slid down his banister that morning and given the bronze backside of Aphrodite on the hall table a smack, as he jogged toward the smell of coffee in his dining room. He might have been compared to a summer's day, particularly the last hours of one, and while he lacked a tennis racket or a sail bag the impression was definitely one of youth, sport, and clement weather. He had been swimming and now he was breathing deeply, stertorously as if he could gulp into his lungs the components of that moment, the heat of the sun, the intenseness of his pleasure. It all seemed to flow into his chest. His own house stood in Bullet Park, eight miles to the south, where his four beautiful daughters would have had their lunch and might be playing tennis. Then it occurred to him that by taking a dogleg to the southwest he could reach his home by water.

His life was not confining and the delight he took in this observation could not be explained by its suggestion of escape. He seemed to see, with a cartographer's eye, that string of swimming pools, that quasi-subterranean stream that curved across the county. He had made a discovery, a contribution to modern geography; he would name the stream Lucinda after his wife. He was not a practical joker nor was he a fool but he was determinedly original and had a vague and modest idea of himself as a legendary figure. The day was beautiful and it seemed to him that a long swim might enlarge and celebrate its beauty.

He took off a sweater that was hung over his shoulders and dove in. He had an inexplicable contempt for men who did not hurl themselves into pools. He swam a choppy crawl, breathing either with every stroke or every fourth stroke and counting somewhere well in the back of his mind the one-two one-two of a flutter kick. It was not a serviceable stroke for long distances but the domestication of swimming had saddled the sport with some customs and in his part of the world a crawl was customary. To be embraced and sustained by the light green water was less a pleasure, it seemed, than the resumption of a natural condition, and he would have liked to swim without trunks, but this was not possible, considering his project. He hoisted himself up on the far curb — he never used the ladder — and started across the lawn. When Lucinda asked where he was going he said he was going to swim home.

The only maps and charts he had to go by were remembered or imaginary but these were clear enough. First there were the Grahams, the Hammers, the Lears, the Howlands, and the Crosscups. He would cross Ditmar Street to the Bunkers and come, after a short portage, to the Levys, the Welchers, and the public pool in Lancaster. Then there were the Hallorans, the Sachses, the Biswangers, Shirley Adams, the Gilmartins, and the Clydes. The day was lovely, and that he lived in a world so generously supplied with water seemed like a clemency, a beneficence. His heart was high and he ran across the grass. Making his way home by an uncommon route gave him the feeling that he was a pilgrim, an explorer, a man with a destiny, and he knew that he would find friends all along the way; friends would line the banks of the Lucinda River.

He went through a hedge that separated the Westerhazys' land from the Grahams', walked under some flowering apple trees, passed the shed that housed their pump and filter, and came out at the Grahams' pool. "Why, Neddy," Mrs. Graham said, "what a marvelous surprise. I've been trying to get you on the phone all morning. Here, let me get you a drink." He saw then, like any explorer, that the hospitable customs and traditions of the natives would have to be handled with diplomacy if he was ever going to reach his destination. He did not want to mystify or seem rude to the Grahams nor did he have the time to linger there. He swam the length of their pool and joined them in the sun and was rescued, a few minutes later, by the arrival of two carloads of friends from Connecticut. During the uproarious reunions he was able to slip away. He went down by the front of the Grahams' house, stepped over a thorny hedge, and crossed a vacant lot to the Hammers'. Mrs. Hammer, looking up from her roses, saw him swim

by although she wasn't quite sure who it was. The Lears heard him splashing past the open windows of their living room. The Howlands and the
Crosscups were away. After leaving the Howlands' he crossed Ditmar Street
and started for the Bunkers', where he could hear, even at that distance, the
noise of a party.

The water refracted the sound of voices and laughter and seemed to
suspend it in midair. The Bunkers' pool was on a rise and he climbed some
stairs to a terrace where twenty-five or thirty men and women were drinking. The only person in the water was Rusty Towers, who floated there on a
rubber raft. Oh, how bonny and lush were the banks of the Lucinda River!
Prosperous men and women gathered by the sapphire-colored waters while
caterer's men in white coats passed them cold gin. Overhead a red de
Haviland trainer was circling around and around and around in the sky with
something like the glee of a child in a swing. Ned felt a passing affection for
the scene, a tenderness for the gathering, as if it was something he might
touch. In the distance he heard thunder. As soon as Enid Bunker saw him
she began to scream: "Oh, look who's here! What a marvelous surprise!
When Lucinda said you couldn't come I thought I'd *die.*" She made her
way to him through the crowd, and when they had finished kissing she led
him to the bar, a progress that was slowed by the fact that he stopped to kiss
eight or ten other women and shake the hands of as many men. A smiling
bartender he had seen at a hundred parties gave him a gin and tonic and he
stood by the bar for a moment, anxious not to get stuck in any conversation
that would delay his voyage. When he seemed about to be surrounded he
dove in and swam close to the side to avoid colliding with Rusty's raft. At
the far end of the pool he bypassed the Tomlinsons with a broad smile and
jogged up the garden path. The gravel cut his feet but this was only unpleasantness. The party was confined to the pool, and as he went toward the
house he heard the brilliant, watery sound of voices fade, heard the noise of
a radio from the Bunkers' kitchen, where someone was listening to a ball
game. Sunday afternoon. He made his way through the parked cars and
down the grassy border of their driveway to Alewives Lane. He did not want
to be seen on the road in his bathing trunks but there was no traffic and he
made the short distance to the Levys' driveway, marked with a PRIVATE
PROPERTY sign and a green tube for *The New York Times.* All the doors
and windows of the big house were open but there were no signs of life; not
even a dog barked. He went around the side of the house to the pool and
saw that the Levys had only recently left. Glasses and bottles and dishes of
nuts were on a table at the deep end, where there was a bathhouse or gazebo, hung with Japanese lanterns. After swimming the pool he got himself
a glass and poured a drink. It was his fourth or fifth drink and he had swum
nearly half the length of the Lucinda River. He felt tired, clean, and pleased
at that moment to be alone; pleased with everything.

It would storm. The stand of cumulus cloud — that city — had risen
and darkened, and while he sat there he heard the percussiveness of thun-

der again. The de Haviland trainer was still circling overhead and it seemed to Ned that he could almost hear the pilot laugh with pleasure in the afternoon; but when there was another peal of thunder he took off for home. A train whistle blew and he wondered what time it had gotten to be. Four? Five? He thought of the provincial station at that hour, where a waiter, his tuxedo concealed by a raincoat, a dwarf with some flowers wrapped in newspaper, and a woman who had been crying would be waiting for the local. It was suddenly growing dark; it was that moment when the pin-headed birds seemed to organize their song into some acute and knowledgeable recognition of the storm's approach. Then there was a fine noise of rushing water from the crown of an oak at his back, as if a spigot there had been turned. Then the noise of fountains came from the crowns of all the tall trees. Why did he love storms, what was the meaning of his excitement when the door sprang open and the rain wind fled rudely up the stairs, why had the simple task of shutting the windows of an old house seemed fitting and urgent, why did the first watery notes of a storm wind have for him the unmistakable sound of good news, cheer, glad tidings? Then there was an explosion, a smell of cordite, and rain lashed the Japanese lanterns that Mrs. Levy had bought in Kyoto the year before last, or was it the year before that?

He stayed in the Levys' gazebo until the storm had passed. The rain had cooled the air and he shivered. The force of the wind had stripped a maple of its red and yellow leaves and scattered them over the grass and the water. Since it was midsummer the tree must be blighted, and yet he felt a peculiar sadness at this sign of autumn. He braced his shoulders, emptied his glass, and started for the Welchers' pool. This meant crossing the Lindleys' riding ring and he was surprised to find it overgrown with grass and all the jumps dismantled. He wondered if the Lindleys had sold their horses or gone away for the summer and put them out to board. He seemed to remember having heard something about the Lindleys and their horses but the memory was unclear. On he went, barefoot through the wet grass, to the Welchers', where he found their pool was dry.

This breach in his chain of water disappointed him absurdly, and he felt like some explorer who seeks a torrential headwater and finds a dead stream. He was disappointed and mystified. It was common enough to go away for the summer but no one ever drained his pool. The Welchers had definitely gone away. The pool furniture was folded, stacked, and covered with a tarpaulin. The bathhouse was locked. All the windows of the house were shut, and when he went around to the driveway in front he saw a FOR SALE sign nailed to a tree. When had he last heard from the Welchers — when, that is, had he and Lucinda last regretted an invitation to dine with them? It seemed only a week or so ago. Was his memory failing or had he so disciplined it in the repression of unpleasant facts that he had damaged his sense of the truth? Then in the distance he heard the sound of a tennis game. This cheered him, cleared away all his apprehensions and let him regard the overcast sky and the cold air with indifference. This was the day that Neddy Merrill swam across the county. That was the day! He started off then for his most difficult portage.

Had you gone for a Sunday afternoon ride that day you might have seen him, close to naked, standing on the shoulders of Route 424, waiting for a chance to cross. You might have wondered if he was the victim of foul play, had his car broken down, or was he merely a fool. Standing barefoot in the deposits of the highway — beer cans, rags, and blowout patches — exposed to all kinds of ridicule, he seemed pitiful. He had known when he started that this was a part of his journey — it had been on his maps — but confronted with the lines of traffic, worming through the summery light, he found himself unprepared. He was laughed at, jeered at, a beer can was thrown at him, and he had no dignity or humor to bring to the situation. He could have gone back, back to the Westerhazys', where Lucinda would still be sitting in the sun. He had signed nothing, vowed nothing, pledged nothing, not even to himself. Why, believing as he did, that all human obduracy was susceptible to common sense, was he unable to turn back? Why was he determined to complete his journey even if it meant putting his life in danger? At what point had this prank, this joke, this piece of horseplay become serious? He could not go back, he could not even recall with any clearness the green water at the Westerhazys', the sense of inhaling the day's components, the friendly and relaxed voices saying that they had *drunk* too much. In the space of an hour, more or less, he had covered a distance that made his return impossible.

An old man, tooling down the highway at fifteen miles an hour, let him get to the middle of the road, where there was a grass divider. Here he was exposed to the ridicule of the northbound traffic, but after ten or fifteen minutes he was able to cross. From here he had only a short walk to the Recreation Center at the edge of the village of Lancaster, where there were some handball courts and a public pool.

The effect of the water on voices, the illusion of brilliance and suspense, was the same here as it had been at the Bunkers' but the sounds here were louder, harsher, and more shrill, and as soon as he entered the crowded enclosure he was confronted with regimentation. "ALL SWIMMERS MUST TAKE A SHOWER BEFORE USING THE POOL. ALL SWIMMERS MUST USE THE FOOTBATH. ALL SWIMMERS MUST WEAR THEIR IDENTIFICATION DISKS." He took a shower, washed his feet in a cloudy and bitter solution, and made his way to the edge of the water. It stank of chlorine and looked to him like a sink. A pair of lifeguards in a pair of towers blew police whistles at what seemed to be regular intervals and abused the swimmers through a public address system. Neddy remembered the sapphire water at the Bunkers' with longing and thought that he might contaminate himself — damage his own prosperousness and charm — by swimming in this murk, but he reminded himself that he was an explorer, a pilgrim, and that this was merely a stagnant bend in the Lucinda River. He dove, scowling with distaste, into the chlorine and had to swim with his head above water to avoid collisions, but even so he was bumped into, splashed, and jostled. When he got to the shallow end both lifeguards were shouting at him: "Hey, you, you without the identification disk, get outa the water." He did, but they had no way of pursuing him and he went through the reek of suntan oil and chlorine out through the hurricane fence and passed the handball courts. By crossing the road he entered the wooded part of the Halloran estate. The woods were not cleared and the footing was treacherous and difficult until he reached the lawn and the clipped beech hedge that encircled their pool.

The Hallorans were friends, an elderly couple of enormous wealth who seemed to bask in the suspicion that they might be Communists. They were zealous reformers but they were not Communists, and yet when they were accused, as they sometimes were, of subversion, it seemed to gratify and excite them. Their beech hedge was yellow and he guessed this had been blighted like the Levys' maple. He called hullo, hullo, to warn the Hallorans of his approach, to palliate his invasion of their privacy. The Hallorans, for reasons that had never been explained to him, did not wear bathing suits. No explanations were in order, really. Their nakedness was a detail in their uncompromising zeal for reform and he stepped politely out of his trunks before he went through the opening in the hedge.

Mrs. Halloran, a stout woman with white hair and a serene face, was reading the *Times*. Mr. Halloran was taking beech leaves out of the water with a scoop. They seemed not surprised or displeased to see him. Their pool was perhaps the oldest in the country, a fieldstone rectangle, fed by a brook. It had no filter or pump and its waters were the opaque gold of the stream.

"I'm swimming across the county," Ned said.

"Why, I didn't know one could," exclaimed Mrs. Halloran.

"Well, I've made it from the Westerhazys'," Ned said. "That must be about four miles."

He left his trunks at the deep end, walked to the shallow end, and swam this stretch. As he was pulling himself out of the water he heard Mrs. Halloran say, "We've been *terribly* sorry to hear about all your misfortunes, Neddy."

"My misfortunes?" Ned asked. "I don't know what you mean."

"Why we heard that you'd sold the house and that your poor children. . . ."

"I don't recall having sold the house," Ned said, "and the girls are at home."

"Yes," Mrs. Halloran sighed. "Yes. . . . " Her voice filled the air with an unseasonable melancholy and Ned spoke briskly. "Thank you for the swim."

"Well, have a nice trip," said Mrs. Halloran.

Beyond the hedge he pulled on his trunks and fastened them. They were loose and he wondered if, during the space of an afternoon, he could have lost some weight. He was cold and he was tired and the naked Hallorans and their dark water had depressed him. The swim was too much for his strength but how could he have guessed this, sliding down the banister that morning and sitting in the Westerhazys' sun? His arms were lame. His legs felt rubbery and ached at the joints. The worst of it was the cold in his bones and the feeling that he might never be warm again. Leaves were falling down around him and he smelled wood smoke on the wind. Who would be burning wood at this time of the year?

He needed a drink. Whiskey would warm him, pick him up, carry him through the last of his journey, refresh his feeling that it was original and valorous to swim across the county. Channel swimmers took brandy. He needed a stimulant. He crossed the lawn in front of the Hallorans' house and went down a little path to where they had built a house for their only daughter, Helen, and her husband, Eric Sachs. The Sachses' pool was small and he found Helen and her husband there.

"Oh, *Neddy*," Helen said. "Did you lunch at Mother's?"

"Not *really*," Ned said. "I *did* stop to see your parents." This seemed to be explanation enough. "I'm terribly sorry to break in on you like this but I've taken a chill and I wonder if you'd give me a drink."

"Why, I'd *love* to," Helen said, "but there hasn't been anything in this house to drink since Eric's operation. That was three years ago."

Was he losing his memory, had his gift for concealing painful facts let him forget that he had sold his house, that his children were in trouble, and that his friend had been ill? His eyes slipped from Eric's face to his abdomen, where he saw three pale, sutured scars, two of them at least a foot long. Gone was his navel, and what, Neddy thought, would the roving hand, bed-checking one's gifts at 3 A.M., make of a belly with no navel, no link to birth, this breach in the succession?

"I'm sure you can get a drink at the Biswangers'," Helen said. "They're having an enormous do. You can hear it from here. Listen!"

She raised her head and from across the road, the lawns, the gardens, the woods, the fields, he heard again the brilliant noise of voices over water. "Well, I'll get wet," he said, still feeling that he had no freedom of choice about his means of travel. He dove into the Sachses' cold water, and gasping, close to drowning, made his way from one end of the pool to the other. "Lucinda and I want *terribly* to see you," he said over his shoulder, his face set toward the Biswangers'. "We're sorry it's been so long and we'll call you *very* soon."

He crossed some fields to the Biswangers' and the sounds of revelry there. They would be honored to give him a drink, they would be happy to give him a drink. The Biswangers invited him and Lucinda for dinner four times a year, six weeks in advance. They were always rebuffed and yet they continued to send out their invitations, unwilling to comprehend the rigid and undemocratic realities of their society. They were the sort of people who discussed the price of things at cocktails, exchanged market tips during dinner, and after dinner told dirty stories to mixed company. They did not belong to Neddy's set — they were not even on Lucinda's Christmas card list. He went toward their pool with feelings of indifference, charity, and some unease, since it seemed to be getting dark and these were the longest days of the year. The party when he joined it was noisy and large. Grace Biswanger was the kind of hostess who asked the optometrist, the veterinarian, the real-estate dealer, and the dentist. No one was swimming and the twilight, reflected on the water of the pool, had a wintry gleam. There was a bar and he started for this. When Grace Biswanger saw him she came toward him, not affectionately as he had every right to expect, but bellicosely.

"Why, this party has everything," she said loudly, "including a gate crasher."

She could not deal him a social blow — there was no question about this and he did not flinch. "As a gate crasher," he asked politely, "do I rate a drink?"

"Suit yourself," she said. "You don't seem to pay much attention to invitations."

She turned her back on him and joined some guests, and he went to the bar and ordered a whiskey. The bartender served him but he served him rudely. His was a world in which the caterer's men kept the social score, and to be rebuffed by a part-time barkeep meant that he had suffered some loss of social esteem. Or perhaps the man was new and uninformed. Then he heard Grace at his back say: "They went for broke overnight — nothing but income — and he showed up drunk one Sunday and asked us to loan him five thousand dollars. . . . " She was always talking about money. It was worse than eating your peas off a knife. He dove into the pool, swam its length and went away.

The next pool on his list, the last but two, belonged to his old mistress, Shirley Adams. If he had suffered any injuries at the Biswangers' they would be cured here. Love — sexual roughhouse in fact — was the supreme elixir, the pain killer, the brightly colored pill that would put the spring back into his step, the joy of life in his heart. They had had an affair last week, last month, last year. He couldn't remember. It was he who had broken it off, his was the upper hand, and he stepped through the gate of the wall that surrounded her pool with nothing so considered as self-confidence. It seemed in a way to be his pool, as the lover, particularly the illicit lover, enjoys the possessions of his mistress with an authority unknown to holy matrimony. She was there, her hair the color of brass, but her figure, at the edge of the lighted, cerulean water, excited in him no profound memories. It had been, he thought, a lighthearted affair, although she had wept when he broke it off. She seemed confused to see him and he wondered if she was still wounded. Would she, God forbid, weep again?

"What do you want?" she asked.

"I'm swimming across the county."

"Good Christ. Will you ever grow up?"

"What's the matter?"

"If you've come here for money," she said, "I won't give you another cent."

"You could give me a drink."

"I could but I won't. I'm not alone."

"Well, I'm on my way."

He dove in and swam the pool, but when he tried to haul himself up onto the curb he found that the strength in his arms and shoulders had gone, and he paddled to the ladder and climbed out. Looking over his shoulder he saw, in the lighted bathhouse, a young man. Going out onto the dark lawn he smelled chrysanthemums or marigolds — some stubborn autumnal fragrance — on the night air, strong as gas. Looking overhead he saw that the stars had come out, but why should he seem to see Andromeda, Cepheus, and Cassiopeia? What had become of the constellations of midsummer? He began to cry.

It was probably the first time in his adult life that he had ever cried, certainly the first time in his life that he had ever felt so miserable, cold, tired, and bewildered. He could not understand the rudeness of the caterer's barkeep or the rudeness of a mistress who had come to him on her knees and showered his trousers with tears. He had swum too long, he had been immersed too long, and his nose and his throat were sore from the water. What he needed then was a drink, some company, and some clean, dry clothes, and while he could have cut directly across the road to his home he went on to the Gilmartins' pool. Here, for the first time in his life, he did not dive but went down the steps into the icy water and swam a hobbled sidestroke that he might have learned as a youth. He staggered with fatigue on his way to the Clydes' and paddled the length of their pool, stopping again and again with his hand on the curb to rest. He climbed up the ladder and wondered if he had the strength to get home. He had done what he wanted, he had swum the county, but he was so stupefied with exhaustion that his triumph seemed vague. Stooped, holding on to the gateposts for support, he turned up the driveway of his own house.

The place was dark. Was it so late that they had all gone to bed? Had Lucinda stayed at the Westerhazys' for supper? Had the girls joined her there or gone someplace else? Hadn't they agreed, as they usually did on Sunday, to regret all their invitations and stay at home? He tried the garage doors to see what cars were in but the doors were locked and rust came off the handles onto his hands. Going toward the house, he saw the force of the thunderstorm had knocked one of the rain gutters loose. It hung down over the front door like an umbrella rib, but it could be fixed in the morning. The house was locked, and he thought that the stupid cook or the stupid maid must have locked the place up until he remembered that it had been some time since they had employed a maid or a cook. He shouted, pounded on the door, tried to force it with his shoulder, and then, looking in at the windows, saw that the place was empty.

[1964]

TILLIE OLSEN (b. 1913) was born in Omaha, Nebraska, the daughter of political refugees from the Russian Czarist repression after the revolution of 1905. Her father was a farmer, packing-house worker, house painter, and jack-of-all-trades; her mother was a factory worker who also laundered, sewed, and took care of other people's children. At the age of fifteen, Olsen dropped out of high school to help support her family during the Depression. She was a member of the Young Communist League, involved in the Warehouse Union's labor disputes among packing-house workers in Kansas City, and she was jailed briefly. Shortly thereafter she became ill with pleurisy. When she recovered her health at age nineteen, she began to write her first novel, Yonnondio. Four chapters of this book about a poverty-stricken working-class family were completed in the next four years, during which time she married, gave birth to her first child, and was left with the baby by her husband because, as she later wrote in her autobiographical story "I Stand Here Ironing," he "could no longer endure sharing want with them." In 1934 a section of the first chapter of her novel was published in Partisan Review, but she abandoned the unfinished book in 1937. The year before she had married Jack Olsen, also a political activist, with whom she had three more children; raising the children and working for political causes took up all her time. She also always held a full-time job in addition to the "caring, nurturing, and maintaining of other human beings" as a mother and wife. In the 1940s she was a factory worker, in the 1950s a secretary, and not until 1953, when her youngest daughter started school, could she begin writing again.

That year Olsen enrolled in a class in fiction-writing at San Francisco State College. She was awarded a Stanford University creative writing fellowship for 1955 and 1956. During the 1950s she wrote the four stories collected in Tell Me a Riddle, which established her reputation when they were published as a paperback in 1961. Identified as a champion of the re-emerging feminist movement, Olsen wrote a biographical introduction to Rebecca Harding Davis's nineteenth-century proletarian novel, Life in the Iron Mills, published by the Feminist Press in 1972. Two years later, after several grants and creative writing fellowships, she published the still-unfinished Yonnondio. In 1978 Silences appeared, a collection of essays exploring the different circumstances that obstruct or silence literary creation.

Olsen cites her own life circumstances as the cause for publishing so little. As the Canadian novelist Margaret Atwood understood, "Few writers have gained such wide respect on such a small body of published work. . . . Among women writers in the United States, 'respect' is too pale a word: 'reverence' is more like it. This is presumably because women writers, even *more than their male counterparts, recognize what a heroic feat it is to have held down a job, raised four children, and still somehow managed to become and to remain a writer." A radical feminist, Olsen has said that she felt no personal guilt as a single parent over her daughter's predicament, as described in her confessional narrative "I Stand Here Ironing," since "guilt is a word used far too sloppily, to cover up harmful situations in society that must be changed." Her four stories have appeared in over fifty anthologies and have been translated into different languages all over the world.*

Tillie Olsen

ଷଷ

I STAND HERE IRONING

I stand here ironing, and what you asked me moves tormented back and forth with the iron.

"I wish you would manage the time to come in and talk with me about your daughter. I'm sure you can help me understand her. She's a youngster who needs help and whom I'm deeply interested in helping."

"Who needs help." . . . Even if I came, what good would it do? You think because I am her mother I have a key, or that in some way you could use me as a key? She has lived for nineteen years. There is all that life that has happened outside of me, beyond me.

And when is there time to remember, to sift, to weigh, to estimate, to total? I will start and there will be an interruption and I will have to gather it all together again. Or I will become engulfed with all I did or did not do, with what should have been and what cannot be helped.

Why do I put that first? I do not even know if it matters, or if it explains anything.

She was a beautiful baby. She blew shining bubbles of sound. She loved motion, loved light, loved color and music and textures. She would lie on the floor in her blue overalls patting the surface so hard in ecstasy her hands and feet would blur. She was a miracle to me, but when she was eight months old I had to leave her daytimes with the woman downstairs to whom she was no miracle at all, for I worked or looked for work and for Emily's father, who "could no longer endure" (he wrote in his good-bye note) "sharing want with us."

I was nineteen, it was the pre-relief, pre-WPA world of the Depression. I would start running as soon as I got off the streetcar, running up the stairs, the place smelling sour, and awake or asleep to startle awake, when she saw me she would break into a clogged weeping that could not be comforted, a weeping I can hear yet.

After a while I found a job hashing at night so I could be with her days, and it was better. But it came to where I had to bring her to his family and leave her.

It took a long time to raise the money for her fare back. Then she got chicken pox and I had to wait longer. When she finally came, I hardly knew her, walking quick and nervous like her father, looking like her father, thin, and dressed in a shoddy red that yellowed her skin and glared at the pockmarks. All the baby loveliness gone.

She was two. Old enough for nursery school they said, and I did not know then what I know now — the fatigue of the long day, and the lacerations of group life in the kinds of nurseries that are only parking places for children.

Except that it would have made no difference if I had known. It was the only place there was. It was the only way we could be together, the only way I could hold a job.

And even without knowing, I knew. I knew the teacher that was evil because all these years it has curdled into my memory, the little boy hunched in the corner, her rasp, "why aren't you outside, because Alvin hits you? that's no reason, go out, scaredy." I knew Emily hated it even if she did not clutch and implore "don't go Mommy" like the other children, mornings.

She always had a reason why we should stay home. Momma, you look sick, Momma. I feel sick. Momma, the teachers aren't there today, they're sick. Momma, we can't go, there was a fire there last night. Momma, it's a holiday today, no school, they told me.

But never a direct protest, never rebellion. I think of our others in their three-, four-year-oldness — the explosions, the tempers, the denunciations, the demands — and I feel suddenly ill. I put the iron down. What in me demanded that goodness in her? And what was the cost, the cost to her of such goodness?

The old man living in the back once said in his gentle way: "You should smile at Emily more when you look at her." What was in my face when I looked at her? I loved her. There were all the acts of love.

It was only with the others I remembered what he said, and it was the face of joy, and not of care or tightness or worry I turned to them — too late for Emily. She does not smile easily, let alone almost always as her brothers and sisters do. Her face is closed and sombre, but when she wants, how fluid. You must have seen it in her pantomimes, you spoke of her rare gift for comedy on the stage that rouses a laughter out of the audience so dear they applaud and applaud and do not want to let her go.

Where does it come from, that comedy? There was none of it in her when she came back to me that second time, after I had had to send her away again. She had a new daddy now to learn to love, and I think perhaps it was a better time.

Except when we left her alone nights, telling ourselves she was old enough.

"Can't you go some other time, Mommy, like tomorrow?" she would ask. "Will it be just a little while you'll be gone? Do you promise?"

The time we came back, the front door open, the clock on the floor in the hall. She rigid awake. "It wasn't just a little while. I didn't cry. Three times I called you, just three times, and then I ran downstairs to open the door so you could come faster. The clock talked loud. I threw it away, it scared me what it talked."

She said the clock talked loud again that night I went to the hospital to have Susan. She was delirious with the fever that comes before red measles, but she was fully conscious all the week I was gone and the week after we were home when she could not come near the new baby or me.

She did not get well. She stayed skeleton thin, not wanting to eat, and night after night she had nightmares. She would call for me, and I would rouse from exhaustion to sleepily call back: "You're all right, darling, go to sleep, it's just a dream," and if she still called, in a sterner voice, "now go to sleep, Emily, there's nothing to hurt you." Twice, only twice, when I had to get up for Susan anyhow, I went in to sit with her.

Now when it is too late (as if she would let me hold and comfort her like I do the others) I get up and go to her at once at her moan or restless stirring. "Are you awake, Emily? Can I get you something?" And the answer is always the same: "No, I'm all right, go back to sleep, Mother."

They persuaded me at the clinic to send her away to a convalescent home in the country where "she can have the kind of food and care you can't manage for her, and you'll be free to concentrate on the new baby." They still send children to that place. I see pictures on the society page of sleek young women planning affairs to raise money for it, or dancing at the affairs, or decorating Easter eggs or filling Christmas stockings for the children.

They never have a picture of the children so I do not know if the girls still wear those gigantic red bows and the ravaged looks on the every other Sunday when parents can come to visit "unless otherwise notified" — as we were notified the first six weeks.

Oh it is a handsome place, green lawns and tall trees and fluted flower beds. High up on the balconies of each cottage the children stand, the girls in their red bows and white dresses, the boys in white suits and gigantic red ties. The parents stand below shrieking up to be heard and the children shriek down to be heard, and between them the invisible wall "Not To Be Contaminated by Parental Germs or Physical Affection."

There was a tiny girl who always stood hand in hand with Emily. Her parents never came. One visit she was gone. "They moved her to Rose

Cottage," Emily shouted in explanation. "They don't like you to love anybody here."

She wrote once a week, the labored writing of a seven-year-old. "I am fine. How is the baby. If I write my letter nicly I will have a star. Love." There never was a star. We wrote every other day, letters she could never hold or keep but only hear read — once. "We simply do not have room for children to keep any personal possessions," they patiently explained when we pieced one Sunday's shrieking together to plead how much it would mean to Emily, who loved so to keep things, to be allowed to keep her letters and cards.

Each visit she looked frailer. "She isn't eating," they told us.

(They had runny eggs for breakfast or mush with lumps, Emily said later, I'd hold it in my mouth and not swallow. Nothing ever tasted good, just when they had chicken.)

It took us eight months to get her released home, and only the fact that she gained back so little of her seven lost pounds convinced the social worker.

I used to try to hold and love her after she came back, but her body would stay stiff, and after a while she'd push away. She ate little. Food sickened her, and I think much of life too. Oh she had physical lightness and brightness, twinkling by on skates, bouncing like a ball up and down up and down over the jump rope, skimming over the hill; but these were momentary.

She fretted about her appearance, thin and dark and foreign-looking at a time when every little girl was supposed to look or thought she should look a chubby blonde replica of Shirley Temple. The doorbell sometimes rang for her, but no one seemed to come and play in the house or be a best friend. Maybe because we moved so much.

There was a boy she loved painfully through two school semesters. Months later she told me how she had taken pennies from my purse to buy him candy. "Licorice was his favorite and I brought him some every day, but he still liked Jennifer better'n me. Why, Mommy?" The kind of question for which there is no answer.

School was a worry to her. She was not glib or quick in a world where glibness and quickness were easily confused with ability to learn. To her overworked and exasperated teachers she was an overconscientious "slow learner" who kept trying to catch up and was absent entirely too often.

I let her be absent, though sometimes the illness was imaginary. How different from my now-strictness about attendance with the others. I wasn't working. We had a new baby, I was home anyhow. Sometimes, after Susan grew old enough, I would keep her home from school, too, to have them all together.

Mostly Emily had asthma, and her breathing, harsh and labored, would fill the house with a curiously tranquil sound. I would bring the two old dresser mirrors and her boxes of collections to her bed. She would select beads and single earrings, bottle tops and shells, dried flowers and pebbles, old postcards and scraps, all sorts of oddments; then she and Susan would play Kingdom, setting up landscapes and furniture, peopling them with action.

Those were the only times of peaceful companionship between her and Susan. I have edged away from it, that poisonous feeling between them, that terrible balancing of hurts and needs I had to do between the two, and did so badly, those earlier years.

Oh there are conflicts between the others too, each one human, needing, demanding, hurting, taking — but only between Emily and Susan, no, Emily toward Susan that corroding resentment. It seems so obvious on the surface, yet it is not obvious. Susan, the second child, Susan, golden- and curly-haired and chubby, quick and articulate and assured, everything in appearance and manner Emily was not; Susan, not able to resist Emily's precious things, losing or sometimes clumsily breaking them; Susan telling jokes and riddles to company for applause while Emily sat silent (to say to me later: that was *my* riddle, Mother, I told it to Susan); Susan, who for all the five years' difference in age was just a year behind Emily in developing physically.

I am glad for that slow physical development that widened the difference between her and her contemporaries, though she suffered over it. She was too vulnerable for that terrible world of youthful competition, of preening and parading, of constant measuring of yourself against every other, of envy, "If I had that copper hair," "If I had that skin. . . ." She tormented herself enough about not looking like the others, there was enough of the unsureness, the having to be conscious of words before you speak, the constant caring — what are they thinking of me? without having it all magnified by the merciless physical drives.

Ronnie is calling. He is wet and I change him. It is rare there is such a cry now. That time of motherhood is almost behind me when the ear is not one's own but must always be racked and listening for the child cry, the child call. We sit for a while and I hold him, looking out over the city spread in charcoal with its soft aisles of light. "*Shoogily*," he breathes and curls closer. I carry him back to bed, asleep. *Shoogily*. A funny word, a family word, inherited from Emily, invented by her to say: *comfort*.

In this and other ways she leaves her seal, I say aloud. And startle at my saying it. What do I mean? What did I start to gather together, to try and make coherent? I was at the terrible, growing years. War years. I do not remember them well. I was working, there were four smaller ones now, there was not time for her. She had to help be a mother, and housekeeper, and shopper. She had to set her seal. Mornings of crisis and near hysteria trying to get lunches packed, hair combed, coats and shoes found, everyone to school or Child Care on time, the baby ready for transportation. And always the paper scribbled on by a smaller one, the book looked at by Susan then mislaid, the homework not done. Running out to that huge school where she was one, she was lost, she was a drop; suffering over the unpreparedness, stammering and unsure in her classes.

There was so little time left at night after the kids were bedded down. She would struggle over books, always eating (it was in those years she developed her enormous appetite that is legendary in our family) and I would be ironing, or preparing food for the next day, or writing V-mail to Bill, or tending the baby. Sometimes, to make me laugh, or out of her despair, she would imitate happenings or types at school.

I think I said once: "Why don't you do something like this in the school amateur show?" One morning she phoned me at work, hardly understandable through the weeping: "Mother, I did it. I won, I won; they gave me first prize; they clapped and clapped and wouldn't let me go."

Now suddenly she was Somebody, and as imprisoned in her difference as she had been in anonymity.

She began to be asked to perform at other high schools, even in colleges, then at city and statewide affairs. The first one we went to, I only recognized her that first moment when thin, shy, she almost drowned herself into the curtains. Then: Was this Emily? The control, the command, the convulsing and deadly drowning, the spell, then the roaring, stamping audience, unwilling to let this rare and precious laughter out of their lives.

Afterwards: You ought to do something about her with a gift like that — but without money or knowing how, what does one do? We have left it all to her, and the gift has as often eddied inside, clogged and clotted, as been used and growing.

She is coming. She runs up the stairs two at a time with her light graceful step, and I know she is happy tonight. Whatever it was that occasioned your call did not happen today.

"Aren't you ever going to finish the ironing, Mother? Whistler painted his mother in a rocker. I'd have to paint mine standing over an ironing board." This is one of her communicative nights and she tells me everything and nothing as she fixes herself a plate of food out of the icebox.

She is so lovely. Why did you want me to come in at all? Why were you concerned? She will find her way.

She starts up the stairs to bed. "Don't get me up with the rest in the morning." "But I thought you were having midterms." "Oh, those," she comes back in, kisses me, and says quite lightly, "in a couple of years when we'll all be atom-dead they won't matter a bit."

She has said it before. She *believes* it. But because I have been dredging the past, and all that compounds a human being is so heavy and meaningful in me, I cannot endure it tonight.

I will never total it all. I will never come in to say: She was a child seldom smiled at. Her father left me before she was a year old. I had to work her first six years when there was work, or I sent her home and to his relatives. There were years she had care she hated. She was dark and thin and foreign-looking in a world where the prestige went to blondeness and curly hair and dimples, she was slow where glibness was prized. She was a child of anxious, not proud, love. We were poor and could not afford for her the soil of easy growth. I was a young mother, I was a distracted mother. There were the other children pushing up, demanding. Her younger sister seemed all that she was not. There were years she did not want me to touch her. She kept too much in herself, her life was such she had to keep too much in herself. My wisdom came too late. She has much to her and probably little will come of it. She is a child of her age, of depression, of war, of fear.

Let her be. So all that is in her will not bloom — but in how many does it? There is still enough left to live by. Only help her to know — help make it so there is cause for her to know — that she is more than this dress on the ironing board, helpless before the iron.

[1961]

RALPH ELLISON (*b.* 1914) *was born in Oklahoma City, Oklahoma. When he was three his father died, and thereafter his mother worked as a domestic servant to support herself and her son. She often brought home discarded books and phonograph records from the white households where she worked, and as a boy Ellison developed an interest in literature and music. He played trumpet in his high school band, at the same time that he began to relate the works of fiction he was reading to real life. "I began to look at my own life through the lives of fictional characters. When I read Stendhal, I would search until I began to find patterns of a Stendhalian novel within the Negro communities in which I grew up. I began, in other words, quite early to connect the worlds projected in literature . . . with the life in which I found myself."*

In 1933 Ellison entered Tuskegee Institute in Alabama, where he studied music for three years. Then he went to New York City and met the black writers Langston Hughes and Richard Wright, whose encouragement helped him to become a writer. Wright turned Ellison's attention to "those works in which writing was discussed as a craft . . . to Henry James's prefaces, to Conrad," and to other authors. In 1939 Ellison's short stories, essays, and reviews began to appear in periodicals. After World War II, aided by a Rosenwald Fellowship, he settled down to work on the novel In- visible Man. *Published in 1952, it received the National Book Award for fiction; and, in 1965, a Book Week poll listed it as the most distinguished American novel of the preceding twenty years. In addition to* Invisible Man, *Ellison has published only a few short stories and a book of essays,* Shadow and Act *(1964). He has also taught at such universities as Yale, Harvard, and Rutgers, and has been Albert Schweitzer Professor of Contemporary Literature and Culture at New York University since 1970.*

"Battle Royal" is an excerpt from Invisible Man, *often anthologized in collections of short stories. It appears early in the novel, after the prologue describing the underground chamber to which the protagonist has retreated from the chaos of life above ground. "Battle Royal" is written in a simple, naturalistic style. It is the first step in the quest of an unnamed young black man for personal and community identity as he travels from South to North and from innocence to experience. Ellison meant his central character to dramatize more than just a personal ritual initiation in this story of his encounter with racial prejudice. Believing that modern American writers were handicapped by "the triumph of industrialism . . . with the blatant hypocrisy between its ideals and its acts," Ellison feels that artistic individualism (for example, the amoral violence described by Hemingway) has led writers to reject broad social responsibility. Seeking technical perfection rather*

than moral insight, most American writers have forgotten that "art by its nature is social." While Ellison gives no program for the improvement of the situation, his fiction and essays present a depiction of contemporary American social problems remarkable for its intellectual perception, emotional balance, and moral depth.

Ralph Ellison

ත౦ත

Battle Royal

It goes a long way back, some twenty years. All my life I had been looking for something, and everywhere I turned someone tried to tell me what it was. I accepted their answers too, though they were often in contradiction and even self-contradictory. I was naïve. I was looking for myself and asking everyone except myself questions which I, and only I, could answer. It took me a long time and much painful boomeranging of my expectations to achieve a realization everyone else appears to have been born with: That I am nobody but myself. But first I had to discover that I am an invisible man!

And yet I am no freak of nature, nor of history. I was in the cards, other things having been equal (or unequal) eighty-five years ago. I am not ashamed of my grandparents for having been slaves. I am only ashamed of myself for having at one time been ashamed. About eighty-five years ago they were told that they were free, united with others of our country in everything pertaining to the common good, and, in everything social, separate like the fingers of the hand. And they believed it. They exulted in it. They stayed in their place, worked hard, and brought up my father to do the same. But my grandfather is the one. He was an odd old guy, my grandfather, and I am told I take after him. It was he who caused the trouble. On his deathbed he called my father to him and said, "Son, after I'm gone I want you to keep up the good fight. I never told you, but our life is a war and I have been a traitor all my born days, a spy in the enemy's country ever since I give up my gun back in the Reconstruction. Live with your head in the lion's mouth. I want you to overcome 'em with yeses, undermine 'em with grins, agree 'em to death and destruction, let 'em swoller you till they vomit or bust wide open." They thought the old man had gone out of his mind. He had been the meekest of men. The younger children were rushed from the room, the shades drawn and the flame of the lamp turned so low that it sputtered on the wick like the old man's breathing. "Learn it to the younguns," he whispered fiercely; then he died.

But my folks were more alarmed over his last words than over his dying. It was as though he had not died at all, his words caused so much anxiety. I was warned emphatically to forget what he had said and, indeed, this is the first time it has been mentioned outside the family circle. It had a tremendous effect upon me, however. I could never be sure of what he meant. Grandfather had been a quiet old man who never made any trouble, yet on his deathbed he had called himself a traitor and a spy, and he had spoken of his meekness as a dangerous activity. It became a constant puzzle which lay unanswered in the back of my mind. And whenever things went well for me I remembered my grandfather and felt guilty and uncomfortable. It was as though I was carrying out his advice in spite of myself. And to make it worse, everyone loved me for it. I was praised by the most lily-white men of the town. I was considered an example of desirable conduct — just as my grandfather had been. And what puzzled me was that the old man had defined it as *treachery.* When I was praised for my conduct I felt a guilt that in some way I was doing something that was really against the wishes of the white folks, that if they had understood they would have desired me to act just the opposite, that I should have been sulky and mean, and that that really would have been what they wanted, even though they were fooled and thought they wanted me to act as I did. It made me afraid that some day they would look upon me as a traitor and I would be lost. Still I was more afraid to act any other way because they didn't like that at all. The old man's words were like a curse. On my graduation day I delivered an oration in which I showed that humility was the secret, indeed, the very essence of progress. (Not that I believed this — how could I, remembering my grandfather? — I only believed that it worked.) It was a great success. Everyone praised me and I was invited to give the speech at a gathering of the town's leading white citizens. It was a triumph for our whole community.

It was in the main ballroom of the leading hotel. When I got there I discovered that it was on the occasion of a smoker, and I was told that since I was to be there anyway I might as well take part in the battle royal to be fought by some of my schoolmates as part of the entertainment. The battle royal came first.

All of the town's big shots were there in their tuxedoes, wolfing down the buffet foods, drinking beer and whiskey and smoking black cigars. It was a large room with a high ceiling. Chairs were arranged in neat rows around three sides of a portable boxing ring. The fourth side was clear, revealing a gleaming space of polished floor. I had some misgivings over the battle royal, by the way. Not from a distaste for fighting, but because I didn't care too much for the other fellows who were to take part. They were tough guys who seemed to have no grandfather's curse worrying their minds. No one could mistake their toughness. And besides, I suspected that fighting a battle royal might detract from the dignity of my speech. In those pre-invisible days I visualized myself as a potential Booker T. Washington. But the other fellows didn't care too much for me either, and there were nine of them. I felt superior to them in my way, and I didn't like the manner in which we were all crowded together into the servants' elevator. Nor did they like my being there. In fact, as the warmly lighted floors flashed past the elevator we had words over the fact that I, by taking part in the fight, had knocked one of their friends out of a night's work.

We were led out of the elevator through a rococo hall into an ante-room and told to get into our fighting togs. Each of us was issued a pair of boxing gloves and ushered out into the big mirrored hall, which we entered looking cautiously about us and whispering, lest we might accidentally be heard above the noise of the room. It was foggy with cigar smoke. And already the whiskey was taking effect. I was shocked to see some of the most important men of the town quite tipsy. They were all there — bankers, lawyers, judges, doctors, fire chiefs, teachers, merchants. Even one of the more fashionable pastors. Something we could not see was going on up front. A clarinet was vibrating sensuously and the men were standing up and moving eagerly forward. We were a small tight group, clustered together, our bare upper bodies touching and shining with anticipatory sweat; while up front the big shots were becoming increasingly excited over something we still could not see. Suddenly I heard the school superintendent, who had told me to come, yell, "Bring up the shines gentlemen! Bring up the little shines!"

We were rushed up to the front of the ballroom, where it smelled even more strongly of tobacco and whiskey. Then we were pushed into place. I almost wet my pants. A sea of faces, some hostile, some amused, ringed around us, and in the center, facing us, stood a magnificent blonde — stark naked. There was dead silence. I felt a blast of cold air chill me. I tried to back away, but they were behind me and around me. Some of the boys stood with lowered heads, trembling. I felt a wave of irrational guilt and fear. My teeth chattered, my skin turned to goose flesh, my knees knocked. Yet I was strongly attracted and looked in spite of myself. Had the price of looking been blindness, I would have looked. The hair was yellow like that of a circus kewpie doll, the face heavily powdered and rouged, as though to form an abstract mask, the eyes hollow and smeared a cool blue, the color of a baboon's butt. I felt a desire to spit upon her as my eyes brushed slowly over her body. Her breasts were firm and round as the domes of East Indian temples, and I stood so close as to see the fine skin texture and beads of pearly perspiration glistening like dew around the pink and erected buds of her nipples. I wanted at one and the same time to run from the room, to sink through the floor, or go to her and cover her from my eyes and the eyes of the others with my body; to feel the soft thighs, to caress her and destroy her, to love her and murder her, to hide from her, and yet to stroke where below the small American flag tatooed upon her belly her thighs formed a capital V. I had a notion that of all in the room she saw only me with her impersonal eyes.

And then she began to dance, a slow sensuous movement; the smoke of a hundred cigars clinging to her like the thinnest of veils. She seemed like a fair bird-girl girdled in veils calling to me from the angry surface of some gray and threatening sea. I was transported. Then I became aware of the clarinet playing and the big shots yelling at us. Some threatened us if we looked and others if we did not. On my right I saw one boy faint. And now a man grabbed a silver pitcher from a table and stepped close as he dashed ice water upon him and stood him up and forced two of us to support him as his head hung and moans issued from his thick bluish lips. Another boy began to plead to go home. He was the largest of the group, wearing dark red fighting trunks much too small to conceal the erection which projected from him as though in answer to the insinuating low-registered moaning of the clarinet. He tried to hide himself with his boxing gloves.

And all the while the blonde continued dancing, smiling faintly at the big shots who watched her with fascination, and faintly smiling at our fear. I noticed a certain merchant who followed her hungrily, his lips loose and drooling. He was a large man who wore diamond studs in a shirtfront which swelled with the ample paunch underneath, and each time the blonde swayed her undulating hips he ran his hand through the thin hair of his bald head and, with his arms upheld, his posture clumsy like that of an intoxicated panda, wound his belly in a slow and obscene grind. This creature was completely hypnotized. The music had quickened. As the dancer flung herself about with a detached expression on her face, the men began reaching out to touch her. I could see their beefy fingers sink into her soft flesh. Some of the others tried to stop them and she began to move around the floor in graceful circles, as they gave chase, slipping and sliding over the polished floor. It was mad. Chairs went crashing, drinks were spilt, as they ran laughing and howling after her. They caught her just as she reached a door, raised her from the floor, and tossed her as college boys are tossed at a hazing, and above her red, fixed-smiling lips I saw the terror and disgust in her eyes, almost like my own terror and that which I saw in some of the other boys. As I watched, they tossed her twice and her soft breasts seemed to flatten against the air and her legs flung wildly as she spun. Some of the more sober ones helped her to escape. And I started off the floor, heading for the anteroom with the rest of the boys.

Some were still crying and in hysteria. But as we tried to leave we were stopped and ordered to get into the ring. There was nothing to do but what we were told. All ten of us climbed under the ropes and allowed ourselves to be blindfolded with broad bands of white cloth. One of the men seemed to feel a bit sympathetic and tried to cheer us up as we stood with our backs against the ropes. Some of us tried to grin. "See that boy over there?" one of the men said. "I want you to run across at the bell and give it to him right in the belly. If you don't get him, I'm going to get you. I don't like his looks." Each of us was told the same. The blindfolds were put on. Yet even then I had been going over my speech. In my mind each word was as bright as flame. I felt the cloth pressed into place, and frowned so that it would be loosened when I relaxed.

But now I felt a sudden fit of blind terror. I was unused to darkness. It was as though I had suddenly found myself in a dark room filled with poisonous cottonmouths. I could hear the bleary voices yelling insistently for the battle royal to begin.

"Get going in there!"

"Let me at that big nigger!"

I strained to pick up the school superintendent's voice, as though to squeeze some security out of that slightly more familiar sound.

"Let me at those black sonsabitches!" someone yelled.

"No, Jackson, no!" another voice yelled. "Here, somebody, help me hold Jack."

"I want to get at that ginger-colored nigger. Tear him limb from limb," the first voice yelled.

I stood against the ropes trembling. For in those days I was what they called ginger-colored, and he sounded as though he might crunch me between his teeth like a crisp ginger cookie.

Quite a struggle was going on. Chairs were being kicked about and I could hear voices grunting as with a terrific effort. I wanted to see, to see more desperately than ever before. But the blindfold was as tight as a thick skin-puckering scab and when I raised my gloved hands to push the layers of white aside a voice yelled, "Oh, no you don't, black bastard! Leave that alone!"

"Ring the bell before Jackson kills him a coon!" someone boomed in the sudden silence. And I heard the bell clang and the sound of the feet scuffling forward.

A glove smacked against my head. I pivoted, striking out stiffly as someone went past, and felt the jar ripple along the length of my arm to my shoulder. Then it seemed as though all nine of the boys had turned upon me at once. Blows pounded me from all sides while I struck out as best I could. So many blows landed upon me that I wondered if I were not the only blindfolded fighter in the ring, or if the man called Jackson hadn't succeeded in getting me after all.

Blindfolded, I could no longer control my motions. I had no dignity. I stumbled about like a baby or a drunken man. The smoke had become thicker and with each new blow it seemed to sear and further restrict my lungs. My saliva became like hot bitter glue. A glove connected with my head, filling my mouth with warm blood. It was everywhere. I could not tell if the moisture I felt upon my body was sweat or blood. A blow landed hard against the nape of my neck. I felt myself going over, my head hitting the floor. Streaks of blue light filled the black world behind the blindfold. I lay prone, pretending that I was knocked out, but felt myself seized by hands and yanked to my feet. "Get going, black boy! Mix it up!" My arms were like lead, my head smarting from blows. I managed to feel my way to the ropes and held on, trying to catch my breath. A glove landed in my midsection and I went over again, feeling as though the smoke had become a knife jabbed into my guts. Pushed this way and that by the legs milling around me, I finally pulled erect and discovered that I could see the black, sweat-washed forms weaving in the smoky-blue atmosphere like drunken dancers weaving to the rapid drum-like thuds of blows.

Everyone fought hysterically. It was complete anarchy. Everybody fought everybody else. No group fought together for long. Two, three, four, fought one, then turned to fight each other, were themselves attacked. Blows landed below the belt and in the kidney, with the gloves open as well as closed, and with my eye partly opened now there was not so much terror. I moved carefully, avoiding blows, although not too many to attract attention, fighting from group to group. The boys groped about like blind, cautious crabs crouching to protect their mid-sections, their heads pulled in short against their shoulders, their arms stretched nervously before them, with their fists testing the smoke-filled air like the knobbed feelers of hypersensitive snails. In one corner I glimpsed a boy violently punching the air and heard him scream in pain as he smashed his hand against a ring post. For a second I saw him bent over holding his hand, then going down as a blow caught his unprotected head. I played one group against the other, slipping in and throwing a punch then stepping out of range while pushing the others into the melee to take the blows blindly aimed at me. The smoke was agonizing and there were no rounds, no bells at three minute intervals to relieve our exhaustion. The room spun round me, a swirl of lights, smoke, sweating bodies surrounded by tense white faces. I bled from both nose and mouth, the blood spattering upon my chest.

The men kept yelling, "Slug him, black boy! Knock his guts out!"

"Uppercut him! Kill him! Kill that big boy!"

Taking a fake fall, I saw a boy going down heavily beside me as though we were felled by a single blow, saw a sneaker-clad foot shoot into his groin as the two who had knocked him down stumbled upon him. I rolled out of range, feeling a twinge of nausea.

The harder we fought the more threatening the men became. And yet, I had begun to worry about my speech again. How would it go? Would they recognize my ability? What would they give me?

I was fighting automatically and suddenly I noticed that one after another of the boys was leaving the ring. I was surprised, filled with panic, as though I had been left alone with an unknown danger. Then I understood. The boys had arranged it among themselves. It was the custom for the two men left in the ring to slug it out for the winner's prize. I discovered this too late. When the bell sounded two men in tuxedoes leaped into the ring and removed the blindfold. I found myself facing Tatlock, the biggest of the gang. I felt sick at my stomach. Hardly had the bell stopped ringing in my ears than it clanged again and I saw him moving swiftly toward me. Thinking of nothing else to do I hit him smash on the nose. He kept coming, bringing the rank sharp violence of stale sweat. His face was a black blank of a face, only his eyes alive — with hate of me and aglow with a feverish terror from what had happened to us all. I became anxious. I wanted to deliver my speech and he came at me as though he meant to beat it out of me. I smashed him again and again, taking his blows as they came. Then on a sudden impulse I struck him lightly and as we clinched, I whispered, "Fake like I knocked you out, you can have the prize."

"I'll break your behind," he whispered hoarsely.

"For *them?*"

"For *me*, sonofabitch!"

They were yelling for us to break it up and Tatlock spun me half around with a blow, and as a joggled camera sweeps in a reeling scene, I saw the howling red faces crouching tense beneath the cloud of blue-gray smoke. For a moment the world wavered, unraveled, flowed, then my head cleared and Tatlock bounced before me. That fluttering shadow before my eyes was his jabbing left hand. Then falling forward, my head against his damp shoulder, I whispered,

"I'll make it five dollars more."

"Go to hell!"

But his muscles relaxed a trifle beneath my pressure and I breathed, "Seven!"

"Give it to your ma," he said, ripping me beneath the heart.

And while I still held him I butted him and moved away. I felt myself bombarded with punches. I fought back with hopeless desperation. I wanted to deliver my speech more than anything else in the world, because I felt that only these men could judge truly my ability, and now this stupid clown was ruining my chances. I began fighting carefully now, moving in to punch him and out again with my greater speed. A lucky blow to his chin and I had him going too — until I heard a loud voice yell, "I got my money on the big boy."

Hearing this, I almost dropped my guard. I was confused: Should I try to win against the voice out there? Would not this go against my speech, and was not this a moment for humility, for nonresistance? A blow to my head as I danced about sent my right eye popping like a jack-in-the-box and settled my dilemma. The room went red as I fell. It was a dream fall, my body languid and fastidious as to where to land, until the floor became impatient and smashed up to meet me. A moment later I came to. An hypnotic voice said FIVE emphatically. And I lay there, hazily watching a dark red spot of my own blood shaping itself into a butterfly, glistening and soaking into the soiled gray world of the canvas.

When the voice drawled TEN I was lifted up and dragged to a chair. I sat dazed. My eye pained and swelled with each throb of my pounding heart and I wondered if now I would be allowed to speak. I was wringing wet, my mouth still bleeding. We were grouped along the wall now. The other boys ignored me as they congratulated Tatlock and speculated as to how much they would be paid. One boy whimpered over his smashed hand. Looking up front, I saw attendants in white jackets rolling the portable ring away and placing a small square rug in the vacant space surrounded by chairs. Perhaps, I thought, I will stand on the rug to deliver my speech.

Then the M.C. called to us, "Come on up here boys and get your money."

We ran forward to where the men laughed and talked in their chairs, waiting. Everyone seemed friendly now.

"There it is on the rug," the man said. I saw the rug covered with coins of all dimensions and a few crumpled bills. But what excited me, scattered here and there, were the gold pieces.

"Boys, it's all yours," the man said. "You get all you grab."

"That's right, Sambo," a blond man said, winking at me confidentially.

I trembled with excitement, forgetting my pain. I would get the gold and the bills, I thought. I would use both hands. I would throw my body against the boys nearest me to block them from the gold.

"Get down around the rug now," the man commanded, "and don't anyone touch it until I give the signal."

"This ought to be good," I heard.

As told, we got around the square rug on our knees. Slowly the man raised his freckled hand as we followed it upward with our eyes.

I heard, "These niggers look like they're about to pray!"

Then, "Ready," the man said. "Go!"

I lunged for a yellow coin lying on the blue design of the carpet, touching it and sending a surprised shriek to join those rising around me. I tried frantically to remove my hand but could not let go. A hot, violent force tore through my body, shaking me like a wet rat. The rug was electrified. The hair bristled up on my head as I shook myself free. My muscles jumped, my nerves jangled, writhed. But I saw that this was not stopping the other boys. Laughing in fear and embarrassment, some were holding back and scooping up the coins knocked off by the painful contortions of the others. The men roared above us as we struggled.

"Pick it up, goddamnit, pick it up!" someone called like a bass-voiced parrot. "Go on, get it!"

I crawled rapidly around the floor, picking up the coins, trying to avoid the coppers and to get greenbacks and the gold. Ignoring the shock by laughing, as I brushed the coins off quickly, I discovered that I could contain the electricity — a contradiction, but it works. Then the men began to push us onto the rug. Laughing embarrassedly, we struggled out of their hands and kept after the coins. We were all wet and slippery and hard to hold. Suddenly I saw a boy lifted into the air, glistening with sweat like a circus seal, and dropped, his wet back landing flush upon the charged rug, heard him yell and saw him literally dance upon his back, his elbows beating a frenzied tatoo upon the floor, his muscles twitching like the flesh of a horse stung by many flies. When he finally rolled off, his face was gray and no one stopped him when he ran from the floor amid booming laughter.

"Get the money," the M.C. called. "That's good hard American cash!"

And we snatched and grabbed, snatched and grabbed. I was careful not to come too close to the rug now, and when I felt the hot whiskey breath descend upon me like a cloud of foul air I reached out and grabbed the leg of a chair. It was occupied and I held on desperately.

"Leggo, nigger! Leggo!"

The huge face wavered down to mine as he tried to push me free. But my body was slippery and he was too drunk. It was Mr. Colcord, who owned a chain of movie houses and "entertainment palaces." Each time he grabbed me I slipped out of his hands. It became a real struggle. I feared the rug more than I did the drunk, so I held on, surprising myself for a moment by trying to topple *him* upon the rug. It was such an enormous idea that I found myself actually carrying it out. I tried not to be obvious, yet when I grabbed his leg, trying to tumble him out of the chair, he raised up roaring with laughter, and, looking at me with soberness dead in the eye, kicked me viciously in the chest. The chair leg flew out of my hand. I felt myself going and rolled. It was as though I had rolled through a bed of hot coals. It seemed a whole century would pass before I would roll free, a century in which I was seared through the deepest levels of my body to the fearful breath within me and the breath seared and heated to the point of explosion. It'll all be over in a flash, I thought as I rolled clear. It'll all be over in a flash.

But not yet, the men on the other side were waiting, red faces swollen as though from apoplexy as they bent forward in their chairs. Seeing their fingers coming toward me I rolled away as a fumbled football rolls off the receiver's fingertips, back into the coals. That time I luckily sent the rug sliding out of place and heard the coins ringing against the floor and the boys scuffling to pick them up and the M.C. calling, "All right, boys, that's all. Go get dressed and get your money."

I was limp as a dish rag. My back felt as though it had been beaten with wires.

When we had dressed the M.C. came in and gave us each five dollars, except Tatlock, who got ten for being last in the ring. Then he told us to leave. I was not to get a chance to deliver my speech, I thought. I was going out into the dim alley in despair when I was stopped and told to go back. I returned to the ballroom, where the men were pushing back their chairs and gathering in groups to talk.

The M.C. knocked on a table for quiet. "Gentlemen," he said, "we almost forgot an important part of the program. A most serious part, gentlemen. This boy was brought here to deliver a speech which he made at his graduation yesterday. . . ."

"Bravo!"

"I'm told that he is the smartest boy we've got out there in Greenwood. I'm told that he knows more big words than a pocket-sized dictionary."

Much applause and laughter.

"So now, gentlemen, I want you to give him your attention."

There was still laughter as I faced them, my mouth dry, my eye throbbing. I began slowly, but evidently my throat was tense, because they began shouting, "Louder! Louder!"

"We of the younger generation extol the wisdom of that great leader and educator," I shouted, "who first spoke these flaming words of wisdom: 'A ship lost at sea for many days suddenly sighted a friendly vessel. From the mast of the unfortunate vessel was seen a signal: "Water, water; we die of thirst!" The answer from the friendly vessel came back: "Cast down your bucket where you are." The captain of the distressed vessel, at last heeding the injunction, cast down his bucket, and it came up full of fresh sparkling water from the mouth of the Amazon River.' And like him I say, and in his words, 'To those of my race who depend upon bettering their condition in a foreign land, or who underestimate the importance of cultivating friendly relations with the Southern white man, who is his next-door neighbor, I would say: "Cast down your bucket where you are" — cast it down in making friends in every manly way of the people of all races by whom we are surrounded. . . .' "

I spoke automatically and with such fervor that I did not realize that the men were still talking and laughing until my dry mouth, filling up with blood from the cut, almost strangled me. I coughed, wanting to stop and go to one of the tall brass, sand-filled spittoons to relieve myself, but a few of the men, especially the superintendent, were listening and I was afraid. So I gulped it down, blood, saliva and all, and continued. (What powers of endurance I had during those days! What enthusiasm! What a belief in the rightness of things!) I spoke even louder in spite of the pain. But still they talked and still they laughed, as though deaf with cotton in dirty ears. So I spoke with greater emotional emphasis. I closed my ears and swallowed blood until I was nauseated. The speech seemed a hundred times as long as before, but I could not leave out a single word. All had to be said, each memorized nuance considered, rendered. Nor was that all. Whenever I uttered a word of three or more syllables a group of voices would yell for me to repeat it. I used the phrase "social responsibility" and they yelled:

"What's the word you say, boy?"

"Social responsibility," I said.

"What?"

"Social . . ."

"Louder."

". . . responsibility."

"More!"

"Respon — "

"Repeat!"

" — sibility."

The room filled with the uproar of laughter until, no doubt, distracted by having to gulp down my blood, I made a mistake and yelled a phrase I had often seen denounced in newspaper editorials, heard debated in private.

"Social . . ."

"What?" they yelled.

". . . equality — "

The laughter hung smokelike in the sudden stillness. I opened my eyes, puzzled. Sounds of displeasure filled the room. The M.C. rushed forward. They shouted hostile phrases at me. But I did not understand.

A small dry mustached man in the front row blared out, "Say that slowly, son!"

"What sir?"

"What you just said!"

"Social responsibility, sir," I said.

"You weren't being smart, were you, boy?" he said, not unkindly.

"No, sir!"

"You sure that about 'equality' was a mistake?"

"Oh, yes, sir," I said. "I was swallowing blood."

"Well, you had better speak more slowly so we can understand. We mean to do right by you, but you've got to know your place at all times. All right, now, go on with your speech."

I was afraid. I wanted to leave but I wanted also to speak and I was afraid they'd snatch me down.

"Thank you, sir," I said, beginning where I had left off, and having them ignore me as before.

Yet when I finished there was a thunderous applause. I was surprised to see the superintendent come forth with a package wrapped in white tissue paper, and, gesturing for quiet, address the men.

"Gentlemen, you see that I did not overpraise this boy. He makes a good speech and some day he'll lead his people in the proper paths. And I don't have to tell you that that is important in these days and times. This is a good, smart boy, and so to encourage him in the right direction, in the name of the Board of Education I wish to present him a prize in the form of this . . ."

He paused, removing the tissue paper and revealing a gleaming calf-skin brief case.

". . . in the form of this first-class article from Shad Whitmore's shop."

"Boy," he said, addressing me, "take this prize and keep it well. Consider it a badge of office. Prize it. Keep developing as you are and some day it will be filled with important papers that will help shape the destiny of your people."

I was so moved that I could hardly express my thanks. A rope of bloody saliva forming a shape like an undiscovered continent drooled upon the leather and I wiped it quickly away. I felt an importance that I had never dreamed.

"Open it and see what's inside," I was told.

My fingers a-tremble, I complied, smelling the fresh leather and finding an official-looking document inside. It was a scholarship to the state college for Negroes. My eyes filled with tears and I ran awkwardly off the floor.

I was overjoyed; I did not even mind when I discovered that the gold pieces I had scrambled for were brass pocket tokens advertising a certain make of automobile.

When I reached home everyone was excited. Next day the neighbors came to congratulate me. I even felt safe from grandfather, whose deathbed curse usually spoiled my triumphs. I stood beneath his photograph with my brief case in hand and smiled triumphantly into his stolid black peasant's face. It was a face that fascinated me. The eyes seemed to follow everywhere I went.

That night I dreamed I was at a circus with him and that he refused to laugh at the clowns no matter what they did. Then later he told me to open my brief case and read what was inside and I did, finding an official envelope stamped with the state seal; and inside the envelope I found another and another, endlessly, and I thought I would fall of weariness. "Them's years," he said. "Now open that one." And I did and in it I found an engraved document containing a short message in letters of gold. "Read it," my grandfather said. "Out loud."

"To Whom It May Concern," I intoned. "Keep This Nigger-Boy Running."

I awoke with the old man's laughter ringing in my ears.

(It was a dream I was to remember and dream again for many years after. But at the time I had no insight into its meaning. First I had to attend college.)

[1952]

ALEKSANDR SOLZHENITSYN (b. 1918) *was born in Kislovodsk, Russia, a health resort in the northern Caucasus. His father, a philology student at Moscow University, was killed on the German front during World War I six months before Solzhenitsyn was born. His mother never remarried. She moved with her son to Rostov-on-Don, where she worked as a typist and stenographer. After Solzhenitsyn completed his secondary education, he studied physics and mathematics at Rostov University, graduating with honors in 1941. There was little opportunity to read literature, yet he remembers that "the desire to write, and the unconscious idea (unprompted by anyone) that I ought for some reason to become a writer, arose in me at a very early age, at nine or ten, when I was not even capable of understanding what it was like to be a writer or why one wrote." Because of the poverty of his experience, he had no idea what to write about, and although he "wrote a great deal of nonsense in various genres," it was not until after World War II that he began to write seriously.*

Solzhenitsyn served as a commander of a reconnaissance battery in the Russian army at the front from 1943 to 1945. In 1945 he was arrested suddenly in East Prussia on the charge of criticizing Stalin in a letter to an old friend. He served his full eight-year sentence in hard labor at prison camps, and in 1953 he was sent into "permanent" exile in central Russia to work as a science and mathematics teacher in secondary schools. All through the following years he wrote prose and poetry, but not until 1961 did he attempt to have any of it published. In that year, the short novel One Day in the Life of Ivan Denisovich *appeared in the Soviet literary magazine* Novy Mir. *With this he sprang from obscurity as a provincial teacher to immediate fame as a writer. Publication of the novel had been ordered by Soviet Premier Nikita Khrushchev himself as part of his anti-Stalinist campaign. The work was a sensation because it gave a realistic account, based on Solzhenitsyn's own experience, of life in a Soviet labor camp. Afterward the only other works by him that were permitted to appear in the Soviet Union were four stories, including "Zakhar-the-Pouch" in 1966 — a story that showed his deep feeling for the history of ancient Russia.*

*In May 1967 Solzhenitsyn wrote his famous letter to the Fourth National Congress of Soviet Writers, protesting the censorship of his novels, plays, and stories. Two years later he was expelled from the Soviet Writers' Union, and his outspoken letter of protest received worldwide publicity. The authorities cited his publication of two novels abroad (*Cancer Ward *and* The First Circle, *in 1968), as well as his criticism of Soviet society, as unacceptable. They also condemned his being awarded the Nobel Prize for Literature in 1970 as a hostile political gesture. In 1971 he published another major novel abroad,* August 1914, *which had been rejected sight un-*

seen by Soviet publishers. Two years later he authorized publication in the West of his Gulag Archipelago, *a factual account, ultimately amounting to three massive volumes, of the "archipelago" system of Soviet prison camps organized between 1918 and 1956. This literary project has been called "the most heavy and relentless book of our time." Its publication precipitated a major attack on Solzhenitsyn by the Communist Party, and in 1974 he was deprived against his will of his Soviet citizenship and deported from the country. He currently lives with his wife and family in rural Vermont.*

"Zakhar-the-Pouch" was published in the United States in 1971 as part of the book Stories and Prose Poems. *Interested in longer prose forms, Solzhenitsyn has not written many stories, but the construction of his novels is often episodic, dependent on an intricate interlocking of incidents that resemble short stories. He usually writes from his own experience, believing like the great nineteenth-century Russian novelist Fyodor Dostoevsky that "Beauty will save the world." As he proclaimed in his Nobel award speech, "The simple act of an ordinary courageous man is not to take part, not to support lies. Let that come into the world and even reign over it, but not through me. Writers and artists can do more: they can VANQUISH LIES! In the struggle against lies, art has always won and always will. Conspicuously, incontestably for everyone. Lies can stand up against much in the world, but not against art."*

Aleksandr Solzhenitsyn

ಐಐ

ZAKHAR-THE-POUCH

– translated by Michael Glenny

You asked me to tell you something about my cycling holiday last summer. Well, if it's not too boring, listen to this one about Kulikovo Field.

We had been meaning to go there for a long time, but it was somehow a difficult place to reach. There are no brightly painted notices or signposts to show you the way, and you won't find it on a single map, even though this battle cost more Russian lives in the fourteenth century than Borodino[1] did in the nineteenth. There has been only one such encounter for fifteen hundred years, not only in Russia but in all Europe. It was a battle not merely between principalities or nation-states, but between continents.

---

[1] Battle between the Russians and the invading French under Napoleon, on August 26, 1812. The French won, but at such great cost in lives and morale that they were forced to begin a retreat from Russia not long after. Tolstoy describes the battle movingly and at great length in *War and Peace*, Book III.

Perhaps we chose a rather roundabout way to get there: from Epiphania through Kazanovka and Monastirshchina. It was only because there had been no rain till then that we were able to ride instead of pushing our bikes; to cross the Don, which was not yet in full spate, and its tributary, the Nepriadva, we wheeled them over narrow, two-plank footbridges.

After a long trek, we stood on a hill and caught sight of what looked like a needle pointing into the sky from a distant flat-topped rise. We went downhill and lost sight of it. Then we started to climb again, and the grey needle reappeared, this time more distinct, and next to it we saw what looked like a church. There seemed to be something uniquely strange about its design, something never seen except in fairy tales: its domes looked transparent and fluid; they shimmered deceptively in the cascading sunlight of the hot August day — one minute they were there and the next they were gone.

We guessed rightly that we would be able to quench our thirst and fill our water bottles at the well in the valley, which proved to be invaluable later on. But the peasant who handed us the bucket, in reply to our question: "Where's Kulikovo Field?" just stared at us as if we were idiots.

"You don't say Kulikóvo, you say Kulíkovo. The village of Kulíkovka is right next to the battlefield, but Kulikóvka's over there, on the other side of the Don."

After our meeting with this man, we travelled along deserted country lanes, and until we reached the monument several kilometers away, we did not come across a single person. It must have been because no one happened to be around on that particular day, for we could see the wheel of a combine harvester flailing somewhere in the distance. People obviously frequented this place and would do so again, because all the land had been planted with crops as far as the eye could see, and the harvest was almost ready — buckwheat, clover, sugar beet, rye, and peas (we had shelled some of those young peas); yet we saw no one that day and we passed through what seemed like the blessed calm of a reservation. Nothing disturbed us from musing on the fate of those fair-haired warriors, nine out of every ten of whom lay seven feet beneath the present topsoil, and whose bones had now dissolved into the earth, in order that Holy Russia might rid herself of the heathen Mussulman.[2]

The features of the land — this wide slope gradually ascending to Mamai Hill — could not have greatly changed over six centuries, except that the forest had disappeared. Spread out before us was the very place where they had crossed the Don in the evening and the night of September 7, 1380, then settled down to feed their horses (though the majority were foot soldiers), sharpen their swords, restore their morale, pray, and hope — almost a quarter of a million Russians, certainly more than two hundred

[2] Moslem.

thousand. The population of Russia then was barely a seventh of what it is now, so that an army of that size staggers the imagination.

And for nine out of every ten warriors, that was to be their last morning on earth.

On that occasion our men had not crossed the Don from choice, for what army would want to stand and fight with its retreat blocked by a river? The truth of history is bitter but it is better to admit it: Mamai had as allies not only Circassians, Genoese, and Lithuanians but also Prince Oleg of Ryazan. (One must understand Oleg's motives also: he had no other way of protecting his territory from the Tartars,[3] as it lay right across their path. His land had been ravaged by fire three times in the preceding seven years.) That is why the Russians had crossed the Don — to protect their rear from their own people, the men of Ryazan: in any other circumstances, Orthodox Christians would not have attacked them.

The needle loomed up in front of us, though it was no longer a needle but an imposing tower, unlike anything I had ever seen. We could not reach it directly: the tracks had come to an end and we were confronted by standing crops. We wheeled our bicycles round the edges of the fields and, finally, starting nowhere in particular, there emerged from the ground an old, neglected, abandoned road, overgrown with weeds, which grew more distinct as it drew nearer to the monument and even had ditches on either side of it.

Suddenly the crops came to an end and the hillside became even more like a reservation, a piece of fallow land overgrown with tough rye-grass instead of the usual feather-grass. We paid homage to this ancient place in the best way possible — just by breathing the pure air. One look around, and behold! — there in the light of sunrise the Mongol chief Telebei is engaged in single combat with Prince Peresvet, the two leaning against each other like two sheaves of wheat; the Mongolian cavalry are shooting their arrows and brandishing their spears; with faces contorted with blood lust, they trample on the Russian infantry, breaking through the core of their formation and driving them back to where a milky cloud of mist has risen from the Nepriadva and the Don.

Our men were mown down like wheat, and we were trampled to death beneath their hoofs.

Here, at the very axis of the bloody carnage, provided that the person who guessed the spot did so correctly, are the monument and the church with the unearthly domes which had so amazed us from afar. There turned out to be a simple solution to the puzzle: the local inhabitants have ripped off the metal from all five domes for their own requirements, so the domes have become transparent; their delicate structure is still intact, except that

---

[3] natives and inhabitants of Tatary, a region near Turkey that is now part of the Soviet Union, famed for their fierceness in battle.

it now consists of nothing but the framework, and from a distance it looks like a mirage.

The monument, too, is remarkable at close quarters. Unless you go right up to it and touch it, you will not understand how it was made. Although it was built in the last century, in fact well over a hundred years ago, the idea — of piecing the monument together from sections of cast iron — is entirely modern, except that nowadays it would not be cast in iron. It is made up of two square platforms, one on top of another, then a twelve-sided structure which gradually becomes round; the lower part is decorated in relief with iron shields, swords, helmets, and Slavonic inscriptions. Farther up, it rises in the shape of a fourfold cylinder cast so that it looks like four massive organ pipes welded together. Then comes a capping piece with an incised pattern, and above it all a gilded cross triumphing over a crescent. The whole tower — fully thirty meters high — is made up of figured slabs so tightly bolted together that not a single rivet or seam is visible, just as if the monument had been cast in a single piece — at least until time, or more likely the sons and grandsons of the men who put it up, had begun to knock holes in it.

After the long route to the monument through empty fields, we had assumed that the place would be deserted. As we walked along, we were wondering why it was in this state. This was, after all, a historic spot. What happened here was a turning point in the fate of Russia. For our invaders have not always come from the West. . . . Yet this place is spurned, forgotten.

How glad we were to be mistaken! At once, not far from the monument, we caught sight of a grey-haired old man and two young boys. They had thrown down their rucksacks and were lying in the grass, writing something in a large book the size of a class register. When we approached, we found that he was a literature teacher who had met the boys somewhere nearby, and that the book was not a school exercise book, but none other than the Visitors' Comments Book. But there was no museum here; where, then, in all this wild field was the book kept?

Suddenly a massive shadow blotted out the sun. We turned. It was the Keeper of Kulikovo Field — the man whose duty it was to guard our glorious heritage.

We did not have time to focus the camera, and in any case it was impossible to take a snapshot into the sun. What is more, the Keeper would have refused to be photographed (he knew what he was worth and refused to let himself be photographed all day). How shall I set about describing him? Should I begin with the man himself? Or start with his sack? (He was carrying an ordinary peasant's sack, only half full and evidently not very heavy since he was holding it without effort).

The Keeper was a hot-tempered muzhik[4] who looked something of a

---

[4] peasant.

ruffian. His arms and legs were hefty, and his shirt was dashingly unbuttoned. Red hair stuck out from under the cap planted sideways on his head, and although it was obviously a week since he had shaved, a fresh reddish scratch ran right across his cheek.

"Ah!" he greeted us in a disapproving voice as he loomed over us. "You've just arrived, have you? How did you get here?"

He seemed puzzled, as if the place were completely fenced in and we had found a hole to crawl through. We nodded towards the bicycles, which we had propped up in the bushes. Although he was holding the sack as though about to board a train, he looked as if he would demand to see our passports. His face was haggard, with a pointed chin and a determined expression.

"I'm warning you! Don't damage the grass with your bicycles!"

With this, he let us know immediately that here, on Kulikovo Field, you were not free to do as you liked.

The Keeper's unbuttoned coat was long-skirted and enveloped him like a parka; it was patched in a few places and was the color you read about in folk tales — somewhere between grey, brown, red, and purple. A star glinted in the lapel of his jacket; at first we thought it was a medal, but then we realized it was just the ordinary little badge, with Lenin's head in a circle, that everyone buys on Revolution Day. A long blue-and-white-striped linen shirt, obviously home-made, was hanging out from underneath his jacket and was gathered at the waist by an army belt with a five-pointed star on the buckle. His second-hand officer's breeches were tucked into the frayed tops of his canvas boots.

"Well?" he asked the teacher, in a much gentler tone of voice. "How's the writing going?"

"Fine, Zakhar Dmitrich," he replied, calling him by name. "We've nearly finished."

"Will *you*" — more sternly again — "be writing too?"

"Later on." We tried to escape from his insistent questions by cutting in: "Do you know when this monument was built?"

"Of course I do!" he snapped, offended, coughing and spluttering at the insult. "What do you think I'm here for?"

And carefully lowering his sack (which clinked with what sounded like bottles), the Keeper pulled a document out of his pocket and unfolded it; it was a page of an exercise book on which was written, in capital letters and in complete disregard of the ruled lines, a copy of the monument's dedication to Dmitry Donskoi and the year — 1848.

"What is that?"

"Well, comrades," sighed Zakhar Dmitrich, revealing by his frankness that he was not quite the tyrant that he had at first pretended to be, "it's like this. I copied it myself from the plaque because everyone asks when it was built. I'll show you where the plaque was, if you like."

"What became of it?"

"Some rogue from our village pinched it — and we can't do anything about it."

"Do you know who it was?"

"Of course I know. I scared off some of his gang of louts, I dealt with them all right, but he and the rest got away. I'd like to lay my hands on all those vandals, I'd show 'em."

"But why did he steal the plaque?"

"For his house."

"Can't you take it back?"

"Ha, ha!" Zakhar threw back his head in reply to our foolish question. "That's the problem! I don't have any authority. They won't give me a gun. I need a machine gun in a job like this."

Looking at the scratch across his cheek, we thought to ourselves it was just as well they didn't give him a gun.

Then the teacher finished what he was writing and handed back the Comments Book. We thought that Zakhar Dmitrich would put it under his arm or into his sack, but we were wrong. He opened the flap of his dirty jacket and revealed, sewn inside, a sort of pocket or bag made of sacking (in fact, it was more like a pouch than anything else), the exact size of the Comments Book, which fitted neatly into it. Also attached to the pouch was a slot for the blunt indelible pencil which he lent to visitors.

Convinced that we were not suitably intimidated, Zakhar-the-Pouch picked up his sack, (the clinking *was* glass) and went off with his long, loping stride into the bushes. Here the brusque forcefulness with which he had first met us vanished. Hunching himself miserably, he sat down, lit a cigarette, and smoked with such unalleviated grief, with such despair, that one might have thought all those who had perished on this battlefield had died only yesterday and had been his closest relatives, and that now he did not know how to go on living.

We decided to spend the whole day and night here: to see whether nighttime at Kulikovo really was as Blok described it in his poem. Without hurrying, we walked over to the monument, inspected the abandoned church, and wandered over the field, trying to imagine the dispositions of the battlefield on that eighth of September; then we clambered up onto the iron surface of the monument.

Plenty of people had been here before us. It would be quite wrong to say that the monument had been forgotten. People had been busy carving the iron surface of the monument with chisels and scratching it with nails, while those with less energy had written more faintly on the church walls with charcoal: "Maria Polyneyeva and Nikolai Lazarev were here from 8/5/50[5] to 24/5. . . ." "Delegates of the regional conference were here. . . ." "Workers from the Kimovskaya Postal Administration were here 23/6/52. . . ." And so on and so on.

---

[5] The dates are written in the European style, with the day preceding the month.

Then three young working lads from Novomoskovsk drove up on motorbikes. Jumping off lightly onto the iron surface, they started to examine the warm grey-black body of the monument and slapped it affectionately; they were surprised at how well made it was and explained to us how it had been done. In return, from the top platform we pointed out everything we knew about the battle.

But who can know nowadays exactly where and how it took place? According to the manuscripts, the Mongol-Tartar cavalry cut into our infantry regiments, decimated them, and drove them back toward the crossings over the Don, thus turning the Don from a protective moat against Oleg into a possible death trap. If the worst had happened, Dmitry would have been called "Donskoi" for the opposite reason.[6] But he had taken everything into careful account and stood his ground, something of which not every grand duke was capable. He left a boyar[7] dressed in his, Dmitry's, attire, fighting beneath his flag, while he himself fought as an ordinary foot soldier, and he was once seen taking on four Tartars at once. But the grand-ducal standard was chopped down and Dmitry, his armor severely battered, barely managed to crawl to the wood, when the Mongols broke through the Russian lines and drove them back. But then another Dmitry, Volinsky-Bobrok, the governor of Moscow, who had been lying in ambush with his army, attacked the ferocious Tartars from the rear. He drove them back, harrying them as they galloped away. Then he wheeled sharply and forced them into the river Nepriadva. From that moment the Russians took heart; they re-formed and turned on the Tartars, rose from the ground and drove all the khans, the enemy commanders, even Mamai himself, forty versts[8] away across the river Ptan as far as Krasivaya Mech. (But here one legend contradicts another. An old man from the neighboring village of Ivanovka had his own version: the mist, he said, had not lifted, and in the mist Mamai, thinking a broad oak tree beside him was a Russian warrior, took fright — "Ah, mighty is the Christian God!" — and so fled.)

Afterwards the Russians cleared the field of battle and buried the dead: it took them eight days.

"There's one they didn't pick up — they left him behind!" the cheerful fitter from Novomoskovsk said accusingly.

We turned around and could not help but burst out laughing. Yes! — one fallen warrior was lying there this very day, not far from the monument, face down on mother earth — his native land. His bold head had dropped to the ground and his valiant limbs were spread-eagled; he was without his shield or sword and, in place of his helmet, wore a threadbare cap, and near his hand lay a sack. (All the same, he was careful not to crush the edge of

---

[6] After winning the battle, Prince Dmitry of Moscow was honored with the name *Donskoi*, meaning "of the Don." Solzhenitsyn punningly implies that he might have become "Dmitry of the Don" in another, more literal sense.

[7] a high-ranking aristocrat.

[8] One verst is about two-thirds of a mile.

his jacket with the pouch in it, where he kept the Comments Book; he had pulled it out from underneath his stomach and it lay on the grass beside him.) Perhaps he was just lying there in a drunken stupor, but if he was sleeping or thinking, then the way he was sprawled across the ground was very touching. He went perfectly with the field. They should cast an iron figure like that and place it here.

However, for all his height, Zakhar was too skinny to be a warrior.

"He doesn't want to work on the kolkhoz,[9] so he found himself a soft government job where he can get a suntan," one of the lads growled.

What we disliked most of all was the way Zakhar flew at all the new arrivals, especially those who looked as if they might cause him trouble. During the day a few more people arrived; when he heard their cars he would get up, shake himself, and pounce on them with threats, as if they, not he, were responsible for the monument. Before they had time to be annoyed, Zakhar himself would give vent to violent indignation about the desolation of the place. It seemed incredible that he could harbor such passion.

"Don't you think it's a disgrace?" he said, waving his arms aggressively, to four people who got out of a Zaporozhetz car. "I'll bide my time, then I'll walk right through the regional department of culture." (With those long legs he could easily have done it.) "I'll take leave and I'll go to Moscow, right to Furtseva, the Minister of Culture herself. I'll tell her everything."

Then, as soon as he noticed that the visitors were intimidated and were not standing up to him, he picked up his sack with an air of importance, as an official picks up his briefcase, and went off to have a smoke and a nap.

Wandering here and there, we met Zakhar several times during the day. We noticed that when he walked he limped in one leg, and we asked him what had caused this.

He replied proudly: "It's a souvenir from the war!"

Again we did not believe him: he was just a practiced liar.

We had drunk our water bottles dry, so we went up to Zakhar and asked him where we could get some water. Wa-ater? The whole trouble was, he explained, that there was no well here and they wouldn't allocate any money to dig one. The only source of drinking water in the whole field was the puddles. The well was in the village.

After that, he no longer bothered to get up to talk to us, as if we were old friends.

When we complained about the inscriptions having been hacked away or scratched over, Zakhar retorted: "Have a look and see if you can read any of the dates. If you find any new damage, then you can blame me. All this vandalism was done before my time; they don't dare try it when I'm

---

[9] collective farm.

around! Well, perhaps some scoundrel hid in the church and then scribbled on the walls — I've only got one pair of legs, you know!"

The church, dedicated to St. Sergei of Radonezh, who united the Russian forces and brought them to battle and soon afterwards effected the reconciliation between Dmitry Donskoi and Oleg of Ryazan, was a sturdy fortresslike building with tightly interlocking limbs: the truncated pyramid of the nave, a cloister surmounted by a watchtower, and two round castellated towers. There were a few windows like loopholes.

Inside it, everything had been stripped and there wasn't even a floor — you walked over sand. We asked Zakhar about it.

"Ha, ha, ha! It was all pinched!" He gloated over us. "It was during the war. Our people in Kulikovo tore up all the slabs from the floors and paved their yards, so they wouldn't have to walk in the muck. I made a list of who took the slabs. . . . Then the war ended, but they still went on pinching the stuff. Even before that, our troops had used all the ikon screens to put round the edges of dugouts and for heating their stoves."

As the hours passed and he got used to us, Zakhar was no longer embarrassed to delve into his sack in front of us, and we gradually found out exactly what was inside it. It contained five empty bottles (twelve kopecks) and jam jars (five kopecks) left behind by visitors — he picked them up in the bushes after their picnics — and also a full bottle of water, because he had no other access to drinking water during the day. He carried two loaves of rye bread, which he broke bits off of now and again and chewed for his frugal meals.

"People come here in crowds all day long. I don't have any time to go off to the village for a meal."

On some days he probably carried a precious half-bottle of vodka in there or some canned fish; then he would clutch the sack tightly, afraid to leave it anywhere. That day, when the sun had already begun to set, a friend on a motorbike came to see him; they sat in the bushes for an hour and a half. Then the friend went away and Zakhar came back without his sack. He talked rather more loudly, waved his arms more vigorously, and, noticing that I was writing something, warned us: "I'm in charge here, let me tell you! In '57 they decided to put a building up here. See those posts over there, planted round the monument? They've been here since then. They were cast in Tula. They were supposed to join up the posts with chains, but the chains never came. So they gave me this job and they pay me for it. Without me, the whole place would be in ruins!"

"How much do you get paid, Zakhar Dmitrich?"

After a sigh like a blacksmith's bellows, he was speechless for a moment. He mumbled something, then said quietly: "Twenty-seven roubles."

"What? The minimum's thirty."

"Well, maybe it is. . . . And I don't get any days off, either. Morning to dusk I'm on the job without a break, and I even have to come back late at night too."

What an incorrigible old liar he is, we thought.

"Why do you have to be here at night?"

"Why d'you think?" he said in an offended voice. "How can I leave the place at night? Someone's got to watch it all the time. If a car comes, I have to make a note of its number."

"Why the number?"

"Well, they won't let me have a gun. They say I might shoot the visitors. The only authority I've got is to take their number. And supposing they do some damage?"

"What do you do with the number afterwards?"

"Nothing. I just keep it. . . . Now they've built a house for tourists, have you seen it? I have to guard that too."

We had, of course, seen the house. Single-story, with several rooms, it was near completion but was still kept locked. The windows had been put in, and several were already broken; the floors were laid, but the plastering was not yet finished.

"Will you let us stay the night there?" (Towards sunset, it had begun to get cold; it was going to be a bitter night.)

"In the tourist house? No, it's impossible."

"Then who's it for?"

"No, it can't be done. Anyway, I haven't got the keys. So you needn't bother to ask. You can sleep in my shed."

His low shed with its sloping roof was designed for a half a dozen sheep. Bending down, we peered inside. Broken, trampled straw was scattered around; on the floor there was a cooking pot with some leftovers in it, a few more empty bottles, and a desiccated piece of bread. However, there was room for our bikes, and we could lie down and still leave enough space for Zakhar to stretch out.

He made use of our stay to take some time off.

"I'm off to Kulikovo to have supper at home. Grab a bite of something hot. Leave the door on the hook."

"Knock when you want to come in," we said, laughingly.

"O.K."

Zakhar-the-Pouch turned back the other flap of his miraculous jacket, to reveal two loops sewn into it. Out of his inexhaustible sack he drew an axe with a shortened handle and placed it firmly into the loops.

"Well," he said gloomily, "that's all I have for protection. They won't allow me anything else."

He said this in a tone of the deepest doom, as if he were expecting a horde of infidels to gallop up one of these nights and overthrow the monument, and he would have to face them alone with his little hatchet. We even shuddered at his voice as we sat there in the half-light. Perhaps he wasn't a buffoon at all? Perhaps he really believed that if he didn't stand guard every night the battlefield and the monument were doomed?

Weakened by drink and a day of noisy activity, stooping and barely managing to hobble, Zakhar went off to his village and we laughed at him once more.

As had been our wish, we were left alone on Kulikovo Field. Night set in, with a full moon. The tower of the monument and the fortress-like church were silhouetted against it like great black screens. The distant lights of Kulikovka and Ivanovka competed faintly with the light of the moon. Not one aeroplane flew overhead; no motorcar rumbled by, no train rattled past in the distance. By moonlight the pattern of the nearby fields was no longer visible. Earth, grass, and moonlit solitude were as they had been in 1380. The centuries stood still, and as we wandered over the field we could evoke the whole scene — the campfires and the troops of dark horses. From the river Nepriadva came the sound of swans, just as Blok had described.

We wanted to understand the battle of Kulikovo in its entirety, grasp its inevitability, ignore the infuriating ambiguities of the chronicles; nothing had been as simple or as straightforward as it seemed; history had repeated itself after a long time-lag, and when it did, the result was disastrous. After the victory, the warriors of Russia faded away. Tokhtamysh immediately replaced Mamai, and two years after Kulikovo, he crushed the power of Muscovy; Dmitry Donskoi fled to Kostroma, while Tokhtamysh again destroyed both Ryazan and Moscow, took the Kremlin by ruse, plundered it, set it afire, chopped off heads, and dragged prisoners back in chains to the Golden Horde, the Tartar capital.

Centuries pass and the devious path of history is simplified for the distant spectator until it looks as straight as a road drawn by a cartographer.

The night turned bitterly cold, but we shut ourselves in the shed and slept soundly right through it. We had decided to leave early in the morning. It was hardly light when we pushed our bicycles out and, with chattering teeth, started to load up.

The grass was white with hoarfrost; wisps of fog stretched from the hollow in which Kulikovka village lay and across the fields, dotted with haycocks. Just as we emerged from the shed to mount our bicycles and leave, we heard a loud, ferocious bark coming from one of the haycocks, and a shaggy grey dog ran out and made straight for us. As it bounded out, the haycock collapsed behind it; wakened by the barking, a tall figure arose from beneath it, called for the dog, and began to shake off the straw. It was already light enough for us to recognize him as our Zakhar-the-Pouch, still wearing his curious short-sleeved overcoat.

He had spent the night in the haycock, in the bone-chilling cold. Why? Was it anxiety or was it devotion to the place that had made him do it?

Immediately our previous attitude of amused condescension vanished. Rising out of the haycock on that frosty morning, he was no longer the ridiculous Keeper but rather the Spirit of the Field, a kind of guardian angel who never left the place.

He came towards us, still shaking himself and rubbing his hands together, and with his cap pushed back on his head, he seemed like a dear old friend.

"Why didn't you knock, Zakhar Dmitrich?"

"I didn't want to disturb you." He shrugged his shoulders and yawned. He was covered all over in straw and fluff. As he unbuttoned his coat to shake himself, we caught sight of both the Comments Book and his sole legal weapon, the hatchet, in their respective places.

The grey dog by his side was baring its teeth.

We said goodbye warmly and were already pedalling off as he stood there with his long arm raised, calling out: "Don't worry! I'll see to it! I'll go right to Furtseva! To Furtseva herself!"

That was two years ago. Perhaps the place is tidier now and better cared for. I have been a bit slow about writing this, but I haven't forgotten the Field of Kulikovo, or its Keeper, its red-haired tutelary spirit.

And let it be said that we Russians would be very foolish to neglect that place.

[1971]

DORIS LESSING (*b.* 1919) *was born in Persia (now Iran), where her father managed a bank. When she was five her family moved to a farm in Rhodesia (now Zimbabwe), in an isolated part of Africa that had not been settled before by white people. "Looking back now at that enormous tract of bush, dotted with lonely farms, it seems as if we all lived on brightly lit stages where the dramas of our lives were played out to a chorus of comment and gossip. As a girl I watched these lives unfolding epically in the logic of their natures — a relentless and pitiless process it seemed then, as it still does." Lessing left school at the age of fourteen in rebellion against her mother, who had conventional ambitions for her. She lived on the farm and wrote two "bad" novels, then married at nineteen and had two children. After this marriage failed, she married again and had one son. She was a Communist for some years in her twenties, when she "learned a great deal, chiefly about the nature of political power, how groups of people operate." Then in 1949 she left her husband in Rhodesia and came with her son to London, where she has lived as a professional writer ever since, "at first rather poor, but now comfortable."*

After Lessing left Africa, it remained in her consciousness as "an inexplicable majestic silence lying just over the border of memory or of thought. Africa gives you the knowledge that man is a small creature, among other creatures, in a large landscape." Her first two books, the novel The Grass Is Singing *(1950) and a volume of short stories,* This Was the Old Chief's Country *(1951), were based on her experiences in Rhodesia. They developed the theme of the exploitation of blacks by white people — although Lessing also places racial prejudice in a larger context as being "only one aspect of the atrophy of the imagination that prevents us from seeing ourselves in every creature that breathes under the sun." Her books were recognized as work by a gifted young writer, and her next collection of African stories,* Five, *received the 1953 Somerset Maugham Award. Her third collection of stories,* The Habit of Loving *(1957), dramatized another of her themes as a writer: the destructive relationship between men and women. While her female characters have achieved a degree of intellectual, professional, and sexual freedom, they are still victims of their own emotional vulnerability to men who continue to exploit them. In 1962 Lessing published the experimental novel* The Golden Notebook, *which critics read as an exploration of the emotional problems faced by intelligent women who wish to live in the kind of freedom men take for granted. Lessing, however, said that she had shaped the book to explore a theme that went beyond the status of women: the perilous situation of human beings in a fragmented, materialistic society. Her later novels have included the five volumes in the series* Children of Violence, *and several recent science fiction works,* Canopus in Argos Archives.

Considered one of the most accomplished novelists now writing in English, Lessing is also praised for her short stories, which have often been compared to those of D. H. Lawrence. Like Lawrence, she is not always confident of rational solutions to the political and sexual problems of modern life. In her fiction she goes beyond Lawrence to explore the possibilities for psychological reorientation that exist in states of temporary insanity and in religious experience. Lessing is highly receptive to emotions that surface during the process of writing fiction: "This question of I, who am I, what different levels there are inside of us, is very relevant to writing, to the process of creative writing about which we know nothing whatsoever. Every writer feels when he, she, hits a different level. A certain kind of writing or emotion comes from it. But you don't know who it is who lives there. It is very frightening to write a story like 'To Room 19,' for instance, a story soaked in emotions that you don't remember as your own."

Lessing's story "Homage for Isaac Babel," on the other hand, can be traced more directly to one of her political concerns, the idea that young people today have no understanding of the Russian revolution (the period of early Soviet history that Babel described so brilliantly in his stories) and could not care less about it. As Lessing has observed in her essay "A Small Personal Voice" (1957), "The mental climate created by the Cold War has produced a generation . . . who totally reject everything communism stands for; they cut themselves off imaginatively from a third of mankind, and impoverish themselves by doing so."

Doris Lessing

ᘛᘚ

TO ROOM 19

This is a story, I suppose, about a failure in intelligence: the Rawlings' marriage was grounded in intelligence.

They were older when they married than most of their married friends: in their well-seasoned late twenties. Both had had a number of affairs, sweet rather than bitter; and when they fell in love — for they did fall in love — had known each other for some time. They joked that they had saved each other "for the real thing." That they had waited so long (but not too long) for this real thing was to them a proof of their sensible discrimination. A good many of their friends had married young, and now (they felt) probably regretted lost opportunities; while others, still unmarried, seemed to them arid, self-doubting, and likely to make desperate or romantic marriages.

Not only they, but others, felt they were well-matched: their friends' delight was an additional proof of their happiness. They had played the same roles, male and female, in this group or set, if such a wide, loosely connected, constantly changing constellation of people could be called a set. They had both become, by virtue of their moderation, their humour, and their abstinence from painful experience, people to whom others came for advice. They could be, and were, relied on. It was one of those cases of a man and a woman linking themselves whom no one else had ever thought of linking, probably because of their similarities. But then everyone exclaimed: Of course! How right! How was it we never thought of it before!

And so they married amid general rejoicing, and because of their foresight and their sense for what was probable, nothing was a surprise to them.

Both had well-paid jobs. Matthew was a subeditor on a large London newspaper, and Susan worked in an advertising firm. He was not the stuff of which editors or publicised journalists are made, but he was much more than "a subeditor," being one of the essential background people who in fact steady, inspire, and make possible the people in the limelight. He was content with this position. Susan had a talent for commercial drawing. She was humorous about the advertisements she was responsible for, but she did not feel strongly about them one way or the other.

Both, before they married, had had pleasant flats, but they felt it unwise to base a marriage on either flat, because it might seem like a submission of personality on the part of the one whose flat it was not. They moved into a new flat in South Kensington on the clear understanding that when their marriage had settled down (a process they knew would not take long, and was in fact more a humorous concession to popular wisdom than what was due to themselves) they would buy a house and start a family.

And this is what happened. They lived in their charming flat for two years, giving parties and going to them, being a popular young married couple, and then Susan became pregnant, she gave up her job, and they bought a house in Richmond. It was typical of this couple that they had a son first, then a daughter, then twins, son and daughter. Everything right, appropriate, and what everyone would wish for, if they could choose. But people did feel these two had chosen; this balanced and sensible family was no more than what was due to them because of their infallible sense for *choosing* right.

And so they lived with their four children in their gardened house in Richmond and were happy. They had everything they had wanted and had planned for.

And yet. . . .

Well, even this was expected, that there must be a certain flatness. . . .

Yes, yes, of course, it was natural they sometimes felt like this. Like what?

Their life seemed to be like a snake biting its tail. Matthew's job for the sake of Susan, children, house, and garden — which caravanserai needed a well-paid job to maintain it. And Susan's practical intelligence for the sake of Matthew, the children, the house, and the garden — which unit would have collapsed in a week without her.

But there was no point about which either could say: "For the sake of *this* is all at rest." Children? But children can't be a centre of life and a reason for being. They can be a thousand things that are delightful, interesting, satisfying, but they can't be a wellspring to live from. Or they shouldn't be. Susan and Matthew knew that well enough.

Matthew's job? Ridiculous. It was an interesting job, but scarcely a reason for living. Matthew took pride in doing it well, but he could hardly be expected to be proud of the newspaper; the newspaper he read, *his* newspaper, was not the one he worked for.

Their love for each other? Well, that was nearest it. If this wasn't a centre, what was? Yes, it was around this point, their love, that the whole extraordinary structure revolved. For extraordinary it certainly was. Both Susan and Matthew had moments of thinking so, of looking in secret disbelief at this thing they had created: marriage, four children, big house, garden, charwomen, friends, cars . . . and this *thing*, this entity, all of it had come into existence, been blown into being out of nowhere, because Susan loved Matthew and Matthew loved Susan. Extraordinary. So that was the central point, the wellspring.

And if one felt that it simply was not strong enough, important enough, to support it all, well whose fault was that? Certainly neither Susan's nor Matthew's. It was in the nature of things. And they sensibly blamed neither themselves nor each other.

On the contrary, they used their intelligence to preserve what they had created from a painful and explosive world: they looked around them, and took lessons. All around them, marriages collapsing, or breaking, or rubbing along (even worse, they felt). They must not make the same mistakes, they must not.

They had avoided the pitfall so many of their friends had fallen into — of buying a house in the country *for the sake of the children*, so that the husband became a weekend husband, a weekend father, and the wife always careful not to ask what went on in the town flat which they called (in joke) a bachelor flat. No, Matthew was a full-time husband, a full-time father, and at night, in the big married bed in the big married bedroom (which had an attractive view of the river), they lay beside each other talking and he told her about his day, and what he had done, and whom he had met; and she told him about her day (not as interesting, but that was not her fault), for both knew of the hidden resentments and deprivations of the woman who has lived her own life — and above all, has earned her own living — and is now dependent on a husband for outside interests and money.

Nor did Susan make the mistake of taking a job for the sake of her independence, which she might very well have done, since her old firm, missing her qualities of humour, balance, and sense, invited her often to go back. Children needed their mother to a certain age, that both parents knew and agreed on; and when these four healthy wisely brought up children were of the right age, Susan would work again, because she knew, and so did he, what happened to women of fifty at the height of their energy and ability, with grownup children who no longer needed their full devotion.

So here was this couple, testing their marriage, looking after it, treating it like a small boat full of helpless people in a very stormy sea. Well, of course, so it was. . . . The storms of the world were bad, but not too close — which is not to say they were selfishly felt: Susan and Matthew were both well-informed and responsible people. And the inner storms and quicksands were understood and charted. So everything was all right. Everything was in order. Yes, things were under control.

So what did it matter if they felt dry, flat? People like themselves, fed on a hundred books (psychological, anthropological, sociological), could scarcely be unprepared for the dry, controlled wistfulness which is the distinguishing mark of the intelligent marriage. Two people, endowed with education, with discrimination, with judgement, linked together voluntarily from their will to be happy together and to be of use to others — one sees them everywhere, one knows them, one even is that thing oneself: sadness because so much is after all so little. These two, unsurprised, turned towards each other with even more courtesy and gentle love: this was life, that two people, no matter how carefully chosen, could not be everything to each other. In fact, even to say so, to think in such a way, was banal; they were ashamed to do it.

It was banal, too, when one night Matthew came home late and confessed he had been to a party, taken a girl home, and slept with her. Susan forgave him, of course. Except that forgiveness is hardly the word. Understanding, yes. But if you understand something, you don't forgive it, you are the thing itself: forgiveness is for what you *don't* understand. Nor had he *confessed* — what sort of word is that?

The whole thing was not important. After all, years ago they had joked: Of course I'm not going to be faithful to you, no one can be faithful to one other person for a whole lifetime. (And there was the word "faithful" — stupid, all these words, stupid, belonging to a savage old world.) But the incident left both of them irritable. Strange, but they were both bad-tempered, annoyed. There was something unassimilable about it.

Making love splendidly after he had come home that night, both had felt that the idea that Myra Jenkins, a pretty girl met at a party, could be even relevant was ridiculous. They had loved each other for over a decade, would love each other for years more. Who, then, was Myra Jenkins?

Except, thought Susan, unaccountably bad-tempered, she was (is?) the first. In ten years. So either the ten years' fidelity was not important, or she isn't. (No, no, there is something wrong with this way of thinking, there must be.) But if she isn't important, presumably it wasn't important either when Matthew and I first went to bed with each other that afternoon whose delight even now (like a very long shadow at sundown) lays a long, wandlike finger over us. (Why did I say sundown?) Well, if what we felt that afternoon was not important, nothing is important, because if it hadn't been for what we felt, we wouldn't be Mr. and Mrs. Rawlings with four children, et cetera, et cetera. The whole thing is *absurd* — for him to have come home and told me was absurd. For him not to have told me was absurd. For me to care or, for that matter, not to care, is absurd . . . and who is Myra Jenkins? Why, no one at all.

There was only one thing to do, and of course these sensible people did it; they put the thing behind them, and consciously, knowing what they were doing, moved forward into a different phase of their marriage, giving thanks for the past good fortune as they did so.

For it was inevitable that the handsome, blond, attractive, manly man, Matthew Rawlings, should be at times tempted (oh, what a word!) by the attractive girls at parties she could not attend because of the four children; and that sometimes he would succumb (a word even more repulsive, if possible) and that she, a goodlooking woman in the big well-tended garden at Richmond, would sometimes be pierced as by an arrow from the sky with bitterness. Except that bitterness was not in order, it was out of court. Did the casual girls touch the marriage? They did not. Rather it was they who knew defeat because of the handsome Matthew Rawlings' marriage body and soul to Susan Rawlings.

In that case why did Susan feel (though luckily not for longer than a few seconds at a time) as if life had become a desert, and that nothing mattered, and that her children were not her own?

Meanwhile her intelligence continued to assert that all was well. What if her Matthew did have an occasional sweet afternoon, the odd affair? For she knew quite well, except in her moments of aridity, that they were very happy, that the affairs were not important.

Perhaps that was the trouble? It was in the nature of things that the adventures and delights could no longer be hers, because of the four children and the big house that needed so much attention. But perhaps she was secretly wishing, and even knowing that she did, that the wildness and the beauty could be his. But he was married to her. She was married to him. They were married inextricably. And therefore the gods could not strike him with the real magic, not really. Well, was it Susan's fault that after he came home from an adventure he looked harassed rather than fulfilled? (In fact, that was how she knew he had been *unfaithful*, because of his sullen air, and his glances at her, similar to hers at him: What is it that I share with this person that shields all delight from me?) But none of it by anybody's fault. (But what did they feel ought to be somebody's fault?) Nobody's fault, nothing to be at fault, no one to blame, no one to offer or to take it . . . and nothing wrong, either, except that Matthew never was really struck, as he wanted to be, by joy; and that Susan was more and more often threatened by emptiness. (It was usually in the garden that she was invaded by this feeling: she was coming to avoid the garden, unless the children or Matthew were with her.) There was no need to use the dramatic words "unfaithful," "forgive," and the rest: intelligence forbade them. Intelligence barred, too, quarrelling, sulking, anger, silences of withdrawal, accusations, and tears. Above all, intelligence forbids tears.

A high price has to be paid for the happy marriage with the four healthy children in the large white gardened house.

And they were paying it, willingly, knowing what they were doing. When they lay side by side or breast to breast in the big civilised bedroom overlooking the wild sullied river, they laughed, often, for no particular reason; but they knew it was really because of these two small people, Susan and Matthew, supporting such an edifice on their intelligent love. The laugh comforted them; it saved them both, though from what, they did not know.

They were now both fortyish. The older children, boy and girl, were ten and eight, at school. The twins, six, were still at home. Susan did not have nurses or girls to help her: childhood is short; and she did not regret the hard work. Often enough she was bored, since small children can be boring; she was often very tired; but she regretted nothing. In another decade, she would turn herself back into being a woman with a life of her own.

Soon the twins would go to school, and they would be away from home from nine until four. These hours, so Susan saw it, would be the preparation for her own slow emancipation away from the role of hub-of-the-family into woman-with-her-own-life. She was already planning for the hours of freedom when all the children would be "off her hands." That was the phrase used by Matthew and by Susan and by their friends, for the moment when the youngest child went off to school. "They'll be off your hands, darling Susan, and you'll have time to yourself." So said Matthew, the intelligent husband, who had often enough commended and consoled Susan, standing by her in spirit during the years when her soul was not her own, as she said, but her children's.

What it amounted to was that Susan saw herself as she had been at twenty-eight, unmarried; and then again somewhere about fifty, blossoming from the root of what she had been twenty years before. As if the essential Susan were in abeyance, as if she were in cold storage. Matthew said something like this to Susan one night: and she agreed that it was true — she did feel something like that. What, then, was this essential Susan? She did not know. Put like that it sounded ridiculous, and she did not really feel it. Anyway, they had a long discussion about the whole thing before going off to sleep in each other's arms.

So the twins went off to their school, two bright affectionate children who had no problems about it, since their older brother and sister had trodden this path so successfully before them. And now Susan was going to be alone in the big house, every day of the school term, except for the daily woman who came in to clean.

It was now, for the first time in this marriage, that something happened which neither of them had foreseen.

This is what happened. She returned, at nine-thirty, from taking the twins to the school by car, looking forward to seven blissful hours of freedom. On the first morning she was simply restless, worrying about the twins "naturally enough" since this was their first day away at school. She was hardly able to contain herself until they came back. Which they did happily, excited by the world of school, looking forward to the next day. And the next day Susan took them, dropped them, came back, and found herself reluctant to enter her big and beautiful home because it was as if something was waiting for her there that she did not wish to confront. Sensibly, however, she parked the car in the garage, entered the house, spoke to Mrs. Parkes, the daily woman, about her duties, and went up to her bedroom. She was possessed by a fever which drove her out again, downstairs, into the kitchen, where Mrs. Parkes was making cake and did not need her, and into the garden. There she sat on a bench and tried to calm herself looking at trees, at a brown glimpse of the river. But she was filled with tension, like a panic: as if an enemy was in the garden with her. She spoke to herself severely, thus: All this is quite natural. First, I spent twelve years of my adult life working, *living my own life.* Then I married, and from the moment I became pregnant for the first time I signed myself over, so to speak, to other people. To the children. Not for one moment in twelve years have I been alone, had time to myself. So now I have to learn to be myself again. That's all.

And she went indoors to help Mrs. Parkes cook and clean, and found some sewing to do for the children. She kept herself occupied every day. At the end of the first term she understood she felt two contrary emotions. First: secret astonishment and dismay that during those weeks when the house was empty of children she had in fact been more occupied (had been careful to keep herself occupied) than ever she had been when the children were around her needing her continual attention. Second: that now she knew the house would be full of them, and for five weeks, she resented the fact she would never be alone. She was already looking back at those hours of sewing, cooking (but by herself) as at a lost freedom which would not be hers for five long weeks. And the two months of term which would succeed the five weeks stretched alluringly open to her — freedom. But what freedom — when in fact she had been so careful *not* to be free of small duties during the last weeks? She looked at herself, Susan Rawlings, sitting in a big chair by the window in the bedroom, sewing shirts or dresses, which she might just as well have bought. She saw herself making cakes for hours at a time in the big family kitchen: yet usually she bought cakes. What she saw was a woman alone, that was true, but she had not felt alone. For instance, Mrs. Parkes was always somewhere in the house. And she did not like being in the garden at all, because of the closeness there of the enemy — irritation, restlessness, emptiness, whatever it was — which keeping her hands occupied made less dangerous for some reason.

Susan did not tell Matthew of these thoughts. They were not sensible. She did not recognise herself in them. What should she say to her dear friend and husband, Matthew? "When I go into the garden, that is, if the children are not there, I feel as if there is an enemy there waiting to invade me." "What enemy, Susan darling?" "Well I don't know, really. . . ." "Perhaps you should see a doctor?"

No, clearly this conversation should not take place. The holidays began and Susan welcomed them. Four children, lively, energetic, intelligent, demanding: she was never, not for a moment of her day, alone. If she was in a room, they would be in the next room, or waiting for her to do something for them; or it would soon be time for lunch or tea, or to take one of them to the dentist. Something to do: five weeks of it, thank goodness.

On the fourth day of these so welcome holidays, she found she was storming with anger at the twins; two shrinking beautiful children who (and this is what checked her) stood hand in hand looking at her with sheer dismayed disbelief. This was their calm mother, shouting at them. And for what? They had come to her with some game, some bit of nonsense. They looked at each other, moved closer for support, and went off hand in hand, leaving Susan holding on to the windowsill of the livingroom, breathing deep, feeling sick. She went to lie down, telling the older children she had a headache. She heard the boy Harry telling the little ones: "It's all right, Mother's got a headache." She heard that *It's all right* with pain.

That night she said to her husband: "Today I shouted at the twins, quite unfairly." She sounded miserable, and he said gently: "Well, what of it?"

"It's more of an adjustment than I thought, their going to school."

"But Susie, Susie darling. . . . " For she was crouched weeping on the bed. He comforted her: "Susan, what is all this about? You shouted at them? What of it? If you shouted at them fifty times a day it wouldn't be more than the little devils deserve." But she wouldn't laugh. She wept. Soon he comforted her with his body. She became calm. Calm, she wondered what was wrong with her, and why she should mind so much that she might, just once, have behaved unjustly with the children. What did it matter? They had forgotten it all long ago: Mother had a headache and everything was all right.

It was a long time later that Susan understood that that night, when

she had wept and Matthew had driven the misery out of her with his big
solid body, was the last time, ever in their married life, that they had
been — to use their mutual language — with each other. And even that
was a lie, because she had not told him of her real fears at all.

The five weeks passed, and Susan was in control of herself, and good
and kind, and she looked forward to the holidays with a mixture of fear and
longing. She did not know what to expect. She took the twins off to school
(the elder children took themselves to school) and she returned to the house
determined to face the enemy wherever he was, in the house, or the garden
or — where?

She was again restless, she was possessed by restlessness. She cooked
and sewed and worked as before, day after day, while Mrs. Parkes remonstrated: "Mrs. Rawlings, what's the need for it? I can do that, it's what you
pay me for."

And it was so irrational that she checked herself. She would put the
car in the garage, go up to her bedroom, and sit, hands in her lap, forcing
herself to be quiet. She listened to Mrs. Parkes moving around the house.
She looked out into the garden and saw the branches shake the trees. She
sat defeating the enemy, restlessness. Emptiness. She ought to be thinking
about her life, about herself. But she did not. Or perhaps she could not. As
soon as she forced her mind to think about Susan (for what else did she
want to be alone for?), it skipped off to thoughts of butter or school clothes.
Or it thought of Mrs. Parkes. She realised that she sat listening for the
movements of the cleaning woman, following her every turn, bend,
thought. She followed her in her mind from kitchen to bathroom, from
table to oven, and it was as if the duster, the cleaning cloth, the saucepan,
were in her own hand. She would hear herself saying: No, not like that,
don't put that there. . . . Yet she did not give a damn what Mrs. Parkes did,
or if she did it at all. Yet she could not prevent herself from being conscious
of her, every minute. Yes, this was what was wrong with her: she needed,
when she was alone, to be really alone, with no one near. She could not endure the knowledge that in ten minutes or in half an hour Mrs. Parkes
would call up the stairs: "Mrs. Rawlings, there's no silver polish. Madam,
we're out of flour."

So she left the house and went to sit in the garden where she was
screened from the house by trees. She waited for the demon to appear and
claim her, but he did not.

She was keeping him off, because she had not, after all, come to an
end of arranging herself.

She was planning how to be somewhere where Mrs. Parkes would not
come after her with a cup of tea, or a demand to be allowed to telephone
(always irritating, since Susan did not care who she telephoned or how
often), or just a nice talk about something. Yes, she needed a place, or a
state of affairs, where it would not be necessary to keep reminding herself:
In ten minutes I must telephone Matthew about . . . and at half past three I

must leave early for the children because the car needs cleaning. And at ten o'clock tomorrow I must remember. . . . She was possessed with resentment that the seven hours of freedom in every day (during weekdays in the school term) were not free, that never, not for one second, ever, was she free from the pressure of time, from having to remember this or that. She could never forget herself; never really let herself go into forgetfulness.

Resentment. It was poisoning her. (She looked at this emotion and thought it was absurd. Yet she felt it.) She was a prisoner. (She looked at this thought too, and it was no good telling herself it was a ridiculous one.) She must tell Matthew — but what? She was filled with emotions that were utterly ridiculous, that she despised, yet that nevertheless she was feeling so strongly she could not shake them off.

The school holidays came round, and this time they were for nearly two months, and she behaved with a conscious controlled decency that nearly drove her crazy. She would lock herself in the bathroom, and sit on the edge of the bath, breathing deep, trying to let go into some kind of calm. Or she went up into the spare room, usually empty, where no one would expect her to be. She heard the children calling "Mother, Mother," and kept silent, feeling guilty. Or she went to the very end of the garden, by herself, and looked at the slow-moving brown river; she looked at the river and closed her eyes and breathed slow and deep, taking it into her being, into her veins.

Then she returned to the family, wife and mother, smiling and responsible, feeling as if the pressure of these people — four lively children and her husband — were a painful pressure on the surface of her skin, a hand pressing on her brain. She did not once break down into irritation during these holidays, but it was like living out a prison sentence, and when the children went back to school, she sat on a white stone near the flowing river, and she thought: It is not even a year since the twins went to school, since *they were off my hands* (What on earth did I think I meant when I used that stupid phrase?), and yet I'm a different person. I'm simply not myself. I don't understand it.

Yet she had to understand it. For she knew that this structure — big white house, on which the mortgage still cost four hundred a year, a husband, so good and kind and insightful; four children, all doing so nicely; and the garden where she sat; and Mrs. Parkes, the cleaning woman — all this depended on her, and yet she could not understand why, or even what it was she contributed to it.

She said to Matthew in their bedroom: "I think there must be something wrong with me."

And he said: "Surely not, Susan? You look marvellous — you're as lovely as ever."

She looked at the handsome blond man, with his clear, intelligent, blue-eyed face, and thought: Why is it I can't tell him? Why not? And she said: "I need to be alone more than I am."

At which he swung his slow blue gaze at her, and she saw what she had been dreading: Incredulity. Disbelief. And fear. An incredulous blue stare from a stranger who was her husband, as close to her as her own breath.

He said: "But the children are at school and off your hands."

She said to herself: I've got to force myself to say: Yes, but do you realize that I never feel free? There's never a moment I can say to myself: There's nothing I have to remind myself about, nothing I have to do in half an hour, or an hour, or two hours. . . .

But she said: "I don't feel well."

He said: "Perhaps you need a holiday."

She said, appalled: "But not without you, surely?" For she could not imagine herself going off without him. Yet that was what he meant. Seeing her face, he laughed, and opened his arms, and she went into them, thinking: Yes, yes, but why can't I say it? And what is it I have to say?

She tried to tell him, about never being free. And he listened and said: "But Susan, what sort of freedom can you possibly want — short of being dead! Am I ever free? I go to the office, and I have to be there at ten — all right, half past ten, sometimes. And I have to do this or that, don't I? Then I've got to come home at a certain time — I don't mean it, you know I don't — but if I'm not going to be back home at six I telephone you. When can I ever say to myself: I have nothing to be responsible for in the next six hours?"

Susan, hearing this, was remorseful. Because it was true. The good marriage, the house, the children, depended just as much on his voluntary bondage as it did on hers. But why did he not feel bound? Why didn't he chafe and become restless? No, there was something really wrong with her and this proved it.

And that word "bondage" — why had she used it? She had never felt marriage, or the children, as bondage. Neither had he, or surely they wouldn't be together lying in each other's arms content after twelve years of marriage.

No, her state (whatever it was) was irrelevant, nothing to do with her real good life with her family. She had to accept the fact that, after all, she was an irrational person and to live with it. Some people had to live with crippled arms, or stammers, or being deaf. She would have to live knowing she was subject to a state of mind she could not own.

Nevertheless, as a result of this conversation with her husband, there was a new regime next holidays.

The spare room at the top of the house now had a cardboard sign saying: PRIVATE! DO NOT DISTURB! on it. (This sign had been drawn in coloured chalks by the children, after a discussion between the parents in which it was decided this was psychologically the right thing.) The family and Mrs. Parkes knew this was "Mother's Room" and that she was entitled to her privacy. Many serious conversations took place between Matthew and the children about not taking Mother for granted. Susan overheard the first, between father and Harry, the older boy, and was surprised at her irritation over it. Surely she could have a room somewhere in that big house and retire into it without such a fuss being made? Without it being so solemnly discussed? Why couldn't she simply have announced: "I'm going to fit out the little top room for myself, and when I'm in it I'm not to be disturbed for anything short of fire"? Just that, and finished; instead of long earnest discussions. When she heard Harry and Matthew explaining it to the twins with Mrs. Parkes coming in — "Yes, well, a family sometimes gets on top of a woman" — she had to go right away to the bottom of the garden until the devils of exasperation had finished their dance in her blood.

But now there was a room, and she could go there when she liked, she used it seldom: she felt even more caged there than in her bedroom. One day she had gone up there after a lunch for ten children she had cooked and served because Mrs. Parkes was not there, and had sat alone for a while looking into the garden. She saw the children stream out from the kitchen and stand looking up at the window where she sat behind the curtains. They were all — her children and their friends — discussing Mother's Room. A few minutes later, the chase of children in some game came pounding up the stairs, but ended as abruptly as if they had fallen over a ravine, so sudden was the silence. They had remembered she was there, and had gone silent in a great gale of "Hush! Shhhhhh! Quiet, you'll disturb her. . . ." And they went tiptoeing downstairs like criminal conspirators. When she came down to make tea for them, they all apologised. The twins put their arms around her, from front and back, making a human cage of loving limbs, and promised it would never occur again. "We forgot, Mummy, we forgot all about it!"

What it amounted to was that Mother's Room, and her need for privacy, had become a valuable lesson in respect for other people's rights. Quite soon Susan was going up to the room only because it was a lesson it was a pity to drop. Then she took sewing up there, and the children and Mrs. Parkes came in and out: it had become another family room.

She sighed, and smiled, and resigned herself — she made jokes at her own expense with Matthew over the room. That is, she did from the self she liked, she respected. But at the same time, something inside her howled with impatience, with rage. . . . And she was frightened. One day she found herself kneeling by her bed and praying: "Dear God, keep it away from me, keep him away from me." She meant the devil, for she now thought of it, not caring if she was irrational, as some sort of demon. She imagined him, or it, as a youngish man, or perhaps a middleaged man pretending to be young. Or a man young-looking from immaturity? At any rate, she saw the young-looking face which, when she drew closer, had dry lines about mouth and eyes. He was thinnish, meagre in build. And he had a reddish complexion, and ginger hair. That was he — a gingery, energetic man, and he wore a reddish hairy jacket, unpleasant to the touch.

Well, one day she saw him. She was standing at the bottom of the garden, watching the river ebb past, when she raised her eyes and saw this person, or being, sitting on the white stone bench. He was looking at her, and grinning. In his hand was a long crooked stick, which he had picked off the ground, or broken off the tree above him. He was absent-mindedly, out of an absent-minded or freakish impulse of spite, using the stick to stir around in the coils of a blindworm or a grass snake (or some kind of snake-like creature: it was whitish and unhealthy to look at, unpleasant). The snake was twisting about, flinging its coils from side to side in a kind of dance of protest against the teasing prodding stick.

Susan looked at him, thinking: Who is the stranger? What is he doing in our garden? Then she recognised the man around whom her terrors had crystallised. As she did so, he vanished. She made herself walk over to the bench. A shadow from a branch lay across thin emerald grass, moving jerkily over its roughness, and she could see why she had taken it for a snake, lashing and twisting. She went back to the house thinking: Right, then, so I've seen him with my own eyes, so I'm not crazy after all — there *is* a danger because I've seen him. He is lurking in the garden and sometimes even in the house, and he wants to *get into me and to take me over.*

She dreamed of having a room or a place, anywhere, where she could go and sit, by herself, no one knowing where she was.

Once, near Victoria, she found herself outside a news agent that had Rooms to Let advertised. She decided to rent a room, telling no one. Sometimes she could take the train into Richmond and sit alone in it for an hour or two. Yet how could she? A room would cost three or four pounds a week, and she earned no money, and how could she explain to Matthew that she needed such a sum? What for? It did not occur to her that she was taking it for granted she wasn't going to tell him about the room.

Well, it was out of the question, having a room; yet she knew she must.

One day, when a school term was well established, and none of the children had measles or other ailments, and everything seemed in order, she did the shopping early, explained to Mrs. Parkes she was meeting an old school friend, took the train to Victoria, searched until she found a small quiet hotel, and asked for a room for the day. They did not let rooms by the day, the manageress said, looking doubtful, since Susan so obviously was not the kind of woman who needed a room for unrespectable reasons. Susan made a long explanation about not being well, being unable to shop without frequent rests for lying down. At last she was allowed to rent the room provided she paid a full night's price for it. She was taken up by the manageress and a maid, both concerned over the state of her health ... which must be pretty bad if, living at Richmond (she had signed her name and address in the register), she needed a shelter at Victoria.

The room was ordinary and anonymous, and was just what Susan needed. She put a shilling in the gas fire, and sat, eyes shut, in a dingy armchair with her back to a dingy window. She was alone. She was alone. She was alone. She could feel pressures lifting off her. First the sounds of traffic came very loud; then they seemed to vanish; she might even have slept a little. A knock on the door: it was Miss Townsend, the manageress, bringing her a cup of tea with her own hands, so concerned was she over Susan's long silence and possible illness.

Miss Townsend was a lonely woman of fifty, running this hotel with all the rectitude expected of her, and she sensed in Susan the possibility of understanding companionship. She stayed to talk. Susan found herself in the middle of a fantastic story about her illness, which got more and more impossible as she tried to make it tally with the large house at Richmond, well-off husband, and four children. Suppose she said instead: Miss Townsend, I'm here in your hotel because I need to be alone for a few hours, above all *alone and with no one knowing where I am*. She said it mentally, and saw, mentally, the look that would inevitably come on Miss Townsend's elderly maiden's face. "Miss Townsend, my four children and my husband are driving me insane, do you understand that? Yes, I can see from the gleam of hysteria in your eyes that comes from loneliness controlled but only just contained that I've got everything in the world you've ever longed for. Well, Miss Townsend, I don't want any of it. You can have it, Miss Townsend. I wish I was absolutely alone in the world, like you. Miss Townsend, I'm besieged by seven devils, Miss Townsend, Miss Townsend, let me stay here in your hotel where the devils can't get me. . . . " Instead of saying all this, she described her anaemia, agreed to try Miss Townsend's remedy for it, which was raw liver, minced, between whole-meal bread, and said yes, perhaps it would be better if she stayed at home and let a friend do shopping for her. She paid her bill and left the hotel, defeated.

At home Mrs. Parkes said she didn't really like it, no, not really, when Mrs. Rawlings was away from nine in the morning until five. The teacher had telephoned from school to say Joan's teeth were paining her, and she hadn't known what to say; and what was she to make for the children's tea, Mrs. Rawlings hadn't said.

All this was nonsense, of course. Mrs. Parkes's complaint was that Susan had withdrawn herself spiritually, leaving the burden of the big house on her.

Susan looked back at her day of "freedom" which had resulted in her becoming a friend of the lonely Miss Townsend, and in Mrs. Parkes's remonstrances. Yet she remembered the short blissful hour of being alone, really alone. She was determined to arrange her life, no matter what it cost, so that she could have that solitude more often. An absolute solitude, where no one knew her or cared about her.

But how? She thought of saying to her old employer: I want you to back me up in a story with Matthew that I am doing part-time work for you. The truth is that. . . . But she would have to tell him a lie too, and which lie? She could not say: I want to sit by myself three or four times a week in a rented room. And besides, he knew Matthew, and she could not really ask him to tell lies on her behalf, apart from being bound to think it meant a lover.

Suppose she really took a part-time job, which she could get through fast and efficiently, leaving time for herself. What job? Addressing envelopes? Canvassing?

And there was Mrs. Parkes, working widow, who knew exactly what she was prepared to give to the house, who knew by instinct when her mistress withdrew in spirit from her responsibilities. Mrs. Parkes was one of the servers of this world, but she needed someone to serve. She had to have Mrs. Rawlings, her madam, at the top of the house or in the garden, so that she could come and get support from her: "Yes, the bread's not what it was when I was a girl. . . . Yes, Harry's got a wonderful appetite, I wonder where he puts it all. . . . Yes, it's lucky the twins are so much of a size, they can wear each other's shoes, that's a saving in these hard times. . . . Yes, the cherry jam from Switzerland is not a patch on the jam from Poland, and three times the price. . . . " And so on. That sort of talk Mrs. Parkes must have, every day, or she would leave, not knowing herself why she left.

Susan Rawlings, thinking these thoughts, found that she was prowling through the great thicketed garden like a wild cat: she was walking up the stairs, down the stairs, through the rooms into the garden, along the brown running river, back, up through the house, down again. . . . It was a wonder Mrs. Parkes did not think it strange. But, on the contrary, Mrs. Rawlings could do what she liked, she could stand on her head if she wanted, provided she was *there*. Susan Rawlings prowled and muttered through her house, hating Mrs. Parkes, hating poor Miss Townsend, dreaming of her hour of solitude in the dingy respectability of Miss Townsend's hotel bedroom, and she knew quite well she was mad. Yes, she was mad.

She said to Matthew that she must have a holiday. Matthew agreed with her. This was not as things had been once — how they had talked in each other's arms in the marriage bed. He had, she knew, diagnosed her finally as *unreasonable*. She had become someone outside himself that he had to manage. They were living side by side in this house like two tolerably friendly strangers.

Having told Mrs. Parkes — or rather, asked for her permission — she went off on a walking holiday in Wales. She chose the remotest place she knew of. Every morning the children telephoned her before they went off to school, to encourage and support her, just as they had over Mother's Room. Every evening she telephoned them, spoke to each child in turn, and then to Matthew. Mrs. Parkes, given permission to telephone for instructions or advice, did so every day at lunchtime. When, as happened three times, Mrs. Rawlings was out on the mountainside, Mrs. Parkes asked that she should ring back at such-and-such a time, for she would not be happy in what she was doing without Mrs. Rawlings' blessing.

Susan prowled over wild country with the telephone wire holding her to her duty like a leash. The next time she must telephone, or wait to be telephoned, nailed her to her cross. The mountains themselves seemed trammelled by her unfreedom. Everywhere on the mountains, where she met no one at all, from breakfast time to dusk, excepting sheep, or a shepherd, she came face to face with her own craziness, which might attack her in the broadest valleys, so that they seemed too small, or on a mountain top from which she could see a hundred other mountains and valleys, so that they seemed too low, too small, with the sky pressing down too close. She would stand gazing at a hillside brilliant with ferns and bracken, jewelled with running water, and see nothing but her devil, who lifted inhuman eyes at her from where he leaned negligently on a rock, switching at his ugly yellow boots with a leafy twig.

She returned to her home and family, with the Welsh emptiness at the back of her mind like a promise of freedom.

She told her husband she wanted to have an *au pair* girl.

They were in their bedroom, it was late at night, the children slept. He sat, shirted and slippered, in a chair by the window, looking out. She sat brushing her hair and watching him in the mirror. A time-hallowed scene in the connubial bedroom. He said nothing, while she heard the arguments coming into his mind, only to be rejected because every one was *reasonable*.

"It seems strange to get one now; after all, the children are in school most of the day. Surely the time for you to have help was when you were stuck with them day and night. Why don't you ask Mrs. Parkes to cook for you? She's even offered to — I can understand if you are tired of cooking for six people. But you know that an *au pair* girl means all kinds of problems; it's not like having an ordinary char in during the day. . . ."

Finally he said carefully: "Are you thinking of going back to work?"

"No," she said, "no, not really." She made herself sound vague, rather stupid. She went on brushing her black hair and peering at herself so as to be oblivious of the short uneasy glances her Matthew kept giving her. "Do you think we can't afford it?" she went on vaguely, not at all the old efficient Susan who knew exactly what they could afford.

"It's not that," he said, looking out of the window at dark trees, so as not to look at her. Meanwhile she examined a round, candid, pleasant face with clear dark brows and clear grey eyes. A sensible face. She brushed thick healthy black hair and thought: Yet that's the reflection of a madwoman. How very strange! Much more to the point if what looked back at me was the gingery green-eyed demon with his dry meagre smile. . . . Why wasn't Matthew agreeing? After all, what else could he do? She was breaking her part of the bargain and there was no way of forcing her to keep it: that her spirit, her soul, should live in this house, so that the people in it could grow like plants in water, and Mrs. Parkes remain content in their service. In return for this, he would be a good loving husband, and responsible towards the children. Well, nothing like this had been true of either of them for a long time. He did his duty, perfunctorily; she did not even pretend to do hers. And he had become like other husbands, with his real life in his work and the people he met there, and very likely a serious affair. All this was her fault.

At last he drew heavy curtains, blotting out the trees, and turned to force her attention: "Susan, are you really sure we need a girl?" But she would not meet his appeal at all. She was running the brush over her hair again and again, lifting fine black clouds in a small hiss of electricity. She was peering in and smiling as if she were amused at the clinging hissing hair that followed the brush.

"Yes, I think it would be a good idea, on the whole," she said, with the cunning of a madwoman evading the real point.

In the mirror she could see her Matthew lying on his back, his hands behind his head, staring upwards, his face sad and hard. She felt her heart (the old heart of Susan Rawlings) soften and call out to him. But she set it to be indifferent.

He said: "Susan, the children?" It was an appeal that *almost* reached her. He opened his arms, lifting them palms up, empty. She had only to run across and fling herself into them, onto his hard, warm chest, and melt into herself, into Susan. But she could not. She would not see his lifted arms. She said vaguely: "Well, surely it'll be even better for them? We'll get a French or a German girl and they'll learn the language."

In the dark she lay beside him, feeling frozen, a stranger. She felt as if Susan had been spirited away. She disliked very much this woman who lay here, cold and indifferent beside a suffering man, but she could not change her.

Next morning she set about getting a girl, and very soon came Sophie Traub from Hamburg, a girl of twenty, laughing, healthy, blue-eyed, intending to learn English. Indeed, she already spoke a good deal. In return for a room — "Mother's Room" — and her food, she undertook to do some light cooking, and to be with the children when Mrs. Rawlings asked. She was an intelligent girl and understood perfectly what was needed. Susan said: "I go off sometimes, for the morning or for the day — well, sometimes the children run home from school, or they ring up, or a teacher rings up. I should be here, really. And there's the daily woman. . . ." And Sophie laughed her deep fruity *Fräulein's* laugh, showed her fine white teeth and her dimples, and said: "You want some person to play mistress of the house sometimes, not so?"

"Yes, that is just so," said Susan, a bit dry, despite herself, thinking in secret fear how easy it was, how much nearer to the end she was than she thought. Healthy Fräulein Traub's instant understanding of their position proved this to be true.

The *au pair* girl, because of her own commonsense, or (as Susan said to herself, with her new inward shudder) because she had been *chosen* so well by Susan, was a success with everyone, the children liking her, Mrs. Parkes forgetting almost at once that she was German, and Matthew finding her "nice to have around the house." For he was now taking things as they came, from the surface of life, withdrawn both as a husband and a father from the household.

One day Susan saw how Sophie and Mrs. Parkes were talking and laughing in the kitchen, and she announced that she would be away until tea time. She knew exactly where to go and what she must look for. She took the District Line to South Kensington, changed to the Circle, got off at Paddington, and walked around looking at the smaller hotels until she was satisfied with one which had FRED'S HOTEL painted on windowpanes that needed cleaning. The facade was a faded shiny yellow, like unhealthy skin. A door at the end of a passage said she must knock; she did, and Fred appeared. He was not at all attractive, not in any way, being fattish, and run-down, and wearing a tasteless striped suit. He had small sharp eyes in a white creased face, and was quite prepared to let Mrs. Jones (she chose the farcical name deliberately, staring him out) have a room three days a week from ten until six. Provided of course that she paid in advance each time she came? Susan produced fifteen shillings (no price had been set by him) and held it out, still fixing him with a bold unblinking challenge she had not known until then she could use at will. Looking at her still, he took up a ten-shilling note from her palm between thumb and forefinger, fingered it; then shuffled up two half-crowns, held out his own palm with these bits of money displayed thereon, and let his gaze lower broodingly at them. They were standing in the passage, a red-shaded light above, bare boards beneath, and a strong smell of floor polish rising about them. He shot his gaze up at her over the still-extended palm, and smiled as if to say: What do you take me for? "I shan't," said Susan, "be using this room for the purposes of making money." He still waited. She added another five shillings, at which he nodded and said: "You pay, and I ask no questions." "Good," said Susan. He now went past her to the stairs, and there waited a moment: the light from the street door being in her eyes, she lost sight of him momentarily. Then she saw a sober-suited, white-faced, white-balding little man trotting up the stairs like a waiter, and she went after him. They proceeded in utter silence up the stairs of this house where no questions were asked — Fred's Hotel, which could afford the freedom for its visitors that poor Miss Townsend's hotel could not. The room was hideous. It had a single window, with thin green brocade curtains, a three-quarter bed that had a cheap green satin bedspread on it, a fireplace with a gas fire and a shilling meter by it, a chest of drawers, and a green wicker armchair.

"Thank you," said Susan, knowing that Fred (if this was Fred, and not George, or Herbert or Charlie) was looking at her, not so much with curiosity, an emotion he would not own to, for professional reasons, but with a philosophical sense of what was appropriate. Having taken her money and shown her up and agreed to everything, he was clearly disapproving of her for coming here. She did not belong here at all, so his look said. (But she knew, already, how very much she did belong: the room had been waiting for her to join it.) "Would you have me called at five o'clock, please?" and he nodded and went downstairs.

It was twelve in the morning. She was free. She sat in the armchair, she simply sat, she closed her eyes and sat and let herself be alone. She was alone and no one knew where she was. When a knock came on the door she was annoyed, and prepared to show it: but it was Fred himself; it was five o'clock and he was calling her as ordered. He flicked his sharp little eyes over the room — bed, first. It was undisturbed. She might never have been in the room at all. She thanked him, said she would be returning the day after tomorrow, and left. She was back home in time to cook supper, to put the children to bed, to cook a second supper for her husband and herself later. And to welcome Sophie back from the pictures where she had gone with a friend. All these things she did cheerfully, willingly. But she was thinking all the time of the hotel room; she was longing for it with her whole being.

Three times a week. She arrived promptly at ten, looked Fred in the eyes, gave him twenty shillings, followed him up the stairs, went into the room, and shut the door on him with gentle firmness. For Fred, disapproving of her being here at all, was quite ready to let friendship, or at least acquaintanceship, follow his disapproval, if only she would let him. But he was content to go off on her dismissing nod, with the twenty shillings in his hand.

She sat in the armchair and shut her eyes.

What did she *do* in the room? Why, nothing at all. From the chair, when it had rested her, she went to the window, stretching her arms, smiling, treasuring her anonymity, to look out. She was no longer Susan Rawlings, mother of four, wife of Matthew, employer of Mrs. Parkes and of Sophie Traub, with these and those relations with friends, school-teachers, tradesmen. She no longer was mistress of the big white house and garden, owning clothes suitable for this and that activity or occasion. She was Mrs. Jones, and she was alone, and she had no past and no future. Here I am, she thought, after all these years of being married and having children and playing those roles of responsibility — and I'm just the same. Yet there have been times I thought that nothing existed of me except the roles that went with being Mrs. Matthew Rawlings. Yes, here I am, and if I never saw any of my family again, here I would still be . . . how very strange that is! And she leaned on the sill, and looked into the street, loving the men and women who passed, because she did not know them. She looked at the down-trodden buildings over the street, and at the sky, wet and dingy, or sometimes blue, and she felt she had never seen buildings or sky before. And then she went back to the chair, empty, her mind a blank. Sometimes she talked aloud, saying nothing — an exclamation, meaningless, followed by a comment about the floral pattern on the thin rug, or a stain on the green satin coverlet. For the most part, she wool-gathered — what word is there for it? — brooded, wandered, simply went dark, feeling emptiness run deliciously through her veins like the movement of her blood.

This room had become more her own than the house she lived in. One morning she found Fred taking her a flight higher than usual. She stopped, refusing to go up, and demanded her usual room, Number 19. "Well, you'll have to wait half an hour, then," he said. Willingly she descended to the dark disinfectant-smelling hall, and sat waiting until the two, man and woman, came down the stairs, giving her swift indifferent glances before they hurried out into the street, separating at the door. She went up to the room, *her* room, which they had just vacated. It was no less hers, though the windows were set wide open, and a maid was straightening the bed as she came in.

After these days of solitude, it was both easy to play her part as mother and wife, and difficult — because it was so easy: she felt an imposter. She felt as if her shell moved here, with her family, answering to Mummy, Mother, Susan, Mrs. Rawlings. She was surprised no one saw through her, that she wasn't turned out of doors, as a fake. On the contrary, it seemed the children loved her more; Matthew and she "got on" pleasantly, and Mrs. Parkes was happy in her work under (for the most part, it must be confessed) Sophie Traub. At night she lay beside her husband, and they made love again, apparently just as they used to, when they were really married. But she, Susan, or the being who answered so readily and improbably to the name of Susan, was not there: she was in Fred's Hotel, in Paddington, waiting for the easing hours of solitude to begin.

Soon she made a new arrangement with Fred and with Sophie. It was for five days a week. As for the money, five pounds, she simply asked Matthew for it. She saw that she was not even frightened he might ask what for: he would give it to her, she knew that, and yet it was terrifying it could be so, for this close couple, these partners, had once known the destination of every shilling they must spend. He agreed to give her five pounds a week. She asked for just so much, not a penny more. He sounded indifferent about it. It was as if he were paying her, she thought: *paying her off* — yes, that was it. Terror came back for a moment when she understood this, but she stilled it: things had gone too far for that. Now, every week, on Sunday nights, he gave her five pounds, turning away from her before their eyes could meet on the transaction. As for Sophie Traub, she was to be somewhere in or near the house until six at night, after which she was free. She was not to cook, or to clean; she was simply to be there. So she gardened or sewed, and asked friends in, being a person who was bound to have a lot of friends. If the children were sick, she nursed them. If teachers telephoned, she answered them sensibly. For the five daytimes in the school week, she was altogether the mistress of the house.

One night in the bedroom, Matthew asked: "Susan, I don't want to interfere — don't think that, please — but are you sure you are well?"

She was brushing her hair at the mirror. She made two more strokes on either side of her head, before she replied: "Yes, dear, I am sure I am well."

He was again lying on his back, his blond head on his hands, his elbows angled up and part-concealing his face. He said: "Then Susan, I have to ask you this question, though you must understand, I'm not putting any sort of pressure on you." (Susan heard the word "pressure" with dismay, because this was inevitable; of course she could not go on like this.) "Are things going to go on like this?"

"Well," she said, going vague and bright and idiotic again, so as to escape: "Well, I don't see why not."

He was jerking his elbows up and down, in annoyance or in pain, and, looking at him, she saw he had got thin, even gaunt; and restless angry movements were not what she remembered of him. He said: "Do you want a divorce, is that it?"

At this, Susan only with the greatest difficulty stopped herself from laughing: she could hear the bright bubbling laughter she *would* have emitted, had she let herself. He could only mean one thing: she had a lover, and that was why she spent her days in London, as lost to him as if she had vanished to another continent.

Then the small panic set in again: she understood that he hoped she did have a lover, he was begging her to say so, because otherwise it would be too terrifying.

She thought this out as she brushed her hair, watching the fine black stuff fly up to make its little clouds of electricity, hiss, hiss, hiss. Behind her head, across the room, was a blue wall. She realised she was absorbed in watching the black hair making shapes against the blue. She should be answering him. "Do *you* want a divorce, Matthew?"

He said: "That surely isn't the point, is it?"

"You brought it up, I didn't," she said, brightly, suppressing meaningless tinkling laughter.

Next day she asked Fred: "Have enquiries been made for me?"

He hesitated, and she said: "I've been coming here a year now. I've made no trouble, and you've been paid every day. I have a right to be told."

"As a matter of fact, Mrs. Jones, a man did come asking."

"A man from a detective agency?"

"Well, he could have been, couldn't he?"

"I was asking you. . . . Well, what did you tell him?"

"I told him a Mrs. Jones came every weekday from ten until five or six and stayed in Number 19 by herself."

"Describing me?"

"Well, Mrs. Jones, I had no alternative. Put yourself in my place."

"By rights I should deduct what that man gave you for the information."

He raised shocked eyes: she was not the sort of person to make jokes like this! Then he chose to laugh: a pinkish wet slit appeared across his white crinkled face; his eyes positively begged her to laugh, otherwise he might lose some money. She remained grave, looking at him.

He stopped laughing and said: "You want to go up now?" — returning to the familiarity, the comradeship, of the country where no questions are asked, on which (and he knew it) she depended completely.

She went up to sit in her wicker chair. But it was not the same. Her husband had searched her out. (The world had searched her out.) The pressures were on her. She was here with his connivance. He might walk in at any moment, here, into Room 19. She imagined the report from the detective agency: "A woman calling herself Mrs. Jones, fitting the description of your wife (et cetera, et cetera, et cetera), stays alone all day in Room No. 19. She insists on this room, waits for it if it is engaged. As far as the proprietor knows, she receives no visitors there, male or female." A report something on these lines Matthew must have received.

Well, of course he was right: things couldn't go on like this. He had put an end to it all simply by sending a detective after her.

She tried to shrink herself back into the shelter of the room, a snail pecked out of its shell and trying to squirm back. But the peace of the room had gone. She was trying consciously to revive it, trying to let go into the dark creative trance (or whatever it was) that she had found there. It was no use, yet she craved for it, she was as ill as a suddenly deprived addict.

Several times she returned to the room, to look for herself there, but instead she found the unnamed spirit of restlessness, a pricking fevered hunger for movement, an irritable self-consciousness that made her brain feel as if it had coloured lights going on and off inside it. Instead of the soft dark that had been the room's air, were now waiting for her demons that made her dash blindly about, muttering words of hate; she was impelling herself from point to point like a moth dashing itself against a windowpane, sliding to the bottom, fluttering off on broken wings, then crashing into the invisible barrier again. And again and again. Soon she was exhausted, and she told Fred that for a while she would not be needing the room, she was going on a holiday. Home she went, to the big white house by the river. The middle of a weekday, and she felt guilty at returning to her own home when not expected. She stood unseen, looking in at the kitchen window. Mrs. Parkes, wearing a discarded floral overall of Susan's, was stooping to slide something into the oven. Sophie, arms folded, was leaning her back against a cupboard and laughing at some joke made by a girl not seen before by Susan — a dark foreign girl, Sophie's visitor. In an armchair Molly, one of the twins, lay curled, sucking her thumb and watching the grownups. She must have some sickness, to be kept from school. The child's listless face, the dark circles under her eyes, hurt Susan: Molly was looking at the three grownups working and talking in exactly the same way Susan looked at the four through the kitchen window: she was remote, shut off from them.

But then, just as Susan imagined herself going in, picking up the little girl, and sitting in an armchair with her, stroking her probably heated forehead, Sophie did just that: she had been standing on one leg, the other knee flexed, its foot set against the wall. Now she let her foot in its ribbon-tied red shoe slide down the wall, stood solid on two feet, clapping her hands before and behind her, and sang a couple of lines in German, so that the child lifted her heavy eyes at her and began to smile. Then she walked, or rather skipped, over to the child, swung her up, and let her fall into her lap at the same moment she sat herself. She said "Hopla! Hopla! Molly . . ." and began stroking the dark untidy young head that Molly laid on her shoulder for comfort.

Well. . . . Susan blinked the tears of farewell out of her eyes, and went quietly up through the house to her bedroom. There she sat looking at the river through the trees. She felt at peace, but in a way that was new to her. She had no desire to move, to talk, to do anything at all. The devils that had haunted the house, the garden, were not there; but she knew it was because her soul was in Room 19 in Fred's Hotel; she was not really here at all. It was a sensation that should have been frightening: to sit at her own bedroom window, listening to Sophie's rich young voice sing German nursery songs to her child, listening to Mrs. Parkes clatter and move below, and to know that all this had nothing to do with her: she was already out of it.

Later, she made herself go down and say she was home: it was unfair to be here unannounced. She took lunch with Mrs. Parkes, Sophie, Sophie's Italian friend Maria, and her daughter Molly, and felt like a visitor.

A few days later, at bedtime, Matthew said: "Here's your five pounds," and pushed them over at her. Yet he must have known she had not been leaving the house at all.

She shook her head, gave it back to him, and said, in explanation, not in accusation: "As soon as you knew where I was, there was no point."

He nodded, not looking at her. He was turned away from her: thinking, she knew, how best to handle this wife who terrified him.

He said: "I wasn't trying to. . . . It's just that I was worried."

"Yes, I know."

"I must confess that I was beginning to wonder. . . ."

"You thought I had a lover?"

"Yes, I am afraid I did."

She knew that he wished she had. She sat wondering how to say: "For a year now I've been spending all my days in a very sordid hotel room. It's the place where I'm happy. In fact, without it I don't exist." She heard herself saying this, and understood how terrified he was that she might. So instead she said: "Well, perhaps you're not far wrong."

Probably Matthew would think the hotel proprietor lied: he would want to think so.

"Well," he said, and she could hear his voice spring up, so to speak, with relief, "in that case I must confess I've got a bit of an affair on myself."

She said, detached and interested: "Really? Who is she?" and saw Matthew's startled look because of this reaction.

"It's Phil. Phil Hunt."

She had known Phil Hunt well in the old unmarried days. She was thinking: No, she won't do, she's too neurotic and difficult. She's never been happy yet. Sophie's much better. Well, Matthew will see that himself, as sensible as he is.

This line of thought went on in silence, while she said aloud: "It's no point telling you about mine, because you don't know him."

Quick, quick, invent, she thought. Remember how you invented all that nonsense for Miss Townsend.

She began slowly, careful not to contradict herself: "His name is Michael" (*Michael What?*) — "Michael Plant." (What a silly name!) "He's rather like you — in looks, I mean." And indeed, she could imagine herself being touched by no one but Matthew himself. "He's a publisher." (Really? Why?) "He's got a wife already and two children."

She brought out this fantasy, proud of herself.

Matthew said: "Are you two thinking of marrying?"

She said, before she could stop herself: "Good God, *no!*"

She realised, if Matthew wanted to marry Phil Hunt, that this was too emphatic, but apparently it was all right, for his voice sounded relieved as he said: "It is a bit impossible to imagine oneself married to anyone else, isn't it?" With which he pulled her to him, so that her head lay on his shoulder. She turned her face into the dark of his flesh, and listened to the blood pounding through her ears saying: I am alone, I am alone, I am alone.

In the morning Susan lay in bed while he dressed.

He had been thinking things out in the night, because now he said: "Susan, why don't we make a foursome?"

Of course, she said to herself, of course he would be bound to say that. If one is sensible, if one is reasonable, if one never allows oneself a base thought or an envious emotion, naturally one says: Let's make a foursome!

"Why not?" she said.

"We could all meet for lunch. I mean, it's ridiculous, you sneaking off to filthy hotels, and me staying late at the office, and all the lies everyone has to tell."

What on earth did I say his name was? — she panicked, then said: "I think it's a good idea, but Michael is away at the moment. When he comes back, though — and I'm sure you two would like each other."

"He's away, is he? So that's why you've been. . . ." Her husband put his hand to the knot of his tie in a gesture of male coquetry she would not before have associated with him; and he bent to kiss her cheek with the expression that goes with the words: Oh you naughty little puss! And she felt its answering look, naughty and coy, come onto her face.

Inside she was dissolving in horror at them both, at how far they had both sunk from honesty of emotion.

So now she was saddled with a lover, and he had a mistress! How ordinary, how reassuring, how jolly! And now they would make a foursome of it, and go about to theatres and restaurants. After all, the Rawlings could well afford that sort of thing, and presumably the publisher Michael Plant could afford to do himself and his mistress quite well. No, there was nothing to stop the four of them developing the most intricate relationship of civilised tolerance, all enveloped in a charming afterglow of autumnal passion. Perhaps they would all go off on holidays together? She had known people who did. Or perhaps Matthew would draw the line there? Why should he, though, if he was capable of talking about "foursomes" at all?

She lay in the empty bedroom, listening to the car drive off with Matthew in it, off to work. Then she heard the children clattering off to school to the accompaniment of Sophie's cheerfully ringing voice. She slid down into the hollow of the bed, for shelter against her own irrelevance. And she stretched out her hand to the hollow where her husband's body had lain, but found no comfort there: he was not her husband. She curled herself up in a small tight ball under the clothes: she could stay here all day, all week, indeed, all her life.

But in a few days she must produce Michael Plant, and — but how? She must presumably find some agreeable man prepared to impersonate a publisher called Michael Plant. And in return for which she would — what? Well, for one thing they would make love. The idea made her want to cry with sheer exhaustion. Oh no, she had finished with all that — the proof of it was that the words "make love," or even imagining it, trying hard to revive no more than the pleasures of sensuality, let alone affection, or love, made her want to run away and hide from the sheer effort of the thing. . . . Good Lord, why make love at all? Why make love with anyone? Or if you are going to make love, what does it matter who with? Why shouldn't she simply walk into the street, pick up a man and have a roaring sexual affair with him? Why not? Or even with Fred? What difference did it make?

But she had let herself in for it — an interminable stretch of time with a lover, called Michael, as part of a gallant civilised foursome. Well, she could not, and she would not.

She got up, dressed, went down to find Mrs. Parkes, and asked her for the loan of a pound, since Matthew, she said, had forgotten to leave her money. She exchanged with Mrs. Parkes variations on the theme that husbands are all the same, they don't think, and without saying a word to Sophie, whose voice could be heard upstairs from the telephone, walked to the underground, travelled to South Kensington, changed to the Inner Circle, got out at Paddington, and walked to Fred's Hotel. There she told Fred that she wasn't going on holiday after all, she needed the room. She would have to wait an hour, Fred said. She went to a busy tearoom-cum-restaurant around the corner, and sat watching the people flow in and out the door that kept swinging open and shut, watched them mingle and merge, and separate, felt her being flow into them, into their movement. When the hour was up, she left a half-crown for her pot of tea, and left the place without looking back at it, just as she had left her house, the big, beautiful white house, without another look, but silently dedicating it to Sophie. She returned to Fred, received the key of Number 19, now free, and ascended the grimy stairs slowly, letting floor after floor fall away below her, keeping her eyes lifted, so that floor after floor descended jerkily to her level of vision, and fell away out of sight.

Number 19 was the same. She saw everything with an acute, narrow, checking glance: the cheap shine of the satin spread, which had been replaced carelessly after the two bodies had finished their convulsions under it; a trace of powder on the glass that topped the chest of drawers; an intense green shade in a fold of the curtain. She stood at the window, looking down, watching people pass and pass and pass until her mind went dark from the constant movement. Then she sat in the wicker chair, letting herself go slack. But she had to be careful, because she did not want, today, to be surprised by Fred's knock at five o'clock.

The demons were not here. They had gone forever, because she was buying her freedom from them. She was slipping already into the dark fructifying dream that seemed to caress her inwardly, like the movement of her blood . . . but she had to think about Matthew first. Should she write a letter for the coroner? But what should she say? She would like to leave him with the look on his face she had seen this morning — banal, admittedly, but at least confidently healthy. Well, that was impossible, one did not look like that with a wife dead from suicide. But how to leave him believing she was dying because of a man — because of the fascinating publisher Michael Plant? Oh, how ridiculous! How absurd! How humiliating! But she decided not to trouble about it, simply not to think about the living. If he wanted to believe she had a lover, he would believe it. And he *did* want to believe it. Even when he had found out that there was no publisher in London called Michael Plant, he would think: Oh poor Susan, she was afraid to give me his real name.

And what did it matter whether he married Phil Hunt or Sophie? Though it ought to be Sophie, who was already the mother of those children . . . and what hypocrisy to sit here worrying about the children, when she was going to leave them because she had not got the energy to stay.

She had about four hours. She spent them delightfully, darkly, sweetly, letting herself slide gently, gently, to the edge of the river. Then, with hardly a break in her consciousness, she got up, pushed the thin rug against the door, made sure the windows were tight shut, put two shillings in the meter, and turned on the gas. For the first time since she had been in the room she lay on the hard bed that smelled stale, that smelled of sweat and sex.

She lay on her back on the green satin cover, but her legs were chilly. She got up, found a blanket folded in the bottom of the chest of drawers, and carefully covered her legs with it. She was quite content lying there, listening to the faint soft hiss of the gas that poured into the room, into her lungs, into her brain, as she drifted off into the dark river.

[1963]

Doris Lessing

ဢ

HOMAGE FOR ISAAC BABEL

The day I had promised to take Catherine down to visit my young friend Philip at his school in the country, we were to leave at eleven, but she arrived at nine. Her blue dress was new, and so were her fashionable shoes. Her hair had just been done. She looked more than ever like a pink and gold Renoir[1] girl who expects everything from life.

Catherine lives in a white house overlooking the sweeping brown tides of the river. She helped me clean up my flat with a devotion which said that she felt small flats were altogether more romantic than large houses. We drank tea, and talked mainly about Philip, who, being fifteen, has pure stern tastes in everything from food to music. Catherine looked at the books lying around his room, and asked if she might borrow the stories of Isaac Babel[2] to read on the train. Catherine is thirteen. I suggested she might find them difficult, but she said: "Philip reads them, doesn't he?"

During the journey I read newspapers and watched her pretty frowning face as she turned the pages of Babel, for she was determined to let nothing get between her and her ambition to be worthy of Philip.

At the school, which is charming, civilised, and expensive, the two children walked together across green fields, and I followed, seeing how the sun gilded their bright friendly heads turned towards each other as they talked. In Catherine's left hand she carried the stories of Isaac Babel.

After lunch we went to the pictures. Philip allowed it to be seen that he thought going to the pictures just for the fun of it was not worthy of intelligent people, but he made the concession, for our sakes. For his sake we chose the more serious of the two films that were showing in the little town. It was about a good priest who helped criminals in New York. His goodness, however, was not enough to prevent one of them from being sent to

---

[1] Pierre Auguste Renoir (1841–1919), French Impressionist painter.
[2] For a biographical note on Isaac Babel, see page 686.

the gas chamber; and Philip and I waited with Catherine in the dark until she had stopped crying and could face the light of a golden evening.

At the entrance of the cinema the doorman was lying in wait for anyone who had red eyes. Grasping Catherine by her suffering arm, he said bitterly: "Yes, why are you crying? He had to be punished for his crime, didn't he?" Catherine stared at him, incredulous. Philip rescued her by saying with disdain: "Some people don't know right from wrong even when it's *demonstrated* to them." The doorman turned his attention to the next redeyed emerger from the dark; and we went on together to the station, the children silent because of the cruelty of the world.

Finally Catherine said, her eyes wet again: "I think it's all absolutely beastly, and I can't bear to think about it." And Philip said: "But we've got to think about it, don't you see, because if we don't it'll just go on and *on*, don't you see?"

In the train going back to London I sat beside Catherine. She had the stories open in front of her, but she said: "Philip's awfully lucky. I wish I went to that school. Did you notice that girl who said hullo to him in the garden? They must be great friends. I wish my mother would let me have a dress like that, it's *not* fair."

"I thought it was too old for her."

"Oh, *did* you?"

Soon she bent her head again over the book, but almost at once lifted it to say: "Is he a very famous writer?"

"He's a marvellous writer, brilliant, one of the very best."

"Why?"

"Well, for one thing he's so simple. Look how few words he uses, and how strong his stories are."

"I see. Do you know him? Does he live in London?"

"Oh no, he's dead."

"Oh. Then why did you — I thought he was alive, the way you talked."

"I'm sorry, I suppose I wasn't thinking of him as dead."

"When did he die?"

"He was murdered. About twenty years ago, I suppose."

"*Twenty years.*" Her hands began the movement of pushing the book over to me, but then relaxed. "I'll be fourteen in November," she stated, sounding threatened, while her eyes challenged me.

I found it hard to express my need to apologise, but before I could speak, she said, patiently attentive again: "You said he was murdered?"

"Yes."

"I expect the person who murdered him felt sorry when he discovered he had murdered a famous writer."

"Yes, I expect so."

"Was he old when he was murdered?"

"No, quite young really."

"Well, that was bad luck, wasn't it?"

"Yes, I suppose it was bad luck."

"Which do you think is the very best story here? I mean, in your honest opinion, the very very best one."

I chose the story about killing the goose. She read it slowly, while I sat waiting, wishing to take it from her, wishing to protect this charming little person from Isaac Babel.

When she had finished she said: "Well, some of it I don't understand. He's got a funny way of looking at things. Why should a man's legs in boots look like *girls*?" She finally pushed the book over at me, and said: "I think it's all morbid."

"But you have to understand the kind of life he had. First, he was a Jew in Russia. That was bad enough. Then his experience was all revolution and civil war and. . . ."

But I could see these words bouncing off the clear glass of her fiercely denying gaze; and I said: "Look, Catherine, why don't you try again when you're older? Perhaps you'll like him better then?"

She said gratefully: "Yes, perhaps that would be best. After all, Philip is two years older than me, isn't he?"

A week later I got a letter from Catherine.

> *Thank you very much for being kind enough to take me to visit Philip at his school. It was the most lovely day in my whole life. I am extremely grateful to you for taking me. I have been thinking about the Hoodlum Priest. That was a film which demonstrated to me beyond any shadow of doubt that Capital Punishment is a Wicked Thing, and I shall never forget what I learned that afternoon, and the lessons of it will be with me all my life. I have been meditating about what you said about Isaac Babel, the famed Russian short story writer, and I now see that the conscious simplicity of his style is what makes him, beyond the shadow of a doubt, the great writer that he is, and now in my school compositions I am endeavouring to emulate him so as to learn a conscious simplicity which is the only basis for a really brilliant writing style. Love, Catherine. P.S. Has Philip said anything about my party? I wrote but he hasn't answered. Please find out if he is coming or if he just forgot to answer my letter. I hope he comes, because sometimes I feel I should die if he doesn't. P.P.S. Please don't tell him I said anything, because I should die if he knew. Love, Catherine.*

[1963]

SHIRLEY JACKSON (1919–1965) *was born in San Francisco, California, her mother a housewife and her father an employee of a lithographing company. Most of her early life was spent in Burlingame, California, which she later used as the setting for her first novel,* The Road through the Wall *(1948). As a child she was interested in writing; she won a poetry prize at age twelve, and in high school she began keeping a diary to record her writing progress. Her family moved to Rochester, New York, when she was a teenager. After high school she briefly attended the University of Rochester, but left because of an attack of the mental depression that was to recur periodically in her later years. She recovered her health by living quietly at home and writing, conscientiously turning out 1,000 words of prose a day. In 1937 she entered Syracuse University, where she published stories in the student literary magazine. There she also met Stanley Edgar Hyman, who was to become a noted literary critic. They were married in 1940, the year she received her degree from Syracuse. They had four children while both continued active literary careers, settling to raise their family in a large Victorian house in Vermont, where Hyman taught literature at Bennington College.*

Jackson's first national publication was a humorous story written after a job at a department store during the Christmas rush: "My Life with R. H. Macy," which appeared in The New Republic *in 1941. Her first child was born the next year, but she wrote every day on a disciplined schedule, selling stories to* The New Yorker, American Mercury, Harper's, *and* The Hudson Review. *Her work was included in* Best American Stories *of 1944 and 1956. In the 1940s and 1950s she also published many stories in women's magazines, especially* Good Housekeeping *and* Woman's Home Companion, *where her talent for casual, humorous storytelling and her straightforward, conversational prose style turned anecdotes about her own and her husband's eccentricities and the problems of raising four children into blithe domestic narratives. These stories were collected in her books* Life among the Savages *(1953) and* Raising Demons *(1957). She regarded these two books as her "potboilers," preferring her psychological suspense novels,* Hangsman *(1951),* The Haunting of Hill House *(1959), and* We Have Always Lived in the Castle *(1962). Jackson refused to take herself too seriously as a writer: "I can't persuade myself that writing is honest work. It is a very personal reaction, but 50 percent of my life is spent washing and dressing the children, cooking, washing dishes and clothes, and mending. After I get it all to bed, I turn around to my typewriter and try to — well, to create concrete things again. It's great fun, and I love it. But it doesn't tie any shoes."*

Best known as a story writer, Jackson published only one collection of short fiction in her lifetime, The Lottery: Or, The Adventures of James Harris *(1949). After her death in 1965 her husband issued twenty-five of her stories in two anthologies,* The Magic of Shirley Jackson *(1966) and* Come Along with Me *(1968). "The Lottery" is often anthologized, dramatized, and televised. Jackson regarded it as a tale in the sense that Hawthorne used the term — a moral allegory revealing the hidden evil of the human soul, which in her narrative is illustrated in the injustice performed in blindly observing a social ritual. She wrote later that "Explaining just what I had hoped the story to say is very difficult. I supposed, I hoped, by setting a particularly brutal ancient rite in the present and in my own village, to shock the story's readers with a graphic dramatization of the pointless violence and general inhumanity in their own lives." Most of Jackson's best fiction explored extreme psychological states, juxtaposing the familiar and the bizarre. Her work is most absorbing when the reader feels in the presence of an inexplicable, genuine sense of evil, like the exploration of the social nature of human evil in "The Lottery."*

Shirley Jackson

ຕຕ

THE LOTTERY

The morning of June 27th was clear and sunny, with the fresh warmth of a full-summer day; the flowers were blossoming profusely and the grass was richly green. The people of the village began to gather in the square, between the post office and the bank, around ten o'clock; in some towns there were so many people that the lottery took two days and had to be started on June 26th, but in this village, where there were only about three hundred people, the whole lottery took less than two hours, so it could begin at ten o'clock in the morning and still be through in time to allow the villagers to get home for noon dinner.

The children assembled first, of course. School was recently over for the summer, and the feeling of liberty sat uneasily on most of them; they tended to gather together quietly for a while before they broke into boisterous play, and their talk was still of the classroom and the teacher, of books and reprimands. Bobby Martin had already stuffed his pockets full of stones, and the other boys soon followed his example, selecting the smoothest and roundest stones; Bobby and Harry Jones and Dickie Delacroix — the villagers pronounced this name "Dellacroy" — eventually made a great pile of stones in one corner of the square and guarded it against the raids of the other boys. The girls stood aside, talking among themselves, looking over their shoulders at the boys, and the very small children rolled in the dust or clung to the hands of their older brothers or sisters.

Soon the men began to gather, surveying their own children, speaking of planting and rain, tractors and taxes. They stood together, away from the pile of stones in the corner, and their jokes were quiet and they smiled rather than laughed. The women, wearing faded house dresses and sweaters, came shortly after their menfolk. They greeted one another and exchanged bits of gossip as they went to join their husbands. Soon the women, standing by their husbands, began to call to their children, and the children came reluctantly, having to be called four or five times. Bobby Martin ducked under his mother's grasping hand and ran, laughing, back to the pile of stones. His father spoke up sharply, and Bobby came quickly and took his place between his father and his oldest brother.

The lottery was conducted — as were the square dances, the teen-age club, the Halloween program — by Mr. Summers, who had time and energy to devote to civic activities. He was a round-faced, jovial man and he ran the coal business, and people were sorry for him, because he had no children and his wife was a scold. When he arrived in the square, carrying the black wooden box, there was a murmur of conversation among the villagers, and he waved and called, "Little late today, folks." The postmaster, Mr. Graves, followed him, carrying a three-legged stool, and the stool was put in the center of the square and Mr. Summers set the black box down on it. The villagers kept their distance, leaving a space between themselves and the stool, and when Mr. Summers said, "Some of you fellows want to give me a hand?" there was a hesitation before two men, Mr. Martin and his oldest son, Baxter, came forward to hold the box steady on the stool while Mr. Summers stirred up the papers inside it.

The original paraphernalia for the lottery had been lost long ago, and the black box now resting on the stool had been put into use even before Old Man Warner, the oldest man in town, was born. Mr. Summers spoke frequently to the villagers about making a new box, but no one liked to upset even as much tradition as was represented by the black box. There was a story that the present box had been made with some pieces of the box that had preceded it, the one that had been constructed when the first people settled down to make a village here. Every year, after the lottery, Mr. Summers began talking again about a new box, but every year the subject was allowed to fade off without anything's being done. The black box grew shabbier each year; by now it was no longer completely black but splintered badly among one side to show the original wood color, and in some places faded or stained.

Mr. Martin and his oldest son, Baxter, held the black box securely on the stool until Mr. Summers had stirred the papers thoroughly with his hand. Because so much of the ritual had been forgotten or discarded, Mr.

Summers had been successful in having slips of paper substituted for the chips of wood that had been used for generations. Chips of wood, Mr. Summers had argued, had been all very well when the village was tiny, but now that the population was more than three hundred and likely to keep on growing, it was necessary to use something that would fit more easily into the black box. The night before the lottery, Mr. Summers and Mr. Graves made up the slips of paper and put them in the box, and it was then taken to the safe of Mr. Summers's coal company and locked up until Mr. Summers was ready to take it to the square next morning. The rest of the year, the box was put away, sometimes one place, sometimes another; it had spent one year in Mr. Graves's barn and another year underfoot in the post office, and sometimes it was set on a shelf in the Martin grocery and left there.

There was a great deal of fussing to be done before Mr. Summers declared the lottery open. There were the lists to make up — of heads of families, heads of households in each family, members of each household in each family. There was the proper swearing-in of Mr. Summers by the postmaster, as the official of the lottery; at one time, some people remembered, there had been a recital of some sort, performed by the official of the lottery, a perfunctory, tuneless chant that had been rattled off duly each year; some people believed that the official of the lottery used to stand just so when he said or sang it, others believed that he was supposed to walk among the people, but years and years ago this part of the ritual had been allowed to lapse. There had been, also, a ritual salute, which the official of the lottery had had to use in addressing each person who came up to draw from the box, but this also had changed with time, until now it was felt necessary only for the official to speak to each person approaching. Mr. Summers was very good at all this; in his clean white shirt and blue jeans, with one hand resting carelessly on the black box, he seemed very proper and important as he talked interminably to Mr. Graves and the Martins.

Just as Mr. Summers finally left off talking and turned to the assembled villagers, Mrs. Hutchinson came hurriedly along the path to the square, her sweater thrown over her shoulders, and slid into place in the back of the crowd. "Clean forgot what day it was," she said to Mrs. Delacroix, who stood next to her, and they both laughed softly. "Thought my old man was out back stacking wood," Mrs. Hutchinson went on, "and then I looked out the window and the kids was gone, and then I remembered it was the twenty-seventh and came a-running." She dried her hands on her apron, and Mrs. Delacroix said, "You're in time, though. They're still talking away up there."

Mrs. Hutchinson craned her neck to see through the crowd and found her husband and children standing near the front. She tapped Mrs. Delacroix on the arm as a farewell and began to make her way through the crowd. The people separated good-humoredly to let her through; two or three people said, in voices just loud enough to be heard across the crowd,

"Here comes your Missus, Hutchinson," and "Bill, she made it after all." Mrs. Hutchinson reached her husband, and Mr. Summers, who had been waiting, said cheerfully, "Thought we were going to have to get on without you, Tessie." Mrs. Hutchinson said, grinning, "Wouldn't have me leave m'dishes in the sink, now, would you, Joe?" and soft laughter ran through the crowd as the people stirred back into position after Mrs. Hutchinson's arrival.

"Well, now," Mr. Summers said soberly, "guess we better get started, get this over with, so's we can go back to work. Anybody ain't here?"

"Dunbar," several people said. "Dunbar, Dunbar."

Mr. Summers consulted his list. "Clyde Dunbar," he said. "That's right. He's broke his leg, hasn't he? Who's drawing for him?"

"Me, I guess," a woman said, and Mr. Summers turned to look at her. "Wife draws for her husband," Mr. Summers said. "Don't you have a grown boy to do it for you, Janey?" Although Mr. Summers and everyone else in the village knew the answer perfectly well, it was the business of the official of the lottery to ask such questions formally. Mr. Summers waited with an expression of polite interest while Mrs. Dunbar answered.

"Horace's not but sixteen yet," Mrs. Dunbar said regretfully. "Guess I gotta fill in for the old man this year."

"Right," Mr. Summers said. He made a note on the list he was holding. Then he asked, "Watson boy drawing this year?"

A tall boy in the crowd raised his hand. "Here," he said. "I'm drawing for m'mother and me." He blinked his eyes nervously and ducked his head as several voices in the crowd said things like "Good fellow, Jack," and "Glad to see your mother's got a man to do it."

"Well," Mr. Summers said, "guess that's everyone. Old Man Warner make it?"

"Here," a voice said, and Mr. Summers nodded.

A sudden hush fell on the crowd as Mr. Summers cleared his throat and looked at the list. "All ready?" he called. "Now, I'll read the names — heads of families first — and the men come up and take a paper out of the box. Keep the paper folded in your hand without looking at it until everyone has had a turn. Everything clear?"

The people had done it so many times that they only half listened to the directions; most of them were quiet, wetting their lips, not looking around. Then Mr. Summers raised one hand high and said, "Adams." A man disengaged himself from the crowd and came forward. "Hi, Steve," Mr. Summers said, and Mr. Adams said, "Hi, Joe." They grinned at one another humorlessly and nervously. Then Mr. Adams reached into the black box and took out a folded paper. He held it firmly by one corner as he turned and went hastily back to his place in the crowd, where he stood a little apart from his family, not looking down at his hand.

"Allen," Mr. Summers said, "Anderson. . . . Bentham."

"Seems like there's no time at all between lotteries any more," Mrs. Delacroix said to Mrs. Graves in the back row. "Seems like we got through with the last one only last week."

"Time sure goes fast," Mrs. Graves said.

"Clark. . . . Delacroix."

"There goes my old man," Mrs. Delacroix said. She held her breath while her husband went forward.

"Dunbar," Mr. Summers said, and Mrs. Dunbar went steadily to the box while one of the women said, "Go on, Janey," and another said, "There she goes."

"We're next," Mrs. Graves said. She watched while Mr. Graves came around from the side of the box, greeted Mr. Summers gravely, and selected a slip of paper from the box. By now, all through the crowd there were men holding the small folded papers in their large hands, turning them over and over nervously. Mrs. Dunbar and her two sons stood together, Mrs. Dunbar holding the slip of paper.

"Harburt. . . . Hutchinson."

"Get up there, Bill," Mrs. Hutchinson said, and the people near her laughed.

"Jones."

"They do say," Mr. Adams said to Old Man Warner, who stood next to him, "that over in the north village they're talking of giving up the lottery."

Old Man Warner snorted. "Pack of crazy fools," he said. "Listening to the young folks, nothing's good enough for *them*. Next thing you know, they'll be wanting to go back to living in caves, nobody work any more, live *that* way for a while. Used to be a saying about 'Lottery in June, corn be heavy soon.' First thing you know, we'd all be eating stewed chickweed and acorns. There's *always* been a lottery," he added petulantly. "Bad enough to see young Joe Summers up there joking with everybody."

"Some places have already quit lotteries," Mrs. Adams said.

"Nothing but trouble in *that*," Old Man Warner said stoutly. "Pack of young fools."

"Martin." And Bobby Martin watched his father go forward. "Overdyke. . . . Percy."

"I wish they'd hurry," Mrs. Dunbar said to her older son. "I wish they'd hurry."

"They're almost through," her son said.

"You get ready to run tell Dad," Mrs. Dunbar said.

Mr. Summers called his own name and then stepped forward precisely and selected a slip from the box. Then he called, "Warner."

"Seventy-seventh year I been in the lottery," Old Man Warner said as he went through the crowd. "Seventy-seventh time."

"Watson." The tall boy came awkwardly through the crowd. Someone said. "Don't be nervous, Jack," and Mr. Summers said, "Take your time, son."

"Zanini."

After that, there was a long pause, a breathless pause, until Mr. Summers, holding his slip of paper in the air, said, "All right, fellows." For a minute, no one moved, and then all the slips of paper were opened. Suddenly, all the women began to speak at once, saying, "Who is it?" "Who's got it?" "Is it the Dunbars?" "Is it the Watsons?" Then the voices began to say, "It's Hutchinson. It's Bill," "Bill Hutchinson's got it."

"Go tell your father," Mrs. Dunbar said to her older son.

People began to look around to see the Hutchinsons. Bill Hutchinson was standing quiet, staring down at the paper in his hand. Suddenly, Tessie Hutchinson shouted to Mr. Summers, "You didn't give him time enough to take any paper he wanted. I saw you. It wasn't fair!"

"Be a good sport, Tessie," Mrs. Delacroix called, and Mrs. Graves said, "All of us took the same chance."

"Shut up, Tessie," Bill Hutchinson said.

"Well, everyone," Mr. Summers said, "that was done pretty fast, and now we've got to be hurrying a little more to get done in time." He consulted his next list. "Bill," he said, "you draw for the Hutchinson family. You got an other households in the Hutchinsons?"

"There's Don and Eva," Mrs. Hutchinson yelled. "Make *them* take their chance!"

"Daughters drew with their husbands' families, Tessie," Mr. Summers said gently. "You know that as well as anyone else."

"It wasn't *fair*," Tessie said.

"I guess not, Joe," Bill Hutchinson said regretfully. "My daughter draws with her husband's family, that's only fair. And I've got no other family except the kids."

"Then, as far as drawing for families is concerned, it's you," Mr. Summers said in explanation, "and as far as drawing for households is concerned, that's you, too. Right?"

"Right," Bill Hutchinson said.

"How many kids, Bill?" Mr. Summers asked formally.

"Three," Bill Hutchinson said. "There's Bill, Jr., and Nancy, and little Dave. And Tessie and me."

"All right, then," Mr. Summers said. "Harry, you got their tickets back?"

Mr. Graves nodded and held up the slips of paper. "Put them in the box, then," Mr. Summers directed. "Take Bill's and put it in."

"I think we ought to start over," Mrs. Hutchinson said, as quietly as she could. "I tell you it wasn't *fair*. You didn't give him time enough to choose. *Every*body saw that."

Mr. Graves had selected the five slips and put them in the box, and he dropped all the papers but those onto the ground, where the breeze caught them and lifted them off.

"Listen, everybody," Mrs. Hutchinson was saying to the people around her.

"Ready, Bill?" Mr. Summers asked, and Bill Hutchinson, with one quick glance around at his wife and children, nodded.

"Remember," Mr. Summers said, "take the slips and keep them folded until each person has taken one. Harry, you help little Dave." Mr. Graves took the hand of the little boy, who came willingly with him up to the box. "Take a paper out of the box, Davy," Mr. Summers said. Davy put his hand into the box and laughed. "Take just *one* paper," Mr. Summers said. "Harry, you hold it for him." Mr. Graves took the child's hand and removed the folded paper from the tight fist and held it while little Dave stood next to him and looked up at him wonderingly.

"Nancy next," Mr. Summers said. Nancy was twelve, and her school friends breathed heavily as she went forward, switching her skirt, and took a slip daintily from the box. "Bill, Jr.," Mr. Summers said, and Billy, his face red and his feet overlarge, nearly knocked the box over as he got a paper out. "Tessie," Mr. Summers said. She hesitated for a minute, looking around defiantly, and then set her lips and went up to the box. She snatched a paper out and held it behind her.

"Bill," Mr. Summers said, and Bill Hutchinson reached into the box and felt around, bringing his hand out at last with the slip of paper in it.

The crowd was quiet. A girl whispered, "I hope it's not Nancy," and the sound of the whisper reached the edges of the crowd.

"It's not the way it used to be," Old Man Warner said clearly. "People ain't the way they used to be."

"All right," Mr. Summers said. "Open the papers. Harry, you open little Dave's."

Mr. Graves opened the slip of paper and there was a general sigh through the crowd as he held it up and everyone could see that it was blank. Nancy and Bill, Jr., opened theirs at the same time, and both beamed and laughed, turning around to the crowd and holding their slips of paper above their heads.

"Tessie," Mr. Summers said. There was a pause, and then Mr. Summers looked at Bill Hutchinson, and Bill unfolded this paper and showed it. It was blank.

"It's Tessie," Mr. Summers said, and his voiced was hushed. Show us her paper, Bill."

Bill Hutchinson went over to his wife and forced the slip of paper out of her hand. It had a black spot on it, the black spot Mr. Summers had made the night before with the heavy pencil in the coal-company office. Bill Hutchinson held it up and there was a stir in the crowd.

"All right, folks," Mr. Summers said. "Let's finish quickly."

Although the villagers had forgotten the ritual and lost the original black box, they still remembered to use stones. The pile of stones the boys had made earlier was ready; there were stones on the ground with the blowing scraps of paper that had come out of the box. Mrs. Delacroix selected a stone so large she had to pick it up with both hands and turned to Mrs. Dunbar. "Come on," she said. "Hurry up."

Mrs. Dunbar had small stones in both hands, and she said, gasping for breath, "I can't run at all. You'll have to go ahead and I'll catch up with you."

The children had stones already, and someone gave little Davy Hutchinson a few pebbles.

Tessie Hutchinson was in the center of a cleared space by now, and she held her hands out desperately as the villagers moved in on her. "It isn't fair," she said. A stone hit her on the side of the head.

Old Man Warner was saying, "Come on, come on, everyone." Steve Adams was in the front of the crowd of villagers, with Mrs. Graves beside him.

"It isn't fair, it isn't right," Mrs. Hutchinson screamed and then they were upon her.

[1948]

GRACE PALEY (b. 1922) was born in New York City. She studied at Hunter College and New York University, and in 1942 she married for the first time. She had two children from that marriage. In the 1950s she turned from writing poetry to try her hand at short fiction. Her first book of stories, The Little Disturbances of Man (1959), established her reputation as a writer with a remarkably supple gift for language. As a reviewer said, her characters were "delicately manipulated; they approach each other, perhaps touch for an instant, and then back away. [Paley] deals with elaborate surfaces, scarcely ever with developed interiors. Her characters barely jostle one another." When the book went out of print in 1965, its reputation survived, strengthened by the infrequent appearances of her new stories in magazines like The Atlantic Monthly, Esquire, The Noble Savage, Genesis West, The New American Review, Ararat, and Fiction.

During the 1960s and 1970s Paley was prominent as a nonviolent activist protesting the Vietnam War. She was secretary of the Greenwich Village Peace Center, spent time in jail for her antiwar activities, and visited Hanoi and Moscow as a member of peace delegations, defining her politics as "anarchist, if that's politics." Courageously speaking out during the World Peace Congress in Moscow in 1973, she condemned the Soviet Union for silencing political dissidents, and the World Congress dissociated itself from her statement. In recent years she has been active in the antinuclear movement. In 1974 her second volume of stories, Enormous Changes at the Last Minute, was published — a quieter, more openly personal collection of seventeen stories, many of them autobiographical, like "A Conversation with My Father."

Although Paley has published only two books of short stories, she refuses to blame her teaching jobs or her involvement in antinuclear demonstrations and other peace movement activities for her relatively low productivity as a writer. She says she writes "from distress." What Paley tries to get at in her stories is "a history of everyday life," and her subject matter and prose style are unmistakable. From the windows of her apartment on the Lower West Side of Manhattan, she is an acute and honest observer of private and public chaos — the passing show of drug addicts, thieves, rapists, muggers, and corrupt city officials. Using the form of short fiction to reflect on the disintegration of moral values in the society around her, she makes sardonic observations that are always tinged with compassion and humor; her spare dissection of her characters is never performed at the expense of sympathy for the human condition. It is likely that, as with her Jewish counterpart Isaac Babel, her production of fiction will continue to be limited; as she puts it, "There is a long time in me between knowing and telling."

Grace Paley

ღღ

A CONVERSATION WITH MY FATHER

My father is eighty-six years old and in bed. His heart, that bloody motor, is equally old and will not do certain jobs any more. It still floods his head with brainy light. But it won't let his legs carry the weight of his body around the house. Despite my metaphors, this muscle failure is not due to his old heart, he says, but to a potassium shortage. Sitting on one pillow, leaning on three, he offers last-minute advice and makes a request.

"I would like you to write a simple story just once more," he says, "the kind de Maupassant wrote, or Chekhov, the kind you used to write. Just recognizable people and then write down what happened to them next."

I say, "Yes, why not? That's possible." I want to please him, though I don't remember writing that way. I *would* like to try to tell such a story, if he means the kind that begins: "There was a woman . . . " followed by plot, the absolute line between two points which I've always despised. Not for literary reasons, but because it takes all hope away. Everyone, real or invented, deserves the open destiny of life.

Finally I thought of a story that had been happening for a couple of years right across the street. I wrote it down, then read it aloud. "Pa," I said, "how about this? Do you mean something like this?"

> Once in my time there was a woman and she had a son. They lived nicely, in a small apartment in Manhattan. This boy at about fifteen became a junkie, which is not unusual in our neighborhood. In order to maintain her close friendship with him, she became a junkie too. She said it was part of the youth culture, with which she felt very much at home. After a while, for a number of reasons, the boy gave it all up and left the city and his mother in disgust. Hopeless and alone, she grieved. We all visit her.

"O.K., Pa, that's it," I said, "an unadorned and miserable tale."

"But that's not what I mean," my father said. "You misunderstood me on purpose. You know there's a lot more to it. You know that. You left everything out. Turgenev wouldn't do that. Chekhov wouldn't do that. There are in fact Russian writers you never heard of, you don't have an inkling of, as good as anyone, who can write a plain ordinary story, who would not leave out what you have left out. I object not to facts but to people sitting in trees talking senselessly, voices from who knows where. . . . "

"Forget that one, Pa, what have I left out now? In this one?"

"Her looks, for instance."

"Oh. Quite handsome, I think. Yes."

"Her hair?"

"Dark, with heavy braids, as though she were a girl or a foreigner."

"What were her parents like, her stock? That she became such a person. It's interesting, you know."

"From out of town. Professional people. The first to be divorced in their county. How's that? Enough?" I asked.

"With you, it's all a joke," he said. "What about the boy's father? Why didn't you mention him? Who was he? Or was the boy born out of wedlock?"

"Yes," I said. "He was born out of wedlock."

"For Godsakes, doesn't anyone in your stories get married? Doesn't anyone have the time to run down to City Hall before they jump into bed?"

"No," I said. "In real life, yes. But in my stories, no."

"Why do you answer me like that?"

"Oh, Pa, this is a simple story about a smart woman who came to N.Y.C. full of interest love trust excitement very up to date, and about her son, what a hard time she had in this world. Married or not, it's of small consequence."

"It is of great consequence," he said.

"O.K.," I said.

"O.K. O.K. yourself," he said, "but listen. I believe you that she's good-looking, but I don't think she was so smart."

"That's true," I said. "Actually that's the trouble with stories. People start out fantastic. You think they're extraordinary, but it turns out as the work goes along, they're just average with a good education. Sometimes the other way around, the person's a kind of dumb innocent, but he outwits you and you can't even think of an ending good enough."

"What do you do then?" he asked. He had been a doctor for a couple of decades and then an artist for a couple of decades and he's still interested in details, craft, technique.

"Well, you just have to let the story lie around till some agreement can be reached between you and the stubborn hero."

"Aren't you talking silly now?" he asked. "Start again," he said. "It so happens I'm not going out this evening. Tell the story again. See what you can do this time."

"O.K.," I said. "But it's not a five-minute job." Second attempt:

> Once, across the street from us, there was a fine handsome woman, our neighbor. She had a son whom she loved because she'd known him since birth (in helpless chubby infancy, and in the wrestling, hugging ages,

seven to ten, as well as earlier and later). This boy, when he fell into the fist of adolescence, became a junkie. He was not a hopeless one. He was in fact hopeful, an ideologue and successful converter. With his busy brilliance, he wrote persuasive articles for his high-school newspaper. Seeking a wider audience, using important connections, he drummed into Lower Manhattan newsstand distribution a periodical called *Oh! Golden Horse!*

In order to keep him from feeling guilty (because guilt is the stony heart of nine tenths of all clinically diagnosed cancers in America today, she said), and because she had always believed in giving bad habits room at home where one could keep an eye on them, she too became a junkie. Her kitchen was famous for a while — a center for intellectual addicts who knew what they were doing. A few felt artistic like Coleridge[1] and others were scientific and revolutionary like Leary.[2] Although she was often high herself, certain good mothering reflexes remained, and she saw to it that there was lots of orange juice around and honey and milk and vitamin pills. However, she never cooked anything but chili, and that no more than once a week. She explained, when we talked to her, seriously, with neighborly concern, that it was her part in the youth culture and she would rather be with the young, it was an honor, than with her own generation.

One week, while nodding through an Antonioni film, this boy was severely jabbed by the elbow of a stern and proselytizing girl, sitting beside him. She offered immediate apricots and nuts for his sugar level, spoke to him sharply, and took him home.

She had heard of him and his work and she herself published, edited, and wrote a competitive journal called *Man Does Live by Bread Alone*. In the organic heat of her continuous presence he could not help but become interested once more in his muscles, his arteries, and nerve connections. In fact he began to love them, treasure them, praise them with funny little songs in *Man Does Live*. . . .

> the fingers of my flesh transcend
> my transcendental soul
> the tightness in my shoulders end
> my teeth have made me whole

To the mouth of his head (that glory of will and determination) he brought hard apples, nuts, wheat germ, and soybean oil. He said to his old friends, From now on, I guess I'll keep my wits about me. I'm going on the natch. He said he was about to begin a spiritual deep-breathing journey. How about you too, Mom? he asked kindly.

His conversion was so radiant, splendid, that neighborhood kids his age began to say that he had never been a real addict at all, only a journalist along for the smell of the story. The mother tried several times to give up

[1] Samuel Taylor Coleridge (1772–1834), English Romantic poet, who was an opium addict.
[2] Timothy Leary (b. 1920), sometime Harvard professor of psychology and early advocate of the use of LSD.

what had become without her son and his friends a lonely habit. This effort only brought it to supportable levels. The boy and his girl took their electronic mimeograph and moved to the bushy edge of another borough. They were very strict. They said they would not see her again until she had been off drugs for sixty days.

At home alone in the evening, weeping, the mother read and reread the seven issues of *Oh! Golden Horse!* They seemed to her as truthful as ever. We often crossed the street to visit and console. But if we mentioned any of our children who were at college or in the hospital or dropouts at home, she would cry out, My baby! My baby! and burst into terrible, face-scarring, time-consuming tears. The End.

First my father was silent, then he said, "Number One: You have a nice sense of humor. Number Two: I see you can't tell a plain story. So don't waste time." Then he said sadly, "Number Three: I suppose that means she was alone, she was left like that, his mother. Alone. Probably sick?"

I said, "Yes."

"Poor woman. Poor girl, to be born in a time of fools, to live among fools. The end. The end. You were right to put that down. The end."

I didn't want to argue, but I had to say, "Well, it is not necessarily the end, Pa."

"Yes," he said, "what a tragedy. The end of a person."

"No, Pa," I begged him. "It doesn't have to be. She's only about forty. She could be a hundred different things in this world as time goes on. A teacher or a social worker. An ex-junkie! Sometimes it's better than having a master's in education."

"Jokes," he said. "As a writer that's your main trouble. You don't want to recognize it. Tragedy! Plain tragedy! Historical tragedy! No hope. The end."

"Oh, Pa," I said. "She could change."

"In your own life, too, you have to look it in the face." He took a couple of nitroglycerin. "Turn to five," he said, pointing to the dial on the oxygen tank. He inserted the tubes into his nostrils and breathed deep. He closed his eyes and said, "No."

I had promised the family to always let him have the last word when arguing, but in this case I had a different responsibility. That woman lives across the street. She's my knowledge and my invention. I'm sorry for her. I'm not going to leave her there in that house crying. (Actually neither would Life, which unlike me has no pity.)

Therefore: She did change. Of course her son never came home again. But right now, she's the receptionist in a storefront community clinic in the East Village. Most of the customers are young people, some old friends. The head doctor has said to her, "If we only had three people in this clinic with your experiences. . . ."

"The doctor said that?" My father took the oxygen tubes out of his nostrils and said, "Jokes. Jokes again."

"No, Pa, it could really happen that way, it's a funny world nowadays."

"No," he said. "Truth first. She will slide back. A person must have character. She does not."

"No, Pa," I said. "That's it. She's got a job. Forget it. She's in that storefront working."

"How long will it be?" he asked. "Tragedy! You too. When will you look it in the face?"

[1974]

NADINE GORDIMER (*b. 1923*) *was born in the small town of Springs, near Johannesburg, South Africa. Her mother was English, and her father, a Jewish watchmaker, emigrated to Africa from the Baltic states. Gordimer attended a convent school and studied at the University of Witwatersrand, getting what she called "a scrappy and uninspiring minimal education." At an early age she turned to books to enrich her experience. "Life was prefigured in them; without knowing quite how I should bring this about, I felt that I should live it for myself someday. I began, quite unconsciously, through writing; passing from the passive act of reading to the creative act of writing brought me to life. Walls fell down; one of the biggest was the colour bar. I discovered that although the law of my country and the custom of white people kept them huddled together with their skirts drawn up away from what Africa really is, I in myself was free of their prejudices and their fears. . . . This discovery was a joyous personal one, not a political one, at first; but, of course, as time has gone by it has hardened into a sense of political opposition to abusive white power. The core of it remains a personal freedom, to me."*

Gordimer began to write stories before she attempted a novel. She acknowledges three writers as her guides: D. H. Lawrence, who influenced her way of looking at the natural world; Henry James, who gave her a consciousness of form; and Ernest Hemingway, who taught her to hear what is essential in dialogue. Her early stories appeared in The New Yorker, Harper's, *and other American magazines, and were first collected in* Face to Face *(1949) and* The Soft Voice of the Serpent *(1952). Publishing her first novel,* The Lying Days, *in 1953, she has continued since that time alternating books of long and short fiction. She rarely experiments beyond the realistic rendering of her subject in her stories, but her decision to write in the form of the short story or the novel depends on the shape the material takes as a narrative. "Whether it sprawls or neatly bites its own tail, a short story is a concept that the writer can 'hold' fully realized in his imagination at one time. A novel is, by comparison, staked out, and must be taken possession of stage by stage; it is impossible to contain, all at once, the proliferation of concepts it ultimately may use. For this reason I cannot understand how people can suppose one makes a conscious choice, after knowing what one wants to write about, between writing a novel or a short story. A short story occurs, in the imaginative sense. To write one is to express from a situation in the exterior or interior world the life-giving drop — sweat, tear, semen, saliva — that will spread an intensity on the page; burn a hole in it."*

"A Chip of Glass Ruby" is from the volume Not for Publication *(1965), and was reprinted in* Selected Stories *(1978), gathered from five*

story collections. It is a realistic narrative about a courageous Indian house-wife who involves herself in the blacks' struggle against oppression in South Africa, an example of Gordimer's use of fiction over the last thirty years to mirror the significant changes in social attitudes in her country. She feels herself "selected" by her subject, and in her latest story collection, A Sol-dier's Embrace (1980), and her latest novels, Burger's Daughter (1979) and July's People (1981), she continues to explore the ramifications of racial strife in South Africa. Gordimer's achievement as a writer is further proof of Flaubert's insight, "One is not at all free to write this or that. One does not choose one's subject. This is what the public and the critics do not un-derstand. The secret of masterpieces lies in the concordance between the subject and the temperament of the author."

Nadine Gordimer

‍ಬಌ

A Chip of Glass Ruby

When the duplicating machine was brought into the house, Bamjee said, "Isn't it enough that you've got the Indians' troubles on your back?" Mrs. Bamjee said, with a smile that showed the gap of a missing tooth but was confident all the same, "What's the difference, Yusuf? We've all got the same troubles."

"Don't tell me that. We don't have to carry passes; let the natives protest against passes on their own, there are millions of them. Let them go ahead with it."

The nine Bamjee and Pahad children were present at this exchange as they were always; in the small house that held them all there was no room for privacy for the discussion of matters they were too young to hear, and so they had never been too young to hear anything. Only their sister and half-sister, Girlie, was missing; she was the eldest, and married. The children looked expectantly, unalarmed and interested, at Bamjee, who had neither left the dining-room nor settled down again to the task of rolling his own cigarettes which had been interrupted by the arrival of the duplicator. He looked at the thing that had come hidden in a wash-basket and conveyed in a black man's taxi, and the children turned on it too, their black eyes sur-rounded by thick lashes like those still, open flowers with hairy tentacles that close on whatever touches them.

"A fine thing to have on the dining-room table," was all he said at last. They smelled the machine among them; a smell of cold black grease. He went out, heavily on tiptoe, in his troubled way.

"It's going to go nicely on the sideboard!" Mrs. Bamjee was busy making a place by removing the two pink glass vases filled with plastic carnations and the hand-painted velvet runner with the picture of the Taj Mahal.

After supper she began to run off leaflets on the machine. The family lived in the dining-room — the three other rooms in the house were full of beds — and they were all there. The older children shared a bottle of ink while they did their homework, and the two little ones pushed a couple of empty milk bottles in and out the chair legs. The three-year-old fell asleep and was carted away by one of the girls. They all drifted off to bed eventually; Bamjee himself went before the older children — he was a fruit and vegetable hawker and was up at half past four every morning to get to the market by five. "Not long now," said Mrs. Bamjee. The older children looked up and smiled at him. He turned his back on her. She still wore the traditional clothing of a Moslem woman, and her body, which was scraggy and unimportant as a dress on a peg when it was not host to a child, was wrapped in the trailing rags of a cheap sari, and her thin black plait was greased. When she was a girl, in the Transvaal town where they lived still, her mother fixed a chip of glass ruby in her nostril; but she had abandoned that adornment as too old-style, even for her, long ago.

She was up until long after midnight, turning out leaflets. She did it as if she might have been pounding chillies.

Bamjee did not have to ask what the leaflets were. He had read the papers. All the past week Africans had been destroying their passes and then presenting themselves for arrest. Their leaders were jailed on charges of incitement, campaign offices were raided — someone must be helping the few minor leaders who were left to keep the campaign going without offices or equipment. What was it the leaflets would say — "Don't go to work tomorrow," "Day of Protest," "Burn Your Pass for Freedom"? He didn't want to see.

He was used to coming home and finding his wife sitting at the dining-room table deep in discussion with strangers or people whose names were familiar by repute. Some were prominent Indians, like the lawyer, Dr. Abdul Mohammed Khan, or the big businessman, Mr. Moonsamy Patel, and he was flattered, in a suspicious way, to meet them in his house. As he came home from work next day he met Dr. Khan coming out of the house, and Dr. Khan — a highly educated man — said to him, "A wonderful woman." But Bamjee had never caught his wife out in any presumption; she behaved properly, as any Moslem woman should, and once her business with such gentlemen was over would never, for instance, have sat down to eat with them. He found her now back in the kitchen, setting about the preparation of dinner and carrying on a conversation on several different wave lengths with the children. "It's really a shame if you're tired of lentils, Jimmy, because that's what you're getting — Amina, hurry up, get a pot of water going — don't worry, I'll mend that in a minute, just bring the yellow cotton, and there's a needle in the cigarette box on the sideboard."

"Was that Dr. Khan leaving?" said Bamjee.

"Yes, there's going to be a stay-at-home on Monday. Desai's ill, and he's got to get the word around by himself. Bob Jali was up all last night printing leaflets, but he's gone to have a tooth out." She had always treated Bamjee as if it were only a mannerism that made him appear uninterested in politics, the way some woman will persist in interpreting her husband's bad temper as an endearing gruffness hiding boundless goodwill, and she talked to him of these things just as she passed on to him neighbors' or family gossip.

"What for do you want to get mixed up with these killings and stonings and I don't know what? Congress should keep out of it. Isn't it enough with the Group Areas?"

She laughed. "Now, Yusuf, you know you don't believe that. Look how you said the same thing when the Group Areas started in Natal. You said we should begin to worry when we get moved out of our own houses here in the Transvaal. And then your own mother lost her house in Noorddorp, and there you are; you saw that nobody's safe. Oh, Girlie was here this afternoon, she says Ismail's brother's engaged — that's nice, isn't it? His mother will be pleased; she was worried."

"Why was she worried?" asked Jimmy, who was fifteen, and old enough to patronize his mother.

"Well, she wanted to see him settled. There's a party on Sunday week at Ismail's place — you'd better give me your suit to give to the cleaners tomorrow, Yusuf."

One of the girls presented herself at once. "I'll have nothing to wear, Ma."

Mrs. Bamjee scratched her sallow face. "Perhaps Girlie will lend you her pink, eh? Run over to Girlie's place now and say I say will she lend it to you."

The sound of commonplaces often does service as security, and Bamjee, going to sit in the armchair with the shiny armrests that was wedged between the dining-room table and the sideboard, lapsed into an unthinking doze that, like all times of dreamlike ordinariness during those weeks, was filled with uneasy jerks and starts back into reality. The next morning, as soon as he got to market, he heard that Dr. Khan had been arrested. But that night Mrs. Bamjee sat up making a new dress for her daughter; the sight disarmed Bamjee, reassured him again, against his will, so that the resentment he had been making ready all day faded into a morose and accusing silence. Heaven knew, of course, who came and went in the house during the day. Twice in that week of riots, raids, and arrests, he found black women in the house when he came home; plain ordinary native women in doeks,[1] drinking tea. This was not a thing other Indian women would have in their homes, he thought bitterly; but then his wife was not like other people, in a way he could not put his finger on, except to say what it was not: not scandalous, not punishable, not rebellious. It was, like the attraction that had led him to marry her, Pahad's widow with five children, something he could not see clearly.

When the Special Branch knocked steadily on the door in the small hours of Thursday morning, he did not wake up, for his return to consciousness was always set in his mind to half past four, and that was more than an hour away. Mrs. Bamjee got up herself, struggled into Jimmy's raincoat, which was hanging over a chair, and went to the front door. The clock on the wall — a wedding present when she married Pahad — showed three o'clock when she snapped on the light, and she knew at once who it was on the other side of the door. Although she was not surprised, her hands shook like a very old person's as she undid the locks and the complicated catch on the wire burglar-proofing. And then she opened the door and they were there — two colored policemen in plain clothes. "Zanip Bamjee?"

"Yes."

As they talked, Bamjee woke up in the sudden terror of having overslept. Then he became conscious of men's voices. He heaved himself out of bed in the dark and went to the window, which, like the front door, was covered with a heavy mesh of thick wire against intruders from the dingy lane it looked upon. Bewildered, he appeared in the dining-room, where the policemen were searching through a soapbox of papers beside the duplicating machine. "Yusuf, it's for me," Mrs. Bamjee said.

At once, the snap of a trap, realization came. He stood there in an old shirt before the two policemen, and the woman was going off to prison because of the natives. "There you are!" he shouted, standing away from her. "That's what you've got for it. Didn't I tell you? Didn't I? That's the end of it now. That's the finish. That's what it's come to." She listened with her head at the slightest tilt to one side, as if to ward off a blow, or in compassion.

Jimmy, Pahad's son, appeared at the door with a suitcase; two or three of the girls were behind him. "Here, Ma, you take my green jersey." "I've found your clean blouse." Bamjee had to keep moving out of their way as they helped their mother to make ready. It was like the preparation for one of the family festivals his wife made such a fuss over; wherever he put himself, they bumped into him. Even the two policemen mumbled, "Excuse

---

[1] scarves tied about the head.

me," and pushed past into the rest of the house to continue their search. They took with them a tome that Nehru[2] had written in prison; it had been bought from a persevering travelling salesman and kept, for years, on the mantelpiece. "Oh, don't take that, please," Mrs. Bamjee said suddenly, clinging to the arm of the man who had picked it up.

The man held it away from her.

"What does it matter, Ma?"

It was true that no one in the house had ever read it; but she said, "It's for my children."

"Ma, leave it." Jimmy, who was squat and plump, looked like a merchant advising a client against a roll of silk she had set her heart on. She went into the bedroom and got dressed. When she came out in her old yellow sari with a brown coat over it, the faces of the children were behind her like faces on the platform at a railway station. They kissed her good-bye. The policemen did not hurry her, but she seemed to be in a hurry just the same.

"What am I going to do?" Bamjee accused them all.

The policemen looked away patiently.

"It's all right. Girlie will help. The big children can manage. And Yusuf — " The children crowded in around her; two of the younger ones had awakened and appeared, asking shrill questions.

"Come on," said the policemen.

"I want to speak to my husband." She broke away and came back to him, and the movement of her sari hid them from the rest of the room for a moment. His face hardened in suspicious anticipation against the request to give some message to the next fool who would take up her pamphleteering until he, too, was arrested. "On Sunday," she said. "Take them on Sunday." He did not know what she was talking about. "The engagement party," she whispered, low and urgent. "They shouldn't miss it. Ismail will be offended."

They listened to the car drive away. Jimmy bolted and barred the front door, and then at once opened it again; he put on the raincoat that his mother had taken off. "Going to tell Girlie," he said. The children went back to bed. Their father did not say a word to any of them; their talk, the crying of the younger ones and the argumentative voices of the older, went on in the bedrooms. He found himself alone; he felt the night all around him. And then he happened to meet the clock face and saw with a terrible sense of unfamiliarity that this was not the secret night but an hour he should have recognized: the time he always got up. He pulled on his trou-

---

[2] Jawaharlal Nehru (1889–1964), champion of Indian independence and first prime minister of India (1947–1964). Nehru spent almost nine years in prison because of his political activities against the British colonial power. The "tome" referred to is probably his *Glimpses of World History* (1938), a work of almost 1,000 pages written in the form of letters to his young daughter Indira (b. 1917), who later, as Indira Gandhi, became prime minister of India as well.

sers and his dirty white hawker's coat and wound his grey muffler up to the stubble on his chin and went to work.

The duplicating machine was gone from the sideboard. The policemen had taken it with them, along with the pamphlets and the conference reports and the stack of old newspapers that had collected on top of the wardrobe in the bedroom — not the thick dailies of the white men, but the thin, impermanent-looking papers that spoke up, sometimes interrupted by suppression or lack of money, for the rest. It was all gone. When he had married her and moved in with her and her five children, into what had been the Pahad and became the Bamjee house, he had not recognized the humble, harmless, and apparently useless routine tasks — the minutes of meetings being written up on the dining-room table at night, the government blue books that were read while the latest baby was suckled, the employment of the fingers of the older children in the fashioning of crinkle-paper Congress rosettes — as activity intended to move mountains. For years and years he had not noticed it, and now it was gone.

The house was quiet. The children kept to their lairs, crowded on the beds with the doors shut. He sat and looked at the sideboard, where the plastic carnations and the mat with the picture of the Taj Mahal were in place. For the first few weeks he never spoke of her. There was the feeling, in the house, that he had wept and raged at her, that boulders of reproach had thundered down upon her absence, and yet he had said not one word. He had not been to inquire where she was; Jimmy and Girlie had gone to Mohammed Ebrahim, the lawyer, and when he found out that their mother had been taken — when she was arrested, at least — to a prison in the next town, they had stood about outside the big prison door for hours while they waited to be told where she had been moved from there. At last they had discovered that she was fifty miles away, in Pretoria. Jimmy asked Bamjee for five shillings to help Girlie pay the train fare to Pretoria, once she had been interviewed by the police and had been given a permit to visit her mother; he put three two-shilling pieces on the table for Jimmy to pick up, and the boy, looking at him keenly, did not know whether the extra shilling meant anything, or whether it was merely that Bamjee had no change.

It was only when relations and neighbors came to the house that Bamjee would suddenly begin to talk. He had never been so expansive in his life as he was in the company of these visitors, many of them come on a polite call rather in the nature of a visit of condolence. "Ah, yes, yes, you can see how I am — you see what has been done to me. Nine children, and I am on the cart all day, I get home at seven or eight. What are you to do? What can people like us do?"

"Poor Mrs. Bamjee. Such a kind lady."

"Well, you see for yourself. They walk in here in the middle of the night and leave a houseful of children. I'm out on the cart all day. I've got a living to earn." Standing about in his shirt sleeves, he became quite animated; he would call for the girls to bring fruit drinks for the visitors. When they were gone, it was as if he, who was orthodox if not devout and never drank liquor, had been drunk and abruptly sobered up; he looked dazed and could not have gone over in his mind what he had been saying. And as he cooled, the lump of resentment and wrongedness stopped his throat again.

Bamjee found one of the little boys the center of a self-important group of championing brothers and sisters in the dining-room one evening. "They've been cruel to Ahmed."

"What has he done?" said the father.

"Nothing! Nothing!" The little girl stood twisting her handkerchief excitedly.

An older one, thin as her mother, took over, silencing the others with a gesture of her skinny hand. "They did it at school today. They made an example of him."

"What is an example?" said Bamjee impatiently.

"The teacher made him come up and stand in front of the whole class, and he told them, 'You see this boy? His mother's in jail because she likes the natives so much. She wants the Indians to be the same as natives.'"

"It's terrible," he said. His hands fell to his sides. "Did she ever think of this?"

"That's why Ma's *there*," said Jimmy, putting aside his comic and emptying out his schoolbooks upon the table. "That's all the kids need to know. Ma's there because things like this happen. Petersen's a colored teacher, and it's his black blood that's brought him trouble all his life, I suppose. He hates anyone who says everybody's the same, because that takes away from him his bit of whiteness that's all he's got. What d'you expect? It's nothing to make too much fuss about."

"Of course, you are fifteen and you know everything," Bamjee mumbled at him.

"I don't say that. But I know Ma, anyway." The boy laughed.

There was a hunger strike among the political prisoners, and Bamjee could not bring himself to ask Girlie if her mother was starving herself too. He would not ask; and yet he saw in the young woman's face the gradual weakening of her mother. When the strike had gone on for nearly a week one of the elder children burst into tears at the table and could not eat. Bamjee pushed his own plate away in rage.

Sometimes he spoke out loud to himself while he was driving the vegetable lorry. "What for?" Again and again. "What for?" She was not a modern woman who cut her hair and wore short skirts. He had married a good plain Moslem woman who bore children and stamped her own chillies. He had a sudden vision of her at the duplicating machine, that night just before she was taken away, and he felt himself maddened, baffled, and hopeless. He had become the ghost of a victim, hanging about the scene of a crime whose motive he could not understand and had not had time to learn.

The hunger strike at the prison went into the second week. Alone in the rattling cab of his lorry, he said things that he heard as if spoken by someone else, and his heart burned in fierce agreement with them. "For a crowd of natives who'll smash our shops and kill us in our houses when their time comes." "She will starve herself to death there." "She will die there." "Devils who will burn and kill us." He fell into bed each night like a stone, and dragged himself up in the mornings as a beast of burden is beaten to its feet.

One of these mornings, Girlie appeared very early, while he was wolfing bread and strong tea — alternate sensations of dry solidity and stinging heat — at the kitchen table. Her real name was Fatima, of course, but she had adopted the silly modern name along with the clothes of the young factory girls among whom she worked. She was expecting her first baby in a week or two, and her small face, her cut and curled hair, and the sooty arches drawn over her eyebrows did not seem to belong to her thrust-out body under a clean smock. She wore mauve lipstick and was smiling her cocky little white girl's smile, foolish and bold, not like an Indian girl's at all.

"What's the matter?" he said.

She smiled again. "Don't you know? I told Bobby he must get me up in time this morning. I wanted to be sure I wouldn't miss you today."

"I don't know what you're talking about."

She came over and put her arm up around his unwilling neck and kissed the grey bristles at the side of his mouth. "Many happy returns! Don't you know it's your birthday?"

"No," he said. "I didn't know, didn't think — " He broke the pause by swiftly picking up the bread and giving his attention desperately to eating and drinking. His mouth was busy, but his eyes looked at her, intensely black. She said nothing, but stood there with him. She would not speak, and at last he said, swallowing a piece of bread that tore at his throat as it went down, "I don't remember these things."

The girl nodded, the Woolworth baubles in her ears swinging. "That's the first thing she told me when I saw her yesterday — don't forget it's Bajie's birthday tomorrow."

He shrugged over it. "It means a lot to children. But that's how she is. Whether it's one of the old cousins or the neighbor's grandmother, she always knows when the birthday is. What importance is my birthday, while she's sitting there in a prison? I don't understand how she can do the things she does when her mind is always full of woman's nonsense at the same time — that's what I don't understand with her."

"Oh, but don't you see?" the girl said. "It's because she doesn't want anybody to be left out. It's because she always remembers; remembers everything — people without somewhere to live, hungry kids, boys who can't get educated — remembers all the time. That's how Ma is."

"Nobody else is like that." It was half a complaint.

"No, nobody else," said his stepdaughter.

She sat herself down at the table, resting her belly. He put his head in his hands. "I'm getting old" — but he was overcome by something much more curious, by an answer. He knew why he had desired her, the ugly widow with five children; he knew what way it was in which she was not like the others; it was there, like the fact of the belly that lay between him and her daughter.

[1965]

FLANNERY O'CONNOR (1925–1964) *was born in Savannah,
Georgia, the only child of Roman Catholic parents. When she was thirteen
her father was found to have disseminated lupus, an incurable disease in
which antibodies in the immune system attack the body's own substances.
During her father's medical treatment the family moved to her mother's
family home in Milledgeville, Georgia, where her ancestors had lived since
before the Civil War. There O'Connor attended high school and began to
write. After her father's death in 1941, she finished high school and studied
social science and English at the Georgia State College for Women in Milledgeville, where she also published stories and edited the literary magazine.
On the strength of these stories, she was awarded a fellowship at the
Writer's Workshop at the University of Iowa. In 1946 she sold her first
story to* Accent *magazine and earned her M.F.A. degree at Iowa. Two years
later she moved to New York City and published chapters of a novel in
progress,* Wise Blood, *in magazines. Late in 1950 she became ill with what
was diagnosed as lupus, and she returned to Milledgeville to start a series of
treatments which temporarily arrested the progress of the disease. Living
with her mother on the family's 500-acre dairy farm, she began to work
again, writing from nine to twelve in the mornings and spending the rest of
the day resting, reading, writing letters, and raising her peacocks, whose
proud beauty enthralled her and whose regular cycles of growing, shedding,
and regrowing their wondrous plumage served as a symbol to her of Christ's
divinity and the resurrection.*

O'Connor's first book, Wise Blood, *a complex comic novel attacking
the contemporary secularization of religion, was published in 1952. It was
followed in 1955 by her first collection of stories,* A Good Man Is Hard to
Find. *O'Connor was able to see a second novel,* The Violent Bear It Away,
*through to publication in 1960, but she died of lupus in 1964, having com-
pleted enough stories for a second collection,* Everything That Rises Must
Converge *(1965). Her total output of just thirty-one stories, collected in her*
Complete Stories, *won the National Book Award for fiction in 1972.*

*Despite her illness, O'Connor was never a recluse; she accepted as
many lecture invitations as her health would permit. A volume of her lectures and occasional pieces was published in 1969 as* Mystery and Manners.
*It is a valuable companion to her stories and novels, because she often re-
flected on her writing and interpreted her fiction. As a devout Roman
Catholic, O'Connor was uncompromising in her religious views:* "For I am
no disbeliever in spiritual purpose and no vague believer. This means that
for me the meaning of life is centered in our Redemption by Christ and
what I see in the world I see in relation to that." *Her own favorite story was*
"The Artificial Nigger," *where she moves Mr. Head into a frightening con-*

frontation with his own nature during his journey to Atlanta with his grandson so that the old man can receive a glimpse of the need and the chance for redemption. Her fiction has been criticized for relying on violence for its emotional effect, but O'Connor defended her use of violence in stories like "A Good Man Is Hard to Find," saying that to a serious writer, "violence is never an end in itself." As Joyce Carol Oates recognized in her essay "The Visionary Art of Flannery O'Connor," O'Connor is one of the greatest religious writers of modern times, unique "in her celebration of the necessity of succumbing to the divine through violence that is immediate and irreparable. There is no mysticism in her work that is only spiritual; it is physical as well." O'Connor's stories are not meant to be realistic or naturalistic. She wrote them as parables, as she explained in her lecture on "A Good Man Is Hard to Find," which is reprinted on pages 1196–1199. It is her artistic arrangement of the fates of her grotesque characters that leads to the construction of a vision that is harshly and defiantly spiritual.

Flannery O'Connor

ᘏᘏ

A Good Man Is Hard to Find

> *The dragon is by the side of the road, watching those who pass. Beware lest he devour you. We go to the Father of Souls, but it is necessary to pass by the dragon.*
>
> — St. Cyril of Jerusalem

The grandmother didn't want to go to Florida. She wanted to visit some of her connections in east Tennessee and she was seizing at every chance to change Bailey's mind. Bailey was the son she lived with, her only boy. He was sitting on the edge of his chair at the table, bent over the orange sports section of the *Journal*. "Now look here, Bailey," she said, "see here, read this," and she stood with one hand on her thin hip and the other rattling the newspaper at his bald head. "Here this fellow that calls himself The Misfit is aloose from the Federal Pen and headed toward Florida and you read here what it says he did to these people. Just you read it. I wouldn't take my children in any direction with a criminal like that aloose in it. I couldn't answer to my conscience if I did."

Bailey didn't look up from his reading so she wheeled around then and faced the children's mother, a young woman in slacks, whose face was as broad and innocent as a cabbage and was tied around with a green head-kerchief that had two points on the top like a rabbit's ears. She was sitting on the sofa, feeding the baby his apricots out of a jar. "The children have been to Florida before," the old lady said. "You all ought to take them somewhere else for a change so they would see different parts of the world and be broad. They never have been to east Tennessee."

The children's mother didn't seem to hear her but the eight-year-old boy, John Wesley, a stocky child with glasses, said, "If you don't want to go to Florida, why dontcha stay at home?" He and the little girl, June Star, were reading the funny papers on the floor.

"She wouldn't stay at home to be queen for a day," June Star said without raising her yellow head.

"Yes and what would you do if this fellow, The Misfit, caught you?" the grandmother asked.

"I'd smack his face," John Wesley said.

"She wouldn't stay at home for a million bucks," June Star said. "Afraid she'd miss something. She has to go everywhere we go."

"All right, Miss," the grandmother said. "Just remember that the next time you want me to curl your hair."

June Star said her hair was naturally curly.

The next morning the grandmother was the first one in the car, ready to go. She had her big black valise that looked like the head of a hippopotamus in one corner, and underneath it she was hiding a basket with Pitty Sing, the cat, in it. She didn't intend for the cat to be left alone in the house for three days because he would miss her too much and she was afraid he might brush against one of the gas burners and accidentally asphyxiate himself. Her son, Bailey, didn't like to arrive at a motel with a cat.

She sat in the middle of the back seat with John Wesley and June Star on either side of her. Bailey and the children's mother and the baby sat in front and they left Atlanta at eight forty-five with the mileage on the car at 55890. The grandmother wrote this down because she thought it would be interesting to say how many miles they had been when they got back. It took them twenty minutes to reach the outskirts of the city.

The old lady settled herself comfortably, removing her white cotton gloves and putting them up with her purse on the shelf in front of the back window. The children's mother still had on slacks and still had her head tied up in a green kerchief, but the grandmother had on a navy blue straw sailor hat with a bunch of white violets on the brim and a navy blue dress with a small white dot in the print. Her collars and cuffs were white organdy trimmed with lace and at her neckline she had pinned a purple spray of cloth violets containing a sachet. In case of an accident, anyone seeing her dead on the highway would know at once that she was a lady.

She said she thought it was going to be a good day for driving, neither too hot nor too cold, and she cautioned Bailey that the speed limit was fifty-five miles an hour and that the patrolmen hid themselves behind billboards and small clumps of trees and sped out after you before you had a chance to slow down. She pointed out interesting details of the scenery: Stone Mountain; the blue granite that in some places came up to both sides of the highway; the brilliant red clay banks slightly streaked with purple; and the various crops that made rows of green lace-work on the ground. The trees were full of silver-white sunlight and the meanest of them sparkled. The children were reading comic magazines and their mother had gone back to sleep.

"Let's go through Georgia fast so we won't have to look at it much," John Wesley said.

"If I were a little boy," said the grandmother, "I wouldn't talk about my native state that way. Tennessee has the mountains and Georgia has the hills."

"Tennessee is just a hillbilly dumping ground," John Wesley said, "and Georgia is a lousy state too."

"You said it," June Star said.

"In my time," said the grandmother, folding her thin veined fingers, "children were more respectful of their native states and their parents and everything else. People did right then. Oh look at the cute little picka-ninny!" she said and pointed to a Negro child standing in the door of a shack. "Wouldn't that make a picture, now?" she asked and they all turned and looked at the little Negro out of the back window. He waved.

"He didn't have any britches on," June Star said.

"He probably didn't have any," the grandmother explained. "Little niggers in the country don't have things like we do. If I could paint, I'd paint that picture," she said.

The children exchanged comic books.

The grandmother offered to hold the baby and the children's mother passed him over the front seat to her. She set him on her knee and bounced him and told him about the things they were passing. She rolled her eyes and screwed up her mouth and stuck her leathery thin face into his smooth bland one. Occasionally he gave her a faraway smile. They passed a large cotton field with five or six graves fenced in the middle of it, like a small island. "Look at the graveyard!" the grandmother said, pointing it out. "That was the old family burying ground. That belonged to the planta-tion."

"Where's the plantation?" John Wesley asked.

"Gone with the Wind," said the grandmother. "Ha. Ha."

When the children finished all the comic books they had brought, they opened the lunch and ate it. The grandmother ate a peanut butter sandwich and an olive and would not let the children throw the box and the paper napkins out the window. When there was nothing else to do they played a game by choosing a cloud and making the other two guess what shape it suggested. John Wesley took one the shape of a cow and June Star guessed a cow and John Wesley said, no, an automobile, and June Star said he didn't play fair, and they began to slap each other over the grandmother.

The grandmother said she would tell them a story if they would keep quiet. When she told a story, she rolled her eyes and waved her head and was very dramatic. She said once when she was a maiden lady she had been courted by a Mr. Edgar Atkins Teagarden from Jasper, Georgia. She said he was a very good-looking man and a gentleman and that he brought her a watermelon every Saturday afternoon with his initials cut in it, E. A. T. Well, one Saturday, she said, Mr. Teagarden brought the watermelon and there was nobody at home and he left it on the front porch and returned in his buggy to Jasper, but she never got the watermelon, she said, because a nigger boy ate it when he saw the initials, E. A. T.! This story tickled John Wesley's funny bone and he giggled and giggled but June Star didn't think it was any good. She said she wouldn't marry a man that just brought her a watermelon on Saturday. The grandmother said she would have done well to marry Mr. Teagarden because he was a gentleman and had bought Coca-Cola stock when it first came out and that he had died only a few years ago, a very wealthy man.

They stopped at The Tower for barbecued sandwiches. The Tower was a part stucco and part wood filling station and dance hall set in a clearing outside of Timothy. A fat man named Red Sammy Butts ran it and there were signs stuck here and there on the building and for miles up and down the highway saying, TRY RED SAMMY'S FAMOUS BARBECUE. NONE LIKE FAMOUS RED SAMMY'S! RED SAM! THE FAT BOY WITH THE HAPPY LAUGH. A VETERAN! RED SAMMY'S YOUR MAN!

Red Sammy was lying on the bare ground outside The Tower with his head under a truck while a gray monkey about a foot high, chained to a small chinaberry tree, chattered nearby. The monkey sprang back into the tree and got on the highest limb as soon as he saw the children jump out of the car and run toward him.

Inside, The Tower was a long dark room with a counter at one end and tables at the other and dancing space in the middle. They all sat down at a board table next to the nickelodeon and Red Sam's wife, a tall burnt-brown woman with hair and eyes lighter than her skin, came and took their order. The children's mother put a dime in the machine and played "The Tennessee Waltz," and the grandmother said that tune always made her want to dance. She asked Bailey if he would like to dance but he only glared at her. He didn't have a naturally sunny disposition like she did and trips made him nervous. The grandmother's brown eyes were very bright. She swayed her head from side to side and pretended she was dancing in her chair. June Star said play something she could tap to so the children's mother put in another dime and played a fast number and June Star stepped out onto the dance floor and did her tap routine.

"Ain't she cute?" Red Sam's wife said, leaning over the counter. "Would you like to come be my little girl?"

"No I certainly wouldn't," June Star said. "I wouldn't live in a broken-down place like this for a million bucks!" and she ran back to the table.

"Ain't she cute?" the woman repeated, stretching her mouth politely.

"Aren't you ashamed?" hissed the grandmother.

Red Sam came in and told his wife to quit lounging on the counter and hurry up with these people's order. His khaki trousers reached just to his hip bones and his stomach hung over them like a sack of meal swaying under his shirt. He came over and sat down at a table nearby and let out a combination sigh and yodel. "You can't win," he said. "You can't win," and he wiped his sweating red face off with a gray handkerchief. "These days you don't know who to trust," he said. "Ain't that the truth?"

"People are certainly not nice like they used to be," said the grandmother.

"Two fellers come in here last week," Red Sammy said, "driving a Chrysler. It was a old beat-up car but it was a good one and these boys looked all right to me. Said they worked at the mill and you know I let them fellers charge the gas they bought? Now why did I do that?"

"Because you're a good man!" the grandmother said at once.

"Yes'm, I suppose so," Red Sam said as if he were struck with this answer.

His wife brought the orders, carrying the five plates all at once without a tray, two in each hand and one balanced on her arm. "It isn't a soul in this green world of God's that you can trust," she said. "And I don't count nobody out of that, not nobody," she repeated, looking at Red Sammy.

"Did you read about that criminal, The Misfit, that's escaped?" asked the grandmother.

"I wouldn't be a bit surprised if he didn't attact this place right here," said the woman. "If he hears about it being here, I wouldn't be none surprised to see him. If he hears it's two cent in the cash register, I wouldn't be a tall surprised if he. . . ."

"That'll do," Red Sam said. "Go bring these people their Co'-Colas," and the woman went off to get the rest of the order.

"A good man is hard to find," Red Sammy said. "Everything is getting terrible. I remember the day you could go off and leave your screen door unlatched. Not no more."

He and the grandmother discussed better times. The old lady said that in her opinion Europe was entirely to blame for the way things were now. She said the way Europe acted you would think we were made of money and Red Sam said it was no use talking about it, she was exactly right. The children ran outside into the white sunlight and looked at the monkey in the lacy chinaberry tree. He was busy catching fleas on himself and biting each one carefully between his teeth as if it were a delicacy.

They drove off again into the hot afternoon. The grandmother took cat naps and woke up every few minutes with her own snoring. Outside of Toombsboro she woke up and recalled an old plantation that she had visited in this neighborhood once when she was a young lady. She said the house had six white columns across the front and that there was an avenue of oaks leading up to it and two little wooden trellis arbors on either side in front where you sat down with your suitor after a stroll in the garden. She recalled exactly which road to turn off to get to it. She knew that Bailey would not be willing to lose any time looking at an old house, but the more she talked about it, the more she wanted to see it once again and find out if the little twin arbors were still standing. "There was a secret panel in this house," she said craftily, not telling the truth but wishing that she were, "and the story went that all the family silver was hidden in it when Sherman came through but it was never found. . . ."

"Hey!" John Wesley said. "Let's go see it! We'll find it! We'll poke all the woodwork and find it! Who lives there? Where do you turn off at? Hey Pop, can't we turn off there?"

"We never have seen a house with a secret panel!" June Star shrieked. "Let's go to the house with the secret panel! Hey Pop, can't we go see the house with the secret panel!"

"It's not far from here, I know," the grandmother said. "It won't take over twenty minutes."

Bailey was looking straight ahead. His jaw was as rigid as a horseshoe. "No," he said.

The children began to yell and scream that they wanted to see the house with the secret panel. John Wesley kicked the back of the front seat and June Star hung over her mother's shoulder and whined desperately into her ear that they never had any fun even on their vacation, that they could never do what THEY wanted to do. The baby began to scream and John Wesley kicked the back of the seat so hard that his father could feel the blows in his kidney.

"All right!" he shouted and drew the car to a stop at the side of the road. "Will you all shut up? Will you all just shut up for one second? If you don't shut up, we won't go anywhere."

"It would be very educational for them," the grandmother murmured.

"All right," Bailey said, "but get this: this is the only time we're going to stop for anything like this. This is the one and only time."

"The dirt road that you have to turn down is about a mile back," the grandmother directed. "I marked it when we passed."

"A dirt road," Bailey groaned.

After they had turned around and were headed toward the dirt road, the grandmother recalled other points about the house, the beautiful glass over the front doorway and the candle-lamp in the hall. John Wesley said that the secret panel was probably in the fireplace.

"You can't go inside this house," Bailey said. "You don't know who lives there."

"While you all talk to the people in front, I'll run around behind and get in a window," John Wesley suggested.

"We'll all stay in the car," his mother said.

They turned onto the dirt road and the car raced roughly along in a swirl of pink dust. The grandmother recalled the times when there were no paved roads and thirty miles was a day's journey. The dirt road was hilly and there were sudden washes in it and sharp curves on dangerous embankments. All at once they would be on a hill, looking down over the blue tops of trees for miles around, then the next minute, they would be in a red depression with the dust-coated trees looking down on them.

"This place had better turn up in a minute," Bailey said, "or I'm going to turn around."

The road looked as if no one had traveled on it for months.

"It's not much farther," the grandmother said and just as she said it, a horrible thought came to her. The thought was so embarrassing that she turned red in the face and her eyes dilated and her feet jumped up, upsetting her valise in the corner. The instant the valise moved, the newspaper top she had over the basket under it rose with a snarl and Pitty Sing, the cat, sprang onto Bailey's shoulder.

The children were thrown to the floor and their mother, clutching the baby, was thrown out the door onto the ground; the old lady was thrown into the front seat. The car turned over once and landed right-side-up in a gulch off the side of the road. Bailey remained in the driver's seat with the cat — gray-striped with a broad white face and an orange nose — clinging to his neck like a caterpillar.

As soon as the children saw they could move their arms and legs, they scrambled out of the car, shouting, "We've had an ACCIDENT!" The grandmother was curled up under the dashboard, hoping she was injured so that Bailey's wrath would not come down on her all at once. The horrible thought she had before the accident was that the house she had remembered so vividly was not in Georgia but in Tennessee.

Bailey removed the cat from his neck with both hands and flung it out the window against the side of a pine tree. Then he got out of the car and started looking for the children's mother. She was sitting against the side of the red gutted ditch, holding the screaming baby, but she only had a cut down her face and a broken shoulder. "We've had an ACCIDENT!" the children screamed in a frenzy of delight.

"But nobody's killed," June Star said with disappointment as the grandmother limped out of the car, her hat still pinned to her head but the broken front brim standing up at a jaunty angle and the violet spray hanging off the side. They all sat down in the ditch, except the children, to recover from the shock. They were all shaking.

"Maybe a car will come along," said the children's mother hoarsely.

"I believe I have injured an organ," said the grandmother, pressing her side, but no one answered her. Bailey's teeth were clattering. He had on a

yellow sport shirt with bright blue parrots designed in it and his face was as
yellow as the shirt. The grandmother decided that she would not mention
that the house was in Tennessee.

The road was about ten feet above and they could see only the tops of
the trees on the other side of it. Behind the ditch they were sitting in there
were more woods, tall and dark and deep. In a few minutes they saw a car
some distance away on top of a hill, coming slowly as if the occupants were
watching them. The grandmother stood up and waved both arms dramati-
cally to attract their attention. The car continued to come on slowly, disappeared around a bend and appeared again, moving even slower, on top of
the hill they had gone over. It was a big black battered hearse-like automobile. There were three men in it.

It came to a stop just over them and for some minutes, the driver
looked down with a steady expressionless gaze to where they were sitting,
and didn't speak. Then he turned his head and muttered something to the
other two and they got out. One was a fat boy in black trousers and a red
sweat shirt with a silver stallion embossed on the front of it. He moved
around on the right side of them and stood staring, his mouth partly open
in a kind of loose grin. The other had on khaki pants and a blue striped coat
and a gray hat pulled down very low, hiding most of his face. He came
around slowly on the left side. Neither spoke.

The driver got out of the car and stood by the side of it, looking down
at them. He was an older man than the other two. His hair was just beginning to gray and he wore silver-rimmed spectacles that gave him a scholarly
look. He had a long creased face and didn't have on any shirt or undershirt.
He had on blue jeans that were too tight for him and was holding a black
hat and a gun. The two boys also had guns.

"We've had an ACCIDENT!" the children screamed.

The grandmother had the peculiar feeling that the bespectacled man
was someone she knew. His face was as familiar to her as if she had known
him all her life but she could not recall who he was. He moved away from
the car and began to come down the embankment, placing his feet carefully
so that he wouldn't slip. He had on tan and white shoes and no socks, and
his ankles were red and thin. "Good afternoon," he said. "I see you all had
you a little spill."

"We turned over twice!" said the grandmother.

"Oncet," he corrected. "We seen it happen. Try their car and see will
it run, Hiram," he said quietly to the boy with the gray hat.

"What you got that gun for?" John Wesley asked. "Whatcha gonna
do with that gun?"

"Lady," the man said to the children's mother, "would you mind calling them children to sit down by you? Children make me nervous. I want
all you all to sit down right together there where you're at."

"What are you telling US what to do for?" June Star asked.

Behind them the line of woods gaped like a dark open mouth. "Come here," said their mother.

"Look here now," Bailey said suddenly, "we're in a predicament! We're in. . . ."

The grandmother shrieked. She scrambled to her feet and stood staring. "You're The Misfit!" she said. "I recognized you at once!"

"Yes'm," the man said, smiling slightly as if he were pleased in spite of himself to be known, "but it would have been better for all of you, lady, if you hadn't of reckernized me."

Bailey turned his head sharply and said something to his mother that shocked even the children. The old lady began to cry and The Misfit reddened.

"Lady," he said, "don't you get upset. Sometimes a man says things he don't mean. I don't reckon he meant to talk to you thataway."

"You wouldn't shoot a lady, would you?" the grandmother said and removed a clean handkerchief from her cuff and began to slap at her eyes with it.

The Misfit pointed the toe of his shoe into the ground and made a little hole and then covered it up again. "I would hate to have to," he said.

"Listen," the grandmother almost screamed, "I know you're a good man. You don't look a bit like you have common blood. I know you must come from nice people!"

"Yes mam," he said, "finest people in the world." When he smiled he showed a row of strong white teeth. "God never made a finer woman than my mother and my daddy's heart was pure gold," he said. The boy with the red sweat shirt had come around behind them and was standing with his gun at his hip. The Misfit squatted down on the ground. "Watch them children, Bobby Lee," he said. "You know they make me nervous." He looked at the six of them huddled together in front of him and he seemed to be embarrassed as if he couldn't think of anything to say. "Ain't a cloud in the sky," he remarked, looking up at it. "Don't see no sun but don't see no cloud neither."

"Yes, it's a beautiful day," said the grandmother. "Listen," she said, "you shouldn't call yourself The Misfit because I know you're a good man at heart. I can just look at you and tell."

"Hush!" Bailey yelled. "Hush! Everybody shut up and let me handle this!" He was squatting in the position of a runner about to sprint forward but he didn't move.

"I pre-chate that, lady," The Misfit said and drew a little circle in the ground with the butt of his gun.

"It'll take a half a hour to fix this here car," Hiram called, looking over the raised hood of it.

"Well, first you and Bobby Lee get him and that little boy to step over yonder with you," The Misfit said, pointing to Bailey and John Wesley.

"The boys want to ast you something," he said to Bailey. "Would you mind stepping back in them woods there with them?"

"Listen," Bailey began, "we're in a terrible predicament! Nobody realizes what this is," and his voice cracked. His eyes were as blue and intense as the parrots in his shirt and he remained perfectly still.

The grandmother reached up to adjust her hat brim as if she were going to the woods with him but it came off in her hand. She stood staring at it and after a second she let it fall to the ground. Hiram pulled Bailey up by the arm as if he were assisting an old man. John Wesley caught hold of his father's hand and Bobby Lee followed. They went off toward the woods and just as they reached the dark edge, Bailey turned and supporting himself against a gray naked pine trunk, he shouted, "I'll be back in a minute, Mamma, wait on me!"

"Come back this instant!" his mother shrilled but they all disappeared into the woods.

"Bailey Boy!" the grandmother called in a tragic voice but she found she was looking at The Misfit squatting on the ground in front of her. "I just know you're a good man," she said desperately. "You're not a bit common!"

"Nome, I ain't a good man," The Misfit said after a second as if he had considered her statement carefully, "but I ain't the worst in the world neither. My daddy said I was a different breed of dog from my brothers and sisters. 'You know,' Daddy said, 'it's some that can live their whole life out without asking about it and it's others has to know why it is, and this boy is one of the latters. He's going to be into everything!'" He put on his black hat and looked up suddenly and then away deep into the woods as if he were embarrassed again. "I'm sorry I don't have on a shirt before you ladies," he said, hunching his shoulders slightly. "We buried our clothes that we had on when we escaped and we're just making do until we can get better. We borrowed these from some folks we met," he explained.

"That's perfectly all right," the grandmother said. "Maybe Bailey has an extra shirt in his suitcase."

"I'll look and see terreckly," The Misfit said.

"Where are they taking him?" the children's mother screamed.

"Daddy was a card himself," The Misfit said. "You couldn't put anything over on him. He never got in trouble with the Authorities though. Just had the knack of handling them."

"You could be honest too if you'd only try," said the grandmother. "Think how wonderful it would be to settle down and live a comfortable life and not have to think about somebody chasing you all the time."

The Misfit kept scratching in the ground with the butt of his gun as if he were thinking about it. "Yes'm, somebody is always after you," he murmured.

The grandmother noticed how thin his shoulder blades were just behind his hat because she was standing up looking down on him. "Do you ever pray?" she asked.

He shook his head. All she saw was the black hat wiggle between his shoulder blades. "Nome," he said.

There was a pistol shot from the woods, followed closely by another. Then silence. The old lady's head jerked around. She could hear the wind move through the tree tops like a long satisfied insuck of breath. "Bailey Boy!" she called.

"I was a gospel singer for a while," The Misfit said. "I been most everything. Been in the arm service, both land and sea, at home and abroad, been twict married, been an undertaker, been with the railroads, plowed Mother Earth, been in a tornado, seen a man burnt alive oncet," and he looked up at the children's mother and the little girl who were sitting close together, their faces white and their eyes glassy; "I even seen a woman flogged," he said.

"Pray, pray," the grandmother began, "pray, pray. . . ."

"I never was a bad boy that I remember of," The Misfit said in an almost dreamy voice, "but somewheres along the line I done something wrong and got sent to the penitentiary. I was buried alive," and he looked up and held her attention to him by a steady stare.

"That's when you should have started to pray," she said. "What did you do to get sent to the penitentiary that first time?"

"Turn to the right, it was a wall," The Misfit said, looking up again at the cloudless sky. "Turn to the left, it was a wall. Look up it was a ceiling, look down it was a floor. I forget what I done, lady. I set there and set there, trying to remember what it was I done and I ain't recalled it to this day. Oncet in a while, I would think it was coming to me, but it never come."

"Maybe they put you in by mistake," the old lady said vaguely.

"Nome," he said. "It wasn't no mistake. They had the papers on me."

"You must have stolen something," she said.

The Misfit sneered slightly. "Nobody had nothing I wanted," he said. "It was a head-doctor at the penitentiary said what I had done was kill my daddy but I known that for a lie. My daddy died in nineteen ought nineteen of the epidemic flu and I never had a thing to do with it. He was buried in the Mount Hopewell Baptist churchyard and you can see for yourself."

"If you would pray," the old lady said, "Jesus would help you."

"That's right," The Misfit said.

"Well then, why don't you pray?" she asked trembling with delight suddenly.

"I don't want no hep," he said. "I'm doing all right by myself."

Bobby Lee and Hiram came ambling back from the woods. Bobby Lee was dragging a yellow shirt with bright blue parrots in it.

"Throw me that shirt, Bobby Lee," The Misfit said. The shirt came flying at him and landed on his shoulder and he put it on. The grandmother couldn't name what the shirt reminded her of. "No, lady," The Misfit said while he was buttoning it up, "I found out the crime don't matter. You can do one thing or you can do another, kill a man or take a tire off his car, because sooner or later you're going to forget what it was you done and just be punished for it."

The children's mother had begun to make heaving noises as if she couldn't get her breath. "Lady," he asked, "would you and that little girl like to step off yonder with Bobby Lee and Hiram and join your husband?"

"Yes, thank you," the mother said faintly. Her left arm dangled helplessly and she was holding the baby, who had gone to sleep, in the other. "Hep that lady up, Hiram," The Misfit said as she struggled to climb out of the ditch, "and Bobby Lee, you hold onto that little girl's hand."

"I don't want to hold hands with him," June Star said. "He reminds me of a pig."

The fat boy blushed and laughed and caught her by the arm and pulled her off into the woods after Hiram and her mother.

Alone with The Misfit, the grandmother found that she had lost her voice. There was not a cloud in the sky nor any sun. There was nothing around her but woods. She wanted to tell him that he must pray. She opened and closed her mouth several times before anything came out. Finally she found herself saying, "Jesus, Jesus," meaning, Jesus will help you, but the way she was saying it, it sounded as if she might be cursing.

"Yes'm," The Misfit said as if he agreed. "Jesus thown everything off balance. It was the same case with Him as with me except He hadn't committed any crime and they could prove I had committed one because they had the papers on me. Of course," he said, "they never shown me my papers. That's why I sign myself now. I said long ago, you get your signature and sign everything you do and keep a copy of it. Then you'll know what you done and you can hold up the crime to the punishment and see do they match and in the end you'll have something to prove you ain't been treated right. I call myself The Misfit," he said, "because I can't make what all I done wrong fit what all I gone through in punishment."

There was a piercing scream from the woods, followed closely by a pistol report. "Does it seem right to you, lady, that one is punished a heap and another ain't punished at all?"

"Jesus!" the old lady cried. "You've got good blood! I know you wouldn't shoot a lady! I know you come from nice people! Pray! Jesus, you ought not to shoot a lady. I'll give you all the money I've got!"

"Lady," The Misfit said, looking beyond her far into the woods, "there never was a body that give the undertaker a tip."

There were two more pistol reports and the grandmother raised her head like a parched old turkey hen crying for water and called, "Bailey Boy, Bailey Boy!" as if her heart would break.

"Jesus was the only One that ever raised the dead," The Misfit continued, "and He shouldn't have done it. He thown everything off balance.

If He did what He said, then it's nothing for you to do but throw away everything and follow Him, and if He didn't, then it's nothing for you to do but enjoy the few minutes you got left the best way you can — by killing somebody or burning down his house or doing some other meanness to him. No pleasure but meanness," he said and his voice had become almost a snarl.

"Maybe He didn't raise the dead," the old lady mumbled, not knowing what she was saying and feeling so dizzy that she sank down in the ditch with her legs twisted under her.

"I wasn't there so I can't say He didn't," The Misfit said. "I wisht I had of been there," he said, hitting the ground with his fist. "It ain't right I wasn't there because if I had of been there I would of known. Listen lady," he said in a high voice, "if I had of been there I would of known and I wouldn't be like I am now." His voice seemed about to crack and the grandmother's head cleared for an instant. She saw the man's face twisted close to her own as if he were going to cry and she murmured, "Why you're one of my babies. You're one of my own children!" She reached out and touched him on the shoulder. The Misfit sprang back as if a snake had bitten him and shot her three times through the chest. Then he put his gun down on the ground and took off his glasses and began to clean them.

Hiram and Bobby Lee returned from the woods and stood over the ditch, looking down at the grandmother who half sat and half lay in a puddle of blood with her legs crossed under her like a child's and her face smiling up at the cloudless sky.

Without his glasses, The Misfit's eyes were red-rimmed and pale and defenseless-looking. "Take her off and throw her where you thrown the others," he said, picking up the cat that was rubbing itself against his leg.

"She was a talker, wasn't she?" Bobby Lee said, sliding down the ditch with a yodel.

"She would of been a good woman," The Misfit said, "if it had been somebody there to shoot her every minute of her life."

"Some fun!" Bobby Lee said.

"Shut up, Bobby Lee," The Misfit said. "It's no real pleasure in life."

[1955]

Flannery O'Connor

ɷ

THE ARTIFICIAL NIGGER

Mr. Head awakened to discover that the room was full of moonlight. He sat up and stared at the floor boards — the color of silver — and then at the ticking on his pillow, which might have been brocade, and after a second, he saw half of the moon five feet away in his shaving mirror, paused as if it were waiting for his permission to enter. It rolled forward and cast a dignifying light on everything. The straight chair against the wall looked stiff and attentive as if it were awaiting an order and Mr. Head's trousers, hanging to the back of it, had an almost noble air, like the garment some great man had just flung to his servant; but the face on the moon was a grave one. It gazed across the room and out the window where it floated over the horse stall and appeared to contemplate itself with the look of a young man who sees his old age before him.

Mr. Head could have said to it that age was a choice blessing and that only with years does a man enter into that calm understanding of life that makes him a suitable guide for the young. This, at least, had been his own experience.

He sat up and grasped the iron posts at the foot of his bed and raised himself until he could see the face on the alarm clock which sat on an overturned bucket beside the chair. The hour was two in the morning. The alarm on the clock did not work but he was not dependent on any mechanical means to awaken him. Sixty years had not dulled his responses; his physical reactions, like his moral ones, were guided by his will and strong character, and these could be seen plainly in his features. He had a long tube-like face with a long rounded open jaw and a long depressed nose. His eyes were alert but quiet, and in the miraculous moonlight they had a look of composure and of ancient wisdom as if they belonged to one of the great guides of men. He might have been Vergil summoned in the middle of the night to go to Dante, or better, Raphael, awakened by a blast of God's light to fly to the side of Tobias. The only dark spot in the room was Nelson's pallet, underneath the shadow of the window.

Nelson was hunched over on his side, his knees under his chin and his heels under his bottom. His new suit and hat were in the boxes that they had been sent in and these were on the floor at the foot of the pallet where he could get his hands on them as soon as he woke up. The slop jar, out of the shadow and made snow-white in the moonlight, appeared to stand guard over him like a small personal angel. Mr. Head lay back down, feeling entirely confident that he could carry out the moral mission of the coming day. He meant to be up before Nelson and to have the breakfast cooking by the time he awakened. The boy was always irked when Mr. Head was the first up. They would have to leave the house at four to get to the railroad junction by five-thirty. The train was to stop for them at five forty-five and they had to be there on time for this train was stopping merely to accommodate them.

This would be the boy's first trip to the city though he claimed it would be his second because he had been born there. Mr. Head had tried to point out to him that when he was born he didn't have the intelligence to determine his whereabouts but this had made no impression on the child at all and he continued to insist that this was to be his second trip. It would be Mr. Head's third trip. Nelson had said, "I will've already been there twict and I ain't but ten."

Mr. Head had contradicted him.

"If you ain't been there in fifteen years, how you know you'll be able to find your way about?" Nelson had asked. "How you know it hasn't changed some?"

"Have you ever," Mr. Head had asked, "seen me lost?"

Nelson certainly had not but he was a child who was never satisfied until he had given an impudent answer and he replied, "It's nowhere around here to get lost at."

"The day is going to come," Mr. Head prophesied, "when you'll find you ain't as smart as you think you are." He had been thinking about this trip for several months but it was for the most part in moral terms that he conceived it. It was to be a lesson that the boy would never forget. He was to find out from it that he had no cause for pride merely because he had been born in a city. He was to find out that the city is not a great place. Mr. Head meant him to see everything there is to see in a city so that he would be content to stay at home for the rest of his life. He fell asleep thinking how the boy would at last find out that he was not as smart as he thought he was.

He was awakened at three-thirty by the smell of fatback frying and he leaped off his cot. The pallet was empty and the clothes boxes had been thrown open. He put on his trousers and ran into the other room. The boy had a corn pone on cooking and had fried the meat. He was sitting in the half-dark at the table, drinking cold coffee out of a can. He had on his new suit and his new gray hat pulled low over his eyes. It was too big for him but they had ordered it a size large because they expected his head to grow. He didn't say anything but his entire figure suggested satisfaction at having arisen before Mr. Head.

Mr. Head went to the stove and brought the meat to the table in the skillet. "It's no hurry," he said. "You'll get there soon enough, and it's no guarantee you'll like it when you do neither," and he sat down across from the boy whose hat teetered back slowly to reveal a fiercely expressionless face, very much the same shape as the old man's. They were grandfather and grandson but they looked enough alike to be brothers and brothers not too far apart in age, for Mr. Head had a youthful expression by daylight, while the boy's look was ancient, as if he knew everything already and would be pleased to forget it.

Mr. Head had once had a wife and daughter and when the wife died, the daughter ran away and returned after an interval with Nelson. Then one morning, without getting out of bed, she died and left Mr. Head with sole care of the year-old child. He had made the mistake of telling Nelson that he had been born in Atlanta. If he hadn't told him that, Nelson couldn't have insisted that this was going to be his second trip.

"You may not like it a bit," Mr. Head continued. "It'll be full of niggers."

The boy made a face as if he could handle a nigger.

"All right," Mr. Head said. "You ain't ever seen a nigger."

"You wasn't up very early," Nelson said.

"You ain't ever seen a nigger," Mr. Head repeated. "There hasn't been a nigger in this county since we run that one out twelve years ago and that was before you were born." He looked at the boy as if he were daring him to say he had ever seen a Negro.

"How you know I never saw a nigger when I lived there before?" Nelson asked. "I probably saw a lot of niggers."

"If you seen one you didn't know what he was," Mr. Head said, completely exasperated. "A six-month-old child don't know a nigger from anybody else."

"I reckon I'll know a nigger if I see one," the boy said and got up and straightened his slick sharply creased gray hat and went outside to the privy.

They reached the junction some time before the train was due to arrive and stood about two feet from the first set of tracks. Mr. Head carried a paper sack with some biscuits and a can of sardines in it for their lunch. A coarse-looking orange-colored sun coming up behind the east range of mountains was making the sky a dull red behind them, but in front of them it was still gray and they faced a gray transparent moon, hardly stronger than a thumbprint and completely without light. A small tin switch box and a black fuel tank were all there was to mark the place as a junction; the tracks were double and did not converge again until they were hidden behind the bends at either end of the clearing. Trains passing appeared to emerge from a tunnel of trees and, hit for a second by the cold sky, vanish terrified into the woods again. Mr. Head had had to make special arrangements with the ticket agent to have this train stop and he was secretly afraid it would not, in which case, he knew Nelson would say, "I never thought no train was going to stop for you." Under the useless morning moon the tracks looked white and fragile. Both the old man and the child stared ahead as if they were awaiting an apparition.

Then suddenly, before Mr. Head could make up his mind to turn back, there was a deep warning bleat and the train appeared, gliding very slowly, almost silently around the bend of trees about two hundred yards down the track, with one yellow front light shining. Mr. Head was still not certain it would stop and he felt it would make an even bigger idiot of him if it went by slowly. Both he and Nelson, however, were prepared to ignore the train if it passed them.

The engine charged by, filling their noses with the smell of hot metal and then the second coach came to a stop exactly where they were standing. A conductor with the face of an ancient bloated bulldog was on the step as if he expected them, though he did not look as if it mattered one way or the other to him if they got on or not. "To the right," he said.

Their entry took only a fraction of a second and the train was already speeding on as they entered the quiet car. Most of the travelers were still sleeping, some with their heads hanging off the chair arms, some stretched across two seats, and some sprawled out with their feet in the aisle. Mr. Head saw two unoccupied seats and pushed Nelson toward them. "Get in there by the winder," he said in his normal voice which was very loud at this hour of the morning. "Nobody cares if you sit there because it's nobody in it. Sit right there."

"I heard you," the boy muttered. "It's no use in you yelling," and he sat down and turned his head to the glass. There he saw a pale ghost-like face scowling at him beneath the brim of a pale ghost-like hat. His grandfather, looking quickly too, saw a different ghost, pale but grinning, under a black hat.

Mr. Head sat down and settled himself and took out his ticket and started reading aloud everything that was printed on it. People began to stir. Several woke up and stared at him. "Take off your hat," he said to Nelson and took off his own and put it on his knee. He had a small amount of white hair that had turned tobacco-colored over the years and this lay flat across the back of his head. The front of his head was bald and creased. Nelson took off his hat and put it on his knee and they waited for the conductor to come ask for their tickets.

The man across the aisle from them was spread out over two seats, his feet propped on the window and his head jutting into the aisle. He had on a light blue suit and a yellow shirt unbuttoned at the neck. His eyes had just opened and Mr. Head was ready to introduce himself when the conductor came up from behind and growled, "Tickets."

When the conductor had gone, Mr. Head gave Nelson the return half of his ticket and said, "Now put that in your pocket and don't lose it or you'll have to stay in the city."

"Maybe I will," Nelson said as if this were a reasonable suggestion. Mr. Head ignored him. "First time this boy has ever been on a train," he explained to the man across the aisle, who was sitting up now on the edge of his seat with both feet on the floor.

Nelson jerked his hat on again and turned angrily to the window.

"He's never seen anything before," Mr. Head continued. "Ignorant as the day he was born, but I mean for him to get his fill once and for all."

The boy leaned forward, across his grandfather and toward the stranger. "I was born in the city," he said. "I was born there. This is my second trip." He said it in a high positive voice but the man across the aisle didn't look as if he understood. There were heavy purple circles under his eyes.

Mr. Head reached across the aisle and tapped him on the arm. "The thing to do with a boy," he said sagely, "is to show him all it is to show. Don't hold nothing back."

"Yeah," the man said. He gazed down at his swollen feet and lifted the left one about ten inches from the floor. After a minute he put it down and lifted the other. All through the car people began to get up and move about and yawn and stretch. Separate voices could be heard here and there and then a general hum. Suddenly Mr. Head's serene expression changed. His mouth almost closed and a light, fierce and cautious both, came into his eyes. He was looking down the length of the car. Without turning, he caught Nelson by the arm and pulled him forward. "Look," he said.

A huge coffee-colored man was coming slowly forward. He had on a light suit and a yellow satin tie with a ruby pin in it. One of his hands rested on his stomach which rode majestically under his buttoned coat, and in the other he held the head of a black walking stick that he picked up and set down with a deliberate outward motion each time he took a step. He was proceeding very slowly, his large brown eyes gazing over the heads of the passengers. He had a small white mustache and white crinkly hair. Behind him there were two young women, both coffee-colored, one in a yellow dress and one in a green. Their progress was kept at the rate of his and they chatted in low throaty voices as they followed him.

Mr. Head's grip was tightening insistently on Nelson's arm. As the procession passed them, the light from a sapphire ring on the brown hand that picked up the cane reflected in Mr. Head's eye, but he did not look up nor did the tremendous man look at him. The group proceeded up the rest of the aisle and out of the car. Mr. Head's grip on Nelson's arm loosened. "What was that?" he asked.

"A man," the boy said and gave him an indignant look as if he were tired of having his intelligence insulted.

"What kind of a man?" Mr. Head persisted, his voice expressionless.

"A fat man," Nelson said. He was beginning to feel that he had better be cautious.

"You don't know what kind?" Mr. Head said in a final tone.

"An old man," the boy said and had a sudden foreboding that he was not going to enjoy the day.

"That was a nigger," Mr. Head said and sat back.

Nelson jumped up on the seat and stood looking backward to the end of the car but the Negro had gone.

"I'd of thought you'd know a nigger since you seen so many when you was in the city on your first visit," Mr. Head continued. "That's his first nigger," he said to the man across the aisle.

The boy slid down into the seat. "You said they were black," he said in an angry voice. "You never said they were tan. How do you expect me to know anything when you don't tell me right?"

"You're just ignorant is all," Mr. Head said and he got up and moved over in the vacant seat by the man across the aisle.

Nelson turned backward again and looked where the Negro had disappeared. He felt that the Negro had deliberately walked down the aisle in order to make a fool of him and he hated him with a fierce raw fresh hate; and also, he understood now why his grandfather disliked them. He looked toward the window and the face there seemed to suggest that he might be inadequate to the day's exactions. He wondered if he would even recognize the city when they came to it.

After he had told several stories, Mr. Head realized that the man he was talking to was asleep and he got up and suggested to Nelson that they walk over the train and see the parts of it. He particularly wanted the boy to see the toilet so they went first to the men's room and examined the plumbing. Mr. Head demonstrated the ice-water cooler as if he had invented it and showed Nelson the bowl with the single spigot where the travelers brushed their teeth. They went through several cars and came to the diner.

This was the most elegant car in the train. It was painted a rich egg-yellow and had a wine-colored carpet on the floor. There were wide windows over the tables and great spaces of the rolling view were caught in miniature in the sides of the coffee pots and in the glasses. Three very black Negroes in white suits and aprons were running up and down the aisle, swinging trays and bowing and bending over the travelers eating breakfast. One of them rushed up to Mr. Head and Nelson and said, holding up two fingers, "Space for two!" but Mr. Head replied in a loud voice, "We eaten before we left!"

The waiter wore large brown spectacles that increased the size of his eye whites. "Stan' aside then please," he said with an airy wave of the arm as if he were brushing aside flies.

Neither Nelson nor Mr. Head moved a fraction of an inch. "Look," Mr. Head said.

The near corner of the diner, containing two tables, was set off from the rest by a saffron-colored curtain. One table was set but empty but at the other, facing them, his back to the drape, sat the tremendous Negro. He was speaking in a soft voice to the two women while he buttered a muffin. He had a heavy sad face and his neck bulged over his white collar on either side. "They rope them off," Mr. Head explained. Then he said, "Let's go see the kitchen," and they walked the length of the diner but the black waiter was coming fast behind them.

"Passengers are not allowed in the kitchen!" he said in a haughty voice. "Passengers are NOT allowed in the kitchen!"

Mr. Head stopped where he was and turned. "And there's good reason for that," he shouted into the Negro's chest, "because the cockroaches would run the passengers out!"

And the travelers laughed and Mr. Head and Nelson walked out, grinning. Mr. Head was known at home for his quick wit and Nelson felt a sudden keen pride in him. He realized the old man would be his only support in the strange place they were approaching. He would be entirely alone in the world if he were ever lost from his grandfather. A terrible excitement shook him and he wanted to take hold of Mr. Head's coat and hold on like a child.

As they went back to their seats they could see through the passing windows that the countryside was becoming speckled with small houses and shacks and that a highway ran alongside the train. Cars sped by on it, very small and fast. Nelson felt that there was less breath in the air than there had been thirty minutes ago. The man across the aisle had left and there was no one near for Mr. Head to hold a conversation with so he looked out the window, through his own reflection, and read aloud the names of the buildings they were passing. "The Dixie Chemical Corp!" he announced. "Southern Maid Flour! Dixie Doors! Southern Belle Cotton Products! Patty's Peanut Butter! Southern Mammy Cane Syrup!"

"Hush up!" Nelson hissed.

All over the car people were beginning to get up and take their luggage off the overhead racks. Women were putting on their coats and hats. The conductor stuck his head in the car and snarled, "Firstopppppmry," and Nelson lunged out of his sitting position, trembling. Mr. Head pushed him down by the shoulder.

"Keep your seat," he said in dignified tones. "The first stop is on the edge of town. The second stop is at the main railroad station." He had come by this knowledge on his first trip when he had got off at the first stop and had had to pay a man fifteen cents to take him into the heart of town. Nelson sat back down, very pale. For the first time in his life, he understood that his grandfather was indispensable to him.

The train stopped and let off a few passengers and glided on as if it had never ceased moving. Outside, behind rows of brown rickety houses, a line of blue buildings stood up, and beyond them a pale rose-gray sky faded away to nothing. The train moved into the railroad yard. Looking down, Nelson saw lines and lines of silver tracks multiplying and criss-crossing. Then before he could start counting them, the face in the window started out at him, gray but distinct, and he looked the other way. The train was in the station. Both he and Mr. Head jumped up and ran to the door. Neither noticed that they had left the paper sack with the lunch in it on the seat.

They walked stiffly through the small station and came out of a heavy door into the squall of traffic. Crowds were hurrying to work. Nelson didn't know where to look. Mr. Head leaned against the side of the building and glared in front of him.

Finally Nelson said, "Well, how do you see what all it is to see?"

Mr. Head didn't answer. Then as if the sight of people passing had given him the clue, he said, "You walk," and started off down the street. Nelson followed, steadying his hat. So many sights and sounds were flooding in on him that for the first block he hardly knew what he was seeing. At the second corner, Mr. Head turned and looked behind him at the station they had left, a putty-colored terminal with a concrete dome on top. He thought that if he could keep the dome always in sight, he would be able to get back in the afternoon to catch the train again.

As they walked along, Nelson began to distinguish details and take note of the store windows, jammed with every kind of equipment — hardware, drygoods, chicken feed, liquor. They passed one that Mr. Head called his particular attention to where you walked in and sat on a chair with your feet upon two rests and and let a Negro polish your shoes. They walked slowly and stopped and stood at the entrances so he could see what went on in each place but they did not go into any of them. Mr. Head was determined not to go into any city store because on his first trip here, he had got lost in a large one and had found his way out only after many people had insulted him.

They came in the middle of the next block to a store that had a weighing machine in front of it and they both in turn stepped up on it and put in a penny and received a ticket. Mr. Head's ticket said, "You weigh 120 pounds. You are upright and brave and all your friends admire you." He put the ticket in his pocket, surprised that the machine should have got his character correct but his weight wrong, for he had weighed on a grain scale not long before and knew he weighed 110. Nelson's ticket said, "You weight 98 pounds. You have a great destiny ahead of you but beware of dark women." Nelson did not know any women and he weighed only 68 pounds but Mr. Head pointed out that the machine had probably printed the number upside down, meaning the 9 for a 6.

They walked on and at the end of five blocks the dome of the terminal sank out of sight and Mr. Head turned to the left. Nelson could have stood in front of every store window for an hour if there had not been another more interesting one next to it. Suddenly he said, "I was born here!" Mr. Head turned and looked at him with horror. There was a sweaty brightness about his face. "This is where I come from!" he said.

Mr. Head was appalled. He saw the moment had come for drastic action. "Lemme show you one thing you ain't seen yet," he said and took him to the corner where there was a sewer entrance. "Squat down," he said, "and stick you head in there," and he held the back of the boy's coat while he got down and put his head in the sewer. He drew it back quickly, hearing a gurgling in the depths under the sidewalk. Then Mr. Head explained the sewer system, how the entire city was underlined with it, how it contained all the drainage and was full of rats and how a man could slide into it and be sucked along down endless pitchblack tunnels. At any minute any man in the city might be sucked into the sewer and never heard from again. He described it so well that Nelson was for some seconds shaken. He connected the sewer passages with the entrance to hell and understood for the first time how the world was put together in its lower parts. He drew away from the curb.

Then he said, "Yes, but you can stay away from the holes," and his face took on that stubborn look that was so exasperating to his grandfather. "This is where I come from!" he said.

Mr. Head was dismayed but he only muttered, "You'll get your fill," and they walked on. At the end of two more blocks he turned to the left, feeling that he was circling the dome; and he was correct for in a half-hour they passed in front of the railroad station again. At first Nelson did not notice that he was seeing the same stores twice but when they passed the one where you put your feet on the rests while the Negro polished your shoes, he perceived that they were walking in a circle.

"We done been here!" he shouted. "I don't believe you know where you're at!"

"The direction just slipped my mind for a minute," Mr. Head said and they turned down a different street. He still did not intend to let the dome get too far away and after two blocks in their new direction, he turned to the left. This street contained two and three-story wooden dwellings. Anyone passing on the sidewalk could see into the rooms and Mr. Head, glancing through one window, saw a woman lying on an iron bed, looking out, with a sheet pulled over her. Her knowing expression shook him. A fierce-looking boy on a bicycle came driving down out of nowhere and he had to jump to the side to keep from being hit. "It's nothing to them if they knock you down," he said. "You better keep closer to me."

They walked on for some time on streets like this before he remembered to turn again. The houses they were passing now were all unpainted and the wood in them looked rotten; the street between was narrower. Nelson saw a colored man. Then another. Then another. "Niggers live in these houses," he observed.

"Well come on and we'll go somewheres else," Mr. Head said. "We didn't come to look at niggers," and they turned down another street but they continued to see Negroes everywhere. Nelson's skin began to prickle and they stepped along at a faster pace in order to leave the neighborhood as soon as possible. There were colored men in their undershirts standing in the doors and colored women rocking on the sagging porches. Colored children played in the gutters and stopped what they were doing to look at them. Before long they began to pass rows of stores with colored customers in them but they didn't pause at the entrances of these. Black eyes in black faces were watching them from every direction. "Yes," Mr. Head said, "this is where you were born — right here with all these niggers."

Nelson scowled. "I think you done got us lost," he said.

Mr. Head swung around sharply and looked for the dome. It was nowhere in sight. "I ain't got us lost either," he said. "You're just tired of walking."

"I ain't tired, I'm hungry," Nelson said. "Give me a biscuit."

They discovered then that they had lost the lunch.

"You were the one holding the sack," Nelson said. "I would have kepaholt of it."

"If you want to direct this trip, I'll go on by myself and leave you right here," Mr. Head said and was pleased to see the boy turn white. However, he realized they were lost and drifting farther every minute from the station. He was hungry himself and beginning to be thirsty and since they had been in the colored neighborhood, they had both begun to sweat. Nelson had on his shoes and he was unaccustomed to them. The concrete sidewalks were very hard. They both wanted to find a place to sit down but this was impossible and they kept on walking, the boy muttering under his breath, "First you lost the sack and then you lost the way," and Mr. Head growling from time to time, "Anybody wants to be from this nigger heaven can be from it!"

By now the sun was well forward in the sky. The odor of dinners cooking drifted out to them. The Negroes were all at their doors to see them pass. "Whyn't you ast one of these niggers the way?" Nelson said. "You got us lost."

"This is where you were born," Mr. Head said. "You can ast one yourself if you want to."

Nelson was afraid of the colored men and he didn't want to be laughed at by the colored children. Up ahead he saw a large colored woman leaning in a doorway that opened onto the sidewalk. Her hair stood straight out from her head for about four inches all around and she was resting on bare brown feet that turned pink at the sides. She had on a pink dress that showed her exact shape. As they came abreast of her, she lazily lifted one hand to her head and her fingers disappeared into her hair.

Nelson stopped. He felt his breath drawn up by the woman's dark eyes. "How do you get back to town?" he said in a voice that did not sound like his own.

After a minute she said, "You in town now," in a rich low tone that made Nelson feel as if a cool spray had been turned on him.

"How do you get back to the train?" he said in the same reed-like voice.

"You can catch you a car," she said.

He understood she was making fun of him but he was too paralyzed even to scowl. He stood drinking in every detail of her. His eyes traveled up from her great knees to her forehead and then made a triangular path from the glistening sweat on her neck down and across her tremendous bosom and over her bare arm back to where her fingers lay hidden in her hair. He suddenly wanted her to reach down and pick him up and draw him against her and then he wanted to feel her breath on his face. He wanted to look down and down into her eyes while she held him tighter and tighter. He had never had such a feeling before. He felt as if he were reeling down through a pitchblack tunnel.

"You can go a block down yonder and catch you a car take you to the railroad station, Sugarpie," she said.

Nelson would have collapsed at her feet if Mr. Head had not pulled him roughly away. "You act like you don't have any sense!" the old man growled.

They hurried down the street and Nelson did not look back at the woman. He pushed his hat sharply forward over his face which was already burning with shame. The sneering ghost he had seen in the train window and all the foreboding feelings he had on the way returned to him and he remembered that his ticket from the scale had said to beware of dark women and that his grandfather's had said he was upright and brave. He took hold of the old man's hand, a sign of dependence that he seldom showed.

They headed down the street toward the car tracks where a long yellow rattling trolley was coming. Mr. Head had never boarded a streetcar and he let that one pass. Nelson was silent. From time to time his mouth trembled slightly but his grandfather, occupied with his own problems, paid him no attention. They stood on the corner and neither looked at the Negroes who were passing, going about their business just as if they had been white, except that most of them stopped and eyed Mr. Head and Nelson. It occurred to Mr. Head that since the streetcar ran on tracks, they could simply follow the tracks. He gave Nelson a slight push and explained that they would follow the tracks on into the railroad station, walking, and they set off.

Presently to their great relief they began to see white people again and Nelson sat down on the sidewalk against the wall of a building. "I got to rest myself some," he said. "You lost the sack and the direction. You can just wait on me to rest myself."

"There's the tracks in front of us," Mr. Head said. "All we got to do is keep them in sight and you could have remembered the sack as good as me. This is where you were born. This is your old home town. This is your second trip. You ought to know how to do," and he squatted down and continued in this vein but the boy, easing his burning feet out of his shoes, did not answer.

"And standing there grinning like a chim-pan-zee while a nigger woman gives you direction. Great Gawd!" Mr. Head said.

"I never said I was nothing but born here," the boy said in a shaky voice. "I never said I would or wouldn't like it. I never said I wanted to come. I only said I was born here and I never had nothing to do with that. I want to go home. I never wanted to come in the first place. It was all your big idea. How you know you ain't following the tracks in the wrong direction?"

This last had occurred to Mr. Head too. "All these people are white," he said.

"We ain't passed here before," Nelson said. This was a neighborhood of brick buildings that might have been lived in or might not. A few empty automobiles were parked along the curb and there was an occasional passerby. The heat of the pavement came up through Nelson's thin suit. His eyelids began to droop, and after a few minutes his head tilted forward. His shoulders twitched once or twice and then he fell over on his side and lay sprawled in an exhausted fit of sleep.

Mr. Head watched him silently. He was very tired himself but they could not both sleep at the same time and he could not have slept anyway because he did not know where he was. In a few minutes Nelson would wake up, refreshed by his sleep and very cocky, and would begin complaining that he had lost the sack and the way. You'd have a mighty sorry time if I wasn't here, Mr. Head thought; and then another idea occurred to him. He looked at the sprawled figure for several minutes; presently he stood up. He justified what he was going to do on the grounds that it is sometimes necessary to teach a child a lesson he won't forget, particularly when the child is always reasserting his position with some new impudence. He walked without a sound to the corner about twenty feet away and sat down on a covered garbage can in the alley where he could look out and watch Nelson wake up alone.

The boy was dozing fitfully, half conscious of vague noises and black forms moving up from some dark part of him into the light. His face worked in his sleep and he had pulled his knees up under his chin. The sun shed a dull dry light on the narrow street; everything looked like exactly what it was. After a while Mr. Head, hunched like an old monkey on the garbage can lid, decided that if Nelson didn't wake up soon, he would make a loud noise by bamming his foot against the can. He looked at his watch and discovered that it was two o'clock. Their train left at six and the possibility of missing it was too awful for him to think of. He kicked his foot backwards on the can and a hollow boom reverberated in the alley.

Nelson shot up onto his feet with a shout. He looked where his grandfather should have been and stared. He seemed to whirl several times and then, picking up his feet and throwing his head back, he dashed down the street like a wild maddened pony. Mr. Head jumped off the can and galloped after but the child was almost out of sight. He saw a streak of gray disappearing diagonally a block ahead. He ran as fast as he could, looking both ways down every intersection, but without sight of him again. Then as he passed the third intersection, completely winded, he saw about half a block down the street a scene that stopped him altogether. He crouched behind a trash box to watch and get his bearings.

Nelson was sitting with both legs spread out and by his side lay an elderly woman, screaming. Groceries were scattered about the sidewalk. A crowd of women had already gathered to see justice done and Mr. Head distinctly heard the old woman on the pavement shout, "You've broken my ankle and your daddy'll pay for it! Every nickel! Police! Police!" Several of the women were plucking at Nelson's shoulder but the boy seemed too dazed to get up.

Something forced Mr. Head from behind the trash box and forward, but only at a creeping pace. He had never in his life been accosted by a policeman. The women were milling around Nelson as if they might suddenly all dive on him at once and tear him to pieces, and the old woman continued to scream that her ankle was broken and to call for an officer. Mr. Head came on so slowly that he could have been taking a backward step after each forward one, but when he was about ten feet away, Nelson saw him and sprang. The child caught him around the hips and clung panting against him.

The women all turned on Mr. Head. The injured one sat up and shouted, "You sir! You'll pay every penny of my doctor's bill that your boy has caused. He's a juve-nile delinquent! Where is an officer? Somebody take this man's name and address!"

Mr. Head was trying to detach Nelson's fingers from the flesh in the back of his legs. The old man's head had lowered itself into his collar like a turtle's; his eyes were glazed with fear and caution.

"Your boy has broken my ankle!" the old woman shouted. "Police!"

Mr. Head sensed the approach of the policeman from behind. He stared straight ahead at the women who were massed in their fury like a solid wall to block his escape. "This is not my boy," he said. "I never seen him before."

He felt Nelson's fingers fall out of his flesh.

The women dropped back, staring at him with horror, as if they were so repulsed by a man who would deny his own image and likeness that they could not bear to lay hands on him. Mr. Head walked on, through a space they silently cleared, and left Nelson behind. Ahead of him he saw nothing but a hollow tunnel that had once been the street.

The boy remained standing where he was, his neck craned forward and his hands hanging by his sides. His hat was jammed on his head so that there were no longer any creases in it. The injured woman got up and shook her fist at him and the others gave him pitying looks, but he didn't notice any of them. There was no policeman in sight.

In a minute he began to move mechanically, making no effort to catch up with his grandfather but merely following at about twenty paces. They walked on for five blocks in this way. Mr. Head's shoulders were sagging and his neck hung forward at such an angle that it was not visible from behind. He was afraid to turn his head. Finally he cut a short hopeful glance over his shoulder. Twenty feet behind him, he saw two small eyes piercing into his back like pitchfork prongs.

The boy was not of a forgiving nature but this was the first time he had ever had anything to forgive. Mr. Head had never disgraced himself before. After two more blocks, he turned and called over his shoulder in a high desperately gay voice, "Let's us go get us a Co' Cola somewheres!"

Nelson, with a dignity he had never shown before, turned and stood with his back to his grandfather.

Mr. Head began to feel the depth of his denial. His face as they walked on became all hollows and bare ridges. He saw nothing they were passing but he perceived that they had lost the car tracks. There was no dome to be seen anywhere and the afternoon was advancing. He knew that if dark overtook them in the city, they would be beaten and robbed. The speed of God's justice was only what he expected for himself, but he could not stand to think that his sins would be visited upon Nelson and that even now, he was leading the boy to his doom.

They continued to walk on block after block through an endless section of small brick houses until Mr. Head almost fell over a water spigot sticking up about six inches off the edge of a grass plot. He had not had a drink of water since early this morning but he felt he did not deserve it now. Then he thought that Nelson would be thirsty and they would both drink and be brought together. He squatted down and put his mouth to the nozzle and turned a cold stream of water into his throat. Then he called out in the high desperate voice, "Come on and getcher some water!"

This time the child stared through him for nearly sixty seconds. Mr. Head got up and walked on as if he had drunk poison. Nelson, though he had not had water since some he had drunk out of a paper cup on the train, passed by the spigot, disdaining to drink where his grandfather had. When Mr. Head realized this, he lost all hope. His face in the waning afternoon light looked ravaged and abandoned. He could feel the boy's steady hate, traveling at an even pace behind him and he knew that (if by some miracle they escaped being murdered in the city) it would continue just that way for the rest of his life. He knew that now he was wandering into a black strange place where nothing was like it had ever been before, a long old age without respect and an end that would be welcome because it would be the end.

As for Nelson, his mind had frozen around his grandfather's treachery as if he were trying to preserve it intact to present at the final judgment. He walked without looking to one side or the other, but every now and then his mouth would twitch and this was when he felt, from some remote place inside himself, a black mysterious form reach up as if it would melt his frozen vision in one hot grasp.

The sun dropped down behind a row of houses and hardly noticing, they passed into an elegant suburban section where mansions were set back from the road by lawns with birdbaths on them. Here everything was entirely deserted. For blocks they didn't pass even a dog. The big white houses were like partially submerged icebergs in the distance. There were no sidewalks, only drives, and these wound around and around in endless ridiculous circles. Nelson made no move to come nearer to Mr. Head. The old man felt that if he saw a sewer entrance he would drop down into it and let himself be carried away; and he could imagine the boy standing by, watching with only a slight interest, while he disappeared.

A loud bark jarred him to attention and he looked up to see a fat man approaching with two bulldogs. He waved both arms like someone shipwrecked on a desert island. "I'm lost!" he called. "I'm lost and can't find my way and me and this boy have got to catch this train and I can't find the station. Oh Gawd I'm lost! Oh hep me Gawd I'm lost!"

The man, who was bald-headed and had on golf knickers, asked him what train he was trying to catch and Mr. Head began to get out his tickets, trembling so violently he could hardly hold them. Nelson had come up to within fifteen feet and stood watching.

"Well," the fat man said, giving him back the tickets, "you won't have time to get back to town to make this but you can catch it at the suburb stop. That's three blocks from here," and he began explaining how to get there.

Mr. Head stared as if he were slowly returning from the dead and when the man had finished and gone off with the dogs jumping at his heels, he turned to Nelson and said breathlessly, "We're going to get home!"

The child was standing about ten feet away, his face bloodless under the gray hat. His eyes were triumphantly cold. There was no light in them, no feeling, no interest. He was merely there, a small figure, waiting. Home was nothing to him.

Mr. Head turned slowly. He felt he knew now what time would be like without seasons and what heat would be like without light and what man would be like without salvation. He didn't care if he never made the train and if it had not been for what suddenly caught his attention, like a cry out of the gathering dusk, he might have forgotten there was a station to go to.

He had not walked five hundred yards down the road when he saw, within reach of him, the plaster figure of a Negro sitting bent over on a low yellow brick fence that curved around a wide lawn. The Negro was about Nelson's size and he was pitched forward at an unsteady angle because the putty that held him to the wall had cracked. One of his eyes was entirely white and he held a piece of brown watermelon.

Mr. Head stood looking at him silently until Nelson stopped at a little distance. Then as the two of them stood there, Mr. Head breathed, "An artificial nigger!"

It was not possible to tell if the artificial Negro were meant to be young or old; he looked too miserable to be either. He was meant to look happy because his mouth was stretched up at the corners but the chipped eye and the angle he was cocked at gave him a wild look of misery instead.

"An artificial nigger!" Nelson repeated in Mr. Head's exact tone.

The two of them stood there with their necks forward at almost the same angle and their shoulders curved in almost exactly the same way and their hands trembling identically in their pockets. Mr. Head looked like an ancient child and Nelson like a miniature old man. They stood gazing at the artificial Negro as if they were faced with some great mystery, some monument to another's victory that brought them together in their common defeat. They could both feel it dissolving their differences like an action of mercy. Mr. Head had never known before what mercy felt like because he had been too good to deserve any, but he felt he knew now. He looked at Nelson and understood that he must say something to the child to show that he was still wise and in the look the boy returned he saw a hungry need for that assurance. Nelson's eyes seemed to implore him to explain once and for all the mystery of existence.

Mr. Head opened his lips to make a lofty statement and heard himself say, "They ain't got enough real ones here. They got to have an artificial one."

After a second, the boy nodded with a strange shivering about his mouth, and said, "Let's go home before we get ourselves lost again."

Their train glided into the suburb stop just as they reached the station and they boarded it together, and ten minutes before it was due to arrive at the junction, they went to the door and stood ready to jump off if it did not stop; but it did, just as the moon, restored to its full splendor, sprang from a cloud and flooded the clearing with light. As they stepped off, the sage grass was shivering gently in shades of silver and the clinkers under their feet glittered with a fresh black light. The treetops, fencing the junction like the protecting walls of a garden, were darker than the sky which was hung with gigantic white clouds illuminated like lanterns.

Mr. Head stood very still and felt the action of mercy touch him again but this time he knew that there were no words in the world that could name it. He understood that it grew out of agony, which is not denied to any man and which is given in strange ways to children. He understood it was all a man could carry into death to give his Maker and he suddenly burned with shame that he had so little of it to take with him. He stood appalled, judging himself with the thoroughness of God, while the action of mercy covered his pride like a flame and consumed it. He had never thought himself a great sinner before but he saw now that his true depravity had been hidden from him lest it cause him despair. He realized that he was forgiven for sins from the beginning of time, when he had conceived in his own heart the sin of Adam, until the present, when he had denied poor Nelson. He saw that no sin was too monstrous for him to claim as his own, and since God loved in proportion as He forgave, he felt ready at that instant to enter Paradise.

Nelson, composing his expression under the shadow of his hat brim, watched him with a mixture of fatigue and suspicion, but as the train glided past them and disappeared like a frightened serpent into the woods, even his face lightened and he muttered, "I'm glad I've went once, but I'll never go back again!"

[1955]

GABRIEL GARCÍA MÁRQUEZ (b. 1928) *was born in the re-mote small town of Aracataca in Magdalena province, near the Caribbean seacoast of Colombia. As the oldest of twelve children of a poverty-stricken telegraph operator and his wife, he was raised in the home of his maternal grandparents. When he was eight years old he was sent away to school near Bogotá, and after his graduation in 1946 he studied law until civil war in Colombia closed the university. A writer from childhood, García Márquez published his first stories in 1947. After he began to earn his living as a re-porter and film critic, he worked on a novel and short fiction. His first book was* Leaf Storm and Other Stories *(1955), which included "A Very Old Man with Enormous Wings," originally published in English translation in* The New American Review. *García Márquez spent the next few years in Paris, where he wrote two short novels,* No One Writes to the Colonel *(1958) and* In Evil Hour *(1961). After the Cuban Revolution, he returned to Central America and worked as a journalist and screenwriter. His great comic masterpiece, the novel* One Hundred Years of Solitude *(1967), was written while he lived in Mexico City; it received several major interna-tional literary prizes. In 1972 he published a new collection of stories,* The Incredible and Sad Tale of Innocent Erendira and Her Heartless Grand-mother. The Autumn of the Patriarch *(1975), a novel about the life of a Latin American dictator, was acclaimed as a work at least as important as the earlier* One Hundred Years of Solitude. *In 1982 García Márquez re-ceived the Nobel Prize for Literature.*

García Márquez's fiction has been compared by the London Times Literary Supplement *to Cervantes'* Don Quixote, *because, like Cervantes, he writes allegories in which his characters are placed "in a hybrid world in which the imaginary and the marvelous are weighted down by drab and sordid reality." He mingles realistic and fabulous details in all of his fiction, including "A Very Old Man with Enormous Wings," to suggest a sense of the world's mystery. As the novelist and essayist Paul Theroux recognized, "Religion is often seen as barren and stultifying, a stubborn and constrict-ing preoccupation, but there are minds which find release in it and then soar to tremendous heights of imagination. Gabriel García Márquez may not be pious in the traditional sense; however, there is in his stories . . . a pervasive tone of imaginative religiosity, a mystical lyricism in even the simplest exchange."*

The book Leaf Storm and Other Stories *was written after García Márquez returned from a visit to the house in Aracataca where he had spent his early childhood. As he later explained to an interviewer from* The Paris Review:

I'm not sure whether I had already read Faulkner or not, but I know now that only a technique like Faulkner's could have enabled me to write down what I was seeing. The atmosphere, the decadence, the heat in the village were roughly the same as what I had felt in Faulkner. It was a banana plantation region inhabited by a lot of Americans from the fruit companies which gave it the same sort of atmosphere I had found in the writers of the Deep South. Critics have spoken of the literary influence of Faulkner but I see it as a coincidence: I had simply found material that had to be dealt with in the same way that Faulkner had treated similar material. . . .

What really happened to me in that trip to Aracataca was that I realized that everything that had occurred in my childhood had a literary value that I was only now appreciating. From the moment I wrote Leaf Storm *I realized I wanted to be a writer and that nobody could stop me and that the only thing left for me to do was to be the best writer in the world.*

Gabriel García Márquez

ოჱ

A VERY OLD MAN
WITH ENORMOUS WINGS

– translated by Gregory Rabassa

On the third day of rain they had killed so many crabs inside the house that Pelayo had to cross his drenched courtyard and throw them into the sea, because the newborn child had a temperature all night and they thought it was due to the stench. The world had been sad since Tuesday. Sea and sky were a single ash-gray thing and the sands of the beach, which on March nights glimmered like powdered light, had become a stew of mud and rotten shellfish. The light was so weak at noon that when Pelayo was coming back to the house after throwing away the crabs, it was hard for him to see what it was that was moving and groaning in the rear of the courtyard. He had to go very close to see that it was an old man, a very old man, lying face down in the mud, who, in spite of his tremendous efforts, couldn't get up, impeded by his enormous wings.

Frightened by that nightmare, Pelayo ran to get Elisenda, his wife, who was putting compresses on the sick child, and he took her to the rear of the courtyard. They both looked at the fallen body with mute stupor. He was dressed like a ragpicker. There were only a few faded hairs left on his bald skull and very few teeth in his mouth, and his pitiful condition of a drenched great-grandfather had taken away any sense of grandeur he might have had. His huge buzzard wings, dirty and half-plucked, were forever entangled in the mud. They looked at him so long and so closely that Pelayo and Elisenda very soon overcame their surprise and in the end found him familiar. Then they dared speak to him, and he answered in an incomprehensible dialect with a strong sailor's voice. That was how they skipped over the inconvenience of the wings and quite intelligently concluded that he was a lonely castaway from some foreign ship wrecked by the storm. And yet, they called in a neighbor woman who knew everything about life and death to see him, and all she needed was one look to show them their mistake.

"He's an angel," she told them. "He must have been coming for the child, but the poor fellow is so old that the rain knocked him down."

On the following day everyone knew that a flesh-and-blood angel was held captive in Pelayo's house. Against the judgment of the wise neighbor woman, for whom angels in those times were the fugitive survivors of a celestial conspiracy, they did not have the heart to club him to death. Pelayo watched over him all afternoon from the kitchen, armed with his bailiff's club, and before going to bed he dragged him out of the mud and locked him up with the hens in the wire chicken coop. In the middle of the night, when the rain stopped, Pelayo and Elisenda were still killing crabs. A short time afterward the child woke up without a fever and with a desire to eat. Then they felt magnanimous and decided to put the angel on a raft with fresh water and provisions for three days and leave him to his fate on the high seas. But when they went out into the courtyard with the first light of dawn, they found the whole neighborhood in front of the chicken coop having fun with the angel, without the slightest reverence, tossing him things to eat through the openings in the wire as if he weren't a supernatural creature but a circus animal.

Father Gonzaga arrived before seven o'clock, alarmed at the strange news. By that time onlookers less frivolous than those at dawn had already arrived and they were making all kinds of conjectures concerning the captive's future. The simplest among them thought that he should be named mayor of the world. Others of sterner mind felt that he should be promoted to the rank of five-star general in order to win all wars. Some visionaries hoped that he could be put to stud in order to implant on earth a race of winged wise men who could take charge of the universe. But Father Gonzaga, before becoming a priest, had been a robust woodcutter. Standing by the wire, he reviewed his catechism in an instant and asked them to open the door so that he could take a close look at that pitiful man who looked more like a huge decrepit hen among the fascinated chickens. He was lying in a corner drying his open wings in the sunlight among the fruit peels and breakfast leftovers that the early risers had thrown him. Alien to the impertinences of the world, he only lifted his antiquarian eyes and murmured something in his dialect when Father Gonzaga went into the chicken coop and said good morning to him in Latin. The parish priest had his first suspicion of an impostor when he saw that he did not understand the language of God or know how to greet His ministers. Then he noticed that seen close up he was much too human: he had an unbearable smell of the outdoors, the back side of his wings was strewn with parasites and his main feathers had been mistreated by terrestrial winds, and nothing about him measured up to the proud dignity of angels. Then he came out of the chicken coop and in a brief sermon warned the curious against the risks of being ingenuous. He reminded them that the devil had the bad habit of making use of carnival tricks in order to confuse the unwary. He argued that if wings were not the essential element in determining the difference between a hawk and an airplane, they were even less so in the recognition of angels. Nevertheless, he promised to write a letter to his bishop so that the latter would write to his primate so that the latter would write to the Supreme Pontiff in order to get the final verdict from the highest courts.

His prudence fell on sterile hearts. The news of the captive angel spread with such rapidity that after a few hours the courtyard had the bustle of a marketplace and they had to call in troops with fixed bayonets to disperse the mob that was about to knock the house down. Elisenda, her spine all twisted from sweeping up so much marketplace trash, then got the idea of fencing in the yard and charging five cents admission to see the angel.

The curious came from far away. A traveling carnival arrived with a flying acrobat who buzzed over the crowd several times, but no one paid any attention to him because his wings were not those of an angel but, rather, those of a sidereal[1] bat. The most unfortunate invalids on earth came in search of health: a poor woman who since childhood had been counting her heartbeats and had run out of numbers; a Portuguese man who couldn't sleep because the noise of the stars disturbed him; a sleepwalker who got up at night to undo the things he had done while awake; and many others with less serious ailments. In the midst of that shipwreck disorder that made the earth tremble, Pelayo and Elisenda were happy with fatigue, for in less than a week they had crammed their rooms with money and the line of pilgrims waiting their turn to enter still reached beyond the horizon.

The angel was the only one who took no part in his own act. He spent his time trying to get comfortable in his borrowed nest, befuddled by the hellish heat of the oil lamps and sacramental candles that had been placed along the wire. At first they tried to make him eat some mothballs, which, according to the wisdom of the wise neighbor woman, were the food prescribed for angels. But he turned them down, just as he turned down the papal lunches that the penitents brought him, and they never found out whether it was because he was an angel or because he was an old man that in the end he ate nothing but eggplant mush. His only supernatural virtue

[1] coming from the stars.

seemed to be patience. Especially during the first days, when the hens pecked at him, searching for the stellar parasites that proliferated in his wings, and the cripples pulled out feathers to touch their defective parts with, and even the most merciful threw stones at him, trying to get him to rise so they could see him standing. The only time they succeeded in arousing him was when they burned his side with an iron for branding steers, for he had been motionless for so many hours that they thought he was dead. He awoke with a start, ranting in his hermetic language and with tears in his eyes, and he flapped his wings a couple of times, which brought on a whirlwind of chicken dung and lunar dust and a gale of panic that did not seem to be of this world. Although many thought that his reaction had been one not of rage but of pain, from then on they were careful not to annoy him, because the majority understood that his passivity was not that of a hero taking his ease but that of a cataclysm in repose.

Father Gonzaga held back the crowd's frivolity with formulas of maidservant inspiration while awaiting the arrival of a final judgment on the nature of the captive. But the mail from Rome showed no sense of urgency. They spent their time finding out if the prisoner had a navel, if his dialect had any connection with Aramaic, how many times he could fit on the head of a pin, or whether he wasn't just a Norwegian with wings. Those meager letters might have come and gone until the end of time if a providential event had not put an end to the priest's tribulations.

It so happened that during those days, among so many other carnival attractions, there arrived in town the traveling show of the woman who had been changed into a spider for having disobeyed her parents. The admission to see her was not only less than the admission to see the angel, but people were permitted to ask her all manner of questions about her absurd state and to examine her up and down so that no one would ever doubt the truth of her horror. She was a frightful tarantula the size of a ram and with the head of a sad maiden. What was most heart-rending, however, was not her outlandish shape but the sincere affliction with which she recounted the details of her misfortune. While still practically a child she had sneaked out of her parents' house to go to a dance, and while she was coming back through the woods after having danced all night without permission, a fearful thunderclap rent the sky in two and through the crack came the lightning bolt of brimstone that changed her into a spider. Her only nourishment came from the meatballs that charitable souls chose to toss into her mouth. A spectacle like that, full of so much human truth and with such a fearful lesson, was bound to defeat without even trying that of a haughty angel who scarcely deigned to look at mortals. Besides, the few miracles attributed to the angel showed a certain mental disorder, like the blind man who didn't recover his sight but grew three new teeth, or the paralytic who didn't get to walk but almost won the lottery, and the leper whose sores sprouted sunflowers. Those consolation miracles, which were more like mocking fun, had already ruined the angel's reputation when the woman who had been changed into a spider finally crushed him completely. That was how Father Gonzaga was cured forever of his insomnia and Pelayo's courtyard went back to being as empty as during the time it had rained for three days and crabs walked through the bedrooms.

The owners of the house had no reason to lament. With the money they saved they built a two-story mansion with balconies and gardens and high netting so that crabs wouldn't get in during the winter, and with iron bars on the windows so that angels wouldn't get in. Pelayo also set up a rabbit warren close to town and gave up his job as bailiff for good, and Elisenda bought some satin pumps with high heels and many dresses of iridescent silk, the kind worn on Sunday by the most desirable women in those times. The chicken coop was the only thing that didn't receive any attention. If they washed it down with creolin and burned tears of myrrh inside it every so often, it was not in homage to the angel but to drive away the dungheap stench that still hung everywhere like a ghost and was turning the new house into an old one. At first, when the child learned to walk, they were careful that he not get too close to the chicken coop. But then they began to lose their fears and got used to the smell, and before the child got his second teeth he'd gone inside the chicken coop to play, where the wires were falling apart. The angel was no less standoffish with him than with other mortals, but he tolerated the most ingenious infamies with the patience of a dog who had no illusions. They both came down with chicken pox at the same time. The doctor who took care of the child couldn't resist the temptation to listen to the angel's heart, and he found so much whistling in the heart and so many sounds in his kidneys that it seemed impossible for him to be alive. What surprised him most, however, was the logic of his wings. They seemed so natural on that completely human organism that he couldn't understand why other men didn't have them too.

When the child began school it had been some time since the sun and rain had caused the collapse of the chicken coop. The angel went dragging himself about here and there like a stray dying man. They would drive him out of the bedroom with a broom and a moment later find him in the kitchen. He seemed to be in so many places at the same time that they grew to think that he'd been duplicated, that he was reproducing himself all through the house, and the exasperated and unhinged Elisenda shouted that it was awful living in that hell full of angels. He could scarcely eat and his antiquarian eyes had also become so foggy that he went about bumping into posts. All he had left were the bare cannulae[2] of his last feathers. Pelayo threw a blanket over him and extended him the charity of letting him sleep in the shed, and only then did they notice that he had a temperature at night, and was delirious with the tongue twisters of an old Norwegian. That was one of the few times they became alarmed, for they thought he

---

[2] the tubular pieces by which feathers are attached to a body.

was going to die and not even the wise neighbor woman had been able to tell them what to do with dead angels.

And yet he not only survived his worst winter, but seemed improved with the first sunny days. He remained motionless for several days in the farthest corner of the courtyard, where no one would see him, and at the beginning of December some large, stiff feathers began to grow on his wings, the feathers of a scarecrow, which looked more like another misfortune of decrepitude. But he must have known the reason for those changes, for he was quite careful that no one should notice them, that no one should hear the sea chanteys that he sometimes sang under the stars. One morning Elisenda was cutting some bunches of onions for lunch when a wind that seemed to come from the high seas blew into the kitchen. Then she went to the window and caught the angel in his first attempts at flight. They were so clumsy that his fingernails opened a furrow in the vegetable patch and he was on the point of knocking the shed down with the ungainly flapping that slipped on the light and couldn't get a grip on the air. But he did manage to gain altitude. Elisenda let out a sigh of relief, for herself and for him, when she saw him pass over the last houses, holding himself up in some way with the risky flapping of a senile vulture. She kept watching him even when she was through cutting the onions and she kept on watching until it was no longer possible for her to see him, because then he was no longer an annoyance in her life but an imaginary dot on the horizon of the sea.

[1955]

MILAN KUNDERA (b. 1929) was born in Brno, Czechoslovakia. As a child he intended to become a musician, following the example of his father Ludvík Kundera, a pianist and pupil of the great Czech composer Leoš Jandcek, but in 1948 Kundera decided this was not his true vocation. Instead he studied scriptwriting and directing at the Prague Academy of Music and Dramatic Arts. Four years later he joined the film faculty there. Writing poetry since the age of fourteen, Kundera published his first book in 1953, a volume of verse entitled Man a Broad Garden. Two more poetry collections followed, and a play in 1961, but he felt he discovered his voice as a writer when, at nearly thirty, he wrote the first short stories of the cycle Laughable Loves. "The Hitchhiking Game" is from the second of the three volumes of that cycle, published in 1969.

Like other Czech students of his generation, Kundera had joined the Communist Party — when he was eighteen — but he was expelled from it in 1950, reinstated in 1956, and expelled yet again in 1970, after he made a speech in front of the congress of Czech writers in 1967 advocating greater artistic freedom. This act caused him trouble when the Soviets invaded the country in 1968. He was charged with being a "counterrevolutionary" and forced to leave his teaching job at the Academy of Music and Dramatic Arts. In 1975 he was given an extended travel visa by the Czech government so he could accept a position as professor at the University of Rennes, France, where he continues to live while retaining his Czech citizenship. (As one of his first official acts, France's Socialist President François Mitterand — himself a writer — granted Kundera and several other exiled writers honorary French citizenship in 1981.) Kundera's novels include The Joke (1969), Life Is Elsewhere (1974), and The Farewell Party (1976) — the last two published only in Europe and America, because after he left his native country his works were forbidden to be published there. The Book of Laughter and Forgetting (1980), generally considered his best work, is a collection of interrelated stories, mixing fantasy and nostalgia with brutal realism to create a picture of modern man in a world of alienation and political oppression which victimizes him for no apparent reason.

Kundera has also completed a study of Franz Kafka. He feels that although the drama of politics is often present in his books, his fictional characters are not taking part in any particular politics, but acting in more general realms of humor, irony, and imagination. "It's in this sense that I don't much like the idea of committed literature. For me the only commitment of the novelist ought to be to oppose the ironic wisdom of the novel to ideological simplifications of every sort." Unlike Solzhenitsyn, another dissident writer who lives in the West, Kundera believes that "Ideology is a

*school of intolerance. . . . Today, when politics have become a religion, I
see the novel as one of the last forms of atheism."*

In Philip Roth's introduction to the English edition of Laughable
Loves, he discusses Kundera as a writer so attuned to the harsh role that
contemporary politics has played in his life that he has become intrigued
"by the startling consequences that can flow from playing around." Erotic
play and power are the subjects at the center of Kundera's stories, dramatizing the way in which, as in "The Hitchhiking Game," the most cun-
ningly woven net of sexual intrigue is likely to descend around the plotter.
"Simply by fooling around and indulging their curiosity," Roth notes, "the
lovers find they have managed to deepen responsibility as well as passion. . . . What is so often laughable, in the stories of Kundera's Czechoslovakia, is how grimly serious just about everything turns out to be, jokes and
games and pleasure included; what's laughable is how terribly little there is
to laugh at with any joy."

Milan Kundera

ཀྱ

THE HITCHHIKING GAME

– translated by Suzanne Rappaport

I

The needle on the gas gauge suddenly dipped toward empty and the
young driver of the sports car declared that it was maddening how much gas
the car ate up. "See that we don't run out of gas again," protested the girl
(about twenty-two), and reminded the driver of several places where this
had already happened to them. The young man replied that he wasn't worried, because whatever he went through with her had the charm of adventure for him. The girl objected; whenever they had run out of gas on the
highway it had, she said, always been an adventure only for her. The young
man had hidden and she had had to make ill use of her charms by thumbing a ride and letting herself be driven to the nearest gas station, then
thumbing a ride back with a can of gas. The young man asked the girl
whether the drivers who had given her a ride had been unpleasant, since she
spoke as if her task had been a hardship. She replied (with awkward flirtatiousness) that sometimes they had been *very* pleasant but that it hadn't
done her any good as she had been burdened with the can and had had to
leave them before she could get anything going. "Pig," said the young man.

The girl protested that she wasn't a pig, but that he really was. God knows how many girls stopped him on the highway, when he was driving the car alone! Still driving, the young man put his arm around the girl's shoulders and kissed her gently on the forehead. He knew that she loved him and that she was jealous. Jealousy isn't a pleasant quality, but if it isn't overdone (and if it's combined with modesty), apart from its inconvenience there's even something touching about it. At least that's what the young man thought. Because he was only twenty-eight, it seemed to him that he was old and knew everything that a man could know about women. In the girl sitting beside him he valued precisely what, until now, he had met with least in women: purity.

The needle was already on empty, when to the right the young man caught sight of a sign, announcing that the station was a quarter of a mile ahead. The girl hardly had time to say how relieved she was before the young man was signaling left and driving into a space in front of the pumps. However, he had to stop a little way off, because beside the pumps was a huge gasoline truck with a large metal tank and a bulky hose, which was refilling the pumps. "We'll have to wait," said the young man to the girl and got out of the car. "How long will it take?" he shouted to the man in overalls. "Only a moment," replied the attendant, and the young man said: "I've heard that one before." He wanted to go back and sit in the car, but he saw that the girl had gotten out the other side. "I'll take a little walk in the meantime," she said. "Where to?" the young man asked on purpose, wanting to see the girl's embarrassment. He had known her for a year now but she would still get shy in front of him. He enjoyed her moments of shyness, partly because they distinguished her from the women he'd met before, partly because he was aware of the law of universal transience, which made even his girl's shyness a precious thing to him.

II

The girl really didn't like it when during the trip (the young man would drive for several hours without stopping) she had to ask him to stop for a moment somewhere near a clump of trees. She always got angry when, with feigned surprise, he asked her why he should stop. She knew that her shyness was ridiculous and old-fashioned. Many times at work she had noticed that they laughed at her on account of it and deliberately provoked her. She always got shy in advance at the thought of how she was going to get shy. She often longed to feel free and easy about her body, the way most of the women around her did. She had even invented a special course in self-persuasion: she would repeat to herself that at birth every human being received one out of the millions of available bodies, as one would receive an allotted room out of the millions of rooms in an enormous hotel. Consequently, the body was fortuitous and impersonal, it was only a ready-made, borrowed thing. She would repeat this to herself in different ways, but she could never manage to feel it. This mind-body dualism was alien to her. She was too much one with her body; that is why she always felt such anxiety about it.

She experienced this same anxiety even in her relations with the young man, whom she had known for a year and with whom she was happy, perhaps because he never separated her body from her soul and she could live with him *wholly*. In this unity there was happiness, but right behind the happiness lurked suspicion, and the girl was full of that. For instance, it often occurred to her that the other women (those who weren't anxious) were more attractive and more seductive and that the young man, who did not conceal the fact that he knew this kind of woman well, would someday leave her for a woman like that. (True, the young man declared that he'd had enough of them to last his whole life, but she knew that he was still much younger than he thought.) She wanted him to be completely hers and she to be completely his, but it often seemed to her that the more she tried to give him everything, the more she denied him something: the very thing that a light and superficial love or a flirtation gives to a person. It worried her that she was not able to combine seriousness with lightheartedness.

But now she wasn't worrying and any such thoughts were far from her mind. She felt good. It was the first day of their vacation (of their two-week vacation, about which she had been dreaming for a whole year), the sky was blue (the whole year she had been worrying about whether the sky would really be blue), and he was beside her. At his, "Where to?" she blushed, and left the car without a word. She walked around the gas station, which was situated beside the highway in total isolation, surrounded by fields. About a hundred yards away (in the direction in which they were traveling), a wood began. She set off for it, vanished behind a little bush, and gave herself up to her good mood. (In solitude it was possible for her to get the greatest enjoyment from the presence of the man she loved. If his presence had been continuous, it would have kept on disappearing. Only when alone was she able to *hold on* to it.)

When she came out of the wood onto the highway, the gas station was visible. The large gasoline truck was already pulling out and the sports car moved forward toward the red turret of the pump. The girl walked on along the highway and only at times looked back to see if the sports car was coming. At last she caught sight of it. She stopped and began to wave at it like a hitchhiker waving at a stranger's car. The sports car slowed down and stopped close to the girl. The young man leaned toward the window, rolled it down, smiled, and asked, "Where are you headed, miss?" "Are you going to Bystritsa?" asked the girl, smiling flirtatiously at him. "Yes, please get in," said the young man, opening the door. The girl got in and the car took off.

III

The young man was always glad when his girl friend was gay. This didn't happen too often; she had a quite tiresome job in an unpleasant environment, many hours of overtime without compensatory leisure and, at home, a sick mother. So she often felt tired. She didn't have either particularly good nerves or self-confidence and easily fell into a state of anxiety and fear. For this reason he welcomed every manifestation of her gaiety with the tender solicitude of a foster parent. He smiled at her and said: "I'm lucky today. I've been driving for five years, but I've never given a ride to such a pretty hitchhiker."

The girl was grateful to the young man for every bit of flattery; she wanted to linger for a moment in its warmth and so she said, "You're very good at lying."

"Do I look like a liar?"

"You look like you enjoy lying to women," said the girl, and into her words there crept unawares a touch of the old anxiety, because she really did believe that her young man enjoyed lying to women.

The girl's jealousy often irritated the young man, but this time he could easily overlook it for, after all, her words didn't apply to him but to the unknown driver. And so he just casually inquired, "Does it bother you?"

"If I were going with you, then it would bother me," said the girl and her words contained a subtle, instructive message for the young man; but the end of her sentence applied only to the unknown driver, "but I don't know you, so it doesn't bother me."

"Things about her own man always bother a woman more than things about a stranger" (this was now the young man's subtle, instructive message to the girl), "so seeing that we are strangers, we could get on well together."

The girl purposely didn't want to understand the implied meaning of his message, so she now addressed the unknown driver exclusively:

"What does it matter, since we'll part company in a little while?"

"Why?" asked the young man.

"Well, I'm getting out at Bystritsa."

"And what if I get out with you?"

At those words the girl looked up at him and found that he looked exactly as she imagined him in her most agonizing hours of jealousy. She was alarmed at how he was flattering her and flirting with her (an unknown hitchhiker), and *how becoming it was to him.* Therefore she responded with defiant provocativeness, "What would *you* do with me, I wonder?"

"I wouldn't have to think too hard about what to do with such a beautiful woman," said the young man gallantly and at this moment he was once again speaking far more to his own girl than to the figure of the hitchhiker.

But this flattering sentence made the girl feel as if she had caught him at something, as if she had wheedled a confession out of him with a fraudulent trick. She felt toward him a brief flash of intense hatred and said, "Aren't you rather too sure of yourself?"

The young man looked at the girl. Her defiant face appeared to him to be completely convulsed. He felt sorry for her and longed for her usual, familiar expression (which he used to call childish and simple). He leaned toward her, put his arm around her shoulders, and softly spoke the name with which he usually addressed her and with which he now wanted to stop the game.

But the girl released herself and said: "You're going a bit too fast!"

At this rebuff the young man said: "Excuse me, miss," and looked silently in front of him at the highway.

IV

The girl's pitiful jealousy, however, left her as quickly as it had come over her. After all, she was sensible and knew perfectly well that all this was merely a game. Now it even struck her as a little ridiculous that she had repulsed her man out of a jealous rage. It wouldn't be pleasant for her if he found out why she had done it. Fortunately women have the miraculous ability to change the meaning of their actions after the event. Using this ability, she decided that she had repulsed him not out of anger but so that she could go on with the game, which, with its whimsicality, so well suited the first day of their vacation.

So again she was the hitchhiker, who had just repulsed the overenterprising driver, but only so as to slow down his conquest and make it more exciting. She half turned toward the young man and said caressingly:

"I didn't mean to offend you, mister!"

"Excuse me, I won't touch you again," said the young man.

He was furious with the girl for not listening to him and refusing to be herself when that was what he wanted. And since the girl insisted on continuing in her role, he transferred his anger to the unknown hitchhiker whom she was portraying. And all at once he discovered the character of his own part: he stopped making the gallant remarks with which he had wanted to flatter his girl in a roundabout way, and began to play the tough guy who treats women to the coarser aspects of his masculinity: willfulness, sarcasm, self-assurance.

This role was a complete contradiction of the young man's habitually solicitous approach to the girl. True, before he had met her, he had in fact behaved roughly rather than gently toward women. But he had never resembled a heartless tough guy, because he had never demonstrated either a particularly strong will or ruthlessness. However, if he did not resemble such a man, nonetheless he had *longed* to at one time. Of course it was a quite naive desire, but there it was. Childish desires withstand all the snares of the adult mind and often survive into ripe old age. And this childish desire quickly took advantage of the opportunity to embody itself in the proffered role.

The young man's sarcastic reserve suited the girl very well — it freed her from herself. For she herself was, above all, the epitome of jealousy. The moment she stopped seeing the gallantly seductive young man beside her and saw only his inaccessible face, her jealousy subsided. The girl could forget herself and give herself up to her role.

Her role? What was her role? It was a role out of trashy literature. The hitchhiker stopped the car not to get a ride, but to seduce the man who was driving the car. She was an artful seductress, cleverly knowing how to use her charms. The girl slipped into this silly, romantic part with an ease that astonished her and held her spellbound.

V

There was nothing the young man missed in his life more than light-heartedness. The main road of his life was drawn with implacable precision. His job didn't use up merely eight hours a day, it also infiltrated the remaining time with the compulsory boredom of meetings and home study, and, by means of the attentiveness of his countless male and female colleagues, it infiltrated the wretchedly little time he had left for his private life as well. This private life never remained secret and sometimes even became the subject of gossip and public discussion. Even two weeks' vacation didn't give him a feeling of liberation and adventure; the gray shadow of precise planning lay even here. The scarcity of summer accommodations in our country compelled him to book a room in the Tatras six months in advance, and since for that he needed a recommendation from his office, its omnipresent brain thus did not cease knowing about him even for an instant.

He had become reconciled to all this, yet all the same from time to time the terrible thought of the straight road would overcome him — a road along which he was being pursued, where he was visible to everyone, and from which he could not turn aside. At this moment that thought returned to him. Through an odd and brief conjunction of ideas the figurative road became identified with the real highway along which he was driving — and this led him suddenly to do a crazy thing.

"Where did you say you wanted to go?" he asked the girl.

"To Banska Bystritsa," she replied.

"And what are you going to do there?"

"I have a date there."

"Who with?"

"With a certain gentleman."

The car was just coming to a large crossroads. The driver slowed down so he could read the road signs, then turned off to the right.

"What will happen if you don't arrive for that date?"

"It would be your fault and you would have to take care of me."

"You obviously didn't notice that I turned off in the direction of Nove Zamky."

"Is that true? You've gone crazy!"

"Don't be afraid, I'll take care of you," said the young man.

So they drove and chatted thus — the driver and the hitchhiker who did not know each other.

The game all at once went into a higher gear. The sports car was moving away not only from the imaginary goal of Banska Bystritsa, but also from the real goal, toward which it had been heading in the morning: the Tatras and the room that had been booked. Fiction was suddenly making an assault upon real life. The young man was moving away from himself and from the implacable straight road, from which he had never strayed until now.

"But you said you were going to the Low Tatras!" The girl was surprised.

"I am going, miss, wherever I feel like going. I'm a free man and I do what I want and what it pleases me to do."

VI

When they drove into Nove Zamky it was already getting dark.

The young man had never been here before and it took him a while to orient himself. Several times he stopped the car and asked the passersby directions to the hotel. Several streets had been dug up, so that the drive to the hotel, even though it was quite close by (as all those who had been asked asserted), necessitated so many detours and roundabout routes that it was almost a quarter of an hour before they finally stopped in front of it. The hotel looked unprepossessing, but it was the only one in town and the young man didn't feel like driving on. So he said to the girl, "Wait here," and got out of the car.

Out of the car he was, of course, himself again. And it was upsetting for him to find himself in the evening somewhere completely different from his intended destination — the more so because no one had forced him to do it and as a matter of fact he hadn't even really wanted to. He blamed himself for this piece of folly, but then became reconciled to it. The room in the Tatras could wait until tomorrow and it wouldn't do any harm if they celebrated the first day of their vacation with something unexpected.

He walked through the restaurant — smoky, noisy, and crowded — and asked for the reception desk. They sent him to the back of the lobby near the staircase, where behind a glass panel a superannuated blonde was sitting beneath a board full of keys. With difficulty, he obtained the key to the only room left.

The girl, when she found herself alone, also threw off her role. She didn't feel ill-humored, though, at finding herself in an unexpected town. She was so devoted to the young man that she never had doubts about anything he did, and confidently entrusted every moment of her life to him. On the other hand the idea once again popped into her mind that perhaps — just as she was now doing — other women had waited for her man in his car, those women whom he met on business trips. But surprisingly enough this idea didn't upset her at all now. In fact, she smiled at the thought of how nice it was that today she was this other woman, this irresponsible, indecent other woman, one of those women of whom she was so jealous. It seemed to her that she was cutting them all out, that she had learned how to use their weapons; how to give the young man what until now she had not known how to give him: lightheartedness, shamelessness, and dissoluteness. A curious feeling of satisfaction filled her, because she alone had the ability to be all women and in this way (she alone) could completely captivate her lover and hold his interest.

The young man opened the car door and led the girl into the restaurant. Amid the din, the dirt, and the smoke he found a single, unoccupied table in a corner.

VII

"So how are you going to take care of me now?" asked the girl provocatively.

"What would you like for an aperitif?"

The girl wasn't too fond of alcohol, still she drank a little wine and liked vermouth fairly well. Now, however, she purposely said: "Vodka."

"Fine," said the young man. "I hope you won't get drunk on me."

"And if I do?" said the girl.

The young man did not reply but called over a waiter and ordered two vodkas and two steak dinners. In a moment the waiter brought a tray with two small glasses and placed it in front of them.

The man raised his glass, "To you!"

"Can't you think of a wittier toast?"

Something was beginning to irritate him about the girl's game. Now sitting face to face with her, he realized that it wasn't just the *words* which were turning her into a stranger, but that her *whole persona* had changed, the movements of her body and her facial expression, and that she unpalatably and faithfully resembled that type of woman whom he knew so well and for whom he felt some aversion.

And so (holding his glass in his raised hand), he corrected his toast: "O.K., then I won't drink to you, but to your kind, in which are combined so successfully the better qualities of the animal and the worse aspects of the human being."

"By 'kind' do you mean all women?" asked the girl.

"No, I mean only those who are like you."

"Anyway it doesn't seem very witty to me to compare a woman with an animal."

"O.K.," the young man was still holding his glass aloft, "then I won't drink to your kind, but to your soul. Agreed? To your soul, which lights up when it descends from your head into your belly, and which goes out when it rises back up to your head."

The girl raised her glass. "O.K., to my soul, which descends into my belly."

"I'll correct myself once more," said the young man. "To your belly, into which your soul descends."

"To my belly," said the girl, and her belly (now that they had named it specifically), as it were, responded to the call; she felt every inch of it.

Then the waiter brought their steaks and the young man ordered them another vodka and some water (this time they drank to the girl's breasts), and the conversation continued in this peculiar, frivolous tone. It irritated the young man more and more how *well able* the girl was to become the lascivious miss. If she was able to do it so well, he thought, it meant that she really *was* like that. After all, no alien soul had entered into her from somewhere in space. What she was acting now was she herself; perhaps it was the part of her being which had formerly been locked up and which the pretext of the game had let out of its cage. Perhaps the girl supposed that by means of the game she was *disowning* herself, but wasn't it the other way around? Wasn't she becoming herself only through the game? Wasn't she freeing herself through the game? No, opposite him was not sitting a strange woman in his girl's body; it was his girl, herself, no one else. He looked at her and felt growing aversion toward her.

However, it was not only aversion. The more the girl withdrew from him *psychically*, the more he longed for her *physically*. The alien quality of her soul drew attention to her body, yes, as a matter of fact it turned her body into a body for *him* as if until now it had existed for the young man hidden within clouds of compassion, tenderness, concern, love, and emotion, as if it had been lost in these clouds (yes, as if this body had been lost!). It seemed to the young man that today he was seeing his girl's body for the first time.

After her third vodka and soda the girl got up and said flirtatiously, "Excuse me."

The young man said, "May I ask you where you are going, miss?"

"To piss, if you'll permit me," said the girl and walked off between the tables back toward the plush screen.

VIII

She was pleased with the way she had astounded the young man with this word, which — in spite of all its innocence — he had never heard from her. Nothing seemed to her truer to the character of the woman she was playing than this flirtatious emphasis placed on the word in question. Yes, she was pleased, she was in the best of moods. The game captivated her. It allowed her to feel what she had not felt till now: a *feeling* of *happy-go-lucky irresponsibility.*

She, who was always uneasy in advance about her every next step, suddenly felt completely relaxed. The alien life in which she had become involved was a life without shame, without biographical specifications, without past or future, without obligations. It was a life that was extraordinarily free. The girl, as a hitchhiker, could do anything, *everything was permitted her.* She could say, do, and feel whatever she liked.

She walked through the room and was aware that people were watching her from all the tables. It was a new sensation, one she didn't recognize: *indecent joy caused by her body.* Until now she had never been able to get rid of the fourteen-year-old girl within herself who was ashamed of her breasts and had the disagreeable feeling that she was indecent, because they stuck out from her body and were visible. Even though she was proud of being pretty and having a good figure, this feeling of pride was always immediately curtailed by shame. She rightly suspected that feminine beauty functioned above all as sexual provocation and she found this distasteful. She longed for her body to relate only to the man she loved. When men stared at her breasts in the street it seemed to her that they were invading a piece of her most secret privacy which should belong only to herself and her lover. But now she was the hitchhiker, the woman without a destiny. In this role she was relieved of the tender bonds of her love and began to be intensely aware of her body. And her body became more aroused the more alien the eyes watching it.

She was walking past the last table when an intoxicated man, wanting to show off his worldliness, addressed her in French: "*Combien, mademoiselle?*"

The girl understood. She thrust out her breasts and fully experienced every movement of her hips, then disappeared behind the screen.

IX

It was a curious game. This curiousness was evidenced, for example, in the fact that the young man, even though he himself was playing the unknown driver remarkably well, did not for a moment stop seeing his girl in the hitchhiker. And it was precisely this that was tormenting. He saw his girl seducing a strange man, and had the bitter privilege of being present, of seeing at close quarters how she looked and of hearing what she said when she was cheating on him (when she had cheated on him, when she would cheat on him). He had the paradoxical honor of being himself the pretext for her unfaithfulness.

This was all the worse because he worshipped rather than loved her. It had always seemed to him that her inward nature was *real* only within the bounds of fidelity and purity, and that beyond these bounds it simply didn't exist. Beyond these bounds she would cease to be herself, as water ceases to be water beyond the boiling point. When he now saw her crossing this horrifying boundary with nonchalant elegance, he was filled with anger.

The girl came back from the rest room and complained: "A guy over there asked me: *Combien, mademoiselle?*"

"You shouldn't be surprised," said the young man, "after all, you look like a whore."

"Do you know that it doesn't bother me in the least?"

"Then you should go with the gentleman!"

"But I have you."

"You can go with him after me. Go and work out something with him."

"I don't find him attractive."

"But in principle you have nothing against it, having several men in one night."

"Why not, if they're good-looking."

"Do you prefer them one after the other or at the same time?"

"Either way," said the girl.

The conversation was proceeding to still greater extremes of rudeness; it shocked the girl slightly but she couldn't protest. Even in a game there lurks a lack of freedom; even a game is a trap for the players. If this had not been a game and they had really been two strangers, the hitchhiker could long ago have taken offense and left. But there's no escape from a game. A team cannot flee from the playing field before the end of the match, chess pieces cannot desert the chessboard: the boundaries of the playing field are fixed. The girl knew that she had to accept whatever form the game might take, just because it was a game. She knew that the more extreme the game became, the more it would be a game and the more obediently she would have to play it. And it was futile to evoke good sense and warn her dazed soul that she must keep her distance from the game and not take it seriously. Just because it was only a game her soul was not afraid, did not oppose the game, and narcotically sank deeper into it.

The young man called the waiter and paid. Then he got up and said to the girl, "We're going."

"Where to?" The girl feigned surprise.

"Don't ask, just come on," said the young man.

"What sort of way is that to talk to me?"

"The way I talk to whores," said the young man.

X

They went up the badly lit staircase. On the landing below the second floor a group of intoxicated men was standing near the rest room. The young man caught hold of the girl from behind so that he was holding her breast with his hand. The men by the rest room saw this and began to call out. The girl wanted to break away, but the young man yelled at her: "Keep still!" The men greeted this with general ribaldry and addressed several dirty remarks to the girl. The young man and the girl reached the second floor. He opened the door of their room and switched on the light.

It was a narrow room with two beds, a small table, a chair, and a washbasin. The young man locked the door and turned to the girl. She was standing facing him in a defiant pose with insolent sensuality in her eyes. He looked at her and tried to discover behind her lascivious expression the familiar features which he loved tenderly. It was as if he were looking at two images through the same lens, at two images superimposed one upon the other with the one showing through the other. These two images showing through each other were telling him that *everything* was in the girl, that her soul was terrifyingly amorphous, that it held faithfulness and unfaithfulness, treachery and innocence, flirtatiousness and chastity. This disorderly jumble seemed disgusting to him, like the variety to be found in a pile of garbage. Both images continued to show through each other and the young man understood that the girl differed only on the surface from other women, but deep down was the same as they: full of all possible thoughts, feelings, and vices, which justified all his secret misgivings and fits of jealousy. The impression that certain outlines delineated her as an individual was only a delusion to which the other person, the one who was looking, was subject — namely himself. It seemed to him that the girl he loved was a creation of his desire, his thoughts, and his faith and that the *real* girl now standing in front of him was hopelessly alien, hopelessly *ambiguous*. He hated her.

"What are you waiting for? Strip," he said.

The girl flirtatiously bent her head and said, "Is it necessary?"

The tone in which she said this seemed to him very familiar; it seemed to him that once long ago some other woman had said this to him, only he no longer knew which one. He longed to humiliate her. Not the hitchhiker, but his own girl. The game merged with life. The game of humiliating the hitchhiker became only a pretext for humiliating his girl. The young man had forgotten that he was playing a game. He simply hated the woman standing in front of him. He stared at her and took a fifty-crown bill from his wallet. He offered it to the girl. "Is that enough?"

The girl took the fifty crowns and said: "You don't think I'm worth much."

The young man said: "You aren't worth more."

The girl nestled up against the young man. "You can't get around me like that! You must try a different approach, you must work a little!"

She put her arms around him and moved her mouth toward his. He put his fingers on her mouth and gently pushed her away. He said: "I only kiss women I love."

"And you don't love me?"

"No."

"Whom do you love?"

"What's that got to do with you? Strip!"

XI

She had never undressed like this before. The shyness, the feeling of inner panic, the dizziness, all that she had always felt when undressing in front of the young man (and she couldn't hide in the darkness), all this was gone. She was standing in front of him self-confident, insolent, bathed in light, and astonished at where she had all of a sudden discovered the gestures, heretofore unknown to her, of a slow, provocative striptease. She took in his glances, slipping off each piece of clothing with a caressing movement and enjoying each individual stage of this exposure.

But then suddenly she was standing in front of him completely naked and at this moment it flashed through her head that now the whole game would end, that, since she had stripped off her clothes, she had also stripped away her dissimulation, and that being naked meant that she was now herself and the young man ought to come up to her now and make a gesture with which he would wipe out everything and after which would follow only their most intimate love-making. So she stood naked in front of the young man and at this moment stopped playing the game. She felt embarrassed and on her face appeared the smile, which really belonged to her — a shy and confused smile.

But the young man didn't come to her and didn't end the game. He didn't notice the familiar smile. He saw before him only the beautiful, alien body of his own girl, whom he hated. Hatred cleansed his sensuality of any sentimental coating. She wanted to come to him, but he said: "Stay where you are, I want to have a good look at you." Now he longed only to treat her like a whore. But the young man had never had a whore and the ideas he had about them came from literature and hearsay. So he turned to these ideas and the first thing he recalled was the image of a woman in black underwear (and black stockings) dancing on the shiny top of a piano. In the little hotel room there was no piano, there was only a small table covered with a linen cloth leaning against the wall. He ordered the girl to climb up on it. The girl made a pleading gesture, but the young man said, "You've been paid."

When she saw the look of unshakable obsession in the young man's eyes, she tried to go on with the game, even though she no longer could and no longer knew how. With tears in her eyes she climbed onto the table. The top was scarcely three feet square and one leg was a little bit shorter than the others so that standing on it the girl felt unsteady.

But the young man was pleased with the naked figure, now towering above him, and the girl's shy insecurity merely inflamed his imperiousness. He wanted to see her body in all positions and from all sides, as he imagined other men had seen it and would see it. He was vulgar and lascivious. He used words that she had never heard from him in her life. She wanted to refuse, she wanted to be released from the game. She called him by his first name, but he immediately yelled at her that she had no right to address him so intimately. And so eventually in confusion and on the verge of tears, she obeyed, she bent forward and squatted according to the young man's wishes, saluted, and then wiggled her hips as she did the Twist for him. During a slightly more violent movement, when the cloth slipped beneath her feet and she nearly fell, the young man caught her and dragged her to the bed.

He had intercourse with her. She was glad that at least now finally the unfortunate game would end and they would again be the two people they had been before and would love each other. She wanted to press her mouth against his. But the young man pushed her head away and repeated that he only kissed women he loved. She burst into loud sobs. But she wasn't even allowed to cry, because the young man's furious passion gradually won over her body, which then silenced the complaint of her soul. On the bed there were soon two bodies in perfect harmony, two sensual bodies, alien to each other. This was exactly what the girl had most dreaded all her life and had scrupulously avoided till now: love-making without emotion or love. She knew that she had crossed the forbidden boundary, but she proceeded across it without objections and as a full participant — only somewhere, far off in a corner of her consciousness, did she feel horror at the thought that she had never known such pleasure, never so much pleasure as at this moment — beyond that boundary.

XII

Then it was all over. The young man got up off the girl and, reaching out for the long cord hanging over the bed, switched off the light. He didn't want to see the girl's face. He knew that the game was over, but didn't feel like returning to their customary relationship. He feared this return. He lay beside the girl in the dark in such a way that their bodies would not touch.

After a moment he heard her sobbing quietly. The girl's hand diffidently, childishly touched his. It touched, withdrew, then touched again, and then a pleading, sobbing voice broke the silence, calling him by his name and saying, "I am me, I am me. . . ."

The young man was silent, he didn't move, and he was aware of the sad emptiness of the girl's assertion, in which the unknown was defined in terms of the same unknown quantity.

And the girl soon passed from sobbing to loud crying and went on endlessly repeating this pitiful tautology: "I am me, I am me, I am me. . . ."

The young man began to call compassion to his aid (he had to call it from afar, because it was nowhere near at hand), so as to be able to calm the girl. There were still thirteen days' vacation before them.

[1969]

JOHN BARTH (b. 1930) was born in Cambridge, Maryland, on the Eastern Shore of the Chesapeake Bay. He has an older brother and a twin sister. He regards being born a twin as influential in his development as a writer. Having an "established sidekick" from birth, he has written, "one might reasonably therefore expect a twin who becomes a storyteller never to take language for granted; to be ever at it, tinkering, foregrounding it, perhaps unnaturally conscious of it. Language is for relating to the Others." Music was Barth's first vocation. He was a student of orchestration for a year at the Juilliard School in New York City before he enrolled as a journalism major on a scholarship at Johns Hopkins University, earning his B.A. in 1951 and his M.A. in 1952. Barth's job as a book filer in the university library stacks developed his taste for fiction: "I was permanently impressed with the size of literature and its wild variety; likewise, as I explored the larger geography of the stacks, with the variety of temperaments, histories, and circumstances from which came the literature I came to love." In his writing class as an undergraduate he began but did not finish a cycle of 100 stories about Dorchester County, Maryland. He has said that his "affair with Scheherazade is an old and continuing one." Scheherazade — the storyteller in Tales of an Arabian Night, and a character Barth himself called on in the three long stories that make up his book Chimera (1972) — can be taken as a figure for "the estate of the fictioner in general and the particular endeavors and aspirations of this one, at least, who can wish for nothing better than to spin like the vizier's excellent daughter, through what nights remain to him tales within tales within tales."

In 1953 Barth joined the faculty of Pennsylvania State University as an instructor in English. He began to publish his novels a few years later. The Floating Opera (1956) and The End of the Road (1958) are conventional in form and language, but The Sot-Weed Factor (1960) and Giles Goat-Boy (1966) are very long, experimental comic novels, indebted to the fiction of Borges and Nabokov, which reviewers praised for their display of erudition and bawdy wit. His later novels include Letters (1979) and Sabbatical: A Romance (1982). Barth's talent for parody is evident in all his works. "At heart I'm an arranger still, whose chiefest literary pleasure is to take a received melody — an old narrative poem, a classical myth, a shopworn literary convention, a shard of my experience . . . and, improvising like a jazzman within its constraints, reorchestrate it to present purpose."

Barth has published only one book of short stories so far, Lost in the Funhouse (1968), subtitled Fiction for Print, Tape, Live Voice. It was influenced by his friendships with the philosopher Marshall McLuhan and the scholar and critic Leslie Fiedler, formed after he began to teach at the State University of New York at Buffalo in 1965. The title story, "Lost in

1020

the Funhouse," like the other short pieces in the collection, suggests that Barth has lost faith in fiction, and instead is self-consciously concerned with what happens when a writer writes, and what happens when a reader reads — "the metaphysical plight of imagination engaging with imagination." As John Updike observed, Barth "hit the floor of nihilism hard and returns to us covered with coal dust. . . . [He] seems to me a very strong-minded and inventive and powerful voice from another planet."

John Barth

ಎಲ

LOST IN THE FUNHOUSE

For whom is the funhouse fun? Perhaps for lovers. For Ambrose it is *a place of fear and confusion.* He has come to the seashore with his family for the holiday, *the occasion of their visit is Independence Day, the most important secular holiday of the United States of America.* A single straight underline is the manuscript mark for italic type, *which in turn* is the printed equivalent to oral emphasis of words and phrases as well as the customary type for titles of complete works, not to mention. Italics are also employed, in fiction stories especially, for "outside," intrusive, or artificial voices, such as radio announcements, the texts of telegrams and newspaper articles, et cetera. They should be used *sparingly.* If passages originally in roman type are italicized by someone repeating them, it's customary to acknowledge the fact. *Italics mine.*

Ambrose was "at that awkward age." His voice came out high-pitched as a child's if he let himself get carried away; to be on the safe side, therefore, he moved and spoke with *deliberate calm* and *adult gravity.* Talking soberly of unimportant or irrelevant matters and listening consciously to the sound of your own voice are useful habits for maintaining control in this difficult interval. *En route* to Ocean City he sat in the back seat of the family car with his brother Peter, age fifteen, and Magda G———, age fourteen, a pretty girl and exquisite young lady, who lived not far from them on B——— Street in the town of D———, Maryland. Initials, blanks, or both were often substituted for proper names in nineteenth-century fiction to enhance the illusion of reality. It is as if the author felt it necessary to delete the names for reasons of tact or legal liability. Interestingly, as with other aspects of realism, it is an *illusion* that is being enhanced, by purely artificial means. Is it likely, does it violate the principle of verisimilitude, that a thirteen-year-old boy could make such a sophisticated observation? A girl of fourteen is *the psychological coeval* of a boy of fifteen or sixteen; a thirteen-year-old boy, therefore, even one precocious in some other respects, might be three years *her emotional junior*.

Thrice a year — on Memorial, Independence, and Labor Days — the family visits Ocean City for the afternoon and evening. When Ambrose and Peter's father was their age, the excursion was made by train, as mentioned in the novel *The 42nd Parallel* by John Dos Passos. Many families from the same neighborhood used to travel together, with dependent relatives and often with Negro servants; schoolfuls of children swarmed through the railway cars; everyone shared everyone else's Maryland fried chicken, Virginia ham, deviled eggs, potato salad, beaten biscuits, iced tea. Nowadays (that is, in 19—, the year of our story) the journey is made by automobile — more comfortably and quickly though without the extra fun though without the *camaraderie* of a general excursion. It's all part of the deterioration of American life, their father declares; Uncle Karl supposes that when the boys take *their* families to Ocean City for the holidays they'll fly in Autogiros. Their mother, sitting in the middle of the front seat like Magda in the second, only with her arms on the seat-back behind the men's shoulders, wouldn't want the good old days back again, the steaming trains and stuffy long dresses; on the other hand she can do without Autogiros, too, if she has to become a grandmother to fly in them.

Description of physical appearance and mannerisms is one of several standard methods of characterization used by writers of fiction. It is also important to "keep the senses operating"; when a detail from one of the five senses, say visual, is "crossed" with a detail from another, say auditory, the reader's imagination is oriented to the scene, perhaps unconsciously. This procedure may be compared to the way surveyors and navigators determine their positions by two or more compass bearings, a process known as triangulation. The brown hair on Ambrose's mother's forearms gleamed in the sun like. Though right-handed, she took her left arm from the seat-back to press the dashboard cigar lighter for Uncle Karl. When the glass bead in its handle glowed red, the lighter was ready for use. The smell of Uncle Karl's cigar smoke reminded one of. The fragrance of the ocean came strong to the picnic ground where they always stopped for lunch, two miles inland from Ocean City. Having to pause for a full hour almost within sound of the breakers was difficult for Peter and Ambrose when they were younger; even at their present age it was not easy to keep their anticipation, *stimulated by the briny spume*, from turning into short temper. The Irish author James Joyce, in his unusual novel entitled *Ulysses*, now available in this country, uses the adjectives *snot-green* and *scrotum-tightening* to describe the sea. Visual, auditory, tactile, olfactory, gustatory. Peter and Ambrose's father, while steering their black 1936 LaSalle sedan with one hand, could with the other remove the first cigarette from a white pack of Lucky Strikes and, more remarkably, light it with a match forefingered from its book and thumbed against the flint paper without being detached. The matchbook cover merely advertised U.S. War Bonds and Stamps. A fine metaphor, simile, or other figure of speech, in addition to its obvious "first-order" relevance to the thing it describes, will be seen upon reflection to have a second order of significance: it may be drawn from the *milieu* of the action, for example, or be particularly appropriate to the sensibility of the narrator, even hinting to the reader things of which the narrator is unaware; or it may cast further and subtler lights upon the things it describes, sometimes ironically qualifying the more evident sense of the comparison.

To say that Ambrose's and Peter's mother was *pretty* is to accomplish nothing; the reader may acknowledge the proposition, but his imagination is not engaged. Besides, Magda was also pretty, yet in an altogether different way. Although she lived on B—— Street she had very good manners and did better than average in school. Her figure was very well developed for her age. Her right hand lay casually on the plush upholstery of the seat, very near Ambrose's left leg, on which his own hand rested. The space between their legs, between her right and his left leg, was out of the line of sight of anyone sitting on the other side of Magda, as well as anyone glancing into the rear-view mirror. Uncle Karl's face resembled Peter's — rather, vice versa. Both had dark hair and eyes, short husky statures, deep voices. Magda's left hand was probably in a similar position on her left side. The boys' father is difficult to describe; no particular feature of his appearance or manner stood out. He wore glasses and was principal of a T—— County grade school. Uncle Karl was a masonry contractor.

Although Peter must have known as well as Ambrose that the latter, because of his position in the car, would be first to see the electrical towers of the power plant at V——, the halfway point of their trip, he leaned forward and slightly toward the center of the car and pretended to be looking for them through the flat pinewoods and tuckahoe creeks along the highway. For as long as the boys could remember, "looking for the Towers" had been a feature of the first half of their excursions to Ocean City, "looking for the standpipe" of the second. Though the game was childish, their mother preserved the tradition of rewarding the first to see the Towers with a candy-bar or piece of fruit. She insisted now that Magda play the game; the prize, she said, was "something hard to get nowadays." Ambrose decided not to join in; he sat far back in his seat. Magda, like Peter, leaned forward. Two sets of straps were discernible through the shoulders of her sun dress; the inside right one, a brassiere-strap, was fastened or shortened with a small safety pin. The right armpit of her dress, presumably the left as well, was damp with perspiration. The simple strategy for being first to espy the Towers, which Ambrose had understood by the age of four, was to sit on the right-hand side of the car. Whoever sat there, however, had also to put up with the worst of the sun, and so Ambrose, without mentioning the matter, chose sometimes the one and sometimes the other. Not impossibly Peter had never caught on to the trick, or thought that his brother hadn't simply because Ambrose on occasion preferred shade to a Baby Ruth or tangerine.

The shade-sun situation didn't apply to the front seat, owning to the windshield; if anything the driver got more sun, since the person on the passenger side not only was shadowed below by the door and dashboard but might swing down his sunvisor all the way too.

"Is that them?" Magda asked. Ambrose's mother teased the boys for letting Magda win, insinuating that "somebody [had] a girlfriend." Peter and Ambrose's father reached a long thin arm across their mother to butt his cigarette in the dashboard ashtray, under the lighter. The prize this time for seeing the Towers first was a banana. Their mother bestowed it after chiding their father for wasting a half-smoked cigarette when everything was so scarce. Magda, to take the prize, moved her hand from so near Ambrose's that he could have touched it as though accidentally. She offered to share the prize, things like that were so hard to find; but everyone insisted it was hers alone. Ambrose's mother sang an iambic trimeter couplet from a popular song, femininely rhymed:

> "What's good is in the Army;
> What's left will never harm me."

Uncle Karl tapped his cigar ash out the ventilator window; some particles were sucked by the slipstream back into the car through the rear window on the passenger side. Magda demonstrated her ability to hold a banana in one hand and peel it with her teeth. She still sat forward; Ambrose pushed his glasses back onto the bridge of his nose with his left hand, which he then negligently let fall to the seat cushion immediately behind her. He even permitted the single hair, gold, on the second joint of his thumb to brush the fabric of her skirt. Should she have sat back at that instant, his hand would have been caught under her.

Plush upholstery prickles uncomfortably through gabardine slacks in the July sun. The function of the *beginning* of a story is to introduce the principal characters, establish their initial relationships, set the scene for the main action, expose the background of the situation if necessary, plant motifs and foreshadowings where appropriate, and initiate the first complication or whatever of the "rising action." Actually, if one imagines a story called "The Funhouse," or "Lost in the Funhouse," the details of the drive to Ocean City don't seem especially relevant. The *beginning* should recount the events between Ambrose's first sight of the funhouse early in the afternoon and his entering it with Magda and Peter in the evening. The *middle* would narrate all relevant events from the time he goes in to the time he loses his way; middles have the double and contradictory function of delaying the climax while at the same time preparing the reader for it and fetching him to it. Then the *ending* would tell what Ambrose does while he's lost, how he finally finds his way out, and what everybody makes of the experience. So far there's been no real dialogue, very little sensory detail, and nothing in the way of a *theme*. And a long time has gone by already without anything happening; it makes a person wonder. We haven't even reached Ocean City yet: we will never get out of the funhouse.

The more closely an author identifies with the narrator, literally or metaphorically, the less advisable it is, as a rule, to use the first-person narrative viewpoint. Once three years previously the young people *aforementioned* played Niggers and Masters in the backyard; when it was Ambrose's turn to be Master and theirs to be Niggers Peter had to go serve his evening papers; Ambrose was afraid to punish Magda alone, but she led him to the whitewashed Torture Chamber between the woodshed and the privy in the Slaves Quarters; there she knelt sweating among bamboo rakes and dusty Mason jars, pleadingly embraced his knees, and while bees droned in the lattice as if on an ordinary summer afternoon, purchased clemency at a surprising price set by herself. Doubtless she remembered nothing of this event; Ambrose on the other hand seemed unable to forget the least detail of his life. He even recalled how, standing beside himself with awed impersonality in the reeky heat, he'd stared the while at an empty cigar box in which Uncle Karl kept stone-cutting chisels: beneath the words *El Producto*, a laureled, loose-toga'd lady regarded the sea from a marble bench; beside her, forgotten or not yet turned to, was a five-stringed lyre. Her chin reposed on the back of her right hand; her left depended negligently from the bench-arm. The lower half of scene and lady was peeled away; the words EXAMINED BY ——— were inked there into the wood. Nowadays cigar boxes are made of pasteboard. Ambrose wondered what Magda would have done, Ambrose wondered what Magda would do when she sat back on his hand as he resolved she should. Be angry. Make a teasing joke of it. Give no sign at all. For a long time she leaned forward, playing cow-poker with Peter against Uncle Karl and Mother and watching for the first sign of Ocean City. At nearly the same instant, picnic ground and Ocean City standpipe hove into view; an Amoco filling station on their side of the road cost Mother and Uncle Karl fifty cows and the game; Magda bounced back, clapping her right hand on Mother's right arm; Ambrose moved clear "in the nick of time."

At this rate our hero, at this rate our protagonist will remain in the funhouse forever. Narrative ordinarily consists of alternating dramatization and summarization. One symptom of nervous tension, paradoxically, is repeated and violent yawning; neither Peter nor Magda nor Uncle Karl nor Mother reacted in this manner. Although they were no longer small children, Peter and Ambrose were each given a dollar to spend on boardwalk amusements in addition to what money of their own they'd brought along. Magda too, though she protested she had ample spending money. The boys' mother made a little scene out of distributing the bills; she pretended that her sons and Magda were small children and cautioned them not to spend the sum too quickly or in one place. Magda promised with a merry laugh and, having both hands free, took the bill with her left. Peter laughed also and pledged in a falsetto to be a good boy. His imitation of a child was not clever. The boys' father was tall and thin, balding, fair-complexioned. Assertions of that sort are not effective; the reader may acknowledge the proposition, but. We should be much farther along than we are; something has gone wrong; not much of the preliminary rambling seems relevant. Yet everyone begins in the same place; how is it that most go along without difficulty but a few lose their way?

"Stay out from under the boardwalk," Uncle Karl growled from the side of his mouth. The boys' mother pushed his shoulder *in mock annoyance.* They were all standing before Fat May the Laughing Lady who advertised the funhouse. Larger than life, Fat May mechanically shook, rocked on her heels, slapped her thighs while recorded laughter — uproarious, female — came amplified from a hidden loudspeaker. It chuckled, wheezed, wept; tried in vain to catch its breath; tittered, groaned, exploded raucous and anew. You couldn't hear it without laughing yourself, no matter how you felt. Father came back from talking to a Coast-Guardsman on duty and reported that the surf was spoiled with crude oil from tankers recently torpedoed offshore. Lumps of it, difficult to remove, made tarry tidelines on the beach and stuck on swimmers. Many bathed in the surf nevertheless and came out speckled; others paid to use a municipal pool and only sunbathed on the beach. We would do the latter. We would do the latter. We would do the latter.

Under the boardwalk, matchbook covers, grainy other things. What is the story's theme? Ambrose is ill. He perspires in the dark passages, candied apples-on-a-stick, delicious-looking, disappointing to eat. Funhouses need men's and ladies' rooms at intervals. Others perhaps have also vomited in corners and corridors; may even have had bowel movements liable to be stepped in in the dark. The word *fuck* suggests suction and/or and/or flatulence. Mother and Father; grandmothers and grandfathers on both sides; great-grandmothers and great-grandfathers on four sides, et cetera. Count a generation as thirty years: in approximately the year when Lord Baltimore was granted charter to the province of Maryland by Charles I, five hundred twelve women — English, Welsh, Bavarian, Swiss — of every class and character, received into themselves the penises the intromittent organs of five hundred twelve men, ditto, in every circumstance and posture, to conceive the five hundred twelve ancestors of the two hundred fifty-six ancestors of the et cetera et cetera et cetera et cetera et cetera et cetera et cetera et cetera of the author, of the narrator, of this story, *Lost in the Funhouse.* In alleyways, ditches, canopy beds, pinewoods, bridal suites, ship's cabins, coach-and-fours, coaches-and-four, sultry toolsheds; on the cold sand under boardwalks, littered with *El Producto* cigar butts, treasured with Lucky Strike cigarette stubs, Coca-Cola caps, gritty turds, cardboard lollipop sticks, matchbook covers warning that A Slip of the Lip Can Sink a Ship. The shluppish whisper, continuous as seawash round the globe, tidelike falls and rises with the circuit of dawn and dusk.

Magda's teeth. She *was* left-handed. Perspiration. They've gone all the way, through, Magda and Peter, they've been waiting for hours with Mother and Uncle Karl while Father searches for his lost son; they draw french-fried potatoes from a paper cup and shake their heads. They've named the children they'll one day have and bring to Ocean City on holidays. Can spermatozoa properly be thought of as male animalcules when there are no female spermatozoa? They grope through hot, dark windings, past Love's Tunnel's fearsome obstacles. Some perhaps lose their way.

Peter suggested then and there that they do the funhouse; he had been through it before, so had Magda, Ambrose hadn't and suggested, his voice cracking on account of Fat May's laughter, that they swim first. All were chuckling, couldn't help it; Ambrose's father, Ambrose's and Peter's father came up grinning like a lunatic with two boxes of syrup-coated popcorn, one for Mother, one for Magda; the men were to help themselves. Ambrose walked on Magda's right; being by nature left-handed, she carried the box in her left hand. Up front the situation was reversed.

"What are you limping for?" Magda inquired of Ambrose. He supposed in a husky tone that his foot had gone to sleep in the car. Her teeth flashed. "Pins and needles?" It was the honeysuckle on the lattice of the former privy that drew the bees. Imagine being stung there. How long is this going to take?

The adults decided to forgo the pool; but Uncle Karl insisted they change into swimsuits and do the beach. "He wants to watch the pretty girls," Peter teased, and ducked behind Magda from Uncle Karl's pretended wrath. "You've got all the pretty girls you need right here," Magda declared, and Mother said: "Now that's the gospel truth." Magda scolded Peter, who reached over her shoulder to sneak some popcorn. "Your brother and father aren't getting any." Uncle Karl wondered if they were going to have fireworks that night, what with the shortages. It wasn't the shortages, Mr. M—— replied; Ocean City had fireworks from pre-war. But it was too risky on account of the enemy submarines, some people thought.

"Don't seem like Fourth of July without fireworks," said Uncle Karl. The inverted tag in dialogue writing is still considered permissible with proper names or epithets, but sounds old-fashioned with personal pronouns. "We'll have 'em again soon enough," predicted the boys' father. Their mother declared she could do without fireworks: they reminded her too much of the real thing. Their father said all the more reason to shoot off a few now and again. Uncle Karl asked *rhetorically* who needed reminding, just look at people's hair and skin.

"The oil, yes," said Mrs. M——.

Ambrose had a pain in his stomach and so didn't swim but enjoyed watching the others. He and his father burned red easily. Magda's figure was exceedingly well developed for her age. She too declined to swim, and got mad, and became angry when Peter attempted to drag her into the pool.

She always swam, he insisted; what did she mean not swim? Why did a person come to Ocean City?

"Maybe I want to lay here with Ambrose," Magda teased.

Nobody likes a pedant.

"Aha," said Mother. Peter grabbed Magda by one ankle and ordered Ambrose to grab the other. She squealed and rolled over on the beach blanket. Ambrose pretended to help hold her back. Her tan was darker than even Mother's and Peter's. "Help out, Uncle Karl!" Peter cried. Uncle Karl went to seize the other ankle. Inside the top of her swimsuit, however, you could see the line where the sunburn ended and, when she hunched her shoulders and squealed again, one nipple's auburn edge. Mother made them behave themselves. "*You* should certainly know," she said to Uncle Karl. Archly. "that when a lady says she doesn't feel like swimming, a gentleman doesn't ask questions." Uncle Karl said excuse *him*; Mother winked at Magda; Ambrose blushed; stupid Peter kept saying "Phooey on *feel like!*" and tugging at Magda's ankle; then even he got the point, and cannonballed with a holler into the pool.

"I swear," Magda said, in mock *in feigned* exasperation.

The diving would make a suitable literary symbol. To go off the high board you had to wait in a line along the poolside and up the ladder. Fellows tickled girls and goosed one another and shouted to the ones at the top to hurry up, or razzed them for bellyfloppers. Once on the springboard some took a great while posing or clowning or deciding on a dive or getting up their nerve; others ran right off. Especially among the younger fellows the idea was to strike the funniest pose or do the craziest stunt as you fell, a thing that got harder to do as you kept on and kept on. But whether you hollered *Geronimo!* or *Sieg heil!*, held your nose or "rode a bicycle," pretended to be shot or did a perfect jackknife or changed your mind halfway down and ended up with nothing, it was over in two seconds, after all that wait. Spring, pose, splash. Spring, neat-o, splash. Spring, aw fooey, splash.

The grown-ups had gone on; Ambrose wanted to converse with Magda; she was remarkably well developed for her age; it was said that that came from rubbing with a turkish towel, and there were other theories. Ambrose could think of nothing to say except how good a diver Peter was, who was showing off for her benefit. You could pretty well tell by looking at their bathing suits and arm muscles how far along the different fellows were. Ambrose was glad he hadn't gone in swimming, the cold water shrank you up so. Magda pretended to be uninterested in the diving; she probably weighed as much as he did. If you knew your way around in the funhouse like your own bedroom, you could wait until a girl came along and then slip away without ever getting caught, even if her boyfriend was right with her. She'd think *he* did it! It would be better to be the boyfriend, and act outraged, and tear the funhouse apart.

Not act; *be.*

"He's a master diver," Ambrose said. In feigned admiration. "You really have to slave away at it to get that good." What would it matter anyhow if he asked her right out whether she remembered, even teased her with it as Peter would have?

There's no point in going farther; this isn't getting anybody anywhere; they haven't even come to the funhouse yet. Ambrose is off the track, in some new or old part of the place that's not supposed to be used; he strayed into it by some one-in-a-million chance, like the time the roller-coaster car left the tracks in the nineteen-teens against all the laws of physics and sailed over the boardwalk in the dark. And they can't locate him because they don't know where to look. Even the designer and operator have forgotten this other part, that winds around on itself like a whelk shell. That winds around the right part like the snakes on Mercury's caduceus. Some people, perhaps, don't "hit their stride" until their twenties, when the growing-up business is over and women appreciate other things besides wisecracks and teasing and strutting. Peter didn't have one-tenth the imagination *he* had, not one-tenth. Peter did this naming-their-children thing as a joke, making up names like Aloysius and Murgatroyd, but Ambrose knew *exactly* how it would feel to be married and have children of your own, and be a loving husband and father, and go comfortably to work in the mornings and to bed with your wife at night, and wake up with her there. With a breeze coming through the sash and birds and mockingbirds singing in the Chinese-cigar trees. His eyes watered, there aren't enough ways to say that. He would be quite famous in his line of work. Whether Magda was his wife or not, one evening when he was wise-lined and gray at the temples he'd smile gravely, at a fashionable dinner party and remind her of his youthful passion. The time they went with his family to Ocean City; the *erotic fantasies* he used to have about her. How long ago it seemed, and childish! Yet tender, too, *n'est-ce pas?* Would she have imagined that the world-famous whatever remembered how many strings were on the lyre on the bench beside the girl on the label of the cigar box he'd stared at in the toolshed at age ten while, she, age eleven. Even then he had felt *wise beyond his years;* he'd stroked her hair and said in his deepest voice and correctest English, as to a dear child: "I shall never forget this moment."

But though he had breathed heavily, groaned as if ecstatic, what he'd really felt throughout was an odd detachment, as though someone else were Master. Strive as he might to be transported, he heard his mind take notes upon the scene: *This is what they call* passion. *I am experiencing it.* Many of the digger machines were out of order in the penny arcades and could not be repaired or replaced for the duration. Moreover the prizes, made now in USA, were less interesting than formerly, pasteboard items for the most part, and some of the machines wouldn't work on white pennies. The gypsy fortune-teller machine might have provided a foreshadowing of the climax of this story if Ambrose had operated it. It was even dilapidateder than most: the silver coating was worn off the brown metal handles, the glass windows around the dummy were cracked and taped, her kerchiefs and silks long-faded. If a man lived by himself, he could take a department-store mannequin with flexible joints and modify her in certain ways. *However:* by the time he was that old he'd have a real woman. There was a machine that stamped your name around a white-metal coin with a star in the middle: *A* ——— . His son would be the second, and when the lad reached thirteen or so he would put a strong arm around his shoulder and tell him calmly: "It is perfectly normal. We have all been through it. It will not last forever." Nobody knew how to be what they were right. He'd smoke a pipe, teach his son how to fish and softcrab, assure him he needn't worry about himself. Magda would certainly give, Magda would certainly yield a great deal of milk, although guilty of occasional solecisms. It don't taste so bad. Suppose the lights came on now!

The day wore on. You think you're yourself, but there are other persons in you. Ambrose gets hard when Ambrose doesn't want to, *and obversely.* Ambrose watches them disagree; Ambrose watches him watch. In the funhouse mirror room you can't see yourself go on forever, because no matter how you stand, your head gets in the way. Even if you had a glass periscope, the image of your eye would cover up the thing you really wanted to see. The police will come; there'll be a story in the papers. That must be where it happened. Unless he can find a surprise exit, an unofficial backdoor or escape hatch opening on an alley, say, and then stroll up to the family in front of the funhouse and ask where everybody's been; *he's* been out of the place for ages. That's just where it happened, in that last lighted room: Peter and Magda found the right exit; he found one that you weren't supposed to find and strayed off into the works somewhere. In a perfect funhouse you'd be able to go only one way, like the divers off the highboard; getting lost would be impossible; the doors and halls would work like minnow traps or the valves in veins.

On account of German U-boats, Ocean City was "browned out": streetlights were shaded on the seaward side; shop-windows and boardwalk amusement places were kept dim, not to silhouette tankers and Liberty-ships for torpedoing. In a short story about Ocean City, Maryland, during World War II, the author could make use of the image of sailors on leave in the penny arcades and shooting galleries, sighting through the crosshairs of toy machine guns at swastika'd subs, while out in the black Atlantic a U-boat skipper squints through his periscope at real ships outlined by the glow of penny arcades. After dinner the family strolled back to the amusement end of the boardwalk. The boys' father had burnt red as always and was masked with Noxzema, a minstrel in reverse. The grownups stood at the end of the boardwalk where the Hurricane of '33 had cut an inlet from the ocean to Assawoman Bay.

"Pronounced with a long *o*," Uncle Karl reminded Magda with a wink. His shirt sleeves were rolled up; Mother punched his brown biceps with the arrowed heart on it and said his mind was naughty. Fat May's laugh came suddenly from the funhouse, as if she'd just got the joke; the family laughed too at the coincidence. Ambrose went under the boardwalk to search for out-of-town matchbook covers with the aid of his pocket flashlight; he looked out from the edge of the North American continent and wondered how far their laughter carried over the water. Spies in rubber rafts; survivors in lifeboats. If the joke had been beyond his understanding, he could have said: *"The laughter was over his head."* And let the reader see the serious wordplay on second reading.

He turned the flashlight on and then off at once even before the woman whooped. He sprang away, heart athud, dropping the light. What had the man grunted? Perspiration drenched and chilled him by the time he scrambled up to the family. "See anything?" his father asked. His voice wouldn't come; he shrugged and violently brushed sand from his pants legs.

"Let's ride the old flying horses!" Magda cried. I'll never be an author. It's been forever already, everybody's gone home, Ocean City's deserted, the ghost-crabs are tickling across the beach and down the littered cold streets. And the empty halls of clapboard hotels and abandoned funhouses. A tidal wave; an enemy air raid; a monster-crab swelling like an island from the sea. *The inhabitants fled in terror.* Magda clung to his trouser leg; he alone knew the maze's secret. "He gave his life that we might live," said Uncle Karl with a scowl of pain, as he. The fellow's hands had been tattooed; the woman's legs, the woman's fat white legs had. *An astonishing coincidence.* He yearned to tell Peter. He wanted to throw up for excitement. They hadn't even chased him. He wished he were dead.

One possible ending would be to have Ambrose come across another lost person in the dark. They'd match their wits together against the funhouse, struggle like Ulysses past obstacle after obstacle, help and encourage each other. Or a girl. By the time they found the exit they'd be closest friends, sweethearts if it were a girl; they'd know each other's inmost souls, be bound together *by the cement of shared adventure*; then they'd emerge into the light and it would turn out that his friend was a Negro. A blind girl. President Roosevelt's son. Ambrose's former archenemy.

Shortly after the mirror room he'd groped along a musty corridor, his heart already misgiving him at the absence of phosphorescent arrows and other signs. He'd found a crack of light — not a door, it turned out, but a seam between the plyboard wall panels — and squinting up to it, espied a small old man, *in appearance not unlike* the photographs at home of Ambrose's late grandfather, nodding upon a stool beneath a bare, speckled bulb. A crude panel of toggle- and knife-switches hung beside the open fuse box near his head; elsewhere in the little room were wooden levers and ropes belayed to boat cleats. At the time, Ambrose wasn't lost enough to rap or call; later he couldn't find that crack. Now it seemed to him that he'd possibly dozed off for a few minutes somewhere along the way; certainly he was exhausted from the afternoon's sunshine and the evening's problems; he couldn't be sure he hadn't dreamed part or all of the sight. Had an old black wall fan droned like bees and shimmied two flypaper streamers? Had the funhouse operator — gentle, somewhat sad and tired-appearing, in expression not unlike the photographs at home of Ambrose's late Uncle Konrad — murmured in his sleep? Is there really such a person as Ambrose, or is he a figment of the author's imagination? Was it Assawoman Bay or Sinepuxent? Are there other errors of fact in this fiction? Was there another sound besides the little slap slap of thigh on ham, like water sucking at the chine-boards of a skiff?

When you're lost, the smartest thing to do is stay put till you're found, hollering if necessary. But to holler guarantees humiliation as well as rescue; keeping silent permits some saving of face — you can act surprised at the fuss when your rescuers find you and swear you weren't lost, if they do. What's more you might find your own way yet, *however belatedly.*

"Don't tell me your foot's still asleep!" Magda exclaimed as the three young people walked from the inlet to the area set aside for ferris wheels, carrousels, and other carnival rides, they having decided in favor of the vast and ancient merry-go-round instead of the funhouse. What a sentence, everything was wrong from the outset. People don't know what to make of him, he doesn't know what to make of himself, he's only thirteen, *athletically and socially inept,* not astonishingly bright, but there are antennae; he has . . . some sort of receivers in his head; things speak to him, he understands more than he should, the world winks at him through its objects, grabs grinning at his coat. Everybody else is in on some secret he doesn't know; they've forgotten to tell him. Through simple *procrastination* his mother put off his baptism until this year. Everyone else had it done as a baby; he'd assumed the same of himself, as had his mother, so she claimed, until it was time for him to join Grace Methodist-Protestant and the oversight came out. He was mortified, but pitched sleepless through his private catechizing, intimidated by the ancient mysteries, a thirteen year old would never say that, resolved to experience conversion like St. Augustine. When the water touched his brow and Adam's sin left him, he contrived by a strain like defecation to bring tears into his eyes — but felt nothing. There was some simple, radical difference about him; he hoped it was genius, feared it was madness, devoted himself to amiability and inconspicuousness. Alone on the seawall near his house he was seized by the terrifying transports he'd thought to find in toolshed, in Communion-cup. The grass was alive! The town, the river, himself, were not imaginary; time roared in his ears like wind; the world was *going on!* This part ought to be dramatized. The Irish author James Joyce once wrote. Ambrose M —— is going to scream.

There is no *texture of rendered sensory detail,* for one thing. The faded distorting mirrors beside Fat May; the impossibility of choosing a mount when one had but a single ride on the great carrousel; the *vertigo attendant on his recognition* that Ocean City was worn out, the place of fathers and grandfathers, straw-boatered men and parasoled ladies survived by their amusements. Money spent, the three paused at Peter's insistence beside Fat May to watch the girls get their skirts blown up. The object was to tease Magda, who said: "I swear, Peter M——, you've got a one-track mind! Amby and me aren't *interested* in such things." In the tumbling-barrel, too, just inside the Devil's-mouth entrance to the funhouse, the girls were upended and their boyfriends and others could see up their dresses if they cared to. Which was the whole point, Ambrose realized. Of the entire funhouse! If you looked around, you noticed that almost all the people on the boardwalk were paired off into couples except the small children; in a way, that was the whole point of Ocean City! If you had X-ray eyes and could see everything going on at that instant under the boardwalk and in all the hotel rooms and cars and alleyways, you'd realize that all that normally *showed*, like restaurants and dance halls and clothing and test-your-strength machines, was merely preparation and intermission. Fat May screamed.

Because he watched the going-ons from the corner of his eye, it was Ambrose who spied the half-dollar on the boardwalk near the tumbling-barrel. Losers weepers. The first time he'd heard some people moving through a corridor not far away, just after he'd lost sight of the crack of light, he'd decided not to call to them, for fear they'd guess he was scared and poke fun; it sounded like roughnecks; he'd hoped they'd come by and he could follow in the dark without their knowing. Another time he'd heard just one person, unless he imagined it, bumping along as if on the other side of the plywood; perhaps Peter coming back for him, or Father, or Magda lost too. Or the owner and operator of the funhouse. He'd called out once, as though merrily: "Anybody know where the heck we are?" But the query was too stiff, his voice cracked, when the sounds stopped he was terrified: maybe it was a queer who waited for fellows to get lost, or a longhaired filthy monster that lived in some cranny of the funhouse. He stood rigid for hours it seemed like, scarcely respiring. His future was shockingly clear, in outline. He tried holding his breath to the point of unconsciousness. There ought to be a button you could push to end your life absolutely without pain; disappear in a flick, like turning out a light. He would push it instantly! He despised Uncle Karl. But he despised his father too, for not being what he was supposed to be. Perhaps his father hated *his* father, and so on, and his son would hate him, and so on. Instantly!

Naturally he didn't have nerve enough to ask Magda to go through the funhouse with him. With incredible nerve and to everyone's surprise he invited Magda, quietly and politely, to go through the funhouse with him. "I warn you, I've never been through it before," he added, *laughing easily*; "but I reckon we can manage somehow. The important thing to remember, after all, is that it's meant to be a *fun*house; that is, a place of amusement.

If people really got lost or injured or too badly frightened in it, the owner'd go out of business. There'd even be lawsuits. No character in a work of fiction can make a speech this long without interruption or acknowledgment from the other characters."

Mother teased Uncle Karl: "Three's a crowd, I always heard." But actually Ambrose was relieved that Peter now had a quarter too. Nothing was what it looked like. Every instant, under the surface of the Atlantic Ocean, millions of living animals devoured one another. Pilots were falling in flames over Europe; women were being forcibly raped in the South Pacific. His father should have taken him aside and said: "There is a simple secret to getting through the funhouse, as simple as being first to see the Towers. Here it is. Peter does not know it; neither does your Uncle Karl. You and I are different. Not surprisingly, you've often wished you weren't. Don't think I haven't noticed how unhappy your childhood has been! But you'll understand, when I tell you, why it had to be kept secret until now. And you won't regret not being like your brother and your uncle. *On the contrary!*" If you knew all the stories behind all the people on the boardwalk, you'd see that *nothing* was what it looked like. Husbands and wives often hated each other; parents didn't necessarily love their children; et cetera. A child took things for granted because he had nothing to compare his life to and everybody acted as if things were as they should be. Therefore each saw himself as the hero of the story, when the truth might turn out to be that he's the villain, or the coward. And there wasn't one thing you could do about it!

Hunchbacks, fat ladies, fools — that no one chose what he was was unbearable. In the movies he'd meet a beautiful young girl in the funhouse; they'd have hairs-breadth escapes from real dangers; he'd do and say the right things; she also; in the end they'd be lovers; their dialogue lines would match up; he'd be perfectly at ease; she'd not only like him well enough, she'd think he was *marvelous*; she'd lie awake thinking about *him*, instead of vice versa — the way *his* face looked in different lights and how he stood and exactly what he'd said — and yet that would be only one small episode in his wonderful life, among many many others. Not a *turning point* at all. What had happened in the toolshed was nothing. He hated, he loathed his parents! One reason for not writing a lost-in-the-funhouse story is that either everybody's felt what Ambrose feels, in which case it goes without saying, or else no normal person feels such things, in which case Ambrose is a freak. "Is anything more tiresome, in fiction, than the problems of sensitive adolescents?" And it's all too long and rambling, as if the author. For all a person knows the first time through, the end could be just around any corner; perhaps, *not impossibly* it's been within reach any number of times. On the other hand he may be scarcely past the start, with everything yet to get through, an intolerable idea.

Fill in: His father's raised eyebrows when he announced his decision to do the funhouse with Magda. Ambrose understands now, but didn't then, that his father was wondering whether he knew what the funhouse was *for* — especially since he didn't object, as he should have, when Peter decided to come along too. The ticket-woman, witchlike, mortifying him when inadvertently he gave her his name-coin instead of the half-dollar, then unkindly calling Magda's attention to the birthmark on his temple: "Watch out for him, girlie, he's a marked man!" She wasn't even cruel, he understood, only vulgar and insensitive. Somewhere in the world there was a young woman with such splendid understanding that she'd see him entire, like a poem or story, and find his words so valuable after all that when he confessed his apprehensions she would explain why they were in fact the very things that made him precious to her . . . and to Western Civilization! There was no such girl, the simple truth being. Violent yawns as they approached the mouth. Whispered advice from an old-timer on a bench near the barrel: "Go crabwise and ye'll get an eyeful without upsetting!" Composure vanished at the first pitch: Peter hollered joyously, Magda tumbled, shrieked, clutched her skirt; Ambrose scrambled crabwise, tight-lipped with terror, was soon out, watched his dropped name-coin slide among the couples. Shame-faced he saw that to get through expeditiously was not the point; Peter feigned assistance in order to trip Magda up, shouted "I see Christmas!" when her legs went flying. The old man, his latest betrayer, cackled approval. A dim hall then of black-thread cobwebs and recorded gibber: he took Magda's elbow to steady her against revolving discs set in the slanted floor to throw your feet out from under, and explained to her in a calm, deep voice his theory that each phase of the funhouse was triggered either automatically, by a series of photoelectric devices, or else manually by operators stationed at peepholes. But he lost his voice thrice as the discs unbalanced him; Magda was anyhow squealing; but at one point she clutched him about the waist to keep from falling, and her right cheek pressed for a moment against his belt-buckle. Heroically he drew her up, it was his chance to clutch her close as if for support and say: "I love you." He even put an arm lightly about the small of her back before a sailor-and-girl pitched into them from behind, sorely treading his left big toe and knocking Magda asprawl with them. The sailor's girl was a string-haired hussy with a loud laugh and light blue drawers; Ambrose realized that he wouldn't have said "I love you" anyhow, and was smitten with self-contempt. How much better it would be to be that common sailor! A wiry little Seaman 3rd, the fellow squeezed a girl to each side and stumbled hilarious into the mirror room, closer to Magda in thirty seconds than Ambrose had got in thirteen years. She giggled at something the fellow said to Peter; she drew her hair from her eyes with a movement so womanly it struck Ambrose's heart; Peter's smacking her backside then seemed particularly coarse. But Magda made a pleased indignant face and cried, "All right for *you* mister!" and pursued Peter into the maze without a backward glance. The sailor followed after, leisurely, drawing his girl against his hip; Ambrose understood not only that they were all so relieved to be rid of his burdensome company that they didn't even notice his absence, but that he himself shared their relief. Stepping from the treacherous passage at last into the mirror-maze, he saw once again, more clearly than ever, how readily he deceived himself into supposing he was a person. He even foresaw, wincing at his dreadful self-knowledge, that he would repeat the deception, at ever-rarer intervals, all his wretched life, so fearful were the alternatives. Fame, madness, suicide; perhaps all three. It's not believable that so young a boy could articulate that reflection, and in fiction the merely true must always yield to the plausible. Moreover, the symbolism is in places heavy-footed. Yet Ambrose M—— understood, as few adults do, that the famous loneliness of the great was no popular myth but a general truth — furthermore, that it was as much cause as effect.

All the preceding except the last few sentences is exposition that should've been done earlier or interspersed with the present action instead of lumped together. No reader would put up with so much with such *prolixity.* It's interesting that Ambrose's father, though presumably an intelligent man (as indicated by his role as grade-school principal), neither encouraged nor discouraged his sons at all in any way — as if he either didn't care about them or cared all right but didn't know how to act. If this fact should contribute to one of them's becoming a celebrated but wretchedly unhappy scientist, was it a good thing or not? He too might someday face the question; it would be useful to know whether it had tortured his father for years, for example, or never once crossed his mind.

In the maze two important things happened. First, our hero found a name-coin someone else had lost or discarded: *AMBROSE,* suggestive of the famous lightship and of his late grandfather's favorite dessert, which his mother used to prepare on special occasions out of coconut, oranges, grapes, and what else. Second, as he wondered at the endless replication of his image in the mirrors, second, as he *lost himself in the reflection* that the necessity for an observer makes perfect observation impossible, better make him eighteen at least, yet that would render other things unlikely, he heard Peter and Magda chuckling somewhere together in the maze. "Here!" "No, here!" they shouted to each other; Peter said, "Where's Amby?" Magda murmured. "Amb?" Peter called. In a pleased, friendly voice. He didn't reply. The truth was, his brother was a *happy-go-lucky youngster* who'd've been better off with a regular brother of his own, but who seldom complained of his lot and was generally cordial. Ambrose's throat ached; there aren't enough different ways to say that. He stood quietly while the two young people giggled and thumped through the glittering maze, hurrah'd their discovery of its exit, cried out in joyful alarm at what next beset them. Then he set his mouth and followed after, as he supposed, took a wrong turn, strayed into the pass *wherein he lingers yet.*

The action of conventional dramatic narrative may be represented by a diagram called Freitag's Triangle:

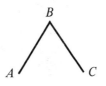

or more accurately by a variant of that diagram:

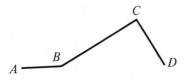

in which *AB* represents the exposition, *B* the introduction of conflict, *BC* the "rising action," complication, or development of the conflict, *C* the climax, or turn of the action, *CD* the dénouement, or resolution of the conflict. While there is no reason to regard this pattern as an absolute necessity, like many other conventions it became conventional because great numbers of people over many years learned by trial and error that it was effective; one ought not to forsake it, therefore, unless one wishes to forsake as well the effect of drama or has clear cause to feel that deliberate violation of the "normal" pattern can better can better effect that effect. This can't go on much longer; it can go on forever. He died telling stories to himself in the dark; years later, when that vast unsuspected area of the funhouse came to light, the first expedition found his skeleton in one of its labyrinthine corridors and mistook it for part of the entertainment. He died of starvation telling himself stories in the dark; but unbeknownst unbeknownst to him, an assistant operator of the funhouse, happening to overhear him, crouched just behind the plyboard partition and wrote down his every word. The operator's daughter, an exquisite young woman with a figure unusually well developed for her age, crouched just behind the partition and transcribed his every word. Though she had never laid eyes on him, she recognized that here was one of Western Culture's truly great imaginations, the eloquence of whose suffering would be an inspiration to unnumbered. And her heart was torn between her love for the misfortunate young man (yes, she loved him, though she had never laid though she knew him only — but how well! — through his words, and the deep, calm voice in which he spoke them) between her love et cetera and her womanly intuition that only in suffering and isolation could he give voice et cetera. Lone dark dying. Quietly she kissed the rough plyboard, and a tear fell upon the page. Where she had written in shorthand *Where she had written in shorthand* Where she had written in shorthand *Where she* et cetera. A long time ago we should have passed the apex of Freitag's Triangle and made brief work of the *dénouement;* the plot doesn't rise by meaningful steps but winds upon itself, digresses, retreats, hesitates, sighs, collapses, expires. The climax of the story must be its protagonist's discovery of a way to get through the funhouse. But he had found none, may have ceased to search.

What relevance does the war have to the story? Should there be fireworks outside or not?

Ambrose wandered, languished, dozed. Now and then he fell into his habit of rehearsing to himself the unadventurous story of his life, narrated from the third-person point of view, from his earliest memory parenthesis of maple leaves stirring in the summer breath of tidewater Maryland end of parenthesis to the present moment. Its principal events, on this telling, would appear to have been A, B, C, and D.

He imagined himself years hence, successful, married, at ease in the world, the trials of his adolescence far behind him. He has come to the seashore with his family for the holiday: how Ocean City has changed! But at one seldom at one ill-frequented end of the boardwalk a few derelict amusements survive from times gone by: the great carrousel from the turn of the century, with its monstrous griffins and mechanical concert band; the roller coaster rumored since 1916 to have been condemned; the mechanical shooting gallery in which only the image of our enemies changed. His own son laughs with Fat May and wants to know what a funhouse is; Ambrose hugs the sturdy lad close and smiles around his pipestem at his wife.

The family's going home. Mother sits between Father and Uncle Karl, who teases him good-naturedly who chuckles over the fact that the comrade with whom he'd fought his way shoulder to shoulder through the funhouse had turned out to be a blind Negro girl — to their mutual discomfort, as they'd opened their souls. But such are the walls of custom, which even. Whose arm is where? How must it feel. He dreams of a funhouse vaster by far than any yet constructed; but by then they may be out of fashion, like steamboats and excursion trains. Already quaint and seedy: the draperied ladies on the frieze of the carrousel are his father's father's mooncheeked dreams; if he thinks of it more he will vomit his apple-on-a-stick.

He wonders: will he become a regular person? Something has gone wrong; his vaccination didn't take; at the Boy-Scout initiation campfire he only pretended to be deeply moved, as he pretends to this hour that it is not so bad after all in the funhouse, and that he has a little limp. How long will it last? He envisions a truly astonishing funhouse, incredibly complex yet utterly controlled from a great central switchboard like the console of a pipe organ. Nobody had enough imagination. He could design such a place himself, wiring and all, and he's only thirteen years old. He would be its operator: panel lights would show what was up in every cranny of its cunning of its multivarious vastness; a switch-flick would ease this fellow's way, complicate that's, to balance things out; if anyone seemed lost or frightened, all the operator had to do was.

He wishes he had never entered the funhouse. But he has. Then he wishes he were dead. But he's not. Therefore he will construct funhouses for others and be their secret operator — though he would rather be among the lovers for whom funhouses are designed.

[1968]

*J*OHN UPDIKE (*b. 1932*) *was born in Shillington, Pennsylvania, an only child. His father taught algebra in a local high school, and his mother wrote short stories and novels, none of them ever published. From her Updike says he gathered that "either drawing or writing would be a noble and gay way of making a living; and I think I was very young when image-making dawned on me as a way of defying mortality." His mother's consciousness of a special destiny, combined with his family's near poverty — they lived with his mother's parents for the first thirteen years of Updike's life — made him both arrogant and shy as a teenager, writing stories, drawing cartoons, and clowning for the approval of his peers. After getting straight As in high school, he went to Harvard on a full scholarship, studying English and graduating summa cum laude in 1954. He spent a year at Oxford on a fellowship, then joined the staff of* The New Yorker. *In 1959 Updike published both his first book of short fiction,* The Same Door, *and his first novel,* The Poorhouse Fair. *That year he also decided to move from New York City to Ipswich, the Massachusetts coastal town where he has lived most of the time since then.*

In the 1960s, 1970s, and early 1980s, Updike continued to alternate novels and collections of stories, also adding occasional volumes of verse, two collections of essays, and one play. His novels include Rabbit, Run (*1960*), The Centaur (*1963*), Of the Farm (*1965*), Couples (*1968*), Rabbit Redux (*1971*), A Month of Sundays (*1975*), *and* Marry Me! (*1976*). *In* The Coup (*1978*), *an account of an American-educated revolutionary leader in a fictitious African country, Updike turned his attention beyond the contemporary American urban and suburban people who had been his subjects until then, and won great critical acclaim.* Rabbit Is Rich (*1981*), *continuing the story of Harry "Rabbit" Angstrom, a suburban Pennsylvanian whom Updike has traced through adolescence, marriage, fatherhood, and middle age, won virtually every major American literary award for that year. Updike's collections of stories include* Pigeon Feathers (*1962*), The Music School (*1966*), Museums and Women (*1972*), *and* Problems and Other Stories (*1981*).

The majority of Updike's early stories, like "Flight," refer to his youth in Pennsylvania, and he says he is indebted to J. D. Salinger's stories for the literary form he adopted to describe the painful experience of adolescence. "I learned a lot from Salinger's short stories; he did remove the short narrative from the wise-guy, slice-of-life stories of the thirties and forties. Like most innovative artists, he made new room for shapelessness, for life as it is lived." Updike writes realistic narrative, believing that "Fiction is a tissue of lies that refreshes and informs our sense of actuality. Reality is — chemically, atomically, biologically — a fabric of microscopic accuracies." His fiction concentrates on these "microscopic accuracies," tiny details of char-acterization and setting brilliantly described, as in "Wife-wooing." This story appeared in the book Too Far to Go *(1979), a collection of related stories about the disintegration of the marriage of a suburban couple named Joan and Richard Maple.*

John Updike

ಬಬ

FLIGHT

At the age of seventeen I was poorly dressed and funny-looking, and went around thinking about myself in the third person. "Allen Dow strode down the street and home." "Allen Dow smiled a thin sardonic smile." Consciousness of a special destiny made me both arrogant and shy. Years before, when I was eleven or twelve, just on the brink of ceasing to be a lit-tle boy, my mother and I, one Sunday afternoon — my father was busy, or asleep — hiked up to the top of Shale Hill, a child's mountain that formed one side of the valley that held our town. There the town lay under us, Olinger, perhaps a thousand homes, the best and biggest of them climbing Shale Hill toward us, and beyond them the blocks of brick houses, one- and two-family, the homes of my friends, sloping down to the pale thread of the Alton Pike, which strung together the high school, the tennis courts, the movie theatre, the town's few stores and gasoline stations, the elementary school, the Lutheran church. On the other side lay more homes, including our own, a tiny white patch placed just where the land began to rise toward the opposite mountain, Cedar Top. There were rims and rims of hills be-yond Cedar Top, and looking south we could see the pike dissolving in other towns and turning out of sight amid the patches of green and brown farmland, and it seemed the entire country was lying exposed under a thin veil of haze. I was old enough to feel embarrassment at standing there alone with my mother, beside a wind-stunted spruce tree, on a long spine of shale. Suddenly she dug her fingers into the hair on my head and announced, "There we all are, and there we'll all be forever." She hesitated before the word "forever," and hesitated again before adding, "Except you, Allen. You're going to fly." A few birds were hung far out over the valley, at the level of our eyes, and in her impulsive way she had just plucked the image from them, but it felt like the clue I had been waiting all my childhood for. My most secret self had been made to respond, and I was intensely embarrassed, and irritably ducked my head out from under her melodramatic hand.

She was impulsive and romantic and inconsistent. I was never able to develop this spurt of reassurance into a steady theme between us. That she continued to treat me like an ordinary child seemed a betrayal of the vision she had made me share. I was captive to a hope she had tossed off and forgotten. My shy attempts to justify irregularities in my conduct — reading late at night or not coming back from school on time — by appealing to the image of flight were received with a startled blank look, as if I were talking nonsense. It seemed outrageously unjust. Yes, but, I wanted to say, yes, but it's *your* nonsense. And of course it was just this that made my appeal ineffective: her knowing that I had not made it mine, that I cynically intended to exploit both the privileges of being extraordinary and the pleasures of being ordinary. She feared my wish to be ordinary; once she did respond to my protest that I was learning to fly, by crying with red-faced ferocity, "You'll never learn, you'll stick and die in the dirt just like I'm doing. Why should you be better than your mother?"

She had been born ten miles to the south, on a farm she and her mother had loved. Her mother, a small fierce woman who looked more like an Arab than a German, worked in the fields with the men, and drove the wagon to market ten miles away every Friday. When still a tiny girl, my mother rode with her, and my impression of those rides is of fear — the little girl's fear of the gross and beery men who grabbed and hugged her, her fear of the wagon breaking, of the produce not selling, fear of her mother's possible humiliation and of her father's condition when at nightfall they returned. Friday was his holiday, and he drank. His drinking is impossible for me to picture; for I never knew him except as an enduring, didactic, almost Biblical old man, whose one passion was reading the newspapers and whose one hatred was of the Republican Party. There was something public about him; now that he is dead I keep seeing bits of him attached to famous politicians — his watch chain and his plump square stomach in old films of Theodore Roosevelt, his high-top shoes and the tilt of his head in a photograph of Alfalfa Bill Murray. Alfalfa Bill is turning his head to talk, and holds his hat by the crown, pinching it between two fingers and a thumb, a gentle and courtly grip that reminded me so keenly of my grandfather that I tore the picture out of *Life* and put it in a drawer.

Laboring in the soil had never been congenial to my grandfather, though with his wife's help he prospered by it. Then, in an era when success was hard to avoid, he began to invest in stocks. In 1922 he bought our large white home in the town — its fashionable section had not yet shifted to the Shale Hill side of the valley — and settled in to reap his dividends. He believed to his death that women were foolish, and the broken hearts of his two must have seemed specially so. The dignity of finance for the indignity of farming must have struck him as an eminently advantageous exchange. It strikes me that way, too, and how to reconcile my idea of those fear-ridden wagon rides with the grief that my mother insists she and her mother felt at being taken from the farm? Perhaps prolonged fear is a ground of love. Or perhaps, and likelier, the equation is long and complex, and the few factors I know — the middle-aged woman's mannish pride of land, the adolescent girl's pleasure in riding horses across the fields, their common feeling of rejection in Olinger — are enclosed in brackets and heightened by coefficients that I cannot see. Or perhaps it is not love of land but its absence that needs explaining, in my grandfather's fastidiousness and pride. He believed that as a boy he had been abused, and bore his father a grudge that my mother could never understand. Her grandfather to her was a saintly slender giant, over six feet tall when this was a prodigy, who knew the names of everything, like Adam in Eden. In his old age he was blind. When he came out of the house, the dogs rushed forward to lick his hands. When he lay dying, he requested a Gravenstein apple from the tree on the far edge of the meadow, and his son brought him a Krauser from the orchard near the house. The old man refused it, and my grandfather made a second trip, but in my mother's eyes the outrage had been committed, a savage insult insanely without provocation. What had his father done to him? The only specific complaint I ever heard my grandfather make was that when he was a boy and had to fetch water for the men in the fields, his father would tell him sarcastically, "Pick up your feet; they'll come down themselves." How incongruous! As if each generation of parents commits atrocities against their children which by God's decree remain invisible to the rest of the world.

I remember my grandmother as a little dark-eyed woman who talked seldom and who tried to feed me too much, and then as a hook-nosed profile pink against the lemon cushions of the casket. She died when I was seven. All the rest I know about her is that she was the baby of thirteen children, that while she was alive she made our yard one of the most beautiful in town, and that I am supposed to resemble her brother Pete.

My mother was precocious; she was fourteen when they moved, and for three years had been attending the county normal school. She graduated from Lake College, near Philadelphia, when she was only twenty, a tall handsome girl with a deprecatory smile, to judge from one of the curling photographs kept in a shoebox that I was always opening as a child, as if it might contain the clue to the quarrels in my house. My mother stands at the end of our brick walk, beside the elaborately trimmed end of our privet hedge — in shape a thick square column mounted by a rough ball of leaf. The ragged arc of a lilac bush in flower cuts into the right edge of the photograph, and behind my mother I can see a vacant lot where there has been a house ever since I can remember. She poses with a kind of country grace in a long fur-trimmed coat, unbuttoned to expose her beads and a short yet somehow demure flapper dress. Her hands are in her coat pockets, a beret sits on one side of her bangs, and there is a swank about her that seemed incongruous to me, examining this picture on the stained carpet of an ill-lit old house in the evening years of the thirties and in the dark of the warring forties. The costume and the girl in it look so up-to-date, so formidable. It was my grandfather's pleasure, in his prosperity, to give her a generous clothes allowance. My father, the penniless younger son of a Presbyterian minister in Passaic, had worked his way through Lake College by waiting on tables, and still speaks with mild resentment of the beautiful clothes that Lillian Baer wore. This aspect of my mother caused me some pain in high school; she was a fabric snob, and insisted on buying my slacks and sports shirts at the best store in Alton, and since we had little money, she bought me few, when of course what I needed was what my classmates had — a wide variety of cheap clothes.

At the time the photograph was taken, my mother wanted to go to New York. What she would have done there, or exactly what she wanted to do, I don't know; but her father forbade her. "Forbid" is a husk of a word today, but at that time, in that quaint province, in the mouth of an "indulgent father," it apparently was still viable, for the great moist weight of that forbidding continued to be felt in the house for years, and when I was a child, as one of my mother's endless harangues to my grandfather screamed toward its weeping peak, I could feel it around and above me, like a huge root encountered by an earthworm.

Perhaps in a reaction of anger my mother married my father, Victor Dow, who at least took her as far away as Wilmington, where he had made a beginning with an engineering firm. But the depression hit, my father was laid off, and the couple came to the white house in Olinger, where my grandfather sat reading the newspapers that traced his stocks' cautious decline into worthlessness. I was born. My grandmother went around as a cleaning lady, and grew things in our quarter-acre yard to sell. We kept chickens, and there was a large plot of asparagus. After she had died, in a frightened way I used to seek her in the asparagus patch. By midsummer it would be a forest of dainty green trees, some as tall as I was, and in their frothy touch a spirit seemed to speak, and in the soft thick net of their intermingling branches a promise seemed to be caught, as well as a menace. The asparagus trees were frightening; in the center of the patch, far from the house and the alley, I would fall under a spell, and become tiny, and wander among the great smooth green trunks expecting to find a little house with a smoking chimney, and in it my grandmother. She herself had believed in ghosts, which made her own ghost potent. Even now, sitting alone in my own house, a board creaks in the kitchen and I look up fearing she will come through the doorway. And at night, just before I fall asleep, her voice calls my name in a penetrating whisper, or calls, *"Pete."*

My mother went to work in an Alton department store, selling inferior fabric for $14 a week. During the daytime of my first year of life it was my father who took care of me. He has said since, flattering me as he always does, that it was having me on his hands that kept him from going insane. It may have been this that made my affection for him so inarticulate, as if I were still a wordless infant looking up into the mothering blur of his man's face. And that same shared year helps account, perhaps, for his gentleness with me, for his willingness to praise, as if everything I do has something sad and crippled in it. He feels sorry for me; my birth coincided with the birth of a great misery, a national misery — only recently has he stopped calling me by the nickname "Young America." Around my first birthday he acquired a position teaching arithmetic and algebra in the Olinger high school, and though he was so kind and humorous he couldn't enter a classroom without creating uproarious problems of discipline, he endured it day by day and year by year, and eventually came to occupy a place in this alien town, so that I believe there are now one or two dozen ex-students, men and women nearing middle age, who carry around with them some piece of encouragement my father gave them, or remember some sentence of his that helped shape them. Certainly there are many who remember the antics with which he burlesqued his discomfort in the classroom. He kept a confiscated cap pistol in his desk, and upon getting an especially stupid answer, he would take it out and, wearing a preoccupied, regretful expression, shoot himself in the head.

My grandfather was the last to go to work, and the most degraded by it. He was hired by the borough crew, men who went around the streets shoveling stones and spreading tar. Bulky and ominous in their overalls, wreathed in steam, and associated with dramatic and portentous equipment, these men had grandeur in the eyes of a child, and it puzzled me, as I walked to and from elementary school, that my grandfather refused to wave to me or confess his presence in any way. Curiously strong for a fastidious man, he kept at it well into his seventies, when his sight failed. It was my task then to read his beloved newspapers to him as he sat in his chair by the bay window, twiddling his high-top shoes in the sunshine. I teased him, reading too fast, then maddeningly slow, skipping from column to column to create one long chaotic story; I read him the sports page, which did not interest him, and mumbled the editorials. Only the speed of his feet's twiddling betrayed vexation. When I'd stop, he would plead mildly in his rather beautiful, old-fashioned, elocutionary voice, "Now just the obituaries, Allen. Just the names to see if anyone I know is there." I imagined, as I viciously barked at him the list of names that might contain the name of a friend, that I was avenging my mother; I believed that she hated him, and for her sake I tried to hate him also. From her incessant resurrection of mysterious grievances buried far back in the confused sunless earth of the time before I was born, I had been able to deduce only that he was an evil man, who had ruined her life, that fair creature in the beret. I did not understand. She fought with him not because she wanted to fight but because *she could not bear to leave him alone.*

Sometimes, glancing up from the sheet of print where our armies swarmed in retreat like harried insects, I could catch the old man's head in the act of lifting slightly to receive the warm sunshine on his face, a dry frail face ennobled by its thick crown of combed cornsilk hair. It would dawn on me then that his sins as a father were likely no worse than any father's. But my mother's genius was to give the people closest to her mythic immensity. I was the phoenix. My father and grandmother were legendary invader-saints, she springing out of some narrow vein of Arab blood in the German race and he crossing over from the Protestant wastes of New Jersey, both of them serving and enslaving their mates with their prodigious powers of endurance and labor. For my mother felt that she and her father alike had been destroyed by marriage, been made captive by people better yet less than they. It was true, my father had loved Mom Baer, and her death made him seem more of an alien than ever. He, and her ghost, stood to one side, in the shadows but separate from the house's dark core, the inheritance of frustration and folly that had descended from my grandfather to my mother to me, and that I, with a few beats of my grown wings, was destined to reverse and redeem.

At the age of seventeen, in the fall of my senior year, I went with three girls to debate at a high school over a hundred miles away. They were, all three, bright girls, A students; they were disfigured by A's as if by acne. Yet even so it excited me to be mounting a train with them early on a Friday morning, at an hour when our schoolmates miles away were slumping into the seats of their first class. Sunshine spread broad bars of dust down the length of the half-empty car, and through the windows Pennsylvania unravelled in a long brown scroll scribbled with industry. Black pipes raced beside the tracks for miles. At rhythmic intervals one of them looped upward, like the Greek letter Ω. "Why does it do that?" I asked. "Is it sick?"

"Condensation?" Judith Potteiger suggested in her shy, transparent voice. She loved science.

"No," I said. "It's in pain. It's withering! It's going to grab the train! Look out!" I ducked, honestly a little scared. All the girls laughed.

Judith and Catharine Miller were in my class, and expected me to be amusing; the third girl, a plump small junior named Molly Bingaman, had not known what to expect. It was her fresh audience I was playing to. She was the best dressed of us four, and the most poised; this made me suspect that she was the least bright. She had been substituted at the last moment for a sick member of the debating team; I knew her just by seeing her in the halls and in assembly. From a distance she seemed dumpy and prematurely adult. But up close she was gently fragrant, and against the weary purple cloth of the train seats her skin seemed luminous. She had beautiful skin, heartbreaking skin a pencil dot would have marred, and large blue eyes equally clear. Except for a double chin, and a mouth too large and thick, she would have been perfectly pretty, in a little woman's compact and cocky way. She and I sat side by side, facing the two senior girls, who more and more took on the wan slyness of matchmakers. It was they who had forced the seating arrangements.

We debated in the afternoon, and won. Yes, the German Federal Republic *should* be freed of all Allied control. The school, a posh castle on the edge of a miserable coal city, was the site of a statewide cycle of debates that was to continue into Saturday. There was a dance Friday night in the gym. I danced with Molly mostly, though to my annoyance she got in with a set of Harrisburg boys while I conscientiously pushed Judith and Catharine around the floor. We were stiff dancers, the three of us; only Molly made me seem good, floating backward from my feet fearlessly as her cheek rumpled my moist shirt. The gym was hung with orange and black crepe paper in honor of Hallowe'en, and the pennants of all the competing schools were fastened to the walls, and a twelve-piece band pumped away blissfully on the year's sad tunes — "Heartaches," "Near You," "That's My Desire." A great cloud of balloons gathered in the steel girders was released. There was pink punch, and a local girl sang.

Judith and Catharine decided to leave before the dance was over, and I made Molly come too, though she was in a literal sweat of pleasure; her perfect skin in the oval above her neckline was flushed and glazed. I realized, with a little shock of possessiveness and pity, that she was unused to attention back home, in competition with the gorgeous Olinger ignorant.

We walked together to the house where the four of us had been boarded, a large white frame owned by an old couple and standing with lonely decency in a semi-slum. Judith and Catharine turned up the walk, but Molly and I, with a diffident decision that I believe came from her initiative, continued, "to walk around the block." We walked miles, stopping off after midnight at a trolley-car-shaped diner. I got a hamburger, and she impressed me by ordering coffee. We walked back to the house and let ourselves in with the key we had been given; but instead of going upstairs to our rooms we sat downstairs in the dark living room and talked softly for more hours.

What did we say? I talked about myself. It is hard to hear, much less remember, what we ourselves say, just as it might be hard for a movie projector, given life, to see the shadows its eye of light is casting. A transcript, could I produce it, of my monologue through the wide turning point of that night, with all its word-by-word conceit, would distort the picture: this living room miles from home, the street light piercing the chinks in the curtains and erecting on the wallpaper rods of light the size of yardsticks, our hosts and companions asleep upstairs, the incessant sigh of my voice, coffee-primed Molly on the floor beside my chair, her stockinged legs stretched out on the rug; and this odd sense in the room, a tasteless and odorless aura unfamiliar to me, as of a pool of water widening.

I remember one exchange. I must have been describing the steep waves of fearing death that had come over me ever since early childhood, about one every three years, and I ended by supposing that it would take great courage to be an atheist. "But I bet you'll become one," Molly said. "Just to show yourself that you're brave enough." I felt she overestimated me, and was flattered. Within a few years, while I still remembered many of her words, I realized how touchingly gauche our assumption was that an atheist is a lonely rebel; for mobs of men are united in atheism, and oblivion — the dense lead-like sea that would occasionally sweep over me — is to them a weight as negligible as the faint pressure of their wallets in their hip pockets. This grotesque and tender misestimate of the world flares in my memory of our conversation like one of the innumerable matches we struck.

The room filled with smoke. Too weary to sit, I lay down on the floor beside her, and stroked her silver arm in silence, yet still was too timid to act on the wide and negative aura that I did not understand was of compliance. On the upstairs landing, as I went to turn into my room, Molly came forward with a prim look and kissed me. With clumsy force I entered the negative space that had been waiting. Her lipstick smeared in little unflattering flecks into the skin around her mouth; it was as if I had been given a face to eat, and the presence of bone — skull under skin, teeth behind lips — impeded me. We stood for a long time under the burning hall light, until my neck began to ache from bowing. My legs were trembling when we finally parted and sneaked into our rooms. In bed I thought, "Allen Dow tossed restlessly," and realized it was the first time that day I had thought of myself in the third person.

On Saturday morning, we lost our debate. I was sleepy and verbose and haughty, and some of the students in the audience began to boo whenever I opened my mouth. The principal came up on the stage and made a scolding speech, which finished me and my cause, untrammeled Germany. On the train back, Catharine and Judith arranged the seating so that they sat behind Molly and me, and spied on only the tops of our heads. For the first time, on the ride home, I felt what it was to bury a humiliation in the body of a woman. Nothing but the friction of my face against hers drowned out the echo of those boos. When we kissed, a red shadow would well under my lips and eclipse the hostile hooting faces of the debate audience, and when our lips parted, the bright inner sea would ebb, and there the faces would be again, more intense than ever. With a shudder of shame I'd hide my face on her shoulder and in the warm darkness there, while a frill of her prissy collar gently scratched my nose, I felt united with Hitler and all the villains, traitors, madmen, and failures who had managed to keep, up to the moment of capture or death, a woman with them. This had puzzled me. In high school, females were proud and remote; in the newspapers they were fantastic monsters of submission. And now Molly administered reassurance to me with small motions and bodily adjustments that had about them a strange flavor of the practical.

Our parents met us at the station. I was startled at how tired my mother looked. There were deep blue dents on either side of her nose, and her hair seemed somehow dissociated from her head, as if it were a ragged, half-gray wig she had put on carelessly. She was a heavy woman, and her weight, which she usually carried upright, like a kind of wealth, had slumped away from her ownership and seemed, in the sullen light of the railway platform, to weigh on the world. I asked, "How's Grandpa?" He had taken to bed several months before with pains in his chest.

"He still sings," she said rather sharply. For entertainment in his increasing blindness my grandfather had long ago begun to sing, and his shapely old voice would pour forth hymns, forgotten comic ballads, and camp-meeting songs at any hour. His memory seemed to improve the longer he lived.

My mother's irritability was more manifest in the private cavity of the car; her heavy silence oppressed me. "You look so tired, Mother," I said, trying to take the offensive.

"That's nothing to how you look," she answered. "What happened up there? You stoop like an old married man."

"Nothing happened," I lied. My cheeks were parched, as if her high steady anger had the power of giving sunburn.

"I remember that Bingaman girl's mother when we first moved to town. She was the smuggest little snip south of the pike. They're real old Olinger stock, you know. They have no use for hillbillies."

My father tried to change the subject. "Well, you won one debate, Allen, and that's more than I would have done. I don't see how you do it."

"Why, he gets it from you, Victor. I've never won a debate with you."

"He gets it from Pop Baer. If that man had gone into politics, Lillian, all the misery of his life would have been avoided."

"Dad was never a debater. He was a bully. Don't go with little women, Allen. It puts you too close to the ground."

"I'm not *going* with *any*body, Mother. Really, you're so fanciful."

"Why, when she stepped off the train from the way her chins bounced I thought she had eaten a canary. And then making my poor son, all skin and bones, carry her bag. When she walked by me I honestly was afraid she'd spit in my eye."

"I had to carry somebody's bag. I'm sure she doesn't know who you are." Though it was true I had talked a good deal about my family the night before.

My mother turned away from me. "You see, Victor — he defends her. When I was his age that girl's mother gave me a cut I'm still bleeding from, and my own son attacks me on behalf of her fat little daughter. I wonder if her mother put her up to catching him."

"Molly's a nice girl," my father interceded. "She never gave me any trouble in class like some of those smug bastards." But he was curiously listless, for so Christian a man, in pronouncing this endorsement.

I discovered that nobody wanted me to go with Molly Bingaman. My friends — for on the strength of being funny I did have some friends, classmates whose love affairs went on over my head but whom I could accompany, as clown, on communal outings — never talked with me about Molly, and when I brought her to their parties gave the impression of ignoring her, so that I stopped taking her. Teachers at school would smile an odd tight smile when they saw us leaning by her locker or hanging around in the stairways. The eleventh-grade English instructor — one of my "boosters" on the faculty, a man who was always trying to "challenge" me, to "exploit" my "potential" — took me aside and told me how stupid she was. She just couldn't grasp the principles of syntax. He confided her parsing mistakes to me as if they betrayed — as indeed in a way they did — an obtuseness her social manner cleverly concealed. Even the Fabers, an ultra-Republican couple who ran a luncheonette near the high school, showed malicious delight whenever Molly and I broke up, and persistently treated my attachment as being a witty piece of play, like my pretense with Mr. Faber of being a Communist. The entire town seemed ensnarled in my mother's myth, that escape was my proper fate. It was as if I were a sport that the ghostly elders of Olinger had segregated from the rest of the livestock and agreed to donate in time to the air; this fitted with the ambiguous sensation I had always had in the town, of being simultaneously flattered and rejected.

Molly's parents disapproved because in their eyes my family was virtually white trash. It was so persistently hammered into me that I was too good for Molly that I scarcely considered the proposition that, by another scale, she was too good for me. Further, Molly herself shielded me. Only once, exasperated by some tedious, condescending confession of mine, did she state that her mother didn't like me. "Why not?" I asked, genuinely surprised. I admired Mrs. Bingaman — she was beautifully preserved — and I always felt gay in her house, with its white woodwork and matching furniture and vases of iris posing before polished mirrors.

"Oh, I don't know. She thinks you're flippant."

"But that's not true. Nobody takes himself more seriously than I do."

While Molly protected me from the Bingaman side of the ugliness, I conveyed the Dow side more or less directly to her. It infuriated me that nobody allowed me to be proud of her. I kept, in effect, asking her, Why was she stupid in English? Why didn't she get along with my friends? Why did she look so dumpy and smug? — this last despite the fact that she often, especially in intimate moments, looked beautiful to me. I was especially angry with her because this affair had brought out an ignoble, hysterical, brutal aspect of my mother that I might never have had to see otherwise. I had hoped to keep things secret from her, but even if her intuition had not been relentless, my father, at school, knew everything. Sometimes, indeed, my mother said that she didn't care if I went with Molly; it was my father who was upset. Like a frantic dog tied by one leg, she snapped in any direction, mouthing ridiculous fancies — such as that Mrs. Bingaman had sicked Molly on me just to keep me from going to college and giving the Dows something to be proud of — that would make us both suddenly start laughing. Laughter in that house that winter had a guilty sound. My grandfather was dying, and lay upstairs singing and coughing and weeping as the mood came to him, and we were too poor to hire a nurse, and too kind and cowardly to send him to a "home." It was still his house, after all. Any noise he made seemed to slash my mother's heart, and she was unable to sleep upstairs near him, and waited the nights out on the sofa downstairs. In her desperate state she would say unforgivable things to me even while the tears streamed down her face. I've never seen so many tears as I saw that winter.

Every time I saw my mother cry, it seemed I had to make Molly cry. I developed a skill at it; it came naturally to an only child who had been surrounded all his life by adults ransacking each other for the truth. Even in the heart of intimacy, half-naked each of us, I would say something to humiliate her. We never made love in the final, coital sense. My reason was a mixture of idealism and superstition; I felt that if I took her virginity she would be mine forever. I depended overmuch on a technicality; she gave herself to me anyway, and I had her anyway, and have her still, for the longer I travel in a direction I could not have taken with her, the more clearly she seems the one person who loved me without advantage. I was a homely, comically ambitious hillbilly, and I even refused to tell her I loved her, to pronounce the word "love" — an icy piece of pedantry that shocks me now that I have almost forgottten the context of confusion in which it seemed wise.

In addition to my grandfather's illness, and my mother's grief, and my waiting to hear if I had won a scholarship to the one college that seemed good enough for me, I was burdened with managing too many petty affairs of my graduating class. I was in charge of yearbook writeups, art editor of the school paper, chairman of the Class Gift Committee, director of the Senior Assembly, and teachers' workhorse. Frightened by my father's tales of nervous breakdowns he had seen, I kept listening for the sounds of my brain snapping, and the image of that gray, infinitely interconnected mass seemed to extend outward, to become my whole world, one dense organic dungeon, and I felt I had to get out; if I could just get out of this, into June, it would be blue sky, and I would be all right for life.

One Friday night in spring, after trying for over an hour to write thirty-five affectionate words for the yearbook about a dull girl in the Secretarial Course I had never spoken a word to, I heard my grandfather begin coughing upstairs with a sound like dry membrane tearing, and I panicked. I called up the stairs, "Mother! I must go out."

"It's nine-thirty."

"I know, but I have to. I'm going insane."

Without waiting to hear her answer or to find a coat, I left the house and got our old car out of the garage. The weekend before, I had broken up with Molly again. All week I hadn't spoken to her, though I had seen her once in Faber's, with a boy in her class, averting her face while I, hanging by the side of the pinball machine, made wisecracks in her direction. I didn't dare go up to her door and knock so late at night; I just parked across the street and watched the lit windows of her house. Through their living-room window I could see one of Mrs. Bingaman's vases of hothouse iris standing on a white mantel, and my open car window admitted the spring air, which delicately smelled of wet ashes. Molly was probably out on a date with that moron in her class. But then the Bingamans' door opened, and her figure appeared in the rectangle of light. Her back was toward me, a coat was on her arm, and her mother seemed to be screaming. Molly closed the door and ran down off the porch and across the street and quickly got into the car, her eyes downcast in their sockets of shadow. *She came.* When I have finally forgotten everything else, her powdery fragrance, her lucid cool skin, the way her lower lip was like a curved pillow of two cloths, the dusty red outer and wet pink inner, I'll still be grieved by this about Molly, that she came to me.

After I returned her to her house — she told me not to worry, her mother enjoyed shouting — I went to the all-night diner just beyond the Olinger town line and ate three hamburgers, ordering them one at a time, and drank two glasses of milk. It was close to two o'clock when I got home, but my mother was still awake. She lay on the sofa in the dark, with the radio sitting on the floor murmuring Dixieland piped up from New Orleans by way of Philadelphia. Radio music was a steady feature of her insomniac life; not only did it help drown out the noise of her father upstairs but she seemed to enjoy it in itself. She would resist my father's pleas to come to bed by saying that the New Orleans program was not over yet. The radio was an old Philco we had always had; I had once drawn a fish on the orange disc of its celluloid dial, which looked to my child's eyes like a fishbowl.

Her loneliness caught at me; I went into the living room and sat on a chair with my back to the window. For a long time she looked at me tensely out of the darkness. "Well," she said at last, "how was little hot-pants?" The vulgarity this affair had brought out in her language appalled me.

"I made her cry," I told her.

"Why do you torment the girl?"

"To please you."

"It doesn't please me."

"Well, then, stop nagging me."

"I'll stop nagging you if you'll solemnly tell me you're willing to marry her."

I said nothing to this, and after waiting she went on in a different voice, "Isn't it funny, that you should show this weakness?"

"Weakness is a funny way to put it when it's the only thing that gives me strength."

"Does it really, Allen? Well. It may be. I forget, you were born here."

Upstairs, close to our heads, my grandfather, in a voice frail but still melodious, began to sing, "There is a happy land, far, far away, where saints in glory stand, bright, bright as day." We listened; and his voice broke into coughing, a terrible rending cough growing in fury, struggling to escape, and loud with fear he called my mother's name. She didn't stir. His voice grew enormous, a bully's voice, as he repeated, "Lillian! Lillian!" and I saw my mother's shape quiver with the force coming down the stairs into her; she was like a dam; and then the power, as my grandfather fell momentarily silent, flowed toward me in the darkness, and I felt intensely angry, and hated that black mass of suffering, even while I realized, with a rapid light calculation, that I was too weak to withstand it.

In a dry tone of certainty and dislike — how hard my heart had become! — I told her. "All right. You'll win this one, Mother; but it'll be the last one you'll win."

My pang of fright following this unprecedentedly cold insolence seemed to blot my senses; the chair ceased to be felt under me, and the walls and furniture of the room fell away — there was only the dim orange glow of the radio dial down below. In a husky voice that seemed to come across a great distance my mother said, with typical melodrama, "Goodbye, Allen."

[1962]

John Updike

ಗಿಲ

WIFE-WOOING

Oh my love. Yes. Here we sit, on warm broad floorboards, before a fire, the children between us, in a crescent, eating. The girl and I share one halfpint of French-fried potatoes; you and the boy share another; and in the center, sharing nothing, making simple reflections within himself like a jewel, the baby, mounted in an Easybaby, sucks at his bottle with frowning mastery, his selfish, contemplative eyes stealing glitter from the center of the flames. And you. You. You allow your skirt, the same black skirt in which this morning you with woman's soft bravery mounted a bicycle and sallied forth to play hymns in difficult keys on the Sunday school's old piano — you allow this black skirt to slide off your raised knees down your thighs, slide *up* your thighs in your body's absolute geography, so the parallel whiteness of their undersides is exposed to the fire's warmth and to my sight. Oh. There is a line of Joyce. I try to recover it from the legendary, imperfectly explored grottoes of *Ulysses:* a garter snapped, to please Blazes Boylan, in a deep Dublin den. What? Smackwarm. That was the crucial word. Smacked smackwarm on her smackable warm woman's thigh. Something like that. A splendid man, to feel that. Smackwarm woman's. Splendid also to feel the curious and potent, inexplicable and irrefutably magical life language leads within itself. What soul took thought and knew that adding "wo" to man would make a woman? The difference exactly. The wide w, the receptive o. Womb. In our crescent the children for all their size seem to come out of you toward me, wet fingers and eyes, tinted bronze. Three children, five persons, seven years. Seven years since I wed wide warm woman, white-thighed. Wooed and wed. Wife. A knife of a word that for all its final bite did not end the wooing. To my wonderment.

We eat meat, meat I wrested warm from the raw hands of the hamburger girl in the diner a mile away, a ferocious place, slick with savagery, wild with chrome; young predators snarling dirty jokes menaced me, old men reached for me with coffee-warmed paws; I wielded my wallet, and won my way back. The fat brown bag of buns was warm beside me in the cold car; the smaller bag holding the two tiny cartons of French-fries emitted an even more urgent heat. Back through the black winter air to the fire, the intimate cave, where halloos and hurrahs greeted me, the deer, mouth agape and its cotton throat gushing, stretched dead across my shoulders. And now you, beside the white O of the plate upon which the children discarded with squeals of disgust the rings of translucent onion that came squeezed in the hamburgers — you push your toes an inch closer to the blaze, and the ashy white of the inside of your deep thigh is lazily laid bare, and the eternally elastic garter snaps smackwarm against my hidden heart.

Who would have thought, wide wife, back there in the white tremble of the ceremony (in the corner of my eye I held, despite the distracting hail of ominous vows, the vibration of the cluster of stephanotis clutched against your waist), that seven years would bring us no distance, through all those warm beds, to the same trembling point, of beginning? The cells change every seven years, and down in the atom, apparently, there is a strange discontinuity; as if God wills the universe anew every instant. (Ah God, dear God, tall friend of my childhood, I will never forget you, though they say dreadful things. They say rose windows in cathedrals are vaginal symbols.) Your legs, exposed as fully as by a bathing suit, yearn deeper into the amber wash of heat. Well: begin. A green jet of flame spits out sideways from a pocket of resin in a log, crying, and the orange shadows on the ceiling sway with fresh life. Begin.

"Remember, on our honeymoon, how the top of the kerosene heater made a great big rose window on the ceiling?"

"Vnn." Your chin goes to your knees, your shins draw in, all is retracted. Not much to remember, perhaps, for you; blood badly spilled, clumsiness of all sorts. "It was cold for June."

"Mommy, what was cold? What did you say?" the girl asks, enunciating angrily, determined not to let language slip on her tongue and tumble her so that we laugh.

"A house where Daddy and I stayed one time."

"I don't like dat," the boy says, and throws a half bun painted with chartreuse mustard onto the floor.

You pick it up and with beautiful sombre musing ask, "Isn't that funny? Did any of the others have mustard on them?"

"I *hate* dat," the boy insists; he is two. Language is to him thick vague handles swirling by; he grabs what he can.

"Here. He can have mine. Give me his." I pass my hamburger over, you take it, he takes it from you, there is nowhere a ripple of gratitude. There is no more praise of my heroism in fetching Sunday supper, saving you labor. Cunning, you sense, and sense that I sense your knowledge, that I had hoped to hoard your energy toward a more ecstatic spending. We sense everything between us, every ripple, existent and nonexistent; it is tiring. Courting a wife takes tenfold the strength of winning an ignorant girl. The fire shifts, shattering fragments of newspaper that carry in lighter gray the ghost of the ink of their message. You huddle your legs and bring the skirt back over them. With a sizzling noise like the sighs of the exhausted logs, the baby sucks the last from his bottle, drops it to the floor with its distasteful hoax of vacant suds, and begins to cry. His egotist's mouth opens; the delicate membrane of his satisfaction tears. You pick him up and stand. You love the baby more than me.

Who would have thought, blood once spilled, that no barrier would be broken, that you would be each time healed into a virgin again? Tall, fair, obscure, remote, and courteous.

We put the children to bed, one by one, in reverse order of birth. I am limitlessly patient, paternal, good. Yet you know. We watch the paper bags and cartons ignite on the breathing pillow of embers, read, watch television, eat crackers, it does not matter. Eleven comes. For a tingling moment you stand on the bedroom rug in your underpants, untangling your nightie; oh, fat white sweet fat fatness. In bed you read about Richard Nixon. He fascinates you; you hate him. You know how he defeated Jerry Voorhis, martyred Mrs. Douglas, how he played poker in the Navy despite being a Quaker, every fiendish trick, every low adaptation. Oh my Lord. Let's let the poor man go to bed. We're none of us perfect. "Hey let's turn out the light."

"Wait. He's just about to get Hiss convicted. It's very strange. It says he acted honorably."

"I'm sure he did." I reach for the switch.

"No. Wait. Just till I finish this chapter. I'm sure there'll be something at the end."

"Honey, Hiss was guilty. We're all guilty. Conceived in concupiscence, we die unrepentant." Once my ornate words wooed you.

I lie against your filmy convex back. You read sideways, a sleepy trick. I see the page through the fringe of your hair, sharp and white as a wedge of crystal. Suddenly it slips. The book has slipped from your hand. You are asleep. Oh cunning trick, cunning. In the darkness I consider. Cunning. The headlights of cars accidentally slide fanning slits of light around our walls and ceiling. The great rose window was projected upward through the petal-shaped perforations in the top of the black kerosene stove, which we stood in the center of the floor. As the flame on the circular wick flickered, the wide soft star of interlocked penumbrae moved and waved as if it were printed on a silk cloth being gently tugged or slowly blown. Its color soft blurred blood. We pay dear in blood for our peaceful homes.

In the morning, to my relief, you are ugly. Monday's wan breakfast light bleaches you blotchily, drains the goodness from your thickness, makes the bathrobe a limp stained tube flapping disconsolately, exposing sallow décolletage. The skin between your breasts a sad yellow. I feast with the coffee on your drabness. Every wrinkle and sickly tint a relief and a revenge. The children yammer. The toaster sticks. Seven years have worn this woman.

The man, he arrows off to work, jousting for right-of-way, veering on the thin hard edge of the legal speed limit. Out of domestic muddle, softness, pallor, flaccidity: into the city. Stone is his province. The winning coin. The maneuvering of abstractions. Making heartless things run. Oh the inanimate, adamant joys of job!

I return with my head enmeshed in a machine. A technicality it would take weeks to explain to you snags my brain; I fiddle with phrases and numbers all the blind evening. You serve me supper as a waitress — as less than a waitress, for I have known you. The children touch me timidly, as they would a steep girder bolted into a framework whose height they don't understand. They drift into sleep securely. We survive their passing in calm parallelity. My thoughts rework in chronic right angles the same snagging circuits on the same professional grid. You rustle the book about Nixon; vanish upstairs into the plumbing; the bathtub pipes cry. In my head I seem to have found the stuck switch at last: I push at it; it jams; I push; it is jammed. I grow dizzy, churning with cigarettes. I circle the room aimlessly.

So I am taken by surprise at a turning when at the meaningful hour of ten you come with a kiss of toothpaste to me moist and girlish and quick; the momentous moral of this story being, An expected gift is not worth giving.

[1962]

PHILIP ROTH (b. 1933) *was born in Newark, New Jersey, and grew up in a Jewish neighborhood there. His father was an insurance salesman whose parents had emigrated from Austria-Hungary. Roth is remembered by his teachers as a quiet, studious boy. He worked on the high school newspaper and studied literature at Rutgers and at Bucknell University before receiving his M.A. in literature from the University of Chicago, where he later taught English. While he was teaching he also began publishing stories in such little magazines as* Epoch, Chicago Review, *and* Paris Review, *and in such large-circulation periodicals as* The New Yorker, Esquire, *and* Harper's. *He launched his career as a writer with a short novel,* Goodbye Columbus, *published together with five short stories in 1959. It was so successful — it won a National Book Award — that he decided to give up teaching. Three years later he followed it with his first full-length novel,* Letting Go, *and he continued publishing novels during the 1960s, 1970s, and 1980s. In 1975 a second collection of stories appeared,* Reading Myself and Others, *which included " 'I Always Wanted You to Admire My Fasting': Or, Looking at Kafka."*

Over the years Roth's work has developed from realistic, serious depictions of characters and events, to surreal, comic attacks on such favorite American institutions as the cult of success and baseball, to bittersweet, introspective examinations of the personal and moral dilemmas of a writer living among the people he writes about. Portnoy's Complaint (1969) *a semiautobiographical novel about a young Jewish boy growing up in Newark, caused something of a scandal because of its frank depiction of Alexander Portnoy's sexual fantasies. A similar autobiographical character, the writer Nathan Zuckerman, is the main character in two of Roth's finer recent novels,* The Ghost Writer (1979) *and* Zuckerman Unbound (1981).

Roth's interest in Franz Kafka is apparent in his novel The Breast (1972), *in which a professor of literature experiences a Kafkaesque metamorphosis — "a massive hormonal influx" — which transforms him overnight into a spongy, sightless, six-foot-wide female breast. In the later novel* The Professor of Desire (1977), *Roth's main character goes to Prague largely because he is devoted to Kafka, visits the writer's home, and discusses him with a Czech professor.*

Roth's susceptibility to Kafka's literary influence is integrated into his larger view of himself as a writer. His story " 'I Always Wanted You to Admire My Fasting': Or, Looking at Kafka" is about Kafka's fictional arrival in Newark in 1942 to become a Hebrew teacher. Roth was actually nine years old at the time, attending Hebrew school in Newark, and the story of their imaginary encounter implies a dramatic contrast between the self-denying and self-defeating Kafka, spiritual and ascetic, and Roth himself — the grandson of emigrants, "the Jew who got away" from Hitler's concentration camps, whose fiction as a second-generation American writer is indebted to the culture around him, even as he plaintively criticizes it. Playing games with his reader, Roth uses his wit as the evasive strategy of a writer who, like his character Alexander Portnoy, complains that he is "the son in the Jewish joke — only it ain't no joke!" Roth's story is the dramatization of his endless questioning of himself, reflecting on what he sees as his predicament as a Jew in America.

Philip Roth

ಬಬ

"I ALWAYS WANTED YOU TO ADMIRE MY FASTING"

Or, Looking at Kafka

> *"I always wanted you to admire my fasting," said the hunger artist. "We do admire it," said the overseer, affably. "But you shouldn't admire it," said the hunger artist. "Well, then we don't admire it," said the overseer, "but why shouldn't we admire it?" "Because I have to fast, I can't help it," said the hunger artist. "What a fellow you are," said the overseer, "and why can't you help it?" "Because," said the hunger artist, lifting his head a little and speaking, with his lips pursed, as if for a kiss, right into the overseer's ear, so that no syllable might be lost, "because I couldn't find the food I liked. If I had found it, believe me, I should have made no fuss and stuffed myself like you or anyone else." These were his last words, but in his dimming eyes remained the firm though no longer proud persuasion that he was still continuing to fast.*
>
> *   –Franz Kafka, "A HUNGER ARTIST"*

I

I am looking, as I write of Kafka, at the photograph taken of him at the age of forty (my age) — it is 1924, as sweet and hopeful a year as he may ever have known as a man, and the year of his death. His face is sharp and skeletal, a burrower's face: pronounced cheekbones made even more conspicuous by the absence of sideburns; the ears shaped and angled on his head like angel wings; an intense, creaturely gaze of startled composure — enormous fears, enormous control; a black towel of Levantine hair pulled close around the skull the only sensuous feature; there is a familiar Jewish flare in the bridge of the nose, the nose itself is long and weighted slightly at the tip — the nose of half the Jewish boys who were my friends in high school. Skulls chiseled like this one were shoveled by the thousands from the ovens; had he lived, his would have been among them, along with the skulls of his three younger sisters.

Of course it is no more horrifying to think of Franz Kafka in Auschwitz than to think of anyone in Auschwitz — it is just horrifying in its own way. But he died too soon for the holocaust. Had he lived, perhaps he would have escaped with his good friend Max Brod, who found refuge in Palestine, a citizen of Israel until his death there in 1968. But *Kafka* escaping? It seems unlikely for one so fascinated by entrapment and careers that culminate in an anguished death. Still, there is Karl Rossmann, his American greenhorn.[1] Having imagined Karl's escape to America and his mixed luck here, could not Kafka have found a way to execute an escape for himself? The New School for Social Research in New York becoming *his* Great Nature Theatre of Oklahoma? Or perhaps, through the influence of Thomas Mann,[2] a position in the German department at Princeton. . . . But then, had Kafka lived, it is not at all certain that the books of his which Mann celebrated from *his* refuge in New Jersey would ever have been published; eventually Kafka might either have destroyed those manuscripts that he had once bid Max Brod to dispose of at his death or, at the least, continued to keep them his secret. The Jewish refugee arriving in America in 1938 would not then have been Mann's "religious humorist" but a frail and bookish fifty-five-year-old bachelor, formerly a lawyer for a government insurance firm in Prague, retired on a pension in Berlin at the time of Hitler's rise to power — an author, yes, but of a few eccentric stories, mostly about animals, stories no one in America had ever heard of and only a handful in Europe had read; a homeless K.,[3] but without K.'s willfulness and purpose, a homeless Karl, but without Karl's youthful spirit and resilience; just a Jew lucky enough to have escaped with his life, in his possession a suitcase containing some clothes, some family photos, some Prague mementos, and the manuscripts, still unpublished and in pieces, of *Amerika, The Trial, The Castle,* and (stranger things happen) three more fragmented novels, no less remarkable than the bizarre masterworks that he keeps to himself out of

---

[1] Character in Kafka's unfinished novel *Amerika.* For some biographical information on Franz Kafka, see the headnote to "The Metamorphosis," pp. 553–554.

[2] German novelist (1875–1955) whose works include *Buddenbrooks, The Magic Mountain,* and *Death in Venice.* Mann fled Hitler's Germany and lived his last years in the United States and Switzerland.

[3] Nameless main character in Kafka's novel *The Castle.* The main character in his *The Trial* is also named "K.," but is given a first name, Joseph.

oedipal timidity, perfectionist madness, and insatiable longings for solitude and spiritual purity.

July 1923: Eleven months before he will die in a Vienna sanatorium, Kafka somehow finds the resolve to leave Prague and his father's home for good. Never before has he even remotely succeeded in living apart, independent of his mother, his sisters, and his father, nor has he been a writer other than in those few hours when he is not working in the legal department of the Workers' Accident Insurance Office in Prague; since taking his law degree at the university, he has been by all reports the most dutiful and scrupulous of employees, though he finds the work tedious and enervating. But in June of 1923 — having some months earlier been pensioned from his job because of his illness — he meets a young Jewish girl of nineteen at a seaside resort in Germany, Dora Dymant, an employee at the vacation camp of the Jewish People's Home of Berlin. Dora has left her Orthodox Polish family to make a life of her own (at half Kafka's age); she and Kafka — who has just turned forty — fall in love. . . . Kafka has by now been engaged to two somewhat more conventional Jewish girls — twice to one of them — hectic, anguished engagements wrecked largely by his fears. "I am mentally incapable of marrying," he writes his father in the forty-five-page letter he gave to his mother to deliver. ". . . the moment I make up my mind to marry I can no longer sleep, my head burns day and night, life can no longer be called life." He explains why. "Marrying is barred to me," he tells his father, "because it is your domain. Sometimes I imagine the map of the world spread out and you stretched diagonally across it. And I feel as if I could consider living in only those regions that are not covered by you or are not within your reach. And in keeping with the conception I have of your magnitude, these are not many and not very comforting regions — and marriage is not among them." The letter explaining what is wrong between this father and this son is dated November 1919; the mother thought it best not even to deliver it, perhaps for lack of courage, probably, like the son, for lack of hope.

During the following two years, Kafka attempts wage an affair with Milena Jesenká-Pollak, an intense young woman of twenty-four who has translated a few of his stories into Czech and is most unhappily married in Vienna; his affair with Milena, conducted feverishly, but by and large through the mails, is even more demoralizing to Kafka than the fearsome engagements to the nice Jewish girls. They aroused only the paterfamilias longings that he dared not indulge, longings inhibited by his exaggerated awe of his father — "spellbound," says Brod, "in the family circle" — and the hypnotic spell of his own solitude; but the Czech Milena, impetuous, frenetic, indifferent to conventional restraints, a woman of appetite and anger, arouses more elemental yearnings and more elemental fears. According to a Prague critic, Rio Preisner, Milena was "psychopathic"; according to Margaret Buber-Neumann, who lived two years beside her in the German concentration camp where Milena died following a kidney operation in 1944, she was powerfully sane, extraordinarily humane and courageous. Milena's obituary for Kafka was the only one of consequence to appear in the Prague press; the prose is strong, so are the claims she makes for Kafka's accomplishment. She is still only in her twenties, the dead man is hardly known as a writer beyond his small circle of friends — yet Milena writes: "His knowledge of the world was exceptional and deep, and he was a deep and exceptional world in himself.... [He had] a delicacy of feeling bordering on the miraculous and a mental clarity that was terrifyingly uncompromising, and in turn he loaded on to his illness the whole burden of his mental fear of life.... He wrote the most important books in recent German literature." One can imagine this vibrant young woman stretched diagonally across the bed, as awesome to Kafka as his own father spread out across the map of the world. His letters to her are disjointed, unlike anything else of his in print; the word "fear" appears on page after page. "We are both married, you in Vienna, I to my Fear in Prague." He yearns to lay his head upon her breast; he calls her "Mother Milena"; during at least one of their two brief rendezvous, he is hopelessly impotent. At last he has to tell her to leave him be, an edict that Milena honors, though it leaves her hollow with grief. "Do not write," Kafka tells her, "and let us not see each other; I ask you only to quietly fulfill this request of mine; only on those conditions is survival possible for me; everything else continues the process of destruction."

Then, in the early summer of 1923, during a visit to his sister, who is vacationing with her children by the Baltic Sea, he finds young Dora Dymant, and within a month Franz Kafka has gone off to live with her in two rooms in a suburb of Berlin, out of reach at last of the "claws" of Prague and home. How can it be? How can he, in his illness, have accomplished so swiftly and decisively the leave-taking that was beyond him in his healthiest days? The impassioned letter writer who could equivocate interminably about which train to catch to Vienna to meet with Milena (if he should meet with her for the weekend at all); the bourgeois suitor in the high collar, who, during his drawn-out agony of an engagement with the proper Fräulein Bauer, secretly draws up a memorandum for himself, countering the arguments "for" marriage with the arguments "against"; the poet of the ungraspable and the unresolved, whose belief in the immovable barrier separating the wish from its realization is at the heart of his excruciating visions of defeat; the Kafka whose fiction refutes every easy, touching, humanish daydream of salvation and justice and fulfillment with densely imagined counterdreams that mock all solutions and escapes — this Kafka *escapes*. Overnight! K. penetrates the Castle walls — Joseph K. evades his indictment — "a breaking away from it altogether, a mode of living completely outside the jurisdiction of the Court." Yes, the possibility of which Joseph

K. has just a glimmering in the Cathedral, but can neither fathom nor effectuate — "not . . . some influential manipulation of the case, but . . . a circumvention of it" — Kafka realizes in the last year of his life.

Was it Dora Dymant or was it death that pointed the new way? Perhaps it could not have been one without the other. We know that the "illusory emptiness" at which K. gazed, upon first entering the village and looking up through the mist and the darkness to the Castle, was no more vast and incomprehensible than the idea of himself as husband and father was to the young Kafka; but now, it seems, the prospect of a Dora forever, of a wife, home, and children everlasting, is no longer the terrifying, bewildering prospect it would once have been, for now "everlasting" is undoubtedly not much more than a matter of months. Yes, the dying Kafka is determined to marry, and writes to Dora's Orthodox father for his daughter's hand. But the imminent death that has resolved all contradictions and uncertainties in Kafka is the very obstacle placed in his path by the young girl's father. The request of the dying man Franz Kafka to bind to him in his invalidism the healthy young girl Dora Dymant is — denied!

If there is not one father standing in Kafka's way, there is another — and another behind him. Dora's father, writes Max Brod in his biography of Kafka, "set off with [Kafka's] letter to consult the man he honored most, whose authority counted more than anything else for him, the 'Gerer Rebbe.' The rabbi read the letter, put it to one side, and said nothing more than the single syllable, 'No.'" No. Klamm[4] himself could have been no more abrupt — or any more removed from the petitioner. No. In its harsh finality, as telling and inescapable as the curselike threat delivered by his father to Georg Bendemann,[5] that thwarted fiancé: "Just take your bride on your arm and try getting in my way. I'll sweep her from your very side, you don't know how!" No. Thou shalt not have, say the fathers, and Kafka agrees that he shall not. The habit of obedience and renunciation; also, his own distaste for the diseased and reverence for strength, appetite, and health. "'Well, clear this out now!' said the overseer, and they buried the hunger artist, straw and all. Into the cage they put a young panther. Even the most insensitive felt it refreshing to see this wild creature leaping around the cage that had so long been dreary. The panther was all right. The food he liked was brought him without hesitation by the attendants; he seemed not even to miss his freedom; his noble body, furnished almost to the bursting point with all that it needed, seemed to carry freedom around with it too; somewhere in his jaws it seemed to lurk; and the joy of life streamed with such ardent passion from his throat that for the onlookers it was not easy to stand the shock of it. But they braced themselves, crowded round the cage, and did not want ever to move away."[6] So no is no; he knew

---

[4] character in *The Castle*.
[5] main character in Kafka's story "The Judgment."
[6] closing paragraph of Kafka's story "A Hunger Artist."

as much himself. A healthy young girl of nineteen cannot, *should* not, be given in matrimony to a sickly man twice her age, who spits up blood ("I sentence you," cries Georg Bendemann's father, "to death by drowning!") and shakes in his bed with fevers and chills. What sort of un-Kafka-like dream had Kafka been dreaming!

And those nine months spent with Dora have still other "Kafkaesque" elements: a fierce winter in quarters inadequately heated; the inflation that makes a pittance of his own meager pension, and sends into the streets of Berlin the hungry and needy whose suffering, says Dora, turns Kafka "ash-gray"; and his tubercular lungs, flesh transformed and punished. Dora cares for the diseased writer as devotedly and tenderly as Gregor Samsa's sister does for her brother, the bug. Gregor's sister plays the violin so beautifully that Gregor "felt as if the way were opening before him to the unknown nourishment he craved"; he dreams, in his condition, of sending his gifted sister to the Conservatory! Dora's music is Hebrew, which she reads aloud to Kafka, and with such skill that, according to Brod, "Franz recognized her dramatic talent; on his advice and under his direction she later educated herself in the art. . . ."

Only Kafka is hardly vermin to Dora Dymant, *or to himself.* Away from Prague and his father's home, Kafka, at forty, seems at last to have been delivered from the self-loathing, the self-doubt, and those guilt-ridden impulses to dependence and self-effacement that had nearly driven him mad throughout his twenties and thirties; all at once he seems to have shed the pervasive sense of hopeless despair that informs the great punitive fantasies of *The Trial,* "In the Penal Colony," and "The Metamorphosis." Years earlier, in Prague, he had directed Max Brod to destroy all his papers, including three unpublished novels, upon his death; now, in Berlin, when Brod introduces him to a German publisher interested in his work, Kafka consents to the publication of a volume of four stories, and consents, says Brod, "without much need of long arguments to persuade him." With Dora to help, he diligently resumes the study of Hebrew; despite his illness and the harsh winter, he travels to the Berlin Academy for Jewish Studies to attend a series of lectures on the Talmud — a very different Kafka from the estranged melancholic who once wrote in his diary, "What have I in common with the Jews? I have hardly anything in common with myself and should stand very quietly in a corner, content that I can breathe." And to further mark the change, there is ease and happiness with a woman: with this young and adoring companion, he is playful, he is pedagogical, and, one would guess, in light of his illness (*and* his happiness), he is chaste. If not a husband (such as he had striven to be to the conventional Fräulein Bauer), if not a lover (as he struggled hopelessly to be with Milena), he would seem to have become something no less miraculous in his scheme of things: a father, a kind of father to this sisterly, mothering daughter. *As Franz Kafka awoke one morning from uneasy dreams he found himself transformed in his bed into a father, a writer, and a Jew.*

"I have completed the construction of my burrow," begins the long, exquisite, and tedious story that he wrote that winter in Berlin, "and it seems to be successful. . . . Just at the place where, according to my calculations, the Castle Keep should be, the soil was very loose and sandy and had literally to be hammered and pounded into a firm state to serve as a wall for the beautifully vaulted chamber. But for such tasks the only tool I possess is my forehead. So I had to run with my forehead thousands and thousands of times, for whole days and nights, against the ground, and I was glad when the blood came, for that was proof that the walls were beginning to harden; in that way, as everybody must admit, I richly paid for my Castle Keep."

"The Burrow" is the story of an animal with a keen sense of peril whose life is organized around the principle of defense, and whose deepest longings are for security and serenity; with teeth and claws — *and* forehead — the burrower constructs an elaborate and ingeniously intricate system of underground chambers and corridors that are designed to afford it some peace of mind; however, while this burrow does succeed in reducing the sense of danger from without, its maintenance and protection are equally fraught with anxiety: "these anxieties are different from ordinary ones, prouder, richer in content, often long repressed, but in their destructive effects they are perhaps much the same as the anxieties that existence in the outer world gives rise to." The story (whose ending is lost) terminates with the burrower fixated upon distant subterranean noises that cause it "to assume the existence of a great beast," itself burrowing in the direction of the Castle Keep.

Another grim tale of entrapment, and of obsession so grand that no distinction is possible between character and predicament. Yet this fiction imagined in the last "happy" months of his life is touched by a spirit of personal reconciliation and sardonic self-acceptance, by a tolerance of one's own brand of madness, that is not apparent in "The Metamorphosis." The piercing masochistic irony of the earlier animal story — as of "The Judgment" and *The Trial* — has given way here to a critique of the self and its preoccupations that, though bordering on mockery, no longer seeks to resolve itself in images of the uttermost humiliation and defeat. . . . Yet there is more here than a metaphor for the insanely defended ego, whose striving for invulnerability produces a defensive system that must in its turn become the object of perpetual concern — there is also a very unromantic and hardheaded fable about how and why art is made, a portrait of the artist in all his ingenuity, anxiety, isolation, dissatisfaction, relentlessness, obsessiveness, secretiveness, paranoia, and self-addiction, a portrait of the magical thinker at the end of his tether, Kafka's Prospero.[7] . . . It is an endlessly suggestive story, this story of life in a hole. For, finally, remember the prox-

---

[7] main character in Shakespeare's *The Tempest*, the deposed Duke of Milan, who uses magic to recover his dukedom and reconcile himself to the brother who had usurped it.

imity of Dora Dymant during the months that Kafka was at work on "The Burrow" in the two underheated rooms that were their illicit home. Certainly a dreamer like Kafka need never have entered the young girl's body for her tender presence to kindle in him a fantasy of a hidden orifice that promises "satisfied desire," "achieved ambition," and "profound slumber," but that, once penetrated and in one's possession, arouses the most terrifying and heartbreaking fears of retribution and loss. "For the rest I try to unriddle the beast's plans. Is it on its wanderings, or is it working on its own burrow? If it is on its wanderings then perhaps an understanding with it might be possible. If it should really break through to the burrow I shall give it some of my stores and it will go on its way again. It will go on its way again, a fine story! Lying in my heap of earth I can naturally dream of all sorts of things, even of an understanding with the beast, though I know well enough that no such thing can happen, and that at the instant when we see each other, more, at the moment when we merely guess at each other's presence, we shall blindly bare our claws and teeth. . . ."

He died of tuberculosis of the lungs and larynx on June 3, 1924, a month before his forty-first birthday. Dora, inconsolable, whispers for days afterward, "My love, my love, my good one. . . ."

II

1942. I am nine; my Hebrew-school teacher, Dr. Kafka, is fifty-nine. To the little boys who must attend his "four-to-five" class each afternoon, he is known — in part because of his remote and melancholy foreignness, but largely because we vent on him our resentment at having to learn an ancient calligraphy at the very hour we should be out screaming our heads off on the ball field — he is known as Dr. Kishka. Named, I confess, by me. His sour breath, spiced with intestinal juices by five in the afternoon, makes the Yiddish word for "insides" particularly telling, I think. Cruel, yes, but in truth I would have cut out my tongue had I ever imagined the name would become legend. A coddled child, I do not yet think of myself as persuasive, or, quite yet, as a literary force in the world. My jokes don't hurt, how could they, I'm so adorable. And if you don't believe me, just ask my family and the teachers in my school. Already at nine, one foot in college, the other in the Catskills. Little borscht-belt comic that I am outside the classroom, I amuse my friends Schlossman and Ratner on the dark walk home from Hebrew school with an imitation of Kishka, his precise and finicky professorial manner, his German accent, his cough, his gloom. "Doctor *Kishka!*" cries Schlossman, and hurls himself savagely against the newsstand that belongs to the candy-store owner whom Schlossman drives just a little crazier each night. "Doctor Franz — Doctor Franz — Doctor Franz — *Kishka!*" screams Ratner, and my chubby little friend who lives upstairs from me on nothing but chocolate milk and Mallomars does not stop laughing until, as is his wont (his mother has asked me "to keep an eye on him" for just this reason), he wets his pants. Schlossman takes the occasion of Ratner's humiliation to pull the little boy's paper out of his notebook and wave it in the air — it is the assignment Dr. Kafka has just returned to us, graded; we were told to make up an alphabet of our own, out of straight lines and curved lines and dots. "That is all an alphabet is," he had explained. "That is all Hebrew is. That is all English is. Straight lines and curved lines and dots." Ratner's alphabet, for which he received a C, looks like twenty-six skulls strung in a row. I received my A for a curlicued alphabet, inspired largely (as Dr. Kafka seems to have surmised, given his comment at the top of the page) by the number eight. Schlossman received an F for forgetting even to do it — and a lot he seems to care. He is content — he is *overjoyed* — with things as they are. Just waving a piece of paper in the air and screaming, "Kishka! Kishka!" makes him deliriously happy. We should all be so lucky.

At home, alone in the glow of my goose-necked "desk" lamp (plugged after dinner into an outlet in the kitchen, my study), the vision of our refugee teacher, sticklike in a fraying three-piece blue suit, is no longer very funny — particularly after the entire beginners' Hebrew class, of which I am the most studious member, takes the name Kishka to his heart. My guilt awakens redemptive fantasies of heroism, I have them often about the "Jews in Europe." I must save him. If not me, who? The demonic Schlossman? The babyish Ratner? And if not now, when? For I have learned in the ensuing weeks that Dr. Kafka lives in a room in the house of an elderly Jewish lady on the shabby lower stretch of Avon Avenue, where the trolley still runs and the poorest of Newark's Negroes shuffle meekly up and down the street, for all they seem to know, still back in Mississippi. A *room*. And *there*! My family's apartment is no palace, but it is ours at least, so long as we pay the $38.50 a month in rent; and though our neighbors are not rich, they refuse to be poor and they refuse to be meek. Tears of shame and sorrow in my eyes, I rush into the living room to tell my parents what I have heard (though not that I heard it during a quick game of "aces up" played a minute before class against the synagogue's rear wall — worse, played directly beneath a stained-glass window embossed with the names of the dead): "My Hebrew teacher lives in a *room*."

My parents go much further than I could imagine anybody going in the real world. Invite him to dinner, my mother says. *Here*? Of course here — Friday night; I'm sure he can stand a home-cooked meal, she says, and a little pleasant company. Meanwhile, my father gets on the phone to call my Aunt Rhoda, who lives with my grandmother and tends her and her potted plants in the apartment house at the corner of our street. For nearly two decades my father has been introducing my mother's "baby" sister, now forty, to the Jewish bachelors and widowers of north Jersey. No luck so far. Aunt Rhoda, an "interior decorator" in the dry-goods department of the Big Bear, a mammoth merchandise and produce market in industrial Elizabeth, wears falsies (this information by way of my older brother) and sheer frilly blouses, and family lore has it that she spends hours in the bathroom every day applying powder and sweeping her stiffish hair up into a dramatic pile on her head; but despite all this dash and display, she is, in my father's words, "still afraid of the facts of life." He, however, is undaunted, and administers therapy regularly and gratis: "Let 'em squeeze ya, Rhoda — it *feels* good!" I am his flesh and blood, I can reconcile myself to such scandalous talk in our kitchen — *but what will Dr. Kafka think?* Oh, but it's too late to do anything now. The massive machinery of matchmaking has been set in motion by my undiscourageable father, and the smooth engines of my proud homemaking mother's hospitality are already purring away. To throw my body into the works in an attempt to bring it all to a halt — well, I might as well try to bring down the New Jersey Bell Telephone Company by leaving our receiver off the hook. Only Dr. Kafka can save me now. But to my muttered invitation, he replies, with a formal bow that turns me scarlet — who has ever seen a person do such a thing outside of a movie house? — he replies that he would be *honored* to be my family's dinner guest. "My aunt," I rush to tell him, "will be there too." It appears that I have just said something mildly humorous; odd to see Dr. Kafka smile. Sighing, he says, "I will be delighted to meet her." Meet her? He's supposed to *marry* her. How do I warn him? And how do I warn Aunt Rhoda (a very great admirer of me and my marks) about his sour breath, his roomer's pallor, his Old World ways, so at odds with her up-to-dateness? My face feels as if it will ignite of its own — and spark the fires that will engulf the synagogue, Torah and all — when I see Dr. Kafka scrawl our address in his notebook, and beneath it, some words *in German*. "Good night, Dr. Kafka!" "Good night, and thank you, thank you." I turn to run, I go, but not fast enough: out on the street I hear Schlossman — that fiend! — announcing to my classmates, who are punching one another under the lamplight down from the synagogue steps (where a card game is also in progress, organized by the bar mitzvah boys): "Roth invited Kishka to his *house!* To *eat!*"

Does my father do a job on Kafka! Does he make a sales pitch for familial bliss! What it means to a man to have two fine boys and a wonderful wife! Can Dr. Kafka imagine what it's like? The thrill? The satisfaction? The pride? He tells our visitor of the network of relatives on his mother's side that are joined in a "family association" of over two hundred people located in seven states, including the state of Washington! Yes, relatives even in the Far West: here are their photographs, Dr. Kafka; this is a beautiful book we published entirely on our own for five dollars a copy, pictures of every member of the family, including infants, and a family history by "Uncle" Lichtblau, the eighty-five-year-old patriarch of the clan. This is our family newsletter, which is published twice a year and distributed nationwide to all the relatives. This, in the frame, is the menu from the banquet of the family association, held last year in a ballroom of the "Y" in Newark, in honor of my father's mother on her seventy-fifth birthday. My mother, Dr.

Kafka learns, has served *six consecutive years* as the secretary-treasurer of the family association. My father has served a two-year term as president, as have each of his three brothers. We now have fourteen boys in the family in uniform. Philip writes a letter on V-mail stationery to five of his cousins in the army every single month. "Religiously," my mother puts in, smoothing my hair. "I firmly believe," says my father, "that the family is the corner-stone of everything."

Dr. Kafka, who has listened with close attention to my father's spiel, handling the various documents that have been passed to him with great delicacy and poring over them with a kind of rapt absorption that reminds me of myself over the watermarks of my stamps, now for the first time ex-presses himself on the subject of family; softly he says, "I agree," and inspects again the pages of our family book. "Alone," says my father, in conclusion, "alone, Dr. Kafka, is a stone." Dr. Kafka, setting the book gently down upon my mother's gleaming coffee table, allows with a nod that that is so. My mother's fingers are now turning in the curls behind my ears; not that I even know it at the time, or that she does. Being stroked is my life; stroking me, my father, and my brother is hers.

My brother goes off to a Boy Scout meeting, but only after my father has him stand in his neckerchief before Dr. Kafka and describe to him the skills he has mastered to earn each of his badges. I am invited to bring my stamp album into the living room and show Dr. Kafka my set of triangular stamps from Zanzibar. "Zanzibar!" says my father rapturously, as though I, not even ten, have already been there and back. My father accompanies Dr. Kafka and me into the "sun parlor," where my tropical fish swim in the aer-ated, heated, and hygienic paradise I have made for them with my weekly allowance and my Hanukkah *gelt*.[8] I am encouraged to tell Dr. Kafka what I know about the temperament of the angelfish, the function of the catfish, and the family life of the black mollie. I know quite a bit. "All on his own he does that," my father says to Kafka. "He gives me a lecture on one of those fish, it's seventh heaven, Dr. Kafka." "I can imagine," Kafka replies.

Back in the living room my Aunt Rhoda suddenly launches into a rather recondite monologue on "Scotch plaids," intended, it would appear, for the edification of my mother alone. At least she looks fixedly at my mother while she delivers it. I have not yet seen her look directly at Dr. Kafka; she did not even turn his way at dinner when he asked how many employees there were at the Big Bear. "How would I know?" she had re-plied, and then continued right on conversing with my mother, about a butcher who would take care of her "under the counter" if she could find him nylons for his wife. It never occurs to me that she will not look at Dr. Kafka because she is shy — nobody that dolled up could, in my estimation, be shy. I can only think that she is outraged. *It's his breath. It's his accent. It's his age.*

---

[8] money (Yiddish).

I'm wrong — it turns out to be what Aunt Rhoda calls his "superiority complex." "Sitting there, sneering at us like that," says my aunt, somewhat superior now herself. "Sneering?" repeats my father, incredulous. "Sneering and laughing, yes!" says Aunt Rhoda. My mother shrugs. "I don't think he was laughing." "Oh, don't worry, by himself there he was having a very good time — *at our expense.* I know the European-type man. Underneath they think they're all lords of the manor," Rhoda says. "You know something, Rhoda?" says my father, tilting his head and pointing a finger, "I think you fell in love." "With *him?* Are you *crazy?*" "He's too quiet for Rhoda," my mother says. "I think maybe he's a little bit of a wallflower. Rhoda is a very lively person, she needs lively people around." "Wallflower? He's not a wallflower! He's a gentleman, that's all. And he's lonely," my father says assertively, glaring at my mother for going over his head like this *against* Kafka. My Aunt Rhoda is forty years old — it is not exactly a shipment of brand-new goods that he is trying to move. "He's a gentleman, he's an educated man, and I'll tell you something, he'd give his eyeteeth to have a nice home and a wife." "Well," says my Aunt Rhoda, "let him find one then, if he's so educated. Somebody who's his equal, who he doesn't have to look down his nose at with his big sad refugee eyes!" "Yep, she's in love," my father announces, squeezing Rhoda's knee in triumph. "With *him?*" she cries, jumping to her feet, taffeta crackling around her like a bonfire. "With *Kafka?*" she snorts. "I wouldn't give an old man like him the time of day!"

Dr. Kafka calls and takes my Aunt Rhoda to a movie. I am astonished, both that he calls and that she goes; it seems there is more desperation in life than I have come across yet in my fish tank. Dr. Kafka takes my Aunt Rhoda to a play performed at the "Y." Dr. Kafka eats Sunday dinner with my grandmother and my Aunt Rhoda and, at the end of the afternoon, accepts with that formal bow of his the mason jar of barley soup that my grandmother presses him to carry back to his room with him on the No. 8 bus. Apparently he was very taken with my grandmother's jungle of potted plants — and she, as a result, with him. Together they spoke in Yiddish about gardening. One Wednesday morning, only an hour after the store has opened for the day, Dr. Kafka shows up at the dry-goods department of the Big Bear; he tells Aunt Rhoda that he just wants to see where she works. That night he writes in his diary: "With the customers she is forthright and cheery, and so managerial about 'taste' that when I hear her explain to a chubby young bride why green and blue do not 'go,' I am myself ready to believe that Nature is in error and R. is correct."

One night, at ten, Dr. Kafka and Aunt Rhoda come by unexpectedly, and a small impromptu party is held in the kitchen — coffee and cake, even a thimbleful of whiskey all around, to celebrate the resumption of Aunt Rhoda's career on the stage. I have only heard tell of my aunt's theatrical ambitions. My brother says that when I was small she used to come to entertain the two of us on Sundays with her puppets — she was at that time

employed by the W.P.A. to travel around New Jersey and put on mario-
nette shows in schools and even in churches; Aunt Rhoda did all the voices
and, with the help of a female assistant, manipulated the manikins on their
strings. Simultaneously she had been a member of the Newark Collective
Theater, a troupe organized primarily to go around to strike groups to perform *Waiting for Lefty*.[9] Everybody in Newark (as I understood it) had had
high hopes that Rhoda Pilchik would go on to Broadway — everybody except my grandmother. To me this period of history is as difficult to believe
in as the era of the lake dwellers, which I am studying in school; people say
it was once so, so I believe them, but nonetheless it is hard to grant such
stories the status of the real, given the life I see around me.

Yet my father, a very avid realist, is in the kitchen, schnapps glass in
hand, toasting Aunt Rhoda's success. She has been awarded one of the
starring roles in the Russian masterpiece *The Three Sisters*, to be performed six weeks hence by the amateur group at the Newark "Y." Everything, announces Aunt Rhoda, everything she owes to Franz and his
encouragement. One conversation — "One!" she cries gaily — and Dr.
Kafka had apparently talked my grandmother out of her lifelong belief
that actors are not serious human beings. And what an actor *he* is,
in his own right, says Aunt Rhoda. How he had opened her eyes to the
meaning of things, by reading her the famous Chekhov play — yes, read
it to her from the opening line to the final curtain, all the parts, and actually left her in tears. Here Aunt Rhoda says, "Listen, listen — this is the
first line of the play — it's the key to everything. Listen — I just think
about what it was like the night Pop passed away, how I wondered and wondered what would become of us, what would we all do — and, and,
listen — "

"We're listening," laughs my father. So am *I* listening, from my bed.

Pause; she must have walked to the center of the kitchen linoleum.
She says, sounding a little surprised, " 'It's just a year ago today that father
died.' "

"Shhh," warns my mother, "you'll give the little one nightmares."

I am not alone in finding my aunt a "changed person" during the
weeks of rehearsal. My mother says this is just what she was like as a little
girl. "Red cheeks, always those hot, red cheeks — and everything exciting,
even taking a bath." "She'll calm down, don't worry," says my father, "and
then he'll pop the question." "Knock on wood," says my mother. "Come
on," says my father, "he knows what side his bread is buttered on — he sets
foot in this house, he sees what a family is all about, and believe me, he's
licking his chops. Just look at him when he sits in that club chair. This is his
dream come true." "Rhoda says that in Berlin, before Hitler, he had a

---

[9] play by Clifford Odets (1906–1963), very popular — and very controversial — during the Great Depression because of its highly sympathetic portrayal of radical left-wing elements of the labor movement.

young girl friend, years and years it went on, and then she left him. For somebody else. She got tired of waiting." "Don't worry," says my father, "when the time comes I'll give him a little nudge. He ain't going to live forever, either, and he knows it."

Then one weekend, as a respite from the "strain" of nightly rehearsals — which Dr. Kafka regularly visits, watching in his hat and coat at the back of the auditorium until it is time to accompany Aunt Rhoda home — they take a trip to Atlantic City. Ever since he arrived on these shores Dr. Kafka has wanted to see the famous boardwalk and the horse that dives from the high board. But in Atlantic City something happens that I am not allowed to know about; any discussion of the subject conducted in my presence is in Yiddish. Dr. Kafka sends Aunt Rhoda four letters in three days. She comes to us for dinner and sits till midnight crying in our kitchen. She calls the "Y" on our phone to tell them (weeping) that her mother is still ill and she cannot come to rehearsal again — she may even have to drop out of the play. No, she can't, she can't, her mother is too ill, she herself is too upset! goodbye! Then back to the kitchen table to cry. She wears no pink powder and no red lipstick, and her stiff brown hair, down, is thick and spiky as a new broom.

My brother and I listen from our bedroom, through the door that silently he has pushed ajar.

"Have you ever?" says Aunt Rhoda, weeping. "Have you *ever?*"

"Poor soul," says my mother.

"*Who?*" I whisper to my brother. "Aunt Rhoda or — "

"Shhhh!" he says. "Shut *up!*"

In the kitchen my father grunts. "Hmm. Hmm." I hear him getting up and walking around and sitting down again — and then grunting. I am listening so hard that I can hear the letters being folded and unfolded, stuck back into their envelopes, then removed to be puzzled over one more time.

"Well?" demands Aunt Rhoda. "*Well?*"

"Well what?" answers my father.

"Well, what do you want to say *now?*"

"He's *meshugeh,*"[10] admits my father. "Something is wrong with him all right."

"But," sobs Aunt Rhoda, "no one would believe me when *I* said it!"

"Rhody, Rhody," croons my mother in that voice I know from those times that I have had to have stitches taken, or when I have awakened in tears, somehow on the floor beside my bed. "Rhody, don't be hysterical, darling. It's over, kitten, it's all over."

I reach across to my brother's twin bed and tug on the blanket. I don't think I've ever been so confused in my life, not even by death. The speed of things! Everything good undone in a moment! But what? "*What?*" I whisper. "*What is it?*"

[10] crazy (Yiddish).

My brother, the Boy Scout, smiles leeringly and, with a fierce hiss that is no answer and enough answer, addresses my bewilderment: "Sex!"

Years later, a junior at college, I receive an envelope from home containing Dr. Kafka's obituary, clipped from *The Jewish News*, the tabloid of Jewish affairs that is mailed each week to the homes of the Jews of Essex County. It is summer, the semester is over, but I have stayed on at school, alone in my room in the town, trying to write short stories. I am fed by a young English professor and his wife in exchange for babysitting; I tell the sympathetic couple, who are also loaning me the money for my rent, why it is I can't go home. My tearful fights with my father are all I can talk about at their dinner table. "Keep him away from me!" I scream at my mother. "But, darling," she asks me, "what is going on? What is this all about?" — the very same question with which I used to plague my older brother, asked now of me and out of the same bewilderment and innocence. "He *loves* you," she explains.

But that, of all things, seems to me precisely what is blocking my way. Others are crushed by paternal criticism — I find myself oppressed by his high opinion of me! Can it possibly be true (and can I possibly admit) that I am coming to hate him for loving me so? praising me so? But that makes no sense — the ingratitude! the stupidity! the contrariness! Being loved is so obviously a blessing, *the* blessing, praise such a rare bequest. Only listen late at night to my closest friends on the literary magazine and in the drama society — they tell horror stories of family life to rival *The Way of All Flesh*,[11] they return shell-shocked from vacations, drift back to school as though from the wars. What they would give to be in my golden slippers! "What's going on?" my mother begs me to tell her; but how can I, when I myself don't fully believe that this is happening to us, or that I am the one who is making it happen. That they, who together cleared all obstructions from my path, should seem now to be my final obstruction! No wonder my rage must filter through a child's tears of shame, confusion, and loss. All that we have constructed together over the course of two century-long decades, and look how I must bring it down — in the name of this tyrannical need that I call my "independence"! My mother, keeping the lines of communication open, sends a note to me at school: "We miss you" — and encloses the brief obituary notice. Across the margin at the bottom of the clipping, she has written (in the same hand with which she wrote notes to my teachers and signed my report cards, in the very same handwriting that once eased my way in the world), "Remember poor Kafka, Aunt Rhoda's beau?"

"Dr. Franz Kafka," the notice reads, "a Hebrew teacher at the Talmud Torah of the Schley Street Synagogue from 1939 to 1948, died on June 3 in the Deborah Heart and Lung Center in Browns Mills, New Jersey. Dr. Kafka had been a patient there since 1950. He was 70 years old. Dr.

---

[11] novel by Samuel Butler (1835–1902).

Kafka was born in Prague, Czechoslovakia, and was a refugee from the Nazis. He leaves no survivors."

He also leaves no books: no *Trial*, no *Castle*, no Diaries. The dead man's papers are claimed by no one, and disappear — all except those four "*meshugeneh*" letters that are, to this day, as far as I know, still somewhere in among the memorabilia accumulated by my spinster aunt, along with a collection of Broadway Playbills, sales citations from the Big Bear, and transatlantic steamship stickers.

Thus all trace of Dr. Kafka disappears. Destiny being destiny, how could it be otherwise? Does the Land Surveyor reach the Castle? Does K. escape the judgment of the Court, or Georg Bendemann the judgment of his father? " 'Well, clear this out now,' said the overseer, and they buried the hunger artist, straw and all." No, it simply is not in the cards for Kafka ever to become *the* Kafka — why, that would be stranger even than a man turning into an insect. No one would believe it, Kafka least of all.

[1975]

IMAMU AMIRI BARAKA (b. 1934) was born Everett Leroi Jones in Newark, New Jersey. His father was a postal supervisor and his mother a social worker, and he was raised with a younger sister in a middle-class family. Jones attended integrated public schools in Newark. He began to write — comic strips and science fiction — when he was nine or ten. After a year at Rutgers, he switched to Howard University, which disappointed him because, he felt, it tried to teach "the Negro how to make out in the white society, using the agonizing over-compensation of pretending he's also white." After his graduation from Howard University at the age of nineteen, Jones served for three years with the Strategic Air Command as an aerial gunner and climatographer, stationed most of the time in Puerto Rico. In 1957 he was discharged and settled in Greenwich Village, making friends with poet Allen Ginsberg and other Beat writers who sought an alternative to what they considered the cant and hypocrisy of establishment America in the Cold War years between the Korean and Vietnam conflicts. Ginsberg also influenced his view of how to write poetry. "Ginsberg let me in on poetry as a living phenomenon, a world of human concern, and literature as a breathing force in one's life, the task of a lifetime." At first Jones published books of poetry, Preface to a Twenty-Volume Suicide Note (1961) and The Dead Lecturer (1964), and plays, The Dutchman and The Slave (1964). Then in 1965 he left Greenwich Village, his white friends, and his white wife, and lived briefly in Harlem. His political ideas had changed after a trip to Cuba. He became a Black Nationalist follower of Malcolm X, founding the Black Arts Repertory Theater in Harlem. The following year he moved back to Newark to direct a new black theater and community center, Spirit House. "No amount of pacifism is going to break Charlie's back," Jones has said. "We must eliminate the white man before we will ever be able to draw a free breath on this planet." The extremity of his views has gotten him into conflicts with law enforcement agencies, but his power and influence in Newark have grown steadily. In 1968 Jones assumed the name Imamu Amiri Baraka (after Ameer "prince" and Baraka "the blessed one"), given to him by Heshaam Jaaber, an orthodox Muslim and the man who buried Malcolm X. Baraka and his followers at the Temple of Kawaida in Newark are dedicated to the creation of a new value system for the black community free from the spirit of materialist-individualist white America.

As a writer, Baraka has made the most impact as a playwright, especially through his play The Dutchman, which won a 1964 Obie Award. It is performed all over the world and frequently shown in a film version to college audiences in the United States. His early plays attempted to shock white audiences into an awareness of the racial disaster toward which he

*felt society was heading. Now he is a Marxist-Leninist, believing in commu-
nal art and a revolutionary theater. "The revolutionary theater should force
change: itself should be change. . . . Basically I want to write plays that will
make good people happy and will frighten evil people. In America, it
usually turns out to be black and white . . . through no doing of my own."
Baraka has also written highly acclaimed studies of black music,* Blues People *(1963) and* Black Music *(1968), and allusions to music are central to
his work. "There has never been an equivalent to Duke Ellington or Louis
Armstrong in Negro writing, and even the best of contemporary literature
written by Negroes cannot be compared to the fantastic beauty of the
music of Charlie Parker."*

Baraka's novel, The System of Dante's Hell *(1965), was conceived
with a musical-literary scheme, as was his book of short stories,* Tales
*(1967), which included "Uncle Tom's Cabin: Alternate Ending." Based on
what he calls "association complexes," his phrases build to form prose
motifs that are jammed together "to make straighter narrative." The conflict between the black schoolboy and the white teacher in this story is
based on an incident that occurred during Baraka's childhood in Newark.
Since 1970, Baraka has published more than fifteen books of essays, poetry,
and plays reflecting his radical political commitments.*

Imamu Amiri Baraka

༖

UNCLE TOM'S CABIN:
ALTERNATE ENDING

"6½" *was* the answer. But it seemed to irritate Miss Orbach. Maybe
not the answer — the figure itself, but the fact it should be there, and in
such loose possession.

"OH who is he to know such a thing? That's really improper to set up
such liberations. And moreso."

What came into her head next she could hardly understand. A breath
of cold. She did shudder, and her fingers clawed at the tiny watch she wore
hidden in the lace of the blouse her grandmother had given her when she
graduated teacher's college.

Ellen, Eileen, Evelyn . . . Orbach. She could be any of them. Her personality was one of theirs. As specific and as vague. The kindly menace of
leading a life in whose balance evil was a constant intrigue but grew uglier

and more remote as it grew stronger. She would have loved to do something really dirty. But nothing she had ever heard of was dirty enough. So she contented herself with good, i.e., purity, as a refuge from mediocrity. But being unconscious, or largely remote from her own sources, she would only admit to the possibility of grace. Not God. She would not be trapped into *wanting* even God.

So remorse took her easily. For any reason. A reflection in a shop window, of a man looking in vain for her ankles. (Which she covered with heavy colorless woolen.) A sudden gust of warm damp air around her legs or face. Long dull rains that turned her from her books. Or, as was the case this morning, some completely uncalled-for shaking of her silent doctrinaire routines.

"6½" had wrenched her unwillingly to exactly where she was. Teaching the 5th grade, in a grim industrial complex of northeastern America; about 1942. And how the social doth pain the anchorite.[1]

Nothing made much sense in such a context. People moved around, and disliked each other for no reason. Also, and worse, they said they loved each other, and usually for less reason, Miss Orbach thought. Or would have if she did.

And in this class sat 30 dreary sons and daughters of such circumstance. Specifically, the thriving children of the thriving urban lower middle classes. Postmen's sons and factory-worker debutantes. Making a great run for America, now prosperity and the war had silenced for a time the intelligent cackle of tradition. Like a huge grey bubbling vat the country, in its apocalyptic version of history and the future, sought now, in its equally apocalyptic profile of itself as it had urged swiftly its own death since the Civil War. To promise. Promise. And that to be that all who had ever dared to live here would die when the people and interests who had been its rulers died. The intelligent poor now were being admitted. And with them a great many Negroes . . . who would die when the rest of the dream died not even understanding that they, like Ishmael, should have been the sole survivors. But now they were being tricked. "6½" the boy said. After the fidgeting and awkward silence. One little black boy, raised his hand, and looking at the tip of Miss Orbach's nose said 6½. And then he smiled, very embarrassed and very sure of being wrong.

I would have said "No, boy, shut up and sit down. You are wrong. You don't know anything. Get out of here and be very quick. Have you no idea what you're getting involved in? My God . . . you nigger, get out of here and save yourself, while there's time. Now beat it." But those people had already been convinced. Read Booker T. Washington one day, when there's time. What that led to. The 6½'s moved for power . . . and there seemed no other way.

So three elegant Negroes in light grey suits grin and throw me through

[1] hermit.

the window. They are happy and I am sad. It is an ample test of an idea.
And besides "6½" is the right answer to the woman's question.

[The psychological and the social. The spiritual and the practical.
Keep them together and you profit, maybe, someday, come out on top. Separate them, and you go along the road to the commonest of Hells. The one
we westerners love to try to make art out of.]

The woman looked at the little brown boy. He blinked at her, trying
again not to smile. She tightened her eyes, but her lips flew open. She
tightened her lips, and her eyes blinked like the boy's. She said, "How do
you get that answer?" The boy told her. "Well, it's right," she said, and the
boy fell limp, straining even harder to look sorry. The Negro in back of the
answerer pinched him, and the boy shuddered. A little white girl next to
him touched his hand, and he tried to pull his own hand away with his
brain.

"Well, that's right, class. That's exactly right. You may sit down now
Mr. McGhee."

Later on in the day, after it had started exaggeratedly to rain very hard
and very stupidly against the windows and soul of her 5th-grade class, Miss
Orbach became convinced that the little boy's eyes were too large. And in
fact they did bulge almost grotesquely white and huge against his bony
heavy-veined skull. Also, his head was much too large for the rest of the
scrawny body. And he talked too much, and caused too many disturbances.
He also stared out the window when Miss Orbach herself would drift off
into her sanctuary of light and hygiene even though her voice carried the
inanities of arithmetic seemingly without delay. When she came back to
the petty social demands of 20th-century humanism the boy would be
watching something walk across the playground. OH, it just would not
work.

She wrote a note to Miss Janone, the school nurse, and gave it to the
boy, McGhee, to take to her. The note read: "Are the large eyes a sign of
————?"

Little McGhee, of course, could read, and read the note. But he didn't
of course understand the last large word which was misspelled anyway. But
he tried to memorize the note, repeating to himself over and over again
its contents . . . sounding the last long word out in his head, as best he
could.

Miss Janone wiped her big nose and sat the boy down, reading the
note. She looked at him when she finished, then read the note again, crum-
pling it on her desk.

She looked in her medical book and found out what Miss Orbach
meant. Then she said to the little Negro, Dr. Robard will be here in 5 minutes. He'll look at you. Then she began doing something to her eyes and
fingernails.

When the doctor arrived he looked closely at McGhee and said to
Miss Janone, "Miss Orbach is confused."

McGhee's mother thought that too. Though by the time little McGhee had gotten home he had forgotten the "long word" at the end of the note.

"Is Miss Orbach the woman who told you to say sangwich instead of sammich," Louise McGhee giggled.

"No, that was Miss Columbe."

"Sangwich, my christ. That's worse than sammich. Though you better not let me hear you saying sammich either . . . like those Davises."

"I don't say sammich, mamma."

"What's the word then?"

"Sandwich."

"That's right. And don't let anyone tell you anything else. Teacher or otherwise. Now I wonder what that word could have been?"

"I dunno. It was very long. I forgot it."

Eddie McGhee Sr. didn't have much of an idea what the word could be either. But he had never been to college like his wife. It was one of the most conspicuously dealt with factors of their marriage.

So the next morning Louise McGhee, after calling her office, the Child Welfare Bureau, and telling them she would be a little late, took a trip to the school, which was on the same block as the house where the McGhees lived, to speak to Miss Orbach about the long word which she suspected might be injurious to her son and maybe to Negroes In General. This suspicion had been bolstered a great deal by what Eddie Jr. had told her about Miss Orbach, and also equally by what Eddie Sr. had long maintained about the nature of White People In General. "Oh well," Louise McGhee sighed, "I guess I better straighten this sister out." And that is exactly what she intended.

When the two McGhees reached the Center Street school the next morning Mrs. McGhee took Eddie along with her to the principal's office, where she would request that she be allowed to see Eddie's teacher.

Miss Day, the old, lady principal, would then send Eddie to his class with a note for his teacher, and talk to Louise McGhee, while she was waiting, on general problems of the neighborhood. Miss Day was a very old woman who had despised Calvin Coolidge. She was also, in one sense, exotically liberal. One time she had forbidden old man Seidman to wear his pince-nez anymore, as they looked too snooty. Center Street sold more war stamps than any other grammar school in the area, and had a fairly good track team.

Miss Orbach was going to say something about Eddie McGhee's being late, but he immediately produced Miss Day's note. Then Miss Orbach looked at Eddie again, as she had when she had written her own note the day before.

She made Mary Ann Fantano the monitor and stalked off down the dim halls. The class had a merry time of it when she left, and Eddie won an extra 2 Nabisco graham crackers by kissing Mary Ann while she sat at Miss Orbach's desk.

When Miss Orbach got to the principal's office and pushed open the door she looked directly into Louise McGhee's large brown eyes, and fell deeply and hopelessly in love.

[1967]

JOYCE CAROL OATES (*b.* 1938) *was born in Lockport, New York, one of three children in a Roman Catholic family. She dismisses her childhood as "dull, ordinary, nothing people would be interested in." There was nothing ordinary, however, about her desire to express her imagination. She began to put picture stories down on paper even before she could write, and she remembers that her parents "dutifully" supplied her with lined tablets for her stories and gave her a typewriter at the age of fourteen. She had written thousands of pages of prose by the time she discovered Hemingway's* In Our Time *in the public library as a high school sophomore. She proceeded to write several novels in imitation of his book, though not of his prose style, "that ironic burnt-out voice being merely monotonous to my adolescent ear." In 1956, after Oates graduated from high school, she went on a scholarship to major in English at Syracuse University, where she resumed writing short stories and graduated Phi Beta Kappa and class valedictorian in 1960. The previous year she won the 1959* Mademoiselle *college fiction award with her story "In the Old World." Other stories began to be published in* Cosmopolitan, Prairie Schooner, *and* The Literary Review, *but she did not devote most of her time to writing until after she received her M.A. at the University of Wisconsin in 1961. Discovering by chance that one of her stories had been cited in the honor roll of Martha Foley's annual* Best American Short Stories, *Oates assembled the fourteen stories in her first book,* By the North Gate *(1963). Her first novel,* With Shuddering Fall, *written during her renunciation of Catholicism, was published the next year. This was followed in 1966 by a second collection of stories,* Upon the Sweeping Flood. *A "thematic trilogy" of novels came next, the third of which —* them *— won the National Book Award for fiction in 1970 and established her reputation as one of the most prolific authors of her time. Later memorable novels include* Do with Me What You Will *(1973),* Childwold *(1976),* Bellefleur *(1980), and* A Bloodsmoor Romance *(1982).*

Oates had published almost forty books by 1982, including about 100 stories. She also writes poetry and literary criticism, including the volume New Heaven, New Earth *(1974), analyzing the "visionary experience in literature" as exemplified in the work of Henry James, Virginia Woolf, D. H. Lawrence, Franz Kafka, Flannery O'Connor, and others. As a writer, critic, and professor at Princeton University, she dedicates her life to "promoting and exploring literature. . . . I am not conscious of being in any particular literary tradition, though I share with my contemporaries an intense interest in the formal aspects of writing; each of my books is an experiment of a kind, an investigation of the relationship between a certain consciousness and its formal aesthetic expression. My method has always been to combine* the 'naturalistic' world and the 'symbolic' method of expression, so that I am always — or usually — writing about real people in a real society, but the means of expression may be naturalistic, realistic, surreal, or parodistic. In this way I have, to my own satisfaction at least, solved the old problem — should one be faithful to the 'real' world, or to one's imagination?"

The story "Where Are You Going, Where Have You Been?" was first published in Epoch in 1966; it was included in The Best American Stories of 1967 and Prize Stories: The O. Henry Awards 1968. Oates has said that this story has been "constantly misunderstood by one generation, and intuitively understood by another," and that she sees it as dealing with a human being "struggling heroically to define personal identity in the face of incredible opposition, even in the face of death itself." "The Lady with the Pet Dog," included in Marriages and Infidelities (1972), is her reworking of the Chekhov story. The same volume also includes her version of Kafka's "The Metamorphosis."

Joyce Carol Oates

ಞ

WHERE ARE YOU GOING, WHERE HAVE YOU BEEN?

For Bob Dylan

Her name was Connie. She was fifteen and she had a quick nervous giggling habit of craning her neck to glance into mirrors, or checking other people's faces to make sure her own was all right. Her mother, who noticed everything and knew everything and who hadn't much reason any longer to look at her own face, always scolded Connie about it. "Stop gawking at yourself, who are you? You think you're so pretty?" she would say. Connie would raise her eyebrows at these familiar complaints and look right through her mother, into a shadowy vision of herself as she was right at that moment: she knew she was pretty and that was everything. Her mother had been pretty once too, if you could believe those old snapshots in the album, but now her looks were gone and that was why she was always after Connie.

"Why don't you keep your room clean like your sister? How've you got your hair fixed — what the hell stinks? Hair spray? You don't see your sister using that junk."

Her sister June was twenty-four and still lived at home. She was a secretary in the high school Connie attended, and if that wasn't bad enough — with her in the same building — she was so plain and chunky and steady that Connie had to hear her praised all the time by her mother and her mother's sisters. June did this, June did that, she saved money and helped clean the house and cooked and Connie couldn't do a thing, her mind was all filled with trashy daydreams. Their father was away at work most of the time and when he came home he wanted supper and he read the newspaper at supper and after supper he went to bed. He didn't bother talking much to them, but around his bent head Connie's mother kept picking at her until Connie wished her mother was dead and she herself was dead and it was all over. "She makes me want to throw up sometimes," she complained to her friends. She had a high, breathless, amused voice which made everything she said a little forced, whether it was sincere or not.

There was one good thing: June went places with girl friends of hers, girls who were just as plain and steady as she, and so when Connie wanted to do that her mother had no objections. The father of Connie's best girl friend drove the girls the three miles to town and left them off at a shopping plaza, so that they could walk through the stores or go to a movie, and when he came to pick them up again at eleven he never bothered to ask what they had done.

They must have been familiar sights, walking around that shopping plaza in their shorts and flat ballerina slippers that always scuffed the sidewalk, with charm bracelets jingling on their thin wrists; they would lean together to whisper and laugh secretly if someone passed by who amused or interested them. Connie had long dark blond hair that drew anyone's eye to it, and she wore part of it pulled up on her head and puffed out and the rest of it she let fall down her back. She wore a pullover jersey blouse that looked one way when she was at home and another way when she was away from home. Everything about her had two sides to it, one for home and one for anywhere that was not home: her walk that could be childlike and bobbing, or languid enough to make anyone think she was hearing music in her head, her mouth which was pale and smirking most of the time, but bright and pink on these evenings out, her laugh which was cynical and drawling at home — "Ha, ha, very funny" — but high-pitched and nervous anywhere else, like the jingling of the charms on her bracelet.

Sometimes they did go shopping or to a movie, but sometimes they went across the highway, ducking fast across the busy road, to a drive-in restaurant where older kids hung out. The restaurant was shaped like a big bottle, though squatter than a real bottle, and on its cap was a revolving figure of a grinning boy who held a hamburger aloft. One night in midsummer they ran across, breathless with daring, and right away someone leaned out a car window and invited them over, but it was just a boy from high school they didn't like. It made them feel good to be able to ignore him. They went up through the maze of parked and cruising cars to the bright-lit, fly-infested restaurant, their faces pleased and expectant as if they were entering a sacred building that loomed out of the night to give them what haven and what blessing they yearned for. They sat at the counter and crossed their legs at the ankles, their thin shoulders rigid with excitement and listened to the music that made everything so good: the music was always in the background like music at a church service, it was something to depend upon.

A boy named Eddie came in to talk with them. He sat backwards on his stool, turning himself jerkily around in semi-circles and then stopping and turning again, and after a while he asked Connie if she would like something to eat. She said she did and so she tapped her friend's arm on her way out — her friend pulled her face up into a brave droll look — and Connie said she would meet her at eleven, across the way. "I just hate to leave her like that," Connie said earnestly, but the boy said that she wouldn't be alone for long. So they went out to his car and on the way Connie couldn't help but let her eyes wander over the windshields and faces all around her, her face gleaming with the joy that had nothing to do with Eddie or even this place; it might have been the music. She drew her shoulders up and sucked in her breath with the pure pleasure of being alive, and just at that moment she happened to glance at a face just a few feet from hers. It was a boy with shaggy black hair, in a convertible jalopy painted gold. He stared at her and then his lips widened into a grin. Connie slit her eyes at him and turned away, but she couldn't help glancing back and there he was still watching her. He wagged a finger and laughed and said, "Gonna get you, baby," and Connie turned away again without Eddie noticing anything.

She spent three hours with him, at the restaurant where they ate hamburgers and drank Cokes in wax cups that were always sweating, and then down an alley a mile or so away, and when he left her off at five to eleven only the movie house was still open at the plaza. Her girl friend was there, talking with a boy. When Connie came up the two girls smiled at each other and Connie said, "How was the movie?" and the girl said, "You should know." They rode off with the girl's father, sleepy and pleased, and Connie couldn't help but look at the darkened shopping plaza with its big empty parking lot and its signs that were faded and ghostly now, and over at the drive-in restaurant where cars were still circling tirelessly. She couldn't hear the music at this distance.

Next morning June asked her how the movie was and Connie said, "So-so."

She and that girl and occasionally another girl went out several times a week that way, and the rest of the time Connie spent around the house — it was summer vacation — getting in her mother's way and thinking, dreaming, about the boys she met. But all the boys fell back and dissolved into a single face that was not even a face, but an idea, a feeling, mixed up with the urgent insistent pounding of the music and the humid night air of

July. Connie's mother kept dragging her back to the daylight by finding things for her to do or saying suddenly, "What's this about the Pettinger girl?"

And Connie would say nervously, "Oh, her. That dope." She always drew thick clear lines between herself and such girls, and her mother was simple and kindly enough to believe her. Her mother was so simple, Connie thought, that it was maybe cruel to fool her so much. Her mother went scuffling around the house in old bedroom slippers and complained over the telephone to one sister about the other, then the other called up and the two of them complained about the third one. If June's name was mentioned her mother's tone was approving, and if Connie's name was mentioned it was disapproving. This did not really mean she disliked Connie and actually Connie thought that her mother preferred her to June because she was prettier, but the two of them kept up a pretense of exasperation, a sense that they were tugging and struggling over something of little value to either of them. Sometimes, over coffee, they were almost friends, but something would come up — some vexation that was like a fly buzzing suddenly around their heads — and their faces went hard with contempt.

One Sunday Connie got up at eleven — none of them bothered with church — and washed her hair so that it could dry all day long, in the sun. Her parents and sister were going to a barbecue at an aunt's house and Connie said no, she wasn't interested, rolling her eyes, to let mother know just what she thought of it. "Stay home alone then," her mother said sharply. Connie sat out back in a lawn chair and watched them drive away, her father quiet and bald, hunched around so that he could back the car out, her mother with a look that was still angry and not at all softened through the windshield, and in the back seat poor old June all dressed up as if she didn't know what a barbecue was, with all the running yelling kids and the flies. Connie sat with her eyes closed in the sun, dreaming and dazed with the warmth about her as if this were a kind of love, the caresses of love, and her mind slipped over onto thoughts of the boy she had been with the night before and how nice he had been, how sweet it always was, not the way someone like June would suppose but sweet, gentle, the way it was in movies and promised in songs; and when she opened her eyes she hardly knew where she was, the back yard ran off into weeds and a fence-line of trees and behind it the sky was perfectly blue and still. The asbestos "ranch house" that was now three years old startled her — it looked small. She shook her head as if to get awake.

It was too hot. She went inside the house and turned on the radio to drown out the quiet. She sat on the edge of her bed, barefoot, and listened for an hour and a half to a program called XYZ Sunday Jamboree, record after record of hard, fast, shrieking songs she sang along with, interspersed by exclamations from "Bobby King": "An' look here you girls at Napoleon's — Son and Charley want you to pay real close attention to this song coming up!"

And Connie paid close attention herself, bathed in a glow of slow-pulsed joy that seemed to rise mysteriously out of the music itself and lay languidly about the airless little room, breathed in and breathed out with each gentle rise and fall of her chest.

After a while she heard a car coming up the drive. She sat up at once, startled, because it couldn't be her father so soon. The gravel kept crunching all the way in from the road — the driveway was long — and Connie ran to the window. It was a car she didn't know. It was an open jalopy, painted a bright gold that caught the sun opaquely. Her heart began to pound and her fingers snatched at her hair, checking it, and she whispered "Christ. Christ," wondering how bad she looked. The car came to a stop at the side door and the horn sounded four short taps as if this were a signal Connie knew.

She went into the kitchen and approached the door slowly, then hung out the screen door, her bare toes curling down off the step. There were two boys in the car and now she recognized the driver: he had shaggy, shabby black hair that looked crazy as a wig and he was grinning at her.

"I ain't late, am I?" he said.

"Who the hell do you think you are?" Connie said.

"Toldja I'd be out, didn't I?"

"I don't even know who you are."

She spoke sullenly, careful to show no interest or pleasure, and he spoke in a fast bright monotone. Connie looked past him to the other boy, taking her time. He had fair brown hair, with a lock that fell onto his forehead. His sideburns gave him a fierce, embarrassed look, but so far he hadn't even bothered to glance at her. Both boys wore sunglasses. The driver's glasses were metallic and mirrored everything in miniature.

"You wanta come for a ride?" he said.

Connie smirked and let her hair fall loose over one shoulder.

"Don'tcha like my car? New paint job," he said. "Hey."

"What?"

"You're cute."

She pretended to fidget, chasing flies away from the door.

"Don'tcha believe me, or what?" he said.

"Look, I don't even know who you are," Connie said in disgust.

"Hey, Ellie's got a radio, see. Mine's broke down." He lifted his friend's arm and showed her the little transistor the boy was holding, and now Connie began to hear the music. It was the same program that was playing inside the house.

"Bobby King?" she said.

"I listen to him all the time. I think he's great."

"He's kind of great," Connie said reluctantly.

"Listen, that guy's *great*. He knows where the action is."

Connie blushed a little, because the glasses made it impossible for her to see just what this boy was looking at. She couldn't decide if she liked him or if he was just a jerk, and so she dawdled in the doorway and wouldn't come down or go back inside. She said, "What's all that stuff painted on your car?"

"Can'tcha read it?" He opened the door very carefully, as if he was afraid it might fall off. He slid out just as carefully, planting his feet firmly on the ground, the tiny metallic world in his glasses slowing down like gelatine hardening and in the midst of it Connie's bright green blouse. "This here is my name, to begin with," he said. ARNOLD FRIEND was written in tar-like black letters on the side, with a drawing of a round grinning face that reminded Connie of a pumpkin, except it wore sunglasses. "I wanta introduce myself, I'm Arnold Friend and that's my real name and I'm gonna be your friend, honey, and inside the car's Ellie Oscar, he's kinda shy." Ellie brought his transistor up to his shoulder and balanced it there. "Now these numbers are a secret code, honey," Arnold Friend explained. He read off the numbers 33, 19, 17 and raised his eyebrows at her to see what she thought of that, but she didn't think much of it. The left rear fender had been smashed and around it was written, on the gleaming gold background: DONE BY CRAZY WOMAN DRIVER. Connie had to laugh at that. Arnold Friend was pleased at her laughter and looked up at her. "Around the other side's a lot more — you wanta come and see them?"

"No."

"Why not?"

"Why should I?"

"Don'tcha wanta see what's on the car? Don'tcha wanta go for a ride?"

"I don't know."

"Why not?"

"I got things to do."

"Like what?"

"Things."

He laughed as if she had said something funny. He slapped his thighs. He was standing in a strange way, leaning back against the car as if he were balancing himself. He wasn't tall, only an inch or so taller than she would be if she came down to him. Connie liked the way he was dressed, which was the way all of them dressed: tight faded jeans stuffed into black, scuffed boots, a belt that pulled his waist in and showed how lean he was, and a white pull-over shirt that was a little soiled and showed the hard small muscles of his arms and shoulders. He looked as if he probably did hard work, lifting and carrying things. Even his neck looked muscular. And his face was a familiar face, somehow: the jaw and chin and cheeks slightly darkened, because he hadn't shaved for a day or two, and the nose long and hawk-like, sniffing as if she were a treat he was going to gobble up and it was all a joke.

"Connie, you ain't telling the truth. This is your day set aside for a ride with me and you know it," he said, still laughing. The way he straightened and recovered from his fit of laughing showed that it had been all fake.

"How do you know what my name is?" she said suspiciously.

"It's Connie."

"Maybe and maybe not."

"I know my Connie," he said, wagging his finger. Now she remembered him even better, back at the restaurant, and her cheeks warmed at the thought of how she sucked in her breath just at the moment she passed him — how she must have looked to him. And he had remembered her. "Ellie and I come out here especially for you," he said. "Ellie can sit in back. How about it?"

"Where?"

"Where what?"

"Where're we going?"

He looked at her. He took off the sunglasses and she saw how pale the skin around his eyes was, like holes that were not in shadow but instead in light. His eyes were like chips of broken glass that catch the light in an amiable way. He smiled. It was as if the idea of going for a ride somewhere, to some place, was a new idea to him.

"Just for a ride, Connie sweetheart."

"I never said my name was Connie," she said.

"But I know what it is. I know your name and all about you, lots of things," Arnold Friend said. He had not moved yet but stood still leaning back against the side of his jalopy. "I took a special interest in you, such a pretty girl, and found out all about you like I know your parents and sister are gone somewheres and I know where and how long they're going to be gone, and I know who you were with last night, and your best friend's name is Betty. Right?"

He spoke in a simple lilting voice, exactly as if he were reciting the words to a song. His smile assured her that everything was fine. In the car Ellie turned up the volume on his radio and did not bother to look around at them.

"Ellie can sit in the back seat," Arnold Friend said. He indicated his friend with a casual jerk of his chin, as if Ellie did not count and she should not bother with him.

"How'd you find out all that stuff?" Connie said.

"Listen: Betty Schultz and Tony Fitch and Jimmy Pettinger and Nancy Pettinger," he said, in a chant. "Raymond Stanley and Bob Hutter — "

"Do you know all those kids?"

"I know everybody."

"Look, you're kidding. You're not from around here."

"Sure."

"But — how come we never saw you before?"

"Sure you saw me before," he said. He looked down at his boots, as if he were a little offended. "You just don't remember."

"I guess I'd remember you," Connie said.

"Yeah?" He looked up at this, beaming. He was pleased. He began to mark time with the music from Ellie's radio, tapping his fists lightly together. Connie looked away from his smile to the car, which was painted so bright it almost hurt her eyes to look at it. She looked at that name, ARNOLD FRIEND. And up at the front fender was an expression that was familiar — MAN THE FLYING SAUCERS. It was an expression kids had used the year before, but didn't use this year. She looked at it for a while as if the words meant something to her that she did not yet know.

"What're you thinking about? Huh?" Arnold Friend demanded. "Not worried about your hair blowing around in the car, are you?"

"No."

"Think I maybe can't drive good?"

"How do I know?"

"You're a hard girl to handle. How come?" he said. "Don't you know I'm your friend? Didn't you see me put my sign in the air when you walked by?"

"What sign?"

"My sign." And he drew an X in the air, leaning out toward her. They were maybe ten feet apart. After his hand fell back to his side the X was still in the air, almost visible. Connie let the screen door close and stood perfectly still inside it, listening to the music from her radio and the boy's blend together. She stared at Arnold Friend. He stood there so stiffly relaxed, pretending to be relaxed, with one hand idly on the door handle as if he were keeping himself up that way and had no intention of ever moving again. She recognized most things about him, the tight jeans that showed his thighs and buttocks and the greasy leather boots and the tight shirt, and even that slippery friendly smile of his, that sleepy dreamy smile that all the boys used to get across ideas they didn't want to put into words. She recognized all this and also the singsong way he talked, slightly mocking, kidding, but serious and a little melancholy, and she recognized the way he tapped one fist against the other in homage to the perpetual music behind him. But all these things did not come together.

She said suddenly, "Hey, how old are you?"

His smile faded. She could see then that he wasn't a kid, he was much older — thirty, maybe more. At this knowledge her heart began to pound faster.

"That's a crazy thing to ask. Can'tcha see I'm your own age?"

"Like hell you are."

"Or maybe a coupla years older, I'm eighteen."

"Eighteen?" she said doubtfully.

He grinned to reassure her and lines appeared at the corners of his mouth. His teeth were big and white. He grinned so broadly his eyes became slits and she saw how thick the lashes were, thick and black as if painted with a black tar-like material. Then he seemed to become embarrassed, abruptly, and looked over his shoulder at Ellie. "*Him*, he's crazy," he said. "Ain't he a riot, he's a nut, a real character." Ellie was still listening to the music. His sunglasses told nothing about what he was thinking. He wore a bright orange shirt unbuttoned halfway to show his chest, which was a pale, bluish chest and not muscular like Arnold Friend's. His shirt collar was turned up all around and the very tips of the collar pointed out past his chin as if they were protecting him. He was pressing the transistor radio up against his ear and sat there in a kind of daze, right in the sun.

"He's kinda strange," Connie said.

"Hey, she says you're kinda strange! Kinda strange!" Arnold Friend cried. He pounded on the car to get Ellie's attention. Ellie turned for the first time and Connie saw with shock that he wasn't a kid either — he had a fair, hairless face, cheeks reddened slightly as if the veins grew too close to the surface of his skin, the face of a forty-year-old baby. Connie felt a wave of dizziness rise in her at this sight and she stared at him as if waiting for something to change the shock of the moment, make it all right again. Ellie's lips kept shaping words, mumbling along with the words blasting his ear.

"Maybe you two better go away," Connie said faintly.

"What? How come?" Arnold Friend cried. "We come out here to take you for a ride. It's Sunday." He had the voice of the man on the radio now. It was the same voice, Connie thought. "Don'tcha know it's Sunday all day and honey, no matter who you were with last night today you're with Arnold Friend and don't you forget it! — Maybe you better step out here," he said, and this last was in a different voice. It was a little flatter, as if the heat was finally getting to him.

"No. I got things to do."

"Hey."

"You two better leave."

"We ain't leaving until you come with us."

"Like hell I am — "

"Connie, don't fool around with me. I mean, I mean, don't fool *around*," he said, shaking his head. He laughed incredulously. He placed his sunglasses on top of his head, carefully, as if he were indeed wearing a wig, and brought the stems down behind his ears. Connie stared at him, another wave of dizziness and fear rising in her so that for a moment he wasn't even in focus but was just a blur, standing there against his gold car, and she had the idea that he had driven up the driveway all right but had come from nowhere before that and belonged nowhere and that everything about him and even the music that was so familiar to her was only half real.

"If my father comes and sees you — "

"He ain't coming. He's at a barbecue."

"How do you know that?"

"Aunt Tillie's. Right now they're — uh — they're drinking. Sitting around," he said vaguely, squinting as if he were staring all the way to town and over to Aunt Tillie's back yard. Then the vision seemed to clear and he nodded energetically. "Yeah. Sitting around. There's your sister in a blue dress, huh? And high heels, the poor sad bitch — nothing like you, sweetheart! And your mother's helping some fat woman with the corn, they're cleaning the corn — husking the corn — "

"What fat woman?" Connie cried.

"How do I know what fat woman. I don't know every goddam fat woman in the world!" Arnold Friend laughed.

"Oh, that's Mrs. Hornby. . . . Who invited her?" Connie said. She felt a little light-headed. Her breath was coming quickly.

"She's too fat. I don't like them fat. I like them the way you are, honey," he said, smiling sleepily at her. They stared at each other for a while, through the screen door. He said softly, "Now what you're going to do is this: you're going to come out that door. You're going to sit up front with me and Ellie's going to sit in the back, the hell with Ellie, right? This isn't Ellie's date. You're my date. I'm your lover, honey."

"What? You're crazy — "

"Yes, I'm your lover. You don't know what that is but you will," he said. "I know that too. I know all about you. But look: it's real nice and you couldn't ask for nobody better than me, or more polite. I always keep my word. I'll tell you how it is, I'm always nice at first, the first time. I'll hold you so tight you won't think you have to try to get away or pretend anything because you'll know you can't. And I'll come inside you where it's all secret and you'll give in to me and you'll love me — "

"Shut up! You're crazy!" Connie said. She backed away from the door. She put her hands against her ears as if she'd heard something terrible, something not meant for her. "People don't talk like that, you're crazy," she muttered. Her heart was almost too big now for her chest and its pumping made sweat break out all over her. She looked out to see Arnold Friend pause and then take a step toward the porch lurching. He almost fell. But, like a clever drunken man, he managed to catch his balance. He wobbled in his high boots and grabbed hold of one of the porch posts.

"Honey?" he said. "You still listening?"

"Get the hell out of here!"

"Be nice, honey. Listen."

"I'm going to call the police — "

He wobbled again and out of the side of his mouth came a fast spat curse, an aside not meant for her to hear. But even this "Christ!" sounded forced. Then he began to smile again. She watched this smile come, awkward as if he were smiling from inside a mask. His whole face was a mask, she thought wildly, tanned down onto his throat but then running out as if he had plastered make-up on his face but had forgotten about his throat.

"Honey — ? Listen, here's how it is. I always tell the truth and I promise you this: I ain't coming in that house after you."

"You better not! I'm going to call the police if you — if you don't — "

"Honey," he said, talking right through her voice, "honey, I'm not coming in there but you are coming out here. You know why?"

She was panting. The kitchen looked like a place she had never seen before, some room she had run inside but which wasn't good enough, wasn't going to help her. The kitchen window had never had a curtain, after three years, and there were dishes in the sink for her to do — probably — and if you ran your hand across the table you'd probably feel something sticky there.

"You listening, honey? Hey?"

" — going to call the police — "

"Soon as you touch the phone I don't need to keep my promise and can come inside. You won't want that."

She rushed forward and tried to lock the door. Her fingers were shaking. "But why lock it," Arnold Friend said gently, talking right into her face. "It's just a screen door. It's just nothing." One of his boots was at a strange angle, as if his foot wasn't in it. It pointed out to the left, bent at the ankle. "I mean, anybody can break through a screen door and glass and wood and iron or anything else if he needs to, anybody at all and specially Arnold Friend. If the place got lit up with a fire honey you'd come running out into my arms, right into my arms and safe at home — like you knew I was your lover and'd stopped fooling around. I don't mind a nice shy girl but I don't like no fooling around." Part of those words were spoken with a slight rhythmic lilt, and Connie somehow recognized them — the echo of a song from last year, about a girl rushing into her boy friend's arms and coming home again —

Connie stood barefoot on the linoleum floor, staring at him. "What do you want?" she whispered.

"I want you," he said.

"What?"

"Seen you that night and thought, that's the one, yes sir. I never needed to look any more."

"But my father's coming back. He's coming to get me. I had to wash my hair first — " She spoke in a dry, rapid voice, hardly raising it for him to hear.

"No, your daddy is not coming and yes, you had to wash your hair and you washed it for me. It's nice and shining and all for me, I thank you, sweetheart," he said, with a mock bow, but again he almost lost his balance. He had to bend and adjust his boots. Evidently his feet did not go all the way down; the boots must have been stuffed with something so that he would seem taller. Connie stared out at him and behind him Ellie in the car, who seemed to be looking off toward Connie's right, into nothing. This Ellie said, pulling the words out of the air one after another as if he were just discovering them, "You want me to pull out the phone?"

"Shut your mouth and keep it shut," Arnold Friend said, his face red from bending over or maybe from embarrassment because Connie had seen his boots. "This ain't none of your business."

"What — what are you doing? What do you want?" Connie said. "If I call the police they'll get you, they'll arrest you — "

"Promise was not to come in unless you touch that phone, and I'll keep that promise," he said. He resumed his erect position and tried to force his shoulders back. He sounded like a hero in a movie, declaring something important. He spoke too loudly and it was as if he were speaking to someone behind Connie. "I ain't made plans for coming in that house where I don't belong but just for you to come out to me, the way you should. Don't you know who I am?"

"You're crazy," she whispered. She backed away from the door but did not want to go into another part of the house, as if this would give him permission to come through the door. "What do you. . . . You're crazy, you. . . . "

"Huh? What're you saying, honey?"

Her eyes darted everywhere in the kitchen. She could not remember what it was, this room.

"This is how it is, honey: you come out and we'll drive away, have a nice ride. But if you don't come out we're gonna wait till your people come home and then they're all going to get it."

"You want that telephone pulled out?" Ellie said. He held the radio away from his ear and grimaced, as if without the radio the air was too much for him.

"I toldja shut up, Ellie." Arnold Friend said, "you're deaf, get a hearing aid, right? Fix yourself up. This little girl's no trouble and's gonna be nice to me, so Ellie keep to yourself, this ain't your date — right? Don't hem in on me. Don't hog. Don't crush. Don't bird dog. Don't trail me," he said in a rapid meaningless voice, as if he were running through all the expressions he'd learned but was no longer sure which one of them was in style, then rushing on to new ones, making them up with his eyes closed, "Don't crawl under my fence, don't squeeze in my chipmunk hole, don't sniff my glue, suck my popsicle, keep your own greasy fingers on yourself!" He shaded his eyes and peered in at Connie, who was backed against the kitchen table. "Don't mind him honey he's just a creep. He's a dope. Right? I'm the boy for you and like I said you come out here nice like a lady and give me your hand, and nobody else gets hurt, I mean, your nice old bald-headed daddy and your mummy and your sister in her high heels. Because listen: why bring them in this?"

"Leave me alone," Connie whispered.

"Hey, you know that old woman down the road, the one with the chickens and stuff — you know her?"

"She's dead!"

"Dead? What? You know her?" Arnold Friend said.

"She's dead — "

"Don't you like her?"

"She's dead — she's — she isn't here any more — "

"But don't you like her, I mean, you got something against her? Some grudge or something?" Then his voice dipped as if he were conscious of rudeness. He touched the sunglasses on top of his head as if to make sure they were still there. "Now you be a good girl."

"What are you going to do?"

"Just two things, or maybe three," Arnold Friend said. "But I promise it won't last long and you'll like me that way you get to like people you're close to. You will. It's all over for you here, so come on out. You don't want your people in any trouble, do you?"

She turned and bumped against a chair or something, hurting her leg, but she ran into the back room and picked up the telephone. Something roared in her ear, a tiny roaring, and she was so sick with fear that she could do nothing but listen to it — the telephone was clammy and very heavy and her fingers groped down to the dial but were too weak to touch it. She began to scream into the phone, into the roaring. She cried out, she cried for her mother, she felt her breath start jerking back and forth in her lungs as if it were something Arnold Friend were stabbing her with again and again with no tenderness. A noisy sorrowful wailing rose all about her and she was locked inside it the way she was locked inside this house.

After a while she could hear again. She was sitting on the floor, with her wet back against the wall.

Arnold Friend was saying from the door, "That's a good girl. Put the phone back."

She kicked the phone away from her.

"No, honey. Pick it up. Put it back right."

She picked it up and put it back. The dial tone stopped.

"That's a good girl. Now you come outside."

She was hollow with what had been fear, but what was now just an emptiness. All that screaming had blasted it out of her. She sat, one leg cramped under her, and deep inside her brain was something like a pinpoint of light that kept going and would not let her relax. She thought, I'm not going to see my mother again. She thought, I'm not going to sleep in my bed again. Her bright green blouse was all wet.

Arnold Friend said, in a gentle-loud voice that was like a stage voice, "The place where you came from ain't there any more, and where you had in mind to go is cancelled out. This place you are now — inside your daddy's house — is nothing but a cardboard box I can knock down any time. You know that and always did know it. You hear me?"

She thought, I have got to think. I have to know what to do.

"We'll go out to a nice field, out in the country here where it smells so nice and it's sunny," Arnold Friend said. "I'll have my arms tight around you so you won't need to try to get away and I'll show you what love is like, what it does. The hell with this house! It looks solid all right," he said. He ran a fingernail down the screen and the noise did not make Connie shiver, as it would have the day before. "Now put your hand on your heart, honey. Feel that? That feels solid too but we know better, be nice to me, be sweet like you can because what else is there for a girl like you but to be sweet and pretty and give in? — and get away before her people come back?"

She felt her pounding heart. Her hands seemed to enclose it. She thought for the first time in her life that it was nothing that was hers, that belonged to her, but just a pounding, living thing inside this body that wasn't hers either.

"You don't want them to get hurt," Arnold Friend went on. "Now get up, honey. Get up all by yourself."

She stood.

"Now turn this way. That's right. Come over here to me — Ellie, put that away, didn't I tell you? You dope. You miserable creepy dope," Arnold Friend said. His words were not angry but only part of an incantation. The incantation was kindly. "Now come out through the kitchen to me honey and let's see a smile, try it, you're a brave sweet little girl and now they're eating corn and hotdogs cooked to bursting over an outdoor fire, and they don't know one thing about you and never did and honey you're better than them because not one of them would have done this for you."

Connie felt the linoleum under her feet; it was cool. She brushed her hair back out of her eyes. Arnold Friend let go of the post tentatively and opened his arms for her, his elbows pointing up toward each other and his wrists limp, to show that this was an embarrassed embrace and a little mocking, he didn't want to make her self-conscious.

She put out her hand against the screen. She watched herself push the door slowly open as if she were safe back somewhere in the other doorway, watching this body and this head of long hair moving out into the sunlight where Arnold Friend waited.

"My sweet little blue-eyed girl," he said, in a half-sung sigh that had nothing to do with her brown eyes but was taken up just the same by the vast sunlit reaches of the land behind him and on all sides of him, so much land that Connie had never seen before and did not recognize except to know that she was going to it.

[1970]

Joyce Carol Oates

ᖇᕐᕐ

THE LADY WITH THE PET DOG

I

Strangers parted as if to make way for him.

There he stood. He was there in the aisle, a few yards away, watching her.

She leaned forward at once in her seat, her hand jerked up to her face as if to ward off a blow — but then the crowd in the aisle hid him, he was gone. She pressed both hands against her cheeks. He was not there, she had imagined him.

"My God," she whispered.

She was alone. Her husband had gone out to the foyer to make a telephone call; it was intermission at the concert, a Thursday evening.

Now she saw him again, clearly. He was standing there. He was staring at her. Her blood rocked in her body, draining out of her head . . . she was going to faint. . . . They stared at each other. They gave no sign of recognition. Only when he took a step forward did she shake her head *no — no — keep away.* It was not possible.

When her husband returned, she was staring at the place in the aisle where her lover had been standing. Her husband leaned forward to interrupt that stare.

"What's wrong?" he said. "Are you sick?"

Panic rose in her in long shuddering waves. She tried to get to her feet, panicked at the thought of fainting here, and her husband took hold of her. She stood like an aged woman, clutching the seat before her.

At home he helped her up the stairs and she lay down. Her head was like a large piece of crockery that had to be held still, it was so heavy. She was still panicked. She felt it in the shallows of her face, behind her knees, in the pit of her stomach. It sickened her, it made her think of mucus, of something thick and gray congested inside her, stuck to her, that was herself and yet not herself — a poison.

She lay with her knees drawn up toward her chest, her eyes hotly open, while her husband spoke to her. She imagined that other man saying, *Why did you run away from me?* Her husband was saying other words. She tried to listen to them. He was going to call the doctor, he said, and she tried to sit up. "No, I'm all right now," she said quickly. The panic was like lead inside her, so thickly congested. How slow love was to drain out of her, how fluid and sticky it was inside her head!

Her husband believed her. No doctor. No threat. Grateful, she drew her husband down to her. They embraced, not comfortably. For years now they had not been comfortable together, in their intimacy and at a distance, and now they struggled gently as if the paces of this dance were too rigorous for them. It was something they might have known once, but had now outgrown. The panic in her thickened at this double betrayal: she drew her husband to her, she caressed him wildly, she shut her eyes to think about that other man.

A crowd of men and women parting, unexpectedly, and there he stood — there he stood — she kept seeing him, and yet her vision blotched at the memory. It had been finished between them, six months before, but he had come out here . . . and she had escaped him, now she was lying in her husband's arms, in his embrace, her face pressed against his. It was a kind of sleep, this love-making. She felt herself falling asleep, her body falling from her. Her eyes shut.

"I love you," her husband said fiercely, angrily.

She shut her eyes and thought of that other man, as if betraying him would give her life a center.

"Did I hurt you? Are you — ?" her husband whispered.

Always this hot flashing of shame between them, the shame of her husband's near failure, the clumsiness of his love —

"You didn't hurt me," she said.

II

They had said good-by six months before. He drove her from Nantucket, where they had met, to Albany, New York, where she visited her sister. The hours of intimacy in the car had sealed something between them, a vow of silence and impersonality: she recalled the movement of the highways, the passing of other cars, the natural rhythms of the day hypnotizing her toward sleep while he drove. She trusted him, she could sleep in his presence. Yet she could not really fall asleep in spite of her exhaustion, and she kept jerking awake, frightened, to discover that nothing had changed — still the stranger who was driving her to Albany, still the highway, the sky, the antiseptic odor of the rented car, the sense of a rhythm behind the rhythm of the air that might unleash itself at any second. Everywhere on this highway, at this moment, there were men and women driving together, bonded together — what did that mean, to be together? What did it mean to enter into a bond with another person?

No, she did not really trust him; she did not really trust men. He would glance at her with his small cautious smile and she felt a declaration of shame between them.

Shame.

In her head she rehearsed conversations. She said bitterly, "You'll be relieved when we get to Albany. Relieved to get rid of me." They had spent so many days talking, confessing too much, driven to a pitch of childish excitement, laughing together on the beach, breaking into that pose of laughter that seems to eradicate the soul, so many days of this that the silence of the trip was like the silence of a hospital — all these surface noises, these rattles and hums, but an interior silence, a befuddlement. She said to him in her imagination, "One of us should die." Then she leaned over to touch him. She caressed the back of his neck. She said, aloud, "Would you like me to drive for a while?"

They stopped at a picnic area where other cars were stopped — couples, families — and walked together, smiling at their good luck. He put his arm around her shoulders and she sensed how they were in a posture together, a man and a woman forming a posture, a figure, that someone might sketch and show to them. She said slowly, "I don't want to go back. . . ."

Silence. She looked up at him. His face was heavy with her words, as if she had pulled at his skin with her fingers. Children ran nearby and distracted him — yes, he was a father too, his children ran like that, they tugged at his skin with their light, busy fingers.

"Are you so unhappy?" he said.

"I'm not unhappy, back there. I'm nothing. There's nothing to me," she said.

They stared at each other. The sensation between them was intense, exhausting. She thought that this man was her savior, that he had come to her at a time in her life when her life demanded completion, an end, a permanent fixing of all that was troubled and shifting and deadly. And yet it was absurd to think this. No person could save another. So she drew back from him and released him.

A few hours later they stopped at a gas station in a small city. She went to the women's rest room, having to ask the attendant for a key, and when she came back her eye jumped nervously onto the rented car — why? did she think he might have driven off without her? — onto the man, her friend, standing in conversation with the young attendant. Her friend was as old as her husband, over forty, with lanky, sloping shoulders, a full body, his hair thick, a dark, burnished brown, a festive color that made her eye twitch a little — and his hands were always moving, always those rapid conversational circles, going nowhere, gestures that were at once a little aggressive and apologetic.

She put her hand on his arm, a claim. He turned to her and smiled and she felt that she loved him, that everything in her life had forced her to this moment and that she had no choice about it.

They sat in the car for two hours, in Albany, in the parking lot of a Howard Johnson's restaurant, talking, trying to figure out their past. There was no future. They concentrated on the past, the several days behind them, lit up with a hot, dazzling August sun, like explosions that already belonged to other people, to strangers. Her face was faintly reflected in the green-tinted curve of the windshield, but she could not have recognized that face. She began to cry; she told herself: *I am not here, this will pass, this is nothing.* Still, she could not stop crying. The muscles of her face were springy, like a child's, unpredictable muscles. He stroked her arms, her shoulders, trying to comfort her. "This is so hard . . . this is impossible . . ." he said. She felt panic for the world outside this car, all that was not herself and this man, and at the same time she understood that she was free of him, as people are free of other people, she would leave him soon, safely, and within a few days he would have fallen into the past, the impersonal past. . . .

"I'm so ashamed of myself!" she said finally.

She returned to her husband and saw that another woman, a shadow-woman, had taken her place — noiseless and convincing, like a dancer performing certain difficult steps. Her husband folded her in his arms and talked to her of his own loneliness, his worries about his business, his health, his mother, kept tranquillized and mute in a nursing home, and her spirit detached itself from her and drifted about the rooms of the large house she lived in with her husband, a shadow-woman delicate and imprecise. There was no boundary to her, no edge. Alone, she took hot baths and sat exhausted in the steaming water, wondering at her perpetual exhaustion. All that winter she noticed the limp, languid weight of her arms, her veins bulging slightly with the pressure of her extreme weariness. *This is fate*, she thought, to be here and not there, to be one person and not another, a certain man's wife and not the wife of another man. The long, slow pain of this certainty rose in her, but it never became clear, it was baffling and imprecise. She could not be serious about it; she kept congratulating herself on her own good luck, to have escaped so easily, to have freed herself. So much love had gone into the first several years of her marriage that there wasn't much left, now, for another man. . . . She was certain of that. But the bath water made her dizzy, all that perpetual heat, and one day in January she drew a razor blade lightly across the inside of her arm, near the elbow, to see what would happen.

Afterward she wrapped a small towel around it, to stop the bleeding. The towel soaked through. She wrapped a bath towel around that and walked through the empty rooms of her home, lightheaded, hardly aware of the stubborn seeping of blood. There was no boundary to her in this house, no precise limit. She could flow out like her own blood and come to no end.

She sat for a while on a blue love seat, her mind empty. Her husband telephoned her when he would be staying late at the plant. He talked to her always about his plans, his problems, his business friends, his future. It was obvious that he had a future. As he spoke she nodded to encourage him, and her heartbeat quickened with the memory of her own, personal shame, the shame of this man's particular, private wife. One evening at dinner he leaned forward and put his head in his arms and fell asleep, like a child. She sat at the table with him for a while watching him. His hair had gone gray, almost white, at the temples — no one would guess that he was so quick, so careful a man, still fairly young about the eyes. She put her hand on his head, lightly, as if to prove to herself that he was real. He slept, exhausted.

One evening they went to a concert and she looked up to see her lover there, in the crowded aisle, in this city, watching her. He was standing there, with his overcoat on, watching her. She went cold. That morning the telephone had rung while her husband was still home, and she had heard him answer it, heard him hang up — it must have been a wrong number — and when the telephone rang again, at 9:30, she had been afraid to answer it. She had left home to be out of the range of that ringing, but now, in this public place, in this busy auditorium, she found herself staring at that man, unable to make any sign to him, any gesture of recognition. . . .

He would have come to her but she shook her head. No. Stay away.

Her husband helped her out of the row of seats, saying, "Excuse us, please. Excuse us," so that strangers got to their feet, quickly, alarmed, to let them pass. Was that woman about to faint? What was wrong?

At home she felt the blood drain slowly back into her head. Her husband embraced her hips, pressing his face against her, in that silence that belonged to the earliest days of their marriage. She thought, He will drive it out of me. He made love to her and she was back in the auditorium again, sitting alone, now that the concert was over. The stage was empty; the heavy velvet curtains had not been drawn; the musicians' chairs were empty, everything was silent and expectant; in the aisle her lover stood and smiled at her — Her husband was impatient. He was apart from her, working on her, operating on her; and then, stricken, he whispered, "Did I hurt you?"

The telephone rang the next morning. Dully, sluggishly, she answered it. She recognized his voice at once — that "Anna?" with its lifting of the second syllable, questioning and apologetic and making its claim — "Yes, what do you want?" she said.

"Just to see you. Please — "

"I can't."

"Anna, I'm sorry, I didn't mean to upset you — "

"I can't see you."

"Just for a few minutes — I have to talk to you — "

"But why, why now? Why now?" she said.

She heard her voice rising, but she could not stop it. He began to talk again, drowning her out. She remembered his rapid conversation. She remembered his gestures, the witty energetic circling of his hands.

"Please don't hang up!" he cried.

"I can't — I don't want to go through it again — "

"I'm not going to hurt you. Just tell me how you are."

"Everything is the same."

"Everything is the same with me."

She looked up at the ceiling, shyly. "Your wife? Your children?"

"The same."

"Your son?"

"He's fine — "

"I'm glad to hear that. I — "

"Is it still the same with you, your marriage? Tell me what you feel. What are you thinking?"

"I don't know. . . ."

She remembered his intense, eager words, the movement of his hands, that impatient precise fixing of the air by his hands, the jabbing of his fingers.

"Do you love me?" he said.

She could not answer.

"I'll come over to see you," he said.

"No," she said.

What will come next, what will happen?

Flesh hardening on his body, aging. Shrinking. He will grow old, but not soft like her husband. They are two different types: he is nervous, lean, energetic, wise. She will grow thinner, as the tension radiates out from her backbone, wearing down her flesh. Her collarbones will jut out of her skin. Her husband, caressing her in their bed, will discover that she is another woman — she is not there with him — instead she is rising in an elevator in a downtown hotel, carrying a book as a prop, or walking quickly away from that hotel, her head bent and filled with secrets. Love, what to do with it? . . . Useless as moths' wings, as moths' fluttering. . . . She feels the flutterings of silky, crazy wings in her chest.

He flew out to visit her every several weeks, staying at a different hotel each time. He telephoned her, and she drove down to park in an underground garage at the very center of the city.

She lay in his arms while her husband talked to her, miles away, one body fading into another. He will grow old, his body will change, she thought, pressing her cheek against the back of one of these men. If it was her lover, they were in a hotel room: always the propped-up little booklet describing the hotel's many services, with color photographs of its cocktail lounge and dining room and coffee shop. Grow old, leave me, die, go back to your neurotic wife and your sad, ordinary children, she thought, but still her eyes closed gratefully against his skin and she felt how complete their silence was, how they had come to rest in each other.

"Tell me about your life here. The people who love you," he said, as he always did.

One afternoon they lay together for four hours. It was her birthday and she was intoxicated with her good fortune, this prize of the afternoon, this man in her arms! She was a little giddy, she talked too much. She told him about her parents, about her husband. . . . "They were all people I believed in, but it turned out wrong. Now, I believe in you. . . ." He laughed as if shocked by her words. She did not understand. Then she understood. "But I believe truly in you. I can't think of myself without you," she said. . . . He spoke of his wife, her ambitions, her intelligence, her use of the children against him, her use of his younger son's blindness, all of his words gentle and hypnotic and convincing in the late afternoon peace of this hotel room . . . and she felt the terror of laughter, threatening laughter. Their words, like their bodies, were aging.

She dressed quickly in the bathroom, drawing her long hair up around the back of her head, fixing it as always, anxious that everything be the same. Her face was slightly raw, from his face. The rubbing of his skin. Her eyes were too bright, wearily bright. Her hair was blond but not so blond as it had been that summer in the white Nantucket air.

She ran water and splashed it on her face. She blinked at the water. Blind. Drowning. She thought with satisfaction that soon, soon, he would be back home, in that house on Long Island she had never seen, with that woman she had never seen, sitting on the edge of another bed, putting on his shoes. She wanted nothing except to be free of him. Why not be free? Oh, she thought suddenly, *I will follow you back and kill you. You and her and the little boy. What is there to stop me?*

She left him. Everyone on the street pitied her, that look of absolute zero.

III

A man and a child, approaching her. The sharp acrid smell of fish. The crashing of waves. Anna pretended not to notice the father with his son — there was something strange about them. That frank, silent intimacy, too gentle, the man's bare feet in the water and the boy a few feet away, leaning away from his father. He was about nine years old and still his father held his hand.

A small yipping dog, a golden dog, bounded near them.

Anna turned shyly back to her reading; she did not want to have to speak to these neighbors. She saw the man's shadow falling over her legs, then over the pages of her book, and she had the idea that he wanted to see what she was reading. The dog nuzzled her; the man called him away.

She watched them walk down the beach. She was relieved that the man had not spoken to her.

She saw them in town later that day, the two of them brown-haired and patient, now wearing sandals, walking with that same look of care. The man's white shorts were soiled and a little baggy. His pullover shirt was a faded green. His face was broad, the cheekbones wide, spaced widely apart, the eyes stark in their sockets, as if they fastened onto objects for no reason, ponderous and edgy. The little boy's face was pale and sharp; his lips were perpetually parted.

Anna realized that the child was blind.

The next morning, early, she caught sight of them again. For some reason she went to the back door of her cottage. She faced the sea breeze eagerly. Her heart hammered. . . . She had been here, in her family's old house, for three days, alone, bitterly satisfied at being alone, and now it was a puzzle to her how her soul strained to fly outward, to meet with another person. She watched the man with his son, his cautious, rather stooped shoulders above the child's small shoulders.

The man was carrying something, it looked like a notebook. He sat on the sand, not far from Anna's spot of the day before, and the dog rushed up to them. The child approached the edge of the ocean, timidly. He moved in short jerky steps, his legs stiff. The dog ran around him. Anna heard the child crying out a word that sounded like "Ty" — it must have been the dog's name — and then the man joined in, his voice heavy and firm.

"Ty — "

Anna tied her hair back with a yellow scarf and went down to the beach.

The man glanced around at her. He smiled. She stared past him at the waves. To talk to him or not to talk — she had the freedom of that choice. For a moment she felt that she had made a mistake, that the child and the dog would not protect her, that behind this man's ordinary, friendly face there was a certain arrogant maleness — then she relented, she smiled shyly.

"A nice house you've got there," the man said.

She nodded her thanks.

The man pushed his sunglasses up on his forehead. Yes, she recognized the eyes of the day before — intelligent and nervous, the sockets pale, untanned.

"Is that your telephone ringing?" he said.

She did not bother to listen. "It's a wrong number," she said.

Her husband calling: she had left home for a few days, to be alone.

But the man, settling himself on the sand, seemed to misinterpret this. He smiled in surprise, one corner of his mouth higher than the other. He said nothing. Anna wondered: *What is he thinking?* The dog was leaping about her, panting against her legs, and she laughed in embarrassment. She bent to pet it, grateful for its busyness. "Don't let him jump up on you," the man said. "He's a nuisance."

The dog was a small golden retriever, a young dog. The blind child, standing now in the water, turned to call the dog to him. His voice was shrill and impatient.

"Our house is the third one down — the white one," the man said.

She turned, startled. "Oh, did you buy it from Dr. Patrick? Did he die?"

"Yes, finally. . . ."

Her eyes wandered nervously over the child and the dog. She felt the nervous beat of her heart out to the very tips of her fingers, the fleshy tips of her fingers: little hearts were there, pulsing. *What is he thinking?* The man had opened his notebook. He had a piece of charcoal and he began to sketch something.

Anna looked down at him. She saw the top of his head, his thick brown hair, the freckles on his shoulders, the quick, deft movement of his hand. Upside down, Anna herself being drawn. She smiled in surprise.

"Let me draw you. Sit down," he said.

She knelt awkwardly a few yards away. He turned the page of the sketch pad. The dog ran to her and she sat, straightening out her skirt beneath her, flinching from the dog's tongue. "Ty!" cried the child. Anna sat, and slowly the pleasure of the moment began to glow in her; her skin flushed with gratitude.

She sat there for nearly an hour. The man did not talk much. Back and forth the dog bounded, shaking itself. The child came to sit near them, in silence. Anna felt that she was drifting into a kind of trance while the man sketched her, half a dozen rapid sketches, the surface of her face given up to him. "Where are you from?" the man asked.

"Ohio. My husband lives in Ohio."

She wore no wedding band.

"Your wife — " Anna began.

"Yes?"

"Is she here?"

"Not right now."

She was silent, ashamed. She had asked an improper question. But the man did not seem to notice. He continued drawing her, bent over the sketch pad. When Anna said she had to go, he showed her the drawings — one after another of her, Anna, recognizably Anna, a woman in her early thirties, her hair smooth and flat across the top of her head, tied behind by a scarf. "Take the one you like best," he said, and she picked one of her with the dog in her lap, sitting very straight, her brows and eyes clearly defined, her lips girlishly pursed, the dog and her dress suggested by a few quick irregular lines.

"Lady with pet dog," the man said.

She spent the rest of the day reading, nearer her cottage. It was not really a cottage — it was a two-story house, large and ungainly and weathered. It was mixed up in her mind with her family, her own childhood, and she glanced up from her book, perplexed, as if waiting for one of her parents or her sister to come up to her. Then she thought of the man, the man with the blind child, the man with the dog, and she could not concentrate on her reading. Someone — probably her father — had marked a passage that must be important, but she kept reading and rereading it: *We try to discover in things, endeared to us on that account, the spiritual glamour which we ourselves have cast upon them; we are disillusioned, and learn that they are in themselves barren and devoid of the charm that they owed, in our minds, to the association of certain ideas. . . .*

She thought again of the man on the beach. She lay the book aside and thought of him: his eyes, his aloneness, his drawings of her.

They began seeing each other after that. He came to her front door in the evening, without the child; he drove her into town for dinner. She was shy and extremely pleased. The darkness of the expensive restaurant released her; she heard herself chatter; she leaned forward and seemed to be offering her face up to him, listening to him. He talked about his work on a Long Island newspaper and she seemed to be listening to him, as she stared at his face, arranging her own face into the expression she had seen in that charcoal drawing. Did he see her like that, then? — girlish and withdrawn and patrician? She felt the weight of his interest in her, a force that fell upon her like a blow. A repeated blow. Of course he was married, he had children — of course she was married, permanently married. This flight from her husband was not important. She had left him before, to be alone, it was not important. Everything in her was slender and delicate and not important.

They walked for hours after dinner, looking at the other strollers, the weekend visitors, the tourists, the couples like themselves. Surely they were mistaken for a couple, a married couple. *This is the hour in which everything is decided,* Anna thought. They had both had several drinks and they talked a great deal. Anna found herself saying too much, stopping and starting giddily. She put her hand to her forehead, feeling faint.

"It's from the sun — you've had too much sun — " he said.

At the door to her cottage, on the front porch, she heard herself asking him if he would like to come in. She allowed him to lead her inside, to close the door. *This is not important, she thought clearly, he doesn't mean it, he doesn't love me, nothing will come of it.* She was frightened, yet it seemed to her necessary to give in; she had to leave Nantucket with that act completed, an act of adultery, an accomplishment she would take back to Ohio and to her marriage.

Later, incredibly, she heard herself asking: "Do you . . . do you love me?"

"You're so beautiful!" he said, amazed.

She felt this beauty, shy and glowing and centered in her eyes. He stared at her. In this large, drafty house, alone together, they were like accomplices, conspirators. She could not think: how old was she? which year was this? They had done something unforgivable together, and the knowledge of it was tugging at their faces. A cloud seemed to pass over her. She felt herself smiling shrilly.

Afterward, a peculiar raspiness, a dryness of breath. He was silent. She felt a strange, idle fear, a sense of the danger outside this room and this old, comfortable bed — a danger that would not recognize her as the lady in that drawing, the lady with the pet dog. There was nothing to say to this man, this stranger. She felt the beauty draining out of her face, her eyes fading.

"I've got to be alone," she told him.

He left, and she understood that she would not see him again. She stood by the window of the room, watching the ocean. A sense of shame overpowered her: it was smeared everywhere on her body, the smell of it, the richness of it. She tried to recall him, and his face was confused in her memory: she would have to shout to him across a jumbled space, she would have to wave her arms wildly. *You love me! You must love me!* But she knew he did not love her, and she did not love him; he was a man who drew everything up into himself, like all men, walking away, free to walk away, free to have his own thoughts, free to envision her body, all the secrets of her body. . . . And she lay down again in the bed, feeling how heavy this body had become, her insides heavy with shame, the very backs of her eyelids coated with shame.

"This is the end of one part of my life," she thought.

But in the morning the telephone rang. She answered it. It was her lover: they talked brightly and happily. She could hear the eagerness in his voice, the love in his voice, that same still, sad amazement — she understood how simple life was, there were no problems.

They spent most of their time on the beach, with the child and the dog. He joked and was serious at the same time. He said, once, "You have defined my soul for me," and she laughed to hide her alarm. In a few days it was time for her to leave. He got a sitter for the boy and took the ferry with her to the mainland, then rented a car to drive her up to Albany. She kept thinking: *Now something will happen. It will come to an end.* But most of the drive was silent and hypnotic. She wanted him to joke with her, to say again that she had defined his soul for him, but he drove fast, he was serious, she distrusted the hawkish look of his profile — she did not know him at all. At a gas station she splashed her face with cold water. Alone in the grubby little rest room, shaky and very much alone. In such places are women totally alone with their bodies. The body grows heavier, more evil, in such silence. . . . On the beach everything had been noisy with sunlight and gulls and waves; here, as if run to earth, everything was cramped and silent and dead.

She went outside, squinting. There he was, talking with the station attendant. She could not think as she returned to him whether she wanted to live or not.

She stayed in Albany for a few days, then flew home to her husband. He met her at the airport, near the luggage counter, where her three pieces of pale-brown luggage were brought to him on a conveyer belt, to be claimed by him. He kissed her on the cheek. They shook hands, a little embarrassed. She had come home again.

"How will I live out the rest of my life?" she wondered.

In January her lover spied on her: she glanced up and saw him, in a public place, in the DeRoy Symphony Hall. She was paralyzed with fear. She nearly fainted. In this faint she felt her husband's body, loving her, working its love upon her, and she shut her eyes harder to keep out the certainty of his love — sometimes he failed at loving her, sometimes he succeeded, it had nothing to do with her or her pity or her ten years of love for him, it had nothing to do with a woman at all. It was a private act accomplished by a man, a husband or a lover, in communion with his own soul, his manhood.

Her husband was forty-two years old now, growing slowly into middle age, getting heavier, softer. Her lover was about the same age, narrower in the shoulders, with a full, solid chest, yet lean, nervous. She thought, in her paralysis, of men and how they love freely and eagerly so long as their bodies are capable of love, love for a woman; and then, as love fades in their bodies, it fades from their souls and they become immune and immortal and ready to die.

Her husband was a little rough with her, as if impatient with himself. "I love you," he said fiercely, angrily. And then, ashamed, he said, "Did I hurt you? . . ."

"You didn't hurt me," she said.

Her voice was too shrill for their embrace.

While he was in the bathroom she went to her closet and took out that drawing of the summer before. There she was, on the beach at Nantucket, a lady with a pet dog, her eyes large and defined, the dog in her lap hardly more than a few snarls, a few coarse soft lines of charcoal . . . her dress smeared, her arms oddly limp . . . her hands not well drawn at all. . . . She tried to think: did she love the man who had drawn this? did he love her? The fever in her husband's body had touched her and driven her temperature up, and now she stared at the drawing with a kind of lust, fearful of seeing an ugly soul in that woman's face, fearful of seeing the face suddenly through her lover's eyes. She breathed quickly and harshly, staring at the drawing.

And so, the next day, she went to him at his hotel. She wept, pressing against him, demanding of him, "What do you want? Why are you here? Why don't you let me alone?" He told her that he wanted nothing. He expected nothing. He would not cause trouble.

"I want to talk about last August," he said.

"Don't — " she said.

She was hypnotized by his gesturing hands, his nervousness, his obvious agitation. He kept saying, "I understand. I'm making no claims upon you."

They became lovers again.

He called room service for something to drink and they sat side by side on his bed, looking through a copy of *The New Yorker*, laughing at the cartoons. It was so peaceful in this room, so complete. They were on a holiday. It was a secret holiday. Four-thirty in the afternoon, on a Friday, an ordinary Friday: a secret holiday.

"I won't bother you again," he said.

He flew back to see her again in March, and in late April. He telephoned her from his hotel — a different hotel each time — and she came down to him at once. She rose to him in various elevators, she knocked on the doors of various rooms, she stepped into his embrace, breathless and guilty and already angry with him, pleading with him. One morning in May, when he telephoned, she pressed her forehead against the doorframe and could not speak. He kept saying, "What's wrong? Can't you talk? Aren't you alone?" She felt that she was going insane. Her head would burst. Why, why did he love her, why did he pursue her? Why did he want her to die?

She went to him in the hotel room. A familiar room: had they been here before? "Everything is repeating itself. Everything is stuck," she said. He framed her face in his hands and said that she looked thinner — was she sick? — what was wrong? She shook herself free. He, her lover, looked about the same. There was a small, angry pimple on his neck. He stared at her, eagerly and suspiciously. Did she bring bad news?

"So you love me? You love me?" she asked.

"Why are you so angry?"

"I want to be free of you. The two of us free of each other."

"That isn't true — you don't want that — "

He embraced her. She was wild with that old, familiar passion for him, her body clinging to his, her arms not strong enough to hold him. Ah, what despair! — what bitter hatred she felt! — she needed this man for her salvation, he was all she had to live for, and yet she could not believe in him. He embraced her thighs, her hips, kissing her, pressing his warm face against her, and yet she could not believe in him, not really. She needed him in order to live, but he was not worth her love, he was not worth her dying. . . . She promised herself this: when she got back home, when she was alone, she would draw the razor more deeply across her arm.

The telephone rang and he answered it: a wrong number.

"Jesus," he said.

They lay together, still. She imagined their posture like this, the two of them one figure, one substance; and outside this room and this bed there was a universe of disjointed, separate things, blank things, that had nothing to do with them. She would not be Anna out there, the lady in the drawing. He would not be her lover.

"I love you so much. . . ." she whispered.

"Please don't cry! We have only a few hours, please. . . ."

It was absurd, their clinging together like this. She saw them as a single figure in a drawing, their arms and legs entwined, their heads pressing mutely together. Helpless substance, so heavy and warm and doomed. It was absurd that any human being should be so important to another human being. She wanted to laugh: a laugh might free them both.

She could not laugh.

Sometime later he said, as if they had been arguing, "Look. It's you. You're the one who doesn't want to get married. You lie to me — "

"Lie to you?"

"You love me but you won't marry me, because you want something left over — Something not finished — All your life you can attribute your misery to me, to our not being married — you are using me — "

"Stop it! You'll make me hate you!" she cried.

"You can say to yourself that you're miserable because of *me*. We will never be married, you will never be happy, neither one of us will ever be happy — "

"I don't want to hear this!" she said.

She pressed her hands flatly against her face.

She went to the bathroom to get dressed. She washed her face and part of her body, quickly. The fever was in her, in the pit of her belly. She would rush home and strike a razor across the inside of her arm and free that pressure, that fever.

The impatient bulging of the veins: an ordeal over.

The demand of the telephone's ringing: that ordeal over.

The nuisance of getting the car and driving home in all that five o'clock traffic: an ordeal too much for a woman.

The movement of this stranger's body in hers: over, finished.

Now, dressed, a little calmer, they held hands and talked. They had to talk swiftly, to get all their news in: he did not trust the people who worked for him, he had faith in no one, his wife had moved to a textbook publishing company and was doing well, she had inherited a Ben Shahn painting from her father and wanted to "touch it up a little" — she was crazy! — his blind son was at another school, doing fairly well, in fact his children were all doing fairly well in spite of the stupid mistake of their parents' marriage — and what about her? what about her life? She told him in a rush the one thing he wanted to hear: that she lived with her husband lovelessly, the two of them polite strangers, sharing a bed, lying side by side in the night in that bed, bodies out of which souls had fled. There was no longer even any shame between them.

"And what about me? Do you feel shame with me still?" he asked.

She did not answer. She moved away from him and prepared to leave.

Then, a minute later, she happened to catch sight of his reflection in the bureau mirror — he was glancing down at himself, checking himself mechanically, impersonally, preparing also to leave. He too would leave this room: he too was headed somewhere else.

She stared at him. It seemed to her that in this instant he was breaking from her, the image of her lover fell free of her, breaking from her . . . and she realized that he existed in a dimension quite apart from her, a mysterious being. And suddenly, joyfully, she felt a miraculous calm. This man was her husband, truly — they were truly married, here in this room — they had been married haphazardly and accidentally for a long time. In another part of the city she had another husband, a "husband," but she had not betrayed that man, not really. This man, whom she loved above any other person in the world, above even her own self-pitying sorrow and her own life, was her truest lover, her destiny. And she did not hate him, she did not hate herself any longer; she did not wish to die; she was flooded with a strange certainty, a sense of gratitude, of pure selfless energy. It was obvious to her that she had, all along, been behaving correctly; out of instinct.

What triumph, to love like this in any room, anywhere, risking even the craziest of accidents!

"Why are you so happy? What's wrong?" he asked, startled. He stared at her. She felt the abrupt concentration in him, the focusing of his vision on her, almost a bitterness in his face, as if he feared her. What, was it beginning all over again? Their love beginning again, in spite of them? "How can you look so happy?" he asked. "We don't have any right to it. Is it because. . . ?"

"Yes," she said.

[1972]

ANN BEATTIE (b. 1947) was born in Washington, D.C. She grew up in Chevy Chase, Maryland, the only child of parents who sent her to a suburban school that she called "a civilized concentration camp" because of its strict dress code and stern disciplinary system. She rebelled by bleaching her hair, wearing fishnet stockings, smoking cigarettes, and graduating in the bottom tenth of her class: "That took a little effort on my part." In 1969 she received a B.A. from American University, and the following year she went on to the University of Connecticut as a graduate student in English literature. Her short stories attracted the interest of Professor J. D. O'Hara there. "He said that he heard that I wrote, and if I was so good at it, why didn't I let him see what I was doing? So I took one of the few stories I had and put it in his mailbox, and it came back with comments all over it — more comments than I'd ever seen, more words than there were in the story. I would put something in his mailbox every few days and he would return it. He taught me a lot . . . about the technical process of writing." Beattie began to send her stories to magazines, and her first publication, "A Rose for Judy Garland's Casket," appeared in the Western Humanities Review in 1972. The next year another story won an Atlantic Monthly "first" award, and shortly thereafter she began publishing in The New Yorker. Beattie estimates that she sent thirteen stories to that magazine before one was accepted. "You see, I was living in Eastford, Connecticut, at the time and I was bored. You either wrote a story every night or watched television. I wrote a story every night."

Her first book of nineteen stories, Distortions, was published in 1976, the same year as her first novel, Chilly Scenes of Winter, which was later made into a film. In 1978 she published her second collection of stories, Secrets and Surprises. She published a second novel, Falling in Place, in 1980, and a third collection, The Burning House, in 1982. Critics have compared her fiction to the work of John Cheever and John Updike for its exploration of American suburban life and its "weird domesticities." Beattie herself sees little resemblance: "I think they're fine writers, but I don't see any comparison in the world between us. . . . Updike's style, that learned elegance, that intrusion of self into the material and that very careful way he orchestrates everything, and the same thing with Cheever — they're writing traditionally well-made stories." She says she writes about chaos, "and many of the simple flat statements that I bring together are usually non sequiturs or bordering on being non sequiturs — which reinforces the chaos. I write in these flat simple sentences because that's the way I think."

A common theme in Beattie's fiction, including "Waiting," from The

Burning House, is one of lives wrenched out of shape by bad timing or faulty perception; yet her sense of the world is that "you can take the correct steps and obtain the correct answers and a tree will fall on your head." Although she admires the stories of Flannery O'Connor, Beattie resists a religious answer to the "huge questions" of life, preferring the "surprises" that emerge in the creation of her work and tell her things she did not know before.

Ann Beattie

ಬಿ

WAITING

"It's beautiful," the woman says.

"How did you come by this?"

She wiggles her finger in the mousehole. It's a genuine mousehole: sometime in the eighteenth century a mouse gnawed its way into the cupboard, through the two inside shelves, and out the bottom.

"We bought it from an antique dealer in Virginia," I say.

"Where in Virginia?"

"Ruckersville. Outside of Charlottesville."

"That's beautiful country," she says. "I know where Ruckersville is. I had an uncle who lived in Keswick."

"Keswick was nice," I say. "The farms."

"Oh," she says. "The tax writeoffs, you mean? Those mansions with one sheep grazing out front?"

She is touching the wood, stroking lightly in case there might be a splinter. Even after so much time, everything might not have been worn down to smoothness. She lowers her eyes. "Would you take eight hundred?" she says.

"I'd like to sell it for a thousand," I say. "I paid thirteen hundred, ten years ago."

"It's beautiful," she says. "I suppose I should try to tell you it has some faults, but I've never seen one like it. Very nice. My husband wouldn't like my spending more than six hundred to begin with, but I can see that it's worth eight." She is resting her index finger on the latch. "Could I bring my husband to see it tonight?"

"All right."

"You're moving?" she says.

"Eventually," I say.

"That would be something to load around." She shakes her head. "Are you going back South?"

"I doubt it," I say.

"You probably think I'm kidding about coming back with my husband," she says suddenly. She lowers her eyes again. "Are other people interested?"

"There's just been one other call. Somebody who wanted to come out Saturday." I smile. "I guess I should pretend there's great interest."

"I'll take it," the woman says. "For a thousand. You probably could sell it for more and I could probably resell it for more. I'll tell my husband that."

She picks up her embroidered shoulder bag from the floor by the corner cabinet. She sits at the oak table by the octagonal window and rummages for her checkbook.

"I was thinking, What if I left it home? But I didn't." She takes out a checkbook in a red plastic cover. "My uncle in Keswick was one of those gentleman farmers," she says. "He lived until he was eighty-six, and enjoyed his life. He did everything in moderation, but the key was that he did *everything*." She looks appraisingly at her signature. "Some movie actress just bought a farm across from the Cobham store," she says. "A girl. I never saw her in the movies. Do you know who I'm talking about?"

"Well, Art Garfunkel used to have a place out there," I say.

"Maybe she bought his place." The woman pushes the check to the center of the table, tilts the vase full of phlox, and puts the corner of the check underneath. "Well," she says. "Thank you. We'll come with my brother's truck to get it on the weekend. What about Saturday?"

"That's fine," I say.

"You're going to have some move," she says, looking around at the other furniture. "I haven't moved in thirty years, and I wouldn't want to."

The dogs walks through the room.

"What a well-mannered dog," she says.

"That's Hugo. Hugo's moved quite a few times in thirteen years. Virginia. D.C. Boston. Here."

"Poor old Hugo," she says.

Hugo, in the living room now, thumps down and sighs.

"Thank you," she says, putting out her hand. I reach out to shake it, but our hands don't meet and she clasps her hand around my wrist. "Saturday afternoon. Maybe Saturday evening. Should I be specific?"

"Any time is all right."

"Can I turn around on your grass or no?"

"Sure. Did you see the tire marks? I do it all the time."

"Well," she says. "People who back into traffic. I don't know. I honk at them all the time."

I go to the screen door and wave. She is driving a yellow Mercedes, an old one that's been repainted, with a license that says "RAVE-1." The car stalls. She re-starts it and waves. I wave again.

When she's gone, I go out the back door and walk down the driveway. A single daisy is growing out of the foot-wide crack in the concrete. Somebody has thrown a beer can into the driveway. I pick it up and marvel at how light it is. I get the mail from the box across the street and look at it as cars pass by. One of the stream of cars honks a warning at me, although I am not moving, except for flipping through the mail. There is a C.L.&P. bill, a couple of pieces of junk mail, a postcard from Henry in Los Angeles, and a letter from my husband in — he's made it to California. Berkeley, California, mailed four days ago. Years ago, when I visited a friend in Berkeley we went to a little park and some people wandered in walking two dogs and a goat. An African pygmy goat. The woman said it was housebroken to urinate outside and as for the other she just picked up the pellets.

I go inside and watch the moving red band on the digital clock in the kitchen. Behind the clock is an old coffee tin decorated with a picture of a man and a woman in a romantic embrace; his arms are nearly rusted away, her hair is chipped, but a perfectly painted wreath of coffee beans rises in an arc above them. Probably I should have advertised the coffee tin, too, but I like to hear the metal top creak when I lift it in the morning to take the jar of coffee out. But if not the coffee tin, I should probably have put the tin breadbox up for sale.

John and I liked looking for antiques. He liked the ones almost beyond repair — the kind that you would have to buy twenty dollars' worth of books to understand how to restore. When we used to go looking, antiques were much less expensive than they are now. We bought them at a time when we had the patience to sit all day on folding chairs under a canopy at an auction. We were organized; we would come and inspect the things the day before. Then we would get there early the next day and wait. Most of the auctioneers in that part of Virginia were very good. One, named Wicked Richard, used to lace his fingers together and crack his knuckles as he called the lots. His real name was Wisted. When he did classier auctions and there was a pamphlet, his name was listed as Wisted. At most of the regular auctions, though, he introduced himself as Wicked Richard.

I cut a section of cheese and take some crackers out of a container. I put them on a plate and carry them into the dining room, feeling a little sad about parting with the big corner cupboard. Suddenly it seems older and bigger — a very large thing to be giving up.

The phone rings. A woman wants to know the size of the refrigerator that I have advertised. I tell her.

"Is it white?" she says.

The ad said it was white.

"Yes," I tell her.

"This is your refrigerator?" she says.

"One of them," I say. "I'm moving."

"Oh," she says. "You shouldn't tell people that. People read these ads to figure out who's moving and might not be around, so they can rob them. There were a lot of robberies in your neighborhood last summer."

The refrigerator is too small for her. We hang up.

The phone rings again, and I let it ring. I sit down and look at the corner cupboard. I put a piece of cheese on top of a cracker and eat it. I get up and go into the living room and offer a piece of cheese to Hugo. He sniffs and takes it lightly from my fingers. Earlier today, in the morning, I ran him in Putnam Park. I could hardly keep up with him, as usual. Thirteen isn't so old, for a dog. He scared the ducks and sent them running into the water. He growled at a beagle a man was walking, and tugged on his leash until he choked. He pulled almost as hard as he could a few summers ago. The air made his fur fluffy. Now he is·happy, slowly licking his mouth, getting ready to take his afternoon nap.

John wanted to take Hugo across country, but in the end we decided that, as much as Hugo would enjoy terrorizing so many dogs along the way, it was going to be a hot July and it was better if he stayed home. We discussed this reasonably. No frenzy — nothing like the way we had been swept in at some auctions to bid on things that we didn't want, just because so many other people were mad for them. A reasonable discussion about Hugo, even if it was at the last minute: Hugo, in the car, already sticking his head out the window to bark goodbye. "It's too hot for him," I said. I was standing outside in my nightgown. "It's almost July. He'll be a hassle for you if campgrounds won't take him or if you have to park in the sun." So Hugo stood beside me, barking his high-pitched goodbye, as John backed out of the driveway. He forgot: his big battery lantern and his can opener. He remembered: his tent, the cooler filled with ice (he couldn't decide when he left whether he was going to stock up on beer or Coke), a camera, a suitcase, a fiddle, and a banjo. He forgot his driver's license, too. I never understood why he didn't keep it in his wallet, but it always seemed to get taken out for some reason and then be lost. Yesterday I found it leaning up against the Excedrin in the medicine cabinet.

Bobby calls. He fools me with his imitation of a man with an English accent who wants to know if I also have an avocado-colored refrigerator for sale. When I say I don't, he asks if I know somebody who paints refrigerators.

"Of course not," I tell him.

"That's the most decisive thing I've heard you say in five years," Bobby says in his real voice. "How's it going, Sally?"

"Jesus," I say. "If you'd answered this phone all morning, you wouldn't think that was funny. Where are you?"

"New York. Where do you think I am? It's my lunch hour. Going to

Le Relais to get tanked up. A little *le pain et le beurre*,[1] put down a few
Scotches."

"Le Relais," I say. "Hmm."

"Don't make a bad eye on me," he says, going into his Muhammad
Ali imitation. "Step on my foot and I kick you to the moon. Glad-hand me
and I shake you like a loon." Bobby clears his throat. "I got the company
twenty big ones today," he says. "Twenty Gs."

"Congratulations. Have a good lunch. Come out for dinner, if you feel
like the drive."

"I don't have any gas and I can't face the train." He coughs again. "I
gave up cigarettes," he says. "Why am I coughing?" He moves away from
the phone to cough loudly.

"Are you smoking grass in the office?" I say.

"Not this time," he gasps. "I'm goddam dying of something." A
pause. "What did you do yesterday?"

"I was in town. You'd laugh at what I did."

"You went to the fireworks."

"Yeah, that's right. I wouldn't hesitate to tell you that part."

"What'd you do?" he says.

"I met Andy and Tom at the Plaza and drank champagne. They
didn't. I did. Then we went to the fireworks."

"Sally at the *Plaza*?" He laughs. "What were they doing in town?"

"Tom was there on business. Andy came to see the fireworks."

"It rained, didn't it?"

"Only a little. It was O.K. They were pretty."

"The fireworks," Bobby says. "I didn't make the fireworks."

"You're going to miss lunch, Bobby," I say.

"God," he says. "I am. Bye."

I pull a record out from under the big library table, where they're kept
on the wide mahogany board that connects the legs. By coincidence, the
record I pull out is the Miles Davis Sextet's "Jazz at the Plaza." At the
Palm Court on the Fourth of July, a violinist played "Play Gypsies, Dance
Gypsies" and "Oklahoma!" I try to remember what else and can't.

"What do you say, Hugo?" I say to the dog. "Another piece of cheese,
or would you rather go on with your siesta?"

He knows the word "cheese." He knows it as well as his name. I love
the way his eyes light up and he perks his ears for certain words. Bobby tells
me that you can speak gibberish to people, ninety percent of the people, as
long as you throw in a little catchword now and then, and it's the same
when I talk to Hugo: "Cheese." "Tag." "Out."

No reaction. Hugo is lying where he always does, on his right side,
near the stereo. His nose is only a fraction of an inch away from a plant in a

[1] bread and butter.

basket beneath the window. The branches of the plant sweep the floor. He seems very still.

"Cheese?" I whisper. "Hugo?" It is as loud as I can speak.

No reaction. I start to take a step closer, but stop myself. I put down the record and stare at him. Nothing changes. I walk out into the back yard. The sun is shining directly down from overhead, striking the dark-blue doors of the garage, washing out the color to the palest tint of blue. The peach tree by the garage, with one dead branch. The wind chimes tinkling in the peach tree. A bird hopping by the iris underneath the tree. Mosquitoes or gnats, a puff of them in the air, clustered in front of me. I sink down into the grass. I pick a blade, split it slowly with my fingernail. I count the times I breathe in and out. When I open my eyes, the sun is shining hard on the blue doors.

After a while — maybe ten minutes, maybe twenty — a truck pulls into the driveway. The man who usually delivers packages to the house hops out of the United Parcel truck. He is a nice man, about twenty-five, with long hair tucked behind his ears, and kind eyes.

Hugo did not bark when the truck pulled into the drive.

"Hi," he says. "What a beautiful day. Here you go."

He holds out a clipboard and a pen.

"Forty-two," he says, pointing to the tiny numbered block in which I am to sign my name. A mailing envelope is under his arm.

"Another book," he says. He hands me the package.

I reach up for it. There is a blue label with my name and address typed on it.

He locks his hands behind his back and raises his arms, bowing. "Did you notice that?" he says, straightening out of the yoga stretch, pointing to the envelope. "What's the joke?" he says.

The return address says "John F. Kennedy."

"Oh," I say. "A friend in publishing." I look up at him. I realize that that hasn't explained it. "We were talking on the phone last week. He was — People are still talking about where they were when he was shot, and I've known my friend for almost ten years and we'd never talked about it before."

The U.P.S. man is wiping sweat off his forehead with a handkerchief. He stuffs the handkerchief into his pocket.

"He wasn't making fun," I say. "He admired Kennedy."

The U.P.S. man crouches, runs his fingers across the grass. He looks in the direction of the garage. He looks at me. "Are you all right?" he says.

"Well — " I say.

He is still watching me.

"Well," I say, trying to catch my breath. "Let's see what this is."

I pull up the flap, being careful not to get cut by the staples. A large paperback called "If Mountains Die." Color photographs. The sky above the Pueblo River gorge in the book is very blue. I show the U.P.S. man.

"Were you all right when I pulled in?" he says. "You were sitting sort of funny."

I still am. I realize that my arms are crossed over my chest and I am leaning forward. I uncross my arms and lean back on my elbows. "Fine," I say. "Thank you."

Another car pulls into the driveway, comes around the truck, and stops on the lawn. Ray's car. Ray gets out, smiles, leans back in through the open window to turn off the tape that's still playing. Ray is my best friend. Also my husband's best friend.

"What are you doing here?" I say to Ray.

"Hi," the U.P.S. man says to Ray. "I've got to get going. Well." He looks at me. "See you," he says.

"See you," I say. "Thanks."

"What am I doing here?" Ray says. He taps his watch. "Lunchtime. I'm on a business lunch. Big deal. Important negotiations. Want to drive down to the Redding Market and buy a couple of sandwiches, or have you already eaten?"

"You drove all the way out here for lunch?"

"Big business lunch. Difficult client. Takes time to bring some clients around. Coaxing. Takes hours." Ray shrugs.

"Don't they care?"

Ray sticks out his tongue and makes a noise, sits beside me and puts his arm around my shoulder and shakes me lightly toward him and away from him a couple of times. "Look at that sunshine," he says. "Finally. I thought the rain would never stop." He hugs my shoulder and takes his arm away. "It depresses me, too," he says. "I don't like what I sound like when I keep saying that nobody cares." Ray sighs. He reaches for a cigarette. "Nobody cares," he says. "Two-hour lunch. Four. Five."

We sit silently. He picks up the book, leafs through. "Pretty," he says. "You eat already?"

I look behind me at the screen door. Hugo is not there. No sound, either, when the car came up the driveway and the truck left.

"Yes," I say. "But there's some cheese in the house. All the usual things. Or you could go to the market."

"Maybe I will," he says. "Want anything?"

"Ray," I say, reaching my hand up. "Don't go to the market."

"What?" he says. He sits on his heels and takes my hand. He looks into my face.

"Why don't you — There's cheese in the house," I say.

He looks puzzled. Then he sees the stack of mail on the grass underneath our hands. "Oh," he says. "Letter from John." He picks it up, sees that it hasn't been opened. "O.K.," he says. "Then I'm perplexed again. Just that he wrote you? That he's already in Berkeley? Well, he had a bad winter. We all had a bad winter. It's going to be all right. He hasn't called? You don't know if he hooked up with that band?"

I shake my head no.

"I tried to call you yesterday," he says. "You weren't home."

"I went into New York."

"And?"

"I went out for drinks with some friends. We went to the fireworks."

"So did I," Ray says. "Where were you?"

"Seventy-sixth Street."

"I was at Ninety-eighth. I knew it was crazy to think I might run into you at the fireworks."

A cardinal flies into the peach tree.

"I did run into Bobby last week," he says. "Of course, it's not really running into him at one o'clock at Le Relais."

"How was Bobby?"

"You haven't heard from him, either?"

"He called today, but he didn't say how he was. I guess I didn't ask."

"He was O.K. He looked good. You can hardly see the scar above his eyebrow where they took the stitches. I imagine in a few weeks when it fades you won't notice it at all."

"You think he's done with dining in Harlem?"

"Doubt it. It could have happened anywhere, you know. People get mugged all over the place."

I hear the phone ringing and don't get up. Ray squeezes my shoulder again. "Well," he says. "I'm going to bring some food out here."

"If there's anything in there that isn't the way it ought to be, just take care of it, will you?"

"What?" he says.

"I mean — If there's anything wrong, just fix it."

He smiles. "Don't tell me. You painted a room what you thought was a nice pastel color and it came out electric pink. Or the chairs — you didn't have them reupholstered again, did you?" Ray comes back to where I'm sitting. "Oh, God," he says. "I was thinking the other night about how you'd had that horrible chintz you bought on Madison Avenue put onto the chairs and when John and I got back here you were afraid to let him into the house. God — that awful striped material. Remember John standing in back of the chair and putting his chin over the back and screaming, 'I'm innocent!' Remember him doing that?" Ray's eyes are about to water, the way they watered because he laughed so hard the day John did that. "That was about a year ago this month," he says.

I nod yes.

"Well," Ray says. "Everything's going to be all right, and I don't say that just because I want to believe in one nice thing. Bobby thinks the same thing. We agree about this. I keep talking about this, don't I? I keep coming out to the house, like you've cracked up or something. You don't want to keep hearing my sermons." Ray opens the screen door. "Anybody can take a trip," he says.

I stare over at him.

"I'm getting lunch," he says. He is holding the door open with his foot. He moves his foot and goes into the house. The door slams behind him.

"Hey!" he calls out. "Want iced tea or something?"

The phone begins to ring.

"Want me to get it?" he says.

"No. Let it ring."

"Let it ring?" he hollers.

The cardinal flies out of the peach tree and onto the sweeping branch of a tall fir tree that borders the lawn — so many trees so close together that you can't see the house on the other side. The bird becomes a speck of red and disappears.

"Hey, pretty lady!" Ray calls. "Where's your mutt?"

Over the noise of the telephone, I can hear him knocking around in the kitchen. The stuck drawer opening.

"You *honestly* want me not to answer the phone?" he calls.

I look back at the house. Ray, balancing a tray, opens the door with one hand, and Hugo is beside him — not rushing out, the way he usually does to get through the door, but padding slowly, shaking himself out of sleep. He comes over and lies down next to me, blinking because his eyes are not yet accustomed to the sunlight.

Ray sits down with his plate of crackers and cheese and a beer. He looks at the tears streaming down my cheeks and shoves over close to me. He takes a big drink and puts the beer on the grass. He pushes the tray next to the beer can.

"Hey," Ray says. "Everything's cool, O.K.? No right and no wrong. People do what they do. A neutral observer, and friend to all. Same easy advice from Ray all around. Our discretion assured." He pushes my hair gently off my wet cheeks. "It's O.K.," he says softly, turning and cupping his hands over my forehead. "Just tell me what you've done."

[1982]

PART TWO

THE COMMENTARIES

THE SECOND PART of this book consists of critical comments on the short story form and on various individual stories. In the preface to his story collection Twice-told Tales, Nathaniel Hawthorne wrote that a writer "would have reason to be ashamed if he could not criticize his own work as fairly as another man's; and — though it is little his business, and perhaps still less his interest — he can hardly resist a temptation to achieve something of the sort. If writers were allowed to do so, and would perform the task with perfect sincerity and unreserve, their opinions of their own productions would often be more valuable and instructive than the works themselves." While Hawthorne was not entirely serious in this last statement, there is some truth in what he is saying. Writers' attitudes about creating short fiction can often clarify their work, place their stories in a larger context of literary history, and shed light on the creative process.

The first ten selections in this section are statements by writers whose stories appear in this book, about the form of the short story and their own process of writing short fiction. The next twenty selections are comments by writers on specific short stories included in the first part of this anthology.

*E*DGAR ALLAN POE *was one of the earliest writers to discuss the aesthetic qualities of the short story as a distinct prose narrative form. In his day literary criticism was still a new, unformed field of thought, lacking a terminology and developed critical concepts. His two long reviews praising the tales of Nathaniel Hawthorne were published in* Graham's Magazine *in 1842 and* Godey's Ladies' Book *in 1847; they are pioneering examples of the analytical literary essay. The following excerpt is taken from the 1847 piece, where Poe amplified his theory of the short story and his views on the nature of originality in literature.*

❧ 1 ❧

Edgar Allan Poe

on the Importance of the Single Effect

in a Prose Tale

Were I called upon . . . to designate that class of composition which, next to such a poem as I have suggested, should best fulfill the demands and serve the purposes of ambitious genius, should offer it the most advantageous field of exertion, and afford it the fairest opportunity of display, I should speak at once of the brief prose tale. . . . The ordinary novel is objectionable, from its length, for reasons analogous to those which render length objectionable in the poem. As the novel cannot be read at one sitting, it cannot avail itself of the immense benefit of *totality*. Worldly interests, intervening during the pauses of perusal, modify, counteract, and annul the impressions intended. But simple cessation in reading would, of itself, be sufficient to destroy the true unity. In the brief tale, however, the author is enabled to carry out his full design without interruption. During the hour of perusal, the soul of the reader is at the writer's control.

A skilful artist has constructed a tale. He has not fashioned his thoughts to accommodate his incidents, but having deliberately conceived a certain *single effect* to be wrought, he then invents such incidents, he then combines such events, and discusses them in such tone as may best serve him in establishing this preconceived effect. If his very first sentence tend not to the out-bringing of this effect, then in his very first step has he committed a blunder. In the whole composition there should be no word written of which the tendency, direct or indirect, is not to the one preestablished design. And by such means, with such care and skill, a picture is at length painted which leaves in the mind of him who contemplates it with a kindred art, a sense of the fullest satisfaction. The idea of the tale, its thesis, has been presented unblemished, because undisturbed — an end absolutely demanded, yet, in the novel, altogether unattainable.   [1847]

*H*ENRY JAMES *was a prolific critic of fiction and fiction writers. It has been estimated that his book reviews, critical articles, introductions, prefaces, and journalistic columns would fill ten volumes. In reading other writers of fiction, he was gaining insight into himself, and he emphasized other writers' artistic intentions — "What are they trying to do?" — as a way of discovering "How shall I do it?" His essay on Ivan Turgenev was published in* The Art of Fiction *in 1884, along with discussions of several other European writers, including Gustave Flaubert and Guy de Maupassant. James was most impressed by Turgenev's emphasis on character in his fiction.*

᪷ 2 ᪷

Henry James

on Turgenev's Idea of

the Germ of a Story

Nothing that Turgenev had to say could be more interesting than his talk about his own work, his manner of writing. What I have heard him tell of these things was worthy of the beautiful results he produced; of the deep purpose, pervading them all, to show us life itself. The germ of a story, with him, was never an affair of plot — that was the last thing he thought of: it was the representation of certain persons. The first form in which a tale appeared to him was as the figure of an individual, or a combination of individuals, whom he wished to see in action, being sure that such people must do something very special and interesting. They stood before him definite, vivid, and he wished to know, and to show, as much as possible of their nature. The first thing was to make clear to himself what he did know, to begin with; and to this end, he wrote out a sort of biography of each of his characters, and everything that they had done and that had happened to them up to the opening of the story. He had their *dossier*, as the French say, and as the police has that of every conspicuous criminal. With this material in his hand he was able to proceed; the story all lay in the question, What shall I make them do? He always made them do things that showed them completely; but, as he said, the defect of his manner and the reproach that was made him was his want of "architecture" — in other words, of composition. The great thing, of course, is to have architecture as well as precious material. . . . If one reads Turgenev's stories with the knowledge that they were composed — or rather that they came into being — in this way, one can trace the process in every line. Story, in the conventional sense of the word — a fable constructed, like Wordsworth's phantom, "to startle and waylay"[1] — there is as little as possible. The thing consists of the motions of a group of selected creatures, which are not the result of a preconceived action, but a consequence of the qualities of the actors.   [1884]

---

[1] The quotation is from "She Was a Phantom of Delight," by English Romantic poet William Wordsworth (1770–1850).

*K*ATE CHOPIN *made a number of translations, mostly of stories by Guy de Maupassant, and she published several essays on literature in St. Louis periodicals. She wrote about the influence of Maupassant on her fiction in response to an invitation of the editor of* The Atlantic Monthly *in 1896. He returned her first version of the essay, however, advising her to "set forth the matter directly." Her revised version was later included in the magazine with the title "In the Confidence of a Story-Teller," but the section describing how she first encountered Maupassant's tales and the impression they made on her was dropped, perhaps because she spoke so enthusiastically about the French writer's escape "from tradition and authority." This portion of the essay is reprinted from the manuscript included in volume 2 of* The Complete Works of Kate Chopin (1969).

`⌐э3⌐`

Kate Chopin

on How She Stumbled upon

Maupassant

About eight years ago there fell accidentally into my hands a volume of Maupassant's tales. These were new to me. I had been in the woods, in the fields, groping around; looking for something big, satisfying, convincing, and finding nothing but — myself; a something neither big nor satisfying but wholly convincing. It was at this period of my emerging from the vast solitude in which I had been making my own acquaintance, that I stumbled upon Maupassant. I read his stories and marvelled at them. Here was life, not fiction; for where were the plots, the old fashioned mechanism and stage trapping that in a vague, unthinking way I had fancied were essential to the art of story making? Here was a man who had escaped from tradition and authority, who had entered into himself and looked out upon life through his own being and with his own eyes; and who, in a direct and simple way, told us what he saw. When a man does this, he gives us the best that he can; something valuable for it is genuine and spontaneous. He gives us his impressions. Someone told me the other day that Maupassant had gone out of fashion. I was not grieved to hear it. He has never seemed to me to belong to the multitude, but rather to the individual. He is not one whom we gather in crowds to listen to — whom we follow in procession —

with beating of brass instruments. He does not move us to throw ourselves into the throng — having the integral of an unthinking whole to shout his praise. I even like to think that he appeals to me alone. You probably like to think that he reaches you exclusively. A whole multitude may be secretly nourishing the belief in regard to him for all I know. Someway I like to cherish the delusion that he has spoken to no one else so directly, so intimately as he does to me. He did not say, as another might have done, "do you see these are charming stories of mine? take them into your closet — study them closely — mark their combination — observe the method, the manner of their putting together — and if ever you are moved to write stories you can do no better than to imitate. . . ." [1896]

ANTON CHEKHOV *described his theories of literature and his practice as a storyteller in countless letters to his family and friends. He was not a systematic critic, and he did not always follow his own advice to other writers. Brevity and concentration on a few essentials of scene and character were the essence of his technique, but he was not always as drastically laconic in his stories as his letters suggest. What is always clear in his advice to other writers is his own unwearying compassion and his desire to speak honestly in his efforts to help them. He wrote in his notebook, "Man will only become better when you make him see what he is like."*

These letters are to his older brother, his publisher, and a younger author whose work he admired.

❧ 4 ❧

Anton Chekhov

on Technique in Writing

a Short Story

From a Letter to Alexander P. Chekhov

In my opinion a true description of Nature should be very brief and have a character of relevance. Commonplaces such as, "the setting sun bathing in the waves of the darkening sea, poured its purple gold, etc." — "the swallows flying over the surface of the water twittered merrily" — such commonplaces one ought to abandon. In descriptions of Nature one ought to seize upon the litttle particulars, grouping them in such a way that, in reading, when you shut your eyes, you get a picture.

For instance, you will get the full effect of a moonlight night if you write that on the mill-dam a little glowing star-point flashed from the neck of a broken bottle, and the round, black shadow of a dog, or a wolf, emerged and ran, etc. Nature becomes animated if you are not squeamish about employing comparisons of her phenomena with ordinary human activities, etc.

In the sphere of psychology, details are also the thing. God preserve us from commonplaces. Best of all is it to avoid depicting the hero's state of mind; you ought to try to make it clear from the hero's actions. It is not necessary to portray many characters. The center of gravity should be in two persons: him and her. [1886]

From a Letter to Aleksey S. Suvorin

You abuse me for objectivity, calling it indifference to good and evil, lack of ideals and ideas, and so on. You would have me, when I describe horse-thieves, say: "Stealing horses is an evil." But that has been known for ages without my saying so. Let the jury judge them; it's my job simply to show what sort of people they are. I write: You are dealing with horse-thieves, so let me tell you that they are not beggars but well-fed people, that they are people of a special cult, and that horse-stealing is not simply theft but a passion. Of course it would be pleasant to combine art with a sermon, but for me personally it is extremely difficult and almost impossible, owing to the conditions of technique. You see, to depict horse-thieves in seven hundred lines I must all the time speak and think in their tone and feel in their spirit, otherwise, if I introduce subjectivity, the image becomes blurred and the story will not be as compact as all short stories ought to be. When I write, I reckon entirely upon the reader to add for himself the subjective elements that are lacking in the story.   [1890]

From a Letter to Maxim Gorky

More advice: when reading the proofs, cross out a host of terms qualifying nouns and verbs. You have so many such terms that the reader's mind finds it a task to concentrate on them, and he soon grows tired. You understand it at once when I say, "The man sat on the grass"; you understand it because it is clear and makes no demands on the attention. On the other hand, it is not easily understood, and it is difficult for the mind, if I write, "A tall, narrow-chested, middle-sized man, with a red beard, sat on the green grass, already trampled by pedestrians, sat silently, shyly, and timidly looked about him." That is not immediately grasped by the mind, whereas good writing should be grasped at once — in a second.   [1899]

꒰ 5 ꒱

Edith Wharton

"Every Subject Must Contain within Itself

Its Own Dimensions"

It is sometimes said that a "good subject" for a short story should always be capable of being expanded into a novel.

The principle may be defendable in special cases; but it is certainly a misleading one on which to build any general theory. Every "subject" (in the novelist's sense of the term) must necessarily contain within itself its own dimensions; and one of the fiction-writer's essential gifts is that of discerning whether the subject which presents itself to him, asking for incarnation, is suited to the proportions of a short story or of a novel. If it appears to be adapted to both the chances are that it is inadequate to either.

It would be as great a mistake, however, to try to base a hard-and-fast theory on the denial of the rule as on its assertion. Instances of short stories made out of subjects that could have been expanded into a novel, and that are yet typical short stories and not mere stunted novels, will occur to everyone. General rules in art are useful chiefly as a lamp in a mine, or a handrail down a black stairway; they are necessary for the sake of the guidance they give, but it is a mistake, once they are formulated, to be too much in awe of them.

There are at least two reasons why a subject should find expression in novel-form rather than as a tale; but neither is based on the number of what may be conveniently called incidents, or external happenings, which the narrative contains. There are novels of action which might be condensed into short stories without the loss of their distinguishing qualities. The marks of the subject requiring a longer development are, first, the gradual unfolding of the inner life of its characters, and secondly the need of producing in the reader's mind the sense of the lapse of time. Outward events of the most varied and exciting nature may without loss of probability be crowded into a few hours, but moral dramas usually have their roots deep in the soul, their rise far back in time; and the suddenest-seeming clash in which they culminate should be led up to step by step if it is to explain and justify itself.

There are cases, indeed, when the short story may make use of the moral drama at its culmination. If the incident dealt with be one which a single retrospective flash sufficiently lights up, it is qualified for use as a short story; but if the subject be so complex, and its successive phases so interesting, as to justify elaboration, the lapse of time must necessarily be suggested, and the novel-form becomes appropriate.

The effect of compactness and instantaneity sought in the short story is attained mainly by the observance of two "unities" — the old traditional one of time, and that other, more modern and complex, which requires that any rapidly enacted episode shall be seen through only one pair of eyes. . . .

One thing more is needful for the ultimate effect of probability; and that is, never to let the character who serves as reflector record anything not naturally within his register. It should be the story-teller's first care to choose this reflecting mind deliberately, as one would choose a building-site, or decide upon the orientation of one's house, and when this is done, to live inside the mind chosen, trying to feel, see and react exactly as the latter would, no more, no less, and, above all, no otherwise. Only thus can the writer avoid attributing incongruities of thought and metaphor to his chosen interpreter.   [1925]

GERTRUDE STEIN came back to the United States to give a series of lectures after the success of her book The Autobiography of Alice B. Toklas *in 1933. She had described her own life in that book, as well as that of her companion Alice B. Toklas, and she moved on to a more theoretical examination of her practice as a prose writer in the talks later published as* Lectures in America *(1935). "Portraits and Repetition" was Stein's favorite lecture, as sustained and coherent a piece of prose as she ever wrote. In it she justified her own decision to ignore plot in what she called her "verbal portraits," and compared her major work,* The Making of Americans, *to the two other "important things written in this generation" which she claimed also lacked a story — Marcel Proust's* Remembrance of Things Past *and James Joyce's* Ulysses.

⤳6⤝

Gertrude Stein

on Technique in Portraits

and Repetition

And so I am trying to tell you what doing portraits meant to me, I had to find out what it was inside any one, and by any one I mean every one I had to find out inside every one what was in them that was intrinsically exciting and I had to find out not by what they said not by what they did not by how much or how little they resembled any other one but I had to find it out by the intensity of movement that there was inside in any one of them. And of course do not forget, of course I was interested in any one. I am. Of course I am interested in any one. And in any one I must or else I must betake myself to some entirely different occupation and I do not think I will, I must find out what is moving inside them that makes them them, and I must find out how I by the thing moving excitedly inside in me can make a portrait of them.

You can understand why I did it so often, why I did it in so many ways why I say that there is no repetition because, and this is absolutely true, that the exciting thing inside in any one if it is really inside in them is not a remembered thing, if it is really inside in them, it is not a confused thing, it is not a repeated thing. And if I could in any way and I have done it in every way if I could make a portrait of that inside them without any description of

what they are doing and what they are saying then I too was neither repeating, nor remembering nor being in a confusion.

You see what I mean by what I say. But I know you do.

Will you see it as clearly when I read you some of the portraits that I
have written. Maybe you will but I doubt it. But if you do well then if you
do you will see what I have done and do do.

A thing you all know is that in the three novels written in this generation that are the important things written in this generation, there is, in
none of them a story. There is none in Proust[1] in The Making of Americans[2] or in Ulysses.[3] And this is what you are now to begin to realize in this
description I am giving you of making portraits.   [1935]

---

[1] Marcel Proust (1871–1922), *À la Recherche du Temps Perdu* (usually translated,
after a phrase from Shakespeare, as *Remembrance of Things Past*, though the last two words
are more accurately translated as "lost time"). Proust spent almost his entire life laboring on
this massive autobiographical novel, published in seven volumes between 1913 and 1926.

[2] *The Making of Americans* is Stein's own novel, written between 1906 and 1908 but
not published until 1925.

[3] James Joyce, *Ulysses* (1922). For information on Joyce, see the introduction to his
stories on page 507.

SHERWOOD ANDERSON commented on his practice of writing short stories in his autobiography, A Story Teller's Story, published in 1924. This book was his first attempt to write his memoirs and authenticate his "legend"— an improverished childhood, a revolt against business life, and an entrance into the avant-garde literary circles of Chicago, New Orleans, and New York. He was more concerned with the meaning than with the facts of his life. In his rejection of the "plot" story (a story emphasizing plot over character, setting, or theme), which he considered contrived fiction, he became a strong influence on many subsequent American writers of short stories.

❧ 7 ☙

Sherwood Anderson

on Form, Not Plot, in

the Short Story

For such men as myself you must understand there is always a great difficulty about telling the tale after the scent has been picked up. . . . Having, from a conversation overheard or in some other way, got the tone of a tale, I was like a woman who has just become impregnated. Something was growing inside me. At night when I lay in my bed I could feel the heels of the tale kicking against the walls of my body. Often as I lay thus every word of the tale came to me quite clearly but when I got out of bed to write it down the words would not come.

I had constantly to seek in roads new to me. Other men had felt what I had felt, had seen what I had seen — how had they met the difficulties I faced? My father when he told his tales walked up and down the room before his audience. He pushed out little experimental sentences and watched his audience narrowly. There was a dull-eyed old farmer sitting in a corner of the room. Father had his eyes on the fellow. "I'll get him," he said to himself. He watched the farmer's eyes. When the experimental sentence he had tried did not get anywhere he tried another and kept trying. Beside words he had — to help the telling of his tales — the advantage of being able to act out those parts for which he could find no words. He could frown, shake his fists, smile, let a look of pain or annoyance drift over his face.

These were his advantages that I had to give up if I was to write my tales rather than tell them and how often I had cursed my fate.

How significant words had become to me! At about this time an American woman living in Paris, Miss Gertrude Stein, had published a book called *Tender Buttons* and it had come into my hands. How it had excited me! Here was something purely experimental and dealing in words separated from sense — in the ordinary meaning of the word sense — an approach I was sure the poets must often be compelled to make. Was it an approach that would help me? I decided to try it.

A year or two before the time of which I am now writing an American painter, Mr. Felix Russman, had taken me one day into his workshop to show me his colors. He laid them out on a table before me and then his wife called him out of the room and he stayed for half an hour. It had been one of the most exciting moments of my life. I shifted the little pans of color about, laid one color against another. I walked away and came near. Suddenly there had flashed into my consciousness, for perhaps the first time in my life, the secret inner world of the painters. Before that time I had wondered often enough why certain paintings, done by the old masters, and hung in our Chicago Art Institute, had so strange an effect upon me. Now I thought I knew. The true painter revealed all of himself in every stroke of his brush. Titian made one feel so utterly the splendor of himself; from Fra Angelico and Sandro Botticelli there came such a deep human tenderness that on some days it fairly brought tears to the eyes; in a most dreadful way and in spite of all his skill Bouguereau gave away his own inner nastiness while Leonardo made one feel all of the grandeur of his mind just as Balzac[1] had made his readers feel the universality and wonder of his mind.

Very well then, the words used by the tale-teller were as the colors used by the painter. Form was another matter. It grew out of the materials of the tale and the teller's reaction to them. It was the tale trying to take form that kicked about inside the tale-teller at night when he wanted to sleep.

And words were something else. Words were the surfaces, the clothes of the tale. I thought I had begun to get something a little clearer now. I had smiled to myself a little at the sudden realization of how little native American words had been used by American story-writers. When most American writers wanted to be very American they went in for slang. Surely we American scribblers had paid long and hard for the English blood in our veins. The English had got their books into our schools, their ideas of correct forms of expression were firmly fixed in our minds. Words as commonly used in our writing were in reality an army that marched in a certain array and the generals in command of the army were still English. One saw the words as marching, always just so — in books — and came to think of them so — in books.

---

[1] Honoré de Balzac (1799–1850), French novelist, one of the earliest realists.

But when one told a tale to a group of advertising men sitting in a barroom in Chicago or to a group of laborers by a factory door in Indiana one instinctively disbanded the army. There were moments then for what have always been called by our correct writers "unprintable words." One got now and then a certain effect by a bit of profanity. One dropped instinctively into the vocabulary of the men about, was compelled to do so to get the full effect sought for the tale. Was the tale he was telling not just the tale of a man named Smoky Pete and how he caught his foot in the trap set for himself? — or perhaps one was giving them the Mama Geigans story. The devil. What had the words of such a tale to do with Thackeray[2] or Fielding?[3] Did the men to whom one told the tale not know a dozen Smoky Petes and Mama Geigans? Had one ventured into the classic English models for tale-telling at that moment there would have been a roar. "What the devil! Don't you go high-toning us!"

And it was sure one did not always seek a laugh from his audience. Sometimes one wanted to move the audience, make them squirm with sympathy. Perhaps one wanted to throw an altogether new light on a tale the audience already knew.

Would the common words of our daily speech in shops and offices do the trick? Surely the Americans among whom one sat talking had felt everything the Greeks had felt, everything the English felt? Deaths came to them, the tricks of fate assailed their lives. I was certain none of them lived felt or talked as the average American novel made them live feel and talk and as for the plot short stories of the magazines — those bastard children of de Maupassant, Poe, and O. Henry[4] — it was certain there were no plot short stories ever lived in any life I had known anything about.   [1924]

---

[2] William Makepeace Thackeray (1811–1863), English novelist.
[3] Henry Fielding (1707–1754), one of the first English novelists.
[4] O. Henry, pseudonym of William Sydney Porter (1862–1910), famous American author of short stories with elaborate plots and often "trick" endings.

A. E. COPPARD rarely discussed his theory of the short story form. This statement is from the foreword to his Collected Tales (1948). Coppard disliked playing the role of writer, never making — as Doris Lessing expressed it in her short memoir of him — "big statements about literature." Instead of abstract theory, he preferred the concrete anecdote. With his roots in the English countryside, it is fitting that he should refer to the folk tale as the earliest tradition of short narrative and insist on its relevance to the success of short stories written today.

ᢛ 8 ᢘ

A. E. Coppard
on the Story's Principles
of Manufacture

There are just two things I really must say about short stories in general and their principles of manufacture. First, I want to crush the assumption that the short story and the novel are manifestations of one principle of fiction, differentiated merely by size, that the novel is inherently and naturally the substantial and therefore the important piece of work, the bale of tweed — you may suppose — out of which your golfer gets his plus-four suit, the short story being merely a remnant, the rag or two left over to make the caddie a cap. In fact the relationship of the short story to the novel amounts to nothing at all. The novel is a distinct form of art having a pedigree and practice of hardly more than a couple of hundred years; the short story, so far from being its offspring, is an ancient art originating in the folk tale, which was a thing of joy even before writing, not to mention printing, was invented. Put the beginning of English printing in the last quarter of the fifteenth century and you light on a date when the folk tale lost its oral or spoken form and issued as a printed short story. Moreover, it was only through that same device of printing that the novel became even a possibility; it did not materialize until the eighteenth century, its forerunners being *Pilgrim's Progress*[1] and *Gulliver's Travels*.[2]

The folk tale ministered to an apparently inborn and universal desire to hear tales, and it is my feeling that the closer the modern short story

---

[1] religious allegory by John Bunyan (1628–1688).
[2] long satirical narrative by Jonathan Swift (1667–1745).

conforms to that ancient tradition of being spoken to you, rather than being read at you, the more acceptable it becomes. One of the earliest delights of childhood is to be told a tale, and the queer pleasure does not lessen or leave us until we ourselves are left in the grave. Cut off a person from all contact with tales and he will assuredly begin to invent some — probably about himself. I don't know why this is, or what is the curious compulsion that urges some to take to the job of telling the tale, that unconscionable lying which is styled the Art of Fiction, but for good or ill I seem to have been that sort of liar. It has been a pleasant business for me, and I hope it will not be too bad for those about to receive these fabrications.

The second principle I would like to urge is that unity, verisimilitude, and completeness of contour are best obtained by plotting your story through the mind or consciousness of only one of your characters, a process that I used to think might be the secret hinted at in Henry James's tale "The Figure in the Carpet."

Of course one does not adhere to literary principles any more than one does to political or moral ones — we accept them for guidance, not for use in dictatorship. As long as mine served and were not too difficult to embody, I was virtuous; whenever they became irksome or incurred some loss of interest, I took the primrose path and hoped for the best.   [1948]

*F*RANK O'CONNOR *was a skilled teacher of the short story, and his comments on the literary form can be as irreverent as they are profound. In this interview in the* Paris Review, *reprinted from the first volume of* Writers at Work, *collections of interviews from that journal, in 1958, O'Connor compares himself to Maupassant and Coppard and then goes on to discuss his own practice as a writer. His analysis of the history of the short story appeared in more extended form in his book* The Lonely Voice, *published in 1963.*

❧ 9 ❧

Frank O'Connor

"The Nearest Thing to Lyric Poetry

Is the Short Story"

Interviewer: Why do you prefer the short story for your medium?

O'Connor: Because it's the nearest thing I know to lyric poetry — I wrote lyric poetry for a long time, then discovered that God had not intended me to be a lyric poet, and the nearest thing to that is the short story. A novel actually requires far more logic and far more knowledge of circumstances, whereas a short story can have the sort of detachment from circumstances that lyric poetry has. . . .

Interviewer: What about working habits? How do you start a story?

O'Connor: "Get black on white" used to be Maupassant's advice — that's what I always do. I don't give a hoot what the writing's like, I write any sort of rubbish which will cover the main outlines of the story, then I can begin to see it. When I write, when I draft a story, I never think of writing nice sentences about, "It was a nice August evening when Elizabeth Jane Moriarty was coming down the road." I just write roughly what happened, and then I'm able to see what the construction looks like. It's the design of the story which to me is most important, the thing that tells you there's a bad gap in the narrative here and you really ought to fill that up in some way or another. I'm always looking at the design of the story, not the treatment. Yesterday I was finishing off a piece about my friend A. E. Coppard, the greatest of all the English storytellers, who died about a fortnight ago. I was describing the way Coppard must have written these stories, going around with a notebook, recording what the lighting looked like, what that house looked like, and all the time using metaphor to suggest it to himself, "The road looked like a mad serpent going up the hill," or something of the kind, and "She said so-and-so, and the man in the pub said something else." After he had written them all out, he must have got the outline of his story, and he'd start working in all the details. Now, I could never do that at all. I've got to see what these people did, first of all, and *then* I start thinking of whether it was a nice August evening or a spring evening. I have to wait for the theme before I can do anything.

Interviewer: Do you rewrite?

O'Connor: Endlessly, endlessly, endlessly. And keep on rewriting, and after it's published, and then after it's published in book form, I usually rewrite it again. I've rewritten versions of most of my early stories and one of these days, God help, I'll publish these as well.

Interviewer: Do you keep notes as a source of supply for future stories?

O'Connor: Just notes of themes. If somebody tells me a good story, I'll write it down in my four lines; that is the secret of the theme. If you make the subject of a story twelve or fourteen lines, that's a treatment. You've already committed yourself to the sort of character, the sort of surroundings, and the moment you've committed yourself, the story is already written. It has ceased to be fluid, you can't design it any longer, you can't model it. So I always confine myself to my four lines. If it won't go into four, that means you haven't reduced it to its ultimate simplicity, reduced it to the fable.

[1958]

❧ 10 ☙

Joyce Carol Oates
on the Making of a Writer

Telling stories, I discovered at the age of three or four, is a way of being told stories. One picture yields another; one set of words, another set of words. Like our dreams, the stories we tell are also the stories we are told. If I say that I write with the enormous hope of altering the world — and why write without that hope? — I should first say that I write to discover what it is *I will have written.* A love of reading stimulates the wish to write — so that one can read, as a reader, the words one has written. Storytellers may be finite in number but stories appear to be inexhaustible.

For many days — in fact for weeks — I have been tormented by the proposition that if I could set down, in reasonably lucid prose, the story of "the making of the writer Joyce Carol Oates," I might in some rudimentary way be defined, at least to myself. Stretched upon a grammatical framework, who among us does not appear to make sense? But the story will not cohere. The necessary words will not arrange themselves. Of the forty-odd pages I have written (each, I should confess, with the rapt, naïve certainty, *At last I have it*) very little strikes me as useful. The miniature stories I have told myself, by way of analyzing "myself," are not precisely lies; but, since each contains so small a fraction of the truth, it is untrue. Each angle of vision, each voice, yields (by way of that process of fictional abiogenesis[1] all storytellers know) a separate writer-self, an alternative Joyce Carol Oates. Each miniature story exerts so powerful an appeal (to the author, that is) that it could, in time, evolve into a novel — for me the divine form, the ultimate artwork, toward which all the arts aspire. Consequently this "story" you are reading is an admission of failure, or, at the very most, a record of

[1] creation of life from lifeless material.

failed attempts. If knowing oneself is an alphabet, I seem to be stuck at A, and take solace from the elderly Yeats's remark in a letter: "Man can embody truth but he cannot know it."

One of the stories I tell myself has to do with the dream of a "sacred text."

Perhaps it is a dream, an actual dream: to set down words with such talismanic[2] precision, such painstaking love, that they cannot be altered — that they constitute a reality of their own, and are not merely referential. It is one of the enigmas of our craft (so my writer friends agree) that, with the passage of time, *how* becomes an obsession, rather than *what:* It becomes increasingly more difficult to say the simplest things. Content yields to form, theme to "voice." But we don't know what voice is.

The story of the elusive sacred text has something to do with a child-like notion of omnipotent thoughts, a wish for immortality through language, a command that time stand still. What is curious is that writing, the act of writing, often satisfies these demands. We throw ourselves into it with such absorption, writing eight or ten hours at a time, writing in our daydreams, composing in our sleep; we enter that fictional world so deeply that time seems to warp or to fold back in upon itself. Where do you find the time, people ask, to write so much? But the time I inhabit is protracted; my interior clock moves with frustrating slowness.

The melancholy secret at the heart of all creative activity (we are not talking here of quality, that ambiguous term) has something to do with our desire to complete a work and to perfect it — this very desire bringing with it our exclusion from that phase of our lives. Though a novel must be begun, often with extraordinary effort, it eventually acquires its own rhythm, its own voice, and begins to write itself; and when it is completed, the writer is expelled — the door closes slowly upon him or her, but it does close. A work of prose may be many things to many people, but to the author it is a monument to a certain chunk of time: so many pulsebeats, so much effort.   [1982]

---

[2] like an object that magically produces good fortune and wards off evil.

*H*ERMAN MELVILLE *wrote an eloquent essay on Hawthorne's volume of short stories,* Mosses from an Old Manse, *for the New York periodical* The Literary World *in August 1850. Unlike Poe in his review of Hawthorne's short fiction, Melville did not use the opportunity to theorize about the form of the short story. Instead, he conveyed his enthusiasm for Hawthorne's "blackness," the aspect of Hawthorne's work that seemed most congenial to his own genius while he continued work that summer on his novel-in-progress,* Moby Dick.

⌁ 11 ⌁

Herman Melville

on Blackness in Hawthorne's

Young Goodman Brown

It is curious, how a man may travel along a country road, and yet miss the grandest or sweetest of prospects, by reason of an intervening hedge so like all other hedges as in no way to hint of the wide landscape beyond. So has it been with me concerning the enchanting landscape in the soul of this Hawthorne, this most excellent Man of Mosses. His *Old Manse* has been written now four years, but I never read it till a day or two since. I had seen it in the bookstores — heard of it often — even had it recommended to me by a tasteful friend, as a rare, quiet book, perhaps too deserving of popularity to be popular. But there are so many books called "excellent" and so much unpopular merit, that amid the thick stir of other things, the hint of my tasteful friend was disregarded; and for four years the Mosses on the Old Manse never refreshed me with their perennial green. It may be, however, that all this while, the book, like wine, was only improving in flavor and body. . . .

But it is the least part of genius that attracts admiration. Where Hawthorne is known, he seems to be deemed a pleasant writer, with a pleasant style — a sequestered, harmless man, from whom any deep and weighty thing would hardly be anticipated: a man who means no meanings. But there is no man, in whom humor and love, like mountain peaks, soar to such a rapt height, as to receive the irradiations of the upper skies; there is no man in whom humor and love are developed in that high form called genius — no such man can exist without also possessing, as the indispensable complement of these, a great, deep intellect, which drops down into the universe like a plummet. Or, love and humor are only the eyes, through which such an intellect views this world. The great beauty in such a mind is but the product of its strength. . . .

For spite of all the Indian-summer sunlight on the hither side of Hawthorne's soul, the other side — like the dark half of the physical sphere — is shrouded in a blackness, ten times black. But this darkness but gives more effect to the ever-moving dawn, that forever advances through it, and circumnavigates his world. Whether Hawthorne has simply availed himself of this mystical blackness as a means to the wondrous effects he makes it to produce in his lights and shades; or whether there really lurks in him, perhaps unknown to himself, a touch of Puritanic gloom — this I cannot altogether tell. Certain it is, however, that this great power of blackness in him derives its force from its appeals to that Calvinistic sense of Innate Depravity and Original Sin, from whose visitations, in some shape or other, no deeply thinking mind is always and wholly free. For, in certain moods, no man can weigh this world, without throwing in something, somehow like Original Sin, to strike the uneven balance. . . .

But with whatever motive, playful or profound, Nathaniel Hawthorne has chosen to entitle his pieces in the manner he has, it is certain that some of them are directly calculated to deceive — egregiously deceive — the superficial skimmer of pages. To be downright and candid once more, let me cheerfully say that two of these titles did dolefully dupe no less an eagle-eyed reader than myself; and that, too, after I had been impressed with a sense of the great depth and breadth of this American man. "Who in the name of thunder" (as the country people say in this neighborhood), "who in the name of thunder," would anticipate any marvel in a piece entitled "Young Goodman Brown"? You would of course suppose that it was a simple little tale, intended as a supplement to "Goody Two-Shoes." Whereas it is deep as Dante; nor can you finish it, without addressing the author in his own words: "It is yours to penetrate, in every bosom, the deep mystery of sin." And with Young Goodman, too, in allegorical pursuit of his Puritan wife, you cry out in your anguish,

> "Faith!" shouted Goodman Brown, in a voice of agony and despera-
> tion; and the echoes of the forest mocked him, crying — "Faith! Faith!" as
> if bewildered wretches were seeking her, all through the wilderness.

Now this same piece, entitled "Young Goodman Brown," is one of the two that I had not at all read yesterday; and I allude to it now, because it is, in itself, such a strong positive illustration of that blackness in Hawthorne which I had assumed from the mere occasional shadows of it, as revealed in several of the other sketches. But had I previously perused "Young Goodman Brown," I should have been at no pains to draw the conclusion which I came to at a time when I was ignorant that the book contained one such direct and unqualified manifestation of it. . . .   [1850]

DAVID HERBERT LAWRENCE *published* Studies in Classic American Literature *in 1923. It included his responses to the writings of Poe, Hawthorne, Melville, and the poet Walt Whitman, among others. As an Englishman, Lawrence read American authors for their contribution to the cultural life of the Western world, and not merely as writers of children's books, which he said was the opinion of most European readers of American fiction at the time. Lawrence's judgments are often startling, sometimes extreme, but never dull. They reflect the same moral passion exhibited in the rest of his work, especially his abhorrence of possessive love.*

❧ 12 ❧

D. H. Lawrence

on the Lust of Hate in Poe's

THE CASK OF AMONTILLADO

The best [of Poe's] tales all have the same burden. Hate is as inordinate as love, and as slowly consuming, as secret, as underground, as subtle. All this underground vault business in Poe only symbolizes that which takes place *beneath* the consciousness. On top, all is fair-spoken. Beneath, there is the awful murderous extremity of burying alive. Fortunato, in "The Cask of Amontillado," is buried alive out of perfect hatred, as the lady Madeline of Usher[1] is buried alive out of love. The lust of hate is the inordinate desire to consume and unspeakably possess the soul of the hated one, just as the lust of love is the desire to possess, or to be possessed by, the beloved, utterly. But in either case the result is the dissolution of both souls, each losing itself in transgressing its own bounds.

The lust of Montresor is to devour utterly the soul of Fortunato. It would be no use killing him outright. If a man is killed outright his soul remains integral, free to return into the bosom of some beloved, where it can enact itself. In walling-up his enemy in the vault, Montresor seeks to bring about the indescribable capitulation of the man's soul, so that he, the victor, can possess himself of the very being of the vanquished. Perhaps this can actually be done. Perhaps, in the attempt, the victor breaks the bonds of his own identity, and collapses into nothingness, or into the infinite. Becomes a monster. [1923]

[1] in Poe's story "The Fall of the House of Usher."

1146

VLADIMIR NABOKOV delivered lectures on Russian literature to his classes at Cornell University from 1948 to 1958. Forced to leave his native country at the age of twenty to escape what he called "the bloated octopus of the state" after the Russian Revolution, he took with him a passionate love for his homeland and for the "fiery, fanciful, free" literature of pre-revolutionary Russia. For Nabokov, the great Russian writers of the nineteenth century (he began his lecture series with Gogol) were more than artists: They were the last free voices in Russia for whom the government did not dictate absolute limits of imagination.

❧ 13 ☙

Vladimir Nabokov

on Gogol's Genius in

THE OVERCOAT

Gogol was a strange creature, but genius is always strange; it is only your healthy second-rater who seems to the grateful reader to be a wise old friend, nicely developing the reader's own notions of life. Great literature skirts the irrational. *Hamlet* is the wild dream of a neurotic scholar. Gogol's *The Overcoat* is a grotesque and grim nightmare making black holes in the dim pattern of life. The superficial reader of that story will merely see in it the heavy frolics of an extravagant buffoon; the solemn reader will take for granted that Gogol's prime intention was to denounce the horrors of Russian bureaucracy. But neither the person who wants a good laugh, nor the person who craves for books "that make one think" will understand what *The Overcoat* is really about. Give me the creative reader; this is a tale for him.

Steady Pushkin,[1] matter-of-fact Tolstoy, restrained Chekhov have all had their moments of irrational insight which simultaneously blurred the sentence and disclosed a secret meaning worth the sudden focal shift. But with Gogol this shifting is the very basis of his art, so that whenever he tried to write in the round hand of literary tradition and to treat rational ideas in a logical way, he lost all trace of talent. When, as in his immortal *The*

---

[1] Aleksandr Pushkin (1789–1837), considered by many (including Nabokov) the greatest Russian poet. Nabokov has translated his novel in verse, *Eugene Onegin*, into English. For introductions to Leo Tolstoy and Anton Chekhov, see pages 151 and 357.

Overcoat, he really let himself go and pottered happily on the brink of his private abyss, he became the greatest artist that Russia has yet produced.

The sudden slanting of the rational plane of life may be accomplished of course in many ways, and every great writer has his own method. With Gogol it was a combination of two movements: a jerk and a glide. Imagine a trap-door that opens under your feet with absurd suddenness, and a lyrical gust that sweeps you up and then lets you fall with a bump into the next traphole. The absurd was Gogol's favorite muse — but when I say "the absurd," I do not mean the quaint or the comic. The absurd has as many shades and degrees as the tragic has, and moreover, in Gogol's case, it borders upon the latter. It would be wrong to assert that Gogol placed his characters in absurd situations. You cannot place a man in an absurd situation if the whole world he lives in is absurd; you cannot do this if you mean by "absurd" something provoking a chuckle or a shrug. But if you mean the pathetic, the human condition, if you mean all such things that in less weird worlds are linked up with the loftiest aspirations, the deepest sufferings, the strongest passions — then of course the necessary breach is there, and a pathetic human, lost in the midst of Gogol's nightmarish, irresponsible world would be "absurd," by a kind of secondary contrast.

On the lid of the tailor's snuff-box there was "the portrait of a General; I do not know what general because the tailor's thumb has made a hole in the general's face and a square of paper had been gummed over the hole." Thus with the absurdity of Akaki Akakievich Bashmachkin. We did not expect that, amid the whirling masks, one mask would turn out to be a real face, or at least the place where that face ought to be. The essence of mankind is irrationally derived from the chaos of fakes which form Gogol's world. Akaki Akakievich, the hero of *The Overcoat*, is absurd *because* he is pathetic, *because* he is human, and *because* he has been engendered by those very forces which seem to be in such contrast to him.

He is not merely human and pathetic. He is something more, just as the background is not mere burlesque. Somewhere behind the obvious contrast there is a subtle genetic link. His being discloses the same quiver and shimmer as does the dream world to which he belongs. The allusions to something else behind the crudely painted screens, are so artistically combined with the superficial texture of the narration that civic-minded Russians have missed them completely. But a creative reading of Gogol's story reveals that here and there in the most innocent descriptive passage, this or that word, sometimes a mere adverb or a preposition, for instance the word "even" or "almost," is inserted in such a way as to make the harmless sentence explode in a wild display of nightmare fireworks; or else the passage that had started in a rambling colloquial manner all of a sudden leaves the tracks and swerves into the irrational where it really belongs; or again, quite as suddenly, a door bursts open and a mighty wave of foaming poetry rushes in only to dissolve in bathos,[2] or to turn into its own parody, or to be checked by the sentence breaking and reverting to a conjuror's patter, that patter which is such a feature of Gogol's style. It gives one the sensation of something ludicrous and at the same time stellar, lurking constantly around the corner — and one likes to recall that the difference between the comic side of things, and their cosmic side, depends upon one sibilant.

So what is that queer world, glimpses of which we keep catching through the gaps of the harmless looking sentences? It is in a way the *real* one but it looks wildly absurd to us, accustomed as we are to the stage setting that screens it. It is from these glimpses that the main character of *The Overcoat*, the meek little clerk, is formed, so that he embodies the spirit of that secret but real world which breaks through Gogol's style. He is, that meek little clerk, a ghost, a visitor from some tragic depths who by chance happened to assume the disguise of a petty official. Russian progressive critics sensed in him the image of the underdog and the whole story impressed them as a social protest. But it is something much more than that. The gaps and black holes in the texture of Gogol's style imply flaws in the texture of life itself. Something is very wrong and all men are mild lunatics engaged in pursuits that seem to them very important while an absurdly logical force keeps them at their futile jobs — this is the real "message" of the story. In this world of utter futility, of futile humility and futile domination, the highest degree that passion, desire, creative urge can attain is a new cloak which both tailors and customers adore on their knees. I am not speaking of the moral point or the moral lesson. There can be no moral lesson in such a world because there are no pupils and no teachers: this world *is* and it excludes everything that might destroy it, so that any improvement, any struggle, any moral purpose or endeavor, are as utterly impossible as changing the course of a star. It is Gogol's world and as such wholly different from Tolstoy's world, or Pushkin's, or Chekhov's or my own. But after reading Gogol one's eyes may become gogolized and one is apt to see bits of his world in the most unexpected places. I have visited many countries, and something like Akaki Akakievich's overcoat has been the passionate dream of this or that chance acquaintance who never had heard about Gogol.

[1981]

---

[2] One source has defined *bathos* as "pathos [the evoking of sympathy, sorrow, or pity] so overdone that it evokes laughter rather than pity."

*F*RANK O'CONNOR *wrote his essay on Turgenev as part of the section entitled "The Quest for Integral Truth" in his study of the modern novel* The Mirror in the Roadway *(1956). Growing up in an old-fashioned Irish provincial town, O'Connor felt that he knew nineteenth-century fiction as a contemporary art form, "incomparably the greatest of modern art forms . . . greater perhaps than any other popular literary form since the Greek theater," because it was shared by the whole community in a way inconceivable in the twentieth century. O'Connor defined himself as a realist and a liberal, and he was profoundly satisfied by the simple, clear moral ethic that sounded the "note of deep human feeling" in Turgenev's story.*

⇒ 14 ⇐

Frank O'Connor

on Narrative in Turgenev's

BYEZHIN PRAIRIE

What Turgenev did in *A Sportsman's Sketches* was to graft on to the dynamic narrative line the formal static quality of an essay or a poem. Actually, it would seem as if the modern short story derives from the sort of travel book which flourished during the Enlightenment[1] and afterward, and which had titles like *Manners and Customs of the Scottish Highlanders* and *Traits and Stories of the Irish Peasantry*. *A Sportsman's Sketches* is the sublimation of such a book, for it has a vague general subject that enables the writer to take the when, where, and how of the novelist and tale-teller for granted. At a pinch, one can say that the stories illustrate the life of a huntsman or the lives of peasants in a particular area of Russia in the beginning of the nineteenth century. The stories require no particular formal structure; they are assimilated to the essay form. Of all story-tellers before Turgenev one may say that their work is an imaginative rearrangement of historic material. There seems to be no *a priori*[2] reason why one should assume that Turgenev's work is anything but historic material, and it is clear that this is the meaning he attributes to "integral truth."

[1] term for a period in Western life and thought (roughly, the eighteenth century) when individualism, reason, realism, science, and skepticism flourished; also called the Age of Reason.

[2] "from the beginning" — that is, there is no inherent reason inside or outside the story.

If we take the most beautiful of these stories, written in 1851, "Bye-zhin Prairie," we find that it contains only a shadow of narrative line. Mainly, it is a lengthy description of the narrator alone with a group of small boys who are herding the family horses on the prairie during the summer nights, and who pass the long hours telling ghost stories. They scare themselves with these, and when one of the boys, Paul, goes to the river for water, he fancies he hears the voice of a drowned comrade calling him. Even this dramatic episode is deliberately written in a low key.

> "Well, boys," he began after a silence, "there's something bad."
> "What?" asked Kostya hurriedly.
> "I heard Vassily's voice."
> Everyone shuddered.
> "What's that you say?" whispered Kostya.
> "So help me God. I'd just begun to bend down to the water and suddenly I heard my name being called in Vassily's voice, as if it was from under the water. 'Pavel, Pavel, come here!' I went away. I got the water, though."
> "Good Lord!" said the boys, crossing themselves.
> "That was a water-goblin calling you, Pavel," added Fedya. "And we were just talking about Vassily."
> "Oh, that's a bad sign," said Ilyusha with deliberation.
> "Well, never mind, forget about it," said Pavel resolutely, and sat down again. "You can't escape your fate."[3]

One cannot help noticing how all through the key is deliberately lowered, effect after effect is thrown away, and how even the slight surprise of the climax is passed over with studied nonchalance. "I am sorry to say that Pavel died before the year was out. He was not drowned, but killed by a fall from a horse. A pity, he was a splendid lad." Turgenev almost gives away his method in a single sentence: "He was not drowned, but killed by a fall from a horse." Here we can see him discounting the narrative shock to prevent the reader's attention straying from the real effect he is trying to make. This is eerie, too, but of a different order of eeriness from that of the corpse on the stair or the ghost in the cellar. His theme is the mystery of human existence, of humanity faced with the spectacle of infinity. *Le silence éternel de ces espaces infinis m'effraie.*[4]

All the Russians did not adopt this technique — Leskov,[5] for instance, continued to write the old-fashioned tale with great originality and beauty — but those, like Chekhov, who did adopt it have an artistry that is

---

[3] O'Connor quotes a 1950 translation by Charles and Natasha Rubin, not the Constance Garnett translation used in this book.
[4] "The eternal silence of these infinite spaces terrifies me." The quote is from *Pensées*, by the great French Christian apologist Blaise Pascal (1623–1662).
[5] Nikolai Leskov (1831–1895), Russian novelist and short story writer.

lacking in other nineteenth-century story-tellers, and compose stories with the very minimum of episodic interest. "To do something with the least possible number of movements is the definition of grace," according to Chekhov. It isn't, but it is the definition of the peculiar grace we find in the stories of Turgenev and himself.   [1956]

*H*ENRY JAMES *described the origin of his story "The Real Thing" in his notebook entry for February 22, 1891. He kept a record of his works-in-progress for more than thirty years, his notes often written hastily, simply for his own eyes. In 1947 the scholars F. O. Matthiessen and Kenneth Murdock published* The Notebooks of Henry James, *a carefully edited volume that is invaluable for any study of James's fiction. It is also of interest to the aspiring writer, because it is full of James's insights into the process of literary creation.*

❧ 15 ❦

Henry James

on the Genesis of

THE REAL THING

In pursuance of my plan of writing some very short tales — things of from 7,000 to 10,000 words, the easiest length to "place," I began yesterday the little story that was suggested to me some time ago by an incident related to me by George du Maurier — the lady and gentleman who called upon him with a word from Frith, an oldish, faded, ruined pair — he an officer in the army — who unable to turn a penny in any other way, were trying to find employment as models. I was struck with the pathos, the oddity and typicalness of the situation — the little tragedy of good-looking gentlefolk, who had been all their life stupid and well-dressed, living, on a fixed income, at country-houses, watering places and clubs, like so many others of their class in England, and were now utterly unable to *do* anything, had no cleverness, no art nor craft to make use of as a *gagne-pain*[1] — could only *show* themselves, clumsily, for the fine, clean, well-groomed animals that they were, only hope to make a little money by — in this manner — just simply *being*. I thought I saw a subject for very brief treatment in this *donnée*[2] — and I think I do still; but to do anything worth while with it I must (as always, great Heavens!) be very clear as to what is in it and what I wish to get out of it. I tried a beginning yesterday, but I instantly became conscious that I must straighten out the little idea. It must be an idea — it can't be a "story" in the vulgar sense of the word. It must be a picture; it

---

[1] a way to earn their bread.
[2] literally, "given"; the situation or assumption with which one begins an argument.

must illustrate something. God knows that's enough — if the thing *does* illustrate. To make little anecdotes of this kind real *morceaux de vie*[3] is a
plan quite inspiring enough. *Voyons un peu,*[4] therefore, what one can put
into this one — I mean how much of life. One must put a little action —
not a stupid, mechanical, arbitrary action, but something that is of the real
essence of the subject. I thought of representing the husband as jealous of
the wife — that is, jealous of the artist employing her, from the moment
that, in point of fact, she begins to sit. But this is vulgar and obvious —
worth nothing. What I wish to represent is the baffled, ineffectual, incom-
petent character of their attempt, and how it illustrates once again the
everlasting English amateurishness — the way superficial, untrained, un-
professional effort goes to the wall when confronted with trained, competitive, intelligent, *qualified* art — in whatever line it may be a question of. It
is out of *that* element that my little action and movement must come; and
now I begin to see just how — as one always *does* — Glory be to the Highest — when one begins to look at a thing hard and straight and seriously —
to fix it — as I am so sadly lax and desultory about doing. What subjects I
should find — for *everything* — if I could only achieve this more as a habit!
Let my contrast and complication here come from the opposition — to my
melancholy Major and his wife — of a couple of little vulgar professional
people *who know*, with the consequent bewilderment, vagueness, depression of the former — their failure to understand how such people can
be better than *they* — their failure, disappointment, disappearance —
going forth into the vague again. *Il y a bien quelque chose à tirer de ça.*[5]
They have no pictorial sense. They are only clean and stiff and stupid. The
others are dirty, even — the melancholy Major and his wife remark on it,
wondering. The artist is beginning a big illustrated book, a new edition of a
famous novel — say *Tom Jones:*[6] and he is willing to try to work them
in — for he takes an interest in their predicament, and feels — skeptically,
but, with his flexible artistic sympathy — the appeal of their type. He is
willing to give them a trial. Make it out that *he* himself is on trial — he is
young and "rising," but he has still his golden spurs to win. He can't afford,
en somme,[7] to make many mistakes. He has regular work in drawing every
week for a serial novel in an illustrated paper; but the great project — that
of a big house — of issuing an illustrated Fielding promises him a big lift.
He has been intrusted with (say) *Joseph Andrews,*[8] experimentally; he will
have to do this brilliantly in order to have the engagement for the rest confirmed. He has already two models in his service — the "complication"
must come from *them.* One is a common, clever, London girl, of the

[3] slice of life.
[4] "Let us examine for a bit. . . ."
[5] "There is indeed something to draw from that."
[6] novel by Henry Fielding (1707–1754).
[7] in sum.
[8] another, earlier novel by Fielding.

smallest origin and without conventional beauty, but of aptitude, of perceptions — knowing thoroughly *how*. She says "lydy" and "plice" but she has the pictorial sense; and can look like anything he wants her to look like. She poses, in short, in perfection. So does her colleague, a professional Italian, a little fellow — ill dressed, smelling of garlic, but admirably serviceable, quite universal. They must be contrasted, confronted, *juxtaposed* with the others; whom they take for people who *pay*, themselves, till they learn the truth when they are overwhelmed with derisive amazement. The denouncement simply that the melancholy Major and his wife won't do — they're not "in it." Their surprise — their helpless, proud assent — without other prospects: yet at the same time *their* degree of more silent amazement at the success of the two inferior people — who are so much less nice-looking than themselves. Frankly, however, is this contrast enough of a *story*, by itself? It seems to me Yes — for it's an IDEA — and how the deuce should I get *more* into 7,000 words? It must be simply fifty pp. of my manuscript. The little tale of *The Servant* (*Brooksmith*) which I did the other day for *Black and White* and which I thought of at the same time as this, proved a very tight squeeze into the same tiny number of words, and I probably shall find that there is much more to be done with this than the compass will admit of. Make it tremendously succinct — with a very short pulse or rhythm — and the closest selection of detail — in other words *summarize* intensely and keep down the lateral development. It *should* be a little gem of bright, quick, vivid form. I shall get every grain of "action" that the space admits of if I make something, for the artist, hang in the balance — depend on the way he does this particular work. It's when he finds that he shall lose his great opportunity if he keeps on with them, that he has to tell the gentlemanly couple, that, frankly, they won't serve his turn — and make them wander forth into the cold world again. I must keep them the age I've made them — fifty and forty — because it's more touching; but I must bring up the age of the two real models to almost the same thing. That increases the incomprehensibility (to the amateurs) of their usefulness. Picture the immanence, in the latter, of the idle, provided-for, country-house habit — the blankness of their *manière d'être*.[9] But in how tremendously few words I must do it. This is a lesson — a *magnificent* lesson — if I'm to do a good many. Something as admirably compact and *selected* as Maupassant.   [1891]

[9] manner of being.

*S*EAN O'FAOLAIN *defined the qualities of the successful short story as "punch" and "poetry," in the sense of a combination of realistic plausibility and personal voltage which "does something to the material . . . it makes it fume in the memory as an aroma or essence which clings to us even when we have forgotten the details of the yarn." In his literary study* The Short Story (1951) *he analyzes the fiction of Guy de Maupassant, "the relentless realist," as opposed to Anton Chekhov, "the persistent moralist." O'Faolain also quotes Maupassant saying, "The short story is but scantily relished in England, where readers take their fiction rather by the volume than by the page, and the novelist's idea is apt to resemble one of those old fashioned carriages which require a wide court to turn around. In America . . . the short tale has had a better fortune."*

ᵔ❧ 16 ❦ᵔ

Sean O'Faolain

on Maupassant's Interest in Elemental Passion in

Miss Harriet

As to our specific point — Maupassant's refusal to indulge in elaborate psychology: somebody has called this picture of Miss Harriet "a bizarre silhouette" and the adjective seems fair, but "silhouette" is less just. The woman is persuasive; her emotions are sufficiently elaborate; her conflict sufficiently disturbing. What prompted the word was, probably, Maupassant's interest in elemental passion and his almost savage insistence on keeping to that plane. This is where he pursues his path to the cliff's edge, as he does consistently throughout his work. . . . This is where, at the end, we are in a position to appraise his power and measure his weakness — his price that he willingly pays, believing it to be not a weakness but a final and irrefragable[1] strength.

The truth is that Maupassant saw life as a puritan moralist: he saw it, as he believed, without sentiment, and saw it therefore as evil; he saw what a Christian would call the seven deadly sins, and he saw little else. He saw men and women ridden by pride, covetousness, lust, anger, gluttony, envy, and sloth: Norman farmers, Parisian civil-servants, small-town bourgeoisie. What he denied was the slightest trace of soul in any one of them, the least

---

[1] impossible to deny or refute.

speck of godliness, all hope of redemption here or hereafter. That was *his* reality, and it was in pursuit of it that he reduced human nature to its most elemental passions. Miss Harriet might be a Pantheist; she would die as a dog dies; the most that even an artist could strew on her grave was pity and flowers, and the thought that she would persist as a flower or as grass and as the flesh of an ox and the flesh of those after her who would eat her body and drink her blood. He reduced life to the senses and he revelled in them as a man and as a writer. . . .

The mass of his work is clean and classical in its raillery, its optimism, its stoical acceptance of a most ascetic and uncompromising view of life.

One's quarrel with such a writer, and one's admiration of him, will never be purely literary: They will be colored by what, for short, one may call our philosophies, our own personal view of life, and we will approve or disapprove of Maupassant not as a writer but as a man with a similar, or with another (and unacceptable) view of life. It would not have troubled him, but the fact remains that he challenges such approvals and disapprovals more than any other writer of short stories. There is room in the house of Chekhov, Stevenson,[2] or Henry James for men of many philosophies. Maupassant invites a select company, or else a very tolerant one. That was his choice. He chose his way; he never diverged from it; he succeeded in it. He defined his own notion of reality early in his career — in "*Boule de Suif*," his first published story; which is to say he defined his own temperament and its needs. When he had finished he looked into the abyss and it received him.]1951]

---

[2] Robert Louis Stevenson (1850–1894), whose stories include "The Strange Case of Dr. Jekyll and Mr. Hyde" and "The Bottle Imp."

*V*LADIMIR NABOKOV *was a skillful guide to fiction in his* Lectures on Russian Literature. *As this excerpt from his analysis of Chekhov's stories shows, he blends wit, irreverence, and critical insight in his summary of the intricacies of plot and character, illuminating the artistic achievements of the author. Nabokov felt that Chekhov's books were "sad books for humorous people" — that is, only a reader with a sense of humor could really appreciate their sadness. Chekhov's subtle humor pervades the grayness of the lives he creates, flickering through his prose style: "He did it," says Nabokov, "by keeping all his words in the same dim light and of the same exact tint of gray, a tint between the color of an old fence and that of a low cloud."*

❧ 17 ☙

Vladimir Nabokov

on Anton Chekhov's

THE LADY WITH THE LITTLE DOG

Chekhov comes into the story "The Lady with the Little Dog" without knocking. There is no dilly-dallying. The very first paragraph reveals the main character, the young fair-haired lady followed by her white Spitz dog on the waterfront of a Crimean resort, Yalta, on the Black Sea. And immediately after, the male character Gurov appears. His wife, whom he has left with the children in Moscow, is vividly depicted: her solid frame, her thick black eyebrows, and the way she has of calling herself "a woman who thinks." One notes the magic of the trifles the author collects — the wife's manner of dropping a certain mute letter in spelling and her calling her husband by the longest and fullest form of his name, both traits in combination with the impressive dignity of her beetle-browed face and rigid poise forming exactly the necessary impression. A hard woman with the strong feminist and social ideas of her time, but one whom her husband finds in his heart of hearts to be narrow, dull-minded and devoid of grace. The natural transition is to Gurov's constant unfaithfulness to her, to his general attitude toward women — "that inferior race" is what he calls them, but without that inferior race he could not exist. It is hinted that these Russian romances were not altogether as light-winged as in the Paris of Maupassant. Complications and problems are unavoidable with those decent hesitating

1158

people of Moscow who are slow heavy starters but plunge into tedious difficulties when once they start going.

Then with the same neat and direct method of attack, with the bridging formula "and so . . ." (or perhaps still better rendered in English by that "Now" which begins a new paragraph in straightforward fairy tales), we slide back to the lady with the dog. Everything about her, even the way her hair was done, told him that she was bored. The spirit of adventure — though he realized perfectly well that his attitude toward a lone woman in a fashionable sea town was based on vulgar stories, generally false — this spirit of adventure prompts him to call the little dog, which thus becomes a link between her and him. They are both in a public restaurant.

> He beckoned invitingly to the Spitz, and when the dog approached him, shook his finger at it. The Spitz growled; Gurov threatened it again.
> The lady glanced at him and at once dropped her eyes.
> "He doesn't bite," she said and blushed.
> "May I give him a bone?" he asked; and when she nodded he inquired affably, "Have you been in Yalta long?"
> "About five days."

They talk. The author has hinted already that Gurov was witty in the company of women; and instead of having the reader take it for granted (you know the old method of describing the talk as "brilliant" but giving no samples of the conversation), Chekhov makes him joke in a really attractive, winning way. "Bored, are you? An average citizen lives in . . . (here Chekhov lists the names of beautifully chosen, super-provincial towns) and is not bored, but when he arrives here on his vacation it is all boredom and dust. One could think he came from Granada" (a name particularly appealing to the Russian imagination). The rest of their talk, for which this sidelight is richly sufficient, is conveyed indirectly. Now comes a first glimpse of Chekhov's own system of suggesting atmosphere by the most concise details of nature, "the sea was of a warm lilac hue with a golden path for the moon"; whoever has lived in Yalta knows how exactly this conveys the impression of a summer evening there. This first movement of the story ends with Gurov alone in his hotel room thinking of her as he goes to sleep and imagining her delicate weak-looking neck and her pretty gray eyes. It is to be noted that only now, through the medium of the hero's imagination, does Chekhov give a visible and definite form to the lady, features that fit perfectly with her listless manner and expression of boredom already known to us.

> Getting into bed he recalled that she had been a schoolgirl only recently, doing lessons like his own daughter; he thought how much timidity and angularity there was still in her laugh and her manner of talking with a stranger. It must have been the first time in her life that she was alone in a setting in which she was followed, looked at, and spoken to for

one secret purpose alone, which she could hardly fail to guess. He thought of her slim, delicate throat, her lovely gray eyes.

"There's something pathetic about her, though," he thought, and dropped off.

The next movement (each of the four diminutive chapters or movements of which the story is composed is not more than four or five pages long), the next movement starts a week later with Gurov going to the pavilion and bringing the lady iced lemonade on a hot windy day, with the dust flying; and then in the evening when the sirocco subsides, they go on the pier to watch the incoming steamer. "The lady lost her lorgnette in the crowd," Chekhov notes shortly, and this being so casually worded, without any direct influence on the story — just a passing statement — somehow fits in with that helpless pathos already alluded to.

Then in her hotel room her awkwardness and tender angularity are delicately conveyed. They have become lovers. She was now sitting with her long hair hanging down on both sides of her face in the dejected pose of a sinner in some old picture. There was a watermelon on the table. Gurov cut himself a piece and began to eat unhurriedly. This realistic touch is again a typical Chekhov device.

She tells him about her existence in the remote town she comes from and Gurov is slightly bored by her naiveté, confusion, and tears. It is only now that we learn her husband's name: von Dideritz — probably of German descent.

They roam about Yalta in the early morning mist.

> At Oreanda they sat on a bench not far from the church, looked down at the sea, and were silent. Yalta was barely visible through the morning mist; white clouds rested motionlessly on the mountaintops. The leaves did not stir on the trees, the crickets chirped, and the monotonous muffled sound of the sea that rose from below spoke of the peace, the eternal sleep awaiting us. So it rumbled below when there was no Yalta, no Oreanda here; so it rumbles now, and it will rumble as indifferently and hollowly when we are no more. . . . Sitting beside a young woman who in the dawn seemed so lovely, Gurov, soothed and spellbound by these magical surroundings — the sea, the mountains, the clouds, the wide sky — thought how everything is really beautiful in this world when one reflects: everything except what we think or do ourselves when we forget the higher aims of life and our own human dignity.
>
> A man strolled up to them — probably a watchman — looked at them and walked away. And this detail, too, seemed so mysterious and beautiful. They saw a steamer arrive from Feodosia, its lights extinguished in the glow of dawn.
>
> "There is dew on the grass," said Anna Sergeievna, after a silence.
>
> "Yes, it's time to go home."

Then several days pass and then she has to go back to her home town.

" 'Time for me, too, to go North,' thought Gurov as he returned after seeing her off." And there the chapter ends.

The third movement plunges us straight into Gurov's life in Moscow. The richness of a gay Russian winter, his family affairs, the dinners at clubs and restaurants, all this is swiftly and vividly suggested. Then a page is devoted to a queer thing that has happened to him: he cannot forget the lady with the little dog. He has many friends, but the curious longing he has for talking about his adventure finds no outlet. When he happens to speak in a very general way of love and women, nobody guesses what he means, and only his wife moves her dark eyebrows and says: "Stop that fatuous posing; it does not suit you."

And now comes what in Chekhov's quiet stories may be called the climax. There is something that your average citizen calls romance and something he calls prose — though both are the meat of poetry for the artist. Such a contrast has already been hinted at by the slice of watermelon which Gurov crunched in a Yalta hotel room at a most romantic moment, sitting heavily and munching away. This contrast is beautifully followed up when at last Gurov blurts out to a friend late at night as they come out of the club: If you knew what a delightful woman I met in Yalta! His friend, a bureaucratic civil servant, got into his sleigh, the horses moved, but suddenly he turned and called back to Gurov. Yes? asked Gurov, evidently expecting some reaction to what he had just mentioned. By the way, said the man, you were quite right. That fish at the club was decidedly smelly.

This is a natural transition to the description of Gurov's new mood, his feeling that he lives among savages where cards and food are life. His family, his bank, the whole trend of his existence, everything seems futile, dull, and senseless. About Christmas he tells his wife he is going on a business trip to St. Petersburg, instead of which he travels to the remote Volga town where the lady lives.

Critics of Chekhov in the good old days when the mania for the civic problem flourished in Russia were incensed with his way of describing what they considered to be trivial unnecessary matters instead of thoroughly examining and solving the problems of bourgeois marriage. For as soon as Gurov arrives in the early hours to that town and takes the best room at the local hotel, Chekhov, instead of describing his mood or intensifying his difficult moral position, gives what is artistic in the highest sense of the word: he notes the gray carpet, made of military cloth, and the inkstand, also gray with dust, with a horseman whose hand waves a hat and whose head is gone. That is all: it is nothing but it is everything in authentic literature. A feature in the same line is the phonetic transformation which the hotel porter imposes on the German name von Dideritz. Having learned the address Gurov goes there and looks at the house. Opposite was a long gray fence with nails sticking out. An unescapable fence, Gurov says to himself, and here we get the concluding note in the rhythm of drabness and grayness already suggested by the carpet, the inkstand, the illiterate accent of the porter. The unexpected little turns and the lightness of the touches are what places Chekhov, above all Russian writers of fiction, on the level of Gogol and Tolstoy.

Presently he saw an old servant coming out with the familiar little white dog. He wanted to call it (by a kind of conditional reflex), but suddenly his heart began beating fast and in his excitement he could not remember the dog's name — another delightful touch. Later on he decides to go to the local theatre, where for the first time the operetta *The Geisha* is being given. In sixty words Chekhov paints a complete picture of a provincial theatre, not forgetting the town-governor who modestly hid in his box behind a plush curtain so that only his hands were visible. Then the lady appeared. And he realized quite clearly that now in the whole world there was none nearer and dearer and more important to him than this slight woman, lost in a small-town crowd, a woman perfectly unremarkable, with a vulgar lorgnette in her hand. He saw her husband and remembered her qualifying him as a flunkey — he distinctly resembled one.

A remarkably fine scene follows when Gurov manages to talk to her, and then their mad swift walk up all kinds of staircases and corridors, and down again, and up again, amid people in the various uniforms of provincial officials. Neither does Chekhov forget "two schoolboys who smoked on the stairs and looked down at him and her."

> "You must leave," Anna Sergeievna went on in a whisper. "Do you hear, Dmitri Dmitrich? I will come and see you in Moscow. I have never been happy; I am unhappy now, and I never, never shall be happy, never! So don't make me suffer still more! I swear I'll come to Moscow. But now let us part. My dear, good, precious one, let us part!"
>
> She pressed his hand and walked rapidly downstairs, turning to look round at him, and from her eyes he could see that she really was unhappy. Gurov stood for a while, listening, then when all grew quiet, he found his coat and left the theatre.

The fourth and last little chapter gives the atmosphere of their secret meetings in Moscow. As soon as she would arrive she used to send a red-capped messenger to Gurov. One day he was on his way to her and his daughter was with him. She was going to school, in the same direction as he. Big damp snowflakes were slowly coming down.

The thermometer, Gurov was saying to his daughter, shows a few degrees above freezing point (actually 37° above, Fahrenheit), but nevertheless snow is falling. The explanation is that this warmth applies only to the surface of the earth, while in the higher layers of the atmosphere the temperature is quite different.

And as he spoke and walked, he kept thinking that not a soul knew or would ever know about these secret meetings.

What puzzled him was that all the false part of his life, his bank, his club, his conversations, his social obligations — all this happened openly, while the real and interesting part was hidden.

> He had two lives: an open one, seen and known by all who needed to know of it, full of conventional truth and conventional falsehood, exactly like the lives of his friends and acquaintances; and another life that went on in secret. And through some strange, perhaps accidental, combination of circumstances, everything that was of interest and importance to him, everything that was essential to him, everything about which he felt sincerely and did not deceive himself, everything that constituted the core of his life, was going on concealed from others; while all that was false, the shell in which he hid to cover the truth — his work at the bank for instance, his discussions at the club, his references to the "inferior race," his appearances at anniversary celebrations with his wife — all that went on in the open. Judging others by himself, he did not believe what he saw, and always fancied that every man led his real, most interesting life under cover of secrecy as under cover of night. The personal life of every individual is based on secrecy, and perhaps it is partly for that reason that civilized man is so nervously anxious that personal privacy should be respected.

The final scene is full of that pathos which has been suggested in the very beginning. They meet, she sobs, they feel that they are the closest of couples, the tenderest of friends, and he sees that his hair is getting a little gray and knows that only death will end their love.

> The shoulders on which his hands rested were warm and quivering. He felt compassion for this life, still so warm and lovely, but probably already about to begin to fade and wither like his own. Why did she love him so much? He always seemed to women different from what he was, and they loved in him not himself, but the man whom their imagination had created and whom they had been eagerly seeking all their lives; and afterwards, when they saw their mistake, they loved him nevertheless. And not one of them had been happy with him. In the past he had met women, come together with them, parted from them, but he had never once loved; it was anything you please, but not love. And only now when his head was gray he had fallen in love, really, truly — for the first time in his life.

They talk, they discuss their position, how to get rid of the necessity of this sordid secrecy, how to be together always. They find no solution and in the typical Chekhov way the tale fades out with no definite full-stop but with the natural motion of life.

> And it seemed as though in a little while the solution would be found, and then a new and glorious life would begin; and it was clear to both of them that the end was still far off, and that what was to be most complicated and difficult for them was only just beginning.

All the traditional rules of story telling have been broken in this wonderful short story of twenty pages or so. There is no problem, no regular climax, no point at the end. And it is one of the greatest stories ever written. [1981]

THOMAS STEARNS ELIOT was an American-born English poet; he won the Nobel Prize for Literature in 1948. He compiled a volume of Rudyard Kipling's poetry, A Choice of Kipling's Verse, published in 1941. Eliot felt the initial appeal of doing the book was that Kipling's genius was so different from his own; but he also was trying to show that a knowledge of Kipling's verse is essential to an understanding of Kipling's fiction. In his introduction to the book, Eliot said that "The Wish House" was one of his favorite Kipling stories about the Sussex countryside, because of Kipling's inspired vision of the local people. He also pointed out that it was originally published with two long, enigmatic poems — one placed at the beginning of the story and the other at the end. These poems are reprinted with the story in volume 8 of The Collected Works of Rudyard Kipling (1941).

❧ 18 ☙

T. S. Eliot

on the Element of the Supernatural in Kipling's

THE WISH HOUSE

To think of Kipling as a writer who could turn his hand to any subject, who wrote of Sussex because he had exhausted his foreign and imperial material, or had satiated the public demand for it, or merely because he was a chameleon who took his color from environment, would be to miss the mark completely: This later work is the continuation and consummation of the earlier. The second peculiarity of Kipling's Sussex stories I have already touched upon, the fact that he brings to his work the freshness of a mind and a sensibility developed and matured in quite different environment: He is discovering and reclaiming a lost inheritance. . . .

What is most important in . . . "The Wish House". . . is Kipling's vision of the people of the soil. It is not a Christian vision, but it is at least a pagan vision — a contradiction of the materialistic view: It is the insight into a harmony with nature which must be re-established if the truly Christian imagination is to be recovered by Christians. What he is trying to convey is, again, not a program of agrarian reform, but a point of view unintelligible to the industrialized mind. Hence the artistic value of the *obviously* incredible element of the supernatural in "The Wish House" which is exquisitely combined with the sordid realism of the women of the dialogue, the country bus, the suburban villa, and the cancer of the poor.

This hard and obscure story has to be studied in relation to the two hard and obscure poems (not here included) which precede and follow it, and which would be still more hard and obscure without the story. We have gone a long way, at this stage, from the mere story teller: a long way even from the man who felt it his duty to try to make certain things plain to his countrymen who would not see them. He could hardly have thought that many people in his own time or at any time would take the trouble to understand the parables, or even to appreciate the precision of observation, the calculating pains in selecting and combining elements, the choice of word and phrase, that were spent in their elaboration. He must have known that his own fame would get in the way, his reputation as a story teller, his reputation as a "Tory journalist," his reputation as a facile writer who could dash off something about what happened yesterday, his reputation even as a writer of books for children which children liked to read and hear.

[1941]

*F*RANK O'CONNOR *analyzed the stories in James Joyce's* Dubliners *in a chapter entitled "Work in Progress" in his 1963 study of the short story,* The Lonely Voice. *O'Connor addresses himself to the question of why Joyce gave up writing stories after* Dubliners; *he understands that "It is as difficult to think of a real storyteller, like Chekhov, who had experienced the thrill of the completed masterpiece, giving up short stories forever as it is to think of Keats giving up lyric poetry." The answer, for O'Connor, can be found by comparing the formal differences between the stories at the beginning of the book and "The Dead" at the end. That is where his analysis begins.*

·≈ 19 ≈·

Frank O'Connor

on the Elaboration of Style and Form in Joyce's

THE DEAD

"The Dead," Joyce's last story, is entirely different from all the others. It is also immensely more complicated, and it is not always easy to see what any particular episode represents, though it is only too easy to see that it represents something. The scene is the annual dance of the Misses Morkan, old music teachers on Usher's Island, and ostensibly it is no more than a report of what happened at it, except at the end, when Gabriel Conroy and his wife Gretta return to their hotel room. There she breaks down and tells him of a youthful and innocent love affair between herself and a boy of seventeen in Galway, who had caught his death of cold from standing under her bedroom window. But this final scene is irrelevant only in appearance, for in effect it is the real story, and everything that has led up to it has been simply an enormously expanded introduction, a series of themes all of which find their climax in the hotel bedroom.

The setting of the story in a warm, vivacious lighted house in the midst of night and snow is an image of life itself, but every incident, almost every speech, has a crack in it through which we perceive the presence of death all about us, as when Gabriel says that Gretta "takes three *mortal* hours to dress herself," and the aunts say that she must be "perished alive" — an Irishism that ingeniously suggests both life and death. Several times the warmth and gaiety give rise to the idea of love and marriage, but each time it is knocked dead by phrase or incident. At the very opening of the story Gabriel suggests to the servant girl, Lily, that they will soon be attending her wedding, but she retorts savagely that "the men that is now is only all palaver and what they can get out of you," the major theme of the story, for all grace is with the dead: The younger generation have not the generosity of the two old sisters, the younger singers (Caruso, for instance!) cannot sing as well as some long dead English tenor. Gabriel's aunt actually sings "Arrayed for the Bridal," but she is only an old woman who has been dismissed from her position in the local church choir.

Gabriel himself is fired by passion for his wife, but when they return to their hotel bedroom the electric light has failed, and his passion is also extinguished when she tells him the story of her love for a dead boy. Whether it is Gabriel's quarrel with Miss Ivors, who wants him to spend his summer holiday patriotically in the West of Ireland (where his wife and the young man had met), the discussion of Cistercian monks who are supposed to sleep in their coffins, "to remind them of their last end," or the reminiscences of old singers and old relatives, everything pushes Gabriel toward that ultimate dissolution of identity in which real things disappear from about us, and we are as alone as we shall be on our deathbeds.

But it is easy enough to see from "The Dead" why Joyce gave up storytelling. One of his main passions — the elaboration of style and form — had taken control, and the short story is too tightly knit to permit expansion like this. And — what is much more important — it is quite clear from "The Dead" that he had already begun to lose sight of the submerged population that was his original subject. There are little touches of it here and there, as in the sketches of Freddy Malins and his mother — the old lady who finds everything "beautiful" — "beautiful crossing," "beautiful house," "beautiful scenery," "beautiful fish" — but Gabriel does not belong to it, nor does Gretta nor Miss Ivors. They are not characters but personalities, and Joyce would never again be able to deal with characters, people whose identity is determined by their circumstances. His own escape to Trieste, with its enlargement of his own sense of identity, had caused them to fade from his mind or — to put it more precisely — had caused them to reappear in entirely different guises. This is something that is always liable to happen to the provincial storyteller when you put him into a cosmopolitan atmosphere.   [1963]

GUSTAV JANOUCH *published his recollections of Kafka in* Conversa-
*tions with Kafka (1953). Janouch's father worked in the Workers' Accident
Insurance Institute with Kafka, and he introduced his son to Kafka in 1920
because they were both "scribblers." Janouch was only seventeen at the
time, and very impressionable. Having read* The Metamorphosis, *he was
disappointed by his first sight of Kafka: " 'So this is the creator of the mysterious bug, Samsa,' I said to myself, disillusioned to see before me a simple,
well-mannered man." But when their conversation was over that day —
after Kafka had told Janouch that he wrote at night because daytime was a
"great enchantment . . . it distracts from the darkness within" — Janouch
asked himself, "Is he not himself the unfortunate bug in* The Metamorphosis?" *Their acquaintance ripened into a friendship, which lasted until
Kafka's death in 1924.*

❧ 20 ❧

Gustav Janouch

on Franz Kafka's View of

THE METAMORPHOSIS

–translated by Goronwy Rees

I spent my first week's wages on having Kafka's three stories — *The
Metamorphosis, The Judgement,* and *The Stoker* — bound in a dark
brown leather volume, with the name *Franz Kafka* elegantly tooled in gold
lettering.

The book lay in the brief-case on my knee as I told Kafka about the
warehouse-cinema. Then I proudly took the volume out of the case and
gave it across the desk to Kafka.

"What is this?" he asked in astonishment.

"It's my first week's wages."

"Isn't that a waste?"

Kafka's eyelids fluttered. His lips were sharply drawn in. For a few seconds he contemplated the name in the gold lettering, hastily thumbed
through the pages of the book and — with obvious embarrassment —
placed it before me on the desk. I was about to ask why the book offended
him, when he began to cough. He took a handkerchief from his pocket,

1169

held it to his mouth, replaced it when the attack was over, stood up and went to the small washstand behind his desk and washed his hands, then said as he dried them: "You overrate me. Your trust oppresses me."

He sat himself at his desk and said, with his hands to his temples: "I am no burning bush. I am not a flame."

I interrupted him. "You shouldn't say that. It's not just. To me, for example, you are fire, warmth and light."

"No, no!" he contradicted me, shaking his head. "You are wrong. My scribbling does not deserve a leather binding. It's only my own personal spectre of horror. It oughtn't to be printed at all. It should be burned and destroyed. It is without meaning."

I became furious. "Who told you that?" I was forced to contradict him — "How can you say such a thing? Can you see into the future? What you are saying to me is entirely your subjective feeling. Perhaps your scribbling, as you call it, will tomorrow represent a significant voice in the world. Who can tell today?"

I drew a deep breath.

Kafka stared at the desk. At the corners of his mouth were two short, sharp lines of shadow.

I was ashamed of my outburst, so I said quietly, in a low, explanatory tone: "Do you remember what you said to me about the Picasso exhibition?"

Kafka looked at me without understanding.

I continued: "You said that art is a mirror which — like a clock running fast — foretells the future. Perhaps your writing is, in today's *Cinema of the Blind*, only a mirror of tomorrow."

"Please, don't go on," said Kafka fretfully, and covered his eyes with both hands.

I apologized. "Please forgive me, I didn't mean to upset you. I'm stupid."

"No, no — you're not that!" Without removing his hands, he rocked his whole body to and fro. "You are right. You are certainly right. Probably that's why I can't finish anything. I am afraid of the truth. But can one do otherwise?" He took his hands away from his eyes, placed his clenched fists on the table and said in a low, suppressed voice: "One must be silent, if one can't give any help. No one, through his own lack of hope, should make the condition of the patient worse. For that reason, all my scribbling is to be destroyed. I am no light. I have merely lost my way among my own thorns. I'm a dead end."

Kafka leaned backwards. His hands slipped lifelessly from the table. He closed his eyes.

"I don't believe it," I said with utter conviction, yet added appeasingly: "And even if it were true, it would be worthwhile to display the dead end to people."

Kafka merely shook his head slowly. "No, no ... I am weak and tired."

"You should give up your work here," I said gently, to relax the tension which I felt between us.

Kafka nodded. "Yes, I should. I wanted to creep away behind this office desk, but it only increased my weakness. It's become — ," Kafka looked at me with an indescribably painful smile, " — a cinema of the blind."

Then he closed his eyes again.

I was glad at this moment there was a knock on the door behind me. [1953]

WILLA CATHER read the fiction of other writers with a shrewd and discriminating eye. In the volume On Writing (1949), *a collection of her critical essays on literature as art, she analyzed the stories of Sarah Orne Jewett and Katherine Mansfield, among other authors. Cather essentially wrote in praise of the simplest spirit in human beings. There was no theory about the art of fiction in her discussion, but instead "a vision as level and wide as the landscapes and skyscapes of the West" where she grew up.*

ᵕ๋ 21 ๕ᵕ

Willa Cather
on Katherine Mansfield

Every writer and critic of discernment who looked into Katherine Mansfield's first volume of short stories must have felt that here was a very individual talent. At this particular time few writers care much about their medium except as a means for expressing ideas. But in Katherine Mansfield one recognized virtuosity, a love for the medium she had chosen.

The qualities of a second-rate writer can easily be defined, but a first-rate writer can only be experienced. It is just the thing in him which escapes analysis that makes him first-rate. One can catalogue all the qualities that he shares with other writers, but the thing that is his very own, his timbre, this cannot be defined or explained any more than the quality of a beautiful speaking voice can be.

It was usually Miss Mansfield's way to approach the major forces of life through comparatively trivial incidents. She chose a small reflector to throw a luminous streak out into the shadowy realm of personal relationships. I feel that personal relationships, especially the uncatalogued ones, the seemingly unimportant ones, interested her most. To my thinking, she never measured herself up so fully as in the two remarkable stories about an English family in New Zealand, "Prelude" and "At the Bay."

I doubt whether any contemporary writer has made one feel more keenly the many kinds of personal relationships which exist in an everyday "happy family" who are merely going on living their daily lives, with no crises or shocks or bewildering complications to try them. Yet every individual in that household (even the children) is clinging passionately to his individual soul, is in terror of losing it in the general family flavour. As in most families, the mere struggle to have anything of one's own, to be one's self at all, creates an element of strain which keeps everybody almost at the breaking-point.

One realizes that even in harmonious families there is this double life: the group life, which is the one we can observe in our neighbour's household, and, underneath, another — secret and passionate and intense — which is the real life that stamps the faces and gives character to the voices of our friends. Always in his mind each member of these social units is escaping, running away, trying to break the net which circumstances and his own affections have woven about him. One realizes that human relationships are the tragic necessity of human life; that they can never be wholly satisfactory, that every ego is half the time greedily seeking them, and half the time pulling away from them. In those simple relationships of loving husband and wife, affectionate sisters, children and grandmother, there are innumerable shades of sweetness and anguish which make up the pattern of our lives day by day, though they are not down in the list of subjects from which the conventional novelist works.

Katherine Mansfield's peculiar gift lay in her interpretation of these secret accords and antipathies which lie hidden under our everyday behavior, and which more than any outward events make our lives happy or unhappy. Had she lived, her development would have gone on in this direction more than in any other. When she touches this New Zealand family and those faraway memories ever so lightly, as in "The Doll's House," there is a magic one does not find in the other stories, fine as some of them are. With this theme the very letters on the page become alive. She communicates vastly more than she actually writes. One goes back and runs through the pages to find the text which made one know certain things about Linda or Burnell or Beryl, and the text is not there — but something was there, all the same — is there, though no typesetter will ever set it. It is this overtone, which is too fine for the printing press and comes through without it, that makes one know that this writer had something of the gift which is one of the rarest things in writing, and quite the most precious. That she had not the happiness of developing her powers to the full is sad enough. She wrote the truth from Fontainebleau a few weeks before she died: *"The old mechanism isn't mine any longer, and I can't control the new."* She had lived through the first stage, had outgrown her young art, so that it seemed false to her in comparison with the new light that was breaking within. The "new mechanism," big enough to convey the new knowledge, she had not the bodily strength to set in motion.

Katherine Mansfield's published *Journal* begins in 1914 and ends in 1922, some months before her death. It is the record of a long struggle with illness, made more cruel by lack of money and by the physical hardships that war conditions brought about in England and France. At the age of twenty-two (when most young people have a secret conviction that they are immortal), she was already ill in a Bavarian *pension*. From the time when she left New Zealand and came back to England to make her own way, there was never an interval in which she did not have to drive herself beyond her strength. She never reached the stage when she could work with a relaxed elbow. In her story "Prelude," when the family are moving, and the storeman lifts the little girl into the dray and tucks her up, he says: "Easy does it." She knew this, long afterward, but she never had a chance to put that method into practice. In all her earlier stories there is something fierce about her attack, as if she took up a new tale in the spirit of overcoming it. "Do or die" is the mood, — indeed, she must have faced that alternative more than once: a girl come back to make her living in London, without health or money or influential friends, — with no assets but talent and pride.

In her volume of stories entitled *Bliss*, published in 1920 (most of them had been written some years before and had appeared in periodicals), she throws down her glove, utters her little challenge in the high language which she knew better than did most of her readers:

> But I tell you, my lord fool, out of this nettle, danger, we pluck this flower, safety.

A fine attitude, youthful and fiery: out of all the difficulties of life and art we will snatch *something*. No one was ever less afraid of the nettle; she was defrauded unfairly of the physical vigour which seems the natural accompaniment of a high and daring spirit.

At thirteen Katherine Mansfield made the long voyage to England with her grandmother, to go to school in London. At eighteen she returned to her own family in Wellington, New Zealand. It was then the struggle against circumstances began. She afterward burned all her early diaries, but it is those I should have liked to read. Exile may be easy to bear for those who have lived their lives. But at eighteen, after four years of London, to be thrown back into a prosperous commercial colony at the end of the world was starvation. There is no homesickness and no hunger so unbearable. Many a young artist would sell his future, all his chances, simply to get back to the world where other people are doing the only things that, to his inexperience, seem worth doing at all.

Years afterward, when Katherine Mansfield had begun to do her best work but was rapidly sinking in vitality, her homesickness stretched all the other way — backwards, for New Zealand and that same crude Wellington. Unpromising as it was for her purpose, she felt that it was the only territory she could claim, in the deepest sense, as her own. The *Journal* tells us how often she went back to it in her sleep. She recounts these dreams at some length: but the entry which makes one realize that homesickness most keenly is a short one, made in Cornwall in 1918:

> *June 20th.* The twentieth of June 1918.
> C'est de la misère.

Non, pas ça exactement. Il y a quelque chose — une profonde mal-
aise me suive comme un ombre.

Oh, why write bad French? Why write at all? 11,500 miles are so
many — too many by 11,499¾ for me.

Eleven thousand five hundred miles is the distance from England to New
Zealand.

By this, 1918, she had served her apprenticeship. She had gone
through a succession of enthusiasms for this master and that, formed
friendships with some of the young writers of her own time. But the person
who had freed her from the self-consciousness and affectations of the ex-
perimenting young writer, and had brought her to her realest self, was not
one of her literary friends but, quite simply, her own brother.

He came over in 1915 to serve as an officer. He was younger than she,
and she had not seen him for six years. After a short visit with her in London he went to the front, and a few weeks later was killed in action. But he
had brought to his sister the New Zealand of their childhood, and out of
those memories her best stories were to grow. For the remaining seven years
of her life (she died just under thirty-five) her brother seems to have been
almost constantly in her mind. A great change comes over her feelings
about art; what it is, and why it is. When she prays to become "humble," it
is probably the slightly showy quality in the early stories that she begs to be
delivered from — and forgiven for. The *Journal* from 1918 on is a record of
a readjustment to life, a changing sense of its deepest realities. One of the
entries in 1919 recounts a dream in which her brother, "Chummie," came
back to her:

> I hear his hat and stick thrown on to the hall-table. He runs up the stairs,
> three at a time. 'Hullo, darling!' But I can't move — I can't move. He
> puts his arm round me, holding me tightly, and we kiss — a long, firm,
> family kiss. And the kiss means: We are of the same blood; we have abso-
> lute confidence in each other; we love; all is well; nothing can ever come
> between us.

In the same year she writes:

> Now it is May 1919. Six o'clock. I am sitting in my own room thinking of
> Mother: I want to cry. But my thoughts are beautiful and full of gaiety. I
> think of *our* house, *our* garden, *us* children — the lawn, the gate and
> Mother coming in. "Children! Children!" I really only ask for time to
> write it all.

But she did not find too late the things she cared for most. She could
not have written that group of New Zealand stories when she first came to
London. There had to be a long period of writing for writing's sake. The
spontaneous untutored outpouring of personal feeling does not go very far
in art. It is only the practiced hand that can make the natural gesture, —

and the practiced hand has often to grope its way. She tells us that she made four false starts on "At the Bay," and when she finished the story it took her nearly a month to recover.

The *Journal*, painful though it is to read, is not the story of utter defeat. She had not, as she said, the physical strength to write what she now knew were, to her, the most important things in life. But she had found them, she possessed them, her mind fed on them. On them, and on the language of her greatest poet. (She read Shakespeare continually, when she was too ill to leave her bed.) The inexhaustible richness of that language seems to have been like a powerful cordial, warmed her when bodily nourishment failed her.

Among the stories she left unfinished there is one of singular beauty, written in the autumn of 1922, a few months before her death, the last piece of work she did. She called it "Six Years After": Linda and Burnell grown old, and the boy six years dead. It has the same powerful slightness which distinguishes the other New Zealand stories, and an even deeper tenderness.

Of the first of the New Zealand stories, "Prelude," Miss Mansfield wrote an answer to the inquiries of an intimate friend:

> This is about as much as I can say about it. You know, if the truth were known, I have a perfect passion for the island where I was born. Well, in the early morning there I always remember feeling that this little island has dipped back into the dark blue sea during the night only to rise again at gleam of day, all hung with bright spangles and glittering drops. (When you ran over the dewy grass you positively felt that your feet tasted salt.) I tried to catch that moment — with something of its sparkle and its flavour. And just as on those mornings white milky mists rise and uncover some beauty, then smother it again and then again disclose it, I tried to lift that mist from my people and let them be seen and then to hide them again. . . . It's so difficult to describe all this and it sounds perhaps over-ambitious and vain.

An unpretentious but very suggestive statement of how an artist sets to work, and of the hazy sort of thing that almost surely lies behind and directs interesting or beautiful design. And not with the slighter talents only. Tolstoy himself, one knows from the different lives and letters, went to work in very much the same way. The long novels, as well as the short tales, grew out of little family dramas, personal intolerances and predilections, — promptings not apparent to the casual reader and incomprehensible to the commercial novel-maker.   [1949]

*K*ATHERINE ANNE PORTER *gave an interview to the* Paris Review *that was published in the second volume of* Writers at Work, *in 1963. She spoke at great length of her beginnings as a writer and of the difficulty of learning her craft during the long period of her apprenticeship. Her comments on "Flowering Judas" give the background of the story, and suggest her commitment as a writer who had taken up her vocation with the highest seriousness: "Practice an art for love and the happiness of your life — you will find it outlasts almost everything but breath!"*

⌇⌇ 22 ⌇⌇

Katherine Anne Porter

on the Origins of

FLOWERING JUDAS

Interviewer: Has a story never surprised you in the writing? A character suddenly taken a different turn?

Porter: Well, in the vision of death at the end of "Flowering Judas" I knew the real ending — that she was not going to be able to face her life, what she'd done. And I knew that the vengeful spirit was going to come in a dream to tow her away into death, but I didn't know until I'd written it that she was going to wake up saying, "No!" and be afraid to go to sleep again.

Interviewer: That was, in a fairly literal sense, a "true" story, wasn't it?

Porter: The truth is, I have never written a story in my life that didn't have a very firm foundation in actual human experience — somebody else's experience quite often, but an experience that became my own by hearing the story, by witnessing the thing, by hearing just a word perhaps. It doesn't matter, it just takes a little — a tiny seed. Then it takes root, and it grows. It's an organic thing. That story had been on my mind for years, growing out of this one little thing that happened in Mexico. It was forming and forming in my mind, until one night I was quite desperate. People are always so sociable, and I'm sociable too, and if I live around friends. . . . Well, they were insisting that I come and play bridge. But I was very firm, because I knew the time had come to write that story, and I had to write it.

Interviewer: What was that "little thing" from which the story grew?

Porter: Something I saw as I passed a window one evening. A girl I knew had asked me to come and sit with her, because a man was coming to see her, and she was a little afraid of him. And as I went through the court-yard, past the flowering judas tree, I glanced in the window and there she was sitting with an open book on her lap, and there was this great big fat man sitting beside her. Now Mary and I were friends, both American girls living in this revolutionary situation. She was teaching at an Indian school, and I was teaching dancing at a girls' technical school in Mexico City. And we were having a very strange time of it. I was more skeptical, and so I had already begun to look with a skeptical eye on a great many of the revolutionary leaders. Oh, the idea was all right, but a lot of men were misapplying it.

And when I looked through the window that evening, I saw something in Mary's face, something in her pose, something in the whole situation, that set up a commotion in my mind. Because until that moment I hadn't really understood that she was not able to take care of herself, because she was not able to face her own nature and was afraid of everything. I don't know why I saw it. I don't believe in intuition. When you get sudden flashes of perception, it is just the brain working faster than usual. But you've been getting ready to know it for a long time, and when it comes, you feel you've known it always.

Interviewer: You speak of a story "forming" in your mind. Does it begin as a visual impression, growing to a narrative? Or how?

Porter: All my senses were very keen; things came to me through my eyes, through all my pores. Everything hit me at once, you know. That makes it very difficult to describe just exactly what is happening. And then, I think the mind works in such a variety of ways. Sometimes an idea starts completely inarticulately. You're not thinking in images or words or — well, it's exactly like a dark cloud moving in your head. You keep wondering what will come out of this, and then it will dissolve itself into a set of — well, not images exactly, but really thoughts. You begin to think directly in words. Abstractly. Then the words transform themselves into images. By the time I write the story my people are up and alive and walking around and taking things into their own hands. They exist as independently inside my head as you do before me now. I have been criticized for not enough detail in describing my characters, and not enough furniture in the house. And the odd thing is that I see it all so clearly.

Interviewer: What about the technical problems a story presents — its formal structure? How deliberate are you in matters of technique? For example, the use of the historical present in "Flowering Judas"?

Porter: The first time someone said to me, "Why did you write 'Flowering Judas' in the historical present?" I thought for a moment and said, "Did I?" I'd never noticed it. Because I didn't *plan* to write it any way. A story forms in my mind and forms and forms, and when it's ready to go, I strike it down — it takes just the time I sit at the typewriter. I never think about form at all. In fact, I would say that I've never been interested in anything about writing after having learned, I hope, to write. That is, I mas-

tered my craft as well as I could. There is a technique, there is a craft, and
you have to learn it. Well, I did as well as I could with that, but now all in
the world I am interested in is telling a story. I have something to tell you
that I, for some reason, think is worth telling, and so I want to tell it as
clearly and purely and simply as I can. But I had spent fifteen years at least
learning to write. I practiced writing in every possible way that I could. I
wrote a pastiche of other people, imitating Dr. Johnson and Laurence
Sterne, and Petrarch and Shakespeare's sonnets, and then I tried writing my
own way. I spent fifteen years learning to trust myself: that's what it comes
to. Just as a pianist runs his scales for ten years before he gives his concert:
because when he gives that concert, he can't be thinking of his fingering or
of his hands; he has to be thinking of his interpretation, of the music he's
playing. He's thinking of what he's trying to communicate. And if he hasn't
got his technique perfected by then, he needn't give the concert at all.

[1963]

WILLIAM FAULKNER *was writer in residence at the University of Virginia in the springs of 1957 and 1958. During that time he encouraged students to ask questions about his writing. He answered more than 2,000 queries on everything from spelling to the nature of man, including a series of questions about "A Rose for Emily" addressed to him at different interviews by students of Frederick Gwynn and Joseph Blotner. These professors later edited the book* Faulkner in the University (1959), *in which the following excerpt first appeared.*

⤙ 23 ⤚

William Faulkner

on the Meaning of

A ROSE FOR EMILY

Q. What is the meaning of the title "A Rose for Emily"?

A. Oh, it's simply the poor woman had had no life at all. Her father had kept her more or less locked up and then she had a lover who was about to quit her, she had to murder him. It was just "A Rose for Emily" — that's all.

Q. I was wondering, one of your short stories, "A Rose for Emily," what ever inspired you to write this story. . . ?"

A. That to me was another sad and tragic manifestation of man's condition in which he dreams and hopes, in which he is in conflict with himself or with his environment or with others. In this case there was the young girl with a young girl's normal aspirations to find love and then a husband and a family, who was brow-beaten and kept down by her father, a selfish man who didn't want her to leave home because he wanted a housekeeper, and it was a natural instinct of — repressed which — you can't repress it — you can mash it down but it comes up somewhere else and very likely in a tragic form, and that was simply another manifestation of man's injustice to man, of the poor tragic human being struggling with its own heart, with others, with its environment, for the simple things which all human beings want. In that case it was a young girl that just wanted to be loved and to love and to have a husband and a family.

Q. And that purely came from your imagination?

A. Well, the story did but the condition is there. It exists. I didn't in-

vent that condition, I didn't invent the fact that young girls dream of someone to love and children and a home, but the story of what her own particular tragedy was was invented, yes. . . .

Q. Sir, it has been argued that "A Rose for Emily" is a criticism of the
North, and others have argued saying that it is a criticism of the South.
Now, could this story, shall we say, be more properly classified as a criticism
of the times?

A. Now that I don't know, because I was simply trying to write about
people. The writer uses environment — what he knows — and if there's a
symbolism in which the lover represented the North and the woman who
murdered him represents the South, I don't say that's not valid and not
there, but it was no intention of the writer to say, Now let's see, I'm going
to write a piece in which I will use a symbolism for the North and another
symbol for the South, that he was simply writing about people, a story
which he thought was tragic and true, because it came out of the human
heart, the human aspiration, the human — the conflict of conscience with
glands, with the Old Adam. It was a conflict not between the North and the
South so much as between, well you might say, God and Satan.

Q. Sir, just a little more on that thing. You say it's a conflict between
God and Satan. Well, I don't quite understand what you mean. Who is —
did one represent the ——

A. The conflict was in Miss Emily, that she knew that you do not murder people. She had been trained that you do not take a lover. You marry,
you don't take a lover. She had broken all the laws of her tradition, her
background, and she had finally broken the law of God too, which says you
do not take human life. And she knew she was doing wrong, and that's why
her own life was wrecked. Instead of murdering one lover, and then to go
and take another and when she used him up to murder him, she was ex-
piating her crime.

Q. Was the "Rose for Emily" an idea or a character? Just how did you
go about it?

A. That came from a picture of the strand of hair on the pillow. It was
a ghost story. Simply a picture of a strand of hair on the pillow in the abandoned house.   [1959]

*J*ORGE LUIS BORGES *was invited to talk several times to the students in the graduate writing program at Columbia University in the spring of 1971. At one of these meetings, those present were provided with the text of one of Borges's stories, "The End of the Duel." Translator Norman Thomas di Giovanni read it line by line, with Borges interrupting when he wished to comment. Then there was a general conversation in which Borges explained how he gradually transformed his material into a story. A transcript of the entire meeting was included in the book* Borges on Writing (1973), *edited by Norman Thomas di Giovanni, Daniel Halpern, and Frank MacShane.*

❧ 24 ❧

Jorge Luis Borges

on the Meaning and Form of

THE END OF THE DUEL

di Giovanni: Spurts of blood gushed from the men's throats. They dashed forward a number of steps before tumbling face down. Cardoso, as he fell, stretched out his arms. Perhaps never aware of it, he had won.

Borges: This is what always happens: We never know whether we are victors or whether we are defeated.

di Giovanni: Borges, how long did you carry this story around in your head before you set it down?

Borges: I must have carried it some twenty-five or thirty years. When I first heard it, I thought it was striking. The man who told it to me published it in *La Nación* under the title *"Crepúsculo rojo"* — "Reddish Twilight" — but as he wrote it in a style full of purple patches, I felt I could hardly compete with him. After his death I wrote it down in as straightforward a way as possible. In between times, I carried it around in my memory for years, boring my friends with it. . . .

di Giovanni: But can you say something about how you sift the material and take only what you want? For instance, can you remember any facts that you didn't use from the anecdote you were told?

Borges: No, because I was told it in a very bare way, and then Reyles wrote it down in a way full of purple patches and fine writing — the kind of thing I do my best to avoid. I can't write like that; I only went in for what might be called circumstantial invention. For example, I had to make them play *truco*, and I invented the episode about the sheep dog, and I gave him the right name — Treinta y Tres — because that's the kind of name a dog might have, although they are generally called Jazmín.

MacShane: Do you sometimes take one factual episode and combine it with another to make something new — a new story from two completely disconnected and different sources?

Borges: Yes. In this story, for example, I witnessed the *truco* game not in Uruguay, but in the old Northside of Buenos Aires. . . .

Question: I believe that in one of your essays you wrote that a short story can be centered either on the characters or on the situation. In this story, characterization is at a minimum . . .

Borges: It had to be minimal because the two characters are more or less the same character. They are two gauchos, but they could be two hundred or two thousand. They are not Hamlets or Raskolnikovs or Lord Jims.[1] They are just gauchos.

Question: Then the situation is what counts?

Borges: Yes, in this case. And generally speaking, what I think is most important in a short story is the plot or situation, while in a novel what's important are the characters. You may think of *Don Quixote* as being written with incidents, but what is really important are the two characters, Don Quixote and Sancho Panza. In the Sherlock Holmes saga, also, what is really important is the friendship between a very intelligent man and a rather dumb fellow like Dr. Watson. Therefore — if I may be allowed a sweeping statement — in writing a novel, you should know all about the characters, and any plot will do, while in a short story it is the situation that counts. That would be true for Henry James, for example, or for Chesterton.[2]

Question: Do you find some special vision of life in the anecdotes you use?

Borges: I find that most of my stories come from anecdotes, although I distort or change them. Some, of course, come from characters, from people I know. In the short story, I think an anecdote may serve as a beginning point.

Question: Do you think the changes you make are inherent in the anecdote?

Borges: Well, that's a hard nut to crack. I don't know if they're inherent in the anecdote or not, but I know that I need them. If I told a story swiftly and curtly, it wouldn't be effective at all. I have tried to make this

---

[1] Raskolnikov is the main character in the novel *Crime and Punishment* by Russian writer Fyodor Dostoevsky (1821–1881). Lord Jim is the title character in a novel by Joseph Conrad; for information on Conrad, see the introduction to his stories on page 271.

[2] G. K. Chesterton (1874–1936), English critic, theologian, and short story writer. Like Borges, Chesterton experimented with the detective story.

one effective by slowing it down. I couldn't begin by saying, "Two gauchos hated each other," because nobody would believe it. I had to make the hatred seem real. . . .

MacShane: Do you think [political and social issues] should be dealt with in fiction?

Borges: In this story, there was nothing of the kind.

di Giovanni: But there is.

Borges: There may have been, for all I know, but I wasn't concerned about that. I was concerned with the idea of the two men running a race with their throats cut and of the whole thing's being thought of as a joke or prank. Naturally, this story is wound up with the history of Argentina and of Uruguay and of the gauchos. It has associations with the whole of South American history, the wars of liberation, and so on. But I wasn't concerned about that. I was merely trying to tell my story in a convincing way. That was all I was concerned about, although you can link it to anything you like.

di Giovanni: And in spite of your aims, it's a hell of a statement about politics at that time and in that place. It should satisfy anybody.

Borges: And perhaps it's about the politics of any time or any place, I don't know. Of course, these politics are a bit picturesque.

Question: How do you think the artist should relate to his own time?

Borges: Oscar Wilde said that modernity of treatment and subject should be carefully avoided by the modern artist. Of course, he was being witty, but what he was saying was based on an obvious truth. Homer, for example, wrote several centuries after the Trojan war. The idea that a writer should be contemporaneous is itself modern, but I should say it belongs more to journalism than to literature. No real writer ever tried to be contemporary.   [1973]

*L*ANGSTON HUGHES *wrote an introduction entitled "Who Is Simple?" for the 1961 collection* The Best of Simple. *There he said, "I cannot truthfully state, as some novelists do at the beginning of their books, that these stories are about 'nobody living or dead.' The facts are that these tales are about a great many people — although they are stories about no specific persons as such. But it is impossible to live in Harlem and not know at least a hundred Simples. . . ."*

⚜ 25 ⚜

Langston Hughes

"Who Is Simple?"

Simple Speaks His Mind had hardly been published when I walked into a Harlem cafe one night and the proprietor said, "Listen, I don't know where you got that character, Jesse B. Semple, but I want you to meet one of my customers who is *just* like him." He called to a fellow at the end of the bar. "Watch how he walks," he said, "exactly like Simple. And I'll bet he won't be talking to you two minutes before he'll tell you how long he's been standing on his feet, and how much his bunions hurt — just like your book begins."

The barman was right. Even as the customer approached, he cried, "Man, my feet hurt! If you want to see me, why don't you come over here where I am? I stands on my feet all day."

"And I stand on mine all night," said the barman. Without me saying a word, a conversation began so much like the opening chapter in my book that even I was a bit amazed to see how nearly life can be like fiction — or vice versa.

Simple, as a character, originated during the war. His first words came directly out of the mouth of a young man who lived just down the block from me. One night I ran into him in a neighborhood bar and he said, "Come on back to the booth and meet my girl friend." I did and he treated me to a beer. Not knowing much about the young man, I asked where he worked. He said, "In a war plant."

I said, "What do you make?"

He said, "Cranks."

I said, "What kind of cranks?"

He said, "Oh, man, I don't know what kind of cranks."

I said, "Well, do they crank cars, tanks, buses, planes or what?"

He said, "I don't know what them cranks crank."

Whereupon, his girl friend, a little put out at this ignorance of his job, said, "You've been working there long enough. Looks like by now you ought to know what them cranks crank."

"Aw, woman," he said, "you know white folks don't tell colored folks what cranks crank."

That was the beginning of Simple. I have long since lost track of the fellow who uttered those words. But out of the mystery as to what the cranks of this world crank, to whom they belong and why, there evolved the character in this book, wondering and laughing at the numerous problems of white folks, colored folks, and just folks — including himself. He talks about the wife he used to have, the woman he loves today, and his one-time play-girl, Zarita. Usually over a glass of beer, he tells me his tales, mostly in high humor, but sometimes with a pain in his soul as sharp as the occasional hurt of that bunion on his right foot. Sometimes, as the old blues says, Simple might be "laughing to keep from crying." But even then, he keeps you laughing, too. If there were not a lot of genial souls in Harlem as talkative as Simple, I would never have these tales to write down there that are "just like him." He is my ace-boy, Simple. I hope you like him, too.

[1961]

*E*UDORA WELTY *included this discussion of her story "The Worn Path" in her book* The Eye of the Story (1977). *It appeared there in the section called "On Writing," along with her most extensive essays on the art of short fiction — essays that take up such general topics as place and time in fiction, and the art of reading and writing stories. Her reviews of the work of Isak Dinesen, Virginia Woolf, Ralph Ellison, and William Faulkner, from the* New York Times, *are also included in this collection of essays.*

~❦ 26 ❦~

Eudora Welty

"Is Phoenix Jackson's Grandson

Really Dead?"

A story writer is more than happy to be read by students; the fact that these serious readers think and feel something in response to his work he finds life-giving. At the same time he may not always be able to reply to their specific questions in kind. I wondered if it might clarify something, for both the questioners and myself, if I set down a general reply to the question that comes to me most often in the mail, from both students and their teachers, after some classroom discussion. The unrivaled favorite is this: "Is Phoenix Jackson's grandson really *dead?*"

It refers to a short story I wrote years ago called "A Worn Path," which tells of a day's journey an old woman makes on foot from deep in the country into town and into a doctor's office on behalf of her little grandson; he is at home, periodically ill, and periodically she comes for his medicine; they give it to her as usual, she receives it and starts the journey back.

I had not meant to mystify readers by withholding any fact; it is not a writer's business to tease. The story is told through Phoenix's mind as she undertakes her errand. As the author at one with the character as I tell it, I must assume that the boy is alive. As the reader, you are free to think as you like, of course: The story invites you to believe that no matter what happens, Phoenix for as long as she is able to walk and can hold to her purpose will make her journey. The *possibility* that she would keep on even if he were dead is there in her devotion and its single-minded, single-track errand. Certainly the *artistic* truth, which should be good enough for the fact, lies in Phoenix's own answer to that question. When the nurse asks, "He isn't dead, is he?" she speaks for herself: "He still the same. He going to last."

The grandchild is the incentive. But it is the journey, the going of the errand, that is the story, and the question is not whether the grandchild is in reality alive or dead. It doesn't affect the outcome of the story or its meaning from start to finish. But it is not the question itself that has struck me as much as the idea, almost without exception implied in the asking, that for Phoenix's grandson to be dead would somehow make the story "better."

It's *all right*, I want to say to the students who write to me, for things to be what they appear to be, and for words to mean what they say. It's all right, too, for words and appearances to mean more than one thing — ambiguity is a fact of life. A fiction writer's responsibility covers not only what he presents as the facts of a given story but what he chooses to stir up as their implications; in the end, these implications, too, become facts, in the larger, fictional sense. But it is not all right, not in good faith, for things *not* to mean what they say.

The grandson's plight was real and it made the truth of the story, which is the story of an errand of love carried out. If the child no longer lived, the truth would persist in the "wornness" of the path. But his being dead can't increase the truth of the story, can't affect it one way or the other. I think I signal this, because the end of the story has been reached before old Phoenix gets home again: she simply starts back. To the question "Is the grandson really dead?" I could reply that it doesn't make any difference. I could also say that I did not make him up in order to let him play a trick on Phoenix. But my best answer would be: "*Phoenix is alive.*"

The origin of a story is sometimes a trustworthy clue to the author — or can provide him with the clue — to its key image; maybe in this case it will do the same for the reader. One day I saw a solitary old woman like Phoenix. She was walking; I saw her, at middle distance, in a winter country landscape, and watched her slowly make her way across my line of vision. That sight of her made me write the story. I invented an errand for her, but that only seemed a living part of the figure she was herself: What errand other than for someone else could be making her go? And her going was the first thing, her persisting in her landscape was the real thing, and the first and the real were what I wanted and worked to keep. I brought her up close enough, by imagination, to describe her face, make her present to the eyes, but the full-length figure moving across the winter fields was the indelible one and the image to keep, and the perspective extending into the vanishing distance the true one to hold in mind.

I invented for my character, as I wrote, some passing adventures — some dreams and harassments and a small triumph or two, some jolts to her pride, some flights of fancy to console her, one or two encounters to scare her, a moment that gave her cause to feel ashamed, a moment to dance and preen — for it had to be a *journey*, and all these things belonged to that, parts of life's uncertainty.

A narrative line is in its deeper sense, of course, the tracing out of a meaning, and the real continuity of a story lies in this probing forward. The real dramatic force of a story depends on the strength of the emotion that has set it going. The emotional value is the measure of the reach of the story. What gives any such content to "A Worn Path" is not its circumstances but its *subject*: the deep-grained habit of love.

What I hoped would come clear was that in the whole surround of this story, the world it threads through, the only certain thing at all is the worn path. The habit of love cuts through confusion and stumbles or contrives its way out of difficulty, it remembers the way even when it forgets, for a dumfounded moment, its reason for being. The path is the thing that matters.

Her victory — old Phoenix's — is when she sees the diploma in the doctor's office, when she finds "nailed up on the wall the document that had been stamped with the gold seal and framed in the gold frame, which matched the dream that was hung up in her head." The return with the medicine is just a matter of retracing her own footsteps. It is the part of the journey, and of the story, that can now go without saying.

In the matter of function, old Phoenix's way might even do as a sort of parallel to your way of work if you are a writer of stories. The way to get there is the all-important, all-absorbing problem, and this problem is your reason for undertaking the story. Your only guide, too, is your sureness about your subject, about what this subject is. Like Phoenix, you work all your life to find your way, through all the obstructions and the false appearances and the upsets you may have brought on yourself, to reach a meaning — using inventions of your imagination, perhaps helped out by your dreams and bits of good luck. And finally too, like Phoenix, you have to assume that what you are working in aid of is life, not death.

But you would make the trip anyway — wouldn't you? — just on hope.   [1977]

*R*ALPH ELLISON *gave an interview for the "Art of Fiction" series of the* Paris Review *that was reprinted in his volume of essays,* Shadow and Act *(1964). In the introduction to that book he said that what is basic to the fiction writer's confrontation with the world is "converting experience into symbolic action. Good fiction is made of that which is real, and reality is difficult to come by. So much of it depends upon the individual's willingness to discover his true self, upon his defining himself—for the time being at least—against his background."*

⚝ 27 ⚝

Ralph Ellison

on the Influence of Folklore on

BATTLE ROYAL

Interviewers: Can you give us an example of the use of folklore in your own novel?

Ellison: Well, there are certain themes, symbols and images which are based on folk material. For example, there is the old saying amongst Negroes: If you're black, stay back; if you're brown, stick around; if you're white, you're right. And there is the joke Negroes tell on themselves about their being so black they can't be seen in the dark. In my book this sort of thing was merged with the meanings which blackness and light have long had in Western mythology: evil and goodness, ignorance and knowledge, and so on. In my novel the narrator's development is one through blackness to light; that is, from ignorance to enlightenment: invisibility to visibility. He leaves the South and goes North; this, as you will notice in reading Negro folktales, is always the road to freedom — the movement upward. You have the same thing again when he leaves his underground cave for the open.

It took me a long time to learn how to adapt such examples of myth into my work — also ritual. The use of ritual is equally a vital part of the creative process. I learned a few things from Eliot, Joyce, and Hemingway, but not how to adapt them. When I started writing, I knew that in both *The Waste Land*[1] and *Ulysses* ancient myth and ritual were used to give form and significance to the material; but it took me a few years to realize

[1] long, extremely influential poem (1922) by T. S. Eliot (1888–1965).

1190

that the myths and rites which we find functioning in our everyday lives could be used in the same way. In my first attempt at a novel — which I was unable to complete — I began by trying to manipulate the simple structural unities of *beginning, middle,* and *end,* but when I attempted to deal with the psychological strata — the images, symbols, and emotional configurations — of the experience at hand, I discovered that the unities were simply cool points of stability on which one could suspend the narrative line — but beneath the surface of apparently rational human relationships there seethed a chaos before which I was helpless. People rationalize what they shun or are incapable of dealing with; these superstitions and their rationalizations become ritual as they govern behavior. The rituals become social forms, and it is one of the functions of the artist to recognize them and raise them to the level of art.

I don't know whether I'm getting this over or not. Let's put it this way: Take the "Battle Royal" passage in my novel, where the boys are blindfolded and forced to fight each other for the amusement of the white observers. This is a vital part of behavior pattern in the South, which both Negroes and whites thoughtlessly accept. It is a ritual in preservation of caste lines, a keeping of taboo to appease the gods and ward off bad luck. It is also the initiation ritual to which all greenhorns are subjected. This passage which states what Negroes will see I did not have to invent; the patterns were already there in society, so that all I had to do was present them in a broader context of meaning. In any society there are many rituals of situation which, for the most part, go unquestioned. They can be simple or elaborate, but they are the connective tissue between the work of art and the audience.

Interviewers: Do you think a reader unacquainted with this folklore can properly understand your work?

Ellison: Yes, I think so. It's like jazz; there's no inherent problem which prohibits understanding but the assumptions brought to it. We don't all dig Shakespeare uniformly, or even *Little Red Riding Hood.* The understanding of art depends finally upon one's willingness to extend one's humanity and one's knowledge of human life. I noticed, incidentally, that the Germans, having no special caste assumptions concerning American Negroes, dealt with my work simply as a novel. I think the Americans will come to view it that way in twenty years — if it's around that long.

Interviewers: Don't you think it will be?

Ellison: I doubt it. It's not an important novel. I failed of eloquence, and many of the immediate issues are rapidly fading away. If it does last, it will be simply because there are things going on in its depth that are of more permanent interest than on its surface. I hope so, anyway.

[1964]

SHIRLEY JACKSON wrote this "biography of a story" in 1960 as a lecture to be delivered before reading "The Lottery" to college audiences. After her death it was included in Come Along with Me *(1968), edited by her husband, Stanley Edgar Hyman. The lecture also contained extensive quotations from letters she had received from readers of the story who took it literally, which so disgusted Jackson that she promised her listeners at the conclusion of her talk, "I am out of the lottery business for good."*

❧ 28 ❦

Shirley Jackson
on the Morning of June 28, 1948, and
THE LOTTERY

On the morning of June 28, 1948, I walked down to the post office in our little Vermont town to pick up the mail. I was quite casual about it, as I recall — I opened the box, took out a couple of bills and a letter or two, talked to the postmaster for a few minutes, and left, never supposing that it was the last time for months that I was to pick up the mail without an active feeling of panic. By the next week I had had to change my mailbox to the largest one in the post office, and casual conversation with the postmaster was out of the question, because he wasn't speaking to me. June 28, 1948, was the day *The New Yorker* came out with a story of mine in it. It was not my first published story, nor my last, but I have been assured over and over that if it had been the only story I ever wrote or published, there would be people who would not forget my name.

I had written the story three weeks before, on a bright June morning when summer seemed to have come at last, with blue skies and warm sun and no heavenly signs to warn me that my morning's work was anything but just another story. The idea had come to me while I was pushing my daughter up the hill in her stroller — it was, as I say, a warm morning, and the hill was steep, and beside my daughter the stroller held the day's groceries — and perhaps the effort of that last fifty yards up the hill put an edge to the story; at any rate, I had the idea fairly clearly in my mind when I put my daughter in her playpen and the frozen vegetables in the refrigerator, and, writing the story, I found that it went quickly and easily, moving from beginning to end without pause. As a matter of fact, when I read it over later I decided that except for one or two minor corrections, it needed no changes, and the story I finally typed up and sent off to my agent the next day was almost word for word the original draft. This, as any writer of stories can tell you, is not a usual thing. All I know is that when I came to read the story over I felt strongly that I didn't want to fuss with it. I didn't think it was perfect, but I didn't want to fuss with it. It was, I thought, a serious, straightforward story, and I was pleased and a little surprised at the ease with which it had been written; I was reasonably proud of it, and hoped that my agent would sell it to some magazine and I would have the gratification of seeing it in print.

My agent did not care for the story, but — as she said in her note at the time — her job was to sell it, not to like it. She sent it at once to *The New Yorker*, and about a week after the story had been written I received a telephone call from the fiction editor of *The New Yorker*; it was quite clear that he did not really care for the story, either, but *The New Yorker* was going to buy it. He asked for one change — that the date mentioned in the story be changed to coincide with the date of the issue of the magazine in which the story would appear, and I said of course. He then asked, hesitantly, if I had any particular interpretation of my own for the story; Mr. Harold Ross, then the editor of *The New Yorker*, was not altogether sure that he understood the story, and wondered if I cared to enlarge upon its meaning. I said no. Mr. Ross, he said, thought that the story might be puzzling to some people, and in case anyone telephoned the magazine, as sometimes happened, or wrote in asking about the story, was there anything in particular I wanted them to say? No, I said, nothing in particular; it was just a story I wrote.

I had no more preparation than that. I went on picking up the mail every morning, pushing my daughter up and down the hill in her stroller, anticipating pleasurably the check from *The New Yorker*, and shopping for groceries. The weather stayed nice and it looked as though it was going to be a good summer. Then, on June 28, *The New Yorker* came out with my story.

Things began mildly enough with a note from a friend at *The New Yorker*: "Your story has kicked up quite a fuss around the office," he wrote. I was flattered; it's nice to think that your friends notice what you write. Later that day there was a call from one of the magazine's editors; they had had a couple of people phone in about my story, he said, and was there anything I particularly wanted him to say if there were any more calls? No, I said, nothing particular; anything he chose to say was perfectly all right with me; it was just a story.

I was further puzzled by a cryptic note from another friend: "Heard a man talking about a story of yours on the bus this morning," she wrote. "Very exciting. I wanted to tell him I knew the author, but after I heard what he was saying I decided I'd better not."

One of the most terrifying aspects of publishing stories and books is the realization that they are going to be read, and read by strangers. I had never fully realized this before, although I had of course in my imagination dwelt lovingly upon the thought of the millions and millions of people who were going to be uplifted and enriched and delighted by the stories I wrote. It had simply never occurred to me that these millions and millions of people might be so far from being uplifted that they would sit down and write me letters I was downright scared to open; of the three-hundred-odd letters that I received that summer I can count only thirteen that spoke kindly to me, and they were mostly from friends. Even my mother scolded me: "Dad and I did not care at all for your story in *The New Yorker*," she wrote sternly; "it does seem, dear, that this gloomy kind of story is what all you young people think about these days. Why don't you write something to cheer people up?"

By mid-July I had begun to perceive that I was very lucky indeed to be safely in Vermont, where no one in our small town had ever heard of *The New Yorker*, much less read my story. Millions of people, and my mother, had taken a pronounced dislike to me.

The magazine kept no track of telephone calls, but all letters addressed to me care of the magazine were forwarded directly to me for answering, and all letters addressed to the magazine — some of them addressed to Harold Ross personally; these were the most vehement — were answered at the magazine and then the letters were sent me in great batches, along with carbons of the answers written at the magazine. I have all the letters still, and if they could be considered to give any accurate cross section of the reading public, or the reading public of *The New Yorker*, or even the reading public of one issue of *The New Yorker*, I would stop writing now.

Judging from these letters, people who read stories are gullible, rude, frequently illiterate, and horribly afraid of being laughed at. Many of the writers were positive that *The New Yorker* was going to ridicule them in print, and the most cautious letters were headed, in capital letters: NOT FOR PUBLICATION or PLEASE DO NOT PRINT THIS LETTER, or, at best, THIS LETTER MAY BE PUBLISHED AT YOUR USUAL RATES OF PAYMENT. Anonymous letters, of which there were a few, were destroyed. *The New Yorker* never published any comment of any kind about the story in the magazine, but did issue one publicity release saying that the story had received more mail than any piece of fiction they had ever published; this was after the newspapers had gotten into the act, in midsummer, with a front-page story in the San Francisco *Chronicle* begging to know what the story meant, and a series of columns in New York and Chicago papers pointing out that *New Yorker* subscriptions were being canceled right and left.

Curiously, there are three main themes which dominate the letters of that first summer — three themes which might be identified as bewilderment, speculation, and plain old-fashioned abuse. In the years since then, during which the story has been anthologized, dramatized, televised, and even — in one completely mystifying transformation — made into a ballet, the tenor of letters I receive has changed. I am addressed more politely, as a rule, and the letters largely confine themselves to questions like what does this story mean? The general tone of the early letters, however, was a kind of wide-eyed, shocked innocence. People at first were not so much concerned with what the story meant; what they wanted to know was where these lotteries were held, and whether they could go there and watch.

[1968]

*F*LANNERY O'CONNOR *made the following remarks at Hollins College, Virginia, to introduce a reading of her story in October 1963. They were later included in* Mystery and Manners (1969), *a collection of her essays and lectures. The style of this talk is informal, and O'Connor experimented with it, changing the organization and delivery of the material when she appeared before different audiences. Her own interpretation of the themes in her fiction is essential to understanding her stories. As she says, "There are perhaps other ways than my own in which this story could be read, but none other by which it could have been written."*

⁓⋟ 29 ⋞⁓

Flannery O'Connor

on the Element of Suspense in

A GOOD MAN IS HARD TO FIND

A story really isn't any good unless it successfully resists paraphrase, unless it hangs on and expands in the mind. Properly, you analyze to enjoy, but it's equally true that to analyze with any discrimination, you have to have enjoyed already, and I think that the best reason to hear a story read is that it should stimulate that primary enjoyment.

I don't have any pretensions to being an Aeschylus or Sophocles and providing you in this story with a cathartic experience out of your mythic background, though this story I'm going to read certainly calls up a good deal of the South's mythic background, and it should elicit from you a degree of pity and terror, even though its way of being serious is a comic one. I do think, though, that like the Greeks you should know what is going to happen in this story so that any element of suspense in it will be transferred from its surface to its interior.

I would be most happy if you had already read it, happier still if you knew it well, but since experience has taught me to keep my expectations along these lines modest, I'll tell you that this is the story of a family of six which, on its way driving to Florida, gets wiped out by an escaped convict who calls himself the Misfit. The family is made up of the Grandmother and her son, Bailey, and his children, John Wesley and June Star and the baby, and there is also the cat and the children's mother. The cat is named Pitty Sing, and the Grandmother is taking him with them, hidden in a basket.

1196

Now I think it behooves me to try to establish with you the basis on which reason operates in this story. Much of my fiction takes its character from a reasonable use of the unreasonable, though the reasonableness of my use of it may not always be apparent. The assumptions that underlie this use of it, however, are those of the central Christian mysteries. These are assumptions to which a large part of the modern audience takes exception. About this I can only say that there are perhaps other ways than my own in which this story could be read, but none other by which it could have been written. Belief, in my own case anyway, is the engine that makes perception operate.

The heroine of this story, the Grandmother, is in the most significant position life offers the Christian. She is facing death. And to all appearances she, like the rest of us, is not too well prepared for it. She would like to see the event postponed. Indefinitely.

I've talked to a number of teachers who use this story in class and who tell their students that the Grandmother is evil, that in fact, she's a witch, even down to the cat. One of these teachers told me that his students, and particularly his southern students, resisted this interpretation with a certain bemused vigor, and he didn't understand why. I had to tell him that they resisted it because they all had grandmothers or great-aunts just like her at home, and they knew, from personal experience, that the old lady lacked comprehension, but that she had a good heart. The southerner is usually tolerant of those weaknesses that proceed from innocence, and he knows that a taste for self-preservation can be readily combined with the missionary spirit.

This same teacher was telling his students that morally the Misfit was several cuts above the Grandmother. He had a really sentimental attachment to the Misfit. But then a prophet gone wrong is almost always more interesting than your grandmother, and you have to let people take their pleasures where they find them.

It is true that the old lady is a hypocritical old soul; her wits are no match for the Misfit's, nor is her capacity for grace equal to his; yet I think the unprejudiced reader will feel that the Grandmother has a special kind of triumph in this story which instinctively we do not allow to someone altogether bad.

I often ask myself what makes a story work, and what makes it hold up as a story, and I have decided that it is probably some action, some gesture of a character that is unlike any other in the story, one which indicates where the real heart of the story lies. This would have to be an action or a gesture which was both totally right and totally unexpected; it would have to be one that was both in character and beyond character; it would have to suggest both the world and eternity. The action or gesture I'm talking about would have to be on the anagogical level, that is, the level which has to do with the Divine life and our participation in it. It would be a gesture that transcended any neat allegory that might have been intended or any pat moral categories a reader could make. It would be a gesture which somehow made contact with mystery.

There is a point in this story where such a gesture occurs. The Grandmother is at last alone, facing the Misfit. Her head clears for an instant and she realizes, even in her limited way, that she is responsible for the man before her and joined to him by ties of kinship which have their roots deep in the mystery she has been merely prattling about so far. And at this point, she does the right thing, she makes the right gesture.

I find that students are often puzzled by what she says and does here, but I think myself that if I took out this gesture and what she says with it, I would have no story. What was left would not be worth your attention. Our age not only does not have a very sharp eye for the almost imperceptible intrusions of grace, it no longer has much feeling for the nature of the violences which precede and follow them. The devil's greatest wile, Baudelaire has said, is to convince us that he does not exist.

I suppose the reasons for the use of so much violence in modern fiction will differ with each writer who uses it, but in my own stories I have found that violence is strangely capable of returning my characters to reality and preparing them to accept their moment of grace. Their heads are so hard that almost nothing else will do the work. This idea, that reality is something to which we must be returned at considerable cost, is one which is seldom understood by the casual reader, but it is one which is implicit in the Christian view of the world.

I don't want to equate the Misfit with the devil. I prefer to think that, however unlikely this may seem, the old lady's gesture, like the mustard-seed, will grow to be a great crow-filled tree in the Misfit's heart, and will be enough of a pain to him there to turn him into the prophet he was meant to become. But that's another story.

This story has been called grotesque, but I prefer to call it literal. A good story is literal in the same sense that a child's drawing is literal. When a child draws, he doesn't intend to distort but to set down exactly what he sees, and as his gaze is direct, he sees the lines that create motion. Now the lines of motion that interest the writer are usually invisible. They are lines of spiritual motion. And in this story you should be on the lookout for such things as the action of grace in the Grandmother's soul, and not for the dead bodies.

We hear many complaints about the prevalence of violence in modern fiction, and it is always assumed that this violence is a bad thing and meant to be an end in itself. With the serious writer, violence is never an end in itself. It is the extreme situation that best reveals what we are essentially, and I believe these are times when writers are more interested in what we are essentially than in the tenor of our daily lives. Violence is a force which can be used for good or evil, and among other things taken by it is the kingdom of heaven. But regardless of what can be taken by it, the man in the violent situation reveals those qualities least dispensable in his personality, those qualities which are all he will have to take into eternity with him; and since the characters in this story are all on the verge of eternity, it is appropriate to think of what they take with them. In any case, I hope that if you consider these points in connection with the story, you will come to see it as something more than an account of a family murdered on the way to Florida. [1969]

*J*OHN UPDIKE *gave an interview to the* Paris Review *that was later reprinted in the fourth volume of* Writers at Work *(1976). His meticulous craftsmanship as a writer was evident in his handling of the interview. On his guard when first approached by the* Paris Review, *he initially refused to be interviewed, saying, "Perhaps I have written fiction because everything unambiguously expressed seems somehow crass to me; and when the subject is myself, I want to jeer and weep. Also, I really don't have a great deal to tell interviewers; the little I learned about life and the art of fiction I try to express in my work." When he agreed to do the interview the following year, he insisted that written questions had to be submitted to him before the* Paris Review *representative came to see him. Finally, Updike revised the transcript of his spoken comments to bring them into line with the style of his written answers before agreeing to publication. In the interview, he disavowed any important connection between the facts of his life and the fiction he created on paper, although he acknowledged a "submerged thread" of autobiography in stories like "Flight."*

❦ 30 ❦

John Updike

on Writing about Adolescence in

FLIGHT

Interviewer: What I meant to ask is . . . why you write so much about what most people take to be your own adolescence and family. . . .

Updike: I suppose there's no avoiding it — my adolescence seemed interesting to me. In a sense my mother and father, considerable actors both, were dramatizing my youth as I was having it so that I arrived as an adult with some burden of material already half formed. There is, true, a submerged thread connecting certain of the fictions, and I guess the submerged thread is the autobiography. . . .

When I was little, I used to draw disparate objects on a piece of paper — toasters, baseballs, flowers, whatnot — and connect them with lines. But every story, really, is a fresh start for me, and these little connections — recurrences of names, or the way, say, that Piet Hanema's insomnia takes him back into the same high school that John Nordholm, and

David Kern, and Allen Dow[1] sat in — are in there as a kind of running, oblique coherence. Once I've coined a name, by the way, I feel utterly hidden behind that mask, and what I remember and what I imagine become indistinguishable. I feel no obligation to the remembered past; what I create on paper must, and for me does, soar free of whatever the facts were. Do I make any sense?

Interviewer: Some.

Updike: In other words, I disavow any essential connection between my life and whatever I write. I think it's a morbid and inappropriate area of concern, though natural enough — a lot of morbid concerns are natural. But the work, the words on the paper, must stand apart from our living presences; we sit down at the desk and become nothing but the excuse for these husks we cast off. But apart from the somewhat teasing little connections, there is in these three novels and the short stories of *Pigeon Feathers* a central image of flight or escape or loss, the way we flee from the past, a sense of guilt. . . .

The sense that in time as well as space we leave people as if by volition and thereby incur guilt and thereby owe them, the dead, the forsaken, at least the homage of rendering them. The trauma or message that I acquired in Olinger had to do with suppressed pain, with the amount of sacrifice I suppose that middle-class life demands, and by that I guess I mean civilized life. The father, whatever his name, is sacrificing freedom of motion, and the mother is sacrificing in a way — oh, sexual richness, I guess; they're all stuck, and when I think back over these stories (and you know, they *are* dear to me and if I had to give anybody one book of me it would be the Vintage *Olinger Stories*), I think especially of that moment in "Flight" when the boy, chafing to escape, fresh from his encounter with Molly Bingaman and a bit more of a man but not enough quite, finds the mother lying there buried in her own peculiar messages from far away, the New Orleans jazz, and then the grandfather's voice comes tumbling down the stairs singing, "There is a happy land far far away." This is the way it was, is. There has never been anything in my life quite as compressed, simultaneously as communicative to me of my own power and worth and of the irremediable grief in just living, in just going on.

I really don't think I'm alone among writers in caring about what they experienced in the first eighteen years of life. Hemingway cherished the Michigan stories out of proportion, I would think, to their merit. Look at Twain. Look at Joyce. Nothing that happens to us after twenty is as free from self-consciousness because by then we have the vocation to write. Writers' lives break into two halves. At the point where you get your

---

[1] The names are all of characters in Updike's fiction.

writerly vocation you diminish your receptivity to experience. Being able to write becomes a kind of shield, a way of hiding, a way of too instantly transforming pain into honey — whereas when you're young, you're so impotent you cannot help but strive and observe and feel.   [1976]

WRITING
ABOUT SHORT STORIES

In writing an essay about literature, you clarify your relationship to what you have read. This relationship goes beyond a basic emotional response to the story, whether you enjoyed it or not. You write to reveal what Ernest Hemingway referred to as "the measure of what you brought to the reading." As soon as you ask the smallest question about the meaning or structure of a story and try to answer it, you are beginning a critical inquiry that involves your intellect as well as your emotions. This activity is called the interpretation of the text. What makes it valuable is that it reveals to you and to others how you responded to the stories after they have entertained, instructed, and perhaps enchanted you. Now it is your turn to explain their effect on you, and to analyze how they did it. Once you have asked yourself what there is about a story that gives you pleasure — the style, the form, the meaning — you have begun the process of discovering "the measure of what you brought to the reading." The next stage is to communicate your ideas to someone else. Turning yourself from a reader into a writer takes time, but if you understand the various steps involved, the process becomes much easier.

Writing the Paper

An essay about literature can take various forms and lengths, depending on the nature of the assignment. Whatever the case, whether you are writing a paper of only a few paragraphs or a research paper of several thousand words, the basic requirement is always the same. You must keep in mind that an essay on short stories (or on any subject, for that matter) is a type of expository writing, and *expository* means "serving to clarify, set forth, or explain in detail" an idea about the subject. Writing about literature helps you clarify your ideas. If you want your essay to communicate these ideas clearly to a reader, you must understand that it always requires two things to be effective: a strong thesis sentence, or central idea about your topic; and an adequate development of your thesis sentence. How you organize your paper will depend on the way you choose to develop your central idea. The three principal ways of organizing essays about short stories — explication, analysis, and comparison and contrast — will be taken up after a discussion of ways to find a thesis sentence.

GETTING IDEAS FOR YOUR TOPIC AND THESIS SENTENCE

Most effective short papers (about 500 words) usually treat one aspect of the story: its theme, characterization, setting, point of view, or literary style. These are some of the possible *topics* for your paper, the general subject you are going to write about in your interpretive essay. Usually your first response to a story is a jumble of impressions that do not separate themselves into neat categories of *topics* and *thesis sentences.* You must sort through your first impressions to select a topic on which to concentrate in order to get ideas for your thesis sentence.

Before you can start your essay, you should feel that you understand the story thoroughly as a whole. Read it again to remind yourself of the passages that strike you with particular force. Underline the words and sentences you feel are significant — or even better, make a list of what seems important while you are reading the story. These can be outstanding descriptions of the characters or settings, passages of meaningful dialogue, details showing the way the author builds toward the story's climax, or hints that foreshadow the conclusion. To stimulate ideas about topics, you may want to jot down answers to the following questions about the elements of the story as you reread it.

Plot. Does the plot depend on chance or coincidence, or does it grow out of the personalities of the characters? Are any later incidents foreshadowed early in the story? Are the episodes presented in chronological order? If not, why not? Does the climax indicate a change in a situation or a change in a character? How dramatic is this change? Or is there no change at all?

Character. Are the characters believable? Are they stereotypes? Do they suggest real people, or abstract qualities? Is there one protagonist or several? Does the story have an antagonist? How does the author tell you about the main character — through description of physical appearance, actions, thoughts, and emotions, or through contrast with a minor character? Does the main character change in the course of the story? How? Why?

Point of View. How does the point of view shape the theme? Would the story change if told from a different viewpoint? In first-person narration, can you trust the narrator?

Setting. How does the setting influence the plot and the characters? Does it help to suggest or develop the meaning of the story?

Style. Is the author's prose style primarily literal or figurative? Can you find examples of irony in dialogue or narrative passages? If dialect or colloquial speech is used, what is its effect? Does the author call attention to the way he or she uses words, or is the literary style inconspicuous?

Theme. Does the story's title help explain its meaning? Can you find a suggestion of the theme in specific passages of dialogue or description? Are certain symbols or repetitions of images important in revealing the author's intent in the story?

Now put the text aside and look over your notes. Can you see any pattern in them? You may find that you have been most impressed by the way the author developed characterizations, for example. Then you will have a possible topic for your paper. Certainly if you have a choice, you should pick whatever appeals to you most in the story and concentrate on it.

If you still cannot come up with a topic, ask for help in your next English class. Perhaps your instructor will suggest something: "Why don't you discuss the way Hawthorne uses irony in 'Young Goodman Brown'?" Often the class will be assigned one topic to write about in the first place. Some students think assigned topics make writing more difficult; others find they make it easier to begin to write.

A topic, however, is not the same as a thesis sentence. A topic is a general subject (for example, the character of Goodman Brown). A thesis, on the other hand, makes a statement about a topic, usually the result of thinking about the topic and narrowing it down to focus on some relationship of the topic to the story as a whole. A good thesis sentence has two important functions. First, it suggests a way for you to write about the story. Second, it makes clear to your reader the approach you have taken toward the topic. To *write* critically about short fiction, you must *think* critically about it. You start with an interpretation of the entire story and then show how some particular aspect of it contributes to what you think is its overall pattern and meaning.

NARROWING IDEAS TO A THESIS

A thesis sentence states the central idea you will develop in your paper. It should be easy for the reader of your essay to recognize — even if it's sometimes hard for you to formulate at first. A thesis sentence is a complete sentence that points the way you will take to clarify your interpretation of the story. In Hawthorne's story, for example, you might decide to write about the character of Goodman Brown (*topic*). You interpret the story to be a warning about the danger of losing religious faith (*theme*). If you think about the way your topic relates to the theme, your analysis might lead you to the idea that Goodman Brown lost his religious faith through the sin of pride. This thought process narrows the topic into a thesis, which you can state as the sentence "The story 'Young Goodman Brown' shows how a man can lose his religious faith through the sin of pride."

The test of a good thesis sentence is whether your *subject* ("The story 'Young Goodman Brown'") is followed by a clearly focused *predicate* ("shows how a man can lose his faith through the sin of pride"). What you want is a statement of an idea that you can then develop in your essay.

Finding a thesis sentence is often the biggest stumbling block for writers of expository prose. How do you know if your idea is worth developing in a paper? Generally speaking, a thesis will work if it expresses a specific idea about the story that you want to develop. If you are not interested to begin with, or do not like the story you are writing about, you probably will not write effectively. You almost always write better about a story you have enjoyed reading. Certainly you will feel more sympathetic to the intent of the author if you are not hostile to the assignment in the first place. Remember also that as a literary critic you must always keep an open mind when interpreting a story. Your ideas about it are as valid as anyone else's, so long as you can support your interpretation with examples from the text. There can be many possible ways to read a story, although the author may have felt the original impulse to write it because of a particular idea or feeling about the subject.

Sometimes the thesis sentence occurs to you while you are thinking about the story; then you can jot it down as a fully formed idea right away. Other times you may find that you are unable to formulate any definite idea about the story until you start to write. No single procedure works for all writers at all times. You might begin writing with a trial thesis in mind, putting down rough ideas or a string of sentences as you think about the general topic you have chosen. Or you might decide to go back to the notes you took while reading the story and try to organize them into a simple outline about your topic, looking for connections between things that might suggest a direction to take in a trial essay and then hoping a thesis sentence will emerge while you free-associate with paper and pencil in hand. You might also get an idea for a thesis sentence by talking about the story with a friend. Whatever way you start, do not settle for anything quick and easy. "Hawthorne's use of irony in 'Young Goodman Brown' is interesting" is much too general to be of use to you in writing a good essay. Keep thinking or scribbling away at your first rough draft until you find an idea that gives you a specific direction to take in your paper. "Hawthorne's use of irony in 'Young Goodman Brown' suggests his judgment of the Puritan moral code" is a thesis sentence that has a clearly focused predicate. It states a definite relationship of the topic to the meaning of the thesis you want to explore. Then you know you are on your way to writing a good essay.

WRITING AND REVISING

If you begin the first paragraph of your essay with a strong thesis sentence, your ideas will usually flow in writing and revising the paper. You will often discover further possibilities for refining your thesis while using it to interpret the text. That is one reason you should allow plenty of time to complete a writing assignment. It's an unusual first draft in which the central idea is developed coherently and fully enough to be turned in as a finished paper. Revision often stimulates further thought, sharpening and strengthening the development of your thesis. In the process of writing, you will come to understand the story more fully as your thesis takes you closer to its meaning.

Try not to become discouraged about writing by visualizing some distant final product — a well-organized essay, neatly typed on clean, white paper, shimmering on the page in what looks like pristine perfection. Remember that it took time to get that way on paper. It originated in half-formed, often confused thoughts that had to be coaxed in halting steps to arrange themselves into coherent paragraphs linked by what only much later appear to be inevitable transitions. More often than not, the 500 words you might think are a perfect essay when you turn in your final paper will be the end result — if you took enough time in writing — of winnowing down 1,000 or more words from your rough drafts. You must amplify and clarify your thesis, editing your sentences and paragraphs so that each one relates coherently to your central idea. Then your essay will express your insights about the story so clearly that they can be understood as you intended.

At the beginning, the best procedure is to forget about the end result and give all your thought and effort to the *process* of writing. If you find it useful, make an outline and try to follow it, but this practice varies with different writers. Some people find it valuable to organize their notes about the story into a formal outline, while others prefer to make a rough sketch of the steps they plan to follow in developing their central idea. You may find that you do not want to use an outline at all, although in general it can help to keep you from straying too far from the point you are trying to make. Remember, too, that there is no fixed rule about the number of drafts or the amount of revision necessary before you have a finished essay. Every essay changes from the first rough draft through the various revisions, often gone over several times in the days or weeks between getting the assignment and bringing the finished paper to class. In the various stages of writing, different aspects of the central idea often reveal themselves and are integrated into the paper, depending on your degree of concentration and involvement in the assignment. Even if you scrap sentences or whole paragraphs that do not relate to your final discussion, you have not wasted your time, because your early efforts to put your thoughts down on paper bring you to the point where you have better insights.

You will probably have to rewrite your opening paragraph many times to tailor your thesis sentence to the final shape your ideas have taken. Some writers just sketch in the first paragraph and go back to polish it when the rest of the essay is finished. Often you will want to amplify and refine your thesis sentence, dividing it into several sentences in your introductory remarks. Then it becomes a thesis statement, rather than a single sentence.

DEVELOPING THE THESIS

While it is possible to write many different kinds of papers about short fiction, most college instructors assign students the task of interpreting the text. The literary terms used in the headnotes to each writer in this anthology and defined in the glossary (pages 1227–1236) can help you find a vocabulary to express your ideas when writing about the stories. You cannot write intelligently about any subject without using the special vocabulary of that subject, whether you are writing a paper for an English class or for a class in economics, psychology, or engineering. At the same time, dropping the terms in your paper the way a person might drop names at a party will not impress your readers. Understand what the terms mean so you can use them to think and write critically about the elements of a story when you begin to interpret the text in the light of your central idea. You will usually develop your thesis statement in the body of your essay by following one or more of the three common methods of writing about literature: *explication, analysis,* and *comparison and contrast.*

Types of Literary Papers

EXPLICATION

The word *explication* is derived from a Latin word that means "unfolding." When you explicate a text, you unfold its meaning in an essay, proceeding carefully to interpret it passage by passage, sometimes even line by line or word by word. A good explication concentrates on details, quoting the text of the story to bring them to the attention of a reader who might have missed them reading the story from a different perspective. An entire story is usually too long to explicate completely — the explication would be far longer than the story — so you will usually select a short passage or section that relates to the idea that you are developing. Often this short section is a key scene, a crucial conversation, or an opening or closing paragraph where the implications of the text can be revealed to develop the central idea of your essay.

Although explication does not concern itself with the author's life or times, the author's historical period may determine the definitions of words or the meaning of concepts that appear in the passage being interpreted. If the story is a century or more old, the meanings of some words may have changed. The explication is supposed to reveal what the author might have meant when he or she wrote the story, not assuming conscious intentions, but aware of possibilities. In older stories, you will have to do a little research if the passage chosen for explication contains words whose meanings have changed since the author's time. The *Oxford English Dictionary,* available in the reference section of your college library, will give you the meaning of a word in a particular historical era. The philosophical, religious, scientific, or political beliefs of the author, or of the author's age, may also enter into your interpretation of the text. The main emphasis in explication, however, is on the meaning of the words — both *denotative* and *connotative* — and the way those words affect the reader.

The following student paper is an example of how explication is used to develop a central idea in an essay.

The Devil's Tricks in "Young Goodman Brown"

Hawthorne's "Young Goodman Brown" is the story of a man whose
life is ruined because of the sin of pride, which makes him lose his
faith in God. Goodman Brown agrees to meet the devil in the forest,
and his faith is destroyed when he sees a pink ribbon fluttering to
earth. He believes this ribbon could only have fallen from his
beloved wife's hair. It is this scene in the story that reveals his
weakness. His pride makes him trust the evidence of his own senses
more than his faith in God.

Hawthorne begins the scene in which Goodman Brown loses his
faith by leaving him alone, without other characters around him, for
the first time in the story. Alone with his soul, he has only himself to depend on. The devil has abandoned him in the middle of the
dark woods with the maple staff that became a witch's broomstick when
it was borrowed by Goody Cloyse earlier in the evening. Thus the
reader has already seen the devil's tricks before this scene begins.

Other black magic is in store for Goodman Brown. Gazing upward
"into the deep arch of the firmament," he lifts his hands to pray.
The word "firmament," with its biblical connotations, suggests that
Goodman Brown has set his mind on God. He has scarcely begun his
prayer, however, when his concentration is broken: "a cloud, though
no wind was stirring, hurried across the zenith, and hid the brightening stars." The devil's magic show has begun, although Goodman Brown
is not aware of it.

He accepts the appearance of the "black mass" of the cloud overhead and forgets his prayer, listening instead to a "confused and
doubtful sound of townspeople. . . . The next moment, so indistinct
were the sounds, he doubted whether he had heard aught. . . ." The
adjectives and verbs I have underlined in Hawthorne's description
suggest the lack of substance in what Goodman Brown hears and sees;
he is, after all, standing under a dark cloud. The next moment he
believes he hears the voice "of a young woman, uttering lamentations,
yet with an uncertain sorrow, and entreating for some favor, which,
perhaps, it would grieve her to obtain. And all the unseen multitude,
both saints and sinners, seemed to encourage her onward."

At this point Goodman Brown believes not only that he hears the
voice of a young woman, but also that the woman is his wife, Faith.
By now he is completely deluded. When he shouts his wife's name he
is mocked by the ghosts he senses around him: "The echoes of the
forest mocked him, crying 'Faith! Faith!' as if bewildered wretches
were seeking her, all through the wilderness." Here Hawthorne has

*Use quotes for
titles of stories.*

*Start with general
thesis sentence.*

*Narrow the thesis
to show specific
direction your
paper will take.*

*Transition:
Repeat key words
of thesis.*

*Suggest
background of
scene before you
begin explication.*

*Start to quote
from the story.*

*Main section of
the explication:
Text quoted in
the order it
appears*

*OK to use I;
italics are not in
original.*

Good active verbs

built his description out of thin air. The <u>echoes</u> of Goodman Brown's

voice sound <u>as if</u> bewildered, which is certainly ironic, since he him-

self is <u>truly</u> bewildered here.

    Goodman Brown's temptation leads to his fall in the next para-

graph, when "the dark cloud swept away, leaving the clear and silent

sky above Goodman Brown. But something fluttered lightly down through

the air, and caught on the branch of a tree. The young man seized it,

and <u>beheld</u> a pink ribbon." Hawthorne's language has changed, becoming

simple and stark. It suggests the physicality of what he describes.

Goodman Brown might have doubted the evidence of his eyes and ears if

he stopped to reflect on what he had been shown in the "clear and

silent sky" above his head, but before he could reflect, the devil

gave him what he took to be something tangible to hold onto, something

that looks like a pink ribbon.

    On the evidence of what he sees as a ribbon, Goodman Brown jumps

to the conclusion that Faith has joined in the worship of the devil.

He surrenders his trust in God forever. He becomes a victim of his

own pride, believing in the evidence of his own senses more than in

God. As a Puritan, Goodman Brown believes in the devil as much as

he believes in God. Hawthorne might be suggesting that this belief

contributed to his downfall. The story shows that it is but a short

step from believing in the devil to being taken in by him.

Paragraph concludes with a strong idea about Hawthorne's use of irony in the scene.

Do not set off short quote.

Good insight into change in language

Thoughtful analysis of character's motivation

End explication; start conclusion, tying back to thesis.

Conclusion goes one step further, to a wider implication of the thesis (logically connected).

Whether you accept the student's interpretation of the scene with the pink ribbon or not, it is a good example of the use of explication to show a way to read the text that develops the central idea of an essay. The thesis statement is clearly presented in the opening paragraph, so the reader knows what the essay will be about. At first the student approached the explication with the idea that Goodman Brown's essential weakness was his pride in trusting his senses more than his faith in God. He felt from the start that the entire scene with the ribbon was a trick played on the protagonist. Rereading the story, he found evidence in Hawthorne's words to support this interpretation. Then, in writing the essay, he developed this thesis a step further, concluding the paper with two sentences about the "short step from believing in the devil to being taken in by him." This is an example of how the writing process itself can clarify and develop ideas. Just be sure the ideas are closely related, so your reader can follow you. Do not get sidetracked or introduce a new topic.

    Quotation of passages from the story is always more effective than a simple summary of events. Giving a plot summary is a common error of inexperienced essay writers. Most stories are so short that the reader remembers them without a summary. Some instructors assign plot summaries as a writing exercise, but they should not be confused with interpretive essays. An essay is organized according to logic, not simply the sequence of the plot.

Give evidence that develops your thesis statement logically by quoting from the text. Explication — at its simplest, a quotation followed by your interpretation of the words — should develop an *idea* about the story, which is the reason you were asked to write your interpretation in the first place.

ANALYSIS

An *analysis* of a story is the result of the process of separating it into its parts in order to study the whole. Analysis is a process commonly applied in thinking about almost any complex subject. When you are asked to analyze a story, you must think analytically about it, breaking it down into various parts and then usually selecting a single aspect for close study. If you are writing a short essay, try to keep the topic small enough to handle in a few paragraphs. Often what you are analyzing is one of the elements of fiction, an aspect of style, characterization, setting, or symbolism, for example.

While explication deals with a specific section of the text, analysis can range further, discussing details throughout the narrative that are related to your thesis. It is not possible to analyze an entire story, any more than you would attempt to explicate an entire work. You may begin with a general idea, or arrive at one by thinking about some smaller detail that catches your attention in the story.

Perhaps you begin by noticing the path through the forest as you read "Young Goodman Brown." When you stop to think about it later, you realize that Hawthorne's various descriptions of this path contribute to the pattern of the story. You sense a connection of the path with the effect of "blackness" you feel building up in the narrative. This single detail of the setting can suggest a central idea that you might want to investigate. You could write, for example, about the path the protagonist takes on his walk through the forest and analyze the way its use in the different sections of the narrative develops what Melville called Hawthorne's "power of blackness."

Regardless of where you start to think analytically — with the whole or with one of its parts — you will usually begin to write an essay that is developed by analysis by moving from a general thesis statement to the particular part of the story being analyzed. Here is an example of a student essay that analyzes "Young Goodman Brown" by following Hawthorne's references to the path through the forest.

The Path toward Evil

The path's purpose in "Young Goodman Brown" is to show that "evil is the nature of mankind," which is the dominent theme of Hawthorne's story. It is a very black theme, as Herman Melville realized in his 1850 review of Hawthorne's <u>Mosses from an Old Manse</u>. Satan has been with the Puritans since they came to America. "The dreary. . .narrow" path Goodman Brown follows through the gloomy forest is proof that

Thesis sentence, supported by evidence from supplementary reading.

human beings have frequently walked with the devil in the new land.
Goodman Brown's journey on the path makes him realize there are two
kinds of evil: social and personal. He meets social evil first, and is
confused by it. Then he meets the "blackness" that is the evil within
himself, and he is totally destroyed.

 When he begins to walk on the path with the devil, Goodman Brown
is too innocent to understand what he hears. He does not realize that
the religious intolerance of the early Puritan settlers is wrong. So
his companion, the devil, enlightens him further, telling him about
present-day corruption in the community. The church deacons have drunk
the communion wine, and the lawyers "are firm supporters of my interest." Now Goodman Brown is horrified because he understands the
meaning of the devil's remarks. He takes the first step along the
path from innocence to disillusionment when he recognizes hypocrisy in
the respected village elders.

 He proceeds a step further when he sees his own catechism teacher,
the deacon, and the minister on the forest path, too. He does not
understand what they are doing there. He asks himself, "Whither, then,
could these holy men be journeying so deep into the heathen wilderness?" While Goodman Brown now recognizes social evil, he does not
understand it. He must go further along the path to discover his own
evil nature.

 Goodman Brown finds the answer to his question in the story's
climax. The path takes him and the "holy men" to the same destination.
After he has come to believe that his wife is about to become one of
the devil's accomplices, he runs desperately down the path which
"grew wilder and more faintly traced, and vanished at length, leaving
him in the heart of the dark wilderness, still rushing onward, with
the instinct that guides mortal man to evil." Although the trail is
a path toward evil, it is, paradoxically, his last connection with the
familiar Puritan life that has sustained him. When it stops, he is
lost.

 The path terminates in the forest clearing, with its altar dedicated to the worship of Satan. Here he learns "to behold the whole
earth one stain of guilt, one mighty bloodspot." There are no paths
out of the wilderness now for Goodman Brown. The whole earth is bathed
in blood, with no firm ground upon which to fix a path that will lead
him safely home. Overwhelmed by his visions in the forest, he is a
lost soul. He has realized his own personal evil nature.

 As Hawthorne knew, the Puritan settlers of Salem felt the forest
was evil. They had to make paths in order to live in it. They would

*Analysis narrows
thesis and points
to direction of
paper's
development.*

*Analysis is
coherent —
organized from
beginning of story
to end.*

*Quote from story
to illustrate idea.*

*Good transition:
One step leads to
another.*

*Quote evidence
for assertion.*

*End of first part
(social evil)*

*Begin second part
(personal evil).*

*Good comment
on the quote —
relates it to
central idea*

*Evidence to
support the
analysis of the
personal evil in
Goodman Brown*

```
die of exposure if left alone in the woods, and they needed paths to
other nearby settlements.  To journey alone in the forest was, as
Goodman Brown learned, to leave the clearly defined, if hypocritical,
moral path of the established religious community and so to invite
damnation.  Hawthorne dramatizes his dark theme of man's essentially
evil nature by showing Goodman Brown's fate.  He leaves the apparently
straight and narrow path of the religious settlement for the twisting,
crooked path of the forest.  It is a dark journey of his soul to meet
"the deep mystery" of original sin.
```

*Begin conclusion:
Historical
background
relates to
particular details
of the story.*

*Restatement of
thesis*

Here the thesis sentence opens the essay, and the analysis follows from it. The student separated the story into various parts, analyzing the way the path figured in it at each stage of narration. You will notice that explication also plays a role in this essay. Even when analysis is your chosen method of developing your central idea, you should quote examples from the story to support your main points. Each time you use a quotation, comment on it to integrate it smoothly into your discussion.

COMPARISON AND CONTRAST

If you were asked to write about the two Hawthorne stories in this anthology, or to develop an idea about any two stories, you would probably use the method of comparison and contrast. When using the technique of comparison, you place the two stories side by side and comment on their similarities. In contrasting two stories, you point out their differences. Most of the time you will use both methods in writing your essay, since no two stories are ever exactly the same. It is always more meaningful to compare and contrast two stories that have something in common than two that are unrelated. As you work on your essay you will find that if there are no important similarities in the stories, your discussion will be as strained and pointless as any attempt to link together two dissimilar objects, whether mismatched stories or apples and oranges.

You can also compare and contrast two or more elements within a single story. For example, in Poe's "The Cask of Amontillado," you could discuss the character of Montresor as he sees himself and as he is viewed by the reader, or the differences between the two characters, Fortunato and Montresor. If your topic calls for you to use the method of comparison and contrast to elucidate your central idea, it is usually smoother to mingle your treatment of the two stories or elements as you go along than to write the first half of your paper about one and the second half about the other. The result of such a fifty-fifty split is rarely a unified essay; rather, it tends to be an essay that gives the impression of two separate commentaries flimsily linked together.

Here is an example of a paper whose thesis is developed by the method of comparison and contrast.

The Single Effect in

Hawthorne's "Young Goodman Brown"

and Poe's "The Cask of Amontillado"

In addition to writing short fiction, Edgar Allan Poe also published literary criticism, in which he explained his own standards for writing prose tales. Poe stated that the primary goal in creating works in this literary genre should be the development of a "certain single effect." According to Poe, an author invents such incidents in the story as will establish this "preconceived effect." Poe introduced this theory in one of his reviews of a collection of Nathaniel Hawthorne's tales. The theory was conceived by Poe and based on the work of Hawthorne; so the stories of both men emphasize the creation of such a "single effect."

Hawthorne's "Young Goodman Brown" and Poe's "The Cask of Amontillado" show each author's use of the method of "single effect." Poe's story examines the psychological processes in a madman's plot for revenge, and Hawthorne's story describes a man's fall from innocence, but both tales are constructed similarly. The action of both stories features a single character. Both stories are unified by a central theme. Every word, phrase, and image used by the author moves the theme closer to complete development. Neither story is realistic--that is, the events described are not plausible as real-life experiences. When Goodman Brown walks with a flesh-and-blood devil, for example, it is immediately clear that the story is a fantasy because flesh-and-blood devils did not exist in Puritan Salem. A similar world of fantasy operates in "The Cask of Amontillado." The ease with which the narrator is able to lead Fortunato to his death is not true to life as we know it.

Both stories feature a single character, and both emphasize a unity of single effect in developing their themes, but there are some fundamental differences between the stories. The first is created by the nature of the two literary forms the authors use. Hawthorne is writing a moral allegory. Every aspect of the story symbolizes something else. Goodman Brown's wife, for example, is the embodiment of morality and simple faith; even her name, "Faith," contributes to this symbolic meaning. The story would have a different effect if she were named "Gertrude." Poe is writing a psychological fantasy. Fortunato is shown dressed in a cap similar to one that would be worn by a court jester. By calling attention to this outfit, the narrator Montresor adds to the degradation of Fortunato which is part of the aim of his plan for revenge. Poe's fantasy is based on human emotions, while Hawthorne's allegory is based on intellect.

General background information on topic

Summary of most important facts about topic

Topic narrowed to thesis sentence

Important similarities

Single protagonist

Central theme

Not realistic

Specific examples

Begin analyzing differences.

Hawthorne's form

Good example

Contrast with Poe's form.

Summarize differences.

There is another major difference in the style of the two stories. *Another feature of Poe's theory related to another difference in the stories.*

Poe says that the first sentence of any tale should bring out the effect on which the rest depends. Although Poe set up the rules, Hawthorne did not keep to them. The opening sentence of "Young Goodman Brown" is in no hurry: "Young Goodman Brown came forth, at sunset, into the street of Salem village, but put his head back, after crossing the threshold, to exchange a parting kiss with his young wife." Goodman Brown is going on a journey, but the nature of the journey—which is central to the theme—is not clear. The concise opening of Poe's tale, however, reveals the theme: "The thousand injuries of Fortunato I had borne as I best could, but when he ventured upon insult I vowed revenge." This sentence leaves no doubt in the reader's mind about the meaning of the story. The narrator declares that revenge is foremost in his mind, and the action that follows develops the idea of a character obsessed by the desire for revenge. *Quote to give evidence of difference.* *Contrast with Hawthorne.*

Both Poe and Hawthorne were artists deeply interested in creating works of fiction. Despite their differences of form and literary style, both created unified stories based on a "single effect," as shown in the two classic tales, "Young Goodman Brown" and "The Cask of Amontillado." *Concluding summary clear, but a little brief*

In this essay the student shaped the first paragraph to conclude with the central idea, serving as an introduction to the comparison and contrast of the two stories. The stories' similarities were discussed in the next paragraph, and their differences analyzed in the rest of the paper. Throughout, elements of both stories were compared and contrasted side by side, sometimes with general analytical comments, at other times with explication and interpretation of the text. The technique of comparison and contrast is also a way to analyze stories. Quoting or paraphrasing from the texts always helps the reader get a clearer idea of the points being made in the analysis.

WRITING ABOUT THE CONTEXT OF THE STORIES

In addition to developing an idea about short fiction by explication, analysis, or comparison and contrast — all methods primarily involving a close reading of the text — there are other ways to write about short stories. The *context* of short fiction is important as well as the text, as the headnotes to each author's work in this anthology have stressed. The context of literature is usually defined as the biographical and historical background of the work. Literature does not exist in a vacuum. Created by a human being at some particular time in history, it is intended to speak to other human beings about ideas that have human relevance. Any critical method that clarifies the meaning and the pattern of a short story is valuable, and often literary critics use more than one method in their approach to a text.

A paper on the context of a story is also an expository essay based on the development of a central idea or thesis statement. Usually this kind of critical essay develops the thesis of the paper by suggesting the connection of *cause and effect.* That is to say, you maintain that the story has characteristics that originate from causes or sources in the author's background — personal life, historical period, or literary influences. For example, you can use Kate Chopin's statement on her discovery of Maupassant's stories (on page 1127) to show something about her own method of writing short fiction. To establish this connection between the life and work of a writer, you could also analyze or explicate a Chopin story, or compare one of her stories with one of Maupassant's. The amount of time you spend on the context or the text of the story will depend on the emphasis you wish to make in your paper. You have already read two student essays that briefly mention the context of the stories, referring in one case to Melville's recognition of the power of blackness in Hawthorne's short fiction, and in another to Poe's theory of the single effect.

In your experience, you have probably written term papers about literature in a biographical context. A favorite high-school term paper project is for the teacher to assign the student an author to write about, requiring library research into his or her life or historical period. If you wrote this kind of a paper, you may have organized your material chronologically, tracing the life of your author and briefly describing his or her most important literary works, often with no clearly defined thesis in mind. In writing an essay based on a unified central idea, on the other hand, you must ask yourself how knowing the facts of an author's life can help you understand that author's story. You should never assume a connection between a writer's life and the literary work. A story can reflect the life of the man or woman who wrote it, but there are often disparities between the work of fiction and the realities of the life that are as important as the connections you can draw between them. If you decide to give a biographical analysis of Melville's "Bartleby the Scrivener," for example, showing how it illustrates Melville's own decline and fall as a writer, you must remember that he wrote the story in 1853, several years before he decided to give up writing fiction for a popular audience. In 1853, Bartleby's "I prefer not to" was not yet Melville's conscious choice. This particular biographical reading of the story will not take you very far in your interpretation of its psychological, sociological, or philosophical complexities.

Remember that D. H. Lawrence advised us to trust the tale, not the teller. A biographical approach to literature requires at least as much care as textual criticism of the story, care in discovering and presenting the facts of an author's life and in using a sensitive interpretation of them to show relevant connections between a writer and a story. Writers often use their own experience as the basis for their fiction, as Fitzgerald did in "Babylon Revisited" and Hemingway in "The Snows of Kilimanjaro." Your task as a critic is to show how an awareness of Fitzgerald's experiences in Paris or Hemingway's safari in Africa helps you to understand the stories.

You will usually be proceeding on firmer ground when you combine biographical facts with a discussion of an author's thematic or aesthetic intentions in writing fiction, and then relate this material to specific stories. Here again, be cautious. Statements by writers about how and why they created short stories are not necessarily the same as what a given story may show. Use your judgment carefully. Poe wrote model stories based on his theory of the "single effect," but Anton Chekhov did not always follow his own advice about how to write fiction. In "The Lady with the Dog" (page 363) he wrote beautifully about the physical setting of Yalta, instead of restricting himself to the barest description, as he advised another writer to do in his letters (page 1130).

The contexts supplied by the writers themselves in the commentaries on the short story form and on particular stories included in this anthology are meant to stimulate ideas for your essays. They give the historical and biographical backgrounds of some of the stories. These excerpts can furnish a perspective from which you may view the individual stories, as did the students who used the quotations of Melville and Poe in two of the sample essays here (pages 1213 and 1216). Or you can write about the commentaries as a subject in themselves, part of the wider context of short story literature. You can report on the entire books they came from (Frank O'Connor and Sean O'Faolain's studies of the short story form, for example, or Eudora Welty's *The Eye of the Story*), if they are available in your college library.

OTHER PERSPECTIVES

Material from other classes can also be used in papers about short stories. If you major in history or psychology, for example, you can investigate the way stories are sometimes read to give valuable psychological or historical information about the world they describe. You are not limited to writing about remote times when considering essays that take this approach. Joyce Carol Oates's story "Where Are You Going, Where Have You Been" is about modern teenage life. A paper about it could investigate the connection between Oates's fantasy and psychological theories about adolescence in contemporary America. Characters in literature are often used in psychological and sociological textbooks to illustrate pathological symptoms or complexes. Sociology textbooks, for example, cite Oates's fictional characters as representing tendencies toward *anomie* in contemporary society, a condition in which normative standards of conduct have weakened or disappeared. It is possible in writing about literature to illustrate philosophical, historical, sociological, or psychological material you are familiar with through your work in other college courses.

Finally, you can argue a particular ideological point of view in writing about literature. You can read a story, for example, from a feminist, Marxist, or Freudian point of view (though not usually from all three in the same paper). A reader committed to a particular ideology may feel that literature contributes insights into conditioned cultural patterns of thought, whether they are consciously or unconsciously held by the writer. Needless to say, you must take no less care in using this critical approach to writing about stories than you would take in reading the text closely as an aesthetic statement in itself. At times the background of the author can suggest an ideological approach: Jack London was a Socialist, Flannery O'Connor a Catholic, Tillie Olsen a feminist, and so forth. At other times an ideology held by the student but not necessarily by the author can lead to a fresh reading of the stories. Proceed with great care, realizing that the bias of an ideology might make you insensitive to nuances of meaning other than those you are predisposed to find in a doctrinaire interpretation of the text. At the same time, this critical approach can illuminate aspects of a story that are valid and relevant for contemporary readers. A feminist interpretation of "Young Goodman Brown," for example, must not take the story literally, since Hawthorne wrote it as a moral allegory; but a feminist could use the story to argue provocatively about implied sexual stereotyping in Hawthorne's characterization of women.

Woman as Victim in "Young Goodman Brown"

In these feminist times, Hawthorne can be accused of portraying his female characters not as powerful individuals but rather as innocent victims. In "Young Goodman Brown," the women characters are clearly powerless to prevent the eventual destruction of the protagonist, Goodman Brown.

Introduction to thesis statement

While Hawthorne never intended any of the characters in his moral allegory to be read realistically (their names clearly indicate that they function on an abstract, symbolic level of meaning in the story), his attitude toward women as weak and pitiful creatures is apparent in every scene in which they appear. In the exposition of the story, Goodman Brown is kissing his Faith goodbye. It is no coincidence that he then begins his journey to the forest where he loses his faith in mankind. Faith is described as sweet and pretty. The pinkness of her hair ribbons blatantly advertises her youth and innocence. When she pleads with her husband to remain home with her, he speaks to her as if she were a small child and bids her say her bedtime prayers. Then, to add insult to injury, Hawthorne describes her as "peeping" (not looking) after him with a dependent, "melancholy air," as if she were incapable of spending a night alone. This marriage is plainly not one of equals. Goodman Brown seems more like a father than a

Narrow thesis.

Begin analysis.

newlywed husband in this scene. "Poor little Faith!" he thought, the

Quote and interpretation

diminutive "little" emphasizing his attitude that a wife is someone to

be looked after, not listened to.

Even when "sweet" Faith was surrounded by the unholy coven later

in the story, she was not portrayed as being evil. She "uncertainly"

uttered lamentations. Had this married woman no mind of her own?

Didn't she, like her husband, have to agree to come to this meeting on

her own? Instead, she is portrayed as an innocent victim, which makes

sense on an allegorical level, but hardly does credit to women in   *Repetition of central idea*

general.

Finally, at the end of the story when Goodman Brown is busy living

More evidence

out his life in gloomy thought, Faith's happy nature has absolutely no

power to combat his cynicism. How could she be happy to live the rest

of her life with such a man? Hawthorne never explained how Faith

reacted to her husband's changed outlook after his night in the forest.

Are we to believe that she merely accepted his change, docile as ever?

Two other women appear in the story--Goody Cloyse and Goodman   *Analysis of minor characters*

Brown's mother--but neither is portrayed as powerful or worthy of more

than brief consideration. Goody Cloyse was shown to be so frail that

she had to enlist the help of a male (the devil) to get to the meeting.

Goodman Brown's mother, who "threw out her arm to warn him back" at

the witches' coven, has no more power over him than poor little Faith.

These three women nourished the brief portion of this earthly life

that Goodman Brown enjoyed, but were unable to save his blind masculine

soul in the end. Taking the longer view, who was the true victim--the   *Conclusion*

women in the story or Goodman Brown?

As this student essay shows, arguments based on independent judgments about literature are acceptable as long as they are supported by evidence from the text of the story. Contemporary feminist criticism can produce insights into a Hawthorne text. Writers do not intend their readers to
worship literature like priests at an altar, never questioning it. As Vladimir
Nabokov once advised, the ideal reader should keep a psychological distance from the story. Try to express your own ideas *through* the text. You
misread stories if you think of them as absolute, perfect, final statements far
removed from the commonplaces of life. Through their aesthetic patterns,
stories show us what life is like. What they are ultimately saying, in their
affirmation of life and human creativity, is — in the words of Henry
James — "Live! Live!"

Some Common Problems in Writing about Stories

Intepret, don't summarize. Summarizing the plot in an essay is not the same as giving insights into a story's pattern and meaning. Occasionally you can summarize the plot in a sentence if you are making a transition from one part of your paper to another, but keep in mind that the reader of your paper is usually your teacher, who has already read the story and will get the impression that you do not know much about what you are doing the longer you ramble on about the plot.

Write about how you read the story. If you find yourself summarizing the story in more than a couple of sentences, it is probably because you did not organize your essay to develop a strong thesis. Your impressions and ideas are the measure of your encounter with literature. Writing about stories is designed to encourage your clarification of these ideas. Be sure to state your central idea in a sentence in your paper. It does not matter where it appears, although if you include it in your opening paragraph it will help you keep to the point in your discussion.

Avoid long personal anecdotes. Writing a paper based on your personal experience can result in a fine memoir, but such an essay is usually not about the literature you were asked to discuss. You may want to introduce an analysis of D. H. Lawrence's "The Rocking Horse Winner" with a short anecdote about a relevant experience you had as a child with a rocking horse, but make sure your anecdote goes on for only a few sentences before you connect it explicitly with your central idea about Lawrence's story.

Use the text to check your interpretation. Opinions about literature can be wrong. Do not insist on ideas that will not fit the details of the story. You may stumble on a central idea for your paper with an intuitive leap or a hunch about the story's meaning, but be sure the specific details of the story support your interpretation. The student who had an intuition that Goodman Brown was being tricked by the devil in the scene with the pink ribbon went back to Hawthorne's words for evidence to support his theory (see page 1211). You may decide that Hawthorne's story is a heavily veiled nineteenth-century treatment of a wife's infidelity and her husband's resulting nervous breakdown, but can you prove it by quoting from the text? "Whatever I discover in the story is right for me," you may say, but that will not take you very far when writing a paper for an English class. Stories are tough, tangible constructions of language, not shifting tea leaves in the bottom of an empty cup into which you can project whatever meaning you like.

Make good use of quotations. You must quote from the story to give evidence for your interpretation. Usually a sentence should introduce and follow each quotation, linking it to the idea being developed in your paper. In the comparison and contrast essay on page 1216, for example, the student discussed the opening sentences of the Hawthorne and Poe tales to make a point about their differences. Each time she quoted, she introduced the quotation and followed it by a comment of her own to explain how the quotation related to her main idea. Never drop quotations into the body of your essay without a comment.

Be careful not to quote too much. Use only those passages that are relevant to your discussion. Overquoting can weaken an essay, easily turning it into a string of short quotations choppily connected by a few insufficient words from you. Be sure to make it clear to the reader why the passage you are quoting is important.

When the quotation is short (four lines or less), it should be enclosed in quotation marks and included within the regular text, as you have seen in the sample essays. When typing a quotation longer than four lines, separate it from the preceding typewritten line with a double space. Then indent ten spaces, *omit quotation marks*, and type with single spacing (unless your instructor tells you differently). If you had a reason to include the entire opening paragraph of "Young Goodman Brown" in your essay, for example, you would type it like this:

```
     Young Goodman Brown came forth at sunset into the street at Salem
village; but put his head back, after crossing the threshold, to
exchange a parting kiss with his young wife. And Faith, as the wife
was aptly named, thrust her own pretty head into the street, letting
the wind play with the pink ribbons of her cap while she called to
Goodman Brown.
```

In a shorter passage in which you use a quotation within a quotation, such as a line of dialogue inside an excerpt from a story, use double and single quotation marks: "The echoes of the forest mocked him, crying 'Faith! Faith!' as if bewildered wretches were seeking her all through the forest."

If you wish to leave out words in a quoted passage, use ellipsis points, that is, three periods (or four periods if the omitted material includes the end of a sentence): "And Faith . . . thrust her own pretty head into the street. . . ."

Always quote the exact wording, punctuation, and capitalization of the original text. If you underline words in a quotation for emphasis, say so, as the writer of the first student paper did in his explication of Hawthorne's text (see page 1211).

If you find an error, for example a misspelled word in a quotation, indicate that the error is in the original by inserting *sic*, a Latin word meaning "thus," in brackets after the error itself.

Last but not least, punctuate sentences that appear in quotation marks correctly. Commas and periods always belong *inside* the quotation marks, whether or not they appeared in the original text. Semicolons, question marks, colons, and exclamation points, however, belong *outside* the quotation, unless they are part of the quoted material.

Avoid plagiarism. Any material you borrow from other sources and include in your paper must be documented. If you present someone else's material (other than factual information) as if it were your own, you may be open to the charge of plagiarism. Even with factual information, if you use the exact wording of a source, you must indicate that it is a quotation. To be on the safe side, it is always better to footnote your original source, or give credit by working into your essay the name of the author and the title of the work in which you found the material you borrowed.

The one exception to the principle of acknowledging the original source of borrowed material is when the information is considered *common knowledge*. Common knowledge is material that is repeated in a number of sources, so that it is difficult to tell what the original source might have been. Such material as the basic biographical facts about an author or information about the publication of specific stories does not need footnoting, unless you quote someone's exact words at length in your essay.

Know when and how to footnote. Footnotes may be placed at the bottom of the page of your paper on which the reference appears, or they may be gathered together on a separate *notes* page at the end of your essay. Try to avoid a flurry of unnecessary footnotes by integrating information about the source of your quotation into the body of your essay whenever possible. You might, for example, write:

> In Richard J. Jacobson's study, Hawthorne's Conception of the Creative Process (1965), we learn that Hawthorne feared the artist might become "insulated from the common business of life" (page 27).

When you footnote a source, indent the first line of each footnote five spaces before listing the author's first and last name, the title of the book, the city of publication, publisher, and date in parentheses, and the page number cited:

> [1] Richard J. Jacobson, Hawthorne's Conception of the Creative Process (Cambridge, Mass.: Harvard University Press, 1965), p. 27.

Instructions for basic footnote and bibliography form for different sources — books, magazines, encyclopedias, and so on — appear in every handbook and guide to writing college papers. They may also be found in various manuals of style and style sheets that should be available in the reference section of your college library.

Summary: How to Write
an Essay about Short Stories

1. Do not wait until the last minute to start. Allow plenty of time to write and revise.

2. Be sure you have a clear idea of what you want to say about the story. Can you state this idea as a sharply focused thesis sentence? Remember that all expository writing serves to clarify, set forth, or explain in detail an idea about a topic.

3. Read the story over again, taking notes that will help you amplify your central idea. It might help at this point to assemble a short outline, to stake out the ground you intend your essay to cover. Look for an approach that is distinctive enough to be worth your time and effort, yet manageable enough to be handled in a paper of the length you are assigned.

4. Decide how you want to proceed to develop your thesis. Will you use explication, analysis, or comparison and contrast? Is it appropriate to show a cause in an author's life or times and its effect on the work? If you have notes from your reading or research, assemble and number them in the order you intend to use them to develop your central idea.

5. Write a rough draft of your essay. Be sure to state your central idea as a thesis sentence somewhere — depending on how you organize your discussion of the story. If you are using an outline, try to follow it, but allow yourself the possibility of discovering something new that you did not know you had to say about the story while you are writing about it. If you have taken notes or jotted down quotations from your reading, try to introduce such material smoothly into your discussion. Remember that the heart of literary criticism is good quotation. Brief, accurate examples from the text that illustrate the points you are trying to make about your thesis are essential in writing about stories.

6. Allow some time to pass before you look over your rough draft — at least a day. Then make at least one thorough revision before you copy or type a finished draft of your paper. Some students find they need several revisions before they are satisfied with what they have written. When you read your rough draft, concentrate and read critically. Remember that Isaac Babel would sometimes write 100 drafts of a story before he was satisfied with what he had written. Let your words stimulate a flow of ideas about your topic; this will lead you to find more ways to illustrate your thesis or develop your train of thought. Fill out paragraphs that seem thin. Be sure transitions between paragraphs are smooth, and quotations are integrated into the discussion. If you sense that your sentences are wordy, try to be more concise. Eliminate repetition. Be sure your general organization is coherent and your discussion proceeds in a clear, logical order.

7. Check over your rough draft one last time to make sure you have always used complete sentences and correct spelling and punctuation. Avoid sentence fragments and exclamation points, unless they are part of a quotation.

8. Type the paper or write it neatly in its final form. If your instructor requires some particular style for class papers, such as extra-wide margins or triple-spacing, follow those instructions. Use 8½-by-11-inch paper. Type if you can, double spacing between lines. If you write by hand, use ink and write on only one side of each piece of paper. Leave generous margins at the top, bottom, and sides. Number the pages, beginning with the number 2 (not the word *two*) in the upper right-hand corner of the second page. (Your title on the first page will indicate that it is the first page.) Clip or staple your pages together in the upper left-hand corner. Be sure your name, your instructor's name, your class and section number, and the date appear on your paper.

9. Read your essay over one last time for typographical errors. Make legible corrections, in ink. Have you put quotation marks around titles of short stories ("The Snows of Kilimanjaro") and underlined the title of books (The Snows of Kilimanjaro and Other Stories)? Have you placed commas and periods *within* quotation marks in the titles and quotations that appear in your essay? Have you inadvertently left out any words or sentences when you went from the rough draft to the final version of your essay?

10. Finally, make a copy of your paper — a carbon or a photocopy — before you hand it in, and keep it. It is a good idea to save your notes and rough drafts as well, in case the accuracy of a quotation or the originality of your work is called into question.

What do you do after you hand in your paper? You have probably spent so much time on it, thinking, organizing, writing, and rewriting, that you feel you may never want to read it again. The act of writing the essay will have clarified your thinking about the story, so you carry with you an intangible benefit of something learned in the writing process. Returning to your essay in the future might have one final benefit: Your paper will refresh your memory, reminding you of what you did not know you knew, both about yourself and the short story.

GLOSSARY
OF LITERARY TERMS

ABSTRACT LANGUAGE Language that describes ideas or qualities rather than specific, observable people, places, and things, which are described in CONCRETE LANGUAGE.

ACTION At its simplest, the thing or things that happen in a story's PLOT — what the CHARACTERS do and what is done to them. A story may have more than one action (a plot and one or more SUBPLOTS), but a successful short story usually has one identifiable central action.

ALLEGORY A narrative in which CHARACTERS, places, things, and events represent general qualities, and their interactions are meant to reveal a general or abstract truth. Such characters, places, things, and events thus often function as SYMBOLS of the concepts or ideas referred to.

AMBIGUITY A situation expressed in such a way as to admit more than one possible interpretation; also, the way of expressing such a situation. Many short story writers intend some element of their work to be ambiguous, but careless or sloppy writing often creates unintentional ambiguity, or *vagueness*.

ANECDOTE A brief, unified NARRATION of one incident or EPISODE, often humorous and often based on an actual event. Some very good short stories may consist of nothing more than an anecdote; others may be made up of several anecdotes strung together, or may use one or more anecdotes as a way of advancing the PLOT or developing a CHARACTER.

ANTAGONIST A CHARACTER in some stories who is in real or imagined opposition to the PROTAGONIST or HERO. The CONFLICT between these characters makes up the ACTION, or PLOT, of the story. It is usually resolved in some way, but it need not be.

ANTICLIMAX An unexpected, insignificant RESOLUTION to a narrative, sometimes appearing in the place of a CLIMAX, sometimes after a true climax. Many anticlimaxes are the unintended result of inept writing, but often — especially in modern works — they are used intentionally to indicate the randomness, futility, or boredom of human life and action.

ANTI-STORY An experimental short story that attempts to convey objective reality by avoiding what its authors consider the false CONVENTIONS of PLOT, CHARACTER, and THEME, relying instead on seemingly uninterpreted and unarranged fragments of direct experience and language.

ATMOSPHERE The MOOD, feeling, or quality of life in a story as conveyed by the author's choices of language and organization in describing the SETTING in which the speech and activity of the CHARACTERS takes place. The atmosphere in which an author makes characters appear and events occur is often important in determining the TONE of the author in the particular work.

CENTRAL INTELLIGENCE A CHARACTER (often but not always the NARRATOR) through whose perception the author observes the ACTION of a story, and whose perspective thus shapes the reader's view of that action. The term was coined by Henry James, who felt, essentially, that the true subject matter of FICTION was the effect of the action on the understanding of this central intelligence.

CHARACTER Any person who plays a part in a narrative. Characters may be FLAT — simple, one-dimensional, unsurprising, and usually unchanging or *static* — or ROUND — complex, full, described in detail, often contradictory, and usually *dynamic*, i.e., changing in some way during the story. The main character in the story can usually be labeled the PROTAGONIST or HERO; he or she is often in CONFLICT with some other character, an ANTAGONIST. Other characters who affect the action slightly or only indirectly may be called *minor* characters; but, depending on the intention or the skill of the author, the main characters need not be round, nor the minor characters flat. Minor characters are often as full and complex as major characters, or fuller.

CLIMAX The turning point or point of highest interest in a narrative; the point at which the most important part of the ACTION takes place and the final outcome or RESOLUTION of the PLOT becomes inevitable. Leading up to the climax is the RISING ACTION of the story; after the climax, the FALLING ACTION takes the reader to the DENOUEMENT or conclusion, in which the results of the climactic action are presented.

COINCIDENCE An event or situation that arises for no apparent reason and with little or no preparation, and then has a significant effect on the working out of the PLOT or the lives of one or more of the CHARACTERS of a work; a chance happening that has an important consequence or result; an accident of fate.

COMPLICATION The introduction and development of a CONFLICT between CHARACTERS or between a character and his or her situation. A complication moves the PLOT forward by exciting the reader's expectation that the conflict so introduced must lead to a CLIMAX and reach some ultimate RESOLUTION as a result of that climax.

COMPRESSION The use of few or short words, sentences, or paragraphs, or of very brief descriptions of CHARACTERS and SETTINGS and narrations of incidents, to tell a story as clearly and simply as possible; in general, an economical use of language.

CONCRETE LANGUAGE Language that describes or portrays specific, observable persons, places, and things rather than general ideas or qualities, which are described in ABSTRACT LANGUAGE.

CONFLICT The opposition presented to the main CHARACTER (or PROTAGONIST) of a narrative by another character (an ANTAGONIST), by events or situations, by fate, or by some aspect of the protagonist's own personality or nature. The conflict is introduced by means of a COMPLICATION that sets in motion the RISING ACTION, usually toward a CLIMAX and eventual RESOLUTION.

CONNOTATION The meaning of a word (or words) that is implied or suggested by the specific associations the word calls to mind and by the TONE in which it is used, as opposed to its literal meaning or DENOTATION.

CONVENTION A traditional or commonly accepted technique of writing or device used in writing, often an unbelievable device that the reader agrees to believe — such as, for example, the very fact that a FIRST-PERSON NARRATOR is addressing the reader in a friendly and intimate manner.

CONVENTIONAL Following or observing CONVENTIONS; often used in a derogatory manner to indicate a certain overreliance on such conventions and thus a lack of originality or failure of imagination on the part of the writer.

CRISIS The turning point in a narrative; the point at which the ACTION reaches its CLIMAX and its RESOLUTION becomes inevitable.

DENOUEMENT The conclusion of an ACTION or PLOT, in which the FALLING AC-

TION is brought to a close and the outcome or outcomes of the CLIMAX are presented to the reader; from a French word meaning "the untying of a knot."

DESCRIPTION The use of language to present the features of a person, place, or thing.

DIALOGUE The written presentation of words spoken by CHARACTERS in a narrative; used to introduce the CONFLICT, give some impressions of the lives and personalities of the characters who are speaking, and advance the action to its CLIMAX and RESOLUTION.

DICTION The choice and arrangement of specific words and types of words to tell a story. A writer's diction is an important element of STYLE, and has a significant effect on the meaning of a story: The same ACTION will leave a different impression on the reader when it is narrated in street slang, in the simple, precise language of an old schoolteacher, or in the professional jargon of a lawyer or a social scientist.

DIDACTIC A term used to describe a narrative or other work of art that is presented in order to teach a specific lesson, convey a MORAL, or inspire and provide a model for proper behavior.

DISTANCE An author's or a narrator's spatial or temporal — and hence emotional — removal or aloofness from the ACTION of a narrative, and hence from its CHARACTERS.

DRAMATIC IRONY The reader's awareness of a discrepancy between a CHARACTER's perception of his or her own situation or activities, or of the consequences of such activities, and the true nature of that situation or those consequences.

EPIPHANY A sudden revelation of the true nature of a CHARACTER or a situation through a specific event — a word, gesture, or other action — that causes the reader to see that character or situation in a new light. The term was first popularized in modern criticism by James Joyce.

EPISODE A specific, usually very brief incident, often complete in itself and usually narrated at once and as a whole (as in an ANECDOTE). A story may consist of the NARRATION of one episode, or of several episodes strung together and united by a common SETTING or common CHARACTERS, or proceeding toward a single CLIMAX and RESOLUTION; the latter kind of story is referred to as an *episodic* narrative.

EXPOSITION The presentation of background information that a reader must be aware of, especially of situations that exist and events that have occurred before the ACTION of a story begins.

FABLE A very short, often humorous narrative told to present a MORAL. A fable's CHARACTERS are often animals, and specific animals have CONVENTIONAL uses representing specific abstract qualities or values — the fox representing wiliness, the ant industry, and the lion nobility, for example.

FALLING ACTION The events of a narrative that follow the CLIMAX and resolve the CONFLICT that reached its highest point in that climax before bringing the story to its conclusion or DENOUEMENT.

FANTASY A narrative or events in a narrative that have no possible existence in reality and could not have occurred in the real world; used sometimes to amuse or delight readers, sometimes to comment on or illustrate by contrast some aspect of reality, and sometimes, as in a FABLE, to present a clear MORAL that will not be complicated or diminished by the untidiness or inconsistency of reality.

FICTION A narrative drawn from an author's imagination, made up of an ACTION or PLOT of imagined events involving imagined CHARACTERS in imagined or imaginatively reconstructed SETTINGS; lies told with the tolerance, consent, and even complicity of the listener or reader.

FIGURATIVE LANGUAGE The use of a word or a group of words that is literally inaccurate to describe or define a person, event, or thing vividly by calling forth the sensations or responses that person, event, or thing evokes. Such language often takes the form of METAPHORS, in which one thing is equated with another, or of SIMILES, in which one thing is compared to another by using *like, as,* or some other such connecting word.

FIRST-PERSON NARRATION The telling of a story by a person who was involved in or directly observed the ACTION narrated. Such a NARRATOR refers to himself or herself as *I* and becomes a CHARACTER in the story, with his or her understanding shaping the reader's perception of the events and characters.

FLASHBACK A technique of EXPOSITION in which the flow of events in a narrative is interrupted to present to the reader an earlier incident or situation that has a bearing on the story or its CHARACTERS.

FLAT CHARACTER A simple, one-dimensional, usually unchanging CHARACTER who shows none of the human depth, complexity, and contrariness of a ROUND CHARACTER or of most real people.

FOLK TALE A narrative that comes out of the tradition — usually the oral tradition — of a specific culture, and is used to communicate that culture's beliefs, values, history, and MYTHS from generation to generation.

FORESHADOWING The introduction of specific words, IMAGES, or events into a narrative to suggest or anticipate later events that are central to the ACTION and its RESOLUTION.

HERO/HEROINE The PROTAGONIST of a story or other narrative; the main CHARACTER, whose CONFLICT is presented and resolved in the ACTION or PLOT. Traditionally, *heroine* has been used to refer to a female hero, but *hero* may be used, and is more and more being used, to refer to a protagonist of either sex.

IMAGE A word or group of words used to give a CONCRETE representation, either literal or FIGURATIVE, of a sensory experience or an object that is perceived by the senses.

IMAGERY The use of IMAGES, especially of a consistent pattern of related images — often FIGURATIVE ones — to convey an overall sensory impression.

IMPARTIAL OMNISCIENCE The telling of a story by a THIRD-PERSON NARRATOR whose OMNISCIENCE does not allow for any evaluation or judgment of the CHARACTERS and their activities.

IMPRESSIONISM A way of writing in which an author presents CHARACTERS and events in a highly subjective and personal light, freely admitting an authorial POINT OF VIEW and effectively denying any claim to OBJECTIVITY or disinterestedness; after the style of the French Impressionist painters of the middle and late years of the nineteenth century, who sought to free painting from the REALISTIC, representational CONVENTIONS of the day.

IRONY The reader's or audience's awareness of a reality that differs from the reality the characters perceive (DRAMATIC IRONY) or the literal meaning of the author's words (VERBAL IRONY).

LIMITED OMNISCIENCE The ability of a THIRD-PERSON NARRATOR to tell the reader directly about any events that have occurred, are occurring, or will occur in the PLOT of a story, and about the thoughts and feelings of one particular CHARACTER, or a few characters; distinguished from simple OMNISCIENCE, whereby such a NARRATOR can tell the reader directly about the thoughts and feelings of any character.

METAPHOR An implied comparison of two different things that is achieved by a FIGURATIVE verbal equation of those things. "Love is a rose," "War is hell," and "The exam was a killer" are all metaphors, intended not to define the first terms mentioned but to attribute certain qualities to the things being discussed.

MODERNISM A label loosely applied to the work of certain writers of the twentieth century, and especially its first half, who investigated the structure and texture of literature and challenged its CONVENTIONS.

MOOD The ATMOSPHERE that is created by the author's choice of details and the words with which to present them.

MORAL The lesson to be drawn from a story, especially from a FABLE or (in this sense the word is often used disparagingly) from a heavily DIDACTIC story.

MOTIVATION The external forces (SETTING, circumstance) and internal forces (personality, temperament, morality, intelligence) that compel a CHARACTER to act as he or she does in a narrative.

MYTH A traditional story, often a FOLK TALE arising out of a culture's oral tradition and involving gods or superhumanly heroic figures, that is used to explain the way things are and the way things happen, and to transmit the culture's values and beliefs from generation to generation.

NARRATION The dramatic telling of the events that make up the ACTION or PLOT of a story. FIRST-PERSON NARRATION is the telling of a story by a NARRATOR who participated in or directly observed the events being recounted, and who is thus a CHARACTER in the story, identifying himself or herself as I. THIRD-PERSON NARRATION is the telling of a story by a detached, almost always anonymous voice who refers to the characters as *he, she,* and *they.* A third-person narrator may or may not be OMNISCIENT.

NARRATOR The teller of a story; usually either a character who participates in the story's ACTION (see FIRST-PERSON NARRATION) or a detached, anonymous observer who may or may not present himself or herself as omniscient of the story's action from the beginning (see THIRD-PERSON NARRATION).

NATURALISM An extreme form of REALISM in which authors present their work as a scientific observation of a world in which people's acts are strictly determined by their nature and the nature of their surroundings.

NOVEL A long fictional prose narrative.

NOVELLA A short novel; a work of prose fiction whose length falls somewhere between that of a SHORT STORY and that of a NOVEL; sometimes (though infrequently today) referred to as a *novelette.* Different critics have attempted to specify different standards of length for a novella or short novel — some saying 15,000 to 50,000 words, others 50 to 125 ordinary book pages — but there is no universal agreement on such a standard.

OBJECTIVITY An attempt on the part of an author to remove himself or herself from any personal involvement with the CHARACTERS and ACTIONS of a story, to tell the story without bias and without expressing any personal opinions or making any personal judgments of the characters.

OMNISCIENCE Literally, "all-knowingness"; the ability of an author or a NARRA-

TOR (usually a THIRD-PERSON NARRATOR) to tell the reader directly about any events that have occurred, are occurring, or will occur in the PLOT of a story, and about the thoughts and feelings of any CHARACTER.

PACE The rate at which the ACTION of a story progresses. Pace may be affected by varying the lengths of words, sentences, and paragraphs, by COMPRESSING or expanding the NARRATION of certain incidents or EPISODES, or by introducing and repeating certain key words and formulaic phrases.

PARABLE A narrative, usually short, that is told to answer a difficult moral question or teach a moral truth; often a form of ALLEGORY, because each person, event, or thing in the parable represents a literally unrelated person, event, thing, or quality that is involved in the moral dilemma being examined.

PARODY A humorous imitation of another, usually serious, work or type of work, in which the parodist adopts the quirks of STYLE or the CONVENTIONS of the work or works being imitated and uses them in extreme and ridiculous ways, or applies them to a comically inappropriate subject matter.

PATHOS The quality in a work that evokes sorrow or pity. Inappropriate pathos, or a too-frequent resorting to pathetic effects, can reduce a work to SENTIMEN-TALITY or *bathos*.

PLOT The series of events in a narrative that form the ACTION of the story, in which a CHARACTER or characters face an internal or external CONFLICT that propels the story to a CLIMAX and an ultimate RESOLUTION.

POINT OF VIEW The perspective from which an author lets the reader view the ACTION of a narrative; thus, the choice of who tells the story. In FIRST-PERSON NARRATION the NARRATOR tells a story he or she took part in or observed directly; such a narrator usually knows only what has been explicitly revealed, or what he or she has been able to deduce from that. In THIRD-PERSON NARRATION the narrator is not directly involved in the story, and so views it from a certain DISTANCE. Such a narrator may be OMNISCIENT about the CHARACTERS and their actions and MOTIVATIONS, or his or her knowledge may be LIMITED to what one or a few characters know, or even to the plainly observable speeches and acts of the characters.

PROTAGONIST The main CHARACTER of a narrative; its HERO. The ACTION of the story is usually the presentation and RESOLUTION of some internal or external CONFLICT of this protagonist; if the conflict is with another major character, that character may be called the ANTAGONIST.

REALISM The telling of a story in a manner that is faithful to the reader's experience of real life, limiting events in the PLOT to things that might actually happen and CHARACTERS to people who might actually exist.

RESOLUTION The FALLING ACTION of a narrative, in which the CONFLICT, set in motion during the RISING ACTION and reaching its high point in the CLIMAX, is settled, or at least significantly altered, and the story moves swiftly toward its conclusion or DENOUEMENT.

REVERSAL Any turnabout in the fortunes of a CHARACTER, especially of the PROTAGONIST.

RISING ACTION The event or events that present and develop the CONFLICT whose dramatization is the story's ACTION; the COMPLICATION (or set of complications) that leads up to the CLIMAX.

ROMANTICISM A literary movement that flourished in the nineteenth century, valuing individuality, imagination, and the truth revealed in nature.

ROUND CHARACTER A full, complex, multidimensional character whose personality reveals some of the richness and contradictoriness we are accustomed to observing in most actual people, rather than the transparent obviousness of a FLAT CHARACTER.

SATIRE A work that ridicules some aspect of human behavior by portraying it at its most extreme; distinguished from PARODY, which burlesques the STYLE or content of another *work* or type of work.

SENTIMENTALITY An overreliance on emotional effect or PATHOS so great as to strain the reader's willingness to believe; also referred to as *bathos*.

SETTING The place and time in which a story's ACTION takes place; also, in a broader sense, the culture and the ways of life of the CHARACTERS, and the shared beliefs and assumptions that guide their lives.

SHORT STORY A short fictional prose narrative. Critics have attempted to discover distinctions between the short story and the NOVEL — that the short story is more unified, say, or involves fewer CHARACTERS or incidents, or covers a shorter time, or narrates a more specific and independent ACTION — but short stories and novels can always be found that violate any such rules. The only distinction that can be safely drawn between a short story and a novel is that a short story is — well, *shorter*.

SIMILE A FIGURATIVE comparison of one thing to another, especially to one that is not usually thought of as similar. The comparison is achieved by using such connecting words as *like* or *as*. An old country song says, "Life is like a mountain railway," and then goes on to describe the narrow, tortuous paths a person must pass through in dealing with life's moral dilemmas, and the steep fall that awaits those who are not careful. The simile makes possible this figurative comparison of two such dissimilar things as *life*, a very large abstraction, and *mountain railway*, a very specific and seemingly unrelated object.

STEREOTYPE A generalized, oversimplified CHARACTER (often a STOCK CHARACTER) whose thoughts and actions are excessively predictable because they are used so frequently that they have become CONVENTIONAL.

STOCK CHARACTERS CONVENTIONAL CHARACTERS who appear in numerous works, especially in works of the same type, and behave in predictable ways. Examples include the cruel stepmother in fairy tales, or the hard-boiled detective in certain mystery stories.

STREAM OF CONSCIOUSNESS The narrative technique by which an author attempts to capture the flow of a CHARACTER's thoughts, often in a series of separate and apparently unrelated passages that unite to give an IMPRESSIONISTIC view of reality as seen by that character.

STYLE The habitual manner of expression of an author. An author's style is the product of choices, made consciously or unconsciously, about such things as vocabulary, organization, DICTION, IMAGERY, PACE, and even certain recurring THEMES or subjects.

SUBPLOT A minor PLOT, often involving one or more secondary CHARACTERS, that may add an additional COMPLICATION to the ACTION of a narrative, or may reinforce that action, or provide an enlightening contrast to it or a welcome relief from its tension.

SURREALISM A way of writing that involves the presentation of a super-real, dreamlike world where CONVENTIONS are upended and rationality is dispensed with. The spontaneous creations of the unconscious are depicted in a surrealistic work through the use of fantastic and incongruous IMAGERY.

SUSPENSE The anxious uncertainty an author creates in a reader about the outcome of a story's ACTION. Suspense is often resolved when the action reaches a CLIMAX, after which the RESOLUTION is more or less inevitable.

SYMBOL A person, event, or thing that stands for or represents by association some other, usually broader, idea or range of ideas, in addition to maintaining its own literal meaning.

THEME The central, unifying point or idea that is made concrete, developed, and explored in the ACTION and the IMAGERY of a work of FICTION.

THIRD-PERSON NARRATION The telling of a story by a detached, usually anonymous NARRATOR, a voice who refers to all the characters as *he, she,* and *they.* Such a third-person narrator may view his story with full OMNISCIENCE, which may or may not be IMPARTIAL OMNISCIENCE; or he or she may have only LIMITED OMNISCIENCE, seeing through the eyes of only one or a few CHARACTERS.

TONE The expression of the author's attitude toward his or her subject matter — the CHARACTERS, their SETTING, and the ACTION they undertake or undergo. Tone is revealed in the author's DICTION, IMAGERY, organization, vocabulary, and various other choices that contribute to the making of a STYLE.

UNITY The relationship of all parts of a work to one central unifying or organizing principle that forms them into a complete and coherent whole.

VERBAL IRONY The reader's awareness of a discrepancy between the real meaning of the situation being presented and the literal meaning of the author's words in presenting it.

VERISIMILITUDE The use of certain lifelike details to give an imaginative narrative work the semblance of reality or actuality.

Acknowledgments (continued from page iv)

Anton Chekhov. "A Trifle from Real Life," in *Russian Silhouettes: More Stories of Russian Life*, translated by Marian Fell. Copyright 1915 by Charles Scribner's Sons. "The Lady with the Dog" from *The Portable Chekhov*, edited and translated by Avrahm Yarmolinsky. Copyright 1947 by The Viking Press, Inc. Copyright renewed 1974 by Avrahm Yarmolinsky. Reprinted by permission of Viking Penguin Inc. "On Technique in Writing a Short Story" excerpted from *Letters on the Short Story, the Drama, and Other Literary Topics* (1924), by Anton Chekhov, trans. Constance Garnett. Reprinted by permission of the Estate of the late Constance Garnett.

A. E. Coppard. "The Higgler" and "On the Story's Principles of Manufacture" both copyright © 1948 by A. E. Coppard. Copyright renewed 1976 by C. D. Coppard. Reprinted by permission of the Harold Matson Company.

Isak Dinesen. "The Old Chevalier" copyright 1934 and renewed 1962 by Isak Dinesen. Reprinted from *Seven Gothic Tales*, by Isak Dinesen, by permission of Random House, Inc.

T. S. Eliot. "On the Element of the Supernatural in Kipling's 'The Wish House.'" Reprinted by permission of Faber and Faber Ltd. from *A Choice of Kipling's Verse* introduced by T. S. Eliot.

Ralph Ellison. "Battle Royal" copyright 1947 by Ralph Ellison. Reprinted from *Invisible Man*, by Ralph Ellison, by permission of Random House, Inc. "On the Influence of Folklore on 'Battle Royal'" from *Writers at Work: The Paris Review Interviews*, second series, edited by George Plimpton. Copyright © 1963 by The Paris Review, Inc. Reprinted by permission of Viking Penguin Inc.

William Faulkner. "A Rose for Emily" and "Dry September" copyright 1930 and renewed 1958 by William Faulkner. Reprinted from *Selected Short Stories of William Faulkner*, by William Faulkner by permission of Random House, Inc. "On the Meaning of 'A Rose for Emily'" from *Faulkner in the University*, ed. Gwynn & Blotner. Reprinted by permission of the University Press of Virginia.

F. Scott Fitzgerald. "Babylon Revisited" (Copyright 1931 The Curtis Publishing Company; renewed 1959 Charles Scribner's Sons), in *Taps at Reveille*. Copyright 1935, Charles Scribner's Sons; copyright renewed. Reprinted with the permission of Charles Scribner's Sons.

Gustave Flaubert. "A Simple Heart" from *Flaubert: Three Tales*, trans. Robert Baldick (Penguin Classics 1961). Copyright © Robert Baldick, 1961. Reprinted by Permission of Penguin Books Ltd.

Nikolai Gogol. "The Overcoat," from *A Treasury of Russian Literature* (1943), trans. Bernard G. Guerney. Reprinted by permission of Vanguard Press, Inc.

Nadine Gordimer. "A Chip of Glass Ruby" from *Selected Stories* by Nadine Gordimer. Copyright © 1961 by Nadine Gordimer. Reprinted by permission of Viking Penguin Inc.

Ernest Hemingway. "The Snows of Kilimanjaro" (Copyright 1936 Ernest Hemingway; copyright renewed 1964 Mary Hemingway), in *The Short Stories of Ernest Hemingway*. Copyright 1938 Ernest Hemingway; copyright renewed 1966 Mary Hemingway. Reprinted with the permission of Charles Scribner's Sons.

Langston Hughes. "Conversation on the Corner" and "Who is Simple?" Reprinted by permission of Hill and Wang, a division of Farrar, Straus and Giroux, Inc. From *The Best of Simple* by Langston Hughes. Copyright © 1961 by Langston Hughes.

Shirley Jackson. "The Lottery." Reprinted by permission of Farrar, Straus and Giroux, Inc. "The Lottery" from *The Lottery* by Shirley Jackson. Copyright 1948, 1949 by Shirley Jackson. Copyright renewed © 1976, 1977 by Laurence Hyman, Barry Hyman, Mrs. Sarah Webster, and Mrs. Joanne Schnurer. "The Lottery" originally appeared in *The New Yorker*. "On the Morning of June 28, 1948, and 'The Lottery,'" from "Biography of a Story" from *Come along with Me* by Shirley Jackson. Copyright © 1968 by Stanley Edgar Hyman. Reprinted by permission of Viking Penguin Inc.

Henry James. "On the Genesis of 'The Real Thing'" (editor's title) from *The Notebooks of Henry James*, edited by F. O. Matthiessen and Kenneth B. Murdock. Copyright 1947 by Oxford University Press, Inc.; renewed 1974 by Kenneth B. Murdock and Mrs. Peters Putnam. Reprinted by permission.

Gustav Janouch. "On Franz Kafka's View of 'The Metamorphosis'" from Gustav Janouch, *Conversations with Kafka*. Copyright © 1968 by Fischer Verlag GmbH, Frankfurt-am-Main. Reprinted by permission of New Directions Publishing Corporation and Joan Daves.

James Joyce. "An Encounter" and "The Dead" from *Dubliners* by James Joyce. Originally published in 1916 by B. W. Huebsch. Definitive Text Copyright © 1967 by The Estate of James Joyce. Reprinted by permission of Viking Penguin Inc.

Franz Kafka. "The Metamorphosis." Reprinted by permission of Schocken Books Inc. from *The Metamorphosis* by Franz Kafka, copyright © 1946, 1948 by Schocken Books Inc.

Rudyard Kipling. "The Wish House" as it appears in *The Best Short Stories of Rudyard Kipling* edited by Randall Jarrell. Copyright 1924 by Rudyard Kipling. Reprinted by permission of Doubleday & Company, Inc. and The National Trust and Macmillan, London Ltd.

Milan Kundera. "The Hitchhiking Game" from *Laughable Loves*, by Milan Kundera, translated by Suzanne Rappaport. Copyright © 1974 by Alfred A. Knopf, Inc. Reprinted by permission of the publisher.

D. H. Lawrence. "The Primrose Path" by D. H. Lawrence from *The Complete Short Stories of D. H. Lawrence*. Copyright 1922 by Thomas Seltzer, Inc., copyright renewed 1950 by Frieda Lawrence. "The Rocking-Horse Winner" by D. H. Lawrence from *The Complete Short Stories of D. H. Lawrence*. Copyright 1933 by The Estate of D. H. Lawrence. Copyright renewed 1961 by Angelo Ravagli and C. M. Weekley, Executors of the Estate of Frieda Lawrence Ravagli. "On the Lust of Hate in Poe's 'The Cask of Amontillado' " from "Edgar Allan Poe" in *Studies in Classic American Literature* by D. H. Lawrence. Copyright 1923, 1951 by Frieda Lawrence. Copyright © 1961 by the Estate of the late Mrs. Frieda Lawrence. All reprinted by permission of Viking Penguin Inc.

Doris Lessing. "To Room 19" and "Homage for Isaac Babel" from *A Man and Two Women* by Doris Lessing. Copyright © 1958, 1962, 1963 by Doris Lessing. Reprinted by permission of Simon & Schuster, a division of Gulf & Western Corporation. © 1963 Doris Lessing. Reprinted by permission of Curtis Brown Ltd., London, on behalf of Doris Lessing.

Katherine Mansfield. "Bliss" and "The Doll's House" copyright 1920, 1923 by Alfred A. Knopf, Inc. and renewed 1948, 1951 by J. Middleton Murry. Reprinted from *The Short Stories of Katherine Mansfield*, by Katherine Mansfield, by permission of the publisher.

Gabriel García Márquez. "A Very Old Man with Enormous Wings" from *Leaf Storm and Other Stories* by Gabriel García Márquez, translated by Gregory Rabassa. English translation copyright © 1971 by Gabriel García Márquez. Reprinted by permission of Harper & Row, Publishers, Inc.

Guy de Maupassant. "The String" and "Miss Harriet" copyright 1923 and renewed by Alfred A. Knopf, Inc. Reprinted from *The Collected Novels and Stories of Guy de Maupassant*, by Guy de Maupassant, translated by Ernest Boyd and others, by permission of the publisher.

Vladimir Nabokov. "First Love" from *Nabokov's Dozen* by Vladimir Nabokov. Copyright 1948 by Vladimir Nabokov. Reprinted by permission of Doubleday & Company, Inc. "On Gogol's Genius in 'The Overcoat' " from *Nikolai Gogol* by Vladimir Nabokov. Copyright © 1944 by New Directions. Reprinted by permission of Mrs. Vladimir Nabokov. "On Anton Chekhov's 'The Lady with the Little Dog' " from *Lectures on Russian Literature* by Vladimir Nabokov, copyright © 1981 by the Estate of Vladimir Nabokov. Reprinted by permission of Harcourt Brace Jovanovich, Inc.

Joyce Carol Oates. "Where Are You Going, Where Have You Been?" reprinted from *The Wheel of Love* by Joyce Carol Oates by permission of the publisher, Vanguard Press, Inc. Copyright © 1970, 1969, 1968, 1967, 1966, 1965 by Joyce Carol Oates. "The Lady with the Pet Dog" reprinted from *Marriages and Infidelities* by Joyce Carol Oates by permission of the publisher, Vanguard Press, Inc. Copyright © 1968, 1969, 1970, 1971, 1972 by Joyce Carol Oates. "On the Making of a Writer" © 1982 by the New York Times Company. Reprinted by permission.

Flannery O'Connor. "A Good Man Is Hard to Find" copyright 1953 by Flannery O'Connor; copyright renewed 1981 by Regina O'Connor. "The Artificial Nigger" copyright © 1955 by Flannery O'Connor. Both stories reprinted from her volume, *A Good Man Is Hard to Find and Other Stories* by permission of Harcourt Brace Jovanovich, Inc. "On the Element of Suspense in 'A Good Man Is Hard to Find' " (editor's title) from the selection "On Her Own Fiction" in *Mystery and Manners* by Flannery O'Connor, selected and edited by Sally and Robert Fitzgerald. Copyright © 1957, 1961, 1963, 1964, 1966, 1967, 1969 by the Estate of Mary Flannery O'Connor. Reprinted by permission of Farrar, Straus & Giroux, Inc.

Frank O'Connor. "Guests of the Nation" from *Collected Stories*, by Frank O'Connor. Copyright © 1981 by Harriet O'Donovan Sheehy, Executrix of the Estate of Frank O'Connor. Reprinted by permission of Alfred A. Knopf, Inc. and Joan Daves. "My Oedipus Complex" copyright 1950 by Frank O'Connor. Reprinted from *Collected Stories*, by Frank O'Connor, by permission of Alfred A. Knopf, Inc. and by permission of Joan Daves. "The Nearest Thing to Lyric Poetry Is the Short Story" from *Writers at Work: The Paris Review Interviews*, first series, edited by Malcolm Cowley. Copyright © 1957, 1958 by The Paris Review, Inc. Reprinted by permission of Viking Penguin, Inc. "On Narrative in Turgenev's 'Byezhin Prairie' " from *The Mirror in the Roadway*, by Frank O'Connor. Copyright © by Frank O'Connor. "On the Elaboration of Style and Form in Joyce's 'The Dead' " from *The Lonely Voice* by Frank O'Connor. Copyright © 1963 by Frank O'Connor. Both reprinted by permission of Joan Daves.

Sean O'Faolain, "How to Write a Short Story" from *Foreign Affairs and Other Stories* by Sean O'Faolain. Copyright © 1974, 1976 by Sean O'Faolain. By permission of Little, Brown and Company in association with the Atlantic Monthly Press. "On Maupassant's Interest in Elemental Passion in 'Miss Harriet' " from *The Short Story* by Sean O'Faolain. Copyright © 1951 by the Devin Adair Co. Reprinted by permission of the Devin Adair Co.

Tillie Olsen. "I Stand Here Ironing" excerpted from the book *Tell Me a Riddle* by Tillie Olsen. Copyright © 1956 by Tillie Olsen. Reprinted by permission of Delacorte Press/Seymour Lawrence.

Grace Paley. "A Conversation with My Father" reprinted by permission of International Creative Management Inc. Copyright © 1972 by Grace Paley.

Katherine Anne Porter. "María Concepción" and "Flowering Judas" copyright 1930, 1958 by Katherine Anne Porter. Reprinted from her volume *Flowering Judas and Other Stories* by permission of Harcourt Brace Jovanovich, Inc. "On the Origins of 'Flowering Judas' " from *Writers at Work: The Paris Review Interviews*, second series, edited by George Plimpton. Copyright © 1963 by the Paris Review, Inc. Reprinted by permission of Viking Penguin Inc.

Philip Roth. " 'I Always Wanted You to Admire My Fasting': Or, Looking at Kafka" from *Reading Myself and Others* by Philip Roth. Copyright © 1973, 1975 by Philip Roth. Reprinted by permission of Farrar, Straus & Giroux, Inc.

Isaac Bashevis Singer. "A Crown of Feathers" from *A Crown of Feathers* by Isaac Bashevis Singer. Copyright © 1972, 1973 by Isaac Bashevis Singer. "A Crown of Feathers" originally appeared in *The New Yorker*. Reprinted by permission of Farrar, Straus & Giroux, Inc.

Aleksandr Solzhenitsyn. "Zakhar-the-Pouch" from *Stories and Prose Poems* by Aleksandr Solzhenitsyn, translated by Michael Glenny. Translation copyright © 1970, 1971 by Michael Glenny. Reprinted by permission of Farrar, Straus & Giroux, Inc. and The Bodley Head.

Gertrude Stein. "As a Wife Has a Cow: A Love Story" from *Selected Writings of Gertrude Stein*, by Gertrude Stein. Copyright 1946 by Random House, Inc. Reprinted by permission of the publisher. "On Technique in Portraits and Repetition" from *Lectures in America*, by Gertrude Stein. Copyright 1935 and renewed 1963 by Alice B. Toklas. Reprinted by permission of Random House, Inc.

James Thurber. "The Secret Life of Walter Mitty" copyright © 1942 James Thurber. Copyright © 1970 Helen W. Thurber. From *My World — and Welcome to It*, published by Harcourt Brace Jovanovich. Reprinted by permission of Mrs. James Thurber.

Leo Tolstoy. "The Death of Ivan Ilych" from *The Death of Ivan Ilych and Other Stories* by Leo Tolstoy, translated by Louise and Aylmer Maude (1935). Reprinted by permission of Oxford University Press.

John Updike. "Flight" and "Wife-wooing" copyright © 1960, 1962 by John Updike. Reprinted from *Pigeon Feathers and Other Stories*, by John Updike, by permission of Alfred A. Knopf, Inc. Originally appeared in *The New Yorker*. "On Writing about Adolescence in 'Flight' " from *Writers at Work: The Paris Review Interviews*, fourth series, edited by George Plimpton. Copyright © 1974, 1976 by The Paris Review, Inc. Reprinted by permission of Viking Penguin, Inc.

Eudora Welty. "Petrified Man" copyright 1939, 1967 by Eudora Welty. "A Worn Path" copyright 1941, 1969 by Eudora Welty. Both stories reprinted from her volume *A Curtain of Green and Other Stories* by permission of Harcourt Brace Jovanovich, Inc. "Is Phoenix Jackson's Grandson Really Dead?" copyright © 1974 by Eudora Welty. Reprinted from *The Eye of the Story: Selected Essays and Reviews*, by Eudora Welty, by permission of Random House, Inc.

Edith Wharton. "Roman Fever" copyright 1934 (Liberty Magazine; copyright renewed 1962 William R. Tyler) in *The Collected Stories of Edith Wharton*. Copyright © 1968 William R. Tyler. Reprinted with the permission of Charles Scribner's Sons. "Every Subject Must Contain within Itself Its Own Dimensions" excerpted from *The Writing of Fiction*. Copyright 1925 Charles Scribner's Sons; copyright renewed 1953 Frederic R. King. Reprinted with the permission of Charles Scribner's Sons.

Virginia Woolf. "Moments of Being" from *A Haunted House and Other Stories* by Virginia Woolf, copyright 1944, 1972 by Harcourt Brace Jovanovich, Inc. Reprinted by permission of the publisher.

Richard Wright. "The Man Who Was Almost a Man" from *Eight Men* by Richard Wright (World Publishing Company). Copyright 1940, © 1961 by Richard Wright. Reprinted by permission of Harper & Row, Publishers, Inc.